PRAISE FOR ED GREENWOOD

"An old wizard with the power to delight youngsters and horrify adults reveals his early beginnings in this strong fantasy, which traces the evolution of a mage's powers. This joins others in the Forgotten Realms series: readers with a prior familiarity will be the best bets for this strong winner."

—Midwest Book Review
(on *Elminster: The Making of a Mage*)

"With memorable characters and unforgettable settings, Ed Greenwood will take you on an adventure you will not soon forget."

—BC Books Review
(on *The Annotated Elminster*)

"A nonstop adventure story filled with life lessons."

—Fantasy Book Critic
(on *Elminster: The Making of a Mage*)

". . . this is sword and sorcery at the next level."

—John Ottinger III, Grasping for the Wind
(on *Swords of Dragonfire*)

SAGE OF SHADOWDALE

Elminster, the Old Mage, the Chosen of Mystra. Across the face of Faerûn and throughout her history, the Sage of Shadowdale, by whatever name, has always stood firm against the tide of darkness.

Elminster: The Making of a Mage
Elminster in Myth Drannor
The Temptation of Elminster
Elminster in Hell
Elminster's Daughter
The Annotated Eliminster
Elminster Ascending
Elminster Must Die
Bury Elminster Deep
[August 2011]

THE KNIGHTS OF MYTH DRANNOR

From the pastoral village of Espar to a road fraught with danger, magic, and the dubious attentions of villains and royalty alike, the rise of the Knights of Myth Drannor is a remarkable adventure.

Book I
Swords of Eveningstar

Book II
Swords of Dragonfire

Book III
The Sword Never Sleeps

ALSO BY ED GREENWOOD

The City of Splendors: A Waterdeep Novel
(with Elaine Cunningham)

The Best of the Realms, Book II
The Stories of Ed Greenwood
Edited by Susan J. Morris

ED GREENWOOD
SAGE OF SHADOWDALE

ELMINSTER
ASCENDING

ELMINSTER
THE MAKING OF A MAGE

ELMINSTER
IN MYTH DRANNOR

THE TEMPTATION OF
ELMINSTER

Sage of Shadowdale
Elminster Ascending

Published by Wizards of the Coast LLC

FORGOTTEN REALMS, WIZARDS OF THE COAST, and their respective logos are trademarks of Wizards of the Coast LLC in the U.S.A. and other countries.

Printed in the U.S.A.

Cover art by Kekai Kotaki
Map by Todd Gamble
This Edition First Printing: November 2010
Elminster: The Making of a Mage First Printing: December 1994
Elminster in Myth Drannor First Printing: November 1997
The Temptation of Elminster First Printing: December 1998

9 8 7 6 5 4 3 2 1

ISBN: 978-0-7869-5618-0
620-24754000-001-EN

U.S., CANADA,
ASIA, PACIFIC, & LATIN AMERICA
Wizards of the Coast LLC
P.O. Box 707
Renton, WA 98057-0707
+1-800-324-6496

EUROPEAN HEADQUARTERS
Hasbro UK Ltd
Caswell Way
Newport, Gwent NP9 0YH
GREAT BRITAIN
Save this address for your records.

Visit our web site at www.wizards.com

ELMINSTER
THE MAKING OF A MAGE

To Jenny
For Love
And Understanding
And Being There
...As Always

ELMINSTER
THE MAKING OF A MAGE

For Cheryl Freedman
And
Merle von Thorn,
Two ladies Elminster wanted at his side
(blades, good humor, and all)
When he was in Myth Drannor

ELMINSTER
THE MAKING OF A MAGE

To
Steven & Jenny Helleiner
Great friends, good people, champions of gaming and
The gamers who play.
Let all your triumphs together not be in Another World.

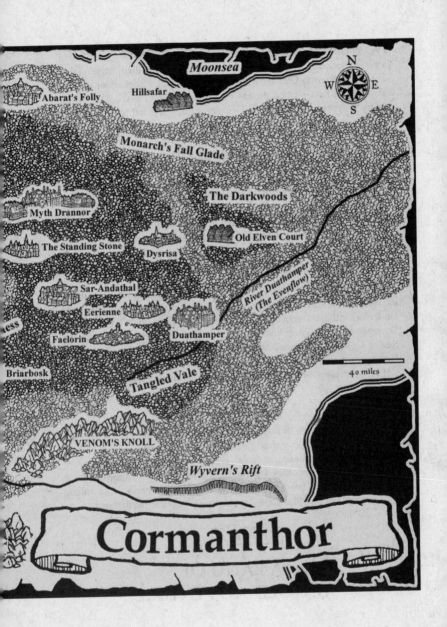

Cormanthor

Welcome to Faerûn, a land of magic and intrigue, brutal violence and divine compassion, where gods have ascended and died, and mighty heroes have risen to fight terrifying monsters. Here, millennia of warfare and conquest have shaped dozens of unique cultures, raised and leveled shining kingdoms and tyrannical empires alike, and left long forgotten, horror-infested ruins in their wake.

A LAND OF MAGIC

When the goddess of magic was murdered, a magical plague of blue fire—the Spellplague—swept across the face of Faerûn, killing some, mutilating many, and imbuing a rare few with amazing supernatural abilities. The Spellplague forever changed the nature of magic itself, and seeded the land with hidden wonders and bloodcurdling monstrosities.

A LAND OF DARKNESS

The threats Faerûn faces are legion. Armies of undead mass in Thay under the brilliant but mad lich king Szass Tam. Treacherous dark elves plot in the Underdark in the service of their cruel and fickle goddess, Lolth. The Abolethic Sovereignty, a terrifying hive of inhuman slave masters, floats above the Sea of Fallen Stars, spreading chaos and destruction. And the Empire of Netheril, armed with magic of unimaginable power, prowls Faerûn in flying fortresses, sowing discord to their own incalculable ends.

A LAND OF HEROES

But Faerûn is not without hope. Heroes have emerged to fight the growing tide of darkness. Battle-scarred rangers bring their notched blades to bear against marauding hordes of orcs. Lowly street rats match wits with demons for the fate of cities. Inscrutable tiefling warlocks unite with fierce elf warriors to rain fire and steel upon monstrous enemies. And valiant servants of merciful gods forever struggle against the darkness.

A LAND OF UNTOLD ADVENTURE

ELMINSTER
THE MAKING OF A MAGE

There are only two precious things on earth:
the first is love; the second, a long way behind it,
is intelligence.

—Gaston Berger

Life has no meaning but what we give it.
I wish a few more of ye would give it a little.
—Elminster of Shadowdale

verba volant, scripta manent

PRELUDE

O f course, Lord Mourngrym," Lhaeo replied, gesturing up the stairs with a ladle that was still dripping jalanth sauce. "He's in his study. You know the way."

Mourngrym nodded his thanks to Elminster's scribe and took the dusty stairs two at a time, charging urgently up into the gloom. The Old Mage's instructions had been quite—

He came to a halt, dust swirling around him mockingly. The cozy little room held the usual crammed shelves, worn carpet, and comfortable chair . . . and Elminster's pipe was floating, ready, above the side table. But of the Old Mage himself, there was no sign.

Mourngrym shrugged and dashed on up the next set of stairs, to the spell chamber. A glowing circle pulsed alone on the floor there, cold and white. The small circular room was otherwise empty.

The Lord of Shadowdale hesitated a moment, and then mounted the last flight of stairs. He'd never dared disturb the Old Mage in his bedchamber before, but . . .

The door was ajar. Mourngrym peered in cautiously, hand going to his sword hilt out of long habit. Stars twinkled silently and endlessly in the dark domed ceiling over the circular bed that filled the room—but that resting place hadn't been slept in since the dust had settled. The room was as empty of life as the others. Unless he was invisible or had taken on the shape of a book or something of the sort, Elminster was nowhere in his tower.

Mourngrym looked warily all around, hairs prickling on the backs of his hands. The Old Mage could be anywhere, on worlds and planes only he and the gods knew of. Mourngrym frowned—and then shrugged. After all, what did anyone in the Realms—besides the Seven Sisters, perhaps—really know about Elminster's plans or his past?

"I wonder," the Lord of Shadowdale mused aloud as he started the long walk back down to Lhaeo, "where Elminster came from, anyway? Was he *ever* a young lad? Where . . . ? And what was the world like then?"

It must have been great fun, growing up as a powerful wizard. . . .

PROLOGUE

It was the hour of the Casting of the Cloak, when the goddess Shar hurled her vast garment of purple darkness and glittering stars across the sky. The day had been cool, and the night promised to be clear and cold. The last rosy embers of day glimmered on the long hair of a lone rider from the west, and lengthening shadows crept ahead of her.

The woman looked around at the gathering night as she rode. Her liquid black eyes were large and framed by arched brows—stern power and keen wits at odds with demure beauty. Whether for the power or the beauty there, most men did not look past the honey-brown tresses curling around her pert white face, and even queens lusted after her beauty—one at least did, of a certainty. Yet as she rode along, her large eyes held no pride, only sadness. In the spring, wildfires had raged across all these lands, leaving behind legions of charred and leafless spars instead of the lush green beauty she recalled. Such fond memories were all that was left of Halangorn Forest now.

As dusk came down on the dusty road, a wolf howled somewhere away to the north. The call was answered from near at hand, but the lone rider showed no fear. Her calm would have raised the eyebrows of the hardened knights who dared ride this road only in large, well-armed patrols—and their wary surprise would not have ended there. The lady rode easily, a long cloak swirling around her, time and again flapping around her hips and hampering her sword arm. Only a fool would allow such a thing—but this tall, lean lady rode the perilous road without even a sword at her hip. A patrol of knights would have judged her either a madwoman or a sorceress and reached for their blades accordingly. They'd not have been wrong.

She was Myrjala "Darkeyes," as the silvern sigil on her cloak proclaimed. Myrjala was feared for her wild ways as much as for the might of her magic, but though all folk feared her, many farmers and townsfolk loved her. Proud lords in castles did not; she'd been known to hurl down cruel barons and plundering knights like a vengeful whirlwind, leaving blazing bodies in dark warning to others. In some places she was most unwelcome.

As night's full gloom fell on the road, Myrjala slowed her horse, twisted in her saddle, and did off her cloak. She spoke a single soft word, and the cloth twisted in her hands, changing from its usual dark green to a russet hue. The silver mage-sigil slithered and writhed like an angry snake and became a pair of entwined golden trumpets.

The transformation did not end with the cloak. Myrjala's long curls darkened and shrank about her shoulders—shoulders suddenly alive and broadening with roiling humps of muscle. The hands that donned the cloak again had become hairy and stubby fingered. They plucked a scabbarded blade out from the pack behind the saddle and belted it on. Thus armed, the man in the saddle arranged his cloak so its newly shaped herald badge could be clearly seen, listened to the wolf howl again—closer now—and calmly urged his mount forward at a trot, over one last hill. Ahead lay a castle where a spy dined this night—a spy for the evil wizards bent on seizing the Stag Throne of Athalantar. That realm lay not far off to the east. The man in the saddle stroked his elegant beard and spurred his horse onward. Where the most feared sorceress in these lands might be met with arrows and ready blades, a lord herald was always welcome. Yet magic was the best blade against a wizard's spy.

The guards were lighting the lamps over the gate as the herald's horse clottered over the wooden drawbridge. The badge on his cloak and tabard were recognized, and he was greeted with quiet courtesy by the gate guards. A bell tolled once within, and the knight of the gate bade him hasten in to the evening feast.

"Be welcome in Morlin Castle, if ye come in peace."

The herald bowed his head in the usual silent response.

" 'Tis a long way from Tavaray, Lord Herald; ye must know hunger," the knight added less formally, helping him down from his mount. The herald took a few slow steps, awkward with saddle stiffness, and smiled thinly.

Startling dark eyes rose to meet those of the knight. "Oh, I've come much farther than that," the herald said softly, nodded a wordless farewell, and strode away into the castle. He walked like a man who knew his way—and welcome—well.

The knight watched him go, face expressionless in puzzlement. An armsman nearby leaned close and murmured, "No spurs . . . and no esquires or armsmen. What manner of herald is this?"

The knight of the gate shrugged. "If he lost them on the road or there's some other tale of interest, we'll know it soon enough. See to his horse." He turned, then stiffened in fresh surprise. The herald's horse was standing near and watching him, for all the world as if it were listening to their talk. It nodded and took a half step to bring its reins smoothly to the armsman's hand. The men exchanged wary glances before the armsman led it away.

The knight watched them for a moment before shrugging and striding back to the mouth of the gate. There'd be much talk on watch later, whatever befell. Out in the night nearby, a wolf howled again. One of the horses snorted and stamped nervously.

Then a window in the castle above flickered with sudden light—*magical* light from a battle spell, and the battle was joined. There was a terrific commotion within, scattering plates and overturned tables, shrieks of serving maids and roars of flame. Next moment, these sounds were joined by the shouts of the knights in the courtyard below.

That had been no herald, and from the sound and smell of it, others within the castle were not what they seemed, either. The knight gritted his teeth and clenched his sword, starting for the keep. If Morlin fell to these wicked spell-slingers, would the Stag King fall next? And if all Athalantar fell, there would be years upon years of sorcerous tyranny. Aye, there would be ruin and misery ahead . . . And who could ever rise to oppose these magelords?

PART
I

BRIGAND

ONE

DRAGON FIRE—AND DOOM

Dragons? Splendid things, lad—so long as ye look upon them only in tapestries,
or in the masks worn at revels, or from about three realms off. . . .

ASTRAGARL HORNWOOD, MAGE OF ELEMBAR
SAID TO AN APPRENTICE
YEAR OF THE TUSK

The sun beat down bright and hot on the rock pile that crowned the high pasture. Far below, the village, cloaked in trees, lay under a blue-green haze of mist—magic mist, some said, conjured by the mist-mages of the Fair Folk, whose magic worked both good and ill. The ill things were spoken of more often, of course, for many folk in Heldon did not love elves.

Elminster was not one of them. He hoped to meet the elves someday—really meet, that is—to touch smooth skin and pointed ears, to converse with them. These woods had once been theirs, and they yet knew the secret places where beasts laired and suchlike. He'd like to know all that, someday, when he was a man and could walk where he pleased.

El sighed, shifted into a more comfortable position against his favorite rock, and from habit glanced at the falling slopes of the meadow to be sure his sheep were safe. They were.

Not for the first time, the bony, beak-nosed youth peered south, squinting. Brushing unruly jet-black hair aside with one slim hand, he kept his fingers raised to shade his piercing blue-gray eyes, trying vainly to see the turrets of far off, splendid Athalgard, in the heart of Hastarl, by the river. As always, he could see the faint bluish haze that marked the nearest curve of the Delimbiyr, but no more. Father told him often that the castle was much too far off to be seen from here—and, from time to time, added that the fair span of distance between it and their village was a good thing.

Elminster longed to know what that meant, but this was one of the many things his father would not speak of. When asked, he settled his oft smiling lips into a stony line, and his level gray eyes would meet Elminster's own with a sharper look than usual but no words ever emerged. El hated secrets—at least those he didn't know. He'd learn all the secrets someday, somehow. Someday, too, he'd see the castle the minstrels said was so splendid . . . mayhap even walk its battlements . . . aye. . . .

A breeze ghosted gently over the meadow, bending the weed heads briefly. It was the Year of Flaming Forests, in the month of Eleasias, a few days short of Eleint. Already the nights were turning very cold. After six seasons of minding sheep on the high meadow, El knew it'd not be long before leaves were blowing about, and the Fading would truly begin.

The shepherd-lad sighed and shrugged his worn, patched leather jerkin closer about him. It had once belonged to a forester. Under a patch on the back, it still bore a ragged, dark-stained hole where an arrow—an elfin arrow, some said—had taken the man's life. Elminster wore the old jack—scabbard buckles, tears from long-gone lord's badges, and worn edges from past adventures—for all the dash its history made him feel. Sometimes, though, he wished it fit him a little better.

A shadow fell over the meadow, and he looked up. From behind him came a sharp, rippling roar of wind he'd never heard before. He spun around, his shoulder against the rock, and sprang up for a better view. He needn't have bothered. The sky above the meadow was filled with two huge, batlike wings— and between them, a dark red scaled bulk larger than a house! Long-taloned claws hung beneath a belly that rose into a long, long neck, which ended in a head that housed two cruel eyes and a wide-gaping jaw lined with jagged teeth as long as Elminster was tall! Trailing back far behind, over the hill, a tail switched and swung. . . .

A dragon! Elminster forgot to gulp. He just stared.

Vast and terrible, it swept toward him, slowing ponderously with wings spread to catch the air, looming against the blue northern sky. And there was a man on its back!

"Dragon at the gate," Elminster whispered the oath unthinkingly, as that gigantic head tilted a little, and he found himself gazing full into the old, wise, and cruel eyes of the great wyrm.

Deep they were, and unblinking; pools of dark evil into which he plunged, sinking, sinking. . . .

The dragon's claws bit deeply into the rock pile with a shriek of riven stone and a spray of sparks. It reared up twice as high as the tallest tower in the village, and those great wings flapped once. In their deafening thunderclap Elminster was flung helplessly back and away, head over heels down the slope as sheep tumbled and bleated their terror around him. He landed hard, rolling painfully on one shoulder. He should run, should—

"Swords!" He spat the strongest oath he knew as he felt his frantic run being dragged to a halt by something unseen. A trembling, quivering boiling arose in his veins—magic! He felt himself turning, being pulled slowly around to face the dragon. Elminster had always hoped to see magic at work up close, but instead of the wild excitement he'd expected, El found he didn't like the feel of magic at all. Anger and fear awoke in him as his head was forced up. No, did not like it at all.

The dragon had folded its wings, and now sat atop the rock pile like a vulture—a vulture as tall as a keep, with a long tail that curled half around the western slope of the meadow. Elminster gulped; his mouth was suddenly dry.

The man had dismounted and stood on a sloping rock beside the dragon, an imperious hand raised to point at Elminster.

Elminster felt his gaze dragged—that horrible, helpless feeling in his body again, the cruel control of another's will moving his own limbs—to meet the man's eyes. Looking into the eyes of the dragon had been terrible but somehow splendid. This was worse. These eyes were cold and promised pain and death . . . perhaps more. El tasted the cold tang of rising fear.

There was cruel amusement in the man's almond eyes. El forced himself to look a little down and aside, and saw the dusky skin around those deadly eyes, and coppery curls, and a winking pendant on the man's hairless breast. Under it were markings on the man's skin, half-hidden by his robe of darkest green. He wore rings, too, of gold and some shining blue metal, and soft boots finer than any El had ever seen. The faint blue glow of magic—something Father had said only Elminster could see, and must never speak of—clung to the pendant, the rings, the robes, and the markings on the man's breast, as well as to what looked like the ends of smoothed wooden sticks, protruding from high slits on the outside of the man's boots. That rare glow rippled more brightly around the man's outstretched arm . . . but Elminster didn't need any other secret sign to know that this was a wizard.

"What is the name of the village below?" The question was cold, quick.

"Heldon." The name left Elminster's lips before he could think. He felt spittle flooding his mouth, and with it a hint of blood.

"Is its lord there now?"

Elminster struggled, but found himself saying, "A-Aye."

The wizard's eyes narrowed. "Name him." He raised his hand, and the blue glow flared brighter.

Elminster felt a sudden eagerness to tell this rude stranger everything—*everything*. Cold fear coiled inside him. "Elthryn, Lord." He felt his lips trembling.

"Describe him."

"He's tall, Lord, and slim. He smiles often, and always has a kind w—"

"What hue is his hair?" the wizard snapped.

"B-Brown, Lord, with gray at the sides and in his beard. He's—"

The wizard made a sharp gesture, and Elminster felt his limbs moving by themselves. He tried to fight against them, whimpering, but already he was wheeling about and running. He pounded hard through the grass, helpless against the driving magic, stumbling in haste, charging down the grassy slope to where the meadow ended—in a sheer drop into the ravine.

As he churned along through the weeds and tall grass, El clung to a small victory; at least he'd not told the wizard that Elthryn was his father.

Small victory, indeed. The cliff edge seemed to leap at him; the wind of his breathless run roared past his ears. The rolling countryside of Athalantar, below, looked beautiful in the mists.

Headlong, Elminster rushed over the edge—and felt the terrible trembling compulsion leave him. As the rocks rushed up to meet him, he struggled against fear and fury, trying to save his life.

Sometimes, he could move things with his mind. Sometimes—please, gods, let it be now!

The ravine was narrow, the rocks very near. Only last month a lamb had fallen in, and the life had been smashed from it long before its broken, loll-limbed body had settled at the bottom. Elminster bit his lip. And then the white glow he was seeking rose and stole over his sight, veiling his view of rushing rocks. He clawed at the air with desperate fingers and twisted sideways as if he'd grown wings for an instant.

Then he was crashing through a thornbush, skin burning as it was slashed open a dozen times. He struck earth and stone, then something springy—a vine?—and was flung away, falling again.

"Uhhh!" Onto rocks this time, hard. The world spun. El gasped for breath he could not find, and the white haze rose around his eyes.

Gods and goddesses preserve . . .

The haze rose and then receded—and then, from above, came a horrible snapping sound.

Something dark and wet fell past him, to the rocks unseen in the gloom below. El shook his head to clear it and peered around. Fresh blood dappled the rocks close by. The sunlight overhead dimmed; Elminster froze, head to one side, and tried to look dead. His arms and ribs and one hip throbbed and ached . . . but he'd been able to move them all. Would the wizard or the dragon come down to make sure he was dead?

The dragon wheeled over the meadow, one limb of a sheep dangling from its jaws, and passed out of his view. When its next languid circle brought it back over the ravine, two sheep were struggling in its mouth. The crunching sounds began again as it passed out of sight.

Elminster shuddered, feeling sick and empty. He clung to the rock as if its hard, solid strength could tell him what to do now. Then the rippling roar of the dragon's wings rose again. El lay as still as possible, head still twisted awkwardly. Letting his mouth fall open, he stared steadily off into the cloudless sky.

The wizard in his high saddle gave the huddled boy a keen look as the dragon rushed past, and then leaned forward and shouted something Elminster couldn't catch, which echoed and hissed in the mouth of the ravine. The dragon's powerful shoulders surged in response, and it rose slightly—only to drop down out of sight in a dive so swift that the raw sound of its rushing wings rose to a shrill scream. A dive toward Heldon.

El found his feet, wincing and staggering, and stumbled along the ravine to its end, hissing as every movement made him ache. There was a place he'd climbed before . . . his fingers bled as they scraped over sharp rocks. A terrible fear was rising inside him, almost choking him.

At last he reached the grassy edge of the meadow, rolled onto it, gasping, and looked down on Heldon. Then Elminster found he still had breath enough to scream.

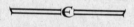

A woman shrieked outside. A moment later, the incessant din of hammering from the smithy came to a sudden, ragged stop. Frowning, Elthryn Aumar rose from the farm tallies in haste, scattering clay tiles. He sighed at his own clumsiness as he snatched his blade down from the wall and strode out into the street, tearing the steel free of the scabbard as he went. Tallies that wouldn't balance all morning, and now this . . . what was it *now*?

The Lion Sword, oldest treasure of Athalantar, shone its proud flame as he came out into the sunlight. Strong magics slumbered in the old blade, and as always, it felt solid in Elthryn's hand, hungry for blood. It flashed as he looked quickly about. Folk were shrieking and running wildly south down the street, faces white in sheer terror. Elthryn had to duck out of the way of a woman so fat that he was astonished she could run at all—one of Tesla's seamstresses—and turned to look north at the dark bulk of the High Forest. The street was full of his neighbors, running south down the road, past him. Some were weeping as they came. A haze—smoke—was in the air whence they'd come.

Brigands? Orcs? Something out of the woods?

He ran up the road, the enchanted blade that was his proudest possession naked in his hand. The sharp reek of burning came to him. A sick fear was already rising in his throat when he rounded the butcher's shop and behind it found the fire.

His own cottage was an inferno of leaping flame. Perhaps she'd been out—but no . . . no . . .

"Amrythale," he whispered. Sudden tears blinded him, and he wiped at them with his sleeve. Somewhere in all that roaring were her bones.

He knew some folk had whispered that a common forester's lass must have used witchery to find a bridal bed with one of the most respected princes of Athalantar—but Elthryn had loved her. And she him. He gazed in horror at her pyre, and in his memory saw her smiling face. As the tears rolled down his cheeks, the prince felt a black rage build inside him.

"Who has done this thing?" he roared. His shout echoed back from the now-empty shops and houses of Heldon, but was answered only by crackling flames . . . and then by a roar so loud and deep that the shops and houses around trembled, and the very cobbles of the street shifted under his boots. Amid the dust that curled up from them, the prince looked up and saw it, aloft, wheeling with contemptuous laziness over the trees: an elder red dragon of great size, its scales dark as dried blood. A man rode it, a man in robes who held a wand ready, a man Elthryn did not know but a wizard without a doubt, and that could mean only one thing: the cruel hand of his eldest brother Belaur was finally about to close on him.

Elthryn had been his father's favorite, and Belaur had always hated him for it. The king had given Elthryn the Lion Sword—it was all he had left of his father, now. It had served him often and well . . . but it was a legacy, not a miracle-spell. As he heard the wizard laugh and lean out to hurl lightning down at some villager fleeing over the back fields, Prince Elthryn looked up into the sky and saw his own death there, wheeling on proud wings.

He raised the Lion Sword to his lips, kissed it, and summoned the lean, serious face of his son to mind: beak-nosed and surrounded by an unruly mane of jet-black hair. Elminster, with all his loneliness, seriousness, and homeliness, and with his secret, the mind powers the gods gave few folk in Faerûn. Perhaps the gods had something special in mind for him. Clinging to that last, slim hope, Elthryn clutched the sword and spoke through tears.

"Live, my son," he whispered. "Live to avenge thy mother and restore honor to the Stag Throne. Hear me!"

Panting his slithering way down a tree-clad slope, still a long way above the village, Elminster stiffened and fetched up breathless against a tree, his eyes blazing. The ghostly whisper of his father's voice was clear in his ears; he was calling on a power of his enchanted sword that El had seen him use only once, when his mother had been lost in a snow squall. He knew what those words meant. His father was about to die.

"I'm coming, Father!" he shouted at the unhearing trees around. "I'm coming!" And he stumbled on, recklessly leaping deadfalls and crashing through thickets, gasping for breath, knowing he'd be too late. . . .

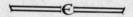

Grimly, Elthryn Aumar set his feet firmly on the road, raised his sword, and prepared to die as a prince should. The dragon swept past, ignoring the lone man with the sword as its rider pointed two wands and calmly struck down the fleeing folk of Heldon with hurled lightning and bolts of magical death. As he swept over the prince, the wizard carelessly aimed one wand at the lone swordsman below.

There was a flash of white light, and then the whole world seemed to be dancing and crawling. Lightning crackled and coiled around Elthryn, but he felt no pain; the blade in his hands drew the magic into itself in angrily crawling arcs of white fire until it was all gone.

The prince saw the wizard turn in his saddle and frown back at him. Holding the Lion Sword high so that the mage could see it, hoping he could lure the wizard down to seize it—and knowing that hope vain—Elthryn lifted his head to curse the man, speaking the slow, heavy words he'd been taught so long ago.

The wizard made a gesture—and then his mouth fell open in surprise: the curse had shattered whatever spell he'd cast at Elthryn. As the dragon swept on, he aimed his other wand at the prince. Bolts of force leaped from it—and were swept into the enchanted blade, which sang and glowed with their fury, thrumming in Elthryn's hands. Spells it could stop . . . but not dragon fire. The prince knew he had only a few breaths of life left.

"O Mystra, let my boy escape this," he prayed as the dragon turned in the air with slow might and swept down on him, "and let him have the sense to flee far." Then he had no time left for prayers.

Bright dragon fire roared around Elthryn Aumar, and as he snarled defiance and swung his blade at the raging flames, he was overwhelmed and swept away.

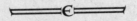

Elminster burst out onto the village street by the miller's house, now only a smoking heap of shattered timbers and tumbled stones. A single hand, blackened by fire that had breathed death through the house and swept on, protruded from under the collapsed chimney, clutching vainly at nothing.

Elminster looked down at it, swallowed, and hurried on around the heap of ruin. After only a few paces, however, his running steps faltered, and he stood staring. There was no need for haste; every building in Heldon was smashed flat or in flames. Thick smoke hid the lower end of the village from him, and small fires blazed here and there, where trees or woodpiles had caught fire. His home was only a blackened area and drifting ashes; beyond, the butcher's shop had fallen into the street, a mass of half-burnt timbers and smashed belongings. The dragon had gone; Elminster was alone with the dead.

Grimly, Elminster searched the village. He found corpses, tumbled or fried among the ruins of their homes, but not a soul that yet lived. Of his mother and father there was no sign . . . but he knew they'd not have fled. It was only when he turned, sick at heart, toward the meadow—where else could he go?—that he stepped on something amid the ashes that lay thick on the road: the half-melted hilt of the Lion Sword.

He took it up in hands that trembled. All but a few fingers of the blade were burnt away, and most of the proud gold; blue magic coursed no longer about this remnant. Yet he knew the feel of the worn hilt. El clutched it to his breast, and the world suddenly wavered.

Tears fell from his sightless eyes for a long time as he knelt among the ashes in the street and the patient sun moved across the sky. At some point he must have fallen senseless, for he roused at the creeping touch of cold to feel hard cobbles under his cheek.

Sitting up, he found dusk upon the ruin of Heldon, and full night coming down from the High Forest. His numb hands tingled as he fumbled with the sword hilt. Elminster got to his feet slowly, looking around at what was left of his home. Somewhere nearby, a wolf called and was answered. Elminster looked at the useless weapon he held, and he shivered. It was time to be gone from this place, before the wolves came down to feed.

Slowly he raised the riven Lion Sword to the sky. For an instant it caught the last feeble glow of sunset, and Elminster stared hard at it and muttered, "I shall slay that wizard, and avenge ye all—or die in the trying. Hear me . . . Mother, Father. This I *swear*."

A wolf howled in reply. Elminster bared his teeth in its direction, shook the ruined hilt at it, and started the long run back up to the meadow.

As he went, Selûne rose serenely over the dying fires of Heldon, bathing the ruins in bright, bone-white moonlight. Elminster did not look back.

He awoke suddenly, in the close darkness of a cavern he'd hidden in once when playing seek-the-ogre with other lads. The hilt of the Lion Sword lay, hard and unyielding, beneath him. Elminster remained still, listening. Someone had said something, very nearby.

"No sign of a raid . . . no one sworded," came the sudden grave words, loud and close. Elminster tensed, lying still and peering into the darkness.

"I suppose all the huts caught fire by themselves, then," another, deeper man's voice said sarcastically. "And the rest fell over just because they were tired of standing up, eh?"

"Enough, Bellard. Everyone's dead, aye—but there's no sword work, not an arrow to be seen. Wolves have been at some of the bodies, but not a one's been rummaged. I found a gold ring on one lady's hand that shone at me clear down the street."

"What kills with fire, then—an' knocks down cottages?"

"Dragons," said another voice, lower still, and grim.

"Dragons? And we saw it not?" The sarcastic voice rose almost jestingly.

"More'n one thing befalls up an' down the Delimbiyr that ye see not, Bellard. What else could it be? A mage, aye—but what mage has spells enough to scorch houses an' haystacks an' odd patches of meadow, as well as every stone-built building in the place?" There was a brief silence, and the voice went on. "Well, if ye think of any other good answer, speak. Until then, if ye've sense, we'll raid only at dawn, before we can be well seen from the air—an' not stray far from the forest, for cover."

"Nay! I'll not sit here like some old woman while others pick over all the coins and goods, only to be left fighting with wolves over the refuse."

"Go then, Bellard. I stay here."

"Aye—with the sheep."

"Indeed. That way there may be something for you to eat—besides cooked villager—when you're done . . . or were you going to herd them all down there an' watch over them as you pick through the rubble?"

There was a disgusted snort, and someone else laughed. "Helm's right, as usual, Bel. Now belt up; let's go. He'll probably have some cooked for us by nightfall, if you speak to him as a lover would instead of always wagging the sharp tongue . . . what say, Helm?"

The grim voice answered, "No promises. If I think something's lurking that might be drawn by a smoke plume, the meat'll be cold. If any of ye sees a good cauldron there—big and stout, mind—have the sense to bring it back, will ye? Then I can boil enough food for us to eat all at once."

"And your helm'll smell less like beans for a while, eh?"

"That, too. Forget not, now."

"I'll not waste my hands on a pot," Bellard said sullenly, "if there's coins or good blades to be had."

"No, no, helmhead—carry thy loot in the pot, see? Then ye can bring that much more, nay?"

There were chuckles. "He's got ye there, Bel."

"Again."

"Aye, let's be off." Then there came the sounds of scrambling and scuffling; stones turned and rolled by the mouth of the cave, and then clattered and were still. Silence fell.

Elminster waited for a long time, but heard only the wind. They must have all gone. Carefully he rose, stretched his stiff arms and legs, and crept forward in the darkness, around the corner—and almost onto the point of a sword. The man at the other end of it said calmly, "An' who might ye be, lad? Run from the village down there?" He wore tattered leather armor, rusty gauntlets, a dented, scratched helm, and a heavy, stubbly beard. This close, Elminster could smell the stench of an unwashed man in armor, the stink of oil and wood smoke.

"Those are my sheep, Helm," he said calmly. "Leave them be."

"Thine? Who be ye herding them for, with all down there dead?"

Elminster met the man's level gaze and was ashamed when sudden tears welled up in his own eyes. He sprang back, wiping at his eyes, and drew the Lion Sword out of the breast of his jerkin.

The man regarded him with what might have been pity and said, "Put that away, boy. I've no interest in crossing blades with ye, even if ye had proper steel to wield. Ye had folk down"—he pointed with a sideways tilt of his head, never taking his eyes from Elminster—"in Heldon?"

"Aye," El managed to say, voice trembling only a little.

"Where will ye go now?"

Elminster shrugged. "I was going to stay here," he said bitterly, "and eat sheep."

Helm's eyes met the young, angry gaze calmly. "A change of plans must needs be in order, then. Shall I save ye one to get ye started?"

Sudden rage rose up inside Elminster at that. "Thief!" he snarled, backing away. "Thief!"

The man shrugged. "I've been called worse."

Elminster found his hands were trembling; he thrust them and the ruined sword back into the front of his jerkin. Helm stood across the only way out. If there were a rock large enough . . .

"You'd not be so calm if there were knights of Athalantar near! They kill brigands, you know," Elminster said, biting off his words as he'd heard his father do when angry, putting a bark of authority in his tone.

The response astonished him. There was a sudden scuffling of boots on rock, and the man had him by the throat, one worn old gauntlet bunching up the jerkin under Elminster's nose. "I *am* a knight of Athalantar, boy—sworn to the Stag King himself, gods and goddesses watch over him. If there weren't so gods-cursed many wizards down in Hastarl, kinging it over the lot of us with the hired brigands they call 'loyal armsmen,' I'd be riding a realm at peace—an' doubtless ye'd still have a home, an' thy folks an' neighbors'd be alive!"

The old gray eyes burned with an anger equal to Elminster's own. El swallowed but looked steadily into them.

"If ye're a true knight," he said, "then let go."

Warily, with a little push that left them both apart, the man did so. "Right, then, boy—why?"

Elminster dragged out the sword hilt again and held it up. "Recognize ye this?" he said, voice wavering.

Helm squinted at it, shook his head—and then froze. "The Lion Sword," he said roughly. "It should be in Uthgrael's tomb. How came you by it, boy?" He held out his hand for it.

Elminster shook his head and thrust the ruined stub of blade back into his jerkin. "'Tis mine—it was my father's, and ..." He fought down a tightness of unshed tears in his throat, and went on, " ... and I think he died wielding it, yestereve."

He and Helm stared into each other's eyes for a long moment, and then El asked curiously, "Who's this Uthgrael? Why would he be buried with my father's sword?"

Helm was staring at him as if he had three heads, and a crown on each one. "I'll answer that, lad, if ye'll tell me thy father's name first." He leaned forward, eyes suddenly dark and intent.

Elminster drew himself up proudly and said, "My father is—was—Elthryn Aumar. Everyone called him the uncrowned lord of Heldon."

Helm let out his breath in a ragged gasp. "Don't—don't tell *anyone* that, lad," he said quickly. "D'ye hear?"

"Why?" Elminster said, eyes narrowing. "I know my father was someone important, and he—" His voice broke, but he snarled at his own weakness and went on "—he was killed by a wizard with two wands, who rode on the back of a dragon. A dark red dragon." His eyes became bleak. "I shall never forget what they look like." He drew out what was left of the Lion Sword again, made a thrusting motion with it, and added fiercely, "One day ..."

He was startled to see the dirty knight grin—not a sneering grin, but a smile of delight.

"What?" El demanded, suddenly embarrassed. He thrust the blade out of sight again. "What amuses ye so?"

"Lad, lad," the man said gently, "sit down here." He sheathed his own sword and pointed at a rock not far away. Elminster eyed him warily, and the man sighed, sat down himself, and unclipped a stoppered trail-flask of chased metal from his belt. He held it out. "Will ye drink?"

Elminster eyed it. He was very thirsty, he realized suddenly. He took a step nearer. "If ye give me some answers," he said, "and promise not to slay me."

Helm regarded him almost with respect and said, "Ye have my word on it—the word of Helm Stoneblade, knight of the Stag Throne." He cleared his throat and said, "An' answers I'll give, too, if ye'll favor me with just one more." He leaned forward. "What is thy name?"

"Elminster Aumar, son of Elthryn."

"Only son?"

"Enough," Elminster said, taking the flask. "Ye've had your one answer; give me mine."

The man grinned again. "Please, Lord Prince? Just one answer more?"

Elminster stared at him. "D'ye mock me? 'Lord Prince'?"

Helm shook his head. "No, lad—Prince Elminster. I pray ye, I must know. Have ye brothers? Sisters?"

Elminster shook his head. "None, alive or dead."

"Thy mother?"

Elminster spread his hands. "Did ye find anyone alive down there?" he asked, suddenly angry again. "I'd like my answers now, Sir Knight." He took a long, deliberate drink from the flask.

His nose and throat exploded in bubbling fire. Elminster choked and gasped. His knees hit the stony ground, hard; through swimming eyes he saw Helm lean swiftly forward to rescue him—and the flask. Strong hands helped him to his seat and gently shook him.

"Firewine not to thy liking, lad? All right now?"

Elminster managed a nod, head bowed. Helm roughly patted him on the arm and said, "Well enough. Seems thy parents thought it safest to tell ye nothing. I agree with them."

Elminster's head came up in anger—but through swimming eyes he saw Helm holding up one gauntleted hand in the gesture that meant "halt."

"Yet I gave my word . . . an' you are a prince of Athalantar. A knight keeps his promises, however rashly made."

"So, speak," Elminster said.

"How much d'ye know of thy parents? Thy lineage?"

Elminster shrugged. "Nothing," he said bitterly, "beyond the names of my parents. My mother was Amrythale Goldsheaf; her father was a forester. My father was proud of this sword—it had magic—and was glad that we couldn't see Athalgard from Heldon. That's all."

Helm rolled his eyes, sighed, and said, "Well, then. Sit an' learn. If ye'd live, keep what I tell thee to thyself. Wizards hunt folk of thy blood in Athalantar, these days."

"Aye," Elminster told him bitterly, "I know."

Helm sighed. "I—my forgiveness, Prince. I forgot." He spread gauntleted hands as if to clear away underbrush before him, and said, "This realm, Athalantar, is called the Kingdom of the Stag after one man: Uthgrael Aumar, the Stag King; a mighty warrior—an' thy grandsire."

Elminster nodded. "That much, I suspected from all thy 'prince' talk. Why then am I not in rich robes right now in some high chamber of Athalgard?"

Helm gave him that grin of delight again and chuckled. "Ye are as quick—an' as iron of nerves—as he was, lad." He reached an arm behind him, found a battered canvas pack, and rummaged in it as he went on. "The best answer to that is to tell things as they befell. Uthgrael was my lord, lad, and the greatest swordsman I've ever seen." His voice sank to a whisper, all traces of his smile gone. "He died in the Year of Frosts, going up against orcs near Jander. Many of us died that wolfwinter—an' the spine of Athalantar went with us."

Helm found what he was looking for: a half loaf of hard, gray bread. He held it out wordlessly. Elminster took it, nodded his thanks, and gestured for the knight to say on. That brought the ghost of a smile to Helm's lips.

"Uthgrael was old an' ready to die; after Queen Syndrel went to her grave, he fell to grimness an' waited for a chance to fall in battle; I saw it in his eyes more than once. The orc chieftain who cut him down left the realm in the hands of his seven sons. There were no daughters."

Helm stared into the depths of the cavern, seeing other times and places—and faces Elminster did not know. "Five princes were ruled by ambition, an' were ruthless, cruel men, all. One of these, Felodar, was interested in gold above all else an' traveled far in its pursuit—to hot Calimshan and beyond, lad, where he still is, for all I know—but the others all stayed in Athalantar."

The knight scratched himself for a moment, eyes still far away, and added, "There were two sons more. One was too young an' timid to be a threat to anyone. The other—thy father, Elthryn—was calm an' just, an' preferred the life of a farmer to the intrigue of the court. He retired here an' married a commoner. We thought that signified his renunciation of the crown. So, I fear, did he."

Helm sighed, met Elminster's intent gaze, and went on. "The other princes fought for control of the realm. Folk as afar from here as Elembar, on the coast, call them The Warring Princes of Athalantar.' There're even songs about them. The winner, thus far, has been the eldest son, Belaur."

The knight leaned forward suddenly to grip Elminster's arms. "Ye must hear me in this," he said urgently. "Belaur bested his brothers—but his victory has cost him, an' all of us, the realm. He bought the services of mages from all over Faerûn to win him the Stag Throne. He sits on it today—but his wits are so clouded by drink an' by their magic that he doesn't even know he barks only when they kick him: his magelords are the true rulers of Athalantar. Even the beggars in Hastarl know it."

"How many of these wizards are there? What are their names?" Elminster asked quietly.

Helm released him and sat back, shaking his head. "I know not—an' I doubt any folk in Athalantar do, below swordcaptains of the Stag, except perhaps the house servants of Athalgard." He cast a keen look at Elminster. "Sworn to avenge thy parents, Prince?"

Elminster nodded.

"Wait," the knight told him bluntly. "Wait until ye're older, an've gathered coins enough to buy mages of thy own. Ye'll need them—unless ye want to spend the rest of your days as a purple frog swimming in some palace perfume-bowl for the amusement of some minor apprentice of the magelords. Though it took all of them to do it, an' they had to split apart Wyrm Tower stone by stone, they slew old Shandrath—as powerful an archmage as ye'll find in all the lands of men—two summers back." He sighed. "An' those they couldn't smash with spells, they slew with blades or poison, Theskyn the court mage, for one. He was the oldest an' most trusted of Uthgrael's friends."

"I will avenge them all," Elminster said quietly. "Before I die, Athalantar will be free of these magelords—every last one, if I have to tear them apart with my bare hands. This I swear."

Helm shook his head. "No, Prince, swear no great oaths. Men who swear oaths are doomed to die by them. One thing hunts and hounds them—an' so, they waste and stunt their lives."

Elminster regarded him darkly. "A wizard took my mother and father—and all my friends, and the other folk I knew. It is my life, to spend how I will."

Helm's face split in that delighted grin again. He shook his head. "Ye're a fool, Prince—a prudent man'd foot it out of Athalantar and never look back, nor breathe a word of his past, his family, or the Lion Sword to a soul . . . mayhap to live a long an' happy life somewhere else." He leaned forward to clasp Elminster's forearm. "But ye could not do that an' still be an Aumar, prince of Athalantar. So ye will die in the trying." He shook his head again. "At least listen to me, then—an' wait until ye have a chance before letting anyone else in all Faerûn know ye live or ye'll not give one of the magelords more than a few minutes of cruel sport."

"They know of me?"

Helm gave him a pitying look. "Ye are a lamb to the ways of court, indeed. The wizard ye saw over Heldon doubtless had orders to eliminate Prince Elthryn an' all his blood before the son they knew he'd sired could grow old and well-trained enough to have royal ambitions of his own."

There was a little silence as the knight watched the youth grow pale. When the lad spoke again, however, Helm got another surprise.

"Sir Helm," Elminster said calmly, "Tell me the names of the magelords and ye can have my sheep."

Helm guffawed. "In faith, lad, I know them not—an' the others I run with'll have thy sheep whate'er befalls. I will give thee the names of thy uncles; ye'll need to know them."

Elminster's eyes flickered. "So tell."

"The eldest—thy chief enemy—is Belaur. A big, bellowing bully of a man, for all he's seen but nine-and-twenty winters. Cruel in the hunt and on the field, but the best trained to arms of all the princes. He's shorter of wits than he thinks he is, an' was Uthgrael's favorite until he showed his cruel ways an', o'er and o'er again, his short temper. He proclaimed himself king six summers ago, but many folk up and down the Delimbiyr don't recognize his title. They know what befell."

Elminster nodded. "And the second son?"

" 'Tis thought he's dead. Elthaun was a soft-tongued womanizer whose every third word was false. All the realm knew him for a master of intrigue, but he fled Hastarl a step ahead of Belaur's armsmen. The word is, some of the magelords found him in Calimshan later that year, hiding in a cellar in some city—an' used spells to make his death long and lingering."

"The third." Elminster was marking them off on his fingers; Helm grinned at that.

"Cauln was killed before Belaur claimed the throne. He was a sneaking, suspicious sort an' always liked watching wizards hurl fire an' the like. He fancied himself a wizard—an' was tricked into a spell duel by a mage commonly thought to be hired for the purpose by Elthaun. The mage turned Cauln into a snake—fitting—an' then burst him apart from within with a spell I've never recognized or heard named. Then the first magelords Belaur had brought in struck him down in turn, 'for the safety of the realm.' I recall them proclaiming 'Death for treason!' in the streets of Hastarl when the news was cried."

Helm shook his head. "Then came your father. He was always quiet an' insisted on fairness among nobles and common folk. The people loved him for that, but there was little respect for him at court. He retired to Heldon early on, an' most folk in Hastarl forgot him. I never knew Uthgrael thought highly of him—but that sword ye bear proves he did."

"Four princes, thus far," Elminster said, nodding as if to nail them down in memory. "The others?"

Helm counted on his own grubby fingers. "Othglas was next—a fat man full of jolly jests, who stuffed himself at feasts every night he could. He was stouter than a barrel an' could barely wheeze his way around on two feet. He liked to poison those who displeased him an' made quite a push through the ranks of those at court, downing foes an' any who so much as spoke a word aloud against him, and advancing his own supporters."

Elminster stared at him, frowning. "Ye make my uncles seem like a lot of villains."

Helm looked steadily back at him. "That was the common judgment up an' down the Delimbiyr, aye. I but report to ye what they did; if ye come to the same judgment as most folk did, doubtless the gods will agree with ye."

He scratched himself again, took a pull from his flask, and added, "When Belaur took the throne, his pet mages made it clear they knew what Othglas was up to an' threatened to put him to death before all the court for it. So he fled to Dalniir an' joined the Huntsmen, who worship Malar. I doubt the Beastlord has ever had so fat a priest before—or since."

"Does he still live?"

Helm shook his head. "Most of Athalantar knows what befell; the magelords made sure we all heard. They turned him into a boar during a hunt, an' he was slain by his own underpriests."

Elminster shuddered despite himself, but all he said was, "The next prince?"

"Felodar—the one who went off to Calimshan. Gold and gems are his love; he left the realm before Uthgrael died, seeking them. Wherever he went, he fostered trade betwixt there and here, pleasing the king very much—an' bringing Athalantar what little name an' wealth it has in Faerûn beyond the Delimbiyr valley today. I think the king'd have been less pleased if he'd known Felodar was raking in gold coins as fast as he could close his hands on them . . . trading in slaves, drugs, an' dark magic. He's still doing that, as far as I know, at least chin deep in the intrigues of Calimshan." Helm chuckled suddenly "He's even hired mages an' sent them here to work spells against Belaur's magelords."

"Not one to turn thy back on, for even a quick breath?" Elminster asked wryly, and Helm grinned and nodded.

"Last, there's Nrymm, the youngest. A timid, frail, sullen little brat, as I recall. He was brought up by women of the court after the queen's death, an' may never have stepped outside the gates of Athalgard in his life. He disappeared about four summers ago."

"Dead?"

Helm shrugged. "That, or held captive somewhere by the magelords so they have another blood heir of Uthgrael in their power should anything happen to Belaur."

Elminster reached for the flask; Helm handed it over. The youth drank carefully, sneezed once, and handed it back. He licked his lips, and said, "Ye don't make it sound a noble thing to be a prince of Athalantar."

Helm shrugged. "It's for every prince, himself, to make it a noble thing; a duty most princes these days seem to forget."

Elminster looked down at the Lion Sword, which had somehow found its way into his hands again. "What should I do now?"

Helm shrugged. "Go west, to the Horn Hills, and run with the outlaws there. Learn how to live hard, an' use a blade—an' kill. Your revenge, lad, isn't catching one mage in a privy an' running a sword up his backside—the gods have set ye up against far too many princes an' wizards an' hired lickspittle armsmen for that. Even if they all lined up and presented their behinds, your arm'd grow tired before the job was done."

He sighed and added, "Ye spoke truth when ye said it'll be your life's work. Ye have to be less the dreamy boy an' more the knight, an' somehow keep well clear of magelords until ye've learned how to stay alive more'n one battle, when the armsmen of Athalantar come looking to kill ye. Most of 'em aren't much in a fight—but right now, neither are ye. Go to the hills and offer your blade to the outlaws at least two winters. In the cities, everything is under the hand—an' the taint—of wizards. Evil rules, and good men must needs be outlaws—or corpses—if they're to stay good. So be ye an outlaw an' learn to be a good one." He did not quite smile as he added, "If ye survive, travel Faerûn until ye find a weapon sharp enough to slay Neldryn—and then come back, and do it."

"Slay who?"

"Neldryn Hawklyn—probably the most powerful of the magelords."

Elminster eyed him with sudden fire in his blue-gray eyes. "Ye said ye knew no names of magelords! Is this what a knight of Athalantar calls 'truth'?"

Helm spat aside, into the darkness. "Truth?" He leaned forward. "Just what is 'truth,' boy?"

Elminster frowned. "It is what it is," he said icily. "I know of no hidden meanings."

"'Truth,'" Helm said, "is a weapon. Remember that."

Silence hung between them for a long moment, and then Elminster said, "Right, I've learned thy clever lesson. Tell me then, O wise knight: how much else of all ye've said can I trust? About my father and my uncles?"

Helm hid a smile. When this lad's voice grew quiet, it betokened danger. No bluster about this one. He deserved a fair answer, well enough. The knight said simply, "All of it. As best I know. If ye're still hungry for names to work revenge on, add these to thy tally: Magelords Seldinor Stormcloak and Kadeln Olothstar—but I'd not know the faces of any of the three if I bumped noses with them in a brothel bathing pool."

Elminster regarded the unshaven, stinking man steadily. "Ye are not what I expected a knight of Athalantar to be."

Helm met his gaze squarely. "Ye thought to see shining armor, Prince? Astride a white horse as tall as a cottage? Courtly manners? Noble sacrifices? Not in this world, lad—not since the Queen of the Hunt died."

"Who?"

Helm sighed and looked away. "I forget ye know naught of your own realm. Queen Syndrel Hornweather; your granddam, Uthgrael's queen, an' mistress of all his stag hunts." He looked into the darkness, and added softly, "She was the most beautiful lady I've ever seen."

Elminster got up abruptly. "My thanks for this, Helm Stoneblade. I must be on my way before any of thy fellow wolves return from plundering Heldon. If the gods smile, we shall meet again."

Helm looked up at him. "I hope so, lad. I hope so—an' let it be when Athalantar is free of magelords again, an' my 'fellow wolves,' the true knights of Athalantar, can ride again."

He held out his hands. The flask was in one, and the bread in the other.

"Go west, to the Horn Hills," he said roughly, "an' take care not to be seen. Move at dusk an' dawn, and keep to fields and forest. Ware armsmen at patrol. Out there, they slay first, an' ask thy corpse its business after. Never forget: the blades the wizards hire are not knights; today's armsmen of Athalantar have no honor." He spat to one side thoughtfully and added, "If ye meet with outlaws, tell them Helm sent ye, an' ye're to be trusted."

Elminster took the bread and the flask. Their eyes met, and he nodded his thanks.

"Remember," Helm said, "tell no one thy true name—an' don't ask fool questions about princes or magelords, either. Be someone else 'til 'tis time."

Elminster nodded. "Have my trust, Sir Knight, and my thanks." He turned with all the gravity of his twelve winters and strode away to the mouth of the cavern.

The knight came after, grinning. Then he said, "Wait, lad—take my sword; ye'll need it. Best ye keep that hilt of thine out of sight."

The boy stopped and turned, trying not to show his excitement. A blade of his own! "What will ye use?" Elminster asked, taking the heavy, plain sword that the knight's dirty hands put into his. Buckles clinked and leather flapped, and a scabbard followed it.

Helm shrugged. "I'll loot me another. I'm supposed to serve any prince of the realm with my sword, so . . ."

Elminster smiled suddenly and swung the sword through the air, holding it with both hands. It felt reassuringly deadly; with it in his hands, he was powerful. He thrust at an imaginary foe, and the point of the blade lifted a little.

Helm gave him a fierce grin. "Aye—take it, and go!"

Elminster took a few steps out into the meadow . . . and then spun around and grinned back at the knight. Then he turned again to the sunlit meadow, the scabbarded blade cradled carefully in his hands, and ran.

Helm took a dagger from his belt and a stone from the floor, shook his head, and went out to kill sheep, wondering when he'd hear of the lad's death. Still, the first duty of a knight is to make the realm shine in the dreams of small boys—or where else will the knights of tomorrow arise, and what will become of the realm?

At that thought, his smile faded. What will become of Athalantar, indeed?

TWO
WOLVES IN WINTER

Know that the purpose of families, in the eyes of the Morninglord at least, is to make each generation a little better than the one before: stronger, perhaps, or wiser; richer, or more capable. Some folk manage one of these aims; the best and the most fortunate manage more than one. That is the task of parents. The task of a ruler is to make, or keep, a realm that allows most of its subjects to see better in their striving, down the generations, than a single improvement.

THORNDAR ERLIN, HIGH PRIEST OF LATHANDER
TEACHINGS OF THE MORNING'S GLORY
YEAR OF THE FALLEN FURY

He was huddled in the icy white heart of a swirling snowstorm, in the Hammer of Winter, that cruel month when men and sheep alike were found frozen hard and the winds howled and shrieked through the Horn Hills night and day, blowing snows in blinding clouds across the barren highlands. It was the Year of the Loremasters, though Elminster cared not a whit. All he cared about was that it was another cold season, his fourth since Heldon burned—and he was growing very weary of them.

A hand clapped him on one thick-clad shoulder. He patted it in reply. Sargeth had the keenest eyes of them all; his touch meant he'd spotted the patrol through the curtain of driving snow. El watched him reach the other way to pass on another warning. The six outlaws, bundled up in layers upon layers of stolen and corpse-stripped cloth until they looked like the fat and shuffling rag golems of fireside fear-tales, kicked their way out of the warmth of their snowbank, fumbled to draw blades with hands clad in thick-bound rags, and waddled down into the cleft.

Wind struck hard as they came down into the narrow space between the rocks, howling billowing snow around and past them. Engarl struggled to keep his feet as the wind tugged at the long lance he bore. He'd taken it from an armsman who'd needed it no more—Engarl had brought him down with a carefully slung stone before the leaves had started to fall.

The outlaws chose their spots, flopped down to kneel in the snows, and dug in. Snow streamed around and past them, and as they settled into stillness, it cloaked them in concealing whiteness, making them mere lumps and billows of snow in the storm.

"Gods *damn* all wizards!" The voice, borne by the winds, seemed startlingly close.

So did the reply. "None o' that. Ye know better than such talk."

"I might. My frozen feet don't. They'd much prefer to be next to a crackling fire, back in—"

"*All* of our feet'd rather be there. They will be, gods willing, soon enough. Swording outlaws'll warm ye, if ye're sharp-eyed enough to find any. Now belt up!"

"Perhaps," Elminster commented calmly, knowing the wind would sweep his words behind him, away from the armsmen, "the gods have other plans."

He could just hear an answering chuckle from off to his left: Sargeth. A moment more . . . Then he heard a sharp query, crunching snow, and the high whinny of a startled horse. The brothers had attacked. Arghel struck first, and then Baerold gave the call—from behind, if he could get there.

It came, a roar as much like the triumph-call of a wolf as Baerold could make it. Horses reared, cried out, and bucked in the deep snows on all sides. The patrol was on top of them.

Elminster rose up out of the snow like a vengeful ghost, sword drawn. To lie still could mean being ridden over and trampled. He saw a flicker of light through the whirling whiteness, as the nearest armsman drew steel.

A moment later, Engarl's awkwardly bobbing lance took the armsman in the throat. He choked, sobbed wetly around blood as the horse under him plunged on, and then he fell, head flopping, taking the lance with him. Elminster wasted no time on the dying man; another armsman off to the right in the swirling storm was trying to spur past him through the cleft.

El ran through the slithery snow as fast as he could, the way the outlaws had shown him, rocking comically from side to side to keep from slipping in the light drifts. All of the outlaws looked like drunken bears when they ran in deep snow. As slow as he was, the horse was even slower; its hooves were slipping in the potholes that marked the trail here, and it danced and stamped for footing, nearly tossing its rider.

The armsman saw Elminster and leaned forward to hack the outlaw. Elminster ducked back, let the blade sing past, and charged in at the man's leg, clawing with one hand as he blocked a return of the man's blade with the edge of his own.

The overbalanced man in armor howled in rising despair, waved his free arm wildly in a vain attempt to find a handhold in empty air—and crashed heavily from his saddle, bouncing in the snow at Elminster's feet. El drove his blade into the man's neck while the spray of snow still shielded the man's face, shuddered as the man spasmed under his steel, and then flopped back into the snow, limp. Four years ago he'd discovered he had no love of killing . . . and it hadn't grown much easier since.

Yet it was slay or be slain out here in the outlaw-haunted hills; Elminster sprang away from the man, glancing about in the confusion of swirling snows and muffled tumult of churning hooves.

There was a grunt, a roar of pain, and the heavy thudding of body and armor striking snow-cloaked ground off to the left, followed by a wail that ended abruptly. Elminster shuddered again, but kept his blade up warily. This was when outlaws who'd grown tired of their fellows sometimes decided to make a mistake, under the cloak of the storming snow, and bring down someone who was not an armsman of Athalantar.

El expected no such treachery from his companions . . . but only the gods knew the hearts of men. Like most in the Horn Hills—those who revered Helm Stoneblade and hated the magelords, at least—this band made no war on common folk. Not wanting to bring down the wrath of the wizards on farmers whose stable straw sometimes served as warm beds and whose frozen and forgotten pot roots could be dug up by men near starvation, the outlaws avoided their neighbors out here in the hills. Even so, they had learned never to trust them. The armsmen of Athalantar paid fifty pieces of gold per head to folk who'd guide them to outlaws. More than one outlaw had been taken by trusting overmuch.

The cold lesson was to trust nothing that lived, from birds and foxes whose alarmed flight could draw the eyes of patrols, to peddlers who might go after the gold and speak of fires or watching men they'd seen deep in the hills where outlaws were known to lurk.

Sargeth strode up through the endless fall of snow, which drifted straight down now as there came a sudden lull in the winds. He was grinning through the cloud of vapor that curled about his mouth. "All dead, El: a dozen armsmen . . . and one of them was carrying a full pack of food!"

Elminster, called Eladar among the outlaws, grunted. "No mages?"

Sargeth chuckled and laid a hand on El's arm. He left bloody marks—the gore of some armsman now lying still in the snows. "Patience," he said. "If it's wizards you want to kill, let us slay enough armsmen—and by all the gods, the mages will come."

Elminster nodded. "Anything else?" Around them, the wind screamed with fresh strength, and it was hard to see through the driven snow.

"One horse hurt. We'll butcher it and wrap it in their cloaks here. Haste, now; the wolves are as hungry as we. Engarl's found a dozen daggers or more—and at least one good helm. Baerold's collecting boots, as usual. Go you and help Nind with the cutting."

Elminster sniffed. "Blood work, as always."

Sargeth laughed and clapped him on the back. "We all have to do it to live. Look upon it as preparing yerself several good feasts, and try not to gnaw on too much raw meat as you usually do . . . unless you *like* icing yer backside in the snow and feeling kitten weak, that is."

Elminster grunted and headed through the snow where Sargeth pointed. A happy shout jerked his head around. It was Baerold, leading back a snorting horse by the reins. Good; it could drag their spoils some way before they would have to kill it to end the trail its hooves would leave.

Around them, the whistle of the wind began to die, and with it the snowfall faltered. Curses came from all around; the outlaws knew they'd have to work fast indeed if it turned cold and clear—for even the weak wizards posted to the keeps out here had magic that could find them from afar when the weather was clear.

By the favor of the gods, another squall came in soon after they left the cleft; even someone already tracking them wouldn't be able to follow. The outlaws struggled on, following Sargeth and Baerold, who knew every slope of the hills here even in blinding snows. When they came to the deep spring that never froze, a place they knew the wizards watched by magic, from afar, Baerold spoke a few soothing words to the horse—and then swung his forester's axe with brutal strength, and leaped clear of its kicking hooves as it fell.

The outlaws left the steaming remnants of the carcass for the wolves to find. Then they rolled in deep drifts to clean off the worst of the gore and went on. North into the driving storm, up ravines narrow and dark, to Wind Cavern, where icy breezes moaned endlessly into a lightless cleft. Each man in turn bent and ducked through the narrow opening, by memory crossed the uneven cave beyond, and found the faint glowstone rock that marked the mouth of the next passage. They walked into the hollow dark until they saw the faint light ahead of another glowstone. Sargeth tapped the wall of the passage slowly and deliberately six times, paused, and then tapped once more. There came an answering tap, and Sargeth took two steps and turned into an unseen side passage. The outlaws followed him into the narrow tunnel. It smelled of earth and damp stone, and descended steeply beneath the Horn Hills.

Light grew somewhere ahead, ale-hued faint light from a cavernful of luminous fungi. As they came out into it, Sargeth said his name calmly to the darkness beyond, and the men who stood there set down their crossbows and replied. "All back safe?"

"All safe—and with meat to roast," Sargeth said triumphantly.

"Horse," a second voice asked sourly, "or chopped armsman?"

They exchanged chuckles before proceeding down another passage, through a cavern where daggers of rock jutted from floor and ceiling like the frozen jaws of some great monster, to a shaft in which vivid red light glowed. A stout ladder led down the hole into a large cavern always wreathed in steam. The light and the vapor came from rocky clefts at its far end, where folk sat huddled in blankets or lay snoring. With each step, the dank air grew warmer until the weary warriors stood beside the scalding waters of the hot spring and welcoming hands reached up to pat or clasp theirs. They were home, in the place proudly called Lawless Castle.

It was a good place, furnished with heaped blankets and old cloaks. Dwarves had shown it to Helm Stoneblade long ago, and from time to time the outlaws still found firewood, prepared torches, or cases of quarrels left in the deeper side passages, next to the privies the outlaws used. The wrinkled old outlaw woman Mauri had told El once that they'd never seen the dwarves, "But they want us here. The Stout Folk like anything that weakens the wizards, for they see their doom in men growing overstrong. . . . We already outbreed them like rabbits, an' if ever we o'ermatch elven magic, they'll be staring at their graves. . . ."

Now she looked up through her warts and bristles at the arriving band, grinned toothlessly at them, and said, "Food, valiant warriors?"

"Aye," Engarl joked, "and when we've feasted, we'll give ye some to replace it." He chuckled at his jest, but the dozen or so ragged outlaws awake around them only snorted sourly in reply; they'd no food left but four shriveled potatoes Mauri had kept safe in the filthy folds of her gargantuan bosom for the last two days, and had taken to chewing on the bitter glow-fungi to still aching stomachs while they waited for one of the bands to bring back meat.

Now they hustled to get a fire going and drag out the cooking frame of rusting sword blades woven together in a rough square. The band stamped the last snows from their boots and unwrapped their bloody bundles. Mauri leaned forward, slapping outlaw hands away to see what had been brought to her table.

Sargeth's band was the best; all of them knew that. El, the worst blade in it but the fastest on his feet, was glad to be a part of it and kept silent when his fellows fought or blustered. They were too cold and exhausted most of the winters to afford dispute among themselves. Once a wizard had found Wind Cavern and died in a hail of crossbow quarrels—but otherwise, Elminster had seen the hated mages of Athalantar little in the passing years; the outlaws struck at patrols of armsmen so often that the magelings had stopped riding with them.

A smiling, red-bearded rogue they all knew as Javal blew to make the fire catch and said with satisfaction, "We caught another two coming from Daera's earlier this night."

"That'd best be enough for a time," Sargeth grunted in reply as he and his companions shed gauntlets, headgear, and the heaviest of the furs and scraps of scavenged leather they wore, "or they'll think her night-comfort lasses are working with us an' burn them out, or lie ready with a mage to work our own trap on us."

Javal's smile went away. He made a face and nodded slowly. "Ye see the right road as usual, Sar."

Sargeth merely grunted and held his hands to the growing warmth of the kindling fire. Armsmen from Heldreth's Horn, the outermost fortress of Athalantar, had gone out to buy the favors of village lasses for as long as the keep had stood. A dozen summers back, some maids had converted an old farm into a house of pleasure and sold their guests wildflower wine besides; the outlaws had slain more than a few armsmen riding home from there drunken and alone. "Aye, 'tis best we leave the lustlorn alone for a time, an' catch 'em again in spring."

"What, and leave them to slay and pillage until spring? How many more warriors can you afford to lose?"

The wizard's voice was cold—colder than the chill battlements where they stood, looking out over the ice-cloaked waters of the Unicorn Run. The swordmaster of Sarn Torel spread strong, hairy hands and said helplessly, "None, Lord Mage. That's why I dare send no more—every man who rides west out of here's going to his death and knows it. They're *that* close to open defiance now ... and I've the law to keep in the streets here, too. If caravan merchants and peddlers are fool enough to go from realm to realm in the deep snows, let 'em look to their own hides, I say—and leave the bandits to freeze in the Hills without our swords to entertain 'em."

The wizard's gaze then was even colder than his voice had been.

The swordmaster quailed inwardly and firmly took hold of the stone merlon in front of him to keep from stepping back a pace or two and showing his fear. He dropped his own gaze to the frozen moss clinging to cracks and chips in the stone and wished he were somewhere else. Somewhere warmer, where they'd never heard of wizards.

"I do not recall the king asking for your view of your duties—though I've no doubt he'll be most interested to find how . . . creatively . . . they cleave from his own," came the mage's voice, silken soft now.

The swordmaster forced himself to turn and stare into dark eyes that glittered with malice. "'Tis *your* wish then, Lord Mage," he asked, stressing the word just enough that the wizard would know that the swordmaster thought the king a wiser warrior than all his strutting magelords, and would have no such view of his swordmaster's prudence, "that I send more armsmen to patrol from the Horn?"

The wizard hesitated, then as softly as before, asked, "Let me know *your* wish, Swordmaster. Perhaps we can come to some agreement."

The swordmaster took a deep breath and held those dark, deadly eyes with his own. "Send to the Horn a cutter full of mages, apprentices even, providing that one mage of experience commands them. Twenty armsmen—all I dare spare—ride with them to the Horn, and from there act as necessary to hunt these outlaws with magic and destroy them."

They stared at each other for a long, chill moment, and then, slowly, Magelord Kadeln Olothstar smiled—thinly, but the swordmaster had wondered if the man knew how. "A stout plan, indeed, Swordmaster. I *knew* we could agree on something this day." He looked north over the snow-clad farms across the river for a moment, then added, "I hope a suitable sledge can be speedily found rather than one that comes not or must be built and finds us still preparing come spring."

The swordmaster pointed down over the battlements with one gauntleted hand. "See the logs there by the mill? One of those cutters beneath 'em can be free by tonight, and a pair of the huts we use to cover the wells lashed atop it before morn."

The wizard smiled softly, a snake contemplating prey that cannot escape. "Then in the morn they'll set out. You shall have twelve mages, Swordmaster— one of them Magelord Landorl Valadarm."

The warrior nodded, wondering privately whether Landorl was a fumbling dolt or someone who had simply earned Kadeln's displeasure. He hoped for the latter. Then this Landorl might at least be useful if the gods-cursed outlaws attacked the cutter.

The two men smiled tightly at each other, there on the battlements, and then both turned their backs deliberately to show they dared to and strode slowly away with a show of casual unconcern. Their every step told the world they were strong men, free of all fear.

The battlements of Sarn Torel stood still and silent, unimpressed, as they would stand when both men were long in their graves. It takes a lot to impress a castle wall.

Elminster was happily blowing on scorched fingers, licking the last scraps of horseflesh from them, when one of the watchers burst into the cavern and gasped out, "Patrol! Found the way in—killed Aghelyn, an' prob'ly more. Some o' them ran straight back to tell where we lair!"

All over the cavern men swore and scrambled to their feet, shouting. Sargeth cut through the din with a bellow. "Crossbows and blades; all but Mauri. The lads and the wounded, stand guard in the glowcavern—all others with me, *now!*"

As they ran through the darkness, swearing and ringing their weapons off the unseen stone in their haste, Sargeth added, "Brerest! Eladar! Try to get clear of the fight here and go after those who're running back to the wizards—you're the fastest afoot of all here old enough to swing a real blade. I need those armsmen *all* dead—or *we* will be."

"Aye," Elminster and Brerest panted, and went through the mouth of Wind Cavern in a roll. The quarrel that sought their lives hissed past and struck the rock within easy reach of Sargeth's head. The second one missed entirely—but Elminster came to a stop behind a snow-cloaked boulder in time to see the third take Sargeth in the eye, and drive him back like a crumpled bag of bones, to slide down the rock wall, twitching.

Elminster laid his drawn dagger beside him in the snow, snatched up the old, mended crossbow that had fallen from Sargeth's hands, and cranked at it for all he was worth. The windlass clattered loudly, but outlaws were rushing past and firing their own bows now, and shouts told him that some of their bolts were finding their marks.

Loaded at last. "Tempus aid my aim," Elminster murmured, scratching his finger on his dagger tip until blood came to seal the prayer to the war god. Then he laid the ready bow down, whipped off the helm he wore, and waved it on one side of the boulder.

A quarrel hissed past. Elminster scooped up the bow and was around the boulder in an instant. As he'd expected, the armsman was standing to watch his target die—so Elminster had a clear shot at his face, past a knot of howling, hacking outlaws and coolly slaying armsmen.

El aimed carefully—and missed. Cursing, he leaped back—but Brerest came past him with a loaded crossbow of his own, set himself, and fired carefully.

The armsman had started to turn away, seeking cover. His face sprouted a quarrel, his head spun around, and he staggered back and fell.

Elminster threw down his bow, snatched up his dagger, and sprinted through the snow, dodging desperately fighting men. He was still a few hard-running paces short of the first rock large enough to shelter behind when an armsman rose from behind the second rock, ready crossbow in hand, to aim into the fray in front of the cavern. Seeing Elminster, he swung his weapon around hurriedly. There was no way he could miss.

Elminster skidded to a desperate stop, then changed direction and dived into the nearest snowbank. He landed hard in a flurry of snow, slid across unseen smooth rock, and flipped over, expecting to feel the thump of death striking home at any moment.

It didn't come. El wiped snow from his face and looked up.

Brerest or one of the other outlaws had been lucky The armsman was curled over the top of his rock, barehanded and groaning, a shaft through his shoulder.

"Thankee, Tempus," Elminster said with feeling, took two running steps, and flung himself right over the top of the first boulder, heels first, to crash down on whomever might be there. The armsman was on his knees, struggling with a jammed windlass; Elminster's landing smashed him to the ground like a rag doll, and El dragged his dagger across the man's throat a breath later. "For Elthryn, prince of Athalantar!" he whispered, and found himself blinking back sudden tears as his father's face came to mind.

Not *now*, he told himself desperately, and ran on toward the next boulder. The wounded man saw him and struggled to get aside, groaning. Elminster drove his dagger home and snarled, "For Amrythale, his princess!" Then he ducked down, scooped up the man's loaded bow from where it had fallen—and looked up in time to fire it into another armsman, who had just risen from cover with a spear in his hand. Ahead, another armsman took an outlaw quarrel in the hand, screamed, and fell back behind his rock, sobbing.

The clash of arms back by the cavern had ceased. El risked a look back and saw only dead men. They lay in bloody heaps in front of the cavern . . . and just a few paces away lay Brerest, both hands clutching forever at a quarrel that stood out of his heart.

Gods! Sargeth and Brerest both . . . and everyone, if those armsmen got word back to the wizards. How many armsmen were there? Four dead, for sure, Elminster thought as he ran forward, crouching low, plus all those by the cavern. The hail of quarrels hissing up and down the ravine had ceased—was everyone dead?

No, the sobbing armsman and perhaps two more lay ahead, somewhere in these rocks. There had to be at least two patrols here, and they'd not have sent more than three from each patrol—perhaps only three in all—to report to the wizards. To have any hope of catching them, he had to find the horses these'd come on, and . . . of course! Some of the missing armsmen, two at least, were holding the horses below.

Elminster crawled around the boulder, keeping low, and took four daggers and a spear from the two dead men. An outlaw quarrel hissed out of the cavern and almost took him from behind; he sighed and crawled on in the snow.

He had almost reached the sobbing armsman when another rose from behind a rock to aim carefully at the cavern mouth. Elminster cast the spear; it was in the air before the man caught sight of him.

The armsman didn't have time to change his aim. His bow hurled a quarrel harmlessly down the ravine as the spear took him in the breast, plucking him away from his rock, and flung him back to crash down on his shoulders in the snow, bouncing and arching in agony.

Elminster's charge took him onto the armsman's bloody chest, and he stabbed down again with his bloody dagger. "For Elthryn, prince of Athalantar!" he snarled as he dealt death, and the warrior under his knees managed a startled look before all light fled from behind his eyes.

Elminster flung himself aside in a roll. Quarrels and spears from both ends of the ravine crossed in the air above the dead warrior where he'd been kneeling. Scrabbling in the snow, Elminster slew the man who was still clutching his bleeding hand. "For my mother, Amrythale!"

Panting, he took up the man's bow and ducked behind a rock to catch his breath and ready the weapon. His boots bristled with spare daggers now, and the bow was soon loaded. He crouched low, cradled it in his arms, and came around the last rock with his finger on the trigger.

No one was there. Elminster stood frozen for a moment, and then knelt down. Another outlaw quarrel hummed past to fall into the empty snows below the ravine. El watched it go, and then looked up. He could climb the shoulder of the ravine and from above see where the armsmen had gone; the snow had stopped falling and the wind had died, leaving the hills around white and smooth with fresh-fallen snow

Everyone could see him as he climbed, too, aye—but then, Tyche put a little hazard into everyone's life.

Elminster sighed as he plucked the quarrel from its groove and slid it down into one of his boots. He left the bow cocked as he slung it across his back by the carry strap and scrambled up the slope.

He'd not climbed more than his own height before a quarrel tore into the snow a handspan away from his head. El snatched at it, kicked himself free of the snowy rocks and frozen grass, and slid back down the slope, feigning lifelessness. The quarrel came with him as he crashed on his face in the snow, trying to keep his bow unbroken.

Tears blinded him for a moment, but his nose didn't seem broken. He blinked them away and spat out snow while he slid the bow free. It was unbroken; he loaded it, emitting a drawn out rattling groan to cover the sounds he made.

An armsman with a second crossbow ready rose out of a snowy thicket nearby, looking for the man he'd hit. He and Elminster saw each other at the same instant. Both fired. And both missed. Elminster found his feet as the quarrel sang past him—would he *forever* be running around this ravine, panting and slipping?—snatched daggers from his boots, and ran toward the thicket, blades flashing in both fists. He was afraid the warrior had a third bow cocked and ready. . . .

He was right. The armsman rose again with a triumphant smile on his face—and Elminster flung a dagger at him. The man's smile tightened in fear, and he fired in haste.

The quarrel leaped at Elminster, who flung himself desperately over backward. As he fell, his knife met the quarrel with a clang and a spark. The dagger spun wildly away, and the quarrel burned past Elminster, ripping open his chin and thrusting his head around.

El roared in pain and fell on his knees, hearing the crunching of the armsman's boots behind him as the warrior came running. Elminster turned, shaking his head to clear it and growling at the pain. The man was scant paces away, sword raised to slay, when El flung the dagger in his other hand into the man's face.

It clanged harmlessly off the nose guard of the armsman's helm, but the man's swing missed the diving youth, the sword striking the snowy ground and the rocks beneath. The warrior roared and fell heavily on top of Elminster's left hand.

Elminster screamed. Gods, the *pain!* The man rolled about atop his hand, kicking at the snow to get a grip with his boots. Elminster sobbed, and the world turned green and yellow and swam fuzzily. He grabbed at his belt with his free hand. Nothing there. The man grunted; Elminster felt the hot breath of the armsman turning to face him and bring his blade down. His weight drove the hidden bulk of the Lion Sword, on its thong, bruisingly into Elminster's chest.

Desperate, Elminster tore at the throat of his jerkin. His fingers found the hilt of the sword. Over long nights in his first winter in the hills, he'd sharpened the broken stub of the blade until it had a keen, raw edge and point—but beyond the quillons, the weapon wasn't even as long as his hand. Its puny length saved him now. As the armsman's face glared into his, inches away, and his elbow swept his sword up for a gutting thrust, Elminster thrust the Lion Sword up and into his eye.

"For Elthryn, prince of Athalantar!" he hissed—and as the hot rush of blood drenched him, found himself sinking into red, wet darkness. . . .

He was floating somewhere dark and still. Whispers rose and fell around him, half-heard through a slow, rhythmic thudding. . . . Elminster felt the pain of his hand and an answering ache all around. In his head? Yes, and the white glow was rising and pulsing, now—the one he saw when he gathered his mind. The glow grew, and the pain lessened.

Ah, *thus!* Elminster *pushed* with his mind, and the white radiance faded. He felt a little tired, but the pain receded . . . he pushed again, and again felt weaker, but now the pain was almost gone.

So. He could push pain aside. Could he truly heal himself? Elminster bent his will . . . and suddenly all his aches and hurts returned, and he could feel cold, hard ground beneath his shoulders, and the wet stickiness of sweat all over. From the place of whispers, he swam up, up, and burst out into the light.

The sky was blue and cloudless overhead. Elminster lay on his back on snowy rocks, stiff, cold, and aching. Gingerly, he rolled to one side and looked around. No sign of anyone or any movement—good, because his head swam and pounded and he had to duck down again to catch his breath. The darkness again rushed up to claim him . . . and it felt so good, his head so heavy. . . .

A little later, he rolled over. Snow vultures flapped heavily into the air, circled over the ravine, and squalled complaints at him.

The last armsman lay dead beside him, the Lion Sword in his face. Elminster winced at the sight, but put his hand to the blade, turned his head away, and pulled it free. Wiping it in the snow, he squinted at the dimming sky—steel-gray now, with the last light of day ebbing behind full clouds—and got up. He had a task to finish if he wanted to live.

He felt weak and a little numb. Down the ravine in the open space in front of the Wind Cavern, eight or more armsmen and more than twice that many outlaws lay dead, quarrels protruding from most of the still forms. The vultures were circling overhead, and wolves would be here soon. Hopefully they'd find enough to feed on without entering the caves, where the weak would guard until armsmen came to hack them down. He'd have to slay more armsmen to prevent that . . . and he was getting sick of killing. El grinned weakly as he went down the ravine, averting his eyes from the sprawled dead he passed. Some brave outlaw warrior he was!

At the mouth of the ravine was a large trampled area trailing off into tracks of horses coming and leaving. The armsmen must have given their fellows up for dead. Elminster's shoulders sagged. He couldn't outrun horses in this deep snow. He and the other survivors were doomed . . . unless he gathered all the bows and blades he could, took them to the last outlaws waiting in the darkness, and made the caves a deathtrap for the armsmen. Still, some would survive to identify the lair for later forays, and besides, what if they began by hurling a fire spell into the caves? No.

Elminster flopped down onto a boulder to think. His sudden descent saved his life; a crossbow quarrel hummed just over his head to vanish into a snowbank close by. The youngest prince of Athalantar—perhaps the *last* prince of Athalantar—dived hastily off his boulder into the snow, face first, and floundered about in the chilly stuff until he was huddled behind the rock. He peered up whence the bolt had come.

Sure enough. High on the shoulder of the ridge, overlooking the ravine, was one armsman. They'd left one behind to pin the outlaws in their lair—or track them if they burst out in numbers. Of course—that was why so many of the outlaws wore crossbow quarrels!

Elminster sighed. Some crafty woods-warrior *he* was. Well, this armsman's horse would be somewhere just below him, around the other side of the ridge. If he could get to it and ride out of bowshot, in time . . .

Aye, and frogs might fly, too . . . Elminster frowned and tried to recall where the crossbows had fallen. That last armsman, who'd almost slain him . . . yes! He'd had three bows, and dropped them *all* after firing—in that thicket, there! El sighed once, and then started to crawl on his belly in the snow. A quarrel hissed past him again—close, but hopefully there'd be no time for a second shot.

"Tempus and Tyche aid me; I feel the need of both of ye," Elminster muttered, hurrying in the cold powdery snow. And then he was in the thicket, crouching low as a third crossbow bolt rattled snow off the trunks around him, cracked against a sapling, and fell broken into the snow somewhere off to the left. How different battle was from what the traveling minstrels sang about!

That thought brought him to the first and second bows, lying in deep snow. They were wet—but if the gods smiled would still fire true until they dried; they'd doubtless twist a bit then. A belt-box and the scattered quarrels it had held were strewn beside the bows.

Elminster calmly worked the dead man's windlass. From the ridge above, he could hear the faint clatter of the living armsman's own bow-winch. The third bow lay fallen a few paces in front of the thicket; Elminster didn't dare go out to get it. When both bows were loaded and full-ready, Elminster started to worm his way sideways in the thicket.

A quarrel dusted snow from a tree back where he'd been. Elminster grinned tightly and stepped forward for a good look. The armsman had just bobbed down to get his second bow. El set down one of his own and raised the other, aimed at where the man had sunk out of view

The moment he saw movement there, he fired.

Tyche was with him. The man rose right into the path of the quarrel; Elminster heard his startled gasp, saw him throw his hands up, and watched the man's crossbow crash and cartwheel down the snow-clad slope into the ravine. A moment later, thudding heavily, the body of the armsman followed it.

Elminster unloaded his second bow, fired it empty to leave its workings loose, then snatched up all three bows and the belt-box of quarrels and hurried around the ridge.

There was the horse—alone and unguarded, thank the gods! In a few breaths, Elminster had tied his gear to a seemingly endless collection of saddle straps and thongs, and was in the saddle, urging the patrol mount to follow the armsmen's trail. It went willingly enough, but slipped and slid in the snow in something a little faster than a trot and a lot slower than a gallop. The tracks ahead were clear and easy to follow so Elminster kicked his heels at the horse's flanks and urged it on. He had to get to Heldreth's Horn before any wizard there caught sight of him by some sort of scrying spell and dealt death from afar.

Soon he was riding hard, the crossbows bouncing bruisingly at his back, and the mist of his breath streaming back behind him into the darkening air. Night was coming down fast over the hills. He had to succeed; the lives of the outlaws trapped back at Lawless Castle depended on it.

As he rode, he smiled at a sudden memory: his father's careful lessons on the duty of every man and maid in the kingdom, from farmer to king. If Elthryn had dwelt longer on the duties of king and prince than on those of a farmer or miller, Elminster had thought this only right—the duties were so much grander, the power mightier, the responsibilities heavier than those of all others. He'd not for a moment suspected that he was a prince or would become one when Elthryn died. He recalled clearly his father's words: "A king's first duty is to his subjects. Their lives are *in* his hands, and he must always look to their brightest, surest future in what he does. All depend on him—and all are lost if he neglects his duties, or governs by whim or willful heart. Obedience is his due, aye, but he must earn loyalty. Some kings never learn this. And what are princes but young willful lads learning to be kings?"

"What indeed, Father?" Elminster asked the wind of his passing as he rode hard for the Horn. The wind did not deign to reply.

THREE
ALL TOO MUCH DEATH
IN THE SNOWS

If in winter ye walk
When snow is deep
Beware when ye talk—
For afar echoes creep.

OLD SWORD COAST SNOW-RUNE

Tyche, at least, had heard his prayers. As Elminster rode down a dusky valley along the clear trail the armsmen had left, he caught sight of them gathered below, building fires—and the trails in the snow made it clear they'd met with and joined another patrol instead of going down to the keep . . . which was still a good ride away. Night would find them very soon, deep in the hills, and they'd halted to make camp.

"Thankee, Tyche," El told the wind wryly, as he pulled his weary mount to a halt. All his foes were gathered together and would soon halt within his reach.

As with all the gifts of Lady Luck, this one was double-edged. All he had to do was kill the five armsmen who'd fled from Lawless Castle—and *all* the others they'd met with down there. For a fleeting moment, he wished he were some great mage to send swift death screaming down upon the gathered camp below—or to ride a dragon down to rake, burn, and scatter.

Elminster shivered at that memory of Heldon and touched the Lion Sword where it rode on its thong inside his jerkin. "Prince Elminster is a *warrior*," he told the wind with grand dignity—and then chuckled. More soberly, he added, "He kills a man to warm up, helps cut up his horse and eat it, and then goes out into a battle and slaughters eight more. As if that's not enough, he's now about to sweep down alone on a score or more ready-armed armsmen. What else could he be but a warrior?"

"A fool, of course," a cold voice answered from very near. Elminster whirled around in his saddle. A dark-robed man was standing watching him—standing on empty air, booted feet well above the unbroken snow.

El's hand stabbed to his belt, found one of the salvaged daggers he'd thrust there, and hurled it. It spun end over end, flashing as it caught the light of the newly kindled campfires below, and plunged straight through the man to bury itself deep in the snows beyond.

Only half the man's mouth smiled. "This is but a spell-image, fool," he said coldly. "You come riding hard, following the trail to our camp—who are you and why come you here?"

Elminster frowned, feigning ignorance as his thoughts raced. "Have I reached Athalantar yet?" He eyed the mage and added, "I seek a magelord, to pass on a message. Are ye such a one?"

"Unfortunately for you, I am," the man replied, "*Prince* Elminster. Oh, yes, I heard your proud little speech. You are Elthryn's son, then, the one we've been seeking."

Elminster sat very still, thinking. Could a wizard send a spell through his image? A cold inner voice answered: Why not?

Best keep moving, in case . . . He urged the horse with his knees until it trotted ahead, then turned it, circling. "That is the name I have taken to bring doom down on a certain magelord," he said, passing the image. It turned in the air and watched him in easy silence. Hmmm . . .

"Other magelords," Elminster added darkly, "have plans of their own."

The watching wizard laughed. "Well, of *course* they do, boastful boy—always have had. See me shiver at your sinister words? Do you dance and play cards, too?"

Elminster felt himself flush with anger. To ride so hard only to be taunted by a wizard from afar while armsmen no doubt rode out to encircle him and bring him down at leisure . . . He spurred away from the wizard, flinging only the calm reply, "Yes, *of course* I do," over his shoulder as he went.

He rode hard back the way he'd come but turned up the nearest easy slope to gain a height to look back. The wizard's image hadn't moved—but as he watched, it winked out and was gone, leaving behind only the circle of beaten snow where he'd ridden around it. Aye, there, below—two bands of mounted armsmen were setting out, riding hard in different directions to curve about and ring him in with swords and bows.

Full night was falling, but the stars were bright overhead, and Selûne would rise all too soon. How far could that wizard see him?

Two plans sprang to mind: somehow ride wide around them all on his weary mount and sweep down on the camp, hoping to find the wizard and take him with quarrels before he could loose a spell. That's what a bard or teller-of-tales would expect him to do, to be sure. It sounded the work of a reckless fool even to his own ears.

The other plot was to get into the path of one band, dig into the snow with all his bows ready, and let his horse run free. If one band of armsmen followed it—he'd have time, perhaps, to take those coming toward him down with his bows, somehow get one of their mounts, and *then* attack the camp. Then, somehow victorious over a wizard who knew he was coming, he'd set forth on the trail of the other armsmen and take them down one by one with quarrels . . . it sounded almost as wild.

He quoted a line of a ballad he'd once heard, "Princes rush in, shouldering fools aside, and find glory," and turned his horse to the right to intercept the band of armsmen he could see better. He thought he counted nine riders, no telling how many were in the other group.

His tired horse stumbled twice on the ride and nearly fell when they blundered into a pocket of deep, loose snow.

"Gently," El murmured to it, suddenly feeling his own aches and weariness in full. All he could do in his mind was numb the pain for a time, and—he touched his chin thoughtfully—stop bleeding. He was no invincible warrior.

So? This attack required a fool, not an invincible warrior . . . but then, riding away would be a fool's act, too, without even the comfort of standing up for the memory of his mother and father and for a day when wizards would not rule Athalantar, and the knights would ride again. . . .

"The knights *will* ride again," he told the wind; it whirled his words away unheard behind him as he came to a good place for the ambush he planned, a narrow gully on the lee slope of a snow-swept rise, and brought his horse to a halt.

Getting down stiffly—he'd not been on a horse much since Heldon burned, and his legs were reminding him of that all too sharply—El unslung his bows and took what he'd need. "Grant me luck," he told the wind, but as before, it made no reply. Taking a deep breath of the sharp air, he slapped the horse's rump and roared. The beast bolted, paused to look back, and then trotted off into the snow. Elminster was alone in the night.

Not for long, by the gods. Nine armsmen in full armor were riding this way, after his blood. Elminster knelt in the snow just below the crest of the rise and worked his windlass like a frenzied-wits.

By the time he had all three bows loaded and ready, he was gasping for breath and could hear the creak of leather and jangle of metal on the wind. The armsmen were coming down upon him. Lying in the snow, breath streaming back over his shoulder, he arranged the bows, planted four daggers in the snow for ready snatching, and waited.

His life hung on the hope that they'd not have bows ready themselves—and wouldn't see him in time. Elminster shook his head at his own recklessness and found his mouth suddenly dry. Well, whatever befell, it wouldn't be long now.

There was a sudden thunder of hooves, shouts, and the clash of arms. What could be—? And suddenly Elminster had no time for speculation as an armsman burst into view, galloping hard, crouched low over the neck of his horse. The prince of Athalantar raised his bow carefully, steadied it, and fired.

The horse plunged on, rearing and giving a high grunt of alarm as it saw the steep descending slope. With no time to veer or slow, it felt the man on its back fall sideways, hard, pulling on its reins. It reared, fighting the reins that were tugging its head around. Its hooves skidded in the snow, and it crashed atop its rider. Together they slid down the hill. The horse sprang up and pranced away, shaking its head as if to clear it. The man lay still in the trampled snow.

No more horsemen rode into view, and from over the brow of the snow-clad rise came the shouts and steely skirl of battle. Elminster frowned in puzzlement, and then took up his daggers, thrusting them back into his belt. Holding his second bow ready, he advanced cautiously until he could see over the crest.

Mounted men were circling and hacking at each other in the nightgloom atop the hill. One group was clad in motley garb, the odds and ends of half a hundred mismatched armors it seemed, and where by all the gods had they come from? The other group were armsmen, outnumbered more than two to one and fast losing. As Elminster watched, one soldier of Athalantar broke free of the fray, spurring his horse desperately, and set off across the hills at a gallop.

The prince of Athalantar set his feet in the snow, raised his bow, and fired. The quarrel passed over the armsman's shoulder, and fleeing warrior galloped on. Elminster cursed and ran back for his third bow. Scooping it up, he sprinted along the edge of the hill. The distant armsman was smaller now, but coming into clear view as his horse climbed the unbroken snow of the next slope. Elminster aimed carefully, fired—and saw his quarrel speed true.

The armsman threw up his arms, tried to clutch at his back with both hands, and fell out of his saddle. The horse went on without him.

"I didn't *think* we had any bowmen with us, this night!"

Elminster turned in delighted recognition at that cheery voice. "Helm!"

The leather-jawed knight wore the same tattered leather armor, rusty gauntlets, dented helm, and stubbly beard El remembered—and probably, by the smell of him, hadn't taken them off or washed any part of him since that day on the meadow above Heldon. He rode a mean-looking black horse that was as scarred as its rider, and the long, curved sword in his fist was nicked and shining darkly with fresh blood.

"How came you here?" Elminster asked, grinning with the sudden hope that he might not die this night after all.

The knight of Athalantar leaned forward in his saddle. "We've just come from Lawless Castle," he said with raised brows. "Quite a few good men lying dead back there, but Mauri couldn't find Eladar among them."

"When I ran out of armsmen to kill, I came here," Elminster replied gravely. "They'd found the castle, and I had to slay the rest before they had a chance to report it. They went to a camp—those fires, there—and there's another band of armsmen, probably larger than this one, over there somewhere." He pointed into the night. "They were circling to take me."

Helm bellowed, "Onthrar! *To me!*" over his shoulder, and then said, "Join us, then, an' we'll ride 'em down together There're empty saddles in plenty to spare!"

Elminster shook his head. "My business lies yonder," he said, pointing with a nod of his head toward the unseen camp. "With wizards."

Helm's fierce grin faded. "Are ye ready yet?" he asked quietly. "*Really*, lad?"

Elminster spread his hands, crossbow in one. "There's one down there, at least, who knows who I am and what I look like."

Helm frowned and nodded, urged his mount forward, and clapped Elminster on the shoulder "Then I hope to see ye alive again, Prince." As his horse circled, be asked, "Would a wild outlaw charge into camp be any help?"

El shook his head. "Nay, Helm—just ride down those armsmen. If ye get every last one of them, Lawless Castle may be safe for a winter or two yet—so long as all outlaws have the sense to abandon it this summer. When the snows are gone, the wizards'll be sure to scour these hills with all the spells and swords they can muster."

Helm nodded. "Wise talk. Let us meet again among the living." He raised his blade in salute—Elminster lifted his bow in response—and spurred away as the snow began to fall again.

Soft flakes drifted down endlessly. Elminster ate a handful of snow to get a drink, recovered his bows and readied them, and set out over the hills toward the camp. He walked in a wide curve to the right, hoping to come on it from the other side . . . though with spells, couldn't wizards see in all directions?

Well, no doubt they run out of magic the same way armsmen run out of quarrels. He'd just have to count on their not scrying for a lone boy on foot in the snows. If he saw this night through, El reflected, he'd owe the gods much, indeed. . . .

Tripods of halberds held the flickering storm lanterns high. Snow whirled endlessly down into their bright radiance where, at the heart of the camp, the wizard Caladar Thearyn frowned down at a sphere of glowing light that hung in the air before him. Though the night was cold, sweat beaded his brow from the effort of keeping the sphere in existence—and in a breath or two, he'd have to hold it together while he cast another spell into it . . . a spell of many leaping lightnings that, if he managed the casting, would burst forth from the distant sphere linked to this one, a sphere bobbing like a pale ghost over the snow-clad hills not far away, just in front of the hard-riding outlaw band.

The magelord muttered the incantation that would link the two spells and felt the power rising within him. He spread his hands in exultation and noted without looking the awed faces and hasty retreat of his bodyguards.

He almost grinned as he began calling up the lightnings. Two intricate gestures, a grand flourish, and the speaking of a single word. Now for the taking up of the pins, then a rub of the rod of crystal with the fur, and last, the crowning incantation. . . . His hand swept down.

The crossbow bolt intended for his heart struck him in the shoulder, numbing his arm and spinning him around. The sphere collapsed in a crackling burst of lightnings that drowned out the magelord's startled scream of pain. The wizard sank down, clutching at his shoulder as another quarrel hissed past him. An armsman flung himself headlong in the well-trodden snow to avoid it, and his fellows drew their blades and ran toward the source of the quarrels.

Coolly, Elminster watched them come, his last bow raised. There, as he suspected . . . out of a tent came another robed man; not much older than he was but with a wand in his hand, looking around for the source of all the commotion. Carefully Elminster put his last ready quarrel in the man's throat. Then he dropped his bow, unbuckled the bulky belt-box of quarrels and let it fall, and drew his own steel.

Angry armsmen were rushing to meet him. Elminster charged them, a sword in one hand and a dagger in the other. The first man tried to beat his blade aside and run him through, but Elminster locked their blades together, pushed until they were face to face, steel shrieking in their ears, and drove his dagger into one of the man's eyes.

Shoving the convulsing corpse away, the prince ran on toward the next man, shouting, "For Athalantar!" This armsman stepped to the left, yelling to a companion to head to the right and close. El flung a dagger at the second man's face. Helm was right; some of these warriors weren't much good. This one threw up both gauntleted hands to shield his face, and Elminster's low thrust left him groaning over the blade in his guts. As El tugged his steel free, the next armsman approached warily. Elminster bent, plucked a dagger from the belt of the feebly moving man he'd just felled, and ran to one side. The surviving foe was still circling when Elminster sped away, back toward the camp.

A man in gleaming armor met him just inside the circle of light, a halberd in his hands. Elminster ran for the blade, batted it aside with his own, and stabbed. The armor turned his point aside, but then he was past, charging right into a tripod of halberds. They toppled, and the lantern they held shattered and set a tent ablaze with a sudden roar.

Men shouted. In the intense, leaping light, El saw the magelord stagger away, the quarrel still in his shoulder, but men with gleaming swords were running toward him, between him and the wizard.

Elminster snarled and turned sharply to the right, dodging between tents and away from the light. He blundered right into a man coming out of one tent and stabbed frantically; the surprised armsman toppled onto the canvas without a sound. Wearily, Elminster headed out into the night. If he could circle back to his bows, and . . . but armsmen were close behind him and running hard. Well, at least there were no bowmen in camp, or he'd be dead already.

Elminster hurried over a hill and dropped down out of sight of the raging flames that now marked the camp. Looking back, he could see two men following. He slowed to a walk, and began his wide circle. Let them draw nearer, and save him the breath. Panting, he topped another ridge and saw men gathered below, and horses: Helm's band. Some of them looked up and started toward him with swords drawn, but Helm saw him and waved. "Eladar! Done?"

"One wizard dead, but the other just wounded," El managed to gasp. "Half . . . the camp . . . is after me too."

Helm grinned. "We were resting our horses—and looting armsmen. Some o' them were wearing armor much too good for 'em. Change yer mind about that charge?"

El nodded wearily. "Seems . . . a better idea . . . now," he said, breathing heavily.

Helm grinned, turned and gave quick orders, and then pointed out a horse. "Take ye that one, Eladar, and follow me."

Leaving four outlaws behind with the loot and extra horses, the ragged knights of Athalantar rode along the way Elminster had come. One had scrounged a short horse bow; as they crested the bill, he drew and loosed, shoulders rolling smoothly, and one of the armsmen who'd been following Elminster clutched at his throat and fell over in the snow, kicking.

The others turned and fled. With a whoop one of the knights broke into a gallop, waving his sword as he urged his horse on, riding an armsman down and chopping another with his blade. The man fell and did not rise.

"Ye seem to bring us luck," Helm shouted as they rode. "Care to lead us to break down the walls of Hastarl?"

Elminster shook his head. "I grow tired of death, Helm," he shouted back, "and I fear the better ye do, the more the wizards'll hurl this way come spring. A few dead outlander merchants are one thing; entire patrols of armsmen slaughtered are another. They dare not let it go unpunished, or folk all o'er the realm will know, and remember, and get ideas."

Helm nodded. "All the same, it feels good to hit out an' really do some damage to these wolves. Ah, ye did quite a job!" He delightedly pointed ahead at the blazing tents. "Hope ye left the food tents alone!"

Elminster could only chuckle as they galloped in among the running, shouting defenders. The knights hacked armsmen as their horses reared, trampled the wounded and the fleeing—and the camp soon grew quiet.

Helm shouted for order. "Let us have watchguards there an' there an' there, in pairs an' in the saddle, well out beyond the light. The rest of ye: six to a tent, an' report back what ye find. No destroying stuff, mind. If ye find a live wizard or someone else to fight, call it out!"

The knights bent willingly to work. There were glad shouts when the kitchen tent was found to have several full metal sledges of meat, potatoes, and keg beer. Grim-faced knights also brought Helm some spellbooks and scrolls, but of the wounded wizard there was no sign, and there was no man who served magelords left alive in the camp.

"Right . . . we stay here this night," Helm said. "Picket all the horses ye can find, and let's make a feast and eat. In the morn we'll take all we can, scuttle back to the castle, and rig these tents in the ravine by Wind Cavern, as shelter for the horses. Then, all pray to Auril and Talos for fresh snows to cover our tracks!"

There was a general roar of approval, and Helm leaned close to Elminster and said, "Ye wanted to leave the hills, lad—an' I can't help but think ye've read the wizards aright. I need these books an' other mage-stuff hidden, an' I was thinking of that cavern in the meadow above Heldon. There's loose stones enough to wall 'em in, there—ye know where . . . an' ye can hunt deer and the like until summer, when I'll come looking for ye again. If armsmen sniff about, go into the High Forest an' hide there; they never dare go very far in."

He scratched his chin. "Ye'll never carry the brawn to be a horse warrior, lad, an' I'd say ye've done better than most at learning to shoot quarrels an' swing swords an' shiver in caves as an outlaw . . . P'raps the alleys and crowds of Hastarl'll do ye better as a place to hide, now—an' be closer to magelords who aren't alert for yer blood, to learn what ye can of 'em before ye decide ye must strike out." The knight turned keen eyes on the young prince. "What say?"

Elminster nodded slowly. "Aye . . . good plan," he murmured.

Helm grinned, clapped him on the shoulder, and then caught him, as Elminster sagged over sideways into the snow, the world spinning in a sudden green and yellow haze again. . . . The darkness of utter exhaustion rushed up to claim him, and El felt himself swept away. . . .

"Damned soft ride, these armsmen have," Helm commented briskly the next morning as they sat eating smoked beef and hard bread spread with garlic butter. Groans and satisfied belches from all around them told them that most of the long-hungry knights had gorged themselves. Snores from among empty casks betrayed how certain others had spent the dark hours.

Elminster nodded.

Helm looked at him sharply. "What's on yer mind, lad?"

"If I never have to kill a man again, 'twill be too soon," Elminster said quietly, looking around at bloodstains in the trampled snow.

The knight nodded. "I could see it in yer eyes last night." He grinned suddenly and added, "Yet ye took care of more trained and ready warriors yestereve than many men manage to slay in a long career of soldiering."

Elminster waved a hand. "I'm trying to forget it."

"Sorry, lad. Feeling up to the trip afoot, or would ye rather ride? The one's easier—as long as ye can find hay enough for the horse, an' they eat like proper pigs, mind. But they'll draw eyes yer way in a hurry, especially when ye cross the Run in Upshyn. Try to do that with a few wagons an' look like ye're part of the group, howe'er ye go. If anyone sees the spellbooks and scrolls ye're carrying, 'twill mean yer death." The knight scratched at his beard and went on. "The other way, though, is slow and hard, even if ye can keep warm—an' mind; to get feet wet is death in this weather. . . ."

"I'll walk," Elminster said. "I'll take a bow and as much food as I can stagger along with, as well . . . no armor, so long as I can get good gloves and a better scabbard."

Helm grinned. "A legion of dead armsmen will graciously provide."

Elminster could not manage to return the grin. He'd killed more than a few of them, men who should be riding proudly for Athalantar right now—free from the orders of wizards. It all came back to the magelords.

"They are the ones who have to die," he whispered to himself, "for Athalantar to live."

Helm nodded. "Nice phrase, that: 'They must die, for Athalantar to live!' A good battle cry; think I'll use it."

Elminster smiled. "Just be sure the folk hearing it know who the 'they' is."

Helm gave back a twisted smile. "That's a problem many have had, down the years."

The fox that had followed him for the last few miles took a final look at Elminster, its dark eyes glistening, and then scampered away through frozen ferns. El listened to its retreat, wondering if the fox were a magelord spy, but somehow knowing it was not. When the creature was long gone, he moved on as quietly as he could through the trees, around the back of the inn paddock.

Seek the feed hatch by the haystack, Helm had said, and there was the hay, against the back wall of the stables. The structure kept out most of the snow by means of a long sagging roof on pillars that had only a nodding acquaintance with the word "straight." Just as Helm had described it: the back way into Woodsedge Inn.

Elminster moved closer, hoping there were no dogs awake to sound an alarm. None yet. Elminster silently thanked the gods as he crept over the low gate on the inn side of the paddock, slipped around the haystack, and found the hatch. Only its own weight held it shut; he didn't even have to put down his sword to open it and climb in.

When he'd drawn the hatch dosed behind him, the stable was very still, and warmer than the night outside. A horse shifted and kicked idly against the side of its stall. Elminster studied the stable and noted one stall filled with shovels, rakes, buckets, and hanging coils of lead-rein, another with straw. Sheathing his blade and taking down a long-tined fork, El probed carefully into it, but there was nothing solid beneath to wake or snarl, so he lifted the wooden pin and went in.

It was the work of but a few breaths to burrow into the straw. He settled himself so he was hidden from view and shielded against the cold by a thick blanket of hay. Relaxing, Elminster called on his will to take himself down to the floating place of whispers . . . to sink down amid white radiance, and sleep. . . .

Straw rustled and scratched his hands as he lurched up out of it. Elminster's eyes flew open. He was *rising* up through the straw—flying! His head struck a beam overhead, hard.

"My apologies, Prince," came a cold, familiar voice. "I fear I've wakened you." Elminster felt himself being turned in the air to hang in emptiness facing the wizard, who stood in the corridor between the stalls, smiling darkly. The blue glow of magic pulsed brightly around the man's hands and encircled a pendant at his throat.

Anger rose in Elminster as he tried to grab the Lion Sword but found his arms wouldn't move. He was at the mercy of this magelord! He tried to speak and found he could. "Who are ye?" he asked slowly.

The mage sketched an elaborate bow and said pleasantly, "Caladar Thearyn, at your service." Elminster felt himself being pulled forward in the air and at the same time saw a long-tined pitchfork rising from where it leaned against the side of the stall and turning one of its sharp points toward his left eye. Slowly, lazily, it drifted nearer.

Elminster stared past it at the wizard, fighting down an urge to swallow. "There is little of fairness in thy fighting, mage," be said coldly.

The wizard laughed. "*How* old are you, Prince—sixteen winters? And you still expect to find this world a fair place? Well, you *are* a dolt." He sneered. "You fancy yourself a warrior and fight with sharpened pieces of metal . . . well, then: I am a mage, and do *my* fighting with spells. Where's the unfairness in that?"

The blue radiance of magic began to pulse strongly about the magelord's hands, and the fork drifted closer. Elminster's throat was unbearably dry now; he swallowed despite himself.

The wizard laughed. "Not so brave now, are we? Tell me, Prince of Athalantar, how much are you willing to do for me, to be allowed to live?"

"Live? Why won't ye kill me, wizard? I know ye want to," Elminster said, with more stern bravado than he felt.

"Other magelords," the wizard quoted his own words mockingly, "have plans of their own." He laughed coldly. "As a prince of Athalantar, you have great value. If anything happens to Belaur—or it becomes *necessary* that something should happen to him—it would be very handy to have my own pet princeling hidden away, for use in the . . . unpleasantness that would ensue." The fork drifted a little nearer. "Of course, blindness won't hamper you when I transform you into . . . a turtle, perhaps, or a slug. Even better, a maggot! You can feed on the gore of your frends the outlaws when we slay them. If we can't catch any, of course, you'll go hungry. . . ."

The mage's taunting voice trailed off into cold laughter. Elminster found himself drenched with sudden sweat as cold fear wormed its way up into his throat. He hung in the air, trembling and helpless, and closed his eyes.

An instant later, he felt them being forced open—and turned in their sockets until he was staring helplessly at the wizard. He found he couldn't speak any longer or make any sound short of the whistle of his breath.

"No screaming, now," the wizard said pleasantly. "We don't want you rousing the good folk of the inn—but I want to see your face when the fork goes in." Elminster could only stare in horror at the tine of the fork, looming closer, closer. . . .

Behind the wizard, a side door swung silently open, and a stout man with a curling mustache leaned into the room, a heavy axe raised. He brought it down hard. There was a meaty thud, and the wizard's head lolled sideways as it was split. Blood flew—and Elminster and the fork both fell abruptly to the floor.

He was up in an instant, the Lion Sword in his hand, hurrying—

"*Back*, my prince!" the man roared, throwing out one huge hand to ward him away. "He may have spells linked to his death!"

The man himself took a pace back and watched the body narrowly, the bloody axe ready on his shoulder. Elminster watched, too, and saw the faint blue glows faded from everything except the mage's pendant. Then, slowly, he walked out of the stall. "That pendant is magical," he said quietly, "but I can see nothing else. My thanks."

The man bowed. "An honor, if you are what the magelord called you."

"I am," Elminster replied. "I am Elminster, son of Elthryn, who is dead. Helm Stoneblade said I could trust you . . . if you are the one called Broarn."

The man bowed again. "I am. Be welcome in my inn—though I must warn you, lord, that six armsmen sleep under this roof tonight, and at least one merchant who tells all he sees to magelings."

"This stable is palace enough," Elminster said with a smile. "I've run from wizards and armsmen across half the Horn Hills, to here . . . and was beginning to wonder where in the world I could be free of them."

"There *is* no place to hide from strong magic," Broarn said soberly. "'Tis why men hold these lands now, and not the Fair Folk."

"I thought elven magic o'ermatched that of men," Elminster said curiously.

"If elven mages wielded it together, aye—but elves have little taste for war, and spend much of their time feuding with each other. Most of them are also . . . we would call it idle; they trouble themselves more about having a good time and less about doing things." The innkeeper reached back through the door he'd come in by, produced a blanket, and tossed it over the side of a stall.

"Human wizards know less," Broarn went on, stepping into the unseen passage beyond the door and reappearing with a covered serving platter and an old, battered tankard as large as Elminster's head, "but're always trying to find old spells or create new ones. Elven mages only smile, say they already know all they need to—or if they're arrogant, say they know everything there is to know—and do nothing."

Elminster saw a nearby stool and sat down. "Tell me more," he said. Please. What that mage said about my simple ways is true enough. I would hear more of the way of the world, hereabouts."

Broarn smiled and passed him the tray and the tankard. His smile broadened as Elminster lifted the lid, saw cold fowl, and dug in eagerly. "Ah, but you have the wits to know that, lord, where most don't. Here in Athalantar, there's little to say: the magelords have this land by the throat and don't mean to shift their grip. Yet for all their airs, they couldn't hold a magic apprenticeship at some places in the southlands."

Elminster looked up with his mouth full but his eyebrows raised. The innkeeper nodded. "Aye, the lands down there have always been rich, and crowded—fair crawling with folk. The greatest realm is Calimshan; the place those dusky-skinned merchants with their heads wrapped, who come here all bundled up in furs in spring and fall, come from."

"I've never seen them," Elminster said quietly.

The innkeeper scratched at his mustache. "You *have* been hidden away, lad. Well, to tell the tale short, there's a huge lawless land north of Calimshan, all forests and rivers, where their nobles always go to hunt game—or went, that is. An archmage—that's a wizard stronger by far than these magelords—" Broarn paused to spit thoughtfully on the dead wizard at his feet "—set himself up there and now rules most of it. The Calishar, it used to be called; I know not if he's renamed it, as he seems bent on changing all else. The Mad Mage, they call him, because he chases his whims so fiercely, and doesn't care about what he destroys in the doing; Ilhundyl's his name. Since he claimed the land, all the folk as didn't want to be turned into frogs and falcons have moved on—north, most of them."

Elminster sighed. "It sounds as if there's nowhere in all the world at peace from mages."

Broarn smiled. "It feels that way, my lord, it does. If you must hide from the magelords, go up the Unicorn Run, deep into the High Forest. They fear the Fair Folk will rise against them there, and they're right on that . . . the elves fear to lose more land to the axes of Athalantar and will fight for every tree. If you need to hide only from armsmen, Wyrm Wood right behind us here will do—they fear dragons. The mages know better; they slew the last dragon hereabout—and took its hoard—some twenty winters gone, but can't get us simple folk to believe that."

Elminster smiled. "And if I want to stand and fight? How can I best a wizard?"

Broarn spread his large and hairy hands. "Learn—or hire—stronger magic."

El shook his head. "How would ye trust anyone stronger in magic than magelords? What's to stop them from just taking the throne themselves after they've slain these wizards?"

The innkeeper nodded and gave Elminster a nod of approval. "A point, aye. Well, the other way is much slower and less sure."

Elminster leaned forward on the stool, and swept his hand up in a beckoning wave. "So tell."

"Work from within, as a rat gnaws away in the pantry."

"How does a man become a rat?"

"Steal. Be a thief in the back streets and the low taverns and the markets of Hastarl, close to the wizards' backsides, and wait and watch and learn. Warriors have to stand tall and wave blades . . . and be seen and slain by any mageling that points a wand their way, and outlaws must needs come out to seize food all too often. You've probably seen enough of the wilderlands of your realm to satisfy your curiosity. 'Tis time to learn the ways of the city, of thieving. It prepares one for ruling, some say." He lifted a corner of his mouth at his own jest. "Besides, a warrior's way is no more nor less safe than being a thief; any man can be overcome if caught alone—as you learned tonight—and if you wait long enough . . ."

El grinned like a wolf over dinner, rose, and took hold of the magelord's legs. "Have ye a shovel?"

Broarn returned the look. "Aye, and a nice warm manure pile to dig with it, Prince." They clasped each other's arms, as one warrior to another.

"At least get some more food into you before you move on," Broarn grunted, handing a tray into the end stall.

Elminster took it; steam and a delicious smell were rising together from a bowl on the tray. "Nay," he said, "I should be—" And then his stomach growled so loudly that he and the innkeeper both laughed.

"Mind you take that pendant with you when you go, and hide it somewhere else," Broarn said sternly. "I don't want magelords tracing it here, digging it up from whatever clever hiding place you've chosen, and then trying to gently 'question' me with their spells."

"It will leave with me," Elminster promised. "It's under a stone on the road outside right now, where a road-thief might have left it."

"Well enough," said Broarn, "so I—" He broke off and held up a hand to bid Elminster to silence.

Then the innkeeper bent his head to the hatch at the back of the stables, listening intently. After a moment, he slid his hand back through the side door. It reappeared clutching the old axe, raised and ready

Elminster drew the broken Lion Sword and sank down in the stall, holding up a large armload of straw to conceal himself, though betraying steam rose idly from the tray.

The hatch opened in well-oiled silence. Broarn stood calmly just inside it and broke into a smile at about the time a familiar voice said, "Waiting up for me, dearest? Wert expecting me?"

"In with you, Helm, while there's still some warmth in my stables," the innkeeper growled in reply, stepping back.

"I brought friends," the knight said as he stepped into the room, looking dirtier than ever. He scowled as Elminster rose in his stall, straw in his hair and sword in hand.

"Is *this* how far ye've got? I thought ye'd be well across the river by now," he said.

Elminster shook his head, losing his grin fast. "The magelord who escaped us at the camp found me here somehow—probably he can trace the spellbook—and nearly slew me. Broarn cut him down with that axe."

Helm turned to regard the innkeeper with new respect. "A slayer of magelords, now." He circled Broarn as if viewing a lady in a bold new gown, then nodded approvingly. "'Tis a most exclusive brotherhood, ye know . . . besides the lad here an' meself, its only members are the dead, an' a few living magelords. Why, th—"

"Helm," Broarn broke in bluntly, "why are you here? I've armsmen in the house, as you should know."

As they'd been talking, knight after outlaw knight had slipped in through the hatch, crowding into the end stalls. So many of them wore armor scavenged from the soldiery of Athalantar that it looked as if a dozen or more rather scruffy, armsmen stood in the stable now.

"There is a matter of some small urgency, aye," Helm said more soberly. "Which is why Mauri's shivering in a sledge outside, with another twenty-odd brave blades."

"They took Lawless Castle?" The innkeeper sounded shocked.

"Nay. We fled from it before they could trap us there. The magelords sent a large band of armsmen out of Sarn Torel, guarding over a dozen mages. They've slain twenty or more wildswords we know of and tortured at least one with spells—they know where the castle is, by now, and are heading straight for it.",

"So you brought them here. My thanks, Helm," Broarn said bitterly and sketched a courtly bow.

"They'll have no way of knowing we did any more than steal a horse or two," Helm said firmly. "We're leaving very soon, now that ye—and the lad, here, a country boy called Eladar, by the way if he hasn't told ye—" The two men exchanged a fleeting, level look "—know the tidings. Eladar was right, we've been too good at killing armsmen an' now they're determined to slay the lot o' us. The wizards daren't let such defiance succeed or soon the whole realm will be up in arms. We must run. Any suggestions, wise innkeeper?"

Broarn snorted. "Run to the Calishar and get Ilhundyl to teach you to be master mages so you can come back and fight these magelords . . . get a friendly mage to hide all of you as frogs before the magelords can find you and do it swifter . . . go to the depths of the elven realms and get them to hide you somehow . . . call on the gods for miracles . . . I believe that about covers it."

"There's one other place," Elminster said quietly

The silence of utter astonishment fell on both Helm and Broarn. They turned as one to look at the lad in the scorched leather jerkin, standing alone in his stall. He'd slid his sword into hiding and picked up the bowl of turkey soup Broarn had brought him. As they watched, he calmly took a spoonful, smiled, dipped his spoon into the bowl again, drew forth another spoonful, and blew on it to cool it.

"I'll *slay* ye, lad, if ye don't stop playing the fool," Helm growled, taking a step toward him.

"That's more or less what the magelord said to me," Elminster remarked mildly, "and look ye what befell him."

Helplessly, Helm started to laugh, and that set Broarn and the other outlaws off into roars of mirth while Elminster assumed an air of innocence over his bowl and ladled several spoonfuls into his mouth, fearing chances to do so later would be few.

"All right, lad," Broarn managed when he had breath enough, "give. Where to hide?"

"Among a lot of folk that wizards dare not slay or upset too many of, or they'll have no realm left. In Hastarl itself," Elminster said.

Helm—and a lot of the outlaw knights behind him—stared at the youth with open mouths, aghast.

"But ye'll attack the first mage ye see when ye step inside the gates, and we'll all perish right then!" the battered knight protested.

Elminster shook his head. "Nay," he said. "Watching sheep taught me patience . . . and hunting wizards is teaching me guile."

"Ye're crazed," one of the other outlaws muttered.

"Aye," another agreed.

"Wait a bit," still another protested. "The more I think on it, the better it seems."

"Ye want death at yer elbow every day, whene'er ye go out?"

"I've got that *now* . . . an' if I go to Hastarl like the lad says, I might get me a warm house to sleep in o' winters."

Then they were all talking, arguing earnestly, until Broarn hissed, "You will be *quiet!*" to knight after knight, waving his axe under their noses for emphasis. When he had silence, the fat innkeeper said, "If you make that sort of noise, I'll have armsmen up from their beds and in here to see what fun they're missing. Anyone want that?"

He let silence stretch for a moment or two, and then went on quietly, "Some of you will want to remain in the hills or flee to other lands, but some may want to go with the lad here to Hastarl. Whatever you decide, do it well back in the woods; I want all of you away from here before dawn. Helm, bring Mauri and the home-stuffs she's got in by the back door. She stays here. Don't let anyone help you who can't move quietly. Now out, all of you—and may the luck of the gods cloak you and keep you!"

The meeting was breaking up; the time to strike was now. This deed would surely win him a rank among the magelords! No more apprenticeship to fat old Harskur . . . and real power at last!

Saphardin Olen rose from the cold hillside, letting his eavesdropping spell fade away He raised the wands in his hands, aiming at the hatch—best to strike now, before any of them left the place.

"Die, fools!" he said with a smile, and then pitched forward like a felled tree as a stone the size of a war helm smashed into the back of his head.

As the blood-spattered rock settled smoothly into the snow, the two fallen wands rose by themselves and glided in a gentle arc through the trees to the next knoll, where a tall, lean woman stood watching them come with large, dark eyes.

Her face was bone white, and her hair a curling honey-brown. At one glance, a farmer would have bowed to her as a lady. She put out a hand to take the wands as they glided up to her, and her dark green cloak swirled about her, as if moved by unseen hands. Silvern threads on its shoulders were worked in a mage-sigil of linked circles.

The sorceress watched the outlaws stride into the woods, and waved a hand. Her body faded, rippled, and became just another of the shifting shadows here in the winter-stripped trees—cloaked and unseen, save for her large, liquid black eyes.

They blinked once as they watched Elminster hug Helm in farewell before heading south, alone.

"The soul is strong in you, Prince of Athalantar," their owner said quietly. "Live, then, and let us see what you can do."

PART
II

BURGLAR

Four
They Come Out at Night

Thieves? Ah, such an ugly word . . . think of them instead as
kings-in-training. Ye seem upset, even disputatious. Well, then, look
upon them as the most honest sort of merchant.

The character Oglar the Thieflord
in the anonymous play *Shards and Swords*
Year of the Screeching Vole

It was just one more in an endless string of hot, damp days in the early summer of the Year of the Black Flame. Folk in Hastarl had taken to lying more or less unclad on the flat stretches of their rooftops and their balconies after sunset, hoping for a breeze to blow over their skin and bring them some fleeting moments of comfort.

This was good for both pleasure and business—the predictable pleasure, and one business in particular.

"Ah," Farl said softly, leaning forward to peer out of the slit window. "The show of flesh beginneth again, so it doth."

"When ye've finished drooling down the stonework," the slim, beak-nosed youth behind him said dryly, "do ye hold the line while I go down."

"That'll be about dawn, I'd say," was the reply.

"Aye, then, hold the line now and look later." Elminster cast a glance over the head of his fellow thief and squinted professionally "Ah, yes, quite a tattoo there . . . though how the man sees it, with the curve of his belly between his eyes and where it is, only the gods can know."

Farl chuckled. "Think of what it must have felt like, getting it, too." He winced with an exaggerated flourish, and added, "But you're supposed to be looking at the maids, El, not at the men!"

"Ah, I've got to learn to tell the difference. It gets me into more trouble," Elminster replied serenely. Then what he'd been waiting for befell: a large bank of clouds drifted across the moon. Without another word, he slipped through the narrow window, one hand on the rope harness, and was gone.

Farl settled the smooth leather rope slide securely on the sill, and with surprising strength slowed the line gliding through it to a gentle, continuous movement until a sharp jerk told him to stop. He thrust a dagger into one of the holes in the wheel from which the rope unwound, then looked out the window.

Directly under him, in the empty air beneath the outthrust upper room of the tower, Elminster calmly hung suspended outside the window of the room below. One of his hands—the hand wearing a wrapping coated with sticky honeycake—was on the tower wall; El was keeping himself to one side of the window, out of the view of the room's occupants. He peered in for what seemed a very long time before raising his hand in a signal, not looking up.

Farl passed the reachers down on their own lines.

Hanging there in the quickening night breeze, Elminster took hold of them: two long, thin wooden sticks with wrist braces at one end, like crutches, and sticky balls of precious stirge glue on their other ends. A hooked and pad-ended side prong jutted from one stick.

El delicately used that prong to swing the shutters fully back—and then withdrew the reachers and waited patiently No sound came from within, and after several long breaths, he reached out again. One stick slid in until its leather sleeve caught the sill. He balanced its weight there, and then slid it onward through its sleeve, probing delicately inside the room. When he drew it out, a gem gleamed on the sticky end. He backed the stick until he could slide his hand up to its tip, let it dangle from its line while he thrust the gem into the tube-bag of stout canvas be wore around his neck, and then reached into the room with the stick again, slowly . . . smoothly . . . silently.

Thrice more the sticks appeared, were emptied of precious cargo, and returned to the room. Farl saw the youth below wipe sweating hands on dark, dusty leather breeches, and then lean forward again. He held this breath, knowing what *that* gesture meant: Eladar the Dark was about to try something especially reckless. Farl mouthed a silent prayer to Mask, Lord of All Thieves.

Elminster reached into the bedchamber once more. His sticks slid over the bare, slumbering body of the young merchant's wife, only inches above the soft curves of her flesh—and paused over her throat. She wore a dark ribbon there . . . and below it, a pectoral of linked emeralds, topped by a spider of black wire whose body was a single huge ruby.

Elminster watched the jewelry rise and fall, ever so slightly, with her slow and even breathing. If it was like others he'd seen, the spider could be unclasped to be worn alone as a cloak pin. If . . . a touch, just so—a wiggle to be sure it was caught . . . and now so was he (This had to work, or he'd be left with a stick twice as long as a man stuck to the breast of a naked woman who'd not stay asleep for very long) . . . and a little lift, up and back, so. Don't brush her nose with it, now . . . with infinite care and patience El brought the reachers back out of the window.

When he dropped the jewels into the bag and jerked the rope for Farl to pull him up, he felt that the spider was still warm from her breathing. Elminster smelled the musky scent clinging to it, sighed soundlessly and wondered fleetingly what women *were* like. . . .

"With those, we can live like idle rich blades for five tendays, at least," Farl said, eyes shining in the dim light of their hovel hideaway.

"Aye," Elminster said, "and get noticed in three evenings. Just who d'ye think we think we can sell that spider to in *this* city? We'll have to wait for a discreet merchant—who's got something to hide an' knows we know it—leaving the city, and sell it to him then. Nay; we sell the ring with the emerald this night, before word gets out; no marks there to say it's hers for certain. Then we lie low—back to hanging around the Black Boots waiting for hire as dockhands and errand-runners."

Farl stared at him for a moment, mouth open to protest, but then closed it in a smile and nodded. "You've the right of it as usual, Eladar. You've the cunning of an alley cat, to be sure."

Elminster shrugged. "I'm still alive, if that's what ye mean. Let's go discover some place that serves drink to young blades with dry throats and loose purses."

Farl laughed, slid the bag back into the hollow stone block, clambered up the ragged stones of the crumbling chimney, and shoved the block the full length of his arm back into the dark, hollow space between floor and ceiling. Withdrawing his arm from the splinter-edged hole, he replaced the dead, dangling, half-eaten rat they used to deter searchers, and slid back down the chimney to the floor.

Around them, the gloomy back room of the shut-up cobbler's shop stank from its occasional use as a toilet by cats, dogs, drunks, and stray street folk. The cobbler had died of black-tongue fever early in the spring, and sane folk made no plans to disturb the place until at least a season had passed. Then it would be smoked to clear disease-vapors and torn down; by then, Farl and Elminster planned to have a new and better loot cache among the ornamental roof spires of the proud houses near Hastarl's north wall. They had their eyes on a tall residence whose roof sported crouching, snarling sculpted gargoyles; if one could be beheaded and hollowed out without anyone in the grand house beneath noticing, they'd have an ideal place. Aye, "if."

The two youths nodded to each other, knowing their silent thoughts had skulked along the same alley. Farl peered out the watch hole and after a moment waved Elminster on. He stepped unconcernedly out into the narrow, dark passage outside, and slipped away. Farl followed, dagger drawn—just in case. It was a full breath later before any of the rats dared come out into the open to get at the moldy slab of cheese the young thieves had thoughtfully left behind.

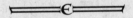

The Kissing Wench was a loud, crowded press of goodfolk—ribaldry and slapping and pinching, pursuit of a night's lust, roared jests and tossed coins, and reckless chase of wine-soaked oblivion. Farl and Eladar took their tankards to their favorite dark corner, just off the bar, where they could see who came in but be seen only by the night-sighted and the determined.

Their spot was occupied already, of course, by ladies whose names they knew well despite a persistent lack of the coinage necessary for more intimate acquaintance. The hour was too early for business to be brisk, so the evening-lasses were sipping from glasses in their hands and rubbing scent into the backs of their knees and the crooks of their elbows, and there was still room to sit down on the benches.

"Game for an early kiss and cuddle?" Ashanda asked disinterestedly, examining her nails. She knew what their reply would be before it came. Nothing from the one with the unruly black hair and the beaky nose, and from Farl—"Nay. We just like to watch." He leered at her over his tankard.

She gave him a mock coquettish look, batting her eyes and putting two delicate fingers to her mouth in a shocked expression, and then replied, "An' most of 'em want a cheering audience, so that's aright. Just be sure to give way when we need the space on the benches, or it's my blade-toe you'll be feeling!"

They'd seen her put her dagger-tipped boot into the shins of many a man, and once into the gut of a sailor who didn't know his own cruel strength; he'd ended up screaming his guts out—literally—on the tavern floor. Both thieves nodded hastily as the other girls tittered.

Farl gave one of them a wink, and she leaned forward to pat his knee. The movement made her low-cut silken bodice slide, smooth and cool, across Elminster's arm. He hastily transferred his tankard out of the way, feeling a stirring in him.

Budaera saw his swift movement and turned her head to smile up at him. Her scent—something of roses, not so strong as some of the reeks the ladies used—wafted to his nostrils. Elminster shivered.

"Anytime you have the coins, love," she breathed huskily. Elminster managed to get the back of his hand over his nose in time. Then his sneeze slopped beer down the side of his tankard, and nearly knocked her sideways to the floor.

Hoots and roars filled the corner. Budaera gave him a glare, and then softened it to an expression of sorrow when she saw that his distress and his stammered apology were genuine. She patted his knee and said, "There, there. 'Tis all a matter of improving your technique—and that, I can teach you."

"If ye can afford her lessons," another girl cackled, and there were chuckles all around. El wiped his streaming eyes on the back of his sleeve and nodded thanks to Budaera, but she was already turning away to ask another girl where that coppery nail daub had come from, and how much it had cost.

Farl ran his fingers through the hair above his ear and drew his hand down to stare in delight at a silver coin in his fingers, as if he'd never seen it before. "Look at *this*," he said to Eladar. "Mayhap there's another!"

There was. He held them up in triumph, and said, "I'm ready, Budaera, an' I'm willing, an' I see you're free of guests at the m—"

"For two silver bits," she said in a flat, cold tone, "that's the way I'm staying, 'my love.'" The laughter of the girls galed around them; men with tall frosted flagons in hand drifted nearer to see what merriment was afoot . . . or abench.

Farl looked crestfallen. "I don't think there's anything more back there, but I didn't comb my hair this morn. . . ." His look changed to hopeful, and he ran his hands through his hair again, then shook his head.

"Nay." One of the girls made a sound of mock sorrow, but he held up his hand. "Wait a bit, wait a bit—I've not checked all me hair, now have I?" Farl leered again and reached inside his dark shirt to scratch at his armpit. His fingers worked lustily, and then paused. Farl frowned, drew out an imaginary—at least, so Elminster hoped—pinch of lice, and examined them critically. Then he pretended to eat them, licked his fingers daintily, and when he was done darted his hand into his shirt again, trying the other armpit.

Almost immediately his eyes grew round and wondering. Slowly he drew out—a gold coin! He sniffed at it, drew back in mock disgust, and then held it up with a laugh of triumph. "See you?"

"Now that," Budaera purred, leaning forward again, "is worth more than a sneeze. Have you another?"

Farl looked hurt. "Just how dirty d'you think my armpits are, anyway?"

Tinkling, genuine laughter surrounded them; the ladies were amused. El watched impassively, only a corner of his mouth crooked upward, as Budaera leaned forward until her darting tongue almost brushed Farl's ear, and breathed, "For just two silver bits more, I might be persuaded to make a pauper's exception . . . just this once. . . ."

"For just two silver bits more," Farl said with elaborate dignity, "I might be compelled to accept your generous offer, good lady. Now, if someone in this august company would be so good as to lend me the trifling sum of—ah, two silver bits?"

There were snorts and lazily rude gestures from the benches beside him. Elminster held out a hand; when he turned it over, two silver coins were stuck to his palm.

Rather dubiously, Farl bent and plucked them free, one after another. Elminster had used only a trifling touch of gum on each; by the time Farl presented them to Budaera with a flourish, they were quite clean.

Budaera beckoned for the gold first. When she had it, she reached into her own armpit and made the coin disappear into the little scented safe pouch most of the ladies wore there. Then she took the pieces of silver, spun them briefly in the air in expert fingers, held up the last one, and kissed it, eyes on Farl's. "We have a deal, then, my lord of love."

She leaned forward, eyes suddenly full of mystery, and like a silent and watchful snake Elminster slid out from his seat beside Farl to give them room. Budaera purred wordless thanks to him as she moved her lithe body into the vacated space, and set to work.

Elminster stepped away shaking his tankard in little circular movements to feel what little was left at the bottom of it—and froze. A slim finger was stroking him, ever so softly. He looked down—and caught his breath.

They called Shandathe "the Shadow" for the silence of her entrances and exits. More than once, El and Farl had agreed she must be an accomplished thief, or if she wasn't, was as accomplished at skulking as the best of them. Her large, dark eyes looked up past his belt buckle at Elminster—and he felt the need to swallow, his throat suddenly dry.

"Coins to lend, Eladar the Dark? Have ye—coins to spend?" Her voice was husky her eyes hungry . . .

Elminster made a helpless little sound of need deep in his throat and dipped his hand to his sleeve, whose cuff was stuffed with gold pieces. "One or two," he managed, in a voice that was not quite steady.

Her eyes danced. "One or two, my lord? I'm sure I heard ye say three or four . . . aye, four gold. One for each of the delights I'll give thee." She licked his hand, the lightest of velvet touches in his palm. Elminster trembled.

Then he was shoved rudely aside. Whirling, he found himself looking into the cold grin of a burly bodyguard in livery. The man held up spiked gauntlets in warning, and El saw another bodyguard beyond him. Between them, in his own little ring of light provided by a small oil lamp held above him on a curving pole by a weary servant, stood a short, pouty-looking man in flame-orange silks. His reddish hair fell in well-oiled ringlets to stain the silken shoulders of his open-fronted shirt. On his hairless chest was a lump of gold as large as a man's fist: a lion's head frozen in an endless, silent snarl, as it hung on a heavy gold chain. Rings of many gems and metals glittered and flashed on his fingers—two and three baubles to each digit, El noted with disgust, and all of it real.

He exchanged glances with Farl over Budaera's shocked face, and then the man thrust his codpiece, adorned with an openwork ivory and gold sheath that made it look like the figurehead of a very decadent Calishite pleasure-barge, right into Shandathe's face.

"Too busy, my little lass?" he drawled, and snapped his fingers. The servant with the lamp put a purse in them, and the man lazily spilled a dozen or so gold pieces down the front of Shandathe's gown. "Or have you time enough for a real man . . . with real gold to spend?"

"How many years does my lord want to spend with me?" Shandathe breathed in reply lifting her hands in welcome. The man grinned tightly, and gestured to his bodyguards. They reached out brutal spiked hands to clear the corner, ignoring the sudden, shrill protests of the other ladies.

One laid hold of Budaera's ankle, and hauled her off Farl to a hard landing on the floor. She squealed in pain, and anger rode high in Farl's face as he rose from the bench.

"Just who in Hastarl do you think *you* are?" he addressed the perfumed man. The bodyguard reached a menacing hand toward him, and Farl snapped his own fingers like the man's master had done, and as if by a spell a dagger gleamed in them. He waved it warningly at the bodyguard's eyes, and the man hesitated.

"Jansibal is my name," came arrogant tones that obviously expected the name to awe everyone within hearing. "Jansibal Otharr."

Farl shrugged. "Heard of any testers of cheap scent by that name, El?" he asked. Elminster waved a dagger of his own under the nose of the bodyguard who'd shoved him, and slipped out from under the man's gauntleted hands.

"No," he said calmly, "but one rat looks quite the same as another." That did bring little gasps and indrawn hisses of breath from around, and a little silence fell. The dandy's face turned dark with anger, and his fingers tightened in Shandathe's hair as she knelt in front of him. Then a sick, lopsided, sneering smile slid onto Jansibal's face, and Elminster felt a little chill inside. This man meant their deaths, here and now. The bodyguards drifted nearer.

"This sounds like the sort of insult that a man of honor"—the loud, new voice that had broken in from behind them dropped little quotes around that last word, and Jansibal paled in recognition and fresh anger—"can answer only with a formal duel, not a distressing brawl that will cost him at least two bodyguards."

Jansibal and his men spun around—to find another dandy, as well garbed as the first, eyeing them with dancing amusement in his eyes. He, too, wore silks, with crawling dragons embroidered on his puffed sleeves. A flagon was in his hand—and to either side of him stood men in matching livery, slim swords in their hands. The needlelike blades were aimed at the crotches of Jansibal's bodyguards. A hush spread across the dark taproom, and men craned their necks to watch.

"Fair even, Jansibal," the newcomer said calmly, rubbing at the thin beginnings of a moustache with the lip of his flagon. "Laryssa spurn you again? Dlaedra insufficiently impressed with your—ah, rampant glory?"

Jansibal snarled. "Get gone, Thelorn! You can't strut in the safety of your sire's shadow forever!"

"His shadow stretches longer than your father's, Janz. My men and I but stopped for a drink . . . but the appalling stench drew us to this corner to see what had died. You really must stop wearing that stuff, Janz; some chamber-maid's likely to empty a pisspot out a window to try and wash your stink away!"

"Your yapping tongue carries you ever closer to a waiting grave, Selemban!" Jansibal spat. "Now begone, or I'll have one of my men spoil that pretty face of yours with a few shards of glass!"

"I love thee too, Jansibal. Which of your two men is it to be? My *six* would dearly love to know." From behind him, another pair of men in livery glided forward, blades raised and glittering in the little dangling lamp that a trembling servant still held aloft on its pole.

"I'll not fight a duel with all these blades of yours around," Jansibal said, drawing himself up. "I know your liking for convenient 'accidents.'"

"While you grandly slash at someone with that blade you've dipped in sleep venom? Aren't you tired of such deceits, Janz? Doesn't using them remind you, every even, that you're a worm? Or is it so much part of your lovely nature that you don't even notice?"

"Shut your lying mouth," Jansibal snarled, "or—"

"Or you'll get away with your little trick, yes? And stab all these lads and lasses around to work off your little rage, no doubt. And what would you be doing with them once they were asleep? Robbing them, of course—you have such *expensive* habits, Janz—but perhaps a little idle butchering . . . or worse? I've noticed the ladies raising their rates down your street, Janz. . . ."

Jansibal snarled wordlessly and charged forward. There was a flash of light and a spray of scattering sparks as the blades of the two nearest bodyguards met some invisible shield of magic around the charging dandy—and then Jansibal came to a sudden halt as Thelorn Selemban, moving without apparent haste, drew a blade and pointed it at Jansibal's nose. Tiny white lightnings spiraled along the steel as its own enchantment cut through Jansibal's shield. Around the two nobles, their bodyguards surged forward, blades out and up.

"Hold, men of Otharr and Selemban, in the name of the king!" came a sudden deep bellow from behind them all, in the direction of the bar. The livened men halted as their masters stiffened—and the crowd around parted as if before a drawn sword.

A man with a short-trimmed, graying beard came into view, a tankard in his hand. "Swordmaster Adarbron," he identified himself flatly. "I'll report any deaths or bloodletting here to the magelords when I see them this night. . . . And I'll also let them know if either of you disobey me, my lords. Now order your men out of this place, and back to your homes—now!"

He stood hard-eyed, and the two dandies saw men drift up to stand at his back. Off-duty armsmen, to be sure, faces not quite masking their glee. If the dandies defied the swordmaster, the soldiers would do their level best to 'accidentally' slay or maim them both—and none of their bodyguards would leave the tavern alive.

"My men have had enough to drink anyway," Thelorn said easily, but a vein was working near his jaw. He did not look in Otharr's direction as he said almost gently to the men around him, "You may go. I shall follow after I drink to the health of this excellent and dedicated officer—whose word I utterly support, for the honor of Athalantar."

"For the honor of Athalantar," half a hundred men muttered in reply, waving their flagons and tankards halfheartedly. Unimpressed, the swordmaster watched the men go. Then, ignoring Thelorn Selemban's smile, he shot a cold look at Jansibal Otharr, and said, "My lord?"

Sullenly, without a reply, Jansibal waved a hand at his men. Then he turned back to the Shadow, who still knelt fearfully in the alcove, and said coldly, "My lords, I was occupied before Selemban took it upon himself to interrupt, if you'll excuse me—?"

"Through there," Elminster murmured, pointing, "is rather more private. I'm sure the folk who were sitting here before thy enthusiastic men shoved them aside would like to resume what they were doing before *thy* interruption, too, my lord."

The dandy snarled at him, promised death again in his eyes, but the sword-master said firmly, "Take the young man's advice, Otharr. He but tries to rescue your family name . . . and remind you of a few simple basics of courtesy."

Otharr did not look around, but his shoulders stiffened, and he turned without a word, fingers firmly wound in Shandathe's hair so that she gave a little shriek and then hurried along on her knees to avoid being dragged.

Elininster took a step forward, but the noble had already halted to fling the curtain wide. "A light in here," he ordered curtly. The young alcove-lass unhooded a slow-wick lamp and blew it into brightness before slipping hurriedly away.

The curtained pleasure-alcove normally cost six gold falcons—but before the fury of the noble and the watchful gaze of the swordmaster, the young girl did not tarry to try for the price . . . and the bodyguards who stood to defend her and her demand kept to the walls and held their silence. Jansibal Otharr surveyed the cushioned, draperied bed that almost filled the niche, nodded in satisfaction, and curtly waved Shandathe to the bed. The curtains fell into place behind them with an angry switch.

Farl reached up the wall with a slow, stealthy hand and dimmed the lamp there by pinching down its wick. He caught the eyes of a lady across the benches, and she did the same, dimming that side of the taproom into darkness again.

The swordmaster turned away, keeping Thelonn Selemban carefully at his side. They went back to the bar together.

Farl and El exchanged glances. Farl sketched the swell of an imaginary bosom with one hand, pointed at the curtain, and then jerked his thumb at himself. El blinked slowly, once, and then pointed toward the jakes and touched his own chest. Farl nodded, and El set out across the room to where he could relieve himself. If there was going to be creeping about or fighting, he'd best be more at ease.

Had it been like this before the magelords came to Hastarl? Shouldering and slipping his way through drunken revelers into the dimly lit privy area, El wondered what the Wench had been like when his grandfather sat on the Stag Throne. Were all men of power as cruel as the two nobles who'd almost begun a battle here? And just how were they more honorable—or more villainous—than Farl and Eladar the Dark, two young and impudent rooftop thieves?

Just who stands better in the eyes of the gods—a magelord, a dandified noble, or a thief? What's the choice between the lot of them? The first two have more influence to do ill, and the thief is at least honest or open about what he does . . . hmm . . . perhaps these would not be safe questions to ask a priest or sage in Hastarl. The foul-smelling trough in front of him had no ready answers either, and he'd best get back out there before Farl did something reckless. If they were going to have all the armsmen in the city out looking for them, he wanted to know about it . . .

When he returned along the far wall, Farl was sitting beside the curtain. He caught El's eye and then slipped smoothly behind it, keeping low. El took his seat, noted that the couple beside him were well beyond noticing what anyone else was doing, and followed.

The two friends lay still, side by side and unseen on the dark carpeted floor, as the gasps in the dimly lit alcove grew louder and more urgent. Farl crawled slowly forward as the amorous sounds built to a height, and reached up silently to lift the glass of wine—complimentary with hire of the alcove, its surface thick with settled dust—from its usual spot. Deftly he tossed its contents over the lamp wick.

The alcove was plunged into sudden, hissing darkness. Elminster rose from the carpet like a vengeful, striking snake and plunged one hand over the dandy's mouth from behind, reaching to stifle the man into slumber with the other.

Farl's hands were already over the Shadow's mouth. She jerked and burbled under him, fighting for breath enough to scream, but her eyes widened when she recognized the man atop her and she stopped struggling. Elminster saw one of her slim hands cease its clawing, and reach up to stroke Farl's shoulder. Then he had no time left to spare for looking at anyone except the noble under him.

Jansibal was oiled and perfumed, slippery under Elminster's hands. He'd never known the hard hours and harsh battle that the youth from Heldon had felt—but he was shorter and heavier, and fury lent him strength. He threw himself sideways, dragging Elminster with him, and tried to bite the fingers that were smothering him.

Elminster drew back one arm, dagger hilt foremost, and slugged the noble hard on the jaw. Jansibal's head snapped around, spittle and blood flying together. The dandy gave a little grunt, shook his head—and toppled over sideways on the bed, knocked senseless. One open eye stared up unseeing at Elminster; satisfied, El spun to look behind them and be sure no one had noticed the sudden dousing of the light behind the curtain, or heard the brief, unloving sounds. The hubbub of folk drinking continued unabated—and sudden soft sounds from beside him proclaimed that Farl was taking full advantage of the noble's generous payment to Shandathe. The gold coins lay on the floor around, freed when Otharr had torn open her bodice; El ignored them to bend closer over the entwined couple, and delicately free a single distinctive earring from where the Shadow's hair curled around her ear.

Shandathe freed her lips from Farl's long enough to whisper a sharp, "What—?"

Elminster put a finger to his lips and murmured, "To lure the other one; ye'll see it again, I promise."

Holding it cupped carefully in his hand, he slipped around the curtain again and made his way unhurriedly across the taproom. As he'd hoped, the swordmaster and Thelonn stood side by side at the bar.

"You'll appreciate," the officer was saying wearily, "that sons of magelords *must* set an example that makes the people feel they're close and among them, not aloof. Magic, and those who wield it, are feared enough; if the kingdom is ever to be strong, th—"

He broke off as Elminster glided up between them, displayed the earring, and murmured, "Cry pardon for the interruption, my lords, but I am sent on a mission of love. The lady Lord Otharr was so anxious to make the acquaintance of confesses herself somewhat disappointed by his . . . ah, brief performance, and hopeful that another man of importance—such as yourself, my lord—would be made of rather sterner stuff. She bade me be sure to tell ye that she found thy tongue and bearing *most* impressive, and would know both better."

Thelorn looked up at Elminster and grinned suddenly; the swordmaster shook his head, rolled his eyes, and turned away. The young noble's eyes went across the room to the curtain. Elminster nodded and strode toward it, Thelorn following through the way that the youth cleared.

When they reached the curtain, El ducked a look around it and held it a little aside; Thelorn peered in.

A heap of clothing and bed draperies lay close by; beyond them, a single flickering stub of candle glimmered in the navel of the lady who lay bare to his sight on the bed. A silk half-mask hooded her face, and she was smiling through the swirl of long hair that lay across her mouth as she lounged with her arms clasped behind her head. "Come in, and be at ease," she murmured, "my lord."

Thelorn's smile widened, and he stepped forward. As the curtain fell into place behind them both, Elminster moved with the noble, raised his trusty dagger hilt, and clubbed down, leaping a little off the floor to put his strength behind the blow.

Thelorn fell forward onto the end of the bed like a chopped sapling; Farl exploded from his concealment under heaped pillows to pull Shandathe's feet away before he crashed down atop them.

Farl and El grinned at each other, working swiftly. Rings that might carry spells they dared not take, and Shandathe was due her coins; they tossed them to her as she swiftly dressed, and were rewarded with an enthusiastic kiss each. She was as beautiful as El had thought she'd be; well, some other night, perhaps.

They quickly stripped Selemban's clothes away, dragged the senseless Jansibal out from under the heap of draperies, and arranged the two naked lordlings in an embrace on the bed for others to find. Supporting the Shadow between them as if she were faint, arms around her shoulders, they helped her out through the taproom, to the alley door by the jakes.

A hopeful slug-and-snatcher glided out from a dark angle of walls, saw Farl's warning gaze and El's dagger gleaming ready, and drew back again. Without a word the trio turned north, toward old Hannibur's.

The grizzled old baker lived alone over his shop. His weathered face, wooden foot, acerbic tongue, and natural stinginess made him unattractive to the ladies of Hastarl. Most days, he tossed drying, unbought bread ends, and sometimes even whole loaves, out his back door to the hopeful and hungry urchins who played there. Tonight his snores rumbled faintly out into the alley through the closed shutters of his bedchamber.

"Where are we going, m'lords?" Shandathe was still amused at the jest—and grateful for the extra gold—but her voice held a note of alarm. She'd heard some things about her two young escorts.

"We must hide you before those beasts awaken and send their bodyguards out to collect what you neglected to give them—and your hide along with it," Farl said in her ear, embracing her.

"Aye, but where?" the Shadow asked, putting her arms around him. Farl pointed up at the window from which the snoring was coming.

Shandathe stared at him. "Are you *crazed?*" she hissed in sudden anger. "If you think I'm g—"

Farl's hands glided to just the right places as he pressed his lips to hers. She struggled angrily for a moment, managing to utter some angry-sounding murmurs . . . and then went limp. Farl promptly passed her to Elminster. "Here," he said brightly.

He turned away and hastily erected a pyramid of crates from the baker's litter of shipping refuse. Elminster stared at him and then down at the girl in his arms. She was soft and beautiful—if heavy—and was stirring already; in a breath or two, she'd return to her senses . . . and if El knew anything about the Shadow, she'd be *very* angry. He looked around gingerly for a place to put her.

"'Tis Hannibur's lucky night," Farl said with a smile, as he swarmed back down the swiftly erected pyramid. Above, the shutters now hung open, and the snores roared out unmuted down the alley. He pointed at Elminster and at Shandathe, and then up at the window again.

"To be sure," El murmured in reply, mounting the crates with the limp Shadow heavy on his back. Her delicate scent played at his nostrils, and he added under his breath, "Luckier than me, I'll warrant."

Then he was climbing carefully through the window, Farl steadying Shandathe's limbs to prevent a fall or noise. She stirred as they crossed the bare board floor to Hannibur's bed.

They drew back the patched woolen covers and laid her carefully beside the sleeping baker. Then they both turned away to stifle rising mirth: the old man wore a daringly cut, frilly wanton wench's robe. Hairy vein-mottled flesh and bony knees protruded from the sheer silk.

El bit his lip and staggered to the window, shoulders shaking silently. Farl mastered himself sooner, and delicately drew aside two sets of garments; their owners stirred. Softly he stroked two bodies, and raced on catlike feet for the window. El was already halfway down the crates, outside.

The two thieves giggled at each other as they hauled out the bottom crates. Everything above tumbled and fell, creating a din that ought to cut through even Hannibur's snores, and they raced away around a corner.

Pausing for breath in a courtyard half Hastarl away, Farl said, "Whew! A good even's work. Pity I hadn't time to empty my tankard before that hippopotamus-ass pushed his way in on you."

Elminster grinned and handed him Shandathe's earring. Farl smiled down at it. "Well, at least we got some pay for all our thoughtful work."

El's own grin widened as he dropped three heavy links of gold chain into Farl's other hand. "Twisted it open and shortened the thing by a few links," he said innocently. "He was wearing his lion too low for the *full* effect, anyway."

Farl burst into delighted laughter, and they clung together, chuckling, until Farl caught sight of a nearby signboard. "Let's go hoist a tankard," he puffed.

"What?" Elminster's blue-gray eyes danced dangerously. "Again?"

Three times Selûne had risen over the high towers of Athalgard since that night, and talk of the two young and very friendly sons of magelords was all over the city. The bodyguards of both were prowling through every tavern and beanpot dining room in the poorer parts of Hastarl, obviously looking for a certain hawk-nosed, black-haired youth and his clever-tongued friend . . . so

Eladar and Farl had judged it prudent to take a brief vacation until the searchers grew careless enough for accidents to happen to them—or until some street thief too desperate to be wise tried to rob one of them, and their search was diverted to new targets.

Lying exposed to the gaze and bows of bored guards on the battlements of Athalgard made both the friends uneasy, so they had taken to chatting, relaxing, and plotting in the seclusion of the old walled burial ground at the other end of the city: an overgrown, disused place where the cracked and leaning stone vaults of wealthy families crumbled into rubble amid stunted trees that burst up through them, and spread concealing branches in all directions.

Proud names and thieves successful enough to buy wealth and station all came here in the end . . . all their boasts and plots and gold coins bought them no more than crumbling gravestones, inscribed with lies about their greatness and good character. Scant comfort, El thought, to the moldering bones beneath.

In the tranquil shade of the tomb trees, the two friends lay atop the sloping roof of Ansildabar's Last Rest, knowing but not caring that the bones of the once-famous explorer lay gnawed and exposed in the pillaged tomb beneath, and passed a wineskin back and forth as they watched the shadows cast by the lowering sun creep across leaning tombs and collapsed mausoleums, heralding dusk.

"I've been thinking," Farl said suddenly, holding out his hand for the skin.

"Usually a bad sign," Elminster agreed affably, handing it over.

"Hah-ha," Farl replied, "between wild orgies, I mean."

"Ah, I'd been wondering what those momentary pauses were," Elminster said, extending his hand for the skin. Farl, who hadn't yet drunk, gave him a hurt look and a 'stay' gesture, and then drank deeply. Sighing with satisfaction, he wiped his mouth and held it out.

"D'you recall how much Budaera was asking me for pleasure together?"

Elminster grinned. "Aye. A low price—just for thee."

Farl nodded. "Exactly. Gold pieces hand over fist, these maids make . . . 'twould be easy, I'm thinking, to find out where some of 'em hide their loot—and help ourselves while they were sleeping, or out 'busy' at the taverns and rich merchants' clubs."

"Nay," El said firmly, "count me out of such plots. Fleece such sheep an' ye'll do it alone."

Farl looked at him. "Right, consider the plot abandoned. Now tell me why."

Elminster set his jaw. "I'll not steal from those who barely have enough coins for food, let alone taxes or saving."

"Principles?" Farl rescued the nearly empty wineskin.

"I've always had 'em. Ye know that." El waved away the skin, and Farl happily drained it.

"I thought ye wanted to slay *all* the wizards in Athalantar."

Elminster nodded. "All the magelords. Aye, I've sworn that oath—and slow, iron-careful, I've set about fulfilling it," he replied, staring out over the river, where a pole barge had just come into view in the distance, heading downstream toward the docks. "Yet sometimes I wonder what else I should do—what more life should be."

"Roast boar feasts every night," Farl said. "So much coin to buy them that I'll never have to feel the bite of a knife or hide in rotting dung while armsmen poke into it with their halberds."

"Nothing more?" El asked. "Nothing—higher?"

"What's the point?" Farl asked with a touch of scorn. "There're priests enough all over Faerûn to worry about things like that—and my empty stomach never tires of telling me what *I* should be tending to." Satisfied that the very last drop of wine had fallen into his open mouth, he lowered the skin, rolled it, and thrust it through his belt. Then he looked across at his friend.

Eladar the Dark was frowning at him. "What gods should I worship?"

Farl shrugged, taken aback, and spread his hands. "A man must find that out for himself—or should. Only fools obey the nearest priest."

Amusement came into the blue-gray eyes locked on his. "What do priests do, then?"

Farl shrugged. "A lot of chanting and angry shouting and sticking swords into people who worship other gods."

In the same quiet, serious voice, El asked, "What use are faiths, then?"

Farl shrugged wildly, adopting a crazed, "Who can know?" expression, but El's serious eyes stayed on him, and after a silence Farl said slowly, "Folk always have to believe there's something better, somewhere, than what they have right now—and that they just *might* get it. And they like to belong, to be part of a group, and feel superior to outlanders. It's why folk join clubs, and companies, and fellowships."

Eladar looked at him. "And go out and stick swords in each other in dark alleys—and then feel superior about it?"

Farl grinned. "Exactly." He watched the pole barge scrape to a stop against a distant dock, and said casually, "If we're going to be facing death together many nights longer, it'd probably be a good thing if I knew this code of yours. I know you prefer shop guarding, dockwork, and errand- and package-running to thieving, but who wouldn't?"

"Crazed-wits out looking for thrills," El said dryly.

Farl laughed. "Leave me out of it for a breath or two, and tell."

Elminster thought for a moment. "I won't slay innocent folk . . . and I don't like stealing from anyone except rich merchants who are grasping, unpleasant, or openly dishonest. Oh, and wizards of course."

"You really hate them, don't you?"

Elminster shrugged. "I—I've contempt for those who hide behind magic and lord it over the rest of us because someone taught them to read, or the gods gave them the power to wield magic, or something. They should be using the Art to help us all, not keep folk down and lord it over them."

"If you were Belaur right now," Farl said softly, "what in the name of the gods could you do but obey the wizards?"

El shrugged. "The king may be trapped, and he may not be. He never shows himself for us unwashed to get to know him—ye know, the subjects he's supposed to be serving—so how can I tell?"

"You said once your parents were killed by a dragon-riding wizard," Farl said.

Elminster looked at him sharply. "Did I?"

"You were drunk. I—not long after we met—I had to know if I could trust you, so I got you drunk. That night at the Ring of Blades, you wouldn't say anything else except 'outlaw' and 'kill magelords.' You kept repeating that."

Elminster stared steadily at the shattered crown of a nearby vault. "Every man needs an obsession," he said. He turned his head. "What's thine?"

Farl shrugged his shoulders. "Excitement. If I'm not in danger or doing high, hidden, and important deeds, I'm not alive."

Elminster nodded, remembering.

It had been a cold, blustery day, muddy slush ankle-deep in the streets of Hastarl. Newly arrived and wandering wide-eyed, El turned down a blind alley only to find, when he spun about, that he was facing a line of hard-eyed, grinning men blocking his way. A balding, burly giant in worn leathers stood at their head, a padded stick in one hand and a canvas sack big enough to enclose Elminster's head—for that was its purpose—in the other. They stalked down the alley toward him.

El backed away, fingering the Lion Sword and wondering if he could fight so many hardened men in such a confined space and hope to win.

He took a stand in a corner, blade out, but they didn't slow their steady, menacing advance. The bald man raised his stick, obviously planning to strike aside the lad's sword while the others wrestled him down, but before he could, a calm voice broke in from overhead.

"I wouldn't do that if I were you, Shildo. He's Hawklyn's meat already, marked and in use; see how bedazed he is?—and you know what Hawklyn does to blades who meddle."

The bald man looked up, face ugly. "And who's going to say we did it?"

The slim youth crouching on the windowsill, hand crossbow sliding gently back and forth to menace one bravo after another, smiled and said, "That's already been done, bald-pate. Two breaths ago Antaerl flew off to report. He left me to dissuade you because he recalls an old debt he owes you—and what happened the *last* time a snatch band took the wrong man. Wasn't pleasant, was it, Shildo? Recall what Undarl said he'd do to you if you made another unfortunate mistake? *I* remember."

Snarling, the bald man spun around and stalked oft, breaking the line of bravos and waving at them to accompany him.

When the alley was empty, Elminster looked up and said, "Thankee for a rescue. My life is thine, Sir—?"

"Farl's the name, an' no 'sir' am I. I'm proud of that, mind." Farl explained that 'meat' was the name given to bumpkins, slaves, and other unfortunates used by magelords for experiments that slew, twisted, transformed, or left them mind-slaves. The wandering, obviously bewildered Elminster had looked like a prime snatch candidate, or a mind-slave already in thrall. "That's what I persuaded him you were," he said warningly.

"Thankee, I think," El replied wryly. "Why did that make a difference?"

"I intimated you were the property of the most powerful magelord. Shildo serves a rival whose power isn't great enough for open challenges yet. Shildo's under *very* strict orders not to provoke anything just now." He shifted on the snowy ledge and added, "Want to put away that blade? We could go somewhere warmer I know of, where they'll overcharge us for some hot turtle soup and burned toast . . . if you'll pay."

"Gladly," Elminster said, "if ye'll tell me where I can find a bed in this city, an' tell me what not to do."

"I'll do that," the laughing youth replied, jumping lightly down. "You need to learn, and I like to talk. Better; you look like you need a friend, and I find myself in short supply of them right now too . . . hey?"

"Lead on," Elminster said.

He'd learned much that day, and in the days since then—but not where Farl had come from. The merry thief seemed part of Hastarl, as if he'd always been there and the city echoed his moods and manner. The two had taken a liking to each other and stolen more than their own weights in gold and gems through a slow spring and much of a long, hot summer.

Musing about this damp city of the magelords around him, Elminster found himself back on the sloping stone of the tomb roof, in the ebbing heat of a long, lazy summer day. He turned to look into his friend's face. "More than once, ye've said ye knew I came from Heldon."

Farl nodded. "The way you speak: up-country, for sure, and east. More—the winter when Undarl joined the magelords, talk went around the city that he'd impressed the others into accepting him in by riding a dragon he could command. At Lord Hawklyn's bidding he went to the village of Heldon to slay a man and wife there—and to show them what he could do, he had it tear the place stone from stone, an' burn all, even dogs running away across the fields."

"Undarl," Elminster repeated softly.

Farl saw that his friend's hands were clenched, white, and trembling. He nodded. "If it makes you feel better, El, I understand how you feel."

The eyes that Elminster turned on him blazed like a fire of blue steel, but his voice came with terrible softness as he asked, "Oh? How?"

"The magelords killed my mother," Farl said calmly.

Elminster looked at him, the fire dying. "What befell thy father then?"

Farl shrugged. "Oh, he's very well indeed."

Elminster looked a silent question, and Farl smiled a little sadly. "In fact, he's probably up in that tower there right now—and if Tyche frowns on us, he'll have magic up that enables him to hear us when I use his name."

Elminster looked up at the tower and said, "Could he strike us with a spell from there?"

Farl shrugged. "Who knows what wizards have learned to do? But I doubt it, or certain men'd be falling on their faces all over Hastarl. Besides, the magelords I know could never resist taunting their foes before smiting them down, face-to-face."

"Then use his name," Elminster said deliberately, "and mayhap he'll come down where I can reach him."

"After I do," Farl replied softly. "After I'm done tearing his tongue out by the roots and breaking all his fingers to stop his spells—then I'll let you have some fun. He shouldn't die in any great haste."

"So who is he?"

Farl lifted one side of his mouth in a mirthless smile. "Lord Hawklyn, master magelord. Mage Royal of Athalantar, to you." He turned his head to watch a fleetwing whirl from one broken pillar to another. "I was illegitimate. Hawklyn had my mother—a lady of the court, loved by many, they say—killed when he learned of my birth."

"Why d'ye still live—outside yon tower?"

Farl stared into the past, not seeing the tombs ahead of him. "His men slaughtered a baby—but the wrong one; some other poor brat. I was stolen by a woman my mother had befriended . . . a lady of the evening."

Elminster raised his brows. "Yet ye proposed stealing from those same night maids?"

Farl shrugged. "One of them strangled my foster mother for a few coins; I've never found out who, but almost certainly one of the girls in the Wench on"—his voice mockingly assumed the pedantic tones of a sage relating a tale of awesome importance—"the night when two magelords' sons revealed their love to all Hastarl."

"Oh, gods," Elminster said quietly, "and I've felt sorry for meself a time or two. Farl, ye—"

"Can tell you to belt up and not say whatever tearful mush you were about to spout," Farl said serenely. "When the feebleness brought on by my advancing dotage requires sympathy from thee, Eladar Mage-Killer, I shall not keep thee unapprised of the fact."

His grandiose tones brought forth a chuckle from Elminster, who asked, "What's it to be now, then?"

Farl grinned and, in one smooth movement, rolled to his feet. "Rest time's over. Back to the wars. So you won't let me take advantage of ladies of the evening or innocent folk—well, that's not a hard bind. There can't be more than two or three of the latter in all Hastarl—an' we've hit the wizards and the high-and-mighty families overmuch. If we roost too often on the same perch, 'tis traps we'll find waiting, not piles of coins ready for the taking. This leaves us with two targets: temples—"

"Nay," Elminster said firmly. "No meddling with the affairs of gods. I'd rather not spend the rest of a short and unhappy life with most of Those Who Hear All furious with me—to say nothing of their priesthoods."

Farl grinned. "I expected that. Well, then, there's but one field we've not touched: rich merchants."

He held up a hand to forestall Elminster's coming protest about plundering hardworking shopkeepers and said quickly, "I mean those who lend coins and invest in back rooms and behind secure doors, working secretly in groups to keep prices high and arrange accidents for competitors ... ever notice how few companies own the barges that actually land here? And the warehouses? Hmmm? We've got to learn how these folk operate, because if we're ever to retire from plucking things out of the pockets of lesser folk—and no one's fingers stay nimble forever, you know—we'll have to join the folk who sit idle and let their coins work for them."

Elminster was frowning thoughtfully. "A hidden world, masked by what most see in the streets."

"Just as our world—the realm of thieves—is hidden," Farl added.

"Right," El said with enthusiasm. "That's our battlefield, then. What now? How to begin?"

"This night," Farl said, "by handsomely bribing a man who owes me an old favor, I plan to attend a dinner I'd never be allowed in to. He'd be serving wine there, but I'll be doing it in his place, and listening to what I should not hear. If I'm right, I'll hear plans and agreements for quite a bit of quiet trade into and out of the city for the rest of the season." He frowned. "There's one problem. You can't come. There's no way you can get close enough to hear anything without being caught; these folk have guards everywhere. I've no excuse for getting you into the place, either."

Elminster nodded. "So I go elsewhere. An evening of idleness, or have ye any suggestions?"

Farl nodded slowly. "Aye, but there's great danger. There's a certain house I've had my eye on for four summers now; 'tis home to three free-spending merchants who deal in exchanging goods and lending coins but never seem to lift a finger to do any real work. They're probably part of this chain of investors. Can you skulk about the place without being seen? We need to know where doors, and approaches, and important rooms and the like are—and if you can overhear anything interesting while they dine. . . ."

El nodded. "Lead me to the place. Just so long as ye don't expect any great tales when we meet on the morrow. I think it's only in minstrels' tales that folk sit around explaining things they already know for eavesdroppers to understand."

Farl nodded. "Just slip in, see where things are, try to find out if there's anything of import befalling—and get you gone again, as quietly as the thing can be done. I want no dead heroes in this partnership; it's too hard to find trustworthy partners."

"Ye prefer live cowards, eh?" Elminster asked as they dropped lightly down from the roof of the tomb and set off through the rubble and tangled plants toward the bough they'd come in by.

Farl stopped him. "Seriously, El—I've never found such fearlessness and honesty in anyone. To find it in one who also has endurance and dexterity . . . I've only one regret."

"Which is?" Elminster was blushing furiously.

"You're not a pretty lass."

Elminster replied with a rude noise, and they both chuckled and clambered up the tree that would afford them exit.

"I see only one worry ahead," Farl added. "Hastarl grows rich under the wizards, and thieves are coming in. Gangs. As they grow larger, you and I will have to join or start one of our own to survive. Besides, we'll need more hands than these four if we're to tackle these back room investors."

"And thy worry?"

"Betrayal."

That word hung in somber silence between them as they leaped down from the crumbling wall into a garbage-choked alley, and watched the rats run. Elminster said softly, "I've found something precious in thee, too, Farl."

"A friend prettier than yourself?"

"A friend, aye. Loyalty, and trust, too—more precious by far than all the gold we've taken together."

"Pretty speech. I've remembered another regret too," Farl added gravely. "I couldn't be there in the room to see Shandathe and old Hannibur waking up and seeing each other!"

They convulsed in shared laughter. "I have noted," Elminster added a few helpless breaths later as they went on down the street, "word of *that* meeting has *not* spread across Hastarl."

"A pity, indeed," Farl replied. They threw their arms around each other's shoulders and strode down the slippery cobbles, the conquest of all Hastarl bright ahead of them.

FIVE
TO CHAIN A MAGE

To chain a mage? Why, the promise of power and knowing secrets ('magic,' if you will), greed, and love—the things that chain all men ... and some of the more foolish women too.

ATHAEAL OF EVERMEET
MUSINGS OF A WITCH-QUEEN IN EXILE
YEAR OF THE BLACK FLAME

The smell wafting up through the high windows was wonderful. In spite of himself, Elminster's stomach growled. He clung to the stone sill, frozen in an awkward head-down pose, and hoped no one would hear.

The feast below was a merry one; glass tinkled and men laughed, short barks of merriment punctuating the general murmur of jests and earnest talk. He was still too distant to hear what was being said. El finished the knot and tugged on it; firm. Aye, then, into the hands of the gods ...

He waited for a burst of laughter and, when it came, slid down the thin cord to the balcony below. For the entire journey he was clearly visible to anyone at the board below who bothered to look up; he was sweating hard as his boots touched the balcony floor, and he could sink thankfully down into a sitting position behind the parapet, completely concealed from those at table. No outcry came. After a moment, he relaxed enough to peer carefully around. The balcony was dark and disused; he tried not to stir up dust that might force a sneeze or leave betraying marks behind.

Elminster then bent his attention to the chatter below—and within a few words was sitting frozen in fear and rising excitement. His hand went unbidden to his breast, where the Lion Sword was hidden.

"I've heard some sly whispers, Havilyn, that you doubt our powers," a cold and proud voice said, words falling into a sudden, tense silence, "that we are meant to scare the common folk into obedience to the Stag Throne and are not real wizards, daring to set foot outside our realm ... that our spells may be showy but would avail little against thieves and the night-work of competitors, leaving our shared investments unprotected."

"I've said no such thing."

"Perhaps not, but your tone now tells me that you believe it. Nay, put your blade away. I intend no harm to you this night. 'Twould be churlish to strike down a man in his own house—and the act of a fool to destroy a good ally and wealthy supporter. All I'd like you to do is watch a little demonstration."

"What sort of magic do you plan to spin, Hawklyn?" Havilyn's tone was wary. "I warn you that some here are not as protected by amulets and shields as I am—and have less reason to love you than I do. It would not be wise to make a man reach for a weapon at this table."

"I have no great violence in mind. I merely wish to reveal the efficacy of my magic by casting for you a spell I've recently perfected, which can compel any mortal whose name and likeness I know into my presence."

"Any mortal?"

"Any living mortal. Yet before you name some old foe you'd like to get your hands on, I want to show you the true power of the magic we wield here in Hastarl . . . the magic you've belittled as mere tricks and flame-balls to cow the common folk."

There was a strange, high ringing and clanking sound. "Behold this chain," came the cold voice of Neldryn Hawklyn, Mage Royal of Athalantar. "Set it down and withdraw; my thanks." There was a glassy shifting sound and then the receding tread of soft and hasty feet.

The clink of moving glass came again, and reflections of flame suddenly danced on the wall above Elminster. He peered at them narrowly and saw that a transparent chain was rising by itself from the floor, rising and coiling upward to hang in the air and turn slowly in a great spiral.

The cold voice of Hawklyn spoke again. "This is the Crystal Chain of Binding, wrought in Netheril long ages ago. Elves, dwarves, and men all searched for it and failed and thought it lost forever. I found it; behold the chain that can imprison any mage—and prevent his use of any magic. Beautiful, is it not?"

There were murmurs of response, and then the mightiest of the magelords continued. "Who is the mightiest mage in all Faerûn, Havilyn?"

"You want me to say you, I suppose . . . in truth, I know not—you're the expert in matters magical, not me . . . this Mad Mage we hear about, I guess. . . .'

"Nay, think greater than that. Recall you nothing of the teachings of Mystra?"

"*Her?* You plan a chain a *goddess?*"

"Nay; a mortal, I said, and it's a mortal I have in mind."

"Stop all this grand questioning and tell us," a sour voice said. "There's a time for cleverness and a time for plain talk—and I think we've fast reached the latter."

"Do you doubt my power?"

"Nay, Magelord, I believe you have magic to spare. I told you to stop lording it over us with arrogant word games and behave more like a great mage and less like a boy trying to impress with his brilliance."

These words ended in a sudden cry of disgust, and a murmur followed. Elminster risked a quick glance above the parapet to peer down, and as quickly ducked back below it again. He'd seen a man sitting at the table gaping in horror at his plate—and on it had been a human head, staring unseeing at him.

"Behold the head of the last man who tried to steal from your warehouse, beheaded by a spell-blade I conjured. There, 'Tis gone now. By all means enjoy the rest of your dinner, Nalith; it was only an illusion."

"I think you should tell us plainly, too, Hawklyn," said another, older voice. "Enough games."

"Well enough," the mage royal replied. "Watch, then, and keep silent."

There was a brief muttering, a flash of light, and a high-pitched sound like the jangle of clashing crystal or tiny ankle bells.

"Tell everyone who you are." There was cold triumph in Hawklyn's voice.

"I am called the Magister," came a new voice, calm but quavering with age. There were gasps from around the table, and Elminster could not restrain himself. This was the wizard who wore the mantle of Mystra's power. The greatest mage of all. He *had* to see. Slowly and cautiously he raised his head to peer over the parapet and froze, chilled by a sudden thought: if the mage-lords controlled the most powerful magic in all Faerûn, how could he ever hope to defeat them?

Below stretched the long, gleaming feast table. All the men seated around it were staring at a thin, bearded and robed man who stood upright in an area of radiance a little way down the hall. The hitherto empty spiral of chain was now revolving slowly around him. Little lightnings leaped and played among its coils as it turned, fed by the radiance around the Magister.

"Do you know where you are?" the mage royal asked coldly.

"This room, I know not—some grand house, surely. In Hastarl, in the Realm of the Stag."

"And what is it that binds you?" Magelord Hawklyn leaned forward as he spoke those eager words. Lamplight caught gem-adorned ward-runes on his dark robes, and they flashed as he moved, drawing eyes to him. He looked lean and dangerous as he spread long-fingered hands before him on the table and half rose to challenge the wizard in the grip of the chain.

The Magister looked at the chain with mild curiosity, rather like a man surveying sale-goods after idly entering a shop with an unspectacular facade. He reached out to touch it, ignoring the sudden lightnings that spat and crackled, blinding white, around his wrinkled hand, tapped it thoughtfully, and said, "It appears to be the Crystal Chain of Binding, forged long ago in Netheril, and thought to be lost. Is it that, or some new chain of thy devising?"

"*I* shall ask the questions," Neldryn Hawklyn commanded grandly, "and you will give answer—or I'll use this crossbow, and Faerûn will have a new Magister." As he spoke, a cocked and loaded crossbow floated into view from behind a curtained door. Startled looks sped between the merchants sitting around the table.

"Oh," the old man said mildly, "is this a challenge, then?"

"Not unless you defy me. Consider it a threat hanging over you. Obey or perish—the same alternatives any king gives his subjects."

"You must live in rather more barbaric lands than I am used to," the Magister said in a dry voice. "Can it be, Neldryn Hawklyn, you have reshaped Athalantar into a tyranny of mages? I have heard things of you and your fellow magelords . . . and they were not good things."

"I don't doubt it," Hawklyn sneered. "Now hold your tongue 'til I bid you speak—or a new Magister will speak, in your stead."

"Do you then seek to control when and how the Magister speaks?" The old man's tone seemed almost sad.

"I do." The crossbow drifted nearer, rising menacingly to hang above the table, aimed at the old man's face.

"Mystra forbids that," the Magister said quietly, "and so I have no choice left. I must answer your challenge."

His body suddenly boiled into billowing vapors, faded, and was gone. The chains hung around emptiness for a moment, and then crashed to the floor.

The crossbow jerked as it fired—but the quarrel sped through emptiness, leaping across the room to strike a hanging shield and rebound. It cracked against the stone wall in a corner, fell, and flew no more.

"Let all that is hidden be *revealed!*" Mage Royal Hawklyn thundered, standing with his arms raised. Then he recoiled; the old man melted out of the air right in front of his face, sitting calmly on nothing in the air just above the table.

Half a dozen spells lashed out as alarmed wizards saw a clear chance to slay. Amid the leaping magic, terrified merchants upset chairs in their haste to bolt from the table. Food sprayed into the air as ravening flame, bolts of lightning, and mist-shedding beams of coldness cut the air, meeting in hissing chaos where the old man—had been. He was gone, instants before deadly magic struck . . . if he'd ever been there at all.

"Those who live by the slaying spell," the Magister said mildly from the balcony—Elminster whirled and gaped in terror as the man in robes suddenly appeared beside him—"must expect, in the end, to die by it."

He raised his wrinkled hands. From each finger a ruby ray of light stabbed out across the room. Solid things they touched boiled silently away. El gulped as he saw legs standing with no body left above them—and beyond, a sobbing wizard crash to the floor as his frantically running feet were suddenly gone from under him. Amid the screams and crashes the rays slowly faded, leaving only spreading flames behind, where they'd scorched wood or singed tapestries.

The rays were still dying away as men all over the room started to rise into the air—whole or in remains, floating slowly straight up, regardless of their struggles or frantic spellcastings. Glass tinkled and sang as the chain also rose into the air, gliding and coiling like a gigantic snake.

From somewhere nearby, Hawklyn snarled an incantation in a high, frightened voice. The old man ignored him.

The rising men came to a smooth halt at the same height as the balcony, and the chain wove its way among them, gleaming in the light of the fires below.

There was a flash and a roar. Elminster dived for his life as Hawklyn's spell smashed half the balcony into a splintered ruin of paneling and shattered stone. Desperately the young thief clawed his way along a stone floor that was crumbling and collapsing under and behind him.

With a shudder and then a gathering roar, most of the tiles of the broken balcony floor slid down to the stones of the feasting hall amid a cloud of dust. The rubble piled up in a heap around a lone, leaning pillar that had supported that end of the balcony moments before. Sprawled on the surviving remnant of the balcony, Elminster turned in haste to see the Magister unconcernedly standing on empty air, surrounded by a ring of helpless, floating, frightened men.

"Is *that* the best you can do, Hawklyn?" The old man shook his head. "You had no business even thinking you could ever grow mighty enough to challenge me, with such feeble powers . . . and dull wits driving them." He sighed. Elminster saw the crystal chain had wrapped itself around the neck of one floating man.

The man's head was turned with slow, terrible, unseen force, until he hung helplessly staring into the old man's eyes. "So you are a magelord, Maulygh . . . of long service, I see, and you fancy yourself too cunning to appear openly ambitious. Yet you desire to rule over all and await any chance to smite down these others, and take the throne for yourself. And you have plans; your reign would not be gentle."

The Magister waved a hand in dismissal, and the crystal links around the wizard's neck burst apart in tinkling shards. Maulygh's headless body jerked once and then hung limp and dripping. The shortened chain glided on to the next man.

"Only a merchant, eh? Othyl Naerimmin, a panderer, smuggler, and dealer in scents and beer." The quavering voice seemed almost hopeful, but when it came again, it was a low, bitter tone of disappointment. "You arrange poisonings." The coil of the chain burst again, leaving another hanging body behind.

Someone wailed in terror, almost drowning out the frantic mutterings of several spellcastings. The Magister ignored it all as he watched the chain wind its deadly way on through the air. One man—a fat merchant, gasping and staring in horror, was spared. He floated gently down to the floor, fell when the magic released him, and then scrambled up, whimpering, and fled from the hall.

The next man was another mage, who spat defiance and went to his death raging. When he was headless, pulses of purple radiance flared around the body. The Magister studied them. "An interesting web of contingencies—don't you think, Hawklyn?

The mage royal spat a word that echoed and rolled around the hall, and there was a sudden burst of flame. Elminster shrank back into the corner and hid his face, feeling a sudden wash of heat. Then it was gone, and amid the creaking of cooling stone and the rush of tortured air, they heard the old man sigh.

"Fireballs . . . always fireballs. Can't the young cast anything else?"

The Magister stood unharmed on empty air, watching the chain—much shortened now, its surface cracked and blackened from fire—move to the next man. He proved to be dead already, of fright or self-spell or a stray glass shard, and the chain drifted on.

Twice more it burst, and then another merchant was spared. He fled sobbing, leaving only the mage royal of Athalantar hanging alive before the Magister. Hawklyn looked right and left at the headless things in the air around him and snarled in fear.

"I must confess that killing you will bring me satisfaction," the old man said. "Yet I'd be more pleased still if you renounced all claims to this realm here and now and agreed to serve Mystra under my direction."

Hawklyn cursed, and with trembling hands tried to shape one last spell. The Magister listened politely and then shook his head, ignoring the shadowy taloned beast that appeared in the air before him.

Its cruel claws passed right through the old man, and then faded away as the last links of the Chain of Binding burst. Blood spattered on the stone floor far below.

Leaving the corpses hanging in grisly array, the Magister turned to regard the youth crouched watching in the surviving corner of the balcony. There was a dangerous glint in his eyes as they met Elminster's awed gaze. "Are you a magelord, boy, or a servant of this house?"

"Neither." Tearing his gaze free with an effort, Elminster leaped from the balcony, landing hard on the blood-spattered stones below. The old man's eyes narrowed, and he lifted a finger. A wall of flames sprang up in a ring around the thief, who spun around, the sharpened stub of an old war-sword suddenly in his hand.

Fear lent Elminster anger; his voice trembled with both as he faced the old man standing on air above him. "Can ye not see I'm no wild-spells wizard? Are ye no better than these cruel mages who rule Athalantar?" He waved his blade at the roaring flames around him. "Or are all who wield magic so twisted by its power that they become tyrants who delight in maiming, destroying, and spreading fear among honest folk?"

"Are you not—with these?" the Magister asked, spreading his hand to indicate the bodies hanging silently around him.

"*With* them?" Elminster spat. "I fight them whenever I dare—and hope one day to destroy them all so men can walk Athalantar free and happy again!" His face twisted at a sudden thought. "I sound a bit like a high minstrel, don't I?" he added, more quietly.

The Magister regarded him thoughtfully. "That's not a bad way to think," he said quietly, "if you survive the dangers of talking the same way." A sudden smile lit his face, and Elminster found himself smiling back.

Unseen by them both, down the hall, a pair of eyes appeared amid swirling points of light, in the flames flickering around the canted wreckage of the collapsed feast table. They watched the boy and the floating mage, and looked thoughtful.

"Can ye really see all that men are, and think?" Elminster asked, awkwardly blurting out the question.

"No," the Magister replied simply. His old brown eyes looked down into unflinching blue-gray ones as he made the crackling wall of flames die away to nothing.

Elminster looked once to see what had befallen, but made no move to flee. Standing on the rubble-strewn, blood-spattered floor, he looked back up at the old wizard. "Are ye going to blast me or let me go?"

"I have no interest in destroying honest folk—and very little at all in the affairs of those who have no magic. I see you have magesight, lad . . . why don't you try your hand at sorcery?"

Elminster gave him a dark look. His voice was scornful as he said, "I've no interest in such things, or in becoming the sort of man who wields magic. Whenever I look upon mages, I see snakes who use their spells to make folk fear them—like a whip to drive others to obey. Hard, arrogant men who can take a life, or"—he raised hard eyes to look at the destruction all around; the eyes watching from the flames shrank down to avoid notice—"destroy a hall in a few breaths, and not care what they've done, so long as their whims are satisfied. Leave me out of the ranks of wizards, lord."

Then, staring up at the old man's calm face, Elminster knew sudden fear. His words had been harsh, and the Magister was a mage like any other. The mild old eyes, though, seemed to hold . . . approval?

"Those who don't love hurling power make the best mages," the Magister replied. His eyes seemed suddenly to bore deep into Elminster's soul like seeking, darting things, and sadness was in his voice again as he added, "And those who live by stealing almost always rob themselves of their own lives, in the end."

"The taking gives me no pleasure," Elminster retorted. "I do it to have enough to eat—and to strike against the magelords where and when I can."

The Magister nodded. "That's why ye might listen," he said. "I'd not have wasted my breath otherwise."

Elminster stared up at him thoughtfully—and then stiffened as he heard the sudden, approaching thunder of running, booted feet echoing in the passages nearby. That sound could mean only one thing: armsmen of Athalantar.

"Save thyself!" he snapped, without stopping to think what a ridiculous warning that was to the mightiest archmage in all the world, and darted toward the nearest archway that did not ring with footfalls.

He was still three running strides short of it when men with halberds and crossbows burst into the room, but the puffing merchant with them stabbed a finger up at the floating mage and bellowed, "There!"

By the time the volley of quarrels and hastily conjured flames had torn through suddenly empty air, both the running boy and the eyes in the licking flames that played about the ruin of Havilyn's once grand table had vanished. A breath later, the floating corpses suddenly fell from the air, striking the stone floor with wet, heavy thuds. White-faced armsmen drew back, calling aloud on Tempus to defend them and Tyche to aid them.

Elminster took one door out of the kitchen, found himself in a dead-end cluster of pantries, and raced frantically back to the kitchen's other, smaller door, offering his own quieter prayer to Tyche that it not be another pantry—when he heard Havilyn's furious voice snarl, "Find that boy! He's no part of my household!"

Cursing aloud, Elminster snatched open the door. Yes, this was the way the terrified cooks had fled. He took the stairs two at time until at a bend in the stair several halberds crashed down together in front of him, striking sparks. Snarling armsmen struggled to tear them free of the stair rails and wrestle them around to stab downward—but El had already seen a third armsman lumbering along the passage above with a ready crossbow. He leaped back down the stairs in a single bound, landed hard on his haunches, and sprang sideways into an evil-smelling alcove.

A breath later, a crossbow quarrel cracked off the wall nearby and rattled down into the kitchens. A second quarrel followed, speeding deep into the throat of the foremost armsman racing up the stairs.

Elminster didn't spare the time to watch the man gurgle and fall; he was looking around the dark alcove for the scullery door. There! Wrenching it open, he skidded across the noisome room, through a maze of sloped boards where meat was washed and buckets where food scraps were thrown, hoping the house was old enough to have . . . *yes!*

El seized the pull ring and hauled up the trapdoor of the refuse pit. He could hear the waters of the Run rushing past in the darkness below as he slid feet first down to join them.

The drop was farther than he'd thought it would be, and the waters numbingly cold. El's heels struck a mucky bottom for a moment, and he twisted to one side to come up off to one side of the door above.

Trying to ignore the unseen slimy lumps floating in the water with him, he came up gasping for breath, in time to hear a quarrel crack off the hatch somewhere above and behind him, followed by the shout, "The sewers! He's gone below!"

Elminster swam with the rushing river, trying not to make noise. He didn't trust the avid armsmen not to come down after him or lower torches and try their archery along the river tunnel. The chill of the waters crept into him as they carried him around a corner and away.

It seemed the first chance he'd had in a long while to collect his wits. The mage royal and at least three other magelords had been swept away in a single night—but the hand of Elminster had done nothing to them. He hadn't even a bite of supper or a spare coin from the house to show for his efforts.

"Elminster gives thee thanks, Tyche," he murmured into the rushing darkness. He'd managed to hang onto his head in that chamber of death; he supposed that was something . . . something even mighty wizards hadn't managed! Prudence stifled the whoop of exultation that suddenly rose within him—but it warmed him as he was swept out of the darkness into the blue, lamplit dimness of evening beneath the docks. He turned his head to look up at the dark spires of Athalgard and grinned his defiance at them.

The feeling lasted until he'd clambered out of the water onto a disused dock and started the cold, dripping walk home. If he'd been Farl, he'd have taken his knowledge of who'd died in that chamber to swoop down on a hand's worth of houses this very night and seize riches their owners would never claim before relatives or lesser vultures knew man or treasure was missing, and be safely gone into the night.

"But I'm not Farl," Elminster told the night, "and not even all that good a thief—what I am is a good runner."

To prove it, he outran the armsman who came around a corner just then, halberd in hand, who with a startled shout recognized the youth he'd almost spitted in a stairway in Havilyn's house not twenty breaths ago. Their pounding pursuit took them along a winding street lined with the walled gardens of the wealthy. As they ran under overhanging trees, a dark shadow reached down from one of them and struck the armsmen hard and accurately in the face with a cobblestone.

The man pitched to the cobbles with a clatter, and Fan dropped lightly down into the road, calling, "Eladar!"

Elminster turned at the top of the road and looked back. His friend stood with hands on hips, shaking his head.

"Can't leave you alone for an evening, I see," Farl said as El puffed his way back down the street.

As he came up, his friend was kneeling on the guard's neck, expertly feeling for purses, spare daggers, medallions, and other items of interest. "Something important's happened," Farl said, not looking up. "Havilyn came running in, all out of breath, and said something to Fentarn—and we were all ordered out of the house, and the armsmen after us to be sure we were turned out into the street—while the lot of them ran somewhere—ran, El, I tell you . . . I didn't know any high-and-mighty merchants *remembered* how to run. . . ."

"I was where the important thing happened," Elminster said quietly. "That's why this one was chasing me."

Farl looked up at him, eyes alight. "Tell," was all he said.

"Later," Elminster replied. "Let me describe the dead first, and once ye've named them, we can visit whichever unsuspecting incipient houses of grief bid fair to have the heaviest loot lying around for the taking."

Farl grinned fiercely. "Suppose we do just that, O prince of thieves." In his excitement and the effort of lifting the guard's body, he did not see Elminster stiffen at the word "prince."

"We're fair out of room in there," Farl said in satisfaction when they were safely away from the boarded-up shop where their takings were cached. "Now let's go somewhere where we can talk and not be seen."

"The burial ground again?"

"Fair enough—once we make sure it's free of lovers."

They did so, and Elminster told Farl the tale. His friend shook his head at El's description of the Magister. "I thought he was just a legend," he protested.

"Nay," El said quietly, "he was frightening—ah, but it was magnificent, the way he ignored their best spells, and calmly judged each and struck them down. The *power!*"

Farl cast a sidelong glance at his friend. Elminster was staring up at the moon, eyes bright. "To have that much power, someday," he murmured, "and never have to run from an armsman again!"

"I thought you hated wizards?"

"I—I do . . . magelords, at least. There's something about seeing spells hurled, though, that—"

"Fascinates, eh? I've felt that." Farl nodded in the moonlight. "You'll get over it once you've tried to fire a wand or speak a spell over and over again and nothing happens. You learn to admire it from a distance and keep well clear—or be swiftly slain. Godsbedamned wizards." He yawned. "Well, a good night's work. . . . Let's get some slumber under Selûne—or we'll be snoring somewhere when full day comes again."

"Here?"

"Nay—two of those dead, at least, have family vaults right here—and what if their servants, sent to clean up the tombs and the brush for a burial, are fearful enough of walking dead to demand an escort of armsmen? Nay, we need to find a roof elsewhere."

A sudden thought came to Elminster, and he grinned. "Hannibur's?"

Farl grinned back. "His snores'd wake a corpse."

"Exactly." They laughed and hastened back through the dark streets and alleys of the city, avoiding aroused bands of armsmen who were tramping aimlessly about in the night, looking for a running youth in dank leathers and an old mage strolling along in the air—and no doubt inwardly hoping they'd find neither.

As the half-light that heralds dawn stole down the river and into Hastarl, El and Farl settled down on Hannibur's roof, wondering at the silence from below. "What's become of his snoring?" El murmured, and Farl shrugged his own puzzlement in reply.

Then they heard the small sound from below that meant Hannibur had slid open the eye panel on his back door. They exchanged raised eyebrows and bent to look down into the alley—in time to see Shandathe Llaerin, called "the Shadow" for her smoothly silent ways, and perhaps the most beautiful woman in all Hastarl, come lightly up the alley to Hannibur's back door. They heard her say softly, "I'm here at last, love."

"At last," the baker rumbled as he drew the door warily open. "I thought ye'd never come. Come to the bed ye belong in, now."

Elminster and Farl exchanged delighted glances, and clasped hands with fierce joy in the night. Then, all thoughts of sleep gone, they settled down to listen to what befell in the room below.

And were fast asleep within seven breaths.

The hot sun woke the two exhausted, filthy thieves sometime late in the morning . . . and once they were awake, the smell of fresh-baked rolls and loaves wafting up from Hannibur's shop made sure they stayed that way.

Stomachs growling, the two thieves peered carefully down at the bedroom below. They could just see Shandathe's elbow as she slept the day peacefully away.

"Don't seem right, that she should sleep when we can't," Farl complained, rubbing his eyes.

"Let her sleep," Elminster replied. "She's doubtless earned it. Come." They climbed carefully down the crumbling back sills and crossbeams of the shop next door and went off to the silver-bit baths—only to find folk lined up.

"Whence this sudden urge for cleanliness, goodsir?" Farl asked a sausage vendor they knew by sight.

He frowned at them. "Haven't ye heard? The mage royal and a dozen other mages were killed last night! The dirge-walk begins at highsun."

"Killed? Just who could manage to slay the mage royal?"

"Ah." The sausage seller leaned close confidentially, pretending not to see the eight or so folk who crowded or leaned out of the line to listen. "There's some who says it was a mage they awakened from sleeping in a tomb all these years since the fall of Netheril!"

"Nay," a woman standing near put in, "'Twas—"

"And there's some," the sausage seller went on, raising his voice to ride over her, "what says it was a poor wretch they caught an' were going to eat, *alive*, so they say, for some foul magic—but when they sat down at the table, he turned into a dragon, and burned 'em all! Others say 'twas a beholder, or a mind flayer, or summat worse!"

"Nay, nay," the woman said, pushing in, "that's not it at all—"

"But meself," the sausage vendor said, elbowing her back and raising his voice again, so that it echoed back off the stone wall across the alley, "I think the first tale I heard is the true one: their wickedness was punished by a visit from Mystra *herself!*"

"Yes! That's it! 'Twas just that as happened, I tell thee!" The woman was hopping up and down in her excitement now; her capacious bosom heaved and rolled like tied bundles on the docks in high winds. "The mage royal thought he had a spell that would bring her to heel like a dog so he could use her power to destroy all wizards but ours and conquer all the lands from here to the Great Sea beyond Elembar! But he was wrong, and she—"

"She turned them all to boars, thrust spits up their behinds, and seared 'em in the hearth fires!" The gleeful voice belonged to a man nearby who stank of fish.

"Nay! I heard she plucked off all their heads—and *ate* 'em!" an old woman said proudly, as if King Belaur personally had told her.

"Ah, get gone wi' ye. Why'd she do that, eh?" The man next to her stepped on her foot, hard.

She hopped in pain, shaking her finger under his nose. "Just you wait, clever-nose! Jus' you wait an' see—if they has carved wooden 'eads when they're borne past us, or their heads covered wi' the burial cloaks, then I'm right! An' there's some folk in Hastarl as'll tell you Berdeece Hettir's *never* wrong! Jus' you wait!"

Farl and Elminster had been trading amused looks, but at this Farl smiled and said out of the side of his mouth, changing his voice so that it sounded gruff and distant: "I suppose as thou wouldn't put *money* on it, hey?"

In an instant, the alley was a bedlam of shouting, red-faced Hastarl folk holding up fingers to indicate their wagers.

"Wait a bit, wait a bit," Elminster said—and silence fell: Eladar the Dark *never* talked. "It always distresses me to see ye wager," he said, looking around earnestly, "because after, there's so much hard talk and people furious at those who didn't pay. So if ye must wager—and ye know *I* don't throw my coins about thus—I'll write down thy claims, and all can be settled fair, after."

There was much talk . . . and then a growing agreement that this was a good idea. Elminster tore the sleeve from the rotten shirt he was wearing, got some ink from the street scribe in trade for a quill that he'd stolen out of a window a tenday ago, and was still carrying in his boot, and set to work, scratching out sums with a rough-pointed needle.

In the rush, none of the folk noticed Farl met several heavy wagers, standing always for the headless side. Elminster worked his way along the line to its head, dodged inside to continue wagering, hung the scribbled sleeve on a high nail, and plunged headlong and fully clothed into the old winepress tub that served as the bath. The water was already gray with filth, and Elminster came out again just as fast, pursued by the furious proprietor. They dodged around the rinse-pump while Farl worked the handle, dousing them both with rather cleaner water—and then Elminster thrust four silver bits into the man's hand, leaped to retrieve the wager sleeve, and scampered out again.

"Gods *blast* thee! 'Tis a gold piece a head this day!" the man bellowed after them.

El spun around, disgusted, and tossed a handful of silver bits in the bath-keeper's direction. "He's a worse thief than we've *ever* been," he muttered to Farl as they headed for a good place to hide the sleeve. It seemed fitting that the folk of Hastarl were willing to pay good gold to see the backs forever of the mage royal and a good handful of magelords besides.

"Or a better," Farl agreed. Word of what had befallen was all over the city; folk talked of nothing else around them as they walked—and something of the air of a festival hung over the city. El shook his head at the open laughter, even among the patrols of armsmen. "Well, of *course* they're happy," Farl explained to his wondering partner. "It's not every night that some helpful young thief—even if he does prefer to give all the credit to some mysterious mage who conveniently came out of thin air and just as helpfully vanished back into it again—downs the most hated and feared man in all Athalantar and many of his fellow mages . . . not to mention a bunch of men that shopkeepers in this city owe a lot of coins to. Wouldn't you be, in their place?"

"They just haven't thought about which cruel magelord will step forward to proclaim himself mage royal, and make them even more fearful than before," Elminster replied darkly.

The wide streets along the route of the dirge-walk were filling already; folk who owned finery (and bath facilities of their own to prepare for its wearing) were pushing for the best positions—unaware of the flood of less polite and poorer neighbors who would shortly be charging in to seize the vantage points they wanted, regardless of who thought they owned it already. In most such processions, a good score of folk ended up crushed under the wheels of the carts, shoved forward by the press of leaning, shouting common folk.

"Are you thinking of what houses may be standing empty this good day, groaning with the weight of coins for the taking, while all Hastarl turns out to watch corpses paraded by?" Farl asked lightly.

"Nay," Elminster said. "I was thinking of switching the bucket that bath-keeper sits on for another—taking the one he's filling up with coins right now, and in its place leaving a bucket of—"

"Dung?" Farl grinned. "Too risky, though, by far—half the folk in line'd see us."

"Ye think they don't know what we do for a living, Farl? Even ye can't be that much the idiot!" Elminster replied.

Farl drew himself up with an air of injured dignity. "'Tis not that, goodsir—'tis that we have a reputation to maintain. Everyone may know that we take, aye—but none should ever see us doing the taking. It shouldst be magic, d'you see? Like those wizards you're so fond of."

El gave him a look. "Let's go take things," he said, and they strolled off to arm themselves for the workday ahead.

One house topped the list of places to loot, and they hastened hence, wearing livery that was not their own but that served to conceal carry bags strapped to their backs and bellies and to hide the handfuls of daggers they both carried.

They dropped over the back wall into a pleasant garden, crossed it like two hungry shadows, and swarmed up a climbing thornflower to a balcony. A servant was asleep in the sun in the room beyond, seizing a prize opportunity while his master was out of the house.

"This is *too* easy," Farl said as they sped up the stairs to a gilded door. He thrust his dagger into the carved snarling lion in its center and waited while the spring-loaded darts flashed away harmlessly down the stairs. "Don't these fools realize that the shops that sell 'em thief-traps are always run by thieves?"

He dug his blade into one of the lion's eyes, and the cut-glass eye popped out of its setting to dangle from the end of a cloth ribbon. Finding the wire in the opening behind the eye, Farl cut it and swung the door open. El looked back down the stairs as they went in, but the house was silent.

The bedchamber was a vision of red and deep pinkish tapestries, cushions, and couches. "I feel as if I'm in someone's stomach," Farl muttered as they crossed this sea of red.

"Or wading around in an open wound," Elminster agreed, striding up to a silver jewel-coffer.

As he reached for it, a hard-thrown dart flashed past his fingers. Farl spun, dagger in hand—to stare into the eyes of two women and a man who were climbing swiftly in through a window. They were all clad in matching black leathers, and bore a sigil on their breasts: a crossed moon and dagger.

"This loot belongs to the Moonclaws," said one woman in a steely whisper, her eyes hard.

"Ah, no," Farl replied disgustedly, hurling his dagger. "Gangs!"

His blade spun through the air to plunge through the hand of the other woman, the hand that had been sweeping up with a dart in it. She screamed and fell to her knees.

Elminster hurled a dagger hilt-first into the man's face, tossed a cushion after it, and then sudden rage took hold of him. He leaped forward to plant a kick so hard in the man's gut that he groaned aloud as his toes struck the armor plate there—but its wearer was driven headlong back out the window to fall screaming to the garden below, a garrote waving uselessly in his hands.

"So noisy . . . so unprofessional," Farl murmured, snatching up the jewel-coffer. The wounded woman was fleeing for the rope at the window she'd come in by, sobbing from the pain and shaking blood all over the red carpets. "Hey— that's one of my good blades!" he complained as the other woman leaped at him, hurling one dagger and raising another.

Farl ducked and swept the coffer up; her blade struck it and shot into the ceiling, where it struck a roof-beam and stood quivering. The woman tried to reach over the coffer and slash his face, but Farl simply stepped around her, keeping the coffer between them, his head low and out of reach, and shoved her away with its end. She slipped on the carpet, and he brought the coffer down hard on her head. She collapsed soundlessly, and Elminster gently laid her unconscious companion atop of her, handing Farl his blade.

Farl examined its bloody tip and wiped it on the woman. "Dead?"

Elminster shook his head. "Just asleep; too hurt to defend herself." They knelt together over the gem-coffer, scooping and snatching in real haste, until Farl said, "Enough! Use their rope—let's begone!"

They paused to check the firmness of the gang's grapnel, and then hastily clambered down, Farl first. The male thief lay sprawled senseless on the turf, with a shocked-looking servant gazing down at him. Seeing the rope dance and jerk, he stared up at them. Then he screamed and ran, and from the window above them, the two thieves heard an angry shout.

"Gods *bedamned!* Let's hope they've no crossbows!" Farl snarled, slipping down the rope as his hands burned.

Then suddenly, sickeningly, the rope was no longer attached, and they were falling. There was a thud and a grunt from below as Farl landed. El tensed at the thought he might soon land atop his partner, but Farl was already up and sprinting out of the way. Elminster tried to relax as the turf swiftly rushed up to meet him.

The landing was hard. He got up, wincing; his right foot hurt, and beside him lay the man he'd kicked, mouth open and face white. A sick feeling rose in him, but as he scrambled to his feet, he saw the man's hand move feebly, grasping for a windowsill that wasn't there. Elminster and Farl sprinted together across the garden and scrabbled hastily up and over the wall. They dropped into the street outside and began strolling nonchalantly toward the nearest cross street, but a heavy clothyard shaft hummed low over the wall and struck the high wooden gate of the house across from them.

Farl stared up at it. "By the gods, a proper archer! Let's begone!"

So it was at an undignified run that the two fetched up, puffing, behind the boarded-up shop to lose loot and gear. Then Farl smote his forehead. "Gangs!" he hissed. "They've always someone to spare, must've set a watcher!" He turned and ran back the way they'd come, motioning to Elminster to hurry on down the alley.

Elminster continued to flee, moving purposefully but not running, looking around warily from time to time. He'd gone two streets farther when Farl dropped down from a nearby rooftop, puffing, and said, "Right . . . let's dump all of this and buy some of Hannibur's hot buttered rolls! We've earned an early even-feast!"

"The watcher?" Elminster asked.

"I threw a blade at him an' missed by half a league—but he was so startled he fell over backward off his roof—and split his head open on the edge of a wagon, below. He'll be watching nothing, forevermore." Elminster shuddered.

Farl shook his head and looked gloomy. "What'd I warn you? Gangs! There goes the high tone of Hastarl!"

Six

Squalor Among Thieves

There is one sort of a city that's worse than one where thieves rule the night streets: the sort where thieves form the government, and rule night and day.

Urkitbaeran of Calimport
The Book of Black Tidings
Year of the Shattered Skulls

The best Calishite silks rarely made the long and perilous way up the pirate-infested and storm-racked coast of the Great Sea in numbers enough that Elembar, Uthtower, and Yarlith did not drink them all in—leaving some for the long, arduous pole-barge journey up the Delimbiyr. It was rarer still for the merchants who owned such barges to stop in tiny, provincial Hastarl, where homespun was the favored wear and a good sword scabbard was more admired than an elegantly cut jerkin. It was rarer yet for the shining, ornamented purple-and-emerald Tahtan weaves from the fabled Cities of the Seabreeze farther south to accompany the silks. Crowds at the docks were heavy. Some of the fat, strutting cloth merchants didn't even bother to climb the streets to the tall, narrow shops of the master tailors, but sold all their wares on the docks.

Farl and Elminster thought themselves subtle indeed not to try for a single thread of that first exciting landing. When a second followed, they left it alone, too, and watched from afar as an unfortunate grab-artist of the Moonclaws was caught stealing silks, whipped skinless, and hanged from the city wall.

The master tailors had no guild because the magelords did not hold with guilds. They did, however, meet earnestly over wine and roast boar in the Dancing Dryad feasting house and come to a business agreement of mutual advantage. A lass who served them at table and collected rather too many pinches for her liking told Farl and Elminster (in return for four gold coins) what had been decided. 'Twas money well spent, Farl judged. Elminster, as was his wont, said nothing.

And so this moonless night found them on the roof of a warehouse overlooking a certain dock, waiting for the creak of oars and surreptitious shining of unshuttered lanterns that would mark the arrival of the private shipment to the master tailors, including (it was rumored) cloth-of-gold and amber buttons.

It was a crisp, breezy night, the first heralding of leaf-fall to come and another cold damp winter, but wrapped in their dark cloaks, they hadn't time to grow stiff and cold before the flashes of lamplight were seen glimmering over the dark waters below.

The two thieves waited in patient silence for their victims-to-be to helpfully load the wagons, four in all and heavy-laden, then slid silently down from their perch, avoiding the lumbering hireguards who clustered around the lead wagon. It was the work of but a moment to hurl a stone over into the heap of rusted metal pans in the alley behind the confectioners' shop, and while heads and blades were turned that way, to slip up into the fourth wagon from the other side of the street. Then they'd have a breath or six to sort before another diversion became necessary to cover their leaving.

It was about the time of the fourth breath that they heard a startled oath from somewhere nearby, the scream of a wounded horse, and the skirl of steel. "Competition?" El breathed into his friend's ear, and Farl nodded.

"Our diversion," he murmured, "provided by the Moonclaws, no doubt. Wait a bit, now—that horse means they've got at least one bow with them. Let the fight get well underway before we go out."

The fight obliged, and the two companions hastened to finish sorting and stowing their loot for carrying. When they were done, they drew their daggers and unlatched the back doors of the wagon to peer cautiously out into the night.

A face with a blade held ready beside it was glaring up at them. Farl leaped high to avoid the man's thrust, landed with both feet atop the blade, and jumped down on the sword-wielder's arm, burying his dagger in that face before the man even had time to cry out.

As El jumped to the cobbles beside them, staggering under the weight of their booty, Farl tugged his dagger free and hurled it into the night, which seemed to be full of running men and drawn swords. It struck the brow of a hireguard, who cursed, clutched at the streaming blood, and ran.

Farl scooped up the long sword that had fallen from the shattered arm of his first victim and hissed, "Come *on*, out o' this!"

They ran to the right, toward one of the rising side streets where folk dwelt who were too respectable to live in hovels but not rich enough to have walls around their homes. Daggers flashed and spun in the night on all sides, but the Moonclaws hadn't a decent blade-tosser among them. It seemed the guards had been inept, or spineless, or paid off: the fight was over. All the other folk yet alive in the street were Moonclaws.

Farl and El didn't waste breath on curses. They dodged from side to side erratically to discourage the Moonclaws' archer and plunged along the street, puffing for breath. The expected humming of a seeking arrow came to their ears accompanied by a startled curse from close behind them. The arrow wobbled past them strangely; Farl frowned at it and looked back. A Moonclaws man who'd been pursuing them was stumbling and rubbing at his shoulder.

"Dare they . . . shoot again?" El gasped. "With . . . their own folk . . ."

"Hasn't stopped 'em yet," Farl puffed. "Keep dodging!"

The next arrow came as they reached the top of the street and turned aside to duck along an alley, crouching low. The humming grew louder, and they both dived to the cobbles. The arrow whipped low over them, and cracked into some shutters across the way just as a patrol of armsmen shouldered out of the alley, halberds held high. The patrol captain peered down in the dimness at the two men sprawled in front of him and snapped, "Get that light up here! Something befalls! Swords ou—"

The Moonclaws had a second archer, it seemed. His shaft hit home with a solid thump—and the captain gurgled, spun around, and plunged to the cobbles, strangling on the long, dark shaft through his throat.

Farl and El rolled to their feet while startled armsmen were still wrestling their halberds down, and ran down the alley past the patrol, hooking the feet out from under the only armsman who tried to block their path.

As the soldier crashed to the cobbles, Farl swarmed up a draper's outside wooden staircase, with El close behind. The roof was an easy leap up from the rail, but slippery with puddles of rainwater. The next roof was thatch, and they burrowed thankfully into its far slope to catch their breaths.

They looked at each other in the darkness, panting. "There's naught for it," Farl said a few frantic breaths later, "but to form our own gang."

"Tyche aid us," El murmured.

Farl looked at him. "Don't you mean Mask, Lord of Thieves?"

"Nay," Elminster replied. "I was praying that this 'gang' does not end our friendship . . . or our lives."

Farl was a silent for a long time. Then Elminster heard him murmur, "Oh, Lady Tyche, hear me. . . ."

"Ah, Naneetha! Those velvet hands . . ." Farl was laughing—and then he stopped. "That's it! We'll call ourselves the 'Velvet Hands'!"

Groans and laughter rang round the tiny room. It was dusty and stank of decades of salted fish—but the owner of the warehouse was dead, and the two broken-down carts they'd carefully jammed together in the mouth of the alley made it unlikely any patrols would get close enough to hear them. Over a dozen folk were in the room, keeping a wary distance apart, with careful eyes on each other and their hands close to their weapons.

Farl eyed them all, and sighed. "I know none of you are delighted at this idea . . . but everyone here knows it's band together or be slain—or leave Hastarl to try our luck elsewhere . . . in strange places where we'll be marked as suspicious outlanders an' find a local gang of thieves waiting to sink knives into us."

"Why not join the Moonclaws?" Klaern rasped. He was one of the Blaenbar brothers, who lounged together by a window where they could give a signal to someone outside.

"On what terms? he asked reasonably. "Every time Eladar or I have crossed paths with 'em, they've tried to put their blades into us before a word was exchanged. We'd start out on the fringes, all of us, untrusted and expendable."

"More than that," Elminster put in, drawing startled looks from all over the room. "I've wondered at all those leathers an' matching badges they wear. Expensive, that—an' right from the outset, before they'd taken two coins to rub together. Good weapons, too. Does that remind all of ye of anything? A private bodyguard, belike? An army in Hastarl that strikes at thieves—us—whenever they see us. That sounds like the work of someone in the hire of a magelord, or the king, or someone rich and important. What better way to rid the city of thieves and arrange 'accidents' for thy rivals but than to put thine own band on the streets?"

There were thoughtful nods all around the room now. "Now *that*," fat old Chaslarla said, scratching herself, "makes more sense o' the mess than I've heard since I first saw 'em. An' it explains why some armsmen seem to look the other way when they strike out—under orders, belike."

"Aye," young Rhegaer said, idly turning a little knife in his fingers as he perched atop a barrel taller than he was. As usual, he was very dirty . . . but then, so was the barrel, and a peering eye might have missed him, but for the flash and turn of the little blade.

"Well, I think it's so much smart lies and fancy-castles talk," Klaern snarled, "an' I'll not listen to more of it. Ye're fools, all of ye, if ye listen to these two dreamers. What have they but smart tongues?" He strode out of his corner to stare around the room, and like a silent wave rolling in his wake his two brothers came to stand at his back in a solid, threatening wall of flesh. "If there's to be a band to rival the Moonclaws, *I'll* lead it. 'Velvet Hands,' indeed! While these two perfumed dancing lads are strutting an' crowing, my brothers 'n' me can make ye rich . . . guaranteed."

"Oh?" A very deep voice rumbled out from one dark corner. "And just how, Blaenbar, are ye going to manage to make me trust *thee*? After watching thy bullying and blustering in the alleys these past three summers, all I know of ye is that I'd best never turn my back—or thy blade'll be in, right sharp."

Klaern sneered. "Jhardin, everyone in Hastarl knows ye're as strong as an ox—but anyone might give ye a good run in a race of wits. What can ye know of planning, or—"

"More than some folk," Jhardin growled. "Where I come from, 'planning' always means some clever jack is going to try to trick me."

"Why don't ye go back there, then?"

"Enough, Klaern," Farl said with cold scorn. "Trust is something the rest of us can never have when you're near, that's for certain. You'd best leave."

The red-maned man turned on him. "Afraid ye'll lose mastery of this little band of Pawing Hands, eh? Well, let's just see who speaks for ye, here?"

Elminster stepped a silent pace forward.

"Yes, yes, we know yer pretty boy does . . . as well as anything else ye ask him to."

Amid his coarse laughter, Jhardin lumbered forward a pace, eyes hard. Rhegaer leaped lightly down from his barrel, and Chaslarla wheezed forward too.

Klaern looked around. "Tassabra?"

The lithe figure in the deepest shadows shifted slightly and said in a low, musical voice, "Sorry, Klaern. I side with Farl too."

"Fah! Gods frown upon all of ye fools!" Klaern spat on the floor, turned, and strode grandly out, his silent brothers Korlar and Othkyn backing watchfully away to guard his going.

"I thought he was thy lover," another man murmured from the shadows.

"Take care, Larrin!" Tassabra's voice was testy. "That rutting boar my lover? Nay, he was but a plaything."

Jhardin looked to Farl, who nodded. The huge man walked out of the room, moving with surprising, silent lightness. Klaern might well have less time left in life than he realized. Farl stepped forward. "Are we agreed, then? Do the Velvet Hands fare forth in Hastarl from this night on?"

"Aye," came the rough voice of one-eyed Tarth. "I'll follow your orders."

"And I," Chaslarla said, wheezing forward, "so long as ye turn not into one of those cold-hearts who thinks himself the true ruler of his city an' sends us out to stab armsmen and magelords all the night through."

There was a general rumble of agreement. Farl grinned and bowed. "We have agreement, then. As our first work together, let's get out of here with blades ready, and as I bid—in case the Moonclaws are waiting for us with bows, or've told a patrol when and where to expect us."

"Can I have first blood?" Rhegaer asked eagerly.

Behind him, they heard Tassabra's low laugh. "Just be sure it's not yours," she said. The darkness covered the look he gave her . . . but they could all feel it. There were chuckles in the night as they went down the stairs together.

All Hastarl knew the noble Athalantan families Glarmeir and Trumpettower had been joined that same night in a true love-match. Peeryst Trumpettower had worn a high-plumed hat and cloth-of-gold doublet specially crafted for the occasion, with his usual bell-trimmed hose and best curl-tip shoes. Strapping on his father's lightest sword, he proudly paraded his lady to the shrines of Sune, Lathander, Helm, and Tyche before the hand-fasting was completed under the sword of Tyr.

The father of the bride had gifted the happy pair with a statue of the rearing Stag of Athalantar (the beast, not the dead king) that had been sculpted from a single gigantic diamond, and was worth more than some large castles. The servant who carried it around all day on a glass-domed platter thought it might well have been heavier than some castles, too. Under a heavy guard, this eminently practical gift had been installed in the bridal bedchamber at the foot of the bed, where, as old Darrigo Trumpettower had put it with a wink and a leer, "'Twould be in a fine position to watch!"

Nanue Glarmeir had worn an exquisite sky-blue gown crafted by the elves of far-off Shantel Othreier; her mother had proudly announced it had cost a thousand pieces of gold. Now it lay crumpled on the floor like so much discarded wrapping—which is precisely what the squeakily excited Peeryst thought it was—as the newly wedded couple toasted each other with sparkling moonbubble wine, and turned to raise their glasses to Selûne, that she might smile down upon the bridal bed. The first pale rays of her radiance had peeked in the window far enough to touch the statue of the stag with moonlight, where it stood rampant and watchful on its own table at the foot of the bed.

Neither man nor wife noticed the deft pair of black-gloved hands reach up from under the bed and take away the gem-headed hairpins Nanue had just drawn out to let her hair cascade unbound down her elegant back (to Peeryst's breathless delight). Both newlyweds, however, did notice the sudden appearance of a pair of booted feet that blotted out the moon and then crashed through the fine glass of the largest arched bed-chamber window, followed by their owner: a woman clad in tight-fitting black leathers with a badge on her breast, who wore a black half-mask.

The shapely intruder smiled at them sweetly as she drew a needle-thin blade from one boot and approached the stag. In all this excitement, none of the three heard an exasperated sigh from under the bed.

"Scream just once," she warned softly, "and I'll slide this into you."

Having been handed the idea, Nanue screamed—just once. Piercingly, too; shards of glass fell from the window frame with a tinkling clatter.

The woman's face darkened into a snarl, and she ran across the room, poniard raised to stab. Seemingly by itself, a footstool beside the bed leaped up from the floor to catch her in the face; she reeled, lost her dagger, and fell heavily sideways into a wardrobe—which promptly toppled, slowly and grandly, over on top of her.

Nanue and Peeryst both boldly seized the initiative, shrieking in unison.

Downstairs, befurred and bejeweled elders of both families heard the mighty crash and the screams. They raised knowing eyes and grins toward the ceiling and then toasted each other.

"Ah, yes," Darrigo Trumpettower said, leering over his glass at a Glarmeir lass almost half his age and blowing his bristling mustache out of his wine with a practiced puff. "I remember well my wedding night—the first one, at least; I was sober for that one. 'Twas back in the Year of the Gorgon Moon, as I recall . . ."

A dark figure rose up from beneath the bed, crept across the room, and ducked behind a lounge onto which Peeryst had grandly tossed his boots, one after the other, not so long ago. The intruder was safely out of sight before the next two thieves in leathers burst in through the other two windows, raining fresh glass onto the thick fur rugs. Peeryst and Nanue clutched each other, naked but not noticing anymore, and howled in fear, clawing at each other's backs in a frantic attempt to get going elsewhere—anywhere!

The two fresh arrivals wore the same masks and tight leathers with breast-badges as the first one had. One was a woman, the other a man, and both were looking wildly about the room.

"Where's she gone, then?"

"*Hush*, Minter—you'll rouse the house."

"*Don't* use my name, gods damn thy tongue!"

They drew daggers from their boots and approached the terrified couple on the bed—who screamed and tried to burrow under the fur-trimmed silk sheets.

"Hold, damn ye!" Minter reached for a fleeing foot, missed, and got hold of an ankle. He pulled. A vainly struggling Peeryst clawed at the sheets and managed to drag them off his wife, who knelt on the bed and screamed again, piercingly. Across the room, a glass figurine shattered, causing the black-gloved hand that had been reaching up from behind the lounge for it to withdraw, with a hasty curse.

Peeryst Trumpettower was hauled from the bed to bounce and then sprawl on the carpet at Minter's feet, gibbering in fear.

Minter flipped him over, reflecting briefly on how ridiculous other naked men look, and snarled, "Where'd she go?" He waved his dagger under the man's nose for effect.

"Wh—Who?" Peeryst shrieked.

Minter pointed with his blade at the whirlwind that was his partner Isparla, who was plucking gem-coffers and silken underthings from the floor and tables around, and tossing them all onto one of the sheets on the floor. As they watched, she scooped up the stag, grunted in surprise under its weight, staggered off-balance, slipped on the carpet, and fell on both elbows atop the piled loot. She moaned in pain—and the stag in her grasp slipped free and thumped down sideways onto one of her hands. She grunted again, louder.

"Another like her, who came in before us!" Minter growled, indicating his partner.

"U—Under the wardrobe," Peeryst panted, pointing. "It fell on her."

Minter turned and saw a ribbon of dank blood running from under the wardrobe, which was as large—and probably as heavy—as a long-haul wagon. He shuddered. He kept on shuddering, all the way to the floor, as a figure rose from under the bed and brought a perfume bottle down on his head.

Isparla clambered to her feet, saw the figure with the shards of the perfume bottle in his hand, obligingly spat, "Velvets! *Again!*" and threw her dagger. The figure obediently dived back behind the bed, and the dagger flashed harmlessly across the room. A titanic sneeze came from behind the bed.

Nanue screamed again—and the woman in black leathers slapped her across the face, backhanded, as she leaped past, grabbing for the elusive sneezing figure. She tripped over the stag in her haste, hopped, and moaned in pain. The stag thumped over onto its other side, and a shard of diamond broke off it.

The mysterious person behind the bed was curled up and shaking in the throes of uncontrollable sneezing, but managed to drive the broken perfume bottle into the Moonclaws woman's face, which she had just stuck around behind the bed. Isparla recoiled, rearing up on the bed, and Nanue slapped her back, hard.

Her masked head whipped around. She snarled, leaned forward, and there was a meaty smack as her face met the brass chamberpot that Peeryst's shaking hands had just swept upward.

Isparla collapsed silently across the bed. Nanue, kneeling beside her, saw blood flowing from the masked woman's mouth onto the silken sheets, and helpfully screamed again.

Peeryst saw what he'd done, threw the chamberpot down in horror—there was a sharp crack as it struck the stag and then a hollow metallic gonging when it skipped across the room and rolled to a stop—and fled across the room, howling. A dark figure burst up from behind the lounge and sprinted to intercept him.

Peeryst was two running paces from the safety of the bedchamber door when the figure caught up with him. They crashed into the door together; it boomed, burst open from the impact, and was instantly smashed shut again by their falling bodies.

Downstairs, the befurred and bejeweled elders of both families heard the crash, raised their eyebrows at each other, and poured another toast.

"Well," Janatha Glarmein said brightly, staring around as color rose prettily into her cheeks, "they certainly seem to be . . . hitting it off, don't they?"

"*Hitting* sounds like it would be about right," Darrigo Trumpettower agreed with a guffaw, leering at her "I remember my second wife was like that. . . ."

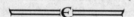

Elminster rose from atop Peeryst's unconscious form, made sure the door was bolted this time, and hurried to where Farl, eyes still streaming from the perfume, was staggering away from the bed.

"We've got to get out of here," he muttered, shaking Farl.

"Damned Moonclaws," his partner snarled. "Grab *something* to make all this worthwhile."

"I have," El said, "now let's *begone!*"

His words rose into an excited shout as a new pair of leather-clad figures swung in the window, using yet more silken lines.

They landed running, blades out. Elminster swept up a small glass-topped table, spilling figurines in all directions, and hurled it hard.

His target ducked, and the table sailed harmlessly out the window—just as one of the figurines landed, hard, on his foot.

Elminster hopped in pain, roaring. The grinning Moonclaws man closed in on him, raising a gleaming blade, as the other one dived to grab the nude, shrieking woman on the bed.

The table fell through the night to explode in shards of glass and twisted spars of brass on the cobbles far below. Some of them clattered on the windows of the feasting-hall and the parlor. The befurred and bejeweled elders of both families turned at the sound, and more eyebrows were raised.

"They wouldn't be *fighting*, would they?" Janatha Glarmeir said anxiously, fanning herself to conceal her burning cheeks. "It certainly seems *lively*."

"Nay," Darrigo Trumpettower roared, "that's just . . . what d'they ca—oh, aye, 'foreplay;' y'know, the fun 'n' games beforehand . . . great big room up there to chase each other around in.

He sighed, looking up at the ceiling. Obligingly, it shook under another sharp, booming crash, and a cloud of dust drifted down. "Wish I were younger and Peeryst was calling for help. . . ."

Promptly there came a faint, quavering cry. "Help!"

"Well," Darrigo said in delight, "if the lad ain't the very shinin' image of his old uncle, indeed! Where're those stairs? Hope I can remember how to do the deed, after all these years. . . ."

Elminster danced backward, wincing. The Moonclaws man lunged at him, blade flashing, and then grunted in surprise as Farl reached out and wrapped himself around the man's leg. The Moonclaws thief toppled like a felled tree, and Farl stabbed him in the throat before he'd even stopped bouncing. The stag statue, cracked and somewhat smaller now, spun away from under the man's sprawled body.

Elminster saw what Farl had done, turned his head away, and promptly emptied his dinner all over a blue-dyed fur rug from Calimshan.

"Well, that's *one* rug we won't be taking back with us," Farl called merrily as he sprinted across the room to where the last Moonclaws woman was struggling with the sobbing bride. Just as he got there, the thief managed to get her hands on Nanue's face and throat, and looked up.

Farl didn't slow. He planted a firm fist in her mask as he ran past.

She hadn't even hit the carpet when he leaped out the window, one of the swing-lines hissing through his gloved hands as he slid down in haste.

Elminster snatched up a hand-sized jewel-coffer to add to the hairpins he'd stowed in his boots, thrust it down the front of his shirt to free his hands for climbing, and ran after Farl. Screaming, Nanue ran the other way, toward the door where her husband lay senseless.

Elminster tripped over the stag, cursed, and ended his flight to the windows in a helpless roll. The statue slid away across slick tiles exposed when rugs were nicked up in the battle, and caromed off a wall, spitting pieces of itself in all directions.

El fetched up against the windowsill in an untidy heap—unseen by the Moonclaws man who swung grandly in the window at that moment and stepped right over the thieving prince. His eyes fixed on the statue, gliding to a gleaming stop in the moonlight.

"Aha! A king's ransom—mine!" the thief bellowed, hurling a dagger out of habit at the nude woman fleeing across the chamber. The flashing fang struck an upright mirror, which pivoted on its pintles, overbalanced, and came crashing down at Nanue. She shrieked and leaped desperately backward, skidding helplessly on the rugs. The mirror crashed down beside it and shattered, shards bouncing on the tiles; Nanue rolled away blindly to escape them, and overturned an ornamental table crowded with scent-bottles. The reek that arose was incredible; it even made the thief, gloved hand about to close on what was left of the stag, recoil.

This sudden movement sent him skidding on a fragment broken off the statue, and he sat down hard, jarring a portrait down off the wall. Roaruld Trumpettower, Scourge of Stirges—depicted holding a glass of blood aloft in one hand and a wrung-out, limp-winged stirge in the other—landed with a crash that shook the room, hopped forward as the frame shivered, and smashed down atop the thief. The stag spun away again, still growing smaller.

Nanue sobbed at the overpowering smell as she wallowed in glass shards and spilled perfume; she was drenched with half a hundred secret oils and glowing daubs, and the tiles were so slippery she couldn't find footing. At length, weeping with frustration—and at the smell—she started to crawl toward the nearest rug. It was the one Elminster had recently decorated. Nanue recoiled from it, selected another as her goal, and crawled in that direction, weeping with fresh energy.

Elminster shook his head in disbelief at the scene of devastation in the room, caught hold of the rope, and was gone into the night. Behind him there was a sharp tearing sound as a gloved hand holding a dagger punched up through the heart of Roaruld Trumpettower, cutting a hole in the massive portrait so that its masked Moonclaws owner could emerge and look wildly around the room for—there!

The stag lay in a serene pool of moonlight near the bed, starred now with many cracks. The thief hastened to scoop it up. "Mine at last!"

"Nay," responded a cold voice from the window. "'Tis *mine!*" A dagger was flung, but missed, coming to quivering rest in a wooden wall carving with a solid thunk.

The first thief sneered as he scooped up the stag—then, realizing the other Moonclaws man couldn't see his expression through the mask, made a rude gesture with the statue. The second thief snarled in rage and threw another dagger. It flashed across the room and passed just in front of Nanue's nose. The crawling bride hastily changed course again, scuttling back across the tiles toward safety behind the lounge.

The thief with the statue strode toward the window. "Keep back!" he warned, waving his dagger.

The second thief scooped up one of the fallen gem-coffers and calmly flung it at the head of the first thief. It hit home and burst open, spilling a glistening rain of gems to the floor. The first thief joined them in the general cascade, the stag flying up from his hand.

End over end it spun through the air—toward the window.

"No!" The second thief lunged desperately after it, slipping and sliding on the bouncing gems. His gloved hands stretched, reaching, reaching—and into the very tips of his straining fingers the proud stag fell.

He clung to it in gloating triumph, skidding across the floor with the momentum of his desperate run. "Hah! I have it! My precious! Oh, my precious stag!"

And then the gems under his boots slid him hard into the low windowsill, and he kicked helplessly, toppled, and with a shriek fell out into the night, wailing, and was gone.

Nanue saw the thief disappear, shivered, and came carefully to her feet, turning again toward the door. She must get out—Another pair of thieves in black leathers swung in through the windows. "Oh, *dungheaps!*" Nanue wailed, and started yet another desperate dash for the door.

The thieves looked around at the wreckage and carnage and swore horribly. One bounded forward into the room, swept up the masked woman from the bed, threw her over his shoulder, and made straight for the window again. The other sprinted down the room after Nanue to snatch her for a ransom.

She screamed, and was slipping on rugs, trying not to crash into the door in her haste and fall on the crumpled Peeryst, when something heavy hit the door from the other side. The bolt twisted and jammed, and Nanue slid helplessly into the wall. Snarled curses echoed through the door from the passage beyond, and then it shook under another thunderous blow. Nanue scrambled aside, shrieking at the thief who grabbed for her kicking legs.

The door splintered then and flew inward, hurling the thief a good distance away across the furs. He rolled to his feet, and two daggers gleamed as he drew them. The Moonclaws thief saluted the nude woman with them, and advanced menacingly. Nanue screamed again.

Darrigo Trumpettower looked around the ruined bedchamber in bewilderment. At his feet lay his nephew and right beside him, his terrified bride on her knees, shrieking as she crawled toward Darrigo.

Darrigo looked up again, mustache bristling. An intruder in black leathers was coming at him in a run, daggers gleaming in both hands. There wasn't even time to leer down at Nanue—who, he couldn't help noticing, looked like a fine wife indeed. He looked up at the onrushing thief again and drew a deep breath. 'Twas time to uphold the honor of the Trumpettowers!

With a roar, Darrigo Trumpettower charged across the room. The thief swept his daggers up to stab—but the old man took one in the arm without flinching, and smashed home a bone-shattering blow to the thief's jaw. Still roaring, he snatched at the reeling man's throat before he could fall, picked the thief up by the neck the same way he carried turkeys in to be cooked at home, and strode across the room, streaming blood.

Straight to the shattered windows he went, lifted the thief, and hurled him out into the empty darkness. He listened for the thud from the cobbles far below, nodded in satisfaction when it came, and went back for another thief.

Nanue decided it was safe to faint now. As the second thief sailed out into the night, the blushing bride sank gracefully down on Peeryst's chest, and knew no more.

Word was all over the city by midmorn how the old, blustering warrior Darrigo Trumpettower had fought a dozen thieves in the bridal bedchamber of his nephew while the unhearing lovers had calmly consummated their match, and how he (Darrigo) hurled every one of the Moonclaws in uniform out the high windows, to their deaths in the courtyard of Trumpettower House.

Farl and El raised eyebrows and tankards of strong ale to the news. "It sounds as though one of them rescued Isparla and got out again," Farl said, sipping.

"How many does that leave?" Elminster asked quietly.

Farl shrugged. "Who knows? The gods and the Moonclaws, alone. But they lost Waera, Minter, Annathe, Obaerig, for certain, and probably Irtil, too. Let's say we're a lot more even after last night—though they did blunder in on a perfectly good grab job and lose us all but the little stuff."

"One of the hairpins broke, too," Elminster reminded him.

"Aye, but we have both pieces; little loss there," Farl said. "Now, if we—"

He broke off, frowned, and bent his head to listen to an excited whisper at a table nearby, laying a hand on El's arm to bid for silence. Elminster, who'd been holding his peace, continued to do so.

"Aye, magic! Doubtless hidden away by King Uthgrael, years agone!" One man was saying, leaning forward almost into his friend's face to avoid being overheard. "In a secret chamber somewheres in the castle, they say!"

Farl and Elminster leaned forward to listen carefully. A moment later, the need to do so passed: a minstrel came in, bounded up onto the nearest table, and cried the tale at the top of his young, excited voice.

In truth, it was a tale straight out of the legends minstrels kept shining: a chest of magical ioun stones had been found in the castle—hidden away years before, probably by (or on the orders of) King Uthgrael. The magelords are, and remain, in heated disagreement about who shall have them, and how they'll be used. By decree of King Belaur himself, the stones—glowing and floating about by themselves, giving off faint chimings and musical sounds like harp-chords from time to time—are on display, guarded by the officers and senior armsmen of Athalgard, in a certain audience chamber no wizards are allowed to approach, until a decision is made. As they left the tavern, the excited minstrel was declaiming in ringing tones that he'd seen the stones himself, and that this was all *true!*

Farl smiled. "You know we *have* to go for those stones."

Elminster shook his head. "Ye couldn't turn thy back on them and still be Farl, Master of the Velvet Hands," he said dryly.

Farl chuckled.

"This time," Elminster told him firmly, "ye should wait, let the Moonclaws spring the trap—and go in only if ye can see a safe, clear way to do so."

"Trap?"

"Don't ye smell the hands of calculating wizards in this wondrous tale? I do."

After a moment, Farl nodded. Their eyes met.

"Why did you say 'ye'?" Farl asked quietly.

"I am done with thieving," Elminster said slowly. "If ye go after these wonderful magical stones, ye must do it alone. I'll be leaving Hastarl after I do one thing more."

Farl stood frozen, eyes very dark. "Why?"

"Robbing and slaying hurts folk I have no quarrel with and brings revenge no closer to the magelords. You saw the stag statue; the grasping hands of thieving only take what's precious and make it battered and broken and worthless. I've learned as much as the street can teach and have had enough." Elminster stared into Farl's stunned eyes and added, "Seasons slip away—and the things I've not done eat at me. I must leave."

"I knew it was coming," Farl admitted, his face going very red. "It's the scruples that assured it. But this 'one thing more'—'twouldn't be a betrayal, would it?"

Elminster shook his head and spoke slowly and deliberately. "I've never had a friend as close and as true as Farl, son of Hawklyn."

Suddenly their arms were around each other in a tight embrace. They stood in the alley and wept, pounding each other on backs and shoulders.

After a time, Farl said, "Ah, El—what'm I to do without you?"

"Take up with Tassabra," Elminster said, and added with a gleam in his eye, "Ye can show her appreciation in a more satisfying way than ye can with me."

They stepped back from each other—and then, slowly, both grinned.

"So we part," Farl said, shaking his head. "Half our wealth is yours."

Elminster shrugged. "I'll take only what I need, for the road."

Farl sighed. "So it's loot for me—and killing magelords for you."

"Mayhap," Elminster said softly, "if the gods are kind."

PRIEST

SEVEN
THE ONE TRUE SPELL

In ancient days, sorcerers sought to learn the One True Spell that would give them power over all the world and understanding of all magic. Some said they'd found it, but such men were usually dismissed as crazed.

I saw one of these "crazed" mages myself. He could ignore spells cast at him as if they did not exist, or work any magic himself by silent thought alone. I did not think he was mad—but at peace, driven by urges and vices no longer. He told me the One True Spell was a woman, that her name was Mystra—and that her kisses were wonderful.

HALIVON THARNSTAR, AVOWED OF MYSTRA
TALES TOLD TO A BLIND WIZARD
YEAR OF THE WYVERN

The night was warm and still. Elminster took a deep breath and counted out most of what Farl had insisted he take. He owed a debt ... and besides, the other matter he meant to see to this night would probably kill him. Then it would be too late to pay any debts.

When he was done, he was looking at a heap of coins—a hundred regals, bright in the moonlight. In the sun, come morn, they'd blaze their true gold color ... but he'd probably not be around to see them, one way or another.

Elminster shrugged. At least his life was his own again, and he was free to pursue any folly he desired. So, of course, he reflected wryly, here he was, bent on one last thiefly act. He slung the coins together in the sack—tight, so they'd not clink—and set off over the rooftops in search of a certain bedchamber.

The shutters were open to let in any breezes that might drift by, to cool a sleeping bridal couple whose furnishings failed by far to match those of the Trumpettowers. Elminster had been delighted to hear of their betrothal, even if it would cost him most of the coins he'd worked for. He stole in over the sill like a purposeful shadow and grinned down at them.

The bridal garter was exquisite, a little thing of lace and silken ribbon. Impishly, Elminster reached down and stroked it. Take it, as a trophy? But no—he was a thief no more.

Shandathe stirred as she felt the light touch high on her thigh. Yet deep in dreams, she stretched out a hand to the familiar warm and hairy bulk of Hannibur, snoring as deep as any drunken tavern-singer could. As Elminster smoothed her new bridal garter back into place where Hannibur had tied it on her hip, she smiled but didn't awaken.

Elminster noted other gifts, too: a stout cudgel and a new apron lying on the carpet on Hannibur's side of the bed ... and the hilt of a dagger protruding, like a winking eye, from beneath Shandathe's pillow.

He laid his bridal gift carefully between them. It was a tight fit between the smooth flank and the hairy one, and it took all his thiefly skills to avoid a clink and rattle as he slid the coins into a smooth sweep of gleaming gold from end to end of the bed. When he'd crammed in all the regals he dared, there were still over a dozen left. He laid the last of his belated bridal gift gently on Shandathe's belly, and left hastily as the touch of cold metal made her stir in earnest.

Selûne was riding high in the deep blue sky over Hastarl as Elminster stood on a rooftop, looking across the empty, silent street at the crumbling front of the disused temple of Mystra.

The place was dark and decaying, and from where he stood Elminster could see the massive lock on the door. The magelords, it seemed, didn't want anyone in Hastarl worshiping the Mistress of All Magic but themselves—and they could do that in the safety and privacy of their own tower inside Athalgard. Yet they hadn't dared desecrate Mystra's temple.

Perhaps their power was rooted in it, and striking here could shake their mastery of sorcery and their grip on the realm. Perhaps he could force Mystra's hand, just as she had forced his when she let his parents be slain. Or perhaps, Elminster admitted to himself as he stared at the temple, he was just weary of doing nothing that mattered, wasting days on rooftops, looking for a chance to steal this bauble or that. Wizards might not dare desecrate Mystra's temple, but Elminster would. Tonight. The world—or at least Athalantar—would be a much better place without any magic at all.

Destroying one temple, though, could hardly hope to do that. But perhaps it might bring down Mystra's curse on the city, so no wizards could work magic within its walk. Or perhaps the temple held some item of magic he could use against the wizards. Or perhaps it just held his death. Any result would be welcome.

Elininster eyed the shabby, peeling paint and the motionless stone bat-things adorning both front corners of the roof. They clutched the tops of the temple's front pillars with many claws, and their beaks hung open hungrily. They did not glow under his magesight—but perhaps the magical gargoyles minstrels sang of didn't glow. . . . The only magic he could see was lower down, and visible to all. Faintly glowing letters over the doors spelled out the words "I Am the One True Spell."

Elminster shook his head, sighed, and began the climb down from the rooftop. Revenge, it seemed, was a demanding business.

He could see no spells on the lock, and it surrendered easily to his metal probes; Farl had taught him well. Elminster looked up and down the silent street one last time, and then eased the door open, stood for a few breaths in its shadow to let his eyes adjust to the darkness, and slipped inside, dagger ready.

Dust and empty darkness. Elminster peered in all directions, but there didn't seem to be any furnishings in the temple of Mystra, only stone pillars.

Cautiously he stepped sideways until he was well away from the door—traps were usually right in front of doors—and stepped forward.

Something was not right about this place. Oh, aye, he'd expected to feel watched, his skin creeping with the singing tension of slumbering spells waiting all around him . . . and that was here, all right. There was something else, though, som—

Of course: a place this big and empty should echo back the sounds he made. Yet there were no echoes. Elminster opened a belt pouch, took one of the dried peas every thief carries to scatter and make pursuers trip, and cast it ahead of him into the darkness.

He did not hear it land. El swallowed and took a cautious step forward. He was in an entry hall, separated from a great open chamber beyond by a row of massive, smooth-curved stone pillars . . . featureless cylinders, as far as he could tell. Nothing moved in the thick blankets of dust over the floor. El cast a last look back at the door he'd drawn closed, and then walked into the darkness.

The great chamber was circular and reached up high overhead to unseen heights—it must go clear to the roof Elminster had looked at outside. There was a circular stone altar in the center of the room and balconies—three tiers of them—curving all around the vast open space. The chamber was dark, empty, and silent.

And that was it. Nothing here to desecrate. No acolytes.

The door behind him suddenly clattered open, and as men with torches came in, Elminster ran toward the back of the temple, seeking pillars to hide behind. Many men; armsmen, at least two patrols, with spears in their hands.

"Spread out," said a cold voice, "and search. No one dares enter a temple of Mystra just on a lark."

The speaker strode forward, lifted a hand, and sketched some sort of salute or respectful gesture toward the altar. Then he said calmly, "We shall have light," and at his words, though he cast no spell, the very stones around Elminster began to glow.

All of the stone in the temple began to shine until a soft, pearly-white radiance filled the room, revealing the young thief for everyone to see. In this case, "everyone" was more than a score of armsmen, advancing across the chamber with grim faces and ready spears. The man who'd spoken stood in their midst and said, "Just a thief. Hold weapons."

"What if he runs, lord?"

The robed man smiled and said, "My magic will force him to walk where I want him to, and nowhere else."

He gestured, and Elminster felt a sudden tugging at his limbs . . . a tingling, numbing trembling akin to what he'd felt on that terrible day in the meadow above Heldon, long ago. His body was no longer his own; he found himself turning, sick despair rising inside, and walking toward the men.

No, toward the altar. A bare circular block of stone, with not even a rune to grace it. The armsmen raised their spears and ringed him in as he came.

"The law holds that those who desecrate temples be put to death," an old armsman growled, "on the spot."

"Indeed," the robed man said, and smiled again. "I, however, shall choose that spot. When this fool's on the altar, you may throw your spears at will. Fresh blood on Mystra's altar will allow me to work a magic I've long wanted to try."

Elminster strode steadily on toward the altar, raging inwardly. He had been a fool to come here. This was it, then. His death, and an end to his futile fight against the magelords. Sorry, Father . . . Mother. . . . Elminster broke into a run and charged the altar, hoping he might somehow break free and knowing he could do nothing else. At least he could die trying to do *something*.

The wizard merely smiled and crooked one finger. Elminster's rush became a smooth trot until he stood in front of the altar. The mage turned him about again, until they stood facing each other.

Then the wizard bowed. "Greetings, thief. I am Lord Ildru, magelord of Athalantar. You may speak. Who are you?"

Elminster found that he could move his jaws. "As you said, Magelord," he responded coldly, "a thief."

The wizard raised an eyebrow. "Why came you here, this night?"

"To speak with Mystra," Elminster said, surprising himself.

Ildru's eyes narrowed. "Why? Are you a mage?"

"No," Elminster spat, "I am proud to say. I came to get Mystra's aid to cast down magelords like you—or curse her if she refused."

The wizard's brows shot up again. "And just what made you think Mystra would aid you?"

Elminster swallowed and found he couldn't shrug. Or move anything except his mouth. "The gods exist," he said slowly, "and their power is real. I have need of that power."

"Oh? The traditional way," the wizard said pleasantly, "is to study—long and hard, for most of a lifetime—and abase oneself as an apprentice, and risk life in trying spells one doesn't understand or in devising one's own new magics. What colossal arrogance, to think Mystra would just give you something when you asked for it!"

"The colossal arrogance in Athalantar," Elminster said softly, "is held by magelords. Your hold on this land is so tight that no other men in it have the luxury of colossal arrogance."

There was a murmur, somewhere among the ring of armsmen. Ildru glared around, and abrupt silence returned. Then the wizard sighed theatrically. "I weary of your bitter words. Be still, unless you want to plead."

Elminster felt himself being forced backward, to clamber up onto the altar.

"No spears yet," the magelord ordered. "I must work a spell first, to learn if this youth is all clever words and deluded dreams . . . or if he holds some secrets yet."

The wizard raised his hands, cast a spell, and then peered narrowly at Elminster, frowning.

"No magic," he said as if to himself, "and yet you have some link to sorcery, some minor ability to shape . . . I've not seen such before." He stepped forward. "What are your powers?"

"I have no magic," Elminster spat. "I abhor magic, and all that is done with it."

"If I freed you and studied what is within you to see where your aptitude lies, would you be loyal to the Stag Throne?"

"Forever!"

The mage's eyes narrowed at that proud, quick answer, and he added, "And to the magelords of Athalantar?"

"Never!" Elminster's shout echoed around the room, and the mage sighed again, watching the raging youth struggle vainly to spring down from the altar. "Enough," he said in a bored voice. "Kill him."

He turned away, and Elminster saw a dozen armsmen—and probably more he couldn't see, behind him—raise their spears, heft them, and take a pace or two back for a good throw.

"Forgive me, Mother . . . Father," Elminster said, through trembling lips, "I—I tried to be a true prince!"

The magelord whirled about. "*What?*"

And then the spears were in the air, and Elminster glared into the wizard's eyes and hissed, "I curse thee, Ildru of the magelords, with my death and the—"

He broke off in confusion. He hadn't expected to get this far in his curse, and he could see the wizard had raised his hands to weave some spell, crying out, "Wait! Stop! No spears!"

He could also see the armsmen staring at him as if he were a dragon—a purple dragon with three heads and a maiden's body, at that!

And the spears . . . they hung in the air, motionless, surrounded by pearly radiance. Elminster found he could move, and whirled around. There were spears on all sides, aye, a deadly ring of points leaping in to transfix him, but they all hung motionless in the air, and by the look on the wizard's face, it was none of his doing.

Elminster flung himself flat before this strange magic faded away. His move brought his facedown low against the altar top, in time to see two floating eyes fade away, and a flame leap up from the bare stone.

Armsmen shouted and backed away, and Elminster heard the magelord cry out in astonishment.

The flame climbed, crackling, and then from it, bolts of flame roared out, consuming the spears where they hung. The spears became spars of flame that curled slowly and faded into smoke.

Elminster watched, openmouthed. A golden radiance was stealing outward from the altar, now, washing over him. Armsmen shouted in real fear and backed away. Elminster saw them turn and reach for blades and try to run, but they seemed to be shimmering and moving slowly, as if they were figures drifting in a dream. Slowly, and more slowly still the armsmen shifted as flames that did not burn them sprang up and surrounded their bodies. Then they stood still and silent, frozen and unseeing . . . frozen in flames.

Elminster spun around to look at the magelord. The wizard stood as still as the rest, golden flames flickering before his staring eyes. His mouth was open, and his hands raised in the gestures of a spell . . . but he moved not.

What had befallen?

The flame pulsed and twisted. Elminster whirled back to face its changing flickering, and it shaped itself into someone . . . someone tall and dark robed and shapely, who strolled calmly over to stand by the brazier. A human woman . . . a sorceress?

Eyes of molten gold met his, and little flames danced in them. "Hail, Elminster Aumar, prince of Athalantar."

Elminster took a pace back, shocked. No, he'd never seen this great lady before—or anyone so beautiful. He swallowed. "Who *are* ye?"

"One who has been watching you for years, hoping to see great things," came the reply.

Elminster swallowed again.

The lady's eyes held dark depths of mystery, and her voice had a musical lilt. She smiled and raised an empty hand—and suddenly, she held a metal scepter. Lights pulsed and winked down its length. Elminster had never seen anything of the like before, but it blazed with blue mage-fire in his gaze, and its very look shouted that it held power.

"With this," the lady said quietly, "you can destroy all your foes here at once. Merely will it and speak the word graven on the grip."

She released the scepter, which rose a little and then drifted smoothly through the air toward Elminster. He watched it come, eyes narrow, then snatched it out of the air. Silent power shuddered in his grasp. Elminster felt it crackle and roil around in him, and his face brightened. He raised it, turning to face the motionless armsmen, feeling a fierce exultation rising in him. The lady watched him. He stood still for a long moment, then carefully bent and set the scepter down on the stone floor at his feet.

"Nay," he said, lifting his eyes to meet hers, " 'twould not be right, to use magic against men who are helpless. That's just what I'm fighting against, Lady."

"Oh?" She raised her head to stare at him in sudden challenge. "Are you afraid of it?"

Elminster shrugged. "A little." He watched her steadily. "More afraid of what I'd do wrongly. Thy scepter burns with power; such magic could do much ill if used carelessly. I'd rather not see the Realms laid waste by mine own hand." He shook his head. "Wielding a little power can be . . . pleasure. No one should have too much."

"What is 'too much'?"

"For me, Lady, anything. I hate magic. A mage slew my parents, on a whim, it seems, or for an afternoon's entertainment. He destroyed a village in less time than it takes me to tell ye what befell. No man should be able to do that."

"Is magic, then, evil?"

"Yes," Elminster snapped, then looked upon her beauty and said, "or perhaps not—but its power twists men to indulge evil."

"Ah," she replied. "Is a sword evil?"

"Nay, Lady—but dangerous. Not all folk should have them to hand."

"Oh? Who is to stop tyrants—and magelords—then?"

Elminster frowned angrily. "Ye seek to trick me with clever words, Lady!"

"Nay," came the soft reply. "I seek to make you think before you offer your own clever words and quick, sure judgments. I ask again: is a sword evil?"

"Nay," Elminster said, "for a sword cannot think."

The lady nodded. "Is a plow evil?"

"Nay," Elminster replied, raising an eyebrow. "What mean ye?"

"If a blade is not evil, but may be used for evil, is not this scepter the same?"

Elminster frowned and shook his head slightly, but did not reply.

Those eyes of light held his steadily. "What if I offered this scepter to a wizard, an innocent apprentice in some other land, not a magelord? What would you say to that?"

Elminster felt anger rising in him. Was everyone who worked sorcery given to fencing with clever words? Why did they always toy with him, as if he were a child, or a beast to be slain or transformed with but a passing thought? "I would say against it, Lady. No one should use such a thing without knowing first *how* to use it—and knowing its work well enough to realize what changes it will work in Faerûn."

"Sober words for one so young. Most youths, and most mages, are so full of whim and pride that they'll dare anything."

Her words calmed him a little. At least she listened and did not dismiss him out of hand. Who *was* she? Did Mystra bind wizards to guard every one of her temples?

Elminster shook his head again. "I am a thief, Lady, in a city ruled by cruel wizards. Whim and pride are luxuries only rich fools can afford. If I want to indulge in them, I must needs do it by night, in bedchambers or on rooftops." He smiled thinly. "Thieves—and indeed farmers, beggars, and folk who own only a small shop or hand-trade, methinks—must keep themselves under rather more control by day, or soon perish."

"What would you do," the sorceress asked curiously, eyes very bright, "if you could work magic and became a wizard as strong as those who dwell here?"

"I'd use my spells to drive all the wizards out of Athalantar so folk could be free. I'd set a few other things right, too, and then renounce magic forever."

"For you hate magic," the lady said softly. "What if you did not and someone gave you the power, and told you that it must be used, that you *must* be a wizard? What then?"

"I'd try to be a good one," Elminster replied, shrugging again. Did temple wizards just *talk* to every intruder all the night through? Still, it felt good to speak openly at last to someone who listened and seemed to understand but not judge.

"Would you make yourself king?"

Elminster shook his head. "I'd not be a good one," he said. "I have not the patience." He smiled suddenly and added, "Yet if I found a man or a maid who'd wear the crown well, I'd stand behind him or her. That, I think, is the true work of a wizard—to make life in the lands he dwells in good for all who dwell there."

Her smile, then, was dazzling. Elminster felt sudden power in the air around him. His hair crackled, and his skin tingled. "Will you kneel to me?" the sorceress asked, striding nearer.

Elminster swallowed, mouth suddenly dry. She was very beautiful, and yet somehow terrifying, her eyes and hair alight with power like flame waiting to burst forth. Trembling, Elminster held his ground and asked, "L—Lady, what is thy name? Who are ye?"

"I am *Mystra*," came a voice that crashed around him like a mighty wave smashing on rocks. Its echoes rolled around the chamber. "*I* am the Lady of Might and the Mistress of Magic! I am *Power Incarnate!* Wherever magic is worked, there am I—from the cold poles of Toril to its hottest jungles, whatever the hand or claw or will that works the sorcery! Behold me and fear me! Yet behold me and love me—as all who deal with me in honesty do. This world is my domain. I *am* magic, mightiest among all those men worship. I am the One True Spell at the heart of all spells. There is no other."

Echoes rolled away. Elminster felt the very pillars of the temple shaking around him. He wavered in awe, like a man struggling in a high wind, but kept his feet. Silence fell, and their eyes met.

Golden flames burned in her gaze. Elminster felt as if he were burning inside; hot fire raced along his veins, pain rising in him like an angry red wave.

"Man," the goddess said, in an awful whisper, "do you defy me?"

Elminster shook his head. "I came here to curse thee or desecrate thy holy place or demand aid from thee, but now—no. I wish ye hadn't let the magelords slay my parents and ruin my realm, and I would . . . know why. But I have no wish to defy ye."

"What do you feel, instead?"

Elminster sighed. Somehow he'd felt he had to speak the truth since her first words to him, and it was still so. "I fear ye, and . . ." He was silent for a time, and then what might have been a smile touched his lips, and he went on. ". . . I think I could learn to love ye."

Mystra was very close to him now, and her eyes were dark pools of mystery. She smiled, and suddenly Elminster felt cool and refreshed, at ease.

"I let mages use spells freely so that all beings who use magic may escape tyranny. But from that freedom come such as the magelords in this land," she said. "If you would overthrow them, why not become a mage yourself? It is but a tool in your hand . . . and it seems to fit your hand better than many I have seen grasping at it."

Elminster took a pace back, lifting his hands in an unconscious warding gesture.

Mystra halted, eyes suddenly stern. "I ask again: will you kneel to me?"

Eyes locked on hers, he knelt slowly. "Lady, I confess I am awed," he said slowly, "but if I serve thee . . . I'd rather do it with my eyes open."

Mystra laughed, eyes sparkling. "Ah, but it is long since I've met such a one as you!"

Then her face was again solemn, and her voice low. "Extend your hand, freely and in trust, or go unharmed; choose."

Elminster extended his hand without hesitation. Mystra smiled and touched it. Fire consumed him, spun him down helplessly into nothing and beyond, and whirled him away into golden depths . . . as a thousand lightning bolts struck through his heart and roared back out of him as consuming flame. . . .

Elminster screamed, or tried to, as he was flung away into many-hued madness, a place of blinding light and blazing pain. He roared, and when darkness rushed up to meet him, he plunged headlong into it, striking it as if it were a stone wall. Dashed against it, he was . . . gone. . . .

It was the cold, again, that awakened him. Elminster sat up, half expecting to see the burial ground slumbering around him, and found instead the temple, still and dark. Power yet flowed in it, though, in a silent, invisible web of stirrings all around him, from the bare altar to the armsmen and the magelord who stood motionless all around the circular chancel.

Now he could feel magic as well as see it!

Awed, Elminster looked all around. He was naked; everything had been burned away to lie in ashes around him except for the Lion Sword, which lay beside him, unchanged from its ruined state. Taking it up with a smile—the Mistress of Magic knew his duty, too, it seemed—he got to his feet. The blue glow of magic was everywhere in this vast chamber, but brightest of all behind him. He turned and beheld the altar.

Mystra was gone, and her scepter with her, but as he looked, words flamed out brightly on the altar. He hurried forward to read them. "Teach thyself magic, and see the Realms. You will know when to come back to Athalantar. Worship me always with that keen mind and that lack of pride, and you will please me well. Serve me first by touching my altar."

As he finished reading, the words faded. When the altar was bare and dark again, he reached forward tentatively—paused in sudden, trembling fear—and then laid a hand firmly on the cold stone.

He thought he heard a faint chuckle, somewhere nearby . . . and then darkness claimed him again.

EIGHT
TO SERVE MYSTRA

Did I ever tell thee how I first came to serve Mystra? No? Ye won't believe a word of it naetheless. The way of the Lady seems strange to most men—but then, most men are sane. Well, more or less.

SUNDRAL MORTHYN
THE WAY OF A WIZARD
YEAR OF SINGING SHARDS

The world was drifting white mists. Elminster shook his head to be free of them and heard a bird calling. A bird? In the depths of the dark, empty temple? He shook his head again, and realized with a start that his bare feet stood on moss and earth, not cold stone. Where *was* he?

El found himself struggling now to break free of the mists . . . clouds in his mind, not the world around. Shaking his head, he heard bird calls again, and a soft rustling, a sound he remembered from long-ago Heldon: breezes blowing through leaves.

He was in a forest somewhere. As the last of the mists fell away, El looked around and caught his breath. He stood in the heart of a deep wood, with duskwoods and shadowtops and blueleaf trees standing all crowded together around him, the ground beneath them a dim and mushroom-studded place stretching off into gloomy, rolling distances.

He stood in sunlight on a little knoll where several old giants of the forest had toppled, leaving a clearing into which the sun could reach. It was a small patch of sunlit moss where a large flat stone lay, and beyond it, a tiny, crystal-clear pool. The Lion Sword lay on the stone. Mystra's magic must have brought it here with him.

Elminster bent forward to take it up. There was an unfamiliar swaying sensation at his chest as he knelt. Frowning, he looked down and saw the breasts and the smooth curves of a maid. Elminster stared down at himself in astonishment, and ran a wondering hand over his body. It was solid and real . . . he looked wildly around, but he was alone. Mystra had turned him into a woman!

Clutching the reassuring, familiar hilt of the Lion Sword, El crawled forward across the rock until he could stare down into the placid waters of the pool. He studied his reflection there, seeing his own sharp nose and black hair, but a rather softer face, with a pert mouth—now frowning in consternation—a long neck and below it, a slim-hipped, rather bony woman. He was Elminster no more.

As he stared down, something seemed to grow in the depths of the pool . . . something blue-white and leaping—a flame.

El sat back. A flame was burning under the water, a flame with nothing to feed on! A flame that was rising, and becoming golden . . . Mystra!

He reached out an eager hand to touch the flame as it broke the surface, never thinking that it might destroy him until it was too late and his slim fingers were already feeling—coolness! A voice seemed to speak in his head. "Elminster becomes Elmara to see the world through the eyes of a woman. Learn how magic is a part of all things and a living force in itself, and pray to me by kindling flame. You will find a teacher in this forest." The flame faded and Elminster shivered. He knew that voice.

He looked down again in wonder. Now he was . . . "Elmara," she said aloud, and repeated it, her voice more musical than before.

She shook her head, suddenly recalling a night in Hastarl bought with stolen coins at Farl's urging. She remembered hot kisses and smooth, cool shoulders sliding soft and curved under his fingers, which wandered with tentative awe.

If he went into such a room now, he'd—she'd—be on the other end of the lovemaking. Hmmm.

So this was Mystra's first trick. Elmara twisted her lips wryly, shivered again, and then drew a deep breath. Elminster, the upstart prince whose failed battles had made him known to at least two magelords, was gone . . . at least for now, perhaps forever. His cause, she vowed, would never die, but end fulfilled. That might take years, though, and for now—Elmara murmured, "So now what?" A breeze rustled the leaves again in answer.

Shrugging, she rose and walked all over the little knoll—noting that her stride was subtly different, shorter and swaying from side to side more—but there was nothing else to be found except moss and dead leaves. She was alone, and nude, the occasional twig sharp under her bare feet. What to do?

There was no food here, and no shelter. The sun already felt hot on her head and shoulders . . . she'd best get into the shade. Mystra's voice had said she'd find a tutor in the forest, but she was reluctant to leave the pool, perhaps her only link to the goddess . . . but no. Mystra had said that El should pray to her by kindling flame, and there was not enough wood or leaves on this knoll to do that. Mystra had also said she'd *find* a tutor, and that implied she'd have to look for one.

Elmara sighed, juggled the Lion Sword thoughtfully, and squinted up at the sun. This forest looked like the High Forest above Heldon. If this was the High Forest, going south would bring her to its edge, and perhaps to food, if she couldn't find anything to eat among the trees, and to some idea of where exactly she was. The ground under the trees was dark and rolling, with sharp slopes and little gullies everywhere. If she left this knoll, she doubted she could ever find it again. That thought made her remember the pool, and she knelt and drank deeply, not knowing when next she'd see water.

Right, then. Time waited on no man—or woman, she reminded herself wryly, wondering how long it would take to get used to this. As she set off down into the trees, she did not look back, and so didn't see the pair of floating eyes that appeared above the pool, watched her go, and seemed to nod approvingly.

She'd walked all day, and her feet were cut to ribbons. She winced as she went and left a bloody trail. She'd have to get into a tree before dark, or some prowling forest cat or wolf would follow her trail. If it bit her throat, she'd be dead before she could wake.

Elmara looked around uneasily. The endless forest seemed dark and menacing now as the small glimpses of sunlight turned amber with sunset, and twilight came creeping . . . should she light a fire? It might attract beasts that could eat her, but yes. Only a little one, and let it die out before she slept. A flame to pray to Mystra. She'd do this every night, she vowed, beginning now.

She bent and gathered a dry tangle of twigs from under a large leaf and spread them on a nearby rock. Then she stopped in confusion. How could she make them burn? With a flint, aye, but she had no flint, nor steel.

A moment later, she smote her forehead and made a disgusted sound. Of course she did: the Lion Sword! She raised it, shaking her head at her slow wits, and rang it off the rock.

A spark jumped. Yes! This was the way. She set about belaboring the edge of the rock with the stoutest part of the blade, the unsharpened length just below the hilt, and pushed kindling in around where she struck, to catch any spark. The ringing sounds she made echoed a long way under the trees . . . and sparks jumped and winked where she didn't want them, disdaining her dry kindling.

Frustration and then anger rose in her . . . could she do *nothing* right? "I'm trying, Mystra," she snarled, "but—"

She broke off as the white glow arose at the back of her mind. Use her mind to call up fire? She'd never done more than nudge things a trifle, or slow falls a bit, or staunch bleeding . . . could she?

Well, why not try? She bent her gaze on the sword and summoned up the white fire within, building it with her anger until it blazed up and filled her mind. Then she brought the sword crashing down on the rock. A spark leaped up—and seemed to grow, expanding into a little ball of light before it arced back down and faded away.

El's eyes widened. She stared down where the spark had been, then shrugged and began the slow process of building the fire in her mind again. This time, the spark glowed white, expanded—and Elmara set her teeth and willed it to drift sideways and keep blazing . . . and it settled down into the kindling.

A curl of smoke drifted up. El watched and grinned in sudden exultation. She blew ever so gently at the kindling, and then shifted some twigs and a leaf so that they'd catch, if only the gods smiled—yes! A tiny flame rose, a tongue of faint amber that licked at the leaf and spread brown over it as it fed, growing higher.

El trembled, suddenly aware that a painful throbbing was beginning in her head, licked her lips, and said over the flame, "My thanks, great Mystra. I shall try to learn, and serve thee well."

The flame soared suddenly, almost burning her nose, and then winked out, gone as if it had never been. Elmara stared at where it wasn't, then sat back, holding her suddenly splitting head. No normal flame would behave that way; Mystra *must* have heard her.

She knelt there for a few breaths, hoping for some sign or word from the goddess, but there was nothing but darkness under the trees, and a faint whiff of woodsmoke. But then, why should she expect anything more? She'd never seen Mystra in all her life before last night . . . and there were other folk and other doings in Faerûn besides Elminster of Athalantar.

Elmara, she corrected herself absently. What *did* gods spend their days at, anyway?

And then a booted foot came down softly on the ground she was staring at, treading firmly on the Lion Sword. She gasped and looked up. Proud eyes—elven eyes—stared down at her, and their gaze was not friendly. A hand was extended toward her, and there was a sudden glow of light from its palm. The bright radiance grew, stretching out straight down at her, until the tip of a sword of light was in front of her chin.

"Tell me," a light, high voice said calmly, "why I should let you live."

Delsaran sniffed suddenly and raised his head. "Fire!" The tree he'd been shaping fell back limply under his hands as his magic faltered. Quick anger turned the tips of his ears red. "Here, in the very heart of the old trees!"

"Yes," Baerithryn agreed, but laid a restraining hand on his friend's arm. "But a small one; tarry." He raised his other hand, sketched a circle in the air with two fingers, and spoke a soft word.

A moment later, an intent face appeared in the air between them, the face of a human woman. Delsaran hissed but said no more as they heard the woman speak: "My thanks, great Mystra. I shall try to learn, and serve thee well."

The flame soared then, and their spell-vision exploded into a tiny twinkling of blue sparks. Delsaran's jaw dropped. "The goddess heard her," he said in grudging disbelief.

Baerithryn nodded. "This must be the one the Lady said would come." He rose, a silent shadow in the gathering night-gloom, and said, "I shall guide her, as I promised. Leave us be . . . as you promised."

Delsaran nodded slowly. "The Lady grant us success"—his lips twisted wryly—"all three." Baerithryn laid a silent hand on his shoulder, then was gone.

Delsaran stared unseeing at the tree he'd been shaping, and then shook his head. Humans had slain his parents and their axes had felled the trees he'd first played in . . . why did the Lady have to send a human? Didn't she want the People to be guided in learning her service and true mastery of magic?

"I guess she thinks elves are wise enough to guide themselves," he said aloud, smiled almost wistfully, and got to his feet. Mystra had never spoken to *him*. He shrugged, set his hand reassuringly on the tree for a moment, and then slipped away into the night.

Elmara stared up at the sword. "There is no special reason," she said at last. "Mystra brought me here, and"—she gestured down at herself, and a sudden blush stole across her face—"changed me, thus. I mean no harm to you or to this place."

The elf regarded her gravely for a moment and said, "Yet there is the will in you to do great harm to many folk."

El stared into his eyes and found her throat suddenly dry. She swallowed and said, "I live to avenge my slain parents. My foes are the magelords of Athalantar."

The elf stood silent, as still and dark as the trees around. The sword of light did not waver. He seemed to be awaiting more words.

Elmara shrugged. "To destroy them, I must master magic—or find some way to destroy theirs. I . . . met with Mystra. She said I'd find a tutor here. . . . Do ye know of a wizard or a priest of Mystra in this wood?"

The sword vanished. Blinking in the sudden darkness, El heard that light voice say simply, "Yes." Silence followed.

Afraid of being left alone in the night in this endless forest, El asked quickly, "Will ye guide me to that person?" To her own astonishment, her voice quavered.

"You have found 'that person,'" the elf replied with an undertone that might have been satisfaction or quiet amusement. "Give me your name."

"El—Elmara," she answered, and something made her add, "I was Elminster until this morn."

The elf nodded. "Baerithryn," he replied. "I was Braer to the last human who knew me."

"Who was that?" El asked, suddenly curious.

Those grave eyes flickered. "A lady mage . . . dead these three hundred summers."

El looked down. "Oh."

"I'm not overfond of questions, you'll find," the elf added. "Look and listen to learn. That is the elven way. You humans have so much less time and always gabble questions and then rush off to do things without waiting for, or truly understanding, the answers. I hope to curb that in you . . . just a little." He leaned forward and added, "Now lie back."

El looked up at him, and then did so, wondering what would come next. Unconsciously, she covered her breasts and loins with her hands.

The elf seemed to smile. "I've seen maids before . . . and all of you, already." He dropped silently into a crouch and said, "Give me your foot."

El looked at him in wonder, and then raised her left foot. The elf cupped it—his touch was feather-soft—and the pain slowly ebbed away. El looked at him in wonder.

"The other," he said simply. She let her healed foot fall and extended the other to him. Again the pain fled. "You've given the forest blood," he said, "which satisfies a ritual some find unpleasant." His grip on her heel became stronger, and he made a surprised sound and let her foot fall.

A moment later—he moved like soundless liquid, or a smooth-flowing shadow—the elf was kneeling by her head. "Allow me," he said, and added, "Lie still." Elmara felt his fingers touch her lightly over each eye, and linger there . . . and slowly, very slowly, the ache in her head subsided, the pain stealing away.

With it went all her weariness, and she was suddenly alert, eager, and awake. "Wh—My thanks, sir—what did you do?"

"Several things. I used simple magic, what you'll need to learn first. Then I winced at being called 'sir' and waited patiently to be called 'Braer' and seen as a person, not some sort of magic-wielding monster." The words were lightly spoken beside her ear, but Elmara felt her answer was very important.

She raised her head slowly, to find those eyes staring into hers from only a finger's length away. "Please forgive me, Braer. Will ye be—my friend?" Impulsively, she leaned forward and kissed the face she could barely see. The elf's eyes blinked into hers as her lips touched—a sharp-boned nose.

Braer did not pull away. His lips did not meet hers, but a moment later Elmara felt soft fingers stroke the length of her chin. "That's better, daughter of a prince. Now sleep."

El was falling down, down into a void of warm darkness before she even had time to wonder how Braer knew his—her—father had been a prince . . . perhaps, she managed to think, as whispering mists rose in her mind, all Faerûn knew it. . . .

"You began as all younglings do: awed by magic. Then you learned to fear it, and hate those who wielded it. After a time, you saw its usefulness as a weapon too powerful to ignore. Mastering it or finding a shield against it then became a necessity."

Braer fell silent and leaned forward, watching intently as blue mage-fire danced at the tips of Elmara's fingers. He gestured, and obediently she made the fire move up and down each finger in turn, racing along her tingling skin.

"You wonder not why I waste so much of your brief life with a child's playing about with magic," Braer said flatly. "It's not to make you familiar with it. You are that, already. It's to make you love magic, for itself, not for what you can do with it."

"Why," Elmara asked in the elven manner, reflected fire dancing in her eyes as her gaze met his, "should a man or a maid love magic?"

Her teacher remained silent, as he did all too often for her liking. They looked into each other's eyes until finally she added, "I would think that leads to bent men who wall themselves up in little rooms and become crabbed and crazed, chasing some elusive spell or detail of magecraft, and wasting their lives away."

"In some, it does," Braer agreed. "But love of magic is more necessary for those who worship Mystra—priests of the goddess, if you will, though most see no difference between such folk and mages—than it is for wizards. One must love magic to properly revere magic."

Elmara frowned a little. There were a few gray hairs in her long, unruly black mane now; she'd studied magic for two winters through at Braer's side, praying to Mystra each night . . . without reply. Hastarl and her days as a thief seemed almost a dream to her now, but she could still remember the faces of the magelords she'd seen.

"Some folk worship out of fear. Is their respect any the less?"

The elf nodded. "It is," he said simply, "even if they do not know it." He rose, as smooth and silent as ever. "Now put away that fire and come and help me find evenfeast."

He strode away through the trees, knowing she'd follow. Elmara rose, smiled a little, and did so. They spent their days thus, talking while she practiced magic under his direction, and then foraging in the forest for food. Once the elf had shown her how to take the shape of a wolf, then bounded off to run down a stag, with her stumbling along behind. In all their days together, she'd never seen him do anything but guide her, though he left her side every nightfall and did not return until dawn. He always chose the spot where she slept, and her magesight told her he cast some sort of magical ring about her.

Braer never seemed tired, or dirty, or less than patient. His garb never changed, and there was never a day when he did not come to her. She saw no other elves, or anyone else . . . though he'd once confirmed they were somewhere in the High Forest, supposedly home to the greatest kingdom of elves in all Faerûn.

On her first morning in the forest, he'd brought her a rough gown of animal hide, glossy high boots of unexpected quality, a thong for tying the Lion Sword around her neck (she kept it wrapped in a skin to avoid cutting her breast), and a trowel for digging her own privy holes. To clean herself, she scrubbed with leaves and moss and washed in the little pools and rivulets that seemed to be everywhere in the endless forest. When she commented that one seemed to find water unexpectedly around every third or fourth hillock or gully, Braer had nodded and replied, "Like magic."

That memory came to Elmara suddenly. She looked ahead at the elf gliding among the trees like a silent shadow, and suddenly scrambled to catch up with him. As always when she hurried, twigs cracked and leaves rustled under her feet. Braer turned and frowned at her.

She matched his frown, and asked the question that had arisen in her. "Braer . . . why do elves love magic?"

For a fleeting moment, a grin of exultation washed across his face. Then it was gone, and his face held its usual expression of calm, open interest. Yet El knew she'd seen that look of delight, and her heart lifted. The elf s next words sent it soaring. "Ah . . . now you begin to think, and to ask the right questions. I can begin teaching you." He turned and walked on.

"*Begin* teaching me?" Elmara asked his back indignantly. "So just *what* have ye been doing these past two seasons?"

"Wasting much time," he told the trees ahead calmly, and her heart came crashing down.

Tears welled up in her, and burst forth. Elmara sank down on her knees and wept. She cried a long time, lonely and lost and feeling worthless, and when the tears were all gone she finally sat up wearily, and looked all around. She was alone.

"Braer!" she cried. "*Braer!* Where are you?" Her shout echoed back at her from the trees, but there came no reply. She sank down again, and whispered, "Mystra, aid me. Mystra . . . help me!"

It was growing dark. Elmara looked wildly in all directions. She was in a part of the forest they'd never walked in before. With sudden urgency she called forth mage-fire, and held up her blazing hand like a lantern. The trees around seemed to rustle and stir for a moment—but then a tense, watchful stillness fell.

"Braer," she said into the darkness. "*Please* . . . come back!"

A tree nearby wavered and bowed—and then stepped forward. It was Baerithryn, looking sad. "Forgive me, Elmara?"

Two running steps later, Elmara crashed into him and threw her arms around him, sobbing. "Where did ye go? Oh, Braer, what did I do?"

"I—am sorry, Lady. I did not mean my words as a judgment." The elf held her gently but firmly, rocking her slightly from side to side as if she were a small child to be soothed. With infinite tenderness, his hands stroked her long, tangled hair.

Elmara pulled her head back, tears bright on her cheeks. "But ye went *away!*"

"You seemed to need a time to grieve . . . a release," the elf said softly. "It seemed churlish to smother what you felt. More than that: sometimes, things must be faced and fought alone."

He took hold of her shoulders and gently pushed her away until they stood facing each other. Then he smiled and raised a hand—and it suddenly held a steaming bowl. A heavenly scent of cooked fowl swirled around them both. "Care to dine?"

Elmara laughed weakly and nodded. Braer whirled his other hand, and out of nowhere a silver goblet appeared in it. He handed it to her with a flourish. When El took it, Braer spun his hand grandly again, and this time two ornate forks and dining knives appeared. He gestured for her to sit.

Elmara discovered she was ravenous. The forest bustards had been cooked in a mushroom sauce and were delicious—and the goblet proved to be full of the best mint wine, incredibly clear and heady. She devoured everything; Braer smiled and shook his head more than once as he watched.

When she was done, another flourish of the elf's hands produced a bowl of warmed vinegar-water and a fine linen cloth for Elmara to wash her face and hands with. As she wiped grease from her chin, she saw his grave expression had returned.

"I ask again, Elmara: do you forgive me? I have wronged you."

"Forgive—of course." El stretched forth her newly cleaned hand to squeeze one of his.

Braer looked down at her hand on his, and then back up at her. "I did to you what we of the forest consider a very bad thing: I misjudged you. I did not mean to upset you . . . nor make it worse by leaving you to your grief. Do you recall just what was said between us?"

Elmara stared at him. "Ye said ye'd wasted much time these past two seasons, and only now could begin to teach me."

Braer nodded. "What question did you ask, to make me say so?"

El wrinkled her brow, and then said slowly, "I asked you why elves love magic."

Braer nodded. "Yes." He waved a hand. All the dinner things vanished, and a vivid ring of blue mage-fire raced into being around them. He settled himself crosslegged, and asked, "Do you feel up to talking the night through?"

El frowned. "Of course . . . why?"

"There are some things you should know . . . and at last are ready to hear."

Elmara met his grave eyes and leaned forward. "Speak, then," she whispered eagerly.

Braer smiled. "To answer one of your questions directly for once: we of the People love magic because we love life. Magic is the life energy of Faerûn, lass, gathered in its raw form and used to power specific effects by those who know how. Elves—and the Stout Folk, too, deep in the rocks beneath us—live close to the land . . . part of it, linked to it—and in balance with it. We grow no more numerous than the land will bear and shape our lives to what the land will support. Forgive me, but humans are different."

Elmara nodded and waved at him to continue.

Braer met her eyes with his own and said steadily, "Like orcs, humans know best how to do four things: breed too rapidly; covet everything around them; destroy anything and everything that stands in the way of any of their desires; and dominate what they can't or won't bother to destroy."

Elmara stared at him. Her face had paled, but she nodded slowly and again gestured for him to continue.

"Harsh words, I know," said the elf gently, "but that is what your kin mean to us. Men seek to change Faerûn around them to suit their own desires. When we—or anything else—stand in their way, they cut us down. Men are quick and clever—I'll give them that—and seem to stumble on new ideas and ways more often and more swiftly than any other people . . . but to us, and to the land, they are a creeping danger. A creeping rot that eats away at this forest and every other untouched part of the realm . . . and at us with it. You are the first of your race to be tolerated here in the depths of the wood for a very long time—and there are some among my folk who would rather you were safely dead, your flesh feeding the trees."

Elmara stared silently at him, face white and eyes very dark.

Braer smiled slightly, and added, "Death is a goal too few of your race strive for, but one more laudable than many they do pursue."

Elmara let out a long, shuddering breath, and asked, "Why then do you . . . tolerate me here?"

The elf reached out a hand slowly and tentatively, and as Elmara watched in wonder, he squeezed one of her hands just as she had done to him earlier. "Out of simple respect for the Lady, I undertook to guide you," he said, "and to turn you into ways that could do us the least damage, down the years, if the gods willed that you should live."

His smile broadened. "I've come to know you . . . and respect you. I know your life's tale, Elminster Aumar, prince of Athalantar. I know what you hope to do—and it would be mere prudence to aid one dedicated to fighting our most powerful and nearest foes, the magelords. Your character—especially your strength in setting aside your hatred of magic long enough to agree to serve the Lady and in clinging to sanity and dignity when she made you a woman without warning—have made my task more than a duty and prudence; you have made it a pleasure."

Elmara swallowed, feeling fresh tears well up and run down her cheeks. "Ye—ye are the kindest and most patient person I've ever known," she whispered. "Please forgive me, for my tears earlier."

Braer patted her hand. "The fault was mine. To answer the question that has just occurred to you: Mystra made you a maid both to hide you from the magelords and to make you able to feel the link between magic, the land, and life; women are able to feel it better than men. In the days ahead, I can show you how to feel and work with that link."

"*Ye can read my thoughts?*" Elmara cried, drawing back from him sharply. "Then why, by all the gods, didn't ye just *tell* me what I needed to know?"

Braer shook his head. "I can only read thoughts when they're charged with strong emotion, and when I'm very close by. More than that: few folk can truly learn by having every idle thought answered in an instant. They don't bother to think about or remember anything, but merely come to rely on the one answering them for all wisdom and direction."

Elmara frowned, nodding very slowly. "Aye," she said softly. "Ye're right."

Braer nodded. "I know. It's the curse of my race."

Elmara looked at him for a moment, and then whooped with laughter. After a few helpless breaths of mirth, she broke off at a sound she'd never heard before: a deep, dry sound . . . Baerithryn of the People was chuckling.

Dawn was stealing through the trees when Braer said, "Too tired to go on?"

Elmara was stiff with sitting and swayed with weariness, but she whispered fiercely, "No! I have to know! Say on!"

Braer inclined his head in salute, and said, "Know then: the High Forest is dying, little by little, year by year, under the axes of men and the spells of magelords. They know our power—and being insecure in their own, feel they can only win the safety of their realm by destroying us."

He waved one hand in a slow arc at the silent trees around them. "Our power is rooted in the shiftings of the seasons. It is drawn from the vitality and endurance of the land—and is not a thing of flashing battle spells and destruction. The magelords know this and how to force us to fight in ways and places where they know they can defeat us, so we often dare not fight them openly . . . and they know that too. I've lost many friends who would not admit the magelords' power rivaled or overmatched our own."

Braer sighed and continued, "You, and others like you, we can aid in your own battles against them . . . and we will. So long as you respect the land and live with it, our ways lie together, and our battles shall, too. When you need aid against the magelords and call to us, we shall come. This we swear."

A moment later, half a dozen trees around them shifted and stepped forward, and his words were echoed by a fierce chorus. "*This we swear.*"

Elmara stared around at all the solemn elven eyes, swallowed, and bowed her head. "And I, in turn, swear not to work against thee or the land. Show me how to do this, please."

The elves bowed in return and melted away again into the forest.

El swallowed. "Are they always here, as trees, around us?"

Braer smiled. "No. You happened to pause and weep in a special place."

El gave him a fierce expression, but it slid into a smile and a weary shake of her head. "I am honored . . . and understand your people enough, now, not to step wrongly with each stride." She yawned helplessly and added, "I think I'm more than ready to sleep now, too. Promise to show me—finally—some earth-shaking spells in the days ahead?"

Baerithryn smiled. "I promise." He reached out and stroked her cheek, and as his spell sent her instantly to sleep, caught her shoulder and lowered her tenderly to the mossy ground.

Then he settled down beside her and stroked her cheek again. In her little time left in the forest, he would keep careful watch over this weapon against the magelords. More than that: he would keep careful watch over this precious friend.

NINE
THE WAY OF A MAGE

The way of a mage is a dark and lonely one. This is why so many wizards fall early into the darkness of the grave—or later into the endless twilight of undeath. Such bright prospects are why the road to mastery of magecraft is always such a crowded one.

JHALIVAR THRUNN
TRAIL TALES OF THE NORTH
YEAR OF THE SUNDERED SHIELDS

A flame was suddenly dancing above the rock, in air that had been empty a moment before. Elmara caught her breath. "Mystra?" she asked, and the flame seemed to brighten for a moment in response—but then it faded away into nothingness, and there was no other reply.

Elmara sighed and knelt beside the pool. "I hoped for something more."

"A little less pride, lass," Braer murmured, touching her elbow. "'Tis more than most of my folk ever see of the Lady."

She looked at him curiously. "Just how many of the People worship Mystra?"

"Not many . . . we have our own gods, and most of us have always preferred to turn our back on the rest of the world and all its unpleasantnesses and keep to the old ways. The problem is that the rest of the world always seems to reach out and thrust blades into our backsides while we're trying to ignore it."

El grinned at his words, despite their tragic meaning. "'Backsides'? I never thought to hear an elf say that."

Braer's mouth crooked. "I never thought to see a human hear an elf say it, if it comes to that. Do you still think of us as unearthly tall and thin noble creatures, gliding around above it all?"

"I—aye, I suppose I do."

The elf shook his head. "We have you fooled with the rest, then. We're as earthy and as untidy as the forest. We *are* the forest, lass. Try not to forget that as you walk out into the world of men."

"'Walk out'?" Elmara frowned at him. "Why d'ye say that?"

"I can't help but read your thoughts, Lady. You've been happier here than ever before in your short life—but you know you've learned all you can here that'll make of yourself a better blade against the magelords . . . and you grow restless to move on."

He held up a hand as she made a small sound of protest, and went on. "Nay, lass; I can see it in you and hear it in you, and for you it is right. You can never be free, never be yourself, until your parents have been avenged and you've set Athalantar back to what you think it should be. You're driven by this, and it's a burden no one in Faerûn can lift but you, by doing the deeds you've set yourself." He smiled wryly. "You didn't want to leave Farl, and now you don't want to leave me. Are you sure you shouldn't stay a woman the rest of your days?"

Elmara made a face and added softly, "I didn't know I had a choice."

"Not yet, perhaps, but you will . . . when you start to become a realm-shattering archmage. Thus far, you've become familiar with magic, and by the grace of Mystra call up and shape what slumbers in the land around. Did you truly think this prayer, now, and all the others each night, were wasted?"

"I—"

"You've begun to fear so, yes. I'm telling you differently," Braer said almost sternly and stood up in a single smooth movement. He reached down a hand to assist her to rise and added, "I'll miss you, but I won't be sad or angry; 'tis time for you to move on. You'll return when you must. My task hasn't been to teach you spells that'll blast magelords and their dragon steeds out of the sky, but to teach you familiarity with magic and wisdom in the use of it. I am a priest of Mystra, yes—but there's a priestess of Mystra greater far than I am. You must go to see her soon, outside the forest. Her temple is at Ladyhouse Falls, and she knows more of the ways of men . . . and of where you should go in the days ahead."

Elmara frowned. "I—ye are right, I do grow restless, but I don't want to leave."

The elf smiled. "Ah, but you do." Then his smile vanished, and he added, "And before you go, I'd like to see that revealment spell cast properly for once!"

Elmara sighed. "It's just a spell I've a little trouble with, one among—what is it?—two score and more?"

Braer raised eyebrows and hands together. "'Just a spell'? Lass, lass. Nothing should ever be just a spell to you. *Revere* magic, remember? Else it's just a faster sword or longer lance to you—only a grubbing after more power than you can grasp by other means."

"It's *not* that to me!" Elmara protested, turning on him angrily. "Oh, before I came here, perhaps! Do you think I've learned nothing from you?"

"Easy, lass, easy. I'm not a magelord, remember?"

El stared at him for a moment, and then managed a laugh. "I did hold my temper and tongue better when I was a thief, didn't I?"

Braer shrugged. "You were a man, then, in a city of men—with a close friend to joke with—and you knew, every moment, that lack of iron control would mean death. Now you're a woman, attuned to the forest, feeling its flows of emotion and energy. Little things are more intense outside the crowded city, more raw, more engaging." He smiled and added, "I can't believe I've started babbling so much—and like a human sage, too!—since you've been here."

Elmara laughed. "I have done some good, then."

Braer flipped the tip of one of his ears back and forth with a finger, a gesture of mild derision among elves, and said, "I believe I mentioned a revealment spell?"

El rolled her eyes. "Didn't think I could lead ye into forgetting about it forever. . . ."

Braer gave her an imperious wave that she knew meant 'get on with it,' and folded his arms across his chest. Elmara assumed an apologetic little-lass smile for a moment, then turned to face the pool. Spreading her arms wide, she closed her eyes and whispered the prayer to Mystra, feeling the power within her surge up her arms and outward, expanding. . . . She opened her eyes, expecting to see the familiar blue glows of magic on the pool, perhaps on the rock where Mystra's flame had manifested, and when she swung around, here and there on Braer's body, where he wore or carried small tokens of magic.

"Ahhh!" Staggered, she stepped back, letting her hands fall. Everything was bright and blinding blue wherever she looked—was the whole world alive with magic?

"Yes," Braer replied calmly, reading her thoughts again. "At *last* you're able to see it. Now," he went on briskly, "you were still having a little trouble with casting a sphere of spells, were you not?"

She turned angry eyes on him, but recoiled again, astonished. The tall, dignified elf she knew stood watching her, but in the special sight the spell gave her was revealed ablaze with magic of great power, and the blue-white glow around him rose into the shadowy shape of a dragon. "Ye—ye're a dragon!"

"Sometimes," Braer shrugged, "I take that shape. But I'm truly an elf who's learned how to take on dragon shape . . . not the other way around. I'm the last reason the magelords did so much dragon hunting in Athalantar."

"The last reason?"

"The others," he said tightly, "are dead. They saw to it very efficiently."

"Oh," Elmara said quietly. "I'm sorry, Braer."

"Why?" he asked lightly. "You didn't do it—'tis the magelords who should be sorry . . . and I and my kin are counting on you to make them so, someday."

Elmara drew herself up. "I intend to. Soon."

The elf shook his head. "No, lass, not yet. You aren't ready . . . and a single archmage, no matter how mighty, can't hope to succeed against all the magelords and their servant creatures, if they whelm against you." He smiled and added, "And you haven't even learned to be an archmage yet. Set aside revenge for a time. 'Tis best savored when one waits a long time for it, anyway."

Elmara sighed. "I may die of old age with the magelords still lording it over Athalantar."

"I've read that fear in your mind often, since we first met," Braer replied, "and I know it will drive you until your death—or theirs. It's why you must leave the High Forest before it starts to feel like a cage around you."

Elmara took a deep breath, then nodded. "When should I go?"

Braer smiled. "As soon as I've conjured up crying towels for us both. Elves hate long, sad farewells even more than humans do."

El tried to laugh, but sudden tears welled up and burst forth.

"You see?" Braer said lightly, stepping forward to embrace her. Elmara saw tears in his own eyes before they embraced fiercely.

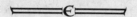

The night was soft and still and deep blue overhead as El left the familiar shade of the forest and headed across the rolling hills toward distant Ladyhouse Falls. She felt suddenly naked, away from the sheltering trees, but fought down the urge to hurry. Folk in too much haste made excellent targets for outlaws with bows . . . and with no foe in sight and a heavy load of sausage, roast fowl, cheese, wine, and bread riding between her shoulder blades, she really had no need to hurry.

She struck the Hastarl road and almost immediately passed by the last marker cairn. It felt marvelous to set foot outside the Kingdom of the Stag for the first time in her life.

Elmara breathed deeply of the crisp air of fast-approaching leaf-fall, and looked at the land around as she went. She was wading through waist-deep brush, where the Great Fires had been set ten years agone to drive the elves out of all these lands and take them for men. But men huddled in ever-more-crowded cities and towns along the Delimbiyr, and summer by summer, the forest crept back to reclaim the hills. Soon the elves—more bitter and swifter with their arrows than they'd once been—would return too.

Here shadowtops rose like a dark stand of halberds; there two hawks circled high in the clear air. She went on with joy in her step, and did not halt until it grew too dark to go on and the wolves began to howl.

She'd expected more than a few ragged stone cottages and a tumbledown barn—but the road ran on and up through the trees toward a distant roar of water; this must be Ladyhouse Falls.

The road narrowed to a deep-rutted cart trail and turned east. A little path led off it into the trees, along which came the sound of water. Elmara took the way it offered and came out in a field broken by a huge, fire-scarred sheet of rock, with the rushing river hard by, and a high-peaked hall in front of her.

Ivy was thick on its old stones, and its door was dark, but to Elmara's magesight it blazed blue, the heart of a web of radiant lines sweeping out across the fields and down the trail she had walked upon. That strand blinked beneath her feet; she stepped aside hastily and advanced thereafter by walking on the mosses beside the trail.

She almost fell over the old woman in dark robes who was kneeling in the dirt, planting small yellow-green things and covering them over deeply.

"I was wondering if you'd stride right through my bed without seeing me at all," she said without looking up, her voice sharp-edged but amused.

Elmara stared, and then swallowed, finding herself shy. "My—pardon, Lady. In truth, I saw thee not. I seek—"

"The glories of Mystra, I know." The wrinkled hands patted another plant into its resting place—like so many tiny graves, El thought suddenly—and the white-haired head came up. Elmara found herself looking into two clear eyes of green flame that seemed to thrust right through her like two emerald blades. "Why?"

El found herself bereft of words. She opened her mouth twice, and then the third time blurted out, "I—Mystra spoke to mé. She said it'd been a long time since she'd met such a one as me. She asked me to kneel to her, and I did." Unable to meet that bright gaze longer, Elmara looked away.

"Aye, so they all say. I suppose she told thee to worship her well."

"She wrote that, aye. I—"

"What has life taught thee thus far, young maid?"

Elmara raised steady blue-gray eyes to meet that glittering green gaze. The old woman's eyes seemed even brighter than before, but she was determined to hold them with her own, and she did.

"I've learned how to hate, steal, grieve, and kill," she said. "I hope there's more to being a priestess of Mystra than that."

The wrinkled old mouth crooked. "For many, not much more. Let's see if we can do better with thee." She looked down at the bed in front of her and tapped thoughtfully at the loose earth.

"What must I do to begin?" Elmara asked, looking down at the dirt. There seemed to be nothing of interest there, but perhaps the priestess meant that she should tend plants, as Braer had wanted her to learn the ways of the woods. She looked around . . . hadn't there been a shovel thrust into the earth nearby?

As if the old woman could read her thoughts (as of course she doubtless could, El thought wryly) the priestess shook her head. "After all these years," she said, "I've learned how to do this right, lass. The last thing I need is eager but careless hands mucking in or a young, impatient tongue asking me questions morn and even through. Nay, get ye gone."

"Gone?"

"Go and walk the world, lass; Mystra doesn't gather toothless, chanting men or maids to kneel to stones carved in her seeming. All Faerûn around us is Mystra's true temple."

She waved a bony hand. "Go and do as I bid, thus; and listen well, lass. Learn from mages, without yourself taking the title or spellhurling habits of a wizard. Spread word of the power of magic, its mysteries and lore; make folk you meet hunger to work magic themselves, and give those who seem most eager a taste of spellcasting, for no more payment than food and a place to sleep. Make maids and men into mages."

El frowned doubtfully. "How shall I know when I'm doing right—is there anything I should not do?"

The priestess shook her head. "Be guided by your own heart—but know that Mystra forbids nothing. Go and experience everything that can befall a man and a maid in Faerûn. *Everything.*"

El frowned again. Slowly, she turned away.

That sharp voice came again. "Sit down and eat first, fool-head. Bitterness lends the weak-witted wings . . . always try to make a stop to eat into a time to think, and you'll think more in a season than most think in all their days."

Elmara smiled slightly, threw her cloak back, and sat, reaching for the shoulder sack Braer had given her.

The old woman shook her head again and snapped her fingers. Out of nowhere, a wooden platter of steaming greens appeared in front of El. Then a silver fork blinked into being above it and hung motionless in the air.

Reluctantly El reached out for it.

The old woman snorted. "Frightened of a little magic? A *fine* advocate of Mystra you'll be."

"I—have seen magic used to slay and destroy and rule through fear," Elmara said slowly. "Wherefore I'm wary of it." She took firm hold of the fork. "I did not choose to look upon Mystra—she came to me."

"Then be more grateful; some wizards dream of seeing her all their lives and die disappointed." The white-haired head bent to regard the dirt again. "If you hate or fear magic so much, why have you come here?"

Silence stretched. "To do a thing I am sworn to do," Elmara said finally, "I'll need strong magic . . . and to understand what it is I wield."

"Well, then . . . eat, and get you going. Mind you try some of that thinking I suggest."

"Thinking of—what?"

"That, I leave to you. Remember, Mystra forbids nothing."

"Think . . . of everything?"

"'Twould be a welcome change."

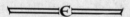

The old woman watched until the young maid in the cloak was gone through the trees. Then she went on watching; a few trees were nothing to her.

Finally she turned and walked to the temple, growing as she went, her shape shifting and rising until a tall and shapely lady in shimmering, iridescent robes strolled to the temple door. She turned once more to look where Elmara had gone. Her eyes were dark and yet golden, and little flames danced in them.

"Seen enough?" The voice from the darkness within the door was a deep rumble.

Mystra tossed her head; long, glossy hair slithered and danced. "This could be the one. His mind has the width, and his heart the depth."

The temple rippled, flowed, and shifted, even as she had done, and split, revealing itself as a bronze dragon rising away from around a much smaller, stone house.

The dragon stretched out gigantic wings with a creak and a sigh and inclined its head until one wise old eye regarded the goddess. Its voice was a purr so deep that the front of the stone house shivered. "As did all the others . . . those many, many others. Having the skill doesn't mean one must or will use it rightly, and take the true path."

"True," Mystra answered, a certain soft bitterness in her tone, and then she smiled and laid a hand on its scales. "My thanks, faithful friend. Until next we fly together."

As gently as if it were brushing her with a feather, the dragon stroked her cheek with one massive claw. Then it drew in its wings and melted, dwindling down into the form of a bent, wrinkled white-haired woman with bright green eyes. Without a backward glance, the priestess went into the temple, moving with the slow gait and bent back of age. Mystra sighed, turned away herself, and became a dazzling web of lights that whirled and spun, faster and faster—until she was gone.

The sack Braer had given her proved to hold over twenty silver coins at the bottom, wrapped in a scrap of hide. That was not so many that she could afford to hurl them away for a warm bed every night, at least before the deep snows came down on the world. Hedges and thickets were her bedchambers, but Elmara usually warmed herself of evenings at an inn with a hot meal and a seat as close to the hearth as she could manage. Lone young women walking the roads were few, but conjuring a little mage-fire and looking mysterious always kept any over-amorous local men at a distance.

This night found her in the latest house of raised flagons, somewhere in the Mlembryn lands. To all who would listen, she spun tales of the glory of magic, tales drawn from what Braer and Helm and the streets of Hastarl had told her. Sometimes these tales won her a few drinks, and on nights when the gods smiled, someone else would tell stories of sorcery to top her own, and thereby tell her more of what most folk thought of magic . . . and win her new marvels to tell on evenings to come.

She had hopes of that happening this night; two men, at least, were edging forward in their chairs, itching to unburden themselves of something, as she warmed to the height of her most splendid tale. ". . . And the last the king and all his court saw of the nine Royal Wizards, they were standing on thin air, facing each other in a circle, already higher than the tallest turret of the castle, and rising!" Elmara drew breath dramatically, looked around at her rapt audience, and went on.

"Lightnings danced ever faster between their hands, weaving a web so bright that it hurt the eyes to look upon it—but the last thing the king saw, ere they rose out of sight, was a dragon appearing in the midst of those lightnings, *fading in*, he said. . . ."

And then a curtain across a booth in the back of the room parted, and Elmara knew she was in trouble. The eager men turned hurriedly away, and the room filled with a sudden tension centered on a splendidly dressed, curl-bearded man who was striding across the room toward her. Rings gleamed on his fingers, and anger shone in his eyes.

"You! Outlander!"

Elmara raised a mild eyebrow. "Goodman?"

" 'Lord,' to you. I am Lord Mage Dunsteen, and I bid you take heed, wench!" The man drew himself up importantly, and Elmara knew that though he looked only at her, he was aware of everyone in the room. "The matters you so idly speak of are not fancies, but sorcery." The lord mage strutted grandly forward and said sharply, "Magic interests everyone with its power—but it is, and rightly, an art of secrets—secrets to be learned only by those fit to know them. If you are wise, you will cease your talk of sorcery at once."

At the end of his words, the room was very still, and into that silence, Elmara said quietly, "I was told to speak of magic, wherever I go."

"Oh? By whom?"

"A priestess of Mystra."

"And why," Lord Mage Dunsteen asked with silken derision, "would a priestess of Mystra waste three words on you?"

Color rose in Elmara's cheeks, but she answered as quietly as before, "She was expecting me."

"Oh? Who sent *you* out into Faerûn to seek priestesses of the Holy Lady of Mysteries?"

"Mystra," Elmara said quietly.

"Oh, *Mystra*. Of course." The wizard scoffed openly. "I suppose she talked to you."

"She did."

"Oh? Then what did she look like?"

"Like eyes floating in flame, and then as a tall woman; dark robed and dark eyed."

Lord Mage Dunsteen addressed the ceiling. "Faerûn is home to many mad folk, some so lost in their wits, I've heard, that they can delude even themselves."

Elmara set down her tankard. "Ye've used many proud, provoking words, Lord Mage, and they tell me ye think thyself a wizard of some . . . *local* importance."

The wizard stiffened, eyes flashing.

Elmara held up a staying hand. "I've heard many times in my life that wizards are seekers after truth. Well, then, so important a wizard as thyself should have spells enough to determine if I speak truly." She sat back in her chair and added, "Ye bade me speak no more of magic. Well, then, I bid ye: use thy spells to see my truth, and stay thy own talk of madness and wild lies."

The lord mage shrugged. "I'll not waste spells on a madwoman."

Elmara shrugged in turn, turned away, and said, "As I was saying, the last the king ever saw of his Royal Wizards, their lightnings were chaining a dragon they'd summoned, and it was spitting fire at them. . . ."

The lord mage glared at the young woman, but Elmara ignored him. The wizard cast angry glances around the room, but men carefully did not meet his eyes, and from where he wasn't glaring, there came chuckles.

After a moment, Lord Mage Dunsteen turned, robes swirling, and stalked back to his private booth. Elmara shrugged, and talked on.

The moon was bright, riding high above the few cold fingers of cloud that crept along above the trees. Elmara drew her cloak closer around herself—clear nights like this brought a frost-chill—and hurried on. Before seeking the inn, she'd chosen a fern-choked hollow ahead to bed down in.

Far behind her, branches snapped. It wasn't the first such sound she'd heard. Elmara paused to listen a moment, and then went on, moving a little faster.

She came to the hollow and darted across it, clambering up its far bank and turning to crouch among the bushes there. Then she did off her cloak and sack and waited. As she'd expected, the stalker was no excited young lad wanting to hear more of magic, but a certain lord mage, moving uncertainly now in the darkness.

Elmara decided to get this over with. "Fair even, Lord Mage," she said calmly, keeping low among the ferns.

The wizard paused, stepped back, and hissed some words.

A breath later, the night exploded in flames. Elmara dived aside as searing heat rolled over her. When she had her feet under her again and her breath back, she forced herself to say laconically, "A campfire would have been sufficient."

Then she tossed a rock to one side, and as it crashed down through the brush, leaped to her feet and ran in the other direction, around the edge of the hollow.

The mage's next fireball exploded well away from her. "*Die*, dangerous fool!"

Elmara pointed at the wizard, who stood clearly outlined by moonlight, and murmured the words of a prayer to Mystra. Her hand tingled, and the lord mage was abruptly hurled backward, crashing roughly through bushes.

"Gods spit on you, outlander!" the wizard cursed, clawing his painful way to his feet. Elmara heard cloth tearing, and another hissed curse.

"*I* don't hurl fire at women whose only offense is not cringing before me," Elmara said coldly. "Why are ye doing this?"

The lord mage stepped forward into the light again. Elmara raised her hands, waiting to ward off magic—but no spell came.

Dunsteen snarled in anger. El sighed and whispered a spell of her own. Blue-white light outlined the mage's head, and she saw his features twist and struggle as he found himself compelled to speak truthfully.

The string of fearful curses he was spitting became the words, "I don't want half the folk in Faerûn to work magic! What price my powers *then*, eh?" Dunsteen's voice rose into a wordless shriek of fear.

"You live now only at my whim, wizard," Elmara told him, pretending a casualness she did not feel. If his fear would just keep him from weaving another fireball . . .

Swallowing her own rising fear, Elmara uttered another prayer to Mystra. When the tingling in her limbs told her its magic had taken effect, she strode off the lip of the hollow, walking on empty air to stand facing the wizard. She pointed down, trembling with the effort to hold herself in midair. "I do not wish to slay ye, Lord Mage. Mystra bade me bring more magic into Faerûn, not rob the Realms of the lives and skills of wizards."

The Lord Mage gulped and took a quick step back. He obviously thought less of his powers than he'd pretended to in the tavern. "And so?"

"Go to thy home and trouble me no more," Elmara said in a voice of doom, "and I shall not bring down the curse of Mystra on thee."

That sounded good—and the priestess had told him to try everything, If Mystra thought her words ill said . . . she'd doubtless say so soon enough.

The night remained still and silent—except for the sounds made by Lord Mage Dunsteen, backing hurriedly away through ferns and brambles.

"*Hold!*" Elmara put the ring of command into her words. She felt herself sinking slowly toward the ground as she turned her will back to her truth-compulsion spell.

Dunsteen froze as if someone had tugged on a leash about his neck.

Elmara said to his moonlit back, "I was told to learn all I could from the mages I met. Where would you suggest I go to learn more about being a mage?"

The magic of her truth-compulsion glowed brightly around the Lord Mage—but he did not turn, so Elmara did not see his twisted smile. "Go see Ilhundyl, ruler of the Calishar, and ask him that . . . and you shall have the best answer any living man can give."

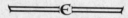

Most intruders wandered in the maze, calling helplessly until Ilhundyl tired of their cries and had them brought to an audience chamber, or released the lions to feed. This young lass, however, strode through the illusory walls and around the portal traps as if she could see them.

Ilhundyl leaned forward to peer out the window in sudden interest as Elmara strode out onto the broad pavement in front of the Great Gate, peered narrowly up at it, and then walked without hesitation toward the hidden door, avoiding the golems and the statues whose welcoming hands could spit lightnings at those who stepped between them.

The Mad Mage valued his privacy, and his life . . . and not many days passed without someone trying to deprive him of either. Thus his Castle of Sorcery was ringed by traps mechanical as well as magical. Now one of his long-fingered hands tapped idly on the table. He seized a slim brass hammer, lifted it, and rapped on a certain bell.

At his signal, unseen men sweated belowground, and the paving stones suddenly opened up under the young woman, who obligingly plunged from view. Ilhundyl smiled tightly and turned to the tall, handsome servant who stood patiently awaiting his orders. Garadic obligingly glided forward. "Lord?"

"Go and see that one's body," he said, "and bring ba—"

"Lord." The servant's rapped word was urgent; Ilhundyl followed his gaze even before he could raise his arm to point. The wizard wheeled around in his chair.

The young intruder was walking on air, treading steadily forward on nothing, and rising up out of the yawning pit. Ilhundyl raised his eyebrows and leaned forward. "Garadic," he said decisively, "go down and bring that maid to me. Alive, if she can stay that way until you get there."

"A priestess of Mystra told me to learn about sorcery from mages . . . and a mage told me you were the best man alive to tell me what it is to work magic."

Ilhundyl smiled thinly. "Why do you want to learn magic—if you don't want to be a mage?"

"I must serve Mystra as best I can," Elmara said steadily, "even as she commanded me."

Ilhundyl nodded. "And so, Elmara, you seek mages to tell you the ways of sorcery, so you can better serve the Lady of Mysteries."

Elmara nodded.

Ilhundyl waved his hands, and darkness enshrouded the chamber, save for two globes of radiance that hung above the Mad Mage and the young intruder. They looked at each other, and when Ilhundyl spoke again, his voice echoed with tones of doom.

"Know then, O Elmara, that you must apprentice yourself to a mage, and once you learn to hurl fire and lightning, slip away without a word to anyone, travel far, and join an adventuring band. Then see the Realms, face danger, and use your spells in earnest."

The ruler of the Calishar leaned forward, voice thinning in urgent precision. "When you can battle a lich spell for spell and prevail, seek out Ondil's Book of Spells and take it to the altar of Mystra on the island called Mystra's Dance. Surrender it to the goddess there."

His voice changed again, thundering once more. "Once you know you hold Ondil's tome in your hands, look no longer on its pages, nor seek to learn the spells therein, for that is the sacrifice Mystra demands! Go, now, and do this."

The light above the Mad Mage's high seat faded, leaving Elmara facing darkness. "My thanks," she said, and turned away. As she walked back down the great chamber, the globe of light moved with her. The light faded beyond the great bronze doors, which ground shut with their usual boom. When the echoes had died away Ilhundyl added quietly, "And once you've got me that book, go and get yourself killed, mageling."

Garadic's handsome features melted soundlessly into the fanged and scaled horror of his true face. The scaled minion stepped forward and asked curiously, "Why, master?"

The Mad Mage frowned. "I've never met anyone with so much latent power before. If she lives, she could grow in magic to master the Realms." He shrugged. "But she'll die."

Garadic took another step, his tail scraping along the floor. "And if she does not, master?"

Ilhundyl smiled and said, "You will see to it that she does."

PART
IU

MAGUS

Ten

In the Floating Tower

Great adventure? Hah! Frantic fear and scrabbling about in tombs or worse, spilling blood or trying to strike down things that can no longer bleed. If ye're a mage, it lasts only until some other wizard hurls a spell faster than thee. Speak to me not of "great adventure."

Theldaun "Firehurler" Ieirson
Teachings of an Angry Old Mage
Year of the Griffon

It was a cold, clear day in early Marpenoth, in the Year of Much Ale. The leaves on the trees all around were touched with gold and flame-orange as the Brave Blades reined in beneath the place they'd sought for so long.

Their destination hung dark and silent above them: the Floating Tower, the lifeless hold of the long-dead mage Ondil, hidden away in this bramble-choked ravine in the wilderlands somewhere well west of the Horn Hills.

Upright it stood, a lone, crumbling stone tower reaching into the bright sky . . . but as the tales had said, its base was a ruin of tumbled stones, and there was a stretch of empty air twelve men or so high between the ground and the dark, empty room of the tower's sixth level. Ondil's tower hung patiently in the air as it had for centuries, held up by an awesome sorcery.

The Blades looked up at it, and then looked away—except for the only woman among them, who stood with a wand raised warily, peering past her hawk nose at the silent, waiting keep hanging above her.

The Blades had come here by a long and perilous road. In a spider-haunted sorcerer's tomb of lost Thaeravel, said by some to be the land of mages from which Netheril sprang, they'd found writings that spoke of the mighty archwizard Ondil and his withdrawal in his later days into a spell-guarded tower to craft many new and powerful sorceries.

Then old Lhangaern of the Blades crafted a potion to make his limbs young again, drank it—and fell screaming into crumbling dust before their eyes . . . and they were without a mage. The Brave Blades dared not take the road again without so much as a light-bringing incantation to aid them. So when a young woman came to their inn and spun tales of the wonders of magic—and proved she could work spells of a sort—they practically dragged this Elmara into their ranks.

She was not a pretty woman. Her fierce hawk nose and dark, serious gaze made many a man and most maids draw back from her, and she rode garbed as a warrior in boots and breeches, avoiding the robes and airs of most mages. None of the Blades felt inclined to lure her to bed, even if the threat of defensive spells weren't hanging around her. Her first demand was for time to study the spellbooks Lhangaern would never read again . . . and the second was for a chance to use them.

The Blades granted her that, riding out to make red war on a band of brigands who oppressed that land. In the crumbling old keep the defeated band used as their stronghold, Elmara found wands they could not use and books of spells they could not read, and bore these out in triumph.

All the next winter, as the howling winds piled up snow deep and cold outside, the Blades sat before fires, sharpened their swords, and told restless tales of what bright deeds they'd done and what brighter things they would do when summer came again. Apart from them, the young sorceress studied.

Her eyes grew deep set and heavy lidded, and her body ever more gaunt. She squinted as she went about and used few words, her wits distant and confused—for all the world as if the spells baffled her. Yet she could conjure fires in rooms that the winter had chilled and light for them all to see by without enduring the smoke of fires and candles or the work of chopping firewood.

The Blades learned to keep out of her way, for their every plan brought from her an earnest torrent of moral questions: "Should we slay such a man? Is it right?" or "But what has the dragon done to us? Would it not be more prudent to leave it in peace?"

Winter passed, and the Blades took to the road again—and fell afoul of the Bright Shields, an arrogant and widely known band of lawless adventurers. They fought in the streets of Baerlith, and the dreams of several Blades died there. Elmara pleaded with the two Bright Shields mages who stood against her not to fight, but to share their spells, "laying the glories of magic before all."

The two mages laughed their derision, and hurled slaying spells—but the wizard of the Blades was no longer there. She reappeared behind the two and struck them down with the hilt of a dagger she held. Then she wept when the other Blades, over her protests, cut their throats while they lay senseless. "But they could have taught me so much!" the maid wailed. "And where is the honor in slaying those who lie asleep?"

Yet at the end of that day, the Bright Shields were no more, and the Blades took coins, armor, horses, and all for their own. Their sorceress found herself the owner of boots and belts and rings and rods and more that glowed with the deep blue of enchantments. She couldn't wait to use them but dared not try to wield most of them—yet. The Blades might think her a sorceress, but she was a priestess of Mystra, with no better magecraft than an eager but untutored apprentice . . . and having seen their hot tempers, she did not reveal this truth.

And so it went as the long hot summer passed. The Blades rode from triumph to triumph, saddlebags bulging with coins, throwing what riches they couldn't carry liberally into the laps of willing ladies wherever they went—all but their dark and serious sorceress, who kept apart, spending her nights wrestling with spells rather than wenches.

Then came the day Tarthe found a merchant's account of a trip across the high hills north of Ong Wood, and of a vale where griffons flew out of a lone keep and drove his band away. They were collared griffons, their breasts bearing shields with the mark of Ondil of the Many Spells.

That excited moment of decision, when they had all leaped at the thought of plundering the Floating Tower, seemed long ago now as they tethered their horses in the shadow of its grim and silent bulk.

Torthe turned to the fierce-eyed woman with the wand. The sun gleamed on the warrior's broad, armored shoulders and danced in his curling, reddish hair and beard. He looked like a lion among men, every inch the proud leader of a famous adventuring band.

"Well, mage?" Tarthe waved one gauntleted hand at the tower floating above them.

Elmara nodded in reply, stepped forward, and made the circling gesture that meant fall back to give her space for a spell. She tossed a long, heavy coil of rope to the turf between her feet.

Her hands dipped to one of the vials at her belt, flicked back its stopper, and tipped it, then deftly restoppered it while holding some of its powder in one cupped hand. A few gestures, a long murmured incantation as the powder was cast aloft, and some lightning-fast work with a strip of parchment—twisting it in the still-falling powder—and the coil of rope on the ground stirred. As the young mage stepped back, the rope rose from the ground like a snake, wavered, and then began to climb steadily, straight up.

Elmara watched it calmly. When the rope ceased to move, hanging motionless and upright in the air, she made a "keep back" gesture and went to the saddles for a second coil of rope. Wearing the coil about her shoulders, she climbed the first rope, slowly and clumsily, making several Blades shake their heads or grin with amusement, and came at last to the top of the rope. Curled around it by the crook of one elbow and the crossed grip of her booted feet, she calmly opened another vial, tapped a drop of something from it, and blew it from her palm while gesturing with the other hand.

Nothing seemed to occur—but when the sorceress stepped off the rope to stand on empty air, it was clear that an unseen platform hung there. It sank a trifle under her boots, but Elmara calmly laid the coil of rope on it and began her first spell over again.

When she was done, the second rope stretched straight up through the air, into the darkness of the riven, floorless chamber at the bottom of the hanging keep. The wizardess spared no breath on any words, but looked down at her fellow Blades as she traced a wide circle with her hands, showing them the limits of the platform. Then she turned, and without another look back, began her slow, awkward climb again.

Sudden lightnings flashed in the air around the wizard, and she slid hastily down the rope, hugging it in pain. She hung there a long time, motionless, while the anxious Blades called up to her. Though she made no reply, she seemed unhurt when at last she stretched forth her arms again and cast something that made the lightnings blaze and crackle, then fade away.

She climbed on, into the darkness of the lowest chamber. Just before disappearing into its gaping gloom, she turned on the rope and beckoned once.

"Right, Blades!" Tarthe was climbing swiftly up the rope while his eager bellow was still echoing around them.

The lean warrior beside the rope shrugged, spat on his hands, and followed. The hard-eyed priest of Tempus elbowed his way past the others in his haste to be next on the rope. The thieves and warriors shrugged and gave way, then calmly took their turns. So did the stout priest of Tyche, his mace dangling at his belt as he puffed and heaved his way up.

The youngest warrior checked his cocked and loaded crossbows again and sat down among the tethered horses. He watched them calmly cropping all the grass and weeds they could reach, and spat thoughtfully off into the dark hollows below, whence came the faint tinkling of running water. More than once he stared up at the ropes above him, straight as iron rods, but his orders were clear. Which is more than many an armsman can say, he thought, and settled down for a long wait.

"Look ye!" The rough whisper held awe and wonder aplenty; even the veteran Blades had not seen the likes of this in their adventures before. Time had touched the tower, but it seemed enchantments held wind, cold, and damp at bay in some places. At the end of a crumbling passage whose very roof blocks fell at his cautious tread, a Blade might step through a curtain of magical gloom into glory.

One room was carpeted in red velvet: a dancing floor ringed with sparkling hanging curtains crafted of gems threaded onto fine wire. Another held smooth whitestone statues, perfectly lifelike in their size and detail and depicting beautiful human maidens with wings arching from their shoulders. Some were speaking statues, who greeted all intruders with soft, sighing voices, uttering poetry a thousand years dead.

"Such shouldst be my only joy, to behold thee, but yet mine eyes see the sun and the moon and cannot but compare them to thee . . . and thou art the brightest ennobled star of my seeing . . ."

"Look to find me no more, where silent towers stare down upon the stars, trapped in still pools of dark water . . ."

"What is this but the mist-dreams of bold faerie, wherein nothing is as it seems and all that one can touch, and kiss, are but dreams?"

Marveling, the Blades stalked among them, careful to touch nothing, as the endless, repetitious sighing of the unfeeling voices echoed all around them. "Gods," even the unshakable Tarthe was heard to mutter, "to see such beauty . . ."

"And not to be able to take it with us," one of the thieves murmured, voice deep with loss and longing. For once, the priests felt as he did, or so their nods and awestruck gawking said, if their mouths did not.

The room beyond the chamber of speaking statues was dark but lit by a rainbow of tiny, glittering lights—sparks of many hues that darted and soared about the chamber like schooling fish, a riot of swirling emerald and gold and ruby that never went out.

Lightning, they all thought, and hung back. Tarthe finally said, "Gralkyn . . . your foray, I fear."

One of the thieves sighed eloquently and set about the long process of divesting himself of every item of metal, from the dozen or so lockpicks behind his ears and elsewhere on his person to the small forest of blades tucked and slid into boots, under clothes, and into nearly every hollow in his slim, almost bony body. When he was done, he stood almost naked. He swallowed, once, said to Tarthe, "This is a very large thing you owe me," and strode forward on catlike feet into the midst of the lights.

They reacted immediately, darting away like frightened minnows and then circling about, faster and faster, until they rushed in on him from all sides with frightening speed, clung—the watching Blades saw Gralkyn wriggle, as if tickled by many unseen hands—and cloaked him in glittering lights.

He looked like an emperor robed all in gems, and stared down at himself in wonder for a time before he said, "Right. Well . . . who's next?"

The other thief, Ithym, came into the chamber hesitantly, but the lights did not move from around Gralkyn, and nothing else seemed to happen. Sighing out a tensely held breath of his own, Ithym glided over to his fellow thief and stretched out a hand toward the lights, but then drew it back. Gralkyn nodded at the wisdom of this.

Ithym went on into the far, dim regions of the room and moved about in soft silence for a time before returning far enough for them to see him trace a square in the air: there was a door beyond.

Tarthe took out his cloak, raked all Gralkyn's discarded metal in it, bundled it onto his shoulder, and strode into the room next, sword drawn. Instantly some of the lights drifted away from the thief in an inquisitive stream, heading for the tall warrior in full armor. The tensely watching Blades saw sudden sweat on Tarthe's forehead as he strode toward the second thief. The lights swirled around Tarthe as buzzing flies survey a walking man . . . and then returned slowly to Gralkyn.

The warrior shook his head in relief, and they heard him whisper hoarsely, "Now, Ithym—where's this door?"

A few scufflings later his voice floated back to them out of the gloom. "Hither, all! The way beyond looks clear!"

Cautiously, one by one, the other Blades hurried or edged past Gralkyn, until at last only the thief in his cloak of lights was left in the room. He walked calmly up to the door, peered through it, and saw the Blades standing anxiously in a little corridor that led into a large, dim, open space beyond. "Back, all of you!" Gralkyn said. "Get well away—right out of the passage! I'm coming through!"

The others obeyed, but waited at the far end of the hall, watching. Gralkyn sprinted toward the door, dived through it, and hit the stone floor hard. As he passed through the opening, the lights halted, as if held by an invisible wall, so he was stripped of all of them. After a moment, he got to his knees and crawled as fast as he could out of the passage. Only then did he look back, at a smooth wall of twinkling lights, solidly filling the doorway.

"Are ye . . . well?" The words were out of Elmara's mouth before she thought about the prudence of asking.

Gralkyn rubbed at his shoulders. "I . . . know not. Everything seems aright . . . now that the tingling's stopped." He was flexing thoughtful fingers when Ithym shrugged, drew a slim dagger from his belt, and flung it at the doorful of floating lights. There was a vicious crackle of tiny lightnings, so bright they all drew their heads back and grunted in pain, and the weapon was gone. There was nothing left to strike the floor. When they could see clearly again, the lights were still filling the doorway, forming a smooth, unbroken barrier.

Tarthe looked at it sourly. "Well," he said, "that's no way back as I'd care to try. So . . . forward."

They all turned and looked about. They stood on a balcony that curved slightly as if on the inside of a vast circle. The waist-high stone railing in front of them opened on to nothingness. Vast, open darkness. They peered along the walls, and could dimly see other balconies nearby—some higher, some lower . . . all of them empty.

Tarthe shrugged. "Well, mage?"

Elmara raised an eyebrow. "Do ye seek my counsel, or a spell?"

"Can you conjure a sphere of light and sail it out into this?" He waved an arm at the great darkness before them, being careful not to extend it beyond the rail.

Elmara nodded. "I can," she said quietly, "but should I? This has the feeling of—something waiting. A trap, belike, awaiting my spell to set it off."

Tarthe sighed. "We're in a wizard's tower! Of *course* there're hanging spells and traps all about . . . and of course we invite danger by working magic here! You think none of us realize that?"

Elmara shrugged. "I . . . strong magic is all about us in webs. I know not what will befall if I disturb it. I want all of ye to be aware of this and be not unprepared to leap aside if . . . the worst comes down on us. So I ask ye again: should I?"

Tarthe exploded. "Why these endless questions about what is right and should you do thus or so? You've got the power—*use it!* When d'you ever hear other mages asking if hurling a spell is to the liking of those around?"

"Not often enough," one of the other warriors murmured, and Tarthe wheeled around to give him a flat glare.

The warrior shrugged and spread empty hands. "Eh, Tarthe," he protested, "I but speak my view of the world."

"Hmmph," Tarthe grunted. "Take care that someone does not alter your view of the world for you—forcefully, and mayhap working on what you view with, not what you see."

"Well enough," Elmara said, raising her hands. "I will give ye light. Be it on thy head, Tarthe, if the result be not pleasant. Stand ye back."

She took something small and glowing from a pouch at her belt, held it up, and muttered over it. It seemed to bubble and grow in her fingers, and she spread them to let it rise up and hang in front of her face, spinning, shaping itself into a sphere of pulsing, ever-growing light. Its flickering radiance gave the mage's sharp-nosed, intent face a brooding appearance.

When the sphere was as large as her head and hung bright and steady, Elmara bent her gaze on it. Obediently it moved away from her, gliding soundlessly through the air, out from the balcony into the darkness beyond. As it went, the darkness parted before it like a tattered curtain, showing them the true size of the vast chamber. Even before it reached the far wall of the great spherical room, other radiances not of Elmara's making appeared, here and there in the air before them, brightening and growing until the Blades could all see their surroundings. Balconies like their own lined the curving wall on all sides, save where darkness lingered above and below. The spherical space within was huge—much larger across than Ondil's tower was on the outside.

"Gods!" one of the warriors gasped.

The priest beside him murmured, "Holy Tyche, be with us."

Four spheres of hitherto dark, slowly brightening radiance floated in the center of the huge chamber. Three of these globes were as tall as two men, and one other, smaller globe hung between them.

The nearest globe held a motionless dragon, its vast bulk coiled up to fit within the radiance, its red scales clear to their gaze. It seemed asleep, yet its eyes were open. It looked strong, healthy, proud—and waiting. The most distant globe held a being they'd heard of in tales: a robed, manlike figure whose skin was a glistening purple, whose eyes were featureless white orbs, and whose mouth was a forest of squid tentacles. It, too, hung motionless in its radiance, standing upright in emptiness, its empty hands having one finger less than their own. A mind flayer! The third globe was partially hidden behind the dragon's bulk . . . but the Blades could see enough to bring the cold, sword-biting taste of fear strongly into all their mouths at last. The globe's dark occupant was a creature whose spherical body was inset with one huge eye and a fanged mouth, and fringed with many snakelike eyestalks: a beholder. Its dread kin were said to rule over many small realms east of Calimshan, each eye tyrant treating all beings who dwelt or came into its territory as its slaves.

Elmara's gaze, however, was drawn to the fourth, smaller globe. In its depths hung a large book held open by two disembodied, skeletal human hands. When Elmara narrowed her eyes against the bright blue glare—everything in this place was magical, making her magesight almost useless—she could see bright webs linking the four globes and wavering between both skeletal hands and the tome. They must be animated guardians, those bones . . . as well as the three monsters.

"So do we turn away from our greatest challenge and live, or go after that book and die gloriously?" Ithym's voice was wry.

"What use is a book?" one of the warriors replied with loud fear.

"Aye," the other agreed. "Just what Faerûn needs—more deadly spells for mages to play with."

"How so?" Gralkyn put in. "Yon book might be prayers to a god, or filled with writings that lead to treasure, or . . ."

The warrior Dlartarnan gave him a sour look. "I know a spellbook when I see one," he grunted.

"I did not ride all this way," Tarthe said crisply, "to turn back now—if there is a way back that won't kill us all. I also have no desire to ride back into that last inn empty handed and have all the tankard-drainers there think us a pack of cowards who did nothing but ride out, eat a few rabbits in the wilderness, and ride home again, our untested blades rusting in their sheaths."

"That's the spirit—" Ithym agreed, then added in a stage whisper "—that'll get us all killed."

"Enough!" Elmara said. "We're here now and face two choices: either we try to find another way onward, or we fight these things, for be in no doubt: all of those globes are spell-linked to the book, and those bone-hands too."

"One death is imminent," the warrior Tharp said in his deep, seldom-heard voice. "The other we can look for later."

One of the priests held up his holy symbol. "Tyche bids the brave and true to chance glory," the Hand of Tyche said sharply.

"Tempus expects adventurers to embrace battle, not slip away when strong foes threaten," agreed the Sword of Tempus. The priests exchanged glances and grim grins as they readied weapons.

The thief Gralkyn sighed. "I knew riding with two battle-mad priests would bring us trouble, in depth and at speed."

"And disappointment came not to you," Tarthe said, "for which you gave much thanks. So you are now at peace, ready to speak of strategies against these globed beasts and not weasel words to try to get out of facing them!"

There was a little silence as the Blades smiled mirthlessly at each other or displayed looks of unconcern, all trying—in vain—to hide the fear in their eyes.

Elmara spoke into that quiet tension. "We are in the house of a mage, and as a worshiper of Mystra, I am closest among us to the mantle of wizardry. It is right that I make the first attack"—she swallowed, and they saw she was trembling with excitement and fear—"as I am the most likely of us to prevail against . . . what we face."

"What are ye, Elmara—the Magister in fool form, perhaps, or the Sorcerer Supreme of all Calimshan, out for a lark? Or are ye really just the soft-witted idiot ye sound to be?" Dlartarnan asked sourly.

"Hold hard, now," Tarthe said warningly. "This is no time for dispute!"

"When I'm dead," the warrior returned darkly, "it'll be just a blade thrust or six too late for me to enjoy one last dispute. . . . I'd just as soon enjoy it *now*."

"Soft-witted idiot I may be," Elmara told him pleasantly, "but sit on thy fear long enough to think . . . and ye can't help but agree that however ill my efforts befall, they are still the best road we can set foot upon."

Several Blades protested at once—and then as one, their voices fell silent. Grim faces looked out at the globes, back at the trembling young mage, and then back at the globes again.

"'Tis madness," Tarthe said at last, "but 'tis just as surely our best hope."

Troubled silence answered him; he raised his voice a little, and asked, "Does anyone here deny this? Or speak against it?"

In the hanging silence after these words, Ithym gave a little shake of his head. As if this had been a signal, the two priests shook their heads together—and one by one, the others followed, Dlartarnan last.

Elmara looked around. "We are agreed, then?" The Blades stared at her in silence until she added, "Well enough; I need every man here to have ready all the weapons he can hurl afar—but to loose *nothing* until I give word, whate'er befalls."

She waved them to one end of the balcony while she went to the other. "I must cast some spells," she said. "Someone keep an eye on those lights behind us and tell me if my work draws them hence."

She stamped and shuffled and murmured for a long time, casting powders into the air, drawing many small objects from various places in her clothing, and from sheaths beneath garments and in and about her well-worn boots.

In wary silence, the Blades watched the young mage trace small signs in the air; each glowed briefly and then faded as she traced the next. Radiances washed over the young mage and then were gone, and though her intent, earnest expression never changed, both she and her companions-at-arms noticed that with each new spell she worked, the four silent globes hanging so menacingly near pulsed and grew brighter. The lights in the doorway winked and drifted around each other, ever faster, but made no move to spill out into the passage.

At last El bent to her boots and drew forth six straight, smooth lengths of wood. She held two end to end so their slightly bulbous tips touched, deftly twisted and pushed, and they became one. In like manner she added length to length, until she held a knobbed staff as tall as she was.

She shook it as if half expecting pieces to fall off, but all held firm. Then she brandished it against an imaginary foe. Dlartarnan snorted; it looked like a toy.

Elmara leaned the toy staff against the balcony rail and came toward them, rubbing her hands thoughtfully. "I'm about ready," she said, casting a keen look at the waiting globes. Her hands trembled slightly.

"We gathered that," Ithym said.

Tarthe nodded, smiling thinly. "Mind telling us just what spells you've worked . . . *before* all the bloodletting begins?"

"I've not much time to chatter; the magics don't last overlong," Elmara replied, "but know ye all: I can fly, flames will harm me not—even dragonfire, though I doubt the mage who wrote the spell had ever faced it when he made his claim—and spells hurled my way will come back upon the sender."

"You can do all that?" Tharp's voice was thoughtful.

"Not every day," Elmara replied. "The spells are woven into a dwaeodem."

"How nice," Gralkyn said with light, lilting sarcasm. "That explains *every-thing* . . . now I can go to my deathbed content."

"The spells are linked in a shield about me," Elmara replied softly. "Its creation took the sacrifice of an enchanted item of power—and it drains the life from me, slowly but inescapably, more the longer I hold it."

"Then enough idle talk," Tarthe said sharply. "Lead us into battle, mage."

Elmara nodded, swallowed, ducked her head just as a helmed warrior does to pull down his visor before a charge—the warriors exchanged looks and smiled—caught up her staff, and scrambled up onto the balcony rail.

Then she leaped off into space—and plunged from view.

The Blades exchanged grim looks and leaned forward over the rail. Far below, Elmara was gliding, arms outstretched, across the chamber, tilting her body as if testing the air. Her flight pulled sharply upward a scant hand's breadth in front of a balcony, and she began to soar toward them. Her face was white and set; they saw her swallow and begin to look green even as she released her staff and moved her hands in intricate passes and finger-linkings. The staff flew along beside her, mirroring her slight shifts of direction as Elmara rose up the far side of the chamber, working a spell. She seemed to cast it twice . . . and drifted to a halt facing them, arms spread above her head, two ghostly circles of radiance flickering about her hands. Then they saw but did not hear her mouth a word that made the chamber itself quiver—and the radiances rushed outward from her hands and vanished.

The four spheres in the center of the space began to move. The Blades watched, warily raising weapons as the globes of light glided around the chamber—and the beings within them stirred. As if awakened from a long sleep, they turned to look about. One of the Blades whispered a heartfelt curse. The thieves ducked low behind the balcony rail, peering at their crazed comrade hanging in the air, hands moving again as she cast yet another spell.

There was a soundless flash. The mind flayer had worked some spell of its own, seeking to break free of its globe, but the glowing magic had prevailed. The tentacled thing crouched down in seeming pain. Elmara frowned and gestured at it, and the mind flayer's prison of light scudded across the chamber, gathering speed as it spun toward the globe that held the dragon. The great wyrm was thrashing its tail, wriggling its shoulders, and roaring silently, trying to shatter the cramped confines of light about it. Its jaws flashed fire as it caught sight of the watching men on the balcony. Hatred glared in its gaze as it snarled at them.

Then the two globes rushed together, and the world shattered.

The Blades roared as a light brighter than they'd ever seen blasted into their eyes. They were staggering back even before the balcony shook beneath them, and they fell, blinded by the flash of the bursting globes. Only Asglyn, the Sword of Tempus, who'd expected spellfury of some sort and had closed his eyes in time, was able to see the mind flayer struggling in the dragon's jaws, hissing and burbling in futile spells before those teeth chomped down, once.

What remained of the purple body fell away in a dark rain of gore as the dragon opened its mouth and roared its rage. The third globe was already rushing in at the dragon, the beholder's eyestalks writhing as it prepared for the battle it knew would come.

Asglyn had a brief glimpse of Elmara, face a mask of sweat, jaw clenched in effort, driving the globe along the path she'd chosen. Then the priest shut his eyes tight, just before the flash of rending globes came again. It was followed by a second flash that lit his face with its heat. When Asglyn dared look, he saw the beholder wreathed in flames as the dragon beat its huge wings and raked at the eye tyrant with reaching claws. Stabbing rays of radiance leaped from the beholder's many eyes. The dragon's answering roars held a rising note of fear amid its fury.

Asglyn looked about him. Gralkyn was slumped almost against him, hands jammed to eyes as he knelt behind the rail. Tarthe was shaking his head, fighting to clear his vision.

"Up, Blades!" the priest hissed urgently, and then stiffened as the voice of Elmara sounded inside his head.

"Hurl everything that can pierce or slash at the tyrant's eyes, as soon as the gods make ye able!"

Asglyn hefted his heavy hammer, his favorite weapon borne through a hundred battles or more, and hurled it with all his might, end over end, in a careful, climbing arc, so that it might fall into the great central eye of the beholder. It spun through the air but he never saw if it struck home; he had turned to scramble about the balcony, shaking and slapping his dazed and groaning companions and hoping somehow they'd escape with their lives.

Elmara's next spell brought whirling blades into being from nothingness. They flashed and spun about the waving eyestalks of the beholder like so many fireflies. El saw more than one eye spurt gore or milky liquid and go dark before the madly spinning eye tyrant blasted the shards into drifting smoke with a ray that leaped on to stab at a certain young mage.

Leaped—and rebounded, slicing silently back into the roiling tangle of dragon wings and scaled shoulders and claws, and the darting, spinning, snarling eye tyrant. The dragon roared in pain, but El could see none harm the beholder.

The dragon spat fire again. As before, the gout of flames seemed to splash away over an invisible shield held in front the eye tyrant. Yet that shield was no barrier to the dragon's claws and tail. As Elmara watched, the tail slapped the beholder end over end across the chamber, its eyestalks curling and struggling vainly. It passed near the balcony where the Blades stood, and more than a few of them hurled daggers, darts, and blades just above and before it so it rushed helplessly into the stream of whirling steel. The monster squalled in pain and fry as it tumbled to a halt. What eyes it had left turned toward the nearby balcony.

Bright beams and flickering rays of feebler radiance flashed, and the Blades cried out and ran vainly about the balcony in terror. It shook and shuddered under them, and most of the rail was suddenly gone, melted away in the fury of the eye tyrant's attack.

Yet no searing spells tore into the men, though the crash and flicker of variegated lights was almost blinding. Magic spat and crawled all along the balcony before rebounding back at the struggling spherical monster; Elmara's last spell was doing its work.

Those Blades who could see well enough hurled more daggers, but in the fury of roiling magic around the balcony, most of these vanished in sparks and fragments or simply sighed into nothingness. Through the hail of blades, the furious dragon clapped its wings and rushed down at the beholder, seeking to slay the thing that had caused it such pain. As it came, it breathed fire again. The blackened eye tyrant rolled over in the streaming storm of flame so all its remaining eyestalks pointed straight at the great wyrm. Rays of magic leaped and thrust, and the oncoming dragon began to scream. The beholder rose a little to get out of the way as the dragon hurtled helplessly past. The wyrm crashed into the wall so hard that the Blades were hurled from their feet. The eye tyrant's eye-rays stabbed mercilessly at the thrashing dragon.

The beast seemed much smaller by the time it managed to flap free of the wall again, smoke rising from its body. Crushed balconies fell away in rubble as the dragon moved, its scream a raw and terrible sound of agony. Then its cries began to fade. The awestruck Blades saw bits of the dragon's straining body vanish as if it were just so much ice melting in the heart of a fire. It dwindled swiftly, lifeblood boiling away into nothing in the face of the cruel powers bent upon it. Beyond the fury of flashing magic, the Blades could see the floating figure of Elmara, arms waving in careful haste as she cast another spell.

When the dragon vanished in a last puff of dark scales and boiling blood, the beholder turned with menacing slowness toward the mage and rolled over so that the broad ray of its central eye could strike at her—the eye that drained all magic.

Caught in that spell-draining field, Elmara fell, arms waving. The watching men heard her sob in fear. The beholder swiftly rolled over again to bring its eyestalks to bear all at once on the sorceress, as it had done to the dragon. As the Blades on the balcony desperately hurled blades, shields, and even boots at it, they heard the cold, cruel thunder of its laughter.

Rays and beams flashed out again. Through that bright fury, the Blades saw Elmara raise one arm as if to lash the beholder with an invisible whip. The wand she held flared into sudden life.

The beholder shuddered under its attack and spun wildly about. The Blades ducked desperately as its rays sizzled across the balcony, but Elmara's barrier still held, and the rending magics rebounded back at the eye tyrant.

Tarthe and Asglyn stood shoulder to shoulder at what was left of the balcony rail, tense and helpless, all their weapons hurled and their foe beyond reach. Through narrowed eyes they saw Elmara draw a dagger from her belt and soar up at the beholder like a vengeful arrow. Eyestalks wriggled, and explosive light burst forth anew. The flying mage was thrown aside by the violent force, and the dagger in her fingers suddenly flared into flames.

She hurled it away, shaking her hand in pain, but in the same motion swept her hand into the front of her bodice. There was another dagger—no, the broken stub of an old sword—in Elmara's hand when she drew it forth. She tumbled in the air through a roiling area of intersecting rays and raced in toward the beholder.

Waiting spells burst into sudden life around the blade in her outstretched hand, coiling and flaring as Elmara struck home—and her tiny steel fang sank into a hard body-plate as if she were thrusting into so much hot stew.

The beholder shrieked like a terrified courtesan and hurled itself away from the sorceress. El was left tumbling alone in the air as the eye tyrant flew blindly into the nearest wall, snarling in pain.

Elmara snatched a wand from her belt and darted after it. Straight among the eyestalks she plunged to touch the thing's rolling body just above the hissing, snapping jaws. Then she kicked herself away and flew clear. Behind her, the beholder began to repeat its actions backward, rolling back to strike the wall again. Then it hurtled back to where Elmara had stabbed it.

It hung there a moment—and then rolled back at the wall again to crash and then roll away in an exact duplication of its previous movements. Fascinated, the watching Blades saw the monster's flight repeat, cycling through its squalling collision with the wall over and over again.

"How long will that go on?" Tarthe asked in wonder.

"The beholder is doomed to smash itself against the wall of the chamber over and over until its body falls apart," Asglyn said grimly. "That's not magic many wizards dare to use."

"I don't doubt it," Ithym put in from beside them. Then he gasped and pointed out into the center of the vast open chamber.

Elmara had retrieved her staff and flown into the heart of the last, smaller globe. One skeletal hand leaped at her eyes, but she smashed it aside. The second hand was already darting in at her from behind; they saw it dig bony digits into her neck as she whirled around, too late.

Elmara flung her staff away and spat the words of another spell, one hand flashing in intricate gestures. The skeletal hand was crawling its steady way around to her throat as she wove the spell—and the hand she'd hit away was flying at her face again, two smashed, bony fingers dangling uselessly.

Tarthe sighed in frustration. Elmara was struggling, a hand at her throat, jerking her head from side to side to keep the other bony claw from piercing her eyes. Her face darkened, but the Blades saw motes of light spring into being around her, growing brighter.

Then, without sound, both skeletal hands fell into dust, and the globe around them faded away entirely. As its magic failed, the Blades heard Elmara gasping for breath in the sudden silence—and the first winking lights drifted past their shoulders from the passage behind them.

The Blades drew aside in wary surprise. The many-hued lights that had cloaked Gralkyn emptied themselves from the doorway in a steady stream, drifting along the passage and out into the open center of the chamber, heading for their sorceress.

"Elmara—beware!" Tarthe called, his voice hoarse and cracked.

Elmara cast a look at him, saw the lights, and stared hard at them for a moment. Then she waved a dismissive hand and turned back to the floating book.

Across the chamber, the trapped beholder threw itself helplessly against the wall again and again, the wet thuds of its impacts marking a steady beat as Elmara bent to peer at the pages.

As her fingers touched the book, the moving lights suddenly rushed forward with a loud sigh. Elmara stiffened as they enveloped her.

The Blades saw the book drift out of her motionless hands and close smoothly. A band of shining metal crawled out of one end of the binding, darted smoothly around the tome, and tightened. There was a flash of light, and the book was bound shut.

The lights around the floating sorceress began to wink out, one by one, until they were all gone. Elmara shook herself, floating in midair, and smiled. She looked fresh, happy, and free of pain as she ran her finger along the metal band, tracing a runic inscription it bore. The Blades heard her gasp excitedly, "This is it! This is *it*! At *last!*"

The mage bound the book to her stomach with the length of climbing-cord she wore wound around her waist and retrieved what weapons she could find before she flew back to the balcony. Her companions eyed her with awe and new respect for a long moment before they stepped forward to reclaim their blades and embrace her sweat-soaked body in rough thanks.

"I hope it's worth all this," Dlartarnan said shortly, eyeing the tome and hefting the familiar weight of his sword. Then he turned away in disgust, striding back down the passage they'd taken to reach the chamber of balconies. "I hope this place holds something I can value as highly—a handful of gems, perhaps, or—"

His voice trailed away, and he lowered his sword in confusion. The room on the other side of the doorway now was not the dark room where they'd first found the lights, but a larger, brighter chamber they'd never seen before.

"More wizard tricks!" he snarled, whirling. "What do we do *now?*"

Tarthe shrugged. "Seek another balcony, perhaps. Ithym, look into yon room first—*without* putting yourself or anything else across the threshold—and tell us what you see."

The thief peered for long breaths, and then shrugged. "A tomb, I think it. That long block, there, is a stone casket, or I'm a dragon. There're at least two other doors I can see—and windows behind those screens . . . they must be: the light changes, like cloud-drifted sunlight, not like conjured light."

They stared at the oval silhouette screens, and the draperies behind them, glowing, backlit. The room was still and empty of life or adornments. Waiting.

"Ondil's tomb," Tharp said in tones of slow doom.

"Aye, but a way out, if all else fails," Tarthe replied, voice calm, eyes darting all round. His gaze fell on Elmara, standing silent in their midst, and he shook his head slightly in disbelief. He'd seen it all happen, but he still wasn't sure he believed it. Perhaps some of those ridiculous tavern tales old adventurers loved to tell were true, after all.

"Let's try to get to another balcony," Gralkyn suggested. "I can reach at least four of them—more if El flies a rope to their rails."

"Aye, we must get out of here, now," Ithym said, "or no one at the inn will ever hear about our wizard destroying a beholder, a mind flayer, and a dragon—just to get something to read!"

As Gralkyn swung over the rail and dropped lightly onto the balcony below, the laughter from above him was a little wild.

ELEUEN
A BLUE FLAME

The most awesome thing a wizard can hope to see in a lifetime of hurling down towers, calling up fiends, and turning rivers into new beds? Why, the blue flame, lad. If ever ye see the blue flame, ye will have looked on the most awesome sight a mage can behold—and the most beautiful.

AUMSHAR URTRAR, MASTER MAGE
SAID TO AN APPRENTICE AT MIDSUMMER
YEAR OF THE WEEPING MOON

The cold hand of doom was tightening around the Brave Blades again. They could all feel it. They'd tried nine balconies now, and every door led somehow into the same silent tomb chamber. It lay across their paths like a waiting pit, patient and inescapable.

"Magic!" Dlartarnan spat, crouching down on a balcony and leaning on his drawn broadsword. "Always magic! Why don't the gods smile on a swung sword and a simple plan?"

"Mind, there!" Asglyn said sharply. "Tempus puts valor of the sword before all else, as well you know, and presuming to know better than any god, Dlar, is a fast leap into the grave!"

"Aye," the priest of Tyche agreed. "My Holy Lady looks well on those who complain little, but take advantage of what befalls and make their own good fortune!"

"Well enough," Dlartarnan grunted. "To please both your gods, I suppose I'd best lead the way into this tomb, and be the first to go down. That will make Tempus and Tyche *both* happy."

Without another word he rose from his haunches and strode into the tomb chamber beyond, his blade gleaming in his hand.

The other Blades exchanged glances and shrugs, and followed.

Dlartarnan was already across the chamber and at the nearest of its two closed doors, prying at the frame with his blade. "'Tis locked," he snarled, putting his weight behind his blade, "but if—"

There was a loud snapping sound. Blue fire burst from the door, racing briefly up and down the frame. Smoke rose from the blackened thing that had been Dlartarnan of Belanchor before it fell to the floor. The warrior's ashes rolled away in dark gray swirls as his bones bounced on the flagstones. The skull rolled over once and came to a stop grinning up at them reproachfully. They stared down at the remains, stunned.

"Tyche watch over his soul," the Hand of Tyche whispered, lips trembling. As if in answer, Dlartarnan's twisted, half-melted sword fell out of the door. With a cry like the sob of a young maiden, it struck the flagstones and shattered.

Elmara swayed, then fell to her knees and was sick. The comforting hand Ithym put on her shoulder trembled violently.

"Perhaps a spell to try to open the other one?" Gralkyn suggested, voice high.

Asglyn nodded. "I have a battleshatter that may serve," he said quietly, "Tempus willing."

He bent his head briefly in prayer, leveled one hand at the remaining door, and murmured a phrase under his breath.

There was a splintering crash. The door shook, but did not burst. Dust fell from the ceiling here and there, and a long, jagged crack split the flagstones with a sharp sound that smote their ears like a hammer. The Blades reeled back, staring, as the crack raced out from the base of the tomb toward the door. Asglyn was running away, face tight with fear, when sudden fire blazed up from his limbs.

"*Nooo!*" he cried, sprinting vainly across the chamber. "*Tempussss!*" Flames roared up to scorch the domed ceiling high overhead, and when they died away, the priest of Tempus was gone.

Into the shocked silence, Tarthe said, "Back—out of this place. That magic came from the tomb!"

Tharp was nearest the passage back to the balcony, so it was only a breath later that he plunged through the doorway—and froze in midstride, limbs trembling under the attack of some unseen force. The Blades watched in horror as the warrior's bones burst up out of his body in a grisly spray of blood and vanished near the ceiling. What was left collapsed in a boneless heap, blood raining down around it as Tharp's helm and armor rang on the floor.

The five remaining Blades looked at each other in horror. Elmara moaned and closed her eyes, face pale—but no less white than Tarthe's, as he reached out a reassuring arm to grip her shoulder. Othbar, the Hand of Tyche, swallowed and said, "Ondil slays us with spells spun from his tomb. Undeath and fell magic will take us all if we do not set our feet right."

Tarthe nodded, face sharp with fear. "What should we do? You and Elmara know more of magic than the rest of us here."

"Dig our way out of the chamber?" Elmara asked faintly. "The doors and windows he must have covered with hanging spells that wait to slay us, but if he's not expected us to pry at the flagstones, he may have to rise from his rest to hurl spells at us."

"And when he rises, what then?" Gralkyn asked fearfully. Ithym nodded grimly, echoing the question.

'We strike with everything we have," Tarthe said, "both spell and blade."

"Let me cast a spell first," said Othbar. His face was very white and his voice shook. "If it works, Ondil will be bound into his tomb for a time, unable to work magic—and we can try to get out."

"To have him sending spells and beasts after us for the rest of our lives?" Ithym asked grimly.

Tarthe shrugged. "We'll have the chance to gather blades and spells enough to fight him if he does, where now he slaughters us at whim. Ready weapons, and I'll try these flagstones. Othbar, say out when you're ready."

The priest of Tyche fell to his knees in fervent prayer, bidding the Lady remember his long and faithful service. Then he pricked his palm with a belt knife, and caught the falling drops of blood in his other hand, intoning something they could not understand.

A moment later, he crumpled to the flagstones, arms flopping loosely. Gralkyn took an involuntary step forward—and then recoiled, as something ghost-white rose in wisps from the priest's body. It roiled in silence, growing taller and thinner—until a ghostly image of Othbar stood facing them. It pointed sternly at the four surviving Blades, and then at the windows. They watched in awe as Othbar's shade strode to the casket and laid its palms on the stone lid.

"What? Is he—?" Ithym was shaken.

Tarthe bent over the body. "Yes." When he straightened, the warrior's face looked older. "He knew the spell would cost him his life, I would guess, by what he said," Tarthe said, and his voice quavered. "Let's begone."

"By the windows?" Ithym asked, tears in his eyes as he looked back at the ghostly figure standing by the tomb.

"It's the way he pointed," Tarthe said heavily. "Ropes first."

The two thieves undid leather jerkins to reveal ropes wound many times around their bellies. Elmara took hold of one end of each rope, and the thieves spun around and around until the ropes lay in loose coils on the floor. Ithym caught up two ends and tied them together.

Then, gingerly, the two thieves approached a window, looking back over to sure there was nothing visible that might spring at them. Ithym carried the coil of rope on his shoulder, and Gralkyn held one end of it in his hands as he approached the window.

He touched the end of the rope to the ornate wrought iron of the window screen, and then to the draperies beyond. Then he followed, gingerly, with one gloved hand. Nothing happened.

The oval window screens depicted scenes of flying dragons, wizards standing atop rocky pinnacles, and rearing pegasi. With a shrug, Gralkyn chose the nearest one with a pegasus on it and swung the screen aside on its hinges. They made a slight squeal of protest, but nothing else befell. His blade parted the draperies beyond—to reveal bubble-pocked glass, and through it, a view of the sky and the wilderlands. Cautiously the thief probed the window opening with his blade, peering about for traps. Then he said, "These were not made to open. The glass is fixed in place."

"Break it, then," Ithym said.

Gralkyn shrugged, reversed his blade, and swung hard. The glass burst apart, shards flashing and tinkling everywhere.

Sudden motes of light shone in the air where the window had been, spiraling, slowly at first . . . and then faster . . .

"Back!" Elmara shouted in sudden alarm. "Get ye back!"

The light of the activating spell flared before her words were half out—and a force of awesome power snatched both thieves out through the small opening, rope and all, smashing their limbs against the walls as they went, as if they were rag dolls being stuffed through a hole too small for them. Ithym had time for one despairing scream—long, raw, and falling—before hitting the rocks.

Tarthe drew a shuddering breath, shook his head, and turned to the young mage. "Just the two of us, now." He nodded at the book strapped to Elmara's chest. "Anything there that might help?"

"Ondil's magic sealed it. I would not like to try to break his spells here in his own keep—not while Othbar's sacrifice holds." Elmara looked at the silent and motionless image holding the coffin shut—and noted its flickering, fading extremities. She pointed. "Even now, the lich tries to break out of its coffin."

Tarthe's eyes went to the flickering hands of the image. "How long do we have?"

Elmara shrugged. "If I knew that, I'd be Ondil."

Tarthe waved his sword. "Don't jest about such things! How can I tell you haven't fallen under some spell or other and become Ondil's slave?"

Elmara stared at him, then slowly nodded. "Ye raise a wise concern."

Tarthe's eyes narrowed, and he drew a dagger, eyes fixed on the young sorceress. Then he turned and threw it back through the opening where Tharp had died. It spun into the passage beyond and was gone—unseen in the sudden flash and whirl of a hundred circling, clanging blades, darting about in the space that had been empty moments before.

"The magic continues," Tarthe said heavily. "Do we try to dig a way out in earnest?"

Elmara thought for a moment, and then shook her head. "Ondil is too strong—these magics can be broken only by destroying him."

"So we must fight him," Tarthe said grimly.

"Aye," Elmara replied, "and I must prepare ye before the fray."

"Oh?" Tarthe raised an eyebrow and his blade as the sorceress approached.

Elmara sighed and came to a halt well beyond his reach. "I can fly yet," she said gently. "If this tower stays aloft through Ondil's own magic, ye too must be able to take wing if we slay him—or ye will fall with the tower, and be crushed when it shatters below."

Tarthe swallowed, then nodded and put his blade on his shoulder. "Cast your spell, then," he said.

Elmara was barely done when sudden radiance flared behind her.

She spun around—in time to see Othbar's image vanish, along with the lid it had been holding down. She sighed again. "Ondil found a way," she murmured. Suddenly she nodded as if answering a question only she could hear, and her hands flashed in frantic haste, working a spell.

Tarthe looked uncertainly at her and risked a step forward, sword raised. Inside the stone casket lay a plain, dark wooden coffin, seemingly new—and on it, three small, thick books.

"Touch them not," Elmara said sharply, "unless ye are ready to kiss a lich!"

The warrior took a step back, blade up and ready. "I doubt I'll ever be ready for that," he said dryly. "Will you?"

"What must be, must be," the sorceress said curtly. "Stand back against yon wall now, as far off as ye can get."

Without looking to see if this direction had been obeyed, she stepped up to the casket and laid one hand firmly on a spellbook.

The dark wooden lid vanished. With inhuman speed, something tall, thin, and robed sprang up from where it had lain, the spellbooks tumbling down around it.

Icy hands clutched at Elmara, caught, and seared the living flesh in their grasp.

Instead of pulling back, Elmara leaned forward, smiled tightly into Ondil's shriveled face and said the last word of her spell. The lich found himself holding nothing—in the brief instant before the ceiling of the chamber smashed down atop him, burying the coffin.

The sorceress reappeared beside Tarthe, shoulders to the wall, eyes on the coffin. Dust and echoes rolled around them both as Elmara rubbed at her seared wrists and watched the stones of the central ceiling begin to rise up in a silent stream, back whence they'd come. Tarthe looked at her, then at the casket, and then back at the mage. His face wore a look of awe—but also, for the first time in quite a while, hope.

Something dusty and shattered rose up out of the casket when the stones were all gone, and it stood facing them, swaying. Slowly it lifted the slivered bones of one arm. Its skull was largely gone, but the jaw remained, chattering something as it fought to move its bent arm to point at them. A cold light burned in the one eyesocket that was whole. The jagged edges of the topless skull turned as the lich looked at Tarthe—and then Elmara whispered a word, and the ceiling came crashing down on it again.

Nothing rose out of the casket this time, and Elmara stepped cautiously forward to peer down into the open coffin.

In the bottom lay dust, smashed and splintered bones among the tatters of once-fine robes and the three spellbooks. Some of the bones shifted, trying to move. A ruined arm rose unsteadily up to point at Elmara—who coolly reached in, grabbed it, and pulled.

When she had the clutching, clawing arm free of the casket, she flung it down on the floor and stamped on it repeatedly until all the bones were shattered. Then she looked into the casket again, seeking other restive remains. Twice more she hauled out bones and stamped on them—and at the sight of her dancing on them, Tarthe broke into sudden shouts of laughter.

Elmara shook her head and reached into the coffin, touching the spellbooks and murmuring the words of one last spell. The books quietly disappeared.

Behind her, Tarthe's laughter ended abruptly. Elmara whirled around in time to see a smiling robed man thicken from a shadowy outline into full solidity above a winking curved thing of metal on the floor . . . Tharp's helm.

It was a cruel smile, and its owner turned to Elmara, who stiffened, recalling a face burned forever into her memories. The magelord who'd ridden the dragon and burned Heldon!

"Ah, yes, Elmara—or should I say Elminster Aumar, *Prince* of Athalantar? Tharp was my spy among the Brave Blades from the very beginning. Very useful you've been, too, finding all sorts of malcontents and hidden magic and gold. Yes, the magelords thank you in particular for the gold . . . one can never have enough, you know." He smiled as Tarthe's hurled dagger spun through him to clash and clatter against the far wall of the chamber.

An instant later, flames roared through the room. The blazing body of Tarthe Maermir, leader of the Brave Blades, was flung into the far wall, and Elmara heard the warrior's neck snap. The magelord looked down at the burning corpse and sneered. "You didn't think I'd be foolish enough to reveal where my true self stood? You did? Ah, well . . ."

Elmara's eyes narrowed, and she spoke a single word. The sound of a body heavily striking a wall came to her ears—and the magelord's image vanished.

A moment later, the man appeared nearby, slumped against the wall. He gazed coldly up at Elmara, who was stammering out a more powerful incantation, and said, "My thanks for destroying Ondil. I shall enjoy augmenting my magic with his. I am in your debt, mageling . . . and so it is my duty and pleasure to rid us of your annoying attacks, once and for all!" A ring on his finger winked once, and the world exploded in flames.

Hands still moving in the feeble, useless gestures of a broken spell, Elmara found herself hurled out the shattered window where the two thieves had gone, a coil of flames crackling and searing around her. She roared in pain, the flames clawing at her, and twisted about as she fell so as to appear helpless for as long as possible before she called on the powers of her still-working flight spell. The book strapped to her stomach seemed to ward off the flames, but her ears were full of the sizzle of her burning hair.

Below lay the shattered bodies of the two thieves, and a large blackened area where lumps still gave off smoke—all Briost had left of the youngest Blade and the horses he'd guarded. Scant feet above them, Elmara bent her will and darted away, soaring just above the ground, smoke trailing from her blackened clothes. She wept as she flew, but not from the growing pain of her burns.

The small open boat held a man and a woman. The old, grizzled man in the stern poled it steadily on through thick sunset mists.

He eyed the young, hawk-nosed woman who stood near the bow, and asked quietly, "Be going to the temple, young lady?"

Elmara nodded. Motes of light sparkled and swam continuously about the large bundle she held with both hands against her chest, veiling its true nature. The old man eyed it anyway, and then looked away and spat thoughtfully into the water.

"Have a care, lass," he said, resting his pole so the boat drifted. "Not many goes, but fewer comes back to the dock next morn. Some we never find at all, some we find only as heaps o' ashes or twisted bones, and others blind or just babbling at nothing, dawn 'til dusk."

The young, hawk-nosed maid turned and looked at him, face expressionless, for a long time. Then she lifted her shoulders, let them fall in a shrug, and said, "This is a thing I must do. I am bidden." She looked ahead into the mists and added quietly, "As are we all, too often, it seems."

The old man shrugged in his turn as the island of Mystra's Dance loomed up out of the scudding mists before them, a dark and silent bulk above the water.

They regarded it, growing larger as they approached. The old man turned the boat slightly. A few breaths later, his craft scraped gently along an old stone dock, and he said, "Mystra's Dance, young lady. Her altar stands atop the hill that's hidden, beyond the one above us. I'll return as we agreed. May Mystra smile upon ye."

Elmara bowed to him and stepped up onto the dock, leaving four gold regals in the old man's hand as she passed. The ferryman steadied his boat in silence, watching the young lady's determined stride as she climbed the hill. The full glory of the setting sun was past now, and purple dusk was coming down swiftly over the clear sky of Faerûn.

Only when Elmara had disappeared over the crest of the bare summit did the boatman move. He turned away and leaned on his pole strongly. The boat pulled away from the dock, and the old, weathered face of its owner split in a sudden grin.

The grin widened horribly as the face above it slid down like rotten porridge. Fangs grew down to pierce the sliding flesh. The flesh dripped off a too-sharp chin and fell away to slop and spatter in the bottom of the boat, and the scaly, grinning face whispered, "Done, master." Garadic knew Ilhundyl was watching.

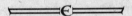

Elmara stopped in front of the altar: a plain, dark block of stone standing alone atop the hill. The wind sighed past her. She offered a heartfelt prayer to Mystra, and the wind seemed to die away for a breath or two. When she was done, she unwrapped Ondil's Book of Spells, its binding still bright around it, and placed it reverently on the cold stone.

"Holy Lady of All Mysteries, please accept my gift," Elmara mumbled, uncertain as to what she should say. She stood watching and waiting, prepared to stand vigil the night through if need be.

A bare moment later, a chill ran down her spine. Two ghostly hands, long-fingered and feminine, were rising up out of the stone. They grasped the tome and began to descend again. Sudden, blinding radiance burst from the book, and there was a high, clear singing sound.

Elmara winced and shaded her eyes. When she could see again, the hands and the book were gone. The breezes blew across the bare stone, just as it had been when she found it.

The young priestess stood before the altar for a long time, feeling strangely empty, and weary—and yet at peace. There would be time to choose a path ahead on the morrow . . . for now, she was content just to stand. And remember.

The folk of Heldon and the outlaws in the ravine outside the Castle, the Velvet Hands lying in the alley, the Brave Blades so many dead. Gone to meet the gods, leaving her alone again. . . .

Lost in reverie, Elmara only gradually became aware of a brightening glow from down the hill, behind the altar.

She stepped forward. The glow was coming from a slim female figure that stood twice as tall as she. The apparition was gowned and regal and stood in the air well clear of the ground. Her eyes were dark pools, and a smile fell across her face as she raised her hand and beckoned. Then she turned and began to walk away, striding on empty air down the hill. After a moment, Elmara followed through the tugging breeze, down the windblown slope, then around another hill, and on. They came out onto a pebble beach on the far side of the isle from the dock, but the glowing figure ahead walked on, straight into—no, above!—the waves, striding out to sea.

Elmara slowed, eyeing the water's edge. Gray waves rolled endlessly up onto the pebbles, and then sucked them back. The water ahead was glowing where Mystra had walked above it. Unbroken by the rolling waves, a shining path lay across the waters ahead of her. The goddess was growing distant now, still striding across the waves.

Gingerly, Elmara walked into the surf, and found her boots still dry. A fine mist covered her, but her feet did not plunge through the waters . . . she was walking on the waves! Emboldened, she began to hurry now, striding along in haste to catch up.

They were walking out to sea, leaving the island well behind. The breezes blew past, cool and steady, driving the sea to shore. Elmara hurried until her breath was coming in gasps, not quite daring to run on the moving waves . . . yet drew no closer to the glowing figure ahead.

El was just beginning to wonder where they were hurrying to when a cold, clear voice from just ahead of her said, "You have failed me."

Ahead, the glowing figure dimmed, fading quickly above the dark waves. Elmara started to run in earnest now, but the radiant waves in front of her grew darker and darker, until the path was gone, and the figure too—and she was suddenly walking on the water no more, but plunged into icy depths.

She rose, struggling, cold water crawling in her throat and nose as she coughed and thrashed . . . and a wave slapped her in the face. She spat out water and clawed her way around, so the next swell lifted her under the shoulders and carried her along.

Back toward the island, now only a dark spot on the running gray seas. She was alone in the chill waters, at night, far from land.

In the breeze howling its way over the hilltop there came a sudden whirl of sparkling lights, rising up into a singing cloud of winking radiance. From its heart stepped a tall, dark-robed figure.

He strode to the bare stone block, looked down at it for a moment, and said coldly, "Rise!"

There was a sigh and a stirring from the stone in front of him, and wisps of pearly light began to stream from it, tugged by the quickening wind. The radiance swirled, thickened, and became a translucent figure—a woman who held a tome. She extended the book to the robed man, who stretched forth his hand in a quick gesture. Brief lightnings played around the book, and then died. Satisfied, the man took it.

The ghostly face leaned close. Its entreating whisper was almost a sob. "Now will ye let me rest, Mage Most Mighty?"

Ilhundyl nodded once. "For a time," he said curtly. "Now—go!" The spirit's shadowy form wavered above the stone block, as if it were whipped in a gale, and her faint voice came again. "Who was the young mage, and what is her fate?"

"Death is her fate, and so she is nothing, of course," Ilhundyl said, and there was a clear edge of anger in his cold tones. "Go!"

The lich moaned and sank back into the stone; the last that could be seen of her before she faded utterly was a pair of spread, beseeching hands.

Ilhundyl ignored them, hefted the weighty book in his hands, and smiled coldly across the breezy night at the third hilltop, where only rubble remained of the shattered True Altar of Mystra. If he had learned one thing in all his years of spell work and ruthless advancement, it was that the Mistress of Magic valued magical might above all. Wherefore Ilhundyl proudly wore the "Mad Mage" title men whispered behind his back. Soon, soon he'd be the most powerful, the Magister over all Faerûn—and then they'd be too busy screaming to whisper and work against him.

He stiffened, peering into the night. A blue flame was rising from the shattered stones on the other hilltop, flickering but growing ever brighter . . . and taller.

Ilhundyl's mouth was suddenly dry. A woman twice as tall as he stood looking across the empty air between them. A tall, regal lady of blue flame, her eyes dark and level as they met his.

Sudden fear rose to choke him. Ilhundyl muttered a hasty word and sketched a sign in the air, and the winking lights rose bright around him, bearing him away.

Elmara groaned, coughed weakly, and opened her eyes. Dawn had come to Faerûn again . . . and, it seemed, had found her still in it. She was lying half in water and half on sand, with the endless crash of the surf all around. Fingers of foaming water ran up the sand past her. El watched its flow, feeling weak and sick, and then tried to lift herself. Sand sucked at her, then she was on hands and knees . . . whole and unhurt, it seemed, just a little dizzy.

The beach was deserted. A cool, salty onshore breeze blew past her and made her shiver. She was naked except for the Lion Sword, still on its thong around her neck. Elmara sighed, and wobbled to her feet. There was no sign of houses or docks or fences . . . just stunted trees, rocks, and a tangle of grasses, old stumps, and bushes where the beach ended and the living things began.

She took a step forward, then froze. In the sand in front of her, someone had scratched one word: "Athalantar."

El looked down at the word in the sand, and then at her bare limbs, and shivered. She coughed, shook her head, lifted her chin, and strode away from the water, heading toward the rising sun.

In a place where guardian spells glowed night and day, deep in the Castle of Sorcery, a man settled down to read.

"Garadic," he said coldly, and sipped his drink.

The scaled minion reluctantly shuffled forward out of the shadows and gingerly opened Ondil's Book of Spells, where it lay on a lectern at the far end of the chamber from his master. Always-vigilant protective spells massed and swirled around the lectern, but no lightnings nor creeping death came. The revealed page was blank.

"Bring it," was the next cold command.

When the lectern stood before his high, padded chair, Ilhundyl set down the goblet of emerald wine and waved the scaled, shambling thing away. He turned the next page himself.

It was as blank and creamy as the flyleaf before it had been. He turned it back. So was the next . . . and the next . . . and the next . . . every one of the pages was blank! Ilhundyl's face froze, and a frown crept in around his eyes.

He spoke a word that made all the radiances in the room dim. The floor glowed briefly, and there came a grating sound, as a flagstone there moved back to reveal a hole. Very quickly, as if it had been waiting, a slyly questing tendril rose from unseen depths below. It touched the book delicately, almost caressingly, and then enfolded it—only to recoil, disappointed, and sink down again. That meant there were no hidden writings, nor portals or linkages to other spaces and other tomes. The book was empty.

Sudden rage seized Ilhundyl then. He rose from his seat in black anger, striding through portals that slid open and curtains that parted at his approach. His furious walk ended half the castle away, before a large sphere of sparkling crystal. It stood atop a black pedestal, alone in a small room of many lamps.

He glared into the depths of the sphere. Flames and flickerings appeared and coiled there, fueled by his anger. Ilhundyl stared into the crystal as the flames within it slowly grew, reaching flickering talons up its curving sides, and suddenly he was shouting. "I'll blast her bones! If she's drowned, I'll raise her—and then smash her bones like hurled eggs, and make her *beg* for release! *No* one tricks Ilhundyl! *No one!*"

He spat a word of summoning, and halfway across the Castle of Sorcery, where he cowered in concealing shadows, the winged and warty shape of Garadic rose hastily and flapped down the swiftest ways to his master's side.

Ilhundyl glared into the crystal, summoning up the young, hawk-nosed face from his memory. The fires swirled and shifted, clearing, and he gathered himself to hurl a scything blade of his will, to chop the young worm's legs off at the knees and let her scream and crawl until Ilhundyl came—and gave her *real* cause to scream and crawl!

But when the fires of the crystal spun into focus, the visage looking calmly back at him was not the one Ilhundyl sought. He gaped in astonishment.

The wrinkled, bearded face dropped its habitual expression of mild curiosity to smile gently at him, nodded in greeting, and said, "Fair day, Ilhundyl; gained a new spellbook, I see."

Ilhundyl spat at the Magister. The spittle hissed and smoked as it struck the crystal. "The pages are blank—and you know it!"

The Magister smiled again, a trifle tightly. "Yes . . . but the young mage who offered it to Mystra did not. You told her not to look inside, and she obeyed you. Such honesty and trust is sadly lacking in this world today—isn't it, Ilhundyl?"

The Mad Mage of the Calishar snarled and hurled a spell into his crystal. The world inside the sphere flashed and rocked, throwing back bright reflections from Ilhundyl's cheeks, but the Magister only smiled a little more tightly—and then the Mad Mage's spell came howling back at him, bursting out of the bobbing, chattering crystal to crash into Ilhundyl and then rage about the chamber. Garadic flapped hastily aloft to avoid the full force of the flaming points of force, only to be tumbled helplessly around the walls, scraping and squawking, by the force of their flights.

"Temper, Ilhundyl, is the downfall of many a foolish young mageling," the Magister said calmly.

Ilhundyl's scream of frustrated fury echoed around the chamber—and then he turned, murder in his eyes, and hurled rending fire. Garadic hadn't even time enough to finish his squawk.

A minstrel was singing in the dimly lit taproom of the Unicorn's Horn as the young hawk-nosed woman stepped wearily inside. The roadside inn stood amid a cluster of sheep farms well west of Athalantar; to reach it, she'd walked all that day with nothing but brook water to drink and nothing at all to eat.

The innkeeper heard the traveler's stomach growl as she stalked past, and greeted her affably. "A table and some stew right off, goodwoman? With a roast and wine to follow, of course . . ."

The young woman nodded, a smile almost rising to her grim lips. "A—quiet corner table, if ye would. Dark and private."

The innkeeper nodded. "I've many such . . . this way, along behind, here. . . ."

The traveler did smile this time and allowed herself to be led to a table. Her dark clothes were worn and nondescript, but by her manner, she'd known both book learning and gentle society, so the innkeeper didn't ask her for coins before service, but was astonished when the slim woman kicked off her boots with a contented sigh and spun a gold regal across the table.

"Let me know when that one needs company," she murmured, and the innkeeper happily assured her that all would be done as she directed.

The wine—a ruby-red dwarven vintage that burned all the way down—was good, the roast excellent, and the singing pleasant. The flagstone floor was cold, so Elmara put her boots back on, pulled her cloak around herself, and settled back against the wall, blowing out the single cup-candle on the table.

Cloaked in darkness, she relaxed, listening to the minstrel singing of she-dragons and brave lady knights rescuing young men who'd been chained out as sacrifices to them. It was good to be warm and full of food again, even if the morrow was sure to bring death and danger (hopefully someone else's, and not her own) as she reached Athalantar's borders.

Yet she would press on. Mystra expected it of her.

The mellow voice of the minstrel rose into words that made Elmara break off thinking about Mystra's disappointment in her, and lean forward to listen with her full attention. The ballad was one Elmara hadn't heard before; a hopeful song of praise to brave King Uthgrael of Athalantar. Listening to the warm words of respect for the grandsire she'd never known, El found her eyes wet with sudden tears. Then the mellow voice changed, thickening, until it trailed off into a croak. Elmara peered through the shadows toward the minstrel's stool beside the hearth, and stiffened.

The minstrel was clutching his throat, eyes staring in fear as he convulsed on his stool. He was goggling at a man who'd risen from his chair at a nearby table—a table of haughty, richly robed men who were laughing at the minstrel's fate. The table in their midst was a forest of already-emptied bottles, goblets, and skins. Elmara saw wands at their belts, as well as daggers . . . wizards.

"What're ye *doing*?" That sharp question came from a fat merchant at another table.

The mage who stood with one outstretched hand slowly clenching, choking the breath out of the minstrel, turned his head to sneer, "We don't allow that dead man to be mentioned in Athalantar."

"You're not *in* Athalantar!" a man at another table protested as the minstrel gagged and gurgled helplessly.

The wizard shrugged as he stared coolly around the room. "We are magelords of Athalantar, and all this land will soon be part of our realm," he said flatly.

Elmara saw the innkeeper, emerging from the kitchens with a steaming platter on his shoulder, come to a shocked halt as he heard the magelord's words.

The wizard smiled silkily around the room. "Is anyone here foolish enough to try to stop me?"

"Yes," Elmara said quietly from her corner, as she broke the strangling spell. Her hands were already moving again as she stepped aside into deeper shadows. The table of magelords—El suspected they were in truth apprentices of little power, here to escort a caravan or do some such lesser work—peered into the darkness, trying to catch sight of her. Then her casting was done. She strode forward, addressing the standing wizard. "Those who wield powerful magic should never use it to bully those who have none. D'ye agree?"

"You are mistaken," the magelord sneered, and raised his hands to work another spell.

Elmara sighed and pointed. The wizard stiffened in midincantation and clutched at his throat.

"Your own spell," Elmara informed the choking wizard pleasantly. "It seems quite effective . . . but then, perhaps I *am* mistaken."

Her words brought a roar of rage from six throats as the self-styled magelords erupted from their seats, snatching at wands and spilling bottles and flagons in their haste. Elmara watched glass topple and roll, smiled, and said the word that brought her waiting spell down upon them.

Wands were leveled and angry hands shaped gestures in the air. Words were spat and strange items flourished as the six able magelords bent malicious magic on their lone foe.

And nothing happened.

Elmara announced calmly to the room, "I can prevent these men from using their magic—for a time. I would enjoy a good spell battle, but I'd rather not destroy this inn doing it. If ye'd care to deal with them . . . ?"

There was a moment of shocked silence. Then chairs scraped back, and men reached for daggers—and the magelords fled. Or tried to. Outthrust boots tripped magelings not used to watching where they walked, and enthusiastic fists laid low apprentices not used to brawling with anything less than fireballs. One wizard's dagger slashed a merchant across the face, and the snarling man hauled out his own knife and made good use of it.

The crash of the mage's body going to the floor amid overturning chairs brought the room to silence again. Only the one magelord was dead; the rest lay senseless, strewn about amid the disarranged tables and chairs.

The innkeeper was the first to say what many of the diners were thinking. "That was all too easy—but who among us will live when their fellow mages come down on us for revenge?"

"Aye—they'll turn us all to snails and grind us under their boots!"

"'They'll blow the inn apart with flame, and us in it!"

"Mayhap," Elmara said, "but only if some tongues here wag too freely." She calmly raised her hands and cast a spell, and then went about the room touching the wizards. Men backed out of her way in haste; it was easy to see they viewed wizards as swift and deadly trouble.

When she was done, she murmured a word, and suddenly, seven stones sat where the sprawled bodies had lain. Elmara made a gesture, and the rocks were gone, leaving only a small, dark pool of blood behind to mark that they'd ever been there.

The nearest merchant turned to Elmara. "You turned them to stones?"

"Aye," she said, and a sudden smile crossed her face. "Ye see—ye *can* get blood from stones." Amid a few uncertain chuckles, she turned to the minstrel. "Have ye breath enough to sing?"

The man nodded uncertainly. "Why?"

"If ye will, I'd like to hear the rest of the tale about King Uthgrael."

The minstrel bowed. "My pleasure, Lady—?"

"Elmara," Elmara told him. "Elmara Aumar—er, descendant of Elthryn of Heldon."

The minstrel looked at her as if Elmara had three heads and crowns on each one. "Heldon is ashes these nine winters past." El did not reply, and after a moment, the man asked curiously, "But tell me: where did you send the stones?"

Elmara shrugged. "A good way offshore near Mystra's Dance, where the water is deep. When my spell wears off and they regain their true forms, they'll have to swim to the surface to survive. I hope they have large and strong lungs."

Silence fell on the room at these words. The minstrel tried to break the mood by beginning the Ballad of the Stag again, but his voice was raw. After it broke the second time, he spread his hands and asked, "Can you wait, Lady Elmara, until the morrow?"

"Of course," El replied, taking a seat at the just-righted table where the wizards had been. "How are ye?"

"Alive, thanks to you," the minstrel said quietly. "May I pay for your dinner?"

"If ye allow me to buy all we drink," Elmara replied. After a moment, they both chuckled.

Elmara set down their third bottle, empty. She eyed it gravely, and asked, "Are any princes left alive?"

The minstrel shrugged. "Belaur, of course, though I've heard he styles himself 'king' now. I know of no others, but there could be, I suppose. It hardly matters now that the magelords rule openly, issuing decrees as if they were all kings. The only entertainment we have is watching them try to outwit each other. I don't go back often."

"How so?" Elmara stared at the last few swallows in her glass. Treacherous stuff.

"It's not a safe land for any who speak openly against the magelords—and that includes minstrels whose clever ballads may not be to the liking of any passing wizards or armsman."

The minstrel thoughtfully drained his own glass. "Athalantar doesn't see any visiting wizards, now, either . . . unless one has the power to defeat all the magelords, why go there? If any mage of power comes to Athalantar, the magelords'd doubtless see it as a threat to their rule and all rise up together against him!"

Elmara laughed quietly. "A prudent mage would go elsewhere, eh?"

The minstrel nodded. "And speedily." His eyes narrowed. "You wear a strange look, Lady. . . . Where will you go on the morrow?"

Elmara looked at him. Fire smoldered deep in eyes gone very dark, and the smile the mage gave the minstrel then had no mirth in it at all. "Athalantar, of course."

TWELVE
HARD CHOICES, EASY DOOMS

Choosing what road to walk in life is a luxury given to few in Faerûn.
Perhaps lack of practice is why so many who do have that choice make
such a gods-cursed mess of it.

GALGARR THORMSPUR, MARSHAL OF MALIGH
A WARRIOR'S VIEWS
YEAR OF THE BLUE SHIELD

The first sign of trouble was the empty road.

At this hour of a bright morning, the way to Narthil should have been crowded with groaning carts, snorting oxen pulling wagons along, any number of peddlers leading mules, laborers and pilgrims trudging along under the weight of their packs, and perhaps even a mounted messenger or two. Instead, Elmara had the road to herself as she topped the last rise and saw that her way was barred by a log swing-gate across the road. In all her days in Hastarl, there'd been no gates on the roads into Athalantar—or she'd surely have heard of it from the tired merchants who complained about every little thing on their journeys.

The guards lounging on benches behind the gate heaved themselves to their feet and picked up their halberds. Armsmen of Athalantar, or she was a magelord. They looked bored and brutal.

Elmara shifted her pack to better conceal the small spell-things she'd taken into her palm, and trudged up to the gate.

"Halt, woman," the swordcaptain of the guard said offhandedly. "Your name and trade?"

Elmara faced the officer across the gate and said politely, "The first is none of thy affair; as to the second, I work magic."

The armsmen drew back, their boredom gone in an instant. Halberds flashed as they came down over the gate to menace the lone woman. The swordcaptain's brows drew together in a frown that had made lesser men turn and run, but the stranger stood her ground.

"Mages who do not serve our king are not welcome here," said the swordcaptain. As he spoke, his men were moving steadily sideways around the ends of the gate, weapons at the ready, moving to encircle Elmara with steel.

El ignored them. "And what king might that be?"

"King Belaur, of course," the swordcaptain snapped, and Elmara felt the cold point of a halberd prodding her lower back.

"On your knees, *now*," the swordcaptain snapped, "and await our local lord mage, who will demand to know further of your business. Best you use a more respectful tongue with him than you did with us."

Elmara smiled tightly and raised one empty hand. She made a small gesture and replied, "Oh, I shall."

Behind him, the first gasps began; and the point probing at her spine was suddenly gone. All around, the guardsmen staggered, cried out or vomited, white-faced, and sank to their knees. One kept going, bonelessly, to the turf, his halberd dropping from loose, empty hands.

"What—what're you doing?" the swordcaptain gulped, face tightening in pain. "Magic—?"

"A small spell that makes ye feel what it is to have a sword sliding through your guts," the young, hawk-nosed maid said calmly. "But if it confuses thee . . ."

The swordcaptain felt a sudden twinge in his stomach, and in the same instant there was a flash in the air before him. He stared down—to see a shining steel blade standing forth from his belly, his own dark red blood running down the blade. He choked, clutched a vain hand to quell the wrenching, searing pain in his stomach—and then the sword and the pain both vanished.

The warrior stared down in astonishment at the unmarked leather over his belly. Then his eyes rose slowly, reluctantly, to meet those of the young woman, who smiled at him pleasantly and raised her other hand.

The guardcaptain paled, opened his mouth to say something, jaw quivering, and then fled, followed a moment later by the rest of the guard. Elmara watched them go, smiling a little, and then walked on along the road, toward the inn.

The sign above the door said Myrkiel's Rest, and merchants had told her it was the best (near the only) inn in Narthil. Elmara found it pleasant enough, and took a chair against a wall at the back of the room, where she could see who came in. She ordered a meal from the stout proprietress and asked if she could use a room for a few breaths, offering a regal if she could do it undisturbed.

The innkeeper's eyebrows rose, but without a word she took Elmara's coin and showed her a room with a door that could be barred. When Elmara returned to her seat, humming the verse "O for an iron guard!" her meal was waiting, hot butter-bread and rabbit stew.

It was good. She was most of the way through it when the front door of the Rest burst open, and armsmen with drawn swords pushed in. An angry-looking man in robes of red and silver strode in their midst.

"Ho, Asmartha!" the splendidly garbed man snapped. "Who is this outlaw you shelter?" With an imperious jerk of his head, he indicated the young woman sitting in the corner. The innkeeper turned angry eyes on Elmara, but the hawk-nosed maid was calmly licking the last sauce from a rabbit bone, and paid no heed.

Motioning his armsmen to stay around him, the man in robes strode grandly toward Elmara's table. Other diners stared and hastily shifted their seats to be well out of the way—but close enough to see and hear all they could.

"A word with you, wench!"

Elmara raised her eyes, over another bone. She inspected it, set it aside, and selected another. "Ye may have several," she decreed calmly and went on eating. There were several sniggers and chuckles from around the tables—quelled by the cold and steady glare of the finely robed man as he turned on one boot heel to survey the room.

"I understand you style yourself a mage," he said coldly to the seated woman.

Elmara put down another bone. "No. I said I worked magic," she replied, not bothering to look up. After a few long breaths more, as she unconcernedly gnawed at a succession of bones, it became clear she had no intention of saying anything more.

"I'm speaking to you, wench!"

"I had noticed, aye," Elmara agreed. "Say on." She picked up another bone, decided it was too bare to suck on a second time, and put it down. "More beer, please," she called, leaning to look past the crowd of armsmen. There were more sounds of mirth from the watching diners.

"Raztan," the robed man said coldly, "run your blade into this arrogant whore."

Elmara yawned and leaned back in her chair, presenting an arched belly to Raztan, who did not fail to miss it, his steel sliding in so smoothly that he overbalanced and fell on his face in the young woman's bowl of stew. Everyone in the suddenly silent room heard the point of the blade scrape the plastered wall behind the young woman. Elmara calmly pushed her plate and bowl aside and selected a toothpick from the pewter holder before her.

"Sorcery!" one of the armsmen spat, and slashed Elmara across the face. No blood spurted—and the blade swung freely through the hawk-nosed face, as if it were only empty air. The watchers gasped.

The robed man curled his lip. "I see you know the ironguard spell," he said, unimpressed.

Elmara smiled up at him, nodded, and wiggled a finger. The drawn swords around her twisted, sang, and became gray serpents. Horrified armsmen watched the fanged heads turn and arch back to strike at the hands that wielded them! With one accord, the armsmen flung down their weapons and leaped back. One man charged for the door, and his run became a thundering rush of booted feet as his comrades joined him. All around the guards, their blades, normal swords once more, clattered to the floor.

The man in robes drew back, face pale. "We shall speak again," he said, his haughty voice a trifle uncertain, "and when we d—"

Elmara raised both her hands to trace an intricate pattern in the air, and the man turned and strode hastily back across the room, toward the door. Halfway there he halted, swaying, and the watchers heard him snarl in fear and frustration. Sudden sweat moistened his brow as he strained to move . . . but could not advance another step. Elmara rose and walked around to face the frozen man. Frightened eyes swiveled to watch her come.

"Who rules here?" she asked.

The man snarled at her wordlessly.

Elmara raised an eyebrow and a hand at the same time.

"M-Mercy," the man gasped.

"There is no mercy for mages," Elmara told him quietly. "I've learned that much." She turned away. "I ask again: who rules?"

"I—ah . . . we hold Narthil for King Belaur."

"Thank you, sir," Elmara murmured politely, and started back to her seat.

The man in robes, suddenly released from magical restraint, lurched and almost fell, took three quick steps toward the door, and then spun around and snarled a spell, his dagger flashing into his hand. The watching townsfolk gasped. The robed wizard's blade and all the discarded swords on the floor leaped up in unison and hurtled through the air toward Elmara's back in a deadly storm of steel. Without turning, El murmured a soft word. The steel points so close to claiming her life swerved away, flying back at the mage.

"No!" the robed wizard cried frantically, snatching at the handle of the door. "Wha—"

The blades thudded home in a deadly rain, lifting the man's body off his feet and carrying him past the door. He fell, kicked once, and then lay still, the blades a shining forest in his back.

Elmara took up her cloak and pack. "Ye see? Mercy continues in short supply. Nor among mages, I've learned, is there overmuch trust," she added and went out into the street.

Watching faces were pressed against the windows of the inn as Elmara walked calmly out into the road and began to peer into shop windows, as if she had coins to spare and a whim to spend them. She had not been strolling long before there was the sound of a horn from north up the road—from the small stone pile of Narthil Keep. A sally port in the keep gate opened, and the clatter of hooves was heard. An old man in a ceremonial tabard rode out, two full-plated armsmen with lances behind him. Elmara watched them turn toward her, saw no signs of crossbows, shrugged, and turned away, heading back to the inn.

The street was rapidly filling with curious townsfolk. "Who are ye, young lass?" asked one scar-nosed man.

"A friend . . . a traveling priestess of Mystra, from Athalantar," said Elmara.

"A magelord?" another man asked, sounding angry.

"A renegade magelord?" the woman beside him offered.

"No magelord at all, ever," Elmara replied, and turned to a big-bosomed, weary-looking woman in apron and patched skirts, who stood gaping at her as if she were a talking fish. "How goes it here in Narthil, goodwoman?"

Taken aback by her words, she stammered for a trice, and then said bitterly, "Bad, lass, since these Athalantan dogs came and took the keep for their own. Since then, they've seized our food and daughters an' all without so much as asking!"

"Aye!" several folk agreed.

"More cruel than most warriors?" Elmara asked, waving a hand at the keep.

The woman shrugged. "Nae so much cruel, as . . . proud. These young bucks'd not prance so free nor be so fast to smash things and upset all, if they had to spend a tenday in my—or any maid's!—place, cleaning up and setting to rights and mending!"

"'Ware!" a man said warningly, and all around Elmara folk drew back as the three horsemen came trotting up. The young woman stood calmly awaiting them.

At her unmoving stance, the old man in the tabard of purple adorned with silver moonflowers reined in his mount and said, "I am Aunsiber, lord steward of Narthil. Who are ye, who here work spells against lawful armsmen and mages of the realm?"

Elmara nodded in polite greeting. "One who would prefer to see wizards help folk, not rule them—who would prefer a king whose rule meant peace, stability, and help in harvesting, not taxes, ceaseless strife, and brutality."

Not surprisingly, there was a murmur of agreement from the watching townsfolk all around. The steward uneasily eyed the crowd, sidestepping his restless mount. His voice, when it came, was derisive. "A dream."

Elmara inclined her head. "As yet, 'tis—and not my only one."

The old man looked down from his high saddle and asked, "And your others, young dreamer?"

"Just one," Elmara replied mildly. "Revenge." She raised both her hands as if to cast a spell—and the old man's face paled. He jerked at his reins, wheeled his mount in a nervous flurry of snorts and hooves, and set off back to the keep at a gallop. There were some hoots and exultant yells from the crowd, but Elmara turned away without another word and went back into the inn.

"What'd she say?" one man was asking as she stepped through the door.

A woman sitting nearby leaned forward and said loudly, "Did ye not hear? *Revenge.*"

Then she saw Elmara was in the room and fell silent, a silence that suddenly hung tense and expectant over the whole room. El gave the woman a gentle smile and went to the bar. "Is that beer ready yet?" she asked calmly, and was pleased to hear at least one man behind her dare to chuckle aloud.

Briost was not having a good day. He burst out of his grand council chamber the moment the messenger had gone. The apprentice who'd been trying to eavesdrop by means of a just-perfected spell stiffened guiltily; his master's face was dark with anger.

"Go and practice hurling fireballs," Briost snapped, "or what spells you will. I'm called away on the king's business. Some mad traveling wizard's had the temerity to slay all of Seldinor's apprentices at an inn west of Narthil—and he's 'too busy' to avenge them. So *I'm* going to reap the idiot's head for the greater glory of the magelords!"

The hand that shook Elmara was soft but insistent. She came awake in the best bed in Myrkiel's Rest and peered at the woman bending over her. The innkeeper wore but a blanket, clutched about her. "Lass, lass," she hissed, hovering over El in the darkness, "ye'd best be gone from here right speedily, out into the woods. Word's come that armsmen are riding here to take thee!"

Elmara yawned, stretched, and said, "My thanks, fair lady. Would there be such a thing as hot cider about, and some sausage?"

The innkeeper stared at her. Then what might almost have been a smile flashed across her face as she turned and hurried out, bare feet flashing in the gloom.

The road fairly shook under their hooves in the gray gloom that comes before dawn. Sixty mounted knights of Athalantar, gleaming dark and deadly in their best battle armor, headed west, bent on battle. In their midst, the man whose helm bore the plumes of a commander turned his head to the man riding beside him.

"Suppose you tell me, mage," he ordered, "what urgent befalling brings us to ride through half the night."

"We go to work revenge, Prince," Magelord Eth snapped. "Is that good enough, or would you question my orders further?"

Prince Gartos appeared to consider the matter for a moment, and then said, "No—revenge is the best reason to make war."

There was a shout from ahead, and the horses broke stride. "Stay on the road, damn you!" Gartos ordered wearily, as the knights' mounts bunched up and snorted and tossed their heads all around him. The band of knights came to an uneasy halt.

"What?" he roared.

"The Narthil road-gate, Lord Prince—and no guard stands here."

Gartos snapped, "Helms on, all! Blades out!" and waved imperiously. The knights around him obeyed, and urged their mounts forward at speed. A breath later, they were thundering down into Narthil.

The gloom-shrouded road ahead was empty and in darkness; no lights glimmered in the houses and shops on either side. The foremost knights slowed their mounts, peering around uncertainly. The town looked asleep, but they'd all heard of knights tumbled from their mounts after riding into cords stretched stiff across streets. There were no cords . . . and no leaping arrows . . . and no one defying them at all. Unless . . .

A lone figure was trudging up the street toward them: a youngish, thin woman in nondescript garb, who held a steaming mug of cider in one hand. She halted calmly in their path and stood sipping and watching. They slowed to a trot and then, in a patter of hooves, swept up to and flowed around her.

Elmara found herself looking up into the hard eyes of a battle-worn warrior who wore magnificent armor and was flanked by a cold-eyed man in robes that bore no device, but somehow had "magelord" limned all over them.

"Fair morn," she offered them mildly, sipping cider. "Who are ye who come in arms to Narthil when honest folk are still abed?"

"*I'll* ask, and *you* will give swift answer," the warrior snapped, turning his mount to one side so he could lean down right over Elmara. "Who are *you?*"

"One who would see proud mages and cruel armsmen taken *down*," El replied, and at the word 'down' her spell went off. Shards of shimmering force flashed out from her in all directions. Where they touched metal, it burst into crackling blue flames—and the man within the armor or holding the blade convulsed and toppled from his saddle.

For a brief instant, the world seemed full of bright light and rearing, crying horses, and then the terrified, riderless mounts were gone in a wild thunder of hooves, leaving Elmara facing just two riders, who sat white-faced in their saddles, a hastily raised protective spell glowing in the air around them.

"My turn," Elmara said, eyes glinting. "Who are ye?"

The warrior slowly and menacingly drew his sword, and Elmara saw magical runes flash and glow down its steely length. "Prince Gartos of Athalantar," he said proudly, "the man who'll slay thee, sorceress, as sure as the sun will rise in the sky o'er Narthil before long." As the warrior spoke, the hands of the silent magelord beside him were moving quickly—but in the next moment his eyes widened: Elmara had suddenly vanished.

Then Magelord Eth's mount was rearing and plunging, and there was a heavy weight behind him. He had just begun to turn when one hand slapped across his nose and mouth, bringing tears—and then another hand came up to punch him hard in the throat.

Gurgling, fighting for air, Magelord Eth reeled in his saddle, and felt something torn from his belt before the dark ground came up hard to hit him in the side of the head, and the Realms spun away from him, forever.

Elmara leaped away from the horse even before the wizard toppled from the saddle; Gartos was very quick. He'd realized where El's magic had taken her, wheeled, and his blade was already cutting the air above the magelord's high-cantled saddle.

Elmara landed hard, jumped to one side to still the speed of her leap, and peered at the wand she'd snatched. Ah, *there!* Hooves were thudding toward her as Elmara looked up, pointed the wand, and carefully spoke the word that was scratched on its butt end. Light pulsed and hissed away from the wand in a pair of bolts that swerved in the air to strike Prince Gartos full in the face. He threw back his head, snarled in pain, and slashed blindly with his blade as his horse galloped forward. Elmara leaped and rolled, and came up well to one side. She pointed the wand at the armored figure rushing past and spoke the word again.

Light flashed again and sped to its target. The gleaming armored arms jerked in pain. The warrior's sword spun away to the turf as his mount bucked under him and then galloped away, fleeing in earnest now. Elmara saw sleepy-eyed folk gaping at her out of their doorways as she dropped the wand to the road at her feet, pointed her hands at the horse, and spoke a few soft words.

The prince fell from his saddle, rolled over once with a mighty crash, and lay still. The horse sped on into the rising dawn.

El retrieved the wand, cast a quick look around for other foes, saw none, and stalked over to where the warrior lay. Gartos lay on his back, face dark with pain and fury.

"I have other questions, warrior," Elmara said. "What brings armsmen of Athalantar to Narthil?"

Gartos snarled angrily and wordlessly up at her. Elmara raised her eyebrow, and lifted her hands warningly to begin the gestures of a spell.

Gartos watched her fingers move, and rumbled, "S-Stay your spell. I was ordered to find the one who slew some magelings at the Unicorn's Horn, west of here . . . you?"

Elmara nodded. "I defeated them and sent them away; they may yet live. How is it that a prince of the realm gets ordered anywhere?"

The warrior's lips twisted wryly. "Even the king does the bidding of the elder magelords—and the king made me a prince."

"Why?"

The fallen man shrugged. "He trusted me . . . and needed to give me the right to command armsmen without having any young fool of a magelord strike down my orders or slay me out of spite."

Elmara nodded. "Who was the wizard with ye?"

"Magelord Eth—my watchdog, set by the magelords to make sure I don't do anything for Belaur that might work against them."

"Ye make Belaur seem a prisoner."

"He is," Gartos said simply, and Elmara saw his eyes dart aside, this way and that, looking for something.

"Tell me more of this Magelord Eth," Elmara said, taking a step forward and drawing the wand from her belt. It would be best to keep this warrior talking and give him no time to plot an attack.

Gartos shrugged again. "I know little; the magelords don't care to say much about themselves. He's called 'Stoneclaw;' he slew an umber hulk with his spells when he was young . . . but that's about all I . . . *Thaerin!*"

At the warrior's shout, magical radiance pulsed. Elmara turned hastily—in time to see the rune-carved blade flashing toward her, point first.

She leaped aside. The warrior snarled, "Osta! Indruu hathan *halarl!*" and the blade veered in the air, darting straight at Elmara.

She let go the wand and raised her hands desperately—and the blade cut right through them, searing aside her fingers to plunge deep into her. Elmara screamed. The dawn sky whirled around her as she staggered back, blood welling up, fought to speak, and fell back onto the turf, greater pain than she'd ever known hissing through her.

She heard a cold chuckle from Gartos as darkness rolled in, and fought with all her will to cling to something . . . anything . . . With her last breath she gasped, "Mystra, aid me . . ."

Prince Gartos struggled to his feet. He felt weak and sick inside and couldn't feel his feet at all . . . but they seemed to obey him. Grunting, he took a few unsteady steps and sat down, armor clanking. Narthil spun around him.

"Easy," he muttered, shaking his head. "Easy, now . . ." His men lay strewn along the road, with not a horse in sight. "Thaerin," he grunted, "*Aglos!*" Gartos extended his hand, watched the blade tug itself free of the dead woman and drift, dark and wet, to his waiting grasp. Young witch, who did she think she was to defy Athalantar's magelords? He fumbled at his gorget, got it aside, and grasped the amulet beneath, closing his eyes and trying to concentrate on the remembered face of Magelord Ithboltar.

Firm fingers swept his aside. His eyes flew open, and he was staring up at the innkeeper's white, frightened face as she thrust a dagger into his throat and drew it firmly across. Blood sprayed. Prince Gartos struggled to swallow, could not, and tried to raise his blade. Its glowing runes dancing before his eyes, mocking him, were the last things he saw as he sank down into darkness.

"Gartos will see that this sorceress dies," Briost said firmly, and a smile slowly crossed his face. "Eth will make sure he does."

"You're confident of Eth's abilities?" Undarl asked. The wizards seated around the table all looked down it to the high seat where the mage royal sat, in time to see his fire-red ring wink with sudden inner light.

Briost shrugged, wondering (not for the first time) just what powers slept in that ring. "He has proven himself able . . . and prudent . . . thus far."

"This was a testing, though, wasn't it?" Galath asked excitedly.

"Of course," Briost replied in a voice dry with patience. Why, he thought privately, did there always have to be one eager puppy at these meetings? Surely work could be found for such as Galath on these evenings—teaching him to unroll a scroll, perhaps, or put on his own robes so the hood was to the back and the tabard facing front? Anything would suffice, so long as it kept him far away. . . .

Galath leaned forward eagerly. "Has he reported in?"

Nasarn the Hooded snorted and looked coldly down the table. "If every mageling we set to a task did that, our ears'd be ringing with their babble every moment of the day—and all night, too!" With his unblinking stare, sharp nose, and dusty black robes, the old man resembled a vulture sitting and watching prey that would soon come its way.

Undarl nodded. "I'd not expect a magelord to waste magic on bothering his fellows just for idle chatter; a report should come only if something serious is amiss . . . if the intruding mage should prove to be a spy for another realm, for instance, or the leader of an invading army."

Galath flushed in embarrassment and looked away from the mage royal's calm face. Several of the other magelords let him see smiles of amusement on their faces as he looked swiftly and involuntarily up and down the table. Briost yawned openly as he smoothed one dark green sleeve of his robes and shifted into a more comfortable position in his chair. Alarashan, ever one to leap onto a popular cart, yawned too, and Galath's gaze fell to the table in front of him in misery.

"Your enthusiasm does you credit, Galath," Undarl Dragonrider added with a straight face. "If Eth asks us for aid or something befalls him, I assign you to act for us all in setting things to rights in Narthil."

Galath straightened with such swift and obvious pride, swelling visibly before their eyes, that more than one magelord at the table sputtered with swiftly repressed mirth. Briost rolled his eyes up to look at the ceiling and asked it silently if Galath knew how to open a spellbook, or if presented with one, he'd peel it like a potato?

The stone vault overhead did not answer . . . but then, it had hung above this high chamber in Athalgard for almost a century, and had learned to be a patient ceiling.

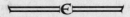

The pain burned and roiled and threatened to sweep her away. In the darkening void, El clung grimly to the white light of her will. She must hold on, somehow. . . .

Pain surged as the enchanted blade shifted and then slid smoothly—oh, so smoothly, *in her own blood!*—out of her, leaving her feeling empty and . . . open. Violated. Faerûn should not see her innards like this, hot blood rushing out of her into the sun . . . but she could do nothing, nothing at all to stop its flow. Her hands moved a bit, she thought, as she tried to clutch at her wound, but now the light and sounds around her were fading, and she was getting colder. Sinking, sinking into a void that was everywhere around her, scornful of her failing life-force . . . and as cold as ice.

Elmara gasped and tried to gather her will. The white radiance she'd always been able to summon flickered feebly before her, like a watchfire in the night. She thrust herself forward into it, enfolding it and clinging to it, until she was adrift in a white haze.

The pain was less, now. Someone seemed to be moving her, rolling her gently over . . . for a moment panic soared within her as the movement shook her hold on the radiance and it seemed to slip from under her. . . . El clawed at the void with her will until the white light surrounded her again.

Something—a voice?—echoed around her, eddying softly and crying afar like a trumpet, but she couldn't make out the words . . . if there were any. The void around seemed to grow darker, and El clung fiercely to her light. It seemed to grow in brightness, and from far away she heard that voice cry out in surprise and draw away, babbling in fear, or was it awe?

She was alone, adrift in a sea of light . . . and out of the pearly mists ahead something she knew swam up to embrace her. Dragonfire! Raging flames framing a street she knew well, and Elmara tried to cry out.

Prince Elthryn stood in the midst of blazing Heldon, the dancing flames gleaming on his mirror-polished black boots, and brandished the Lion Sword, whole and flashing back the flames. He turned, long hair swirling, and looked at Elmara. "Patience, my child."

Then smoke and flames swirled between them, and although she cried her father's name loud and desperately, she saw Elthryn no more, but instead a high hall of stone where cruel mages in rich robes bent over an ornate scrying bowl held up by three winged maidens of glossy polished gold. One was Undarl Dragonrider, the mage royal who'd destroyed Heldon. Another mage was passing his hand over the waters, waving his fingers angrily. "Where *is* he?" he snarled . . . and seemed for just an instant to see Elmara. His eyes narrowed, and then widened—but that chamber whirled and spun away into the void of light, and Elmara was suddenly staring into the eyes of Mystra, who stood in the air in front of her, smiling, her arms open to embrace.

Stumbling in haste, Elmara ran across unseen ground toward her. Tears welled up and burst forth. "Lady Mystra!" she sobbed. "Mystra!" The light around the goddess dimmed, and the smiling Lady of Mysteries was fading . . . fading.

"*Mystra!*" El reached out desperately, tears blurring the darkening scene. She was falling . . . falling . . . into the void once more, chilled and whimpering, alone, her light gone.

She was dying. Elmara Aumar must be dead already, her spirit wandering until it fled and faded . . . but no! In the dark, floating distance El saw a tiny light sparkle and flare—and then rush toward her, bright and spinning. She cried out in wonder and fear as the blinding brightness leaped at her and flooded around her once more. Mystra's smile seemed to be all around her, too, warm and comforting, infinitely wise.

Through thinning mists Elmara saw another vision: she rose from her knees in prayer to Mystra and turned to a table where a large, ornately bound tome lay, surrounded by small items that she recognized as spell components. She sat, opened the spellbook, and began to study . . . mists roiled up, and when they cleared again, El saw herself casting a spell and then watching as a ball of flames burst into bright being in front of her. A fireball? That was a spell wizards commanded, not priestesses. . . .

The mists of light swirled and then parted again, revealing shapes of fire burning, endless and immobile, in emptiness. El stared at them. These fires were magic . . . and familiar. She stared at their coils and leaping tongues of fire . . . and—aye! These were the spells she'd memorized earlier, hanging in her own mind waiting to be released!

Yes, a warm and mighty voice said, echoing all round her, and added, *Watch*. One of the fires moved suddenly, writhing and twisting like a snake unfolding.

It flared in sudden brilliance—too bright to watch, even as the voice said, *Do thus, and behold!*

The fire flared up and was gone, leaving the white mists around a flickering amber. Elmara felt suddenly better, as if tension and pain had lessened . . . and at the same time, the weight in her mind eased, as if a spell had passed from memory.

Again, said the mind-voice of Mystra. Another flame writhed, opened, and flared up. At its passing Elmara felt stronger and more at ease from pain, and hung basking in the growing warmth of the now-golden mists.

Do this yourself now, the voice said, and El trembled in sudden awe and nervousness. She knew somehow that a slip could tear her mind apart . . . but the flames were unfolding, coiling, as her will surged through her and out to guide them. Brighter, now . . . aye! Thus, and—'tis done!

A golden radiance seemed to roll outward through the mists as the fires of the spell dissipated. Elmara felt stronger, as if the pain that numbness had shielded from her was suddenly gone, falling away from her like a tattered cloak that has split asunder . . . and the burning weight of spells in her mind eased again.

Mystra had shown her how to turn her memorized spells into healing energy and guide that raw force to work her own restoration. Hanging in the bright amber mind-void, El gasped at the beauty and intricacy of the process . . . the chill darkness seemed far away now. She found she could identify particular spells if she stared at the flames long enough. She floated, considering, the remaining pain like an aching mantle around her, until she'd chosen the least useful magic.

To spend it was the act of but a brief moment now, and the pain eased still more. She was going to live!

With that thought, El found herself wanting to rise—and then she was in motion, ascending smoothly through golden mists into the light.

There was a sudden rocking burst of noise and radiance. Through a swimming golden haze she could see clouds in the bright blue sky of morning—and darker and nearer, a ring of gawking faces, staring openmouthed at her. El recognized the anxious face of Asmartha the innkeeper, and smiled up at her.

"A-Aye," she said, finding her voice thick with blood, "I live."

There was more than one shriek, and gaps appeared abruptly in the circle of heads. El smiled thinly . . . but her heart swelled when the innkeeper matched her smile, and stretched down one strong hand to touch her.

"I saw it," the woman said, voice husky in wonder. "You were dead—cut open like a slaughtered hog—and now are whole. The gods are *real* . . . they must be. I saw you heal, right in front of me. The gods were *here!*"

Asmartha's face broke into a wide, wild laugh, and tears ran down her face. She traced El's cheek with a gentle finger, shook her head, and said, "I've never seen the like. What god smiles on you, lady?"

"Mystra," Elmara said. "Great Mystra." She struggled to sit up, and there were suddenly strong arms at her shoulders, helping her. "I am a priestess of the Lady of Mysteries," El told the innkeeper—and then, as a sudden realization came to her, added slowly, "Yet I must learn to be more."

"Lady?"

"If I am to battle magelords and their armsmen, face to face and spell to spell," El said softly, frowning, "I must become a mage in truth."

"You're *not* a sorceress?"

Elmara shook her head. "Not yet." Perhaps never, she thought suddenly, if I can't find a wizard willing to train me . . . and where in the world could she find one to trust? Not in Athalantar, where every sorcerer was a magelord . . . nor in the Calishar. There must be wizards in the other lands around, aye, but where to start looking?

Wh—Braer. Of course. Go to the High Forest and ask her teacher. Whatever he said, it would be an answer she could trust. "I must leave," El said, scrambling to her feet.

The world wavered and swam around her, and she swayed, but one of the men of Narthil put a steadying hand on her shoulder, and she stayed upright. "The magelords can find me with their spells," El said urgently. "Every moment I stay here, I endanger ye all." She drew a deep, shuddering breath, and then another, reaching into the mists to uncoil another flame.

Asmartha drew back a pace as Elmara stiffened, and glowing white light emanated from her. Then it faded, and the innkeeper saw that the young, hawk-nosed woman stood at ease despite her blood-drenched clothing and the pale, drawn look on her face.

"My pack," she murmured, and turned back toward the inn. The innkeeper stepped hastily to her side to guard against her falling, but El smiled and said reassuringly, "I'm fine now . . . and happier than I've been in some time. Mystra smiles on me."

"That I can well believe," the stout woman said, as they went into the Rest. The door banged behind them.

Elmara walked off as she had come, alone, her pack on her back, heading northeast over the rolling fields. The innkeeper watched her march out of sight, hoping no ill would befall her. Once Asmartha had dreamed of a life of adventure, seeing all the fabled sights of Faerûn and befriending elves . . . and there went a lass who'd done just that.

The innkeeper smiled at the crest of a far-off hill as the tiny dark figure of her guest disappeared over it. She shook her head. Perhaps the gods would smile enough on the reckless maid to keep her alive through her fight against the mighty magelords, and she'd come back to Narthil one day with time enough to spare to tell a fat and aging innkeeper where she'd gone and what she'd seen . . . but more likely that would never happen.

Asmartha sighed, wiped her hands absently on her apron, and went back into the Rest. She'd best stir some of the men to drag those bodies away, or the whole street'd stink by nightfall, and beasts'd come down into Narthil to feed.

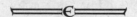

And so, a grumbling goodman of Narthil found himself bending over the dead prince. He reached out to take the warrior's sword for his own—and then hissed in fear, stumbling backward. The sword shivered, moving by itself. The runes on the steel pulsed and rippled with sudden light. Then the blade rose from the ground as if taken up by unseen hands, hung for a moment in front of the terrified townsman's eyes, and flew away, sliding slow and smoothly through the air, point-first and straight, like an arrow shot from a bow. Northeast it went, toward the grazing hills.

The man watched it go, swallowed, and muttered a prayer to Tempus, Lord of Battles. What were things coming to, when even swords held magic? And in the end, what good had that fancy blade done this carrion at his feet? Nay, magic wasn't something to be trusted, ever. The townsman looked down. The dead warrior stared unseeing at the sun. The townsman shook his head, spat on his hands, and took hold of the Athalantan's feet. Hmm . . . the blade might be gone—but those boots, now?

Unseen, the enchanted blade crested a certain hill and flew on, northeast. A spell from afar was bidding it rejoin the being whose blood it had last spilled, a young sorceress hitherto unknown to the magelords. A woman who defied armsmen, heralds, magelords, and princes of Athalantar alike—and for that, she must die. The blade flew on, seeking blood.

Thirteen
Spells Enough to Die

Think on this, arrogant mageling: even the mightiest archmage has no spells strong enough to let him cheat death. Some take the road of lichdom . . . a living death. The rest of us find graves, and our dust is no grander than that of the next man. So when next you lord it over some farmer with your fireballs, remember: we all master spells enough to die.

Ithil Sprandorn, Lord Mage of Saskar
said to the prisoner wizard Thorstel
Year of the Watching Wood

Flamerule had been warm and wet in this Year of Bloodflowers, and if the gods sent rain sparingly in the fall, a plentiful harvest could be expected all down the River Shining.

Phaernos Bauldyn, keeper of the Ambletrees Arms, leaned against his doorpost and watched the last light of the setting sun fade over the hills to the west. A beautiful land, this . . . though he'd be happier if it weren't ruled by wizards who swaggered wherever they went, treating folk as slaves or cattle . . . or worse.

He sighed. So long as they didn't get foolish or arrogant enough to face the elves of the High Forest spell to spell or offended some god sorely enough to all be struck down on the spot, there was no way he could see that Athalantar would ever be free of the magelords. Phaernos frowned, sighed again, and turned back for his candle. It was fast growing dark now. He reached up, with the ease of long habit standing clear of the dripping wax, and lit the over-door lamp. As he drew the candle down and blew it out, he saw her coming wearily up the road to his door: a lone girl, tall, dark haired, slim, and drenched, with her clothes clinging to her and her sodden cloak trailing river water behind.

"Fall in, lass?" he asked, coming forward to offer his arm.

"I had to swim the river," she replied shortly, and then raised her head and smiled at him. She was thin and hollow eyed, but her blue-gray eyes were keen and bright above a sharp nose.

Phaernos nodded as he turned to lead the way in. "A bed for the night?"

"If I can get dry by a fire," she answered, "but my coins are few. Are ye master of this house?"

"I am," Phaernos said, pulling open the wide front door. His guest peered at the old shields nailed to it and seemed almost amused.

"Why d'you ask?" he asked her as they came into the low-beamed taproom. A few farmers and village folk were sitting by the fire, cradling tankards of ale and mugs of broth. They looked up with mild interest.

"I can pay ye with spells," the wet girl said calmly.

Phaernos drew away from her in the sudden silence and said shortly, "We haven't much use for mages hereabouts. Most wizards in this land don't use their magic to help anyone but themselves."

"Then their magic should be stripped from them," she replied.

"And just how d'ye think anyone could do *that*, lass?" one of the drunker farmers demanded from his seat by the fire.

"Take their lives swift enough, and they've seldom any will left to work spells, I've found," the woman said calmly. "I'm no friend of magelords." The silence that followed her words was broken only by the faint, steady drip of river water from her clothes.

No one bothered her—or even spoke to her—after that. Phaernos led her wordlessly into the kitchen, pointed her to a bench by the hearth fire, and brought her a cloak. The kitchen-women bustled over with rags for her to scrub dry with and food to eat, but then went on about their business. Elmara welcomed the peace; she was exhausted. Two hills away from Narthil, she'd made the mistake of using a spell that took her in a single step from where she'd stood to the most distant hilltop she could see. The magic had drawn on her own energy to do its work, leaving her exhausted. After that, the swim across the river hadn't helped—and it'd left her too chilled to just roll herself in her cloak and go to sleep in the open.

Elmara dried off as best she could, wrapped herself in the cloak, and dozed off, dreaming of shivering in a dripping hedge while magelords in the shape of wolves howled and bounded past, seeking her with sharp and hungry jaws agape.

It was much later when, at a gentle touch, she awoke; the innkeeper was bending over her. His guest tensed and looked up alertly as if she might spring up in a moment to give battle or flee.

Phaernos gazed down at her expressionlessly and said, "The house is closed for the night and the drinkers've gone home ... you're the only guest to sleep here tonight. Tell me your name, and what you meant about ... paying me with magic." At his words, two of the women drew nearer to listen.

"I'm Elmara," his guest said, "a traveler from afar. I'm no mage, but I can work a few spells. Would ye like a larger storage cellar?"

Phaernos looked at her silently for a breath or two, and then the beginnings of a smile crept onto his face. "A larger cesspit would be more useful."

"I can do that, or both," Elmara said, rising, "if ye'll let me sleep here this night."

Phaernos nodded. "Done, lady ... if you'll come with me, I'll show you a bed where no magelord will find you."

The woman gave him a sharp look and asked softly, "What d'ye know of me?"

The innkeeper shrugged. "Nothing ... but a friend asked me to watch out for Elmara, if she should pass this way."

"Who was this friend?"

"He goes by the name of Braer," answered the innkeeper, looking steadily into her eyes.

El smiled and relaxed, her shoulders slumping wearily. "Show me the cellar and the pit first," she said. "It may befall that I'll have to slip away before daybreak."

Phaernos nodded again, saying nothing, and they went out together. As the door swung closed, the two kitchen-women exchanged looks—and with one accord made the warding sign against Tyche's disfavor, and turned back to their dishes.

In the morning, Elmara awoke to find her wet things had been dried and hung, and atop her battered pack sat a cloth bundle. It proved to contain sausage, dried fish, and hard bread. She smiled, dressed swiftly, and went out, to find the innkeeper slumped asleep in a chair by the bedchamber door, an old sword across his knees.

Swallowing to drive down the sudden lump in her throat, Elmara slipped down the stairs and out by the kitchen door, past the cesspit and into the trees behind. Perhaps it would have been wiser not to have said anything about magelords or spells last night . . . but she'd been wet and exhausted, and it was done.

It would be best to be well away from Ambletrees before any word of a sorceress spread. Elmara kept to the trees as long as possible before stepping out into the back fields, heading north toward Far Torel. She took care to keep well out of sight of the road. Phaernos had said many armsmen had marched up it this last tenday, gathering for he knew not what—an attack on the elves of the High Forest, he half-hoped and half-feared.

Elmara doubted the magelords would risk themselves as the innkeeper hoped. No, they'd more likely order the woods set afire, and tell their armsmen to use crossbows to fell any elves who came to fight the flames. She sighed and strode on. She might have to spend years slipping across Athalantar like a shadow, evading the clutches of the wizards and their swaggering armsmen while learning all she could of what magelords ruled where. If she were ever to avenge her parents and free the realm, she'd have to find some way to fell a few of the stronger magelords in the backlands so watching eyes would be fewer and she could make their deaths seem the work of enemy magelords or ambitious apprentices.

Perhaps she could seduce a magelord to gain his confidence and learn all he knew before destroying him. Elmara sighed, came to a thoughtful halt for a moment, and then went on. Not only did the idea make her stomach heave, she hadn't the faintest idea of how to act enticing . . . enough that a wizard who could have any maid he wanted would spare her more than a passing glance. A spell to change her shape might be noticed, and she wasn't particularly beautiful. She slowed her customary brisk stride and swayed her hips, gliding along with the lynxlike allure of an evening-lass she'd once seen in Hastarl, and then burst into high, helpless laughter at the very feel of it, shaking her head at how she must look.

Creep up on magelords like a thief, then. . . . Aye, that she still knew how to do, though this lighter, softer body, with its breasts and hips, balanced differently and lacked some of the strength she'd had as a man. She'd need to practice skulking again.

Soon, she thought suddenly. If Far Torel was an armed camp, they'd have patrols and watchers . . . and she'd blunder right into them if she went on walking in the open without a care. On the other hand, if she were seen, someone skulking along would look suspicious indeed, where a traveler who trudged openly would not. Time to walk in and embrace doom again, Elmara thought to herself and smiled wryly. Out of habit she glanced all around, and so saved her life one more time.

A gleaming rune-carved sword was speeding through the air toward her from behind, a sword she'd never forget. The horrible memory of her impalement flashed into her mind, and through the steely taste of fear that rose into her mouth, Elmara shouted the words she'd never forget. "Thaerin! Osta! Indruu hathan *halarl!*"

The blade shivered to a halt, turned aside, and darted uncertainly around in the trees. It reached an open space as El watched, her thoughts racing desperately, and then slowly turned until its glittering point was toward her again.

As the blade leaped at her face, she stammered out the only prayer to Mystra she had left that might work.

"Namaglos!" she shouted its last word desperately—and the blade burst into flashing shards right in front of her. Elmara shuddered in relief and sank to her knees, discovering that tears were running down her cheeks. In angry haste she wiped them away and gasped the words of another prayer.

Tyche smiled upon her, too, it seemed. There was no magelord near. This blade must have been sent after her by someone back in Narthil, or even a wizard distant from that town, perhaps in Athalgard. Whatever its origin, there was no magical scrying upon her, and no intelligent being within spell-sight.

El thanked both goddesses because it seemed the right thing to do, then rose from her knees and went on cautiously. Perhaps she'd best seek a place to hide and pray to Mystra for spells.

Othglar spat thoughtfully into the night, shifted his aching behind on the stump, and then grunted in sudden impatience and got to his feet, kicking at the air to ease the stiffness in his legs. These wizards were all crazed—who in Athalantar would dare to attack almost four thousand swords? Out here in the proverbial chill back of beyond, too, weary miles of marching away from Hastarl and the lower river posts.

Othglar shook his head and walked to the edge of the stone bluff, looking down. Scores of campfires glimmered in the vale below. He reflected on how depressingly familiar they looked as he scratched at his ribs, spat into the night, and then unlaced his codpiece, leaning his halberd against a tree.

He was thoughtfully watering the unseen trees below when someone gave his halberd back to him, swinging it hard into his ear. Othglar's head snapped to one side, and he toppled forward into the night without a sound.

A slim hand propped the halberd back where it had been as the brief, rolling thudding of the guard's landing began, far below.

The owner of the hand drew her dark cloak around herself against the chill of the night and peered out at the same view Othglar had been so unimpressed with. Elmara's magesight found only three small points of blue light—possibly enspelled daggers or rings. None was near, or moving about.

Good. She counted campfires and sighed soundlessly. There were enough armsmen here to start a war against the elves that might ruin both Athalantar and the High Forest. She must act . . . and that meant using one of the most powerful, lengthy, and dangerous prayers she knew.

Crawling cautiously on hands and knees, Elmara found a hollow a little way down the cliff, a place where someone coming to the guard's post wouldn't immediately fall over her. She knelt in it and undressed, putting everything that had metal in or about it in her pack, and then setting her pack well back behind her.

She faced the campfires, softly whispered a supplication to Mystra, spread bare feet for better balance, and began her spell.

Taking up the least favored of her several daggers, she pricked the palms of both her hands so they bled and held the dagger out horizontally before her, pinioned between her bloody palms.

As she murmured the incantation, she could feel blood running down to drip off her elbows and strength ebbing out of her as it was stolen by the spell.

Trembling with weakness, Elmara held the dagger up higher so it gleamed in the moonlight and watched it darken and begin to crumble. When it dissolved into rusty shards, she brushed off her hands and sank down, satisfied. Before dawn, every piece of metal between her and the forest would be useless, powdery rust. That would give the magelords something to think about. If they decided elven magic was the cause, the attack on the High Forest might never come.

Elmara curled her hands into fists and stared up at the moon as she whispered another prayer to Mystra, to heal her slashed flesh. It did not take long, but she was numb with weariness when she was done. She turned back to her pack. Put on cloak and boots, at least, and then best be gone from here, before . . .

"Oho! What've we here, eh?"

The voice was rough but delighted, pitched low so as not to carry far. "Heh," it chuckled, as its owner reached out of the night-shadows by the trees to clutch her firmly by the arm, "I c'n see why Othglar was in no great hurry to report in . . . come here, lass, and give us a kiss."

Elmara felt herself dragged into an embrace. The unseen lips that kissed her were ringed by rough, prickly stubble, but when she could breathe again she did not pull away. At all costs, she must keep this man from raising the alarm.

"Oh, yesss," she moaned, the same way that girl in Hastarl had done so long ago. "He sleeps, now, leaving me so *lonely*. . . ."

"Ho-ho!" the armsman chuckled again. "Truly, the gods smile tonight!" His arms tightened around her.

El fought down a rush of panic and murmured, "Kiss me again, Lord." As those bristled lips sought her own, Elmara put one arm around the corded muscles of his back, shuddered at the taste of the horrible ale the guard had been drinking—and found what she'd been seeking: the dagger sheathed at his belt. She slid the blade free and held the man's lips with her own as she swung the hilt of the dagger as hard as she could against his head.

The armsman made a surprised sound and fell away from her, landing heavily in the brush. The hilt of the dagger was wet and sticky; Elmara fought down a sudden urge to be sick and threw the weapon down. Rolling the senseless man across the rock was hot work, even naked as she was. "Ye were great," she hissed fiercely in his ear as she rolled him over the edge.

Her cloak was around her and her pack on her back by the time she heard the body crash through branches below and start to roll.

El stepped into her boots and carefully went forward onto soft moss before she stamped them firmly onto her feet. Then she crept into the darkness, heading back the way she'd come, hoping no new guardposts or patrols had been set. She'd a few spells left, aye, but scarce the strength to stand and cast them. She dare not try to go through this encamped army to reach the forest—elven patrols might slay her before they knew who she was, even if by some gods-sent miracle she got past all the armsmen.

No, 'twould be best to go back to the place of the goddess, that little pool, and seek Braer from there. It lay well west of here.

Stumbling with weariness, Elmara made her slow way down through the night, wondering how far she'd get before she passed out. It would be interesting to see. . . .

By the end of her second day in the loft, Elmara was still as weak as a newborn kitten. She'd fallen twice on the ladder, and finally struggled up here hissing in pain from a bruised or broken forearm. It was healed now, but the working of that prayer had left her with a splitting headache and a sick, empty feeling within, and she'd lain dreaming for a long time.

She didn't feel ready to move even yet. "Mystra, watch over me," she murmured, and sank again into slumber.

"Gods above!"

The awe-struck voice jerked her awake. Elmara turned her head.

The bearded head of an astonished farmer was staring at her from an arm's reach away, a candle-lantern trembling in his hand. She struggled not to laugh at his expression; she supposed she'd look something like that if she found a lass wearing only a cloak and boots and lying in *her* hayloft. He handled it well, she thought.

As she burst into helpless giggles, he wiped a hand nervously across his mouth, found it was open, closed it, and cleared his throat with the same sort of sound sheep made in the meadow above Heldon. Fresh giggling seized Elmara.

The farmer blinked at her, clearly finding her mirth almost as startling as her presence, and said, "Uh . . . er . . . aghumm. Fair even, uh . . . lass."

"Fair fortune to this farm and all in it," she said formally, rolling over to face him. Redness stole across his face, and he dragged his eyes reluctantly away and hastily descended the ladder.

Oh, aye—these. Elmara pulled the cloak over herself and rolled up to one knee to peer over the edge of the loft. The farmer looked up at her as if he expected her to change shape of a sudden into some sort of forest cat and leap down on him. He caught up a pitchfork and brandished it uncertainly.

"Wh-Who are you, lass? How came you here? Are . . . are you all right?"

The slim, sharp-nosed lady smiled wanly down at him, and said, "I am an enemy of the magelords. Hide me, if you will."

The farmer stared at her in horror, gulped, drew himself up, and said, "Ye'll be as safe here as I can make it." Then he added awkwardly, "If there's anything I . . . or my men . . . can do . . . uh, we daren't fight them, with their magic an' all. . . ."

Elmara smiled at him. "Ye've given me shelter and friendly words, and for me that's enough. It's all most of us need, and lack, in Athalantar."

The man grinned up at her suddenly, as delighted and proud as if she'd knighted him, and shifted his feet. "Be back, Lady," he said hesitantly.

"Tell *no one* I'm here!" Elmara hissed urgently.

The farmer nodded vigorously and went out. Not long after, he returned with a cup of fresh milk, an end of bread, and a slab of cheese.

"Did anyone see ye?" Elmara asked, chin on the edge of the loft.

The farmer shook his head. "Think you I want armsmen or magelords crawling all over my farm, burning down what they don't tear apart, and using magic to make me tell things? No fear, lass!"

Elmara thanked him. He didn't see her hand, glowing with gathered fire inside her cloak, fade again to its normal appearance. "Gods keep ye this night," she said huskily, moved.

The man shifted his feet, bowed a little in embarrassment, and answered, "An' ye, lass. An' ye." He gave her the raised-hand salute that men in fields use, one to another, and hurried out.

When he was gone, Elmara clutched the cloak to her and stared out the loft window, eyes very bright. She watched the moon riding high in the sky, and thought about many things.

She was gone from there before dawn—just in case.

Her way west had been swift, as she fled to get well away from any report of her. Far Torel was emptying of troops, the armsmen returning to safer posts to the south. It seemed the magelords' plans to spill elven blood were abandoned . . . for now at least. That news gave Elmara great satisfaction as she went, earning blisters she healed when she could bear them no more.

She traveled mainly at dawn and at dusk, across country. When she turned north toward Heldon, she found her way blocked by several encampments of armsmen, and a band of magelings being trained by several watchful magelords—and with a weary sigh, decided to go west into the Haunted Vale, and try to reach the High Forest from that direction. She'd never thought fighting magelords would involve so much *walking*. . . .

It was late one day when she found battle again. She trudged up a hill, frowned curiously at a trampled, fresh-broken gap in a farm fence, and went through it. The field was empty, but the hilltop in the field beyond it was a crowded place. A large band of Athalantan armsmen stood in a large ring about a lone figure—a woman in robes—firing at her with crossbow quarrels.

A farmer stood leaning on a stout cane at the gate where the two fields met. His lips quivered in anger as he watched, eyes blazing. He turned his head like an angry lion as Elmara came up beside him, and put out his cane to block her path.

"Stay back, lass," he warned. "Yon dogs are out for blood—and they won't care who they slay. They'd not have dared when I was younger, but the gods and the passing years have taken all from me but my smart mouth and this farm. . . ."

The woman on the hilltop knew sorcery; crossbow quarrels were bounding aside from unseen shields, and she was conjuring small balls of fire, and hurling them to consume some of the bolts leaping at her. Her shoulders sagged in weariness, and when she tossed long, tangled hair out of her eyes, the movement was tired. The armsmen were wearing her down fast.

Elmara patted the old man's arm, stepping around his cane—and strode briskly off into the field, heading for the ring of armsmen. As she approached, a bolt took the sorceress through the shoulder. The woman reeled and then fell to her knees with a sob, clutching at the dark, spreading stain where the quarrel protruded.

"Take her," the battlelord outside the ring snapped, waving at his warriors with one imperious gauntlet.

The armsmen rushed in, but the sorceress was muttering something and gesturing hastily with one bloody hand. The trotting soldiers slowed, and one slumped bonelessly to the trodden turf; followed by another. Then a third, and a fourth.

"Back!" the battlelord roared. "Back, before she has all of you asleep!" When the armsmen were back in an unsteady ring, leaving many of their fellows sprawled on the ground, the commander glared around at them, and snarled, "Shoot her down, then. Bows ready!"

The sorceress knelt with bleak eyes, watching helplessly as crossbows were wound, loaded, and made ready all around her.

Elmara sat down hastily on the muddy ground and spoke one of the most powerful prayers she had, timing it carefully.

"Loose!"

At the battlelord's command, the armsmen let fly their quarrels, and Elmara bent forward, eyes blazing, to watch her spell take hold. Abruptly the battlelord was standing in the midst of the ring, and the sorceress was slumped on the ground where he'd stood, outside it. A score of bolts thudded home. Not a few pierced the opulent armor and found the face that the raised visor did not cover. The battlelord staggered, roared, transfixed by many shafts, lifted his hand—and then slowly toppled onto his face, and lay still.

The arms men were still gaping at the body of their commander when Elmara's hasty second prayer-spell took effect. All around the field, armor glowed a dull red, and men began to grunt, squirm, and cry out, dancing in frantic haste and clawing at their armor.

Hotter it glowed, and hotter. Men were screaming now. The stink of burning flesh and hair joined the metallic reek as armsmen flung their armor desperately in all directions, howling and rolling about naked in the field.

Elmara turned and walked back to the farmer. He flinched at her approach, clutching his cane up in front of his chest like a warding weapon, but stood his ground.

"Ye should be able to deal with them now," she said calmly, looked back at all the writhing, shrieking men, and added, "I fear I've ruined much of your planting."

From empty air she plucked a handful of gems, put them into the astonished old man's hand, and embraced him. Into one large and hairy old ear she murmured, "Ye seem a good man. Try to stay alive; I'll need thy service when this land is mine." Then she turned away.

Darrigo Trumpettower stood with the gems glittering in his hand like so many fallen tears, and stared after her.

The slim woman in the tattered cloak strode off across the field, walking west. The bleeding sorceress floated along in the air behind her, as if she were being towed on an invisible, weightless bed.

Only one armsman moved to stop her, winding his bow into readiness, loading it, and setting it to his shoulder. He felt the hand that struck his bow aside but never felt the stout cane that smashed him to the ground, or anything else. His quarrel leaped toward the sun, and no one saw whether it reached there or not.

Darrigo Trumpettower stood fierce-eyed over the dead armsman and growled, "At least I can be proud of *something* before I die. Come on then, Wolves! Come and cut down an old man, and tell yerselves what mighty heroes ye are!"

This was the time to use a prayer she'd always wanted to try but had never found the right occasion for. Mystra's dictates were quite strict: her priestesses could never call on her for their own benefit, and Braer had warned her how few riches he'd made ready for her to call on. Yet she felt that now was the right time.

The bloodstanch litany was not one Elmara used often, so she had to take time to pray to the goddess for it. Night had come to the Haunted Vale when

Elmara took the fallen sorceress in her arms and said the words of her last useful prayer, the one that would transport them both to the only enclosed refuge she could think of: the cave below the meadow, overlooking ruined Heldon.

As the moon-drenched hills vanished and familiar earthy darkness was suddenly all around, Elmara smiled wearily. She'd never heard of a female magelord, nor were armsmen likely to dare turn on one. If this lady sorceress lived, she could be the teacher and ally El would need in her fight to free Athalantar.

"All alone, I cannot defeat the magelords," she murmured, admitting it at last. "Gods above know, I can barely deal with one enchanted sword!"

Much later, Elmara sighed despairingly. The sorceress hadn't awakened, and her newly healed flesh felt burning hot under El's fingers. Had the crossbow bolt been poisoned? El's prayers had melted that dart away, stopped the bleeding, and drawn together the woman's torn shoulder . . . but in truth, she knew few healing charms—the prayers Mystra gave her faithful included many barriers and spells that blasted foes apart and hurled things down, but were shy on magics that mended and healed.

Still unconscious, the woman lay on a bed of cloaks. Her fevered flesh was drenched with sweat, and from time to time she murmured things El couldn't catch, and moved her limbs feebly about on the sodden cloaks. Her skin—even to her lips—was bone white.

Elmara's best efforts to gather her will and force healing into the body of the sorceress failed utterly. El might be able to turn memorized prayer-spells into healing energy for herself . . . but Mystra hadn't given her the means to aid anyone else.

The sorceress was dying. She might last until morn or a little longer, but . . . perhaps not. Elmara didn't even know her name. The woman's body moved restlessly again, wet with a sheen of sweat that returned however often El wiped it away.

Elmara stared at the woman she'd rescued, and wiped moisture from her own forehead. She must do more, or she'd be sharing her cave with a corpse in the morning. With sudden resolve, she took the woman's purse—which held a good handful of coins—and crawled out of the cave, casting a ward against wolves across its mouth.

There had been a shrine to Chauntea, Mother of Farms and Fields, south of Heldon. Perhaps for wealth enough the priest who tended its plantings could be persuaded to come hence and heal. It was too much to hope he'd keep his mouth closed about the cave and the two women; whatever befell, she'd have to find a new lair.

Elmara sighed grimly and hastened down from the meadow, hurrying as much as she dared in the nightgloom. From days when she'd played here often, her feet easily found gaps in the trees. Just how long ago had those days been?

Then she was out of the trees, into the ruins of Heldon—where she came to an abrupt halt. There were lights ahead: torches burning where there should be none. Not moving as if held by men searching for something, but held fast on high, as if they blazed here always. What had befallen the ashes of Heldon?

Weariness gone, Elmara stole forward in cautious silence, keeping to the deepest shadows. A palisade rose in front of her, a dark wall that ran for a long way, enclosing—what? Looking along it, she saw a helmed head at a corner where the wall turned.

Carefully, El drew back, and retraced her steps in the night until she found a certain boulder she'd climbed often as a child. Shielded from anyone watching from the palisade, she cast a spell that turned her into a silent, drifting shadow, and went to the walls.

In this form, she could glide along swiftly, without worrying about noise. She hurried around the walls. They enclosed a square and were pierced by two gates. The gap under one of them was large enough for her to pass in shadow-shape . . . and she was inside. She reared up in the darkness of the wall and looked around hastily. This spell did not last long, and she had no desire to fight her way out of a camp defended by gods-alone-knew how many aroused armsmen.

For there were armsmen here in plenty: two barracksful, at least, by the look of things . . . guarding loggers, it seemed. Cut timber lay piled everywhere; Elmara shook her head sourly. If she were an angry elf mage, one fireball over the palisade would turn this torchlit camp into a huge funeral pyre. Perhaps someone should suggest it to them.

Later. She had work before her, as always. Where there are lots of armsmen, there were always priests of Tempus, or Helm, or Tyr, or Tyche, or all four . . . Tempus, at least.

The shadow scudded along behind the barracks and warehouses, seeking a corner where a sword would be standing upright in a wooden block as an altar. Ah . . . there. So where was the priest? Elmara drifted toward the nearest building. Within was a plain room hung with battered armor—trophies of Tempus, no doubt—and the unwashed man sleeping beneath them reeked of ale. If that was the priest, she thought in disgust, her venture here had failed, and she'd best be out and seeking the shrine to Chauntea before her spell ended.

But first . . . there was one splendid house in the center of the rest. The lair of the local magelords, doubtless, but she could hear a faint din of laughter and talk from this far off; perhaps they were drinking the night away . . . and a priest might be there.

The house had guards, but they were bored and resentful of the feasting within, and one soon strolled over to the other to share a jest. The shadow slipped through the spot where he'd stood and in at the door. Thence it ghosted past curtains and hurrying servants into a large, noisy room beyond.

A drifting globe of magical radiance competed with many candles to light up this grand chamber, which was crowded with men in rich robes and women in nothing but gems. All of this drunken company were lolling about on pillows and lounges, spilling as much wine as they were quaffing and talking far too loudly and grandly about what they'd do in the days and hours ahead, and how they'd do it.

To Elmara's magesight, the place was awash in the blue light of magic, but an inner room, partly visible past one of the many open doors at the back of the chamber, glowed even more brightly. Not wanting to risk her shadow-shape being stripped from her by some defensive spell or ward, or being seen by someone in the room who had the power to pierce spell-disguises, El glided swiftly around the edge of the feast and made for the beckoning doorway.

The room beyond the door was richly furnished and so overlaid by spells that it seemed one thick blue murk to Elmara's eyes. She stole quickly across the carpet and through an arch, into a bedchamber almost entirely filled by a huge canopied bed.

Now, if I were a mage and had lots of magic to hide, where would I . . . ? Under the bed, of course.

The skirts of the high bed were no barrier to a shadow, and the space within was almost another small room one could sit in. The blue glow was near blinding now, spilling from a chest and two coffers that sat beneath the bed. As Elmara bent forward to peer at them, her shadow-spell ran out, and she thumped down onto the dusty carpet on hands and knees. She froze, listening tensely—but there came no sound of alarm, or of anyone coming into the room.

The small coffer probably held gems and coins; the larger one and the chest were more likely to hold healing potions, if any were to be found here. There were apt to be some, if things she'd heard in Hastarl were true. With them, a magelord could rescue injured men and earn their gratitude, or bargain with them and force their service . . . and without them, a magelord could find himself at the mercy of priests and lesser men who might have healing magic, and could do the same to him.

Which chest or coffer held them, though? Elmara drew her dagger, and felt in the hair over her ear for one of the two lockpicks she still carried. A few deft turns and probes, and the lid of the coffer clicked once. She laid down on the floor beside the coffer, and carefully lifted the lid with the point of her dagger.

Nothing happened. Cautiously she raised her head to peer into it—and saw only coins. Bah!

She was working on the chest when someone came into the room—no, two people, a man who was laughing in anticipation and someone else. A maid for his pleasure, doubtless. The door slammed shut, and a bolt clacked into place.

The bed creaked just over Elmara's head. Ducking involuntarily, she pursed her lips and paused in her work on the lock. It would make a loud clicking sound when she forced it open.

She did not have to wait very long—when the man was roaring with laughter at his own jest, he made more than enough noise to drown out the sound of the chest opening. Unloading it onto the carpet while the couple bounced and rolled around on the bed just above her was a long, sweaty business, but Elmara's care was rewarded: along one side of the chest, under a robe that shimmered blue to her gaze with its own magic, were a row of metal tubes, each stoppered with a wax-sealed cork, and neatly labeled. One gave the power of flight, and the others were all for healing. Aye!

With a triumphant smile, El slid them into her boots and carefully repacked the chest, casting a longing look at the spellbook fastened into the lid. Nay; her task now was to begone from here, as fast as she could without raising an alarm.

Not so easily done. She could hardly hope to cast a spell right underneath a magelord—even a magelord in the throes of passion—without being heard.

And then she heard him grunt, above her head, and say, "Ahhh, yes, by all the gods! Now out, girl—out! I've work to do yet ere I sleep! Stay, mind—I'll be back out for you later!" The bolt was opened, and then the door, and then she heard both being put back again.

Elmara tensed under the bed. She had a few slaying spells—but a sphere of flames is little use if one wants to survive a fight in a small room . . . still less if one wants to do it without alerting a fortress full of armed men.

She also had something smaller: a fleshflame. Hmmm.

And then the curtains in front of her were jerked aside, and a kneeling man thrust his head in under the bed, seeking his riches.

He stared in amazement at Elmara, as her hands shot out and grasped his head by both ears, drawing her toward him.

"Greetings," she purred, murmured the few words that called up the magic, and kissed him.

Flame spat from her parted lips into the incoherently struggling magelord. He stiffened, clutched at her convulsively, and then sagged to the carpet, teeth clicking as his chin hit the floor.

Smoke drifted from the dead wizard's mouth and ears as she dragged the chest over to him, opened it again, and left him kneeling with his head in it. When he was found, perhaps they'd think something inside it slew him.

Coolly, Elmara rose from under the bed. The door was closed and bolted. Good. She ducked back under the bed, and took out the spellbook. Flipping through it rapidly, she found the wizards' spell she wanted.

It was very similar to the prayer-spell that Braer bad taught her. Kneeling with the book open before her, she prayed fervently to the Lady of Mysteries.

Brightness seemed to flare inside her—and abruptly she was standing just outside her ward in the meadow, the spellbook in her hands. "Thanks be, Mystra," she told the stars, and went in.

The spicy scent of turtle soup wafted through the cave. Intent on keeping it from burning, Elmara barely heard the faint voice from behind her.

"Who—who are you?"

She turned to see the sorceress truly awake for the first time. Large, hollow eyes stared into her own. The sorceress reached up a hand to brush matted hair aside, and that hand trembled. There must have been *something* on that crossbow quarrel. Even with the potions, the sorceress had been a long time recovering.

Elmara went on stirring the soup with a long bone—all that was left of a deer her spells had brought down days ago—and said, "Elmara of Athalantar. I...worship Mystra." Those large eyes held her own as if clinging to a last crumbling handhold, and El added, "And I will be a foe of the magelords of this realm until they are all dead, or I am."

The woman let out a long, shuddering breath, and leaned back against the wall of the cave. "Where—what place is this?"

"A cave in the north of Athalantar," El told bet "I brought ye here more than a tenday ago, after I rescued ye from armsmen in the Haunted Vale. How came ye to be there, in a ring of quarrels?"

The woman shrugged. "I...was newly arrived in Athalantar, and met with a patrol of armsmen. They fled, gathered more of their fellows, and came to slay me. From some things they said, it seems they're under orders to slay any wizards they meet who aren't magelords. I was tired and careless...and was overwhelmed."

She smiled and stretched out a hand to touch Elmara's own. "My thanks," she said softly, eyes very large and dark in her beautiful bone-white face. "I am Myrjala Talithyn, of Elvedarr in Ardeep. They call me 'Darkeyes.'"

Elmara nodded. "Soup?"

"Please," Myrjala said, sitting back against the cave wall. "I have been wandering," she said slowly, "in my dreams, and have seen much."

Elmara waited, but the sorceress said no more, so she dipped a drinking jack—all she had—into the soup, wiped its dripping flanks, and handed it to Myrjala. "What brought ye all the way to Athalantar?" she asked.

"I was riding overland to visit elven holds up the Unicorn Run when I first met with the armsmen, and they slew my horse. After, I walked to where you found me," Myrjala replied, and looked around. "Where am I now?"

"Above the ruins of Heldon," Elmara said simply, licking soup from her fingers.

Myrjala nodded, drank deep of the steaming soup, and shuddered at its heat. Then she raised her black, liquid eyes again to meet Elmara's gaze, and said, "I owe you my life. What can I give you in return?"

Elmara looked down at her hands, and found them trembling with sudden excitement. She looked up, and blurted, "Train me. I know some spells, but I'm a priestess, not a mage. I need to master sorcery in my own right, to hope to hurl spells well enough to destroy the magelords."

Myrjala's dark brows arched upward at El's last words, but she said only, "Tell me what you've mastered thus far."

Elmara shrugged. "I've learned to blast foes, and to use their anger against them....I can create and hurl fire, and jump from place to place, take shadow-shape, and rust or master steel. But I know nothing of wise spell-strategies against a clear-headed foe, or the details of just what most wizards' spells do, or how one can best use one spell with another, or..."

Myrjala nodded. "You've learned much . . . most mages never even notice they lack such skills—and if someone dares point it out to them, they lash out in anger to slay the one who revealed it to them, rather than giving thanks."

She took another sip of soup and added, "Aye, I'll train you. Someone had better; there're wild wizards in plenty out roaming Faerûn already. When you've come to trust me, you might tell me why you want to slay all the magelords in this land."

Elmara's thoughts raced. "Ah," she began, "I . . ."

Myrjala held up a restraining hand. "Later," she said with a smile. "When you're ready." She made a face, and added, "And when you've learned just how much salt to put into soup."

They laughed together then, for the first time.

Fourteen
No Greater Fool

*Know this, mageling, and know it well: there is no greater fool than a wizard.
The greater the mage, the greater the fool, because we who work magic live in a
world of dreams, and chase dreams . . . and in the end, dreams undo us.*

Khelben "Blackstaff" Arunsun
Words To Would-Be Apprentices
Year of the Sword and Stars

Fire was born, swirling into furious life where the air had been empty
moments before. Swiftly it grew in two places in the huge cavern, until
Elmara's intent face was lit by two huge spheres of flame. A double-throated
roar began, rising in tone and fury as the spinning spheres grew larger. El
stared from one whirling conflagration to the other, sweat running down
her face like water over rocks and dripping steadily from her chin. Across
the chamber, Myrjala stood unmoving, watching expressionlessly. The twin
fireballs grew even larger, seeming to pluck flames from the air as they rolled
over and over.

"Now!" El whispered, more to herself than to her teacher, and brought her
trembling arms together.

Obediently the two huge spheres of flame moved, pinwheeling across the
cavern toward each other. Elmara took one careful pace backward without
looking away from the flames, and then another. It was as well to be far away
when the two fiery spheres—*touched!*

There was a blinding flash of light as tortured tongues of flame leaped wildly
out in all directions; the cavern rocked with the force of the mighty blast. Heat
rolled over Elmara, and the force of the explosion smashed into her, plucked her
from her feet and hurled her spinning back into—nothing. The fury of the blast
roared past her, and slowly died away. El found herself floating motionless in
midair as the echoes of the explosion boomed and rolled around her and rocks
and dust fell on her from the unseen ceiling far above.

"Myrjala?" she asked the darkness anxiously. "Teacher?"

"I'm fine," a calm voice replied from very near at hand, and El felt herself
turning in the air to look into the dark, intent eyes of the older sorceress,
who was floating upright in midair beside her. Myrjala's bare body was
as dusty and sweat-dewed as her own; around them, the cavern was still
uncomfortably hot.

Myrjala leaned forward and touched El's arm. They began to descend. "To protect us both," she explained, "I had to spin my spell shield around you, then make it pull me into it; my apologies if I startled you."

El waved that away as they sank to the cavern floor together. "My apologies," she said, "for working too powerful an inferno for this space—"

Myrjala smiled, and dismissed those words with a wave of her own. "This was what I intended. You followed my instructions perfectly—something many apprentices never manage in twice the years of study you've had."

"I had experience in following dictates in my time as a priestess," Elmara said, settling to the still-warm stone floor.

Myrjala shrugged. "As much as any adventurer-priestess, perhaps. You were given a goal, and forged your own way toward it." She bent to pluck up her robe from the floor and mop her face with it. "True obedience is learned by folk who spend years drudging away at some endless task, with little hope of betterment or reward, following petty orders issued by small folk who've mastered the tyrant's whip or tongue without any real power to deserve such swagger."

"Was that thy experience?" El asked teasingly, and Myrjala rolled her eyes.

"More than once," she replied. "But seek not to divert my attention from your schooling—you can hurl spells as well as some archmages, but you've not yet mastered them all." She leaned forward, speaking earnestly. "One who has truly mastered sorcery *feels* each magic, almost as a living thing, and so can control its effects precisely, using it in original and unexpected ways or to modify the enchantments of others. I can tell when a pupil develops such a feel for a spell . . . and so far, you've acquired this intimate control over less than half the spells you cast."

Elmara nodded. "I'm not used to talking about magic in this way . . . but I understand ye. Say on."

Myrjala nodded. "When you revert to prayer, calling on Mystra to empower you, I see that attunement in every magic, but that's a feel for the goddess and the flow of raw spell-energy not a mastery of the structure and direction of the unfolding magic."

"And how shall I acquire this mastery over all spells I use?"

"As always, there's only one way," Myrjala said, shrugging. "Practice."

"As in, 'practice until ye're sick of it,'" El said with a wry smile.

"*Now* you understand aright," Myrjala replied. Her answering smile was eager "Let's see how well you can shape a chain lightning to strike and follow the light-spheres I'll conjure . . . green is untouched, and a change to amber means your lightning has found them."

Elmara groaned and gestured down at the bright rivulets of sweat on her dust-coated body. "Is there no rest?"

"Only in death," Myrjala replied soberly. "Only in death. Try not to remember that when most mages do . . . too late."

"Why have we come here?" Elmara asked, staring around into the chill, dank darkness. Myrjala laid a comforting hand on her arm.

"To learn," was all she said.

"Learn what, exactly?" El asked, looking around dubiously at inscriptions she could not read and strangely shaped stone coffers and chests of glassy-smooth stone that bristled with upswept horns. However odd the shapes she was seeing, she knew a tomb when she stood in one.

"When *not* to hurl spells and seek to destroy," Myrjala replied, voice echoing from a distant corner of the room. Motes of light suddenly danced and whirled in a cluster around her body—and when they died away, Myrjala was gone.

"Teacher?" El asked, more calmly than she felt. From the darkness near at hand there came an answer of sorts: inscriptions that had been mere dark grooves in the stone walls and floor filled with sudden emerald light. El turned to face them, wondering if she could puzzle some meaning out of these writings—and then, with a sudden touch of fear, saw wisps of radiance rising from them, thickening and coiling to coalesce into . . .

Elmara hastily readied her mightiest destroying spell—and paused, waiting tensely.

In front of her, the wraith of a man was building itself out of the empty air—tall, thin, and regal, robed in strange garb adorned with upswept horns like the chests, and standing on nothingness well above the rune-graven floor. Eyes that were two emerald flames fixed Elmara with a powerful, deeply wise gaze, and a voice spoke in her head. "Why have ye come to disturb my sleep?"

"To learn," El said quickly, not lowering her hands.

"Students seldom arrive with ready slaying spells," was the reply. "That is more often the style of those who come to steal." Vertical columns of emerald radiance suddenly leaped into being all over the chamber, and from the ceiling jumbled bones descended into each shaft of light, to drift therein lazily. A score or more skulls stared at Elmara. She looked at them and then back at the wraith.

"These are what remains of thieves who've come here?"

"Indeed. They came seeking some glorious treasures of Netheril . . . but the only treasure that lies here is myself." The voice paused, and the wraith drifted a little nearer. "Does this change the purpose of thy visit?"

"I have been a thief, but I did not come here hoping to bear anything away but lessons," Elmara replied.

"I shall let ye keep that much," the cold voice replied.

"Let me keep lessons? Ye can deny them?"

"Of course. I mastered magic in Thyndlamdrivvar . . . not as the wizards of today seem to, plucking spells from tombs or foolish tutors the same way small boys steal apples from others' trees."

"Who are ye?" El whispered, eyes straying to watch the skulls drift and dance.

"I now go by the name of Ander. Before I passed into this state, I was an archwizard of Netheril—but the city where I lived and the great works I wrought seem to have all vanished 'neath the claws of passing years. So much for striving . . . and there's a valuable lesson for ye to bear away, mageling."

El frowned. "What have ye become?"

"I have passed beyond death by means of my art. I understand from such conversations as these—so my knowledge may be clouded by untruths said to me—that all the wizards of today can manage is to preserve their bodies, shuffling about as crumbling, putrefying wreckage until they collapse altogether . . . ye call them 'liches,' I believe?"

Elmara nodded uncertainly. "Aye."

The green eyes of the wraith glowed a little more brightly. "In my day, we mastered our bodies, so we can become solid or as ye see me now, and pass from one state to another at will. With long practice, one even learns to turn only a hand solid, and leave the rest unseen."

"Is this something that can be taught?"

The emerald eyes danced in mirth. "Aye, to those willing to pass beyond death."

"Why," asked Elmara softly, "would anyone want to pass beyond death?"

"To live forever . . . or to finish a task that drives and consumes one's days, as vengeance on magelords consumes thine . . . or to—"

"Ye know that about me?"

"I can read thy thoughts, when ye are this close," the Netherese wraith-wizard replied.

Elmara stepped back, raising her hands with fresh resolve, and the undead sorcerer sighed in her mind.

"Nay, nay—cast not thy petty spell, mageling. I've worked ye no harm."

"Do ye *feed* on thoughts and memories?" El asked in sudden suspicion.

"Nay. I feed on life-force."

El took another step back, and felt a light touch on her shoulder. She turned and stared into the endless grin of a floating skull, bobbing inches away from her nose. She leaped back with a little cry. The sorcerer sighed again.

"Not the life-force of intelligent beings, idiot. Think ye I've no morals, just because ye see bones and all the trappings of death? What is so evil about death? 'Tis something that befalls all of us."

"What life-force, then?" El asked.

"I have a creature imprisoned on the other side of that wall called a deep-spawn, it gives birth to creatures it has devoured—stirge after stirge after stirge, in this case."

"Where's the door to this room of monsters?" El asked suspiciously.

"Door? What need have I of doors? Walls are no barrier to me."

"Why are ye revealing all this to me?"

"Ah, there speaks a living wizard, fearful and mistrustful of all others, jealous of power, hoarding learning like precious stones, to keep it from others. . . . Why not tell ye? Ye're interested, and I'm lonely. While we speak, I learn what I want to hear from your mind, so it matters not what we talk about."

"Ye know all about me?" El whispered, looking around for Myrjala.

"Aye—all thy secrets, and fears. Yet be at ease. I shan't reveal these to others, nor attack thee. Improbable as it seems, I can see ye truly did not intend to steal from me, or hurl magic against me."

"So now what will ye do with me?"

"Let ye go. Mind ye return, in ten seasons or so, and talk with Ander again. Thy mind'll have fresh memories and learning for me by then."

"I—I'll try to return," El said uncertainly. Though she'd now mastered her fear, only the gods above knew if she'd live that long, or still be able to work magic . . . and not be a twisted prisoner of some magelord or other.

"That's all any mortal can promise," Ander said, drifting nearer. "Take this gift from me, sith ye did not come to seize anything."

A shaft of light descended in front of Elmara's nose, and within it hung an open book, a book of circular pages, open at one. As El stared at the crawling runes on that page, they seemed to writhe and reform until she could suddenly read them. It was a spell that completely and permanently transformed the gender of the wizard casting it. El swallowed. She'd almost grown used to being a woman, but . . . The page was tearing itself free of the book, right in front of her eyes. Involuntarily she cried out at this destruction, but the wraith answered her with a laugh.

"What need have I of this spell? I can assume any solid form I choose! Take it!"

Numbly, El reached forth her hand into the light and took the page. As she did so, she was abruptly plunged into darkness. The emerald glows, the wraithwizard, and the bones and all were gone.

All that remained in the silent room was her own feeble mage-fire, and the crumbling page in her hand. She stared around for a moment, and then carefully rolled the parchment and thrust it into her bodice.

Then she stiffened as a quiet chuckle sounded deep in her mind, followed by the words, *Remember Ander, and return. I like thee, man-woman.* El stood for a long time in the gloom, silent and unmoving, before she said, "And I thee, Ander. I *will* come back to visit thee." Then she walked to where Myrjala had disappeared. "Teacher?" she called. "Teacher?"

All was dark and silent. "Myrjala?" she said uncertainly, and at that name, motes of light sparkled into being in front of her, and she saw her tutor's dark and friendly eyes for a moment, before the light specks swirled around her too, and took her from the tomb.

"This is very important to ye," El said, standing on a barren hill in the westernmost reaches of the Haunted Vale.

"And even more to you. This is your greatest test of all," Myrjala replied, "and if you succeed, you'll have done something more useful to Faerûn than most mages ever accomplish. Be warned: this task will take at least a season, and drain some of your life-force."

"What is the task?"

Myrjala waved an arm at the ravine below them—a place of bare stones, weeds, and the ashen stumps of trees consumed in a long-ago fire. "Bring this place back to life, from where this spring rises to where it joins the Darthtil half a day's walk hence."

El stared at her "Bring it to life with spells?"

Her teacher nodded.

"How shall I begin?"

"Ah," Myrjala said, rising into the air. "Trying, and setting right mistakes, and trying again is the best part of the task. I shall meet with ye on this spot, a year from now."

Then brightness flared about her, and she was gone.

El closed her mouth on now-useless protests and questions, then opened it again to say quietly, "Gods smile upon ye, Myrjala," and then looked down at the barren gully. Learning its ways had to be the beginning of the task.

The dragon's talons enfolded Elmara. She calmly watched them close around her, doing nothing . . . and the gigantic claws faded away an instant before touching her Then the quickening breeze blew the last spell-mists away, and she was facing Myrjala across a bare hilltop, on this rainy, windswept day in Eleint, Year of the Disappearing Dragons. Clouds raced past, low in the heavy gray sky.

"Why didn't you strike at me?" her teacher asked, eyebrows raised. "Have you thought of some other way to shatter a dragontalons spell?"

Elmara spread her hands. "I couldn't think of any way not to hurt ye sorely," she said, "with the spells I have left. I knew I could take the harm and survive—just. The other way, I might have lost a teacher . . . and worse, a friend."

Myrjala looked into her eyes. "Yes," she agreed quietly, and waved her hand in an encircling gesture.

Abruptly, the two women were standing in a hollow in the lee of the hill, where their camp was. They were facing each other across a campfire that had lit itself; Myrjala's doing, of course.

Sometimes El mused about how little she knew of her tutor's life and powers, though time and again in their long training together she'd realized just how mighty in magic the sorceress known across Faerûn as 'Darkeyes' must be. Right now, she felt a curious foreboding as she stared across the fire at Myrjala.

The older sorceress stood looking into the flames, sadness in her eyes. "Your work on the ravine was superlative . . . much better than my own when I was set the same task. You are stronger than Myrjala now in might-of-magic." She sighed, and added, "And now you *must* go adventuring on your own to try new ways of using spells, and of altering those you know to make them truly your own . . . so you can come to full mastery of what you wield and not stand forever in the shadow of a mage-mentor."

Unshed tears glimmered in the dark eyes she raised to meet Elmara's horrified stare. "Otherwise," Myrjala added slowly, "the days and the years will pass, and both of us shall be the weaker for it—each forever clutching the other's skirts for support, neither growing in her own right."

Elmara stood staring at her in silence.

"Being a mage is a lonely thing," Myrjala said gently, "and this is why. Do you hear my words and agree?"

Elmara looked at her, trembling, and sighed. "So we must part," she whispered, "and I must go on alone . . . to face the magelords."

"You aren't ready to resume your vengeance yet. Live, and learn a little more first. Find me when you feel ready to challenge for the Stag Throne, and I'll aid you if I can. Yet if we do not part," Myrjala said softly, "you will have won nothing alone, and *that* you must do."

Silence hung heavily over the fire for a long time before Elmara nodded reluctantly. Then she said slowly, "There is a secret I have kept from ye; I would not have it lying between us longer. If we are to go separate ways, it is wrong to keep the truth from thee."

She undid the ties of her gown and let it fall. Myrjala watched as Elmara, standing nude in the firelight, murmured the few words she'd held in her memory since that day in the tomb—and her body changed. Myrjala let fall hands that had risen to weave a swift spell if need be, and stared across the fire at the naked man.

"This is my true self," the hawk-nosed man said slowly. "I am Elminster, son of Elthryn . . . prince of Athalantar."

Myrjala regarded him soberly, her eyes very dark. "Why took you a woman's shape?"

"Mystra did this to me to hide me from magelords, for my likeness had become known to them . . . and, I think, to force me to learn to see the world through a woman's eyes. When I tended ye, ye came to know me as a maid . . . I feared that seeking my true form would upset thee and smash the trust between us."

Myrjala nodded. "I have come to love you," she said quietly, "but this— changes things."

"I love ye, too," Elminster said. "It is one of the reasons I . . . stayed a maid. I did not want to change what we share."

She came around the fire then, and embraced him. "Elminster—or Elmara, or whoever you are—come and eat, one last time. Nothing can change the good work we've done together."

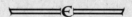

It was dark, and the fire had died down low. Myrjala was a shadow across the flames as she turned her head and asked quietly, "Where will you go?"

Elminster shrugged. "I know not . . . west to see the Calishar, mayhap."

"The Calishar? Take care, Elminster—" her voice caught on the unfamiliar name, forming it with difficulty "—for Ilhundyl the Mad Mage holds sway there."

"I know. It's why I'll go. There's a score I must settle there. I can't go through life leaving *everything* unfinished."

"Many do."

"I am not many, and I cannot." He stared into the fire for a long time. "I will miss ye, Lady . . . take care."

"Gods keep you safe, too, Elminster." Then they both dissolved in tears and reached for each other.

When they parted, the next morn, both of them were weeping.

Ilhundyl let the lions into the maze when he saw the intruder—but they froze in midsnarl as the intruder's spells caught them. The hawk-nosed mage who'd paralyzed the beasts strode on without even slowing, finding his way unerringly through the illusory walls and around portal-traps to stalk across the terrace before the Great Gate, toward the hidden door. Ilhundyl's lips thinned, and he spoke words he never thought he'd have to use.

Stone statues turned, creaking. Clouds of dust fell from their joints as lightnings leaped from their palms. The blue bolts leaped at the hawk-nosed man, who ignored them. The lightnings struck something unseen around the walking man and encircled it, crackling harmlessly.

One of Ilhundyl's long-fingered hands tapped the table before him. Then he raised the other hand, made a certain gesture, and muttered something. Golems stepped out of the solid stone walls of the Castle of Sorcery and lumbered toward the walking wizard. As they came, the lone intruder spoke an incantation. The air in front of the hawk-nosed stranger was suddenly full of whirling blades. In a flashing cloud, they spun over to strike sparks from the armored colossi—who strode stiffly and ponderously through the storm of steel.

Ilhundyl watched the scene expressionlessly, then leaned forward to ring a bell on his table. When a young woman in livery hurried in, face anxious, he said in calm, cold tones, "Order all the archers to the wall by the Great Gate. They are to bring down the intruder by any means necessary."

She hurried out as the golems closed in on the intruder, lifting massive arms to smash him like a rotten grape against the stones. The wizard raised his hands. Invisible forces cut a slice of stone away, severing one moving leg from its foot, and slowly, but with awesome, quickening force, the first golem fell.

The Castle of Sorcery rocked, and Ilhundyl started up from his seat in rage, in time to see the second golem fall over the broken remnants of the first, and topple in its turn.

Gods take this intruder! He was perilously close to the walls already. Where were those archers? And then arrows lashed on the terrace like hard-driven black hail, and the Mad Mage smiled as the wizard's body jerked, spun around, and fell, transfixed.

Ilhundyl's smile collapsed into a frown as the screaming body was suddenly upright again. Another arrow took it through the head, which flopped loosely, and the corpse reeled and fell headlong, only to appear upright again with no shaft standing out of its mouth. Two arrows sped into it and the body spun, legs kicking—to jerk erect again in different garb. . . .

"Stop!" Ilhundyl snarled. "Stop firing!" His hands stabbed for the bell, knowing it was too late. By the time his orders were heard and relayed, all the archers were dead. His foe was using some spell that switched one person or another, in a double teleport!

That was a spell he *had* to learn . . . this young mage must be taken alive. Or at least destroyed in a way that left his spellbook intact.

Ilhundyl strode out of the room and down the Wind Cavern, where smooth shapes of glass stood on all sides, pierced by many holes that sang mournful songs when the wind blew. Taking down this mage might cost him all of his Winged Hands—but it would be done, whatever the price. He could always make more.

He was still a few hurrying paces short of the archway that led into the north tower when the horned suit of armor beside it clanked down from its pedestal and strode toward him, raising its weapons. Ilhundyl spoke a soft word and turned one of the rings on his hand, then cast a spell with a few swift, snarled phrases. Acid burst out from between his fingers in a sphere of acrid purple flames that expanded as it flew. The hissing sphere crashed over the armor and spattered to the floor beyond. Smoke rose from flagstones as it ate away at them; the molten blobs that had been the armor crashed down into the widening pits in the stone, breaking into vapors and droplets.

Another suit of armor was already coming through the door from the next chamber. Ilhundyl sighed at this childishness and hurled his second—and last—acid sphere spell. There was a flash this time as the purple flames struck something in the air and rebounded on the master of the Calishar. Ilhundyl had time for a single pace back before the acid drenched him.

Smoke hissed, and Ilhundyl fell without a sound, dwindling into vapor rather than blood and bone. Out of the air on the far side of the gallery, the Mad Mage faded back into view, and said scornflilly, "Fool! Think yourself the only wizard in all Faerûn to use images and spells of deceit?"

He waved an imperious hand, and stone spikes suddenly erupted from the air to his right. He pointed, and obediently they flew toward the armored figure. Long before they reached it some force dragged them aside—to smash through the many-curved glass figures. Ilhundyl's wind sculptures toppled into ruin, and the Mad Mage's eyes blazed in fury.

"Seven months to fashion those!" he snarled. *"Seven months!"*

Rays of amber radiance leaped from the archwizard's outthrust hands toward the armored figure. His target abruptly vanished, and the rays stabbed past where it had been, to touch the far wall of the chamber. The stones of the wall seemed to boil briefly as the rays sheared through them, opening a large hole, and continued on across empty air to bore through the distant wall of the north tower in the same manner. Outside, an unseen guard shouted a startled warning to his fellows.

The furious ruler of the Calishar was still staring at the destruction he'd caused when the armored figure winked into view a little behind him and well to the right, at the spot the stone spikes had appeared from—and its armored fists swung down, striking apparently empty air with solid smacks. The visible Ilhundyl fell to the floor without a sound and winked out of existence. An instant later, the Mad Mage reappeared at the far end of the gallery in a blind, snarling fury. "You *dare—?*"

He growled out a stream of words that echoed and rolled with power, and the Castle of Sorcery shook around him. Impaling spikes shot up from the floor, transfixing the armored figure from below, and then with a thunderous roar, a score of stone blocks crashed down from the high ceiling and smashed the intruder flat. As the dust of their landings rolled lazily across the floor, wall panels opened all along the gallery. From behind the panels drifted three dead-looking, rotting beholders, eyestalks questing stiffly back and forth for a foe. A glowing cage on a chain plunged down from a ceiling trapdoor, burst open as its spell-glow faded, and six winged green serpents boiled out of it, jaws snapping angrily as they swooped around the gallery, seeking prey. Here and there on the gallery floor, stone blocks turned over with slow uneasiness to reveal glowing magical glyphs.

The hard-eyed Mad Mage waited with hands raised to unleash more destruction as the chamber settled into slow silence. The undead eye tyrants floated menacingly about, finding nothing to turn their beams on, and the flying snakes darted excitedly here and there. One snake dived at Ilhundyl, and he crisped it in the air with a single muttered word. Silence fell again. Perhaps he really had managed to destroy the intruder.

The Mad Mage spoke another spell to raise the stone blocks from the shattered armor. They drifted upward obediently—and then rose to one side. Ilhundyl's jaw dropped. He watched in horror as the blocks, undead beholders, snakes, glass shards, and all began to move in a slow spiral before him.

"Cease!" Ilhundyl cried, and called up the strongest shatter-spell he knew. The spiral's rotation faltered for one breath-stopping moment . . . and then resumed, quickening until things were whirling rapidly around the chamber.

Ilhundyl backed away, for the first time in years knowing the cold taste of fear. More wind-sculptures shattered as the aerial maelstrom swept blocks or undead beholders through them. Their shards glittered in a rising circle to join the spiral, now sweeping down the gallery at Ilhundyl.

The Mad Mage backed away, then turned and ran, hands flashing through hasty and intricate spell-passes. Abruptly there were running Ilhundyls all over the chamber, flickering here and there in a complex dance. The whirlwind swept them all up. One body was promptly dashed against a wall; it crumpled like a broken doll and was gone. Another Ilhundyl suddenly appeared on a balcony high in the gallery, and cast a glowing crystal down into the storm below. The gem flashed once—and in that flash of radiance it and all the whirling items vanished, leaving the chamber empty save for the shattered glass spires on their pedestals.

Ilhundyl looked down on them and said coldly, "Be revealed."

The hawk-nosed mage melted into view—on the balcony beside him, *inside* his protective spellshields!

Ilhundyl recoiled, frantically trying to think of a spell he could safely use against a foe so close. "Why have you come here?" he hissed.

The intruder's eyes met his own coldly. "Ye tricked me, hoping to send me to my death. Like the mages of Athalantar, ye rule by fear and brutal magical might, using thy spells to slay or maim folk—or entrap them in beast-shape."

"So? What do you want of me?"

"Such a question is more appropriately asked *before* attacking," Elminster replied dryly, and then answered, "Thy destruction. I would put an end to all mages who behave as ye do."

"Then you'll have to live a long, long time," said Ilhundyl softly, "and I've no interest in your doing so."

He spoke three words, his fingers moved—and lightning leaped from a shield set high on the far wall of the gallery. Its bright, many-stroked crackling web raked the balcony. Ilhundyl pulled at his magical shieldings as the blue-white bolts danced and spat around him, dragging them aside to expose his foe to the furious energies. The edge of the shield rolled back, lightnings snapping over it viciously, and the Mad Mage saw Elminster stagger.

The ruler of the Calishar roared in triumph and leveled his left hand to unleash a bolt from the ring on his middle finger. There was no way he could miss this upstart wizard, barely three paces away. His life-leeching bolt stabbed out—and rebounded!

Ilhundyl screamed as his own spell tore at his innards, and tried to flee, struggling toward the archway that led off the balcony. Then Elminster's hand touched the stone floor—and the balcony broke off and plunged down the wall. Ilhundyl fell with it, roaring out a desperate word.

A few feet from the floor, his magic took effect; their crashing plummet slowed to a gently drifting descent. In the tumult, neither man noticed a glowing, floating pair of eyes appear low down at one end of the gallery, to calmly survey the battle.

Ilhundyl turned to the wall and raised his hand again. Another ring winked. And the wall slowly sprouted a massive arm, reaching out for Elminster with stony fingers. Elminster spat out a spell, and the hand shuddered in a burst of force and rock shards that hurled the hawk-nosed mage out of the settling balcony. He skidded across the floor, toppling another glass sculpture.

Ilhundyl snarled out an incantation, stabbing his thumbs forward at Elminster. The prince felt himself plucked up from amid the glass and thrown across the room. El spread his hands in a grand, sweeping gesture, and an instant before he would have smashed with bone-shattering force into the gallery wall, the wall suddenly wasn't there any more. With a grinding rumble, the ceiling began to fall. Ilhundyl stared up at tumbling stone blocks for a moment, and then broke into a run, gabbling the words of another spell.

Outside the Castle of Sorcery, Elminster drifted to the ground, upright and alert. His feet touched the stones of the terrace, he turned toward the north tower, and then felt slashing pain as something unseen cut him across the ribs!

It felt like spreading fire! El sprang back, doubling up in agony, and threw up his hands to protect his face. The next sweep of the invisible blade took the tip off one of his fingers. He could see its edge now, a shimmering line of force edged with his own blood. Ilhundyl faded into view behind it, grinning, and slashed down with his conjured blade again at Elminster's hands.

"A handless man casts few spells," the Mad Mage laughed cruelly, chopping and slashing. Elminster hissed out a spell as he dodged and ducked, and with a wild, tortured shriek, the sorcerous blade shattered into bright stars of force.

The blast sent him rolling helplessly away, head ringing. El writhed and groaned. For a breath or two the hawk-nosed prince could do no more than lie on the stones twisting in pain.

Ilhundyl shuddered and wrung his hands, willing away the pain the blast had wrought in them. When he'd mastered control of his trembling fingers again, he raised a shield-spell around himself and stalked forward. His lips curved from a thin line of pain into a cold smile of anticipation.

When he was close enough to touch the writhing intruder, the Mad Mage carefully cast the most powerful and complex spell he knew—and leaned forward to hook one finger into Elminster's ear.

If the soul-drain succeeded, he would gain all the spells and knowledge this intruder possessed. Entering the helpless man's mind, Ilhundyl bore down through the roiling pain he found there, seeking to find and break this upstart's will. Instead, he felt his probe pounced on and slashed at. He threw back his head, hissing in pain, but did not break the contact . . . yet. It would take hours to memorize this spell again, and if his prisoner died, it would all be for nothing—or if the mage recovered, the fight would begin anew.

Suddenly he was falling, plunging into a dark void in the other man's mind, and out of nowhere and everywhere a blade of white flame was stabbing and cutting him, shearing through his very self. Screaming, Ilhundyl fell away from the sprawled mage, breaking contact. Gods, the pain! Shaking his head to clear it, he crawled away through a yellow haze.

When it cleared, he turned . . . and saw Elminster struggling to his own knees, vainly raking through his own gore to recover a ring with fingers that had been chopped away. Angrily, Ilhundyl hissed the words of a short, simple spell and stepped back to watch his foe die.

The spell manifested. Bony claws coalesced out of empty air into sudden, harsh reality, and swarmed over Elminster—a score or more of them, raking and gouging with needle-sharp talons.

Ilhundyl smiled as they did their gruesome work . . . and then his jaw dropped. They were fading away! The claws were ebbing back into the air, leaving the bloody wreck of a man still living.

"What befalls?" the Mad Mage angrily asked Faerûn at large as he strode forward.

"Doom," said a low voice from behind him. Ilhundyl whirled.

A dark-eyed woman was *growing* from his own front door, stepping smoothly out of the dark wood to confront him. She was tall and lithe, and wore robes of dark green. Black, liquid eyes under arched brows met his own ... and Ilhundyl saw his death in them. The Mad Mage was still stammering an incantation when white fire, brighter than anything he'd ever seen, leaped from one of her slim-fingered hands at him.

Ilhundyl stared helplessly at her beautiful, merciless face. And then the roaring flames swept into and through him, and her bone-white face and the sky behind it darkened in his failing gaze.

Through the blood dripping into his eyes, Elminster saw the Mad Mage swept away and consumed in a single roaring moment.

"Wha-What spell was that?" El croaked.

"No spell, but spellfire," Myrjala told him crisply. "Now get up, fool, before all Ilhundyl's rivals arrive to seize what they can. We must be gone by then."

She turned and blasted the Castle of Sorcery with that same all-consuming fire. The Great Gate vanished, and the halls beyond collapsed in flames.

Elminster struggled to his feet somehow, spitting blood. "But his magic! Lost, now, all—"

Myrjala turned back to him. The slim hands that had hurled magical fire an instant before now held a thick, battered old book. She thrust it into Elminster's mangled hands; the pain of the contact nearly made him drop it. "His important work is here—now we must go!"

Elminster's eyes narrowed as he looked at her; somehow her tone seemed different. But perhaps he was just too hurt to hear aright ... he nodded wearily.

Myrjala touched his cheek, and they were suddenly elsewhere: an echoing cavern. Fungi on its walls glowed a faint blue and green here and there.

Elminster stumbled and with an effort caught his balance, cradling the spellbook. "Where—are we?"

"One of my hideaways," Myrjala said, peering around alertly "This was once part of an elven city. We're deep under Nimbral, an island in the Great Sea."

Elminster looked around and then down at the book in his hands. When he raised his watery eyes to meet hers, they held a strange look. "Ye knew him?"

Myrjala's eyes were very dark. "I know many mages, Elminster," she said, almost warningly. "I've been around a long time ... and I did not live this long by recklessly challenging every archmage I heard of."

"Ye don't want me to go to Athalantar yet," Elminster said slowly, eyes on hers.

Myrjala shook her head. "You're not ready. Your magic is still unsubtle, brutal, and predictable—doomed to fail when greater force contests against you."

"Teach me wisdom, then," Elminster said, swaying on his feet.

She turned away. "Separate paths, remember?"

"Ye were watching over me," Elminster said to her back, desperately. "Following me ... why?"

Myrjala turned back to him slowly. Tears glimmered in her eyes. "Because ... I love you," she whispered.

"Stay with me, then," Elminster said. The book fell forgotten from his hands, but it took all his strength to stride forward and put his ravaged arms around her. "Teach me."

She hesitated, her dark eyes seeming to look deep into him.

Then, almost shuddering, she nodded.

A dark, triumphant fire rose in his eyes as their lips met.

Mirtul was a dry, windy month in the Year of the Wandering Leucrotta—especially in the hot, dusty lands of the east.

Elminster stood hard-eyed atop a wind-scoured cliff glaring down at a castle of the sorcerer-kings far below. To reach it, he and Myrjala had ridden for a tenday or more past dead slaves stinking in the sun.

Here at last were their slayers. Through his eagle-eyes spell, Elminster watched bloody whips rise and fall in that courtyard, laying open the bodies of the last slaves. All life had fled already, but the sorcerers flailed on, weaving an evil magic with the fading life-forces of the men and women they'd slain.

In anger, El lashed out with spells of his own devising. The magics fell through the air in a bright web, and Elminster stepped off the cliff to follow them. He was striding along on empty air over the castle when it began to topple. He stopped to watch, standing angrily above the dust, screams, and tumult.

Something rose up out of a shattered window, with men in robes riding it. Elminster fired a bolt down to blast them. The enchanted flyer shattered amid explosive brightness; the men on it jerked like flung dolls and fell back into the ruins. They did not rise again. Stones tumbled to a halt, and the rumble of their falling slowly died. When the dust had settled, Elminster turned, face grim, and walked back through the air to join Myrjala on the heights.

Her dark eyes lifted from the ruined castle, and she asked softly, "And was that the wisest, least wasteful thing to do?"

Anger glinted in Elminster's eyes. "Aye, if it'll make the next band of fools think twice about using such fell magic."

"Yet some wizards'll do so anyway. Will you murder them too?"

Elminster shrugged. "If need be. Who is to stop me?"

"Yourself." Myrjala looked down at the castle again. "Reminds one of Heldon, doesn't it?" she asked quietly, not looking at him.

Elminster opened his mouth to refute her—and then closed his mouth again in silence, watching her step calmly off the height and walk steadily away, treading softly on the air. His gaze fell to the ruin below, and he shivered in sudden shame. Sighing, El turned from what he had wrought—and then looked helplessly down again at the castle. He did not know any spells to put it back up again.

It was a warm night in early Flamerule, in the Year of the Chosen. Elminster awoke drenched with sweat, flinging himself upright to stare with wild eyes at the moon. Myrjala sat up in bed beside him, hair flowing around her shoulders, eyes dark with worry. "You were shouting," she said.

Elminster reached for her, and she folded him into her arms as a mother cradles a frightened child.

"I saw Athalantar," El whispered, staring into the night. "I was walking the streets of Hastarl, and there were sneering wizards wherever I looked. And when I stared at them, they fell over dead . . . terror on their faces. . . ."

Myrjala held him and said calmly, "It sounds as if you're ready for Athalantar at last."

Elminster turned to look at her. "And if I live through purging it of magelords—what then? This vow has driven me for so long . . . what should I do with my life?"

"Why, rule Athalantar, of course."

"Now that the throne comes into my reach," Elminster said slowly, "I find myself wanting it less and less."

The arms around him tightened. "That's good," Myrjala said quietly "I've grown weary waiting for you to grow up."

Elminster looked at her and frowned. "Outgrowing blind vengeance? I suppose . . . why go through with it all, then?"

Myrjala looked at him steadily in the darkness, her dark eyes large and mysterious. "For Athalantar. For your dead mother and father—and all who lived and laughed in Heldon before the dragon came down on them. For the folk in the taproom of the Unicorn's Horn, and those in Narthil . . . and for your outlaw comrades who died in the Horn Hills."

Elminster's lip's thinned. "We'll do it," he said with quiet determination. "Athalantar shall be free of magelords. I swear before Mystra: I'll do this or die in the trying."

Myrjala said nothing as she held him, but he could feel her smile.

PART U

KING

FIFTEEN
AND THE PREY IS MAN

In mighty towers they quake with fright
for the man who kills mages is out tonight.

BENDOGLAER SYNDRATH, BARD OF BARROWHILL,
FROM THE BALLAD *DEATH TO ALL MAGES*
YEAR OF THE BENT COIN

Eleasias was a wet month that year. On the fourth successive stormy night,
Myrjala and Elminster were thankful to duck out of the rain into a tavern
on a muddy back street in Launtok.

"That's the last of the Athalantan envoys put to flight. Their masters have
certainly noticed us by now," Myrjala said with some satisfaction as they settled
into a corner booth with their tankards.

"On to the magelords, then," Elminster said, rubbing his hands together
thoughtfully. He leaned forward. "Ye've warned me often against charging in
with fireballs blazing in both hands . . . so do we spread a few rumors of plots
and unrest, sit back in hiding, and let them kill each other for a while, trying to
see who'll sit in the best spell-tower?"

Myrjala shook her head. "While we sat, they'd destroy Athalantar along
with each other." She sipped her ale, winced, and gave the tankard a dark look.
"Besides, that'd work only if we'd destroyed the most powerful archwizards,
the leaders of the magelords . . . thus far, we've only foiled the buffoons and the
most reckless fools."

"What next, then?" Elminster asked, taking a deep drink of ale.

Myrjala arched one shapely eyebrow. "This is your vengeance."

Ehminster set down his tankard and licked foam from the beginnings of
a mustache. Myrjala looked amused, but her companion was intent on his
thoughts.

"I never thought I'd feel this," he said slowly, "but after Ilhundyl and those
slave-sorcerers . . . I've had a bellyful of vengeance." He looked up. "So how
should we work it? Attack Athalgard, trying to slay all the magelords we can
before they know a foe's come calling?"

Myrjala shrugged and told her tankard, "Some folk get a thrill out of
destroying things. With most, the delight fades quickly. The gods don't suffer
the others to live all that long—if a mage goes about just hurling spells, he

eventually runs into someone else doing the same thing, with just a few more spells up his sleeve."

She lifted her eyes to meet Elminster's. "If you tried a hurl-all-fireballs attack on the magelords, bear in mind how much countryside you'd destroy—and all of it'd be Athalantar, the realm you're fighting for. They won't all obligingly challenge you one after another, each one politely awaiting his turn to die."

Elminster sighed. "Stealth and years in the doing, then." He sipped from his tankard. "So tell me how ye think we should go about this. Ye're the elder of us two; I'll do as ye say."

Myrjala shook her head. "It's past time to think for yourself, Elminster; look at me as your teacher no more, but an ally in your fight."

El looked at her grave expression, nodded slowly, and said, "Ye're right, as always. Well . . . if we're to avoid huge spell battles, magelords must be lured into situations where we can fight them alone and they won't be able to call on all their fellows for aid. We'll have to lay some traps—and if just the two of us go up against them, sooner or later we *will* end up in a mighty spell contest. If we and the magelords both hurl flames at each other, there's going to be a fire."

Myrjala nodded. "And so?" she asked quietly.

"We need allies to fight with us," El said, "but who?" He stared at the table in frowning silence.

Myrjala took up her tankard again and stared thoughtfully at her reflection in it. "You've said more than once you wanted fitting justice to befall the magelords," she said carefully "What could be more right than calling on the elves of the High Forest, and the thieves in Hastarl, and Helm and his knights? 'Tis their realm you're fighting to free, too."

Elminster started to shake his head, then grew very still, as his eyes slowly narrowed. "Ye're right," he said in a small voice. "Why am I always so blind?"

"Lack of attention; I've told you before," Myrjala said crisply—and when he looked at her in irritation, she grinned at him and extended gentle fingers to stroke one of his hands. After a moment, El smiled back at her.

"I'll have to travel about the realm cloaked in magic and speak to them," he said slowly, thinking it through, "because they know ye not." He sipped ale again. "And as a magelord may notice me and 'tis never wise to reveal all one's strengths too soon, ye'd best stay out of sight."

The dark-eyed sorceress nodded. "Yet in case the magelords come down on you in earnest, I'd best accompany you—in other shapes than my own, of course—to fight at your side if need be."

El smiled at her. "I'd not want to be parted from ye now, to be sure. Should we try to raise the common folk of the realm to our cause?" Then he answered his own question. "Nay, they'd flee before the first spell hurled against them, and once roused would strike out blindly until as much ruin is spread across the realm as if enraged magelords were using spells without restraint . . . and whether we won or lost, they'd die by the hundreds, like sheep led to slaughter."

Myrjala nodded. "You were first trained in magic by the elves . . . they would seem the most important allies to gain."

El frowned. "They use their magic to aid, nurture, and reshape, not to blast things in battle."

Myrjala lifted her shoulders in a shrug. "If all you're seeking in allies is folk to stand beside you and add battle-spells to your own, much of the realm *will* be riven in the struggle. You need to find folk with strengths you lack . . . and their decision to aid you or not will shape everything; you need to know if they'll stand with you before you contact the others. Moreover, you know where to find the elves . . . with less likelihood of a magelord watching than in Hastarl or the Horn Hills."

Elminster nodded. "Good sense. When should we begin?"

"Now," Myrjala replied crisply

They traded grins. A moment later, two tankards settled onto an empty table. The tavernkeeper, frowning anxiously, hurried over to the sound—and glumly collected the two tankards from the bare board. They rattled.

He peered in. A silver coin lay at the bottom of each. He brightened, shrugged, and tipped the coins, sticky with beerfoam, into his hand. Juggling them, he headed back for the bar. These wizards' coins'd spend as well as any . . . and as fast, more's the pity . . .

El stopped when he came to the little knoll in the heart of the High Forest, knelt and murmured a prayer to Mystra, and then sat down on the flat stone beside the little pool. Almost immediately his spell-shield flickered as something unseen—an elf, no doubt—tested it, seeking to learn who he was. El stood, looking around at the duskwood, shadowtop, and blueleaf trees that pressed close about the knoll. "Well met!" he called cheerfully and sat down again.

In patient silence he waited, so long a time that even an elf could grow restive. From the gloom beneath the trees strode a silent elf in mottled green, a strung bow in his hand. His face was still, but his eyes were not friendly.

"Magelords aren't welcome here," he said, setting a shaft to his bow.

Elminster made no move. "I am a mage, but no magelord," he replied calmly.

The elf did not lower his bow. "Who else would know of this place?" As he spoke, seven more elven archers stepped out of the trees all around the knoll. The points of their aimed arrows glowed a vivid blue—too much magic for even the strongest shield to withstand.

"I dwelt here a year and more," El replied, "learning magic."

The silvery eyes hardened. "Not so," came the swift reply. "Speak truth, man, if you would live!"

"Yet I dwelt here as I told ye, and what is more, six elves swore to aid me should I try to destroy the magelords."

The elf's eyes narrowed. "I swore such aid, but to a woman, not to a man."

"I am that woman," Elminster said firmly, and kept to his seat amid the merry laughter that followed.

Then he looked mildly around at their scoffing faces. "Ye use magic mightier than most mages but don't believe a wizard can take the shape of a man or a maid?"

The elf's eyes flickered. "Not can't—won't," came his reply. "Humans never do such things for more than a night's lark, or a desperate escape. 'Tis not in their natures to be so strong in themselves."

Elminster spread his empty hands slowly "Tell Braer—Baerithryn—that I am stronger now than I was then . . . and the master of a few more spells."

The elf's eyes flickered again before he turned his head. "Go," he said to one of the other archers, "and bring Baerithryn to us. If this man is who he claims to be, Baerithryn will know it—and tell us all we need to know of him, too." The archer turned and slipped back into the mushroom-studded dimness under the trees.

El nodded and peered into the depths of the crystal-clear pool. For a moment, he thought he saw a pair of thoughtful eyes looking up at him . . . but no, there was nothing there. He sat calmly, ignoring the arrows trained tirelessly on him, until his spell-shield flickered again. He let it drop deliberately, and immediately felt a feather-light touch in his mind. Then the probing contact was gone, and Braer was striding out from under the trees, looking just as he'd done when El had last seen him.

"Time seems to have wrought some small changes in you, Elmara," he said dryly.

"Braer!" El sprang to his feet and rushed down the slope to embrace his old teacher, who kissed him as if he'd still been a maid and then slipped free of Elminster's arms and said, "Easy there, Prince! Elves are far more refined—and delicate—than men."

They laughed together, and the watching elves put away their shafts. Braer looked keenly into Elminster's eyes—and then nodded as if he'd seen something there. "You've come for our aid against the magelords. Sit and tell us your desires."

When they returned to the stone, El found himself surrounded by almost a score of silently watching elves. He looked around at them, found no answering smile to his own, and drew a deep breath. "Well," he began—but got no farther.

The elf who'd first challenged him held up a hand. "First, Prince, be aware that Braer and we who pledged to thee hold it our duty to do whatever you ask of us . . . but we are reluctant indeed to hazard others of the People. Outside the forest, elves are all too easily slain, and when we die, so do the last of our folk in this fair corner of Faerûn. Men—even mages—spring up like so many weeds in spring. Elves are rarer flowers . . . and so the more precious. Do not expect a marching army, or a score of elven archmages flying at your shoulder."

Elminster nodded and looked at Baerithryn. "Braer, d'ye feel the same way?"

His old teacher inclined his head. "I would not like to lead a march on Hastarl under the open skies of day, with mounted hosts of armsmen and dragon-riding magelords waiting to harry us . . . that is not our way of war. What have you in mind?"

"That you shield folk—primarily myself and another mage, but also a few knights and street folk of Hastarl—from slaying spells cast by the magelords . . . and perhaps a few seeking and farspeaking magics too. Shield us, and we'll fight."

"How powerful are you?" one of the archers asked. "There are a lot of magelords, and it would be folly indeed to support you in an attack on Athalgard . . . only to find ourselves beset by all the angry wizards after you've fought one or two—and then fallen."

"I destroyed the archmage who ruled the Calishar not so very long ago," El said calmly.

"We've heard several tales as to how he met his end—even the magelords have claimed to have worked his destruction, though they say several of them had to work together to do it," said another elf. "With respect, we must see your powers for ourselves."

El did not sigh. "What sort of a test d'ye have in mind?"

"Slay a magelord for us," another elf said firmly, and there was a murmured chorus of agreement.

"Any magelord?"

"One—Taraj, he's called—keeps watch over our forest and amuses himself by taking beast-shape to hunt. He slays for the love of killing, and mauls not only his prey, but any creatures of the forest he meets. He seems to have some protection against our spells and arrows. If you could destroy Taraj, most of the People would feel beholden to you . . . and you'd gain more aid than the bows and veiling spells of a handful of foresworn."

"Take me to where Taraj hunts, and I will destroy him," Elminster promised. "What does he like to hunt?"

"Men," Braer replied quietly, as he set off down the slope into the forest. Without ceremony the other elves followed. Elminster rolled his eyes once, but kept pace among them, feeling a strange exultation rising in him. The familiar weight of the Lion Sword bumped against his chest, and El's fingers sought it and gripped it almost fiercely At last—at long last—the scouring of Athalantar had begun.

"Release him," the magelord ordered, swirling the dregs of the wine in the depths of his goblet.

"Sir," the servant said with a bow and hurried away. Taraj watched him go and smiled. He was the magelord who'd come the farthest to rifle in this splendid land of forests and grassgirt hills . . . lovely hunting country. If only Murghôm had been like this, he'd never have to endure these accursed winters.

He went to the window to watch the terrified peddler from far Luthkant flee across the courtyard into the brush beyond. Sometimes he hunted his prisoners as if they were stags, felling them with lances hurled from horseback. He scorned armor, but always rode shielded with warding spells. Today though, he felt like a beast run. He'd take the shape of a lion, perhaps, or . . . yes, a forest cat! 'Panther,' they were called back home.

Taraj set down the empty goblet, threw off his robe, and strode naked into his spell-chamber to study the shape-change spell. It would give the man more time to run.

The spell coiled and burned comfortably in his mind. Taraj felt the same quickening excitement he always did when a hunt was about to begin. He bowed to his reflection in the wall-glass. "Taraj Hurlymm from far Murghôm, magelord and cruel man," he introduced himself to an imaginary feasting-company, smirking. His image smirked back, looking just as satisfied as he was. Taraj winked and moved his arms so the corded muscles of his shoulders rippled. He admired them for a moment, then slid on a robe and rapped with his knuckles on a wall gong. The servant was slow; Taraj told himself to remember to rake her with a claw when he returned, to put a little fear into her.

"See that a feast awaits me at my return," he said, "at moonrise. And at least four women I've not seen before, to share it."

He waved a hand in dismissal, and watched her bow and hurry away. Well, now . . . make her this night's fifth consort, and teach her fear that way. Being abed with a man who can change his shape has its own delights—and dangers.

Taraj grinned and strode down the steps to the garden. He liked to begin every hunt here, under the watchful statue of the Beastlord. As usual, he hung his robe over its snarling head and strolled down the many-flowered grassy paths, speaking the spell slowly, savoring the moment when his body would flow, surge, and change. The moment came. Teeth lengthened to fangs, thighs sank and thickened, shoulders shifted powerfully, and a glossy black panther leaped away into the tall grasses at the end of the garden.

At the garden door, the watching servant shivered. The magelord liked to hunt down and devour men who'd displeased him . . . and deal with women in other ways. She was sure he'd withdrawn from the intrigues of Hastarl to make his home here in far Dalniir at the edges of the realm because it offered him a countryside to hunt in. That peddler was doomed, and any woodcutters or hunters her master met with, too. She hoped he'd find none, and be a long, wearying time at his chase.

She sighed and went in to order the feast made ready . . . and then to the south wing to personally choose the maids who might die tonight. More than once she'd seen that bed and the carpet beneath it awash in blood and torn to shreds . . . sometimes with a gnawed foot or other remnant left tauntingly for the staff to find. She shuddered and prayed silently to whatever gods might be watching that Taraj Hurlymm would meet his own doom this night.

Folk would pray much harder to the gods, she thought to herself as she got up off her knees, if they gave proof that they listened to the fervent desires of mortals more often. Tonight, for instance.

She sighed. That peddler was doomed.

The Calishite's fine silk shirt was soaked through with sweat; it stuck to him, dark and slick, as he puffed wearily up a slope, forced a way through bushes that clawed and tore at his finery, and hurried on, gasping for breath. The man wasn't in very fine form . . . and now, covered with sweat and grime and with his long mustache drooping with sweat and smudged with dust, the magelord liked his looks even less.

The man's appearance had been the reason Taraj had ordered this trader seized in the first place. That and the appeal of the exotic; merchants from as far away as Luthkant found Athalantar seldom and ventured out of Hastarl even more rarely. This exotic prey, however, didn't look to be able to provide him with much sport at all . . . already the trader was wobbling along in exhaustion, his breath coming in fast, sobbing gasps.

Skulking along a ridge not far behind the terrified man, Taraj decided he was becoming increasingly bored. Time to make his kill.

He bounded down into the brush, a sleek black panther feeling fast and deadly and alive! Exulting in his power, he leaped across a narrow, deep gully, his paws scrabbling in crumbling earth for one exciting moment on the far side before they gripped . . . and then he was safely across and into the thicket beyond.

Bursting out of cover atop a bank, he soared right over the Luthkantan, who howled in fear and snatched out a belt knife, slashing uselessly at the air, well in his wake.

So that was the only fang the man had? Well, then . . . Taraj turned, sleek coat rippling, and rushed back at the man, dead leaves rustling as his racing paws hurled them aside.

The Calishite dodged, eyes wide and white with terror, slashed wildly at Taraj's nose—and then turned and ran.

Taraj gave him a throaty snarl and bounded after him. The man heard and spun around to prevent being hamstrung, that tiny blade gleaming again as he brandished it desperately. Taraj snarled and kept coming, not slowing . . . and the terrified man backed away.

After a few hurried, unseeing paces, of course, he stumbled on something underfoot, and fell hard on his behind. Taraj leaped at him, jaws opening wide for that first playful bite, but the man kicked out with frantic savagery—and the magelord felt sudden tearing pain. He snarled and recoiled, bounding away and then whirling back to face his victim.

Gods curse the man! The trader's boots had suddenly sprouted toe daggers. Vicious little blades; one gleamed at him as the exhausted man stayed on his back, feet up—and the other was wet and dark with Taraj's blood.

The magelord snarled again and loped off into the nearest tall grass. Dragon at the gate! You couldn't even trust fat Calishite merchant traders to fight fair these days! Well, you'd never been able to, he admitted wryly as the panther's body fell away, flowing and changing again. A brief visit to the Luthkantan in the shape of an acid-spitting snake should do away with the man's weapons so he could be killed slowly and enjoyably afterward. The snake reared up, coiling experimentally, shaking as the magelord settled into this new shape.

A black crow that had been scudding along unseen behind the panther dived earthward, starting to change even before it struck the grassy ground below.

Something huge and dark rose up out of the grass where it landed, batlike wings unfolding and long tail switching . . . a black dragon crouched amid the crushed grass, leaning forward over the suddenly hissing, coiling snake.

The snake spat. The smoking acid struck the dragon's snout and dripped; black dragons are never harmed by acids. The dragon smiled slowly and opened its own jaws. The acid that streamed from the dragon's maw consumed a tree and left the snake itself smoking and writhing in the scorched grasses beyond, throwing coils about in its agony. The dragon strode forward, slowly, heavily . . . and tauntingly.

From somewhere in the trees ahead came a despairing scream as the Calishite trader saw the dragon, and crashing sounds as he struggled through trees and thick brush in frantic flight.

The snake grew larger and darker, and wings began to sprout from it. As its shape built and stretched, it grew a human hand and mouth for an instant. The ring flashed, and the mouth cried, "Kadeln! Kadeln! Aid me! By our pact, *aid me!*"

The dragon lumbered forward, extending claws to rend the snake that was rapidly becoming another black dragon. Another pace, and another . . . and the dragon that was Elminster reached out and slashed with one black-taloned claw to rend still-forming scales. Blood spattered, and the magelord-turned-dragon squalled in pain.

Elminster extended his head to bite down hard on the other dragon's neck and end this wizard for good—but suddenly a mage stood beside the still-growing dragon, where the only crushed grass had been a moment before. Elminster had a glimpse of this new magelord's dark, glittering eyes as he reared and backed hastily away. The wizard was already casting a spell; there was no time to shift shape into something else.

Elminster beat his wings once to hurl the man off his feet and ruin his spell, but tree limbs got in the way. He was still struggling to lunge forward and bite down on the newcomer when something streaked from the mage's outthrust hand, and roaring fire erupted on all sides and rolled over him.

El's curse of pain came out as a rumble as he hastily backed away, turned, and lashed out with his tail so the magelord had to dive ingloriously into the dirt to avoid being struck. El grunted and bounded aloft.

This body was heavy and ungainly, but the large wings beat strongly. He put some effort into flight, and the wind was whistling past his head when he turned and plunged back down through the air in a dive, waiting for just the right moment to spit acid.

The other dragon was almost fully formed now, but thrashing about in pain, all tangled up under the trees. El could deal with this fire-hurling wizard first!

Snarling, Elminster roared down out of the sky, teeth flashing.

The wizard's hands were making complicated passes—and then he leaped back to watch in triumph ... and Elminster knew sudden fear. He tried to unfold a wing and veer away—but couldn't! His wings were bound by magic!

Helplessly he plunged down into the trees, bracing himself for the crash he knew would come. The wind whistled past him. And then he saw his true doom. Before him a shimmering wall of bright, swirling colors was growing; a rainbow of deadly magic directly in his path. El could only turn his eyes in horror to look at the magelord who stood watching as he fell to death.

"Aid me, Mystra," he whispered, as the swirling colors rushed up to meet him.

Kadeln Olothstar, magelord of Athalantar, laughed coldly. "Ah, I love a good fight! Taming a mageling, too! My thanks, Taraj!"

The dragon hurtled helplessly down into his prismatic wall. Kadeln threw up a hand to shield his eyes from the blast he knew would come as the huge beast passed through his spell and they destroyed each other.

It came. The world rocked, and a blinding flash clawed at his eyes even through his tightly shut lids. Kadeln landed hard on his back and spat a curse at the gods for putting a hard tree root under his spine. Then he blinked his eyes until he could see again and rolled to his feet. Broken trees and smoking grass surrounded him, with nary a dragon in sight ... and stumbling sightlessly out of the smoke came a fat Calishite in tattered silks, a dagger clutched in one trembling hand.

Hah! He could even rob Taraj of his quarry this night! Kadeln smiled a thin, cruel smile and raised his hand to slay the man. It would take only the least of his spells. Then a dark form melted out of the air in front of him—Taraj, tattered and blackened with soot.

"Out of my way, Hurlymm," Kadeln said coldly, but his dazed fellow magelord seemed not to hear him ... perhaps an accident might befall Taraj here, with no watching eyes to speak later of Kadeln's treachery. Or would it be wise to fell this lazy, blood-hungry idiot, and have perhaps a stronger mage rise to take his place in the councils of magelords?

Kadeln made his decision, sighed, and stepped around the bemused Taraj, raising his hand again to hurl a death bolt at the sobbing merchant. As he passed, the dark tatters seemed to ripple. Kadeln Olothstar had been a magelord for many years. He turned to see what shape Taraj was taking—just in case.

Cold blue-gray eyes swam out of the melting form to meet his own, around a hawk-beak of a nose, and a mouth that smiled at him without warmth or mirth.

"Greetings, Magelord," that mouth said, as one dark arm rose up to strike aside Kadeln's raised hand. The dark form's other arm streaked up to his mouth. "I am Elminster. In the name of my father Prince Elthryn and my mother Princess Amrythale, I slay thee."

Kadeln was gabbling the words of a desperate spell as the stranger, still smiling that steely smile, thrust a finger into the magelord's mouth. Flame burst forth in a sphere that rolled down the magelord's throat, and found no ready room to expand.

A moment later, Kadeln Olothstar burst apart in flames that briefly outshone the sun . . . and then swiftly died away into drifting smoke. Silence fell—followed a moment later by the Calishite, who gave a despairing moan as his eyes rolled up and he thudded limply to the scorched turf.

The lady who glided into view atop the nearest ridge made a face at the blood covering Elminster. He looked up at her quickly, raising a hand to blast another foe if need be—and then relaxed, and called, "My thanks—again—for my life?"

Myrjala smiled as she came up to him and spread her hands. "What, after all, are friends for?"

"How did ye do it this time?" El asked, striding forward to embrace her. She whispered something and made a small sign with one hand—and the magelord's gore was abruptly gone. Elminster looked down, shook his head, and then wrapped his arms around her and kissed her.

"Let me breathe, young lion," Myrjala said at last, pulling her head back. "To answer you—I used that spell you're so fond of, switching folk about. Taraj was the dragon who struck the wall-spell, and I guided you into his semblance."

"I needed ye after all," Elminster said, looking into her dark, mysterious eyes.

Myrjala smiled at him. "There's much more to do for Athalantar yet, O Prince . . . and I need you whole to do it."

"I'm—losing my thirst for killing magelords," Elminster said. Myrjala's arms tightened around him.

"I understand, and respect you the more for that, El—but once begun, we must take them all . . . or all we'll achieve for the folk of Athalantar is changing the names and faces of those who rule them iron-hard. Is that all you want to have done to avenge your mother and father?"

When Elminster looked up at her, his eyes were bright and hard. "Who's the next magelord we should slay?" he snapped.

Myrjala almost smiled. "Seldinor," she said, turning away.

"Why he, of them all?"

Myrjala turned back. "You have been a woman. When I tell you his latest schemes, you will understand why, better than most brash young men who call themselves wizards."

Elminster nodded, not smiling. "I was afraid ye'd say something like that."

Elves were suddenly all around them, seeming to melt out the trees. Braer met Elminster's eyes, and asked, "Who is this lady mage?"

Myrjala spoke for herself. "Al hond ebrath, uol tath shantar en tath lalala ol hond ebrath."

El looked at her. "What did ye say?"

"A true friend, as the trees and the water are true friends," Myrjala translated softly, her eyes very dark.

The elf who'd first challenged Elminster by the pool said, "A proud boast, lady, for one who lives and then is gone, while the trees and streams endure forever."

Myrjala turned her head, as tall and as regal as any elf and said, "You may be surprised at my longevity Ruvaen, as others of your folk have been, before."

Ruvaen drew back a pace, frowning. "How is it that you know my name? Who—?"

"Peace," Braer said. "Such things are best spoken of in private, one to another. Now we have much to plan and prepare. The test has been set and passed. Elminster may not have prevailed alone, but two magelords are no more, not one. Do any challenge this?"

Silence answered him, and he turned wordlessly to Ruvaen. The archer looked at Braer, nodded, and then said to Elminster, "The People will fight at your side for Athalantar, if you hold to the pledge you made to us when we swore aid to you."

"I will," Elminster said, and extended his hand.

After a long moment, Ruvaen took it, and they clasped forearms firmly, as one warrior to another. Around them, the gathered elves of the High Forest shouted in exultation—the loudest sound of celebration any elf of Athalantar had made in many a year.

Old, wise eyes watched the elves and humans dwindle into the depths of the crystal, and then slowly fade. What to do?

Aye, what? The lad was just one more young spell weaver with glory in his eyes, but the woman. . . . He'd not seen spellmastery like that since . . . his eyes narrowed, and then he shrugged.

There was no time for idle memories. There never is.

He had to warn everyone, and then s—but no. No. Let these two destroy Seldinor first.

Sixteen
When Mages Go to War

A star rushes past, to crash upon the shore
But the first of many many more
Stoke the fire and stout bar the door
For this is the night mages go to war.

Angarn Dunharp
from the ballad *When Mages Go to War*
Year of the Sword and Stars

Leaves rustled. At that slightest of sounds, Helm whirled, hand going to hilt. Out from behind the tree stepped the silent elven warrior he'd come to know as Ruvaen, the gray cloak that was so hard to see swirling around him. There was another elf with him. Their still faces somehow betrayed a mood darker than usual.

"What news?" Helm asked simply. None of the elves or the knights were wont to waste words.

Ruvaen held out something that filled his hand—something clear and smooth-sided and colorless, like a fist-sized diamond. A few clumps of moss clung to it. Helm looked down at it and raised his brows in an unspoken question.

"A scrying crystal. Used by human wizards," Ruvaen said flatly.

"The magelords," Helm said grimly "Where did ye find this?"

"In a dell, not far from here," said the other elf, pointing off into the forest gloom.

"One of your men hid it under moss," Ruvaen added. "When he wasn't using it?"

Helm Stoneblade let out his breath in a long sigh. "So they may know all our plans and be laughing at us now."

The two elves did not need to answer. Ruvaen put the crystal gently into Helm's callused hand, touched his shoulder, and said, "We'll wait above, in the trees . . . should you need us."

Helm nodded, looking down at the crystal in his hand. Then he lifted his head to stare into the forest. Who most often went off into the woods to relieve himself in that direction?

His battered face changed, hardening. Helm thrust the crystal into the breast of his tunic, turned, and made a short barking sound. One of his men, cutting up a deer some distance away, looked up. Their eyes met through the trees, and Helm nodded. The man turned and barked in his turn.

Soon they were all gathered around: the score or so knights he'd brought with him into the depths of the High Forest. All who still dared swing a blade in defiance of the magelords, clinging to the thin shield of elven mystery and providing the Fair Folk a front line of blades and bows to keep the woodcutter's axes from hewing out a new and larger Athalantar unopposed.

The magic of the elves cloaked them from the wizards who ruled Athalantar, but was ill suited to spell battle . . . beyond quenching fires and hiding Folk, that is. The threat of greater elven spells had kept the magelords largely at bay, thus far, at least. Lending Helm time to plan a rising that might—just might, with the gods' own luck—shatter this rule of wizards, and give him back the carefree Athalantar he'd fought for and loved, so long ago. So they'd fought, by night and the quick blade, and vanished back into the trees or perished under spell-torment, while the long years dragged on and Helm became ever more desperate . . . as the Athalantar of his youth slowly faded away.

The hard winters and the dead friends had hardened him and taught him patience. This crystal, now, changed things. If the magelords knew their numbers, names, schemes, and camps, they'd have to strike swiftly, now, or not at all . . . to have any chance at anything more than an unmarked grave and feeding the wolves.

He waited, silent, stone-faced, until the most restless of his men—Anauviir, of course—spoke. "Aye, Helm, what is it?"

Wordlessly, Helm turned to Halidar, holding out the scrying crystal. Halidar's face went white. He sprang to his feet, whirling to flee—and then gasped and sagged slowly back against Helm. The old knight stood unmoving as the traitor slid slowly down his chest to tumble onto the forest floor. Anauviir's dagger stood out of Halidar's throat, just beneath his contorted mouth. Helm bent to pull it out without a word, wiped it clean, and handed it back to its owner. Halidar had always been quick . . . and Anauviir had always been swifter. Helm held up the crystal for them all to see.

"The magelords have been watching over us," he said flatly. "Mayhap for years." Faces were pale all around him now. "Ruvaen," Helm asked, holding the crystal up, "have ye any use for this?"

Some of his men looked up, involuntarily, though by now they all knew they'd see nothing but leaves and branches, as a quiet, musical voice replied, "Properly used, it can burn out one magelord's mind."

There was an approving murmur, and Helm tossed the crystal straight up, into the branches overhead. It did not come down.

Hand still raised, Helm looked around at his men. Dirty, dark-eyed, and armed like the sort of mercenary bodyguards short, fat men hire to give them grandeur. They looked back at him, haggard and grim. Helm loved them all. If he had another forty blades such as these, he could carve himself out a new Athalantar, magelords or no magelords. But he did not. Forty blades too few, he thought, not for the first time. Nay—forty-one, now . . .

"Stand easy, knights," Ruvaen's lilting voice came unexpectedly from the trees above them. "A man approaches who would speak with you. He means no harm."

Helm looked up, startled. The elves never suffered other humans to venture this far into the woods. . . . And then something faded into view behind a nearby tree. Anauviir saw it even as Helm did and hissed warningly as he raised his blade. Then the shadowy figure stepped forward and mists of magic fell away from it.

The old knight's jaw dropped.

"Well met, Helm," said a voice he'd never thought to hear again.

Out of sight for so long . . . surely the lad had died at the hand of some magelord or other . . . but no. . . . Helm swallowed, lurched, and then went to one knee, proffering his sword as he did so. There were mutters of amazement from his men.

"Who's this, Helm?" Anauviir asked sharply, blade up, peering at the thin, hawk-nosed newcomer. Only a wizard or an upperpriest could step out of empty air like that.

"Rise, Helm," Elminster said quietly, putting a hand on the old knight's forearm.

The old knight got up, turned to his men, and said, "Kneel if you be a true knight of Athalantar . . . for this is Elminster son of Elthryn, the last free prince of the realm!"

"A magelord?" someone asked doubtfully

"No," Elminster said quietly. "A wizard who needs your help to destroy the magelords."

They stared at him unmoving—until, one by one, they caught Helm's furious glare, and went to their knees.

Elminster waited until the last knee—Anauviir's—touched the leaf-strewn ground, and then said, "Rise, all of ye. I am prince of nothing at the moment, and I need allies, not courtiers. I've learned magic enough to defeat any magelord, I believe—but I know that when any magelord gets into trouble, he'll call on another . . . and in a breath or two I'll have forty or more of them on my hands."

There were mirthless chuckles, and the knights unconsciously moved forward. Helm saw it in their faces and felt it himself: for the first time in years, real hope.

"Forty magelords is too many for me," Elminster went on, "and they command far too many armsmen for my liking. The elves have agreed to fight with me in the days ahead, to cleanse this land of the magelords forever—and I hope to find other allies in Hastarl."

"Hastarl?" Anauviir barked, startled.

"Aye . . . before this tenday is out, I plan to attack Athalgard. All I'm lacking is a few good blades." He looked around at the scarred, unshaven warriors. "Are ye with me?"

One of the knights raised hard eyes to meet his. "How do we know this isn't a trap? Or if it isn't, that your spells are strong enough not to fail once we're in that castle, with no way out?"

"I held that same view," Ruvaen's voice came to them from overhead, "and demanded that this man prove himself. He's slain two magelords so far this day—and another mage works with him. Have no fear of their magic failing."

"An' look you," Helm added roughly, "I've known the prince since the day the mage royal's dragon slew his parents, an' he vowed to me—a boy an' all, mind—that he'd see the magelords all dead someday."

"The time has come," Elminster said in a voice of iron. "Can I depend on the last knights of Athalantar?"

There were murmurs and shufflings. "If I may," Anauviir said uneasily, "one question . . . how can you protect *us* against the spells of the magelords? I'd welcome a chance to hew down a few magelings and armsmen—but how'll any of us ever get close enough to *have* that chance?"

"The elves will go to war beside you," Ruvaen's voice came again. "Our magic will hide or shield you whenever we can, so you can stand blade-to-blade against your foes at last." There were rumbles of approval at this, but Helm stepped forward and raised his hand for silence.

"I've led you, but in this every man must choose freely. Death is all too likely, whatever grand words we toss back and forth here." The old knight spat thoughtfully into the leaves at his feet, and added, "Yet think you: death is coming for us if we say no and go on cowering in the forest. The magelords're wearing us down, man by man . . . Rindol, Thanask; you know all of us who've fallen . . . and not a tenday passes that the armsmen aren't seeking us in every cave and thicket we run to. In a summer, or two at most, they'll have hunted down us all. Our lives are lost anyway—why not spend them to forge a blade that might actually take a magelord or two down with us?"

There were many nodding heads and raised blades among the knights, and Helm turned to Elminster with a grin that held no mirth at all.

"Command us, Prince," he said.

El looked around at them all. "Are you with me?" he asked simply. There were nods, and muttered "Ayes."

Elminster leaned forward and said, "I need ye all to go to Hastarl—in small groups or pairs, not all together where ye may attract notice or be all slain together by a vigilant magelord. Just outside the wall, upriver, is a pit where they burn bodies and refuse; traders often camp near it. Gather there before a tenday's out and seek me or a man who gives his name to you as Farl. Dress as peddlers or traders; the elves have mint wine for you to carry as wares." El grinned at them and added dryly, "Try not to drink it all before ye get to Hastarl."

There were real laughs this time and eagerness in their eyes. "There's a supply train bound for the eastern fortresses just leaving the fort at Heldon," Helm said excitedly. "We were debating whether to risk striking at it . . . it'll gain us clothes an' mounts an' pack beasts an' wagons!"

"Good!" Elminster said, knowing he couldn't hold them back now if he wanted to. A hunger for battle was alight in their eyes; a flame he'd lit that would burn now until they—or the magelords—were all dead. There were shouts of eager approval. Helm collected the gazes of all the knights with his own eyes, turning as he drew his old sword and thrust it aloft.

"For Athalantar, and freedom!" he cried, voice ringing through the trees. Twenty blades flashed in reply as they echoed his words in a ragged chorus. And then they were gone, running hard south through the trees with their drawn swords flashing in their hands, Helm at their head.

"My thanks, Ruvaen," Elminster said to the leaves overhead. "Watch over them on their way south, won't ye?"

"Of course," the musical voice replied. "This is a battle no elf or man loyal to Athalantar should miss ... and we must keep sharp watch in case there are other traitors among the knights."

"Aye," Elminster said soberly. "I hadn't thought of that. Well said. I go." He wove a brief gesture with one hand and vanished.

The two elves descended from the tree to make sure one of the knights' cooking fires was truly out. Ruvaen looked south, shook his head, and rose from the last drifting tendrils of smoke.

"Hasty folk," the other elf said, shaking his own head. "No good ever comes of hot haste."

"No good," Ruvaen agreed. "Yet they'll rule this world before our day is done, with recklessness and neverending numbers."

"What will the Realms look like then, I wonder?" the other elf replied darkly, looking south through the trees where the men had gone.

Eight days later, the golden sun of evening saw two crows alight in a stunted tree just inside the walls of Hastarl. The branches danced under the weight of the birds for a moment—and then were suddenly bare. Two spiders scuttled down the scarred and fissured tree trunk, and into cracks in the wall of a certain inn.

The wine cellar beneath the streets was always deserted at highsun—which was a good thing, for the two spiders crawled out into a musty corner, moved a careful distance apart ... and suddenly two short, stout, pox-scarred women of elder years stood facing each other. They surveyed each other's tousled white hair, rotting clothing, and sagging, rotund bodies—and in unison reached to scratch themselves.

"My, but ye look beautiful, my dear," Elminster quavered sardonically.

Myrjala pinched his cheek and cackled, "Oh, you say the *sweetest* things, lass!"

Together they waddled through the cellars, seeking the stairs up into the stables.

Seldinor Stormcloak sat in his study, thick tomes on shelves all around him, and frowned. For two days now he'd been trying to magically graft the cracked, severed lips of a human female—all that was left of the last wench he'd seized for his pleasure—onto the unfinished golem standing before him. He could make them knit with the purple-gray, sagging flesh around the hole wherein he'd set the teeth, yes. ... To make them move again, as they should and not of themselves, though, was proving a problem. Why now, after so many successful golems? *What* had cursed this one?

He sighed, swung his legs down from the desk, and sprang to his feet. If he left the fleshcreep spell hanging and brought it down *as* he sent lightnings through the thing . . . well, now. He raised his hands and began to speak the complicated syllables with the swift sureness of long practice.

Glowing light flashed, and he leaned forward eagerly to watch the lips bind themselves to the raw, knotted flesh of the faceless head. They trembled. Seldinor smiled tightly, remembering the last time he'd seen them do that . . . she'd pleaded for her life. . . .

He brought down his most special spell of all—the one that mated the golem with the intellect of a limbless familiar he'd prepared last night. Hanging in its cage, it stared at him in helpless, mute horror for an instant before the spell took hold and the lights in its eyes went out. Now if things were right at last. . . .

The lips moved on the otherwise blank face, shaped a smile that Seldinor matched delightedly, and breathed the word, "Master!"

Seldinor stood before it triumphantly. "Yes? Do you know me?"

"Well enough," was the breathy, whistling reply. "Well enough." And the arms of the golem came up with frightening speed to grasp his throat. Strangling for air, hands frantically shaping spells out of the air, Seldinor had time for one last horrified glimpse of a magical eye appearing on the blank face of the golem and winking at him, before the golem snapped his neck like a twig—and then, unleashing its awful strength for a moment, tore the wizard's head from his shoulders in a bloody rain of death. . . .

Old, wise eyes watched Seldinor's head sail across his study. The lips of their owner thinned in a smile of satisfaction. He passed a hand of dismissal over his scrying crystal and walked away. It was time to prepare against this threat to them all, now that his hated foe was gone, and in such a fitting manner too. . . .

He chuckled, whispered a word that kept guardian lightnings at bay, and grasped the knob atop a massive wooden stair. It swung open at his touch, and from the hollow within he drew two wands, slid them up his sleeves into the sheaths sewn into his undertunic, and then drew out a small, folded scrap of cloth. Carefully he unfolded it and lowered it onto his head: a skullcap set with many tiny gems. He went back to stand over the crystal, closed his eyes, and gathered his will. Tiny motes of light began to sparkle and pulse in the web of jewels.

Lights played back and forth among the gems as the old man mouthed silent words and traced unseen sigils . . . and the skullcap slowly faded into invisibility. When it was entirely gone, he opened his eyes. The pupils had become a flat, brightly glowing red.

Staring unseeing into the distance, the old man spoke into the crystal. "Undarl. Ildryn. Malanthor. Alarashan. Briost. Chantlarn."

Each name brought an image into the air above his head. Looking up, he saw six mages approach their own crystals and lay hands on them. They were his, now. He smiled, slowly and coldly, as the magic of his crown reached out to grip their wills.

"Speak, Ithboltar," one wizard said abruptly.

"What befalls, Old One?" another asked, more respectfully.

"Colleagues," he began quietly, and then added, "students." It never hurt to remind them. "We are endangered by two stranger-mages." From his mind rose images of the young, hawk-nosed one and the tall, slim woman with the dark eyes.

"Two? A boy and a woman? Old One, have you plunged asudden into your dotage?" Chantlarn asked scornfully.

"Ask yourself, wise young mage," Ithboltar said, his words mild and precise, "where Seldinor is now? Or Taraj? Or Kadeln? And then think again."

"Who are these two?" another magelord asked curtly.

"Rivals from Calimshan, perhaps, or students of Those Who Fled from Netheril and flew far to the south . . . though I've seen the woman a time or two before, riding the lands west of here."

"I've seen the boy," Briost said suddenly, "in Narthil . . . and thought him destroyed."

"And now they are killing us, one by one," Ithboltar said with velvet calm. "Done scoffing, Chantlarn? We must act together against them before others among us fall."

"Ah, Old One—another frantic defense of the realm?" Malanthor's voice was exasperated. "Can it not wait until the morrow?" They all saw him look over his shoulder and smile reassuringly at someone they could not see.

"Amusing your apprentices again, Malanthor?" Briost snorted.

Malanthor made a rude gesture and stepped back from his crystal.

"Until the morrow, then," Ithboltar said quickly. "I'll speak with all of you then." He broke contact, shaking his head. When had all his students, once eager to bend the world to their wills, become such spineless, self-indulgent fools? They'd always been reckless and arrogant, but now . . .

He shrugged. Perhaps they'd learn the error of their ways on the morrow, if the two strangers continued to strike down magelords. At least he could now compel the wizards of Athalantar into battle with the crown . . . so these foes wouldn't find too many more of them alone and unsuspecting. And nothing this side of the archmages' tombs of Netheril, short of a god, could hope to stand against the magical might of the gathered magelords of Athalantir. And gods interested in the Kingdom of the Stag seemed in short supply these days.

"Yes," Elminster said softly. "In this building here." Braer and one of the other elves nodded silently, and stepped forward to touch El's shoulders. As he faded into wraith form, he heard them muttering softly, weaving cloaking magics more powerful than anything he knew.

They alone could still hear him, so he thanked them before stepping off the rooftop and flying through the moonlight to the window below. A single amulet glowed in his magesight, but his experienced eyes saw more: a trap Farl had rigged elsewhere in earlier days. A heavy cleaver had been set on a trap-thread to chop down onto the sill. Elminster's mistlike form drifted past it, and then he was in the room, moving unthinkingly to one side of the window to avoid being silhouetted against the moonglow—and to avoid the sleep-venomed darts set to fire when the floorboard below the sill was stepped on.

The elves had made his insubstantial form completely invisible; Elminster drifted across the room toward familiar snores. They were coming from within a close-canopied bed larger than some coaches El had seen. The prince raised his eyebrows at such wealth. Farl had certainly come up in the world.

There was another trap-thread just inside the draperies. El slipped past it and settled into a comfortable sitting position on the foot of the bed. The sleepers had thrown aside the covers in the warm night, and lay exposed to his view: Farl on his back, one arm spread possessively over the small, sleek woman who lay curled against him: Tassabra.

Elminster looked longingly at her for a moment. Her beauty, sharp wits, and kindness had always stirred him. But . . . we make choices, and he'd chosen to leave this life. At least she and Farl had found happiness together, and hadn't died under the blades of the Moonclaws.

They might well find death in the nights ahead, of course, because of him. Elminster sighed, spoke a word that would let them see and hear him, and said quietly, "Well met, Farl. Well met, Tass." Farl's snores ended abruptly as Tass tensed, coming instantly awake. Her hand slipped under her pillow, seeking the dagger El knew must be there.

"Be at ease," Elminster said, "for I mean ye no hann. 'Tis Eladar, come back to plead with ye to save Athalantar."

By now Farl was awake, too. He sat up and gaped, open mouthed, as Tassabra let out a little shriek of surprise and leaned forward to stare at him. "Eladar! It *is* you!" She lunged forward to embrace him, and fell through his sitting form, to land on her forearms at the end of the bed. "What?"

"A sending—just an image," Farl told her, rising with blade in hand. "El, is that really you?"

"Of course it's really me," El told him. "Were I a magelord, I'd not be just sitting here, would I?"

Tassabra's eyes narrowed. "You're a mage, now?" She passed her hands through his form. "Where are you, truly?"

"Here," El told her. "Aye, I'm something of a mage now. I took this shape to get past all thy, ah, friendly traps."

Tassabra put her hands on her hips. "If you're right here, El," she said severely, "make yourself solid! I want to feel you! How can I kiss a shadow?"

Elminster smiled. "Right then. But for thine own safety, stop waving thy hands about in me."

She did so, he murmured a few words—and was suddenly heavy and solid again. Tassabra embraced him eagerly, smooth skin sliding against his dark leathers. Farl put his arms around them both, hugging tightly "By the *gods* I missed you, El," he said huskily. "I never thought to see you again."

"Where were you?" Tassabra demanded, running her hands along his jaw and through his hair, noting the changes the years had wrought.

"All over Faerûn," El replied, "learning enough magic to destroy the magelords."

"You still hope to—?"

"Before three dawns have come," El told them, "if ye'll help me."

They both gaped at him. "Help how?" Farl asked, frowning. "We spend much of our time just evading casual cruelties cast our way by those wizards. We can't hope to withstand any sort of deliberate attack by even one of them!"

Tassabra nodded soberly. "We've built ourselves a good life here, El," she said. "The Moonclaws are no more; you were right, El—they were tools of the magelords. We run the Velvet Hands together now and shrewd investments and trading make us more coins than we ever got slipping into windows of nights."

Elminster sent a thought to Braer and knew he was cloaked again. He caught an appreciative "Nice lass, there," from the other elf before he turned his attention again to the pair facing him.

"Can ye see me now?" he asked. Farl and Tass shook their heads.

"Nor can ye touch me—even with spells," Elminster told them. "I have powerful allies; they can cloak ye even as they're shielding me now. Ye could steal from magelords and stab at them without fearing their magic!"

Farl stiffened, eyes shining. "No?"

Then his eyes narrowed. "Just who are these allies?"

Elminster flicked a thought at Braer: *May I?*

Leave this to us, came the warm reply. A moment later, he heard the bed hangings rustle behind him. Tass gasped, and Farl's hand tensed on the blade he held beneath the covers.

El knew both elves had appeared behind him even before he heard Braer's musical voice. "Forgive this intrusion, Lord and Lady," the elf said. "We do not make a habit of intruding into bedchambers, but we feel this chance to free the realm is most important. If you'll fight beside us, we would find it an honor."

El saw his old friends blink; the elves must have vanished abruptly. He heard the bed hangings fell back again. Tass closed her gaping mouth with an effort. "An honor?" Farl said wonderingly "*Elves* would take it as an honor to fight with *us*?"

"Elves," Tassabra murmured. "Real elves!"

"Aye," Elminster said with a smile, "and with their magic, we can defeat the magelords."

Farl shook his head. "I want to—gods, I want to!—but . . . all those armsmen . . ."

"Ye would not be fighting alone," El told them. "Beside ye, when it comes to open battle, will stand the Knights of the Stag."

"The lost knights of Athalantar?" Tass gasped.

Farl shook his head in disbelief. "More children's legends! I—this seems a dream . . . you truly intend this. . . ." He shook his head again to clear his wits, and asked, "How did you manage to get the elves and the knights to follow you?"

"They are loyal to Athalantar," El said quietly, "and answered a call from its last prince."

"Who's that?"

"Me," El said flatly "Eladar the Dark is also—Elminster, son of Prince Elthryn. I am a prince of Athalantar."

Farl and Tass stared at him, and then, shakily, Farl swallowed. "I can't believe it," he whispered, "but oh, I want to! A chance to live free, and not have to fear and bow to wizards anywhere in Athalantar . . ."

"We'll do it," Tassabra said firmly. "Count on us, El—Eladar. Prince."

Farl stared at her. "Tass!" he hissed. "What're you saying? We'll be killed!"

Tassabra turned her head to look at him. "And what if we are?" she asked quietly. "We've made a success of things here, yes . . . but a success that could be swept away in an instant at a magelord's whim."

She rose. Moonlight outlined her bare body, but she wore dignity like a grand gown. "More than that," she went on, "we can be satisfied about what we've done . . . but Farl, for once in my life I want to be *proud!* To do something that folk will always respect, whatever befalls! To do something that . . . *matters*. This may be our only chance."

She looked out the window, stiffened as she saw the elves standing on a nearby rooftop, and then made what might have been a sob as they waved to her in salute. Solemnly feeling her heart rising within her, she waved back, and spun from the window in sudden fierceness. "And what better cause can there be? Athalantar needs us! We can be free!"

Farl nodded, a slow smile building on his face. "You speak truth," he said quietly, and looked up at Elminster. "El, you can depend on the Velvet Hands." He raised his blade in salute; it flashed as moonlight leaped down its steely length. "What will you have us do?"

"Tomorrow even," El said, "I'll call on ye. I need Tass to make contact with the knights—'tis best if she looks like a pleasurelass, to go to the camp outside the walls by the burning pit. Then, all the night through, I'll need your folk to work with the elves . . . stealing magic items and the small things they use to work spells—bones and rust flakes and gems and bits of string, ye know—from magelords all over the city. The elves'll cloak ye and guide ye as to what to take."

All three of them grinned at each other. "This is going to be fun," Farl said, eyes shining.

"I hope so," Elminster replied quietly "Oh, I hope so."

"Have they attacked us yet, Old One?" Malanthor's tone and raised eyebrow were sardonic. "Or did I miss it? I did spend a few moments in the jakes this morn."

Ithboltar's smile was thin and wintry. "The threat is real, and remains so. You would do well to set aside a trifling amount of that arrogance, Malanthor. Pride usually precedes disaster, especially for mages."

"And old men start to see things, until the shadows of their dreams seem more real than what is truly around them," Malanthor replied cuttingly, "if we're trading platitudes."

Ithboltar shrugged. "Just be sure to prepare yourself with spells, wands, and the like as if for battle against mage-foes, in the days ahead."

"Athalantar under attack again?" Chantlarn's tone was breezy as he strode into the room. "Armies at our gates and all that?"

"I fear so," Malanthor said, putting a hand to his brow and affecting the broken tones of a hysterical matron. "I fear so."

"And I do too," Chantlarn said heartily. "How does the morning find you, Ithboltar?"

"Surrounded by idiots," the old wizard said sourly, and turned back to the spellbook on the table in front of him. The two younger magelords exchanged amused glances.

"How do I look?" Tassabra asked, lifting her arms and twirling. Small brass bells chimed here and there on the web of leather straps that displayed, rather than clothed, her body. Strips of ruby-hued silk proclaimed her trade to any eye; even her thigh-high boots were trimmed with red.

Elminster licked his lips. "I should never have gone away," he said sadly, and she laughed delightedly.

El rolled his eyes and settled her ruby-red cloak around her shoulders. As he'd suspected, it was pierced by many daring cutouts, and trimmed with lace. Tass strutted, bare knees peeking through the cloak as she approached him.

"Ye're supposed to look as if ye can't make enough coins in Hastarl, and have to go to the traders' camp," El protested, "not bring the whole city to a tongue-dangling halt!"

Tass pouted. "This was supposed to be fun, remember?"

El sighed and took her in his arms. Her eyes widened, and then she reached up her head eagerly and kissed him. Their lips were about to touch when he whispered the word that whirled them away from the dim room to behind a pile of barrels in the garbage-strewn alley along the walls.

Tass clung to him, wrinkled her nose, and then teased, "I've never been kissed like *that* before!"

"Let it be a first, Lady," El said with a bow, as his form faded from view. "My likeness of Helm—'tis still clear in your mind?"

Tass nodded. "Vivid . . . a wonderful spell, that."

"Nay, lass; it takes years to learn magic enough to cast it—and the teleport, too. Tyche smile upon ye . . . try not to get yourself killed or half-crushed under the rush of amorous men before ye find Helm and his knights."

Tass made a very rude gesture in his direction, and then strutted oft through the gathering dusk.

Elminster watched her go and then shook his head. He hoped he'd not be looking at her again sometime soon—and seeing a contorted corpse.

He sighed and turned away. There was much else to do tonight.

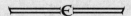

Tass absently slapped aside another groping hand and snapped, "Coins first, great lord."

A rueful chuckle answered her. "Three silver, sister?"

"Your sister is all you'll get for three silver," Tass agreed pleasantly, moving on. This way and that she peered in the gathering shadows, seeking the face Elminster had left hanging in her mind. He wasn't a noble-looking man, this Helm Stoneblade.

"Swords from Sarthryn, Lady?" a voice whined at her.

She looked scathingly in that direction. "What would I want with a sword, man?"

"To go with your tongue, lass?" another voice rumbled in quiet amusement. Tass turned to glare across a campfire at its owner—and stopped dead. This was the man. She looked quickly around at the ill-garbed men oiling and sharpening blades. Of course . . . what better way to account for many weapons, without warriors boldly bearing them?

"It's you I've come for," she said calmly, striding toward Helm. The battered old warrior looked her up and down—and the blade in his lap swept up like a striking snake to touch her breast. Tass came to a sudden halt, swallowing. She'd never seen a sword wielded so fast—and the steel was very cold and firm against her flesh.

"Stand back," its owner ordered, "and tell me who you are, an' who sent you."

Tass stepped smoothly back and parted her cloak to put her hands on her hips. One of the men craned his head for a good look at what she was displaying, but Helm's eyes were fixed on her hands, and his blade was raised and ready.

"I speak for Elminster . . . or for Farl," Tass told him calmly.

The blade flashed in the firelight as it dipped smoothly away. "Well," Helm rumbled, taking up a tankard and offering it to her, "why don't you decide which one, an' we'll talk?"

"The mage royal is elsewhere," Farl whispered, face glistening with sweat. "Or I'd never have kept my life." He was trembling.

"Easy," Elminster said. "Ye did, that's the important thing."

"For now," Farl hissed back. "Who knows if that mage left spells that capture my looks, for him to view later—and come after me?"

The elf beside them shook his head in silence. Elminster indicated the silent elven mage with a nod. "I'd trust him to sense anything this Undarl could cast."

Farl shrugged, but seemed more at ease as he thrust a varied assortment of gems, vials, and pouches into Elminster's hands. "Here. He's got something built into his bed, too, but I couldn't find the way to it, and forgot to bring my axe with me."

"Next time," El replied soothingly, and after a breath or two, Farl grinned at him.

"There were so many thieving apprentices trying to get past Undarl's ward to steal spell scrolls that I kept falling over them! I still don't know how they missed seeing me . . . this shadow of mine must be *good*." He frowned. "How— how're my Hands doing?"

Elminster scratched his nose. "The headstrong lass—Jannath, d'ye call her?— ran into a servant and slew him before she gave herself time to think . . . but her elven shadow flew the body out and gave it to the river. Otherwise, all is quiet, unfolding as we foresaw."

"Who's left to do?"

"We leave the tower of Ithboltar alone," Myrjala's voice came quietly out of the night beside them. "So that leaves only Malanthor for you."

Fan nodded. "Right . . . where's Tass?"

Eiminster grinned. "I made her change out of her ruby-red costume—"

"I'll *bet* you did," Farl and Myrjala said in unison, and then looked at each other and laughed.

"—so she was a trifle late getting started," Elminster continued smoothly, as if the interruption hadn't occurred. "She's in Alarashan's turret now; her shadow hasn't reported anything amiss."

Farl sighed in relief, and sprang to his feet. "Lead me to this Malanthor, then."

Myrjala raised her eyebrows, and gestured at Elminster to cast the first spell. Obediently El stepped forward, pointing across the dark rooftops of the city "See ye that turret, there? We're going to fly you across to the window . . . the smaller one; it's his jakes, whereas the other is sure to have alarm spells and probably traps."

"Fly me?" Farl said, and rolled his eyes. "I'm still not quite used to you being a mighty mage, El—or a prince, for that matter."

"That's all right," Myrjala said soothingly "El's not really used to being either of those things himself, yet."

"You surprise me," Farl said dryly, striding to the edge of the roof. Behind him, the two mages exchanged an amused glance.

Farl reached for the ring. This was almost too easy. "The wine's all gone," a pettish female voice complained, from the bath on the other side of the curtain.

"Well, get some more," the magelord replied from the other end of the bath. "You know where it is."

Water splashed. Farl's fingers closed on the ring—and a wet, long-fingered hand reached through the curtain, closing on . . . Farl's knuckle! Farl snatched his hand away and spun. The time for stealth was past. The woman screamed piercingly. Yes, long past.

Farl heard the magelord's startled curse as he sprinted for the jakes. "Get me *out* of here!" he snarled, vaulting a low chair. "Now!"

There was a chorus of splashing sounds from behind him, and a man's voice, chanting quickly.

Farl cursed despairingly. "Elminster!" he cried, dodging around a table. Then he felt a tingling in his limbs. He faltered, saw light flickering around him like dancing flames, and then fell through the door into the jakes. *Lie still*, a calm elven voice said in his mind. Farl shivered, and did so. What other chance did he have?

"Shielded!" the magelord spat in disbelief. "A spell-shielded thief in my own chambers! What's this realm coming to, anyway?"

Dripping, he strode across the room, tiny blue lightnings playing between his hands. "Well, I think I'll get a few answers before he dies . . . Nanatha, bring me some of that wine too!"

Oh, gods help me, Farl prayed, forehead on the floor. El, where are you? I *knew* this would h—

There was a sudden burst of light, and then a disgusted sigh. "*Right* in the chamberpot," Elminster told the room angrily. "It's not that small a room, but I have to appear right in the—"

"Who in the Nine Blazing Hells are you?"

Malanthor was flabbergasted; there were not one, but two intruders in his jakes, and with no sign of how they got there. He shook his head, but decided not to wait for a reply. Blue lightnings spat from his fingertips. They struck the hawk-nosed man—wait! This was one of the mages Ithboltar had been gibbering about!—and rebounded, leaping back at the magelord before he had time to do anything. They struck home. Malanthor grunted as his body was hurled back, jerking and spasming uncontrollably, and fell backward over a couch. Nanatha screamed again.

"Alabaertha . . . shum*golnar*," he gasped, writhing on the carpet. Chantlarn'd demand a high price for this aid, but it was call on their pact-link or die!

"Myr?" El called. "Are ye ready?"

"I'll come for him," was the soft reply. "We've got a patrol of armsmen up here."

"Is that why I'm visible?" El said, suddenly realizing that the magelord had seen him instantly.

El stepped out of the chamberpot, deciding not to look down at whatever mess he must be making, and strode toward where the magelord had vanished. A bottle sailed across the room at his head; he ducked, and it touched his shoulder and shattered against the door behind him.

"Yes, that's why," Myrjala answered him calmly. "Next time, just pour me a glass, all right?"

El stared at the frightened woman who'd hurled the bottle—did all these magelords walk about naked? Nay, she was dripping wet, just as the man had been: bath time, then—and then turned back to see Myrjala touch Farl.

"Be back," she said to El, and the two of them vanished. El looked back at the woman, and then over to where the magelord was struggling to his feet.

"For the deaths of my parents," he said softly, "die, Magelord!" And a spell roared out of him. Silver spheres poured across the room and began to burst, one after another, shaking the room. The magelord tried to scream.

"My, what a dramatic speech," said a new voice at El's elbow. Elminster turned, and a smug-looking, mustachioed man in purple robes who hadn't been in the room two breaths before smiled pleasantly at him and triggered the wand in his hand. The world went dark, then red. Dimly El heard a splintering crash, his own body striking a wall and demolishing a mirror. He heard bones shattering as he bounced back out into the room, half-crushed, and fell forward into oblivion.

Chantlarn of the magelords nodded in satisfaction and sauntered forward to inspect the stranger's body. Perhaps there'd be some salvageable magic ... he didn't spare a single glance for the sobbing apprentice or the smoking ruin of the couch, where Malanthor's contorted, blackened bones were still writhing in an eerie, futile struggle to stay upright.

"Elminster?" The voice from the doorway of the jakes was low and quiet, but definitely female. Chantlarn turned, and heard the speaker gasp. The other intruder Ithboltar had warned them of! He smiled tightly and triggered his wand again, aiming at her face. The wand flashed again, and Chantlarn opened his eyes. He'd have to stop firing at folk so close to him, or ... it was his turn to gasp.

The woman still stood in the doorway, eyes alight in fury and grief. The magic had done nothing to her! Chantlarn gulped and triggered the wand again. She reached right through its blaze to touch him. Chantlarn had time for one strangled cry before his hurtling body crashed out through the balcony window. He was still high above the castle courtyard when he thrust the wand into his own mouth, thrashing and struggling as he fought the terrible compulsion, and triggered it again.

The bloody explosion set the wand into a wild discharge. Its bolts burst in all directions, hurling flaming spell forces at the castle wall, and scattering a terrified patrol of armsmen.

The apprentice screamed again. Myrjala looked up at her tear-streaked face once, and then turned back to Elminster again, murmuring an incantation. A blue-white glow rose around her hands and flowed out to envelop Elminster's twisted form. She gestured, and he rose into the air, lying limply as if on a bed. The blue-white glow brightened.

Nanatha backed away, moaning in fear. Myrjala turned again to face her ... and smiled. The dumbfounded apprentice watched her features swim and flow, reshaping themselves into—the mage royal! Undarl Dragonrider sneered at her, dropped his cold gaze down her nakedness and then up again, and then waved a mocking salute. The light flared until it blinded her ... and when she could see again, they were gone.

There was a pattering sound from across the room. Nanatha looked there in time to see Malanthor's bones collapse and topple down into the ashes. It seemed like a good time to faint—so she did.

"You'll be all right, my love," Myrjala said softly.

El tried to nod . . . but seemed to be floating back from somewhere far away, on a succession of gently rolling waves that left him powerless to move.

"Lie still," Myrjala said, laying a hand on his brow. Her fingers were cool. . . . Elminster smiled and relaxed.

"Did ye . . . clean my boots?" he managed to ask.

She exploded with laughter, mirth that ended in a sob that betrayed just how worried she'd been.

"Aye," she said, voice steady again, "and more than that. I took the semblance of the mage royal and let Malanthor's apprentice see me. She thinks the whole thing's his work."

"One magelord against another," El murmured, satisfied. "I hear ye. . . ."

A moment later, it was obvious he didn't. Sleep had claimed him, a deep, healing sleep that left him oblivious when Myrjala burst into tears and embraced him. "I almost lost thee," she sobbed, her tears falling onto his face. "Oh, El, what would I have done then? Oh, why couldn't your vengeance have been something lesser?"

Seventeen
For Athalantar

In the name of a kingdom
many fell things are done.
In the name of a love
fairer things are won.

Halindar Droun, Bard of Beregost
rom the ballad *Tears Never Cease*
Year of the Marching Moon

The magelord's words made Tassabra bite her lip. She froze, listening, her fingers only inches away from the glowing armlet.

"I have her with me," the Magelord Alarashan went on almost jovially as he leered at the trembling Nanatha, "and she insists the woman revealed herself as the mage royal—and Undarl even waved farewell to her before he left, taking the other one with him."

"That hardly seems possible." The sour old voice coming from the scrying crystal grew stronger "Bring her to me."

Alarashan bowed his head. "Of course, Old One," he said, taking hold of Nanatha's wrist. "It shall be done."

He touched the crystal, murmured a word, and they both vanished. Tassabra risked a peek around the edge of the table to stare at the empty air where they'd both been a moment before.

She was alone. She sighed and then shrugged, swept the armlet and a scepter she'd been eyeing earlier into her sack, turned away—and then turned back, gave the scrying crystal an impish grin, and tipped it into the sack too.

"All done here," she said gaily and felt the tingling of a spell flood through hen as her elven shadow brought her home. . . .

The last failing rays of moonlight were falling into the cobbled courtyard as Hathan strode across it, toward the tower where his spell chamber waited. Those useless idiots of apprentices had better be standing ready at their places around the circle when he got there. . . . Farjump spells always held risk, even without three ambitious young wild-wands and their clever little plots in—Hathan stiffened in midstride and came to a sudden halt.

His face paled, and then he spun around and stared up at the highest tower of Hornkeep, frowning in concentration. He'd never heard the Old One sound so insistent before; something bad had happened.

In a dark chamber high in that tower, glowing water splashed. Its reflections danced across the intent face of Undarl Dragonrider, mage royal of Athalantar.

The griffons struggled in the water, fighting his spells. If he could ever get them to mate in this vat of enspelled giant crab fluids, a few simple spells afterward should give him what he was after. The offspring would be flying armorplated killers ruled by his will . . . and he'd have taken his first step beyond what the most powerful sorcerers of his family had ever achieved. The gods above knew he was growing weary of waiting, though. Undarl sighed and sat back in his chair, listening to the water surge up over the edge of the vat, the overflow slapping against the wall beyond.

He dare not waste many more days here with that lizard-kisser Seldinor and the others so hungry for his high seat, and . . . Undarl froze as Hathan's mindsend stung him. It was loud because his senior apprentice was only in the courtyard below, and high with excitement and a little fear. He'd have a headache for sure. The mage royal listened, curtly bid Hathan return to his own affairs, and broke the contact.

Forgotten, the creatures splashed and gurgled in the tank behind him as he strode out. Undarl hastened down a dark passage to a certain spot where he laid one hand on the bare wall and murmured a word. The wall swung open with the faintest of rumbles; he reached into the revealed darkness, felt the iron lid, and laid his hand on it. It glowed briefly, tracing his hand, and then swung open, its interior glowing with a faint radiance of its own. Undarl took four wands from it, thrust them into his belt, and reached into a pocket on the lid of the chest. He plucked out the handful of gems he felt there, closed the chest and closet with two quick gestures and a word, and went on down the passage.

One of his junior apprentices looked up, startled, from the scroll he was copying. "Lord Master?" he asked uncertainly.

Undarl strode past him without a word and stepped around a motionless four-armed gargoyle squatting on its block, to mount the stairs beyond. They rose to a dusty, seldom-used balcony, where a bare stone pedestal stood among strange hanging things of wire and curved metal and winking glass. Undarl halted before the pedestal, laid his handful of gems on it, traced a certain sign around them with a finger that left a glowing trail behind, and murmured a long, complicated incantation under his breath.

The apprentice half-rose in his seat to get a better took at what Undarl was doing, and stiffened in that awkward pose, swaying, as the spell took hold.

Undarl smiled tightly and left the chamber. Three rooms away he found another apprentice sprawled on the floor, a key he wasn't supposed to have had fallen from his hand, the other clutching a scroll he'd been forbidden to read. Much good might it do him now.

The spell that brought down the sleep of ages would hold until Undarl ended it, the pedestal broke or crumbled away to break the sigil, or the magic consumed the gems—and that would take a good thousand winters or more. Anyone save

Undarl himself who entered the Dragonrider's Tower would fall into enspelled stasis, a sleep that held them unchanged as the world aged around them.

Perhaps he'd leave them all that long and stay away from his tower for a time to see if Seldinor or other ambitious rivals would be tempted into entering it and be caught in his trap. It would be a simple matter to arrange things so that the spell that broke the stasis also slew them before they could arrange any defenses. ·

Musing, Undarl strode down the winding stone stair and out into the courtyard, the floating, empty suits of armor raising their balberds to let him pass through the door. "Anglathammaroth!" he called. "To me!"

A step later, he was gone. When the huge shadow fell over the courtyard two breaths later, all it found were a few dwindling motes of light. It beat its wings once, the sound of a thunderclap breaking over the Horn Hills, climbed toward the stars, turned, and soared southeast.

The warm, sweet smell of bread rolled out over the armsmen. They sniffed appreciatively and hauled open the door of the bake shop, striding straight over to Shandathe, who was bent over pans of cooling loaves. One grabbed her arm; she looked up and screamed.

Her husband stepped through the door from the kitchens. He took two quick, furious steps toward his struggling wife, and was brought up short by two blades at his throat.

"Keep back, you!" one of the armsmen at the other end of those weapons ordered.

"What're y—"

"Silence! Keep back!" another armsman snarled, snatching up a loaf of bread from the nearest pan. "We'll have this too."

"Shandathe!" the baker roared, as the two jabbing sword tips forced him back a step.

"Keep back, love!" she sobbed as she was dragged roughly toward the door "Back, or they'll slay you!"

"*Why* are you *doing* this?" Hannibur snarled in bewilderment.

"The king has seen your wife and fancies her. Be honored," one of the armsmen said with cruel humor. Another armsman backhanded the baker's head from behind with a heavy, gauntleted fist. Hannibur opened his mouth in a last, trailing snarl, and crashed headlong to the floor. . . .

"Get used to it," Farl said with a grin. "The sewers are the only way under the castle walls."

"Don't you know about the secret passages?" Helm rumbled, glaring around at the dripping walls. Scum floated past his chin; he wrinkled his nose as one of the other knights, to the rear, started to retch.

"Yes," Farl said sweetly, "but I fear the magelords do too. Folk who try to use them always end up in the wizard's spell chambers as part of some fatal magical experiment or other. We lost a lot of competitors that way."

"I don't doubt it, clever-tongue," Helm said sourly, trying to keep his sword dry. Filth swirled and rolled past him as he forged ahead in the chest-high waters, wondering why it was that the elves, who could have pushed back the waters, had chosen to hide nearby, and do their cloaking from their hideaway . . . which was somewhere drier.

"Here's the place," Farl said, pointing up into the darkness. "There're handholds cut into this shaft, because at its top is a chamber where six glory holes meet and things sludge up; it all has to be raked clear every spring. Now remember, Anauviir: the Magelord Briost's chambers can be reached up either of the glory holes off to the left . . . that's *this* hand . . ."

"*Thank* you, thief," Anauviir growled. "I do know right from left, you know."

"Well, you *are* knights," Farl said merrily "And if the nobles of Hastarl are anything to go by . . ."

"Where do the other holes up there lead to?" Anauviir interrupted. Helm grinned at his fellow knight's expression.

"Two rooms used by apprentices," Farl said, "but it's morning; they'll be up preparing morningfest and baths for their masters . . . and the last hole runs to a sort of reading chamber, which should be empty. . . . Helm and I will go on to the next shaft, which leads to Magelord Alarashan's rooms; and Prince Elminster's promised to show himself if the castle is roused, to draw the magelords into attacking him—and *not* attacking *us*. . . . Any questions?"

"Aye," one of the knights said, spitting into the water. "How do thieves ever steal anything in Hastarl? Do they only rob deaf folk?"

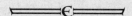

The apprentice let out a little shriek. Alarashan frowned. He preferred willing wenches, but Undarl had forced this one idiot male youth on him . . . doubtless a spy, and the man was hopeless at magic. When he wasn't breaking things, he was busily miscasting spells all over the place, and . . .

The magelord looked into the jakes. Ortran was slumped over on the seat, trousers around his ankles, and . . .

Alarashan stiffened. His apprentice was being thrust aside, by something—someone!—underneath. He strode forward, snatching a wand from his belt, as Ortran's body fell against the wall and the bloody blade that had slain him withdrew down the privy hole.

Alarashan aimed the wand, then stopped. What was to stop someone thrusting a blade into his face, if he showed himself over the hole? No, let them emerge, and slay them as they appear. . . . He crouched low, waiting.

And part of the wall behind him slid smoothly aside. Alarashan had time to whirl around and gape at the secret panel he'd never known about, before the cudgel came down on his shoulder with numbing force, and his wand fell from nerveless, burning fingers.

Briost didn't waste any time being shocked when the man in filthy armor burst out of his garderobe, sword raised. He lifted a hand, triggered his ring, and stepped smoothly aside to give the dying man room to fall.

The second attacker brought a surprised look onto the magelord's face, but his ring winked a second time. Something flashed over the falling man's shoulder, though—*gods!* The hurled dagger nearly took out Briost's eye. He ducked aside and felt a numbing blow on his cheek. The dagger spun on, and as he straightened to meet the men now pouring out of the jakes, he felt wetness on his face.

He'd put his hand up to feel, and brought it away with the fingertips crimson with his own blood, when he realized he hadn't time for such luxuries....

And by then, as the blades came at him from all sides, it was much too late.

The scrying crystal flashed. Ithboltar looked over at it and waved an imperious finger at the thoroughly frightened apprentice, bidding her sit. Nanatha sat in hasty silence as the Old One, one-time tutor of most of the magelords, got up and glared at his crystal.

Obligingly, it flashed again. "Either . . . no . . ." Ithboltar growled and leaned forward to touch something Nanatha could not see, on the underside of his desk. He uttered one soft word, and the room rocked under the sudden tolling of a great bell.

"We're being attacked," the Old One hissed fiercely as a chorus of bells echoed and boomed all over the castle. "Briost? Briost, answer me!" He leaned forward over the crystal, muttering—and then his eyes widened at what he saw in its depths, and he thrust a hand into the breast of his robes, tearing them open in his frantic haste. Nanatha saw white grizzled hair on a sunken chest as Ithboltar found what he was seeking—some sort of gem-adorned skullcap—and pulled it onto his head, hair sticking out wildly in all directions. At another time the apprentice might have giggled inwardly at the old archwizard's ridiculous appearance—but not now. She was too terrified . . . of whatever might put such fear into the Old One, mightiest of all magelords.

Ithboltar fumbled speedily through the gestures of a spell he'd hoped he'd never have to use, and the room whirled amid the ringing sounds of shattering crystals. Nanatha gasped.

Ithboltar's chamber was suddenly full of five startled magelords.

"What did y—?"

"How did you brin—?"

"Why—?"

Ithboltar held up a hand to quell them all. "Together, we stand a chance against this threat. Alone, we are doomed."

The bells boomed again, and the armsmen rose with a chorus of curses. "This *never* happens," Riol protested, his boots scattering dice underfoot as he skidded past the table and raced for the stair.

"Well, it's happening *now*," First Sword Sauvar growled, from right behind him. "And you can bet that anything that can scare a dozen or more magelords is going to be something we should be scared about, too!"

Riol opened his mouth to answer, but someone reached out of a dark side passage and put a sword into it. The blade glistened as it came out of the back of Riol's head; Sauvar ran right into it before he could stop, and reeled back with a startled oath.

"Who in all the—?" he started to ask.

"Tharl Bloodbar, knight of Athalantar," came the crisp reply from a wild-bearded old man whose armor seemed to be made of cast-off, flapping remnants scavenged from a dozen battlefields, which is what in truth it was. "*Sir* Tharl to you."

The bright blade in the old knight's hand skirted against Sauvar's own steel and then leaped over it—and the First Sword joined his fellow armsman on the passage floor. The thunder of hurrying boots coming up the stairs slowed, and the old man grinned fiercely down into the gloom and snarled, "Right then—which one o' you heroes is most eager to die?"

Jansibal Otharr sighed in perfumed exasperation. "Why, in the name of all the gods, does this have to happen *now?*"

He finished at the chamberpot, turned with his elaborate codpiece dangling to look longingly at the woman waiting on the bed, and then sighed and reached down to buckle himself up. He knew what the penalty would be if one of the magelords discovered he'd ignored their precious warning bell for a little rutting.

"Stay," he ordered, "but avail yourself not *over* heavily of the wine, Chlasa. I'll be back soon." Snatching up his bejeweled blade, he strode out.

The torchlit passage beyond, in the part of the castle reserved for noble visitors, was usually deserted except for the occasional scurrying servant. Right now it was crowded with hurrying bodyguards in livery, an envoy in full Athalantan tabard, and Thelorn Selemban, his hated rival. Thelorn was striding along toward him, his slim-filigreed blade drawn.

Jansibal's face darkened, and he struggled to belt on his own blade and get it out into his hand before Selemban reached him—in such chaos, "accidents" could all too easily happen.

Thelorn's eyes were dancing with amusement as he bore down on Jansibal. "Fair even, lover mine," he said tightly, knowing his reference to that little embarrassment in the Kissing Wench would enrage the only scion of the noble house of Otharr.

Jansibal snarled and jerked his blade free—but Thelorn was past him with a mocking laugh, and hurrying down a broad flight of stairs toward the guard room below. A twisted, sneering smile slid onto Jansibal's face, and the perfumed dandy hurried after his rival. Accidents could happen, yes, especially from behind . . .

"What befalls?" Nanue Trumpettower set down her glass, real alarm in her eyes. Ah, thought Darrigo delightedly, the lass is such a delicate little flower . . . wasted on young Peeryst, come to think of it . . .

The old farmer stumped to his feet. "Well, now," he growled, "them's the alarm bells, calling out the guard. I'll just have a—"

"No, uncle," Peeryst interrupted grandly, drawing his blade with a flourish. "I've brought my steel with me . . . *I'll* go and look. Guard Nanue until I return!"

He shouldered past Darrigo without waiting for a reply, jaw set and eyes bright. Aye, trust him to leap on any chance to show off before his wife, Darrigo thought, and reached out to keep the door from banging into a table the magelords might be rather fond of, as Peeryst flung it wide.

Almost immediately, he gave a startled cry. Darrigo saw a rushing armsman crash into the youth, reel, and keep on running. Peeryst wasn't so lucky; he hit the wall nose-first and groaned.

Darrigo groaned. Of *course* blood was leaking from the idiot's over-delicate beak when he got up . . . and of course, little Nanue would have to get up and rush out to see what had befallen her light-o'-love. . . . On cue, Nanue rushed past him, skirts rustling, and shrieked in earnest.

Darrigo peered out in time to see a well-dressed noble shove Nanue off his blade, snarling, "Step *aside*, wench! Can't you hear the alarm?" Nanue felt back against the doorway with a sob of fear. The man's blade had gashed her arm, and blood was running freely down her skirts. That was enough for Darrigo.

Two strides took him to Peeryst. With one hand he snatched the dainty little blade out of his nephew's hand. With the other, he shoved the young hope of the Trumpettowers at his wife. "Bind her wounds," he snarled, setting off down the passage after the hurrying noble.

"But—how?" Peeryst called after him desperately.

"Use yer shirt, man!" Darrigo snarled.

"But, but—'tis new, and—"

"Then use yer hose, stonehead," Darrigo roared back, as he took a flight of stairs three at a time.

He was wheezing and stumbling by the time he reached the bottom, but he caught up with the hurrying noble there. His quarry was just raising his blade, looking for all the world like he was going to plant it in the ribs of another dandified fellow a little farther along the halt. Darrigo smacked him across the back of the head with his sword. Thankfully, the dainty weapon didn't break. The dandy whirled, the reek of his perfume swirling about him.

"You *dare* to touch me, old man?" The noble's blade was darting at his throat before Darrigo could have uttered any reply.

Snarling, the old farmer beat it aside and shouldered forward. "Set steel to a Trumpettower lass, would you? And her unarmed, yet! *You* don't deserve to live three breaths longer!"

Jansibal leaped backward just in time. The old man's ornamental sword hissed past his nose. His urge to laugh died abruptly . . . this graybeard was serious!

Then a clear laugh rang out from behind him: Thelorn, damn him before all the gods! Jansibal snarled and slid aside, forcing his way past the old man to get his unprotected back away from the reach of his rival.

"Attacking old men now, Jansibal? Younger ones starting to refuse you?" Thelorn called interestedly. In sudden fury, Jansibal lunged at Darrigo. Their blades crashed together—once, twice, and thrice . . . and Janisbal's codpiece clanged to the floor, both of its tiny straps cut.

The old man gave him a mirthless smile. "Thought perhaps you'd be able to move a mite faster without all that weight down there," he remarked, advancing again.

Jansibal stared at him in astonishment, and then that little blade was sliding in at him again, and he was forced into a desperate flurry of parries. Thelorn laughed again, enjoying his rival's humiliation. Jansibal snarled and attacked, and almost casually the old man's blade floated in over his guard and drew a line across his nose and cheek.

Jansibal spat out a startled oath and backed away. Darrigo lumbered after him, and the perfumed dandy turned and ran down the dark hall, away from them all. The old man raised an incredulous eyebrow. "Fleeing a challenge? And you think yourself *noble?*"

Jansibal Otharr made no reply but a gasp, and a moment later Darrigo saw why. A blade was protruding from his back, dark with the nobleman's blood. The blade shook, a booted foot kicked, and Jansibal Otharr slid down to his knees on the floor and sagged back into a silent heap.

"*That's* an Athalantan noble?" said the battered old warrior who held the bloody blade. "We should have cleaned out this place earlier!"

Thelorn Selemban strode forward, past the staring Darrigo. "Just who are you?" he demanded.

Helm Stoneblade eyed the noble's ruffed open-to-the-waist silk shirt, its puffed sleeves adorned with many crawling dragons.

"A knight of Athalantar," he growled, "but by the looks of you, it seems I'd've done better down the years as your tailor."

"A knight? What idiocy is this? There are no—" Selemban's eyes narrowed. "Are you loyal to King Belaur and the magelords?"

"I fear not, lad," Helm said, striding forward. There were ten or more warriors in motley armor behind him.

Thelorn Selemban flourished his blade. It glittered in the torchlight as he said excitedly, "Come no farther, rebels, or die!"

"'Tis certainly a day for grand speeches," Helm responded, moving steadily forward. "Let's see if you're any better with that blade than your aromatic friend was . . ."

"Friend?" Thelorn snorted. "He was no friend of mine—despite anything you may have heard. Now stand back, or—"

"Or you'll wave your sword at me?"

Helm's voice was heavy with sarcasm, but it trailed away as Thalorn jerked something from around his neck, raised it to his lips, and sneered, "Or I'll slay you traitors with *this!* I'm told i—"

It was then that Darrigo Trumpettower made his decision. He took two shuffling steps forward and thrust his blade into the young nobleman's ear.

Thelorn gurgled, dropped blade and bauble, reeled, and fell on his face.

Darrigo peered past him at the grim-faced men beyond. "Helm?" he asked, squinting. "Helm Stoneblade?"

"*Darrigo!* You old lion! Well met!"

A moment later they embraced, keeping their swords out of the way with the ease of old veterans.

"I heard you were an outlaw . . . what've you been doing, Helm?"

"Killing armsmen," the knight said, "but I've found killing magelords more fun, so I'm doing that right now. Care to join me?"

"Don't mind if I do," Darrigo Trumpettower growled. "Thank you—I will. Lead the way."

Helm rolled his eyes. "You nobles," he said in disgust, and strode forward. . . .

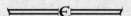

The magelords stared at the Old One and then at each other. There was reluctance in their words of agreement, and suspicious looks in plenty were exchanged. These pleasantries were yet incomplete when the tall window at the far end of Ithboltar's vast spell chamber shattered from top to bottom.

Through the opening strode the grand figure of a mage as tall as two men, white bearded and crowned with fire. He moved purposefully toward them, walking on air and holding high a staff as tall as he was. Its shining length glowed with pulsing, moving radiances. Every magelord shouted out a spell, as one—and the very air seemed to shatter.

The end of the Old One's chamber vanished, raining dust down into the inner courtyard of Athalgard. Unseen behind them all, Ithboltar's crystal winked into life.

El let the crystal Tass had taken fade into darkness once more. "Beautifully done, Myr . . . each one wasted a powerful spell."

Myrjala nodded. "We'll not catch them that way again, though—and they're together now, whisked away from their chambers where the knights and Farl's folk could outnumber them."

El shrugged. "We'll just have to do this the hard way, then."

Armsmen clattered up the stairs by the score. Tass wasn't that good with a crossbow, but it wasn't easy to miss striking *something* in that river of armored humanity. As they watched, an elf spread his hands in a spell, and the foremost armsmen stumbled, clutched at their eyes, and ran on blindly into the wall. Their fellows running right behind them tripped over the sightless, falling armsmen. Curses arose, and a thief leaned out from his perch high on a stair to slip a dagger into one open helm and bellow, "We're under attack!" Another thief uttered a gurgling scream from somewhere near the head of the stair. A breath later, the entire stairway was a tumult of slashing blades and screaming men. Farl watched it with a widening grin on his face.

"How can you *smile* at that?" Tassabra said, waving down at the men mistakenly killing each other.

"Every one dead is one less guard to chase us, Tass—men I've itched to strike down for years, and dared not for fear of magelords' seeking magic. And here they are chopping and hacking at each other—they've no one to blame for their deaths but themselves. Let me enjoy it, will you?"

Braer smiled thinly but kept silence. The tall elf felt much the same way, though he didn't like to admit it even to himself. Whatever befell hereafter, they'd got in a few good sword thrusts right through the might of the magelords this night. Nay . . . this day, by now. . . .

Braer looked up out the great window into the gray sky of breaking dawn—and stiffened. A warning spell he'd set three days ago had just been triggered, sending its cry into his mind. He stepped back in haste; as his battle comrades turned startled faces his way, he waved at them to keep away from him.

"My own battle begins, I fear," he murmured, and started to grow taller, his body darkening swiftly. Wings sprouted and spread, scales shone silver in the flickering torchlight, and a dragon shifted its bulk experimentally for a breath before bounding up through the window. Glass and timber flew in all directions, and a long tail switched once as it slid out of the room.

Tassabra stared openmouthed as those great wings beat once, and the dragon that had been Braer surged up into the sky out of their sight. She turned her head a little to catch the last possible glimpse of him, and then her eyes rolled up in her head, she gave a little sigh, and toppled sideways.

Farl gathered her against him with one long arm. "She never used to do this," he complained to no one in particular. One of the elves—Delsaran was his name, Farl thought—leaned over and stroked her hair tenderly, just once.

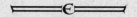

Undarl Dragonrider's face was set in anger as Anglathammaroth flew swift and strong across the realm, heading for Athalgard. Something was seriously amiss. magelords fighting magelords, a rebel mob inside the castle . . . didn't those fools know hated rulers will be attacked by commoners the moment they show weakness? This is what comes of letting ambitious magelings do as they pleased. . . . If it hadn't been for Ithboltar, Undarl could have kept them all in a tight harness!

The mage royal snarled in frustration as the great black dragon dived down over Hastarl, and then gaped in utter astonishment as the breaking dawn showed him a dragon rising to meet them!

A silver dragon . . . Undarl's eyes narrowed. This must be some trick set by a magelord who knew the mage royal would come to the city on dragonback . . . a trap to intercept him. Undarl smiled tightly and cast the strongest spell he carried. Spheres of black, chilling deathflame rolled out from his outflung hands, expanding as they rolled through the air.

The silver dragon sheared away to one side, and Undarl's death flames vanished. The mage royal stared at the empty air in disbelief, and then snatched out one of his wands and fired it. A green bolt of ravening radiance tore along the silver wyrm's side. It shuddered and circled away. With a short laugh of satisfaction, Undarl urged his own dragon after it.

"By all the gods!" a carter swore. Folk around him followed his incredulous gaze, and there was more than one shriek of terror. One man felt to his knees on the cobbles and began babbling a prayer; many others decided to pray on the run, sprinting away down the street—away from the battle raging in the air overhead as two mighty dragons circled and roared in the first bright rays of morning.

Magic flashed, and the carter snarled a bitter oath. Of course one of the two would be the mage royal, not caring if death rained down on the citizens below—but who was the other? A silver wyrm, now! The carter peered up into the sunlight, seeing the black dragon breathe out acid in a curling cloud. That would fall as a stinging rain on . . . the docks, he judged, and wondered if he should be elsewhere, somewhere safer.

But where? There was no place that the two battling wyrms might not imperil . . . no safe place to run to. The carter stared helplessly at the house and shops all around as more screams broke out from their windows. Down on the street folk began to run. He looked at them sprinting in all directions, and then turned his gaze back up to the sky. He shrugged. If fleeing won no safety, he might as well stay here and see all he could. He'd never see such a thing again . . . and if he lived to tell about it, he could always say he'd been there, and watched it through to the end.

The black dragon roared out a challenge. Baerith'ryn of the High Forest wasted no breath in reply. He was working a magic as he rose in a tight spiral, banking and curling his tail to avoid the bolts of death the wizard was firing repeatedly from his wand.

"Stand and fight!" Undarl snarled. A moment later, a bolt caught the wheeling silver dragon's tail. It convulsed and plunged down below him, wind rippling in its wings, followed by the mage royal's triumphant laughter.

Something flickered in the air around him, but Undarl felt no pain: A failed spell, he thought, dismissing it with a shrug, and urged Anglathammaroth into a dive. If its claws could rake the silver wyrm's wings, this battle could be ended right now.

The black wyrm's shoulders surged powerfully. Undarl exulted in its might as the wind streaming past his ears rose into a wail. Aye, let it be *now!*

The silver wyrm was beating its wings frantically, trying to evade Anglathammaroth's dive. Undarl snarled at his steed to turn, turn, and not let their foe escape . . . but the smaller, lighter silver dragon was turning tightly back in and under them. They were going to plunge past it. . . .

Anglathammaroth twisted violently; only the harness kept Undarl from falling helplessly out of his high saddle. The black dragon's limbs curled as he tried to rake or bat at their foe with at least one cruel claw, but the silver wyrm was arching away from them. It was going to slide completely clear! As the rooftops of Hastarl rushed up to meet them, Undarl snarled in anger and triggered his wand again, aiming at the silver dragon's face. Its eyes, proud and sorrowful, met his own: it knew he could not miss.

The green bolt leaped out—and there was a flash as it struck a hitherto unseen barrier, a sphere around Undarl that—*gods!*

The mage royal roared out in helpless fear as the rebounding bolt crashed into him. Faerûn seemed to explode around him. The torn ends of harness straps slapped his face and shoulders, he spun in agony and felt a new, greater pain as one of the other wands in his sleeve exploded, blasting that arm to nothing and flinging him out of the saddle. . . . Then, mercifully, Undarl Dragonrider lost all sight of sky and twisting dragons and rooftops below. . . .

The black dragon screamed, a raw sound of horror and agony that echoed back from the city below, awakening every citizen of Hastarl who still slept. The wyrm arched and writhed, but its back was broken, the torn flesh where the saddle had been streaming gore into the wind. Nerveless wings trembled helplessly. Unable to turn, Anglathammaroth dived on toward Athalgard.

The crash shook all Hastarl. Flying raggedly, curled around his own weary agony, Braer saw those black wings crumple like those of a crushed insect—and the castle tower they'd struck shifted, cracked, and with a thunderous roar, toppled over into the courtyard below. Doomed armsmen screamed as they saw death coming down on them; Braer closed his eyes so as not to see the destruction.

Pain ruled him now. Braer felt his magic failing, his torn and bleeding body shifting and dwindling. As his wings receded back into the slim shoulders of an elf, he began to fall.

The rooftops were very close; he hadn't much time for a last prayer "Mother Mystra," he gasped, fighting to open his eyes. He had a brief glimpse of smoke trailing from his own limbs, and then he was caught by something and cradled gently, the rushing wind around him slowing. Tears were blinding him. Furiously Baerithryn blinked them away and stared up into the face of his rescuer.

Dark eyes glowed with power in the face bent so close over his own. It was Elminster's colleague, Myrjala, and yet—Braer's eyes widened in recognition and awe. "*Lady?*"

It was dark and cold this deep in the dripping cellars of Athalgard. Here below the sewers, the solid stone walls sweated water, and things long undisturbed scuttled or slid away as the sudden fire blazed in their midst. Blood and formless flesh curled and flowed at its heart; flesh that blurred and coiled and spasmed, as all that was left of Undarl Dragonrider fought to rebuild his body. A long time the mage royal struggled, the light flickering and waning as the man shaped one arm onto the shoulder, head, and back that had survived. Then he fought with all his will, panting, to give himself legs again.

Several times he slipped toward his true form, but each time regained the semblance he wanted—a taller, more regal Undarl. The pain ebbed as his confidence grew. . . . He was winning. . . . He could weave all matter to his will, given time enough.

A second arm lengthened into a hand and fingers. Undarl fought to control its thrashing, but could not. Not yet. Give me, gods, just a little more time. . . .

The magelords were arguing bitterly as Elminster rose like a vengeful wraith from Ithboltar's crystal. Bits of the ceiling broke off here and there to fall and shatter on the floor below. Proud wizards stepped back hastily. El's hard eyes were on the Old One as he whispered the last careful words of a mighty incantation.

It ended—and the stone floor of the chamber split from end to end with a crack that deafened them all. Gems, blazing like tiny fireballs, flew in all directions from the Old One's crown.

Ithboltar staggered, screamed in pain, and clutched his head.

A few of the magelords saw Elminster as he vanished back into the crystal, but their angry and disbelieving gazes were caught by the flickering forces spiraling out from the shattered skullcap on Ithboltar's head. Smoke was rising from their staggering ex-tutor's eyes. The crown pulsed, spinning a vortex of gathering force out into the chamber.

Hasty incantations were being chanted all over the shattered chamber as the vortex shivered, throwing off roiling waves of force that swept the wizards into each other and dashed them against the walls . . . and the crown exploded, white bolts of destruction stabbing out in all directions. Magelords wailed and flickered in and out of visibility as contingencies took effect.

Watching the scene from a balcony across the courtyard, Myrjala murmured the last words of a spell of her own. A bloody, disheveled Elminster appeared out of the air beside her, gasping.

They stared together into the shattered chamber. Ithboltar's headless body swayed for a moment, took one unsteady step forward and fell. Over against one wall, a magelord was gibbering on his knees, and another of the mages had become a smoking heap of bones and ashes.

The other wizards were struggling to escape, hands moving in frantic spellcastings. The vortex, adorned with the swirling bolts the crown had spat into it, gathered speed and strength like an angry cyclone as it swept across the chamber toward them. A roar like a deep, unending roll of thunder grew and moved with it, throwing back echoes from the walls and towers of Athalgard. The entire castle began to shake.

Myrjala frowned and made a pulling motion with her hands. The seeing eye she commanded slid through the ragged gap in the wall to hang just outside the tower "The crown," she murmured, "must be holding them in the room."

The vortex struck the mages—and whirled through them to the back wall of Ithboltar's spellchamber It smashed into those old stones, the tower shuddered . . . and slowly, with terrible purpose, the shattered room folded in on itself and collapsed, bringing down the upper reaches of Ithboltar's tower in a titanic crash and roar of falling stone.

An earsplitting explosion burst from where the chamber had been, flinging stones out of the avalanche of falling rock, and among them, one magelord was dashed across the courtyard like a rag doll. He was still struggling weakly to work a spell as his body smashed into another tower. The face of a servant, watching in fascinated horror from a window, was spattered with the wizard's gore. What was left of the mage slid limply down the stone wall . . . and then vanished in a little cluster of winking lights as a last contingency magic awoke. Too late.

Stones were cascading down the walls of the riven tower when the courtyard itself rocked and shuddered. Gratings, paving stones, and dust leaped aloft, borne on sudden geysers of magical radiance, as something exploded in the unseen dungeon depths of the castle.

The shattered stump of Ithboltar's tower swayed, sagged sideways, and crashed into utter ruin. Flames leaped up here and there about the courtyard, amid the frantically running armsmen. The soldiers of Athalantar stumbled on through smoke and dust vainly waving their halberds about as if cleaving the air would fell some invisible foe and set all to rights again.

Somewhere a raw screaming arose and went on and on, amid fresh rumblings.

"Come," Myrjala said, taking Elminster's hand and slipping up to the balcony rail. Elminster followed, and she stepped calmly off it into the air. Hands clasped, they drifted slowly down through the tumult. Athalgard was erupting with running, shouting soldiers. The two mages were still a few feet above the paving stones when a band of armsmen sprinted around a nearby corner and swept down on them.

The guardcaptain saw wizards in his path and slowed, throwing his arms out to signal his men. "What befell?" he bellowed.

Elminster shrugged. "Ithboltar got a word or two of a spell wrong, methinks."

The officer stared at them, and then at the fallen tower, and his eyes narrowed. "I don't know you!" he said sharply. "Who *are* you?"

Elminster smiled. "I am Elminster Aumar, Prince of Athalantar, son of Elthryn.

The guardcaptain gaped at him. Then with a visible effort, he swallowed and asked, "Did you—cause this?"

Elminster gave the wreckage around a pleasant smile, then shifted his gaze to the halberds blocking his way and said, "And if I did?"

He raised his hand. Beside him, Myrjala had already raised her own. Small lights spun and twinkled above her cupped palm.

The armsmen cried out together in fear . . . and an instant later were in full flight, flinging down their halberds and slipping and sliding on the stones underfoot in their headlong haste to get back around the corner.

"You may go," Myrjala grandly told the empty courtyard where they'd stood. Then she chuckled. After a moment, Elminster joined in.

"We can't hold on much longer!" Blood from a gash left by the axe-stroke that had split his helm was dripping into Anauviir's eyes as he shouted desperately at Helm.

The old knight roared back, "Tell me something I don't know!"

Beside him, a red-faced Darrigo Trumpettower was panting as he swung a heavy blade he'd snatched from a dead hand. The old farmer was protecting Helm Stoneblade with his faltering right arm and his life. That was a price, it seemed, soon to be paid.

The surviving knights stood together on the slippery, blood-smeared cobbles of Athalgard's outer courtyard. Armsmen were charging in at them from all sides now, streaming in the gates from barracks and watchtowers. A few old men in motley armor couldn't stand against such numbers for long.

"We can't hold!" one knight cried despairingly, hurling an armsman to the ground and wearily stabbing the man in the face.

"*Stand and fight!*" Helm roared out, his raw voice rising above them all. "Even if we fall, every armsman we take with us is one less to lord it over the realm! Fight and die well for Athalantar!"

A First Sword got through Darrigo's guard, laying the old man's cheek open with the point of his blade. Helm lunged forward and ran the man through, his sword buckling against the man's spine and the armor plate behind it. He let go of his weapon and tore the man's own blade out of failing hands to fight on.

"Where *are* you, Prince?" he muttered as he slew another armsman. Aye, the knights of Athalantar couldn't hold out much longer . . .

King Belaur was wont to partake of evenfeast at about the time lesser men sought their morning meal. He would dine heavily on fresh fish slathered in fresh-frothed cream, and then turn to venison and hare cooked in spiced wine. When he felt full to bursting, he'd retire to the royal chambers to steep his belly's load off. He awoke now, stretched, and strolled naked into his larger, more public bedchamber. Belaur expected to find there fresh minted wine and warmer, livelier entertainment.

This day, rising to the waking world amid the thunders of a strange dream of shakings and rumblings, he was not disappointed. In fact, he was pleased to see two women waiting in the ornate and gigantic bed. One was the woman who'd led that Moonclaws thieving band. Isparla 'Serpenthips' glittered, languorous and dangerous, amid the cushions. Smiling at him in her collar and hip-string of jewels, she looked like a cat strung with diamonds, and trembling beside her was the new wench he'd noticed the evening before outside a midtown bakery. Unclad, the new arrival was even more entrancing than he'd hoped. She wore only the spell-chains magelords used to make defiant prisoners more biddable, and for the occasion someone had polished the links and the collars encircling her wrist, ankles, and throat so they gleamed as bright as Isparla's jewels.

Belaur met her eyes with a savage grin, snatched up a goblet and a decanter from the shining row atop a nearby board, and expressed his approval with a long, rumbling snarl as he strode to the bed. Like a purring lion he lowered himself between them, quaffing wine lazily, and wondered which pleasure to enjoy first. The new treasure . . . or save her, turning first to familiar delights?

Isparla gave a low, throaty purr of her own, and moved her body against him. The king cast a look at Shandathe, lying anxious and still in her chains, and then smiled and turned away from her. He laid a cruel hand on a rope of jewels, and pulled. Serpenthips hissed in pain as the stones cut into her and she was dragged against him. Belaur bent his mouth to hers, intending to bite. He remembered earlier tastes of her warm, salty blood. . . .

There was a sudden flash and a singing sound, and Belaur looked up, startled, into a gaze as frowning as his own. The mage royal of Athalantar stood beside the bed. Belaur cast a quick look down the room at the still-barred doors and back at the master of magelords before he roared, "What are you playing at *now*, wizard?"

"We're under attack," Undarl snarled at the king. "Come! Up and out of here, if you would live!"

"Who *dares*—?"

"We'll have time to ask them who they are later Now *move*, or I'll blast your head from your shoulders . . . all I *need* to take is the crown!"

Face dark with fury, Belaur heaved himself up from the bed, spilling wenches in both directions, and snatched down the sword that hung on the wall. For an instant, he considered thrusting it into the back of the mage royal, who was striding down the room to a painting that could be swung aside to reveal a way up into the old castle. Undarl turned with more speed than the swiftest sword in Belaur's bodyguard, drawing aside from the extended point of the blade, and said in a cold, clear, menacing voice, "Don't. Ever. Even. Think. Of. Such. A. Deed." He leaned closer, and added in a harsh whisper, "Your daily survival depends on my magic."

The blade in the king's hand turned into a snake that reared up and hissed at him, throwing coils around his wrist.

As he stared at it in frozen horror, it slid back into sword shape, and flashed mockingly once, Belaur shuddered, reluctantly turned his gaze to meet the hard points of the magelord's cold eyes, and managed a nod. Then he moved forward obediently as Undarl gestured at the passage door

"Ye know I must do this alone," Elminster said quietly as they stood together in the darkened passage.

Myrjala laid a hand on his arm, and gave him a smile. "I shall not be far. Call if you want me."

El saluted her with the stump of the Lion Sword and strode away down the passage, exchanging the remnant of his father's sword for a more serviceable blade.

The last prince of Athalantar had very few spells left, and lurched in weariness as he went. In his tattered tunic and breeches, drawn sword in hand, he could not have been a usual sight in the grand central rooms and halls of Athalgard as he made his way to the throne room, Servants he passed—and there were many—kept their eyes downcast and stepped smoothly out of his way, as if long used to making way for swaggering warriors. Courtiers tended to stare, and then quickly looked away or turned down another passage or hastened through the door and closed it behind them.

Save for many glances back over his shoulder, Elminster seemed out for a casual walk. Guards stiffened at their posts as he approached, but he'd cast a certain spell before parting from Myrjala. The guards tensed for battle . . . and then froze, held motionless by his magic as he strode past.

When El approached seven armsmen with their backs to high arched double doors, and drawn swords in their hands, he murmured an incantation that sent creatures slumping into slumber beneath a magical cloak that stilled all sound.

The blades raised against him fell to the floor in eerie silence, followed by their owners. El stepped calmly over the doorguards, drew one of the doors open a little, and slipped within.

The high room beyond was hung with banners and encircled by a high gallery; the walls were richly tapestried. Pillars flanked a carpet of deep forest green that ran straight from where he stood to a high seat alone at the other end of the room.

The Stag Throne. What he'd fought his way toward—not just the chair, he reminded himself, but a land around it free of magelords. Men and a handful of women were milling about just within the doors, all around him, talking and shifting their feet rather wearily: courtiers, merchants, and envoys nervously awaiting the return of the king for early court.

Elminster ignored their curious looks, stepped around several in his path, and strode confidently along the green carpet.

The steps leading up to the Stag Throne were guarded by a mountain of a man in gleaming coat-of-plate, standing patiently with a warhammer as long as he was tall in his hands. He wore no helm, and his balding head gleamed in the flickering torchlight as he glared coldly at the intruder, his gray mustache bristling. "Who art thou, stripling?" he asked loudly, taking a step forward, the warhammer sliding up to rest ready on one shoulder.

"Prince Elminster of Athalantar," was the calm reply. "Stand aside, if you would."

The warrior sneered, Elminster slowed his pace and gestured with his blade for the armsman to step aside. The guardian gave him a mirthless, disbelieving smile, and stood his ground, waving the hammer warningly.

El gave the man a brittle smile and lunged with his blade. The warrior smashed it aside with the warhammer, twisting his wrists so the mighty weapon's backspike would lay open this arrogant foot's head on his return sweep. Elminster stepped smoothly back out of his reach and murmured something, raising his free hand as if throwing something light and fragile.

It raced from those delicately spread fingers, and the guardian of the throne blinked, shook his head as if disagreeing violently with something, and crashed to the polished stone tiles beside the carpet. Elminster calmly walked past him and sat on the Stag Throne, laying his blade across his knees.

A murmur arose from the stunned court, then broke off in a fearful hush as sudden light blazed into being from above. In the heart of the pulsing purple-white radiance, the mage royal appeared in the hitherto-empty gallery—flanked by a dozen armsmen or more, loaded crossbows in their hands.

Undarl Dragonrider's hand chopped down. In response, seven crossbow bolts sped at the man on the throne.

The young intruder watched calmly as those bolts cracked and shivered in the air in front of him, striking something unseen and falling aside.

The magelord's hands were moving in the flourishes of a spell as the senior armsman ordered, "Ready bows again!"

Elminster lifted his own hands in quick gestures, but the folk watching saw the air around the throne flicker and dance with sudden tight. El knew no magic would take hold where he sat now; he could raise no barrier to stop missiles or blades seeking his life.

The mage royal laughed and ordered the armsmen who hadn't fired their quarrels yet to loose them. Elminster sprang to his feet.

A fat merchant standing under a pillar suddenly flickered and became a tall, slim woman with bone-white skin and large, dark eyes. One of her hands was raised in a warding gesture—and the crossbow bolts leaping toward the Stag Throne caught sudden fire as they flew. They flared and were gone.

The senior armsman turned and pointed at Myrjala. "Shoot her down!" he ordered, and two crossbows cracked as one.

Dodging around the throne, deciding which spell to use when he got far enough away from Undarl's magic-rending field, Elminster watched those bolts streak across the throne room at his onetime tutor They glowed a vivid blue to his magesight.

He stared in horror; spells flared out angry radiance around them. Undarl laughed coldly as a sudden burst of light marked the destruction of a shield spun around the sorceress. It was followed by a second flash, an instant later, as an inner shield failed—and Myrjala staggered, clutched at her breast where one bolt stood quivering, turned sideways so he saw the second bolt standing in her side—and fell. Undarl's harsh laughter rang out loudly. Elminster started down the steps at a run, his own safety forgotten. He was still three running paces short of Myrjala's sprawled form when she vanished.

The green carpet where she'd lain was empty. Elminster turned from it, eyes blazing, and spat a spell. He was a single snarled word away from the end of the incantation when the mage royal's cruel eyes, fixed triumphantly on his own, faded away into empty air. The wizard had vanished, too.

Elminster's completed spell was already taking effect. Sudden fire raged along the gallery, and armsmen screamed hollowly inside their armor, writhing and staggering. Crossbows crashed down over the rail, followed by one guard, armor blackened and blazing, who toppled over the gallery rail and crashed down atop a merchant, smashing him to the flagstones. There were fresh screams from the courtiers as they rushed for the doors.

The portals they sought were flung open then, bowling over more than one hurrying merchant, and into the throne room strode King Belaur, naked but for a pair of breeches. His face was dark with anger, and a drawn sword glittered in his hand.

Folk fell back before him—and then fled in earnest as they saw who was behind the king. The mage royal was smiling coldly as he walked, his hands weaving another spell. Elminster went white and spat out a word. The air flashed, and that end of the throne room shook, but nothing happened . . . except that a little dust drifted down from above.

Undarl laughed and lowered his hands. His shield had held.

"You're on *my* ground now, Prince—and fool!" he gloated. Then his face changed, he gasped—and felt forward with a howl of pain.

Behind him, belt knife red to the hilt, stood a certain baker, brows trembling in fury. Hannibur had come to Athalgard to find his wife. Courtiers gasped. Hannibur reached down to cut the magelord's throat, but Undarl's hand darted out in a gesture.

The air pulsed and flowed, and the baker's raised dagger shattered. From the whirling sparks of its destruction rays of light leaped out in all directions: a protective spell-cage flashed into being around the fallen mage.

Elminster glared at Undarl and spoke a clipped, precise incantation. A second cage, its glowing bars thicker and brighter than Undarl's, enclosed the first. The mage royal struggled up to one elbow, face pinched in pain, and his hand went to his belt.

Hannibur stared down at the purposeful magelord and the radiances that had just consumed his only blade, shook his head in slow anger, and turned away. It was only two steps to the nearest courtier. A quick jerk freed the startled man's sword from its jeweled scabbard. Holding it like a toy, the baker turned slowly to survey the room, like a heavy-helmed knight peering about in search of foes, Then, implacably, he started down the green carpet toward the king.

A courtier hesitated, and then followed, drawing his own belt knife. Elminster spoke a soft word, and the man froze in midstep, Overbalanced, the motionless man fell over on his face. A second and third courtier, who'd also reached for their blades, stepped back, suddenly losing interest in defending their king.

Elminster sat down again on the Stag Throne to watch his angry uncle come for him. It seemed a fitting place to wait.

King Belaur was furious, but not so rash as to rush right onto the unwavering point of Elminster's waiting sword. He advanced with menacing care, his own blade held high, ready to sweep down and smash aside Elminster's steel. "Who are you?" he snarled. "Get off my throne!"

"I am Elminster, son of Elthryn—whom you had that caged snake over there murder," Elminster replied crisply, "and this seat is as much mine as yours." He sprang down the steps, sword flashing, and went to meet Belaur.

EIGHTEEN
THE PRICE OF A THRONE

How much does a throne cost? Sometimes but one life, when sickness,
old age, or a lucky blade takes the life of a king in a strong kingdom.
Sometimes a throne costs the life of everyone in a kingdom. Most often,
it takes the life of a few ambitious, grasping men, and the more of
those the Realms is rid of the better.

THALDETH FAEROSSDAR
THE WAY OF THE GODS
YEAR OF MOONFALL

Their swords crashed together, ringing loudly. Both men reeled back from the numbing impact, and Elminster carefully declaimed words that echoed and rolled around the room. The two men were suddenly encircled by a wall of white radiance that seemed to be a whirlwind of flashing phantom swords.

Belaur sneered. "More magic?"

"It's the last I'll unleash in Faerûn until ye're dead," Elminster told him calmly, and strode forward.

They met in a whirling clash of steel. Sparks flew as king and prince tried to hack through each other's guard, teeth set and shoulders swinging. Belaur was a heavy-shouldered warrior of long years, run to fat but wary as a wolf. His challenger was younger, smaller, lighter, and quickly on the defensive, as Belaur used his weight to smash through Elminster's parries. Only the young prince's swiftness kept him alive, ducking, dodging, and diving aside from thirsty steel as the furious king rained a flurry of sword blows on his foe.

When Elminster's arms grew too numb to take the onslaught, he was forced to give way. He stepped back and circled to the right. Belaur turned to press him, grinning savagely, but Elminster spun away and ran, heading behind the throne.

"Hah!" Belaur shouted triumphantly, striding forward. He was only a few steps away when Elminster stepped out from behind the throne to hurl a dagger at the king.

Belaur's blade flashed up to smash whirling death aside. The unharmed king did not even slow his rush, He sneered in triumph as he charged in to cut his enemy down.

Elminster parried desperately, dodging around in front of the throne again. The king leaped after him and lunged, but his swifter foe slid out from under the blade. The king snarled, bent to his boot, plucked a dagger from it, and threw it all in one swift flurry and grunt. Elminster ducked away—too slowly.

The dagger burned across his cheek and spun on its way ... and Belaur was at him again, blade flashing.

El's parry was almost too late. The impact jarred his hand, and he shook it to banish numbness and then hastily put both hands to his blade, thrusting it up just in time to smash aside the king's next attack. Belaur's leaping steel seemed to be everywhere.

The Sword of the Stag, Elminster had heard it called—a new-forged blade said to be enchanted by magelords. El was beginning to believe that. Their weapons crashed together again. Sparks flew as steel shrieked and then caught, guard to guard.

The two men snarled into each other's eyes, shoving, both refusing to leap back. Belaur's shoulders, now glistening with sweat, rippled and bunched ... and Elminster's blade was slowly forced back and around. Belaur bellowed exultantly as his greater strength forced the locked blades into Elminster's neck, and blood flowed. Gasping, Elminster dropped suddenly to the floor, wrapping his legs around Belaur's as their blades flashed over his head.

Overbalanced, the king crashed heavily to the tiles, elbows smashing down hard. The locked swords spun far away as Elminster kicked himself free. They were on the floor on their sides now, face to face. Belaur rolled and reached for Elminster's throat. Elminster tried to knock those strong hands aside, and the two men grappled for a moment. Then the prince was overpowered again.

Hard, gouging fingers stabbed at his throat. Spitting in Belaur's face, El arched his head away, struggling. The king smashed his fist against Elminster's forehead, then got a good firm hold on the prince's throat. El clawed vainly at the hairy arms that were choking him and tried to wrench himself free by kicking on the slippery tiles. He managed only to drag the king a little way. Belaur bore down, grunting triumphantly. Elminster's lungs were burning now. The world slowly began to spin and grow dim.

His desperately scrabbling fingers touched a familiar hardness—the Lion Sword! Carefully, as the darkness rushed up to claim him, Elminster drew out the sharpened stub of his father's blade and slid its uneven edge across Belaur's throat. He closed his eyes as the king's hot blood drenched him. Then Belaur was gurgling and thrashing feebly, hands falling from Elminster.

Free to rise at last! Elminster rolled to his feet, shaking his head to clear it, coughing weakly for air, and peering about to make sure no armsmen were near,

A courtier was just retreating from his barrier, hissing in pain from a webwork of cuts welling forth bright fresh blood. Another man who'd tried to breach the barrier lay on his face on the tiles, unmoving. The prince shook his head and turned away.

When he found breath and balance, and stood wiping Belaur's blood from his face, Elminster saw that the courtiers were huddled back along the walls under the gallery. A few had swords out, but none of them wore the faces of men eager for battle. The king made a last wet, rattling sound ... and then it died away, and he lay still, facedown in his own blood. Elminster drew a deep, trembling breath and turned, the Lion Sword in his hand. It seemed a long way down the green carpet to where Undarl Dragonrider, who'd obviously managed a spell to heal himself, was trying everything he knew to break Elminster's spell cage.

A spell flashed out from the caged wizard, clawed vainly at the radiant cage, and then rebounded on him. The mage royal shuddered. Elminster smiled tightly and waded into the cage he'd spun. Its energies raged briefly along his limbs like hungry lightning, surging through him until he trembled uncontrollably.

Undarl's hands were flicking faster than those of any mage El had ever seen, but Elminster had a very short distance to reach. The Lion Sword stabbed down into the wizard's fast-muttering mouth. Undarl made a choking sound, then Elminster leaped on him, sobbing, and stabbed the mage royal repeatedly.

"For Elthryn! For Amrythale!" the last prince of Athalantar cried. "For Athalantar! And—for me, gods blast you!"

The body beneath his blade started to flow and twist. Suddenly fearful of contingencies, Elminster sprang clear. The blood that sprayed from his dripping weapon as he did so was . . . black!

El stared in horror at the bloody ruin of the master of the magelords. The wizard Undarl swayed up to his feet, took one sagging step, and clawed weakly at Elminster—with hands that were suddenly scaled and taloned. His pain-twisted face lengthened into a scaled snout as the wizard fell, and a long, forked tongue flopped onto the tiles before his writhing body was suddenly surrounded by twinkling tights. Amid those lights, the scaly thing slowly and quietly faded from view, leaving behind only a black pool of blood on the tiles.

Elminster stared down at where his greatest enemy had lain, feeling suddenly so weary that he could scarce . . . stand. . . . The prince toppled to the floor, the jagged stub of blade that had slain both the king and the mage royal clattering from his hand, The glowing barrier of blades faded swiftly.

Silence fell. It was several long, still moments before a courtier hesitantly stepped out from behind the pillars, warily drawing his slim court sword. He took a cautious step forward, and then another . . . and raised his blade to stab the fallen stranger.

Steel flashed at his throat, and the courtier leaped back with a scream. The king's blade gleamed in the light as the baker who held it glared around the throne room. "Keep back!" Hannibur snarled, "all of ye!"

Merchants and courtiers alike stared at the stout, disheveled figure standing over the fallen stranger, waving the Sword of the Stag a little uncertainly but with fierce determination . . . until a great light streamed into the room. Their staring faces turned to it, only to goggle all the more.

Through the open double doors walked the source of the radiance: a tall, slim, regal lady with bone-white skin, dark eyes, and a confident manner. She was leading another woman by the hand, a bewildered, barefoot maid wearing a fine gown that did not fit her, who shrieked as she saw the baker and burst into a headlong run. "Hannibur! *Hannibur!*"

"Shan!" he roared, and the Sword of the Stag clattered forgotten to the floor. Sobbing, they rushed into each other's arms.

A bright glow seemed to shine from the regal lady's body as she smiled at the embracing couple and walked calmly along the bloodstained carpet to where Elminster lay on the tiles. She waved her hand, and something suddenly shimmered and sang in the air around them both. Standing there in the light she'd conjured, the woman looked like some sort of sorcerous goddess as she lifted her chin and stared around the chamber with those dark, mysterious eyes. Folk who met that gaze fell still and stared helplessly; Myrjala looked around the chamber until all the watching folk were in her thrall.

Then she spoke, and every man and maid there swore until their dying day that she'd spoken to them, and to them alone.

"This is the dawn of a new day in Athalantar," she said. "I want to see folk who were welcome in this hall when Uthgrael was king. Bring them here to the throne before night falls. If Belaur and his magelords suffered any to live this long, bring them, and bid them fair welcome! A new king summons them!"

Myrjala snapped her fingers, and her eyes darkened. Suddenly folk were moving, pushing toward the doors in urgent haste.

When she snapped her fingers again, only Hannibur and Shandathe, smiling through their tears, were still in the room to turn and see an ornate coffer obediently appear from empty air.

Myrjala looked up, smiled, and waved at them to stay as she drew a flask from the coffer. As she knelt beside Elminster and unstoppered it, the bright glow began to fade from her skin.

The streets were soon full of curious folk, some still smelling of hastily abandoned evenfeast. Hesitantly entering the gates of Athalgard, they skirted a battle between the magelords' armsmen and some unfamiliar warriors and crowded on into the hall of the throne by the score. There were children peering excitedly at everything, shopkeepers looking about warily, and bright-eyed old men and women who tottered and shuffled about, leaning on sticks or the arms of younger folk.

Proud and lowly alike they pushed into the throne room, gawking at the blood and the blackened, dangling bodies of the armsmen, and most of all at King Belaur, sprawled bloody and half-naked by the Stag Throne.

A young, hawk-nosed man they did not know sat on that throne, and a tall, slender woman whose eyes were very large and dark stood beside him. He looked like an exhausted vagabond despite the Sword of the Stag across his knees—but she looked like a queen.

When the room grew so crowded that the press of bodies drove Shandathe up against the shimmering barrier and she gave a little cry of alarm, Myrjala judged the time was right. She stepped forward and gestured at the weary-looking man on the throne. "Folk of Athalantar, behold Elminster, son of Prince Elthryn! He has taken his father's throne by right of arms—do any here deny his right to sit on the Stag Throne and rule the realm that was his grandfather's?"

Silence answered her. Myrjala looked around the chamber. "Speak, or kneel to a new king!"

There were uneasy stirrings, but no one spoke. After a moment, Hannibur the baker knelt, drawing Shandathe down with him. Then a fat wine-merchant went to his knees, and then a horse-trader . . . and then folk were kneeling all over the room.

Myrjala bowed her head in satisfaction, a long labor ended, and said, "So be it."

On the throne, Elminster sighed. "At last, 'Tis over?" Sudden tears spitted down his face.

Myrjala looked out over the kneeling crowd, at the older folk at the back of the chamber, searching among the faces—until she suddenly smiled and raised her hand in greeting.

"Mithtyn," she said to an old, bearded man, "you were herald in Uthgrael's court. Be it so recorded that none contested Elminster's right to the throne."

The old man bowed and said in a voice dry from little use, "Lady, it shall be . . . but who art thou? Ye know me, and yet I swear I've ne'er seen thee before."

Myrjala smiled and said, "I looked different, then. You said once, after you saw me, that you had not known I could dance."

Mithtyn stared at her and turned very pale. He found his mouth had fallen open, swallowed, and staggered back a pace, overcome with awe. Then he fell to his knees, trembling. Myrjala smiled at him and said, "You do remember. Be not afraid, good herald. I mean you no harm. Rise, and be at ease."

She turned back to the throne. "As we agreed, El?"

He nodded, smiling through his tears. "As we agreed."

Myrjala nodded, and strode down the green carpet until she was in the center of the room. The folk of Hastarl parted before her as if she were preceded by a row of leveled lances. "Stand back, folk of the court!" she said pleasantly. "Clear a space, here before me!"

Their retreat became a hasty rush . . . and when a large area of tiles was clear, Myrjala snapped her fingers and spread one hand.

The empty space was suddenly filled. Some twenty sweating, bleeding armed men were standing before her, reddened blades raised, looking around wildly.

"Peace!" Myrjala said. She seemed suddenly taller, and a white radiance pulsed and played again around her. Such was the force of her voice that the warriors did not move. They stood silent, staring around in unmoving wonder at each other and at the halt around them.

"Behold, folk of Hastarl!" Myrjala said. "Here stand men who have remained true to Athalantar—men who want freedom for their realm and an end to the rule of cruel magelords. They are the knights of Athalantar, and mark he who leads them—Helm Stoneblade, a true knight of Athalantar!"

Elminster rose from the throne and came to stand beside her. The two glanced at each other, smiled, nodded—and the hawk-nosed man strode into the midst of the dumbfounded armed band. Blades swung to point his way, but no one struck a blow.

Elminster walked up to Helm. "Surprised, old friend?"

Helm nodded, unspeaking. His dirt-smudged, sweating face wore a look of astonishment and a little awe. Elminster smiled at him, and then looked around at the crowd and said loudly, "By right of arms, and my lineage; the Stag Throne is rightfully mine! Yet I know well that I am not suited for it. One better suited to rule stands here before you! Folk of Athalantar, kneel and do homage to your new king—Helm of Athalantar!"

Helm and his men stood amazed. A ragged cheer rose and then died away again. Even in Hastarl, clasped most tightly in the fist of the magelords, folk had heard of the daring rebel of the backlands.

Elminster embraced Helm, tears in his eyes, and said, "My father is avenged. The land I leave to you."

"But—why?" Helm asked in disbelief. "Why give up yer throne?"

Elminster laughed, traded glances again with Myrjala, and said, "I'm a mage, now, and proud of it. Sorcery is . . . well, it feels right to me. Working with it is what I do, and was meant to do. I'll have little time for the care a realm needs, and even less patience for intrigue and pomp." He smiled crookedly and added, "More than this: I think Athalantar's had enough of wizards ruling things for a long time."

Heartfelt murmurs of agreement were heard all around the chamber, as the doors burst open and a band of ruffians stared into the chamber, swords glittering in their hands. Farl and Tassabra stood at the head of the thieves of the Velvet Hand. El waved merrily to them; Helm shook his head, as if seeing troubles in the days ahead, sighed—and then, as if he could not stop himself, smiled.

"There is one thing we would like before we go," Myrjala purred as she stepped up to them both.

Helm eyed her warily. "Aye, Lady?"

"A feast, of course. If you're of like mind, I'll work a spell that forces all cold iron out of this hall, so that none need fear weapons—even arrows—here tonight, and we can all make merry!"

Helm stared at her. Then he suddenly threw back his head and shouted with laughter. "Of course," he roared, " 'Tis the least I can do!"

Mithtyn was pushing through the crowd toward them, leading a young, trembling page, who bore the crown of Athalantar on a cushion. Elminster smiled, took up the circlet with a bow, and placed it on Helm's head. Then he cried, "Kneel, folk of Athalantar, before Helm Stoneblade, Lord of Athalantar, King of the Stag Throne!" There was a thunder of movement as everyone in the hall—except Elminster and Myrjala—knelt.

Helm bowed his head, grinned at the two of them in thanks, and clapped his hands. "Rise, all!" he roared. "Bring food and wine and tables! Call out the minstrels from all over this city, and let us make merry!" His men threw down their swords and roared back their approval, and the great chamber was suddenly full of happy, shouting people. They wavered in Elminster's sight . . . and he found his face was wet with tears again. "Mother . . . Father . . ." he whispered, unheard in the tumult, "I have done the right thing."

Myrjala's arms were suddenly around him, warm and comforting, and he leaned his face into her bosom and wept. *It is a glorious thing to be free at last.*

More food had vanished than Helm had thought possible. He grinned around at snoring folk sprawled on the benches . . . and his smile broadened as he looked down the carpet to where most of his men were dancing, whirling flush-faced lasses of Hastarl around the floor as weary minstrels played on and on. Among them, the dark-eyed sorceress who'd accompanied Elminster was treading the measures, dancing with first one of his men and then another. She still looked as fresh and as serene as if she were a queen newly arrived from her chambers of a morning.

There on the floor, as they whirled and stepped to the music, a stubbled and dirty warrior bowed over Myrjala's hand and turned her through the intricate steps of the sarad. As he dipped past her, he asked curiously, "Lady, I mean no offence—but why did ye not kneel to the new king?"

"I kneel to no man, Anauviir," Myrjala said and smiled. "If you would know why, ask Mithtyn in the morning."

She left the warrior wondering how she knew his name, and turned away through the dancing folk to find Mithtyn.

He was standing with most of the older folk by the pillars, watching the dance. As she glided toward him out of the whirling dancers, the old man went pale and turned to hasten away, but found himself surrounded by folk pressed forward for a good look. He had nowhere to go.

Myrjala took him firmly by the hand. "After your praise for my dancing, you don't want to measure this floor with me? I'm hurt, brave Mithtyn! You'll not escape me tonight!"

There were chuckles and half-jealous, half-teasing words from the folk standing around as the sorceress dragged the old herald out into the dance—but when he returned to his place later, he stood tall and smiled, and walked as if he were a much younger man.

Elminster was tired, and his throat hurt . . . but Tassabra had firmly whirled him into the midst of the dancers and guided him deftly through a dance of many avid kisses and caresses—and when Farl had smilingly reclaimed her, clapping El on the back so hard that the prince had almost fallen to his knees, the ladies of the court had pressed in.

El found that the night fled slowly before his stumbling feet, but always another beautiful, eager lady of the court, eyes shining with excitement, was waiting for his hand, and the dances went on.

His feet were beginning to hurt as much as his raw throat, and sweat was trickling down his back under his already-soaked shirt . . . and still the music went on, and still he was surrounded by eager ladies. Shaking his head, Elminster peered past whirling shoulders and laughing faces, seeking a tall, regal face with serene dark eyes. Then he was looking into them, and though half a hundred folk were dancing between them, Myrjala's voice seemed a soft whisper in his ear: "Go, and enjoy! Meet me here at dawn!"

Elminster asked the air, "But what will ye be doing?"

A few whirling turns later, Myrjala swept up to and past him and winked. El watched her dance up to Helm, deftly pluck him from the very arms of Isparla, and turn her head back to meet his wondering eyes. "I'll think of something!" Myrjala said to her pupil, and set off across the room, towing Helm by the hand. The old knight shook his head, grinned at Elminster, and shrugged.

Elminster stared across the room at them, astonished at the bubbling laughter in her voice—and then, helplessly, started to laugh. He was still rocking with mirth as smooth hands drew him away through a door into less-well-lit antechambers, where there were couches, and wine, and eager lips to share it with. . . .

In the first gray light of dawn, Elminster staggered back into the throne room. His head was pounding and his mouth very dry. Something seemed to be wrong with his balance, and he was still belting and adjusting the tattered remnants of his clothing when he came through the double doors, and looked straight into Myrjala's amused eyes. She stood in front of the Stag Throne looking immaculate, her dress and regal appearance unchanged from the evening before. "Has Athalantar thanked you property?" she asked teasingly.

Elminster gave her a look. His fingers, still busy fastening and adjusting, encountered smooth silkiness, and he drew a lady's veil from where it been caught up under his belt. Shaking his head, he held it out to Myrjata. "Ye want me to pass this up?" he asked mournfully.

She laughed. "You'd be sick of plots and betrayals inside a tenday. . . . One doesn't have to be king to eat and dance and love a night away, you know."

Elminster sighed and looked around the throne room at the shields and banners of his ancestors. His gaze came very slowly back to her from looking on distant memories, and he stirred.

"Let's to horse, then," he said briskly, "and be out of here before Helm's awake."

Myrjala nodded and stepped forward to link her arm with his. They went out of the throne room together.

The stables were huge and dimly lit, but quiet; it was well before the first feeding. Myrjala calmly chose the two best horses, and ordered a drowsy-eyed groom to saddle them.

"Here, now—" he protested, frowning. "Thos—" He broke off hastily, staring into her stern eyes. His eyes fell to her hands, beginning to shape a spell, and he gulped and said, "A moment, Lady—they'll be ready'n' but a breath or two!"

Myrjala smiled dryly, then turned to Elminster and snapped her fingers. Bulging saddlebags melted slowly out of thin air beside his feet. Elminster gave her a questioning look.

"I took the liberty," she said with a serene and innocent smile, "of assembling these early this morn. Folk who conquer kingdoms and then give them away deserve to eat well, at least."

Elminster hefted one of them and found it was gods-cursed heavy . . . and that it clinked. Coins, or he'd never been a thief. He deftly undid the knots and opened the throat of the bag wide. It was full of gold coins.

Myrjala smiled at him innocently and spread her hands. "How much gold can one king spend? We'll need something to see us along the trail to our next adventure . . ."

"And just where is that, if I may ask?" Elminster cupped his hands, and she put a toe of one soft, pointed boot into them, springing lightly up into the saddle.

"*This* adventure's not quite done yet, I fear," Myrjala replied in a warning tone. Elminster looked at her thoughtfully, but she said no more as she urged her mount on toward the stable gate.

They went out into the mists of the morning and found Mithtyn leaning on his stick waiting for them. He looked up at them, swallowed, and managed a smile. "Someone of Athalantar should thank ye both property. I fear I have not the words . . . but I would not want thee to ride away without even a salute!"

Myrjala gave him a little bow from her saddle, and said, "Our thanks, Mithtyn. Yet I see something troubles you . . . and I would know what it is, if you will."

Mithtyn stared up at her for a moment, and then his words come in a rush. "Alaundo's prophecy, Lady! He's ne'er been wrong yet, and he said 'the Aumar line shall outlive the Stag Throne'! That can only mean Athalantar won't survive without an Aumar as king . . . and yet ye ride away!"

Elminster gave the anxious old man a crooked smile. "While I live, the Aumar line lasts. Let this land grow in strength and happiness, as I hope to, in the days ahead."

Mithtyn said nothing, face troubled, but bowed low. They raised their hands to him in farewell, and rode away up the street in silence. As they went, the risen sun touched the rooftops with rose-red light. The old herald stared after them, still and silent.

They paused at the top of the lane. The hawk-nosed young man looked toward the old burial ground and said something to the tall lady who rode with him, pointing. The herald peered, trying to see what the prince who was giving up his kingdom had indicated . . . and could just make out a lump of cloth.

'Twas . . . a cloak, drawn over a sleeping man and woman. Mithtyn cleared his throat in embarrassment, but by then he'd recognized them: the smiling man called Farl and his lady, the beautiful little one. Aye, Tassabra, that was her name. And behind them, someone was sitting, staring right back at him! An elf! A tall, silent male elf, with a staff of wood across his knees . . . Mithtyn gulped, raised his hand in an awkward salute, and saw it returned.

Then the elf turned his head. Mithtyn looked in the same direction in time to see the prince and the—sorceress, if she wanted to be known so—vanishing around a corner behind the old stone of a proud house. When they were gone, Mithtyn shivered once. Then he turned back into the castle, his eyes wet with tears. He knew he'd not see anything of like importance for the rest of his days. Such knowledge is a heavy thing to bear early in the morning.

Perhaps after a good dawnfry, a few hot mugs, and his wife to tell it all to, Mithtyn hoped—not for the first time—he'd live long enough for his daughter to be old enough to heed, and hear, and appreciate what he told her. He'd tell her about this morning perhaps a hundred times.

As he crossed the courtyard, one of Helm's knights approached and hesitantly told the old herald what the Lady Myrjala had said about herself while dancing the night before. Mithtyn looked into the man's eyes and discovered he did have someone to tell about it, after all. He led Anauviir toward the kitchens, feeling much better.

"Whither now?" Elminster asked, as Myrjala reined in where the trail crossed the shoulder of a little knoll west of the city. He looked around curiously; from Hastarl, one couldn't see this was a grave-knoll. A stone plinth stood within a low wall, overgrown with shrubs and low-branched trees that cloaked the stone from all but the closest eyes.

"In all your struggle, you've gained none of the spells wielded by the magelords," Myrjala replied. "As it befalls, I know where the mage royal kept a cache of magic—spellbooks, healing potions, and items held ready in case he was hounded from Hastarl, or ever found the city held against him. Here in this old shrine of Mystra, where no thieves come for fear of the guardian ghosts of dead mages, is his cache."

"Is it guarded?" Elminster asked warily, as they dismounted amid the trees.

"*Of course it is, fool mageling!*" someone snarled from behind him.

Elminster whirled around—in time to see the rearing body of his horse flow and twist . . . into the familiar shape of Undarl, mage royal of Athalantar. Myrjala's mount screamed in terror, and they heard the frantic drumming of hooves as it fled.

Elminster gulped and plucked at his belt for the things he'd need to cast what paltry battle-spells he had left. Undarl's gloating grin told him he was not going to be in time. The master of the magelords raised his hand and began to murmur something, but Myrjala sprang between them, skirts swirling. The lightning that cracked forth from Undarl split before her upraised hands and splashed harmlessly off to either side.

The mage royal screamed in anger. When he could find words through his fury, he snarled at her, "*You!* Always, it is you! *Die,* then!" His next words were a hissed incantation, and streams of fire burst from his fingertips in a crimson web that crackled and clawed the air, but was turned back by Myrjala's conjured shield. Elminster had no spells left to match such magics; he could only stand anxiously in the lee of Myrjala's barrier.

The web of fire Undarl had spun began to glow a dull, angry red. The mage royal lashed at the shield with his fading flames, and called out a name that echoed among the stones of the shrine.

His call was answered by a vast bestial roar. Something huge and dark rose up from behind the trees behind the mage royal . . . a red dragon! It unfurled batlike wings and hissed, eyes glinting with cruelty. Then its shoulders surged and it leaped through the air toward the prince and the dark-eyed sorceress. It breathed fire as it came, a roaring torrent of flame that poured over Myrjala's shield . . . but could not consume it.

The sorceress said something long and awkward, and the dragon's flame doubled back on itself, coiling and turning from red to an eerie bright blue before it became white hot. To Elminster's magesight it seemed even brighter; Myrjala had transformed it into something awesome. It rushed back at the dragon like a hungry wind. El glimpsed dark wings beating frantically amid the roiling flames for a moment, and then, in an explosion that rocked the knoll and hurled him from his feet, the dragon burst apart.

Scales and blackened scraps of flesh flew past the last prince of Athalantar as he struggled to his feet and saw Undarl snarling and lashing at the sorceress with his whip of flames, seeking to pierce the shield. Fire roared and rumbled.

Myrjala stood unmoving against the fury of the flames, and spoke a single calm word. The edges of her shield began to grow, lengthening into long, lancetike tips that reached toward Undarl, pulsing with power.

The wizard laughed contemptuously. His arms were growing longer, too, stretching into tentacles. The tips of his snakelike limbs hardened into sharp, red, long-taloned claws. The lance-tips of the shield reached him and passed harmlessly through. Undarl's laughter grew more shrill, and his face had begun to stretch forward horribly into a snout. The talons of his hands ended in small bulbous things, now, each with its own snapping mouth.

"My spell can't touch him!" Myrjala exclaimed, amazed.

The mage threw back his head, and his ever-wilder laughter echoed back from the stone plinth behind him. "Of course not! I am no puny mortal of Faerûn, to be mastered by your magic—I walk the shadows where I will on many worlds. Many think themselves mightier than me, only to learn the depths of their folly in the moments before they perish!"

Undarl's ever-larger tentacle-heads suddenly swooped around the shield and were upon her, darting and biting like writhing snakes. Myrjala shrieked as one bit off her raised hand—but her scream was abruptly cut off an instant later when the wizard's head, dragonlike now, breathed out fire that burst through the shield without pause. The sorceress vanished from the waist up, collapsing in a smoking welter of ashes and blackened bones.

"No!" Elminster cried, leaping on the dragon-thing the magelord had become. He clawed at its eyes, kicking and weeping.

Undarl shook him off. El fell heavily, saw the fanged snout turn just above him to breathe down devouring fire, and rolled in under it with desperate speed, rising beneath those snarling jaws.

Undarl's flame roared skyward, useless, as the prince snatched out the stub of the Lion Sword and stabbed at its throat repeatedly, forcing the dragon-thing to recoil. Even as its head arched back away from his blade, hissing, Undarl's biting claws clutched and tore El's back and face. Elminster crooked an arm around the dragon-thing's throat and swung around behind it, scrabbling for balance. Those clattering claws swarmed in on him, but he drove his blade deep into one of the dragon's golden eyes.

Undarl convulsed and shuddered, tearing free. Its newly grown tail smashed El away. He rolled in the dirt as the dragon-thing squalled and thrashed in agony. Elminster scrambled to his feet and carefully cast a lash of lightning, a feeble spell that might not do more to a dragon than singe its scales—but he cast it not at Undarl, but at the hilt of the Lion Sword, where it stood quivering in the dragon's eye.

Lightning leaped and flashed. The dragon-thing stiffened, jerked its tail, and sank limply back across the low stone wall, its brain cooked. Smoke rose in lazy curls from its eyes and nose.

Weeping in fury, Elminster hurled every battle-spell he had left. Before his streaming eyes the scaly body of his foe was chopped apart and then frozen. He stood over the riven carcass until he could force his trembling lips to shape the words of his very last battle-spell. Small, stinging bolts of magic lanced out at the pieces of Undarl, hurling them aloft. El did not stop until only tangled lumps of flesh remained amid blood . . . blood everywhere.

Still weeping, Elminster turned to where Myrjala had fallen. Fallen defending him—again. He tried to embrace her ashen bones, but they crumbled and he was holding only drifting dust . . . and then, nothing.

"No!" he sobbed brokenly, on his knees before Mystra's shrine in the brightening morning. "No!"

He stood up, mouth working, and shouted at the uncaring sun, "Magic brings only *death!* I'll wield magic *no more!*"

The ground rumbled and rocked at his words, and something slithered around his feet. Elminster looked down . . . and froze, watching in stunned silence. The ashes around him began to glow and drift together over the overgrown stone, rising and reshaping themselves into . . . Myrjala!

Honey-brown hair swirled as the glow became her bone-white body, lying on the stones. The hair wavered as if disturbed by an ebbing wave, and fell aside to reveal his teacher's familiar, pert face, and those large, dark eyes. They opened and looked up at him.

Elminster stood gaping in shock as Myrjala said gently, "Please, Elminster . . . never utter such words again—please? For me?"

Dumbly, Elminster fell to his knees again, reaching out wondering hands to touch her shoulders. They were solid, and smooth, and so were the hands that lifted to him and pulled his mouth down to hers. The sharp smell of burnt hair was strong around them as Elminster pulled back in alarm, wary of another magelord trick, and stared down into the eyes of the sorceress.

Their eyes met for a long time, and El *knew* he was facing Myrjala. He swallowed, tears falling from his cheeks onto her own, and said, "I-I promise. I thought ye dead . . . ye *were* dead, burned to ashes! How can this be?"

Fire rose and raged, deep in those dark eyes staring up into his. The ghost of what might have been a smile passed over her lips as she said softly, "For Mystra, anything is possible."

Elminster stared down at her, and then at last, he realized who—what—his teacher truly was.

In real fear, he tried to pull away. A hint of sadness crept into those dark eyes, but then their gaze sharpened and, as much as the firm arms around his neck, held him motionless. The goddess Mystra held him captive with her eyes of dark mystery, and said softly, "Long ago, you said you could learn to love me." Suddenly her eyes held a challenge.

Face white, wordless, Elminster nodded.

"Show me, then, what you've learned," the Lady beneath him said softly, and cool white fire rose up around them both.

Elminster felt clothes and all burn away as they rose into the air amid searing flames, up into the morning sky above the weathered stone plinth. Then her lips met his, and the burning began, as power such as he'd never known before surged into him.

The cart squeaked loud enough to rouse the sleeping dead, as usual. Bethgarl yawned as he pushed it up the bumpy slope before the long descent into Hastarl . . . but then, he was all too used to it.

"Awaken, Hastarl!" he muttered, spreading his arms grandly and yawning again. "For Bethgarl Nreams, famed cheese merchant, cometh, cart loaded high with wheels of sharpcrumble, whitesides, and re—" something moved and caught his eye off to the left, by the old grave-shrine. Bethgarl looked in that direction, then up—and a third yawn died forever as his jaw dropped open in wonder.

He was looking—nay, staring—at a rising ball of blue-white flame, flaring so bright he could scarce bear it . . . but he *had* looked, eyes burning, and seen two folk floating half-hidden in its heart! A man and a maid, and they were. . . . Bethgarl stared, rubbed his watering eyes, stared again, then let fall his cart and ran back the way he'd come, for all he was worth, howling in fear.

Gods, he'd *have* to stop eating those snails! Ammuthe had been right, as usual . . . oh, gods, why had he ever doubted her?

Sated, they floated in each other's arms, hiding from the brightness of highsun in the shade of an old and mighty tree.

The white flames were gone, and Mystra seemed only a languid, beautiful human woman. She rested her head on his shoulder and said softly, "Now your road must be alone, Elminster, for the more I walk Toril in human form, the more power passes from me, and the less I become. Thrice I died as Myrjala, watching over you—here, in Ilhundyl's castle, and in the throne room in Athalgard . . . and with each death I am diminished."

Elminster stared down into her dark eyes. As he opened his mouth to speak, she put fingers over his lips to still him, and went on. "Yet you need not be alone—for I have need of champions in the Realms: men and women who serve me loyally and hold a part of the power over Art that is mine. I would very much like you to be one of my Chosen."

"Anything, Lady," Elminster managed to say. "Command me!"

"No." Mystra's eyes were grave. "This you must freely agree to—and before you speak so quickly, know that I am asking of you service that may last a thousand thousand years. A hard road . . . a long, long doom. You will see Athalantar, with all its folk and proud towers, pass away, crumble into dust, and be forgotten."

Those dark eyes held his, and Elminster floated, looked into them, and was afraid. Staring into his eyes, the goddess went on. "The world will change around you, and I shall command you to do things that are hard, and that will seem cruel or senseless. You will not be welcome in most places . . . and your welcome in others will be born of fawning fear."

She drifted a little apart from him and turned them both, until they hung upright in the air, facing each other. "Moreover, I will not think ill of you if you refuse. You have done far more already than most mortals ever do." Her eyes glowed. "More than that, you fought at my side, trusting me always, and never betraying me or seeking to use me for your own ends. It is a memory I shall always treasure."

Elminster began to weep again. Through the tears, he managed to say huskily, "Lady, I beg of ye—command me! Ye offer me two things that are precious indeed, thy love and a purpose for my life! What more can any man ask than those? I would be honored to serve ye . . . make me, *please*, one of thy Chosen!"

Mystra smiled, and the world around seemed brighter. "I thank you," she said formally. "Would you like to begin now, or have some time to ride your own way and be yourself first?"

"Now," Elminster said firmly. "I want no waiting for doubt to creep in . . . let it be now."

Mystra bowed her head, exultation in her eyes. "This will hurt," she said gravely as her body drifted in to meet his again.

As their lips touched and clung, lightning leaped from her eyes into his, and the white fire was suddenly back, roaring up around them deafeningly, searing him to the bone. Elminster tried to shriek with pain, but found he could not breathe, and then he felt himself torn, tugged, and swept away into the rising flame, and it did not matter anymore. . . .

"Such tales you tell!" Ammuthe was working herself up into a fine temper as she walked. She tossed her head, and that magnificent hair swirled in the sunlight. "Always such fancies—so, well enough, my husband dreams when awake as well as when he snores! I give the gods thanks for that, and in silent despair put up with it! But *this* time—a whole cart of our cheeses let fallen to be snatched up by who knows who? Too much, indeed, my lazy sluggard man! You shall feel more than the edge of my tongue, if every single one of those chee—"

Ammuthe broke off in midtirade, staring up at the grave-shrine on the hill. Trembling with renewed fear, Bethgarl nonetheless allowed himself a small, leaping moment of satisfaction as Ammuthe shrieked, spun about, and ran headlong into his chest.

Bethgarl staggered back, but held her firmly. "None o' that, now," he said, not too loudly, casting a wary eye up at the streaming, roiling sphere of white fire above the shrine of Mystra. "We'd gather up all the cheeses, you said . . . I'd not eat at our table again until you'd seen the money for them, you said . . . well, presently, good wife, I shall grow hungry. I know I will, and—"

"By all the gods, Bethgarl! Shut thy mouth and *run!*"

Ammuthe made as if to jerk free of him. Bethgarl sighed and let her go, and she was off like a rabbit, bounding down the hill again, hair streaming behind her. Bethgarl watched her go, fought down a sudden wild desire to laugh, and turned back to his cart. One of the cheeses had fallen off into the grass. He dusted it thoughtfully, put it back, picked up the handles, and pushed the cart on toward Hastarl, ignoring the sudden cries of his name from far behind.

As he passed the shrine, he looked up at the ball of fire, and winked at it. Then he swallowed. Cold sweat trickled down his back, and he struggled against rising fear. Carefully he pushed the cart on down the hill, not hurrying. He could have sworn that as he stared at the flames, a pair of dark, knowing eyes had met his—and winked back at him!

Bethgarl reached the bottom of the hill and looked back. Fire still pulsed and glowed. Whistling, he pushed his cart on to Hastarl, and frowned curiously at the hubbub by the gates. There seemed to be a lot of folk out in the streets today, all of them excited. . . .

EPILOGUE

There are no endings save death, only pauses for breath, and new beginnings.
Always, new beginnings . . . it's why the world grows ever
more crowded, ye see. So remember, now—there are no endings, only
beginnings. There; simple enough, isn't it? Elegant too.

THARGHIN "THREEBOOTS" AMMATAR
SPEECHES OF A MOST WORTHY SAGE
YEAR OF THE LOST HELM

Elminster floated back from somewhere far away indeed, and found himself lying naked on a slab of cold stone, smoke rising from his limbs. As the last gray wisps curled up and drifted away, he raised his head and looked down. His body was unchanged, unmarked. A shadow fell across him, and he turned his head. Mystra knelt over him, nude and magnificent. Elminster took one of her hands and kissed it.

"My thanks," he said roughly. "I hope I serve thee well."

"Many have said that," Mystra replied a little sadly, "and some have even believed it."

Then she smiled and stroked his arm. "Know, Elminster, that I believe in you far more than most. I felt the Lion Sword's enchantment stripped away by dragonfire that day when Undarl destroyed Heldon, and looked to see what befell, and saw a young lad swear vengeance against all cruel wizards and the magic they wielded. A man of great wits and inner kindness and strength, who might grow to be mighty. So I watched over him as he grew, and liked the choices he made, and what he grew to become . . . until he came to confront me in my temple, as I knew he would in the end. And there he had the courage and the wisdom to debate the ethics of wielding magic with me—and I knew that Elminster could become the greatest mage this world has ever known, if I only led him and let him grow. I have done that~—and El, lovely man, you have delighted me and surprised me and pleased me beyond all my hopes and expectations."

They stared into each other's eyes, and Elminster knew he'd never forget that calm, deep gaze of infinite wildness and love and wisdom, however many years might lie ahead.

Then Mystra smiled a little and bent to kiss his nose, her hair brushing his face and chest. El breathed in her strange, spicy scent anew for a moment and trembled with renewed desire, but Mystra lifted her head and looked southeast, into the quickening breeze. "I need you to go to Cormanthor and learn the rudiments of magic," she said softly.

Elminster raised an eyebrow. "'The rudiments of magic'? What have I been hurling about so far?"

Mystra looked down at him with a quick smile. "Even knowing what I am, you dare to speak so—I love thee for that, El."

"Not *what* you are, Lady," Elminster dared to whisper, "but *who* you are."

Mystra's face lit up with a smile as she went on, "Power, yes, but without discipline or true feeling for the forces you're crafting. Ride south and east from here to the elven city of Cormanthor . . . you'll be needed there in time to come. Apprentice yourself to any archmage of the city who'll have you."

"Aye, Lady," said Elminster, sitting up eagerly. "Will the city be hard to find?"

"Not with my guidance," Mystra said with a smile, "yet be in no haste to rush off. Sit with me this night and talk. I have much to tell you . . . and even gods grow lonely."

Elminster nodded. "I'll stay awake as long as I can!"

Mystra smiled again. "You'll never need to sleep again," she said tenderly, almost sadly, and made a complicated gesture.

A moment later, a dusty bottle stood between them. She wiped its neck clean with one hand, teased out the cork with her teeth like any serving-wench, took a sip, and passed it to him.

"Blue lethe," she said, as Elminster felt coot nectar slide down his throat. "From certain tombs in Netheril."

Elminster raised his eyebrows. "Start telling," he said dryly, and then glowed in the midst of her tinkling laughter.

It was a sound he treasured often in the long years that followed. . . .

Thus it was that Elminster was guided to Cormanthor, the Towers of Song, where Eltargrim was Coronal. There he dwelt for twelve summers and more, studying with many mighty mages, learning to feel magic, and know how it could be bent and directed to his will. His true powers he revealed to few—but it is recorded that when the Mythal was laid, and Cormanthor became Myth Drannor, Elminster was one of those who devised and spun that mighty magic. So the long tale of the doings of Elminster 'Farwalker' began.

Antarn the Sage
from *The High History of Faerûnian Archmages Mighty*
published circa Year of the Staff

ELMINSTER
IN MYTH DRANNOR

PROLOGUE

It was a time of mounting strife in the fair realm of Cormanthor, when the lords and ladies of the oldest, proudest houses felt a threat to their glittering pride. A threat thrust forward by the very throne above them; a threat from their most darkling youthful nightmares. The Stinking Beast That Comes In The Night, the Hairy Lurker who waits his best chance to slay, despoil, violate, and pillage. The monster whose grasp clutches at more realms with each passing day: the terror known as Man.

SHALHEIRA TALANDREN, HIGH ELVEN BARD OF SUMMERSTAR
from *SILVER BLADES AND SUMMER NIGHTS:*
AN INFORMAL BUT TRUE HISTORY OF CORMANTHOR
PUBLISHED IN THE YEAR OF THE HARP

I did indeed promise the prince something in return for the crown," said the king, drawing himself up to his full height and inhaling until his chest trembled. He adjusted the glittering circlet of gems and golden spires that adorned his brows a trifle self-consciously, smiled at his own cleverness in providing himself with this dramatic pause, and added, voice dropping to underline the nobility of his words, "I promised I'd grant his greatest desire."

Those gathered to watch drew in awed breaths in a chorus that was mockingly loud.

The fat monarch paid them no heed, but turned away in a gaudy swirl of cloth of gold and struck a grandly conquering pose, one foot planted on an obviously false dragonskull. The light of the purple-white driftglobes that accompanied him gleamed back from plainly visible wire, where it coiled up through the patchwork skull to hold the royal sword that had supposedly transfixed bone in a mighty, fatal blow.

Every inch the wise old ruler, the king looked out over vast distances for a moment, eyes flashing gravely at things only he could see. Then, almost coyly, he looked back over his shoulder at the kneeling servant.

"And what, pray tell," he purred, "does he most want? Hmmm?"

The steward flung himself full length onto the carpet, striking his head on the stone pave in the process. He rolled his eyes and writhed briefly in pain—as the watchers tittered—ere he dared to lift his gaze for the first time. "Sire," he said at last, in tones of wondering doom, "he wishes to die rich."

The king whirled about again and strode forward. The servant scrambled up on one knee and cowered back from the purposeful monarch—only to freeze, dumbfounded, at the sight of a merry smile upon the regal face.

The king bent to take his hand and raised him up from the carpet, slapping something that jingled into the steward's palm as he did so.

The servant stared down. It was a purse bulging with coins. He looked at the king again, in disbelief, and swallowed.

The royal smile broadened. "Die rich? And so he shall—put that into his hands and then slide your sword through him. Several times is the current fashion, I believe."

The titters of the audience broke into hoots and roars of mirth, laughter that quickly turned to applause as the costume spells cloaking the actors expired in the traditional puffs of red smoke, signaling the end of the scene.

The watchers exploded into motion, swooping and darting away. Some of the older revelers drifted off more sedately, but the young went racing through the night like furious fish chasing each other to eat—or be eaten. They exploded through groups of languid gossipers and danced in the air, flashing along the edge of the perfumed spell field. Only a few remained behind to watch the next coarse scene of *The Fitting End of the Human King Halthor*; such parodies of the low and grasping ways of the Hairy Ones were amusing at first, but very one note,' and above all elves of Cormanthor hated to be bored—or at least, to admit their boredom.

Not that this wasn't a grand revel. The Ereladden had spared no expense in the weaving of the field-spells. A constant array of conjured sounds, smells, and images swirled and wafted over the revelers, and the power of the conjured field allowed everyone to fly, moving through the air to wherever they gazed, and desired to be. Most of the revelers were floating aloft now, drifting down occasionally to take in refreshments.

This night the usually bare garden walls bristled with carved unicorns, pegasi, dancing elven maidens, and rearing stags this night. Every statuette touched by a reveler split apart and drifted open, to reveal teardrop decanters of sparkling moonwine or any one of a dozen ruby-hued Erladden vintages. Amid the spires of the decanters were the shorter spikes of crystal galauntra whose domes covered figurines sculpted of choice cheese, roasted nuts, or sugarstars.

Amid the rainbow-hued lights drifting among the merry elves were vapors that would make any true-blood light-hearted, restless, and full of life. Some abandoned, giggling Cormyth were dodging through the air from cloud to cloud, their eyes gleaming too brightly to see the world around them. Half a hundred giggles rolled amid the branches of the towering trees that rose over all, twinkling magestars winking and slithering here and there among their leaves. As the moon rose to overwhelm such tiny radiances, it shone down on a scene of wild and joyful celebration. Half of Cormanthor was dancing tonight.

"Surprisingly, I still remembered the words that would bring me here."

The voice came out of the night without warning. Its welcoming tone dared him to recall earlier days.

He'd been expecting it, and was even unsurprised to hear its low, melodious tones issuing from the shadows in the deepest part of the bower, where the bed stood.

A bed he still found most restful, even with age beginning to creep into his bones. The Coronal of all Cormanthor turned his head in the moonlight, looking away from the mirror-smooth waters that surrounded this garden isle, and said with a smile that managed to be happier than his heart felt, "Be welcome, Great Lady of the Starym."

There was silence for a moment in the shadows before the voice came again. "I was once more than that," it said, almost wistful.

Eltargrim rose and held out his hand to where his truesight told him she stood. "Come to me, my friend." He stretched out his other hand, almost beseechingly. "My Lyntra."

Shadows shifted, and Ildilyntra Starym came out into the moonlight, her eyes still the dark pools of promise that he recalled so vividly in his dreams. Dreams that had visited him down all the long years to this very night. Dreams built on memories that could still unsettle him. . . .

The Coronal's mouth was suddenly dry, and his tongue felt thick and clumsy. "Will you—?" he mumbled, gesturing toward the Living Seat.

The Starym held themselves to be the eldest and most pure of the families of the One True Realm—and were certainly the proudest. Their matriarch glided toward him, those dark eyes never leaving his.

The Coronal did not have to look to know that the years had not yet touched her flawless white skin, the figure so perfect that it still took his breath away. Her blue tresses were almost black, as always, and Ildilyntra still wore them unbound, falling at her heels to the ground. She was barefoot, the spells of her girdle keeping both hair and feet inches above the dirt of the ground. She wore the full, formal gown of her house, the twin falling dragons of the Starym arms bold in glittering gems upon her stomach, their sculpted wings cupping her breasts in a toothed surround of gold.

Her thighs, revealed through the waist-high slits in the gown as she came, were girt in the black-and-gold spirals of a mantle of honor. The ends of the mantle drew together to support the intricately carved dragontooth scabbard of her honor blade, bobbing like a small lamp, wrapped in the deep, solemn red glow of its awakened power. The Ring of the Watchful Wyvern gleamed upon her hand. This was not an informal visit.

The moon was right for a chat between old friends, but no matriarch comes aglow in all her power for such things. Sadness grew in the Coronal. He knew what must lie ahead.

And so, of course, she surprised him. Ildilyntra came to a halt before him, as he'd known she must. She drew apart her gown, hands on hips, to let him see the light of the full, gathered power of her honor blade. This also he expected, and likewise the deep, shuddering intake of breath that followed.

Now the storm would come, the snarled words of sarcastic fire or cold, biting venom for which she was famous throughout Cormanthor. The twisted words of harmful spells would lurk among them, to be sure, and he'd hav—

In smooth silence, the matriarch of the Starym knelt before him. Her eyes never left his.

Eltargrim swallowed again, looking down at her knees, white tinged with the slightest shade of blue, where they were sunk into the circle of moss at his feet. "Ildilyntra," he said softly. "Lady, I—"

Flecks of gold had always surfaced in her dark eyes when she was moved to strong emotion. Gold glinted in them now.

"I am not one used to begging," that melodious voice came again, bringing back a flood of memories in the Coronal, of other, more tender moonlit nights in this bower, "and yet I've come here to beg you, exalted lord. Reconsider this Opening you speak of. Let no being who is not a trueblood of the People walk in Cormanthor save by our leave. Let that leave be near-never given, that our People endure!"

"Ildilyntra, rise. Please," Eltargrim said firmly, stepping back. "And give me some reasons why I should embrace your plea." His mouth curved into the ghost of a smile. "You can't be unaware that I've heard such words before."

The High Lady of the Starym remained on her knees, cloaked in her hair, and looked into his eyes.

The Coronal smiled openly this time. "Yes, Lyntra, that still works on me. But give me reasons to weigh and work with . . . or speak of lighter things."

Anger snapped in those dark eyes for the first time. "Lighter things? Empty-headed revelry, like those fools indulging themselves over at Erladden Towers?" She rose then, as swift as a coiling serpent, and pulled open her gown. The blue-white sleekness of her bared body was as much a challenge as her level gaze. Ildilyntra added coldly, "Or did you think I'd come for dalliance, lord? Unable to keep myself one night longer from the charms of the ruler of us all, risen to such aged wisdom from the strong and ardent youth I knew?"

Eltargrim let her words fall into silence, as hurled daggers that miss their target spin into empty air. He ended it calmly. "This spitting fury is the High Lady of the Starym I have grown familiar with these past centuries. I admire your taste in undergarments, but I had hoped that you'd set aside some of what your junior kin call your 'cutting bluster' here; there *are* only the two of us on this isle. Let us speak candidly, as befits two elder Cormyth. It saves so much . . . empty courtesy."

Ildilyntra's mouth tightened. "Very well," she said, planting her hands on her hips in a manner he well remembered. "Hear me then, Lord Eltargrim: I, my senior kin, and many other families and folk of Cormanthor besides—I can name the principals if you wish, Lord, but be assured they are neither few nor easily discredited as youths or touch-headed—think that this notion of Opening the realm will doom us all, if it is ever made reality."

She paused, eyes blazing into his, but the Coronal silently beckoned at her to give him more words. She continued, "If you follow your mad dreams of amending the law of Cormanthor to all non-elves into the realm, our long friendship must end."

"With the taking of my life?" he asked quietly.

Again silence fell, as Ildilyntra drew breath, opened her mouth, and then closed it. She strode angrily away across the moon-drenched moss and flagstones before whirling around to face him once more.

"All of House Starym," she said firmly, "must needs take up arms against a ruler so twisted in his head and heart—so tainted in his elven bloodlines—as to preside over, nay, eagerly *embrace* the destruction of the fair realm of Cormanthor."

Their gazes met in silence, but the Coronal seemed carved of patiently smiling marble. Ildilyntra Starym drew in a deep breath and went on, her voice now as imperious as that of any ruling queen. "For make no mistake, Lord: your Opening, if it befalls, will destroy this mightiest realm of the People."

She stalked impatiently across the garden, flinging her hands up at the trees, shrubs, and sculpted banks of flowers. "Where we have dwelt, loved, and nurtured, the beauties of the forests *we* have tended will know the brutal boots and dirty, careless touch of humans." The Starym matriarch turned and pointed at the Coronal, almost spitting in her fury as she advanced upon him, adding a race with each step. "And halflings." She came on, face blazing. "And gnomes." Her voice sank with anger, trembling into a harsh whisper as she delivered the gasp of ultimate outrage: "Even . . . *dwarves!*"

The Coronal opened his mouth to speak, as she thrust her face forward almost to touch his, but she whirled away again, snapping her fingers, and turned back immediately to confront him again, hair swirling. "All we have striven for, all we have fought the beast-men and the orcs and the great wyrms to keep, will be diluted—nay, *polluted*—and in the end swept away, our glory drowned out in the clamoring ambitions, greater numbers, and cunning schemes of the hairy *humans!*"

That last word rose into a ringing shout that tore around their ears, setting the blue glass chimes in the trees around the distant Heartpool singing in response.

As their faint clamor drifted past the Living Seat, Ildilyntra stood facing the Coronal in silence, breast heaving with emotion, eyes blazing. Out of the night a sudden shaft of moonlight struck her shoulders, setting her agleam with cold white light like a vengeful banner.

Eltargrim bowed his head for a moment, as if in respect to her passion, and took a slow step toward her. "I once spoke similar words," he said, "and thought even darker things. Yet I have come to see in our brethren races—the humans, in particular—the life, verve, and energy we lack. Heart and drive we once had; we can only see now in the brief glimpses afforded by visions of days long gone sent by our forebears. Even the proud House of Starym, if all of its tongues spoke bare truth, would be forced to admit that we have lost something—something within ourselves, not merely lives, riches, and forest domains lost to the spreading ambition of others."

The Coronal broke into restless pacing as Ildilyntra had done before him, his white robe swirling as he turned to her in the moonlight and said almost pleadingly, "This may be a way to win back what we have lost. A way where for so long there has been nothing but posturing, denial, and slow decline. I believe true glory can be ours once again, not merely the proud, gilded shell of assumed greatness we cling to now. More than that: the dream of peace between men and elves and dwarves can at last be upon us! Maeral's dream, fulfilled at last!"

The lady with blue-black hair and darker blazing eyes moved from her stillness like a goaded beast, striding past him as a forest cat encircles a foe it remains wary of . . . for a little while yet. Her voice, when it came, was no longer melodious, but instead cut like a lustily waved razor.

"Like all who fall into the grip of elder years, Eltargrim," she snarled, "you begin to long for the world as you want it to be, and not as it is. Maeral's dream is just that—a dream! Only fools could think it might become real, in this savage Faerûn we see around us. The humans rise in magecraft—brutal, grasping, realm-burning magecraft—with each passing year! And you would invite these—these *snakes* into our very bosoms, within our armor . . . into our *homes!*"

Sadness made the Coronal's eyes a little bleak as he looked at what she'd become, revealed now in her fury—far and very far from the gentle elven maid he'd once stroked and comforted, in the shy tears of her youth.

He stepped into the path of her raging stride and asked gently, "And is it not better to invite them in, win friendship and through it some influence to guide, than it would be to fight them, fall, and have them stalk into our homes as smashing, trampling conquerors, striding amid the streaming blood of all our people? Where is the glory in that? What is it you are striving to keep so sacred, if all our people perish? Twisted legends in the minds of the humans and our half-kin? Of a strange, decadent people with pointed ears and upturned noses, whose blinding pride was their fatal folly?"

Ildilyntra had been forced to halt, or her angry progress would have carried her into him. She stood listening to his rain of questions almost nose to nose, white-clenched fists at her sides.

"Will you be the one to let these—these *beast*-races into our secret places and the very seat of our power?" she asked now, her voice suddenly harsh. "To be remembered with hatred by what few of our People will survive your folly, as the traitor who led the citizens he was pledged to serve . . . our very race . . . into ruin?"

Eltargrim shook his head. "I have no choice; I can see only the Opening as a way in which our People may *have* a future. All other roads I've looked down, and even taken this realm a little way along, lead—and speedily, in the seasons just ahead—to red war. War that can only lead to death and defeat for fair Cormanthor, as all the races but the dwarves and gnomes outnumber us twenty to one and more. Humans and orcs overmuster us by thousands to one. If pride leads us to war, it leads us also to the grave—and that is a choice I've no right to make, on behalf of our children, whose lives I'll be crushing before they can fend, and choose, for themselves."

Ildilyntra spat, "That fear-ladling argument can be made from now until forever grows old. There'll *always* be babes too young to choose their own ways!"

She moved again, stepping around him, turning her head to always face him as she went, and added almost casually, "There is an old song that says there is no reasoning with a Coronal of firm purpose . . . and I see the truth of it now. There is nothing I can say that will convince you."

There was something old and very tired in Eltargrim's face as his eyes met hers. "I fear not, Ildilyntra . . . loved and honored Ildilyntra," he said. "A Coronal must do what is right, whate'er the cost."

She gave an exasperated hiss, as he spread his hands a little and told her, "That is what it means to be Coronal—not the pomp and the regalia and the bowing."

Ildilyntra walked away from him across the moss, to where a thrusting shoulder of stone barred her way and gave a home to lavender creepers. She folded her arms with savage grace, and looked south out over the placid water. It was a smooth sheet of white now in the moonlight. The silence she left in her wake grew deep and deafening.

The Coronal let his hands fall and watched her, waiting patiently. In this realm of warring prides and dark, never-forgotten memories, much of a Coronal's work consisted of waiting patiently. Younger elves never realized that.

The High Lady of the Starym looked out into the night for what seemed a very long time, her arms trembling slightly. Her voice was as high and as soft as a sudden breeze when she spoke next. "Then I know what I must do."

Eltargrim raised his hand to let his power lash out and trammel her freedom—the gravest insult one could give to the head of an elven House.

Yet he was too late. Sudden fire blossomed in the night, a line of sparks where his power met hers and wrestled just long enough to let her turn. Her honor blade was in her hand as her eyes met his.

"Oh, that I once loved you," she hissed. "For the Starym! For *Cormanthor!*"

Moongleam flashed once along the keen edge of her blade as she buried it hilt-deep in her breast, and with her other hand thrust its dragon tooth scabbard into the bright fountaining blood there. The carved fang seemed to flicker for a moment, and then, slowly, melted away into the river of gore. More blood was pouring from her than that curvaceous body should have been able to hold.

"Eltar . . ." she gasped then, almost beseechingly, her eyes growing dark as she swayed. The Coronal took a swift step forward and raised his hands, the glow of healing magic blazing along his fingers—but at the sight of it she snatched forth the glistening blade and drove it hard into her throat.

He was running now, across the little space that remained between them, as she choked, stumbled forward—and swept her gore-soaked arm up once more to drive the blade of her honor deep into her own right eye.

She fell into his arms, then, lips frozen trying to whisper his name again, and the Coronal let her down gently onto the moss, despite the growing roar of magic tearing past him, streaming up into the night sky like bloody smoke from where the dragon tooth had been. Magic that he knew sought to claim his life.

"Oh, Lyntra," he murmured. "Was any dispute worth your final death?" He rose from her then, looking at the blood glistening on his hands, and gathered his will.

Her gore was a weakness, a route the magic mustering above him could take past his gathered power if he banished it too late.

As he stared at his spread hands, the dark wetness faded from them, until they blazed blue-white with risen magic, racing along his skin like fire. The Coronal looked up, then, at the sudden darkness above him—and found himself gazing straight into the open, dripping jaws of a blood dragon.

It was the most deadly spell of the elder Houses, a revenge magic that took the life of its awakener. The Doom of the Purebloods, some called it. The dragon towered above him, dark, wet, and terrible in the night, as silent as a breeze and as deadly as a rain of enchanted venom. Living flesh would melt before it, twisting, withering, and shriveling into grey rot and tangled bones and sinew.

The ruler of all Cormanthor stood robed in his aroused power, and watched the dragon strike.

It crashed down around him, in a rain that shook the entire island, setting leaves to rustling all around and shattering the stillness of the lake into a hundred racing wavelets. Rocks rolled and moss scorched away into smoking ash where it touched. Thwarted in its strike by the dome of empty air his risen power guarded, it swirled and roared, flowing in a hungry circle around the elven ruler.

Eltargrim stood unmoving, untouched in the circle his power protected, and watched it run into oblivion. Once more it raised its head to menace him, a tattered shadow of its former self. He stood his ground grimly, and it fell away to drifting smoke against the blue-white fire of the Coronal.

When it was all gone, the old elf ran a trembling hand through his white hair and knelt again at the side of the sprawled lady. "Lyntra," he said sadly, bending to kiss lips where dark blood still bubbled forth. "Oh, Lyntra."

Blood spat into smoke on her throat then, touched by his power just as the slaying spell she'd called up had been. More smokes rose, as his tears began to fall in earnest.

He struggled against them, as the glass chimes sounded again, and the faltering of his shielding spells let in a burst of distant laughter and wild, high music from the Erladden revel. He struggled because he was the Coronal of Cormanthor, and his duty meant he had one more thing to say before the blood stopped flowing, and she grew cold.

Eltargrim threw back his head to look once at the moon, choked back a sob, and managed to say huskily, looking into the one staring eye that remained, "You shall be remembered with honor."

And if his grief overmastered him thereafter, as he cradled the body of the one who was still his beloved, there was no one else on the island to hear.

PART
I

HUMAN

ONE

SAUAGE TRAILS AND SCEPTERS

Nothing is recorded of the journey of Elminster from his native Athalantar across half a world of wild forests to the fabled elven realm of Cormanthor, and it can only be assumed to have been uneventful.

ANTARN THE SAGE
from *THE HIGH HISTORY OF FAERÛNIAN ARCHMAGES MIGHTY*
PUBLISHED CIRCA THE YEAR OF THE STAFF

The young man was busy pondering the last words a goddess had said to him—so the arrow that burst from the trees took him completely by surprise.

It hummed past his nose, trailing leaves, and Elminster peered after it, blinking in surprise. When he looked along the road in front of him again, men in worn and filthy leathers were scrambling down onto it to bar his way, swords and daggers in their hands. There were six or more of them, and none looked kindly.

"Get down or die," one of them announced, almost pleasantly. El cast quick glances right and left, saw no one charging him from behind, and murmured a quick word.

When he flicked his fingers, an instant later, three of the brigands facing him were hurled away as if they'd been struck hard by the empty air. Blades flew spinning aloft, and startled, winded men crashed into brambles and rolled to slow, cursing halts.

"I believe a more traditional greeting consists of the words 'well met,' " Elminster told the man who'd spoken, adding a dry smile to his dignified observation.

The brigand leader's face went white, and he sprinted for the trees. "Algan!" he bellowed. "Drace! A rescue!"

In answer, more arrows came humming out of the deep green forest like angry wasps.

El dived out of his saddle a scant instant before two of them met in his mount's head. The faithful gray horse made an incredulous choking sound, threw up its forelegs as if to challenge an unseen foe, and then rolled over onto its side to kick and die.

It came within a fingerlength of crushing its rider, who rolled away as fast as he could, hissing curses as he tried to think which of his spells would best serve a lone man scrambling through ferns and brambles, surrounded by brigands hiding behind trees with ready bows.

Not that he wanted to leave his saddlebag, anyway. Panting in his frantic haste, El reached the far side of a stout old tree. He noticed in passing that its leaves were beginning to turn, touched gold and brown by the first daring frosts of the Year of the Chosen, and clawed his way up its mossy bark to stand gasping and peering around through the trees.

Crashings marked the routes of the hurrying outlaws as they ran to surround him. Elminster sighed and leaned against his tree, murmuring an incantation he'd been saving for a time when he might be faced with hungry beasts on a night he'd have to spend in the open. Such a night would never come, now, if he didn't put the spell to more immediate use. He finished the casting, smiled at the first brigand to peer warily around a nearby tree at him—and stepped into the duskwood he was leaning against.

The brigand's startled curse was cut off abruptly as El melded into the old, patient silence of the forest giant, and threw his thoughts along its spreading roots to the next tree that was large enough. A shadowtop, in that direction. Well, 'twould have to do.

He sent his shadowy body flowing along the taproot, trying not to feel choked and trapped. The closed-in, buried feeling drove some mages mad when they tried this spell—but Myrjala had considered it one of the most important things for him to master.

Could she have foreseen this day, years later?

That thought sent a chill through the prince of Athalantar as he rose inside the shadowtop. Was everything that happened to him Mystra's will?

And if it was, what would happen when her will clashed with the will of another god, who was guiding someone else?

He'd have been flying in falcon-shape over this forest, after all, if she'd not commanded him to "ride" to the fabled elven realm of Cormanthor. A bird of prey would have been too high for the arrows of these brigands to reach even if they'd felt like wasting shafts.

That thought carried Elminster out into the bright world again. He melted out of the dark, warm wood into the bright sunlight with the Skuldask Road a muddy ribbon on his left—and the dusty leather of a brigand not two paces away to his right. Elminster could not resist doing something he'd once delighted in, years ago, in the streets of Hastarl: he plucked the man's belt dagger out of its sheath so softly and deftly that the brigand didn't notice. Its pommel bore the scratched outline of a serpent, rising to strike.

Then he froze, not daring to take a step for fear of crushing dead leaves underfoot, and betraying his presence. He stood as still as a stone as the man stalked away, moving cautiously toward where the young mage had run to.

Could he get his saddlebag and flee without being noticed? Even if they hadn't had arrows and some skill in firing them, he really didn't want to waste spells on a handful of desperate men, here in the heart of the Skuldaskar. He'd seen bears and great forest cats and sleep-spiders already on his journey, and heard tales of far more fearsome beasts that hunted men along this road. He'd even found the gnawed bones and rotting, overturned wagons of a caravan that had met death along the road, some time ago ... and he didn't want to become just one more grisly trailside warning.

As he stood, undecided, another brigand strode around the tree, head down and hurrying, and walked right into him.

They fell to the leaves in startled unison—but the young Athalantan already had a blade in his hand, and he used it.

The dagger was sharp, and his slash laid open the man's forehead with a single stroke as El rolled to his feet and sprinted away, making sure that he stomped on the bow that the man had dropped. It snapped under his boots, and then he was running hard for the road, startled shouts following him.

The man he'd cut would be blinded by the streaming blood until someone helped him, and that made one less brigand to chase Elminster of Athalantar. The Berduskan Rapids were still days away—longer, now that he had to walk—and Elturel was an even longer trip back. He didn't relish going either way with a band of cutthroats hunting him, day and night.

He reached his horse, scrambling back down onto the road, and used his borrowed dagger to cut free his saddlebag and the loop that held his scabbard. Snatching up both of them, he ran hard along the road, seeking to win a little distance before he'd have to try some other trick.

Another arrow hummed past his shoulder, and he swerved abruptly into the forest on the far side of the road. So much for that brilliant tactic.

He was going to have to stand and fight. Unless ...

In frenzied haste he dropped his burden and snatched out his sword, the daggers from both boots, and the knife sheathed down his back, its hilt hidden under his hair at the nape of his neck. They joined the borrowed dagger on a clump of moss, clattering into a heap—and he added his fire-blackened cooking fork and broad-bladed skinning knife to them even as he began the chant.

Men were leaping and running through the trees, fast approaching, as Elminster muttered his way through the spell, taking each blade in turn and carefully nicking himself so that drops of his blood fell on the steel. He touched each blade to the tangle of feathers and spiderweb strands he'd scooped out of his pouch-lined baldric, thanking Mystra that she'd whispered to him to mark each pouch so he knew their contents at a glance, and then clapped his hands.

The spell was done. Elminster snatched up his saddlebag to use as a shield against any swift arrows that might come his way, and crouched low behind it as the seven weapons he'd enchanted rose restlessly into the air, skirled against each other for a moment as they drifted about as if sniffing for prey—and then leaped away, racing points-first through the forest air.

The first brigand shrieked moments later, and El saw the man spin around, clutching at one eyeball, and fall down the bank onto the road. A second man spat out a curse and swung his blade in frantic haste; there was a ringing of steel on steel, and then the man reeled and fell, blood spurting from his opened throat.

Another man grunted and clutched at his side, snatching out the cooking fork and flinging it down with a groan. Then he joined the frantic retreat, outpaced by some of his fellows who were sprinting desperately to stay ahead of blades that were rushing hungrily after them.

Whenever steel drew blood, his enchantment fled from it. Elminster dropped his saddlebag and went forward cautiously to retrieve his daggers and fork from the men who'd fallen. It would be easy to slip away now, but then he'd never know how many survived to stalk him—and he'd never get his blades back.

The two El had seen fall were both dead, and a heavy trail of blood told him that a third man wouldn't run much farther before the gods gathered him in. A fourth man made it back to Elminster's horse before the young Athalantan's sword plunged itself into his back, and he fell over it onto his face and lay still.

Elminster retrieved all but his borrowed dagger and one of his belt knives, finding two more bodies, before he gave up the grim task and resumed his journey. Both of the dead men had weapons marked with the crudely scratched serpent symbol. El scratched his jaw, where his unshaven stubble was beginning to itch, and then shrugged. He had to go on; what did it matter which gang or fellowship claimed these woods as its own? He was careful to take all the bows he saw with him, and thrust them inside a hollow log a little farther on, startling a young rabbit out of its far end into bounding flight through the trees.

El looked down at the cluster of bloody blades in his hand and shook his head in regret. He never liked to slay, whatever the need. He cleaned the blades on the first thick moss he found and went on, south and east, through the darkening wood.

The skies soon tuned gray, and a chill breeze blew, but the rain that smelled near never came, and Elminster trudged on with his saddlebag growing heavier on his shoulder.

It was with weary relief that he came down into a little hollow just before dusk, and saw chimney smoke and a stockade wall and open fields ahead.

A signboard high on the cornerpost of what looked like a paddock, though it held only mud and trampled grass just now, read: "Be Welcome At The Herald's Horn." Underneath was a bad painting of an almost circular silver trumpet. Elminster smiled at it in relief and walked along the stockade, past several stone buildings that reeked of hops, and in through a gate that was overhung with someone's badly forged iron replica of the looped herald's horn.

This looked to be where he'd be spending the night. El strode across a muddy yard to a door where a bored-looking boy was peeling and trimming radishes and peppers, tossing his work into water-filled barrels, and keeping watch for guests at the same time.

The boy's face sharpened with interest as he surveyed Elminster, but he made no move to strike the gong by his elbow, merely giving the weary, hawk-nosed youth an expressionless nod of acknowledgment. El returned it and went inside.

The place smelled of cedar, and there was a hearthfire somewhere ahead to the left, and voices. Elminster peered about, his shoulder-borne saddlebag swinging, and saw that he stood in the midst of yet another forest—this one a crowded tangle of treetrunk pillars, dim rooms, and flagstones strewn with sawdust, complete with scurrying beetles. Many of the planks around him bore the scars of old fires that had been put out in time, long ago.

And by the smell of things, the place was a brewery. Not just the sour small beer that everyone made, but the source of enough brew to fill the small mountain of barrels El could see through a window whose shutters had been fastened back to let in a little light and air—and a face that stared in at him, wrinkled bushy brows, and growled, "Alone? Afoot? Want a meal and a bed?"

Elminster nodded a silent reply and was rewarded with the gruff addition, "Then be at home. Two silver a bed, two silver for meals, extra tankards a copper apiece, and baths extra. Taproom's on the left, there; keep your bag with you—but be warned: I throw out all who draw steel in my house . . . straightaway, into the night, without their weapons. Got it?"

"Understood," El replied with some dignity.

"Got a name?" the stout owner of the face demanded, resting one fat and hairy arm on the windowsill.

For a brief moment El was moved to reply merely "Aye," but prudence made him say instead, "El, out of Athalantar, and bound for the Rapids."

The face bobbed in a nod. "Mine's Drelden. Built this place myself. Bread, dripping, and cheese on the mantel. Draw yourself a tankard and tell Rose your wants. She's got soup ready."

The face vanished, and as the grunts and thuds of barrels being wrestled about floated in through the window, Elminster did as he'd been bid.

A forest of wary faces looked up as he entered the taproom, and watched in silent interest as the youth quietly adorned his cheese with mustard and settled into a corner seat with his tankard. Elminster gave the room at large a polite nod and Rose an enthusiastic one, and devoted himself to filling his groaning belly and looking back at the folk who were studying him.

In the back corner were a dozen burly, sweaty men and women who wore smocks, big shapeless boots, a lot of dirt, and weary expressions. Local farmers, come for a meal before bed.

There was a table of men who wore leather armor, and were strapped about with weapons. They all sported badges of a scarlet sword laid across a white shield; one of them saw Elminster looking at his and grunted, "We're the Red Blade, bound for the Calishar to find caravan-escort work."

Elminster gave his own name and destination in reply, took a swig from his tankard, and then held silence until folk lost interest in him.

The conversation that had been going on in a desultory way before his entrance resumed. It seemed to be a "have ye heard?" top-this contest between the last two guests: bearded, boisterous men in tattered clothes, who wore stout, well-used swords and small arsenals of clanging cups, knives, mallets, and other small tools.

One, Karlmuth Hauntokh, was hairier, fatter, and more arrogant than the other. As the young prince of Athalantar watched and listened, he waxed eloquent about the "opportunities that be boilin' up right now—just boilin', I tell thee—for prospectors like meself—and Surgath here."

He leaned forward to fix the Red Blades with wise old eyes, and added in a hoarse, confidential whisper that must have carried clear out back to the stables, "It's on account o' the elves, see? They're moving away—no one knows where—jus' gone. They cleared out o' what they called Elanvae . . . that's the woods what the River Reaching runs through, nor'east o' here . . . last winter. Now all that land's ours for the picking. Why, not a tenday back I found a bauble there—gold, and jools stuck in it, clear through—in a house that had fallen in!"

"Aye," one of the farmers said in a voice flat with disbelief, "and how big was it, Hauntokh? Bigger'n my head, this time?"

The prospector scowled, his black brows drawing together into a fierce wall. "Less o' that lip, Naglarn," he growled. "When I'm out there, swingin' m'blade to drive off the wolves, it's right seldom I see *thee* stridin' boldly into the woods!"

"Some of us," Naglarn replied in a voice that dripped scorn, "have honest work to do, Hauntokh . . . but then, y'wouldn't know what that was, now would you?" Many of the farmers chuckled or grinned in tired silence.

"I'll let that pass, farmer," the prospector replied coldly, "seein' as I like the Horn so well, an' plan to be drinkin' here long after they look at thy weed fields an' use thy own plow to put thee under, in a corner somewheres. But I'll show thee not to scoff at them as dares to go where thee won't."

One hairy hand darted into Hauntokh's open shirt-front with snakelike speed, and out of the gray-white hair there drew forth a fist-sized cloth bag. Strong, stubby fingers thrust its drawstrings open, and plucked into view all it held: a sphere of shining gold, inset with sparkling gems. An involuntary gasp of awe came from every throat in the room as the prospector proudly held it up.

It was a beautiful thing, as old and as exquisite as any elven work Elminster had ever seen. It was probably worth a dozen Herald's Horns, or more. Much more, if that glow betokened magics that did more than merely adorn. El watched its inner light play on the ring the prospector wore—a ring that bore the scratched device of a serpent rising to strike.

"Have ye ever seen the like?" Hauntokh gloated. "Aye, Naglarn?" He turned his head, gaze sweeping across the Red Blade adventurers, who were leaning forward so far in their hunger and wonder that they were almost out of their chairs, and looked at his rival prospector.

"And thee, Surgath?" he charged. "Have ye brought back anything to match half o' this, hey?"

"Well, now," the other bearded, weatherbeaten man said, scratching his head. "Well, now." He shifted in his seat, bringing one booted foot up onto the table, while Karlmuth Hauntokh chuckled, enjoying his moment of clear superiority.

And then the ragtag prospector drew something long and thin out of his raised boot, and grew a grin to match Karlmuth's own. He hadn't many teeth left, El noticed.

"I wasn't goin' to lord it over thee, Hauntokh," he said jauntily. "No, that's not Surgath Ilder's road. Quiet and sure, that's my way ... quiet and sure." He held up the long, thin cylinder, and laid his hand on the crumpled black silk that shrouded it. "I've been in the Elanvae too," he drawled, "seein' what pelts—an' treasure—might come my way. Now years ago—probably afore you were born, Hauntokh, I wouldn't doubt—"

The larger prospector snarled, but his eyes never left the silk-shrouded object.

"—I learned that when you're in a hurry, and in elven woods, you can generally find both those things, beasts and loot together, in one place: a tomb."

If the room had been hushed before, that last word made it strainingly silent.

"It's the one place that hunting elves tend to leave be, y'see," Surgath continued. "So if y'don't mind fighting for your life every so often, you might—just might—be lucky enough to find something like *this*." He jerked the silk away.

There was a murmur, and then silence again. The prospector was holding a chased and fluted silver rod. One of its ends tapered into a wavering tongue like a stylized flame, and the other ended in a sky-blue gem as large as the gaping mouth of the nearest Red Blade adventurer. In between, a slender, almost lifelike dragon curled around the barrel of the scepter, its eyes two glowing gems. One was green, and one amber—and at the tip of its curling tail was yet another gemstone, this one ale-brown in hue.

Elminster stared at it for some seconds before remembering to raise his tankard and cover the eagerness in his face. Something like that, now, if he had to duel with elven guards, would come in very handy indeed ... It was elven work, had to be, that smooth and beautiful. What powers did it have, now?

"This here scepter," Surgath said, waving it—there was a gasp and a clatter, then, as Rose came into the room with a platter of hot tarts, and dropped them on her own toes in startled amazement—"was laid to rest with a lord of the elves, I'm thinking, two thousand summers ago, or more. Now, he liked to play at impressing folk—just like certain lazy, loose-tongued retired prospectors I can rest my eyes on, right now! So he could make this here rod do things. Watch."

His awed audience saw him touch one of the dragon's eyes at the same time as he touched the large gem in the butt of the scepter. A light flashed as he pointed it at Karlmuth Hauntokh—who whimpered and dived for the floor, shivering in fear.

Surgath threw back his head and guffawed. "Less fear, Hauntokh," he laughed. "Stop your groveling. That's all it does, y'see: throw off that light."

Elminster shook his head slightly, knowing the scepter must be doing more than that—but only one pair of eyes in that room noticed the unshaven youth's reaction.

As the rival prospector rose into view again, mounting anger in his eyes, Surgath added grandly, "Ah, but there's more."

He pressed the dragon's other eye and the butt-gem in unison—and a beam leaped across the taproom and sent Elminster's tankard spinning. The young man watched it clatter along the wall, smoking, and his eyes narrowed.

"We're not done yet," Surgath said gaily, as the beam died out and the tankard rolled out of the room. "There's this, yet!"

He touched the tail-gem and the butt-gem, this time, and the result was a humming sphere of blue radiance in which small sparks danced and spun.

Elminster's face tightened, and his fingers danced behind his cheese. He looked down, as if peering for his tankard, so that the others wouldn't see him muttering phrases. He had to quell this last unleashing quickly, before real harm was done.

His spell took effect, apparently unnoticed by the other occupants of the taproom, and Elminster sank back in his seat in relief, sweat gathering at his temples. He wasn't done yet; there remained the small matter of somehow getting the scepter away from this old man, too. He *had* to have that scepter.

"Now," Surgath crooned, "I'm thinking that this little toy wouldn't look out of place in a king's fist—and I'm tryin' to decide which one to offer it to, right now. I've got to get there, do the dickering, and get out again without being killed or thrown in a dungeon. I've got to choose me the right king first off, y'see . . . because it's got to be one that can pay me at least fifty rubies, and all of them bigger'n'my thumb!"

The prospector looked smugly around at them, and added, "Oh, and a warning: I also found some useful magic that will take care of anyone who tries to snatch this off me. Permanently take care of 'em, if y'take my meaning."

"Fifty rubies," one of the adventurers echoed, in awed disbelief.

"D'ye mean that?" Elminster blurted out, and something in his tone drew every eye in the room. "Ye'd sell that, right now, for fifty rubies?"

"Well, ah—" Surgath sputtered, and his eyes narrowed. "Why, lad? You have that saddlesack o' yours stuffed with rubies?"

"Perhaps," Elminster said, nervously nibbling on a piece of cheese and almost biting off the tips of his own fingers in the process. "I ask again: is thy offer serious?"

"Well, p'raps I spoke a mite hastily," the prospector said slowly. "I was thinkin' more of a hundred rubies."

"Ye were indeed," Elminster said, his tone dry. "I could feel it, clear over here. Well, Surgath Ilder, I'll buy that scepter from ye, here and now, for a hundred rubies—and all of them bigger than thy thumb."

"Hah!" The prospector leaned back in his chair. "Where would a lad like you get a hundred rubies?"

Elminster shrugged. "Ye know—other people's tombs, places like that."

"No one gets buried with a hundred rubies," Surgath scoffed. "Tell me another, lad."

"Well, I'm the only living prince of a rich kingdom," Elminster began.

Hauntokh's eyes narrowed, but Surgath laughed derisively. Elminster rose, shrugged, and reached into his saddlebag. When his hand came out, he was holding a wadded-up cloak—to conceal the fact that his hand was in fact empty—and to hide the single gesture that would release his waiting, "hanging" spell.

As the adventurers leaned forward, watching him closely, Elminster unrolled the cloth with a flourish—and gems, cherry-red, afire with the reflected flames of the hearth, spilled out across the table before him.

"Pick one up, Surgath," Elminster said gently. "See for thyself that it's real."

Dumbfounded, Surgath did so, holding it up to the light of the whirling scepter. His hands began to shake. Karlmuth Hauntokh snatched one, too, and squinted at it.

Then, very slowly, he set it back on the table in front of the hawk-nosed youth, and turned to look around the taproom.

El dropped his gaze to the man's hairy hands. Yes, his ring definitely matched the symbol borne by the brigands.

"They're real," Hauntokh said hoarsely. "They're more real'n'that." He jerked his thumb at the scepter, looked down at his own golden bauble, and shook his head slowly.

"Boy," Surgath said, "if you're serious . . . this scepter is yours."

Men and women were on their feet all over the room, goggling at the table strewn with sparkling gems. One of the Red Blades strode forward until he loomed above Elminster.

"I wonder where a youngling gets such riches," he said with slow menace. "Have you any more such baubles, to see you down the long, perilous road to the Rapids?"

Elminster smiled slowly, and put something into the warrior's hand.

The man looked down at it. A single coin glimmered in his palm. A large, olden coin of pure platinum.

Elminster took the scepter from its soft midair twirling, and waved his other hand in invitation at the table of gems. Surgath scrambled for it.

The hawk-nosed youth watched him feverishly raking rubies together and leaned forward to speak to the adventurer, in a soft whisper that carried to every corner of the taproom. "There's just one thing to beware of, good sir—and that's coming to look for more."

"Oh?" the man asked, as menacingly as before.

Elminster pointed at the coin—and suddenly it stirred, rising as a hissing serpent in the man's hand. With a curse the man hurled it away. It struck a wall with a metallic ring, dropped, and rolled away, a coin once more.

"They're cursed, ye see," Elminster said sweetly. "All of them. Stolen from a tomb, they were, and that awakened it. And without my magic to keep the curse under control."

"Wait a bit," Surgath said, face darkening. "How do I know these rubies're real, hey?"

"You don't," Elminster told him. "Yet they are, and will remain rubies in the morning. Every morning after that, too. If you want the scepter back—I'll be in the room Rose has ready for me."

He gave them all a polite smile and went out, wondering how many folk, whether they wore serpent rings or not, would try to slay the spell image that would be the only thing sleeping in El's bed tonight, or turn the room inside out searching for a scepter that was not there. The turf-and-tile roof of the Herald's Horn would do well enough for the repose of the last prince of Athalantar.

Of all the eyes in that taproom that wonderingly watched the young man from Athalantar leave, one pair, in a far corner, harbored black, smoldering murder. They did not belong to the man who wore the serpent ring.

"A hundred rubies," Surgath said hoarsely, spilling a small red rain of glittering gems from one hand to the other. "And all of them real." He glanced up at the reassuring glow of the wards, smiled, and stirred his bowl full of rubies once more. It had cost him the same worth as two of these jewels to buy the wardstone, years ago—but it was worth every last copper tonight.

Still smiling, he never saw the wardstone flash once, as a silent spell turned its fiery defenses on its owner.

There was a muted roar, and then the prospector's skeleton toppled slowly sideways onto the bed. Surgath Ilder would grin forever now.

A few rubies, shattered by the heat, tinkled to the floor in blackened fragments. The eyes that watched them fall held a certain satisfaction—but still smoldered with murder yet to be done. Revenge could sometimes reach from beyond the grave.

After a moment, the owner of those eyes smiled, shrugged, and wove the spell that would bring a fistful of those rubies hence.

We must all die in the end—but why not die rich?

Two
Death and Gems

*The passing of the Mage of Many Gems might have doomed the House of
Alastrarra, had it not been for the sacrifice of a passing human. Many elves of
the realm soon wished the man in question had sacrificed everything instead.
Others point out that in more than one sense—he did.*

Shalheira Talandren, High Elven Bard of Summerstar
from *Silver Blades And Summer Nights:
An Informal But True History of Cormanthor*
published in The Year of the Harp

As he went on through the endless wood, the land began to rise again,
sprouting crags and huge mossy overhangs of rock amid the ever-present
trees. There was no trail to follow, but now that Elminster was past the line of
mountains that marked the eastern boundary of the human realm of Cormyr,
wherever south and east the trees rose tallest must be the right direction to head
for Cormanthor. The hawk-nosed youth with the saddlebag on his shoulder
walked steadily toward that unseen destination, knowing he must be getting
close by now. The trees were older and larger, hung with vines and mosses. He'd
long since left all traces of woodsmen's axes behind.

He'd been walking for days—months—but in a way he was glad brigand
arrows had deprived him of his mount. Even in the lands claimed by the men
of Cormyr, now behind him, the hills had been so trackless and heavily wooded
that he'd have had to let his horse go, thus willfully breaking Mystra's directive.

Long before the terrain would've forced that disobedience on him, he'd
have been coinless from buying hay for the beast to eat, and weary-armed
from hacking at tree-limbs to cut a way large enough for the horse to squeeze
onwards—presuming, of course, that the horse would've been willing to be
ridden into woods too thick to move about in. Woods roamed by things that
snarled and howled at night, and caused many unseen things to scream and
wail as they were slain.

El hoped not to join their ranks overly soon.

He kept holding spells handy; they allowed him to freeze rabbits and sometimes deer where they stood, and get close enough to them to use his knife. He
was getting tired of the bloody, messy butcherings that followed, the constant
rustlings and calls that meant he was himself being watched, the loneliness,
and of feeling lost. Sometimes he felt more like a badly aimed arrow rushing
blindly off to nowhere, rather than a powerful, anointed Chosen of Mystra.
Occasionally he hit something, but all too often—though things *seemed* easy

and straightforward enough—he plunged right into one blunder after another. Hmm. No wonder Chosen were rare beasts.

No doubt there were rarer beasts lurking somewhere in all these trees right now, hunting *him*. Why couldn't Mystra have given him a spell that would whisk him right to the streets of the elven city? The Moonsea lay somewhere ahead and to his left, ending these trees that were elven territory—and if his memory of overheard merchant chatter and glimpses of maps in Hastarl served him rightly, it was linked by a river to an arm of the vast and sprawling Sea of Fallen Stars, which formed the eastern boundary of the elven realm he sought. The mountains behind him were the western edge of Cormanthor—so if he kept walking, and turned right whenever he found a river, he'd stay in elven lands. Whether or not he'd ever find the fabled city at its heart was another matter. El sighed; there'd been no glows of torchlight or the like at night to mark a distant city—and he'd not seen an elf since leaving Athalantar, let alone found one since passing the line of mountains. Something as simple as a fall over a tree root out here could kill him, with no one but the wolves and buzzards to know about it. If Mystra attached such importance to his getting himself to the city, couldn't she guide him somehow? Winter could find him still wandering—or long dead, his bones cracked and forgotten by some owlbear or peryton or skulking giant spider!

Elminster sighed and walked on. His feet were beginning to ache so much—a deep bone-ache, that made him feel sick—that the pain overwhelmed the ever-present sting of broken blisters and raw skin. His boots weren't in good shape now, either. In tales heroes just got to wherever the excitement was without delay or hardship—and if he was a Chosen of Mystra, surely he qualified as a hero!

Why couldn't all of this be *easier*? He sighed again. As the wood went on around him, footfall after weary footfall, mushroom-cloaked roots rose out of the earth everywhere, like contorted walls, and full sunlight became rare. Deer were a common sight now, lifting their heads to watch him warily from afar, and rustlings and flutterings in the ever-present shade around told him that other game was growing more plentiful, too.

Elminster ignored most snags and shrubs and clinging creepers, for fear of lurking danger; not wanting to be hunted by anything hungry that had a nose, he'd long ago cast a spell that left him treading air a foot or so clear of the ground. He left no trace of his passage, keeping to where gnarled forest giants choked out saplings and thorn-thickets, and the way was relatively clear. He was making good progress; when he grew weary he rested in the shape of a cloud of mist clinging to high branches in the night. Someone or something was following him, of course.

Something too wary, or cunning, to let him get a look at it. Once he'd even cloaked himself in a spell of invisibility and doubled back on his route. He found the tracks of his pursuer hastily turning aside to end in a stream. All the last prince of Athalantar learned was that the being shadowing him was a lone human—or some other sort of being that wore hard-soled boots. On two feet.

So he'd shrugged and pressed on, heading for the fabled Towers of Song. The elves suffered no human to see their great city and live, but a goddess had commanded El to go thence, in his first service to her. If elves clinging fiercely to their privacy didn't approve, that was just too bad.

Too bad for him, if his alertness or spells failed him. Once already there had been a burst of blue light in the dusk off to his left one evening, as a trap spell claimed the life of an owlbear. Elminster hoped such magics were specific in their triggerings . . . and weren't waiting for humans who used spells to keep clear of the ground.

One thing was increasingly clear to him, now: even elves eager to be friendly, if Cormanthor boasted any such, weren't likely to welcome an intruding human with smiles if that lone visitor was carrying a scepter of power looted from an elven tomb.

The attention he'd attracted back at the Horn had been a mistake, whatever danger that prospector's ignorance of magic had posed. He'd lost a night's sleep, and had to use hasty spells to snatch himself clear, when at least four folk with spells and daggers had separately attacked his sleeping chamber. The last one had come creeping across the roof, blade in hand, right to where El was listening to the sounds of two of the others knifing each other to death in the darkness below.

Now he was carrying a beautiful—and no doubt very recognizable—thing of gems and chased silver that an elf who saw it might be able to awaken from a distance to turn its powers on Elminster . . . a scepter that might bear a curse or spit magics that harmed anyone arousing them. A scepter that had belonged to an elf whose surviving kin might slay any human who dared to touch it. A scepter someone might be tracing even now.

How could he have been so *stupid?* El sighed again. Somewhere on this journey he had to hide the scepter, in a place where he—and, barring tracing spells, only he, not some mysterious follower or elven patrol—could find it again. And that meant a distinctive landmark; in this endless wood, something of the land beneath the trees, not a tree itself. He kept a watch for something suitable.

Soon after sunrise, on the day after Elminster walked above the dark waters of his twelfth swamp, he found it. The land rose sharply in a line of pointed crags, the last one a bare stone needle like the prow of some gigantic ship eager to sail up to the sun.

Elminster chose the crag next to the prow. It was a lower, tree-girt height, with a duskwood tree he liked the look of clinging to one of its edges. 'Twould do. In among its roots he knelt, scooping up a handful of earth and crumbling it in his fingers until it fell away to leave him holding a few stones.

Out of his bag he took the silver scepter, glancing at it briefly as he laid it on his palm amid the stones. It was a beautiful thing, one end tapering into the shape of a tongue of flame. Elminster shook his head in admiration, and whispered a certain spell over his hand. Then he thrust the scepter into the hole he'd created, smoothed dirt over it, and plucked up a nearby clump of moss to lay atop the disturbed earth. A handful of leaves and twigs completed the concealment, and he hurried to the next crag along the line. There he dropped one of the stones, and went on to another three of the tree-clad heights, to leave a stone at each. Pausing at the last, he murmured another spell that left him feeling weak and sick inside, as his limbs tingled with blue-white fire for the space of a long, leisurely breath.

He took that breath, and another, before he felt strong enough to make the second casting. It was a simple thing of gestures, a single phrase, and the melting away of a hair from behind his ear. Done.

The Athalantan kept still for a moment, listening, and peered back the way he'd come for any signs of movement. Nothing met his ears and eyes but the scuttlings of small forest creatures . . . moving in various wrong directions, and ignoring him. El turned and went on with his journey. He didn't feel like waiting for hours just to see who was following him.

Mystra had sent him to Cormanthor on a mission. Just what he was supposed to do there she hadn't revealed yet, but he'd be needed there, she'd said, "in time to come." It didn't sound like anything one had to hurry to, but El wanted to see the legendary ciy of the elves. It was the most beautiful place in all Faerûn, the minstrels said, full of wonders and elven folk so handsome that looking upon them took one's breath away. A place of revels and magical marvels and singing, where fantastic mansions thrust spires to the stars, and the forest and the city grew around each other in a vast, rolling garden. A place where they killed non-elves on sight.

Well, there was a line in an old ballad about stupid brigands that had become a wry saying among Athalantans: "We'll just have to burn that treasure when we get our hands on it." It would have to serve him in the days ahead. El rather suspected that he'd be spending a lot of time drifting around Cormanthor as a watching, listening mist.

Better that, he supposed, than spending the eternal oblivion of death by spells, to sink forgotten into the earth of an elven garden somewhere, his service to Mystra unfulfilled.

The young man paused at the base of a shadowtop as large around as a cottage, swung his saddlebag from one shoulder to another, stretched like a cat, and set off south and east again, walking fast. His boots made no sound as he trod the empty air. He glanced at the still waters of a little pool as he passed, and they reflected back the image of an unshaven, straggle-bearded youth with keen blue eyes, black tangled hair, a sharp beak of a nose, and a long, gangly build. Not unhandsome, but not particularly trustworthy in appearance, either. Well, he was going to have to impress *some* elf, sometime.

Had he looked back at the right moment, El would have seen a cloud of clinging mushrooms rise from the damp forest floor as something unseen disturbed them, and settle softly again as whatever it was whispered a curse and turned hastily aside. Was the young man ahead going to blunder straight into the guarded heart of Cormanthor?

Then the forest gloom to the south and east gave sudden birth to spreading rings of fire, and the ground shook. Yes, it seemed he was.

Elminster hurried forward, running on the air, swinging his saddlebag fore and aft in one hand to give him the momentum to surge forward in earnest. That had been a battle spell, hurled in haste.

Leaves were still flaming in dancing branches ahead, and a tree crashed down somewhere to the west, in answer to the deep, rolling force of the explosion that had shuddered past him moments before.

Elminster dodged around a long side-limb and over a rise, descending into a rocky, fern-filled dell beyond. At its bottom, a spring welled up between old and mossy boulders—one of which was just tumbling back to earth, trailing flames and the spinning bones of something torn apart.

Figures were trotting and scrambling and hacking among those boulders. Elves, El saw, who were fighting burly red-skinned warriors whose mouths jutted tusks, and whose black leather armor bristled with daggers and axes and maces.

Hobgoblins had surprised the elves at the stream and slain most of them. As El raced closer above the ferns, his bag sending them dancing and waving in his wake, an elven sword flashed with spell light as it rose and fell. Its quarry fell away, snarling in pain and clutching at a ravaged neck, as an iron bar wielded by another hobgoblin came down on the head of the elven swordsman with a solid thud that echoed across the dell, sickeningly loud.

The elf"s head collapsed in a spray of gore, and his twitching body fell against his companion. This last survivor of the elven patrol, it seemed, was a tall elf who wore a shoulder mantle adorned with rows of oval, gem-adorned pendants that flashed and sparkled as he dodged. A mage, El guessed, raising a hand to hurl a spell.

The elf was faster. One of his hands blossomed into a ball of fire, which he thrust into the face of the staff-wielding hobgoblin. As his foe staggered backwards, roaring in anger and pain, the fire sprouted two long tongues of flame, like the horns of a bull. The flames stabbed out at the red-skinned ruukha, searing away leather armor to lay bare scorched grey hide. The iron staff clanged to the rocks as the hobgoblin spun away, howling in earnest—and the elven mage swept his horns of flame across the face of another assailant.

Too late. The fire was still sizzling across the bat-eared, snarling face of one ruukha when another reached over it to thrust the dark and wicked tines of a longfork clear through the elven mage's upper body.

The seeking bolts Elminster had hurled were still streaking through the air as the transfixed elf struggled his way clear of the bloody tines, shrieking in agony, and slumped into the stream. Hobgoblins were swarming down around the rocks now, stabbing at the writhing elven mage. El saw his fine-boned face thrown back in agony as he gasped out something—and the air above the stream was suddenly full of countless streaking silver sparks.

Hobgoblins jerked and spasmed, arching in agony, as the elf sank back into the roiling waters. Fallen ruukha weapons crashed down around him as his magic raged. Their former owners were still reeling as Elminster's bolts tore into them, spinning them around and filling them with blue-white fire.

Spellflames roared out from hobgoblin mouths and noses, and the eyes above them bulged and then burst into blue-white, spattering mists. The scorched corpses staggered aimlessly into rocks and trampled ferns until they fell—leaving a moaning elf lying in the waters, and more angry ruukha crashing down the far side of the dell with axes, longforks, and blades in their hands.

Elven bodies lay arched and sprawled around Elminster as he came to a halt above the mage. Pain-wracked emerald eyes blinked up at him through sweat-tangled white hair, and widened in astonishment at seeing a human.

"I'll stand with ye," the Athalantan told the elf, lifting his head clear of the blood-darkened water. That deed caused his airstriding spell to fail, and he promptly discovered that one of his boots leaked, as they settled into the cold, rushing waters.

He also discovered that he really didn't have time to care, as ferns rustled around him and more ruukha rose into view, wearing nasty grins of triumph at their deception. The elven patrol had camped in the midst of a hobgoblin haven, or more likely been carefully and completely surrounded as they slept.

The entire dell, it seemed, was full of yellow-tusked, menacing ruukha, raising shields before them as they crouched low and stumped cautiously forward. They seemed to have already learned that mages are always dangerous . . . and to have survived that lesson. Which meant they'd killed mages before.

Elminster stood over the weakly coughing elf and darted a quick glance behind him. Aye, they were there, closing in slowly, faces grinning in anticipation. There must be seventy or more. And the spells he had left were few enough for that to be a real problem.

The prince cast the only magic that might buy him time to think of a proper way out of this. He tore aside a leathern flap of his saddlebag, plucked forth all six of the revealed daggers in an untidy cluster, and hissed the words he needed as he tossed them into the air, snapping his fingers. They took wing like aroused wasps, darting away in unison to circle the young prince, slashing and spinning across the face of a ruukha who was too close.

That awoke a general yell of rage, and the hobgoblins surged down at Elminster, coming from all sides. The daggers whistled and bit at all who intruded into their tight circle, but there were only five of them, against many burly ruukha shouldering to get at the young mage.

A hurled spear struck El numbingly on the shoulder as it tumbled past, and a stone grazed his nose as he staggered back. The unfortunate thing about the flying blades spell was that its rushing daggers gave the ruukha ideas. Why brave that wall of steel when you can just bury its creator under a hail of hurled weapons?

Another stone hit his forehead, hard. Elminster staggered, dazed. An exultant roar rose from all around him, as the ruukha charged. Shaking his head to drive away the pain, El sank down over the elf and spat out the words of a spell he hadn't expected he'd have to use yet. He hoped he'd be in time.

Eyes that glowed with mage sight looked at the tree-clad crag before it, and then at the next one. And the next. Gods curse the usurper! He'd been to all of them!

Had he left the scepter at the first one, and set the others as decoys? Or did it lie in the second crag, or—?

The owner of those smoldering eyes lost faith in the will of the silent gods to curse the young mage-prince properly, and embarked on a thorough and heartfelt job of personally cursing Elminster.

When the snarling was done, a spell was cast. As expected, it revealed a humming web of force lines linking all the crags, but didn't lay clear the location of the scepter. Breaking the web needed Elminster's assenting will . . . or his death.

Well, if the one was impossible, the other would just have to serve. Hands moved again to weave another enchantment. Something rose like heavy smoke from the forest floor, something that hissed and whispered softly and unceasingly as it took shape. Something whose every movement was a menace that bespoke hunger.

Something that suddenly grew solid, rearing upright as it slithered, and flailing the air before it with dozens of raking claws. A magekiller.

Murderous eyes watched it go forth, seeking the last prince of Athalantar. As it whispered its way out of view through the trees, a smile grew beneath those watching eyes . . . from a mouth that did not often smile. Then the mouth moved again, bestowing more curses on Elminster's head. Had they been listening, the gods would have been pleased at some of the more inventive phrasing.

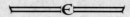

There was an instant of swirling blue mists, and the sensation of falling— and then Elminster's boots scraped on broken rock, and a limp, lolling elven body was in his hands.

They stood on a flat rock partway up the dell, with bent and broken ferns all around, and startled shouts behind them as the ruukha peered this way and that, seeking them—or were sliced by the ring of daggers taking sudden and urgent flight to El's new locale, to take up their protective circling again.

Walking into Cormanthor with a dead or dying elf in his arms might not be such a good idea, either, but right now he had little choice. The prince of Athalantar swung the slim, light body over his shoulder with a grunt and began to walk up out of the dell, trudging carefully amid the ferns to avoid a fall on the uneven ground. There were more shouts from behind him, and Elminster smiled thinly and turned around.

Stones crashed and rolled short, and one spear hissed through the ferns well off to one side, as the ruukha came after him. El chose his spot and made the second journey of his five-jump spell.

Suddenly he was in the very midst of grunting, hurrying hobgoblins, with the elf weighing on his shoulder. Ignoring the sudden oaths and grunts of amazement, El stood tall, turning on one heel to find the next clear spot for the magic to take him to, over—there!

Blades slashed out too late, and he was gone again.

When the swirling mists fell away this time, there were screams from behind him. The whistling daggers had cut a bloody swath through the hobgoblins to reach and encircle El where he'd just been—and now they were trying to reach him again, slashing through the main group of ruukha. The Chosen of Mystra watched hobgoblins see him, turn, and roar out fresh fury as they charged anew—and he awaited them patiently.

None of the ruukha were throwing things now. Their blades and axes were out, each hobgoblin hungry to personally chop and hack this infuriating human. El shifted the elven mage on his shoulder, found the right moment, and jumped again—back to the other side of the rushing ruukha.

There were fresh screams as the daggers swerved to follow him, slicing through the hobgoblins once more. El watched one lumbering warrior lose his throat and spin to the ground not knowing what had slain him, hacking vainly and feebly at an unseen enemy as blood spurted. Many were staggering or limping, now, as they turned to follow their elusive foe. One last jump remained, and Elminster saved it, turning instead to trudge up out of the dell with his dangling burden. Only a few grim ruukha followed.

El went on walking, seeking some vantage point where he could see a distant feature. The ruukha still on his trail were growling back and forth now, reassuring each other that humans tire quickly, and they'd slay this one after dark if he didn't fall earlier.

Elminster ignored them, seeking a long view. It seemed an endless, staggering time before he found one—a thick stand of shadowtop trees across another dell. He made the last jump and left the hobgoblins behind, hoping they'd not care to follow.

His daggers would soon melt away, and when they were gone, he'd little left to fight with.

It was then that a high, faint voice by his ear said in broken Common, "Down. Put—down. Please."

Elminster made sure of his footing in the gloom under the shadowtops, and swung the elf gently down onto a bed of moss. "I speak your tongue," he said in elvish. "I am Elminster of Athalantar, on my way to Cormanthor."

Astonishment touched those green eyes again. "My people will kill you," the elf mage replied, his voice fainter. "There's only one way for you to . . ."

His voice trailed away, and Elminster thrust his hand to the laboring throat and hastily murmured the words of his only healing spell.

The response was a smile. "The pain is less; have my thanks," the mage said with more vigor, "but I am dying. Iymbryl Alastrarra am I, of . . ." His eyes darkened, and he caught at Elminster's arm.

El bent over the elf, helpless to do more healing, and watched long, slim fingers crawl like a shaking spider up his arm, to his shoulder, and thence to touch his cheek.

A sudden vision burst into Elminster's mind. He saw himself on his knees, here under the shadowtops where he knelt now. There was no Iymbryl dying under him, but only dust, and a black gem glistening among it. In the vision, El took it up and touched it to his forehead.

Then the vision was gone, and El was blinking down at the pain-wracked face of Iymbryl Alastrarra, purple at his lips and temples. His hand fell back to twitch like a restless thing on the dead leaves. "You—saw?" the elf gasped.

Trying to catch his breath, Elminster nodded. The elven mage nodded back, and whispered, "On your honor, Elminster of Athalantar, do not fail me." A sudden spasm took him, and he quivered like a dry, curled leaf rocks in winds that will whip it away in a moment. "Oh, Ayaeqlarune!" Iymbryl cried then, no longer seeing the human above him. "Beloved! I come to you at last! Ayaeqlarrr . . ."

The voice trailed away into a long, deep rattle, like the echo of a distant flute. The thin body shook once, and then was still.

Elminster bent nearer—and then recoiled in horror as the flesh under his hands gave forth a queer sigh, and slumped into dust.

It curled and drifted, there in the shade, and at its heart lay a black gem. Just as in the vision. Elminster looked down at it for a long moment, wondering what he was getting himself into, then glanced up and looked at the trees all around. No hobgoblins, no watching eyes. He was alone.

He sighed, shrugged, and picked up the gem.

It was warm, and smooth, altogether pleasant to the touch, and gave off a faint sound, like an echo of harp strings, as he raised it. El looked into its depths, saw nothing—and pressed it to his forehead.

The world exploded into a whirling chaos of sounds and smells and scenes. El was laughing with an elven maiden in a mossy bower; then he *was* the elven maiden, or another one, dancing around a fire whose flames sparkled with swirling gems. Then somehow he was wearing fluted armor and riding a pegasus, swooping down through the trees to drive a lance through a snarling orc . . . its blood blossomed across his view, and then flickered and shifted, becoming the rose-red light of dawn, gleaming from the slender spires of a proud and beautiful castle.

. . . Then he was speaking an elder elven tongue, thick and stilted, in a court where the male elves knelt in silks before warrior-maidens clad in armor that glowed with strange magics, and he heard himself decreeing a war of extermination on humankind . . .

Mystra, aid me! What is this?

His despairing cry seemed to bring back the memory of his name; he was Elminster of Athalantar, Chosen of the goddess, and he was riding through a whirling storm of images. Memories, they were, of the House of Alastrarra. Thinking of that name snatched him back down into the maelstrom of a thousand thousand years, of decrees, family sayings, and beloved places. The faces of a hundred beautiful elven maids—mothers, sisters, daughters, Alastrarrans all—smiled or shouted at him, their deep blue eyes swimming up to his like so many waiting pools . . . Elminster was swept into them and down, down, names and dates and drawn swords flashing like striking whips into his mind.

Why? he cried, and his voice seemed to echo through the chaos until it broke like a wave crashing over rocks on something familiar: the face of vanished Iymbryl, regarding him calmly, a hauntingly beautiful elven maiden at his shoulder.

"Duty," Iymbryl replied. "The gem is the kiira of House Alastrarra, the lore and wisdom held by its heirs down the years. As I was, so Ornthalas of my blood is now. He waits in Cormanthor. Take the gem to him."

"Take the gem—?" Elminster cried, and both the elven heads smiled at him and chanted in unison, "Take the gem to him."

Then Iymbryl said, "Elminster of Athalantar, may I make known to you the Lady Ayaeqlarune of—"

Whatever else he said was swept away, along with his face and hers, under a fresh flood of loud and bright memories—scenes of love, war, and pleasant tree-girt lands. Elminster struggled to remember who he was, and to picture himself on his knees under the shadowtops, here and now—the ground his knees could feel.

He slapped at the ground, and tried to see what his hands felt, but his mind was full of shouting voices, unicorns dancing, and war-horns glinting in the moonlight of other times and distant places. He rose, and staggered blindly with arms outstretched until he ran into a tree trunk.

Clinging to its solid bulk, he tried to see it, but it and the other trunks, so tall and dark around it, felt sickeningly *wrong*. He stared at them, trying to speak, and found himself looking at Iymbryl, who was shrieking as the black tines of the longfork burst through him again—and then he *was* Imbryl, riding a red tide of pain, as ruukha laughed harshly all around and raised cruel blades he could not stop....

They swept down, and he tried to twist away, and—struck something very hard, that drove the breath out of him. Elminster rolled on it, and realized dimly that he was on the ground, amid the treeroots, though he couldn't see the dirt his face was pressed against.

His mind was showing him Iymbryl again, and a young, handsome, haughty-looking elf in rich robes rising from a floating, teardrop-shaped chair that hung in a room where blue webs chimed with music. The young elf was rising with a smile to greet Iymbryl, and into El's mind came the name *Ornthalas*. Of course. He was to make haste to Ornthalas and surrender the gem. Along with his life?

Or would it tear his mind out of his skull, flesh and all, when he pulled on the gem?

Writhing in the dirt, Elminster tried to pry the gem from his forehead, but it seemed part of him, warm, solid, and attached.

He must get up. Hobgoblins could still find him here. He must go on, before a tree spider or owlbear or stirge found him, a helpless and easy meal, and ... he must ... Elminster clawed feebly at the forest floor, trying to remember the name of the goddess he wanted to cry out to. All that came into his head was the name Iymbryl.

Iymbryl Alastrarra. But how could that be? *He* was Iymbryl Alastrarra. Heir of the House, the Mage of Many Gems, leader of the White Raven Patrol, and this fern dell looked like a good place to camp ...

Elminster screamed, and screamed again, but there was no one else in his mind to hear. No one but thousands of Alastrarrans.

THREE
FELL MAGIC AND A FAIR CITY

It is rare for any man to make many foes, and strive against them, only to find a victory so clear and mighty that he vanquishes them forever, and is shut of them cleanly, at a single stroke. Indeed, one may say that such clarity of resolution is found only in the tales of minstrels. In the endlessly unfolding tapestry that is real life in Faerûn, the gods plague folk with far more loose ends—and all too many of these prove as deadly as the decisive battles that preceded them.

ANTARN THE SAGE
FROM *THE HIGH HISTORY OF FAERÛNIAN ARCHMAGES MIGHTY*
PUBLISHED CIRCA THE YEAR OF THE STAFF

"You'd challenge the power of the elves? That is hardly . . . prudent, my lord." The moon elven face that spoke those words was calm inside its dragon helm, but the tone made them a sharp and biting warning.

"And why not?" the man in gilded armor snarled, his eyes flashing in the shadow of his raised lion-head visor as his gauntlets tightened on the hilt of a sword that was longer than the elf he confronted. "Have elves stopped me yet?"

The vision of two armored war captains facing each other on that windswept mountaintop faded, and Elminster moaned. He was so *tired* of this. Each dark or furious or merry scene gave way to the next, exhausting him with the ongoing tide of emotions. His mind felt like it was afire. How by all the gods' mercy did the heir of House Alastrarra stay sane?

Or *did* the heir of House Alastrarra stay sane?

It began then as a gentle whisper; for a moment El thought it was another of the innumerable, softly speaking, caressing elven maidens the visions had brought to him. *Call on me.*

Who, now? El slapped at his own face, or tried to, striving to bring himself back to Faerûn in the present. The present that had hobgoblins, mysterious followers, and magelords and other perils that could so easily slay him.

Call on me; use me. The young mage-prince almost laughed; the seductive whisper reminded him of a certain fat lady night-escort in Hastarl, whose voice was the only thing alluring she had left. She'd sounded like that, whispering huskily out of darkened doorways.

Call on me, use me. Feel my power. Where was the voice coming from?

And then it began; a warm throbbing above his eyes. He probed at it with tentative fingers. The gem was pulsing . . . *Call on me.* The voice was coming from the gem.

"Mystra?" Elminster called aloud, requesting guidance. He felt nothing but warmth. Speaking to it, at least, wasn't forbidden ... it seemed. He cleared his throat.

Call on me.

"How?" As if in response to his exasperated query fresh visions uncoiled in El's mind. Energies flowed endlessly within the gem, stored magics that served to heal and shapeshift and change the heir's body, from weightless to able to see in the dark, to ...

The visions were tugging him away from such revelations now, leading him through scenes of various Alastrarran heirs calling on the gem to shift their shapes. Some merely changed their faces and heights to elude foes; others assumed different genders to lure or eavesdrop; one or two took beast-shape to escape rivals who had blades ready to slay elven heirs with, but no interest in hacking at timid hares or curious cats. El saw how the shift was done, and shown how it could be undone—or would undo itself, regardless of his will. Right, then; he knew how to change shape by calling on the powers of the gem. Why was it showing him this?

Suddenly he was staring at Iymbryl Alastrarra, standing smiling at him in the deep shade under the shadowtops. The face wavered, and became his own—and then shivered again, and was once more the heir of House Alastrarra, emerald eyes under the white hair all Alastrarran heirs had, or quickly acquired. The vision changed again, showing him a rather familiar lanky, raven-haired youth with a hawk-sharp nose and blue eyes, naked above a bathing pool—a body that flowed and sank into the similarly nude body of an elf, all slender hairless sleekness. By its face, Iymbryl. Right; the gem wanted him to change.

With an inward sigh, Elminster called on the powers of the gem to summon up the likeness of Iymbryl. A peculiar surging feeling washed over him, and he *was* Iymbryl, in hopes and memories and ... he looked down at his hands—the rather battered hands of a man who'd lived and fought hard, recently—and willed them to become the long, slim, blue-white, smooth hands that had crawled so laboriously up his arms to touch his cheek, not long ago.

And the hands dwindled, *twisted,* and ... became slim, and delicate, and blue-white in hue. He wiggled them experimentally, and they tingled.

El drew in a deep, shuddering breath, called Iymbryl's face firmly to mind, and willed his body to change. A slow, creeping feeling rose in him, in his back and up his spine. He shivered involuntarily, and grunted in disgust. The visions fell away and he was blinking around at the unchanging, patient trunks of shadowtops that had stood here for centuries.

He looked down. His clothes were hanging from him; he was smaller and slimmer, his smooth skin now blue-white. He was a moon elf. He was Iymbryl Alastrarra.

That had been useful enough. Now was there a teleport or homecalling spell in the gem, perhaps, that could take him right to Cormanthor? He slid into the whirling memories once more, seeking. It was like rushing through a busy battlefield peering for just one familiar face among all the hacking, rushing swordsmen ... no, it didn't seem that there was. El sighed, shook himself, and looked at the ever-present trees. His clothes flapped loosely as he turned, and that reminded him of his saddlebag.

Looking around for it, he suddenly recalled that he'd left it somewhere back in the dell of countless ferns and even more hobgoblins. El shrugged and turned to walk south and east. If the ruukha didn't tear it apart or scatter the contents completely, he'd be able to find it later with a spell; not that he expected to have the leisure for that sort of thing again this year. Nor, perhaps, next season, either. He shrugged again; if that was what service to Mystra meant—well, others endured far worse.

Wearing the shape of an elf would certainly get him into the city of Cormanthor with more ease than he'd taste if he charged in as a human. Elminster sniffed the air; to an elven nose, the woods smelled . . . stronger; his nose took in, or noticed, many more scents. Hmm. Best to think on such things while moving. He set off through the trees, touching the gem on his forehead once to be sure his shifting hadn't loosened or harmed it.

Upon his touch, the kiira made him aware of two things: only braggarts displayed House lore-gems openly—a simple calling on the stone would hide it; and now that he wore Iymbryl's shape, the memories in the gem still awaited him, but no longer overwhelmed.

He hid the kiira first, and then turned to the doorway in his mind that streamed with the vivid lights and colors of waiting memories. This time, they seemed like a sluggish stream through which he waded, going where he desired, and letting the rest slide past. El sought through them for the most recent remembrances of Cormanthor, and for the first time saw its soaring spires, the fluted balconies of homes built in the hearts of living trees, the ornate, free-floating lanterns that drifted about the city, and the bridges that soared from tree to tree, crisscrossing the air. Those spans were arched, and some of them curved as they went. None of them had side railings. El swallowed; it would take some time before he'd feel comfortable strolling along such bold contrivances.

Who ruled this city? The Coronal, the gem showed him—someone chosen rather than born to the office. An "old wise one" and chief judge in all disputes, it seemed, who held sway not only over Cormanthor the city, but its entire deep woods realm. The office carried magical powers, and the current Coronal was one Eltargrim Irithyl—old and overly kindly, in Iymbryl's view, though the Alastrarran heir knew that some of the older, prouder families held far poorer views of their ruler.

Those proud old Houses, in particular the Starym and Echorn, held much of the real power in Cormanthor, and considered themselves the embodiment and guardians of "true" elven character. In their view, a "true" elf was . . .

Elminster broke off that thought as the idea reminded him uncomfortably of what he'd just done. He'd had no choice—unless he'd been a man utterly without mercy. Yet should he have touched the gem at all, since he'd pledged his service to Mystra?

He came to an abrupt halt beside a particularly gigantic shadowtop, drew in a deep breath, and called aloud, "Mystra?"

Then he added in a whisper, "Lady, hear me. Please."

Into his mind he brought his most striking memory of Myrjala, laughing in aroused delight as they soared through the air together, and of the subtle changes in her eyes that betrayed her divinity as her passion rose . . . seizing on that image, he held it, breathed her name again, and bent his will to calling on her.

There came a coldness at the edges of his mind—a thrilling, verge-of-a-shiver tingling—and he asked, "Lady, is this right for me to do? Have I . . . your blessing?"

A surge of loving warmth rolled into his mind, bringing with it a scene of Ornthalas Alastrarra, standing in a fair, sun-dappled chamber whose pillars were living, flower-bedecked trees. The view was out of the eyes of someone approaching the heir—and when they'd drawn very close to the elf, who was looking slightly puzzled, the viewer's hand rose into the image, reaching for an unseen forehead, above.

The eyes of Ornthalas sharpened in astonishment, and the viewer moved closer, and closer still. To . . . kiss? Touch noses? No, to touch foreheads, of course. The eyes of Ornthalas, so close and wide, wavered like a reflection in water disrupted by ripples. When the disturbance passed, the face had become that of the kindly old Coronal, and the viewpoint drew back from him to show Elminster himself, bowing. Somehow, El knew that he was invoking the Coronal's protection against those of the People who were horrified to discover that a human had penetrated into the very heart of their city, wearing the shape of an elf they knew. An elf he might well have murd—

A sudden wash of warning fire blazed across his mind, sweeping the visions away, and Elminster found himself under the trees, being spun around—by Mystra's grace, he supposed—to face . . . something that was sweeping around roots and gliding among the trees like a large and eager snake. Something that hissed bubblingly and tirelessly as it came, whispering what might have been words. Whispering . . . snatches of spell incantations? The body of this strange beast or conjured apparition was sometimes translucent and always indistinct, unfocused. It veered toward him with a triumphant chuckle, raking the empty air with dozens of claws as it came. It was clearly seeking him.

Was this some elven guardian? Or some fell beast-lich kept alive by ancient magic? Whatever its nature, its intent was clear, and those claws looked deadly enough.

El almost retreated, but the thing was so fascinating to watch—one part of it awkward but tirelessly slithering, the other an endless swirling of what looked like the torn, tattered remnants of spells. Eyes in plenty swam and circled in that shifting and reforming body. It had to be a thing of magic. Mystra would take care of it, surely. After all, she was goddess of magic, and he was her Ch—

Claws stabbed out, and though they fell far short of striking, they left in their wake an eerie tingling. His mind felt a little numbed; he couldn't seem to focus his will on his spells.

What spells did he have left, anyway?

Oh, Mystra. *He couldn't remember.*

As those claws swept at him again, closer now, sudden panic blazed up in his mind like a bright bolt of fire. Run! El turned and darted away through the trees, stumbling as shorter legs than he was used to carried along a body that was far lighter than it should be. Gods, but elves could run fast!

He could sprint with ease around and around this slithering whatever-it-was. On impulse he dodged back toward the way he'd come. The monster followed.

He turned around again, risking the time to cast a simple dispel. Almost the last magic of any consequence he had, though the gem seemed to hold much more. A beast so chaotic, so made of tumbling magics, would surely fall apart at the touch of . . .

His magic blazed forth. The many-clawed, slithering thing flickered once, shook itself, and kept coming.

El ducked his head and started to run in earnest, sprinting through the trees, ducking around mossy rock outcrops and leaping over roots and suspicious-looking mushrooms. The hissing and burbling never ceased behind him.

The last prince of Athalantar felt a little chill as he realized how much faster it was than he'd thought it could be.

Well, he had one little weapon of magic left—a spell that sent a jet of flame leaping from the caster's hand. It was a thing for starting fires or singeing beasts into retreating, not a battle magic, but . . .

El stepped behind a tree, caught his breath, and started to climb it. His new longer, slender fingers found fissures in the bark his human hands couldn't have entered, and his lighter body clung to holds that could not have held Elminster the human. The hissing, slithering thing was close behind, now, as El reached a bough he judged large enough.

When the thing came around the tree, it seemed to sense him, looking up without hesitation. Elminster put his little jet of flame right into its many eyes, and swung back up out of the way of any leaps.

He expected a squalling and thrashing, or at least a recoiling—but the thing never hesitated, snapping at his hand right through the flame. If anything, it seemed *larger* and more vigorous, not harmed or in any sort of pain.

Claws cut the air in a whistling frenzy; El took one look and decided a higher branch would be prudent. He'd barely begun to climb when the tree quivered beneath him. The thing had slashed through bark and wood beneath as easily as it had cut the air, carving out a claw-hold. A single raking blow cut another as he watched, and without pause the thing hauled itself up the trunk to cut more. El watched in fascination; it was slashing its way up the tree as fast as an armored man could climb a rope!

It would reach him in a few breaths. In the meantime, it was right under him, and would have to take whatever he dropped on it. Not that he had anything left but a few odd spells not concerned with matters of war at all, nor time to learn what the gem could do.

It looked like he'd be jumping soon. On impulse he dodged around the trunk. The many-clawed thing followed rather clumsily, gouging its way around the curve of the tree. Good; he'd not have to worry about it scrambling across the trunk in time to catch him as he fell past. El went back to his former branch—a better perch—and held tight. When the thing clawed its way back into view around his side of the tree, he hurled a light spell right into its eyes.

Light blazed forth, and then faded instantly. The clawed thing never hesitated, and El's eyes narrowed. Yes, it *did* seem even larger, and somehow more . . . solid.

As it climbed toward him, he cast a minor detection spell at it—to gain lore he did not need.

The spell reached it . . . and faded away, granting him none of the information it was supposed to. The clawed thing grew slightly larger.

It fed on spells! This thing must be a magekiller, something he'd heard of long ago, in his days with the Brave Blades adventuring band. Magekillers were creations of magic, wrought by rare, suppressed spells. Their purpose was to slay wizards who only knew one way to do battle—hurl spells at things.

His magic, no matter how desperate, could only make it stronger, not harm it. Slayer of Magelords and Chosen of Mystra he might be—but he was also unable to stop making mistakes, it seemed, one piled atop another with all-too-fervent energy.

Enough analysis; such thinking was a luxury for mages . . . and just now, he'd best forget about being a mage. He had only a few breaths left to experiment before he'd have to leap down, or die. Carefully El drew one of his belt daggers, and dropped it, point-first, into the many staring eyes of that hissing, burbling head.

It fell freely to the earth far below with a solid thump, leaving a shaft of dark emptiness in its wake right through the heart of the many-clawed thing. The magekiller shuddered and squalled, its tone high and fearful and furious, but somehow fainter than before.

Now it was done keening and was moving again, climbing after Elminster with murder in its eyes. The hole through it had gone, but the entire beast was visibly smaller. The last prince of Athalantar nodded calmly, planted one boot against the trunk below him, and kicked off.

The air whistled past him for a moment before his hands crashed through branchlets, snapping them in a swirling of leaves, and caught hold of the bough he'd aimed for. He clung there for a moment, hearing that urgent squalling sound ringing out again, close above, and then swung out and down, twisting to snatch at a lower branch.

It seemed he wasn't much of a minstrels' hero, either. Instead of the branch they were seeking, his hands found only leaves this time, and tore through them.

An instant later, the Chosen of Mystra hit the ground hard on his behind, rolled over into an unintentional backflip, and found his feet with an involuntary groan. His rear was going to be sore for days.

And his running was going to be an ungainly limp now. Elminster sighed as he watched the slithering thing racing back down the tree in a giddy spiral, to come and kill him.

If he used the lone spell he'd left ready, he'd be whisked back to the scepter ... but that would leave him with all the walking through the woods to do over again, with this hissing monster and perhaps his mysterious follower lurking between him and Cormanthor.

He plucked up his dagger. He had another at his belt, a third sheathed up one sleeve, and one in each boot—but was that enough to do more than annoy this thing?

Spitting out a very human curse, the elf who was not Iymbryl Alastrarra stumbled southward, dagger in hand, wondering how far he could get before the magekiller caught up with him.

If he could only win himself time enough, perhaps there was something the gem could do ...

Preoccupied with his haste and wild plans, Elminster almost ran right out over the edge of the cliff.

It was cloaked in bushes: the crumbling edge of an ancient rockface, where the land dropped away into a tree-filled gorge. A tiny rivulet chuckled over rocks far below. El looked along it and then back at the magekiller—which was coming for him as fast as ever, slithering around trees and their sprawling roots with its tireless claws raking the air.

The prince glanced along the lip of the cliff, and chose a tree that leaned a little way out into space, but seemed large and solid. He ran for it, one hand outspread to test it—and only the whispering warned him.

The magekiller could burst into a charge of astonishing speed when it desired to, it seemed. El looked back in time to see the foremost, lunging claws reaching for his head. He ducked, slipped on the loose stones, and made a desperate grab for a root as he went over the edge.

In a bruising clatter of rolling stones he swung against the cliff, slammed hard into it, and got his other hand onto the root, just as the long, serpentine body hissed past him into the gorge below.

There was a jutting rock some forty feet down, and the magekiller made a twisting grab for it. Claws squealed briefly on rock, trailing sparks, and then the jutting rock pulled free of its ancient berth and fell, its unwilling passenger flailing the air beneath it.

Together boulder and spectral beast crashed into the rocks below. They did not bounce or roll; only the dust they hurled up did that. El watched, eyes narrowed.

When the dust settled again, he saw what he'd been waiting for: a few claws, flailing away tirelessly around the edge of the boulder that had pinned the magekiller against the rocks.

So it was solid enough to slash with its claws, and to be pinned down by rocks—but all that harmed it was metal. Or more probably, just cold iron.

Elminster looked down at the crumbling cliff below him, sighed, and started trotting along it, looking for a way down.

About twenty paces along, the way found him. The ground under his boots muttered, like a man talking in his sleep, and slid sideways. El leaped frantically away from the gorge, and then slid helplessly down into it, bumping along atop a river of moving earth and rolling, bouncing rocks.

When he could see and hear again, he'd been coughing on dust for what seemed like hours, and he hurt all over.

He was back in his own form again. Had he lost the gem?

A quick touch reassured him that it was still there, and its powers were still waiting for him. He must have changed back without thinking, to get more reach and try to ride the moving rocks. Or something.

Elminster got up gingerly, winced at the pain of putting his weight squarely on a foot that seemed to have been hit by several hundred rolling stones during his unintentional journey, and started to pick his way along the rocky bottom of the gorge to where the magekiller had been.

It might, of course, have clawed its way through the rock to freedom by now. It might be waiting for him somewhere among all these rocks, very near. In that case, he'd just have to use that spell, and start off through this dangerous part of the woods all over again . . .

Then he saw it: a forest of spectral claws waving awkwardly around the edge of that massive boulder, in a tumbled forest of rocks ahead. He still—somehow—had his dagger in his hand, and he went to work cautiously, stabbing over the edge of the rocks at one claw and then another, watching them melt away like smoke under his blade.

When they were all gone, he ventured past them, to lie atop the boulder that pinned the strange monster, reaching down again and again to stab at the helpless body beneath. His blade never felt anything, but the frantic whispering from beneath him grew slowly fainter and fainter, until at last it stopped, and the boulder settled against the rocks beneath with a clacking sound.

Elminster straightened slowly, bruised but satisfied, and looked back up at the lip of the gorge.

A man was standing there. A man in robes whom he'd never seen before—but who seemed to know him. He was smiling as he looked down at Elminster of Athalantar, as he raised his hands and made the first careful gestures of what Elminster recognized as a meteor swarm. But the smile wasn't friendly at all.

El sighed, waved to the man in sardonic greeting—and with that gesture released his waiting spell.

When the four balls of raging fire raced down into the gorge and burst, the last prince of Athalantar was gone.

The wizard who'd followed Elminster so far clenched his fists as he watched the fire he'd wrought roar away down the gorge, and cursed bitterly. Now he'd have to spend days over his books, casting tracing spells, and trying to find the young fool again. You'd think the gods themselves watched over him, the way luck seemed to cloak him like a mage-mantle. He'd avoided that slaying spell at the inn . . . old Surgath Ilder had hardly been a fitting alternative. Then he'd somehow trapped the magekiller—and *that* spell had taken days to find components for.

"Gods, look down and curse with me," he muttered, his eyes still murderous, as he turned away from the gorge.

Behind him, unseen, pale shapes rose from half a dozen places in the gorge—stone cairns that the fire had scorched in its passing.

They drifted in eerie silence to where a certain massive boulder lay among the stones, and moved their hands in gestures of spellcasting, though they uttered not a word. The boulder rose unsteadily. The wraithlike, floating forms thrust impossibly long tendrils of themselves into the revealed darkness beneath the lifted stone, and plucked forth a many-eyed something that still clawed at the air with feeble talons.

The muttering wizard heard the boulder thunder back into place, and lifted an eyebrow. Had the Athalantan managed only a short jump spell and now set off something nearby in the gorge? Or had the magekiller finally won free?

He tuned around, pushing back his sleeves. He still had a chain lightning spell, if the need arose . . .

Something was rising out of the gorge—or rather, several somethings. Wraiths—ghostly remnants of men, their legs trailing away into wisps of white mist, their bodies mere white shadows in the shade.

They could slay, yes, but he had the right spell to . . . he peered at them again. Elves? *Were* there elven wraiths? And held between them, still waving its talons as they dragged it along—his magekiller!

It was at that moment that Heldebran, last surviving apprentice to the magelords of Athalantar, felt the first touch of fear.

"And you are?" one of the spectral elves asked, as they swept toward him.

"Keep your distance!" the wizard Heldebran snapped, raising his hands. They did not slow in the slightest, so he hastily spun the spell that would blast all undead to harmless dust, forever, and watched it flash out to enfold them like a web.

And fade away, unheeded.

"Stylish," another of the wraithlike elves commented, as they settled down to the earth in a ring around him. Their feet remained indistinct, and their bodies seemed to pulse, shifting continuously in and out of brightness.

"Oh, I don't know," said a third spectral elf, in heavily accented Common. "These humans always make such a noise and show of things. A simple word and a look would have been enough. They always *exult* so, in the unleashings of their power—like children."

"They *are* children," a fourth replied. "Why, look at this one."

"I don't know who you are," Heldebran of Athalantar snapped, "but I—"

"See? All threats and bluster!" the fourth elf added.

"Well, enough of it," the first elf said commandingly. "Human, fire magics are not tolerated here. You have roused the unsleeping guardians of the Sacred Vale, and must pay the price."

Nervously Heldebran glanced around. The ring did seem tighter, now, though the elves still regarded him calmly, and made no move to lift their arms from their sides. He spat out the words he'd need and raised his hands in hasty claws.

Lightning crackled from the tips of his fingers, dancing bright lines of hungry sparks into the spectral elves. It shot through them, to claw vainly among the trees beyond. Smoke curled up from bark here and there.

One elf turned his head to regard it, and the lightning abruptly vanished, leaving only a few wisps of smoke behind.

The ring stood unchanged. The elves looked, if anything, slightly amused.

"Worse than that," the first elf said sternly, as if the interruption had never occurred, "you created something that feeds on magic and sent it to the very heart of our oldest castings. *This*."

The ghostly guardian's tone was one of utter disgust. His chest bulged, gave off small streams of bright radiance, and then burst as the magekiller drifted into view through it, claws waving feebly at the elves all around. Heldebran felt a sudden, wild surge of hope. Perhaps his creature could be set against these elf-wraiths, and he might yet defeat them, or . . .

"Let the punishment be fitting and final, nameless human," the stern elf added, as the magekiller tuned its head, and saw its creator.

Darkness swam in the many orbs Heldebran stared into, and claws scratched the air with sudden vigor. Whispering faintly, the tattered remnant of his creature drifted forward purposefully.

"No!" the apprentice Magelord shrieked, as those feeble claws cut at his eyes. "Noooo!"

The ring of elven guardians was solid around him now, and their eyes were cold. The human wizard rushed at them, and found himself striking a solid, very hard wall of unseen force. He threw himself along it, sobbing. Then the seeking claws reached him, and dragged him down.

"Anyone important?" one of the elves asked, as the sounds died and they stretched out their hands to drain the magekiller away to nothingness.

"No," another replied simply. "One who might have become a magelord of Athalantar, had their rule not been broken. His name was Heldebran. He knew nothing of interest."

"Was there not another intruder, fighting this hungry thing?" the third guardian asked.

"One of our folk; one who wore a lore-gem."

"And this human was *hunting* such a one, in our vale?" The spectral elf looked down, eyes sudden flames in the ever-present tree gloom, and said, "Call him back to life, that he can be slain again. More slowly."

"Elaethan," the stern elf said, in shocked reproof. "I shall do the reading spells next time. In touching the mind of this human, you become too much like him."

"It's something we all had to guard against, Norlorn, when first they came to the forests where I first saw the sun. Humans always corrupt us; that is their true danger to the People."

"Then perhaps we should destroy any human who passes this way," Norlorn said, drawing himself up into a tower of cold white flame. "That other, who used a spell to escape the flames; he may have borne a lore-gem, but he was human, or seemed so."

"And that is the true danger of such beasts, to themselves," Elaethan said softly. "Many of them seem human, but never manage to become so."

He stood in front of the familiar root. The scepter was beneath it, invisible under the earth and its scattering of twigs, leaves, and clumps of moss he'd arranged so hastily. Elminster peered along the line of crags for nearby danger, found nothing, and used the powers of the lore-gem to check on his spell. Memories swirled briefly, but he wrestled them back from his mind and stood shaking his head to clear it.

He could come back here—or rather, to the scepter— twice more. Not that he wanted to . . . so how to avoid attacks that would drive him here?

The mysterious wizard, or any magekillers he chose to send would be bound to find a certain Chosen of Mystra stupid enough to follow the same route he'd originally taken from this place. So his way from here now would lie east along the crags, then south along the first creek he found heading in that general direction, until it strayed too far from where the trees grew tallest.

In the woods, the light tread and heightened senses of an elf outstripped those of a human, and any elven patrols he encountered would be less likely to attack Iymbryl Alastrarra than an intruding human . . . unless Iymbryl was some personal foe of theirs. Yet he'd seen no trace in the lore-memories, thus far, of Iymbryl being a particular foe of anyone.

It was the work of but a moment to slide into Iymbryl's shape, this time. Elminster thought briefly of the spellbook lost in his saddlebag, and sighed. He was going to have to get used to the lesser, often odd elven spells stored in the gem, which had evidently served the Alastrarran heir as a personal spellbook. He hadn't time to study them now; 'twas best to get well and promptly away from the scepter, in case his wizardly foe came seeking him here.

Elminster sighed again and set out. Would it be best to travel by night, in mist form, and use the daylight hours to study spells? Hmm . . . something to think on as he walked. It could be days before he saw Cormanthor. Did he have days to spend, or did this gem eat at the vitality or mind of its wearer?

If it was eating away at him . . . He smote his elven forehead. "Mystra defend me!" he groaned.

Of course. The unexpected voice in his mind sent him to his knees in thankful awe, but the goddess spoke only eight words more: *The gem is safe. Get on with it.*

After a moment of shocked silence and then a few more spent chuckling weakly, Elminster did so.

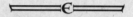

The strange purplish light of the musky grove of giant mushrooms gave way to rising ground at last, and Elminster trudged up it with a full load of spells and a weary heart. He'd been walking for days, and met with no one more exciting than a giant stag, with whom he'd been eyeball-to-eyeball at dusk two days ago. He'd come a long, long way from the modest wharves and towers of Hastarl, and even from holds where farm folk had heard of the realm of Athalantar, but he was getting close to the elven city now, judging by the tinglings of warding spells and the occasional glimpses of elven knights in the sky. Splendid they were, in fluted armor that gleamed purple, blue, and emerald as they swooped past in the saddles of flying unicorns whose hides were blue, and who had no wings nor reins to guide them.

Several such patrols banked close to the lone walking elf, staring closely at him, and El got a good look at their ready javelins and small hand-crossbows. Unsure of what to do, he gave them silent, respectful nods without slowing his travel. All of them nodded back and soared away.

Ahead now, in these trees, there were open clearings cloaked in moss and ferns. Rising silently up from concealment among them, was the first foot patrol he'd seen. Their armor was magnificent, and every one of them held a ready longbow as he stepped toward them, not changing his pace. What else could he do?

One, who was taller than the rest, let go of his bow as El approached. It stayed where he'd released it, floating in the air. The elf stepped forward to meet Elminster, hand lifting in a 'stop' gesture.

Elminster stopped and blinked at him. Best to seem weary and dazed, lest his ignorance put his tongue wrong.

"For some days you've been walking this way," the elven patrol leader said, his voice gentle and melodious, "and yet you give no call of passage to patrols . . . as you have offered none to us. Who are you, and why do you journey?"

"I . . ." Elminster faltered, swaying slightly. "I am Iymbryl Alastrarra, heir of my House. I must return to the city. While on patrol, we were beset by ruukha, and I alone survived—but my spells attracted a human wizard. He set a magekiller on me, and I am . . . not well. I seek my kin, and healing."

"A human mage?" the elven officer snapped. "Where did you meet with such vermin?"

Elminster waved his arm, gesturing back to the northwest. "Many days back, where the land rises and falls much. I . . . I have walked too long to recall clearly."

The elves exchanged glances. "And what if something came upon Iymbryl Alastrarra as he walked, and devoured him, and took his shape?" one of them asked softly. "We've met with such shapeshifters before. They come to prowl in our midst, and feed."

Elminster stared at him with eyes that he hoped looked dull and tired, and raised his hand very slowly to his forehead. "Could one who was not of the People wear this?" he asked, letting weary exasperation sharpen his voice, as the lore-gem faded into view on his brow.

A murmur passed around the patrol, and the elves stepped back without a word from their leader, making way for him to pass. El gave them a weary nod and stumbled forward, trying to look exhausted.

He did not see the patrol leader, behind him, look hard at one of the elven warriors and nod deliberately. The warrior nodded back, knelt in the ferns, touched his hand to the breast of his armor—and faded away.

Now that he was among elves who were afoot, unhurt, and not rushing about in battle, El thought with a shiver, he'd best see how they moved. Did he stand out as an impostor? Or do all who walk upright stagger alike, when weary?

Adding a stumble or two, lest the patrol be watching him, El went on through the trees; huge forest giants soared to the sky, their canopy a hundred feet above him, or more. The ground was rising, and there was an open, sunlit area beyond.

Perhaps here he could . . .

And then he stopped, dumbfounded, and stared. The sun was bright on the fair towers of Cormanthor before him. Their slender spires rose wherever no gigantic tree stood—and there were many such—and stretched away farther than he could see, in a splendor of leaping bridges, hanging gardens, and elves on flying steeds. The blue glows of mighty magic shone everywhere, even in the brightness of full day, and gentle music wafted to him.

El let out a deep sigh of admiration as the music swelled around him, and started walking again. He'd have to be on his guard every moment that he walked amid the Towers of Song.

Now *that* was a change, eh?

FOUR
Home Again the Hunter

More than one ballad of our People tells of Elminster Aumar of Athalantar gawking at the splendors of beautiful Cormanthor upon his first sight of them, and how he was so breathtaken that he spent an entire day just walking the streets, drinking in the glories of the Cormanthor that was. Sometimes 'tis a pity that ballads lie a lot.

Shalheira Talandren, High Elven Bard of Summerstar
from *Silver Blades And Summer Nights:*
An Informal But True History of Cormanthor
published in The Year of the Harp

In the floating dome of varicolored glass, sunlight shot the air through with beams of rose-red, emerald, and blue. A helmed head, turning, flashed back purple, and that burst of light was enough; its wearer did not have to speak to bid his comrade come and look.

Together the two elven guards peered down at the northern edge of the city, beneath their floating post. A lone figure trudged into the streets with the air of dazed weariness usually displayed by captives or exhausted messengers who'd lost their winged steeds days ago, and been forced to continue afoot.

Or rather, not so "lone;" not far behind the staggering elf came a second figure, following the first. This one was a patrol warrior cloaked in magical invisibility that might well serve to fool the eyes of anyone not wearing helms like those of the two watching guards.

Guards who now exchanged meaningful glances waved together at a crystal sphere that floated near at hand, and leaned forward to listen.

The crystal chimed softly, and there was suddenly noise in the dome: a hubbub of various musical airs, soft voices chattering, and the rumble and clatter of a distant cart. The guards inclined their heads intently for a time, and then shrugged in unison. The weary elf wasn't talking to any of the folk hurrying past him. And neither was his shadow.

The guards exchanged glances again. One of them spread his hands in a "what can we do?" gesture. The intruder—if it was someone not of Cormanthor—had an escort already. That meant some patrol leader who'd had a chance to speak with the lone elf, and see him more clearly, had been suspicious. Perhaps two senior members of the Watchful and Vigilant should be too.

Yet this could be no more than a private intrigue, and the lone elf had walked straight through the veil of revelation spell without it reacting in the slightest.

The other guard answered the spread-hands gesture with a dismissive wave, and turned to the querph tree behind him, plucking some of the succulent sapphire-hued berries. The first guard held out his open hand for some, and passed over the duty-bowl of mint water. A moment later, the elf with the invisible escort was forgotten.

He knew what he was looking for. The lore-gem showed it to him: a mansion cloaked in dark pines ("broody affectations," according to the maids of some rival houses, Iymbryl knew), whose tall, narrow windows were masterpieces of sculpted and dyed glass, girt with enchantments that periodically spun ghostly images of minstrelry, dancing unicorns, and rearing stags across the moss-carpeted chambers within. Those casements were the work of Althidon Alastrarra, gone to Sehanine some two centuries and more, and there were no finer in all Cormanthor.

The grounds of House Alastrarra had no walls, but its hedges and plantings spun themselves out to form a continuous barrier along paths marked by irndar trees that bore the falcon sigil of the House. After dusk, these living blazons glowed blue, clear to the eye—there were many such across the proud city—but by day a certain disguised human mage would just have to wander until he found a place that matched the image in his mind.

Most folk thought the servants of gods knew everything and could see all that went on, regardless of how many walls or night glooms were in the way. El smiled wryly at the thought. Mystra herself, perhaps, but not her Chosen.

He stood and marveled amid trees that seemed to have grown into fantastic spired castles of spidery grace. The kiira told him of spells that could combine live trees and shape their growth, though neither Iymbryl nor his forebears knew much of how such magics were worked, or who in the city today was capable of them.

Amid the tree castles were lesser mansions of spired stone and what looked like blown, sculpted glass. However it seemed by the hanging gardens that sprawled over such edifices that elves could not bear to live unless growing plants or trees shared the same space with them. Elminster tried not to stare at the circular windows, the carefully crafted views, and the leaping curves of wood and stone all around him, but he'd never seen anything built for folk to live in that was so beautiful. Not just this building here, or that, but street upon street upon winding lane, a city of growing trees linked overhead, and a lush splendor of plantings and vistas and magically animated sculptures that casually outstripped the most exquisite human-work El had seen, even in the private gardens of the mage-king Ilhundyl.

Gods. With every step he could see new wonders. Over here was a house crafted like a breaking wave, with a glass-bottomed room hanging beneath the overarching curve—itself a garden of carefully shaped shrubs. Over there was a cascade of water plucked up tower-high by magic, so that it could plunge down, laughing, from chamber to chamber of a house whose rooms were all ovoids of tinted glass; within, the elven inhabitants strolled about, glasses in their hands. Down that lane of duskwoods wound a little path, to an ending at a small round pool. Seats circled the water in a gentle, hovering dance, their enchantments making them bob and rise as they went.

El shuffled on, remembering to stagger from time to time. How was he ever going to find House Alastrarra in all this?

Cormanthor was busy this bright afternoon. Its streets of trodden moss and the bridges, aloft, that leaped from tree to tree, held many elves—but none of the dirt and real crowding of human cities . . . and no creature more intelligent than cats and their winged cousins, the tressym, who was not an elf.

It hardly seemed a city. But then, to El, cities meant stone and humans, crammed together in their filth and shouting and seriousnesses, with a scattering of halflings and half-elves and a dwarf or two among the crowd.

Here were only the blue tresses and blue-white, sleek skins of proud elves who glided along in splendid gowns; or in cloaks that seemed entirely fashioned of the quivering green leaves of live plants; or in clinging leathers enspelled so that shifting rainbow hues drifted slowly around wearers' bodies; or in costumes that seemed to be no more than coyly cloaking clouds of lace and baubles drifting around elven forms. These latter were called driftrobes, the kiira let him know, as El tried not to stare at the slender bodies revealed by their circling movements. Driftrobes emitted a constant song of chimings whose descending runs sounded like many tiny, skillfully struck bells falling down the same staircase.

Elminster tried not to stare at anything, or even to look up much, and sighed dolefully from time to time whenever he sensed someone staring at him. This melancholy manner seemed to satisfy the few passersby who spared him much attention. Most seemed lost in their own thoughts or shared enthusiasms. Though the voices tended to be higher, lighter, and more pleasant on the ears, the elves of Cormanthor chattered every bit as much as humans at a market. El was able to covertly watch what he wanted most to see as he went along: how elves walked, so he could imitate them.

Most seemed to have a lilt and swing, like dancers. Ah, that was it—none strode flat-footed; even the tallest and most hurried of the citizenry danced forward on their toes. In his borrowed shape, El did likewise, and wondered when his sense of unease would lighten just a trifle.

It refused to, and as he went on, turning this way and that among the gigantic trees that rose like castle towers from the mossy ways, it began to dawn on him: he was being watched.

Not the countless casual inspections, the glances of laughing elves and sprawled cats and even winged steeds wheeling overhead, but by a single pair of eyes that was always on him, following him.

El began to double back on his route, hoping to catch a glimpse of whoever was following him, but the feeling grew more intense, as if the source of the scrutiny was drawing closer. Once or twice he stopped and wheeled around, as if to take in the view back along a sweeping avenue—but really to see who shared the path under the arching trees with him, trying to notice any face that was there more than once.

Some elves looked at him oddly, and El turned quickly away. Odd looks meant the lookers thought he was behaving oddly. He mustn't earn attention, at all costs. He'd just have to go on as before, trying to shrug off the odd prickling feeling between his shoulder blades that warned him of the ongoing scrutiny.

Did this open city have some sinister means of identifying intruders not of the People? They must, El supposed, or they'd soon be awash in the shape-shifters men called alunsree, or doppelgangers . . . hmm, but wasn't "alunsree" an elven word? The elves must have faced such problems when humans were still grunting at each other in caves and mud huts.

So he'd been spotted by someone. Someone concerned enough to stalk after him all this time, as he wandered down almost every street and lane of Cormanthor. What could he do?

Nothing but what he was doing—seeking House Alastrarra without seeming to be anxiously looking for anything. He dared not ask anyone where it was, or attract enough attention by his manner that someone might ask him if he needed aid . . . and he dared not call on the magic in the lore-gem unless he was desperate.

Desperate: surrounded by angry elven mages, all seeking his death with risen magic blazing in their hands. El glanced around the street as if such perils might come drifting toward him from all sides in a breath or two, but the scene remained almost like the revels of a feast-day. Folk were dancing in small groups or declaiming grandly as they swept along wrapped in their own self-importance. The fluting calls of horns heralded fresh songs, and off to the east a pair of pegasi riders chased each other across the sky in loops, rolls, and dartings that often sent leaves swirling in their wakes.

If he'd dared to, El would have sat on one of the many benches and floating highseats that flanked the mossy ways, and watched Cormanthor's comings and goings, openly fascinated. Yet if his true form were revealed, he might well be slain on the spot, and he had a mission to fulfill for Iymbryl. Where in all these endless trees *was* House Alastrarra, anyway? He'd been walking for hours, it seemed, and the light told him that the sun was sliding down the western sky. With its descent, the feeling grew in El that his mysterious shadow would attack.

After darkness fell? Or whenever things grew private enough? Where he stood now, the network of crossing trails was growing sparse, and the lights, bridges, and sounds were becoming fewer. If he continued on, he'd probably be heading into the deep green heart of the woods beyond the city, to the . . . south-west. Aye, southwest. He peered that way, and saw hanging creepers, and thick stands of gnarled trees, and a dell full of ferns. That decided him. Fern dells weren't high in his personal ranking of scenic beauty spots just now.

El turned around and picked up his pace, dancing softly forward on his toes as it seemed all Cormanthan elves did. He was moving purposefully now, as if heading for a known destination. His hand wasn't far from the hilt of the dagger that rode hidden in his sleeve. Was he charging straight toward an invisible, waiting foe? One who could draw a blade and hold it out, so that a hurrying false Iymbryl Alastrarra impaled himself on it?

The delicate strikings of a harp arose from a garden of hanging plants to his left as he went on. He had to go on; what else could he do?

After the mission the dying Iymbryl had set him stood his first task for Mystra. El shook his head in exasperation. This place was so beautiful; he wanted so much to just stroll and enjoy it.

Just as he'd wanted to grow up in Athalantar with his mother and father, not shiver in the wilds as an orphan outlaw, hunted by magelords. Aye, there was always *someone* with magic lurking about to ruin things. El set his jaw and went northeast. He'd strike clear across the city, and then try to circle around its outermost trails from there—he reckoned he'd trudged most of its labyrinthine heart already, with nary a sign of the falcon sigil of Alastrarra.

No unseen blade felled him, but the feeling of being watched didn't fade, either. The glows of enchanted symbols were growing stronger around El, now, as he walked. The gleam of the setting sun touched the treetops into golden flame, but down here in the dappled gloom its lances never penetrated.

The elven games and music went on unabated as twilight came down over Cormanthor. El walked on, trying not to show how anxious he was becoming. Could the lore-gem have played him false? Had it shown him an older House Alastrarra, or was the mansion well outside the city? Yet it held no scenes of another family holding, nor any sense that it was elsewhere in Cormanthor. *Surely* Iymbryl had known where he lived.

Aye, known too well for it to matter and be set forth clearly in the gem's stored memories. The whereabouts of House Alastrarra were a known, everyday thing to the bearers of the gems, not something . . .

But wait! Wasn't that a—no, *the* falcon symbol he was seeking?

El turned aside, pace quickening. It was!

His call of thanks to Mystra was no less fervent because of its silence.

The arched gate stood open, blue and green spell-glows winking and crawling up and down its filigree of living vines. El stepped inside, took two paces into the gloom of the twilit garden beyond, and then turned to survey the street behind him.

No elf stood there, but the unseen gaze remained unbroken. Slowly El turned around again.

Something gleamed in the air ahead of him, floating above the winding garden path. Something that hadn't been there moments before. It was the gleaming helm, arms, and shoulders of an elf in armor.

Or the semblance of such a guard—because those arms and shoulders and head were all he faced. The body that should have been beneath them was missing, the dark, gleaming armor trailing away like smoke below the breast of the silent apparition. As El stared at it, something rose menacingly from behind a bush off to the left: another armored form, just like the first.

El swallowed. So he'd awakened the magical defenses of this place. Blasting them with spells was probably not the wisest choice. So he turned slowly on his heels as guardian after guardian rose silently out of the dusk-cloaked garden, to ring him in on all sides.

Fire kindled then, behind the eye slits of one helm, as El found himself facing the one who'd first blocked his way. The mansion rose beyond it, just as in the scene the gem had shown him. The soft glows of moving lights showed from the tall, narrow windows the Alastrarrans were so proud of.

Right now, some of them might be glancing out those windows to see what manner of creature their guardians were slaying.

As El stood quietly, wondering what to do, and searching frantically through the gem's visions in search of some guidance, thin beams of amber fire suddenly reached out from the fire raging within the helm before him to touch the disguised prince of Athalantar.

El felt no pain; the beams were sweeping *through* him, leaving behind a tingling, rather than burning or tearing. There was a sudden warmth on his brow and a burst of light that almost blinded him. He narrowed his eyes until he could see again.

The lore-gem had blazed into life, glowing like a leaping flame in the darkness of the garden. Its eruption seemed to satisfy the guardians. The searching beams winked out, and the menacing helms began to sink into the darkness on all sides, until El faced only the first one. It hung, helm dark now, in his way.

Elminster made himself walk calmly toward it, until the smokelike trail that marked where its body faded should have been tickling his nose.

But it wasn't. As he took the step that would have brought him into collision with the silent sentinel, it vanished, winking out of existence and leaving him staring at the front door of House Alastrarra. Music came faintly to him through that portal, and tiny traceries of golden light formed endless and intricate patterns on one of its panels.

The lore-gem told him nothing about traps or door gongs or even servants of the portal, so El strode toward the doors and extended a hand to the crescent-shaped handle that hung like a bar in the air before them. Mystra grant that they be unlocked, he thought.

As he took that last step and laid his hand on the bar, El realized that something felt different. For the first time in hours, the ever-present pressure of those unseen, watching eyes was gone.

A feeling of cool relief washed over him—relief that lasted almost an entire breath before the handle under his hand glowed with sudden savage blue fire, and the doors rolled soundlessly open, to leave him staring into the startled eyes of several elves in the hall beyond.

"Oho," Elminster whispered, almost audibly. "Mother Mystra, if ye love me at all, *be with me now.*"

An old trick practiced by thieves in the city of Hastarl is to act with cool condescension when caught where one has no business being. Lacking time to think, El used it now.

The five elves had frozen in the midst of opening fluted bottles of wine and pouring them over heaps of diced nuts and greens on several platters that seemed content to float in the absence of any table. El stepped around them with a calm, superior nod of recognition—something he was very far from feeling, for the gem held no images of servants; Iymbryl had evidently spent little time noticing underlings—and swept on into the back of the hall, where small indoor gardens sprouted. Behind him, the servants hastily sketched salutes and murmured greetings that he did not stop to acknowledge.

A sudden burst of laughter from an open doorway on the right made the servants hasten in their tasks and forget him. El smiled with relief and at the good fortune Mystra had sent him. Along the passage he hadn't chosen, an array of unattended bottles was flying, approaching at chest height and spectacular speed, in obvious answer to a servant's summons.

His smile froze on his face when an elven maid danced out of a crescentiform archway ahead along the right-hand wall and looked him full in the face. Her large, dark eyes filled with surprise as she gasped, "My lord! We did not expect you home for another three dawns!"

Her tone was eager, and her arms were rising to embrace him. Oh, Mystra.

Again El did what his time in the backstreets of Hastarl bid him. He winked, spun away from her on down the hall, and raised a finger to his lips in a sly "silent, now" gesture.

It worked. The lass chuckled in delight, waved to him in a way that promised future ecstasies, and danced away down the passage toward the front hall. The sash of her brief garment swirled behind her for a moment, displaying its glowing falcon sigil.

Of course. That sigil, like those the five by the doors were wearing, was the livery of the staff; they otherwise wore whatever befitted the situation, not any sort of uniform.

And from the memories he was borrowing swam up the face of the lass who'd now danced out of sight around the corner, and her name: Yalanilue. In Iymbryl's remembrance, she'd been chuckling just like that, face close to his. But she hadn't been wearing any clothes at the time.

El drew in a deep breath, and released it slowly and ruefully. At least the lore-gem steered him through the nuances of elven speech.

He went on down the passage, finding an archway to the left leading into a room where reflected stars glimmered in the deserted waters of a pool, and another to the right opening into a darkened room that seemed to house a sculpture collection. Thereafter the passage displayed closed doors down both walls on its run to an ending in a round room where glowing spheres of light floated, drifting gently about like sleepy fireflies as they lit a slender spiral stair.

El took it, wanting very much to be out of the passage before one of the Alastrarras found him. He ascended past a chamber where dancers were stretching into and out of twists and backflips, obviously warming up for a performance to come. Of both sexes, they wore only their long hair, flowing free.

Tiny bells were woven into some of the locks, and their bodies were painted with intricate and obviously fresh designs.

One of them glanced at the elf hurrying past on the stair, but El put a finger to his chin as if in deep thought and hastened on, pretending not to have noticed the arching bodies of the dancers at all.

The stair took him then to a landing festooned with hanging plants—or rather, with spire-bottomed bowls enspelled so as to float at varying heights above the landing, to let the trailing leaves of their living burdens just brush the iridescent tiles underfoot.

El ducked between them toward an archway visible in the dimness beyond, still affecting his "lost in thought" pose. Then he came to an abrupt halt as something barred his way.

It blossomed into cold, white brightness, curling up to illuminate the chamber from its source: the naked edge of a leveled sword blade.

The blade hung by itself in midair, but a few drifting motes of magical radiance drew El's eye from it to an elven hand—an upraised right hand in a back corner, near the archway.

It belonged to a handsome, almost burly elf who must be accounted a muscle-bound giant among Cormanthans. The elf rose with easy grace from the gleaming black gaming board on the floor at which he'd been playing spellcircles, here in the darkness, against a frail-seeming servant—a maid who'd have been beautiful if there hadn't been so much fear in her eyes. She was losing, badly, and no doubt saw ahead the whipping or other punishment her burly opponent had promised her. El wondered for a moment if winning or losing would grant her the greater pain.

The lore-gem told El that the burly elf facing him was Riluaneth, a cousin taken in by the Alastrarras after his parents died, and a source of trouble ever since. Resentful and with a cruel streak that was seldom far from governing him, Ril had delighted in teasing and occasionally tormenting the two young Alastrarran brothers, Iymbryl and Ornthalas.

"Riluaneth," El greeted him now, voice level. The glowing blade turned slowly in the air to point at him; Elminster ignored it.

There was a spell the kiira urgently wanted him to examine; a spell Iymbryl had linked with his image of Riluaneth, binding the two together with a surge of anger. El followed its bidding, standing motionless as his burly cousin glided toward him. "As always, Iym," purred Riluaneth, "you blunder in where you aren't wanted, and see too much. That'll get you hurt some day . . . possibly sooner."

The glow around the blade faded abruptly, and out of the sudden darkness the blade hissed right at El's face.

He ducked aside, followed by Riluaneth's quiet laughter. The sword swooped overhead and raced off into the gloom, seeking its true quarry. The servant sobbed once, utter terror making her too breathless to do more, as the blade raced at her mouth.

Grimly El bought her life at the possible cost of his own. A quick spell plucked the blade out of its flight and wrestled it around to fly away from the elven maiden. Riluaneth grunted in amazement. His hand swept to his belt, to the hilt of the knife he wore there.

Well, a human intruder could do at least one good deed for House Alastrarra this day. El set his teeth and fought off the burly elf's clawing, clumsy mental attempt to regain control of the blade. The attempt ended abruptly as El lifted the streaking blade a little, over Riluaneth's drawn dagger, and let it slide through the elf's midriff.

Riluaneth staggered, doubled over the hilt lodged against his convulsing belly, and clutched at the hilt of his dagger, trying to snarl out some words. The dagger winked as he began the unleashing of whatever fell magic it held. El, not wanting to be caught in something as deadly as it was likely to be, used the spell Iymbryl had intended for Riluaneth the next time there was "trouble."

The burly elf let out all his breath in a gasp of white smoke, and reeled. More white vapors billowed out of his ears, nose, and eyeballs. Riluaneth's brain was afire inside his head, something that Iymbryl had predicted, with uncharacteristic dark humor, would be "a swiftly ended blaze, to be sure."

It was. Elminster barely got out of the way in time as the big, sleek body toppled past him, starting its headlong plunge down the stair. It bounced twice, wetly, on the way down.

Someone screamed at the bottom of the stair. El sorted impatiently through the magics that the gem was proudly displaying, brushing aside images of the deft castings of elves who wore superior smiles, and found what he needed.

A bloodfire spell, to burn away a burly troublemaker to nothing. A pyre without a barge might be the dwarven way, but Elminster had no time to be fussy about such things; already a triple-chiming gong had struck forth a strident chord on the floor below.

Brief brightness told him Riluaneth's remains had caught fire. El glanced over at the gaming board and found it gone—servant, pieces, and all. He wasn't the only one in this house who could move swiftly.

He might have been the only human ever to slay an elf here, though. Curses upon all cruel and arrogant bloods. Why couldn't he have run into Ornthalas in this corridor, and not into more trouble?

Below, the fire died and the blade clanged to the floor. There must be nothing left of Riluaneth now but trailing smoke and ash.

Time for him to be away from here, elsewhere in this grand house. Word of his part in Riluaneth's passing would spread soon enough. If he could somehow get to the heir first, and pass on the gem . . .

El bounded through the archway and down the passage beyond, sprinting with a lack of grace that would have raised elven eyebrows, but which certainly covered ground faster than they would have cared to. He snatched open a door and leaped into the high-ceilinged chamber beyond, finding himself in a place of floor-to-ceiling screens of filigree-work and lecterns with animated hands sprouting from their tops—hands that proffered open books to him as he darted past.

The Alastrarran library? Or reading room? He'd have liked to spend a winter here, or more, not dash past things without even looking at th—

But there was another door. El dodged around a floating, reclining chair that looked more comfortable than any other seating he'd ever seen and made a dive for the door handle.

He was still two speeding paces away when the door suddenly swung away from him, opening to reveal a startled elven face now inches from his own! He couldn't stop or swerve in time . . .

"He fell right here, Revered Lady!" the dancer gasped, pointing. His oiled body glistened in the flickering light of the brazier-bowls that circled around them both in obedience to the will of the matriarch of House Alastrarra.

The plum-hued gown she wore displayed every tall, curvaceous inch of Namyriitha Alastrarra from time to time, as portions of it flowed like smoke to wreath this part of her or that part of her in glistening rainbow droplets, and left other parts bare. An expert eye could tell she had no longer been young for many centuries, but few eyes bothered to practice any expertise when faced with such smooth-flowing beauty.

Fewer dared to look her way at all, when her face was as dark with fury as it was right now. "Keep back!" she snarled, sweeping an arm out to reinforce her order. Her gown rose into an elaborate sculpture of rising, interlaced spines standing up from her shoulders, but her hair burst through them now, a sure sign of unbridled rage. A servant whimpered softly, somewhere nearby. They'd only seen her thus thrice before—and each time, some part of the mansion had paid dearly to win her calm.

She wove her magic this time, though, with a few curt words. The sword rose obediently, quivering with the power racing through it, and then set off through the air, point first, up the stair. It would lead her, like a sure-strike hunting arrow, to Riluaneth's slayer. No doubt his gambling, dark schemes, or philandering had earned him his fate, but no one entered House Alastrarra and struck down one of her own without paying the price, twice over and speedily.

The Lady Namyriitha undid something as she hastened to the stairs, and the lower half of her gown fell away; she kicked it aside and set off up the stairs, bare legs flashing among wisps of patterned lace. Halfway up, her fingers, gliding along the rail, slid through something dark and sticky.

She looked back at the dark blood on the rail without slowing, and then lifted her dripping fingers and looked at them expressionlessly. She made no move to wipe them clean, or to slow her pursuit of the blade cutting through the air before her.

Below, the dancer picked up the discarded skirt uncertainly, and then handed it to a servant and whirled back to the stair to follow the Lady of the House. In his wake, hesitantly, several servants followed.

By the time they reached the landing at the top of the stair there was no sign of Namyriitha or the sword. The dancer began to run in earnest.

El dropped one arm to touch his knee at the last instant, and so it was his rolling shoulder that smashed into the elven servant and the door. Both flew back against the wall of the passage beyond with a mighty crash and rebounded into the passage in Elminster's wake. The elf sprawled on the furs underfoot in a tangle of limbs and did not move again.

Panting, El caught his balance again and ran on. Somewhere beneath him, the gong chimed its chord again. The passage forked ahead—this mansion was *big*—and El turned left this time. Perhaps he could double back.

A poor choice, it seemed. Two elves in glowing aquamarine armor were hastening down the passage toward him, buckling on their swords as they came. "Intruders," El called, hoping his shout was close enough to Iymbryl's voice to serve. He pointed back the way the guards had come. "Thieves! They ran thence!"

The guards wheeled around, though one gave El a hard, head-to-toe look, and ran back the way they'd come. "At least it wasn't Lady Herself just making sure we were awake," El heard one of them mutter, as they raced along the passage together. Ahead was a chamber dominated by a life-sized statue of a gowned elven lady, arms lifted in exultation. On its far side was another stair, curving down. A cross-corridor ran out of it, flanked by lounges on which the guards had obviously been reclining. Ornate double doors were along this passage; Elminster chose one he liked the look of, and veered toward it. He was into the passage and only a few running steps from its handles when shouts from the stair told him the two guards had noticed he was no longer with them.

He yanked on the ring handles, and twisted. The doors clicked open, and he whirled inside, drawing them closed as swiftly and as quietly as he could.

When he turned to see what manner of peril he'd hurled himself into this time, he found himself staring at an oval bed floating in midair in the middle of a dark, domed chamber. A leafy canopy floated above it, flanked by several platters carrying an array of fluted bottles and glasses, and a soft emerald glow was spreading across those leaves as the occupant of the bed sat bolt upright and stared at the intruder in her bedchamber.

She was slim and exquisitely beautiful, blue-black hair tumbling freely about her. She wore a night shift consisting of a collar and a thin strip of sheer, gauzy blue-green silk that fell from it down her front—and presumably down her back, too. Bare flanks and shoulders gleamed in the growing light as her large eyes changed from alarm to delight, and she somersaulted from the bed in a graceful sweep of bare limbs to bound forward and fling her arms around El.

"Oh, dearest brother!" she breathed, staring up into his eyes. "You're back, and whole! I had the most *terrible* dream about you dying!" She bit at her lip, and tightened her arms around him as if she'd never let him go. Oh, *Mystra*.

"Well," Elminster began awkwardly, "there's something I must tell you . . ."

With a boom, a door on the far side of the room burst inward, and a tall, angry-eyed elven maiden clad in a similar night shift stood in the doorway, conjured fire blazing around her wrists. Behind her crowded guards in glowing armor, the falcon sigil of Alastrarra on their breasts, and the winking lights of ready magic flickering and racing up and down the bared blades in their hands.

"Filaurel!" she cried. "Stand away from yon imposter! He but wears our brother's shape!"

The elven maiden stiffened in El's arms, and tried to draw back. El clung to her as tightly as she'd clutched him, uncomfortably aware of the sleek softness of the body pressed against his, and murmured, "Wait—please!" With one sister held against him, the other might not be so quick to blast him with spells.

Her arms quivered with rage as she lifted them to do just that. She paused, seeing that she'd endanger Filaurel. But if she dared not hurl magic just yet, there was no such constraint on her tongue. "*Murderer!*"

"Melarue," Filaurel said in a small voice, trembling against Elminster's chest, "what shall I do?"

"Bite him! Kick him! Let him have no time to work spells, while we come at him!" Melarue snarled, striding forward.

Another door boomed, and its thunder was out-shouted by a magically augmented voice uttering a clear, crisp command. "Be *still*, all!"

The room fell silent and motionless, but for the heaving bosom of Filaurel, pressed against the one who held her.

And for the sword, gliding smoothly through the air at Elminster. It rose, above the head of the elf maiden, until all it could imperil was the tense face of the false elf, who watched it slide straight for his mouth, nearer . . . and nearer . . .

Beyond it stood an elven matriarch in the upper half of a courtly gown, her face calm. Only her snapping eyes betrayed her outrage, as she stood with her hands raised in the gesture that had accompanied her order. A lady used to her will being absolutely obeyed within this House. This must be the Lady Namyriitha, Iymbryl's mother.

El had no choice—call on the gem, or die. With an inward sigh he awakened the power that would turn the sword to flakes of rust, and then dust ere it hit the floor.

"You are not my son," the matriarch said coldly, her eyes like the points of two daggers as she locked gazes with Elminster.

"But he wears the kiira," Filaurel said, almost pleadingly, staring up at where it glowed on the brow of the one who held her—the one who felt like her brother.

Namyriitha ignored her younger daughter. "Who *are* you?" she demanded, gliding forward.

"Ornthalas," Elminster said wearily. "Bring Ornthalas to me, and ye shall have the answer ye seek."

The lady matriarch stared at him, eyes narrow, for a long, silent time. Then she whirled, exposed lace swirling about her legs, and muttered orders. Two of the guards bent their heads and turned, holding their blades high to ensure they harmed no one in the crowd of bodies, and slipped out the door. Though he could see little of their departure, El did not think they were heading for the same destination.

The tense silence that followed did not last long. As the guards behind Lady Namyriitha spread out into an arc on both sides of her and put away their swords to pluck out hand darts instead, Melarue led her own guards forward to ring Elminster about completely.

"Revered mother," she said, spellflames still chasing each other in circles about her wrists, "what danger do we now dance with? This impostor could be spellbound to slay at all costs—a sacrifice whose body holds magics mighty enough to blast us all, and this house asunder around us! Dare we bring the heir of Alastrarra here, into the very presence of this—this shapeshifter?"

"I am *always* aware of the perils awaiting us all, Melarue," her mother said coldly, not turning her head to take her eyes off Elminster for a second, "and have spent centuries honing my judgment. Never forget that I am head of this house."

"Yes, mother," Melarue replied, in a respectful tone that twisted just enough in weary exasperation that El almost smiled. It seemed humans and elves were not so very different at heart after all.

"Please believe," El said to the elf maid in his arms, "that I mean no harm to you, or to House Alastrarra. I am here because of a promise I made, upon my honor."

"What promise?" Lady Namyriitha asked sharply.

"Revered Lady," El replied, turning his head to her, "I shall reveal all when what I must do is done—it is too precious a thing to endanger with dispute. I assure you that I mean no harm to anyone in this house."

"Surrender unto me your *name!*" the matriarch cried, using magic on the last word to compel him. El shook like a leaf in the thrall of her power, but the gem steadied him, and Mystra's grace kept him standing. He blinked at her, and shook his head. There was a murmur of respect from the ring of warriors, and Namyriitha's face tightened in fresh anger as she heard it.

"I am come," a deep yet musical voice said from the doorway. An old elf stood there, clad in the cape and robes usually affected by human archwizards. The falcon device of the house was worked into the sash he wore, repeated many times, yet El knew this was no servant. Rings gleamed on his ancient fingers, and he bore a short wooden scepter in his hands, its sides carved with spiral grooves.

"Naeryndam," the matriarch said curtly, nodding her head in Elminster's direction, "deal with this."

The old elf met El's gaze, and his eyes were keen and searching. "Unknown one," the elven mage said slowly, "I can tell ye are not Iymbryl, of this House. Yet ye wear the gem that was his. Think ye that possession of it gives ye rightful command over the kin of Alastrarra?"

"Revered elder," El replied, bowing his head, "I have no desire to command anyone in this fair city, or do any harm to ye or thy kin. I am here because of a promise I made to one who was dying."

In his arms, Filaurel started to shake. El knew she was weeping silently, and automatically stroked her hair and shoulders in futile soothings. The Lady

Namyriitha's mouth tightened again, but Melarue and some of the warriors looked more kindly upon the intruder in their midst.

The old elf nodded. "Thy words ring true. Know, then, that I am going to cast a spell that is not an attack, and conduct thyself accordingly."

He lifted his hand, made a circling motion, spread and crooked two fingers, and blew some dust or powder over his wrist. There was a singing in the air, and the warriors on all sides hastily fell back. The singing air—some sort of spell-barrier, El guessed—ringed him around closely.

He merely nodded to the old elf mage, and stood waiting. Filaurel was crying openly now, and he swung her fully against his chest and murmured, "Lady, let me tell ye how thy brother died."

There was suddenly utter stillness in the room. "By chance I came upon a patrol Iymbryl was part of, in the deep wood—"

"A patrol he *led*," Lady Namyriitha almost spat.

El inclined his head gravely. "Lady, indeed; I meant no slight. I saw the last few of his fellows fall, until only he was left, beset on all sides by ruukha, in numbers enough to overwhelm his spells, and mine own."

"*Your* spells?" she sneered, her tone making it clear she doubted his words. Filaurel's face, however, wet with tears, was raised and intent on his every word.

"As I fought my way to him, he was pierced through by a ruukha longfork, and fell into a stream there. My spells took us both away from our foes, but he was dying. Had he lived longer, he could have been my guide to bring him hence. But he had time only to show me that I should put the kiira to my brow before he failed . . . and was gone to dust."

"Did he say anything?" Filaurel sobbed. "His last words: *do you remember them?*" Her voice rose in anguish, to ring in the far corners of her bedchamber.

"He did, Lady," El told her gently. "He cried out a name, and that he was coming at last to its owner. That name was . . . Ayaeqlarune."

There was a general groan, and both Melarue and Filaurel hid their faces. Their mother, however, stood like white-faced stone, and the old elf mage only nodded sadly.

Into this grieving swept new arrivals, slim and straight-backed and proud. Rich were their costumes, and haughty their manner, as they came in at the door and stood staring: four she-elves and two much younger maids, with a proud, youthful elven lord at their head. El recognized him from the gem-visions, though there was no floating chair nor tree-pillars and sun-dappling here. This was Ornthalas, now heir—though he did not yet know it—of House Alastrarra.

Ornthalas looked at El in some puzzlement. "Brother," he asked, one elegant brow lowering in a frown, "what means this?"

He glanced about the chamber. "The House is yours; there's no need to challenge our kin about anything." His gaze fell to Filaurel, and darkened. "Or have you taken our sist—"

"Hold peace, youngling," Naeryndam said sternly. "Such thoughts demean us all. See yon gem upon thy brother's brow?"

Ornthalas looked at his uncle as if the old mage had lost his senses. "Of course," he said. "Is this some sort of game? Be—"

"Still for once," the Lady Namyriitha said crisply, and someone among the ring of warriors chuckled.

At that sound, the young elven lord drew himself up, looked around the room in an attempt at dignified silence (El thought he looked like a fat merchant in the streets of Hastarl who has slipped in horse-droppings and fallen hard on his behind on the cobbles; he has scrambled up, and is now looking around to see if anyone witnessed his pratfall, pretending all the while that there is no horse-dung on his backside—no, none at all, as all well-bred people can plainly see . . .), and announced to his uncle, "Yes, Revered Uncle, I see the kiira."

"Good," the old elf said dryly, and there was another chuckle from the warriors, this one better suppressed. Naeryndam let it die away, and then said, "Ye are sworn to obey the bearer of the kiira, as are we all."

"Yes," Ornthalas nodded, his puzzled frown returning. "I have known this since I was a child, Uncle."

"And remember it yet? Good, good," the old mage replied softly, evoking several chuckles this time. Both Lady Namyriitha and Melarue stirred, exasperation plain on their faces, but said nothing.

"Then do ye swear by the kiira of our House, and all our forebears who live within it, to lift no hand, and cast no spell, upon thy brother as he approaches ye?" Naeryndam asked, his voice suddenly as hard and ringing as a sword blade striking metal.

"I do," Ornthalas said shortly.

The old elf-mage took hold of the young elf's arm, towed him forward through the singing barrier, and then turned to El and said, "Here be he. Do what ye've come to do, sir, before one of my hot-blooded kin does something foolish."

El inclined his head in thanks, took Filaurel gently by the elbows, and said, "My humble apologies, lady, for trammeling thy freedom. It was needful. May the gods grant that it never be so, upon thee, ever again in all thy long days."

Filaurel shrank away from him, eyes very large, and put her knuckles to her lips. Yet as he turned away, she blurted out, "Your honor goes unblemished with you, unknown lord."

El took two quick steps toward Naeryndam, stepped smoothly around him, and bore down upon Ornthalas with a polite smile.

The young elf looked at him. "Brother, are you renouncing—?"

"Sad news, Ornthalas," said Elminster, as their noses crashed together, and then their brows. As the tingling and flashing begun, he held like grim death to the elf's shoulders, and added, "I'm not thy brother."

The memories were surging around him, then, in a maelstrom that was sweeping him away, and Ornthalas was screaming in shock and pain. A white, roaring surge of magic was tugging at him as it rose, and El couldn't hold on any longer.

"May the law of the realm protect me!" he cried, and then gasped in a hoarse whisper, "Mystra, stand by me!"

The room spun around him then, and he had no breath left to cry anything. His body was stretching, everyone was shouting in anger and alarm, and the last thing the prince of Athalantar saw, as he spun down into tentacles of darkness that came sweeping greedily up to take him, was the furious face of the Lady Namyriitha, dwindling away behind the one solid thing in all this: the leveled wooden scepter, held firmly in Naeryndam's old hand. He clung to that image as utter darkness claimed him.

FIVE
TO CALL ON THE CORONAL

And so it befell that Elminster of Athalantar found the elven family he had so inadvertently joined and did that which he was sworn to do. Like many who fulfill an unusual and dangerous duty, he received scant thanks for it. Had it not been for the grace of Mystra, he might easily have died in the Coronal's garden that night.

ANTARN THE SAGE
FROM *THE HIGH HISTORY OF FAERÛNIAN ARCHMAGES MIGHTY*
PUBLISHED CIRCA THE YEAR OF THE STAFF

Ornthalas Alastrarra stumbled across the chamber, clutching his head and screaming, his voice raw and ugly. Crackling lightnings of magic trailed from the gem that shone like a new star upon his brow, back to the one from whom it had come: the sprawled body on the floor, so young, and ugly—and *human*.

Filaurel's bedchamber was in an uproar. Warriors hacked at the barrier that repelled their armor and their blades, and were repulsed. They clawed their way along it, shouting in pain amid bright clouds of sparks, only to stagger back, master their trembling limbs, and try again. Under their high-booted feet Melarue lay sprawled, her hair outflung like a fan around her, stunned from her own attempt to burst through Naeryndam's barrier. She'd forgotten the manyfold enchantments upon her jewelry.

Not so her mother. Lady Namyriitha was standing well clear of the singing air and grimly bringing down the barrier with spell after spell of her own, melting away its essence layer by layer. As those magics crashed and swirled, Filaurel and most of the other women screamed at the sight of Elminster's true nature and at the agony of Ornthalas. Servants crowded in at every door to see what was befalling.

The old elf-mage calmly stepped over the motionless body of the hawk-nosed human and stood astride it, drawing a sword seemingly out of the empty air. Magic winked and chased itself up and down that rune-marked blade as he raised and shook it a little doubtfully, as many an old warrior readies a weapon he finds heavier than he remembered. He raised his scepter in the other hand. When the barrier failed in a wash of white sparks an instant later, and the warriors of House Alastrarra surged forward with an exultant shout, he was ready.

Blue fire swirled out from the tip of Naeryndam's blade, so hot and quick that warriors bent over backward in mid-charge, and fell in awkward, sliding heaps. A sweep of that same blue fire along the furs underfoot, a sweep that left the furs unscorched, sent them rolling and scrambling away again, back to where they'd stood before. One elf flung his blade as he fled, spinning hard and fast through the air at the motionless human. The scepter spat forth its own fire, a stabbing, silvery needle of force, and the thrown blade exploded into a rainbow of snapping sparks that spun and flew until they were no more. One or two of them bounced almost at Naeryndam's feet.

"What treachery is this?" Lady Namyriitha spat at the old mage. "Are you crazed, aged brother? Has the human some sort of spellhold over you?"

"Be still," the old mage replied in calm and pleasant tones—but as she had done earlier; he put his risen power behind his words. The only sounds that followed their rolling, imperious thunder were faint groans from where Ornthalas lay in a corner, his head against the wall, and sobbings here and there where women who'd been screaming struggled to catch their breaths again.

"There's entirely too much shouting and spellhurling in this House, these days," Naeryndam observed, "and not nearly enough listening, caring, and thinking. In a few generations more, we'll be as bad as the Starym."

The warriors and servants stared at the old mage in genuine astonishment; the Starym held themselves to be the pinnacle of all that is noble and fine among the People, and even their age-old rivals acknowledged them first among all the proud Houses of Cormanthor.

The corners of Naeryndam's mouth crooked in what might almost have been a smile as he looked around the room at all the astonished faces. With blade in hand he motioned his kin and the servants all to stand before him, on one side of the room. When no one moved, he let fire roll forth from the blade again, in long, snarling arcs of clear warning. Slowly, almost dazedly, they obeyed.

"Now," the old mage told them, "just for this once, and for a short enough time, ye'll listen—ye too, Ornthalas, risen Heir of House Alastrarra."

A groan was his only reply, but those who turned to look saw Ornthalas nodding, his white face still held in his hands.

"This human youngling," Naeryndam said, pointing down at the body beneath him with his scepter, "invoked the law of the realm. And yet all of ye—save Filaurel and Sheedra and young Nanthleene—attacked him, or tried to. Ye disgust me."

There were murmurs of protest. He quelled them with fire leaping in his old eyes and continued, "Yes, disgust me. This House has an heir right now because this man risked his life, and kept to his honor. He made his way into our city, past a hundred elves or more who might have killed him—would have slain him, had they known his true nature—because Iymbryl asked him to. And because he keeps his word to those not of his kin nor race, those he barely knows, and dared this task, the memories of this House, the thoughts of our forebears, are not lost, and we can keep our rightful place in the realm as a first House. All because of this human, whose name we don't even know."

"Nevertheless," his sister Namyriitha began, "w—"

"*I'm not finished,*" her brother said, in tones that cut like steel. "*Thou* listen even less well than the young ones, sister."

Had the moment been less important, the air less full of tension and awe, the gathered House might have enjoyed the sight of the sharp-tongued matriarch opening and closing her mouth like a gasping fish in silence, as her face flooded crimson and purple. No one, though, so much as looked at her; their eyes were all on Naeryndam, the oldest living Alastrarran.

"The human invoked our law," the old mage said flatly. "Younglings, heed well: the law is just that—the *law*, a thing not permitting of our tampering or setting aside. If we do, we are no better than the most brutal ruukha or the most dishonest human. I will not stand idle and see ye of the blood of Thurruvyn fail the rightful honor of our House . . . and of our race. If ye would attack the human, ye must first defeat *me*."

The silence that followed was broken by a groan from beneath the old mage; the raven-haired, hawk-nosed human youth gave an involuntary cry of pain as he stirred. One tanned and rather dirty hand closed blindly on the booted elven ankle hard by it. At the sight a warrior of House Alastrarra cried out and threw his blade.

End over end it flashed, straight at the tousled head of the human, as he started to claw his way up the leg of the elf who stood over him.

Naeryndam calmly watched it come, and at precisely the right moment swept his own blade down to strike the whirling steel aside into a corner of the room. "Thou listen but poorly, do thou not?" he asked with soft sadness, as the warrior who'd thrown the blade cowered away from him. "When is this House going to start using its wits?"

"*My* wits tell me that Alastrarra shall be forever stained and belittled by Cormanthans from end to end of our fair realm, as the House that harbored a human," the Lady Namyriitha said bitterly, raising her hands dramatically.

"Yes," Melarue chimed in, rising from the floor with the pain of her striving against the barrier still etched on her face. "You've lost *your* wits, Uncle!"

"What say ye, Ornthalas?" the old mage asked, looking past them. "What say—our ancestors?"

The haughty young elf looked sadder and more serious than any in the room remembered him ever seeming. His brow was still pinched with pain, and strange shadows yet swirled in his eyes, as memories that were not his own plunged past them in the endless, bewildering flood. Slowly, reluctantly, he said, "Prudence bids us conduct the human to the Coronal, that no stain be upon us." He looked from one Alastrarran to another. "Yet if we harm so much as a hair upon his head, our honor is bereft. This man has done us more service than any elf living, save you, noble Naeryndam."

"Ah," the old mage said, satisfied. "Ah, now. See, Namyriitha, what a treasure the kiira is? Ornthalas wears it for but moments and gains good sense."

His sister stiffened in fresh annoyance, but Ornthalas smiled ruefully, and said, "I fear you speak bald truth, Uncle. Let us quit this field before battle comes to it, and return to our singing. Let the songs be of our remembrances of Iymbryl my brother, until dawn or slumber. Sisters, will you join me?"

He held out his arms, and after a moment of hesitation Melarue and Filaurel took them, and the three siblings swept out of the chamber together.

As they went out, Filaurel looked back at the human, just as the strange man found his feet, and shook her head. Fresh tears glistened in her eyes as she called, "Have my thanks, human sir."

"Elminster am I," the hawk-nosed man replied, lifting his head, his elvish now strangely accented. "Prince of Athalantar."

He turned his head to look at Naeryndam. "I stand in thy debt, revered lord. I am ready, if ye'd take me to the Coronal."

"Yes, brother," the Lady Namyriitha snarled, face pinched in disgust, "remove *that* from our halls—and stop staring at him, Nanthee; you demean us before an unwashed beast!"

The young lass thus addressed was staring in open awe at the human, with his stubbled face, and stubby ears, and—*otherness*. El winked at her.

That brought gasps of outrage from both Lady Namyriitha and Sheedra, the mother of Nanthleene, who snatched at her daughter's hand, and practically dragged her from the chamber.

"Come, Prince Elminster," the old mage said dryly. "The impressionable young ladies of this House are not for thee. Though 'tis to thy credit that thou're not disgusted when faced with folk of other races than thine own. Many of my kin are not so large of mind and heart, and so there is danger for thee here." He held out his winking sword, hilt first. "Carry my blade, will thou?"

Wondering, Elminster took hold of the enspelled sword, feeling the tingling of strong magics as he hefted the light, supple blade. It was magnificent. He raised it, staring in admiration at its feel and at the way its steel—if it *was* steel—shone bright and blue in the light of the bedchamber. More than one of the warriors gasped in alarm at the sight of the mage arming this human intruder, but Naeryndam paid them no heed.

"There is also a danger to us, if a human should see the glories and defenses of our realm, which is why we suffer few of thy blood to catch even a glimpse of our city, and live. Wherefore my blade will cloud thy sight, even as it binds thee to accompany me."

"It is not needful, Lord Mage. I have no mind to cross thee, or escape thee," El told him truthfully, as mists rose to enclose them both in a world of swirling blueness. "And even less of a mind to storm this fair city, alone, in time to come."

"I know those things, but others of my kind do not," Naeryndam replied calmly, "and some of them are *very* swift with their bows and blades." He took a step forward, and the blue mists rolled away behind them, dwindling to nothingness.

El looked around in wonder; they were now standing not in a crowded bedchamber, but under the night sky in the green heart of a garden. Stars glittered overhead. Beneath their feet two paths of soft, lush moss met beside the statue of a large, winged panther that glowed a vivid blue in the night. Will o'wisps danced and drifted here and there above the beautiful plants around them, swaying above luminous night-flowers to the accompaniment of faint strains of unseen harps.

"The Coronal's garden?" El asked in a soft whisper. The old mage smiled at the wonder in the human's eyes.

"The Coronal's garden," he confirmed, his voice a soft rumble. The words were barely said when something rose out of the ground at their very feet—spectral, and graceful, and yet deadly in appearance.

Blue-white it glowed, all sleek nude curves and long flowing hair, but its eyes were two dark holes against the stars as it said in their minds, *Who comes?*

"Naeryndam, eldest of the House of Alastrarra, and guest," the old mage said firmly.

The watchnorn swayed to meet his gaze, and then back to look into the eyes of Elminster, from only inches away.

A chill crackled between living flesh and undead essence as those dark eyes stared into his, and El swallowed. He'd not want to see that serenely beautiful face angry.

This is a human. Blue-white hair swirled severely.

"Aye," the old elf told the watchnorn in dry tones. "I can recognize them too."

Why bring you a forbidden one where the Coronal walks this night?

"To see the Coronal, of course," Naeryndam told the undead maiden. "This human brought the kiira of my House from our dying heir to his successor, alone and on foot through the deep heart of the forest."

The swirling spirit seemed to look at Elminster with new respect. *That is something a Coronal should see; there can never be too many wonders in the world.* The blue-white, ghostly face came close enough to brush against Elminster's once more. *Can you not speak, human?*

"I did not want to insult a lady," El said carefully, "and know not how to properly address thee. Yet I think now we are well met." He threw back one booted foot and sketched a sweeping bow. "I am Elminster, of the land of Athalantar. Who art thou, Lady of Moonlight?"

Wonder upon wonder, the ghostly thing said, brightening. *A mortal who desires to know my name. I like that "Lady of Moonlight" you entitle me; it is fair upon the ears. Yet know, man called Elminster, that I was in life Braerindra of the House of Calauth, last of my House.*

Her voice began astonished and pleased, yet ended with such sadness that Elminster found tears welling up in him. Roughly, he said, "Yet, Lady Braerindra, look ye: while ye abide here, the House of Calauth yet stands, and is not forgotten."

Ah, but who is to remember it? The voice in their heads was a sad sigh. *The forest grows through roofless chambers that once were fair, and scatter the bones and dust that were my kin, while I am here, far distant. A watchnorn, now. Cormanthans term us "ghosts," and fear us, and keep away. Hence our guardianships here be lonely, and bid fair to remain so.*

"I shall remember the House of Calauth," Elminster said quietly, his tone firm. "And if I live and am allowed to walk fair Cormanthor freely, I will return to talk with thee, Lady Braerindra. Ye shall not be forgotten."

Blue-white hair swirled up around Elminster, and a chill prickled through him. *I never thought to hear a mortal do me honor in the world again*, the voice in his head replied, full of wonder. *Still less a human, to speak so fair. Be welcome whenever ye can find the time to come hence.* Elminster felt a sudden wrenching cold on his cheek, and he shivered involuntarily. Naeryndam caught hold of his shoulder as he reeled.

My thanks to thee also, wise mage, the spirit added, as Elminster struggled to smile. *Truly, you bring wonders to show our Coronal.*

"Aye, and so we must pass on. Fare thee well, Braerindra, until next our paths cross," the old elf replied.

Until next, the voice replied faintly, as blue-white wisps sank into the ground and were gone.

Naeryndam hurried Elminster along one of the mossy paths. "Truly, ye impress me, man, by the way ye take on the weight of others' cares. I begin to hope for the human race yet."

"I—I can scarce speak," El told him, teeth chattering. "Her kiss was so . . . cold."

"Indeed—had she meant it to do so, 'twould have driven the life from thy body, lad," the old elf told him. "It is why she serves thus, she and those of her kind. Yet be of heart; the chill will pass, and ye need not fear the touch of any undead of Cormanthor, forevermore. Or rather, for as long as thy 'forevermore' lasts."

"Our lives must seem fleeting to elves," El murmured, as the path took them up into small bowers of curved seats amid shrubs, and past trickling streamlets and little pools.

"Aye," the elven mage told him, "but I meant rather the peril ye stand in. Speak as fairly in the time just ahead as ye did to the watchnorn, lad, or death may yet find thee this night."

The young man beside him was silent for some time. "Is the Coronal one I should kneel to?" he asked finally, as they came up some stone steps and between two strange, spiral-barked trees out onto a broad patio lit by luminous plants.

"Be guided by his face," the mage replied smoothly as they advanced, not hurrying.

An elf sat on nothing at the center of the paved space, with an open book, a tray of tall, thin bottles, and a footrest floating in the air around him. Two cloaked elves who wore power as if it crowned them stood on either side of him; at the sight of the human they glided swiftly forward to bar Elminster's path to the Coronal, slowing only slightly at the sight of Naeryndam Alastrarra behind the human.

"*You* must have helped this forbidden one win past the watchnorns," one of the elven mages said to the old elf-mage, ignoring Elminster as if he were no more than a post or bird-spotted stone sculpture. His voice was cold with anger. "Why? What treachery, reveal unto us, could reach the heart of one who has served the realm so long? Have your kin sent you hither for punishment?"

"No treachery, Earynspieir," Naeryndam replied calmly, "nor punishment, but a matter of state requiring the judgment of the Coronal. This human invoked our law, and survives to stand here because of it."

"No *human* can claim rights under the laws of Cormanthor," the other mage snapped. "Only those of our People can be citizens of the realm: elves, and elf-kin."

"And how would ye judge a human who has in all honor, and not through battle-spoil, worn a kiira of an elder House of Cormanthor, and walked the streets of our city until he found the rightful heir to surrender it to?"

"I'd believe that tale only when it could be proven to me, beyond doubt," Earynspieir replied. "What House?"

"Mine own," Naeryndam replied.

Into the little silence that his soft words made, the old elf in the chair said, "Enough tongue-fencing, lords. This man is here, that I may judge; bring him to me."

Elminster ducked around the mage who stood nearest and strode boldly toward the Coronal. He never saw the mage wheel and cast a deadly spell at him, or Naeryndam nullify it with a scepter held ready for just such an occurrence.

The second mage was hurling another dark magic when Elminster knelt before the ruler of all Cormanthor. The Coronal raised a hand, and that magic, rushing toward his face like a dark roiling in the air, ceased to be. "Enough spell-hurling, lords all," he commanded gently. "Let us see this man." He looked into Elminster's eyes.

El's mouth was suddenly dry. The eyes of the elven king were like holes opening into the night sky. Stars swam and twinkled in their depths, and one could fall into those dark pools and be dragged down, down, and away . . .

He shook his head to clear it, clenched his teeth at the effort required, and set one booted foot on the pave. It seemed as if he were lifting a castle tower on his shoulders when he tried to straighten that leg, and surge to his feet. He growled, and set about doing so.

Behind him, the three elven mages exchanged looks. Not even they could forge on against the Coronal's will, when mindlocked with the ruler of all Cormanthor.

White-faced and trembling, sweat running in rivers down his cheeks and chin, the raven-haired young man rose slowly, gaze still locked with the Coronal, until he was standing beside the seated elf.

"Do you resist me yet?" the old elf whispered.

The young man's lips moved with agonizing slowness as he tried to shape words. "No," he said at last, slowly and deliberately. "Ye are welcome in my thoughts. Were ye not trying to make me rise?"

"No," the Coronal said, turning his head so that the link between their gazes was cut off, as if by a knife. "I strove to keep you on your knees, to master your will." He frowned, eyes narrowing. "Perhaps another works through you."

"My lord!" the mage Earynspieir cried, thrusting himself between Elminster and the Coronal. "This is precisely the peril you must be shielded against! Who knows what deadly spell could be worked upon you, through this lad?"

"Hold him in thrall, then, if you must," the Coronal said wearily. "All three of you—and Earynspieir, let there be no 'accidentally' broken necks, or frozen lungs, or the like. I shall reveal whom he serves with the scepter, and read his memories of the matter of the kiira thereafter."

From one of the trays floating near at hand the white-robed elf took up what looked like a long claret-hued glass rod, smooth and straight, no thicker than his smallest finger. It seemed almost too delicate to hold together.

El found himself lifted off his feet to hang motionless in the air, hands spread out stiffly from his sides. He could move his eyes, his throat, and his chest; all else was gripped as if by unyielding iron.

A light grew in the glass rod, and raced along its length. The old elf calmly pointed it at Elminster's head, and they both watched the thin ray of radiance slide out of the rod and move through the air, with almost lazy slowness, to touch El's forehead.

A great coldness crashed through the Athalantan, shaking him to his very fingertips. As he quivered there in midair he could hear the clatter of his teeth chattering uncontrollably, and then gasps of amazement from all four elves.

"What is it?" he tried to say, but all that came out through his frozen lips was a confused gurgling. Abruptly he found that his mouth was freed, and that he was turning—being turned—in the air, around to face a ghostly image that was towering over the patio. The spectral outlines of a face he knew.

A calm, serene face regarding them all with mild interest. Its eyes lit upon Elminster, and brightened.

"Is that who I think it is, man?" the Coronal asked gently.

"It is Holy Mystra," El told him simply. "I am her servant."

"So much I had come to suspect," the old elf told him a trifle grimly. A moment later, he and the young human melted away together, leaving the floating chair, and the air above and before it, empty.

The three mages stared at those emptinesses, and then at each other. Earynspieir whirled around to look up into the sky again. The huge human face was fading, the ghostly tresses curling and whipping like restless snakes as it seemed to draw slightly away from the Coronal's garden.

But what made the elf-mages cower and stammer out the names of their gods was the way the beautiful female face looked at each of them in turn, as a broad and satisfied smile grew across it.

A few moments later, the face could no longer be seen at all.

"Some trick of the young human, no doubt," Earynspieir hissed, visibly shaken. Naeryndam only shook his head in silence, but the other court mage plucked at Earynspieir's arm to get his attention, and pointed.

That vast smile had suddenly reappeared. There was no face around it this time, but all three mages knew what it was. They would see it in their memories until their dying days.

As they turned their backs on the stars and hastened toward the nearest doors that led into the palace, another sight made them all pause and stare in silence once more.

All over the gardens, the watchnorns were rising silently to watch that smile fade.

SIX
THE VAULT OF AGES

Beneath the fair city of Cormanthor, in some hidden place, lies the Vault of Ages, sacred storehouse of the lore of our People. 'Let Mythal rise and Myth Drannor fall,' says one ballad, "and still the Vault remembreth all." Some say the Vault lies there yet, unplundered and as splendid as before, though few now know the way to it. Some say 'tis the Srinshee's tomb. Some say she has become a terrible mad thing of clawing rnagics, and has made the Vault her lair. And there are even some who admit that they do not know.

SHALHEIRA TALANDREN, HIGH ELVEN BARD OF SUMMERSTAR
from *SILVER BLADES AND SUMMER NIGHTS:*
AN INFORMAL BUT TRUE HISTORY OF CORMANTHOR
PUBLISHED IN THE YEAR OF THE HARP

There were no mists, this time, only a soft moment of purple-black velvet darkness, and then Elminster was elsewhere.

The white-robed elven ruler stood with him, in a cool, damp stone room whose ceiling arched low overhead. Luminous crystals were set in the places where the crisscrossing stone ribs of its vaults met, one with the next.

The elf and the human stood in the brightest spot, a clear space at the center of the domed chamber. In four places around its circular arc the wall was pierced by ornate arches that gave onto long vaulted passages running— El peered down one, and then another—to other domed chambers.

A narrow, winding path had been left clear down the center of each passage, but all of the rest of the space was crammed with treasure: a spreading sea of gold coins and bars and statuary, holding in its frozen waves ivory coffers that spilled pearls and rainbows of glittering gems.

Chests were stacked six high along the walls, and chased and worked metal banner-poles leaned against them like fallen trees. Nearer at hand, a dragon as tall as Elminster, carved from a single gigantic emerald, leaned amid the branches of a tree of solid sardonyx; its leaves were of electrum covered with tiny cut gems. The prince of Athalantar turned slowly on his heel to survey this treasure, trying to look expressionless and very much aware that the Coronal was watching his face.

There were more riches here, in this one chamber, than he'd ever seen before in all his life. The wealth here was truly staggering. The entire treasury of Athalantar was outshone by what would lie beneath him, were he to simply fall on his face in the nearest heap of coins. Right by his foot gleamed a cut ruby as large as his head.

El dragged his gaze up from all the wealth to meet the searching, starry eyes of the Coronal. "What is all this?" he asked. "I—that is, I know what I'm looking at, but why keep it here, underground? The gems would dazzle far more in sunlight."

The old elf smiled. "My People dislike cold metal, and keep little of it to look at and touch on a daily basis; something gnomes and dwarves and humans never seem able to grasp. The gems we need to serve us as homes for magic, yes, those we keep about us; the remainder rests in various vaults. That which belongs to the Coronal—or rather, to the court, and thus, all Cormanthor—comes here." He looked down one of the passages. "Some call this the Vault of Ages."

"Because ye've been piling up riches here for so long?"

"No. Because of the one who dwells here, guarding it all." The Coronal raised a hand in greeting, and El stared down the passage that the old elf was facing.

There *was* a figure there, tiny in the dim distance, and as thin as a post. A very graceful post, swaying as it came toward them.

"Look at me," the Coronal said suddenly. When Elminster turned, he found himself looking into the full, awakened might of the ruler of Cormanthor. Once again his boots rose helplessly from the floor, and he hung in the air above the old elf as irresistible probes raced through him, calling up memories of a ferny dell, his spellbook left behind, Iymbryl gasping, and a certain scepter.

The Coronal stopped at that, and then sent El's mind racing back, through brigand battles and The Herald's Horn, to a certain encounter outside the city of Hastarl, where—

Now the smiling face of Mystra was back again, blocking the Coronal's probings. She raised a reproving eyebrow at the elf, and smiled to soften her rebuke as the elven ruler reeled and shook his head, grunting in mindshock and pain.

El found himself abruptly back on the floor, dumped like a sack of grain.

When he looked up, he found himself staring into the tiny, shrunken face of the oldest elf he'd ever seen. Her long silver-white hair brushed the tiles below her slippered feet—feet that trod air, inches above the smooth-worn paving stones underfoot—and her skin seemed draped over her bones . . . bones so petite and shapely that she looked exquisite rather than grotesque, despite the fact that except where her diaphanous gown intervened, El could almost see her skeleton.

"Seen enough?" she asked impishly, caressing her hips and turning alluringly, like a tavern dancer.

El dropped his eyes. "I—my apologies for staring," he said quickly. "I've never seen one of the People who looked so old before."

"There are few of us as old as the Srinshee," the Coronal said.

"The Srinshee?"

The old elven lady inclined her head in regal greeting. Then she turned, held out her hand over some empty air, and sat on that air, reclining as if she was lying in a pillow-padded lounge. Another sorceress.

"Her tale is her own to tell you," the Coronal said, holding up a hand to stay further words from Elminster. "First must come my judgment."

He walked a little away from the young man, treading the air above the floor. Then he turned back to face the Athalantan and said, "Your honesty and honor I have never doubted. Your aid to House Alastrarra, without thought of reward or rank, alone is worthy of an armathor—in human words, a knighthood, with citizenship—in Cormanthor. So much I freely grant, and bid you welcome."

"Yet—?" El asked ruefully, at the old elf's guarded tone.

"Yet I cannot help but conclude that you were sent to Cormanthor by the divine one you serve. Whenever *I* try to learn why, she blocks my inquiries."

Elminster took step toward the old elf and looked into his eyes. "Read me now, pray ye, and know that I speak truth, Revered Lord," he said. "I am sent here by Great Mystra to 'learn the rudiments of magic' as she put it, and because she foresaw that I'd be needed here 'in time to come.' She did not reveal to me just when, and how, and needed by whom or what cause."

The white-robed elf nodded. "I doubt not your belief, man; 'tis the goddess I cannot fathom. I well believe she said just those words to you; yet she bars me from learning your true powers, and her true designs . . . and I have a realm to protect. So, a test."

He smiled. "Think you I show every outland intruder riches that could well bring every hungry human from here to the western sea clamoring through the trees of Cormanthor?"

The Srinshee chuckled, and put in, "Elven ways may outstrip the comprehension of men, but that does not make them the ways of fools."

El looked from one of them to the other. "What testing do you plan? I've little stomach left for more spell duels or wrestlings mind-to-mind."

The Coronal nodded. "This I already know; were you such a one, you'd never have been brought here. To risk myself in your presence is to imperil a strong weapon of Cormanthor; to endanger the Srinshee needlessly is to toy with a treasure of the realm."

"Enough flattery, Eltargrim," the sorceress said primly. "You'll have the lad thinking you a poet, and not the rough warrior you are."

El blinked at the old Coronal. "A warrior?"

The white-haired elf sighed. "I did in my time down some orcs—"

"And a hundred thousand men or so, and a dragon or two," the Srinshee put in. The Coronal waved a dismissive hand.

"Speak of such things when I am gone, for if we tarry overlong we'll have the court mages blasting apart half the palace seeking me."

The Srinshee winced. "Those young dolts?"

The Coronal sighed in exasperation. "Oluevaera, how can I pass judgment on this man if you shatter our every attempt at dignity?"

The ancient sorceress shrugged in her airy ease. "Even humans deserve the truth."

"Indeed." The Coronal's tone was dry as he turned to Elminster, assumed a stern face, and said, "Hear, then, the judgment of Cormanthor: that you remain in these vaults for a moon, and search and converse with their guardian as you will; she will feed you and see to your needs. Folk of the court, myself among them, will come for you at the end of that time, and bid you take but one thing out of these vaults to keep."

El inclined his head. "And the dangerous part?"

The Srinshee chuckled at the young human's tone.

"This is hardly the time for levity, young Prince," the Coronal said severely. "If you choose the wrong thing to bring forth—that is, something we judge to be wrong—the penalty will be your death."

In the silence that followed he added, "Think, young human, on what the most fitting thing you can acquire here might be. Think well."

Winking lights were suddenly occurring about the Coronal's body. He raised his hand to the Srinshee in salute, turned within the rising lights, and was gone. The radiances streamed toward the ceiling for a moment more, and then silently faded away.

"Before you ask, young sir, a moon is a human month," the Srinshee said in dry tones, "and no, I'm not his mother."

El chuckled. "Ye tell me what ye are not—tell me, I pray, what ye are."

She adjusted the air until she was sitting upright, facing him. "I am the councilor of Coronals, the secret wisdom at the heart of the realm."

El glanced at her, and decided to dare it. "And are you wise?"

The old sorceress chuckled. "Ah, a sharp-witted human at last!" She drew herself up grandly, eyes flashing, conjured a scepter out of nowhere into her hand, and snarled, "No."

She joined in El's startled shout of laughter, and let herself down to walk toward him, seeming so frail that El found himself reaching out to offer her a steadying arm.

She gave him a look. "I'm not so feeble as all that, lad. Don't overreach yourself, or you'll end up like yonder worm."

El looked about. "'Yonder worm'?" he asked hesitantly, seeing no beast or trophy of one, but only rooms of treasure.

"That passage," the Srinshee told him, "is vaulted with the bones of a deep-worm that rose up from gnawing in the deep places and came tunneling in here, hungry for treasure. They eat metal, you know."

El stared at the vaulting along the indicated passage. It *did* look like bone, come to think of it, but . . . He looked back at the sorceress with new respect. "So if I offer you violence, or try to leave this place, you can slay me by lifting one finger."

The old elf shrugged. "Probably. I don't see it happening, unless you're far more foolish—or brutish—than you look."

El nodded. "I don't think I am. My name is Elminster . . . Elminster Aumar, son of Elthryn. I am—or was—a prince of Athalantar, a small human kingdom that lies—"

The old sorceress nodded. "I know it. Uthgrael must be long dead by now."

El nodded. "He was my grandsire."

The Srinshee tilted her head consideringly. "Hmmm."

El stared at her. "You *knew* the Stag King?"

The Srinshee nodded. "A . . . man of vigor," she said, smiling.

Elminster raised an incredulous eyebrow.

The old sorceress burst out laughing. "No, no, nothing like that . . . though with some of the maids I danced with, such could have befallen. In those days, we amused ourselves by peering at the doings of humans. When we saw someone interesting—a bold warrior, say, or a grasping mageling—we'd show ourselves to him by moonlight, and then lead him on a merry chase through the woods. Some of those chases ended in broken necks; some of us let ourselves be caught. I led Uthgrael through half the southern High Forest until he fell exhausted, at dawn. I did show myself to him once later, when he was wed, just to see his jaw drop."

El shook his head. "I can see that it's going to be a long moon down here," he observed to the ceiling.

"Well!" The Srinshee affected outrage, and then chuckled. "Your turn; what pranks have you played, Elminster?"

"I don't know that we need to go into that, just now . . ." Elminster said in dignified tones.

She caught his eye.

"Well," he added, "I survived for some years by thieving in Hastarl, and there was this . . ."

Elminster was hoarse. They'd been talking for hours. After the second coughing fit took him, the Srinshee waved her hand and said, "Enough. You must be getting tired. Lift the lid of that platter over there." She indicated a silver-domed tray that rested atop a heap of armor, amid a spill of octagonal coins stamped from some bluish metal Elminster had never seen before.

El did so. Beneath the lid was steaming stag meat, in a nut-and-leek gravy. "How came this here?" he asked in astonishment.

"Magic," she replied impishly, plucking a half-buried gilded decanter from the heart of a heap of coins at her elbow. "Drink?" Shaking his head in wonder, El extended his hand for it. She tossed the decanter carelessly in his direction. It spun toward the floor, and then swooped smoothly up into his hand.

"My thanks," El said, taking firm hold of it with both hands. The Srinshee shrugged, and the young man suddenly felt something cold atop his head. Reaching up, he found a crystal glass there.

"Your hands were both full," the sorceress explained mildly.

As El snorted in amusement, a bowl of grapes appeared in his lap. He laughed helplessly, and found himself sliding down the coins he'd been leaning against, as they slumped onto the floor. One rolled away, and he smashed it to the floor with his boot heel, to stop it.

"You're going to get awfully sick of those," the elven sorceress told him.

"I don't want coins," El told her. "Where would I spend them, anyway?"

"Yes, but you'll have to shift them all to get at what's buried," the Srinshee said. "I keep the best stuff packed about with coins, you see."

El stared at her, and then shook his head, smiled wordlessly, and applied himself to eating.

"So what brings an elven sorceress who can advise Coronals and blow away deep-worms and lead crowned kings on wild wood chases to some vaults underground no one ever sees?" he asked, when he'd eaten all he could.

The old sorceress had eaten even more, gorging herself on platter after platter of fried mushrooms and lemon clams without seeming discomfort. She leaned back on empty air again, crossed her legs on some invisible floating footstool, and replied, "A sense of belonging, at last."

"Belonging? With cold coins and the jewels of the dead?"

She regarded him with some respect. "Shrewdly said, man." She set her glass on empty air at her elbow and leaned forward. "Yet you say that because you don't see what is here as I do."

She plucked up a tarnished silver bracelet, chased about with the body of a serpent. "Pay heed, Elminster. This is what you need me for: to make the choice the Coronal charged you to, and win your life. This arm ring is all Cormanthor has left of Princess Elvandaruil, lost in the waves of the Fallen Stars three thousand summers ago, when her flight spell failed. It washed up on Ambral Isle when Waterdeep was yet unborn."

Elminster fished a gleaming piece of shell out of the heap beside him. It was pierced at all four corners, and from there fine chains led to silver medallions set with sea-horses picked out in emeralds, with amethyst eyes. "And this?"

"The pectoral of Chathanglas Siltral, who styled himself Lord of the Rivers And Bays before the founding of your realm of Cormyr. He unwittingly took to wife a shapechanger, and the monstrous descendants of their offspring lurk yet, tentacled and deadly, in the waterways of Marsember and what humans call the Vast Swamp."

El leaned forward. "Ye know the provenance of every last bauble in these vaults?"

The Srinshee shrugged. "Of course. What good is a long life and an adequate memory if you don't *use* them?"

El shook his head in wonder. After a moment, he said, "Yet forgive me . . . the folk who wore or fashioned these can't all be kin to ye—if this Siltral fathered no elves, for instance. Yet you feel you belong . . . to what?"

"To the realm of my kin, and others of the People," the sorceress said calmly. "I am Oluevaera Estelda, the last of my line. Yet I rise above the family rivalries of House against House, and consider all Cormanthans my kin. It gives me a reason for having lived so long, and another to go on living, after those I first loved are gone."

"How lonely is it, at the worst?" El asked quietly, rolling forward to look deep into her eyes.

The withered old elf met his gaze. Her eyes were like blue flames against a storm sky. "You are far kinder, and see far clearer, than any human I've ever met before," she said quietly. "I begin to wish the Coronal's judgment did not hang over you."

El spread his hands. "I'd rather not be here, either," he said with a smile.

The Srinshee answered it with one of her own, and said briskly, "Well, we'd best be getting on with it. Dig out that sword by your knee, there, and I'll tell you of the line of elven lords who bore it . . ."

Some hours later, she said, "Would you like some nightglade tea?"

El looked up. "I've never had such a drink, but if it isn't all mushrooms, aye."

"No, there are other things in it, too," she replied smoothly, and they chuckled together.

"Yes, there are mushrooms in it, and no, it's not harmful, or that different from what haughty ladies drink in Cormyr and Chondath," she added.

"Oh, you mean it's like brandy?" El asked innocently, and she pursed her lips and chuckled again.

"I'll make some for us both," she said, rising. Then she looked back over her shoulder at Elminster, who was patiently digging a breastplate out from yet another pile of coins. It was fashioned of a single piece of copper as thick as his thumb, and sculpted into a pair of fine female breasts with a snarling lion's jaws below them. "Don't you ever sleep, man?" she asked curiously.

El looked up. "I get weary, aye, but I no longer need to sleep."

"Something your goddess did?"

El nodded, and frowned down at the breastplate. "This lion," he said. "It has eyes set into its tongue, here, and—"

The bust of the long-lost Queen Eldratha of the vanished elven realm of Larlotha was of solid marble, and as tall as the length of Elminster's arm. It came flying at him at just the right angle, and struck him almost gently behind his right ear. He never even knew it had hit him.

He awoke with a splitting headache. It felt as if someone were jabbing a dagger into his right ear, pulling it out, and then thrusting it home once more. In. Out. In. Out. Arrrgh.

He rolled around, groaning, hearing coins slither as his boots raked across them. *What* had happened?

His eyes settled on the soft, unchanging lights above him. Gems, set in a vaulted ceiling. Oh, aye—he was in the Vault of Ages. With the Srinshee, until the Coronal came to test him on his choice of what to take out of here.

"Lady? Lady—uh—Srinshee?" he asked, and followed his words with another groan. Speaking had awakened a fresh throbbing in his head. "Lady . . . ah, Oluevaera?"

"Over here," a weak, ragged whisper answered him, and he turned toward the sound.

The old sorceress was lying spreadeagled on a heap of treasure, her gown in tatters and smoke rising lazily from her body. A body, largely bared now, that featured many wrinkles and age-spots, but seemed unmarked by recent violence. El crawled toward her, holding his head.

"Lady?" he asked. "Are ye hurt? What befell?"

"I attacked you," she said ruefully, "and paid the price."

El stared at her, bewildered. "Ye—?"

"Man, I am ashamed," she said, lips quivering. "To find a friend, after so long, and throw friendship aside for loyalty to the realm . . . I did what I thought right—and find my choice was wrong."

El laid his pounding head on the coins beside the Srinshee so that he could look into her eyes. They were full of tears. "Lady," he said gently, stricken by the sadness in her voice, "for the love of thy gods and mine, tell me what happened."

She stared into his eyes, forlorn. "I have done the unforgiveable."

"And that was?" El almost pleaded, gesturing wearily at her to let words pour from her mouth.

She almost smiled at that as she replied sadly, "Eltargrim asked me to try where he failed; to learn all I could from your mind while you slept. But time passed, a day and a night, and still you were sorting through the treasures, with nary a sign of sliding into slumber. So I asked you, and you said you never slept."

El nodded, coins shifting under his cheek. "What did you hit me with?"

"A bust of Eldratha of Larlotha," she muttered. "Elminster, I'm so sorry."

"So am I," he told her feelingly. "Can elven magic banish headaches?"

"Oh," she gasped, putting a hand to her mouth in chagrin. "Here." she reached out with two fingertips, touched the side of his head, and murmured something.

And like cool water lapping down his neck, the pain washed away.

El gasped his thanks, and slid down the coins until he was sitting on the floor again. "So ye set to work on my mind once I was stunned, and—"

Remembering, he whirled and rose to bend anxiously over her. "Lady, there was smoke coming from ye! Were ye hurt?"

"Mystra was waiting for me, just as she waited for the Coronal," the Srinshee told him with the ghost of a smile on her lips. "She cares for you, young man. She thrust me right out of your mind, and told me she'd placed a spell in your mind that could blast me to dust."

El stared at her, and then let his mind sink down to where, for so long, no spells had lain ready. He was going to have to do something about that. Without even a single spell to hurl, and no gem to call on, he was defenseless in the midst of all these proud elves.

Aye, there it was. A deadly magic he'd never known before—so mighty, and so simple. One touch, and elven blood would boil in the body he'd chosen, melting it to dust in a few breaths regardless of armor and defensive magics, and . . .

He shivered. *That* was a slaying spell.

When his senses returned to the here and now, cool fingers as small as a child's were tugging at his wrist, towing his hand to rest on smooth, cool flesh. Flesh that felt like—

He stared down. The Srinshee had bared her breast and placed his hand firmly upon it.

"Lady," he asked, staring into the sad blue flames of her eyes, "what—?"

"Use the spell," she told him. "I deserve no less."

El gently shook his hand free, and lifted what was left of her gown back into place. "And what would the Coronal do to me *then?*" he asked her, in mock despair. "That's the trouble with ye tragic types—no thought for what happens next!"

He smiled, and saw her struggling to give him one in return. After a moment, he saw that she was crying, silent tears welling from her old eyes.

Impulsively he bent and kissed her cheek. "Ye did the unforgiveable, aye," he growled in her ear. "Ye promised me nightglade tea—and I'm *still* waiting!"

She tried to laugh, and burst into sobs. El dragged her up into his arms to comfort her, and found that it was like cradling a crying child. She weighed *nothing.*

She was still sobbing, arms around his neck, when two steaming cups of nightglade tea appeared in the air in front of his nose.

Elminster had long since lost count of the things that he thought most clever. There was a crown that let its wearers appear as they had done when younger, and a glove that could resculpt the skin of battered or marred faces with its fingertips. The Srinshee had set these, and other things he most fancied, aside in a chest in the domed central chamber, but he'd seen less than a twentieth of the treasures held here, and the Srinshee's eyes were growing sad again.

"El," she said, as he tossed aside a flute that had belonged to the elven hero Erglareo of the Long Arrow, "your time grows short."

"I know," he said shortly. "What is this?"

"A cloak that banishes blight from trees whose trunks it is wrapped around, or plants it is draped over, left to us by the elven mage Raeranthur of—"

He was already trudging away from her, toward the chest for things he fancied. The Lady Estelda fell silent and sadly watched him walk away from her. She dared not aid him even by shifting coins, for fear one of the court mages, eager for this human intruder's death, was scrying her from afar.

Elminster returned, looking weary about the eyes. "How much longer?" he asked.

"Perhaps ten breaths," she said softly, "perhaps twenty. It depends on how eager they are."

"For my death," El growled, leaning past her. Was it an accident that she'd rested her hand on this crystal sphere thrice in the last little while?

"What's this?" he asked, scooping it up.

"A crystal through which one can see the course of waterflows through the realm, on the surface or underground; every handspan of their travel, clearly lit for your eye to see beaver dams, snags, and sources of foulness," the Srinshee told him, quickly, almost breathlessly, "crafted for the House of Clatharla, now fallen, by the—"

"I'll take it," El growled, starting past her. He stopped in midstride and kicked at the hilt of a blade buried under the coins. "This?"

"A sword that cuts darkness, and the undead things called shadows—though I believe wraiths and ghosts

also—"

He waved a dismissive hand and set off back down the passage toward the chest. The Srinshee adjusted the jeweled gown he'd unearthed and insisted she put on—it persisted in sliding off one aged shoulder—and sighed. They'd be here at any moment, and they—

Were here now. There was a soundless flash of light in the domed central chamber, and El stiffened, finding himself suddenly ringed with unfriendly looking elven sorceresses. Six of them there were, all holding scepters trained at him. Tiny sparks winked and flowed along those deadly things. Along the passage El saw the Srinshee coming up behind him. She snapped her fingers as she came, and a seventh scepter was suddenly in that hand, leveled and ready.

He turned his back on her slowly, knowing who'd be awaiting him in the other direction. Rulers always liked to make entrances. Behind two of the sorceresses was an old elf in white robes, with eyes like two pools of stars. The women slid sideways smoothly to make a place for him in the ring of death. The Coronal.

"Well met, Revered Lord," Elminster said, and gently set the crystal sphere he held down into the open chest.

The elf looked down at the treasures it held, and raised an approving eyebrow. Things of nurturing, not things of battle. His voice when it rolled forth, however, was stern. "I bade you choose one thing only, to take forth from these vaults. Let us all now witness that choice."

Elminster bowed, and then walked to the Coronal, hands spread and empty.

"Well?" the elven ruler demanded.

"I have made my choice," El said quietly.

"You choose to take nothing?" the Coronal asked, frowning. "'Tis a coward's way of trying to evade death."

"Nay," Elminster replied, voice just as stern. "I've chosen the most precious thing in thy vaults."

Scepters hung quivering in midair all around him, abandoned by sorceresses who were now weaving magics for all they were worth. El turned slowly, one eyebrow raised, as they whispered incantations in a murmuring chorus. Only the Srinshee's hands were still. She held her scepter tipped back so that its point touched her own breast, and her eyes were anxious.

Spells fell upon Elminster Aumar then, spells that searched and proved and scryed, vainly seeking hidden items or disguising magics on the young man's body. One by one they looked to the Coronal and gave small shakes of their heads; they'd found nothing.

"And what is that most precious thing?" the Coronal asked finally, as two of the sorceresses slowly drew in front of him to form a shield, raised scepters in their hands once more.

"Friendship," Elminster replied. "Shared regard, and my fondness for a wise and gracious lady." He turned to face the Srinshee and made a deep bow, such as envoys did to kings they truly respected, in the kingdoms of men.

After a long moment, as the other elves stared at her, the old sorceress smiled and echoed his bow. Her eyes were very bright, with what might be tears.

The Coronal's eyebrows rose. "You've chosen more wisely even than I might have done," he said. More than one of the six court sorceresses looked stunned. There were open gasps of astonished horror around their circle when the ruler of all Cormanthor bowed deeply to Elminster. "I am honored by your presence in this fairest of realms; you are welcome here, as deserving of residence as any of the People. Be one with Cormanthor."

"And Cormanthor shall be one with thee," the sorceresses chanted in unison. There was dumbfounded awe in more than one of those voices. Elminster smiled at the Coronal, but turned to embrace the Srinshee. Tears were shining on her withered cheeks as she looked up at him, so he kissed them away.

As the velvet darkness came down again, and rolled away to reveal a huge and shining hall crowded with elves in their splendor, the Coronal's magic made the chant roll forth again.

Amid the astonished faces of the Court of Cormanthor, all heard it ring clear: "And Cormanthor shall be one with thee."

Part
II

ARMATHOR

SEVEN
EVERY POOL ITS PARTY

When Elminster first saw it, Cormanthor was a city of haughty pretence,
intrigue, strife, and decadence. A place, in fact, very like the proudest human
cities of today.

ANTARN THE SAGE
FROM *THE HIGH HISTORY OF FAERÛNIAN ARCHMAGES MIGHTY*
PUBLISHED CIRCA THE YEAR OF THE STAFF

By the time Ithrythra had clicked her way unsteadily up the wooded path to the pool in her new boots, the party was well under way.

"Frankly, gentlest," Duilya Evendusk confided to someone, loud enough to shake leaves off the moon-bark trees overhead, "I don't care *what* your elders say! The Coronal is mad! *Completely* mad!"

"You'd know madness better than the rest of us," Ithrythra muttered under her breath, setting her own glass on a float-platter to unlace her thigh-high silver boots. It was a relief to step out of them. The spiked heels made her tower over the servants, yes, but ohh, how they hurt. Human fashions were as crazed as they were brazen.

Ithrythra hung her lacy gown over a branch and shook out the ruffles of her undergown until they hung as they were supposed to. She checked her reflection in the hanging glass under the shadowtop tree, an oval mirror taller than she was.

As she stared into its depths and saw just a hint of swirling things there, she recalled that some Cormanth ladies whispered that this mirror sometimes served the Tornglaras as a portal into dark and dirty streets in the cities of men. The Tornglara lords went to do business that Cormanthor frowned upon, trading with humans. The Tornglara ladies, now . . .

She clucked her lips at those thoughts and set them firmly aside. Fashions were what Alaglossa Tornglara went seeking; fashions, and no more.

Ithrythra gave the legendary mirror a little smile. Her new hairdo had held its sideswirl, firmly woven about the hand lyre, sigil of her House. Her ears stood up proudly, their rouged tips unmarred by over-gaudy jewelry. She turned, so as to survey one side of her body, and then the other. The gems glued down her flanks were all in place. She struck a pose, and blew the mirror a pouting kiss. Not bad.

After the highsun meal of every fourth day, the ladies of five Houses gathered at Satyrdance Pool in the private gardens behind the many-towered mansion that was House Tornglara. There they bathed in the warmest of the pools, in which spiced rosewater had been poured for the occasion, and sipped summermint wine from tall, green fluted glasses. The platters of sugared confections and the justly famous Tornglara vintages flowed freely, and so did the real reason the ladies came back to the same place time and time again: the gossip.

Ithrythra Mornmist joined her chattering companions, making her greetings with her usual silent smiles. As she slipped her long legs into the pool, sighing with pleasure at the soothing warmth of the waters, she noted that her glass was the only one not yet empty. Where were the servants?

Her hostess noticed Ithrythra's glances, and halted in midchatter to lean forward conspiratorially and say, "Oh, I've sent them away, dear. We'll have to fill our own glasses this time—but then, 'tisn't every day one discusses *crown treason!*"

"Crown treason? What treachery can the Coronal have practiced? That elf's too old to have any wits left, or stamina either!" Ithrythra exclaimed, evoking shrieks of laughter from the ladies already in the pool.

"Oh, you're *out* of *touch*, dearest Ithrythra! It must be all that time you spend in your cellars grubbing up mushrooms to earn a living!" Duilya Evendusk said cuttingly; Alaglossa Tornglara had the grace to roll her eyes at this rudeness.

"Well, at least it proves to my elders that I *can* work if I have to," Ithrythra replied, "and so escape being a complete loss to my House—you should try it, dear . . . or, well, no, I suppose not . . ."

Cilivren Doedance, the quietest and most polite of them all, sputtered briefly over the glass she was filling, and decided the prudent thing to do was to put it down. Setting the glass back on its float-platter, she stoppered the decanter and slid it back into its usual recess in the little stream in the bushes beside her.

"The word's all over the city," she explained calmly. "The Coronal has named some *human* an armathor of the realm! And a *man* human at that! A thief who stole the kiira of a First House, and broke into their city residence to steal spells and despoil their ladies!"

"It wasn't House Starym, was it?" Ithrythra asked dryly. "There's never been much love lost between old Eltargrim and our haughtiest of Houses."

"House Starym has served Cormanthor a thousand summers longer than a certain House I could name," Phuingara Lhoril said stiffly. "Those Cormanthans of truly noble spirit do not find their pride excessive."

"Cormanthans of truly noble spirit do not indulge in prideful behavior at all," Ithrythra replied silkily.

"Oh, Ithrythra! Always *cutting* at us, as if that tongue of yours was a sword! I don't know why your lord puts up with you!" Duilya Evendusk said pettishly, annoyed at having the center of attention wrenched from her grasp.

"I've heard why," Alaglossa Tornglara observed quietly to the leaves overhead. Ithrythra blushed as the other ladies in the pool tittered. Duilya added her own grating guffaw and then hastened to seize center stage once more. The tips of her ears were almost drooping today under the weight of all the gems dangling from their rows of studs.

"Pride or no pride, 'twasn't the Starym," she said excitedly, "but House Alastrarra. They're saying at court that both the court mages would like to challenge the Eltargrim with blades before the altar of Corellon, rather than let a human walk among us and live—let alone be named armathor! Some of the younger armathors, those not lords of Houses, mind, and with little to lose, have been to the palace already to break their blades and hurl the pieces at the Coronal's feet! One even threw his blade right *at* Eltargrim!"

"So how long will it be, I wonder," Ithrythra pondered aloud, "before this human meets with an . . . accident."

"Not long at all, if the looks of the court elders are anything to go by," Duilya gushed on, eyes bright. "If we're very lucky, they'll challenge him at court—or have seeing-spells cast beforehand, so we can all see him torn apart!"

"How very civilized," Cilivren murmured, her voice just audible to Alaglossa and Ithrythra. Duilya, deafened by her own gleeful words, didn't hear.

"And then," she continued, still in full flood, "the First Houses might call a Hunt, for the first time in centuries, and they'll force old Eltargrim into stag shape and hunt him down! Then we'll have a new Coronal! Oh, what excitement!" In her exuberance, she snatched up a decanter and drained it without benefit of a glass.

Reeling, she promptly slumped back in the pool, shuddering and gagging. "Gods above, dear, don't drown *here*," Phuingara growled, holding her above the waters, "or all our lords'll be at us about talking to those of rival Houses without their leave!"

Ithrythra took great delight in thumping the coughing Duilya solidly in the back. Gems flew across the pool and tinkled against a float-platter.

Alaglossa gave the reigning lady of House Mornmist a tight smile that told Ithrythra her hostess knew quite well that the force of her helpful blow had been quite deliberate—and that silence on that matter might carry a price, later.

"There, there, gentle doe," Alaglossa said solicitously, putting an arm around the shuddering Lady Evendusk. "Better now? The sweetness of our wine often misleads folk into thinking it has no fire—but it's stronger even than that, ah, 'tripleshroom sherry' our lords're always roaring at each other about!"

"Oh," Phuingara purred, "So you've had some of that, have you?"

Alaglossa turned her head and favoured the lady of House Lhoril with a look that had silent daggers in it; Phuingara merely smiled and asked, "Well? How was it?"

"You mean, you want to know what leaves our lords falling into pillars, giggling like younglings and hooting as they lie on the floor and try to shake hands with themselves?" Cilivren said suddenly, laughter in her voice. "Well, it tastes terrible!"

"*You've* drunk tripleshroom?" Phuingara asked, her voice incredulous.

Cilivren gave the Lady Lhoril a catlike smile and said, "Some lords don't leave their ladies out of all the fun."

All of the others, even the still-coughing Duilya, looked at the Lady Doedance as if she'd suddenly grown several extra heads.

"Cilivren," Duilya said in shocked tones, when she could speak again. "I would never have thought . . ."

"That's just the problem," snarled Ithrythra, "you never think!"

Mouths opened in shock all around the pool, but before Duilya could erupt in rage at this insult, the Lady Mornmist leaned forward, her eyes serious, and said into Duilya's face, "*Listen*, Lady Evendusk. How do you think Cormanthor chooses a Coronal? You can't wait for the excitement, you say? Would you feel that way if I told you that naming a new Coronal is likely to mean poisonings, duels in the streets, and mages working nights in their towers to send slaying spells at their rivals all over the city? Human or no human, Eltargrim an addle-brained idiot or not, do you want to die—or see your children slain, and feuds begun that will rend Cormanthor forever, and let *all* the humans into our city over our warring *bones?*"

She gasped for breath, fists clenched in aroused fear and rage, glaring at the four faces that were staring back at her. Couldn't they *see?*

"Gods watch over us all," the Lady Mornmist went on, in a voice that trembled, "I find the idea of a human walking our fair realm revolting. But I'd take that human for a mate if need be, and kiss and serve him day and night, to keep our realm from tearing itself apart!"

She clenched her fists, breast heaving, and almost shouted, "You think Cormanthor stands so splendid and mighty that none can touch us? How so? Our lords strut and sneer and tell tales of what heroics their fathers' fathers did, when the world was young and we fought dragons barehanded moon in and moon out. And our sons boast of how much bolder they'll be, and can't even down a flagon of tripleshroom without falling over! Every year the axes of the humans nibble at the edges of our fair forests, and their mages grow stronger. Every year their adventurers grow bolder, and fewer of our patrols pass through a season without losing blood!"

Alaglossa Tornglara nodded slowly, face white, as Ithrythra caught her breath, swallowed, and added in a whisper, "I don't expect to see the fair towers of our city still standing when I die. Don't any of you ever worry about that?"

In the silence that followed, she defiantly snatched up a full decanter of summermint and drained it, slowly and deliberately, while they all stared at her.

"Really," Duilya said, laughing uneasily, as they watched Ithrythra Mornmist, apparently unaffected by the wine, set aside the empty decanter and pick up another one to delicately refill her glass, "I think you indulge in wild fancies overmuch, Ithrythra—as usual. Cormanthor endangered? Come, now. Who can threaten us? We have the spells to turn any number of barbarians into—into more mushrooms for the making of sherry!"

She laughed merrily at her own jest, but her mirth fell away into thoughtful silence. She whirled around to confront Phuingara for support. "Don't you think so?"

"I think," Phuingara said slowly, "that we gossip and prattle the days away because we don't like to talk of such things. Duilya, listen to me now: I don't agree with everything Ithrythra fears, but just because no one speaks so openly, or we don't like to hear it, doesn't make her *wrong*. If you didn't hear truth in her words, I suggest you kiss her and ask her very nicely to repeat them again . . . and listen harder this time."

And with those words, the Lady Lhoril turned and began to climb out of the pool, leaving a sombre silence in her wake.

"Wait!" Alaglossa said, catching at one of Phuingara's wet wrists. "Stay!"

The Lady Lhoril turned blazing eyes upon her hostess, and said softly, "Lady, by all you hold dear, pray make your case for *handling* me good."

The Lady Tornglara nodded curtly. "Ithrythra's right," she said earnestly, leaning forward. "This is too important to just pass off as an awkward moment, and go on joking and sparring and watching as the city comes to blows over this human. We must work on our lords to keep the peace, telling them over and over again that a mere human isn't worth unseating the Coronal, and drawing blades, and starting feuds."

"My lord never listens to me," Duilya Evendusk said in a tragic whisper. "What can I do?"

"*Make* him listen," Cilivren told her. "Make him notice you, and pay heed."

"He only does that when we're . . ."

"Then, dearest," Phuingara told her in a voice that cut like a whip, "it's time you got a little better at turning your lord to your will. Alaglossa, you were right to keep me from storming off; we've work to do right here. Do you have any tripleshroom sherry?"

The Lady Tornglara stared at her in surprise. "Why, yes," she said, "but why?"

"One of the few ways I can think of that would win the respect of Lord Evendusk," the Lady Lhoril said crisply, "when he's groaning of a forenoon because of what he's drunk the night before—and cursing at his sons because of what they broke the night before, raging and giggling; you did have to choose a prize oaf, didn't you, Duilya?—is to snatch up a full bottle of that sherry, drink it down in front of him, and then sit there *not* roaring or staggering about. While he's gaping at his gentle lady tuned lion, you can tell him off good and proper, and announce that you see no need for all the roistering."

"And then what?" Duilya said, face white at the very thought of facing down her lord.

"And then you could drag him off to bed in front of the whole household," Phuingara said firmly, "and tell him that drinking every night's no excuse for stumbling about like an idiot, making a mockery of the honor of the House, while you're neglected."

There was a moment of silence, and then laughter began around the pool—low at first, but then rising swiftly as the full import of Phuingara's words hit home.

It was Cilivren who stopped first. "You want us to practice drinking tripleshroom sherry until we can drain a bottle without showing it? Phuingara, we'll *die*." She winced. "I mean it; that stuff burns the insides like fire!"

The Lady Lhoril shrugged. "So we'll master it enough to down a few glasses without tears or trembling, and work up a spell, just for ourselves, that'll turn what passes our lips to water as we down it. It's the respect we're after, not to drown our worries about the realm the way our lords do. Why d'you think they drink the way they do? They've seen what Ithrythra has, and just don't want to face it."

"So I get my Ihimbraskar up to the bedchamber, after humiliating him in front of the entire household," Duilya said in a small voice, "and what then? He'll strike me silly, toss my bones out the window, and go seeking a new and younger lady in the morn!"

"Not if you sit him down and give him the same blazing words Ithrythra gave us," Alaglossa told her. "Even if he doesn't agree, he'll be so astonished at your thinking about such things, that he'll probably argue with you like an equal—whereupon you tell him that such disputes are precisely what you're *for*, and then take him to bed."

Duilya stared at her for a moment, and then started to laugh wildly. "Oh, Haṇali bless us all! If I thought I had the strength to carry it through . . ."

"Lady Evendusk," Ithrythra said formally, "would you mind terribly if the four of us were linked to you with a spell or two, to—ah, assist with the words you need, at the awkward moments?"

Duilya gaped at her, and then looked slowly around the pool. "You'd do that?"

"We all might benefit from such a spell," Phuingara said slowly. "Clever, Ithrythra." She turned to Alaglossa. "Get that sherry, Lady Tornglara; I can feel a toast coming on."

"Though in time to come I and others shall teach you some of the spells of our People," the Srinshee said, "a time of great danger awaits you now, Elminster." She smiled. "You didn't need me to tell you that."

El nodded. "That's why ye brought me here." He looked around at the dark and dusty walls and asked, "But what is this place?"

"A sacred tomb of our people—a haunted tower, once the home of the first proud and noble House to try to make themselves greater than the rest of us. The Dlardrageth."

"What happened to them?"

"They courted incubi and succubi, seeking to breed a stronger race. Few survived such dealings, fewer still the birthings that followed, and all elven peoples turned against them. The few survivors were walled in here by our strongest spells, until the end of their days." The Srinshee dusted her hand across a pillar thoughtfully, uncovering a relief carving of a leering face. "Some of those spells still linger, though daring young Cormanthan lords broke in more than a thousand years ago to despoil this castle of the riches of House Dlardrageth. They found little of value, and took away what they did find. They also took back word of the ghosts that linger here."

"Ghosts?" Elminster asked calmly. The Srinshee nodded.

"Oh, there are a few, but nothing that need be feared. What matters most is that we won't be disturbed."

"Ye're going to teach me magic?"

"No," the Srinshee said, drawing close so that she stood looking up at him. "You're going to teach *me* magic."

El raised both brows. "I—?"

"With this," she said calmly, as she spread her empty hands and they suddenly filled with—his spellbook.

She staggered a trifle, under its weight, and he automatically took it from her, peering at it. Aye, it was his. Left in a saddlebag, back in a fern-filled dell in the trackless forest where the White Raven Patrol had met with far too many ruukha.

"My deepest thanks, Lady," Elminster said to her, going to one knee so that he was below her and not towering over her. "Yet at the risk of sounding ungrateful, won't those of the People who are upset by one of my race being named armathor be turning Cormanthor over stone by tree, looking for me? And won't the other elves of thy realm expect me to take up some duties to go with my rank . . . in other words, to be seen?"

"Seen you will be, soon enough," the Srinshee said grimly. "The center of plots and schemes aplenty, even by those who do not wish you ill. We are jaded, in the fair city of Cormanthor, and each new interest becomes something to be sported over by the great Houses. All too often, their sport mars or destroys that which they toy with."

"Elves begin to seem more and more like men," El told her, sitting down on the broken stump of a pillar.

"How dare you!" the old sorceress snarled. He looked up in time to see her smile and reach out to tousle his hair. "How dare you speak truth to me," she murmured. "So few of my race ever do . . . or have done. 'Tis a rare pleasure, to deal in honesty for a change."

"How, now? Are not elves honest?" El asked teasingly, for there was a brightness that might have been rising tears in her old eyes again.

"Let us say that some of us are too worldly for our own good," she said with a smile, strolling away from him on air. She whirled about and added, "And the others are too world-weary."

At her words, a darkness rose behind her, and sudden claws flashed down. El started up with a cry but the claws flashed through her and raced on through the gloom between them, trailing a thin, high wailing that faded away as if into vast distances.

El watched where it had gone, and then turned back to the small sorceress. "One of the ghosts?" he asked, brow raised.

She nodded. "They want to learn your magic too."

He smiled, and then, seeing her expression, let the grin slowly fade from his lips. "Ye're not jesting," he said roughly.

She shook her head. The sadness was back in her eyes. "You begin to see, I hope, just how much my People need you, and others like you, to breathe new ideas into us and awaken the flame of spirit that once made us soar above all others in Faerûn. Consorting with humans, with our half-kin and the little folk, and even with dwarves is the Coronal's dream. He can see so clearly what we must do—and the great Houses refuse so adamantly to see anything except the dreaming days stretching on forever, with themselves at the pinnacle of all."

El shook his head, acquiring a very thin smile. "I seem to bear a heavy burden," he said.

"You can carry it," the Srinshee told him, and winked at him impishly. "'Tis why Mystra chose you."

"Are we not met to decide what best to do?" Sylmae asked coldly. She looked around the circle of solemn faces that hovered above the balefire; her own and the other five sorceresses who'd accompanied the Coronal to the Vault of Ages after the High Court Mages, Earynspieir and Ilimitar, had refused to do so.

Holone shook her head. "No sister; that is the mistake we must leave to the Houses and the other folk of the court. We must wait, and watch, and act for the good of the realm when the rash acts of others make it needful to do so."

"So which rash act requires that we take action in our turn?" Sylmae asked. "The appointment of a human to standing in the realm as an armathor—or the responses that will inevitably follow?"

"Those responses will tell us who stands where," the sorceress Ajhalanda put in. "The next set of actions on the part of those players, as this unfolds, may well require that we act."

"Strike out, you mean," Sylmae said, her voice rising. "Against the Coronal, or one of the great Houses of the realm, or—"

"Or against all of the Houses, or the High Court Mages, or even such as the Srinshee," Holone said calmly. "We know not what, yet—only that it is our duty and desire to meet, and confer, and act as one."

"It is our hope, you mean," the sorceress Yathlanae said, speaking for the first time that night, "that we work together, and not be split asunder, hand against hand and will against will, as we all fear the realm will be."

Holone nodded grimly. "And so we must choose carefully, sisters, very carefully, not to fall into dispute among ourselves."

More than one face above the flames sighed, knowing how difficult that alone was going to be.

Ajhalanda broke the lengthening silence. "Sylmae, you walk among all folk, high and low, more than the rest of us. Which Houses must we watch—who will lead where others follow?"

Sylmae sighed gustily, so that the balefire quivered beneath their chins, and said, "The spine of the old Houses—those who despise and stand against the Coronal, and lady sorceresses, and anything that is new these past three thousand years—are the Starym, of course, and Houses Echorn and Waelvor. The path they cleave, the old Houses and all of the timid new ones will follow. They are the tide: slow, mighty, and predictable."

"Why watch the tide?" Yathlanae asked. "However hard you scrutinize it, it changes not—you only invent new motives and meanings for it, as your watching grows longer."

"Well said," Sylmae replied, "and yet the tide aren't those we must watch. They are the powerful newer proud ones, the rich Houses, led by Maendellyn and Nlossae."

"Are not they just as predictable, in their way?" Holone put in. "They stand for anything new that might break the power of the old Houses, to let them supplant or at least stand as equals. As all elves do, they grow tired of being sneered at."

"There is a third group," Sylmae said, "who bear the closest watching of all. They are a group only in my speaking of them; in Cormanthor they hew their own roads, and walk to differing stars. The reckless upstarts, some term them; they are the Houses who will try anything, merely for the joy of being part of something new. They are Auglamyr and Ealoeth, and lesser families such as the Falanae and Uirthur."

"You and I are Auglamyr, sister," Holone stated calmly. "Are you then telling us we six should or will try anything new?"

"We are already doing so," Sylmae replied, "by meeting thus, and striving to act in concert. It is not something the proud lords of any House but those I've named last would tolerate, if they knew about it. She-elves are only for dancing, bedecking with gems, and begetting young on, know you not?"

"Cooking," Ajhalanda said. "You forgot cooking."

Sylmae shrugged and smiled. "I was ever a poor dutiful she-elf."

Yathlanae shrugged. "There are males in this land who are poor dutiful lords, if it comes to that."

"Aye, too many of them," Holone said, "or making one human an armathor would be no more than idle news."

"I see Cormanthor in peril of destruction, if we act not wisely and swiftly, when the time comes," Sylmae told them.

"Then let us do so," Holone replied, and the others all echoed, "Aye, let us do so."

As if that had been a cue, the balefire went out; someone had sent scrying magic their way. Without another word or light, they parted and slipped away, leaving the air high above the palace to the bats and the glittering stars . . . who seemed quite comfortable there until morning.

Eight
The Uses of a Human

The elves of Cormanthor have always been known for their calm, measured responses to perceived threats. They often consider for half a day or more before going out and killing them.

Shalheira Talandren, High Elven Bard of Summerstar
from *Silver Blades And Summer Nights:*
An Informal But True History of Cormanthor
published in The Year of the Harp

"They're so beautiful," Symrustar murmured. "See, coz?"

Amaranthae bent to look at the silktails, circling and wriggling in the glass cylinder as they danced for the best position below Symrustar's fingers, from which they knew food would soon fall. "I love the way the sun turns their scales into tiny rainbows," she replied diplomatically, having resolved long since that whatever it took, her cousin would never learn just how much Amaranthae hated fish.

Symrustar had over a thousand finned and scaled pets here. From the crowning bowl where she now scattered morsels of the secret food she mixed herself (Amaranthae had heard it said that its chief ingredients were the ground flesh, blood, and bones of unsuccessful suitors), Symrustar's glass fish tank descended more than a hundred feet to the ground, in a fantastic sculpture of pipes, spheres, and larger chambers of hollow glass shaped like dragons and other beasts. Amaranthae wanted to be around—but not too close—on the day Symrustar's father discovered that a certain large tank, out near the end of the branch, resembled him in all-too-unflattering detail.

Lord Auglamyr was not known for his gentle temper. "A thundercloud of towering pride, sweeping all before it" was the way one senior lady of the court had once described him, and her words had been overgentle.

Perhaps that was where Symrustar had acquired her utterly amoral ruthlessness. Amaranthae was very careful to remain supportive and helpful to her ambitious cousin at all times, for she had no doubt that Symrustar Auglamyr would betray her in a twinkling instant, best friends notwithstanding, if Amaranthae ever got in her way in even the smallest degree.

I'm no more free than all these fish, Amaranthae thought, leaning out from the bowl-shaped bower where they sat, at the base of the longest branch left in this westernmost shadowtop of House Auglamyr. Pipe after column after sphere of glass gleamed back the morning light, in the fantastic assemblage that housed

Symrustar's finned pets. The servants knew better than to disturb them—or rather, Symrustar—here, and used the speaking chimes instead.

Morning after morning they spent here, reclining on cushions and sipping cool fermented forest fruit juices, while the Auglamyr heiress schemed and plotted aloud how to further her every ambition—and some of them seemed to heart-weary Amaranthae to be no more than manipulating acquaintances for the sake of deft manipulation—and her cousin listened and said supportive things at the right moments.

This morning Symrustar was truly excited, her eyes flashing as she set aside the food, waving a dismissive hand at the tiny gasping mouths in the bowl as she turned away. *By all the gods, but she's beautiful*, Amaranthae thought, staring at her cousin's fine shoulders and the long, smoothly curving lines of her body in its silk robe. A striking eyes and face, even among the beauties of the court. No wonder so many elven lords straightened their ears at the sight of her.

Symrustar lifted one perfect eyebrow and asked, "Are you thinking along the same lines as I am, coz?"

Amaranthae shrugged, smiled, and said the safe thing. "I was thinking about this human male our Coronal has named armathor . . . and wondering what you'd do with this most unlikely of surprises, most sprightly of ladies!"

Symrustar winked. "You know me well, 'Ranthae. What do you think a human would be like to dally with? Hmmm?"

Amaranthae shuddered. "A man? Ughhh. As heavy and lumbering as a stag, with the stink to match . . . and all that *hair!*"

Her cousin nodded, eyes far away. "True. Yet I hear this unwashed brute has magic—human magic, far inferior to our own, of course, but different. With a little of that in my hands, I could surprise a few of our over-proud young mages. Even if the human's spells are but little wisps of things suitable for impressing gullible younglings, I've one such who could use a little impressing: Lord Heir Most High Elandorr Waelvor."

Amaranthae shook her head in rueful amusement. "Haven't you tormented him enough?"

Symrustar raised one shapely brow again, and her eyes flashed. "Enough? There *is* no enough for Elandorr the Buffoon! When he's not grandly proclaiming to all the city that this or that spell he's created is greater than anything that bad-tempered maid Symrustar Auglamyr can craft, he's crawling in my bedchamber window with fresh blandishments! No matter how firmly—"

"Rudely," Amaranthae corrected with a smile.

"—I refuse him," her cousin continued, "he's back a few nights later trying again! In between, he hints to his drinking companions about the unmatched sweetness of my charms, remarks to ladies in passing that I worship him in secret, and flits about the libraries of men—*men*—stealing bad love poetry to pass off as his own, wooing me with all the style and grace of a laugh-chasing gnome clown!"

"He came last night?"

"As usual! I had three of the guards throw him from my balcony. He had the brazen gall to try transforming spells on them!"

"You countered them, of course," Amaranthae murmured.

"No," Symrustar said scornfully, "I left them as frogs until morning. No guard worthy of my bedchamber balcony should be unprepared for a simple twice-trying transformation!"

"Oh, Symma!" Amaranthae said reproachfully.

Her cousin's eyes flashed again. "You think me harsh? Coz, you spend a night in my bed, and be pestered by the Love Lord of the Waelvors come calling, and we'll see how charitable you feel to the guards who should have kept him out!"

"Symma, he's a master mage!"

"Then let them be master guards, and *wear* the turnback amulets I gave them. What matter if they must draw blood to work? They'll turn back Elandorr's oh-so-masterful spells on himself! A few scars should be worth that—to say nothing of their professed loyalty to House Auglamyr!"

Symrustar rose and paced restlessly across the little bowl-shaped hollow, the morning sun glinting on the gem-adorned chain that spiraled up her left leg from anklet to garter. "Why, three moons ago," she burst out, waving her arms, "when he got as far as the very curtains of my bed, I found a guard hiding and *watching*, by the Hunt! Watching, to see me swoon in the arms of Elandorr! Oh, he claimed he was there to protect me against the 'last humiliation,' but he was lying atop the very canopy of my bed, clad in black velvet so as not to be seen, and wrapped about with so many amulets that he practically staggered! He got them from my father, he said, but I'd not be surprised to find that some of them came from House Waelvor!"

"What did you do to *him?*" Amaranthae asked, turning her head away to hide a yawn.

Symrustar smiled chillingly. "Showed him what he'd been trying to see, took off every last thing he was wearing, too, and—the fish."

Amaranthae shuddered. "You fed him to—?"

Symrustar nodded. "Umm-hmmm, and sent off all his gear in a bundle to Elandorr the next day, with a love note telling him that such trappings were all that was left from the last dozen lords who thought themselves worthy of wooing Symrustar Auglamyr." She sighed theatrically. "He was back trying the next night, of course."

Amaranthae shook her head. "Why don't you just tell your father, and let him go roaring to Lord Waelvor? You know how the old Houses are; Kuskyn Waelvor would be so mortified that a son of his was wooing a lady of such an 'unknown' House as ours—or wooing any high-house lady, without his permission—that Elandorr would find himself in a spell cage for the next decade, before you could draw another breath!"

Symrustar stared at her cousin. "And where, 'Ranthae, would the fun be in that?"

Amaranthae shook her head, smiling. "Of course. Let prudence never get in the way of fun!"

Symrustar smiled. "Of course." She reached for the speaking-chimes. "More dawnberry cordial, coz?"

Amaranthae gave her an answering smile and reclined against the leafy boughs that ringed their bower. "And why not? Hurl all spells behind us, and soar howling into the moon!"

"A fitting sentiment," Symrustar agreed, stretching her magnificent body, "considering my plans for this human, 'Elminster.' Yes, I'll see to it that humans have their uses." Extending her empty cordial glass in her toes, she struck the speaking chimes with it.

As their gentle chord resounded, Amaranthae Auglamyr shuddered at the cold, careless pleasure in her cousin's voice. It sounded somehow *hungry*.

"I'd not be in the boots of this human, no matter how mighty a sorcerer he may be," Taeglyn murmured from below, where he was sorting the gems carefully on velvet with the aid of a magnification spell.

"I care not a whit for this human—a beast of the fields, after all," Delmuth growled, "but it's the boots of the Coronal I'll want to see filled by a new owner, after I do what I must."

" 'Do what you must'? But, Lord, the Lesser Flith is almost complete! It lacks but a ruby for the star Esmel, and two diamonds for the Vraelen!" The servant gestured at the glittering star map filling the domed upper half of the chamber. In response to the star names he uttered, the spell Delmuth had cast earlier awakened two precise points in the empty air into winking life.

They flashed silently, awaiting their gems, but Delmuth Echorn was descending smoothly out of the midst of his life work, the constellations he'd modeled in gems glittering around him. "Yes, do what I must—destroy this human. If we let this go unchallenged, we'll have them in here by the thousands, a sea of rabble around our ankles, begging or threatening us whenever we go out, and despoiling the forest as fast as they so ably know how!" His boots touched the glossy black marble floor. "Why, if they could touch the stars," he snarled, pointing up at his miniature heavens, "we'd have found one or two missing by now!"

Delmuth glared up at the winking points of light, which obediently went out. He handed Taeglyn his gloves, with their long, talonlike metal points, stretched like a great and supple cat of the jungles, and added, still angry, "Yes, our fair and mighty Coronal has gone mad, and none of us seem ready enough to raise our hands and voices against him. Well, I'll take the first step, if no other Cormanthan has the stomach to. The pollution he has allowed to walk right into the very bosom of our fair Cormanthor must be eradicated."

Face set, he strode out of the room, smashing its double doors aside with his enchanted bracers. They boomed, splintered, and shuddered back from where they'd struck the wall, but Delmuth Echorn, striding hard, didn't even hear them.

A few breaths later, he was passing through the high, many-balconied front hall, his best boar sword glowing green in his hands from its many enchantments, when his uncle Neldor leaned down over a stair rail and exclaimed, "By the unseen beard of Corellon, *what* are you about? There's no Hunt called for this even, and it's still morn yet!"

"I'm not going on a Hunt, Uncle," Delmuth replied, without slowing or looking up. "I'm out to cleanse the realm of a human."

"The one named armathor by our Coronal? Lad, where are thy senses? No trumpet has cried your challenge! No charge has been delivered before the court, or to this man! Duels must be formally declared. 'Tis the law!"

Delmuth stopped at the tall front doors to give a scrambling servant time to swing them open, and looked up and back. "I go to slay one who is vermin, not a person with any right to be treated as one of us, whatever the Coronal may say."

He cast the sword spinning up into the air and followed it outside; just before the doors boomed shut behind him, Neldor saw him catch the blade and set off through the mushroom garden, taking the shortest route to the hawthorn gate.

"You're making a mistake, lad," he said sadly, "and taking our House with you." But there was no one left in the forehall of Castle Echorn to hear him except the frightened servant, whose white face was raised to heed Neldor.

Instead of ignoring him or snapping out a curt order, the eldest living elf of the blood of Echorn sadly spread his empty hands in a gesture of helplessness.

By the doors, the servant began to cry.

The elf in black leathers turned an exultant somersault in the air, crashed through the curtain of evercreeper leaves, and flung the sword in his hand exuberantly into the trunk of a blueleaf tree as he fell past. It struck deep and thrummed, neatly cutting an errant leaf in two on its brief journey.

The pieces were still fluttering down when the elf sprang up through them and snatched his sword back, crying joyously, "Ho ho, a cat has certainly been set loose among all the sleepy doves at court *this* time!"

"Easy, Athtar; they can probably hear you right down south by the sea." Galan Goadulphyn was carefully arranging small heaps of glass beads on his cloak, spread out atop the stump of a shadowtop that had fallen when Cormanthor was young. Only he knew that they represented the loans paid out to a certain phantom mushroom-growing concern by several too many proud Houses of the realm. Galan was trying to work out how to pay off some of the stiffer-lipped House keymasters by borrowing more from others.

If he couldn't come up with a deft pattern by nightfall, it might be necessary to leave Toril for a lifetime or two. Or however long it took for elves to find spells enough to build completely different, mind- and spell-fooling identities for themselves. A gloomhunter spider wandered onto the cloak, and Galan scowled at it.

"So? Everyone in the realm knows as much!"

"*I don't*," Galan said, staring intently into the eyes of the spider. They looked at each other for a moment, one eye to a thousand. Then the spider decided that prudence wasn't always only for others, and scrambled off the cloak as fast as its spindly legs could carry it. "Enlighten me."

Athtar drew in a deep and delighted breath. "Well, the Coronal has found a human somewhere, and brought him to court, and named him his heir and an armathor of the realm! Our next Coronal's going to be a *man!*"

"What?" Galan shook his head as if to clear it, spun away from his cloak, and snatched at his friend's throat lacings. "Athtar Nlossae," he snarled, shaking the leather-clad elf as if Athtar was a large and floppy doll, "kindly speak sense! Where in the name of all the bastard gods of the dwarves would the Coronal *find* a human? Under a rock? In his vaults? In a discarded slipper?" He let go of Athtar, who staggered back until he found a tree trunk to lean against, and took refuge there.

Galan advanced on him, growling, "I'm engaged in something very *important*, Athtar, and you come to me with wild tales! The Coronal'd never dare name a human armathor even if someone brought him a hundred humans! Why, he'd have all the stiff-necked young lads and old warriors in the realm lining up to spit on their swords and throw them back at him!"

"That's *just* what they're doing," Athtar replied delightedly, "right now! If you stand up on yon stump and listen, Gal—like this!—you'll—"

"Athtar—*nooo!*"

Galan's clutching hands came down just an instant too late. Beads bounced, rolled, and flew. Breathing heavily, the tall, one-eyed elf found his hands locked around Athtar's throat, and the leather-clad elf looking at him rather reproachfully.

"You're very *intense* these days, Gal," Athtar said in hurt tones. "A simple 'I find I feel deeply for you' would've sufficed."

Galan let his hands fall. What was the use? The beads were scattered, now, save for the few that—

There was a crunching sound under Athtar's right boot.

—remained on the cloak, under their feet. Galan sighed, took a deep breath, and then sighed again. When he spoke again, his tone was wearily pleasant. "You came here to tell me that our next Coronal, a thousand years after they kill the both of us for our deeds and forget where our graves lie, will be a human—is that it? I'm supposed to 'feel deeply' about that?"

"No, dolt! They'll never let a human be Coronal! The realm'll be torn apart first," Athtar said, shaking him by one shoulder. "And with the laws swept away and every House floundering, lowskins like you and me will hold the ready blades at last!" He thrust up his sword in celebration, and laughed again.

Galan shook his head sourly. "It'll never get that far. It never does. Too many mages lurking about to control minds and threaten the high and mighty into obeying whatever they can't force them into supporting. Oh, there'll be an uproar, sure. But the realm torn apart? Over one human? Hah!" He turned away to step down off the stump, trying to shake off Athtar's grip.

Athtar didn't let go. "Even so, Gal," he said urgently, lowering his voice to underscore his excitement. "Even so! This human knows magic, they say, and the folk at court are wild with tales of how he'll shake things up. Whatever happens to him in the end—and it'll happen, never fear; the young blades'll see to that—this is the best chance we'll ever see to break the old guard's strangehold on what's done and not done in Cormanthor! Settle some old scores with the Starym and Echorns, if we don't get trampled in the rush of other Houses trying to do the same thing! Who do you owe the most money to? Who are giving you the hardest time over it? Who can be put down in the forest mud where they belong, forever?"

As the elf in leathers ran out of breath with his last query echoing back from the trees around them, Galan looked at his friend with true enthusiasm for the first time.

"*Now* you're interesting me," he breathed, embracing Athtar. "So settle down, and get yourself some bitterroot ale; it's over by the duskwood that's losing its bark—there. We have to talk."

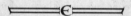

Elminster, aid me. The mind-cry was faint, but somehow familiar. Could it be, after all this time? It sounded like Shandathe of Hastarl, whom El had carried into the bedroom of a certain baker, to find unintended bliss, and later tested the mind powers Mystra had honed in him by eavesdropping on . . .

Elminster sat up, frowning. Though it was highsun, their work together had been exhausting, and the Srinshee was asleep, floating on air across the chamber, the faint glow of her keep-warm spell eddying around her. Were the Dlardrageth ghosts playing tricks on him?

He closed his eyes and shut out the dark chamber and the weight of his full roster of freshly memorized spells, letting all stray thought and distraction drain away, drifting down into the dark place where mind voices were wont to echo.

Elminster? Elminster, can you hear me?

The voice was faint and distant, yet oddly flat. Strange. He sent a single thought toward it: *Where?*

After a time of echoing emptiness an image came swimming up to him, spinning slowly like a bright coin on edge. He plunged into it, and was suddenly at its glowing heart, staring into a dark, stormy scene: somewhere in Faerûn, with wind trailing across a rocky height, and treetops below. A woman was spread-eagled face down on that rock, wrists and ankles bound apart on saplings, her features hidden by the swirl of her unbound hair. It was a place he'd not seen before. The woman could be Shandathe.

The viewpoint could not be made to move. It was time to decide.

El shrugged; as always, there was only one decision he could make, and still be Elminster. The fool wizard.

Smiling in bleak self-mockery at that last thought, he rose, holding firmly to the image of the peak with the bound woman—a striking trap, he'd grant its weaver that much—and crossed the room to touch the Srinshee's teaching crystal. It could store mind images, and so show her where he'd gone. The stone flashed once, and he turned his back on its light and stepped away, calling up the spell he'd need.

When his foot came down again, he stood on the rocky height with the cool breeze sliding past. He was in the center of a vast forest that looked suspiciously like Cormanthor. The bound woman at his feet was fading and shrinking, her form flowing like pale smoke. Of course. Elminster called up what he hoped was the best spell for the occasion, and waited for the attack he knew would come.

In a dark chamber, a floating figure sat up and frowned at where her human charge had last stood. Some battles must be faced alone, but . . . so soon?

She wondered which elven foe was so swift in calling him to battle. Once news of the Coronal's proclaiming spread across the realm, yes, El would find no shortage of opponents, but . . . now?

The Srinshee sighed, called up the spell she'd cast earlier, and gathered her will around the image of Elminster in her mind. In a few breaths' time she'd be seeing him. Gods grant that it not be to witness his death now, before their friendship—along with the Coronal's dream and the trail that led to the best future for Cormanthor—was truly begun.

Without looking at her crystal, she beckoned it, and touched it when it came. The image of a rocky height amid the Cormanthan forest leaped into her mind. Druindar's Rock, a place none but a Cormanthan was likely to choose for a moot or spell duel. The Srinshee sent her spell sight racing toward it, seeing a familiar young, hawk-nosed man standing above a bound woman, who was no bound woman at all, but a . . .

The woman and the spars she'd been bound to were both flowing and dwindling. Elminster calmly stepped back from the changing magic and glanced over the edge of the rock on which he stood. It was a long, long way down on two flanks, with a prow-like point between. In the third direction rocks rose into broken, tree-cloaked ground. It was from the concealing branches of those trees that cold laughter came as the lady captive shrank at last into a long, wavy-bladed boar sword that flickered and glowed green as it rose smoothly from the ground, turned on edge, and flew toward him point first.

Knowing what is about to kill you doesn't always make it easier to evade the waiting death, as a philosopher—dead now—among the outlaws of Athalantar had once said.

There was little space in which to dodge, and almost no time for El to act. This blade might be only animated by a simple spell, or it might well bear enchantments of its own. If he assumed the former and was wrong, he'd be dead. So . . .

Elminster carried in his mind only one of the mighty spells known as Mystra's unraveling, and disliked casting it so soon when he stood in danger, but—

The blade raced at his throat, turning smoothly as he sidestepped, and following his every move as he bobbed and crouched. At the last moment he hissed the single word of the spell and made the necessary flick of his cupped hand.

The swift-flying sword shivered and fell apart in the air in front of him. Green radiance sputtered, tumbled away, and was gone as the blade became falling flakes of rust. Dust kissed Elminster's face as it rushed past . . . and then nothing at all.

The laughter in the trees broke off abruptly, into a shout of, "Corellon aid me—human, *what have you done?*"

A finely dressed, youthful elf lord with hair like white silk and eyes like two red and furious flames came leaping out of the trees with the flames of rising magic growing ever-brighter around his wrists.

As the elf came snarling to a halt on the last rock above Elminster, almost weeping in his rage, Elminster looked up at him, used a spell echo to momentarily call up the image of the glowing green sword's destruction, and calmly asked, "Is this elven humor, or some sort of trick question?"

With a wild shriek of rage the elf sprang at El, flames leaping from his hands.

NINE
DUEL BY DAY, REUEL BY NIGHT

Few who've witnessed a spell battle forget the very old saying among humans:
"When mages duel, honest folk should seek hiding places far away." Though mantles
and araemyths make elven wizardly duels more a matter of anticipation and slowly
unfolding complexity than human struggles, 'tis still a good idea to be at a safe
distance when sorcerers make war. Out of the realm, for instance.

ANTARN THE SAGE
from *THE HIGH HISTORY OF FAERÛNIAN ARCHMAGES MIGHTY*
PUBLISHED CIRCA THE YEAR OF THE STAFF

Y ou—you *wretch!*" the elf snarled, hurling fire from his hands in a web of
snapping flames. "That blade was a treasure of my House! It was old when
humans first learned to speak!"

"My," Elminster replied as his warding spell took effect, sending the flames
splashing down around him in a ring, "that's a lot of dead boars. How old did
any of them live to be, I wonder?"

"Insolent barbarian *human!*" the elf hissed, dancing around Elminster's ring.
His fair hair bounced about his shoulders as he went, flowing in the passing
breeze as if it were the flames of a hungry fire.

Elminster turned to keep himself facing this angry foe, and said calmly, "I
tend not to be overly pleasant to those who try to slay me, but I have no real
quarrel with ye, nameless elf lord. Can we not part in peace?"

"Peace? When you're *dead*, human, perhaps, and the mages of whatever
godless grubbing kingdom spawned you have been compelled to replace the
sacred sword you destroyed!"

The angry elf drew back, raised both arms above his head with his hands
still pointed at Elminster, and spat angry words. El murmured a single word in
response and flicked his fingers, altering his warding into a shield that would
send hostile magics back whence they'd come.

A trio of racing blue bolts, each with its own nimbus of lightning encircling it, roared out of the elf's hands and came screaming at the last prince of
Athalantar. Inside his shield El crouched ready, bringing another spell to mind
but not casting it.

The bolts struck, washed over his shield in a soundless fury of white light,
and raced back at their source.

The elf's eyes widened in amazement, and he shut his eyes and grimaced as
the blue bolts crashed into an invisible shield that surrounded him. Of course,
thought El. Every magic-hurling Cormanthan probably wore a conjured mantle

of defensive magics when he went to war.

And this was war, El thought, as the elven lord fell back a few paces and snarled out another incantation. With an attacker who'd chosen the ground and had a defensive mantle up and ready on one hand, and the freakish and widely hated human intruder on the other. Oh, joy.

This time the spell that came at Elminster consisted of three disembodied jaws, their long fangs snapping as they swerved and split apart to come at him from three directions. El fell flat on his stomach and raised his left hand, waiting, as the first soundless flash marked the meeting of his shield and the foremost maw.

After the flash, it danced and staggered away, heading back for the elf lord. But the second mouth tore asunder his shield with its collision, both spell effects twisting together into a roiling blast that sent a scorching trail of angry purple flames racing along the rocks.

The returning jaws faded away against the elf lord's mantle at about the same time as the third raced at Elminster, gaping low to be sure of scooping him up off the rocks.

From El's patiently waiting hand flashed a dozen globes of light that spat tiny lightnings behind them as they went. The first blasted the jaws into golden-green nothingness, and the others shot through the spreading fire of that explosion and leaped at the elf beyond in a deadly approaching storm.

The elf lord looked anxious for the first time, and worked a hasty spell as the spinning globes flashed toward him. He fell back a few more steps to gain time to finish his spell—and so tasted Elminster's first trap.

The globes that the elf's stabbing defensive magic did not touch struck the unseen mantle and exploded in harmless, spreading sheets of light. Those the elf did strike burst apart into triple lightning bolts that stabbed rocks, trees, and the nearby elf lord with equal vigor.

With a groan of pain the elf staggered backward, smoke rising from him.

"Not a bad defense for a nameless elf," Elminster observed calmly.

His goading promptly had the effect he'd been hoping for. "No nameless one am I, human," the elf snarled, arms folded around himself in pain, "but Delmuth Echorn, of one of the foremost Houses of Cormanthor! Heir of the Echorns am I, and my rank in your human terms would be 'emperor'! Uncultured *dog!*"

"Ye use 'uncultured dog' as a title?" Elminster asked innocently. "It fits ye, aye, but I must warn ye we humans haven't come to expect such candor from elven folk. Ye may achieve unintended hilarity in thy dealings with my kind!"

Delmuth roared in fresh fury; but then his eyes narrowed and he hissed like a snake. "You hope to overmaster me through my temper! No such fortune will I hand to you—nameless human!"

"Elminster Aumar am I," El replied pleasantly, "Prince of Athalant—ah, but ye won't be interested in the titles of pig-sty human realms, will ye?"

"Yes, precisely!" Delmuth snapped. "Er, that is: *no!*" His arms were acquiring flames again. Circles of fire-bursts chased each other endlessly about his wrists, betokening risen but unleashed old elven battle magic.

So was the elf lord's mantle gone entirely, or did it survive still? El silently bent his will to spinning another shield of his own as he waited, suspecting Delmuth would try to ruin the next visible spell his human foe cast by hurling his own spell attack into the midst of El's casting.

When El's shield was complete, he acted out the casting of a false spell. Sure enough, emerald lightnings lashed at him in mid-gibberish, clawing at his shield and rebounding. Delmuth laughed triumphantly, and El saw by the rebounding sparks that the elf's mantle had survived, or had been renewed. He shrugged, smiled, and began his own next spell, at the same time as the fiercely smiling elf undertook his own casting.

Unnoticed by either of them, one of the trees struck by Elminster's lightning fell over the edge of the peak, tearing crumbling stone with it, to plunge down, down through the empty air.

"Oh, be careful, Elminster!" the Lady Oluevaera Estelda breathed, as she sat on empty air in a dark and dusty chamber at the heart of the ghost castle of the Dlardrageth. Her eyes were seeing a distant peak and two figures striving against each other there, as their spells flashed and raged about them. The one just might be the future of Cormanthor, while the other was one of the most haughty and headstrong of its oldest, proudest Houses—and its heir to boot.

Some would call it treachery to the People to intervene in any spell duel—but then, this was no proper duel, but a man lured into a trap by the deceit of an elf. Many more would deem one who aided any human against any elf, in any situation, a traitor to the People. And yet she would do this, if she could. The Srinshee had seen more summers by far—aye, and winters, too—than any other elf who breathed the clear air of Cormanthor today. She was one of those whose judgment would be deferred to, in any high dispute between Houses. Well, then; her judgment would have to be respected as highly in this more personal matter.

Not that anyone but ghosts were in this shunned ruin to stop her.

The only swift link she had with Druindar's Rock was through Elminster himself, and it might well be fatal to him to create any distraction in his mind at the wrong moment. However, she could "ride" through him, exposing herself to the same magics he faced in the process, until he happened to let his eyes fall on some part of the surroundings that wasn't full of erupting magic or a leaping elf lord—whereupon she could hurl herself to that spot, and materialize there.

The spell was a powerful but simple one. The Srinshee murmured the words that released it without taking her eyes off the spell-battle, and felt herself *sliding* into Elminster's mind, as if slipping into warm, tingling waters that carried her swiftly along a dark, narrow tunnel, toward a distant light.

The light grew brighter and larger with terrifying speed, until it became a serenely beautiful face that the Srinshee knew, its long tresses stirring and writing like restless snakes. A face whose eyes were stern as it loomed up like a vast, endless wall before her, a wall she was going to crash helplessly into . . .

"Oh, Lady Goddess, not *again!*" The Srinshee cried, an instant before she struck those gigantic, pursed lips. "Can't you see I'm trying to help—?"

When the whirling world came back again, Oluevaera was staring at a dark, cobwebbed ceiling inches overhead. She was sprawled on her back on a bed of raging black flames that tickled her bare skin—her bare skin? what had become of her gown?—as if it were a thousand moving feathers, but did not burn.

The flames seemed to be slowly sinking away from the ceiling; had she appeared *through* it? Wonderingly she ran her hands up and down her body. Her gown, with its amulets and spell-gems—yes, even those woven into her hair—were gone, but her body was smooth and full and young again!

Great Corellon, Labelas, and Hanali! What had befalle—but no. Great *Mystra!* The human goddess had wrought this!

She sat up abruptly, amid the descending flames. Why? In payment for aiding the young lad, or as an apology for shutting her out? Was it lasting? Or but a taunting taste of youth? She still had her spells, her memories, the—

"So, old whore, you've traded your loyalty to the realm for some spell of youth the human knows! I *wondered* why you aided him!"

The Srinshee turned her head to stare at the speaker, bringing her hands up to cover her breasts without thinking. She knew that cold voice, but how came it here?

"Cormanthor knows how to treat traitors!" he snarled, and a bolt of ravening lightning crackled across the room.

It sank into the black flames and was sucked in without a sound. The black flames hauled every last spark of the bolt from the hands of the astonished High Court Mage Ilimitar. He stared at the now-youthful sorceress.

She looked back at him with sad reproach in her eyes and spoke softly, using her old pet name for him. "So how is it, Limi, that you rise from being my pupil, and learning love for Cormanthor from my lips, to presuming to speak for all the realm as you try to slay me?"

"Seek not to twist my will with words, witch!" Ilimitar snapped, raising a scepter to menace her. The dark flames touched the stone floor of the chamber and faded, and the Srinshee stood facing him, spreading her hands to show that she was nude and unarmed.

He leveled the scepter without hesitation, saying coldly, "Pray to the gods for forgiveness, traitor!"

Emerald fire raced from it as that last hurtful word left his lips; the Srinshee tuned to leap side, stumbled—it had been so long since she'd known a body that could obey swift movements—and then sprawled bruisingly on the stones as the scepter's death roared over her.

Her onetime pupil aimed the scepter lower, but the Srinshee had hissed the words she needed. Its fury splashed in futility along an unseen shield.

Her mantle was up now, and she doubted all the scepters he owned could bring it down. It would be spell to spell, unless she could dissuade him. The

High Court Mage *she'd* trained. Earynspieir might attack her, yes, he'd never been her friend. But she'd not thought Ilimitar could be so quick to do this.

Oluevaera rose and faced the furious mage, standing no taller than his shoulder. "Why did you seek me here, Ilimitar?" she asked.

"This tomb of traitors was always your favored spot to bring pupils to try castings, remember?" he spat at her.

Gods, yes, she'd brought Ilimitar here to Castle Dlardrageth, twice. Tears came at the memory, and as the High Court Mage flung down his scepter and wove a spell to bring the roof down on her, he snarled, "Regretting your folly now, eh? Too late, old witch! Your treachery is clear, and you must die!"

In reply the last Lady Estelda merely shook her head and calmly wove the magic that awakened the ancient enchantments the Dlardrageth had used to raise these halls. When Ilimitar's spell smashed and clawed at the ceiling, instants later, his magic turned to fire that rained back down at him.

He staggered back, coughing and shuddering—his mantle must be weak, she thought—and shouted, "Seek not to escape me, Oluevaera! No part of the realm is safe for you now!"

"By whose decree?" she cried, fresh tears on her cheeks. "Have you slain Eltargrim, too?"

"His folly is not yet open treachery to Cormanthor, but something that can be corrected once the human—and *you*, with your lying tongue—are gone. I will hunt you down wherever you flee to!" He muttered an incantation on the heels of that shout.

"I've no intention of fleeing anywhere, Ilimitar!" the Srinshee told him angrily. "This realm is my home!"

The air before her exploded in flames. From each blossoming ball of fire a beam shot out, to link with the other fireballs. Oluevaera ducked away from one whose heat threatened to blister her shoulder and whispered words that would dissolve a spell into strengthening her mantle.

"Is that why," the High Court Mage snarled in reply, "you protected a *human*, keeping him alive and counseling him into flattering the Coronal enough to win an armathor out of the old fool? He'll just be the first of a scheming, grasping horde of the hairy ones, if we let him live! Can you not see that?"

"No!" the Srinshee shouted, over the crash and roar of his next spell attack. "I fail to see why loving Cormanthor and working to strengthen it must place me in the situation of having to slay one honorable human—who came here to keep a promise to a dying heir, and deliver a kiira to an elder House, Ilimitar!—or be slain by you, unless I destroy you: a mage in whom I awakened mastery of magic, and have been proud of these six centuries!"

"Always you twist folk with clever words!" he shouted back, and went right on into snarling the incantation of another spell.

The Srinshee found herself weeping again. "Why?" she sobbed. "Why do you force me to make this choice?"

Her mantle shuddered then, as purple lightnings of magical force sought to drain its vitality. Through the tumult, as paving stones cracked underfoot in a ragged, deafening chorus, her newfound foe cried, "Your wits are addled by love, old hag, and corrupted by the Coronals' dreams! Can you not understand that the security of the realm *must* be paramount over all other things?"

The Srinshee set her teeth and lashed out with lightnings of her own; his mantle lit up briefly under their strike, and she saw him staggering. "And can you not see," she shouted at him, "that this man *is* the security of our realm, if we but guard him and let him grow into what Eltargrim sees?"

"Bah!" Ilimitar the mage spat derisively. "The Coronal is as corrupt as you are! You and he both stain the good name of our court, and the trust our People have put in you!" The chamber rocked around them as his latest spell clawed its way along every inch of her mantle, but could not break it.

"Ilimitar," the Srinshee asked sadly, "are you mad?"

The chamber fell suddenly silent, with smoke eddying around their feet, as he stared at her in genuine amazement.

"No," he said at last, in almost conversational tones, "but I think I've been mad for years not to see the game you and the Coronal have been playing, moving Cormanthor ever so gently—deftly, like the sly oldlings you both are—toward the day when humans would dwell among us, and outbreed us, and in the end overwhelm us, leaving no Cormanthor at all to serve or be proud of! How much did they offer you? Spells you couldn't find elsewhere? A realm to rule? Or was it this return of your youth, all along?"

"Limi," she said earnestly, "this body you see is not of my doing, and when first you found me here and now, I was but newly aware of it. I know not where it came from—it could be some old joke of the Dlardrageth, for all I know—and the young human certainly didn't give it to me, or promise it; he doesn't even *know* about it!"

Ilimitar waved a dismissive hand. "Words—just words," he said heavily. "Always your sharpest weapons. They don't work with me anymore, witch!" He was panting, now, as he faced her.

"Do you know what this is?" he asked, taking something small from a belt pouch and raising it into view. "It's from the Vault of Ages," he added mockingly. "You should know!"

"It's the Overmantle of Halgondas," the Srinshee said quietly, her face going pale.

"You fear it, don't you?" he snarled, triumph glinting in his eyes again. "And there's nothing you can do to stop me using it! And then, old witch, you are mine!"

"How so?"

"Our mantles will merge, and become one. Not only will you not ward off my spells, but you won't escape; if you flee, you'll drag me with you!" He laughed, his tones high and wild, and the Srinshee knew then that he was mad, and that she would have to kill him here, or perish.

He broke the Overmantle.

The inexorable surging together of their two mantles began, their ragged ends searching for, and attracted to, each other. The Srinshee sighed and began to walk toward her onetime pupil. It was time to use the spell she hated.

"Surrendering?" Ilimitar asked, almost gleefully. "Or are you foolish enough to think you can fight on—and prevail? I'm a High Court Mage, witch, not the youth you showed castings to! Your magic is all trickery and old sly spells and little magics for scaring younglings!"

The Srinshee drew in a deep breath, and lifted her chin. "Well then, grand and mighty sorcerer—destroy me if you must!"

High Court Mage Ilimitar gave her an disbelieving look, raised his hands, and said gruffly, "I'll make it quick."

A trident of spell spears thrust through her. She stood unmoving, though her eyes rolled up in her head and she bit her lip. After the spell began to fade, her body started to tremble.

Ilimitar watched her. Well, it wasn't his fault she'd spun so many preservative and guardian enchantments down the centuries, layer upon layer. She'd just have to endure the pain, now, as they kept her alive longer than was necessary.

She brought her head down, eyes closed, and stood breathing heavily. Blood ran down her face from her closed eyelids, and dripped on the shattered stones underfoot. Ilimitar's nostrils flared in distaste. So it was martyr time, was it? He'd make short work of that.

His next spell was a thrust of pure energy that should have left her in ashes. When it faded and he could see again, the stones were melted away in a neat circle, and she stood ankle-deep in rubble, blackened and with all her hair burnt away—but she still stood, and still shuddered.

What foul pact had the sorceress made with human mages? Ilimitar cast the spell she'd once forbid him utterly to use; the one that summoned the Hungry Worm.

The worm materialized coiled about one of her arms, but it slithered straight for her belly, and began burrowing into the cracked and blackened flesh immediately. Ilimitar sighed and hoped it would be quick; he had to be sure that human was dead, and swiftly, so he could be back at court to denounce the Coronal before nightfall. But he was trapped here with the Srinshee, inside the shared Overmantle, until one of them was dead.

It was a pity, really. She'd been a good teacher—if an overly strict one, with little love for pranks and stealing days in high summer to snatch honey and nibble berries and hunt down new owl eggs—and she should never have sunk to this. She'd been old even then, though, and no doubt tempted to take any means to regain youth. But consorting with humans was unforgivable. If she wanted to do that, why hadn't she just quietly left Cormanthor? Why ruin the realm? Why—

The worm was largely done, now. It never touched the limbs or head when it had a body to feast upon, a body now little more than rags of skin upon hollowed-out, empty bones. How was it that she was still standing?

Ilimitar frowned, and hurled a quartet of small forcebolts into her—the sort one uses to fell woodcutters or running rabbits. Her ravaged body still stood.

He was nearly out of useful battle spells. He shrugged and picked up the fallen scepter, raking her with emerald fire until the scepter sputtered and died, drained away.

The High Court Mage frowned down at it. He hadn't realized, when bringing it here today, just how little magic had been left in it. That could have been disastrous. As it was, well . . .

The ravaged body of the Srinshee still stood. She must still be alive—and he knew better than to touch her directly, even with his dagger. There were tricks the older casters knew. Best to simply blast her to nothingness.

He snapped his finger and said a certain word, and there was suddenly a staff in his hands—long and black, set with many silver runes. He let it wake slowly, thrumming in his hands—ah, that delicious feeling of power—before he poured white-hot death into his motionless foe.

The staff fell silent after only moments. He frowned, tried to send it away again, and found it dead—just so much dark wood, now. In puzzlement he threw it down and summoned a rod. He had two more scepters he could call to him after that, if the rod failed. Perhaps the Overmantle was deadening them. In frantic haste he called on all of its withering and life-draining powers.

The body facing him became a withered bag of skin once more, and what skin was left turned gray and rotten. But still the old sorceress stood.

Grunting in exasperated amazement, Ilimitar called first one scepter, and then the other. When it fizzled into crackling, smoking death, the first cold taste of foreboding filled his mouth, for the Srinshee still stood.

Her shattered head hung askew from a broken neck, but those blackened, bleeding eyes opened—to be revealed as two pools of flickering flame—and the mouth beneath them worked its broken jaw for a grinding moment and then croaked, "Are you done, Limi?"

"Corellon preserve me!" the mage shouted, in real horror, as he shrank away from her. Would she start to move toward him?

Yes! Oh, gods, yes!

He screamed as that broken body shuffled forward, out of its pit of melted rubble, and set footless stumps on the paving stones. He fell back, crying, "Stay back!"

"I don't want to do this, Limi," the mutilated thing said sadly, as it thumped slowly and awkwardly toward him. "The choice was yours, I fear, as it was when you began this battle, Limi."

"Speak not my name, foul witch of darkness!" the High Court Mage howled, snatching out his last item of magic with trembling fingers. It was a ring on a fine chain; he slid it onto one of his fingers and pointed at her. The ring-finger swiftly lengthened into a lone, hooklike talon and began to grow scales. "You serve a foe of the realm," he cried, "and must needs be struck down, that Cormanthor endure!"

The ring flashed. A last beam of black, deadly force shot out.

The shuffling body halted, shuddering with fresh violence, and Ilimitar laughed in crazed relief. Yes! It was finally over! She was falling.

The broken thing crashed into his shoulder and slid down his body, brushing him with its lips as it fell.

There was an instant of crawling magic that made Oluevaera Estelda retch uncontrollably as the Overmantle surged in through every orifice of her body, and then out again.

Then it was gone, like mist before a morning sun, and she was on her knees, whole again, before the body of Ilimitar—who had just simultaneously received every spell and magical discharge he'd poured into her.

She *still* hated that spell. It was as cruel as the long ago elven mage who'd devised it—almost as bad as Halgondas and his Overmantle. Moreover, its caster had to feel the pain of all that was done to them—and Ilimitar had been so enthusiastic in his attempted destruction that the pain would have driven most mages mad. But not this one. Not the old Srinshee.

She looked down at the heap of blasted, smoldering bones in front of her, and started to cry again. Her tears made little hissing sounds as they fell into the dying fires that flickered within what had been Ilimitar.

"Blood of Corellon, it's raining *trees* now!" Galan Goadulphyn snarled, springing back and raising his cloak hastily before his face. The fallen duskwood bounced deafeningly as it shattered in front of him, hurling dust and splinters in all directions.

"There's a spell duel going on up there, for sure," Athtar said, peering upwards. "Hadn't we better get out of here? We can come back for your coins later"

"Later?" Galan groaned, as they hastened away together. "If I know bloody yapping mages, they'll split that mountain apart before they're done, and either leave my cache revealed for every passing sprite to see—or they'll bury it keep-deep under broken rock!"

There was another crash, and Athtar Nlossae looked back in time to see a sheet of rock plunging down the cliff, bouncing and shattering as it struck outcroppings in its fall. "You're right, as usual, Gal—buried it is, or will be!"

As he bent his legs to following the elf in dusty black leathers just as fast as they both could travel, Galan began to sort through his collection of curses. Loudly.

"You can't hope to escape my magics forever, coward!" Delmuth told Elminster, as elven mantle and human shield struck sparks from each other, and yet another mighty old elven spell curled away into harmless smoke.

They stood almost breast to breast, as close as their warring spell-barriers would let them. Elminster went on smiling silently, as the angry elf hurled spell after spell.

Delmuth had discovered that so long as mantle and shield touched, the surging effect of his own spells rebounding on him was minimal; his own defenses didn't crumble away so quickly at each magical onslaught. So he'd advanced, and Elminster hadn't bothered to retreat.

The only place to fall back was over the edge of a cliff, anyway, and the Athalantan mage was weary of running. Let the stand be made here.

The heir of House Echorn hurled another blast—this one past Elminster, avoiding both mage and shield, in hopes that it would rend rock and spray him from behind with stone shards. Instead, it ripped a trench through the rock and spat the stone over the edge of the cliff, away into nothingness below.

El kept his eyes on the elf lord. This had gone on long enough; if Delmuth Echorn wanted to see a death so badly, it'd have to be his own. Safe inside his shield, Elminster carefully made an elaborate casting, and then another that called up his mage-sight, and waited. One advantage to battling elves with human spells was that they largely didn't recognize the castings, and so could be surprised by the final results.

This one was Mruster's Twist, a further modification of Jhalavan's Fond Return. It allowed a mage who could think fast to change spells that were being returned to their caster into different magics. Now if this Delmuth was just foolish enough to try to blast a certain annoying human to dust, and keep close to Elminster as he did it, so he didn't notice that the spreading furies of his spells were left over from their first strikes, and not their rebounds . . .

Delmuth enthusiastically proved he was just foolish enough, hurling a spell El had never seen before that brought into being a tray of acid above the victim's head and let its contents rain down.

The hissings and roilings of El's tormented shield were spectacular. Delmuth never noticed when the rain of acid was twisted into a surging dispel effect that clawed silently at his mantle.

Still angry, and thinking his foe was finally cornered, Delmuth lashed out with a second spell. Elminster put on a scared look this time to distract the elf from noticing that his energy blasts again melted away into something silent, and it worked.

Delmuth raised both hands exultantly and lashed his human foe with bladed tentacles. El reeled and pantomimed pain, as it some part of the fading spell had actually reached him through his shield. And Delmuth's twisted spell ate away the last strength of his own mantle.

To El's mage-sight, the elf was surrounded now only by flickering, darkening wisps of magic, the failing shell of what had once been an impregnable barrier. "Delmuth," he cried, "I ask ye one last time: can't we end this, and part in peace?"

"Certainly, human," the elf replied with a feral grin. "When you are dead, then there'll be *perfect* peace!"

And his slender fingers shaped a casting El did not know. Force flickered, visible only in its settling outline; it seemed to be the same invisible evocation that human mages wove into what were called walls of force.

Delmuth saw El watching intently, and looked up, gloating, as the last radiances shaped an invisible sword, floating before Delmuth with its point toward Elminster. "Behold a spell you cannot send back at me," the elf lord chuckled, leaning low over it. "We call it a 'deadly seeking blade' and all of elven blood are immune to it!" He snapped his fingers and broke into open, rolling laughter as the blade leaped forward.

They were standing only a few paces apart, but El already knew what magic he wanted to turn this unseen blade of force into. Delmuth would have been wiser to have wielded it in his hand, and hacked at El's shield as if it were a real blade, giving El no time to twist it in the brief contacts.

But then, Delmuth would have been wiser never to have lured Elminster here at all.

El twisted the blade into something else and flung it back. As it struck the elf, Delmuth's laughter faltered. The last gasp of his mantle, striving vainly to protect him as it scattered into drifting sparks, lifted him up off the ground to kick his heels in empty air.

He stiffened as Elminster's twisted magic struck him, and then grew still, his hands raised into claws in front of his breast, his legs straining, with the toes of his boots pointed at the ground. The paralysis El had bestowed upon him took firm hold, and all that El could see the elf lord move was his eyes, widening now in terror and rolling around to stare helplessly at the human mage.

Or perhaps not so helplessly. Delmuth could still launch magics that were triggered by act of will alone, like Elminster's shielding spells—and in the elf lord's eyes El saw terror be washed away by fury, and then by cunning.

Delmuth hadn't been so scared for a long time. Fear was like cold iron in his mouth, and his heart raced. That a mere *human* could bring him to this! He could *die* here, floating above some windswept rock in the backwoods of the realm! He—

Yet steady . . . steady, son of Echorn. He had one spell left that no human could anticipate, something more secret and terrible even than the blade. They'd been pressed together mantle-to-mantle; for his own to have failed, the human's must inevitably have collapsed, too. Wasn't that why this Elminster had pleaded for the fight to end? And now the human must think him helpless, and was standing there vainly trying to think of some way of slaying him with a rock or dagger without breaking his paralysis. Yes, if the spell was cast now, the human could not hope to stop it.

The "call bones" spell had been developed by Napraeleon Echorn seven—or was it eight? he'd never paid all that much attention to his tutors—centuries ago, as a way of reducing giant stags to cartloads of ready meat. It could summon a particular assembly of bones to its caster, so that they tore their way right out of the victim's body. If the caster chose to receive the skull, the victim could not hope but die. Though Delmuth couldn't come up with a use, just this moment, for a blood-dripping human skull, there'd be plenty of time to think of one . . .

'Smiling with his eyes, he cast the spell. *Elminster, your skull, please . . .*

He was still gloating—humming to himself, actually—when the world darkened and the brief, incredible pain began. He could not even shriek as red blood bubbled up into his mind and Faerûn went away forever.

Elminster winced as blood fountained. When the grisly, blood-drenched thing came hurtling at him, he used his shield like the warriors' object it was named for, deflecting the bony missile past him and off the peak, into empty air.

The last prince of Athalantar looked at the headless floating body one last time, shook his head sadly, and said the words that would take him back to the room at the heart of the haunted castle, and the Srinshee. He hoped she hadn't wakened and found him gone; he'd no desire to upset her unnecessarily.

The hawk-nosed young man took a step toward the nearest cliff, and vanished into thin air. The buzzards waiting in a tree nearby decided it was safe to dine now, and flapped clumsily aloft. Their long, slow glides would have to be aimed just right; it wasn't every day that the food was floating in midair.

"Gal," Athtar said patiently, as they struggled up the second sheer rockface in a row, "I know you're upset about your cache—gods above, half the *forest* knows it!—but we'll come back for them, really we will, and it isn't serving any useful purpose to—"

Something fast and round and the color of wet blood fell out of the sky and swept Athtar's face away.

The body in black leather, limbs wriggling and twitching, fell past Galan. The thing that had killed Athtar bounced off his chest on the way, rolling to a stop in a tangle of roots beside Galan's face.

He found himself staring into the sockets of an elf skull drowned in fresh blood—for the brief instant before he lost his hold on the crumbling ledge and found himself falling down, down into the darkness that had claimed Athtar.

Elminster took one step into the dark chamber, and saw that something was very wrong. The Srinshee was gone, and a young, naked elven girl was on her knees before a sprawled, ashen skeleton, sobbing uncontrollably. Had his friend caught fire?

The young girl looked up, face streaming, and sobbed, "Oh, Elminster!" As she reached for him, El rushed into her arms, embracing her. Gods look down—*this* was the Srinshee!

"Lady Oluevaera," he asked gently, as he stroked her hair and shoulders, cradling her to his breast, "what befell here?"

She shook her head, and managed to choke out the word, "Later."

El rocked her, murmuring wordless soothings, for some time before her weeping subsided, and she said, "Elminster? Forgive me, but I am exhausted, and in grave danger of failing Cormanthor for the first time in my life."

"Is there anything I can do?"

Oluevaera lifted her youthful face to meet his gaze. She still had those wise, sad old eyes, El noticed. "Yes," she whispered. "Go into danger once more. I cannot ask this; the peril is too great."

"Tell me," Elminster murmured. "I'm beginning to think hurling myself into danger is what Mystra sent me here to do."

The Srinshee tried to smile. Her lips trembled for a moment, and then she said, "You may well be right. I've seen Mystra, while you were gone." She raised a hand to forestall his questions, and said, "So you must stay alive to hear about it later. I've just power enough left to cast a body switch spell."

El's eyes narrowed. "To send me to where someone else stands, and him or her here."

The Srinshee nodded. "The Coronal attends a revel this night, and there is bound to be someone angry enough to try to slay him."

"Cast the spell," El told her firmly. "I'm down a few spells, but I'm ready."

"Will you?" she asked, and shook her head, impatiently brushing away fresh tears. "Oh, El . . . such honor . . ."

She sprang from his lap and ran quickly across the chamber. For the first time Elminster noticed that it was strewn with what looked to be wizards' scepters of power, and even a staff. The Srinshee bent and plucked one up.

"Take this with you," she said. "It has some little power left. One thing it can do is duplicate any spell you see cast by someone else while you are holding it. Handle it, and into your mind it'll whisper its powers."

Elminster took it and nodded. Impulsively she threw her arms around his neck and kissed him. "Go with my good wishes—and, I know, Mystra's blessing, too."

El raised an eyebrow. Just what *had* happened here?

He was still wondering that as the Srinshee cast her spell, and blue mists whirled the world away again.

Ten
Love Oft Astray

The love of an elf is a deep and precious thing. Misused or spurned, it can be deadly. Realms have fallen and been sundered for love, and proud elder houses swept away. Some have said that an elf is the force of his or her love, and all else just flesh and dross. It is certain that elves can love humans, and humans love elves—but in such meetings of the heart, sorrow is never far away.

Shalheira Talandren, High Elven Bard of Summerstar
from *Silver Blades And Summer Nights:
An Informal But True History of Cormanthor*
published in The Year of the Harp

The mists rolled away and Elminster was in a garden he'd never seen before, a place of many tall, straight shadowtops soaring straight up like huge black pillars from a manicured lawn of mosses adorned with small mushroom plantings. High overhead, the leaves of the trees blotted out the sun completely, though El could see shafts of sunlight in the distance where there must be clearings.

Here the only light came from spheres of luminous air—globes that glowed faint blue, green, ruby-red, or gold as they drifted softly and aimlessly through the trees.

Elves in ornate silken robes were strolling among the shadowtops, laughing and chatting, and beneath each luminous globe floated a tray that held an array of tall, thin bottles, and layered platters of delicacies; at a glance, El recognized oysters, mushrooms, and what looked to be forest grubs in a plum or apricot sauce.

There was also an elf standing very near, and looking very startled. An elf Elminster had seen before—one of the High Court Mages who'd been with the Coronal when Naeryndam had taken him to the palace.

"Well met," Elminster said to him, bowing politely. "Lord Earynspieir, is it not?"

The elven mage looked, if anything, more confused and alarmed than before. He nodded, "Earynspieir I am, human sir. Forgive me if I recall not your name, for I am in some anxiousness: where is the Coronal?"

Elminster spread his hands. "I know not. Was he standing a moment or so ago where I am now?"

The elf nodded, eyes narrowing. "He was."

El nodded. "Then that is as it's supposed to be. I am to attend this revel in his place."

Earynspieir scowled. "You are? And did you decide this yourself, young sir?"

"No," Elminster replied gently. "It was decided for me—for the security of the realm. I agreed to it, aye. By the way, the name's Elminster. Elminster Aumar, Prince of Athalantar . . . and, as ye know, Chosen of Mystra."

The elf mage's mouth tightened. His gaze descended to the scepter thrust through Elminster's belt and tightened still further, but he said nothing.

"Perhaps, Lord Mage, we could set aside thy feelings toward me for a moment or three," Elminster murmured, "while ye tell me where we're standing, and what is customary at an elven revel. I have no wish to give offense."

Earynspieir's eyes slid sideways to meet those of Elminster, and his lips curled in distaste. Then he seemed to come to a decision.

"Very well," he said, as softly. "Perhaps my natural reactions toward your kind have governed me overmuch. The Coronal did tell me that 'twould be easier for us all if I regarded you as one of us—one of the People—visiting from a far realm, and wearing a human disguise. I shall assay this, young Elminster. Pray bear with me; I am unsettled just now for other reasons."

"And can ye speak of them to me?" Elminster asked softly.

The elf shot him a sharp glance, and then said shortly, "Let me speak with utter candor—a habit popular with those of your race, I hear. Moreover, I doubt you know any loose-tongued Cormanthans to gossip with, which frees me to speak more plainly than I might otherwise do."

Elminster nodded. The elven mage looked around to make certain no one was within earshot, and then turned to the young prince and said bluntly, "Our Coronal's decision regarding you has not been popular. Many who hold the rank of armathor in the realm have come to the palace to renounce their rank, and break their blades before the Coronal. There has been open talk of deposing and even slaying him, of hunting you down, and of . . . general unpleasantness here this night, and elsewhere until he, ah, comes to his senses. My counterpart, the High Court Mage Ilimitar, has not returned from a visit to several of the elder Houses of the realm, and I know not his fate—or if treason is involved. I thought I held the Coronal's closest confidence, and yet, without word or warning, he vanishes from my side, and you appear, speaking guardedly of 'the security of the realm,' something I've had good reason to believe was entrusted to *me*. Despite the Coronal's earlier confidence in you, I see you as a human mage of unknown but probably great powers, who has a close relationship with a goddess of your race—and thus, whatever your motives, a great danger to Cormanthor, as you stand here at its heart. Do you see why I am less than gracious to you?"

"I do," Elminster replied, "and bear no ill will toward ye, Lord Mage—how could ye do otherwise, in these straits?"

"Precisely," Earynspieir said in a satisfied voice, almost smiling. "I fear I've misjudged your race, sir, and you with it—I never knew that humans cared about the intrigues and the . . . ah, graces and troubles of others. All we see and hear of you here is axes cutting down trees and swords impatiently settling even the slightest dispute."

" 'Tis true that some among us do favor the most swift and direct form of politics," Elminster agreed with a smile. "Yet I must hasten to remind ye and all others of Cormanthor that to judge humans of all lands as one alike mass is no more correct than to judge moon elves by the habits of the dark elven, or vice versa."

The elf beside him turned away and stiffened, eyes blazing, and then relaxed visibly and managed a short laugh. "Your point is taken, human sir—but I must remind *you* that folk of Cormanthor are unused to such boldly blunt speech, and may like it rather less than I do."

"Understood," El said. "My apologies. Someone approaches. Sorry: a pair of someones."

Earynspieir looked at El, startled by this sudden brevity, and then turned to see the elven couple the young human had indicated. They had glasses in their hands and were walking at a leisurely gait, arms linked, but their surprised expressions left no doubt that they were headed hence because of the unexpected sight of the human armathor there'd been so much talk about.

"Ah," Earynspieir said smoothly, "it lacks some hours yet until dusk, when the dancing and ah, less dignified revelries begin. Those who wish to speak candidly with each other or with the Coronal, or to choose new consorts for an evening, often arrive now, when revelers are few and rather less wine has been consumed than will be the case later; these are some such. Allow me to perform the introductions."

El inclined his head, every inch the polite prince, as the couple swept up to the High Court Mage. The young, handsome elven male stared at Elminster as though a forest boar had put on clothes and come to the revel, but the breathtakingly beautiful, gossamer-gowned elven maiden on his arm smiled charmingly at the elf mage and said, "Fair even, Revered Lord. We—ah, expected to see the Coronal with you. Is he indisposed?"

"Our Coronal Most High was called away on urgent business of the realm only a very short time ago. May I introduce to you instead Prince Elminster of the land of Athalantar, our newest armathor?"

The elven male went on staring at Elminster, and said nothing. His lady giggled uneasily and said, "An unexpected and—dare I say it?—unusual pleasure."

She did not extend her hand.

"Prince Elminster," the High Court Mage purred, "be at ease with Lord Qildor, of the House of Revven, and the Lady Aurae of House Shaeremae. May your meeting and parting be of equal pleasure."

Elminster bowed. "My honor is brightened," he said, recalling a phrase from the memories in the kiira. Three sets of elven eyebrows rose in astonished unison at those words of ancient elven courtesy as the human went on, "It is my desire to befriend—yet not alarm or intrude upon—the folk of fair Cormanthor. To such a one as myself, both the land and People of this fair place are so beautiful as to be revered treasures we honor from a distance."

"Does that mean you're not the first spysword of a human army?" the Lord Qildor growled, hand going to the ornate silver hilt of the sword he wore at his hip.

"That and more," Elminster replied mildly. "It is no desire of my realm or any other land of men that I know of to invade Cormanthor or intrude our ways and trade where we are not wanted, and can only do harm. My presence here is a personal matter, not an unfolding affair of state or any harbinger of invasion or prying exploration. No Cormanthan need fear me, or see me as representing more than a lone human who stands in just awe of thy People and their accomplishments."

The Lord Qildor raised his eyebrow again. "Forgive my forward speech," he said, "but would you permit a mage to read the truth of your words?"

"I would, and will," El said, meeting his eyes directly.

"If that is so," the elf said, "I have misjudged you before our meeting, purely on the speculations of others. Yet, Lord Elminster, you should know that I—as most of the People—fear and hate humans; to see one in the heart of our realm is a source of alarm and disgust. I do not know that any noble thing you can do, or fair words you can speak, can ever change that. Have a care for yourself here, sir; others will be less polite than we. Perhaps it would have been better for us both if you had never come to Cormanthor."

He fell silent for a moment, looking grave in his yellow silks, and then added slowly, "I wish I could find fairer words for you, man, but I cannot. It is not in me and I have seen more humans than most."

He nodded a little sadly, and turned away. Gems winked here and there among the hair that spilled down his back, as long and as magnificent as that of any highborn human woman. His lady, who had listened with eyes downcast, lifted her head proudly, gave Elminster and the High Court Mage a shared smile, and said, "It is as my lord says. Fare you well, lords both."

When they'd drawn a safe distance away, and had their covert looks back at the elf and the human standing together, Elminster turned to look Lord Earynspieir full in the face. "The folk of Cormanthor are unused to boldly blunt speech, Lord?" he asked smoothly, raising his own eyebrows. Earynspieir winced.

"Please believe that I meant not to lead you astray, lord sir," he replied. "It seems the sight of a human awakens a spirit of bluntness in Cormanthans I've not seen before."

"Fairly spoken," El granted, "and I—but who comes here?"

Drifting through the trees toward them came two elven ladies—literally drifting, their high-booted feet inches off the ground. Both were tall for elves, and sleekly curved, wearing gowns that showed off every line of their strikingly beautiful bodies. Heads turned as they wound their way through the revelers.

"Symrustar and Amaranthae Auglamyr, ladies and cousins," the High Court Mage murmured smoothly, and El thought he detected more than a little hunger in Lord Earynspieir's tone. As well there might be.

The woman who led was stunning even among all the elven maids El had seen since his arrival in the city. Hair that was almost royal blue flowed freely over her shoulders and down her back, only to be gathered in a silken sash that rode low on her right hip, as the tail of a horse is gathered to keep it from trailing along the ground. Her eyes were a bright, almost electric blue, flashing promises to Elminster under dark and archly raised eyebrows as she swept nearer. A black, unadorned ribbon encircled her throat, and her lips were full and slightly pouting; she ran her tongue openly over them as she surveyed the man standing beside the elven mage. The front of her crimson gown was cut away to show the design of a many-headed dragon worked in gems glued to her flat belly, slim waist, and cleavage; frozen flames of fine wire cupped and displayed her high breasts, and gold dust clung to the coyly-displayed tip of one of her ears. She was achingly beautiful—and knew it.

Her cousin wore a rather less revealing gown of dark blue, though one side of it was parted to above her waist to display a fine webwork of golden chains flowing down her bare, almost brown flank. She had flowing honey-blonde hair, startlingly brown eyes, and a far kinder smile than her blue-haired companion, as well as the most tanned skin and lush curves of any elf Elminster had ever seen. But her cousin outshone her beauty as a sun outblazes a night star.

"That is Symrustar in the lead," Earynspieir muttered. "She is heir of her House—and dangerous, sir; her honor consists solely of what she can get away with."

"You deeply prefer the Lady Amaranthae, do you not?" Elminster murmured back.

The High Court Mage turned his head sharply to regard Elminster with eyes that held both respect and a sharp warning. "You see keener than most elven elders, young lord," he hissed, as the ladies came upon them.

"Well met," the Lady Symrustar purred, tossing her hair aside with easy grace as she leaned forward to kiss Lord Earynspieir on the cheek. "You won't mind, wise old Lord, if I take your guest from you? I've—we've—a great hunger to learn more about humans; this is a rare opportunity."

"I . . . no, of course not, Lady." The elven mage put on a broad smile. "Ladies, may I present to you the lord Elminster of Athalantar? He is a prince in his own land, and newly—as I'm sure you've heard—an armathor of Cormanthor."

Earynspieir turned his head to regard El, a clear warning in his eyes, and continued, "Lord Elminster, it is my great pleasure to make known unto you two of the fairest flowers of our land: the Lady Symrustar, Heir of House Auglamyr, and her cousin, the Lady Amaranthae Auglamyr."

El bowed low, kissing the fingertips of the Lady Symrustar—an unaccustomed gesture, it seemed, from the appreciative purr she gave, and the hesitant way Amaranthae then extended her arm.

"The honor, ladies," he said, "is mine. But surely you cannot think to abandon the guardian of the realm just to talk to me? I am the allure of the unknown, 'tis true, but ladies, I confess I am overwhelmed by just one of ye, and have come to deeply appreciate the attentive wisdom of My Lord Earynspieir since our first meeting; he is a finer speaker than me, by far!"

Something leaped in the High Court Mage's eyes as Elminster spoke so earnestly, but he uttered not a sound as the Lady Symrustar laughed easily and said, "But of course Amaranthae will keep the mightiest mage of Cormanthor close and attentive company while we two talk, Lord Elminster. You are quite right in your estimation of his qualities, and one can accomplish far more face-to-face with just two faces thus engaged. You and Amaranthae can enjoy each other later. How splendidly swift-witted of you! Come, let us away!"

As she laced her fingers with his, Elminster turned to nod a polite farewell to the High Court Mage—whose face was unreadable—and to the Lady Amaranthae, who gave the human a look that was both deeply grateful and a mute warning to him about her cousin; El thanked her for both with a second nod and a smile.

"You seem attracted to my cousin, Lord Elminster," the Lady Symrustar purred in his ear, and El turned swiftly back to her, reminding himself that he was going to have to be very careful with this elven maid.

Very careful. As he turned, she did too, extending one slim leg around his so that they came together, breast to breast. Elminster felt the wire-girded points of her bosom low on his chest, and skin as smooth as silk brushing his breeches. She wore a black lace garter around that leg, and knee-high black boots of leather with spiked heels.

"My apologies for thrusting myself so into your path, Lord," she breathed, sounding completely unapologetic. "I fear I am unused to human company, and find myself quite . . . excited."

"No apology is necessary, fair Lady," El replied smoothly, "when no offense is taken." He glanced quickly back at the revel, and saw several curious faces turned in their direction, but no one moving toward them, or nearby.

"You must know how beautiful males of at least two races find you," he added, glancing ahead to ensure that the garden was similarly empty—and knowing that it almost certainly was; this lady planned things carefully— "but I must confess that I find splendid minds more intriguing than splendid bodies."

Lady Symrustar met his eyes. "Would you prefer I dropped the pretense of breathless excitement then, Lord Elminster?" she asked softly. "Among the People, many males do not believe that their ladies really *have* minds."

Elminster crooked an eyebrow. "With your swift wit gliding through revel after revel to prove them different?"

She laughed, eyes flashing. "Blood to you," she acknowledged. "I think I'm going to enjoy this." She led him on through the garden, walking now, whatever magic had levitated her banished or exhausted. Her hips swayed with every step in a way that left Elminster's mouth dry; he kept his eyes firmly on her eyes and saw a little knowing twinkle growing in them. She knew full well what effect she was having on him.

"I spoke simple truth when first we met," she said, tossing that magnificent hair out of the way again, "I do want to learn all I can about humans. Will you oblige me? My questions may seem witless at times."

"Lady, allow me," El murmured, wondering when her attack would fall on him, and what form it would take. He was mildly surprised, as they walked deeper and deeper into the wild and empty depths of the garden and the last sunlight started to fade, just how thorough her questioning was, and genuine her interest seemed.

They came at last to a pale glow of moonlight in the trees ahead, talking earnestly of how elves dwelt in Cormanthor and humans lived in Athalantar. Symrustar led her exotic human to a stone bench that curved about a circular pool in the center of that clearing. Reflected stars glimmered in its depths as they sat down together in the pleasantly warm night air, and the bright moonlight touched Symrustar's smooth skin with ivory fingers.

Quite naturally and simply, as if this was something elven females always did when sitting on benches in the moonlight, she guided Elminster's hands within the wire breastworks of her gown. She was trembling.

"Tell me more of men," she murmured, her eyes very large now, and seemingly darker. "Tell me . . . how they love."

Elminster almost smiled as a memory flashed through his mind. In the library of a wizard's tomb lost in the High Forest there is a curious book that has no name. It is the diary of a nameless half-elven ranger of long ago, that tells of his thoughts and deeds, and the sorceress Myrjala had made Elminster read it to learn how elves regarded magic. On the subject of giving pleasure to elven maids, it mentioned using one's tongue gently on the palms of the hands and the tips of the ears.

El slipped one of his hands out of where she'd put it, let his fingertips trail down her belly, and then caught hold of her wrist.

"Hungrily," he replied, and bent his tongue to her open palm.

She gasped, trembling in earnest now, and he lifted his head out of long habit to look around.

Moonlight gleamed on a set and furious elven face. A male, there in the trees. El slid his other hand free. There was another, over there. And another. They sat at the heart of a silently closing ring.

"What is it, Lord Elminster?" the Lady Symrustar asked, almost sharply. "Am I—abhorrent in some way?"

"Lady," he replied, "we are about to be attacked." He put his hands on the scepter at his belt, but the elven maid rose and turned with swift, fluid grace, and looked into the trees.

"They'll charge us, now, in silence," she said calmly. "Hold to me, and I'll take us from this place!"

Elminster slipped an arm about her waist and crouched low, scepter out and ready. She murmured something as the lithe shapes leaped at them out of the trees, and did something behind her that Elminster did not see. An instant later they were gone.

The elven warriors rolled and sprang, snarling in disappointment, blades slashing air that was now empty.

"What's this?" one of them hissed, pausing above the bench where the two figures had been entwined. A small obsidian figurine lay on it, rocking slightly. It was shaped like Symrustar Auglamyr, her hands at her sides, and bindings about her to keep them there. A cautious fingertip prodded it and found it still warm from the heat of someone's body.

"The human!" an elf hissed, raising his blade to smash the thing. "He was using dark magic to ensnare her!"

"Wait—destroy it not! It's clear proof of that!"

"To show to *whom?*" another elf snarled. "The Coronal? *He* brought this human viper into our midst, recall you?"

"True!" the first elf said. Two swords flashed down as one, shattering the tiny piece of obsidian so deftly that neither blade touched the bench beneath.

The explosion that followed tore apart bench, pool, and pave, and sent elven heads and limbs spattering through the trees.

Elminster straightened slowly. The garden they were in now held a circular bed, bathed in the moonlight, and a ring of trees. Far off in the distance lights twinkled through tree branches, but there were no buildings or watchful elves in sight.

"We're quite alone, Elminster," the Lady Symrustar said softly. "Those jealous males can't follow us here, and my wards keep the inquisitive out of this end of the family gardens. Besides, what I bring to bed is entirely my own affair."

Her eyes flashed as she turned to him again. Somehow her gown had fallen away to her knees, leaving her body bare in the moonlight.

Elminster almost laughed again. Not at her, for she was so beautiful that he could barely control himself, but at his own quirky mind. *She has splendid shoulders*, it was reporting excitedly to him.

That's nice, he told it, and shoved all thought aside.

She stepped forward out of the spreading puddle of silk that had been her gown and came toward him, gems glittering in the moonlight as she moved.

She glided to a stop in front of him. He kissed her eyelids, and then her chin—but at her lips he found his way barred by two raised fingers. "Leave my mouth for last," she said from behind them. "For elves, that's particularly special."

He murmured a wordless assent and reached his head around to her ears. From the way she quivered in his arms, moaned, and stamped her feet, the book had been right.

He licked them gently, teasingly, not hurrying. They had a deliciously spicy taste. Symrustar moaned as El bent to his task, darting his tongue into them. Her fingers raked at his back, drawing blood through his shirt.

"Elminster," she hissed, and then said his name again, rolling it with her tongue as if it was a sacred thing to be chanted. "Prince of a distant land," she added, voice rising in sudden urgency, "show me what it is to know the love of a man."

Her unbound hair swirled around them, its tresses moving at her unspoken bidding, tearing at his clothing like dozens of small, insistent hands. They were circling each other as his shirt was tugged open, moving toward the bed.

Suddenly Symrustar moaned again and said, "I can wait *no longer*. My mouth—Elminster, kiss my mouth!"

Their lips met, and then their tongues. And El faced the attack he'd been expecting.

The bright sparks of a spell seemed to streak through his mind, with her will racing right behind them. Symrustar was seeking to control him, body and mind, to be her puppet, while she raked through his memories to learn all she could . . . especially human magic. El let her race and pierce and rummage while he read what *he* wanted in her bared, open thoughts.

Gods, but she was a ruthless, evil creature. He saw a little obsidian statuette she'd prepared, and how he'd been blamed for what befell. He saw her tresses coiling up to encircle his throat right now, to throttle him if he tried to use any weapon against her. He saw her schemes to entrap any number of elves at court, from the Coronal to a certain rival and suitor, Elandorr Waelvor, to High Court Mage Earynspieir—the other court mage was already hers, ensnared and manipulated, sent to attack someone she dared not go up against: the Srinshee!

Elminster almost struck her then, knowing that with a simple spell he'd have power enough to break her neck like a twig, hair or no hair. Instead he rode the bright flare of his rage into an iron hold on her mind, clamping down until she screamed soundlessly in shock and horror. He cut off her sight into his own memories with brutal haste, leaving her blinded and dazed, and held her that way as he reached out with the power of the scepter her tresses had so deftly plucked away from him, and duplicated the body switch spell the Srinshee had worked on him earlier.

Then he charged back into her mind, overwhelming all semblance of reserve and control she had left, and forcing her mind to stay open and vulnerable, her schemes, memories, and thoughts bared to anyone who touched her. El brought her back to the peak of lust, aching with need. Then he worked the spell, taking himself to where Elandorr Waelvor stood languidly, glass in hand, in the midst of revelry. He whisked the elf back to the hidden bower, thrusting him into Symrustar's arms, his lips to hers, and her mind, with all its treacheries and plans for *him*, bared to him.

El had a last glimpse of her wild eyes staring at Elandorr as she realized who he was and what he was seeing in her mind as she kissed him, nude and two swift paces from her bed. As both elves stiffened and moaned in horror, their mouths and minds mated and open to each other, Elminster broke contact.

He was standing in a softly lit space where Elandorr had been, in the midst of a handful of very startled elves. Others, who wore only bells on their limbs, were dancing in the air overhead, laughing softly. Glasses of wine were soaring up to them like eager wasps, from trays floating in the midst of a group of jaded, bored elves in finery who'd been chatting about the decay of the realm in general—until his sudden appearance.

"You recall Mythanthar's crazy schemes of 'mythals' to shield us all? Why, ther—"

"When *I* was a youth, we didn't indulge in such outrageous displ—"

"Well, what does she expect? Not every young armathor of the realm ca—"

Silence fell as if every throat there had been cut by the same slash of a sword, and all eyes turned to look at one tall figure in their midst.

El faced them, a human male with his clothes in disarray and a scepter in his hand. He was breathing heavily, and there was a trickle of blood at the corner of his mouth where Symrustar had bitten it.

Elves were staring into his eyes in shock and angry recognition. "What did you do to Elandorr?"

"He's slain Elandorr!"

"Blew him to nothingness—just as he did Arandron and Inchel and the others by the pool!"

"'Ware, all! The human *murderer* is among us!"

"Kill him! Kill him now, before he gets more of us!"

"For the honor of House Waelvor!"

"Slay the human dog!"

Swords were flashing out on all sides, or being magically summoned from distant scabbards and chambers to settle into their owner's hands amid spell glows; El spun around and cried out in a loud, deep voice, "Elandorr lives—I've sent him to confront the murderess who slew everyone by the pool!"

"Hear the human!" sneered one elf, blade glittering in his hand. "He must think us elven folk simple indeed, to believe such a claim!"

"I am innocent," Elminster roared, and triggered the scepter. Bright fire burst forth in a ring around him, striking aside blades and hurling their owners back.

"He has a court scepter! Thief!"

"He must've murdered one of the mages to get it! *Kill the human!*"

El shrugged and used the only spell he could, vanishing an instant before half a dozen hurled blades flashed through the spot where he'd stood.

Into the sudden silence, before the groans of disappointment started, one old elf said clearly, "In *my* time, younglings, we held *trials* before we drew our blades! A simple mindtouch will reveal the truth! If we find him guilty, then will be the time for blades!"

"Fall silent, father," another voice snapped. "We've heard quite enough of how things should be done, or were done in the old dawn days. Cannot you see that the human is guilty?"

"Ivran Selorn," another old voice said in outraged tones, "to think that the day would come when I'd hear you speak to your sire like that! Are you not ashamed?"

"No," Ivran said almost savagely, holding up his sword. Its blade glimmered in the spell light, displaying the scrap of cloth transfixed on it. "We have the human," he said in triumph, holding it high for all present to see. "With this, my magic can trace him. We'll hunt him down before sunrise."

ELEVEN
TO HUNT A HUMAN

There is no beast more dangerous to hunt than a man forewarned—
save one: a human mage forewarned.

ANTARN THE SAGE
FROM *THE HIGH HISTORY OF FAERÛNIAN ARCHMAGES MIGHTY*
PUBLISHED CIRCA THE YEAR OF THE STAFF

He found himself standing in utter darkness, but it was darkness that *smelled* right. It was dank, and there was open space all around. He did something with his mind, and the scepter in his hand blossomed into a soft green radiance.

The chamber at the heart of Castle Dlardrageth was empty. Only an area of cracked and melted rubble—he'd have to ask the Lady Oluevaera about that when the chance befell—remained to show that he and the Srinshee had been here. She'd taken the Coronal elsewhere.

Something flashed in the gloom above him and moaned softly past, swooping toward the far end of the room. El smiled. Hello, ghosts.

He changed the light of the scepter to the purple-white glow that outlined magic. There! She *had* left it!

Invisible inside three nested spheres of magical concealment, floating in the air just low enough for him to reach, a little way along one wall, hung his spellbook. El smiled, said "Oluevaera" aloud as he touched the outermost sphere, and watched it melt silently away. The second descended to his hand, and he spoke the Srinshee's real name again—and a third time. When the last sphere melted away, the book fell into his hands.

El made the scepter glow green again, thrust it between two stones of the wall as high as he could reach, and sat down under its radiance to study his spells. If he was going to be hunted by every bloodthirsty young blood of Cormanthor, 'twas best to have a full roster of ready magic to call upon.

"Tidings grow worse, Revered Lord." Uldreiyn Starym's voice was grave.

Lord Eltargrim looked up. "And how might they do that?" he asked quietly.

"Sixty-three blades were broken before me today." His lips tightened in what might have been the wry beginnings of a smile. "That I know of, thus far."

The burly senior archmage of the Starym family ran a weary hand through his thinning white hair and replied, "Word comes from the Hallows that the human armathor has worked deadly magic there, causing a blast that destroyed the Narnpool and at least a dozen young lords and warriors who were gathered there. Moreover, the Lady Symrustar and the Lord Elandorr have both vanished, and the heir of House Waelvor was snatched by spells out of the midst of folk he was speaking with, to be replaced upon the instant by the human—who protested his innocence but was wielding a court scepter. When menaced by the swords of some of the revelers he teleported away. None know where he is now, but some of the warriors are hunting him with magic."

In the shadows around the table a light-haired head snapped up, eyes catching fire. "My cousin was with the Lord Elminster. They were strolling together when they left us!"

"Gently," the High Court Mage Earynspieir said from beside Amaranthae, putting a soothing hand on her arm. "They could well have parted before these troubles began."

"I know Symma," she said, turning to him, "and she planned to—to . . ." She blushed and looked away, biting her lip.

"To take the human lord to bed, in the private part of the Auglamyr gardens?" the Srinshee asked quietly. Amaranthae stiffened, and the tiny sorceress added gently, "Don't bother to act scandalized, girl: half Cormanthor knows about her career."

"We also know something of the power of Symrustar's magic," Naeryndam Alastrarra said thoughtfully. "In fact, probably far more than she desires we know or suspect. I doubt the human lord has spells enough to do her harm, if they were in her bower, with all the magic she can call to hand there. If the hunt mounted by these young fire brains leads them hence, *they* might be in danger."

Amaranthae turned her head to look at the old mage, white to the lips. "Do you elders know *everything?*"

"Enough to keep ourselves entertained," the Srinshee said dryly, and Uldreiyn Starym nodded.

" 'Tis a common mistake of the young and vigorous," he calmly told the tabletop, "to believe their elders have forgotten to see, or think, or remember things—when what we've really forgotten to do is scare younglings into respecting us, thoroughly and often."

The Lady Amaranthae moaned aloud, anxious and miserable. "Symma could be dead," she whispered, an instant before the High Court Mage gathered her in his arms and said soothingly, "We shall go to the gardens now, to see for ourselves."

"Yet if she's unharmed, she'll be *furious* at our intrusion," Amaranthae protested.

The Coronal looked up. "Tell her the Coronal ordered you to check on her safety, and let her bring her fury to *me.*" He smiled a little sadly and added, "Where she's likely to become lost in the crowd of clamoring complainants."

Lord Earynspieir silently thanked the old ruler with his eyes as he rose and led the distraught Lady Auglamyr away.

Lord Starym said heavily, "The murders done by the human in our midst—or perceived by most Cormanthans to be done by him, which at present holds out to us the same trouble—imperils your plan, Revered Lord, to open the city to other races. You know, Lord, as few can, how deeply my sister Ildilyntra felt against this Opening. We of House Starym still oppose it. By all of our gods, I beseech you, don't drive us into doing so with force."

"Lord Uldreiyn, I respect your counsel," the Coronal said softly, "as I have always done. You are the senior archmage of your House, one of the mightiest sorcerers in all Faerûn. Yet does that make you mighty enough to withstand the swarming vigor of the most greed-goaded humans, whose magic grows apace with each passing year? I still believe—and I urge you to think long and hard upon this, to see if you really can seize to, and hold, any other conclusion— that we must deal with humankind on our terms now, or be overwhelmed and slaughtered by men storming our gates in a century or so."

"I shall think upon this," the Starym archmage said, bowing his head, "again. Yet I have done so before, and not reached the same conclusion as you did. Can it not be that a Coronal might be mistaken?"

"Of course I can be wrong," Eltargrim said with a sigh. "I've been wrong many times before. Yet I know more of the world beyond our forest than any other Cormanthan—save this young human lad, of course. I see forces stirring that to most senior Cormyth, as well as to our youth, seem mere fancies. How often in the past few moons have I heard voices at court saying, 'Oh, but humans could never do *that!*' What do they think humans are, lumps of stone? From time to time men hold something they call a magefair—"

"*Selling* magic? Like a sort of bazaar?" The Starym's lips curled in disbelief and distaste.

"More like a House-gathering attended by many mages: humans, gnomes, halfbloods, and even elves from other lands than ours," the Coronal explained, "though I believe some scrolls and rare magical components do change hands. But the burden of my song is this: at the last magefair I saw, in my days as a far-wandering warrior, two human wizards engaged in a duel. The spells they hurled fell far short of our High Magic, 'tis true. But they would also have awed and shamed most sorcerers of Cormanthor! 'Tis *always* a mistake to dismiss humans."

"All those of House Alastrarra would, I believe, support you on that," Naeryndam put in. "The human Elminster wore the kiira more ably than our heir has yet managed to. I mean no slur upon Ornthalas, who will grow to command it, I'm sure, as ably as did Iymbryl before him ... merely that the human was swiftly capable."

"Too capable, if all these reports of deaths are true," Uldreiyn murmured. "Very well, we shall continue to disagree ami—"

The tabletop glowed with a sudden, sparkling radiance that was laced with the soft, calling notes of a distant horn. Lord Starym stared down at it.

"My herald approaches," the Coronal explained. "When wards are raised, her passage awakens such a warning."

The Starym archmage frowned. "'Her'?" he asked. "But sur—"

The door of the chamber opened by itself, admitting a cloud of swirling flames of the palest green and white. It rose and thinned as Lord Uldreiyn stared at it, dwindling swiftly into a flickering death to reveal at its heart an elven lady who wore a helm and a mottled gray cloak. "Hail, great Coronal," she said in greeting.

"What news, Lady Herald?"

"The heir of House Echorn has been found dead atop Druindar's Rock— slain in spell-battle, 'tis thought," the herald said gravely. "House Echorn beseeches you to allow them vengeance."

The Coronal's lips thinned. "On whom?"

"The human armathor Elminster of Athalantar, slayer of Delmuth Echorn."

The Coronal slapped the table. "He's a lone human, not an elemental whirlwind! How could he deal death in the backlands and in the Hallows, too?"

"Perhaps," Lord Uldreiyn told the tabletop, "being a human, he's swiftly capable."

As Naeryndam Alastrarra gave him a disgusted look, the Srinshee surprised them all by saying, "Delmuth's own spell slew him. I farscryed the fray; he lured Elminster from his studies and sought to slay the human, who worked a magic that returned Delmuth's attacks upon his own head. Knowing this, the Echorn made the mistake of trusting in his own mantle, and proceeded with his attack. Elminster pleaded with him to make peace, but was rebuffed. There is no fault to avenge; Delmuth died through Delmuth's scheme and Delmuth's hurled spell."

"An unheralded human? Defeat an heir of one of the oldest Houses of the realm?" Uldreiyn Starym was clearly shocked. He stared at the Srinshee in disbelief, but when she merely shrugged, he shook his head and said finally, "All the more reason to stop human intrusions now."

"What answer shall I take back to House Echorn?" the herald asked.

"That Delmuth was responsible for his own death," the Coronal replied, "and that this has been attested to by a senior archmage of the realm, but that I shall investigate further."

The Lady Herald went to one knee, called up her whirling flames about herself once more, and went out.

"When you do catch this Elminster, his brains may run like wax merely from all the truth-scrying," Lord Uldreiyn observed.

"If the young bloods leave us enough of him to do *anything* with," Naeryndam replied.

The Starym smiled and shrugged. "When," he asked the Coronal, "did you acquire a Lady Herald? I thought Mlartlar was herald of Cormanthor."

"He was," the Coronal said grimly, "until he thought himself a better swordsman than his Coronal. Your House is not the only one opposed to my plan of Opening, Lord Staryrn."

"So where did you find *her?*" Uldreiyn asked quietly. "With all due respect, the office of herald has always been held by one of the senior families of the realm."

"The herald of Cormanthor," the Srinshee told Uldreiyn's favorite spot on the tabletop, "must bear foremost loyalty to the Coronal—a quality unattainable today, it seems, in the three Houses who hold themselves to be senior in the realm."

"I resent that," the Lord Starym said softly, his face going pale.

"Three of the People were approached," the Srinshee told him firmly. "Two declined, one very rudely. The third—Glarald, of your House, Lord—accepted, and was tested. What we found in his mind is a matter between himself and us, but when he knew we'd learned it, he tried to strike down myself and Lord Earynspieir with spells."

"*Glarald?*" Uldreiyn Starym's voice was flat with disbelief.

"Yes, Uldreiyn: Glarald of the easy smiles. Do you know how he hoped to defeat us and deceive us in the first place? He took one of the forbidden enchantments from the tomb of Felaern Starym, and altered it to control not merely wands and scepters from afar—such as your own storm scepter, which I'm afraid was destroyed in our dispute—but minds. The minds of two unicorns and one young sorceress of House Dree."

Lord Starym's face was ashen now. "I—I can scarce believe . . . his beloved, Alais?"

"I doubt his affections for her ran all that deep," the Srinshee told him dryly, "but he did dally with her long enough to work a blood spell—another forbidden magic, of course—and so enthrall her to cast spells at his bidding. The Lady Aubaudameira Dree, or 'Alais,' as you know her, attacked the Lord Earynspieir in the midst of our investigation."

The Starym lord shook his head in dumbfounded disbelief. The Coronal and Naeryndam both nodded silent confirmation of the words of the sorceress.

"Her spells were formidable," the Srinshee continued. "Our High Court Mage owes his life to my magic. As does Glarald, for Alais wasn't pleased with him after I broke his thrall. 'Twas the unicorns that did it; once my spells shook him, he couldn't control their restive natures, and his entire linkage collapsed. So it was that the Coronal gained a new Lady Herald."

"That was Alais?" Lord Uldreiyn breathed, shaking his head and gesturing at the door whence the Herald had departed. "But she was much more—ah . . .'"

"Lushly curved than our Lady Herald?" the Srinshee finished his question crisply. "Indeed. You saw her when she was already in thrall, and had been forced to change her body to please Glarald's tastes."

The Starym lord closed his eyes and shook his head again, as if to will away this unwelcome news. "Does Glarald yet live?" he asked slowly.

"He does," the Coronal said gravely. "Though wounded deeply in his wits. The unicorns were not gentle, and he seized upon one of the scepters when his control was already failing, and sought to turn it on them; they hurled its effects back upon him. He is currently in hiding, wrestling with his shame, at Thurdan's Tree at the southern edge of the realm."

"But you've not told me of this!" Lord Uldreiyn snapped. "Wh—"

"Hold!" the Srinshee snapped, just as fiercely. His mouth dropped open in surprise.

"I've had quite enough, Lord," she told him in controlled tones, "of the great Houses of the realm snarling about their rights—in this case, privacy of minds and of the doings of their individuals—whenever Coronal or Court require something of them . . . and then expecting us to break those rights whenever it personally suits them. So we are not to pry into your doings, my lord, or those of your warriors or steeds or cats—but we are to reveal the doings of another of your House to you? He's not your son or heir, and if he chooses not to confide in you himself, that—as you and speakers from House Echorn and House Waelvor have so cuttingly reminded us, on several occasions—is none of *our* affair."

Uldreiyn sat staring at her, stunned.

"You," the Srinshee went on, "have been almost panting to ask me about the disappearance of my wrinkles since first we met this even, and cudgeling your wits for a way to politely slide a query into our converse, so that you don't have to ask me directly. You know it is none of your affair. You respect the rule, and expect us to respect it, too, until our observance inconveniences you, whereupon you demand we break it. And yet you wonder why the Court regards the three senior Houses in particular, and all of the important Houses en masse, as foes."

The Starym lord blinked at her, sighed, and sat back. "I-I cannot discount your words, nor parry them," he said heavily. "In this, we are guilty."

"As for Glarald's schemes—in particular, his ambitious, creative, and wholly forbidden use of magic," the Srinshee went on inexorably, "this is the sort of thing our young bloods are up to, My Lord Uldreiyn, while you and your kith sit around decrying our dreams of Opening, and clinging to false notions of the purity and noble nature of our People."

"Do you want to be toppled from within, great Lord, or stormed from without?" Naeryndam Alastrarra asked mildly, tracing a circle on the part of the table-top that had listened so attentively to Uldreiyn earlier.

The Lord Starym glared at him, but then sighed and said, "I'm almost convinced, listening to you three, that the elder Houses of the realm are its chief villains and peril. Almost. The fact remains that you, Revered Lord, allowed a human into our midst, here in the very heart of the realm—and since his arrival we have seen death upon death in a wave of violence unmatched since the last orc horde was foolish enough to test our borders. What are you going to do about it before there are *more* deaths?"

"There is almost nothing I can do before more deaths occur," the Coronal told him sadly. "The fire brains who were at the revel when Elandorr disappeared are hunting the human as we speak. If they find him, *someone* will find death, too."

"And that death will, I fear, be laid at your door," said Uldreiyn Starym. "With the others."

Eltargrim nodded. "That, my lord," he said wearily, "is what it means to be Coronal of Cormanthor. Sometimes I think the elder Houses of the realm forget that."

One of the elves came to a halt so swiftly that his flowing hair swung out in front of him like two tusks. "That's the Ghost Castle of Dlardrageth!"

"And so?" Ivran Selorn asked coolly. "Afraid of ghosts, are we?"

Yet they had stopped, and some of the young bloods were looking at Ivran uneasily.

"My sire told me it bears a terrible curse," Tlannatar Wrathtree said reluctantly, "bringing ill luck—and miscast magics—upon any who enter."

"The ghosts that lurk there," another elf put in, "can claw you no matter what blade or spell you use against them."

"What utter leaf-rotting lies!" Ivran laughed. "Why, Ylyndar Starscatter brought his ladies here for loving six summers running. Who'd do that if the ghosts were a bother?"

"Aye, but Ylyndar's one of the most wild-witted mages in all Cormanthor! He even believes in old Mythanthar's mythals! And didn't one of his ladies try to eat her own hand?"

Ivran made a rude sound. "As if that has anything to do with yon castle!" He laughed again, tossed his blade in the air and caught it, and added, "Well, you weak-knees can please yourselves, but I'm going to cut me a little human into pieces I can present to His High Fool-wits the Coronal, and House Waelvor, and hang up in the Selorn trophy lodge!"

He set off at a run again, waving his sword around his head and hooting. After a few moments of uncertain hesitation, Tlannator followed, and two others trotted off on his heels. Another pair of elves looked at each other, shrugged, and followed more cautiously. That left three. They exchanged looks, shrugged, and followed.

Elminster looked up sharply. A metal sword blade ringing off stone has a particular sound. Distinctive enough to make a hunted human rise, close his spellbook, and stand listening intently. Then he smiled. One elf hissing curses at another has a distinctive sound too.

He tried to remember what the Srinshee had told him about the layout of this place. The castle was . . . nothing, beyond the news that this chamber was "at its heart." Hmm. The elves hunting him could be three breaths away, or an hour's hard climbing and peering. That they were hunting him was certain; why else would one of them want another to keep quiet?

El stood there, spellbook under his arm, thinking hard. He could translocate away—once—by calling on the scepter, but he hadn't had a chance to regain his own teleport spell yet. The only place in Cormanthor he could think of to go was the Vault of Ages, and who knew what defenses it would have to prevent thieves just teleporting in and out? To hide would be best. The more blood that ended up on his hands, the harder for his friends here to stay his friends, to let him stay, and to carry out whatever work Mystra had planned for him. Agile, alert elves, however, weren't the easiest folk to hide from. Mystra had given him one slaying spell, not a dozen. He'd have to plunge into the midst of a roused and ready band of human-hunters, to touch one and slay.

A ghostly form swooped past him, trailing a faint echoing sound that might have been wild laughter, and the last prince of Athalántar grinned suddenly. Of course! Take ghost form!

He took two quick steps to see where the ghost disappeared to this time, and was rewarded: high up on one wall was a crevice. Far too small for him, but not too small for a spellbook.

If he cast the spell as Myrjala had shown him, he could shift back and forth between solid and wraithlike form for brief periods—becoming his solid, normal self for no more than nine breaths at a time, or less. Longer would break the spell, and his fourth time becoming solid would also end the magic.

El became a flitting shadow and soared aloft. As he rose to the crevice, there came a scuffing sound from somewhere nearby, as if a boot had slipped on rock. Evidently he hadn't any time to waste.

Something dark but pale-faced rushed out of the gloom at him, seemingly enraged. El almost tumbled and fell in fright, but then ducked aside. The ghost looped once, impressively, then scudded on out of sight around a corner, heading for other rooms. Evidently the Dlardrageth ghosts liked wraithlike intruders even less than solid mortals.

Reaching the crevice, El drifted inside. It opened into a small, cramped room—the remnants of a much larger chamber whose roof had long ago collapsed. There were bones under the rubble here, elven bones, and El doubted the ghosts would leave him alone if he took up residence in here for long. Still, he hadn't much choice. As he peered around, the air seemed to fill with a faint purplish haze. What was it? Magic, aye, but what?

Whatever it was, he felt no different, and was still a weightless flying shadow. He drifted to the other end of the little room.

Beyond its far wall, through the socket holes that had once held beams, a ghost could reach another huge chamber—this one open to the sky, and holding the first cautious elf, scrambling in over some rubble with sword raised. Ivran Selorn, if El's memory served him rightly; a blood-hungry youngling.

There was a jagged hole at one end of the collapsed room through which he could plunge, if he felt like dying on broken stones below. Through it, El could see the route that linked the open chamber where Ivran was, and the room where he'd been studying. The hole opened onto a cascade of rubble that spilled down into a round room once at the base of a now-fallen tower. A passage ran out of Ivran's room into an antechamber, and thence through the tower room. From there a narrow, rubble-choked passage linked up with the room El's spellbook still lay in. The route was not a long one, and Ivran—bold and eager—was moving swiftly.

That left a certain Athalantan boy very little time. El went to his knees in the room with the bones, turned solid, and yanked down his breeches.

His one legacy of his thieving days was what he always wore under his clothes: a long, thin waxed black cord, wound round and round his midriff.

He uncoiled it now and hurled most of it out the crevice, tying its other end to the splintered end of a ceiling beam in the little room with the bones. Holding his breeches up with one hand, El became a wraith again, and returned to his spellbook.

As he became solid and hastily tied the free end of the cord around and around the book, the stealthy sounds coming along the passages told him that Ivran and the other searchers were already entering the tower room: a few paces in the right direction and they'd be able to see him here, feverishly tying a length of cord around a book with his pants around his ankles.

He became a wraith again and almost leaped into the air, soaring up and into the crevice just as fast as he could fly.

Back in the room with the bones, El turned solid once more and hauled on his cord, gasping in his haste. He didn't have long to work before he'd break the magic, so the moment the spellbook was safely up in the crevice, the dust of its passage still drifting out from the wall in a betraying cloud, he had his breeches belted and was a ghostly shadow again, leaving the book and the tangle of cord to deal with later.

As a thing of gray emptiness, he peered out of the crevice. Ivran was just entering the chamber where he'd been studying. The elf had noticed the dust drifting down. El pulled in his shadowy head hastily before any elf might look up and see him, and floated in the darkness, trying to think what to do next. The elves would probably determine that, of course, by what they did.

A moment later, El was spinning in the collapsed room, shaking and chilled, and the ghost that had caused his upset by rushing through him—the *real* ghost—was moaning its way back down into the chamber full of elves.

There were shouts from below, and the flash of a spell. El smiled grimly and set forth from the beam holes into the other chamber, to drift around the castle and learn just what he was facing.

His discoveries were not heartening. The castle was an impressive ruin, but it was still a ruin. The only unblocked well was in the tower room he'd seen already. No less than nine elves, with swords drawn and an unknown number of spells up their sleeves, were prowling through the once-splendid fortress of the Dlardrageth. At least three ghosts were following them like shadowy bats, ducking and diving but unable to do any real harm.

The real problem, however, were the four elven mages sitting together on a hill not far from the ruin, and the mighty glamer they'd cast over the entire area. It was the source of the haze that had appeared when he'd entered the little room, and the castle was now completely surrounded by it.

El drifted back inside, sought the little room, and turned solid again. His shoulder-blades settled into hard rubble, and he sighed as quietly as he could; his ghost form was gone for good now.

Drawing the scepter from his belt, he thrust it up into the air, and cautiously awakened its powers. The tingling that ran along his fingers told him that the elves were using magic that could detect any use of the scepter something a shout from somewhere below underscored immediately—but the scepter did what he needed it to do. In storing a duplicate of the purplish field enveloping the castle, it told El what the glamer was: a ward field that would twist a teleport spell or any other translocational magic into ravaging fire *inside* the body of the teleport-spell caster.

He was trapped in the castle unless he could slip out on foot or memorize another ghost-shape spell—or *fight* his way out on foot, through all those eager elven swordsmen, to run straight into the waiting spells of those four mages. All of them were ready for the elusive human to appear, eager to destroy him.

El considered what to do next. The scepter was off and in his belt again, and he was lying on his back in near-darkness, amid rubble, crumbling elven bones, and the tangles of a cord tied to his spellbook, with the sagging wreckage of a collapsed ceiling inches from his nose. The exploring elves were back in the room he'd been studying in just below him, now, speculating aloud about where he might be hiding, and stirring around with their blades in the rubble. The use of the scepter had told them he was very near; soon enough they'd think of digging . . . or climbing.

"Mystra," Elminster breathed, closing his eyes, "aid me now. There are too many of them, too much magic; if I seek battle now, many will die. What should I do? Guide me, Great Lady of Mysteries, that I set no foot wrong in this journey to serve ye."

Was it his imagination, or was he floating now, rising an inch or so above the rubble? His prayer seemed to be rolling out into vast, dark distances in his mind—and something black seemed to be coming back to him out of that void, spinning end over end as it approached. Something smooth, glossy, and small, tumbling—the kiira! The lore-gem of House Alastrarra!

Wasn't it firmly on the brow of Ornthalas Alastrarra right now? It raced right at him, growing to impossible size, enveloping him. He was spiraling around its dark interior, now, racing along the inside of its curves. This must be his memory of the kiira, with its sea of memories.

Oh dear Mystra, preserve me! That thought made him see a rushing wave of chaos—ghostly and imperfect, mind-echoes of what he recalled from the gem now torn from him, but plunging at him all the same. He tried to turn and run, but no matter how hard he struggled, everywhere he ran was *toward* the rushing wave of memories. It was almost upon him—it broke over him!

"That babbling—that's human talk! He must be up there somewhere!" The words were elvish; deep, booming echoes that seemed to come from all around him.

In the shrieking, blinding chaos that followed those deafening words Elminster Aumar spat blood from nose and mouth and eyes and ears, and went down, drifting, into dark oblivion . . .

TWELVE
THE STAG AT BAY

The most dangerous moment in the hunt is when the stag turns, at bay, to trade his life for as many hunters as he can. Elven magic customarily turns such moments into mere glimpses of magnificent futility. But what would such moments be, I wonder, if the stag had strong magic, too?

SHALHEIRA TALANDREN, HIGH ELVEN BARD OF SUMMERSTAR
from *SILVER BLADES AND SUMMER NIGHTS:*
AN INFORMAL BUT TRUE HISTORY OF CORMANTHOR
PUBLISHED IN THE YEAR OF THE HARP

I t's coming for me! *Blast* it!"
The voice was elven and terrified; it drew Elminster up out of floating darkness soaked in sweat, to find himself still lying in the little room with the elven bones.

There was a roar of flame off to his right, and a stabbing tongue of fire licked the collapsed ceiling above his nose for one scorching moment. El narrowed his eyes to slits, trying to see; one side of his face felt blistered.

When he trusted his sight again, he looked in that direction. The fire was gone. Three soft globes of radiance were drifting beyond the crevice, high in the air of the room where he'd been studying. By their light he could see the elf who'd cried out. He was standing on empty air, sword in hand, near his crevice. Levitating, not flying freely. Swooping around him, just out of reach of his vainly slashing and stabbing blade, was one of the Dlardrageth ghosts; the fire spell hurled from below had failed to destroy it.

If common or easily crafted spells could fell the ghostly remnants of House Dlardrageth, of course, they'd have all been destroyed long ago, and some ambitious fledgling House would be dwelling in this castle now. There was little chance any of the young elves here today had the power to destroy a Dlardrageth ghost.

On the other hand, the swooping, flitting ghost could probably do little more than frighten living elves—and one of those elves was within easy distance of hurling a deadly spell at Elminster, even if the opening between them was too small to allow any elf to enter.

El reached out and cautiously, quietly picked up his spellbook. He'd just have to drag the tangle of cord attached to it around with him for now, as he crept as far along this room as he could, away from the crevice.

Though he felt like he'd been torn apart and been put back together again, piece by agonizing piece, Mystra had come to his aid. She'd dragged him through a thousand tangled Alastrarran half-memories to what his mage's mind had remembered clearly, at the very depths of his recall: the spells the lore-gem had held.

There'd been one he'd dared not use; its price was too high. Empowering it would strip three of the most powerful spells from his memory and drain something from the scepter as well . . . but now it was needful he do so.

With a sigh, Elminster did what had to be done, shuddering silently as sparks seemed to wash and flow through his mind, stripping spells away. Thankfully, he did not have to awaken the scepter again to drain power from it. When the new spell shone bright and ready within him, El found the deepest niche he could, in a far corner of the collapsed room, and wedged his precious spellbook into it. Taking the cord he'd stripped from his tome, he checked that its other end was still secure about the splintered stub of the ceiling beam, tossed its coils down the cascade of stones into the tower room, and slipped down it as quietly as he could.

Inevitably stones rolled and bounced, but the levitating elf was snarling so much in his battle with the ghost that no one heard the little clatterings. El reached the bottom, rolled up cord until he had a substantial bundle, tied it to itself to keep the mass together, and threw the thing back up the fallen rocks as high and far as he could, hoping it'd not be seen.

Well, not without someone flying, or a very bright light, he judged, studying it. Drawing a deep breath, he started his first casting: a simple shielding, like he'd used against Delmuth. It was time to face Ivran's merry band of blood hunters.

His casting warned the elves that magic was being unleashed, of course, and there was an immediate, excited roar from the room they'd been searching. They'd be coming along the narrow passage soon; it was time to greet them.

Elminster showed himself at the mouth of that passage just long enough to make sure of one thing: the levitating elf wasn't trying to find any ceiling route anywhere, but was descending as fast as he could. Good. El gave the foremost elf a merry wave, and waited.

"He waved at me!" that elf said anxiously, and stopped.

The one behind him—Tlannatar Wrathtree, as it happened—gave him a nudge with the flat of his sword, and snarled, "Go on!"

The elf hesitated. El gave him a grin that must have showed every tooth he possessed, and made an almost amorous beckoning gesture.

The elf stopped, and started to scramble back. "He—"

"I don't *care!*" Ivran barked, from the room behind. "I don't care if he's grown dwarven-dunged gossamer wings! *Move!*"

"Go on!" Tlannatar added, giving another shove with his sword. He did not use the flat this time.

The less-than-brave elf shrieked and stumbled hastily ahead. El took one last glance down that passage—it was *so* tempting to hurl a lightning bolt now, but one of them was sure to have a mantle that would reflect such things—and backed away. He went across the tower room to its other passage, to stand within its opening. Almost none of these noble Cormanthans seemed to have bows;

they left that weapon to their common warriors, thank Mystra. Or Corellon. Or Solonor Thelandira, the hunting god. Or whomever.

Still, he'd have to time this perfectly; he'd committed himself now, and would only get one chance. He waited, smiling grimly, for Tlannatar as well as the fearful elf in the lead to scramble out into the tower room and see him before he turned and sprinted down the linking passages, hurrying for the shattered chamber through which the hunters had first entered the castle.

"If this doesn't work, Mystra," he remarked pleasantly, as he ran, "you'll have to send someone else into Cormanthor to be your Chosen. If you want to be gentle on whoever that is, select an elf, hmm?"

Mystra gave no sign that she'd heard, but by then El was out into the shattered chamber, and heading for a rock pile at its center. The elves, running fast, weren't far behind.

El found his spot and spun to face them, assuming an anxious expression and raising his hands as if uncertain which spell to hurl. The blood hunters came racing into the chamber, waving their blades, and howled their way to a halt.

The elf who'd been first in the narrow passage said uncertainly, "This doesn't look right—he wasn't so fearful before. This must be a tr—"

"Silence!" Ivran Selorn snarled, shoving the speaker aside. The fearful elf slipped on fallen stones and almost fell, but Ivran paid no attention. It was his moment of glory; he was swaggering toward Elminster with leisurely grace, almost dancing on the tips of his toes as he came. "So, human rat," he sneered, "cornered at last, are you?"

"You are," Elminster agreed with a smile. The fearful elf raised a fresh cry of alarm, but Ivran hissed, "*Be still!*" at him, and then turned back to favor Elminster with a mirthless smile.

"You hairy barbarians think yourselves clever," he remarked, eyes glittering, "and you are—too clever. Unfortunately, in the half-witted, cleverness breeds insolence. You've certainly shown us ample supplies of that, being insolent enough to think you can slaughter the heirs of no less than *ten* Houses of Cormanthor— eleven, if we count Alastrarra, whose lore-gem you wore when you came trotting into our midst; who's to say you didn't murder Iymbryl to get it?—and pay no price. Some who hold the rank of armathor serve Cormanthor diligently all their lives and slay fewer foes than you have already."

With exaggerated apparent surprise, Ivran Selorn looked around at his companions, and then back to Elminster. "See? There are many more, here. What a splendid opportunity to add to your score! Why do you not attack? Are you scared, perhaps?"

Elminster lifted his lips in a half-smile. "Violence has never been Mystra's way."

"Oh, so?" Ivran said, his voice high and incredulous. "What then was that blast by the pool? A natural occurrence, perhaps?"

With a tight, wolfish smile, he motioned the other elves to encircle Elminster; keeping a safe distance, they did so, silently and smiling. Then the leader of these blood hunters turned back to his quarry and said, "Let me tell you the heirs you've slain, oh most mighty of armathors: Waelvor, and a bloody harvest by the pool: Yeschant, Amarthen, Ibryiil, Gwaelon, Tassarion, Ortauré, Bellas, and, I hear from our mages, Echorn and Auglamyr, too!"

Ivran advanced again, slowly, tossing his long, slim blade into the air and catching it in a fluid, restless juggling that El knew meant he'd throw it soon. "Just one of those heirs—to say nothing of the dozen or so servants and house blades you've felled, along the way—would be more than enough to buy your death, human. Just one! So now we have you at last, and face the difficult problem of how to fittingly slay you ten times over . . . or should it be eleven?"

Ivran came still closer. "Two of the gallants you slew were close friends of mine. And all of us here are saddened by the loss of the Lady Symrustar, whose promise has warmed us all for three seasons now. You took these from us, human worm. Have you anything futile to say on your own behalf? Something to entertain us as we *hack you down?!*"

As he screamed these last words, Ivran charged, hurling his blade in a silvery blur. It was meant to slash El's hand and ruin any spellcasting, before the other elves—leaping in from all sides now—reached him.

Smiling grimly, Elminster worked the spell, and became a rising, roiling column of white sparks. Charging elves crashed through him and into each other, blades biting deep. Elves arched in agony, and screamed, or coughed around the hilts of deeply driven blades, and poured out their blood upon the stones.

The whirling column of sparks began to drift away, heading for the passage El had entered by. Snarling and panting, with two blades that were not his standing out of his body, Ivran cried, "Slay the human! Use the swordpoint spell!"

His last word was choked off by blood bubbling forth, and an elf who streamed blood from a slash on his forehead—the one who'd been so fearful, earlier—hastened to the staggering Ivran, his hands glowing with healing magic.

Tlannatar Wrathtree followed his leader's bidding, shouting, "I have the spell! Throw your blades *up!*"

Obediently those elves who still could hurled swords and daggers into the air above their heads. The spell, which was making blue-white stars of force flare and twinkle around Tlannatar's hands, snared those hurled blades and sent them across the chamber in a deadly stream, point-first.

The whirling white column of sparks and light paused at the entrance to the passage, and the hurled blades swerved in their flight to go around it, picking up speed, and then spray out back across the room like a deadly hail of darts, flung in random directions. Tlannatar cried out as one took him in the ear, and toppled over with his mouth still open; it would gape, now, forever. Ivran, held up by his healer, took one in the throat and spat blood at the ceiling in a last, dying stream, and another elf fell, far across the room, with a sword right through him. He took two staggering steps toward the rock pile he'd been seeking as cover, then collapsed across it, and did not move again. When the column that had been the human armathor whirled away down the passage and silence fell over the room, the fearful elf looked around. Of them all, only he still stood, though someone was moaning and moving feebly by one wall.

Dazed by grief, he stumbled in that direction, hoping the one healing spell he had left would be enough. By the time he got there, the body was still and silent. He shook it and whispered its name, but life had fled.

"How many of us," he asked the empty room in a trembling voice, "does it take to buy the life of one human? Father Corellon! *How many?*"

Raw power was surging through Elminster—more than he'd ever known outside Mystra's embrace—and he was feeling stronger, warmer, and mightier by the second. As he spun, the purple-hued glamer spun by the mages was being sucked down into him, giving him its energy . . . wild, unleashed, and wonderful!

Laughing uncontrollably, El felt himself growing taller and brighter, as he rose from the shattered base of the fallen tower.

He was conscious of the four mages scrambling up and shouting in fear. He spun in their direction, drunk with power, hungry to slay, and destroy, and—

The mages were casting something in unison. El leaned toward them, trying to get there before they could flee, or do whatever else they were trying to do, but his spinning form couldn't hurry. He tried to bend over, to sweep at them, but couldn't hold the shape, as his spinning whirled him upright again. He was closing on them now, he was—

Too late. The four elves swept their hands down by their sides—hands that trailed fire—and stood watching him expectantly. They were not fleeing or even looking alarmed.

An instant later, Faerûn exploded, and El felt himself being wrenched apart and hurled in all directions, like dry grass spun away by a gale wind. "Mystra!" he cried, or tried to, but there was nothing but the roaring and the light, and he was falling . . . many of him were falling, onto many treetops . . .

"And then what happened?" High Court Mage Earynspieir's voice was thin with anger and exasperation. Why, oh Corellon tell me why, did the younger bloods of the realm have to be such bloodthirsty *fools?*

The trembling elven mage facing him started to cry, and went to his knees, pleading for his life.

"Oh, get *up,*" Lord Earynspieir said disgustedly. "It's done, *now.* You're sure the human is dead?"

"We blasted him to nothing, L-lord," one of the other mages blurted out. "I've been scrying for magic use and invisible creatures since then, and have seen no evidence of either."

Earynspieir nodded almost absently. "Who survived, out of the whole band that went in there?"

"Rotheloe Tyrneladhelu, Lord. He—he bears no wound, but hasn't stopped crying yet. He may not be well in his wits."

"So we have eight dead and a ninth suffering," the High Court Mage said coldly, "and you four unhurt and triumphant." He looked at the ruined castle. "And no body of the foe, to be sure he is dead. Truly, a great victory."

"Well, it *was!*" the fourth mage shouted, erupting in sudden fury. "I didn't see you here, standing boot-to-boot with us, hurling spells at the Heirslayer! He came boiling up out of that castle like some sort of god, a deadly column of fire and sparks a hundred feet high and more, spitting off spells in all directions! Most would've fled, I swear—but we four stood and kept our calm and took him down! And"—he looked around at all of the silent, somber faces around him, court mages and sorceresses and guards, these last all heroes of earlier wars, their aged faces expressionless, and finished lamely—"and I'm proud of what we did."

"I gathered that," Earynspieir said dryly. "Sylmae? Holone? Truth-scry these four . . . and Tyrneladhelu, to see how much of a wreck his mind is. We need to know the truth, not how windy their boasting can be." He turned away as the sorceresses nodded.

As the sorceresses advanced, one of the mages raised his hands. Red rings of fire encircled them, and he said warningly, "Keep back, wenches."

Sylmae's mouth crooked. "You'll look rather less handsome wearing those flame hoops on your backside, puppy. Dispense with this nonsense, or in the next three paces or so Holone and I'll grow weary of it."

"You *dare* to truth-scry *me?* The heir of a House?"

Sylmae shrugged. "Of course. In this, we act with the Coronal's authority."

"What authority?" the mage sneered as he retreated a step, the flamehoops still blazing about his hands. "The whole realm knows that the Coronal's gone mad!"

The High Court Mage turned around slowly, a slim but menacing figure in his black robe, and said gravely, "After your behind eats those flame hoops you're so fond of, Selgauth Cathdeiryn, and you've been thoroughly truth-scryed, you will be conducted under guard to the Coronal. You will then be free to make that observation to our Revered Lord himself. If you're feeling a trifle more prudent than at present, you *may* be wise enough to do so politely."

Galan Goadulphyn looked at the surface of the pool one last time, and sighed. Had he been less proud, there might have been tears, but he was a warrior of Cormanthor, not one of these weak-knees, the prancing and overperfumed lispers whom the high noble Houses of the realm were pleased to call heirs. He was like stone, or old treeroot. He would endure without complaint and rise again. Someday.

The picture the pool displayed was not inspiring. His face was a mask of old, dried blood, the fine line of his jaw marred where a flap of torn skin had bonded in its dangling state, making his chin square as a human's. The tip of one ear was missing, and his hair was as matted as a dead spider's legs, much of it stuck in the dark scabs that covered the raw furrows the rocks had gouged out of his head.

Galan looked back at the pool. His lips curved in an unlovely smile as he—stiffly—made a formal bow in its direction. Then he turned and booted a stone into its tranquil heart, shattering the smooth surface with muddy ripples.

Feeling much better, he checked the hilts of his sword and dagger to be sure they were loose and ready in their scabbards, and set off through the forest once more. His gut growled at him more than once, reminding him that one can't eat coins.

It was two days' steady travel through the trees to the waymoot of Assamboryl, and a day beyond that to Six Thorns. The hours seemed longer without Athtar's endless inanities. Not that he wasn't enjoying the relative quiet, for once—though he was so stiff, and whatever he'd hurt in his right thigh stabbed with such burning pain, that he was stumping along through the moss and dead leaves like a clumsy human.

Thankfully few folk dwelt hereabouts, because of the stirges. There was one flitting along in the trees right now, keeping well away but following his travel.

Hmmph. It must not be thirsty just now—but if he was heading toward all of its relatives, old Galan the Gallant might be no more than a sack of empty skin before nightfall.

Cheery thought, that.

A mushroom float rose up from behind a ferny bank on his left. His nose twitched. It was piled high with fresh limecaps, their mottled brown stems oozing the white sap that meant they'd just been harvested. His stomach growled again—and without thought he snatched a few and thrust them to his mouth.

"Ho!"

In his weary hunger, he'd forgotten that mushroom floats need someone to pull them. Or push them, as the angry-looking elf at the other end of this float was doing, getting his harvest aboveground in good time for washing and sorting. The elf snatched out a dagger, and swept it up for a throw.

Galan took it out of his fingers for him with his own fast-hurled dagger, and followed it up with a duck under the float and a lunge up the other side, sword point first.

The elf screamed and scrambled backwards, fetching up against a tree. Galan rose up in front of him with slow, silent menace, putting the point of his blade to the farmer's throat.

The terrified elf began to gabble, pleading and wildly unfolding all sorts of friendly information about his name, his lineage, his ownership of this mushroom den, the fine 'shrooms it produced, the finer weather they'd been having lately, and—

Galan gave him an unlovely smile, and raised a hand. The elf misinterpreted the gesture.

"Of course, human lord! Please forgive my tardiness in understanding your needs! I have little, being but a poor farmer, but it is yours—all yours!" With frantic fingers the farmer undid his belt, slid off its pouch, and presented it to Galan in trembling fingers, as his loose, baggy mucking-breeches fell to his ankles.

The belt was heavy with coin—small coin, no doubt, but still probably good thalvers and bedoars and thammarchs of the realm. As Galan hefted it in disbelief, the farmer misinterpreted his expression and gabbled, "But of *course* I have more! I would not dream of trifling with or cheating the great human armathor that Corellon himself has sent to our Coronal to scourge the sinful and decadent from the realm! Here!"

This time his fingers brought out a pouch from a thong around his neck . . . a pouch that swelled with gems. Galan took it in wide-eyed incredulity, and the farmer burst into tears and cried, "Slay me *not*, oh mighty armathor! I've no more to give you but my float of 'shrooms and my lunch!"

Galan growled with approval at that last word—well, after all, what *would* a mighty human armathor speak like?—and extended an insistent, beckoning hand. When the farmer staring at it for a moment, he followed it up with an insistent, beckoning blade.

"Ah- ah-'shrooms?" the bewildered farmer cried, in a panic. Galan scowled, shook his head, and made the beckoning gesture again.

"Uh . . . lunch?" the farmer said timidly. Galan nodded slowly and emphatically, treating his guest to a crooked smile.

Mushrooms flew as the farmer burrowed into one corner of the float, cursed tearfully, gabbled apologies, and rushed to another corner, where mushrooms flew again.

Galan took the cloth-wrapped bundle, hefted it, and then slowly held the bag of gems back out to the farmer. Gems were tricky; too many of them, in Cormanthor, bore tracing spells, or even enchantments that could burst forth to do harm when commanded to do so from a safe distance. No, the coins were safer by far.

The farmer burst into tears and went to his knees to loudly thank Corellon, and the volume of his praises was such that Galan was loudly tempted to chop him down where he stood.

Instead, he pointed with his sword, indicating that the farmer should go back down into his mushroom cavern without delay. The tearful farmer neglected to see it, so Galan growled.

In the sudden, total silence that followed he repeated the gesture, swinging his blade grandly—and there was a wet and heavy impact as he was bringing it back down. Galan opened his mouth to emit a startled curse as he saw the slab of stirge fall from one side of his blade, and heard the thump as the rest of it hit the ground somewhere near, but the farmer set up such a deafening storm of fervent praises that the only living Goadulphyn—head of the house, heir, champion, elder, and all—decided he couldn't stand any more of this (it was worse than Athtar), and headed north again. He'd open his bundle and eat when he was well out of whatever territory fervently gullible mushroom farmers dwelt in.

Galan stumped along for quite some time, shaking his head, before he found a tree old enough and large enough to hold Corellon's awareness. He went right up to it and murmured wonderingly, "You do have a sense of humor, Sacred Mother and Father, don't you?"

The tree did not reply—but then, Corellon probably already knew he had a sense of humor. So Galan sat down and devoured the farmer's lunch with gusto. Corellon offered no objections.

"Heirs slaughtered like lajauva birds in spring! Armathors breaking and hurling down their blades in protest! What's Cormanthor coming to?" Lord Ihimbraskar Evendusk was shouting again, face red and eyes redder. A servant who'd frozen into terrified immobility at his sudden and roaring approach found herself uncomfortably in Lord Evendusk's way.

More to the point, so did Lord Evendusk, and he still carried his pegasi goad in his hand. Its leather whip whacked twice, thrice, and then a savage backhand to send the weeping servant pelting down the passage, her platter of pastries fallen and forgotten.

Duilya shuddered. "Oh, gods," she whimpered, "do I really have to go through with this?"

Yes, Duilya—or he'll be carving you up with that goad next!

Duilya sighed.

Don't worry; we're here. Do it just as we agreed.

"It's the Coronal, that's who it is!" Evendusk snarled. "Eltargrim must have got funny ideas into his head while gallivanting off through Faerûn, o'erturning human wenches every night and listening overlong to their sauce . . ."

Lord Evendusk's customary morning rant trailed away into bug-eyed silence. There was his favorite chair, and there on the table beside it—the table that should have held a waiting glass of rubythrymm and a seeing-gem holding scenes of last night's revelry—was a fill bottle of his very best tripleshroom sherry.

His wife was sitting in *his* chair, clad in a gown that would have made his pulses race if Duilya had been forty summers younger, twice as slim as she was, and just a bit less familiar. She didn't seem to have noticed him.

As he watched, rocking slightly from side to side and breathing heavily, she picked up an empty glass from the floor beside her, shrugged at it, and set it aside.

Then she calmly unstoppered the sherry bottle, raised it to the morning light and murmured something appreciative—and drank the *whole* thing down, slowly and steadily, eyes closed and throat moving rhythmically.

Lord Evendusk's silently boiling rage slid sideways, as he noticed what a beautiful throat his wife possessed. He didn't think he'd ever noticed it before.

She set the empty—yes, empty; *she'd drunk the whole thing!*—bottle down, face serene, and said aloud, "That was so good, I think I'll have some more."

She was reaching for the bell when Lord Evendusk found his wits and his breath again. Catching firm hold of both, he gave vent to his now-towering rage.

"Duilya! Just what by all the pits of the spider-worshipping drow d'you think you're doing?" he bellowed.

As she rang the bell, his wife turned that stupid and customarily yawping face toward his, smiled almost timidly, and said, "Good morn, my lord."

"Well?" he bellowed, striding forward. "Just what is the meaning of this?" He waved at the bottle with his goad, and then glared down at his wife.

She was frowning slightly, and seemed to be listening to something.

Lord Evendusk snatched hold of her shoulder and shook her. "Duilya!" he roared into her face. "Answer me, or I'll—"

Red-faced, he raised his goad, holding it aloft, ready to strike, with a trembling hand. Behind him, the room filled with anxious servants.

Duilya smiled up at him, and tore open the front of her gown. His name was emblazoned in gems across her otherwise bare breasts. "Ihimbraskar" was rising and falling as he stared at it, gaping. Into that stunned silence she said clearly, "Wouldn't you prefer to do that in our bedchamber, lord? Where you've room to take a really good swing?"

She gave him a little smile and added, "Though I must confess I prefer it when you just put on my gowns and let *me* use the goad."

Lord Evendusk, who'd been in the process of turning purple, now turned white instead. One of the servants snorted in suppressed mirth, but when their lord wheeled around, wild-eyed, to glare at them all, they presented him with a row of expressionless faces and said in a ragged chorus, "You rang, great Lady?"

Duilya smiled sweetly. "I did, and my thanks for your swift arrival. Naertho, I'd like another bottle of tripleshroom sherry by my bedside, forthwith. There's no need for glasses. The rest of you, attend please, in case my lord needs something."

"Need something?" Lord Evendusk snarled, turning around again. "Aye, and forthwith—an explanation, wench, of your . . . this . . ." he waved his arms wildly, lost for words, while the servants were still gasping at his insulting use of the word "wench," and then finished almost desperately, ". . . behavior!"

"Of course," Duilya said, looking almost scared for a moment. She glanced at the servants, took a deep breath, lifted her chin—almost as though she was following silent instructions—and said crisply, "Night after night you go to revels, leaving your household neglected. Not once have you taken me with you—or any of your servants, if you'd rather not have me witness what you do there. Jhalass, there, and Rubrae—they're much younger and prettier than I am; why don't you show them off and let them enjoy the same fun you do?"

The servants were staring at her as wide-eyed as Lord Evendusk, now. Duilya lay back in the chair and crossed her legs just as he customarily did, and said, gesturing down at herself, "*This* is all I see of you in the mornings, lord. This and a lot of roaring and groaning. So I decided to try this roistering of yours, to see what attractions it might have."

She wrinkled her nose. "Aside from giving me a powerful urge to relieve myself, I can't see that tripleshroom sherry tastes so wonderful that you need go off all night to plow through a bottle of it. Perhaps another bottle would convince me otherwise? So I've summoned that second one to my bedside—where we're going now, Lord."

Lord Evendusk was purple again, and shaking, but his voice was soft as he asked, "We are? Why?"

"Drinking every night's no excuse for spending every morning stumbling about like an idiot, making a mockery of the honor of the House, and leaving me neglected, night after night, and day after day. We are *partners*, my lord, and it's high time you treated me as one."

Ihimbraskar Evendusk raised his head as a stag does, to draw breath before drinking at a forest pool. When he brought it down again, he looked almost calm. "Could you be more specific about what you want me to do in this regard, Lady?" he asked in silken tones.

"Sit down and talk," she snapped. "Here. Now. About the Coronal, and the deaths, and the tumult over the human."

"And just what do you know of that?" her lord asked, still standing. He slapped the palm of his hand gently with the goad.

Duilya pointed at a vacant chair. Lord Evendusk looked at it, and then slowly back to her. She kept her arm motionless, indicating the chair.

Slowly he went to it, planted one boot in it, and stood leaning on it. "Speak," he said softly. There was something in his eyes, as he looked at her, that hadn't been there before.

"I know, Lord, that you—and other lords like you— are the very backbone of Cormanthor," Duilya said, staring right into his eyes. Her lips quivered for a moment, as if she might cry, but she drew in a deep breath and went on carefully, "On your shoulders the greatness and splendor of us all rests, and is carried. Never think for a moment that I do not revere you for the work you do, and the honor that you have won."

One of the servants stirred, but the room had grown very still.

Lady Evendusk went on. "Ihimbraskar, I do not want to lose that honor. I don't want to lose *you*. Lords and their houses are drawing swords, hurling spells, and defying their Coronal openly over one human. I'm afraid someone will stick their blade through My Lord Evendusk."

Lord and lady were both silent for a moment, their eyes locked, and then Duilya continued, her words ringing in the silent room.

"*Nothing* is worth that. No human is worth feuds and blood spilled and Cormanthor torn apart. Here I sit, day after day, talking with other ladies and seeing the life of the realm unfold. Never do you ask me what I've seen and heard, or talk anything over with me. You *waste* me, Lord. You treat me like a chair—or like a clown, to be laughed at for my fripperies, as you boast to your friends how many coins I've thrown away on my latest jewels and gowns!"

Duilya rose, took off her gown, and held it out to him. "I'm more than this, Ihimbraskar. See?"

His eyes flickered; she stepped swiftly toward him, gown in hand, and said passionately, "I'm your *friend*, Lord. I'm the one you should come home and confide in and share rude jokes with and argue with. Have you forgotten what it is to share ideas—not kisses or pinches, but *ideas*, spoken of aloud—with an elf maid? Come with me now, and I'll teach you how. We have a realm to save."

She turned away, walking from the room with a determined stride. Lord Evendusk watched her go, bared swinging hips and all, cleared his throat noisily, and then turned and said to the servants, "Ah . . . you heard my lady. Unless we ring, please don't disturb us. We have much to talk about."

He turned toward the door the Lady Duilya had left by, took two swift steps, and then whirled around to face the servants, tossed his goad onto the table, and said, "One more thing. Uh . . . my apologies."

He turned and left the room, running hard. The servants kept very quiet until they were sure he was out of earshot.

Their cheering and excited converse fell silent again when Naertho came into the room. He was carrying the second bottle of tripleshroom sherry in his hand. "The lord and lady said 'twas for us!" he said gruffly.

When the astonished cheer that evoked had died away, he looked out the window and the trees, his eyes very bright, and added, "Thanks to you, Corellon. Bring us humans every moon, if they cause such as this!"

In a pool in a private garden, four ladies collapsed into each others' arms and wept happy tears. Their glasses of tripleshroom sherry floated, untouched and forgotten, around them.

Thirteen
Adrift in Cormanthor

For a time, Elminster became as a ghost, and wandered unheard and unseen through the very heart of Cormanthor. The elves regarded him not, and he learned much thereby . . . not that he had much of a life left in which to make use of what he gained.

Antarn the Sage
from *The High History of Faerûnian Archmages Mighty*
published circa The Year of the Staff

Faerûn took a very long while to come floating back again. At first Elminster was only dimly aware of himself as a drifting cloud of thoughts—of awareness—in a dark, endless void through which booming, distorted sounds . . . bursts of loudness they were, no more . . . rumbled and echoed from time to time.

After an infinity of floating, only dimly aware of who he was or *what* he was, Elminster saw lights appear—stabbing, momentary flashes of brightness that occurred from time to time as he floated, unwondering, in their midst.

Later, sounds and lights befell more often, and memories began to stir, like restless, uncoiling serpents, in the spark of self-awareness that was the Athalantan prince and Chosen of Mystra. El saw swords rising and falling, and a gem that held a whirling chaos of images, the memories of others, raging like a sea that tossed him up into the presence of a female eidolon in the night gardens of a palace . . . the palace of a kindly one, an old elf in white robes, the ruler of pursuivants who rode unicorns and pegasi, the ruler of . . . of . . .

The Coronal. That title blazed like white fire in his memory, like the great and awesome chord of a fanfare of triumphal doom—the march favored by magelords in the Athalantar of his younger years, that resounded across Hastarl, echoing back from its towers, when wizards were gathering for some decision of import.

The same mages he had defeated in the end, to claim—and then renounce—his throne. He was a prince, the grandson of the Stag King. He was of the royal blood of Athalantar, of the family Aumar, the last of many princes. He was a boy running through the trees of Heldon, an outlaw and a thief of Hastarl, a priest—or was it priestess? Had he not been a woman?—of Mystra. The Lady of Mysteries, the Mother of Magic, Myrjala his teacher who became Mystra his divine ruler and guide, making him her Chosen, making him her—*Elminster!*

He was Elminster! Human armathor of Cormanthor, named so by the Coronal, sent here by Mystra to do something important that remained yet hidden from him—and beset on all sides by the ambitious, ruthless, arrogantly powerful young elves of this realm, chafing under the old ways and unwelcome new decrees of the Coronal and his court ... *ardavanshee*, the elders called them; or "restless young ones." Ardavanshee who may yet have brought about his death ... for if Elminster Aumar was not dead, what was he?

Floating here, in dark chaos ...

He sank back into his thoughts, which were running now like a river. Ardavanshee who defied the will of their elders but stood tall upon the pride of the houses of their birth. Ardavanshee who feared and yet spoke against the power of the High Court Mages and the Coronal and his old advisor the Srinshee.

That title seemed to be another door opening in his mind, letting in a wash of brightness and fresh recollections and a stronger sense of being Elminster. The Lady Oluevaera Estelda, smiling up at him from that noble, wrinkled ruin of a face and then, incongruously, from one that looked like a little elven girl's, yet retained those old and wise eyes ... the Srinshee, older than trees and deeper rooted, treading the crammed Vault of Ages with reverence for the dead and vanished, holding the whole lore and long lineage of the proud Cormanthan elves in her mind—in the vault behind her eyes that was so much larger than the one she trod with an impatient, hawk-nosed young human ...

The hated human intruder sought across the realm for the murders he'd done by the ardavanshee—led by the houses of Echorn and Starym and Waelvor ... Waelvor, whose scion was Elandorr ... suitor and rival of the Lady Symrustar.

Symrustar! That perfect face, those hungrily tugging blue tresses, that dragon on her belly and breast, the eyes like blue flames of promise, and lips parted in a waiting, knowing smile ... that ruthless, ambitious sorceress whose mind was as dark a cesspit as any Magelord's, who thought of elves—and men—as mere stupid beasts to be used as she clawed her way up through them, to some as-yet-unrealized goal.

The lady who had almost torn his mind open to make him her plaything and source of spells. The lady he had in turn betrayed into the grasp of her rival, Elandorr, leaving both their fates unknown to him.

Aye. He knew who he was now. Elminster, set upon by Delmuth Echorn and then by a band of ardavanshee led by Ivran Selorn, who hunted him through Castle Dlardrageth. Elminster the overconfident, careless Chosen. Elminster, who'd been drunk with power as he flew right into the waiting spell of the ardavanshan mages—a spell that had torn him apart.

Was he whole again? Or was he but a ghost, his mortal life over? Perhaps Mystra had kept him alive—if this *was* alive—to carry out her purposes, a failure forced to complete his mission.

Elminster was suddenly aware that he could move in the void, scudding in this direction or that as he thought of movement. Yet that meant little when there was nowhere to move to, dark emptiness on all sides, lights and noise scattering at seeming random, everywhere and nowhere.

The world around him had once been a series of specific "wheres," an unfolding landscape of different and often named locations, from the deep forest of Cormanthor to the outlaw wastes beyond Athalantar.

Perhaps this was death, after all. Faerûn, and a body to walk it in, were what he was lacking. Almost without thinking he sent himself into a racing flight through the void, searching the endless for an end, a boundary, perhaps a rift where the light of Faerûn in all its familiar glory could shine in . . .

And as this swift but vain movement went on and on he raised a prayer to Mystra, a silent cry in his mind: *Mystra, where are ye? Aid me. Be my guide, I beseech thee.*

There was a dark and silent moment as the words in his mind seemed to roll away into endless distance. Then there came a bright, almost blinding burst of light, white and clarioned, with a sennet that echoed stridently through him, hurling him over and over in its brassy tumult. When it faded he was racing back the way he'd come, aimed exactly back upon his former course, though he could not tell how it was he knew that to be so.

At long last, a horizon fell into his void, a line of misty blue with a node of brightness partway along it, like a gem upon the arc of a ring . . . and Elminster of Athalantar was headed for that distant point of brilliance.

It seemed a long way off, but in the end he rushed up to plunge into it with dizzying speed, shedding something as he left the darkness, shooting out into the light. The light of a lowering sun, above the marching treetops of Cormanthor, with the dark ruin of Castle Dlardrageth in the distance, and something urging him in another direction. He followed that urging, unsure even if he could have chosen otherwise, and flew low above shadowtops and duskwoods, rose-needles and beetle palms, rushing as smooth and as swift as if outracing dragons.

Here and there, as he flew, El glimpsed trails and slim wooden bridges that leaped from tree to tree, transforming the forest giants into the living homes of elves. He was crossing Cormanthor in the space of a few breaths. Now he was descending and slowing, as if let fall by a vast and invisible hand.

Thanks to ye, Mystra, he thought, fairly sure whom he should be thanking. He sank past the gardens of the palace, into the many-spired bustle of the central city, Cormanthor itself.

He was slowing greatly now, as if he was but a leaf drifting on a gentle breeze. In truth, he could hear no whistle of wind nor feel any chill or damp as of moving air, at all. Turrets and softly luminous driftglobes rose past him as his plunge ended, and he began to move freely, hither and yon.

He moved from here to there in accordance with wherever he looked that interested him enough to approach. As he flew, he passed among elves who saw him not, and—as he discovered when he blundered right into the path of several floats piled high with mushrooms, and they slid through him without him feeling a thing—felt him not. He was truly a ghost, it seemed; an invisible, silent, undetected drifting thing.

As he drifted this way and that, peering at the busy lives of Cormanthans, he began to hear things as well. At first there was only a faint, confusing rumble broken by louder irregularities, but it grew to a deafening din of interlaced gabbling. It seemed to be the conversations and noises made by thousands of elves at once, as if he could hear all Cormanthor, without regard for distance and walls and cellar depths, laid all at once upon the ears he no longer seemed to have.

He hovered for a time in a little tangle of shrubs growing between three closely spaced duskwoods, waiting for the din to subside or for his wits to flee entirely. Slowly the noises did die, receding to what normal ears would hear: the sounds nearby, with the gentle, incessant sighing of breeze-stirred leaves drowning out all else. He relaxed, able to *think* again, until thinking begat curiosity, and a desire to know what was befalling in Cormanthor.

So he was invisible, silent, and scentless, even to alert elves. Ideal for prying into their doings. But 'twould be best to make sure of his stealth before seeking to enter any heart of watchful peril hereabout.

El undertook to swoop at elves in the streets and on the bridges, screaming for all he was worth as he did so. He even passed through them whilst clawing at them and crying insults. He could hear himself perfectly, and even shape ghostly limbs to stab and slash with—limbs that he at least could feel, enduring painful scrapings as one limb struck another.

His elven targets, however, noticed him not. They laughed and chatted in a way they'd never have done had they known a human was nearby. El drew himself up in midair after hurling himself through a particularly frosty-looking elven lady of high station and reflected that he might not have all that much time to make use of this state. After all, none of his powers since his awakening had remained unchanged for long. So he'd best be about his spying.

One thing to check on, first.

He remembered these streets dimly: he'd passed along that one, he thought, in his first stagger through the city, trying to search for House Alastrarra without seeming to do more than stroll. A particularly proud mansion, in the heart of walled gardens, should lie in that direction.

His memory was correct. It was the work of an instant to pass through the gates unseen, and seek the great house beyond. He could pass through small items, especially wood, he discovered, but stone and metal hurt or deflected him; he could not burst or even seep through solid walls. A window served him amply, however, and he entered into the tapestried splendor of a lavishly decorated home. Furs lay everywhere underfoot, and polished wood sculpted into lounges and chairs rose in flowing shapes on all sides. Wealthy elven families seemed to love varicolored blown glass and chairs that rose into a variety of little armrests and shelves and curved lounging cavities. El passed among these like a purposeful thread of smoke, seeking a particular thing.

He found it in an ornate bedchamber where a nude elven couple were floating in each other's arms, upright above their bed, earnestly—even angrily— discussing the affairs of the realm. Elminster found the arguments advanced and parried by the aroused tongues of Lord and Lady Evendusk so fascinating that he lingered a long time listening, before a purely personal dispute about moderation and the consumption of tripleshroom sherry sent him swooping to the floor, and a little way across the furs there, to the visibly pulsing enchantments surrounding Duilya Evendusk's gem bower.

It was the Cormanthan custom for elven ladies of means to have a pod-shaped, walk-in portable closet, something like the canopy surrounding a sedan chair. In this closet their jewels were hung or kept in little drawers individually carved to fit into the flowing wooden walls. Gem bowers were equipped with little hanging mirrors, tiny glass light-globes that shone when tapped with a forefinger, and little seats. They also contained powerful enchantments to keep out the wandering fingers of those overwhelmed by the beauty of the gems contained therein; enchantments that in theory could be tuned to keep out all except their lady owner. These "veilings" were so strong that they glowed a rich blue, quite visible to the eye, as they crawled and ebbed around their bowers in a close-clinging sphere of magic.

They were strong enough, El recalled dimly from the Srinshee's comments, to hurl intruders across a room, or stand immobile against the charge of the strongest warrior—even a charge preceded by a spear, or augmented by a second or third warrior, racing shoulder to shoulder. Would they likewise rend a drifting human phantom? Or rebuff him?

Gingerly he drifted closer, moving with infinite patience, extending the thinnest thread of himself cautiously outward to touch the pulsing blue glow.

It rippled unchanged, and he felt nothing. He thrust it in further, reaching with the smokelike finger for three gems hanging on fine chains from the curving ceiling of Duilya Evendusk's bower.

He felt nothing, and the enchantment seemed unchanged. Reluctantly he spread himself out along it, brushing against the blueness. No sensation of pain or disruption, and no change in the enchantment. Drawing himself back across the room from the bower, he swirled around Lord and Lady Evendusk for a moment, as they murmured gentle words to each other with slow but building hunger. Then he raced across the room, charging right at the magical barrier.

He was almost up t—he was through!—bursting through the heart of the bower without disturbing so much as a ring and storming on out its other side, piercing the barrier again and flashing into a silent, unseen turn inches shy of a wall.

Behind him the veiling glowed on, unchanging. El turned and regarded it with some satisfaction. Glancing beyond it, at the langorous midair dance of the amorous elven couple, he smiled—or tried to—and soared away, out an oval window into the mossy gardens beyond, seeking information.

He wanted to find the Coronal, to be sure the bloodthirsty ardavanshee—or worse, the elder mages of the haughty houses to which the reckless younglings belonged—hadn't so lost their senses as to strike at the heart and head of the realm.

Then, assuming the Revered Lord Most High of Cormanthor was unharmed, 'twould be time to seek out the Srinshee and get a certain much-maligned human armathor of the realm his body back, if this condition hadn't passed away by then.

El turned in the direction the palace should be, rose until he was among treetops and spired towers, and sped among them, looking down as he passed at the unfolding beauty of Cormanthor.

There were circulâr gardens like little green wells, and trees planted in crescentiform arcs to enclose little moss lawns in their encircling shelter. There were stone spires around which gigantic trees spiraled in living helices of leaves and carefully-shaped branches and little windows opening in the bark, with the forms of young elves at play dancing and wrestling visible within. There were banners of translucent silk that rode the winds as lightly as gossamer threads, and trees that held those banners on boughs shaped like the fingers of an open hand, with a domed upper room squatting like an egg in the palm of that hand. There were houses that revolved, and sparkled back the sun from swirling glass ornaments hanging like frozen raindrops from their balconies and casements.

El looked at it all with fresh wonder. In all his tearing about and fighting, he'd forgotten just how beautiful elven work could be. If the elder elven houses had their way, of course, humans would never see any of this—and those few intruders who did, such as one Elminster Aumar, would not live long enough to tell anyone of such splendors.

After a time he came out of a knot of tree homes and spired, many-windowed houses, passing over a wall that bore several enchantments. Beyond was a garden of many pools and statues. The garden, El realized as he drifted onward and onward, was *big*.

And yet it didn't *look* like the Coronal's palace garden. Where were the . . . ?

No, that wasn't the palace. It was a grand house, yes—a mound of greenery pierced by windows and bristling with slender towers. Its ivy-covered flanks fell away to the lazy curves of a stream that slid placidly past islands that looked like huge clumps of moss linked by little arched bridges.

It was the most beautiful mansion El had ever seen. He veered toward its nearest large upper window. Like most such openings it was bereft of glass, and filled instead by an invisible spell field that prevented the passage of all solid objects, but let breezes blow unchecked. Two well-dressed elves were leaning against the unseen field, goblets in their hands.

"My Lord Maendellyn," someone was saying in thin, superior tones, "you can hardly think it usual for one of my House to so swiftly find common cause with those of younger heritage and lesser concerns; this is truly something that strikes at us all."

"Have we then, Llombaerth, the open support of House Starym?"

"Oh, I don't think that is yet necessary. Those who wish to reshape Cormanthor and stand proud in doing so must occasionally be seen to do things for themselves—and bear the consequences."

"While the Starym watch, smiling, from the sidelines," a third voice said in dry tones, "ready to applaud such bold Houses if they succeed, or decry their foul treachery if they fail. Yes, that would make a House live long and profit much. At the same time, it leaves those of the House in question standing on uneasy ground when presuming to lecture others on tactics, or ethics, or the good of the realm."

"My Lord Yeschant," the thin voice said coldly, "I don't care for the tone of your observations."

"And yet, Lord Speaker of the Starym, you can find it in you to make common cause with us—for, you have the most to lose of us all."

"How so?"

"House Starym now holds the proudest rank of all. If this insane plan the Coronal is urging on Cormanthor is allowed to befall, House Starym has more to lose than, say, House Yridnae."

"*Is* there a House Yridnae?" someone asked, in the background, but El, as he drifted nearer, heard no reply.

"My lords," the Lord Maendellyn was saying hastily, "let us set aside this dissension and pursue the stag we've all seen ahead: to whit, the necessity of ending the rule of our current Coronal, and his folly of Opening, for the good of us all."

"Whatever we pursue," a deep voice said despairingly, "won't bring my son back. The human did it; the Coronal brought the human into the realm—so, the human being dead already, the Coronal must die, that my Aerendyl be avenged."

"I lost a son, too, Lord Tassarion," said another new voice, "but it does not follow that the death of my Leayonadas must needs be paid for by the blood of the ruler of Cormanthor. If Eltargrim must die, let it be a reasoned decision made for the future of Cormanthor, and not a blood evening."

"House Starym knows better than many the pain of loss and the weight of blood price," the thin voice of Llombaerth Starym, Lord Speaker of his House, came again. "We have no desire to belittle the pain of a loss felt by others, and we hear the deep—and undeniable—call for justice. Yet we, too, believe that the matter of the Coronal's continued rule must be treated as an affair of state. The misruler must pay for his shocking ideas and his failure to guide Cormanthor capably, regardless of how many or how few brave sons of the realm have died from his mistakes."

"May I propose," a lisping voice put in, "that we resolve and work toward the slaying of the Coronal? With that as a commonly held goal, those of us who see revenge as part of this—myself, Lord Yeschant, Lord Tassarion, and Lord Ortauré—can agree among ourselves who shall have a hand in the actual killing, so that honor may be satisfied. That in turn allows House Starym and others who'd rather not be part of actual bloodshed to work toward our common goal with hands that remain clean of all but the work of loyally defending Cormanthor."

"Well said, My Lord Bellas," Lord Maendellyn agreed. "Are we then agreed that the Coronal must die?"

"We are," came the rough chorus.

"And are we agreed on when, how, and whom shall ascend to the throne of Coronal after Eltargrim?"

There was a little silence, and then everyone started to speak at once. El could see them, now: the five heads of Houses and the Starym envoy, sitting around a polished table with goblets and bottles between them, the slowly revolving flashes of an anti-poison field winking among those vessels.

"Pray silence!" Lord Yeschant said sharply, after a few moments of babble. "It is clear that we are *not* agreed on these things. I suspect that the matter of who shall be our next Coronal is the issue of most contention, and should be dealt with last—though I must stress, lords, that we do Cormanthor a grave disservice if we do not, before striking, choose a new Coronal and support him with the same united resolve we show in removing the old one. None of us benefits from a realm in chaos." He paused, and then asked in a quiet voice, "My Lord Maendellyn?"

"My thanks, Lord Yeschant—and, may I say, how swiftly and ably spoken. Is the 'how' we remove the Coronal easiest to decide among ourselves, as I judge it?"

"It must be some way that lets us strike him down personally," Lord Tassarion said quickly.

"Yet 'twould be best," the lord speaker of the Starym put in, "if it not be a formal audience or other appointment for which a suspicious Coronal could assemble a formidable defensive force, and thereby increase our losses and personal danger as he delays our success and places the realm in jeopardy of the very war and uncertainty we are all so rightly concerned about."

"How then to trick him into meeting with us?"

"Adopt disguises, so as to come to him as his advisors: those six sorceresses he dallies with, for instance?"

Lord Yeschant and Lord Tassarion frowned in unison. "I dislike the thought of involving such extra complications in what we do," said Yeschant. "Should one of them observe us, she'll be sure to attack, and we'll have a spell battle far greater than what we'll face if we can catch Eltargrim alone."

"Bah! As Coronal, he can call and summon a number of things," the Starym envoy said dismissively.

"Aye, but if such aid arrives and finds him dead," Lord Tassarion said thoughtfully, "things are far different than if we draw one or even all six of the lady sorceresses—members of noble houses themselves, remember, with the blood prices their deaths will inevitably carry—into the fray before we are sure that we can slay the Coronal then and there. I do not want to be caught in a drawn-out battle across half the realm with six hostile sorceresses able to teleport into our laps and then out again, if we can't know that we are buying the Coronal's sure and swift death with whatever price we pay."

"I don't think we are ready to slay a Coronal yet," Lord Bellas lisped. "I see us still standing undecided between three alternatives: publicly challenging the Coronal's rule; or openly slaying him; or merely being nearby when an 'unfortunate accident' befalls our beloved ruler."

"Lords all," their host said firmly, "'tis clear that we'll be some time in reaching agreement on any of these matters. I have engagements ahead this eve, and the longer we six sit gathered here, the greater the chance that someone in the realm will hear or suspect something." The Lord Maendellyn looked around the room and added, "If we part now, and all think on the three matters Lord Yeschant so capably outlined, I trust that when I send word three morns hence, we can meet again armed with what we'll need to strike an agreement."

" 'Strike' is aptly chosen," someone muttered, as the others said, "Agreed" around the table, and they rose swiftly and made for the doors, to depart.

For a moment El was tempted to linger and follow one or more of these conspirators, but their mansions or castles were all easily located in the city, and he had his own needs to attend to. He must see for himself if Cormanthor still had a Coronal to murder, or if someone else had beaten these exalted lords to the deed.

He swooped out of the window and around Castle Maendellyn without delay, racing past its other turrets in the direction he'd originally been heading. The lovely gardens stretched on beneath him as he went. Lovely, and well-guarded; no less than three barriers flashed in front of him as he thrust through them and raced on, seeking the spires he knew.

The gardens ended at last in a high wall cloaked in a thick tangle of trees. A street lay beyond the wall, and a row of houses fronted onto the street. Their back gardens rose through lush plantings and under duskwood trees to another street. On its far side were the walls of the palace gardens.

The watchnorns here might be able to see him, but El had to reach the palace, so he drifted on, cautiously now, for fear that the enchantments that girded the High House of Cormanthor would be more powerful than those he'd encountered thus far.

Perhaps they were, but they saw him not. Nor did any of the ghostly guardians appear. Elminster slipped into the palace by an upper window, and glided up and down its halls, feeling strangely ill at ease. The place was splendid, but its upper floor was almost empty; only a few servants padded about in soft boots, seeing leisurely to the dust with minor spells.

Of the Coronal himself he saw no sign, but in a little outlying turret on the north side of the palace he found a gathering strangely similar to that he'd just witnessed breaking up in Castle Maendellyn: six noble lords sitting around a polished table. This gathering had a seventh grave-faced elf present: the High Court Mage Earynspieir. Elminster did not know any of the others.

Lord Earynspieir was on his feet, pacing. Elminster drifted into the room and took his seat at the table, undetected.

"We know there are plots being hatched even now," an old and rather plump elf down at the end of the table said. "Every gathering, be it revel or formal audience, from now on must be treated as a potential battle."

"More like a series of waiting ambushes," another elf commented.

The High Court Mage turned. "Lord Droth," he said, nodding at the stout elf, "and Lord Bowharp, please believe that we recognize this and are making preparations. We realize we cannot wall away the Coronal behind armathors bristling with weapons, and d—"

"What preparations?" another lord asked bluntly. This one looked every inch a battle commander, from his scars to his ready sword. When he leaned forward to ask that question, his rich voice held the snap of command.

"*Secret* preparations, My Lord Paeral," Earynspieir said meaningfully.

A lord who was sitting beside the head of House Paeral—a gold elf, and quite the most handsome male Elminster had ever seen, of any species—looked up with startlingly silver eyes and said quietly, "If you can't trust us, Lord High Mage, Cormanthor is doomed. The time is well past for keeping coy secrets. If those who are loyal don't know exactly where and when events are unfolding in the realm, our Coronal could well fall."

Earynspieir grimaced as if in pain for a moment, before assuming a sickly smile. "Well said as always, My Lord Unicorn. Yet as Lord Adorellan pointed out earlier, every word let out of our lips that need not be is another chink in the Coronal's armor. The Lord Most High is in hiding at this time, upon my recommendation, and—"

"Guarded by whom?" Lords Droth and Paeral asked in almost perfect unison.

"Mages of the court," Earynspieir replied, in tones that signaled he preferred to say no more.

"'The Six Kissing Sisters'?" the sixth lord asked, lifting an eyebrow. "Are they really a match for a determined attack—considering that some of them belong to houses that may be less than heartbroken to see Eltargrim dead?"

"Lord Siirist," the High Court Mage said severely, "I do not appreciate your description of the ladies who serve the realm so capably. Even less do I admire your open misapprehensions about their loyalty. However, others have shared your concerns, and the six ladies have been truth-scryed by the same expert who even now stands with ready spells at the Coronal's side."

"And that is?" Lord Unicorn prompted firmly.

"The Srinshee," Earynspieir said, a trace of exasperation in his voice. "And if we cannot trust her, lords, who in all Cormanthor can we trust?"

It was clear to Elminster as discussions went on that Lord Earynspieir was going to say as little as possible about whatever preparations he'd made. Instead he was trying to get these lords to agree to muster mages and warriors at various places, under commanders agreeable to obey anyone who gave them certain secret phrases. He wasn't going to say which houses or individuals he knew to be disloyal, and he certainly wasn't going to reveal anything about the current whereabouts of the Coronal and the Srinshee.

Without a means of teleporting, El couldn't even look in the Vault of Ages for himself. It was well underground—and he didn't even know where.

Feeling sudden exasperation himself, he soared up out of that room, hurled himself through the palace like a foe-seeking arrow, and turned north, out of the city. He needed the quiet of the trees again, to drift and think. Probably, in the end, he'd wind up poking and prying into the lives of elves all over the city, just to glean all the useful information he could. He really didn't know how most elves earned coins to spend for things, for inst—

Something moved, under the trees ahead of him. Something that seemed disturbingly familiar.

El slowed swiftly, drifting to one side to circle and thus see it better. He was right out in the woods now, beyond where the regular patrols would pass, on the edge of a region of small, twisting ravines and tangled brambles.

The thing he was looking at was much scratched from those brambles, as it crawled laboriously along, moving aimlessly on hands and knees—or rather, one hand, for the other was bent back into a frozen claw, and the crawling, murmuring thing was leaning on the wrist instead. Sharp sticks or rocks or thorns had long ago torn open that wrist, as well as other places, and the crawler was leaving a trail of blood. Soon something that devoured such helpless things would get wind of it, or happen upon it.

El descended until he was floating chin-down in the dirt, staring through a trailing forest of filthy, matted blue tresses into the tortured, swimming blue eyes of the toast of the ardavanshee: the Lady Symrustar Auglamyr.

FOURTEEN
ANGER AT COURT

Elves today still say "As splendid as the Coronal's Court itself" when describing luxury or work of exquisite beauty, and the memory of that splendor, now taken from us, will never die. The Court of the Coronal was known for its decorum. Even scions of the mightiest houses were known to pause in admiration and awe at the glittering panoply it presented to the eye; and temper their words and deeds with the most courtly graces; and from the Throne of Cormanthor, floating above them, went out the gravest and most noble judgments of that age.

SHALHEIRA TALANDREN, HIGH ELVEN BARD OF SUMMERSTAR
from *SILVER BLADES AND SUMMER NIGHTS:*
AN INFORMAL BUT TRUE HISTORY OF CORMANTHOR
PUBLISHED IN THE YEAR OF THE HARP

There came a skirling, as of many harp strings struck in unison, and the gentle, magically amplified voice of the Lady Herald rolled across the glassy-smooth floor of the vast Chamber of the Court: "Lord Haladavar; Lord Urddusk; Lord Malgath."

There was a stir among the courtiers; quick conversations rose and then died away into a hush of excitement as the three old elven lords glided in, walking on air, clad in their full robes of honor. Their servants fell away to join the armathors at the doors of the court, and in the tense, hanging silence the three heads of Houses traveled down the long, open hall to the Pool.

A rustling grew in their wake as courtiers along both sides of the room shifted their positions to gain the best possible vantage points. Amid this flurry of movement one short, slim, almost childlike figure drifted behind one of the tapestries that hid exits, and slipped away.

Floating above the glowing, circular Pool of Remembrance was the Throne of the Coronal, and at ease in its high-arched splendor sat the aged Lord Eltargrim in his gleaming white robes. "Approach and be welcome," he said, formally but warmly. "What would you speak of, here before all Cormanthor?"

Lord Haladavar spread his hands. "We would speak of your plan of Opening; we have some misgivings about this matter."

"Plainly said, and in like spirit: proceed," Eltargrim said calmly.

In unison, the three lords held aside the sashes of their robes. Lightning crackled around the hilts of three revealed stormswords. There was a gasp of horror from the courtiers at this breach of etiquette as well as at the danger drawn stormswords could bring, were they wielded in this chamber amid all its thickly laid enchantments.

Armathors started forward grimly from their places by the doors, but the Coronal waved them back and raised his hand, palm up, in the gesture for silence. When it fell, he gestured at the twinkling lights winking excitely in the pool beneath him, and said calmly, "We were already aware of your weaponry and have taken the view that it was an error in judgment that you deemed necessary to underscore your solemn resolve."

"Precisely, Revered High Lord," Haladavar replied, and then added what his tone had already made clear: "I am relieved that you see it so."

"I wish I could also take the same view," the Srinshee muttered, settling herself in the ornate ceiling screen high above them all and aiming the Staff of Sundering down through it at the three nobles. "Now that your gesture is made, behave yourselves, lords," she murmured, as if they were children again, and she was their tutor. "Cormanthor will thank you for it."

Glancing up, she saw the row of downward-aimed wands were all in their places, awaiting only her touch to unleash their various perils. "Corellon grant that none of this be needed," the sorceress whispered, and bent her full attention to the events unfolding below.

Unaware of the danger overhead, the three lords ranged themselves in a line facing the Pool, and the head of House Urddusk took up the converse.

"Revered High Lord," he said shortly, "I've not the gift of a sweet or smooth tongue; few and blunt words are my way. I pray ye take no offense at what I say, for it is only right that ye should know: hear us not, or dismiss our concerns out of hand without parley, and we will try to use these swords we have brought against ye. I say this with deep sorrow; I pray it not become necessary. But, Most High, *we shall be heard*. We would fail Cormanthor if we kept silent now."

"I will hear you," the Coronal said mildly. "It is why I am here. Speak."

Lord Urddusk looked to the third lord; Malgath was known as a smooth— some might even have used the word "sly"—speaker. Now, knowing the eyes of all the court were upon him, he couldn't resist striking a pose.

"Most High," he purred, "we fear that the realm as we know it will be swept away if gnomes, halflings, our half-kin, and worse, are let loose to run about Cormanthor, putting trees to the axe and crowding us out. Oh, I've heard that you plan to set all of us lords in stewardship over the forest, decreeing which tree shall be touched, and which shall stand. But, Lord Eltargrim, think on this: when a tree is cut, and falls dead, the deed is done, and no amount of hand-wringing or apologies for choosing the wrong one will restore it. The proper magics will, yes, but too much of the wisdom and energy of our best mages, these past twelve winters, has been set to devising new spells to make trees grow from stumps, and trees to become more vital. Those replenishment magics would be imnecessary if we simply *keep the humans out*. You've said before that the laziness of humans will ensure that most of them will give no trouble. Perhaps that's true, but we see the other sort of humans—the restless, the adventurers, the ones who must explore for the sake of spying, and destroy for the sake of dominating—all too often. We also know that humans are greedy . . . almost as greedy as dwarves. And now you plan to let both into the very heart of Cormanthor. The humans will cut the trees down, and the dwarves will snarl for more *to feed the fires of their forges!*"

As Lord Malgath roared these last words some in the court almost shouted in agreement; the Coronal waited almost three breaths for the noise to die down. When things were relatively quiet again he asked, "Is this your only concern, lords? That the realm as we know it today will be swept away if we let other races settle in this our city, and the other areas we patrol and hold dear? For halflings in particular, many half-elven, and even some humans have dwelt for years on the fringes of the realm and yet we are here today, free to argue. I'll have the armathors check, if you'd like, but I'm sure no humans have overrun this hall today."

There was a ripple of laughter, but Lord Haladavar snarled, "This is not a matter I can find in myself room to laugh about, Revered Lord. Humans and dwarves, in particular, have a way of ignoring or twisting any authority put over them, and of defying our People wherever and whenever they can. If we let them in, they will outbreed us, outtrick us, and outnumber us from the start. Very soon we'll be pushed right out of Cormanthor!"

"Ah, Lord Haladavar," the Coronal said, leaning forward on the throne, "you bring up the very reason I have proposed this Opening: that if we don't allow humans some share of Cormanthor now, under our conditions and rule, they will march in, army after vast army, and overwhelm us before this century, or the next, is done. We'll all be too *dead* to be pushed out of Cormanthor."

"Purest fantasy!" Lord Urddusk protested. "How can you say *humans* can field any army capable of winning even a single skirmish against the pride of Cormanthor?"

"Aye," Lord Haladavar said sternly. "I, too, cannot believe in this peril you threaten us with."

Lord Malgath merely raised a disbelieving eyebrow. The Coronal matched it, raising his hand for silence, and called, "Lady Herald, stand forth!"

Alais Dree stepped forward from the doors of the Chamber of the Court. Her bright robes of office took wing after three paces, and she floated past the three glowering lords to attend the throne. "Great Lord, what is your need?"

"These lords question the strength of human warfare, and doubt my testimony as being bent to the support of my proposal. Unfold to them what you have seen in the lands of men."

Alais bowed and turned. When she was facing the three lords, she caught the eye of each in turn, and said crisply, "I am no puppet of the throne, lords, nor weak-willed because I am young, or a she. I have seen more of the doings of men than all three of you together."

There was another ripple of alarm in the Court as the lords once again pulled aside their robes to reveal stormswords; Alais shrugged. Seven swords faded into view in the air in front of her, hovering with their points toward the elven lords, and then vanished again. She paid them no attention, and went on, "From what I have seen, the humans have their own feuds, and are much disorganized, as well as being what we might call undisciplined and untutored in the ways of the forest. Yet they outnumber us already twenty to one and more. Far more humans have swung swords in earnest than have our People.

They swarm, and fight with more ruthlessness, speed, and ability to adapt and change in battle than we have ever known. If they invade, lords, we shall probably manage two or four victories, perhaps even a decisive slaughter. They will manage the rest, and be hunting us through the streets before two seasons are past. Please believe me now; I don't want the realm to feel the pain of your believing me only as you die, later."

She continued, "'To those who, hearing me, then say: 'Then let us fare forth now, and smite all human realms, that they can never raise armies against us,' I say only: no. Humans invaded will unite to slay a common foe; we shall be slain outside our realm, only to leave it undefended when the counterstrike comes. Moreover, anyone who goes to war with humans makes lasting enemies: they remember grudges, lords, as well as we do. To strike at a land now, even to humble it, is to await its next generation, or the one after that, to come riding back at us for revenge—and humans have a score or more generations for each one of ours."

"Will you accept, lords," the Coronal asked mildly, "the testimony of our Lady Herald? Do you grant that she is probably right?"

The three lords shifted uneasily, until Urddusk snapped, "And if we do?"

"If you do, lords," Alais replied, startling everyone save the Coronal by her interjection, "than you and our Coronal stand agreed, both fighting to save Cormanthor. Your shared dispute is only over the means to do so."

She turned again to face the throne, and the Coronal thanked her with a smile and gestured her dismissal. As she floated past the three lords, he spoke again, saying, "Hear my will, lords. The Opening shall proceed—but only after one thing is in place."

The silence, as everyone waited for his next words, was a tense, straining thing.

"My lords, you have all raised just and grave concerns over the safety of our People in an 'open' Cormanthor. Inviting other races in without the elves of Cormanthor having some sort of overarching, pervasive protection is unthinkable. Yet this cannot be a protection of mere law, for we can be swamped and unable to muster blades enough to enforce our law, precisely as if we made war. We do, however, still outstrip humans in one area, for a few more seasons at least: the magic we weave."

The Coronal made a gesture, and suddenly several of the courtiers glowed with golden auras, up and down the hall. They glanced down at themselves in surprise, as their fellows drew back from them. The Coronal pointed at them with a smile, and said, "Elves who have the means to do so, or the skill, have always crafted, or hired others to craft for them, personal mantles of defensive magic. We need a mantle that will encloak all of Cormanthor. We *shall have* such a mantle before the city is laid open to those not of pure elven blood."

Lord Urddusk sputtered, "But such a thing is impossible!"

The Coronal laughed. "That's not a word I ever like to use in Cormanthor, my lord. 'Tis almost always a swift embarrassment to whomever utters it!"

Lord Haladavar leaned his head over to the ear of Lord Urddusk and murmured, "Be at ease! He says this so he can retreat from his plan with dignity! We've won!"

Unfortunately, the Lady Herald seemed to have left some trace of her voice-hurling magic behind, for the whispered words carried to every corner of the chamber. Lord Haladavar flushed a deep, rich red, but the Coronal laughed merrily and said, "No, lords, I mean it! Opening we shall have—but an Opening with the People well protected!"

"I suppose we'll now waste the best efforts of our young mages on *this* now, for the next twoscore seasons or so," Lord Malgath snapped.

The flash of one of the old-fashioned little globes known as "come hither" signals spilled forth among the courtiers then, and everyone looked to see its source. As a buzz of conversation arose and Lord Malgath's comment hung unanswered, the Lady Herald cut through the gaping ranks of well-dressed elves like a wasp seeking to sting, and came at last to an aged elf in dark, plain robes. She smiled, turned to face the Throne, and announced, "Mythanthar would speak."

The three lords frowned in puzzlement as the courtiers burst again into excited whispers, but the Coronal made the gesture for silence. When it had fallen, the Lady Herald touched the old mage with her sleeve, and by her magic his thin, quavering voice rang clear to every corner of that vast hall. "I would remind Cormanthans of the 'spell fields' I tried to develop from mantles, for use by our war captains, three thousand years agone. Our need passed, and I turned to other things, but I know now what direction to work in, where I was ignorant before. In elder days, our magic weavers could easily alter how magic worked in a given area. I shall craft a spell that does the same, and give Cormanthor its mantle. From end to end of this fair city there shall be a 'mythal.' Give me three seasons to get started, and I shall then be able to give thee a count of how many more I shall need."

There was a momentary silence as everyone waited for him to say more, but Mythanthar waved that he was done, and turned away from the herald; the Court erupted in excited chatter.

"My lord," Lord Malgath snapped, approaching the Throne and raising his arms in his anxiousness to be heard (overhead, the Srinshee aimed two scepters at him, her face set and stern). "please hear me: it is imperative that this 'mythal' deny the working of any magic by all N'Tel'Quess—in fact, by all who are not purebloods of Cormanthor!"

"And it must reveal to all the alignments of folk entering it," Lord Haladavar said excitedly, "to protect us from the shapeshifting beasts and all who dare to impersonate elves, or even specific elven lords!"

"Well said!" Lord Urddusk echoed. "It should also, and for the same reason, make invisible things visible at its boundaries, and prevent teleportation into or out of it, or we'll have invading armies of adventurers in our laps every night!"

Nearly every elf at court was crowding forward now, bobbing their heads, waving their arms, and shouting their own suggestions; as the din mounted, the

Coronal finally spread his hands in resignation and pressed one of the buttons set deep in one arm of the Throne.

There was a blinding brilliance as the Coronal's lightshock wave took effect. It kept almost everyone from seeing the dagger hurled at the Coronal from the ranks of courtiers. That blade struck the field created by the scepter in the Srinshee's left hand and was transported to an empty storage cellar deep under the north wing of the palace.

It also had its intended effect: everyone except the Coronal on his throne staggered backward, stunned into silence.

Into the gentle moaning sounds that followed, as folk fought to clear the swirling lights from their eyes, the ruler of all Cormanthor said gently, "No mythal can hope to include every desire expressed by every Cormanthan, but I intend that it act on as many as are possible and tenable. Please make all of your suggestions to the Lady Herald of the court; she will convey them to the senior mages of the court and to myself. Mythanthar, have my deepest thanks—and my hopes that all Cormanthor will soon echo that thanks. It is my will that you craft an initial version of your mythal—no matter how incomplete or crude—as soon as possible, for presentation to the court."

"Revered Lord, I shall do so," Mythanthar replied, bowing low. He turned away again, and high above him, the Srinshee's eyes widened. Had there, or had there not, been a circle of nine sparks around the old mage's head, just for an instant?

Well, there was none to be seen now. Face thoughtful, the Srinshee watched him totter toward one of the tapestries, face thoughtful. Her eyes widened again an instant later—and this time one of the scepters in her hands leaped slightly as it hurled forth magic.

The old mage passed out among the tapestries, and Oluevaera was pleased to note that two of the Coronal's best young armathors fell into place before and behind him, wearing ornamental half-cloaks that her mage-sight could see were generating a metal-warding field between them. Mythanthar's own mantle should take care of any hurled spells, and he should soon stand in his own tower again, unharmed, now that the first opportunistic attack on him had been foiled.

The Srinshee watched grimly as a courtier in a plum-colored tunic, whose name and lineage she did not know, sagged back against a wall, staring down at his hand. His face was white and his mouth was gaping in soundless shock.

Her aim had been good; that hand was now a withered, clawlike thing mottled with age . . . and too weak to hold the deadly triple-bladed dagger that lay on the floor beneath it.

"I must confess I am still gloating about the success Duilya enjoyed," Alaglossa Tornglara confided, the moment they were out of hearing of their servants. The two parties of uniformed retainers carefully set down the purchases made by their lady masters at the side of the street, and stood patient guard over them.

"They'll not all be that easy, I'm afraid," the Lady Ithrythra Mornmist murmured.

"Indeed; have you seen the Lady Auglamyr? Amaranthae, I mean. She was as still and silent as a statue today; I wonder if the wooing of a certain High Court Mage is troubling her."

"No," Ithrythra said slowly, "it's something else. She's worried for someone, but not herself. She barely notices what she's wearing, and sends Auglamyr pages scurrying on dozens of seeking errands, by the hour. She's lost something . . . or someone."

"I wonder what can have befallen?" Lady Tornglara breathed, a frown drawing down her beautiful features into solemnity. "This must be something serious, I'll be bound."

"Intrigues in the streets, now, is it?" The voice that hailed them was almost exuberantly arrogant; Elandorr Waelvor, flower of the third elder House of the realm, was gleeful about something.

He was resplendent in a jerkin of black velvet trimmed about with white thunderbolts, and a cloak of rich purple with a magenta lining swirled about his shoulders and gleaming black thigh-high boots as he advanced upon them. His slim, elegant fingers bristled with rings, and the jeweled silver scabbard of his sword of honor was so long that it slapped at his ankles with every step. The two ladies watched him strut, their faces expressionless.

Elandorr seemed to sense their unspoken disapproval; he lowered his brows, clasped his hands behind his back, and started to circle them.

"Though 'tis refreshing to see the younger, more vigorous houses of Cormanthor grow into taking an interest in the doings of the realm," he said airily, "I must caution you ladies that overmuch talk about affairs of import would be a bad, nay, a *very* bad thing. It has recently been my painful duty to ah, curb the behavioral excesses of the wayward Lady Symrustar, of the fledgling House of Auglamyr. You may have heard something about it, borne on the lamentable winds of gossip with which our fair city seems so intolerably afflicted . . . ?"

The upward, inquisitorial rise of his voice, and his lifted brows, urged a reply; he was momentarily disconcerted when both ladies silently arched scornful eyebrows of their own, locked gazes with him, and said nothing.

His eyes flashed with irritation as he spun away from the weight of two level stares, swirling his cloak grandly. Then Elandorr put his hand to his breast, sighed theatrically, and turned back toward them. "It would grieve me deeply," he said passionately, "to hear the same tragic sort of news mooted about the city concerning the proud ladies of Mornmist and Tornglara. Yet such misfortunes can all too easily befall any elven she who doesn't know her proper place, and now keep to it—in the new Cormanthor."

"And which 'new Cormanthor' would that be, Lord Waelvor?" Alaglossa asked softly, wide-eyed, two fingers to her chin.

"Why, this realm around us, known and loved by all true Connanthans. This realm as it will be in a moon or so, renewed and set back on the proper path that was good enough for our ancestors, and theirs before them."

"Renewed? By whom, and how?" Ithrythra joined in the dumbfounded game. "Coyly gloating young lordlings?"

Elandorr scowled at her, and drew his lips back from his teeth in an unlovely smile. "I shan't forget your insolence, 'Lady', and shall act appropriately—you may assure yourself of that!"

"Lord, I shall await you," she said, dropping her head in deference. As she did so, she rolled her eyes.

With a growl, Elandorr swept past her, deliberately extending his elbow to strike her head as he did so—but somehow, as she swayed out of his reach, he found himself bearing down on the back of a servant who had appeared out of nowhere to attend to the Lady Tornglara. Elandorr cast an angry look around and saw that servants of both ladies were closing in around him, eyes averted from him but with daggers, goads, and carry-yokes in their hands. The scion of the Waelvors snarled and quickened his pace, striding out of the closing press of bodies.

The servants crowded in around both ladies, who looked at each other and discovered that they were both dark-eyed, quick of breath, and flaring about the nostrils. The tips of their ears were red with anger.

"A dangerous foe, and now one fully aware of you, Ithrythra," Alaglossa said in soft warning.

"Ah, but look how much he blurted out about someone's future plans for the realm, because he lost his temper," Ithrythra replied. Then she looked at the servants all around them both and said, "I thank all of you. 'Twas very brave, walking into our peril when you could—should—have stayed safely away."

"Nay, Lady; 'twas all we could do, and still know any honor in our days," one of the older male stewards muttered.

Ithrythra smiled at him, and replied, "Well, if I ever act so rude as yon lordling, you've my permission to toss me down in the mud and use that goad of yours a time or two on my backside!"

"Best forewarn your lord of his arrival, though," Alaglossa put in with a smile. "This man's one of mine!"

A general roar of mirth erupted, in which all joined—but then died away slowly as, one by one, they turned and looked along the street to discover that Elandorr Waelvor hadn't walked all that far off after all. He obviously thought that their laughter had been at his direct expense, and was standing looking at them all with black murder in his eyes.

Lord Ihimbraskar Evendusk floated at ease several feet above his own bed, naked as his birthing day, smiling at his lady like an admiring young elven lover.

Lady Duilya Evendusk smiled back at him, her chin resting on her hands, and her elbows resting on the same empty air. She wore only fine golden chains studded with gems; they hung down in loops toward the bed below.

"So, my lord, what news today?" she breathed, still delighted that he'd hastened straight home to disrobe after Court emptied—and that he'd reacted with delight, and not irritation, to find her waiting in his bed. The ceremonially ignored bottle of tripleshroom sherry was still on the floor where she'd ordered it set; Duilya doubted her lord had touched a drop since seeing her drain one such bottle. She wondered when—if—she'd ever dare tell him about the magic her lady friends had worked, to enable her to do that drinking.

"Three senior lords," her Ihimbraskar told her, "Haladavar, Urddusk and that serpent Malgath, came to Court and demanded that the Coronal reconsider the Opening. They wore stormswords, and threatened to use them."

"And do they yet live?" Duilya asked dryly.

"They do. Eltargrim chose to view their weapons as 'errors in judgment.'"

Duilya snorted. "The enemy armathor gasped out blood as my error of judgment took him through the vitals," she declaimed grandly, waving a hand. Her lord chuckled.

"Wait, love, there's more," he told her, rolling over. She shrugged at him to continue; her hair slid down over her shoulder and fell free.

Ihimbraskar watched her tresses spread and swing back and forth as he continued, "The Coronal said their concerns were valid, had his Lady Herald scare us all with tales of the battle-might of humans, and said the Opening will go ahead eventually: *after* the city is cloaked in a huge spellmantle!"

Duilya frowned. "What, old crazed Mythanthar's 'mythal' again? What good will that be, if the realm is open to all?"

"Aye, Mythanthar, and it'll give us control over what these nonelven intruders do, and what magic they work, and what they can hide, by the sounds of it," her lord said.

Duilya drifted closer, and as she reached out to stroke his chest, she added softly, "Elves too, my lord—elves too!"

Lord Evendusk started to shake his head dismissively, then froze, looking very thoughtful, and said in a small voice, "Duilya—however have I kept myself from utter stupidity, all these years I ignored you? Spells can be crafted to work only on creatures of certain races, and to ignore others . . . but will they be? What a weapon in the hand of whoever is Coronal!"

"It seems to me, my lord," Duilya said as she rolled over to rest the side of her face against his and fix him with a very solemn eye, "that we'd better work as hard as we can to see that Eltargrim is still our Coronal, and not one of these ambitious ardavanshee—in particular, not one of the oh-so-noble sons of our three highest houses. They may consider humans and the like no better than snakes and ground-slugs, but they look upon the rest of us elven Cormanthans as no better than cattle. The Opening will make them scared for the security of their lofty positions, and so, ruthlessly desperate in their acts."

"Why aren't *you* a court advisor?" Ihimbraskar sighed.

Duilya rolled over atop him and said sweetly, "I am. I advise the court through you."

Lord Evendusk groaned. "Too true. You make me sound like some sort of lackey you send off into danger every day, to put forth your views."

The Lady Duilya Evendusk smiled and said nothing. Their eyes met, and held steady. There was a twinkle in her eyes as she continued to say nothing.

A slow smile crooked Ihimbraskar's usually hard mouth. "Corellon praise you and damn you, Lady," he said, in the breath before he started to laugh helplessly.

Fifteen
A Mythal, Maybe

It came to pass that Elminster was slain by the elves, or nearly so, and by the grace of Mystra drifted about Cormanthor in the shape of a ghost or phantom, powerless and unseen—akin, some have said, to the lot of scullery maids in service to a highborn lady. Like such wenches, woe would likely befall the last prince of Athalantar if he were to come to the notice of the mighty. The master sorcerers of the elves were powerful in those days, and faster to make war and cast forth reckless magics. They saw the world around them, and all humans in it, as rebellious playthings to be tamed often, swiftly, and harshly. Among certain of the elven, that thinking has changed but little to this day.

Antarn the Sage
from *The High History of Faerûnian Archmages Mighty*
published circa The Year of the Staff

Symrustar was naked, her face a dark mask of dried blood. She stared out of the shadow cast by her overhanging hair, seeing neither Elminster nor anything else in Faerûn. Foam bubbled at the corners of her trembling mouth as she panted and whimpered. If there was still a whole mind behind those eyes, Elminster could see no evidence of it.

Elandorr must be an even more vicious rival than Symrustar had thought. El felt sick. He had done this, by whisking Elandorr past her defenses and letting him see into her mind. It was his to undo, if he could.

Lady, he said, or tried to. *Symrustar Auglamyr,* he called softly, knowing that he was making no sound. Perhaps if he drifted right into her head . . . or would that do more harm?

She half-fell on her face then, as she blundered into the top of a gully, and El shrugged. How could she be made any worse? The danger of a predator was very real, and would grow worse as darkness came. He drifted in past her eyes, into the confusing darkness beyond, trying to perceive anything around him as he called her name again. Nothing.

El drifted through the tortured elven lady, and looked sadly at her backside as she lurched away from him, drooling and making confused, wordless noises. He could do nothing.

In his present state, he couldn't even stroke her with a soothing touch, or speak to her. He was truly a phantom . . . and she was possibly dying, and probably mad. The Srinshee might be able to help her, but he knew not where the Lady Oluevaera might be found.

Mystra, he cried again, *aid me! Please!*

He waited, drifting, looking anxiously into Symrustar's unseeing eyes from time to time as she waddled onwards, but no matter how long or often he called, there was no apparent reply. Uncertainly El floated along beside the crawling, moaning elven sorceress, as she made her slow and painful way through the forest.

Once she panted, "Elandorr, no!" and El hoped other lucid words would follow, but she growled, made some yipping sounds, and then burst into tears . . . tears that in the end became the murmuring sound again.

Perhaps even Mystra couldn't hear him now. No, that was foolish; it must have been she who restored him after his folly at the ruined castle. It seemed she wanted him to learn a lesson now, though.

If he flew back across the mountains and desert to that temple of Mystra beyond Athalantar, or one of the other holy places of the goddess he'd heard of, perhaps the priests could give him his body back.

If they could even sense him, that is. Who was to say they could, where the spell-hurling elves of Cormanthor could not?

Perhaps he'd be noticed if he passed through an unfolding spell, or blundered into the chambers of a mage trying to craft a new magic. Yet if he left Symrustar . . .

He whirled in the air in exasperation, coming to a wrenching decision. He could do nothing but watch if she got hurt or attacked or killed right now. If he regained his body, surely he could use spells to find her, or at least send someone else to rescue her; the Srinshee, perhaps. He didn't give much for his chances of convincing House Auglamyr that he, the hated human armathor, somehow knew that Elandorr Waelvor had left their dearest daughter and heir crawling through the forest like a mad-witted animal.

No, he could do nothing for Symrustar. If she died out here, it wasn't as though she was an innocent who'd done nothing to bring this on herself. No, gods above, she'd earned it many times over before the blundering human Elminster had happened along and she'd seen him as a good fit for her clutches.

And yet he was almost as guilty of her present state as if he'd broken her mind and body himself.

He had to get back to the city, and hope that he could communicate with someone. At that thought, El hurled himself through the trees, not caring if he went around or through, racing back to the streets and grand homes of Cormanthor. He thrust himself right through the glowing armor of a patrol leader who was just directing his warriors into the formation he favored for leaving the city.

Dusk was falling. El swooped through a line of glowing globes of air that hung above the second street he came upon, illuminating an impromptu party. Though one of them seemed to bob and flicker after he passed through it, he could feel nothing.

He turned toward the Coronal's palace once more, and saw soft light coming from part way up a tower he'd never noticed before. The last light of day was fading off across the gardens; he slowed near the window and saw, in the chamber within, the Coronal sitting in a chair, apparently asleep. The Srinshee was leaning on one of its arms and speaking to the six court sorceresses, who sat in a ring all around.

If he had any good hope of aid in Cormanthor, it lay in that room. Elminster rushed excitedly along the side of the palace, seeking a way in.

He found a slightly open window almost immediately, but it led to a storeroom so securely sealed off from the rest of the palace that he could go no further. He boiled up out of it again, frustration rising; every moment wasted was more of the conversation in that lighted chamber that he wouldn't hear. He raced along the wall until he found one of those large windows whose "glass" was no glass at all, but an invisible field of magic.

He felt a slight tingling as he darted through it, and almost whirled to go through again, in hopes that this heralded a return to solidity, but no. Later. He had a gathering to eavesdrop on now.

He knew what room he needed to enter, and his sense of direction was supported by the three tinglings he felt as he drew near it, and encountered spell after spell of warding. The Srinshee certainly didn't want anyone to overhear what was going on in that room.

Its door, however, was old and massive, and therefore worn so much by centuries of swinging that there was a sizable chink around the frame. El darted in excitedly, and raced right through the ring of listening sorceresses to circle the tiny figure at their heart.

The Srinshee gave no sign of feeling or hearing him, as he bellowed her name and waved his hands through her. El sighed, resigned himself to more of this silent ghostliness, and settled down to hover above the empty arm of the Coronal's chair, to listen in earnest. He'd arrived, it seemed—thank Mystra—at the best part.

"Bhuraelea and Mladris," the Srinshee was saying, "must shield Mythanthar's body at all times—and themselves besides, for any foe rebuffed in an initial strike at Emmyth will surely seek out the source of his protection and try to eliminate it. His mantle bests any of ours, and I suggest only one augmentation: Sylmae, you cast the web of watching I gave you so as to mesh with Emmyth's mantle. You and Holone must then take turns observing it. It will lash back at anyone seeking to pierce it with spells by itself, yes, but such attackers may be well protected, and suffer no harm at all. I want you two *not* to strike at them, but simply to identify them and inform us all as soon as possible."

"That leaves us idle again," the sorceress Ajhalanda said a little sadly, her gesture taking in herself and Yathlanae, the elven maid who sat at her elbow.

"Not so," the Srinshee said with a smile. "Your shared task is to lay spells that listen for anyone in the realm who utters the names 'Emmyth' or 'Mythanthar' or even 'Lord Iydril,' though I suspect few of the Cormyth of today recall that title. Identify them, try to follow what they're saying, and report back."

"Anything else?" Holone asked, a little wearily.

"I know what it is to be young, and restless to be doing things," the Srinshree said softly. "Watching and waiting is the hardest work, ladies. I think it best if we meet here four morns hence, and switch tasks."

"What will you be doing?" Sylmae asked, nodding in agreement with the Srinshee's plan.

"Guarding the Coronal, of course," the Lady Oluevaera said with a smile. "*Someone* has to."

Mouths crooked with amusement around the circle. A half smile played about the edges of the Srinshee's mouth as she turned slowly to meet the eyes of each of the six in turn, and receive their slight nods of agreement.

"I know it chafes not to be working unfettered, you six," she added softly, "but I suspect the time for that will come soon enough, when the prouder houses of this realm realize that a mythal is going to curb their own spellhurlings and covert activities. Then our troubles will begin in earnest."

"How far may we go, should things come to open spell battle in these 'troubles'?" Holone asked quietly.

"Oh, they will, spellsister, they assuredly will," the Srinshee replied. "You must all feel free to do what you feel needful; blast any foe at will, to death and beyond. Hesitate not to strike out at any Cormanthan whose intent you are sure of, who works against the Coronal or the creation of a mythal. The future of our realm is at stake; no price is too high to pay."

Heads were nodding in somber silence, all round the circle. The Coronal chose that moment to snore; the Srinshee regarded him affectionately as the six sorceresses smiled and rose.

"Hasten!" she bid them, eyes shining. "You are the guardians of Cormanthor, and its future. Go forth, and win victory!"

"Queen of Spells," Sylmae intoned in a male-sounding roar, striking her chest, "we go!"

This was evidently some sort of quotation; there was a general ripple of mirth, and then the six sorceresses were on the move in a graceful swirling of long hair and robes and longer legs. El cast a brief, sad glance at the Srinshee, who still could not hear his loudest cry of her name, and followed the one called Bhuraelea, making careful note of the face and form of Mladris, in case keeping silent escort to her became necessary instead.

As it happened, the two tall, slender sorceresses kept together, striding down a palace corridor with the haste of a storm wind. "Should we eat something, do you think?" Bhuraelea asked her fellow mage, as they stepped out past the last palace ward-field and turned themselves invisible. El, hovering close by, was relieved to see that they remained clearly visible to him, though their bodies now seemed outlined with a bluish gleam, like strong winter starlight reflected off snow.

"I brought some food earlier," Mladris replied. "I'll summon it before we enter his first ward." She wrinkled her nose. "Wait until you see his tower; some old males embrace the idea of 'home as dump' rather too wholeheartedly."

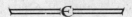

The two sorceresses were passing a jack of mint water and a cold grouse pie back and forth as they slipped through the glowing wards that surrounded the rather ramshackle tower of Mythanthar the mage. Starfall Turret resembled a long, grassy barrow-hill, pierced along one side with windows, and rising at its north end into a squat, rough-walled stone tower. Its yard was an overgrown tangle of stumps, fallen trees, and forest shrubs and creepers. In the dusk, they looked like a dark chaos of giants' fingers stabbing the darkening sky.

"Ye gods and heroes," Bhuraelea murmured. "Defending this against stealthy foes would take an army."

"That's us," Mladris agreed cheerfully, and then added, "Thank the gods, our foes aren't likely to be any too stealthy. They're more apt to try to crush the wards with realm-shaking spells, and then follow up with more."

"Three wards . . . no, four. That'll take a lot of blasting," Bhuraelea observed, as they finished the pie and licked their fingers. A light flared briefly in one of the high windows of the tower.

"He's at it already," Mladris said.

Bhuraelea grimaced. "He's probably been 'at it' since he stepped out of the Chamber of the Court," she replied. "The Lady Oluevaera told me he's apt to be more than a bit single-minded. We could dance nude around him and sing courting songs in his ear, she said, and he'd probably murmur that it was nice to have such energetic young things around, and could we please fetch yon powders for him?"

"Gods," Mladris said feelingly, rolling her eyes, "grant that I never get old enough to be like that."

Out of the empty air very close by a cold voice said smugly, "Granted."

An instant later, Faerûn exploded into many leaping lightnings, bright arcs that raced hungrily through the air to stab through the gasping, staggering sorceresses and snarl onward. Mladris and Bhuraelea were snatched off their daintily booted feet and hurled back over shrubs and brambles, with smoke streaming from their mouths and flames spitting fitfully from their eyes.

Even Elminster was taken by surprise; how had he missed seeing the cruel-faced elven mage who was now rising, a vengeful column of mist turning solid, above the tangled garden? Clouds of radiance were swirling in from all directions to join the thickening form of the sorcerer. As he grew taller and more solid, he calmly continued to lash the coughing, sobbing sorceresses with crackling streams of lightning, allowing them no moment to recover or escape.

Sparks fell in showers from the elf's hands as he stepped forward, treading on the empty air with a mincing swagger of satisfaction. El felt a stinging pain as they drifted through him and winked out. He swirled around the mage, swooping and shouting in silent futility.

The innermost ward had been no ward at all, but the cloudlike, alert form of the mage, awaiting aid, intentional or otherwise!

"Haemir Waelvor, at your service," the elven sorcerer told the two ladies, when their burned and trembling bodies were so enwrapped with lightnings that they couldn't move. "The Starym seem to be delayed—perhaps wanting me to do the dirty work before they deign to appear. It matters little, now that I have your life-energies to feed my shield-sundering. You're here to protect feeble-witted, doddering old Mythanthar, I take it? A pity; you're going to be the death of him instead."

Bhuraelea managed a groan of protest; little black flames leaped from her mouth. Mladris hung limp and silent, her eyes open, staring, and dark. Only a pulse racing in her throat showed that she yet lived.

El felt rage rising in him like a hungry red tide, demanding release. He turned ponderously, letting the anger build into shaking energy that burst out at last in a long, soundless charge that took him through the lightnings that bound the two sorceresses, and straight at the Waelvor mage.

Halfway there he arched and cried out in silent pain and surprise. He could feel the lightnings! Their caster could see and feel his contact, too; Haemir's eyes narrowed at the sight of his suddenly crackling, spitting, somehow dimmed bolts of lightning. What was *dragging* at them so?

Waelvor's lips thinned. Old Mythanthar, or some other meddler? It mattered little. He snarled something, and moved one hand in a quick spell that spun a dozen slicing blades to clash in the air at the point of the disturbance.

El watched the blades appear and tumble down behind him, and rose up out of the lightnings feeling both pain and exhilaration. Some of their energy was racing around inside him, making him tingle unpleasantly, and scattering sparks from his mouth and eyes.

The Waelvor wizard's eyes widened in surprise as he dimly perceived the lightning-lashed outline of an elven—or was it human?—shape, an instant before it smashed into him.

El struck with all his force, lashing and slashing, trying to overwhelm Haemir Waelvor through sheer ferocity. When he "touched" the mage, he felt no solidity, only a tingling as the lightnings rolled out of him, then searing pain as the interlaced spells of the wizard's mantle tried to tear him apart, phantom that he was.

While Elminster rolled in midair screaming soundlessly in agony, Haemir Waelvor shook his head, roaring, his own lightnings spitting and coiling from his mouth in their rude return. The pupils of his eyes suddenly turned as milky and sparkling as a white opal—a look El had last seen years back, in the eyes of a mage who'd just fallen victim to his own confusion spell.

El shook his head and screamed again, trying to gain control of his own pain-wracked form. So, he could hurt—or at least cause pain and confusion to—folk he rushed through, could he?

Shuddering, he drifted away to a distant vantage point to watch, knowing he could do nothing to aid the two sorceresses, who lay slumped where the failing lightnings had released them.

He needed to know how long it would take a wizard to recover—and if swooping through one as a spell was being cast would ruin and waste the magic. He'd have to go through this punishment all over again.

Mystra, let this elf be a long time recovering, El said in fervent prayer. But it seemed Mystra was contrary-minded, or at least hard of hearing, this day: Haemir was already staggering about, feeling for his surroundings with an outstretched hand, holding his head, and cursing weakly. El was sorely tempted to gather himself and plunge through the elven mage again right now, but he needed to know what sort of damage his passing through an elf would do. And hadn't this smug Waelvor mage said something about the Starym showing up? It might be best not to be all that clearly visible whenever a group of cruel elven sorcerers arrived, looking for trouble.

Haemir Waelvor was shaking his head gingerly as if to clear it now, and his curses were gathering force.

He seemed on the verge of recovery while a certain ghostly Elminster certainly still hurt, acutely and all over.

Mystra curse him. He was going to drain these two lady sorceresses to husks while the last prince of Athalantar hovered over him on watch, powerless to stop him!

Of course, Elminster reflected wryly, an instant later, things could get worse—much worse. Right now, for instance.

One after the other, the outer wards were failing, sundering themselves in silent explosions of sparks at a certain point and fading away outwards from there. The center of this disruption was something that looked like a tall black flame, one that promptly split as it glided through the last ward, and died away to—reveal three tall, fine-boned elven males in robes whose sashes of flame-hued silk were adorned with twin falling dragons. The Starym had come.

"Hail, Lord Waelvor," one said in tones of velvet softness, as the three figures strode forward together, treading air with a languid air of cold superiority. "What distress finds you here, in the empty night? Did yon ladies seek to defend themselves?"

"A watchghost," Haemir hissed, his eyes glittering with mingled pain and anger. "It awaited, and struck me. I fought it off, but the pain lingers. And how does this fair night find you, my lords?"

"Bored," one of them said bluntly. "Still, perhaps the old fool can provide us with some sport ere we send him to dust. Let us see."

He strode forward, and the other two Starym drew apart to flank him and follow, moving their fingers in the intricate passes and gestures of mighty battle spells. They strode right past the Waelvor wizard and the crumpled bodies of the two fallen sorceresses. El hovered near Haemir, fearing he might take out his rage on the ladies, and watched the Starym strike.

From the cupped palms of one wizard white fire burst forth, rushing upwards in a sinuous column like an eel seeking the stars, only to burst apart into three long, serpentine necks that grew huge, dragonlike maws at their ends. Those heads shook themselves restlessly, and then bent and bit at the old stone tower. Where their teeth touched, stone silently vanished, melting away into nothingness and laying bare the chambers within.

From the fingertips of the second wizard red lances of racing fire then erupted, leaping into the revealed chambers of Mythanthar's tower to smite certain things of magic. Some of those things exploded into bright showers of sparks, or blasts that rocked Starfall Turret and hurled slivers of its stones far away into the gathering darkness, to crash through trees to unseen distant landings. Others burst into rushing red flames, swirling into fiery pinwheels that hung here and there in the tower, pinned in place by the Starym wizard's magic.

From the hands of the third mage a green cloud billowed, grew teeth and many clawed limbs with frightening speed, and flew forth into the tower, hunting Mythanthar.

A breath or two after its dive into Starfall Turret, something flared a vivid purple deep inside those shattered stones, and a bright bolt of that radiance snarled out, spitting aside the dismembered claws of the green monster as it came. Haemir Waelvor watched them spin down to crash into the shrubbery, and cursed in fear.

The three Starym flinched and scrambled away from the tower on the heels of his oath, as the purple radiance burst into three fingers that stabbed out at them, veering to follow each scrambling elf.

Personal mantles flared into visibility as they were tested; one mage stiffened, threw out his arms as his mantle turned to roiling purple and black smoke around him, and then fell hard on his face, and lay still.

The other two mages spun around and cried something to each other that El couldn't catch; their voices were high and distorted in frantic fear. It seemed the old fool was providing them with just a trifle more sport than they'd expected.

The body of the fallen Starym spat sparks and sputtering wisps of dying spells as he expired. His head remained bent at a sickening angle against the old stump, but the rest of his body slowly melted its way into the ground.

Waelvor stared down at it in gaping amazement, but the two surviving Starym paid their relative no heed as they busily spun magic. Fingers flew and the very air around the two elves crackled and flowed, like oil sliding down the inside of a water-filled bowl. Tiny motes of light flickered here and there as the mages danced the measures of a long and intricate spell.

As the twin magics unfolded, two glowing clouds of pale green radiance faded into being above the heads of the Starym, shedding enough light to show the sweat glistening on corded necks and working jaws.

Then, with a silent flourish, one cloud coalesced into a sphere and began to spin. The second followed an instant later, and two globes of force hung in the air above the busy elven mages.

Haemir swore again, his features as sharp and white as if they'd been quarried out of milky marble.

A red mist streamed out of the riven turret, reaching for the intruders in a long, inexorable wave, and they were almost stumbling in haste as they plucked scepters, wands, gems, and various small and winking items out of their sashes and hurled them up into the spheres above their heads. Each item floated there, drifting lazily around among the other items in the spheres.

The red mist was only feet away when one of the Starym snapped out a single ringing word—or perhaps it was a name—and every item of magic in his sphere went off at once, tearing apart the very air in a darksome rift of glimmering stars that sucked in the sphere, the items, the red mist, and much of the gardens and front face of the tower before it vanished with a high sighing sound.

The other Starym mage laughed in triumph before he said the word that awakened the items in his sphere.

They rose, like flies disturbed from carrion on a hot day, and spat a deadly volley of bright beams into the tower, which burst apart amid deafening thunders, raining down stones all around and releasing a cloud of crimson dust as some ancient magic or other failed.

The rift in the wake of these beams was small, sucking in only the items themselves and the sphere that had contained them before it vanished; no doubt this was the way the spell was supposed to work.

The two surviving Starym were moving their hands again, weaving unfamiliar—but seemingly strong—magics as they stared into the tower. By their shared manner, Mythanthar must be visible to them, and still very much alive and active.

El made his decision. Scudding low across the darkened garden, he built up speed and smashed through Waelvor. This time the impact was like being hit across the chest by a solidly-swung log; it drove all the breath out of him in a soundless scream. He passed through the body of the mage and plunged into the head of the nearest Starym like a hurled spear.

The blow sent him spinning end over end through the night, shuddering in agony so great that it snatched all his breath away again, and a golden haze of dazedness began to swirl around him.

He had the satisfaction, however, of seeing the Starym he'd struck rolling on the ground, clutching his head and whimpering. The other Starym stared at his fellow in disbelief and so didn't see the blackened figure that trudged out of the tower behind him, trailing smoke. An elf who could only be Mythanthar.

The old elf turned and looked back at the tiny flames that were now leaping from every stone of his shattered tower. He shook his head, leveled one finger at the mage who was still standing, and—as the Starym whirled around belatedly—vanished.

An instant later, a golden sphere erupted out of thin air, cutting the Starym neatly in two at chest level as it englobed his torso.

When the sphere imploded again an instant later, it took the upper body of the proud elven mage with it, leaving only two trembling legs behind. They took one staggering step and then parted company, toppling in different directions to the ground.

"*You!*"

The cry was both furious and frightened. El swirled around, still slowed and mind-mazed by his agonies, and realized that the lone surviving Starym, now staggering up from the ground, meant *him*. The elf could see the human!

Now, if he could only survive to reach the Srinshee, and tell her . . .

The Starym spat something malicious, and raised his hands in a casting Elminster had seen before: a spell humans called a "meteor swarm."

"Mystra, be with me *now*," the last prince of Athalantar murmured, as four balls of roiling flame raced to positions around him, and exploded.

The last thing El saw was the body of Haemir Waelvor turning to ashes as it tumbled helplessly toward him, borne on roaring flames that were bursting forth to consume the world all around. Faerûn turned over, spun crazily, and then whirled away into hungry fire.

Sixteen
Masked Mages

The People looked upon Elminster Aumar, and saw, but did not understand what they saw. He was the first gust of the new wind sent by Mystra. And Cormanthor was like an old and mighty wall, that stands against such winds of change for century upon century, until even its builders forget that it was built, and was ever anything else but an unyielding barrier. There will come a day for such a wall when it will topple, and be changed by the unseen, unsolid winds. It always does.

That day came for the proud realm when the Coronal named the human Elminster Aumar a knight of Cormanthor—but the wall knew not that it had been shattered, and waited for its tumbling stones to crash to earth before it would deign to notice. That fall, when it came, would be the laying of the Mythal. But the stones of the wall being elven stones, lingered in the air for an astonishingly long while. . . .

Shalheira Talandren, High Elven Bard of Summerstar
from *Silver Blades And Summer Nights:
An Informal But True History of Cormanthor*
published in The Year of the Harp

Stars swam overhead, and eyeballs gleamed below. Elminster frowned as he fought his way back to awareness. Eyeballs? He rolled over—or thought he did—for a better look. The night around him slowly spun itself clear.

Yes, definitely: eyeballs. Scores of blinking and glistening eyeballs, flickering into being and disappearing again in a constant winking cloud as the bored and jaded elves of Cormanthor heard about the latest excitement and hastened to watch from a safe distance.

A few, by the way they drifted up to peer and blink at him, had definitely noticed the motionless, drifting ripple among the stars that was Ehninster—a ragged cloud of human-shaped mist, thinned from floating so long, senseless, above the riven stump of Mythanthar's tower.

That still-smoking, charred heap of fallen stones was a sea of the little orbs, flitting here and there like curious fireflies as the eyes of distant elves peered at every last detail of the old mage's revealed magic.

As Elminster watched them dart and peer with mild interest, he slowly became aware of his surroundings—and who he was—again.

Two Starym had died here, but of the third there was no sign. The bodies of the two sorceresses had also vanished; El hoped the Srinshee had whisked them away to safety and healing before less kind observers had spotted them.

Two of the floating eyes in the ruins below suddenly veered to look at the same thing, as if it had done something to interest them. Elminster swooped down to catch a look, startling several other blinking orbs.

The two eyes were staring at nothing. Or rather they stared at something blurred and twisted, rotating in the air and creating nothingness.

It was a cone or spiral of smoky strands that moved purposefully among the ruins, poking at a shelf here, and a pile of tumbled stone blocks there. Where it poked its open end, solid items vanished, whisked away to—elsewhere.

El drifted closer, trying to see what was disappearing. Stone blocks, aye, but only to clear a way through rubble to the space beyond. In that space— magic! An item here, a broken fragment of apparatus there, a stand yonder, a crucible just here . . . the helix of smoke was sucking up and stealing away things that Mythanthar had used to work magic, or that held spells stored within them.

Was this a thing Mythanthar himself was directing, to snatch away what could be salvaged before other Cormanthan hands seized what he was not there to defend? Or did it serve some other master?

It certainly seemed to know where magic might be found. El watched it root through a tangle of fallen spars—ceiling-beams—in one corner, to find whatever had rested on the table beneath, and then . . .

He drifted closer, to peer around the wreckage and see what the helix was after. There was—

Suddenly smoky lines were whirling all around Elminster, and Faerûn was twisting between them, rushing away. The magical gatherer must have been lurking below the lip of the overhanging debris, deliberately waiting for him. Everything was whirling, now, and El sighed aloud. Whither *this* time?

Mystra, he called almost plaintively, as he was whirled down and away into a darkening, sickening elsewhere, *when is my task to begin? And what, by all the watching stars, IS it?*

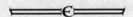

Long, long, he spiraled, until he almost forgot what stillness was, and could scarce remember light. Panic clutched at Elminster's heart and thoughts, and he tried to scream and sob, but could not.

The whirling continued unabated, through a void that went on and on, heedless of the cries he tried to make. It made no difference to the void whether or not the ghost of a human called Elminster was present, silent or agitated.

He was beneath notice, and powerless.

Yet if he could do nothing, what was there to worry about? He had striven, and known the love of a goddess, and his fate now lay in Mystra's hands. Hands that he knew could be gentle, belonging to one too wise by far to throw away a tool that could still see much use.

As if that thought had been a cue, there came a sudden burst of light around Elminster, and with it an explosion of colors. The smoky cage in which he moved veered into a misty blue area, and raced through it toward a lighter, brighter horizon. Was he rising? It seemed so, as he flashed through clouds of blue mist into—

A chamber he'd not seen before, its floor a glistening sea of black marble, its walls high, its ceiling vaulted. A mage's spellhurling chamber, and in it one elven mage, floating upright, thin, and graceful, pale long-fingered hands moving in almost lazy gestures.

A masked mage, whose eyes flashed in surprise at Elminster's sudden appearance.

The vortex of smoky lines was already whirling El across the chamber, to where a sphere of radiant white light floated, trailing mists of its own as if it was weeping.

The mage watched El spin helplessly across the room and plunge into the sphere, the smoky lines vanishing into the stuff of the sphere itself, leaving the human imprisoned. El tried to drift straight on and out through the curving far wall of the sphere, but it was as solid as stone, and his attempt merely took him on a looping journey around the inside of its curves.

He came softly to a stop facing the source of a brightening light outside the sphere: the masked mage was drifting closer, head cocked in obvious curiosity.

"What have we here?" the anonymous elf asked, in a cold, thin voice. "A human undead? Or . . . something more interesting?"

El nodded in grave greeting, as one equal to another, but said nothing.

The mask seemed to cling to the skin around its wearer's eyes, and to move and flex with it. Beneath it, a superior eyebrow rose in amusement. "I require one thing of all thinking beings I encounter: their name," the elf explained flatly. "Those who resist me, I destroy. Choose swiftly, or I shall make the choice for you."

El shrugged. "My name is no precious secret," he said, and his voice seemed to roll out across the chamber. Here, at least, he could be heard perfectly. "I am Elminster Aumar, a prince in the human land of Athalantar, and the Coronal recently named me an armathor of Cormanthor. I work magic. I also seem to have a blundering talent for upsetting elves whom I encounter."

The mage gave Elminster a cold smile and a nod of agreement. "Indeed. Is your present form voluntary? Good for spying out the secrets of elven magic, perhaps?"

"No," said Elminster genially, "and not particularly."

"How is it, then, that you came to be in the ruined home of the noted elven mage Mythanthar? Have you worked with him?"

"No. Nor am I pledged to any sorcerer of Cormanthor." El doubted this masked wizard would consider the Coronal a sorcerer, and the Srinshee was a "sorceress."

"I'm not accustomed to asking questions twice, and you stand very much within my power." The masked mage drifted a foot or so closer.

El raised an eyebrow of his own. "And whose power would that be? A name for a name is the custom among the People as well as in the affairs of men."

The masked mage seemed to smile—almost. "You may call me The Masked. Speak not again save in answer to my query, or I shall blow you away to nameless dust forever."

El shrugged. "The answer is, I fear, as unrevealing as your name: simple curiosity took me thence, along with half the elves in Cormanthor, it seems, for I fairly swam in peering eyes."

The masked mage did smile this time. "What, then, attracted your curious attention to that locale?"

"The beauty of two sorceresses," El replied. "I wanted to see where they'd go, and perhaps learn their names and where they dwelt."

The Masked acquired a cold smile. "You consider elf-shes fitting mates for human men, do you?"

"I've never considered the matter," Elminster replied easily. "Like most men, I'm attracted to beauty wherever I find it. Like most elves, I see no harm in looking at what I cannot have, or where I dare not venture."

The Masked nodded slightly, and remarked, "Most Cormanthans would deem this chamber around you a place they'd dare not venture into. And rightly so: to intrude here would cost them their lives."

"And have ye come to a decision in the matter of my intrusion?" Elminster asked calmly. "Or was that decision made when ye 'harvested' me in the ruins?"

The elven mage shrugged. "I could easily destroy you. As a visible phantom you have little value other than as a spy or herald—one easily swept away by the right spells. As a whole man, however, you could be of service."

"As a willing agent?" El asked, "Or as a dupe?"

The thin mouth of The Masked tightened still further. "I am not accustomed to overmuch impertinence even from rivals, man—let alone apprentices."

Silence hung between them for a long moment. A very long moment.

Well, Mystra? That silent plea for guidance was instantly rewarded by a glimpse of Elminster nodding in this same room, as the masked elven mage demonstrated something. Well enough.

"Apprentices?" Elminster asked, a breath before his hesitation might become fatally overlong. "Would I be correct in discerning a most gracious offer . . . master?"

The Masked smiled. "You would. I take it you accept?"

"I do. I still have much to learn about magic, and in that learning I should like to be guided by someone I can respect."

The elven mage said nothing, and lost his smile, but something about him seemed to radiate satisfaction as he turned away. "Certain exacting spells are necessary for your return to full and normal physical form," he said over his shoulder, as he strode to a wall, touched it, and watched a stained and battered workbench float into view out of suddenly-revealed darkness behind the wall.

His hands darted here and there among the jars and vessels that littered it. "Remain still and quiet until I bid you stir again," he ordered, turning around again with a mottled purple egg and a silver key in his hand. "The spells I am about to cast will not appear to have any effect; they will take hold about the sphere, and reach you only when I cause the field that now encloses you to vanish."

Elminster nodded, and The Masked began to work magic, laying three small but completely unfamiliar enchantments upon the sphere before embarking on the first magic that El could guess the purpose of. Spheres like the one El was floating in seemed to be the form in which elven mages combined magics to work together upon a single target or focus.

The Masked calmly uttered a single unfamiliar word, and the sphere caught fire.

El wriggled just a little as the heat struck him. The elven sorcerer was already crafting another magic as the flames slowed, faltered, and then abruptly went out, leaving a single rope of smoke climbing into the darkness overhead.

When the Masked turned to face the sphere again, he crooked his finger like a harpist plucking a string, and the smoke abruptly bent toward him. He rotated that hand slowly, as if conducting invisible musicians, and the line of smoke snaked around the sphere, settling into the familiar curves of the helix.

El watched, fascinated, as the masked elf danced and swayed in the working of yet another magic—something that caused a faint music to arise out of nowhere and accompany the tall, graceful body as it swung this way and that.

"Nassabrath," the Masked said suddenly, coming to a halt and kneeling. He drew his left hand, fingers uppermost and palm inwards, vertically down in front of his face as he did so. From the tip of each finger tiny lightnings flared.

They curled and spat toward the sphere with almost aimless sloth; as Elminster watched their slow progress, he called on Mystra once more.

A vision appeared in his mind, as bright and as sudden as if someone had snatched aside a curtain. He was standing naked in the forest, face lined with pain, and covered with scrapes and thorn-scratches. Or rather, he was almost naked: at his wrists and ankles were glowing manacles, attached to chains that rose into the air to fade into invisibility a few feet from his limbs. Their links blazed with the same tiny lightnings as were crawling toward the sphere that held him, right now. The Masked suddenly strode through the background of the scene, making an impatient beckoning gesture almost absently as he hurried on his way.

Elminster was jerked around by the chains and forced to follow his master. They went through the trees for quite some distance, stumbling and scraping along, until El fetched up against a jutting rock with bruising force. The elf left him there as he bent down to examine a certain plant, and the vision swept in to show Elminster laying his hand flat on the stone, whispering Mystra's name, and concentrating on a particular symbol—an unfamiliar and complex character of shining golden curves that hung in El's mind and caught fire, as if it was was being branded into his memory.

In the scene, Elminster's bare body changed, arching away from the rock as it flowed into the smooth, full curves of a woman, a form he'd worn before in Mystra's service. "Elmara," he'd been then, and it was Elmara who stepped away from the stone, chains gone, and began a swift casting even as The Masked straightened up and spun around, his face sharp with astonishment and fear. That face that promptly vanished in the bolt of emerald fire Elmara flung through it. The green flames flowed and splashed through his head, and the scene was gone.

El found himself shaking his head to clear his dazed vision. Through the sudden glimmer of tears, he saw the lightnings, back in the here and now, touch the sphere around him at last, and awaken it to fresh fire.

He tried to recall the symbol he'd seen, and it swept back into his mind in all its intricate glory. Well enough; touch stone and think of that while calling aloud of Mystra, and he would wear a woman's shape again—a changing that would be enough to break the bindings this treacherous elven sorcerer was going to lay upon him now. The Masked—a proud elf with a thin, cold voice that he'd heard before, he was sure . . . but where?

El shrugged. Even if he learned who wore the mask, what then? Learning a face and a name meant little when you knew little or nothing of the character behind them. To a Cormanthan born and bred the identity of The Masked might well be a secret as valuable as it was deadly; to Elminster, it was simply something he didn't know yet.

He suspected his very unfamiliarity with the realm was his chief value to this elven mage, and he resolved to reveal as little as possible of his own true powers and nature, belittling even his experience with the kiira. Who was to say what an overwhelmed human mind could even comprehend of its stored memories, let alone retain after the gem was gone?

"Look into my eyes," The Masked commanded crisply. El looked up in time to see one long-fingered hand make an imperious gesture. There was a flash of light from all around, and a high singing sound, as the sphere burst into a sheet of golden sparks.

For an instant El felt as if he was falling—and then there was a sickening surging feeling, as if eels were wriggling through his innards, as the sparks streamed into the midst of his misty form.

Fire followed, and the wracking pain of being caught squarely in the raging, blistering heat of hot flame. Elminster threw back his head and shouted—a sound that echoed back off the high vaulting above as he fell in earnest this time, dropping several feet before he was rudely caught up in a tangle of webs.

The webs were spells spinning themselves down and around him from the smoky helix. He was caught in their coils, their substance melting into his skin and pouring into his nose and mouth, choking him. He gagged, writhed, and tried to vomit, throat shuddering spasmodically. Then it was over, and he was on his knees on cold flagstones, the masked elven sorcerer standing on air not far away, looking down at him with a superior smile.

"Arise," the Masked said coldly. El decided to test things right now. Acting dazed, he hid his face in his hands and groaned, but did not try to get up.

"Elminster!" the elf snapped, but El shook his head, murmuring something wordless. Abruptly he felt a burning sensation in his head, like heat flowing down his neck and shoulders, and an irresistible tugging began, making all of his limbs leap and tremble. He could fight this, El thought, and resist for some time, but it was best to seem entirely in thrall, so he hastened to his feet, to stand as The Masked posed him: upright but with both arms extended, offering his wrists as if for binding.

The elven sorcerer met Elminster's gaze with eyes that were very level and very dark, and El suddenly found his limbs being pulled again. He surrendered utterly this time, and the elf made him wave his arms wide, point downwards, and then slap himself across the face, hard, once with each hand.

It hurt, and as El shook his numbed hands and felt his lips with his tongue where his teeth had rattled under the blows, The Masked smiled again. "Your body seems to work well. Come."

El's limbs were suddenly free to move as he willed. He set aside any urge to strike back, and followed humbly, head bent. A heavy feeling of being watched rode his shoulders, but he didn't bother to look up and back to find the floating eye he knew would be there.

The Masked touched the featureless wall of the spell chamber and an oval doorway suddenly opened in it. The elf turned on its threshold to look his new apprentice up and down and allowed himself a slow, cold smile of triumph.

El decided to act as if it was a smile of welcome, and tremulously matched it. The elven mage shook his head wryly at that and turned away, crooking one hand in a beckoning gesture.

Rolling his eyes inwardly but careful to keep his face looking both dazed and eager, Elminster hastened to follow. Thanks be to Mystra, this was going to be a *long* apprenticeship.

Moonlight touched the trees of Cormanthor, and in the remote distance, somewhere off to the north, a wolf howled.

There was an answering bark from the trees very nearby, but the naked, shivering elf who was crawling aimlessly down a tangled slope did not seem to hear it. She slipped partway down, and plunged most of the rest of the way on her face. Her hair was a muddy mass, and her limbs glistened darkly in a dozen places in the pale blue light, where they were wet with blood.

The wolf padded out onto the mossy rocks at the top of the slope and stood looking down, eyes agleam. Such easy prey. He trotted down the incline by the easiest way, not bothering to hurry; the panting, mumbling woman at the bottom wasn't going anywhere.

As he loped nearer she even rolled over to present her breast and throat to his jaws, and lay back bathed in moonlight, gasping out something wordless. The wolf paused, momentarily suspicious of such fearlessness, and then gathered himself to spring. There'd be plenty of time to sniff around warily for others of her kind after her throat was torn out.

A forest spider who'd been creeping cautiously along above the sobbing elf for some time drew back at the sight of the wolf. Perhaps it could gain two blood-meals this night, rather than just one.

The wolf sprang.

Symrustar Auglamyr never saw the single blue-white star that blazed into being above her parted lips. Nor did she hear the startled, chopped-off yelp as it emptied into the jaws of the wolf, nor the silent disintegration that followed.

A few hairs from the wolf's tail were all that was left of it; they drifted down to settle across her thighs as something unseen said, "Poor proud one. By magic bent. Let you be by magic restored."

A circle of stars spun up from the ground then to flash around Symrustar in a blue-white ring. The spider recoiled from their light and waited. Light meant fire, and sure, sizzling death.

When the whirling ring had faded and only the moonlight remained, the spider moved down the tree again, creeping swiftly now, in little runs and jumps and dodges. Its hunger was exceeded only by its rage when it reached the flattened leaves where the elf-she had rolled, and found her gone. Gone without a trace, and the wolf too. The bewildered spider searched the area for some time and then wandered off into the woods by moonlight, sighing as loudly and gustily as any lost elf—or human.

Humans, now; humans were fat, and full of blood and juices. Long-dimmed memories stirred in the spider, and it climbed a tree in eager haste. Humans dwelt in *that* direction, a long way off, and—

The head of the giant snake shot forward, its jaws snapped once, and the spider was gone. It never even had time to worry about choosing the wrong tree.

PART
III

MYTHAL

SEVENTEEN
APPRENTICED AGAIN

For some years Elminster served the elf known only as The Masked as apprentice. Despite the cruel nature of the high sorcerer, and the spell chains that bound the human in servitude, a respect grew between master and man. It was respect that ignored the differences between them, and the betrayal and battle that both knew lay ahead.

ANTARN THE SAGE
FROM *THE HIGH HISTORY OF FAERÛNIAN ARCHMAGES MIGHTY*
PUBLISHED CIRCA THE YEAR OF THE STAFF

There came a spring day twenty years after the first greening season Elminster had known in service to The Masked, when a golden, shining symbol surfaced in the Athalantan's mind, a symbol he'd almost forgotten. It troubled him; as it revolved slowly inside his head, other long-buried memories stirred. *Mystra*, he heard his own voice calling, and a gaze fell upon him—her gaze. He could not see her, but he could feel the awesome weight of her regard: deep and warm and terrible, more mighty than the most furious glare of the Master, and more loving than . . . than . . .

Nacacia.

He looked down at Nacacia from where he hung in the great glowing spell web they'd spent all morning crafting together, and their gazes met. Her eyes were dark and liquid and very large, and there was longing in them as she looked up at him. Soundlessly, trembling, her lips shaped his name.

It was all she dared do. El fought down a sudden urge to lash out at the masked sorcerer, who was floating with his back to them not far away, weaving spells of his own, and gave her a wink before he quickly turned his head away. The Master delved too much into both their minds to hide their mutual fondness from him. Already the mysterious elven mage had taken to making Nacacia slap his human apprentice, otherwise keep well away from Elminster, and speak harshly when she spoke to the Athalantan at all.

The Masked seldom compelled Elminster to do anything. He seemed to be watching El and waiting for something. One of the things he watched for was any act of defiance, and he took open delight in punishing his human apprentice for all of them. Remembering some of those punishments, El shuddered involuntarily.

He risked another glance at Nacacia, and found that she was doing the same thing. Their eyes met almost guiltily, and they both hurriedly looked away. El set his teeth and started to climb the spell web away from her—anything to be moving, *doing* something.

Mystra, he thought silently, seeking to thrust away his vivid memory of Nacacia's smiling face. Oh, Mystra, I need guidance . . . are all these passing years of my servitude part of your plan?

The world around him seemed to shimmer, and he was suddenly standing in a rocky meadow. It was the field in which he'd watched sheep, above Heldon, as a boy!

A breeze was blowing across it, and he was cold. Small wonder—he was also naked.

Lifting his head, he found himself staring at the sorceress he'd trained under for so long, years ago: Myrjala, she known as "Darkeyes." The great dark eyes for which she was named seemed deeper and more alluring than ever as she reclined on the empty air above the blown grasses, regarding him. The winds did not touch her dark satin gown.

Myrjala had been Mystra. Elminster stretched out a hand to her, tentatively.

"Great Lady," he almost whispered, "is it ye in truth—after all these years?"

"Of course," the goddess said, her eyes dark pools of promise. "How is it that you doubt me?"

El almost shuddered under the sudden wash of shame that he felt. He went to his knees, dropping his eyes. "I—I am wrong to do so, and . . . well, it's just that it's been so *long*, and . . ."

"Not long to an elf," Mystra said gently. "Are you beginning to learn patience at last, or are you truly desperate?"

Elminster looked up at her, eyes bright, as he found himself suddenly hovering on the edge of tears. "No!" he cried. "All I needed was this, to see ye, and know I'm doing what ye intend. I—I need guidance still."

Mystra smiled at him. "At least you know you need it. Some never do, and crash happily through life, laying waste to all they can reach in Faerûn around them, whether they realize it or not." She raised a hand, and her smile changed.

"Yet think on this, dearest of my Chosen: most folk of Faerûn never have such guidance, and still learn to stand on their own feet unaided, and follow their own ideas as their lives run, and make their own mistakes. You've certainly mastered that last talent."

Elminster looked away, fighting back tears again, and Mystra laughed and touched his cheek. Warm fire seemed to race through him.

"Be not downhearted," she murmured, as a mother does to a crying son, "for you *are* learning patience, and your shame is unfounded. Much though you fear you've forgotten me and strayed from the task I set you, I am well pleased."

Her face changed, then, as Heldon darkened and faded around it, and became the face of Nacacia.

Elminster blinked at it, as it winked at him. He was back in the spell web, staring down at the real Nacacia once more. He drew in a deep, tremulous breath, smiled at her, and climbed on through the web. No matter what he did, however, his thoughts stayed on his fellow apprentice. He could see her face as clearly in his mind as his eyes had beheld it, moments ago. Sometimes he wondered how much of such mind-scenes the master could see, and what the elven sorcerer truly thought of his two apprentices.

Nacacia. Ah, leave my thoughts for a moment, leave me in peace! But no . . .

She was a half-elf, brought into the tower as a bright-eyed waif one night, huddled in the arms of The Masked. Elminster suspected he'd raided the village where she lived.

Bright and bubbly, possessed of a pranksome nature that The Masked harshly beat out of her with spanking spells and transformations into toads or earthworms, and a merry nature it seemed nothing he did could crush, Nacacia had swiftly grown into a beauty.

She had auburn hair that flowed down to the backs of her knees in a thick fall, and a surprisingly muscular back and shoulders; from where he'd been standing in the web above her, El had admired the deep, curving line of her spine. Her large eyes, smile and cheekbones bore the classic beauty of her elven blood, and her waist was so slim as to seem almost toylike.

Her master allowed her the black breeches and vest of a thief, and let her grow her hair long. He even taught her the spells to animate it so as to stroke him, when he took her into his chamber of nights and left Elminster floating furiously outside.

She never spoke to him of what went on in the spell-locked bedchamber, save to say that their master never took off his mask. Once, when awakening from a shrieking nightmare, she babbled something about "soft and terrible tentacles."

The Masked not only never removed his mask; he never slept. As far as El could tell, he had no friends or kin, and no Cormanthan ever called on him, for any reason. His days were spent crafting magic, working magic, and teaching magic to his two apprentices. Sometimes he treated them almost as friends, though he never revealed anything about himself. At other times, they were clearly his slaves. Most of the time they worked as drudges, together. In fact, it seemed that the masked mage almost taunted his two apprentices with each other's company, thrusting them into messy, slippery jobs half-naked to help each other lift, sort, or clean. But whenever they reached for each other, even to give innocent aid or comfort, he struck out with punishments.

These visitations of pain were many and varied, but the Master's favorite punishment for apprentices was to paralyze the bared body of the miscreant with spells and set acid leeches on it to feed. The slow, glistening creatures excreted a burning slime as they slid over skin, or bored almost lazily in. The Masked was always careful to use his spells in time to keep his apprentices alive, but Elminster could attest that there are few things in Faerûn as painful as having a sluglike beast eating its way very slowly into your lungs, or stomach, or guts.

Yet El had learned true respect for The Masked during twenty years of learning deep-woven, complex elven magics. The elf was a meticulous crafter of spells and a stylish caster, who left nothing to chance, always thought ahead, and seemed never to be surprised. He had an instinctive understanding of magic, and could modify, combine, or improvise spells with almost effortless ease and no hesitation. He also never forgot where he'd put anything, no matter how trivial, and always kept himself under iron control, never showing weariness, loneliness, or a need to confide in anyone. Even his losses of temper seemed almost planned and scripted.

Moreover, after twenty years of intense contact, Elminster still did not know who the mage was. A male of one of the old, proud families, to be sure, and—judging by the views he evidently held—probably not among the eldest Cormanthans. The Masked spun and projected a false body for himself often, directing it in activities elsewhere with part of his mind, while he devoted some part of the rest to instructing Elminster.

At first, the last prince of Athalantar had been astonished by what powerful spells the anonymous elven mage had let him learn. But then, why should The Masked worry, when he could compel instant obedience from the body he'd given to his human apprentice? Elminster suspected he and Nacacia were among the very few Cormanthan apprentices who never left their master's abode, and they were probably the only apprentices who weren't pureblood elves, and who were never taught how to create their own defensive mantles.

Sometimes El thought about his tumultuous early days in Cormanthor. He wondered if the Srinshee and the Coronal thought him dead, or if they cared about his fate at all. More often he wondered what had become of the elven lady Symrustar, whom he'd left crawling in the woods, when he'd been unable to defend her or even to make her notice him. And what had become of Mythanthar, and his dream of a mythal? Surely they'd have heard from the Master if such a spectacular giant mantle had been spun, and the city opened to other races. But then, why would he tell news of the world outside his tower to two apprentices whom he kept as virtual prisoners?

Recently, even the attentive teaching of magic had stopped. The Masked was absent from his tower more often, or shut away in spell-sealed chambers scrying events elsewhere. Day after day during this most recent winter his apprentices had been left alone to feed themselves and follow a bald list of tasks that appeared written in letters of fire on a certain wall: drudge-work, and the spinning of small spells to keep the Master's tower clean, well-ordered, and strong in its fabric. Yet he kept a watch over them; unauthorized explorations of the tower, or overmuch intimacy between them, brought swift and sharp retributive spells out of the empty air. Only two tendays ago, when Nacacia had dropped a kiss on Elminster's shoulder as she brushed past him, an unseen whip had lashed her lips and face to bloody ribbons, defying El's frantic attempts to dispel it as she staggered back, screaming. She'd awakened the next morning wholly healed. But a row of barbed thorns grew all around her mouth, making kissing impossible. It was more than a tenday before they faded away.

These days, when the masked mage put in one of his rare appearances in the rooms where they dwelt, it was to call on them for magical aid, usually either to drain some of their vital energies in an arcane—and unexplained—spell he was experimenting with, or to help him create a spell web.

Like the one they were working on now. Incredible constructions these were, glowing nets or interwoven cages of glowing force-lines that one could walk along as if striding along a broad wooden beam, regardless of whether one was upside down, or walking tilted sharply sideways. Multiple spells could be cast into the glowing fabric of these cages, placed in particular spots and for specific reasons, so that triggering the collapse of the web would unleash spell after spell at preset targets, in a particular order.

The Master rarely revealed all of the magics he'd placed in a web before its triggering displayed their true natures, and had never shown either apprentice how to start such a web. El and Nacacia didn't even know the primary purpose—or target—of most of the webs they worked on; El suspected The Masked often used the aid of his two largely ignorant apprentices purely to remain hidden, so that the spells striking down a distant rival would bear no hint of who was behind them.

Now the elf turned, his eyes flashing beneath the mask that never left his face. "Elminster, come here," he said coldly, indicating a particular spot in the web with one finger. "We have death to weave, together."

EIGHTEEN
IN THE WEB

There comes a day at last when even the most patient and exacting of schem-ing traitors grows impatient, and breaks forth into open treachery. Hence-forth, he must deal with the world as it is, reacting around him, and not as he sees or desires it to be in his plots and dreams. This is the point at which many treacheries go awry.

The sorcerer known as The Masked was, however, no ordinary traitor—if one may think of an "ordinary traitor." The historian of Cormanthor, reaching back far enough, can do so, finding many ordinary treacheries, but this was not one of them. This was the stuff of which wailing doom-ballads are made.

SHALHEIRA TALANDREN, HIGH ELVEN BARD OF SUMMERSTAR
FROM *SILVER BLADES AND SUMMER NIGHTS:*
AN INFORMAL BUT TRUE HISTORY OF CORMANTHOR
PUBLISHED IN THE YEAR OF THE HARP

Elminster shook his head to try to banish mind-weariness; he'd been spin-ning spells with another, colder mind for too long, and almost staggered in the patiently humming web.

"Get clear now," the thin, cold voice of the Master said into his ear then, though the elven mage was standing in the air at the other side of the spell chamber.

"Nacacia, hie you to the couch in the corner. Elminster, here to stand with me."

Knowing his impatience was apt to flare at such times, both apprentices hastened to obey, dropping lightly out of the webwork as soon as they were low enough to do so without disrupting anything.

El had scarce reached the spot The Masked was pointing at when the elf hissed something and used one finger to bridge the gap between two protruding points at the end of the glowing lines. That set the web to working; its magic snarled forth, trailing sparks as the web dissolved itself, discharging spell after spell. The elven sorcerer looked up expectantly, and El followed his gaze to a spot in the air high above them, where the air, encircled by an arching strand of the web, was flickering into sudden life. A scene appeared there, floating in the emptiness like a bright hanging tapestry, and growing steadily brighter.

It was a view of a house El had never seen before, one of the sprawling country mansions made by elves. A house that lived, growing slowly larger as the centuries passed. This one had been standing for more than a thousand summers, by the looks of it, at the heart of a grove of old and mighty shadowtops, somewhere in the forest deeps. An old house; a proud house.

A house that would be standing only a few moments more.

El watched grimly as the unleashed magics of the spell web shattered its magical shields, set off its attack spells and forced their discharges back inwards to strike at the heart of the old house, and snatched guardian creatures and steeds from their posts and stables, only to dash them back against the walls, right through the full fury of the awakened spells, reducing them to raglike, bloody tatters.

It took only a few minutes to alter the proud, soaring house of mighty branches and lush leaves to a smoking crater flanked by two splintered, precariously wavering fragments of blackened and splintered trunk. Misshapen things that might have been bodies were still raining down around the wreckage when the spell web drank its own scene, and the air went dark again.

Elminster was still blinking at the empty air where the scene had been when sudden mists snatched at him. Before he could even cry out, he was somewhere else. Soft soil and dead leaves were under his boots, and the smells of trees all around.

He was standing in a clearing deep in the forest with The Masked reclining at ease on empty air nearby, and no sign of Nacacia or of any elven habitation. They were somewhere deep in the wild forest.

El blinked at the change in light, drew in a deep breath of the damp air, and looked all around, delighting in being out of the tower at last, and yet filled with foreboding. Had his master espied his meeting with Mystra, or seen it in his mind since? She'd reclined in almost the same way.

The clearing they were standing in was odd. It was a semicircular bare patch perhaps a hundred paces across—completely bare, just earth and rock, with not a stump or lichen or pecking woodbird to enliven its barren lifelessness.

El looked at The Masked and raised inquiring eyebrows in silence.

His master pointed down. "This is what is left behind by a casting of the spell I'm going to teach you now."

El looked at the devastation once more, and then back at the Master, stone-faced. "Aye. Something potent, is it?"

"Something very useful. Properly used, it can make its caster nigh-invincible." The Masked showed his teeth in a mirthless grin and added, "Like myself, for instance." He uncoiled himself from his reclining position and said, "Lie down just here, where the waste ends and the living forest begins. Nose to the ground, hands spread out. Move not."

When the Master spoke like that, one didn't hesitate or argue. Elminster scrambled down onto his face in the dirt.

Once he was there, he felt the icy touch of the Master's fingertips on the back of his head. They only felt so cold when a spell was being slipped into his mind, stealing in without need for studying or instruction or . . .

Gods! This magic would fuel any spell you already possessed, doubling its effects or making a twin of it. To do so, it drained life-force—from a tree.

Or a sentient being.

And it was so *simple*. Powerful, aye, one had to be a very capable mage to wield it, but the actual doing was so hideously easy. It left utter lifelessness in its wake. And *elves* had wrought this?

"When," El asked the moss under his nose, "would I ever dare to use this?"

"In an emergency," the Master said calmly, "when your life—or the realm or holding you were defending—was in the most dire peril. When all else is lost, the only immoral act is to avoid doing something you know can aid your cause. This is such a spell."

El almost turned his head to glance up at the masked elf. His voice, for the first time in twenty years, had sounded eager, almost hungry.

Mystra, El thought, *he loves the thought of utterly smashing a foe, regardless of the cost!*

"I can't think, Master, that I'll ever trust my own judgment enough to be comfortable using this spell," El said slowly.

"Comfortable, no; not one thinking, caring being would be, knowing what this magic can do. Yet capable you can become. That's why we're here. Up, now."

El rose. "I'm going to practice?"

"In a manner of speaking, yes. You'll be unleashing the spell in earnest against an enemy of Cormanthor. By decree of the Coronal, this spell is only to be used in direct defense of the realm or of an imperiled elven elder."

El stared at the ever-present enchanted mask his master wore, wondering for perhaps the ten thousandth time what its true powers were—and just what he'd find beneath it, if he ever dared snatch it away.

As if that thought had crossed the elf's mind, the masked mage stepped back hastily and said, "You've just seen our spell web destroy a high house. It was an abode used by certain conspirators in the realm who desire that we trade with the drow. They are so hungry for the wealth and importance the dark ones have promised will flow to them personally that they'll betray us all into becoming vassals of some matron of Down Below."

"But surely—" Elminster began, and then fell silent. Nothing was sure about this tale beyond the fact that his masked Master was lying. That much Mystra had given him in the meadow. He could now tell when the thin, cold voice of the elven sorcerer was straying from the truth.

It was doing so with almost every word.

"Soon," the Masked went on, "I'll transport us to a place that is specifically warded against me. It is a place I can enter only by blasting my way through its shields, alerting everyone within to my arrival and wasting much magic besides."

The elven sorcerer's pointing finger shot out to indicate El. "You, however, can step right in. My magic will bring a chained orc to your side—a vicious despoiler of human and elven villages whom we captured while he was roasting elven babies on spits for his evening meal. You'll drain him to power your spell, and then hurl your antimagic shell—augmented by this magic in both area and efficacy, of course—into the house you'll be facing. I can then summon a few loyal armathors with ready swords, and the deed will be done. The traitors will lie dead, and Cormanthor will stand safe for a while longer. With that deed under your belt, you should be ready for presentation to the Coronal at last."

"The Coronal?" Elminster felt almost as much excitement as he put into that gasp. 'Twould be good, indeed, to see old Lord Eltargrim again. Still, that did nothing to drive away the uneasy feeling he had about this whole arrangement. Who would he really be slaying?

The Masked saw his dislike in his face. "There is a mage in the house you'll be striking at," he added slowly, "and a capable one at that. Yet I hope that any apprentice of mine will go up against true foes with the same bravery as we transform toadstools and conjure light in dark places. The true mage never allows himself to be awed by magic when he's using it."

The wise mage, Elminster thought silently, recalling the words of Mystra, pretends to know nothing about magic at all.

Then he wryly added the corollary: When he gains true wisdom, he'll know that he wasn't pretending.

"Are you ready, Elminster?" his master asked then, very quietly. "Are you ready to undertake a mission of importance at last?"

Mystra? El asked inwardly. Instantly a vision appeared in his mind: The Masked pointing at him, just as he'd done a moment ago. This time, in the vision, El smiled and nodded enthusiastically. Well, that was clear enough.

"I am," Elminster said, smiling and nodding enthusiastically.

The mask did not hide the slow smile that grew across the face of his master. The Masked raised his hands and murmured, "Let us be about it, then." He made a single gesture toward El, and the world vanished in swirling smoke.

When the smoke curled away to let the human mage see clearly again, they stood together in a wooded valley. It was probably somewhere in Cormanthor, by the looks of the trees and the sun above them. They stood on a little knoll with a well beside them, and across a small dip that held a garden stood a low, rambling house of trees joined by low-roofed wooden chambers. Except for the oval windows visible in the tree trunks, it might have been a human home rather than an abode of elves.

"Strike swiftly," the Masked murmured beside Elminster's ear, and vanished. The air where he'd been standing promptly spun and shimmered. Then an orc was standing beside him, wrapped in a heavy yoke of chains. It stared at him, pleading with its eyes, trying frantically to say something around the thick gag clamped into and over its jaws. All it managed was a soft, high whimpering.

A babe-devourer and raider, eh? El set his lips in distaste over what he had to do, and reached out to touch the orc without hesitation. The Masked was sure to be watching.

He worked the spell, turning to thrust one spread hand at the house, and settle his antimagic over every part of it, willing it to seek down into even the deepest cellar, and blanket even the mightiest of realms-shaking magics. Let that building be dead to all magic, so long as his power lasted.

The orc's keening became a despairing moan; the light in its eyes flickered and went out, and it buckled slowly at the knees and crashed to the ground; El had to step aside hastily as the chained bulk of its corpse rolled under his feet.

The air shimmered again, nearby; he looked up in time to see elven warriors in gleaming, high-collared plate armor rushing out of a rent in the air. None of them wore helms, but they all waved naked long swords—enchanted blades that flickered with ready, reaving magic—in their hands. They spared no glances for El or the surroundings, but charged at the house, hacking at shutters and doors. As the blades breached those barriers and the elves plunged inside, the radiances dancing on their blades and armor winked out. From inside, the muffled shouting and the ringing of striking steel began.

Feeling suddenly sick, El looked down at the orc again and gasped in horror.

As he flung himself to his knees and reached out to touch and make sure, he felt as if Faerûn was opening up into a dark chasm around him. The chains were lying limp and loose around a small and slender form.

An all-too-familiar form, lolling lifelessly in his hands as he rolled it over. The eyes of Nacacia, still wide in sad and vain pleading, stared up at him, dark and empty. They'd be so forever, now.

Shaking, El touched the cruel gag that still filled her gentle mouth, and then he could hold back the tears no longer. He never noticed when the swirling smoke came again to take him.

Nineteen
More Anger at Court

Among the tales and accounts of men, the Court of Cormanthor is portrayed as a glittering, gigantic hall of enchanted wonders, in which richly robed elves drifted quietly to and fro in the ultimate hauteur and decorum. It was so, most of the time, but a certain day in the Year of Soaring Stars was a decidedly noticeable—and notable—exception.

Antarn the Sage
from *The High History of Faerûnian Archmages Mighty*
published circa The Year of the Staff

Hold!" The Masked cried, and there was a hubbub of shocked voices from all around. "I bring a criminal to justice!"

"Really," someone said, severely, "is there any—"

"Peace, Lady Aelieyeeva," broke in a grave but stern voice that El knew. "We shall resume our business later. The human is one I named armathor of the realm; this affair demands my justice."

El blinked up at the throne of the Coronal, where it floated above the glowing Pool of Remembrance. Lord Eltargrim was leaning forward in its high-arched splendor in interest, and elves in splendid robes were hurriedly gliding aside to clear the glassy-smooth floor between El and the ruler of Cormanthor.

"Do you recognize the human, Revered Lord?" The Masked asked, his cold voice echoing to every corner of the vast Chamber of the Court in the sudden stillness.

"I do," the Coronal said slowly, a trace of sadness in his tone. He turned his head from Elminster to regard the masked elf, and added, "but I do not recognize you."

The Masked reached up, slowly and deliberately, and removed the mask from his face. He did not have to untie it or slip off any browband, but merely peeled it off as if it was a skin. El stared up at him, seeing that coldly handsome face for the first time in over twenty years . . . a face he'd seen once before.

"Llombaerth Starym am I, Lord Speaker of my house," the elf who'd been Elminster's master said. "I charge this human—my apprentice, Elminster Aumar, named armathor of the realm by yourself here in this chamber, twenty years ago—murderer and traitor."

"How so?"

"Revered Lord, I thought to teach him the life-quench spell, to make him capable of defending Cormanthor, so he could be presented to you as a full mage of the realm. Having learned it, he made use of it without delay both to slay my other apprentice—the half-blood who lies beside him now, still in the chains in which he trapped her—and to doom one of the foremost mages of the realm: Mythanthar, whom he cloaked in a death-of-magic, so that our wise old sorcerer could not avoid the swords of the drow this human is in league with."

"Drow?" Among the courtiers who lined both sides of the long, glassy-smooth floor of the hall that cry was almost a shriek.

Llombaerth Starym nodded sadly. "They fear the creation of a mythal will hamper their plans to storm us from Below. Later this summer, I suspect."

There was a moment of shocked silence, and then excited voices rose everywhere; through the tears he was fighting to master, El saw the Coronal look down the hall and make a certain gesture.

There came a skirling, as of many harpstrings struck in unison, and the insistent, magically amplified voice of the Lady Herald rolled down the long, open Chamber of the Court. "Peace and order, lords and ladies all. Let us have silence once more."

The hush was slow in coming, but as armathors left the doors of the court and started purposefully down the ranks of the courtiers, silence returned. A tense, hanging silence.

The Starym mage put on his mask again; it clung to his face as he raised it into place.

The Coronal rose from his throne, his white robes gleaming, and stood on empty air, looking down at Elminster. "Justice has been demanded; the realm will have it. Yet in matters between mages there has always been much strife, and I would know the truth before I pass judgment. Does the half-elven yet live?"

El opened his mouth to speak, but the Masked said, "No."

"Then I must call upon the Srinshee, who can speak with the departed," Lord Eltargrim said heavily. "Until her arr—"

"Hold!" The Masked said quickly. "Revered Lord, that is less than wise! This human could not have made contact with the drow without the aid of citizens of Cormanthor, and all here know of the long series of reverses Mythanthar suffered in his work to craft a mythal. One of the traitors powerful enough to work against that wise old mage undetected, and to traffic with the dark ones and survive, is the Lady Oluevaera Estelda!"

His voice rose dramatically. "If you summon her here, not only will her testimony be tainted, but she could well strike out at you and other loyal Cormanthans, seeking to bring the realm down!"

The Coronal's face was pale, and his eyes glittered with anger at the masked mage's accusation, but his voice was level and almost gentle as he asked, "Who, then, Lord Speaker, would you trust to examine the minds of the dead? And of the one you have accused?"

Llombaerth Starym frowned. "Now that the Great Lady, Ildilyntra Starym, is no longer with us," he said slowly, carefully not watching the Coronal's face turn utterly white as all blood drained out of it, "I find myself at a loss to find a mage to turn to; any or all of them could be tainted, you see."

He turned, walking on air, to stride thoughtfully along the edge of the courtiers. Many of them drew back from him, as if he bore a disease. He paid them no heed.

"How, Lord Speaker, would you view the testimony of the mage Mythanthar?" The rolling tones of the Lady Herald, who still stood by the doors at the end of the chamber, startled everyone. The heads of both the Coronal and The Masked jerked up to stare down the long, open Chamber at Aubaudameira Dree.

"He's *dead*, Lady," The Masked said severely, "and anyone who questions him can by their spells conjure up false answers. Do you not see the problem we face?"

"Ah, Starym stripling," said a slight figure, placing his hand on the shoulder of the Lady Herald to gain the use of her voice-throwing magic, "behold your problem solved: I live. No thanks to you."

The Masked stiffened and gaped, just for a moment. Then his voice rang out in anger. "What imposture is this? I saw the human cast the lifequench. I saw the drow, hastening into the house of Mythanthar! He could not have lived!"

"So you planned," said the old mage, striding forward on the silent air, the Lady Herald at his side. "So you hoped. The problem with you younglings is that you're all so lazy, so impatient. You neglect to check every last detail of your spells, and so earn nasty surprises from their side effects. You don't bother to ensure that your victims—even foolish old mages—are truly dead. Like all Starym, young Llombaerth, you *assume* too much."

As he'd spoken, the old elf mage had been walking the length of the Chamber of the Court. He came to a stop beside Elminster, and reached out with his foot toward the body of Nacacia.

"You would blame *me* for the murder of my apprentice?" The Masked shouted, sudden lightnings crawling up and down his arms. "You accuse *me* of trying to work your death? You *dare*?"

"I do," the old mage replied, as he touched the body of the half-elven lady in its chains.

The Lady Herald said formally, "Lord Starym, you stand in violation of the rules of the Court. Stand down your magic. We duel with words and ideas here, not spells."

As she spoke those words, and the Coronal stirred, as if to add something more, the body in the chains vanished. In its place, a moment later, another form melted into view: a half-elven girl with long auburn hair who stood straight, angry, and very much alive.

The Masked recoiled, his face going white. Mythanthar said in dry tones, "A lifequench spell is a potent thing, Starym, but no antimagic shell, however strengthened, can prevail against a spell shear. You need more schooling before you can call yourself any sort of wizard, whether you wear Andrathath's Mask or not."

"Peace, all!" the Coronal thundered. As heads snapped around to him, and the armathors began to gather by the Pool, he turned his head to regard Nacacia, who was embracing a sobbing Elminster, and asked, "Child, who is to blame for all of this?"

Nacacia pointed at the masked Starym mage and said crisply, "He is. It is all his plotting, and the one he truly seeks to slay, Revered Lord, is *you!*"

"Lies!" the Masked shouted, and two bolts of flame burst from his eyes, snarling across the Chamber of the Court at Nacacia. She shrank back, but Mythanthar smiled and lifted his hand. The streaming fire struck something unseen and faded away.

"You'll have to do better than that, Starym," he said calmly, "and I don't think you know how. You didn't even recognize a seeming when it lay before you here, in chains, an—"

"*Starym!*" The Masked bellowed, raising his arms. "Let it be *NOW!*"

Among the courtiers, all over the chamber, bright magic erupted. There were screams, and sudden explosions, and suddenly elves were running everywhere in the hall, swords flashing out.

"*Die*, false ruler!" Llombaerth Starym shouted, wheeling to face the Coronal. "Let the Starym rule at last!"

The roaring white bolt of rending magic that he hurled then was only one of many that lashed out at the old elf standing before his throne, as Starym mages hurled death from many places in the hall.

The Coronal vanished in a blinding white conflagration of meeting, warring spells. The very air roiled and split apart in dark, starry rifts; the Lady Herald screamed and collapsed to the gleaming floor as the shield she'd spun around her ruler was overwhelmed. The hall rocked, and many of the shrieking courtiers were hurled from their feet. A tapestry fell.

Then the bright, roiling radiance above the Pool was thrust back, to reveal Lord Eltargrim standing atop the floating Throne of the Coronal, his drawn sword in his hand. Light flickered down the awakened runes on the flanks of that blade as he growled, "Death take all who practice treachery against fair Cormanthor! Starym, your life is forfeit!"

The old warrior sprang down from his throne and waded forward, swinging his sword like a farmer scything grain, using the enchantments that smoked and streamed along its edges to cleave the magic trained upon him. The swirling flames and lightnings faded in tatters before the bright edges of that blade.

Someone shouted in triumph among the courtiers, and the ghostly outlines of a great green dragon began to take shape in the air above their heads, its wings spread, its jaws open and poised to bite down on the slowly advancing Coronal. As the Starym who'd summoned it wrestled against the wards of the chamber to bring the wyrm wholly into solidity, and its outlines flickered and darkened, El and Nacacia could see the neck of the dragon arching and straining, trying to reach the lone old elf in white robes who stood beneath it.

Mythanthar said two strange words, calmly and distinctly, and the flickering lightnings and smokes of magic the Coronal was hacking his way through suddenly flowed up and over Eltargrim's head, straight into the straining maw of the dragon.

The blast that followed smashed the roof of the chamber apart, and toppled one of its mighty pillars. Dust swirled and drifted, as elves screamed on all sides, and Elminster and Nacacia, still in each other's arms, were hurled to the floor as the magical radiances that gave light to the vast Chamber of the Court winked out.

In the sudden darkness, as they coughed and blinked, only one source of light remained steady: the empty throne of the Coronal, floating serenely above the glowing Pool of Remembrance.

Lightnings clawed and crashed around it, and the body of a hapless elven lady was dashed to bloody ruin against it. She fell like a rag doll into the Pool below, and its radiance went suddenly scarlet.

The Chamber of the Court shook again, as another explosion smashed aside tapestries along the east wall, and sent more broken bodies flying.

"Stop," snapped a voice in the darkness. "This has gone *quite* far enough."

The Srinshee had come at last.

TWENTY
SPELLSTORM AT COURT

And so it was that a spellstorm was unleashed in the Court of Cormanthor that day. A true spellstorm is a fearful thing, one of the most terrible dooms one can behold, even if one lives to remember it. Yet some among our People hold far more hatred and fear in their hearts for what happened after the spellstorm blew apart.

SHALHEIRA TALANDREN, HIGH ELVEN BARD OF SUMMERSTAR
from *SILVER BLADES AND SUMMER NIGHTS:*
AN INFORMAL BUT TRUE HISTORY OF CORMANTHOR
PUBLISHED IN THE YEAR OF THE HARP

Sudden light kindled in the darkness and the dust. Golden motes of light, drifting up from the open hand of a sorceress who seemed no more than an elf-child. Suddenly the Chamber of the Court was no longer lit only by the flashes of spells, the flickering steel of the Coronal's sweeping blade, and the leaping flames of small fires blazing up tapestries here and there.

Like a sunrise in the morning, light returned to the battlefield.

And battlefield the grand Chamber of the Court had become. Bodies lay strewn everywhere, and amid the risen dust, the sky could be seen faintly through the rent in the vaulted roof of the hall. Huge fragments of the toppled pillar lay tumbled behind the floating throne, with dark rivers of blood creeping out from beneath some of them.

Elves still battled each other all over the Court. Armathors struggled with courtiers and Starym mages here, there, and everywhere, in a tangle of flashing blades, curses, winking rings, and small bursting spells.

The Srinshee was floating in front of the throne, conjured light still streaming up from her tiny body. Lightnings played along the fingertips of her other hand, and stabbed out to intercept spells she deemed too deadly, as they howled and snarled above the littered floor of the Court.

As Nacacia and El found their feet and staggered back into each other's arms, they saw something flicker in the hands of their former master. Suddenly The Masked was holding a stormsword conjured from elsewhere, purple lightnings of its own playing up and down its blade. His face no longer looked so desperate as he watched the Coronal hewing slowly through the Starym retainers gathered in front of their lord speaker.

Llombaerth Starym looked over at the human and the half-elf standing in each other's arms then, and his eyes narrowed.

He crooked a hand, and El felt a sudden stirring in his muscles. "No!" he cried desperately, as The Masked jerked him out of Nacacia's grasp, and lifted his hands to work a spell.

As his eyes were dragged up to focus on the Srinshee, El cried out, "Nacacia! Help me! *Stop* me!"

His mind was flashing through magics as The Masked rummaged his spell roster, seeking one particular spell and, with a warm surge of satisfaction, found it.

It was the spell that snatched blades from elsewhere and transported them, flashing in point-first, to where one desired.

Where the Masked desired the points to go was the eyes and the throat and breast and belly of the Srinshee, as she stood on emptiness deflecting the worst magics of the warring elves.

All over the hall fresh spells flared. Elves who'd hated rivals for years took advantage of the fray to settle old scores. One elf so old that the skin of his ears was nearly transparent clubbed another of like age to the ground with a footstool.

The falling elder's body spread its brains over the slippers of a haughty lady in a blue gown, who didn't even notice. She was too busy struggling against another proud lady in an amber dress. The two swayed back and forth, pulling hair, scratching, and spitting. There was blood on their nails as they slapped, kicked, and flailed at each other in panting fury. The lady in amber slashed open one cheek of the lady in blue; her foe responded by trying to throttle her.

As similar battles raged in front of him, El raised his hands and set his gaze upon the Srinshee.

Nacacia screamed as she realized what was happening, and El felt the thudding blows of her small fists. She jostled him, shoved him, and beat at his head, trying to ruin his spell but not hurt him.

Slowly, fighting his own body but unmoved by the pain she was causing, El gathered his will, took out the tiny sword replicas he needed from the pouch at his belt, lifted his hands to make the gesture that would melt them and unleash the spell, opened his lips, and snarled desperately, "Knock me down! Push me against the floor! I need—do *it!*"

Nacacia launched herself into a desperate, clumsy tackle, and they struck the floor hard, bouncing and driving the wind out of El. He convulsed, arching his body on the smooth, bruising stone as he sought to find air, and she fought to keep on top of him, riding him as a farmer tries to hold down a struggling pig.

He shook himself, dragging her this way and that, and tried to lash out at her, but fell hard on that shoulder, needing his arm for support.

Something was spinning in his mind, rising up out of the depths as he struggled. Something golden.

Ah! Aye! The golden symbol Mystra had put in his mind so long ago gleamed, wavering like a coin seen underwater. Then it shone steadily as he bent his will to capturing it.

The image of the Srinshee overlaid its spinning splendor as The Masked struggled to master El's will, but the golden symbol burst through it.

As Nacacia shoved El's head back down against the stone, he held to that blazing image and gasped, "Mystra!"

His body shuddered, squirmed, and . . . *flowed*. Nacacia tried to slap a hand over his mouth, clinging to him desperately, and El gasped, "Enough! Nacacia, let be! I'm free of him!"

They broke apart, and Nacacia rolled over and up again to find herself staring into the eyes of a human woman!

"Well met," El gasped with a weak grin. "Call me Elmara, please!"

The half-elf stared at him—her—in utter disbelief "Are you truly . . . yourself?"

"Sometimes I think so," El said with a crooked smile, and Nacacia flung her arms around her longtime companion with a shout of relieved laughter.

It was drowned out, an instant later, by shouts of, "For the Starym! Starym risen!"

The two former apprentices clambered to their feet, stumbling over the motionless body of the Lady Herald, and saw elves crowding into the east side of the hall from behind a tapestry. The last armathors of the court were dying under their swords—and their slayers were a swarm of elves whose maroon breastplates bore the twin falling dragons of House Starym, blazoned in silver.

"Make a stand," someone snapped, near at hand. "Here. Guard the Herald, and keep *them* out from under the Srinshee."

It was Mythanthar, and the sudden hard grip of his bony hands on their shoulders made it clear he was speaking to Elmara and Nacacia. Barely turning to acknowledge him, they nodded dutifully and raised their hands to weave spells.

As the Starym warriors burst across the hall, carving a bloody path through the fighting courtiers with complete disregard for whoever they might be slaying, El unleashed the bladecall spell into the throats and faces of the foremost.

Nacacia sent lashing lightnings over the falling, dying first rank of Starym warriors, to stab into the second. Elves in maroon armor staggered and danced to death amid the hungry bolts.

Then the Srinshee sent a spell down to aid them, a wall of ghostly elven warriors who hacked and thrust in complete harmlessness, but blocked the living elves from advancing until they'd been hewn down, one by one. El and Nacacia used the time that took to pour magic missiles into specific warriors, slaying many.

New faces peered in at the doors of the great chamber, as the heads of mighty Houses came to see for themselves what new madness was ruling the Coronal this day. Almost all of them gaped, turned pale, and hastily retreated. Some few swallowed, drew blades that were more ceremonial than practical, and picked their way cautiously forward through the blood and dust and tumult.

Across the great chamber, the ruler of Cormanthor was fighting for his life, slaughtering Starym courtiers like an angry lion. He was one against many, as they stood in a desperate, struggling wall against him. His blade sang and flashed around him, and only two thrusts had managed to slip past it to stain his white robes red. He was back in battle, where he belonged.

Lord Eltargrim was happy. At last, after twenty long years of whisperings and elf-slaying "accidents" and rumors of the Coronal's corruption and setbacks in the mythal-work, at last he could find and see a foe. The spells in his blade and shielding the court were both beginning to fail, but if they kept off the worst of the magics these Starym were hurling just a few breaths longer . . .

"Hold him, you fools!" Llombaerth Starym snarled, striking angrily at the backs and shoulders of the retainers who were being driven back against him. The stormsword in his hand whistled as he plied it, using its flat to slap and spank elves who were failing him.

And when the time came, he had one magic no Cormanthan could stop, a dark secret he'd held for years now. He shook it down into his free hand and waited. One clear throw at Eltargrim's face, and the realm would belong to the House of Starym at last.

Then something slapped across his mind, as brutally as he was striking his retainers. The surging scene of the battling Coronal in front of his eyes was blotted out by a scene in his mind—two dark, arresting stars that swam and flowed into the bleak, merciless old face of the mage Mythanthar, wrinkled and spotted with age, but with eyes that held his like two dark flames.

Going somewhere, young traitor?

The mocking words rang louder in his head than the clangor of the Coronal's blade, and Llombaerth Starym found that he could not move, could not look away from the grim old mage who stood facing him in the heart of the chamber, with Starym warriors raging all around and elven blood staining the once-gleaming pave under the old sorcerer's boots.

"Get . . . out . . . of my *head!*" The Masked snarled, thrusting desperately with his will.

He might as well have been trying to push an old duskwood tree aside. Mythanthar held him in an unyielding grip, and gave a smile that promised death.

Go down and feed the worms, worthless Starym. Go down to your doom, and trouble fair Cormanthor no more.

That grim curse was still ringing through Llombaerth Starym's head as Eltargrim Irithyl, Coronal of Cormanthor, burst past the last reeling Starym warrior and thrust his glowing blade over the snarling stormsword. The two blades were outlined in fire as they struck the mantle of The Masked together, and breached it. With a sudden wet fire more terrible than anything he had ever felt before, the Lord Speaker of the Starym felt the blade of the Coronal slide into his left side, and up through his heart, and on through to strike his right arm upwards as it burst out of his body. The last thing he felt, as darkness reached up claws to spin him down into its cold and waiting grip, was an irritating itching washing out from where the hilt of the Fang of Cormanthor was nudging against his ribs.

He had to scratch it, he had to . . . the damned old mage was still watching and smiling . . . take him away, sweep him off, let him be . . .

And then Llombaerth Starym left Faerûn without even time for a proper farewell.

"He's dead," Flardryn said bitterly, watching the masked elf slump down out of sight. He turned away from the scrying sphere, not even bothering to watch as a spell of bright streaking stars rained down from the Srinshee to fell the Starym army, where they struggled to win past the human and the half-elf—too few, too feeble, and too late to win the day, whatever befell now.

Other Starym stared in white-faced, trembling disbelief at the glowing sphere, where it hovered above the pool of enchanted water. Tears ran down some of their chins, but they were older than Flardryn, and so did not think of turning away. The least one could do for those who wore the Starym dragons was watch them until the end, and mark what happened, to avenge them in time to come. It was simple duty.

"Killed—the Lord Speaker *killed* by the Coronal in his own court! The throne of the realm slapping the face of all Starym, that's what it is!" one of the elder Starym hissed, nose and ears quivering in rage.

The eyes of another senior Starym, this one a lady so old that her hair had almost all fallen out, and was mounted now in a jeweled tiara, flickered across to her outraged kins-elf. She sighed and said sadly, "I never thought to see the day when a Starym elf—even an arrogant and foolish youngling, overblown by a rank we should never have given him—would stand in the Court of Cormanthor and denounce its ruler. And then to attack him openly, with spells, and plunge the folk of the court into all this bloodshed!"

"Easy, sister," another Starym murmured, his own lips trembling with holding back the tears.

"*Have you seen?*" a sudden bellow rang off the rafters above them, as a distant door banged open against the wall with booming force. "This means *war!* To spells, Solonor damn you for witless old weak-knees, to spells! We must to court before the murderous Irithyl can escape!"

"Have done, Maeraddyth," the broad-shouldered elf seated closest to the sphere said quietly.

The young elf didn't hear him as he stormed up to the gathered Starym. "*Move,* you gutless elders! Where've you lost your pride, all of you?! Our Lord Speaker *cut down* in his blood, and you all stand around *watching!* What—"

"I said: have done, Maeraddyth," the seated elf said again, just as quietly as before. The raging young male stiffened in mid-growl, and stared down past all the silent faces, each wearing its own shock and sorrow.

The senior archmage of House Starym looked back up at him with mild eyes. "There is a time for throwing lives away," Uldreiyn Starym told his trembling young relative, "and Llombaerth has used it—more than used it—this day. We shall be fortunate if House Starym is not hunted down and slain, to every last trace-blood. Hold your anger, Maeraddyth; if you hurl your life after all those lost in yon chamber"—he inclined his head toward the sphere, where scenes of battle still flickered and flowed—"you will be a fool, and no hero."

"But Elder Lord, how can you *say* that?" Maeraddyth protested, waving at the sphere. "Are you as craven as the rest of these—"

"You are speaking," Uldreiyn said in a voice of sudden steel, "of your elders; Starym who were revered and celebrated for their deeds when your sire's sire was still a babe. Even when he puled and wailed, he never disgusted me by his childishness as you are doing, here and now."

The young warrior stared at him in genuine astonishment. The archmage's eyes thrust into his like twin spears, keen and merciless. Uldreiyn gestured to the floor, and Maeraddyth, swallowing in disbelief, found himself going to his knees.

The mightiest archmage of House Starym looked down at him. "Yes, it is right to be aghast and angry that one of our own has perished. But your fury should be sent to him, wherever what remains of Llombaerth is wandering now, for daring to drag down all of House Starym into his treachery. To work against a misguided Coronal is one thing; to attack and denounce the ruler of all Cormanthor before all his court is quite another. I am ashamed. All of these kin you deem 'craven' are sad, and shocked, and shamed. They are also thrice your quality, for they know above all that a Cormanthan elf—a noble Cormanthan elf—a *Starym* Cormanthan elf—keeps himself under control at all times, and never betrays the honor and pride of this great family. To do so is to spit upon the family name you are so hot to uphold, and besmirch the names and memories of all your ancestors."

Maeraddyth was white, now, and tears glimmered in his eyes.

"If I was cruel," Uldreiyn told him, "I would share with you some of the memories of Starym you've never known, drowning you in their prides and schemes and sorrows. These kin you ridicule carry such weights, when you are too young and stupid to know true duties. Speak to me not of war, and going 'to spells,' Maeraddyth."

The young Starym burst into tears, and the old mage was suddenly out of his chair and kneeling knee-to-knee with the weeping Maeraddyth, enfolding his shaking arms in a grip like old iron. "Yet I know your rage, and grief, and restlessness, youngling," he said into the young warrior's ear. "Your need to do something, your ache to defend the Starym name. I need that ache to be in you. I need that rage to burn in you. I need that grief to make you never forget the foolishness Llombaerth wrought. You are the future of House Starym, and it is my task to make of you a blade that does not fail, a pride that never tarnishes, and an honor that never, *never* forgets."

Maeraddyth drew back in astonishment, and Uldreiyn smiled at him. The shocked young warrior saw tears to match his own glimmering in the giant elf's eyes. "Now heed, young Maeraddyth, and make me proud of you," the archmage growled.

"You—all of us"—the warrior on his knees was suddenly aware that he knelt in the center of a ring of watching faces, and that tears were falling around him like raindrops in a storm—"must put this dark day behind us. Never speak of it, save in the innermost rooms of this abode, when no servants are about. We must work to rebuild the family honor, pledge our fealty anew to the Coronal as soon as is safely possible, and swallow whatever punishments he deems fitting. If we are to pay wealth, or give up our young to the Coronal's raising, or see retainers who fought today put to death, so be it. We must distance our House from the actions of those Starym who have defied the Coronal's wishes. We must show shame, not proud defiance . . . or there may soon be no House Starym, to rise to greatness again."

He rose, his firm grip dragging Maeraddyth to his feet also, and looked around at the ring of silent faces. "Do we have understanding?"

There were silent nods.

"Do we have disagreement? I would know now, so that I can slay or mind-meld as necessary." He looked around, eyes hard, but no one, not even the trembling Maeraddyth, said him nay.

"Good. Disturb me not, but dress in your best and wait my return. The Starym who flees this abode is no longer one of us."

Without another word Uldreiyn Starym, senior archmage of the House, strode out from them and marched across the room, face set.

Servants fled at the sight of his face, on the long walk through the halls to his own spell tower. When its door closed quietly behind them, he laid a hand on it and said the word that released the two ghost dragons from the splendid wyrms of the Starym arms emblazoned on the outer surface of the door.

They prowled up and down the last little stretch of corridor all night, ready to keep even those of House Starym out, but no one came to try to win a way past them. Which was just as well, for ghost dragons are always hungry.

The Pool of Remembrance shone white again, and the Coronal, looking weary, raised his hand to the Srinshee where she stood on air beside the throne. "None of them understand," he said quietly. He touched the gleaming blade that hung at his side. "For twenty years and more the foolish younglings of the great houses struggled to seize the throne. But even had they triumphed, the victor would have gained no more than the opportunity to submit to the blade-right ritual." He looked at Elmara, now Elminster again, standing with Nacacia and the Lady Herald. "Many may try that ritual, but only one will be chosen, surviving tests of talent, head, and heart." He sighed. "They are so young, so foolish." Mythanthar stood listening, a little smile on his face, and said nothing. His eyes were on the elves busily cleaning the Chamber of the Court of blood and bodies.

The Coronal said quietly to the Srinshee, "Do it now. Please."

Above them, the aged child-sorceress touched the floating Throne of Cormanthor, cast a spell, and then stood trembling, her eyes closed, as the great sound of the Calling rolled out through her.

Light lanced from every part of her body. From where those beams touched its walls and ceiling and pillars, the whole vast chamber hummed into a great rising chord.

It built to a soaring height, and then died away as slowly. When it was done, the leaders of all the Houses of Cormanthor stood before the throne, and lesser elves were crowding in the doors.

Eltargrim sheathed his sword and rose slowly through the air until he stood before the throne. When the Srinshee reeled in the aftermath of the mighty magic she'd awakened, he put an arm around her shoulders to support her, and said, "People of Cormanthor, great evil has been done—and undone—here today. Mythanthar declares that he is ready, and I will not wait longer, lest those who seek to control the realm as their private plaything find time to make another attempt, and cost us more Cormanthan lives. Before dusk, this day, the promised Mythal shall be laid, stretching over all the city from the Northpost to Shammath's Pool. When it is deemed stable—which should befall by highsun on the morrow—the gates of the city shall be thrown open to folk of all races who embrace not evil. Envoys shall go out to the known kingdoms of men, and gnomes, and halflings—and yes, dwarves. Henceforth, though our realm shall remain Cormanthor, this city shall be known as Myth Drannor, in honor of the Mythal Mythanthar shall craft for us, and for Drannor, the first elf of Cormanthor known to have married a dwarven lass, long ago though that be."

He looked down and the Lady Herald caught his eye, stepped forward, and announced grandly, "The wizards have been summoned. Let all who abide here keep peace and watch. Let the laying of the Mythal begin!"

EPILOGUE

The Mythal that rose over the city of Cormanthor was not the most powerful ever
spun, but elves still judge it the most important. With love, and out of strife, it was
wrought, and was given many rich and strange powers by the many who wove it.
Elves still sing of them, and vow their names will live forever, despite the fall of Myth
Drannor: the Coronal Eltargrim Irithyl; the Lady Herald Aubaudameira Dree,
known to minstrels as "Alais;" the human armathor Elminster, Chosen of Mystra;
the Lady Oluevaera Estelda, the legendary Srinshee; the human mage known only
as Mentor; the half-elven Arguth of Ambral Isle; High Court Mage Lord Earyn-
spieir Ongluth; the Lords Aulauthar Orbryn and Ondabrar Maendellyn; and the
Ladies Ahrendue Echorn, Dathlue Mistwinter, known to bards as 'Lady Steel' and
High Lady Alea Dahast. These were not all. Many of Cormanthor joined in the
Song that day, and by the grace of Corellon, Sehanine, and Mystra some of their
wants and skills found mysterious ways into the Mythal. Some did not, for treachery
never died in Cormanthor, whether it was called Myth Drannor or not . . .

ANTARN THE SAGE
FROM THE HIGH HISTORY OF FAERÛNIAN ARCHMAGES MIGHTY
PUBLISHED CIRCA THE YEAR OF THE STAFF

Armathors who had run from their guardposts at the Coronal's palace
hastened into the Chamber of the Court, led by the six court sorceresses.
Grim-faced, they drew their blades and made a ring, shoulder to shoulder and
facing outwards, on the pave before the throne.

Into that ring stepped the Coronal, his Lady Herald, Elminster, Nacacia,
Mythanthar, and the Srinshee. The warriors drew their ranks closed.

Their swords lifted in readiness almost immediately, as a mage hesitantly
approached, looking to the Coronal. "Revered Lord?" he asked cautiously, trying
not to let his eyes stray to the bloodstains on Eltargrim's white robes. "Have
you need of me?"

The Coronal looked to the Srinshee, who said gently, "Aye, Beldroth. But
not yet. Those of us here in the ring must die a little, that the Mythal live. Here
is not for you."

The elf lord withdrew, looking a little ashamed, and a little relieved. "Join
in when the web is spun, and shines out over us," the little sorceress added, and
he froze to hear her every word.

"If dying's involved," an ancient and wrinkled elven lady husked then, stepping out of the crowd with a slow hitch to her step, leaning on her cane, "then
I might as well go down at last doing some good for the land."

"Be welcome within, Ahrendue," the Srinshee said warmly. But the guards
did not move to clear a way into the ring until the Lady Herald said crisply into
their ears, "Make way for the Lady Ahrendue Echorn."

Their swords came up, and a murmur rippled across the court, when an elf
standing by a far pillar stepped forth and said, "The time for deception is done,

I think." An instant later, his slim form rose a head taller, and grew bulkier around the shoulders. Many in the Court gasped. Another human—and this one hidden in their midst!

His face was cloaked in conjured darkness; the tense Cormanthan guards saw only two keen eyes peering at them out of its shadow, but the Srinshee said firmly, "Mentor, you are welcome within our ring."

"Move, stalwarts," the Lady Herald murmured, and this time the warriors were quick to obey.

There was another stir in the crowded hall then, as a line of folk pushed through the assembled Cormanthans. The High Court Mage strode along at the head of this procession, and behind him walked Lord Aulauthar Orbryn, Lord Ondabrar Maendellyn, and a half-elven lord whose cloaked shoulders were surrounded by a whirling ring of glowing gemstones, whom the Srinshee identified in a whisper as "the sorcerer Arguth of Ambral Isle." Bringing up the rear was the High Lady of Art Alea Dahast, slim, smiling, and sharp-eyed.

It was becoming crowded in the ring, and as the Coronal embraced the last of these arrivals, he asked the Srinshee, "Is this all Mythanthar needs, do you think?"

"We await one more," the little sorceress told him, peering over the shoulders of the guards, and finally rising so as to stand on air above them. Playfully Mythanthar began to tap her toes, until she commenced to kick.

"Ah," she said then, beckoning at a face among the gathered citizens. "Our last. Come *on*, Dathlue!"

Looking surprised, the slender warrior stepped forth in her armor, unbuckling the slim long sword that swayed at her hip. Surrendering it to the guards, she slipped into the ring, kissed the Coronal full on the mouth, clapped the Srinshee on the arm, and then stood waiting.

They all looked at each other. The Srinshee looked at Mythanthar, who nodded.

"Widen the ring," the little sorceress commanded crisply. "A long way, now, we need as much space again. Sylmae, did you get all the bows brought in here?"

"No," the sorceress in the ring replied, without turning. "I got the arrows. Holone got the bows."

"And I got some *nasty* wands," Yathlanae put in, from her place along the ring. "Some of these ladies were wearing *four* garters just to carry them all!"

The Srinshee sighed theatrically, and said to Mythanthar, "*Don't* say anything—whatever you're thinking, just don't say it."

The old mage assumed a look of exaggerated innocence, and spread his hands.

The little sorceress shook her head and started taking folk in the ring by the elbows and leading them to where she wanted them to stand, until they stood widely spaced in a ring around Mythanthar, facing inward.

Elminster was surprised to find himself trembling. He shot a look at Nacacia, caught her reassuring smile, and answered it. Then he cast a long look all around the hall, from its floating throne to the gap in the ceiling to the huge, rough sections of toppled, broken pillar and, revealed behind it, the statue of a crouching elven hero who was menacing the Court with his outthrust sword.

He stared hard at it for a long moment, but it was just that: a statue, complete with a thin mantle of dust.

He drew in a deep breath, and tried to relax. Mystra, be with us all now, he thought. Shape and oversee this great magic, I pray, that it be what ye saw so long ago, to send me here.

The Srinshee drew in a deep breath then, looked around at them all, and whispered, "Let it begin."

In the excitement, no one in all that vast hall noticed something small and dark and dusty crawling among them, humping and slithering like some sort of inchworm as it made its slow way out across the bloodstained floor of the chamber—heading steadily for the ring.

Within the ring, Mythanthar spread his hands again, eyes closed, and from his fingers thin beams of light forged out, silent and slow, to link with each person in the ring. He murmured something, and the watching Cormanthans gasped in awe and alarm as his body exploded into a roiling cloud of blood and bones.

Elminster gasped, and almost moved from his place, but the Srinshee caught his eye with a stern look. He could tell from the tear that rolled down her cheek that she'd not known Mythanthar's spell required the sacrifice of his own life.

The cloud that had been the old mage rose like smoke from a fire, and became white, then blinding. The white strands still linking it to the others in the ring glowed with fire of their own.

White flames like tongues of snow soared up to the riven ceiling of the Chamber of the Court, as the bodies of all in the ring suddenly burst into white fire.

The Cormanthans crowded into the hall gasped in unison.

"What is it? Are they dying?" the Lady Duilya Evendusk cried, wringing her hands. Her lord put his own hands on her shoulders in silent reassurance, as Beldroth leaned toward her and said, "Mythanthar is dead—or his body is. *He* will become our Mythal, when 'tis done."

"What?" Elves were crowding forward on all sides to hear.

Beldroth lifted his head and his voice to tell them all, "The others should live, though the spell is stealing something of the force of life from all of them now. They'll begin to weave special powers—one chosen by each—into it soon, and we'll start to hear a sort of drone, or singing."

He looked back up at the rising, arching web of white fire, and discovered that tears were streaming down his face. A small hand crept into his, and squeezed reassuringly. He looked down into the eyes of an elf-child he did not know. Her face was very solemn, even when she was smiling back up at him. He squeezed her hand back in thanks, and went on holding it.

In a little glade where a fountain laughed endlessly down into a pool of dancing fish, Ithrythra Mornmist straightened suddenly and looked at her lord.

His scrying-globe and papers tumbled from his lap, forgotten, as he stood up. No, he was rising off the ground, his eyes fixed on something far away!

"What is it, Nelaer?" Ithrythra cried, running over to him. "Are you . . . well?"

"Oh, yes," Lord Mornmist gasped, his eyes still fixed on nothingness. "Oh, gods, yes. It's beautiful . . . it's wonderful!"

"What is it?" Ithrythra cried. "What's happening?"

"The Mythal," Nelaeryn Mornmist said, his voice sounding as if he wanted to cry. "Oh, how could we all have been so *blind?* We should have done this centuries ago!"

And then he started to sing—an endless, wordless song.

His lady stared at him for some minutes, her face white with worry. He drifted a little higher, his bare feet rising past her chin, and in sudden fright she clutched at his ankles, and clung.

The song washed through her, and with it all that he was feeling. And so it was that Ithrythra Mornmist was the first non-mage in Cormanthor to feel what a mythal was. When a servant found them a few minutes later, Lady Mornmist was wrapped around her lord's feet, trembling, her face bright with awe.

Alaglossa Tornglara stiffened and sat up in Satyrdance Pool, water streaming from her every curve. She said to the servant who knelt beside her with scents and brushes, "Something's happening. Can you feel it?"

The servant did not reply. Tingling to her very fingertips now, the Lady Tornglara turned to speak sharply to her maid, and stared instead.

The lass was floating in the air, still bent forward with a scent-bottle in her hand, and her eyes were staring. Tiny lightnings flickered and played about them, and darted in and out of her open mouth. She started to moan, then, as if aroused, and the sound changed to a low, wordless, endless song.

Alaglossa started to scream, and then, as the servant—Nlaea was her name, yes, that was it—started to drift higher, she reached out to take hold of Nlaea's arm.

The servant who heard the scream and sprinted all the long way through the gardens fetched up panting at the pool, and stared at them both: the floating servant and the noble lady who was staring up at her, eyes wide and fixed on something else. They were both nude, and moaning a chant. He looked at them in some detail, swallowed, and then hastened away again. He'd be in trouble if they came back from that humming and saw him staring.

He shook his head more than once, on his way back to his watering. Pleasure spells were certainly becoming powerful things these days . . .

Galan Goadulphyn cursed and felt for his daggers. Just his luck—within sight of the city with all the dwarven gems his boots could hold, and now a patrol was bearing down on him! He looked back at the trees, knowing there was nowhere he could hide, even if he'd been swift enough to outrun them. Gleaming-armored bastards. With weary grace he straightened out of his footsore shuffle and affected a grand manner.

"Ho, guardians! What news?"

"Hold, human," the foremost armathor said sternly. "The city will be open to you at highsun tomorrow, if all goes well. Until then, this is as far as you go."

Galan raised an incredulous eyebrow, and then doffed his dirty head scarf. The strips of false, straggly haired sideburns he was wearing came off with it—rather painfully.

"See these?" he said, flicking one of his ears back and forth with a grubby finger. "I'm no human."

"By the looks of you, you're no elf, either," the armathor said, his eyes hard. "We've seen dopplegangers before."

"No wife jokes, now," Galan told him, waggling a finger. That got him a dirty look (from the armathor) and some chuckles (from the rest of the patrol). "You mean they've *finally* got that mythal thing working? After all these years?"

The guards exchanged looks. "He must be a citizen," one of them said. "None else know about it, after all."

Reluctantly the patrol leader snapped, "Right—you can pass. I suggest you go somewhere you can bathe."

Galan drew himself up. "Why? If you're going to let *humans* in, what does it matter? Hmmph. You'll be telling me dwarves have the run of the city, next!"

"They do," the armathor said, grinding out every word from between clenched teeth. "Now get going."

Galan gave him a cheery wave. "Thank you, 'my *man*,'" he said airily, and flicked a ruby as big as a good grape out of the top of his right boot, to the startled guard. "That's for your trouble."

As he walked on into the city, Galan whistled happily. The gesture—gods above, the looks on their *faces!*—had been worth one ruby. Well, half a ruby. Well . . . was it too late to go and steal it back?

The essence that was Uldreiyn Starym rose up the thin line of flame his careful spell had birthed, touched the web of white fire, and allowed himself to be swept into the growing web of magic. Power surged through him. Yesss . . .

As he flashed along its strands, he deftly spun himself a cloak of fire from a gout of flame here, a strand shaved there, and a node robbed of a flicker of force as he flashed past.

He was just possibly the most powerful worker of magic in all Cormanthor— and if doddering Mythanthar could weave this, then the senior Lord Starym could ride it, and cloak himself in it, and conceal who he was as he rode the glistening white strands across the city and down, down to the gaping hole in the roof of the Court.

His body was still slumped in his chair, at the heart of his dragon-guarded speculum in the tallest tower of House Starym, the one that stood a little apart. Leaving it behind made him vulnerable—not that these rapture-mazed weavers would notice him until he did something drastic. Which, of course, is what he was here for.

A child could ride a spun spell, once shown how, but he wanted to do more than just ride. Much more. In a world where such as Ildilyntra Starym died and foolish puppies like Maeraddyth had to be kept alive, one had to make one's own justice.

He was plunging down, now, moving as fast as he dared. They were all standing together, and he had to strike the right one without any delay, or risk being sensed by that little shrew the Srinshee or perhaps one of the others he did not know.

Ride the white flames—an exhilarating sensation, he admitted—down, down to . . . *yes!* Farewell, Aulauthar!

His passing saddens us greatly, Uldreiyn thought savagely, as he hurled the full force of his will, bolstered by a burst of the white fire, against the timid, carefully perfectionist mind of his chosen victim. It crumbled in an instant, bathing him in chaotic memories as he wallowed and thrust ruthlessly in all directions.

The watchers in the Court saw one of the living pillars of white flame waver for a moment, but witnessed no other sign of the savage spell attack that burned the brain and innards of Lord Aulauthar Orbryn to ashes, leaving his body a mindless shell.

Now he was part of the weave at last, part of the eager flow and growth of new powers. Orbryn had been crafting the part of the future Mythal that identified creatures by their races. Dragons were to be shut out, were they? Dopplegangers, of course, and orcs, too.

Well, why not expand on Aulauthar's excellent work, and make the Mythal deadly to all non-pureblood elves? Deadly by, say, highsun tomorrow. Dearly though he'd have loved to slay that pollution Elminster, awakening the power now would smite down two more of the weavers of the Mythal—Mentor and the halfblood—and would mean his own certain detection. And after Uldreiyn Starym was dust, they'd simply spin another Mythal to replace the one he'd shattered.

Oh, no, best to bide a bit; he had much grander plans than that.

This outstrips everything but knowing the love of a goddess, Elminster thought, as he soared along pathways of white fire, feeling power surge through him. With every passing instant the grandeur grew, as the Mythal expanded in size and scope. Half a hundred minds were at work, now, smoothing and shaping and making it all larger and more intricate; cross-connected here and augmented there, and . . .

Elminster stiffened, where he was floating in the web, and then whirled through an intricate junction and turned back. There had been sharp, very brief pain and a flash of intolerable heat, followed by a whiff of confusion. A death? Something had gone wrong, something now concealed. Treachery, if that's what it was, could doom the Mythal before it was even born.

It had been a long way back, down and deep. Gods, were they under attack, back in the court? As he descended, his mind flashed out to touch that of Beldroth, part of the expanding web now, humming as he floated just clear of the ground, a wide-eyed child floating with him. People all around were murmuring and drawing back from him warily, but there was more wonder than hostility. No, the guards stood watchfully, but peace held in the Chamber of the Court.

So *where*, then . . . ?

He sank down warily, to where the web was anchored, heading for the elves. The High Court Mage was fine, as was Alea Dahast, an—*no!* There! An awareness that did not belong to Lord Aulauthar Orbryn had peered at him along the white fire, just for a moment; a sentience whose regard had been anything but kindly.

The work the false Orbryn was doing on the Mythal was tainted to destroy all non-elven! This must be why he was here, what he'd spent twenty years working toward! To stop this treachery! *Be with me now, Mystra,* El thought, *for now I strike for thee.*

And riding a plume of white fire, Elminster arrowed down into what had once been Lord Aulauthar Orbryn, and lashed out at who he found there.

The wave of white fire rolled through the ruins of what had once been Orbryn's mind, and El drew back from it a little. The mental bolt that would have impaled him flashed out and missed. The body around them shuddered under its searing impact.

Snarling silently, Elminster struck back.

His bolt was rebuffed by a mind as strong and as deep as his own. An elven elder with whom he'd never brushed minds. A Starym? El sped sideways along the lines of fire, so that the next strike—and his counterstroke—both tore through the construct the false Orbryn had woven, wrecking it beyond repair. The Mythal would not now slay non-elves, whatever else befell.

That left nothing to shield Elminster Aumar. The next thrust from the mighty mind he faced pierced and held him no matter how hard he thrashed, bearing down with mindfire.

Red pain erupted, and with it memories began to flow as they were lost, crashing over him one after another in a racing, confusing flood. Elminster tried to scream and break away, but succeeded only in spinning himself around, still transfixed on the shearing probe that was boring deeper and deeper into him.

He saw his attacker for the first time. Uldreiyn Starym, senior lord and archmage of that House, sneering at him in serene triumph as he yielded that identification to the tortured mind he was sundering . . .

Mystra! Elminster cried, writhing in agony. *Mystra, aid me! For Cormanthor, come to me now!*

The human worm was dying, thrashing, weeping for his god. Now was the time; the others would sense something amiss soon enough. Uldreiyn Starym lashed out at Elminster one more time, and then drew back long enough to work the magic that would call his body to himself, to cloak the weakness of his disembodied mind and give him the means to really strike out, if he had to leave this web under the weight of many aroused attackers. There! Done. Exultantly, he surged back to the attack, stabbing again at the shuddering, tumbling human.

There was a stir of fresh excitement in the Court when the large, burly, grandly robed form of Lord UIdreiyn Starym appeared suddenly within the ring, standing near the human Elminster. His boots were firmly on the pave, only inches from something small, dark, and dusty, that was crawling slowly toward the young human mage. It stopped for a moment, and wavered, reaching toward the Starym sorcerer's boot, but then seemed to come to some sort of decision, and resumed its humping, inching progress toward the last prince of Athalantar.

Holone was not a Sorceress of the Court for nothing. Something was happening behind her, something wrong. She spun around. Gods! A Starym!

He was standing still, though, his eyes as vacant as all the rest, and from his mouth and raised hands white fire was streaming, back and forth . . . he was as much a part of the building Mythal as any of them. Starym could never be trusted, but . . . was he a foe?

Holone bit her lip. She was still standing watching, ruled by indecision, when a tapestry and the window behind it burst inward with a crash. Out of the dust and falling rubble a slim figure flew, hands outstretched to spit fire—real fire!

Holone's gasp was echoed by many of the watching Cormanthans. Symrustar Auglamyr—alive? Where had she been these twenty years? Holone swallowed and raised her hands to weave a barrier, knowing there was no time.

That gout of flame was already snarling ahead of the flying lady, headed straight for the unseeing Starym. There were shouts and screams and oaths in the Chamber of the Court once more as fire struck Lord Uldreiyn Starym, and spun him around. He staggered, went to one knee, and his eyes flamed in dark fury. He looked at his foe.

The Lady Symrustar Auglamyr was only a few feet away from him, still plunging down on him at full speed, her lips pulled back from her white teeth in a snarl of anger, her eyes aflame. She was shouting something.

"*For Mystra!* A gift for thee, sorcerer, from Mystra!"

The senior Starym sneered in reply as he activated the full force of his mantle.

Elves had swords in their hands, now, and were uncertainly approaching the ring—while armathors and the court sorceresses warned them to stay *back*, for the love of Cormanthor!

They watched, aghast, as the flying lady smashed into something unseen that splintered her arms like dry branches, flung her head back, and then broke her legs and spine almost casually as it spun her around in the air, in a tangle of unbound hair, and flung her back whence she'd come.

Many of the watching elves groaned as they saw that twisting, arching, shuddering body aimed firmly sideways, toward the statue of the elven hero. Steered, and turned about with cold, exacting precision, to face them in the last moments before it was thrust onto the hero's stone sword.

Symrustar Auglamyr threw back her head to cry out in hoarse agony as the sword burst forth under her breast, dark and wet with her own blood. Lightnings sang and played around her as her magics began to fail.

Uldreiyn Starym put his hands on his hips and laughed. "So perish all who dare to strike a Starym!" he told the Court, and lifted his hands. "Who shall be next? *You*, Holone?"

The court sorceress blanched and fell back, but did not flee from her place in the ring. She drew in a deep breath, tossed her head, and said, voice trembling only a little, "If need be, traitor."

He had called, and Mystra had sent Symrustar, and she was dying for him! Writhing in agony, El could find no time for grief. *Mystra!* he shouted, as a warrior bellows in battle. *Send me something to aid her! The Starym prevails! Mystra!*

Something golden shone in his tattered mind—a thread, a ribbon, moving and turning. His eyes could not help but follow it, and the image of his unleashing it that overlaid it briefly. It twisted, to form a shape *thus*, and so! Set that upon the foe!

Thanks be, Mystra, El thought with all his heart, and seized on the shape firmly as he lashed out with another bolt, straight at Uldreiyn Starym. This would hurt.

The Starym arch-sorcerer stiffened, turned with slow menace, and smilingly dealt a counterblow, sending a mocking message with it.

Not crazed yet, human? You will be. Oh, you will be.

Oh? Eat this, arrogant elf! Elminster replied in Uldreiyn's mind—and unspun Mystra's weaving.

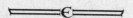

The watching Cormanthans saw Beldroth shriek first, snatching his hand away from the child to clutch at his head with both hands, clawing at his ears and howling in raw pain.

Lord Nelaeryn Mormnist spasmed and kicked out. His lady was hurled back, bowling over two anxiously watching servants. One of the others rushed forward to aid his convulsing lord, who was shrieking like nothing the servant had ever heard before. Droplets of blood were gouting from his mouth, his eyes, and from under his fingernails. He thrashed in midair like a struggling fish, then slumped, crashing to the ground and smashing the servant senseless beneath him.

Ithrythra Mornmist struggled to her feet. "Nelaer!" she cried, tears streaming down her face. "Oh, Nelaer, *speak to me!*" With frantic fingers she rolled him over, staring at the working face of her lord.

"Get a mage!" she snarled at the servants who were still standing. "All of you *go!* Get *twenty* mages! And *hurry!*"

There was a splashing, and a heavy weight tumbling on top of her. Alaglossa Tornglara came back to awareness with a shock as the waters of Satyrdance Pool closed over her head. She kicked out and thrust herself up to the air again, tumbling a stiff body off of her—Nlaea! Gods, what had happened?

"Help!"

The gardener looked up from his watering. That was the lady's voice!

"Help!"

He hastened, kicking over the waterspout he'd just set carefully down in his haste. It was a long run to Satyrdance Pool, Corellon curse it! He got up onto the path and put some leg into it, only to come to a halt, staring.

The Lady Alaglossa Tornglara, naked as the day she was born, staggered along the path toward him, her feet cut open on the flagstones, leaving a trail of blood behind her as she came. She was cradling her maid Nlaea in her arms, her eyes wild. "Help me!" she roared. "We must get her to the house! Move, Corellon curse you!"

The gardener swallowed and scooped Nlaea out of his lady's arms. Corellon, he reflected wryly, as he turned around to run, was going to have a busy day.

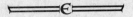

Uldreiyn Starym opened his mouth in surprise—the first time it had worn that expression in earnest in some centuries.

And the last. White fire surged through him and stripped him bare just as he had burned out Lord Orbryn earlier, leaving nothing behind his eyes but a rushing nothingness. A new potency raced through the Mythal, crashing through the heads of mages all over Cormanthor, as the hungry white fire drank the life and wits and power of the Starym archmage.

The elves standing uncertainly in the Court, not knowing where or how to strike, saw the tall, broad body of the great Starym lord blaze forth yellow flames, for all the world as if he were a tree struck by lightning.

He burned like a torch before their shocked faces, while the web of white fire hummed on serenely overhead and profound silence reigned in the Chamber of the Court. Hundreds of elves held their breaths, until the blackened body of the archmage toppled, collapsing into swirling ashes.

The backlash spun Elminster away, whirling him like a leaf in a gale, the golden symbol around him like a protective hand. When the whirling stopped at last, the symbol faded, the light leaving him at last in darkness.

He was floating in a void, a sentience without body. Again.

Mystra? His first call was little more than a whisper. It seemed he'd done a lot of demanding of the goddess recently, managing nothing without her aid or guidance.

Think you so? Her voice, in his mind, was warm, and gentle, and utterly overwhelming. He felt loved and utterly safe, and found himself basking silently in the warmth coiling around him, floating in timeless, endless joy. It might have been hours before Mystra spoke again, or only moments.

You have done well, Chosen One. A brave beginning, but only that: you must abide in Myth Drannor—the new Cormanthor—for a time, to nurture and protect. While you do so, you will also be learning as much as you can of the wielding of magic from those who will come to this bright new fellowship. I am pleased with you, Elminster. Be whole once more.

Abruptly he was elsewhere, floating upright amid many strands of humming white fire, with the shattered stone of a fallen pillar below him and the bloody, pain-etched face of Symrustar Auglamyr in front of him.

There was a chorus of excited whisperings from the elves crowded into the Chamber of the Court, but El scarcely heard it. Mystra had left extra spell energy tingling in his hands, far too much for him to carry for long, and he thought he knew why.

She was a broken thing, her body slumped atop the stone sword that impaled it. Only the failing magics around her had kept her alive this long. With infinite care Elminster lifted the dying elven lady in his arms and drew her off the bloody blade.

She gasped and opened her eyes at his touch, and then sagged against him, her ravaged body quivering once when she slid entirely free of the stone. El thrust a hand against the terrible hole through her ribs and let healing power flow out of him.

She caught her breath and shuddered then, daring to hope—and breathe— for the first time in a long while.

El turned her in the air until he was cradling her in his arms, and drifted very slowly down to the floor. As his knees touched the pave, he could feel the regard of many elven eyes, but he bent his head forward and kissed Symrustar's bloody mouth as if they'd been ardent lovers for years. Holding her lips with his, he thrust life into her, letting all the power Mystra had given him flow into her shattered body. Then he gave of his own vitality, holding his mouth on hers, until trembling weakness made him rise to breathe at last.

She spoke for the first time then, a ragged whisper. " 'Tis you, isn't it, Elminster? I certainly had to wait long enough for that kiss."

El chuckled and held her against him as the light in her eyes came back.

Almost lazily her eyes found Faerûn again, and the shattered ceiling of the Court, and then him. Slowly, wincing and working her mouth, she managed a smile. "I thank you for making my passing easier . . . but I am dying; you cannot stay that. Mystra snatched me from death that night in the woods—the death Elandorr planned for me—for a task. I have served her, and 'tis done. I can die."

Elminster shook his head slowly, aware of the anxious faces and raised hands of the sorceresses Sylmae and Holone waiting above him—waiting to blast Symrustar with spells should she try any last treachery.

"Mystra does not treat folk so," El told her gently.

Symrustar grimaced as a fresh ripple of pain ran through her. A rivulet of bright blood ran from the corner of her mouth. "So you say, Chosen One. I am an elf, and one who misused magic, at that. I tried to enslave you—I would have stolen your magic and slain you. Why should she have a care about my fate?"

"For the same reason I care," El said gently.

Those pain-ridden eyes flickered. "Love? Lust? I know not, man. I cannot tarry to think on it . . . life slips away. . . ."

"One life," Elminster told her urgently, as he realized Mystra's plan at last. "But not all that is Symrustar."

He pulled open the bloodsoaked ruin of her bodice, and upon the ravaged flesh beneath traced the first golden symbol Mystra had put in his mind; the one that would shine there forever.

Her breath caught, and she sat up, eyes shining. "I—I see at last. Oh, human, I have wronged you from the start. I have—"

She wasted no more time on words, as blue-white fire stole out of her skin to claim her, but turned into his embrace to kiss him tenderly.

Her lips were still on his as she faded away. A few motes of blue-white light swirled where she'd been, and then flickered and were gone.

El looked up, and saw four of the weavers, their limbs still ablaze with white fire and linked to the web above, standing above him, looking down with love and concern.

He looked up and told the Srinshee, Lady Steel, the Herald Alais, and the Coronal, "Mystra has claimed her. She will serve the Lady of Mysteries now."

Something crawled up his arm, then, and he snatched at it and held it up, bewildered. A scrap of something dusty, bloodstained, and moving—the mask that Llombaerth Starym had worn for so long. It tingled in his grasp, warm and somehow welcoming.

As he stared at it, there was a sudden flare of rainbow-hued light from overhead, and all the gathered elves gasped in awe. The Mythal was born!

Elminster felt a stirring in his throat, and rose with all the others, to join in what he could already hear echoing through the streets. All over Cormanthor, every elf and half-elf and human was breaking into song. The same swelling, involuntary song of the Mythal's birth—high, radiant, beautiful, and unearthly. And as the singers turned to embrace each other in wonder, every face was wet with tears.

"Yes," Lord Mornmist whispered, his eyes on something far away. The servants looked from his vacant face to that of their lady. Tears ran in floods down her face, dripping from her chin, as she bent over her lord.

"Why?" she whimpered frantically. "*Why* do the mages not come?"

The servants shot anxious looks at each other, not daring to answer. Then Nelaeryn Mornmist rose up out of their gentle hands as if torn aloft by some invisible hand. Ithrythra screamed, but her shrieks turned to sobs of joy an instant later, as her lord opened his eyes and cried out, "Yes! At last! The glory is come to Cormanthor!"

His voice rang like a trumpet as he hung in the air above them, and blue flames spurted from his eyes. He looked down.

"Oh, Ithrythra," he called, "come and share this with me. All of you, come!" He held out his hand, and there were gasps as the Mornmist servants below felt themselves lifted with infinite gentleness, and awesome power, up into the air to join the man whose laughter rang out, then, like triumphal horns.

Nlaea moved in the gardener's arms, and made a small, satisfied sound. He looked down, slipped on the path, and almost dropped her.

"Careful!" the Lady Alaglossa Tornglara snapped at his elbow, her strong arms steadying both him and his burden.

Nlaea moved again, stretching almost luxuriously, and her weight was suddenly gone. The gardener stumbled, overbalanced by its sudden disappearance, and slid into a galamathra bush.

"Nlaea?" Alaglossa cried in terror. "Nlaea!"

Her maid turned in the air and smiled down at her. "Be at peace, Lady," she said softly, and blue flames seemed to blaze in her eyes as she spoke. "Cormanthor is crowned at last."

And as her maid hovered over her, the Lady Alaglossa went to her knees on the path and started to pray through happy floods of tears.

Galan Goadulphyn looked around in disbelief. On all sides, elven bodies were floating up into the air, and there was much laughter, and weeping—happy weeping. Here and there shouts of exultation rose. Had all Cormanthor gone mad at once?

He hastened toward a richly appointed house whose door stood open.

Well, if everyone was going to be lost in celebration, perhaps they'd not notice the loss of a few baubles.

He was almost inside when firm fingers took hold of his left ear. He wrenched himself free and spun around, hand snatching out a dagger. "Who—?" he snarled—and then fell silent, gaping.

The lady some had known as the most beautiful and deadly in all Cormanthor smiled almost dreamily at him as she floated in the doorway, blue fire playing about her limbs. "Why, Galan," Symrustar Auglamyr said delightedly, "you please me greatly. To think that at long last you've put thieving behind you, and have come to the houses of Myth Drannans to repay them in gems for all that you've stolen!"

Galan's face twisted in utter incredulity. "What? Repay? 'Myth Drannans'?"

Those were the last words he uttered before lips that blazed came down on his—and gems started to fly out of his boots like angry wasps leaving a nest, away into the bright air of Myth Drannor.

Moonrise over Myth Drannor that first night was a time of joy. Horns blew and harps were struck in a delighted cacophony, as if a year's festivals and revels had been rolled into one frantic celebration. Thanks to the silent, invisible wonderwork that overlaid the city like a domed shield, those who'd never been able to fly before could do so now, without need of spell or item. The air was full of laughing, embracing elves. Wine flowed freely, and troths were plighted with eager abandon. The moon was full and bright, and spilled down through the riven roof of the Chamber of the Court in a bright flood.

An elven lady glided alone into the empty room, her jeweled slippers treading air above the bloodstained pave. The hems of her low-cut gown glittered with a breathtaking fall of gems, and on her breast diamonds sparkled in the shape of twin falling dragons. Only streaks of white and gray at her temples betrayed her age as she moved sinuously through the stillness, coming at last to where a small pile of ashes lay in the bright pool of moonlight.

She looked down at them in silence for a long time, the quickening rise and fall of her breast the only difference between her and a statue. A tattered song floated in through the rent in the roof above as joyous elves soared past, and the silent lady clenched her fists so tightly that blood dripped from where her long nails pierced her palms.

Lady Sharaera Starym raised her beautiful head to look at the moon riding high above, drew in a deep breath, looked down at what little was left of her Uldreiyn, and hissed fiercely, "The Mythal must fall, and Elminster must be destroyed!"

Only the ghosts were there to hear her.

At the time of the laying of the Mythal, some of the elves of Cormanthor thought opening their realm to other races was a mistake. I'm sure some still do.

There was some small dispute and bother at the time, as there is at the birthing of any new thing that is not a living babe, but nothing that minstrels or sages need be overly concerned about. A matter of a few swords, a handful of spells, and some hasty words, followed by a party. In short, it was very like most of what human heroes are wont to call "adventures."

Elminster the Sage
from a speech to an assembly of Harpers in Twilight Hall,
Berdusk
The Year of the Harp

THE TEMPTATION OF
ELMINSTER

PROLOGUE

There is a time in the unfolding history of the mighty Old Mage of Shadowdale that some sages call "the years when Elminster lay dead." I wasn't there to see any corpse, so I prefer to call them "the Silent Years." I've been vilified and derided as the worst sort of fantasizing idiot for that stance, but my critics and I agree on one thing: whatever Elminster did during those years, all we know of it is—nothing at all.

Antarn the Sage
from *The High History of Faerûnian Archmages Mighty*
published circa The Year of the Staff

The sword flashed down to deal death. The roszel bush made no defense beyond emitting a solid sort of thunking noise as tempered steel sliced through it. Thorny boughs fell away with dry cracklings, a booted foot slipped, and there was a heavy crash, followed, as three adventurers caught their breath in unison, by a tense silence.

"Amandarn?" one of them asked when she could hold her tongue no more, her voice sharp with apprehension. "Amandarn?"

The name echoed back to her from the walls of the ruin—walls that seemed somehow watchful . . . and waiting.

The three waded forward through loose rubble, weapons ready, eyes darting this way and that for the telltale dark ribbon of a snake.

"Amandarn?" came the cry again, lower and more tremulous. A trap could be anywhere, or a lurking beast, and—

"Gods curse these stones and thorns . . . and crazed Netherese builders, too!" a voice more exasperated than pain-wracked snarled from somewhere ahead, somewhere slightly muffled, where the ground gave way into darkness.

"To say nothing of even crazier thieves!" the woman who'd called so anxiously boomed out a reply, her voice loud and warm with relief.

"Wealth redistributors, Nuressa, if you *please*," Amandarn replied in aggrieved tones, as stones shifted and rattled around his clawing hands. "The term 'thief' is such a vulgar, career-limiting word."

"Like the word 'idiot'?" a third voice asked gruffly. "Or 'hero'?" Its gruffness lay like a mock growl atop tones of liquid velvet.

"Iyriklaunavan," Nuressa said severely, "we've had this talk already, haven't we? Insults and provocative comments are for when we're lazing by a fire, safe at home, *not* in the middle of some deadly sorcerer's tomb with unknown Netherese spells and guardian ghosts bristling all around us."

"I thought I heard something odd," a deep, raw fourth voice added with a chuckle. "Ghosts bristle far more noisily than they did in my father's day, I must say."

"Hmmph," Nuressa replied tartly, reaching one long, bronzed and muscled arm down into the gloom to haul the still struggling Amandarn to his feet. The point of the gigantic war sword in her other hand didn't waver or droop for an instant. "Over-clever dwarves, I've heard," she added as she more or less plucked the wealth redistributor into the air like a rather slim packsack, "die just as easily."

"Where do you hear these things?" Iyriklaunavan asked, in light, sardonic tones of mock envy. "I must go drinking there."

"*Iyrik*," Nuressa growled warningly, as she set the thief down.

"Say," Amandarn commented excitedly, waving one black-gloved hand for silence. "That has a ring to it! We could call ourselves . . . The Over-clever Dwarf!"

"We *could*," Nuressa said witheringly, grounding her sword and crossing her forearms on its quillons. It was obvious anything lurking in this crypt—or mausoleum, or whatever it was yawning dark and menacingly just ahead of them—wasn't asleep or unwarned anymore. The need for haste was past and the chance for stealth gone forever. The brawny warrior woman squinted up at the sun, judging how much of the day was left. She was hot in her armor . . . really hot, for the first time since before last harvest.

It was an unexpectedly warm day in Mirtul, the Year of the Missing Blade, and the four adventurers scrambling in the sea of broken, stony rubble were sweating under their shared coating of thick dust.

The shortest, stoutest one chuckled merrily and said in his raw, broken trumpet of a voice, "I can hardly elude my born duty to be the dwarf—so that leaves it to ye three to be 'over-clever.' Even with the triple muster, I'm not before-all-the-gods sure you've wits enough—"

"That'll do," the elf standing beside him said, his tones as gruff as any dwarf could manage. "It's not a name I'm in overmuch favor of, anyway. I don't want a joke name. How can we feel proud—"

"Strut around, you mean," the dwarf murmured.

"—wearing a jest we're sure to become heartily sick of after a month, at most. Why not something exotic, something . . ." He waved his hand as if willing inspiration to burst forth. A moment later, obligingly, it did. "Something like the Steel Rose."

There was a moment of considering silence, which Iyriklaunavan could count as something of a victory, before Folossan chuckled again and asked, "You want me to forge some flowers for us to wear? Belt buckles? Codpieces?"

Amandarn stopped rubbing his bruises long enough to ask witheringly, "Do you have to make a joke of everything, Lossum? I like that name."

The woman who towered over them all in her blackened armor said slowly, "But I don't know that I do, Sir Thief. I was called something similar when I was a slave, thanks to the whippings my disobedience brought me. A 'steel rose' is a welt raised by a steel-barbed whip."

The merry dwarf shrugged. "That makes it a bad name for a brace of bold and menacing adventurers?" he asked.

Amandarn snorted at that description.

Nuressa's mouth tightened into a thin line that the others had learned to respect. "A slaver who makes steel roses is deemed careless with a whip or unable to control his temper. Such a welt lowers the value of a slave. Good slavers have other ways of causing pain without leaving marks. So you'll be saying we're careless and unable to control ourselves."

"Seems even more fitting, then, to me," the dwarf told the nearest stone pillar, then jumped back with a strangled oath as it cracked across and a great shard of stone tumbled down at him, crashing through a sudden flurry of tensely raised weapons.

Dust swirled in the silence, but nothing else moved. After what seemed like a long time, Nuressa lowered her blade and muttered, "We've wasted quite enough time on one more silly argument about what to call ourselves. Let it be spoken of *later*. Amandarn, you were finding us a safe way into yon . . ."

"Waiting tomb," Folossan murmured smoothly, grinning sheepishly under the sudden weight of the three dark, annoyed glares.

In near silence the thief moved forward, hands spread for balance, his soft-soled boots gripping the loose stones. Perhaps a dozen strides ahead lay a dark and gaping opening in the side of a broken-spired bulk of stone that had once been the heart of a mighty palace but now stood like a forlorn and forgotten cottage amid leaning pillars and heaps of fern-girt rubble.

Iyriklaunavan took a few steps forward to better watch Amandarn's slow and careful advance. As the slim, almost child-sized thief came to a halt just outside the ruined walls to peer warily ahead, the maroon-robed elf whispered, "I have a bad feeling about this. . . ."

Folossan waved a dismissive hand and said, "You have a bad feeling about everything, O gruffest of elves."

Nuressa jostled both of them into silence as Amandarn suddenly broke his immobility, gliding forward and out of sight.

They waited. And waited. Iyriklaunavan cleared his throat as quietly as he could, but the sound in his throat still seemed startlingly loud even to him. An eerie, waiting stillness seemed to hang over the ruins. A bird crossed the distant sky without calling, the beats of its wings seeming to measure a time that had grown too long.

Something had happened to Amandarn.

A very quiet doom? They'd heard nothing . . . and as the tense breaths of time dragged on, heard more of it.

Nuressa found herself walking slowly toward the hole where Amandarn had gone, her boots crunching on the shifting stones where the thief had walked with no more noise than a falling leaf. She shrugged and hefted the war sword in her hands. Skulking was for others.

She was almost in under the shadow of the walls when something moved in the waiting darkness ahead of her. Nuressa swept her blade up and back, ready to cut down viciously, but the face grinning at her out of the gloom belonged to Amandarn.

"I knew you were annoyed with me," the thief said, eyeing her raised steel, "but I'm quite short enough already, thank you."

He jerked his thumb at the darkness behind him. "It's a tomb, all right," he said, "old and crawling with runes. They probably say something along the lines of 'Zurmapyxapetyl, a mage of Netheril, sleeps here,' but reading Old High Netherese, or whatever it's properly called, is more Iyrik's skill than mine."

"Any guardians?" Nuressa asked, not taking her eyes off the darkness beyond Amandarn for an instant.

"None that I saw, but a glowblade's pretty dim. . . ."

"Safe to throw in a torch?"

The thief shrugged. "Should be. Everything's made of stone."

Wordlessly Nuressa extended an open, gauntleted hand behind her. After a few scrambling minutes, Folossan put a lit torch into it. The warrior looked at him, dipped her jaw in wordless thanks, and threw.

Flames *whup-whup-whupped* into the darkness. The torchlight guttered when it landed, then recovered and danced brightly once more. Nuressa stepped forward to fill the opening with her body, barring the way, and asked simply, "Traps?"

"None near the entrance," Amandarn replied, "and this place doesn't *feel* like we'll find any. Yet . . . I don't like those runes. You can hide anything in runes."

"True enough," the dwarf agreed in a low voice. "Are you satisfied, Nessa? Are you going to stand aside and let us in or play at being a closed door until nightfall?"

The armored woman gave him a withering look, then silently stood aside and gestured grandly at him to proceed.

Folossan put his head down and scuttled past, not quite daring to whoop. The normally gloomy-looking Iyriklaunavan was hard on his heels, trotting forward with fluid grace and maroon robes held high to avoid tripping. It would not do to tumble and fall helplessly into a tomb where just about any sort of snake or other foe might be lurking.

Amandarn wasn't far behind. In exasperated silence Nuressa watched them storm past and shook her head. Did they think this was some sort of pleasure outing?

She followed more cautiously, looking for doors that might be shut to imprison them, traps Amandarn might have missed, even some sort of lurking foes, hitherto unnoticed. . . .

"Gods on their glittering thrones!" Folossan gasped, somewhere ahead. He made of the curse a slow, measured bricklaying of awe, building a wall of utter astonishment that seemed to echo around the dark tomb chamber for just an instant before something swallowed it.

Nuressa shouldered her way out of the sunlight, war sword ready. Trust them to cry no warning to tell her what peril awaited.

The chamber was high and dusty and dark, the torch dying a slow, sullen death at its heart. There was a space that bore some sort of circular design in the floor tiles, framed by four smooth, dark stone pillars that soared from the pave to the lofty, unseen ceiling.

Away beyond those ever feebler flames rose dark steps crowned by what could only be the casket of someone great and important—or a true giant, so large was the massive black stone, blotched with deep emerald green, its curves aglitter with golden runes that flashed in time with the pulsing, fading light of the torch. Two empty braziers taller than she was flanked this dais, and over it hung the dusty-shrouded ends of what looked like a curtain of mail but could, under the dust, be almost anything that would drape like fabric, hanging motionless from the distant, scarcely seen ceiling.

It was not the tomb that the gruff elf mage, the awed dwarf, and the boyish thief were staring at. It was something else, rather nearer than that, and above them. Nuressa shot a hard glance up at it, then all around the tomb chamber, seeking some other entrance or waiting peril. None offered itself to the tip of her gleaming blade, so she grounded it and joined in the general staring.

High above them, starting perhaps fifty feet up in the air, hung what might be a scarecrow, and might have once been a man. Two worn bootheels they could see, standing on emptiness, and above that a man-sized bulk of gray dust so thick it looked like fur, joined to the ceiling and walls by lazy, dusty arcs of cobwebs that must be as thick as ropes.

"That was a man, once, I think," Iyriklaunavan murmured, voicing what they were all thinking.

"Aye, so, but what's holding him up there?" Folossan asked. "Surely not those webs . . . but I can see naught else."

"So it's magic," Nuressa said reluctantly, and they all nodded in slow and solemn agreement.

"Someone who died in a trap or spell duel," Amandarn said quietly, "or a guardian, who's been waiting all these years, undead or asleep, for the likes of us to intrude?"

"We can't afford to gamble," the elf told him gruffly. "He could well be a mage, and he's above us, where none can hide from him. Stand back, all."

The adventuring band that had no name moved in four different directions, each member taking his own path backward across the ever more dimly lit room. Folossan was fumbling in his voluminous shoulder bags for another torch as Iyriklaunavan raised his hands to cup empty air, murmured something, then spread his hands apart.

Between those hands something shivered and glimmered for a tumbling instant before it flashed, so bright as to sear the watching eye, and leaped through the dark emptiness like a sizzling blade. The spell clove air and all as it smote whatever hung so high above, bringing down a heavy rain of choking dust.

Clods of gray fur fell like snow melting from high branches, pattering down on all sides as the four adventurers coughed and wiped at their eyes and noses, shaking their heads and staggering back.

Something flickered nearby, in several places. Struggling to clear the dust from watering eyes and see, the four adventurers could not help but notice two things through the swirling dust: the booted feet above were still exactly where they had been, and the flickerings were pulsing radiances playing rapidly up and down the four stone pillars.

"He moves!" Iyriklaunavan shouted suddenly, pointing upward. "He moves! I'll . . ."

The rest of his words were lost in a sudden grinding, rumbling noise that shook the floor tiles under their boots. The light dancing down the pillars suddenly flashed into brightness, gleaming back from four tensely raised weapons. Stone facings on all of the pillars slid down into the floor, leaving behind openings that stretched the height of the pillars.

Something filled those openings, dimly seen as the radiances died away, leaving only the ruby embers of the torch on the floor. Folossan dived for that torch, blowing hard on it and coughing in the swirling dust with each breath he took. He thrust a fresh torch against the old one and blew on where they met.

The others were peering suspiciously at what filled the floor-to-ceiling channels in the pillars. It was something pale and glistening that writhed in the channels like maggots crawling over a corpse. Pearly white here, dun-hued there, like rice glistening under a clear sauce but expanding outward, as if flexing and stretching after a long confinement.

The new torch flared, and in the newly leaping light Nuressa saw enough to be certain. "Lossum—*get out of there!*" she shouted. "All of you! Back—out of this place—*now!*"

She had distinctly seen pale flesh peel and wrinkle back to unhood a green-gray eye . . . and there was another, and a third. These were forests of eyestalks!

And the only creatures she knew of that had many eyes on stalks were beholders, the deadly eye tyrants of legend. The others knew the same tales and were sprinting through the settling dust toward her now, all thoughts of tomb plunder and laden sacks of treasure forgotten.

Behind the hurrying adventurers, as Nuressa watched, eyes winked and came to life and began to focus.

"*Hurry!*" she bellowed, drawing in enough dust to make her next words a croak. "Hurry . . . or die!"

A glow suddenly encircled one eye, then another—and burst into beams of golden light that stabbed out through the dust, parting it like smoke, to scorch the heels of hurrying Folossan and the wall beside Iyriklaunavan. Amandarn darted past Nuressa, stinking of fear, and the warrior woman pressed herself against the wall so as not to block the passage of her other two desperately hurrying companions. The elf then the dwarf clattered past, cursing in continuous babblings, but Nuressa kept her eyes on the pillars. Four columns of awake and alert eyes were peering her way now, radiances growing around many of them.

"Gods," she gasped, in utter terror. Oh let them be fixed here, unable to follow. . . .

A ruby beam of light from one eye stabbed at Nuressa and she ducked away, sparks erupting along the edge of her war sword. Sudden heat seared her palm. As a dozen golden beams lanced through the dust at her, she threw the blade over her head, back behind her out of the chamber. She wheeled in the same motion to flee headlong after it, diving for safety as something burst near her left ear with a sound like rolling thunder. Stones began to fall in a hard and heavy rain.

It feels odd, to stand on air, neither solid like stone, nor the slight yielding of turf under one's boots. In dry and dusty darkness . . . where by Mystra's sweet kisses was he?

Memory flowed around him like a river, cloaking him against madness for so long that it would not answer his bidding now. There was a tingling in his limbs. Great power had struck him, forcefully, only moments ago. A spell must have been hurled his way . . . so a foe must be near.

His eyes, so long dry and frozen in place, would not turn in their sockets, so he had to turn his head. His neck proved to be stiff and set in its pose, so he turned his shoulders, wheeling his whole body, as the walls drifted slowly past, and dust fell away from him in wisps and ropes and huge clods.

The walls drifting . . . he was sinking, settling down through the air, released from . . . what?

Something had trapped him here, despite his clever walking on air to avoid traps and guardian spells. Something had seized on the magic holding him aloft and gripped it as if in manacles, holding him immobile in the darkness.

A very long time must have passed.

Yet something had shattered the spell trap, awakening him. He wasn't alone, and he was descending whether he wanted to or not, heading toward . . . what?

He strained to see and found eyes looking back at him from all sides. Malevolent eyes, set in columns of pale eyestalks that danced and swayed with slow grace as they followed his fall, radiances growing around them.

Some strange sort of beholder? No, some of the stalks were darker, or stouter, or larger all around than others . . . these were beholder eyestalks, all right, but they'd come from many different beholders. Those radiances, of course, could only mean him harm.

He still felt oddly . . . detached. Not real, not *here*, but still afloat in the rush of memories that named him . . . Elminster, the Chosen One—or at least *a* Chosen—of Mystra, the dark-eyed lady of all magic. Ah, the warmth and sheer *power* of the silver fire that flowed through her and out of her, pouring from her mouth, locked onto his, to snarl and sear and burn its agonizing, exhilarating way through every inch of him, leaking out nose and ears and his very fingertips.

Light flared and flashed, and Elminster felt new agony. His dry throat struggled to roar, his hands clawed uncontrollably at the air, and his guts seemed afire and yet light and free.

He looked down and found silver fire raging and sputtering around him, spilling restlessly out of his stomach along with something pale, bloody, and ropy that must be his own innards. Fresh fire flashed, and a searing pain and sizzle marked the loss of his hair and the tip of an ear along the right side of his head.

Anger seized him, and without thinking Elminster lashed out, raking the air with silver fire that shattered and scattered a score of reaching magical beams on its way to claw at struggling eyestalks.

Eyes melted away, winking and weeping and thrashing with futile radiances sparking and flickering around them. El wasted no time watching their destruction, but turned to point at another pillar and sear its column of eyestalks from top to bottom.

He knew not what magics preserved all these severed eyestalks, but Mystra's flames could rend all Art, and flesh both alive and undead. Elminster turned to scorch another column of angry eyes. He was still sinking, his guts sagging out in front of him, and with each bolt of silver fire something beyond the pillars glowed in answer. Eyeborn beams of deadly magic were stabbing at him in earnest now, failing before the divine fire of Mystra. The angry crackle and the surflike rising and falling roar of much unleashed magic was howling about the chamber like a full-throated winter storm, shaking the wizard's long-unused limbs.

A last column of eyes darkened and died, to droop and dangle floorward, weeping dark sludge that mirrored Elminster's own tile-drenching flow of vital fluids. He clawed at his own innards, tucking them back inside himself with hands that blazed with silver flames, and was still about it, feeling sick and weak despite the roused, surging divine power, when his boot heels found something solid at last. He stumbled, all balance gone, staggered, and almost fell before he got his feet planted firmly. Dust swirled up anew around him, crackling angrily as it met surging silver fire. Beyond the pillars, runes graven on the steps and casket of what must be a tomb flashed and crackled with flames of their own, mirroring every roar of Mystra's fire.

Gasping as agony caught at him, El bent his efforts to healing the great wound in his middle, ignoring the last few flickering eyes. The flowing silver fire would, he hoped, catch and rend their spells before he was harmed. His blood had fallen in a dark rain on the tiles during his descent, and he felt emptied and torn. The last mage of Athalantar snarled in wordless anger and determination.

He had to get himself whole and out of this place before the stored silver fire faded and failed him, retreating to coil warmly around his heart and rebuild itself. Whatever had entrapped him before could well do so again if he tarried, and his present agony had been caused by only one eyestalk attack. He turned slowly, bent over with silver flames licking between trembling fingers, and held his guts in place as he moved haltingly toward the place where dim daylight was coming from.

Eyestalks flashed forth fresh beams of ravening magic to scorch floor tiles inches behind Elminster's shuffling boots. Sealing the last of his great wound, he slashed behind him with a sheet of silver flame, shielding himself from more attacks.

Behind him, unseen, the surviving eyestalks all went limp and dark in the same instant. In the next breath, the runes on the tomb acquired a steady, strengthening glow. Small radiances winked amid the metallic curtain above it, climbing and descending like curious but excited spiders, flaring forth ever stronger.

Elminster found his way out into the waiting light, half expecting arrows or blades to bite at him while he was still blinking at the dazzling brightness of full daylight. Instead, he found only four frightened faces staring at him over a distant remnant of wall.

He tried to call to them, but all that emerged was a dry, strangled snarl. El coughed, gargled, and tried again, managing a sort of sob.

The elf behind the wall lifted a hand as if to cast a spell, but the dwarf and the human male flanking him struck that hand aside. A furious argument and struggle followed.

El fixed his eyes on the fourth adventurer—a woman watching him warily over the crazed and crumbling edge of a great sword that had been struck by lightning or something of the sort not very long ago—and managed to ask, "What . . . year . . . is this?"

"Year of the Missing Blade, in early Mirtul," she called back, then, seeing his weary lack of comprehension, added, "In Dalereckoning, 'tis seven hundred and fifty-nine."

El nodded and waved his thanks, on his stumbling way to lean against a nearby pillar and shake his head.

He'd been exploring this tomb—a century ago?—seeking to learn how the mightiest archwizards of Netheril had faced death. Some insidious magical trap had ensnared him so cleverly that he'd never even noticed his fall into stasis. For years, it seemed, he'd hung frozen near the ceiling. Elminster the Mighty, Chosen of Mystra, Armathor of Myth Drannor, and Prince of Athalantar stood in midair, a handy anchor for spiderwebs, acquiring a thick cloak of dust and cobwebs.

Careless idiot. Would that ever change, the hawk-nosed mage wondered briefly, if he lived to be a thousand years old or more?

Perhaps not. Ah, well, at least he *knew* he was an idiot. Most wizards never even make it that far. El drew in a deep breath, dodged behind the pillar as he saw the elf glaring at him and raising his hands again, and sorted through his memories. These were the spells—and *that* one would serve. He had a world to see anew, and decades of lost history to catch up on.

"Mystra, forgive me," he said aloud, calling up the spell.

There came no answer, but the spell worked as it was supposed to, plucking him up into a brief maelstrom of blue mists and silver bubbles that would whisk him elsewhere.

Abruptly, the figure behind the pillar was gone.

"I could have had him!" Iyriklaunavan cursed. "Just a few moments longer, and—"

"You could've had us killed in a spell duel, right here," Amandarn hissed. "Shouldn't we be getting away from here? That man was freed from how we found him, those eyes sprouted from the pillars . . . what *else* is waking up, in there?"

Folossan rolled his eyes and said, "Am I hearing rightly? A thief, walking away from treasure?"

The wealth redistributor eyed him coldly. "Try saying it thus," he replied. " 'Hurrying away from likely death, in the interests of staying alive.'"

The dwarf looked up at the silent warrior woman beside him.

"Nessa?"

· She let out a deep, regretful sigh, then said briskly, "We run, away, as swift as we can on these loose stones. Come—*now*." She turned, a hulking figure in blackened armor, and began to shoulder her way around pillars and stub-ends of fallen walls.

"We're barely twenty paces from the strongest magic I've seen in decades," the elf mage protested, waving a hand at the darkness.

Nuressa turned, hands on hips, and said tartly, "Hear my prediction: it's not only the strongest magic you've seen—it's the strongest you'll *ever* see, Iyrik, if you tarry here much longer. Let's get gone before dark . . . and while we still can."

She turned away once more. Folossan and Amandarn cast regretful glances at the hall they'd fled from, but they followed.

The elf in maroon robes cursed, took one longing step around the end of the wall as if to return to the tomb, then turned to follow his companions. A few paces later he stopped and looked back.

He sighed and went on his way, never seeing what came out of the tomb to follow him.

The second torch died down. In the near total darkness that followed, the runes on the steps of the tomb blazed like so many altar candles. From somewhere there came a rhythmic thudding, as if from an unseen, distant drum. The lights winking and playing in the curtain above the dark stone casket began to race about, washing down over the stone tomb as showers of sparks that sank into the runes they touched and caused little flames to flare up briefly from the stone. A mist or wispy smoke came with them, and a faint echo that might have been an exultant chant mingled briefly with the thudding.

The runes flared into blazing brilliance, faded, flashed almost blinding-bright—then abruptly went out, leaving all in darkness and silence.

The embers of the torch gave just enough light, had anyone been in the tomb, to see the massive lid of the casket hovering just above its sides. Through the gap between them, something emerged from the tomb and swirled around the room.

It was more a wind than a body, more a shadow than a presence. Like a chill, chiming whirlwind it gathered itself and drifted purposefully toward where the sunlight beckoned. Living things that had been in the tomb not long ago still walked . . . for a little while yet.

PART
I

THE LADY
OF SHADOWS

ONE
A FIRE AT MIDNIGHT

Azuth remains a mysterious figure—sometimes benevolent, sometimes ruthless, sometimes eager to reveal all, sometimes deliberately cryptic. In other words, a typical mage.

ANTARN THE SAGE
FROM *THE HIGH HISTORY OF FAERÛNIAN ARCHMAGES MIGHTY*
PUBLISHED CIRCA THE YEAR OF THE STAFF

Tempus preserve us!"

"Save the prayers, fool, and *run!* Tempus'll honor your *bones* if you don't hurry!"

Pots clanged together wildly as Larando cast them aside, rucksack and all, and sprinted away through the knee-deep ferns. A low branch took his helm off, and he didn't even pause to try to grab at it.

Panting, the priest of Tempus followed, sweat dripping from his stubbled chin. Ardelnar Trethtran was exhausted, his lungs and thighs aching from all the running—but he dared not collapse yet. The tumbled towers of Myth Drannor were still all around them . . . and so were the lurking fiends.

Deep, harsh laughter rolled out of the trees to Ardelnar's left—followed by a charging trio of barbazu, their beards dripping blood. They were naked, their scaled hides glistening with the gore of victims as well as the usual slime. Broad shoulders rippled, and batlike ears and long, lashing tails bobbed exultantly as they came bounding along like playful orcs, black eyes snapping with glee. They flung away the bloody limbs of some unfortunate adventurer they'd torn apart and swarmed after Larando, shouting exultant jests and boasts in a language Ardelnar was glad he couldn't understand. They waved their heavy, saw-toothed blades like toys as they hooted and snorted and hacked, and it took them only a few moments to draw blood. Larando screamed as one frantically flailing arm went flying away from him, severed cleanly by a shrewd strike.

The competing bearded fiend wasn't so deft; the warrior's other arm was left dangling from his shoulder, attached to his body by a few strips of bloody flesh. When Larando moaned and collapsed, two of the fiends used their saw-toothed blades to lift him in an improvised cradle, and run along with him so the third barbazu could have some sport involving the warrior's innards and carving openings to allow them to briefly see the wider world.

Larando's head was lolling despite the brutal slaps being dealt him, as Ardelnar fled in a different direction. The priest's last glimpse of his friend was of a beautiful winged woman—no, a fiend, an erinyes—swooping down out of the trees with a sickle in her hands.

Giant gray-feathered wings beat above a slender body that was shapely and pale wherever cruel barbed armor didn't cover it. Scowling black brows arched with glee, a pert mouth parted as the she-fiend's tongue licked her lips in anticipation, and she sliced, twisted, and flew on, waving a bloody trophy. Behind her, gore spattered all over the barbazu as they howled their disappointment, a headless corpse thrashing and convulsing in their midst.

"Tempus forgive my fear, I pray," Ardelnar managed to stammer through white and trembling lips, as he fought down nausea and ran on. It had been a mistake to come here, a mistake that looked very much like it was going to cost all of them their lives.

The City of Song was no open treasure pit, but the hunting ground of fiends. These malevolent creatures would hide, letting adventurers venture freely into their midst to wander the very ruins of the riven city. Then they'd trap the intruders and take cruel sport in slaying them as a sort of hunt-and-run game.

Tales of such cruelty were told in taverns where adventurers gather. That was why three famous and very independent companies of adventurers had uneasily joined in a pact and gone into Myth Drannor together. Surely seven mages, two of them archwizards of note, could handle a few bat-winged . . .

Most of those mages had been torn apart already or left to stumble around with eyes and tongues plucked out, for the fiends to tease at leisure later. When the rest of us are dead, Ardelnar thought grimly as he tripped over a fallen statuette, hopped a few awkward steps to keep his footing, and found himself stumbling through the shattered, overgrown remnants of a garden fountain.

Oh, they'd found treasure. His belt pouch was bulging right now with a generous double handful of gems—sapphires and a few rubies—torn from the chest of a mummified elf corpse as its preservative magics faded with a few last glows and sighs. There'd even been a lone erinyes in that crypt; they'd slain her—it—with confidence. With her wings hacked off in a shower of bloody feathers, she'd not lasted long against the blades of a dozen adventurers, for all her hissing and spitting. Ardelnar could still see the spurt of blood from a mouth beautiful enough to kiss, and her blood smoking as it ran along her dusky limbs.

Not long after that, the jaws of the trap had closed, with gloating fiends strolling out of every ruin, glade, and thicket on all sides. The adventurers had broken and fled in all directions to the tune of cold, cruel laughter . . . and the slaughter had begun.

Back in the here and now, he was seeing the erinyes again. Four of them swooping past, gliding low. Ardelnar ducked involuntarily, but found himself ignored as they banked off to his right, giggling like temple-maids—nude, beautiful, and deadly. They'd have passed for dusky-skinned women of the Tashalar without those great gray-feathered wings. They were after the mage he'd been hoping would get them both out of this fiend-haunted ruin. Klargathan Srior was a tall, spade—bearded southerner who seemed the most capable of all the mages, as well as the most arrogant.

All that hauteur was gone now, as the mage ran wearily along on Ardelnar's right, hairy legs stained with blood where he'd gashed himself while slicing off his own robes so he could flee faster. Gold earrings bobbed amid rivers of sweat, and a steady stream of mumbled curses marked the mage's flight for his life. The erinyes glided in, veering apart to come at Klargathan from different directions, razor-sharp daggers in their hands. Sport was in their laughter and their cruel eyes, not outright murder.

Gasping, the mage stopped and took his stand. "Priest!" he bellowed, as a baton from his belt grew of its own accord into a staff. "Aid me, for the love of Tempus!"

Ardelnar almost ran on, leaving the man's death to buy himself a few more breaths of flight, but he stood no chance in this deep and endless wood without Klargathan's spells, and they both knew it. They also both knew that this cold realization carried more weight than the command to serve in the name of the Foehammer. The shame of that was like a cold worm crawling in Ardelnar's heart. Not that there was time to brood or fashion denials.

He swallowed in mid-stride, then almost fell as he wheeled around without slowing and ran to the mage, stumbling over bones half-glimpsed amid the forest plants, old bones—human bones. He had a momentary glimpse of a skull rolling away from his foot, jawless and unable to grin.

Klargathan was whirling his staff over his head with desperate energy, trying to smash aside the gliding erinyes without having one of them slash open his face or pluck the weapon from his hands. They were circling him like sharks, reaching out with their blades to cut at his clothing. One shoulder was already bared—and wet with blood from the dagger cut that had left it so.

Through the desperate chaos of thudding staff and flapping wings, the mage's eyes caught those of the priest. "I need . . ." the southerner gasped, "some time!"

Ardelnar nodded to show he understood and plucked off his own helm to smash at one wing of an erinyes. She flapped aside and he brought his warhammer up from his belt into her beautiful face, hard. Blood sprayed and the fiend squalled. Then she was past them, flying blindly into a tumble along the ground and into a waiting tree, while her three companions descended on Ardelnar in a shrieking, clawing cloud. He jammed the helm over the face of one and ducked under her gliding body so close that her breasts grazed his shoulder, using her as cover against the blades of the others. They struck at both her and the priest, not caring who they cut open, and as Ardelnar ducked away and rolled to his feet to avoid being caught between those last two screaming, spitting she-fiends, he heard Klargathan stammering out an incantation, ignoring the gurgling erinyes who plowed into the ground beside him, her side slashed open and black, smoking blood fountaining forth.

The last two she-fiends soared up into the air to gain height enough to dive back down on this unexpectedly tough pair of humans, and Ardelnar snatched a quick glance back at the overgrown, ruined towers of Myth Drannor. More fiends were coming. Barbazu and barb-covered hamatula, far too many to outfight or outrun, loped along with tails lashing and blood-hunger in their faces. This fern-covered ground would be his grave.

"Tempus, let this last battle be to your glory!" he cried aloud, holding up his bloodied hammer. "Make me worthy of your service, swift in my striking, alert in my fighting, agile and deft!"

One of the erinyes tapped his hammer aside with her dagger, and leaned in to snicker as she swooped past his ear, "My, my—anything else?"

Her voice was low, and lush, full of lusty promise. Its mockery enraged Ardelnar more than anything else ever had in all his life. He bounded after her, almost leaving himself open to easy slaughter at the hands of the other erinyes, but instead she became the first victim of Klargathan's spell.

Black, slimy coils of what looked like a giant serpent or eel erupted from the ferns not far away, spiraling upward with incredible speed. Now they seemed more like taproots, or the boughs of a tree sprouting from nothing to full vigor in mere seconds.

One bough encircled the throat of the erinyes as she turned leisurely to slice at Ardelnar, and another looped about her ankle. The force of her frantic wing beats swung her around to where the black tree was already entwined around both of the previously grounded erinyes. Their bodies were visibly shriveling, sucked dry of blood and innards with the same unnerving speed as everything else this spell-tree did.

Still trying to fly, the snared she-fiend crashed into a tangle of thickening trunks. Her head was driven off, dangling to one side, and thereafter she moved no more.

"By the Lord of Battles, what a spell!" Ardelnar gasped, watching tendrils swarm over the body of the erinyes with that same lightning speed. More were waving in the air above them, encircling the fourth she-fiend. Despite her frightened, wildly slashing struggles, the tendrils caught at her wings, pulled, and slowly dragged her down. The priest of Tempus laughed and waved his hammer at the mage in salute.

Klargathan gave him a lopsided grin. "It won't be enough," he said sadly, "and I haven't another like that. We're going to die for the sake of a few gems and elven gewgaws."

The running fiends were almost upon them now. Ardelnar turned to flee, but the southerner shook his head. "I'm not running," he said. "At least my tree keeps them from taking us from the rear."

A sudden hope lit his features and he added, "Have you any sapphires?"

Ardelnar tore open his pouch and emptied it into the mage's hand. "There must be a dozen there," he said eagerly, no longer caring a whit when Klargathan raked through them and dumped everything that wasn't a sapphire onto the ground.

The southerner swept one arm around the priest and hugged him fiercely. "We're still going to die here," he said, bestowing a firm kiss on the startled priest's lips, "but at least we'll turn a few fiends to smoking bones around us."

He grinned at Ardelnar's expression, and added, "The kiss is for my wife; tell Tempus to deliver it to her for me, if you've time left for another prayer. Hold them off again, please."

He crouched down without another word, and Ardelnar hefted his warhammer in one hand and unhooked his small belt-mace to hold ready in the other, taking a stance in front of the mage as ever-thickening black tendrils curled around and over them like a cupping hand.

The tree shivered under the blows of many barbazu blades even as it grew, and gargoyle-like spinagons, folding their wings and barbed tails flat, scuttled in along the tunnel-like opening in its branches to face the priest, who found fresh happiness—no, *satisfaction*—welling through him. He was going to die here, but die well. Let it befall so.

"Thank you, Tempus," he said, blowing Klargathan's kiss to the air for the god of war to take on. "Let this my last worship please thee."

His warhammer swept up and crashed down. Spinagon claws raked his arm, and he smashed them aside with his mace, being driven back by the sheer force of five charging fiends. "Hurry, mage!" he snarled, struggling to keep from being buried under clawing limbs.

"I have," Klargathan replied calmly, nudging Ardelnar with one knee as he hurled a sapphire down the tunnel of tendrils, and the world exploded in lightning.

From one gem to another held in the mage's cupped hand the lightning bolts blazed, crackling and rebounding in arcs that raced back and forth rather than striking once. Though every hair on both their bodies stood on end, neither the mage nor the priest took harm from the spell.

The biting, clawing fiend wrapped around Ardelnar was protected from the lightning, too, but Klargathan stepped forward and thrust a silver-bladed dagger hilt-deep into one of its eyes, then pulled it out and drove it into the other. It collapsed, slithering down Ardelnar's legs as the two adventurers watched fiends—even one of the tall barb-covered, point-headed hamatulas, its bristling shoulders shedding tendrils with every spasm—dance in the thrall of the lightning. Flesh darkened and eyes sizzled as the bolts flashed back and forth.

Then, as abruptly as it had erupted, the spell ended, leaving Klargathan shaking his hand and blowing on his smoking palm. "Good, large gems," he said with a tight grin, "and we've more to use yet."

"Do we run?" Ardelnar asked, eyeing a pair of erinyes who glared down at him as they swept past overhead, "or bide here?"

The next group of winged she-fiends was struggling under the weight of a broken-off elven statue larger than any of them. They let it go with deft precision. Good Myth Drannan stone crashed through tangled tree limbs, its fall numbing both men despite their dives for safety. They scrambled up to find the falling statuary had left an opening to the sky that spinagons were already circling, aloft, massing to dive into.

The southerner shrugged. "It's death either way," he said. "Moving gives both sides more fun, but tarrying here wins us more time, and we can shed more of their blood before we go down. Not quite the way I'd planned to dance in the ruins of Myth Drannor, but it'll have to do."

Ardelnar's answering laughter was a little wild. "Let's move," he suggested. "I don't want to wind up half crushed under a stone block, with them tormenting my extremities while I die slowly."

Klargathan grinned and clapped the priest on the shoulder. "So be it!" he said and shoved, hard. As the startled Ardelnar crashed headfirst into black tendrils that at least didn't claw at him, half a dozen spinagons slammed down into the space where he'd been standing, their cruel forks stabbing deep into the suddenly vacated ground, too deep to tear free in haste.

"Run!" the mage shouted, pointing up the tunnel. Ardelnar obeyed, steadying himself with his mace against the trampled ground as he stumbled over a forest root, then rushing headlong away from the conjured tree. Behind him raced the mage, a sapphire clenched in his hand and his head cocked to look back as he ran.

When the outstretched claws of the hard-flying, foremost pursuing spinagon were almost touching him, Klargathan held up the gem and said one soft word. Lightning erupted from it right down the fiend's throat. Its struggling gray gargoyle body burst apart in the roar of bolts lashing into it from both in front and behind—for the mage had left another gem on the ground by the fallen statue, where the fiends had swooped down. As the dark, blood-wet tatters fell away behind the rushing men, Ardelnar saw the rest of the spinagons tumbling and shuddering in the grip of those snarling bolts. He followed the mage around a huge duskwood tree, onto a game trail that led more or less in the direction they wanted to go: away from the ruins, in any direction, downright swiftly.

Ardelnar saw the mage toss down another gem as they sprinted on, dodging around standing trees and leaping over fallen ones, out among the barbazu now, in the deep and endless forest now reclaiming the riven city of Myth Drannor.

In the distance they saw another fleeing adventurer cut down. Then a barbed tail swept down out of dark branches overhead to send Klargathan sprawling, and the two men were too busy for any more sightseeing.

The first lash of the cornugon's whip snapped the warhammer from Ardelnar's numbed fingers, and the second laid his shoulder open to the bone, clear through the pauldron and mail shirt that should have protected it. The priest tumbled helplessly away, thrashing in his agony. This was a good thing. It took him well clear of the first howling bolt of lightning.

The bolt crashed into the huge, scale-covered cornugon and toppled it, roaring, right into the pit-of-spikes trap on the trail that it had been guarding. Impaled, it roared more desperately, its cry high and sharp, until a bleeding Klargathan leaped in on top of it, and drove his silver-bladed dagger into another pair of fiend eyes. Those sightless orbs wept streams of smoke as the mage scrambled back out of the thrashing tangle of shuddering bat-wings, long claws, and flailing tail in the pit, and shook the moaning Ardelnar to his feet.

"We'd better run beside the trail, not on it," Klargathan gasped. "I don't suppose you brought any healing-quaffs along? You need one about now."

"My thanks for confirming what a mess I must be," the priest grunted, reeling. "I'm afraid I wasn't the one carrying the potions, but if you'll guard me for a few breaths . . ."

The mage's baton became a staff again, and he stood guard, watching his last fading lightning bolts snap back and forth along the now empty trail as Ardelnar healed himself.

As they stumbled on, the priest felt weak and sick. Ahead, a steep hill rose, forcing them to run around it or try to climb its tree-girt slopes and somehow stay ahead of fiends who could fly. It was no surprise when Klargathan headed around the hill, panting raggedly now. Ardelnar followed, wondering just how long they'd be able to outrun half the vacationing occupants of the Lower Planes.

They came out into a clearing caused by the crashing fall of a shadowtop tree, and Ardelnar had his answer. Unfortunately, it was a very final one.

Klargathan went down under the claws of half a dozen pouncing cornugons. He hurled a handful of gems into the air with his last breath and died in the wild hail of lightning bolts that followed, sending his slayers tumbling away in all directions. The priest saw that, and managed one last, exultant shout. As fiend-talons burst through his chest and his own hot blood welled up to choke him, Ardelnar was briefly glad he'd healed himself before this final fray. It seemed somehow . . . tidy.

His last prayer to Mystra had been answered by a silence as deafening as all the previous ones. A year passed since he'd awakened in a tomb full of malevolent eyes with no words from the goddess Elminster so loved. He'd wept, on his knees, before wearily wrapping his cloak around himself and seeking despondent, lonely slumber out under a sky of rushing, tattered clouds, on a deserted hill out in the rolling wilderlands. He was dozing when the sign had come to him. Unbidden, a scene had swum into his drowsy mind, of him standing on a hilltop he knew . . . and did not know.

It was Halidae's Height, a forest-covered hilltop south and a little west of Myth Drannor that he'd stood on a time or two before, usually with a laughing elf lass on his arm and a warm, star-filled night stretching out before them. In the scene that had come to him there were no elf maidens. Moreover, something had toppled more than one tree on the Height and lit fires here and there, marring it from what he remembered.

He knew he'd journey thence without delay, come morning. He had to know what Mystra desired him to do—and this at least was *something*. For the thousandth time El lamented Mystra's silence and wondered what he'd done to earn it. Surely not getting caught in a trap for a few generations because he'd followed her dictates to seek out ever more magic, in old places and hidden ones.

Yet he retained his powers, some even more vigorous than before—so there must be a Mystra, with her own powers intact and the governance of magic still in her hands. Why was she silent, keeping her face hidden from him?

And just who was he to question what she might do, or not do?

A man, challenging the gods as other men did—and with about as much success. El fell asleep thinking of stars moving about in the heavens as part of a gigantic chess game played among the gods. The last thing he remembered was seeing the sudden, tremulous trail of a shooting star—probably a real one, not a dream's whim—dying, off to the east.

Halidae's Height was as scarred as the vision had shown him. He teleported in to stand beside a duskwood tree that didn't seem to have changed one whit between his memory and the vision. A gentle breeze was blowing, and he was alone on the hilltop. Elminster had barely glanced over its ravaged slope and started to swing his gaze toward Myth Drannor, knowing, by now, the sadness he'd see, when the breeze brought cries to his ears. Shouts of battle.

He sprang to the edge of the Height, where in happier days one could look out and down over the city. Tiny figures were leaping and dying in the thinned-out forest below. Humans and—fiends, monsters from the Lower Planes—were running about, the humans fleeing. Winged she-fiends were swooping here and there. Lightning bolts suddenly stabbed out in all directions from one knot of creatures, in a deadly star of death that sent fiends staggering and screaming. Other devils were slaying humans down there, disemboweling one last adventurer as he watched. Just in case any of the fleeing men escaped, a door in the air—a magical gate—had opened at the foot of the Height, and a steady stream of fiends was pouring forth from it.

El stared at the gate grimly, and raised his hands. "Gates," he told the air softly, "I can handle." He worked a magic that Mystra herself had given him and sent it splashing down on the maw that was still releasing hordes of fiends.

It washed over the gate with a menacing crackle of spell energy, and there were screams and roars from the fiends emerging from it. Yet when the raging fires of the spell fell away, long moments later, the gate stood unchanged.

Elminster gaped at it. How could—?

A moment later, he had an answer . . . of sorts. The last flickering, floating motes of light caused by his spell brightened, rose up to face him, and shaped themselves into letters in one of the elder elvish tongues he'd learned to read in Myth Drannor; it was a language only he and several hundred elf elders could read. Floating in the air, the letters spelled out a blunt message: "Leave alone."

As El stared at them in utter bewilderment, they fell into shapeless tatters of light then faded away, trailing down into wisps of smoke to join the chaos and death below. Fiends looked up, snarling. This could only be from Mystra . . . couldn't it?

Well, if not her, who else?

The last prince of Athalantar looked down at the fiends capering in the ruins of Myth Drannor and asked the world bitterly, "What good is it to be a mage, if ye don't use thy power to do good, by shaping the world around ye?"

The answer came from the air behind Elminster: "What good can it be, save by blind mischance, if you try but lack eyes and wits powerful enough to see the shape you're sculpting?"

The voice was low and calm but filled with a musical hum of raw power that he'd only ever heard before when Mystra spoke. It sounded male and somehow both familiar and wholly new and strange.

Elminster spun around. He stood alone; the Height was empty but for a few trees and the wind stirring them.

He stared hard at the empty air, but it stayed empty.

"Who are ye, who answer me? Reveal thyself," he demanded. "Philosophy comes hard when the lectures are delivered by phantoms."

The empty air chuckled. Suddenly it held two glimmering points of light, miniature stars that circled each other lazily, then whirled around with racing speed and burst into a blinding cascade of starry motes of light.

When the flood of brightness fell away, Elminster beheld a robed man standing behind it. He was white-bearded and black-browed, and his calm eyes shone very blue before they filled with all the colors of the rushing rainbow. As Elminster watched, the man's eyes darkened to black shot through with tiny, slowly moving stars.

"Impressive," Elminster granted amiably. "And ye are . . . ?"

The chuckle came again. "I meant it not as a show, nor yet as a herald's cry of my identity . . . but since we seem to be speaking suchwise, why don't you have a guess?"

El looked the man up and down. Old, ancient even, and yet spry, perhaps as young as some fifty-odd winters. White-haired, save for the brows, forearms, and chest, where the hair was black. He was empty-handed, with no rings in evidence, wearing simple, spare robes with flared sleeves and no belt or purse; bare feet below—feet that could afford to be bare, because they hovered a few inches off the ground, never quite touching.

Elminster looked up from them to the wise face of their owner, and said softly, "Azuth."

"The same," the man replied, and though he did not smile, El thought he seemed somehow pleased.

Elminster took a step forward, and said, "Forgive my boldness, High One, if ye will . . . but I serve Mystra in a manner both close and personal—"

"You are the dearest of her Chosen, yes," Azuth said with a smile. "She speaks often of you and of the joy you've brought her in the times she's spent playing at being mortal."

The prince of Athalantar felt joy and a vast relief. In his sigh of contentment and relaxation he almost stepped backward off the Height. At that moment a barbed whip arced around at his face, from the air off to his left, and something unseen took him around the shoulders as he swayed on the edge of oblivion then snatched him forward, away from the cornugon an instant before its reaching talons could thrust into Elminster's eyes. He found himself skimming across the scorched stones of the hilltop, Azuth receding before him so they always faced each other from the same distance.

"M-my thanks," El stammered, as they came to a gentle halt. He felt himself lowered into a comfortable, lounging position, lying on yielding but somehow solid air. Azuth was also sitting on nothing, facing him, across a fire that suddenly sprang out of nowhere. Flames danced up from air a handspan above the unmarked rock of the Height. El looked at it, then around at a sky now full of bat-winged, scaled, hissing fiends, clawing at the air with widening, many-toothed smiles as they dived nearer.

"I don't wish to seem ungrateful or critical, High One," he said, "but yon fiends can't fail but notice this light, and we'll have them visiting."

Azuth smiled, and for an instant his arms seemed to flow with slowly marching lights, winking and sparkling. "No," he replied in the calm, musical voice that was at once splendid and laced with excitement—and at the same time soothing and reassuring. "This Height, henceforth, is shielded against fiends—of all kinds—so long as my power endures. Now hearken, for there are things you should know."

Elminster nodded, bright-eyed in his eagerness. His manner brought the ghost of a smile to the lips of the Lord of Spells, who caused both of their hands to be suddenly full of goblets of wine that smoked and glowed. The god began to speak.

Over Azuth's left shoulder, a hulking red monster of a fiend flapped huge wings in a booming clap of fury, clawed at air that seemed to resist it, and burst into flames. With fire raging up and down its limbs, it gibbered, fangs spraying green spittle, and a flash of unleashed magic burst from its taloned hands and crawled across an unseen barrier for long moments before rebounding with a flash and roar that plucked the pit fiend from its clawing perch on empty air, sending it tumbling away through the air like a tattered leaf.

The god ignored this, as well as the wails and moans of watching, circling fiends that followed, as he addressed Elminster like a gentle teacher, speaking at ease in a quiet place. "All who work magic serve Mystra whether they will or no," he said. "She is of the Weave, and every use of it strengthens her, reveres her, and exalts her. You and I both know a little of what is left of her mortal side. We've seen traces of the feelings and memories and thoughts she clings to in desperation from time to time, when the wild exultation of power coursing through the Weave—that is the Weave—threatens to overwhelm her sentience entirely. No entity, mortal or divine, can last in her position forever. There will be other Mystras, in time to come."

A hand that trailed tiny stars pointed to Elminster, then back at Azuth's own chest. "We are her treasures, lad—we are what she holds most dear, the rocks she can cling to in the storms of wild Art. She needs us to be strong, far stronger than most mortals . . . tempered tools for her use. Being bound to us by love and linked to us to preserve her very humanity, she finds it hard to be harsh to us—to do the tempering that must be done. She began the tempering of you long ago; you are her 'pet project,' if you will, just as the Magisters are mine. She creates her Chosen and her Magisters, but she gives the training of them to others, chiefly me, once she grows to love them too much or needs them to be distant from her. The Magisters must needs be distant, that creativity in Art be untrammeled. You, she has grown to love too much."

Elminster blushed and ran a finger around the rim of his goblet. Fiends clawed the air in the distance as he looked down—and was abashed as he might not have been at another time—to find the vessel full of wine again after he had drunk deep.

Azuth watched him with a smile and said gently, "You are now wanting to hear much more of how the Lady of Mysteries feels for you, and not daring to ask. Moreover, you are also dying to know more about what 'Magisters' are and can find tongue to say nothing for fear of deflecting me from whatever wonders I was going to reveal if left to speak freely. Wherefore you are riven and will remember but poorly what follows . . . unless I set you at ease."

Elminster found himself wanting to laugh, perhaps cry, and grope for words all at once. He managed a nod almost desperately, and Azuth chuckled once more. Behind him, the air roiled with sudden raging green fire that came out of nowhere, and from its heart boiled two pit fiends, reaching out mighty-thewed and sharp-clawed limbs to clutch at the Lord of Spells . . . limbs that caught fire for all of the time it took Elminster to gasp in alarm before they met with some invisible force that melted them away, boiling off flesh and gore like black smoke. The screams were incredible, but Azuth's gentle, kindly voice cut through them like lantern light stabbing into darkness.

"Mystra loves you as no other," the god told the mage, "but she loves many, including myself and others neither of us know about, some in ways that would astonish or even disgust you. Be content with knowing that among all who share her love, you are the bright spirit and youth she cherishes, and I am the old wise teacher. None of us is better than the other, and she needs us all. Let jealousy of other Chosen—of other mages of any race, station, or outlook— never taint your soul."

Elminster's goblet was full again. He nodded his understanding to the god through its wisps of smoke, as a score of winged she-fiends stabbed at the god with lances that blazed with red flame—and the air, with a silent lack of fuss, ate both weapons and fire.

One of the dusky-skinned fiend-women strayed a little too close to Azuth in her boldness and lost a wing to hungry empty air in a single blurred instant. Shrieking and sobbing, she tumbled away, falling to death below—a death that came rather more swiftly than the waiting ground, as other erinyes, eyes blazing with bloodlust, swooped on her and drove their lances home. Transfixed, the stricken erinyes stiffened, spurted blood in several directions, and fell like a stone.

Ignoring all of this, the god spoke serenely on. "Magisters are wizards who achieve a measure of special recognition—powers, of course, as we spell hurlers measure things—in the eyes of Mystra, by being 'the best' of her mortal worshipers in terms of magical might. Most achieve the title by defeating the incumbent Magister and lose it by the same means—a process often fatal."

As cornugons and pit fiends raged around the Height, watching their spells claw vainly at the god's unseen barrier, Azuth sipped from his own goblet and continued, "Our Lady and I are working to change the nature of the Magister right now—though not overmuch—to make the Magisters less killers-of-rivals and more creators of new spells and ways of employing magic. Only one wizard is the Magister at a time. By serving themselves, they serve to proliferate and develop magic . . . and there is no greater way to serve Mystra. The purpose of her clergy is more to order and instruct, so that novices of the Art don't destroy themselves and Toril many times over before they've mastered basic understandings of magic . . . but were this task not governing them, the priests of Mystra would bend their talents more to what we now leave to the Magister."

Azuth leaned forward, the fire brighter now, and said through the flames, "You serve Mystra differently. She watches you and learns the human side of magic in all its hues from your experiences and the doings of those you meet—foes and friends alike. Yet the time has come for you to change, and grow, to serve as she'll need you to, in the centuries ahead."

"Centuries?" Elminster murmured and discovered suddenly that he needed the contents of his goblet rather urgently. "Watches me?"

Azuth smiled. "Indiscretions with alluring ladies and all. Set all thoughts of that aside—she needs the entertainment 'you just being you' affords her more than she needs someone playacting to impress her. Now attend my words, Elminster Aumar. You are to learn and grow by using as little magic as possible in the year ahead. Use what is needful and no more."

Elminster sputtered over his goblet, opened his mouth to protest—and met Azuth's kindly, knowing, almost mocking gaze. He drew in a deep breath, smiled, and sat back without saying anything.

Azuth smiled at that, and added, "Moreover, you are not to have any deliberate contact with your own pet project, the Harpers, until Mystra advises you otherwise. They must learn to work and think for themselves, not forever looking over their shoulders for praise and guidance from Elminster."

It was Elminster's turn to smile ruefully. "Hard lessons in independent achievements and self-reliance for us all, eh?" he ventured.

"Precisely," the Lord of Spells agreed. "As for me, I shall be learning to guide and minister to the mages of all Toril without Mystra to call upon, for a time."

"She's—'going away'?" El's tone made it clear that he didn't believe a goddess truly could withdraw from contact with her world, her worshipers, and her work.

Azuth's smile deepened. "An inevitable task confronts her," he said, "that she dare not put off longer; contingencies that must be determined and ordered, for the good and stability of the Weave. Neither of us may hear from her or see any manifestation of her presence or powers for some time to come."

"'Dare not'? Does Mystra serve the commands of something higher, or do ye speak of what the Weave requires?"

"The Weave by its very nature places constant demands on those attuned to it and who truly care for it . . . and the nature of all life and stability on this world it dominates. It is a delight and a craft—and something of a game—to anticipate the needs of the Weave, to address those needs, and to make the Weave something greater than it was when you found it."

"I don't believe ye quite revealed the nature of the Lady's 'inevitable task,' or whom—if anything—she answers to and obeys," Elminster said with a smile of his own.

Azuth's own smile broadened. "No, I don't believe I did," he replied softly, merriment dancing in his eyes as he raised his goblet to his lips.

Elminster found himself sinking gently and being brought upright, to stand on the stony ground once more with a landing as soft as a feather landing on velvet. Once, long ago, in Hastarl, the young thief Elminster had spent several minutes watching a scrap of pigeon-down floating down onto a cushion, ever so *slowly* . . . and he still judged those minutes well spent.

Azuth was standing, too, bare feet treading an inch or so of air. It seemed their converse was at an end. Though he hadn't even looked at the raging fiends, they were suddenly tumbling away in all directions, wreathed in white flames, their bodies dwindling in struggling silence as they went. The siege of the Height, it seemed, was at an end.

The High One didn't seem to step forward, but he was suddenly nearer to Elminster. "We may not respond, but call upon us. Look to see us not, but have faith. We do see you."

He reached out a hand; wonderingly, Elminster extended his own.

The god's hand felt like a man's . . . warm and solid, gripping firmly.

A moment later, Elminster roared—or tried to; the breath had been shocked right out of his lungs. Silver fire was surging through him, laced with a peculiarly vivid deep blue streak that must be Azuth's own essence or signature. El saw it clearly as jets of flame burst forth from his own nose, mouth, and ears.

It was surging through him, burning everything it found, wrenching him in spasms of utter agony as organs were consumed, blood blazed away, and skin popped as the flesh beneath boiled away . . . through swimming eyes, Elminster saw Azuth become an upright spindle of flame—a spindle that seemed somehow to watch him closely as it swooped nearer and murmured (despite its lack of any mouth El could see), "The fire cleanses and heals. Awaken stronger, most precious of men."

The spindle whirled nearer, touching the nimbus of magical fire around Elminster, fed by the silver jets still erupting from him—and the world suddenly leaped aloft with a silver-throated roar, whirling Elminster up into ecstasy and ragged ruin, torn apart into dark droplets spewed into a looping river of gold . . . gold too bright to look upon, outshining the sun.

The last Prince of Athalantar lay sprawled on the stones, senseless, with silver fires raging around him and two goblets floating nearby, a cruising spindle of flame between them. The flames touched the goblet Elminster had held, and it jumped a little and vanished into the conflagration, spewing forth fat golden sparks some moments later.

Then the spindle of flame touched the flames raging around Elminster. They rushed into it, and the reinforced, towering Azuth-flames collapsed with a roar that shook all Halidae's Height, washing over Elminster—who convulsed, but did not awaken—then gathered themselves. With sinuous grace and suddenly leisurely speed, the flames rose into a column and flowed up over the edge of Azuth's floating goblet into the steaming wine there. Length after length of roaring flame followed behind, vanishing into the liquid.

In the end, all that was left was that goblet, wisps of wine rising off its brimful contents like smoke whipped by a breeze.

It was the first thing Elminster saw—and drank—the next morning.

The goblet vanished into the air during his last swallow, leaving nothing behind. Elminster smiled at where it had been, got up, and left the Height with a lighter heart and a body that felt new and young again. He stopped at the first still pool of water he came across to peer down to look at his reflection and be sure that it was his. It was, hawk nose and all. He grimaced at his reflection, and it made the face it was supposed to make back at him. Thank Mystra.

TWO
DOOM RIDES A DAPPLE GRAY

And in the days when Mystra revealed herself not, and magic was left to grow as this mage or that saw best or could accomplish, the Chosen called Elminster was left alone in the world—that the world might teach him humility, and more things besides.

ANTARN THE SAGE
FROM *The High History of Faerûnian Archmages Mighty*
PUBLISHED CIRCA THE YEAR OF THE STAFF

When chill ruled mornings, mists lay heavy among the trees. Few folk of the Starn ever ventured this far into Howling Ghost Wood, so the pickings were plentiful—and Immeira had never seen any howling ghosts. Her sack was already half-full of nuts, berries, and alphran leaves. Soon the moontouch blooms would sprout in handfuls among the trees, followed by fiddleheads and butter cones . . . and to think some folk—even some Starneir—claimed that only a hunter who could bring down a stag a tenday could live off the woods.

Immeira rubbed an itch on her cheek thoughtfully, and looked back to where the trees thinned. Over the fields beyond them, down in the vale where Gar's Road crossed the Larrauden, stood Buckralam's Starn.

"Forty cottages full of nosy old women who weave cloaks all day while their sheep wander untended," the bard Talost had once described it. Longtime Starneir were still angry over those words and could be counted on to provide a few new and even more colorfully twisted misfortunes the gods could—and should—visit on the over-critical bard, forthwith. As far as Immeira could tell, Talost had got it about right, but she had already learned, and learned well, that truth wasn't necessarily highly prized around the Starn.

Her father had disappeared while adventuring. He was part of a proper chartered adventuring band who called themselves Taver's Talons after the brawling, always guffawing old warrior Taver who led them with the sun shining back off his bald pate. In Immeira's memory Taver still sat his saddle, bright and bluff, but folk said he was bones and dust these eight years gone. None could tell his bones from those of the next six—her father among them—who'd fallen to the dragon's jaws that day.

The Starn had talked of Taver's Talons for eight winters now, and some of them swore the Talons were fiends in human form, hiding here to better corrupt the women of passing caravans and spread their dark seed over all Faerûn. Others were just as insistent that the Talons had been bandits all along, just lurking hereabouts until they could learn all about Starneir and the forest trails so as to found a bandit realm back in the real woods, not so far off. Some called this kingdom Talontar—to others it was Darkride—but no one knew just where its borders started or who dwelt there or why they'd never come down on the Starn with ready bows and hungry knives in the years since the Talons had fallen or stolen away or committed whatever great crime kept them now in hiding.

Yes, truth was something a wagging tongue or two could change overnight in the Starn. The only exception to that, so far as Immeira could see, was the truth that lurked in the sharp and ready blades of the Iron Fox and his men.

They'd come out of the east on Gar's Road some six springs ago. A handful of hardened mercenaries with cold steel in their hands and a world-weary, merciless set to their colder eyes. The leader was a tall, fat man whose helm peaked with an iron fox head; even his men called him only "the Iron Fox." He rode into the courtyard of the little Shrine of the Sheaf, ordered the feeble old priest Rarendon out into the spring snows at sword point, and taken the place as his home.

Henceforth, he told the silent villagers at the Trough and Plough that evening, services to Chauntea would be held out in the open fields, as was proper. Former keeps were better suited to the purpose they'd been built for: housing men of action such as he and his men, who henceforth would dwell in the Starn and defend it, to the betterment of all.

A little after highsun the next day, a crudely lettered scroll of laws was tacked upon the door of the Trough. It was distressingly short, proclaiming the Iron Fox the sole judge, lawmaker, and authority in Fox's Starn. That very night, a few who'd dared disagree with specific laws, or disapprove of the entire affair, were left sprawled in their blood on the road or on their own steps—or simply disappeared. A few of the best—looking young Starneir ladies were taken from their homes to Fox Tower and installed in scanty gowns there, a cart of stonemasons arrived a tenday later to rebuild it into a fortress, and talk about the hidden evil of the Starn's only heroes, Taver's Talons, began.

Kindly, confused old Rarendon was taken into the old stables behind the mill, where the dwarven millwright allowed orphans of the Starn—including Immeira—to live. In the month that followed, several able-bodied farmers whose lands lay close about Fox Tower died right after planting was done, when their farmhouses mysteriously caught fire by night, their doors were propped shut from outside, and their windows overlooked by hitherto undetected brigands equipped with crossbows of the same sort used by the Fox's men. Two gossipy old Starneir women and blind old Adreim the Carver were flogged in the Market for minor transgressions against the laws. The folk of the Starn started to get used to ever-present patrols of hard-eyed swordsmen, the seizure of not quite half of all the harvests they brought in, and living in fear.

They made their silent, feeble protests. "Fox's Starn" remained Buckralam's Starn in the mouths of one and all, and the Fox's men seemed to ride about in a perpetually silent, nearly deserted valley. Wherever they went, children and goodwives melted away into the woods, leaving toys discarded and pots unwatched, whilst the farmers of the Starn were always in the farthest, muddiest back hollows of their fields, too hard at work to even look up when a plate-armored shadow fell across them.

Like many girls of the Starn on the budding verge of womanhood, Immeira became another sort of shadow—one that lurked in drab old men's clothes and kept to the woods by day, sleeping in barn lofts and on low roofs by night. They'd seen into the eyes of their gowned older sisters, seen their scars and manacles too, and had no desire to join a dance of warmth, good food and ready drink that cost them their freedom and handed them brutality, servility, and pain. Immeira had a figure to equal many of the Fox's "playpretties" now and took care to wear bulky old leather vests and shapeless tunics, keep her hair wild and unkempt—and keep herself hidden in forest gloom or night dark. Even more than the sullen boys of the valley, the she-shadows of the Starn dreamed of the Talons riding up the road someday soon, with bright, bared swords at the ready, to carve the Iron Fox into flight.

Once or twice a tenday Immeira stole through the pheasant-haunted eastern ridges of Howling Ghost Wood to where the Gar's Road topped Hurtle Tor and descended into the Realm of the Iron Fox. The Fox's cruel warriors kept a patrol there to keep watch over who came to the Starn and to exact a toll from peddlers and wagon trains too weary or undermanned to refuse to pay.

Sometimes Immeira kept them occupied by making animal crashings in the underbrush and stealing any crossbow quarrels they were foolish enough to loose into the trees, but more often she simply hunkered down in silence and watched the antics on the road. Word must be getting around the lands beyond the valley. Fewer and fewer peddlers were taking Gar's Road. The Starn hadn't seen anything that could be called a caravan since the season after the coming of the Iron Fox.

This morning there had been a rime of ice along the banks of the Larrauden and frost had touched white sparkles onto many a fallen leaf. Immeira had to keep rubbing her bare fingertips to keep warm, knowing her lips must be blue, but the damp of the slow-warming day kept her footsteps in the forest near-silent, so she was thankful. Once she'd startled a hare into full crashing flight through the trees, but for the most part she moved through the mists like a drifting shadow, dipping gentle fingers to pluck up what food she needed. A little hollow she'd used before afforded her a dirt couch from which to watch the Foxling road patrol with ease. Propped up against a mossy bank with the comforting weight of the tree limb she kept ready there, in case she ever needed a club, ready in her hands, she'd even begun to doze when it happened.

There was a sudden stir among the six black-armored men, a jingling of mail that marked swords sliding out and their owners hurrying back into the roadside trees, to crouch ready while fellow Foxlings swung into their saddles to block the road.

Someone was coming—someone they expected to have either trouble or a bit of fun with. Immeira rubbed her eyes and sat up with quickening interest.

A moment later, a lone man on a dapple gray horse topped the rise, a long sword swaying at his hip as his mount walked unhurriedly down into the valley. He was young and somehow both gentle and hard of face, with a hawklike nose, and black hair pulled back into a shoulder tail. He saw the waiting men, swords and all, but neither hesitated nor checked his mount. Unconcernedly it plodded onward with its rider empty-handed and almost jaunty, humming a tune Immeira did not know.

"Halt!" one of the Foxlings barked. "You stand upon the very threshold of the Realm of the Iron Fox!"

"Wherefore I must—what?" the newcomer inquired with a raised eyebrow, reaching to take up a rolled cloak from his saddle. "Abandon hope? Yield up some toll? Join the local nunnery?"

"Show a lot less smart-jaws first!" the Foxling snarled. "Oh, you'll pay a toll, too—*after* you're done begging our forgiveness . . . and mewling over the loss of your sword hand."

The newcomer raised his brows and brought his mount to a halt. "A rather steep price to cross a threshold," he said. "Don't we get to fight each other first?"

Immeira rubbed her eyes again, in wonder. There was a general roar of rage from the Foxlings, and they surged forward, those afoot springing from the trees. The newcomer backed his horse, and a small knife flashed in his hand. He threw the cloak he'd taken from his saddle into the faces of the oncoming riders, turned the dapple gray, and rode down one of the men on foot, the horse kicking viciously. Its rider kicked at another Foxling to keep him clear, snatched something from his saddle, slashed at it, and threw it at the man. A spurt of sand marked where it burst in the Foxling's face.

Then the newcomer was behind the line of Foxlings. One horse had bolted, throwing its rider. The other two were tangled amid the reason for its flight: the length of barbed chain that had been inside the cloak.

The newcomer leaned back with a matching length of chain in his hand to lash one of the mounted Foxlings across the throat. The man toppled from his saddle without a sound, and the Foxling next to him suddenly sprouted the newcomer's little knife in his eye.

Suddenly riderless, one mount reared and the other jostled it, trampling two fallen Foxlings under its hooves. Another knife flashed into the throat of the Foxling who'd taken the sand in his face. As he fell, another bag of sand wobbled harmlessly past the shoulder of one of the two Foxlings who were left.

Used to bullying frightened men, their faces were white and their steps uncertain. As they advanced slowly on the hawk-nosed man, he plucked another knife from a saddle side sheath and gave them a welcoming smile.

At that, one of the Foxlings moaned in terror and fled. The other listened to booted feet crashing away into the trees, looked into the blue-gray eyes of the man who'd so swiftly and easily slain his fellows, then hurled his sword at that coldly smiling face, wheeled round, and ran.

A bag of sand took the Foxling on the side of the head after he'd managed only a few scrambling strides, and he fell heavily on the road. The dapple gray surged forward to dance on his fallen form, as its owner turned in his saddle, sighed, and leaped for the trees, abandoning Gar's Road to the dead and dying.

The hawk-nosed man ran lightly, another knife in his hand, on the trail of the Foxling who'd fled. It wouldn't be wise to let one foe go free to warn others of his arrival—not if a fifth of what he'd heard of these vicious warriors of the Fox was true.

It wasn't hard to mark where the fleeing man had gone; panting and crashing in plenty were going on among the dancing tree branches up ahead, as the dark-mailed man struggled up a ridge.

A moment later the running man slipped into some sort of hole or gully with a startled yell.

Immeira's scream matched it, as the Foxling warrior suddenly plunged down into her hiding place. She snatched up her tree limb as the sweating man crashed down atop her, struck the side of his helm so hard the wood broke, and somehow got out from under his trembling weight.

She needed only a moment to plant the battered toe of her boot on a projecting tree root and boost herself out, but desperately strong fingers grabbed her before she got that moment, and dragged her back down. She kicked out with her feet and flailed about with her elbows as the man beneath her grunted and snarled half-coherent curses. Then she swung around to claw at his face. Immeira got a momentary glimpse of one furious eye amid grizzled cheeks before a fist out of nowhere crashed into her temple, sending her reeling back against the forest dirt with sun glare and shadows swirling in her eyes.

Immeira was dimly aware of an armored bulk moving toward her. She kicked out and in the same motion rolled over to claw at roots and moss and try to get out of the pit again. One surge, another, and she was on her knees in the forest moss at the lip of the hollow, rising. She came to a quivering halt, with a grip as crushing and cruel as iron around her ankle, dragging her back.

Steel flashed past her head, and the grip was suddenly gone.

Immeira sprawled on her face in damp dead leaves, as a wet gurgling sound slid back down into the hollow behind her. A long sword dark with fresh blood was wiped on the moss to one side of her, and a surprisingly gentle voice said, "Good lady, will ye tarry here by yon duskwood? I have need of thy aid, but urgent battle yet to attend to."

"I—I—yes," Immeira managed to say, shuddering, and a moment later gentle but firm fingers were opening her moss-smeared right hand, laying the hilt of a dagger in her palm, and closing her fingers around it. Immeira stared down at it, a little dazed, as sudden silence descended on this corner of the forest again.

The hawk-nosed man was gone, trotting lightly back through the trees toward the road. Immeira stared after him, licked suddenly dry lips, and could not help but glance back into the hollow.

The Foxling was a huddled heap, his throat drenched crimson with blood, and she suddenly felt very sick.

Retching into the leaves and ferns, Immeira never saw the newcomer busily rolling over bodies, making sure of death and plucking forth weapons. She was waiting by the duskwood when he came back through the trees bearing a large bundle whose innards clashed steel upon steel from time to time as he moved. The stranger gave her a grin. "Well met," he said politely, sketching a courtly bow.

Immeira stared at him, then snorted with sudden, helpless mirth. She found herself trying to manage a low curtsy in return, despite her old breeches and flopping boots, and fell over in the moss. They hooted with laughter together, and a strong arm righted Immeira, leaving her staring into the eyes of the hawk-nosed warrior.

"I—" Immeira began hesitantly.

The newcomer gave her an easy grin, patted her arm reassuringly, and said, "Call me Wanlorn. I've come hunting foxes . . . Iron Foxes. What's thy name?"

"Immeira," she replied, looking down at the dagger he'd given her, then back up at him, scarcely able to believe that the salvation she'd watched for all these years had come to the Starn so quickly and so capably deadly.

"Is it safe to tarry here—not long—and talk?" he asked.

"It is," Immeira granted, then summoned up her wits and will enough to ask a question of her own.

"Are you alone?" she asked, studying the man's face. It was not so young as it had first appeared, and "Wanlorn" was an old folk name for "wanderer searching for something." How could one man—even one so skilled at arms as this one—defeat, or even escape alive, from all the men who raised blades for the Fox?

As if he'd read her mind, the hawk-nosed man took Immeira gently by her upper arms and said urgently, "I am indeed alone—wherefore I need thy help, lass. Not to fight Foxlings with tree limbs . . . or even daggers, but to tell me: do the folk of the Starn wish to be rid of the Iron Fox?"

"Yes," Immeira said, a little bewildered by how fast Faerûn had been turned upside down in front of her eyes. "By the *gods*, yes."

"And how many blades answer the Fox's call? Both ready-armed, like these, and others who may hurl spells or be able to fire a crossbow or hold loyal in some other wise . . . tell me, please."

Immeira found herself spilling out all she knew and could remember or guess about the Iron Fox and his forces. The newcomer's dancing eyes and ready grin never failed, even when she told him that those who wore the dark mail and the fox head badge numbered a dozen more than the six he'd slain, and that no man remained in the Starn with brawn or courage enough to back a lone newcomer against the Iron Fox. Nor could she trust anyone beyond herself to aid him, for fear of tales being carried back by those among the she—shadows who might well, after a hard winter, want to win warmth and fine clothes and good food enough to betray someone they scarcely knew.

His grin broadened when she told him that as far as she'd heard no sorcerer or even priest dwelt in Fox Tower or anywhere near the Starn and that the Fox commanded no magic himself.

Immeira told Wanlorn, or whatever his name truly was, where the guards were posted and how soon the six men would be missed. The half dozen Foxlings were lying in the trees with their helms tossed into the Larrauden and their mounts—plus one unfamiliar dapple gray horse—tethered nearby. She told him as much as she knew—of how the Iron Fox spent his evenings; where his four hunting dogs and the crossbows, lanterns, and horses at Fox Tower were kept; and of life in the Starn both these days and before the fall of the Talons—until she was quite weary of answering questions.

Wanlorn asked her if there were any haystacks in the Starn that could be approached unseen from these woods and that would escape being disturbed by farmers in the next day or two. She told him of three such, and he asked her to guide him to the best of them as stealthily as possible, to hide his bundle of seized weapons.

"What then?" she asked quietly.

" 'Twould be safest, Immeira," Wanlorn said directly, his eyes very steady on hers, "if ye then went to wherever ye're supposed to dwell—not out in the woods where angry armed men with hunting dogs may search—and never went near this hollow or the haystack again until the Fox is gone from the Starn, whatever befalls me."

"And if I refuse?" she almost whispered.

He smiled thinly and said, "I'm no tyrant. In the Faerûn I want to see, lads and lasses should be free to walk and speak as they please. Yet, if ye follow me or step forth to aid me, I cannot protect thee . . . for I am alone in this, with no god to work miracles when battle turns against me."

"Oh, no?" Immeira asked, lifting a hand that trembled rather less than she'd feared it would, to indicate where the Foxling patrol had barred the road. "Was that not a miracle?"

"No," Wanlorn replied, smiling. "Miracles mostly grow when deeds are told of, through years of retelling. If ye speak too freely, it may become a miracle yet"

Who *was* this man, and why had he come here?

Immeira met those calm blue-gray eyes for a moment—just now, they seemed rather more blue than her mind told her they were—and asked simply, "Who are you, really? And why . . . why do you want to face death here? What does the Starn matter to you? Or seek you revenge on the Iron Fox?"

Wanlorn shook his head slightly. "I first heard of him less than a tenday ago. I do as my heart leads me to do, wherefore I am here. I wander to learn and to make the Realms be more as I desire them to be. Unless the Starn proves to be my grave, I cannot stay here but must needs wander onward. I am a man, thrust onto this road by my birth and . . . choices I have made." He fell silent, and as her brows rose and she parted her lips to ask or say more he raised a hand as if to still her and added, "Take me as ye find me."

Immeira held his gaze in silence for a handful of very long moments, then replied, "So then I shall, crazy man—and feel honored to have met you. Come, the haystack awaits."

She turned her back on him—she trusted no other man to so turn her gaze from him, especially one who stood close and armed behind her—and led the way along trails only she and the beasts who'd made them knew. He followed, clanking slightly.

It would be *so* easy to clear the feast hall of Fox Tower with a fireball and strike down the few stray Foxling armsmen with lesser magics, but that was just the temptation Elminster was here to resist. It had been a long summer since he'd talked with a god on a hilltop, but the habit of calling on spells to answer every need or whim, without thinking, was slowly crumbling. Slowly.

The cruelty and butchery of these men of the fox head were so freely and so often practiced that he need not worry about slaying them out of hand. If he could.

One man, fighting fairly and in the open, would have little chance against such dark battle dogs as these.

Hmmm, yes, he thought, those dogs . . .

It was a little shy of highsun now, and the lass Immeira was still at his shoulder. She was a skulking shadow with no less than a dozen daggers strapped and laced all about her and his heavy chain in her hands. Surely the men he'd slain this morn would be found in a very short time, and warning horns would blow. At just about that time a trio of Foxlings would arrive from Fox Tower to relieve this guard post, here at the opposite end of the valley from where he'd met with such a warm and bloody morning reception.

"Relieve" . . . an apt choice of word, that. One of the bored Foxlings who'd been sitting in the roadside shade across the way was now up on his feet, unlacing his codpiece as he headed across the hot, dusty road to this side to answer a call of nature.

This time nature was going to have a little extra to say to him.

Elminster rose out of the shrubbery with unhurried grace and threw one of his knives the moment the man stopped and took up a stance. He cursed soundlessly and hauled out another blade, knowing he'd misjudged his throw. The Foxling lifted his head in sudden alarm as the first knife flashed past—and the second missed the eye it had been meant for, sinking hilt-deep in the man's cheek instead.

As a thick, wet scream arose, El snatched the chain out of Immeira's grasp and sprinted at the man, knowing he hadn't enough time to manage this but had no choice but to try it anyway.

The man was flailing his way blindly back toward the road that both of his fellow Foxlings were crossing now, heading in the direction of the sounds of his distress with drawn swords and wary frowns.

They slowed as they moved out of the bright sun into the dappled shade of the trees, not wanting to be struck down by a ready foe. The two stopped as their fellow Foxling staggered into view. El, running hard, came up right behind him, using his lurching body as a shield as he swung the chain out over it, hard, smashing a sword arm down, then rushing to close with its stunned owner and drive a knife at the man's face.

The man sprang away before El could strike, shaking his numbed arm and shattered fingers. The last prince of Athalantar saw the angry face of the other

Foxling glaring at him across the man he'd first wounded, so he threw his knife hard into it.

The man went down with a yell, more startled than hurt, and El brought the chain up to smash the man he'd disarmed across the face. Blood flew, a head lolled loosely, and the man went down—followed by Elminster, who had to hurl himself into the dirt to avoid the desperate swings of a broadsword wielded by the man he'd first injured at this guard post.

The man had torn El's dagger free and was spitting blood, half-blinded by the tears of pain streaming down his face, but he could see enough to know his danger and mark his foe.

El rolled, trying to get away from the sword that kept slashing at him. As he wallowed in the dust with his assailant staggering and hacking after him, he wondered when the third Foxling would reach him. He knew he'd have to use one of his spells then, Mystra or no Mystra, or die.

The man overbalanced after a particularly vicious swing and stumbled. El put his shoulder into the dirt and spun around, kicking out with both feet. That cursedly persistent sword clanged and bounced by his ear as its owner fell heavily, grunting as the wind was driven from him. El kept spinning, bringing his feet under him and running four paces away before he dared turn to look at his foes. Where was that third Foxling?

Lying still and silent on the road, it seemed, with a white-faced, panting Immeira rising from beside him, bloody dagger in hand. Her eyes met El's through the dust, and she tried to smile . . . not very successfully.

El gave her a wave, then pounced on the man who had chased him with the sword. He stabbed down thrice with his own dagger, and when he looked up again, El saw that both he and Immeira were dusty, sweating, panting, and alive. They traded true smiles this time.

"Lass, lass," El chided her, as they swung each other into an exultant embrace, "I *can't* protect ye!"

Immeira kissed his cheek, then pushed him away, making a face at him through her wild-tangled hair and the Foxling blood spattered across her face. "That's fair enough," she told him. "I can't protect *you*, either!"

El grinned at her and shook his head. He strode to the shade where the three Foxlings had been sitting and chuckled in satisfaction.

"What, Wanlorn?" Immeira asked. "What is it?"

Elminster held up a crossbow and said, "I'd hoped they'd have one of these. Light armor, no lances or horses . . . it stands to reason they'd have something to use against, say, three armsmen guarding a caravan. Here, lass—help me with the windlass. We mayn't have much time."

Immeira ducked past him to scoop up a sling bag bulging with crossbow quarrels. "We don't," she said shortly. "Their relief is riding out here. I just saw them top the last rise . . . the one by Thaermon's farm. They'll be on us in—"

"Then get my chain and take it back the other side of the road," El hissed, cranking the windlass for all he was worth. "Haste, now!"

The Starneir lass showed a little haste, moving with speed and grace despite the heavy, awkward weight of the bloody chain. El crossed the road in a half-crouch right behind her, the bow just about ready.

He had one hand in the sling bag for a quarrel, with Immeira coming to an awkward halt to let him get one out, when the first rider bobbed up over a crest in the road and saw the bodies. The man shouted and hauled on the reins, bringing his horse to a snorting, almost rearing halt. His two companions drew up beside him, and they gaped in unison at the sprawled Foxlings and the trees so close and so innocent on either side of them.

"Drop the chain and *run*," El murmured in Immeira's ear. "Drop this bag soon and go anywhere to avoid being caught. If we lose sight of each other, look for me in that grove west of the haystack. Go!"

Without waiting for her reply, Elminster stepped calmly into the road and shot the most capable-looking Foxling through the throat. Then he sprinted back to the trees, tossing down the bow, and snatched up the chain from where Immeira had let it fall. There was no sign of her but branches dancing in the dim forest distance.

He took two running strides into the woods, then crouched down to listen. He heard the expected curses, but also fear in the furious voices, and hooves pawing as horses were turned.

A moment later, the horn calls Immeira had told him to expect rang out over the valley, fast and strident. The other dead patrol had been discovered. The bugling went on for a long time, and El used the din to cover a quick sprint through the trees beside the road, heading back the way these two horsemen would have to come. Any hopes of felling another on the way past were dashed, however, when they burst past him at a gallop, eager to return to Fox Tower before any more crossbow quarrels came calling.

The riderless mount followed them, depriving El of any chance to rummage in its saddlebag. He stared after it, shrugged, and scurried to retrieve the quarrel from the dead Foxling's throat, then the man's weapons, the crossbow, and its bag of quarrels. Luckily this man's fall had swept his night cloak from its perch on his saddle; it served admirably to bundle everything up in. El's chain, hooked to itself, wrapped the bundle as if it had been made to do so.

The bundle was heavy, but Immeira was waiting for him several trees away to take the crossbow and gaze at him as if he was some great hero.

Elminster hoped she was wrong. In his experience, all the great heroes very soon became dead heroes.

The feast hall in Fox Tower had been in an uproar, but frightened and angry men cannot snap and snarl at each other endlessly without breaking into a brawl or falling into tense, waiting silence.

The silence now hung as heavy as a cloak under the flickering candle wheels. Their hanging chains cast long shadows down the stone walls as the Iron Fox—a great bulk of a man, more like a rotund bear than a fox—and his eight remaining warriors hunkered down over a roast that seemed suddenly tasteless, and drank wine as if they all wanted to drown in it. Servants hardly dared approach the table for fear of being run through, and many a sudden glance was shot up at the dark, empty minstrels' gallery. The ladies waited behind closed doors in the bedchambers beyond, dismissed from the board at the first news. They were all dreading the humor that might govern their men when those who wore the fox head at last came to bed.

Nine men brooded over the long table as the candles guttered lower. The possible identity and allegiance of the lone, briefly glimpsed crossbowman had been endlessly debated, the decision long since made to lock the tower gates, maintain vigilant watch, and sally forth in armed force in the morning. Doors were barred from within, locks checked, and keys retrieved onto this very table. Now all that was left was the waiting, the wondering who this unseen foe was, and the rising fear.

An elbow toppled a goblet, and half a dozen men sprang up shouting, blades half drawn, before the disgusted Iron Fox shouted them to a halt. Men glared around at each other, black murder in their eyes, then slowly sat down again.

Fearful heads drew back from the kitchen doors before someone might see them and go for a whip. The kitchen had grown cold and quiet, but the three serving maids dared not leave.

The last time a lass had dared slip away early she'd been hunted up and down the tower and whipped until long after her clothes had fallen away and the bloody skin beneath was in danger of following it. The Iron Fox had ordered that her bloody footprints not be scrubbed away from the passage floors, so as to serve as ever-present reminders of the reward awaiting laxity and disobedience.

The serving maids cowered sleepily on a bench just inside the kitchen door, more terrified than the men in the hall. The warriors feared the unknown and what might be lurking nearby in night-shrouded Starn, but the servants knew exactly what danger awaited them in the next room and knew they were locked in with it. There'd be a lot of slapping and screaming behind those bedchamber doors soon, if they were any judge, and—

With a sudden loud rattle of chain, one of the candle wheels plunged from its customary height toward the table below. Foxlings boiled up, shouting, their swords flashing into their hands. One of them sprinted across the room with a curse, followed by another. They were through an archway and gone before the Iron Fox's shouted commands could be heard.

The ruler of the Starn had a huge, rough slab of a face, decorated with stubble, a thick and bristling mustache, and eyes as cold and cruel as all bleak midwinter. The body below it, sweating in full armor even to gorget and gauntlets, was no smaller or more dainty. The curved metal plates held in the quivering breasts and belly that would otherwise have shaken and rippled like a pale and obscene sea of flesh as their host rose to his feet and leveled a long and ruthless finger at the rest of the Foxlings. "The next man to leave this room without my leave had best keep going, right off my land and into exile! D'you know how stupid it is to rush off like that, whe—"

He jerked his head around at the high, shrill scream that interrupted him from the passage whence the two men had gone. That hall led to pantries and the back rooms of the tower . . . including Beldrum's Room, a name left over from a long-dead Chauntean priest, where tables were stored and the chains that held the candle wheels were spiked. A room, it seemed, that was suddenly held by foes. The Iron Fox snatched up his helm from the table before him and jammed it down onto his head.

His men followed suit and clustered in close about him to hear his orders. "Durlim and Aawlynson—to the gallery. Shout down that it's clear when you get there. Gondeglus, Tarthane, and Rhen—stand here with me. One of you look under the table; then we'll turn our backs to it and keep watch. Llander, guard yon passage door. When the gallery is secure, all four of us will join you, and we five will scour Beldrum's Room."

The Iron Fox fell silent, and silence followed his orders. His men seemed to be waiting to hear more. Sudden rage almost choked him. Was he leading *sheep?*

"*Move,* you whoresons!" he thundered. "Get gone about it! Move move move, *move!*"

Silence held for a fleeting moment after the echo of his shout died away. Then everyone moved at once.

Gondeglus groaned and reeled backward, followed by Aawlynson, the hissing of the crossbow bolts that had slain them loud in the echoing room. Then it was Rhen's turn to sprout a quarrel in the face and fall. None of them had helms with snout-visors in the southern style. The Iron Fox was wise enough to raise his old and heavy broadsword up in front of his face before he scuttled sideways, turned, and peered up at the gallery.

He was in time to get a glimpse of a black-haired, hawk-nosed man bobbing up from behind the gallery rail with a loaded and ready crossbow in his hands. This time his target was Durlim, but the tall veteran ducked and slapped at the air with his gauntlet, and the quarrel rang off his rerebrace and shattered harmlessly against the far wall.

There were screams of fear from the kitchen, but the Fox didn't have time to see if they heralded an intruder there or just fear at what was happening out here. No matter; the gallery held a known foe, who must have run out of ready-loaded crossbows and be scuttling for cover by now.

"Llander! Tarthane! Up those stairs," the Iron Fox bellowed, brandishing his blade. "Now!"

His most loyal warriors were both noticeably hesitant to obey, but they mounted the stairs as instructed. The Fox took care to back himself in under the edge of the gallery as he watched them ascend, under the guise of ordering Durlim to get down the passage to the bottom of the back stairs to the gallery, in real haste.

He lumbered after Durlim as far as the archway that led into the passage, and crouched there, peering up at the gallery.

Llander and Tarthane were up there, moving cautiously forward.

"Well?" he bellowed. "What news?"

It was then that the tapestry fell on Llander. Tarthane stumbled back to avoid his friend's wild sword thrusts, then lunged, striking past the chaos of heavy cloth with his black war blade, hoping to stab whoever was beyond it and swarming all over the shrouded Llander.

That someone was already flat on the floor, tugging at the runner-rug under all their feet. Tarthane, already off-balance, flailed about, made a grab for the railing to keep upright missed his hold, and toppled over with a crash. The hawk-nosed man bounced up from behind the rolled tapestry and drove a dagger into Tarthane's face.

Llander's sword burst blindly out of the tapestry to stab at the man, who jabbed his dagger through the fabric in response, then vaulted over the railing to land lightly in the feast hall, give the Iron Fox a cheery wave, and race away toward the front of the tower.

Enraged, the Iron Fox gave roaring chase, then stopped two strides short of leaving the hall and put up his blade. No . . . he'd be running alone into a part of the keep he'd sent his men away from, an area offering all too many places where a man with a knife could get above an armored foe and leap down. No, it was time to see if Llander was still alive and go find Durlim, and the three of them could find some defensible room to hold against leaping madmen with knives.

He lumbered back across the feast hall, slashing backhanded behind him twice on the way, and mounted the stairs where Tarthane lay crumpled and the tapestry was rippling slowly and wearily.

"Llander?" he called, hoping not to get a sword thrust in the face. "Llander?"

He heard a small sound behind him and lashed out viciously with his blade, hacking so hard that the steel rang off the stone wall with numbing force, shedding a few tinkling shards of metal in its wake.

He was rewarded with a gasp. When he turned to see who it was, the Iron Fox found himself face to face not with a hawk-nosed man or a bleeding corpse but with a young lass he'd seen a time or two before about the Starn. She was three safe steps down the stair, beyond his sword tip, and looked very stern, a hand at her throat. As the Fox gazed at her, still startled to see this wench here in his locked and barred tower, she brought her hand slowly and deliberately down, and the front of her gown open with it.

His eyes followed her movement until the halberd smashing into his ankles from above sent him cannoning helplessly down the stairs. He screamed out a curse as he swung his blade around to hack away this latest attack. The Fox found himself once more nose to nose with the grinning, hawk-nosed man. A slim dagger driven by a slender but firm arm plunged into the Iron Fox's right eye, and Faerûn whirled away from him forever.

Breathing heavily, Immeira sprang away from the huge armored carcass and let it clang and slither a little way down the stair, gauntlets clutching vainly at empty air.

Then she looked quickly away and up at the man who was smiling down at her. "Wanlorn," she moaned, and found herself trembling—a moment before she burst into tears. "Wanlorn, we've done it!"

"Nay, lass," said the soothing voice that went with the arms that held her then. "We've but done the easiest part. Now the hard and true work begins. Ye've slain a few rats, is all . . . the house they infested must still be set in order."

He plucked the fouled and dripping dagger from her hands and tossed it away; she heard it ring against the floor tiles below.

"The Realm of the Iron Fox is broken, but Buckralam's Starn must be made to live again."

"How?" she moaned into his chest. "Guide me. You said you would not stay. . . ."

"I cannot, lass—not more than a season. 'Twould be better for thee if I left this night."

Her arms tightened around him like a vise.

"No!"

"Easy, lass," he said. "I'll stay long enough to see you take old Rarendon—and whichever of the orphans and farmers ye can trust as an escort on the road—to Saern Hill. I'll write ye a note to give to a man there, a horse breeder named Nantlin; ask him if his harp sounds as sweet as ever, and he'll know who the note is really from. He'll bring folk to dwell here and women and men of honor and ready blades to keep laws all Starneir approve of, to make the Starn strong again. There is a doom laid upon me though, lass . . . I must be gone before he or any of his folk come into the valley."

Immeira stared up at him, her face drenched with tears. She could see plain sorrow in his eyes and tight-set lips, reaching up two timid fingers to trace the set of his jaw.

"Will you tell me your true name, before you go?"

"Immeira," he said solemnly, "I will."

"Good," she said almost fiercely, reaching up her hands to his neck, "for I'll not give myself to a nameless man."

A smile that did not belong to Immeira swam through his dreams and sent Elminster into sudden, coldly sweating wakefulness. "Mystra," he breathed into the darkness, staring up at the cracked stone ceiling of the best bedchamber in Fox Tower. "Lady, have I pleased thee at last?"

Only silence followed—but in it, sudden fire appeared, racing across the ceiling, shaping letters that read: "Serve the one called Dasumia."

Then they were gone, and Elminster was blinking up at darkness. He felt very alone—until he heard the soft whisper against his throat.

"Elminster?" Immeira asked, sounding awed and frightened. "What was that? Do you serve the gods?"

Elminster reached up his hand to touch her face, feeling suddenly close to tears. "We all do, lass," he said huskily. "We all do, if we but know it."

THREE
A Feast in Felmorel

If human, dragon, orc, and elf can in peace sit down anywhere together in these Realms, it must be at a good feast. The trick is to keep them from feasting on each other.

SELBRYN THE SAGE
FROM *MUSINGS FROM A LONELY TOWER IN ATHKATLA*
PUBLISHED IN THE YEAR OF THE WORM

A nd just who," the shortest and loudest of the three gate guards asked with deceptive cheerfulness, "are you?"

The hawk-nosed, neat-bearded man he was staring coldly at—who was standing out in the pelting spring rain, on foot and muddy-booted, yet somehow dry above the tops of his high and well-worn boots—matched the guard's bright, false smile and replied, "A man whom the Lord Esbre will be very sorry to have missed at his table, if ye turn me away."

"A man who has magic and thinks himself clever enough to avoid answering a demand for his name," the guard captain said flatly, crossing his arms across his chest so that the fingers of one hand rested on the high-pommeled dagger sheathed at the right front of his belt, and the fingers of the other could stroke the mace couched in a sling-sheath on the left front. The other two guards also dropped their hands ever so casually to the waiting hilts of their weapons.

The man out in the rain smiled easily and added, "Wanlorn is my name, and Athalantar my country."

The captain snorted, "Never heard of it, and every third brigand calls himself Wanlorn."

"Good," the man said brightly, "that's settled, then."

He strode forward with such calm confidence that he was among the guards before two hard shoves—from gauntlets coming at him from quite different directions—brought him to an abrupt halt.

"Just where d'you think you're going?" the captain snarled, reaching out his hand to add his own shove to Wanlorn's welcome.

The bearded man smiled broadly, seized that hand, and shook it in a warrior's salute. "In to see Lord Esbre Felmorel," he said, "and share some private converse with him, good lad, whilst I partake of one of his superb feasts. Ye may announce me."

THE TEMPTATION OF ELMINSTER
549

"And then again," the captain hissed, leaning forward to glare at the stranger nose-to-nose, "I may not." Blazing green eyes stared into merry blue-gray ones for a long moment, then the captain added shortly, "Go away. Get gone from my gate, or I'll run you through. I don't let rude brigands—or clever-tongued beggars—"

The bearded man smiled and leaned forward to land a resounding kiss on the guard's menacing mouth.

"Ye're as striking as they said ye'd be," the stranger said almost fondly. "Old Glavyn's a fire-lord when he's angry, they said. Get him to spit and snarl and run ye away from his gate—oh, he's a proper little dragon!"

One of the other guards sniggered, and Guard Captain Glavyn abandoned blinking, startled, at the stranger to whirl around with a snarl and thrust his glare down the throat of a more familiar foe. "Do we find something *amusing*, Feiryn? Something that so overwhelms our manhood and training that we must abandon our superiors and fellows in the face of danger whilst we indulge ourselves in a wholly inappropriate and insultingly demeaning display of *mirth?*"

The guard blanched, and a satisfied Glavyn whirled back to fix the hawk-nosed stranger with a look that promised swift and waiting death hovering only inches away. "As for you, goodman . . . if you *ever* dare to—to *violate* my person again, my sword shall be swift and sure in my hand, and not all the gods in this world or the next shall be enough to save you!"

"Ah, Glavyn, Glavyn," the bearded stranger said admiringly, "what flow! What style! Splendid words, stirringly delivered. I'll tell Esbr—the Lord so, when I sit down to dine with him." He clapped the captain on one shoulder and slipped past him in the same movement.

The guard captain exploded into red rage and snatched out his weapons to . . . or, rather, tried to. Somehow, strain and struggle as he might, he couldn't make either mace or dagger budge, or uncross his arms to reach for the short sword slung across his back or his other dagger beside it. He couldn't move his arms at all. Glavyn drew in breath for what would have been a hoarse, incoherent scream, but for—

"My lords, what is all this tumult?" The low, musical voice of the Lady Nasmaerae cut through Glavyn's gathering wind and the rising alarm of his fellow guards like a sword blade sliding through silk. Four men moved in silence to place themselves where they could best—that is, without obstruction—stare at her.

Slender she was, in a gown of green whose tight, pointed sleeves almost hid her fingers but left supple shoulders bare. A stomacher of intricate worked silver caught the gleam of the dying day, even through the rain and mist, as she turned away slightly in the darkness and worked some small cantrip that made the candelabra in her hand burst into warm flame.

By its leaping light eyes that were dark pools grew even larger, and indigo in hue—indigo with flecks of gold. Lady Nasmaerae's mouth and manner seemed all chaste innocence, but those eyes promised old wisdom, dark sensuality, and a smoldering hunger.

A smile rose behind her eyes as she measured her effect on the men at the gate, and she added almost lightly, "Who are we, on a night such as this, to keep a lone traveler standing in the wet? Come in, sir, and be welcome. Castle Felmorel stands open to ye."

The hawk-nosed stranger bowed his head and smiled. "Lady," he said, "ye do me great honor by thy generosity to a stranger—outpouring, as it is, of a trusting and loving manner that thy gate-guards would do well to emulate. Wanlorn of Athalantar am I, and I accept thy hospitality, swearing unreservedly that I mean no harm to ye or to anyone who dwells within, nor to any design or chattel of Felmorel. Folk in the lands around spoke volubly of thy beauty, but I see their words were poor, tattered things compared to the stirring and sublime vision that is—ye."

Nasmaerae dimpled. Still wearing that amused smile, she turned her head and said, "Listen well, Glavyn. *This* is how the racing tongue encompasseth true flattery. Idle and empty it may be—but oh, so pretty."

The guard captain, red-faced and still trembling as he fought with his immobile arms while trying not to appear to be doing so, glowered past her shoulder and said nothing.

The Lady Nasmaerae turned her back on him in a smooth lilt that wasn't quite a flounce and offered her arm to Wanlorn. He took it with a bow and in the same motion he assumed the lofty bearing of the candelabra, their fingers brushing each other for a moment—or perhaps just a lingering instant longer.

As they swept away out of sight down a dark—paneled inner passage, the guards could have collectively sworn that the flames of that bobbing candelabra *winked*. That was when Glavyn found that he could suddenly move his arms again.

One might have expected him to draw forth the weapons he'd so striven to loose these past few breaths—but instead, the captain poured all his energy into a vigorous, snarling-swift, prolonged use of his tongue.

By the time he was finally forced to draw breath, the two guards under his command were regarding him with respect and amazement. Glavyn turned away quickly, so they wouldn't see him blush.

The arms of Felmorel featured at their heart a mantimera rampant, and although no one living had ever seen such an ungainly and dangerous beast (sporting, as it did, three bearded heads and three spike-bristling tails at opposing ends of its bat-winged body), the Lord of Felmorel was known, both affectionately and by those who spoke in fear, as "the Mantimera."

As jovial and as watchfully deadly in manner as his heraldic namesake was reputed to be, Esbre Felmorel greeted his unexpected guest with an easy affability, praising him for a timely arrival to provide light converse whilst his other two guests this night were still a-robing in their apartments. The Lord then offered the obviously weary Wanlorn the immediate hospitality of a suite of rooms for rest and refreshment, but the hawk-nosed man deferred his acceptance until after the feast was done, saying it would be poor repayment of warm generosity to deprive his host of a chance to share that very converse.

The Lady Nasmaerae assumed a couch that was obviously her customary seat with a liquid grace that both men paused to watch. She smiled and silently cupped a fluted elven glass of iced wine beside her cheek, content to listen as the customary opening courtesies were exchanged between the two men, down the long and well-laden, otherwise empty candlelit feasting table.

"Though 'twould be considered overbold in many a hall to ask so bluntly," the Mantimera rumbled, "I would know something out of sheer curiosity, and so will ask: what brings you hither, from a land so distant that I confess I've not heard of it, to seek out one castle in the rain?"

Wanlorn smiled. "Lord Esbre, I am as direct a man as thyself, given my druthers. I am happy to state plainly that I am traveling Faerûn in this Year of Laughter to learn more of it, under holy direction in this task, and am at present seeking news or word of someone I know only as 'Dasumia.' Have ye, perchance, a Dasumia in Felmorel, or perhaps a ready supply of Dasumias in the vicinity?"

The Mantimera frowned slightly in concentration, then said, "I fear not, so far as my knowledge carries me, and must needs cry nay to both your queries. Nasmaerae?"

The Lady Felmorel shook her head slightly. "I have never heard that name." She turned her gaze to meet Wanlorn's eyes directly and asked, "Is this a matter touching on the magic you so ably demonstrated at our gates—or something you'd rather keep private?"

"I know not what it touches on," their guest replied. "As we speak, 'Dasumia' is a mystery to me."

"Perhaps our other guests—one deeply versed in matters magical, and both of them widely traveled—can offer you words to light the dark corners of your mystery," Lord Esbre offered, sliding a decanter closer to Wanlorn. "I've found, down the years, that many useful points of lore lie like gems gleaming in forgotten cellars in the minds of those who sup at my board—gems they're as surprised to recall and bring to light once more as we are that they possess such specific and rare riches."

A fanfare sounded faintly down distant passages, and the Mantimera glanced at servants deftly dragging open a pair of tall, ebon-hued doors with heavy, gilded handles. "Here they both come now," he said, dipping a whellusk, half-shell and all, into a bowl of spiced softcheese. "Pray eat, good sir. We hold to no formality of serving nor waiting on others here. All I ask of my guests is good speech and attentive listening. Drink up!"

Side by side, and striding in careful step—for all the world as if neither wanted the other to enter the hall either first or last—two tall men came into the room then. One was as broad shouldered as a bull, and wore a high-prowed golden belt that reached almost to his bulging breast. Thin purple silk covered his mighty musculature above it and flowed down corded and hairy arms to where gilded bracers encircled forearms larger than the thighs of most men. Both belt and bracers displayed smooth-worked scenes of men wrestling with lions—as did the massive golden codpiece beneath the man's belt. "Ho, Mantimera," he boomed. "Have you more of that venison with the sauce that melts in my memory yet? I starve!"

"No doubt," Lord Felmorel chuckled. "That venison need not live only in memory longer; but lift the dome off yonder great platter, and 'tis thine. Wanlorn of Athalantar, be known to Barundryn Harbright, a warrior and explorer of renown."

Harbright shot a look at the hawk-nosed man without pausing in his determined striding to the indicated platter, and gave a sort of grunt, more noncommittal acknowledgment than welcome or greeting. Wanlorn nodded back, his eyes already turning to the other man, who stood over the table like a cold and dark pillar of fell sorcery. The hawk-nosed guest didn't need the Mantimera's introduction to know that this was a wizard almost as powerful as he was haughty. His eyes held cold sneering as they met Wanlorn's but seemed to acquire a flicker of respect—or was it fear?—as they turned to regard the Lady Nasmaerae.

"Lord Thessamel Arunder, called by some the Lord of Spells," the Mantimera announced. Was his tone just a trifle less enthusiastic than it had been for the warrior?

The archwizard gave Wanlorn a cold nod that was more dismissal than greeting and seated himself with a grand gesture that managed to ostentatiously display the many strangely shaped, glittering rings on his fingers to everyone in the vicinity. To underscore their moment, various of the rings winked in a random scattering of varicolored flashes and glows.

As he looked at the food before him, a brief memory came to Wanlorn of the jaws of wolves snapping in his face, in the deep snows outside the Starn in the hard winter just past. He almost smiled as he put that bloody remembrance from his mind—hunger, it had been simple hunger for those howling beasts; no better and no worse than what had hold of him now—and applied his own gaze to the peppered lizard soup and crusty three-serpent pie within reach. As he cut into the latter and sniffed appreciatively at the savory steam whirling up, Wanlorn knew Arunder had darted a glance his way, to see if this stranger-guest was sufficiently impressed with the show of power. He also knew that the mage must be sitting back now and taking up a glass of wine to hide a mage-sized state of irritation.

Yet he only had to look at himself in a seeing-glass to know that power and accomplishment of Art lures many wizards into childlike petulance, as they expect the world to dance to their whim and are most selfishly annoyed whenever it doesn't. He was Arunder's current source of annoyance; the wizard would lash out at him soon.

All too soon. "You say you hail from Athalantar, good sir—ah, *Wanlorn*. I'd have thought few of your age would proclaim themselves stock of that failed land," the wizard purred, as the warrior Harbright returned to the board bearing a silver platter as broad as his own chest, which fairly groaned under the weight of near a whole roast boar and several dozen spitted fowl, and enthroned himself with the creak of a settling chair and the clatter of shaking decanters. "Where have you dwelt more recently, and what brings you hence, cloaked in secrets and unheralded, to a house so full of riches, if I may ask? Should our hosts be locking away their gem coffers?"

"I've wandered these fair realms for some decades now," Wanlorn replied brightly, seeming not to notice Arunder's sarcasm or unveiled insinuations, "seeking knowledge. I'd hoped that Myth Drannor would teach me much—but it gave me only a lesson in the primal necessity of outrunning fiends. I've poked here and peered there but learned little more than a few secrets about Dasumia."

"Have you so? Seek you lore about magic, then—or is your quest for mere treasure?"

At that last word, the warrior Harbright glanced up from his noisy and nonstop biting and swallowing for a moment, fixing Wanlorn with one level eye to listen to whatever response might be coming.

"Lore is what I chase," Wanlorn said, and the warrior gave a disgusted grunt and resumed eating. "Lore about Dasumia—but instead I seem to find a fair bit about the Art. I suppose its power drives those who can write to set down details of it. As to treasure . . . one can't eat coins. I've enough of them for my needs; alone and afoot, how would I carry more?"

"Use a few of them to buy a horse," Harbright grunted, spraying an arc of table with small morsels of herbed boar. "Gods above—*walking* around the kingdoms! I'd grow old even before my feet wore off at the ankles!"

"Tell me," Lord Felmorel addressed Wanlorn, leaning forward, "how much did you see of the fabled City of Song? Most who even glimpse the ruins are torn apart before they can win clear."

"Or did you just wander about in the woods near where you *imagine* Myth Drannor to be?" Arunder asked silkily, plucking up a decanter to refill his glass.

"The fiends must have been busy hounding someone else," the hawk-nosed man told the Mantimera, "because I spent most of a day clambering through overgrown, largely empty buildings without seeing anything alive that was larger than a squirrel. Beautiful arched windows, curving balconies . . . it must have been very grand. Now there's not much lying about waiting to be carried off. I saw no wineglasses still on tables or books propped open where someone was interrupted in their reading, as the minstrels would have us all believe. No doubt the city was sacked after it fell. Yet I saw, and remember, some sigils and writings. Now if I could just determine what they *mean*. . . ."

"You saw *no* fiends?" Arunder was derisive—but also visibly eager to hear Wanlorn's reply. The hawk-nosed man smiled.

"No, sir mage, they guard the city yet. 'Twill probably be years, if ever, before folk can walk into the ruins without having to worry about anything more dangerous than a stirge, say, or an owlbear."

Lord Felmorel shook his head. "All that power," he murmured, "and yet they fell. All that beauty swept away, the people dead or scattered . . . once lost, it can never be restored again. Not the way it was."

Wanlorn nodded. "Even if the fiends were banished by nightfall," he said, "the place rebuilt in a tenday, and a citizenry of comparable wit and accomplishments assembled the day after, we'd not have the City of Beauty back again. That shared excitement, drive, and the freedom to experiment and freely reason and indulge in whimsy that's founded on the sure knowledge of one's own invulnerability won't be there. One would have a players' stage pretending to be the City of Song, not Myth Drannor once more."

The Mantimera nodded and said, "I've long heard the tales of the fall, and have even faced a fell fiend—not there—and lived to tell the tale. Even divided by their various selfish interests and rivalries, I can scarce believe that so grand and powerful a folk fell as completely and utterly as they did."

"Myth Drannor *had* to fall," Barundryn Harbright rumbled, spreading one massive hand as if holding an invisible skull out over the table for their inspection. "They got above themselves, you see, chasing godhood again . . . like those Netherese. The gods see to it that such dreams end bloodily, or there'd be more gods than we could all remember, and none of 'em with might enough to answer a single prayer. 'Sobvious; so why do all these mages keep making this same mistake?"

The wizard Arunder favored him with a slim, superior smile and said, "Possibly because they don't have you on hand to correct their every little straying from the One True Path."

The warrior's face lit up. "Oh, you've heard of it?" he asked. "The One True Path, aye."

The mage's jaw dropped open. He'd been joking, but by all the gods, this lummox seemed serious.

"There aren't many of us thus far," Harbright continued enthusiastically, waving a whole, gravy-dripping pheasant for emphasis, "but already we wield power in a dozen towns. We need a realm, next, and—"

"So do we all. I'd like several," Arunder said mockingly, swiftly recovered from his astonishment. "Get me one with lots of towering castles, will you?"

Harbright gave him a level look. "The problem with over clever mages," he growled to the table at large, "is their unfamiliarity with *work*—not to mention getting along with all sorts of folk and knowing how to saddle a horse or put a heel back on a boot or even how to kill and cook a chicken. They seldom know how to hold their drink down, or how to woo a wench, or grow turnips . . . but they *always* know how to tell other folk what to do, even about turnip-growing or wringing a chicken's neck!"

Large, hairy, blunt-fingered hands waved about alarmingly, and Arunder shrank away, covering his obvious fear by reaching for a distant decanter. Wanlorn obligingly moved it nearer to the mage but was ignored rather than thanked.

Their host cut into the uncomfortable moment by asking, "Yet, my lords, True Paths or the natures of wizards aside, what see you ahead for all who dwell in this heart of far-sprawling Faerûn? If Myth Drannor the Mighty can be swept away, what can we hold to in the years to come?"

"Lord Felmorel," the wizard Arunder replied hastily, "there has been much converse on this matter among mages and others, but little agreement. Each proposal attracts those who hate and fear it, as well as those who support it. Some have spoken of a council of wizards ruling a land—"

"Ha! A fine tyranny and mess *that'd* be!" Harbright snorted.

"—while others see a bright future in alliances with dragons, so that each human realm is a dragon's domain, with—"

"Everyone as the dragon's slaves and ultimately, its dinner," Harbright told his almost-empty platter.

"—agreements in place to bind both wyrm and people against hostilities practiced on each other."

"As the dragon swept down, its jaws gaping open to swallow, the knight stared into his doom, shouting vainly, 'Our agreement protects me! You can't—' for almost the space of three breaths before the dragon gulped him up and flew away," Harbright said sarcastically. "The surviving folk gathered there solemnly agreed that the dragon had broken the agreement, and the proposal was made that someone should travel to the dragon's lair to inform the wyrm that it had unlawfully devoured the knight. Strangely, no one volunteered."

Silence fell. The hulking warrior thrust his jaw forward and shot the wizard a dark and level gaze, as if daring him to speak, but Thessamel Arunder seemed to have acquired a sudden and abiding interest in peppered lizard soup.

Wanlorn looked up at his host, aware of the Lady Felmorel's continuing and attentive regard, and said, "For my part, Lord, I believe another such shining city will be a long time in coming. Small realms, defended against orcs and brigands more than aught else, will rise as they have always done, standing amid lawless and perilous wilderlands. The bards will keep the hope of Myth Drannor bright while the city is lost to us, now and in foreseeable time to come."

"And this wisdom, young Wanlorn, was written on the walls of the ruined City of Song?" Arunder asked lightly, emboldened to speak once more, but carefully not looking in Harbright's direction. "Or did the gods tell you this, perhaps, in a dream?"

"Sarcasm and derision seems to run away with the tongues of wizards all too often these days," Wanlorn observed in casual tones, addressing Barundryn Harbright. "Have you noticed this, too?"

The warrior grinned, more at the wizard than at the hawk-nosed man, and growled, "I have. A disease of the wits, I think." He waved a quail-lined spit like a scepter and added, "They're all so busy being clever that they never notice when it strikes them personally."

In unspoken unison both Harbright and Wanlorn turned their heads to look hard at the wizard. Arunder opened his mouth with a sneer to say something scathing, seemed to forget what it was, opened his mouth again to say something else, then instead put a glass of wine up to it and drank rather a large amount in a sputteringly short time.

As he choked, burbled, and wheezed, the warrior reached out one shovel-sized hand to slam him solidly between the shoulder-blades. As the mage reeled in his seat, Harbright inquired, "Recovered, are you—in your own small way?"

Into the dangerous silence that followed, as the wizard Arunder struggled for breath and the Lady Nasmaerae lifted a hand both swift and graceful to cover her mouth, Lord Esbre Felmorel said smoothly, "I fear you may have the right of it, good sir Wanlorn. Small holds and fortified towns standing alone are the way of things hereabouts, and things look to stay that way in the years ahead—unless something befalls the Lady of Shadows."

"The Lady—?"

"A fell sorceress," the warrior put in, raising grim eyes to meet those of the hawk-nosed man.

Lord Esbre nodded. "Bluntly put, but yes: the Lady of Shadows is someone we fear and either obey or avoid, whenever possible. None know where she dwells, but she seeks to enforce her will—if not to rule outright—in the lands immediately east of us. She's known to be . . . cruel."

Noticing that the wizard seemed to have recovered, Lord Esbre sought to restore the man's temper by deferring to him with some joviality. "You are our expert on things sorcerous, Lord Arunder—pray unfold for us whatever of import you know about the Lady of Shadows."

It was time for fresh astonishment at Lord Esbre's feast table. Lord Thessamel Arunder stared down at his plate and muttered, "There's no—I have nothing to add on this subject. No."

The tall candles on the feast table danced and flickered in the heart of utter silence for a long time after that.

A dozen candles flickered at the far end of the bedchamber like the tongues of hungry dragon hatchlings. The room was small and high-ceilinged, its walls shrouded in old but still grand tapestries that Elminster was sure hid more than a few secret ways and spy holes. He smiled thinly at the serenity awaiting him, as he strode past the curtained and canopied bed to the nearest flame.

"Wanlorn am I," he told it gently, "and am not. By this seeming, in your service, hear me I pray, O Mystra of the Mysteries, O Lady most precious, O Weaving Flame." He passed two fingers through the flame, and its orange glow became a deep, thrilling blue. Satisfied, he bent forward over it until it almost seemed as if he'd draw the blue flame into his mouth, and whispered, "Hear me, Mystra, I pray, and watch over me in my time of need. *Shammarastra ululumae paerovevim driios.*"

All of the candles suddenly dimmed, sank, guttered, then in unison rose again with renewed vigor, building like spears of the sun to a brighter, warmer radiance than had been in the room before.

As warm firelight danced on his cheek, Elminster's eyes rolled up in his head. He swayed, then fell heavily to his knees, slumping forward into a crawling posture that became a face first slide onto the floor. Lying senseless among the candles, he never saw the flame spit a circle of blue motes that swirled in a circle around him and faded to invisibility, leaving the candle flame its customary amber-white in their wake.

In a chamber that was not far away, yet hidden down dark ways of spell-guarded stone, flames of the same blue were coiling and writhing inches above a floor they didn't scorch, tracing a sigil both intricate and subtly changing as it slowly rotated above the glass-smooth stones. They licked and caressed the ankles of their creator, who danced barefoot in their midst as they rose and fell around her knees. Her white silk nightgown shimmered above the flames as she wove a spell that slowly brought their hue up into her eyes. It spilled out into the air before her face like strange tears as the Lady Nasmaerae whirled and chanted.

The room was bare and dark save for the spell she wove, but it brightened just a trifle when the flames rose into an upright oval that suddenly held the slack face of the hawk-nosed Wanlorn, sprawled on the stones of his bedchamber amid a dozen dancing candles.

The Lady of Felmorel beheld that image and sang something softly that brought the half-lidded eyes of the sleeping man closer, to almost fill the scene between the racing flames. "*Ooundreth*," she chanted then. "*Ooundreth mararae!*"

She spread her hands above the flames and waited for them to well up to lick her palms, bringing with them what she so craved: that dark rush of wit and raw thought she'd drunk so many times before, memories and knowledge stolen from a sleeping mind. What secrets did this Wanlorn hold?

"Give me," she moaned, for the flood was long in coming. "Give . . . me . . ."

Power such as she'd never tasted before suddenly surged through the flames, setting her limbs to trembling and every last hair on her body to standing stiffly out from her crawling, tingling flesh. She struggled to breathe against the sudden tension hanging in her body and the room around her, heavy and somehow *aware*.

Still the dark flood did not come. Who *was* this Wanlorn?

The image in the loop of flame before her was still two half-open, slumberous eyes—but now something was changing in those encircling flames. Tongues of silver fire were leaping among the blue, only a few at first, but faster and more often, now washing over the entire scene for a moment, now blazing up brighter as the wondering dancer watched.

Suddenly the silver flames overwhelmed the blue, and two cold eyes that were not Wanlorn's opened in their midst. Black they were, shot through with twinkling stars, but the flames that swam from them like tears were the same rich blue as were spilling from Nasmaerae's own.

"Azuth am I," a voice that was both musical and terrible rang out of the depths of her mind. "Cease this prying—forever. If you heed not, the means of prying shall be taken from you."

The Lady of Castle Felmorel screamed then—as loud and as long as she knew how, as blue flames whirled her off her feet and held her captive and struggling, upright in their grip. Nasmaerae was lost in fear and horror and self-loathing, as the blue flames of her own thought-stealing spell were hurled forcibly back through her.

She shuddered under their onslaught, fell silent as she writhed in helpless and spasmodic collapse, then howled with a quite different tone, like a lost and wandering thing. All the brightness had gone out of her eyes, and she was drooling, a steady stream plunging from the corner of her twisted mouth.

The eyes that swam with stars regarded the broken woman for several grim moments, then spat forth fresh blue flames to enshroud her in a racing inferno that raged for only moments.

When it receded, the barefoot woman was standing on the stone floor of the spell chamber, her fiery weavings shattered and gone. Her nightgown was plastered to her body with her own sweat, and her hands shook uncontrollably, but the desolate eyes that stared down at them were her own.

"You are Nasmaerae once more, your mind restored. You may consider this no mercy, daughter of Avarae. I've broken all of your bindings—including, of course, the one that holds your Lord in thrall. Consequences will soon be upon you; 'twould be best to prepare yourself."

The sorceress stared into those floating, starry eyes in helpless horror. They looked back at her sternly and steadily even as they began to fade away, dwindling swiftly to nothingness. All of the magical light in the chamber faded and failed with them, leaving only emptiness behind.

Nasmaerae knelt alone in the darkness for a long time, sobbing slightly. Then she arose and padded like a wan-eyed ghost along unseen ways she knew well, feeling turns and archways with her fingertips, seeking the sliding panel that opened into the back of the wardrobe in her own bedchamber.

Thrusting through half-cloaks and gowns, she drew in a deep, tremulous breath, let it out in a sigh, and laid her fingers on her most private of coffers, on the high, hidden shelf right where she'd left it.

The maids had left a single hooded lamp lit on the marble-topped side table; the needle-slim dagger caught and flashed back its faint light as she drew it forth, looked at it almost casually for a moment, then turned it in her hand to menace her own breast.

"Esbre," she told the darkness in a whisper, as she drew back her hand for the stroke that would take her own life, "I'll miss you. Forgive me."

"I already have," said a voice like cold stone, close by her ear. A familiar arm lashed out across her chest to intercept the wrist that held the dagger.

Nasmaerae gave a little startled scream and struggled wildly for a moment, but Lord Esbre's hairy hand was as immovable as iron, yet as gentle as velvet as it encircled her wrist.

His other hand plucked the dagger out of her grasp and threw it away. It flashed across the room to be caught deftly by one of the dozen or so guards who were melting out from behind every tapestry and screen in the room now, unhooding lanterns, lighting torches in wall sconces, and moving grimly to bar any move she might make toward the door or to the wardrobe behind her.

Nasmaerae stared into the eyes of her lord, still too shocked and dazed to speak, wondering when the storm of fury would come. The Mantimera's eyes blazed through a mist of tears, burning into her, but his lips moved slowly and precisely as he asked in tones of quiet puzzlement, "Self-slaying is the answer to misguided sorcery? You had a *good* reason for placing me in a spell-thrall?"

Nasmaerae opened her mouth to plead, to spill forth desperate lies, to protest that her deeds had been misunderstood, but all that came out was a torrent of tears. She threw herself against him and tried to go to her knees, but a strong hand on her hip held her upright. When she could form words through the sobs, it was to beg his forgiveness and offer herself for any punishment he deemed fitting, and to—

He stilled her words with a firm finger laid across her lips and said grimly, "We'll speak no more of what you have done. You shall never enthrall me or anyone else again."

"I—believe me, my Lord, I would never—"

"You *can't*, whatever you may come to desire. This I know. So that others may also know it, you shall try to place me in thrall again—now."

Nasmaerae stared at him. "I—no! No, Esbre, I dare not! I—"

"Lady," the Mantimera told her grimly, "I am uttering a command, not affording you a choice." He made a gesture involving three of his fingers; all around her, swords grated out of scabbards.

The Lady Felmorel darted glances about. She was ringed with drawn steel, the sharp, dark points of well-used war swords menacing her on all sides. She saw a white-faced Glavyn above one of them, trusty old Errart staring grimly at her over another. Then she whirled away, hiding her face in her hands.

"I—I . . . *Esbre!*" she sobbed. "My magic will be shorn from me if I—"

"Your life shall be shorn from you if you do not. Death or obedience, Lady. The same choice warriors who serve me have, every day. It comes not so hard to them."

The Lady Nasmaerae groaned. Slowly her hands fell from her face and she straightened, breathing heavily, her eyes elsewhere. She threw back her head to look at the ceiling and said in a small voice, "I'll need more room. Someone pluck away this rug, lest it be scorched." She walked deliberately onto the point of someone's sword until they gave way before her and she could get off the soft, luxurious rug, then turned to face back into the ring and said softly, "I'll need a knife."

"No," Esbre snapped.

"The spell requires it, Lord," she told the ceiling. "Wield it yourself, if it gives you comfort—but obey me utterly when I begin the casting, lest we both be doomed."

"Proceed," he said, his voice cold stone again.

Nasmaerae strode away from him until she stood in the center of the ring of blades once more, then turned and faced him. "Glavyn," she said, "bring my lord's chamber pot hence. If it be empty, report so back to us."

The guard stared at her, unmoving—but spun from his place and hastened to the door at a curt nod from Lord Felmorel.

While they waited, Nasmaerae calmly tore the soaked nightgown from her body and flung it away, standing nude before them all. She stood flatfooted, neither covering herself modestly nor adopting her usual sensual poses, and licked her lips more than once, looking only at her lord.

"Punish me," she said suddenly, "in any other way but this. The Art means all to me, Esbre, every—"

"Be still," he almost whispered, but she shrank back as if he'd snapped a lash across her lips and said no more.

The door opened; Glavyn returned bearing an earthen pot. Lord Felmorel took it from him, motioned him back into his place in the line, and said to his men, "I trust you all. If you see aught that offers ill to Felmorel, strike accordingly—both of us, if need be." Bearing a small belt knife and the pot, he stepped forward.

"I love you, Esbre," the Lady Nasmaerae whispered, and went to her knees.

He stared at her stonily and said only, "Proceed."

She drew in a deep, shuddering breath and said, "Place the pot so that I can reach within." When he did so, she dipped one hand in and brought it out with a palmful of his urine. Letting her cupped hand rest on the floor, she held out her other hand and said, "Cut my palm—not deeply, but draw blood."

Grimly Lord Felmorel did as he was bid, and she said, "Now withdraw—pot, knife, and all."

As he retreated, the guards grew tense, waiting to leap forward with their steel at the slightest sign from Lord Esbre. As her own dark blood filled her palm, Nasmaerae looked around the ring. Their faces told her just how deeply she was feared and hated. She bit her lip and shook her head slightly.

Then she drew in another deep breath, and with it seemed to gain courage. "I'll begin," she announced, and without pause slipped into a chant that swiftly rose in urgency and seemed fashioned around his name. The words were thick and yet somehow slithering, like aroused serpents. As they came faster and faster, small wisps of smoke issued from between her lips.

Suddenly—very suddenly—she clapped her hands together so that blood and urine mixed, and cried out a phrase that seemed to echo and smite the ears of the men in the chamber like thunderclaps. A white flame flared between her cupped palms, and she lifted her head to look at her lord—only to scream, raw and horrified and desperate, and try to fling herself to her feet and away.

The star-swirling eyes of Azuth, cold and remorseless, were staring at her out of Lord Felmorel's face, and that musical, terrible voice of doom sounded again, telling her, "All magic has its price."

None of the guards heard those five words or saw anything but grim pity in their Lord's face, as the Mantimera held up a hand to stay their blades. The Lady Felmorel had fallen to the floor, her face a mask of despair and her eyes unseeing, dying wisps of smoke rising from her trembling limbs—limbs that withered before their eyes, then were restored to lush vitality, only to wither again in racing waves. All the while, as her body convulsed, rebuilt itself, and shriveled again, her screaming went on, rising and falling in a broken paean of pain and terror.

The guards stared down at her writhing body in shocked silence until the Mantimera spoke again.

"My lady will be abed for some days," he said grimly. "Leave me with her, all of you—but summon her maids-of-chamber hence to see to her needs. Azuth is merciful and shall be worshiped in this house henceforth."

Somewhere a woman was twisting on a bare stone floor, with leveled swords all around her in a ring and her bare body withering in waves as she wailed . . . elsewhere motes of light, like stars in a night sky, were whirling in darkness with a cold chiming sound . . . there followed a confusing, falling instant of mages casting spells and becoming skeletons in their robes as they did so, before Elminster saw himself standing in darkness, moonlight falling around him. He was poised before a castle whose front gate was fashioned in the shape of a giant spiderweb. It was a place he knew he'd never been, or seen before. His hands were raised in the weaving of a spell that took shape an instant later and spell blasted apart the gate in a burst of brilliance. The light whirled away to become the teeth of a laughing mouth that whispered, "Seek me in shadows."

The words were mocking, the voice feminine, and Elminster found himself sitting bolt upright at the foot of his unused bed, cold sweat plastering his clothing to him.

"Mystra has guided me," he murmured. "I'll tarry no longer here, but go out to seek and challenge this Lady of Shadows." He smiled and added, "Or my name isn't Wanlorn."

He'd never unpacked the worn saddlebag that carried his gear. It was the work of moments to make sure no helpful servant had removed anything for washing and he was out the door, striding briskly as if guests always went for late night walks around Castle Felmorel. Skulking is for thieves.

He nodded pleasantly to the one servant he did meet, but he never saw the impassive face of Barundryn Harbright watching him from the depths of a dark corner, with the faintest of satisfied nods. Nor did he see the moving shadow that slipped out from under the staircase he descended to follow him, bearing its own bundle of belongings.

Only a single aged servant was watching the closed castle gate. El peered all around to make sure guards weren't hiding anywhere. Seeing none, he hefted the doused brass lantern he'd borrowed from a hallway moments ago, swung it carefully, and let go.

The lamp plunged to the cobbles well behind the old man, with a crash like the landing of a toppling suit of armor. The man shouted in fear and banged his shin on a door frame trying to get to his pike.

When he reached the shattered lantern, limping and cursing, to menace it with a wobbling pike, El had slipped out the porter's door in the gate, just one more shadow in this wet spring night.

Another shadow followed, conjuring a drift of mist to roll before it in case this wandering Wanlorn looked back for pursuit. The briefest of flashes marked the casting of the shadow's spell—but the servant with the pike was too far away to notice or to have identified the face so fleetingly illuminated. Thessamel Arunder, the Lord of Spells, had also felt the need to suddenly and quietly take his leave of Castle Felmorel in the middle of the night.

The lantern was a bewilderment, the limp painful, and the pike too long and heavy; old Bretchimus was some time getting back to his post. He never felt or heard the chill, chiming whirlwind that was more a wind than a body, more a shadow than a presence, and that, drifting purposefully, became the third shadow that evening to pass out the porter's door. Perhaps it was just as well. As he leaned the pike back against the wall, its head fell off. It was an old pike and had seen enough excitement for one evening.

Torntlar's Farm covered six hills and took a lot of hoeing. Dawn saw Habaertus Ilynker rubbing his aching back and digging into the stony soil of the last hill—the one that adjoined the wolf-prowled wood that stretched all the way to Felmorel. As he did every morning, Habaertus glanced toward Castle Felmorel, though it was too far away to really see, and nodded a greeting to his older brother Bretchimus.

"Yourn the lucky one," he told his absent brother, as he did each morning. "Dwellin' yon, with that vast wine cellar an' that slinking silkhips Lady orderin' y'about, an' all."

He spat on his hands and picked up his hoe once more in time to see a few stray twinklings in the air that told him something strange was arriving. Or rather, passing him by. An unseen, chiming presence swept out of the trees and across the field, swirling like a mist or shadow, yet curiously elusive—for no shadow could be seen if one stared right at it.

Habaertus watched it start to snake past, pursed his lips, then, overcome by curiosity, took a swipe at it with his hoe.

The reaction was immediate. A sparkling occurred in the air where the blade of the hoe had passed through the wind, loud chiming sounded on all sides, then the shadowy wind overwhelmed Habaertus, howling around him like a hound closing on a kill. He hadn't even time for a grunt of astonishment.

As a wind-scoured skeleton collapsed into dust, the whirlwind roused itself with another little chorus of chimings and moved on across Torntlar's Farm. In its wake a battered hoe thumped to the earth beside two empty boots. One of them promptly fell over, and all that was left of Habaertus Ilynker fell out and drifted away.

FOUR
STAG HORNS AND SHADOWS

I wonder: do monsters look different from inside?

CITTA HOTHEMER
FROM *MUSINGS OF A SHAMELESS NOBLE*
PUBLISHED IN THE YEAR OF THE PRINCE

The farmer's eyes were dark with suspicion and sunken with weariness. The fork in his hands, however, pointed very steadily toward Wanlorn's eyes and moved whenever the lone traveler did, to keep that menace on target.

When the farmer finally broke the long, sharp silence that had followed the traveler's question, it was to say, "Yuh can find the Lady of Shadows somewhere over the next hill," a sentence the speaker ended by spitting pointedly into the dirt between them. "Her lands begin there, leastways. I don't want to know why yuh'd *want* to meet her—an' I don't want yuh standing here on *my* land much longer, either. Get yuh boots yonder, and yuh in 'em!"

A feint with the fork underscored the man's words. Wanlorn raised an eyebrow, replied, "Have my thanks," in dry tones, and with neither haste nor delay got his boots yonder.

He did not have to look back to know the farmer was watching him all the way over the crest of the hill; he could feel the man's eyes drilling into his back like two drawn daggers. He made a point of not looking back as he went over the ridge—and in lawless country, no sensible traveler stands long atop any height, visible from afar. Eyes alert enough to be watching for strangers are seldom friendly ones.

As he trotted down the bracken-cloaked hillside that was his first taste of the Lands of the Lady, he briefly considered becoming a falcon or perhaps a prowling beast . . . but no, if this Lady of Shadows was alert and watchful, betraying his magical abilities at the outset would be the height of foolishness.

Not that the man who was Wanlorn, but who'd walked longer under the name of Elminster, cared overmuch about being thought a fool. It was a little late for that he thought wryly, considering the road he'd chosen in life—with his stealthy departure from Castle Felmorel not all that many steps behind him. Mystra was forging him into a weapon, or at least a tool . . . and in all the forging he'd seen, those rains of hammer blows looked to be a little hard on the weapon.

And who was it long ago who'd said, "The task forges the worker"?

It would be so much easier to just do as he pleased, using magic for personal gain and having no care for the consequences or the fates of others. He could have happily ruled the land of his birth, mouthing—as more than one mage he'd met with did—the occasional empty prayer to a goddess of magic who meant nothing to him.

There was that one thing his choice had given him: long life. Long enough to outlive every last friend and neighbor of his youth, every colleague of his early adventures and magical workings and revelry in Myth Drannor . . . and every friend and lover, one after another, of that wondrous city, too.

Elminster's lips twisted in bitterness as remembered faces and laughter and caresses rushed past his mind's regard, one after gods-be-cursed another . . . and the plans with them, the dreams excitedly discussed and well intended, that blow and dwindle away like morning mist in bright sunlight and come to nothing in the end.

So much had come to nothing in the end. . . .

Like the village in front of him, it seemed. Roofs fallen in and overgrown gardens and paths greeted him, with here and there a blackened chimney stabbing up at the sky like a dark and battered dagger to mark where a cottage had stood before fire came, or a vine-choked hump that was once a fieldstone wall or hedgerow between fields. Something that might have been a wolf or may have been another sort of large-jawed hunting beast slunk out of one ruined house as Elminster approached. Otherwise the village of Hammershaws seemed utterly deserted. Was this what Lord Esbre had meant by the Lady of Shadows seeking to "enforce her will" on these lands? Was every such place ahead of him going to be deserted?

What had happened to all the folk who dwelt here?

A few strides later brought him a grim answer. Something dull and yellow-gray cracked under his boots. Not a stone after all, but a piece of skull . . . well, several pieces, now. He turned his head and walked grimly on.

Another stride, another cracking sound; a long bone, this time. And another, a fourth . . . he was walking on the dead. Human bones, gnawed and scattered, were strewn everywhere in Hammershaws. What he'd thought was a collapsed railing on a little log bridge across the meandering creek was actually a tangle of skeletons, their arms dangling down almost to the water. El peered, saw at least eight skulls, sighed, and trudged on, looking this way and that among leaning carts and yard-gates fast vanishing under the brambles and creeping tallgrass that had already reclaimed the yards beyond them.

None but the dead dwelt in Hammershaws now. El poked into one cottage, just to see if anything of interest survived, and was rewarded with a brief glimpse of a slumped human skeleton on a stone chair. The supple mottled coils of an awakened snake glided between the bones as the serpent spiraled up to coil at the top of the chair. It was seeking height to better strike at this overbold intruder. As its hiss rose loud in that ravaged room, Elminster decided not to stay and learn the quality of the serpent's range and aim.

The road beyond Hammershaws looked as overgrown as the village. A lone vulture circled high in the sky, watching the human intruder traverse a fading way across the rolling lands to Drinden.

A mill and busy market town, was Drinden, if the memories of still-vigorous old men could be trusted. Yet this once bustling hamlet proved now to be another ruin, as deserted as the first village had been. El stood at its central crossroads and looked grimly up at a sky that had slowly gone gray with tattered, smoke-like storm clouds. Then he shrugged and walked on. So long as one's paper and components stay dry, what matter a little rain?

Yet no rain came as El took the northwestern way, up a steep slope that skirted a stunted wood that had once been an orchard. The sky started to turn milky-white, but the land remained deserted.

He'd been told the Lady of Shadows rode or walked the land in the company of dark knights he'd do well to fear, with their ready blades and eager treacheries and vicious disregard for surrenders or agreements. Yet as he walked on into the heart of the domain of the Lady of Shadows, he seemed utterly alone in a deserted realm. No hoofbeats or trumpets sounded, and no hooves came thundering down into the road bearing folk to challenge one man walking along with a saddlebag slung over his shoulder.

It was growing late and the skies had just cleared to reveal a glorious sunset like melted coins glimmering in an amber sky as Elminster reached the valley that held the town of Tresset's Ringyl, once and perhaps still home to the Lady of Shadows. He found that it, too, was a deserted, beast-roamed ruin.

Forty or more buildings, at his first glance from the heights, still stood amid the trees that in the end would tear them all apart. Sitting amidst the clustered ruins were the crumbling walls of a castle whose soaring battlements probably afforded something winged and dangerous with a lair. El peered at it as the amber sky became a ruby sea, and the stars began to show overhead.

The long-dead Tresset had been a very successful brigand who'd tried his hand at ruling and built a slender-spired castle—the Ringyl—here to anchor his tiny realm. Tressardon had fallen within days of his death.

Elminster's lips twisted wryly. 'Twould be an act of supremely arrogant self-importance to try to read lesson or message for himself out of such local history. Moreover, from here at least he could see no spiderweb gate like the one in his dream set into the walls of the ruined castle. It could take days to explore all of what was left of the town—assuming, of course, that nothing lived here that would want to eat him or drive him away sooner than that—and nothing he could see but the Ringyl itself stood tall or grand enough to possibly incorporate the gate in his dream. Or at least, he reminded himself with a sigh, so it looked from here.

He'd time for just one foray before true nightfall, by which time it'd probably be most prudent to be elsewhere . . . perhaps on one of those grassy hilltops in the distance, beyond the shattered and overgrown town. A wise man would be setting up camp thereon right now, not scrambling down a slope of loose stones—and more human bones—for a quick peer around before full night came down. But then Elminster Aumar had no intention of becoming a wise man for some centuries yet. . . .

The shadows were already long and purple by the time Elminster reached the valley floor. Thigh-high grass cloaked what had once been the main road through the town, and El waded calmly into it. Dark, gaping houses stood like graying giants' skulls on either side as he walked quietly forward, sweeping the grass side to side with a staff he'd cut earlier to discourage snakes from striking and to uncover any obstacles before his feet or shins made their own, more painful discoveries.

Night was coming down fast as Elminster walked through the heart of deserted Ringyl. A tense, heavy silence seemed to live at its heart, a hanging, waiting stillness that swallowed echoes like heavy fog. El tapped on a stone experimentally but firmly with his staff. He could hear the grating thud of each strike, but no answering echo came from the walls now close around.

Twice he saw movement out of the corner of his eye, but when he whirled he was facing nothing but trees and crumbling stone walls.

Something watchful dwelt or lurked here, he was sure. Twilight was stealing into the gaps between the roofless buildings now, and into the tangles where trees, vines, and thorn bushes all grew thickly entwined. El moved along more briskly, looking only for walls lofty enough to hold the spiderweb gates of his dream. He found nothing so tall . . . except the Ringyl itself.

Gnawed bones, most brown and brittle enough to crack and crumble underfoot, were strewn in plenty along the grass-choked street. Human bones, of course. They grew in abundance to form almost a carpet in front of the riven walls of the castle. Cautiously Elminster forged ahead, turning over bones with his staff and sending more than one rock viper into a swift, ribbonlike retreat. Darkness was closing down around him now, but he had to look through one of these gaps in the wall, to see if . . .

Whatever had torn entire sections of wall as thick as a cottage and as tall as twenty men was still inside, waiting.

Well, perhaps one need not be *quite* so dramatic. El smiled thinly. It's a weakness of archmages to think the fate of Toril rests in their palm or on their every movement and pronouncement. A spiderweb-shaped gate would be sufficient unto his present needs.

He was looking into a chapel or at least a high-ceilinged hall, its vaulted ceiling intact and painted to look like many trees with gilded fruit on their branches though strips of that limning were hanging down in tongues of ruin. All this stood over a once polished floor in which wavy bands of malachite were interwoven between bands of quartz or marble—a floor now mantled in dust, fallen stone rubble, birds' nests and the tiny bones of their perished makers, and less identifiable debris.

It was very dark in the hall. El thought it prudent not to conjure any light, but he could hardly miss seeing the huge oval of black stone facing him in the far wall. Sparkling white quartz had been set into that wall to form a circle of many stars—fourteen or a dozen irregularly shaped twinklings, none of them the long-spindled star of Mystra—and in the center of that circle a carving as broad as Elminster's outstretched arms stood out from the wall: a sculpted pair of feminine lips.

They were closed, slightly curved in a secret smile, and El had a gnawing feeling that he'd seen them, or something very like them, before. Perhaps this was a speaking mouth, an enchanted oracle that could tell him more—if he could unlock its words at all, or understand a message not meant for him. Perhaps it was something less friendly than that.

Well, such investigations could wait until the full light of morning. It was time, and past time, to leave Tresset's Ringyl and its watchful shadows. El backed out of the gaping ruin, saw nothing lunging at him out of the darkness, and with more haste than dignity headed for the hills.

The heights on the far side of the Ringyl weren't yet touched by moonlight, but the glittering stars cast enough light to make their grassy flanks seem to glow. El looked back several times on his determined march up out of the town, but nothing seemed to stir or follow him, and the many eyes that peered at him out of the darkness were no larger than those of rats.

Perhaps he would have time to win some sort of slumber, after all. The hilltop he chose was small and bare of all but the ever-present long grass. He walked it in a smallish ring, then opened his pack, took out a cloth scrip full of daggers that glowed a brief, vivid stormy blue when unwrapped—radiance that promptly seemed to leak out of them, dripping and dancing to the ground—and retraced his steps around the ring. He drove a dagger hilt-deep into the soil at intervals and muttered something that sounded suspiciously like an old and rather bawdy dance rhyme. When the ring was complete, the Athalantan turned back along it and drove a second ring of daggers in, angling each of these additional blades into the turf on the inside of the ring, so that its blade touched the vertical steel of an already-buried dagger. He held out his hand, palm downward and fingers spread, said a single, soft word over them, wrapped his cloak around himself, and went to bed.

"What, pray tell, are you reading?"

The balding, bearded mage set aside a goblet whose contents frothed and bubbled, looked up unhurriedly over his spectacles, elevated one eyebrow at a fashionably slow pace, and replied, "A play . . . of sorts."

The younger wizard standing over him—more splendidly dressed and still possessing some of his own hair—blinked. "A 'play,' Baerast? And 'of sorts'? Not an obscure spellbook or one of Nabraether's meaty grimoires?"

Tabarast of the Three Sung Curses peered up over his spectacles again, more severely this time. "Let there be no impediment to your dawning understanding, dearest Droon," he said. "I am currently immersed in a play, to whit 'The Stormy Knight, Or, The Brazen Butcherer.' A work of some energy."

"And more spilled blood," Beldrune of the Bent Finger replied, sweeping aside an untidy stack of books that had almost buried a high-backed chair and planting himself firmly in it before it even had time to wheeze at its sudden freedom. The crash of tomes that followed was impressive in both room-shaking solidity and in the amount of dust it raised. It almost drowned out the two smaller thunderings that followed, the first occasioned by the clearance of the footstool of its own tower of tomes by means of a hearty two-footed kick, and the second caused by the collapse of both back legs of the old chair.

As Beldrune abruptly settled lower amid scattered literature, Tabarast laid a dust-warding hand over the open top of his goblet and asked through the roiling cloud of dancing motes, "Are you *quite* finished? I begin to weary of this nuisance."

Beldrune made a sound that some folk would have deemed rude and others might judge impressive and by way of elaborating on this reply uttered the words, "My dear fellow, is this—this burgeoning panoply of literary chaos *my* achievement? I think not. There's not a chair or table left on this entire floor that isn't guarding its own ever-growing fortress of magical knowledge at your behest, and—"

Tabarast made a sound like a serpent's skull being crushed under an eager boot heel. "My behest? Do you now deny the parcenary of this disarray around us? I can confute any claims to the contrary, if you've a day or two to spare."

"Meaning my wits are that slow, or words so slow and laborious to come to your lips that—*atch*, never mind. I came not to bandy bright phrases all evening but to banish a little lonely befuddlement by talking a while."

"A prolusion I've heard before," Tabarast observed dryly. "Have a drink."

He pulled on the lever that made the familiar cabinet rise from the floor-boards to stand between them and listened to Beldrune pounce on its contents from the far side with an absence of continued speech that meant young Droon must be *very* thirsty.

"All right . . . have two," he amended his offer.

The sounds of swallowing continued. Tabarast opened his mouth to say something, remembered that a certain topic was by mutual agreement forbidden, and shut it again. Then another thought came to him.

"Have you ever read 'The Stormy Knight?'" he asked the cabinet, judging Beldrune's head to be inside it.

The younger wizard raised his head from clinkings and uncorkings and gurglings, looking hurt. "Have I not?" he asked, then cleared his throat and recited:

> What knight is that
> who yonder comes riding
> bright-arrayed in armor of gold
> his sash the dripping blood of his foes?

There was a pause, then, "I did it in Ambrara, once."

"*You* were the Stormy Knight?" Tabarast asked in open disbelief, his small round spectacles sliding down his nose in search of unknown destinations.

"Second Undergardener," Beldrune snapped, looking even more hurt. "We all have to start somewhere."

Taking a large and dusty bottle firmly in one fist, he plucked its cork and hurled the stopper back over his shoulder where it hit the Snoring Shield of Antalassiter with a bright *ping*, glanced off the Lost Hunting Horn of the Mavran Maidens, and fell somewhere behind the man-high, dust-covered mound of scrolls and books that Tabarast considered his "Urgent Reading of the Moment." He drained the contents of the bottle in one long and loud swallowing that left him gasping, with tears trailing down his face, and in urgent need of something that tasted better.

A knowing Tabarast silently handed him the bowl of roast halavan nuts. Beldrune dug in with both hands until the bowl was empty, then smiled apologetically, burped, and took his worry stone from its drawstring pouch. Thumbing its smooth, familiar curves seemed to calm him.

Settling back in his chair, he added, "I've always preferred 'Broderick Betrayed, Or, The Wizard Woeful.'"

"This would be my turn," the older mage replied with a dignified nod, and in the manner of an actor on center stage threw out his hand and grandly declaimed:

> That so fat and grasping a man
> Should have the very stars bright in his hands
> To blind us all with their shining
> Blotting out his faults in plenty.
> His huge and howling ghost
> Doth prowl the world entire
> but loves and lingers most
> upon this very same and lonesome spot
> Where gods loved, men killed, and careless elves forgot.

"Well," Beldrune said after a little silence, "not to deny your impressive performance—your usual paraph, and then some!—but it seems we've returned again to the subject we agreed was forbidden: the One Who Walks, and just what Mystra meant by creating a Chosen One as her most esteemed mortal servant."

Tabarast shrugged, his long and slender fingers tracing the wisps of his own beard thoughtfully. "Men collect what is forbidden," he said. "Always have, always will."

"And mages more so," Beldrune agreed. "What does that tell us about those who follow our profession, I wonder?"

The older mage snorted. "That no shortage of witty fools has yet fallen over Faerûn."

"Hah!" Beldrune leaned forward, stroking one splendid silk lapel eagerly between forefinger and thumb, the worry stone momentarily forgotten. "Then you grant that Our Lady will take more than one Chosen? At last?"

"I grant no such thing," Tabarast replied rather testily. "I can see a succession of Chosen, one raised after another falls, but I've yet been shown no evidence of the dozen or more you champion, still less of this Bright Company of star-harnessing, mountain-splitting archwizards some of the more romantic mages keep babbling about. They'll be begging Holy Mystra to issue merit badges next."

The younger mage ran one hand through his wavy brown hair, utterly ruining the styling the tower's maid-of-chamber had struggled to achieve, and said, "I quite agree with you that such things are ridiculous—and yet could they not be used as a mark of accomplishment? Meet a mage and see seven stars and a scroll on his sash, and you know where he stands?"

"I know how much time he's willing to waste on impressing folk and sewing little gewgaws onto his undergarments, more like," Tabarast replied sourly. "Just how many upstart magelings would add a few unearned stars to grant themselves rank and hauteur accruing to power and accomplishments they do not in fact possess? Every third one who knows how to sew, that's how many! If we must talk about this—this young elf-loving jackanapes, who seems to have been a prince and the slayer of the mighty Ilhundyl and the bed mate of half a hundred slim elf lasses besides, the object of our discourse shall not be his latest conquest or idle utterance, but his import to us all. I care not which boot he puts on first of mornings, what hue of cloak he favors, or whether he prefers to kiss elf lips or human ones—have we understanding and agreement?"

"Of course," Beldrune replied, spreading his hands. "But why such heat? His achievements—as a Chosen One favored by the goddess Herself, mind—do nothing to belittle yours."

Tabarast thumbed his spectacles back up to the bridge of his nose and muttered, "I grow no younger. I've not the years left to encompass what that young—but enough; I'll say no more. I beg leave to impart to you, my young friend, things about this One Who Walks of rather more importance to us both. The priests of the Mantle, for ins—"

"The priests of the which?"

"The Mantle . . . Mystra's Mantle, the temple to Our Lady in Haramettur. I don't suppose you've ever been therein."

Beldrune shook his head. "I try to avoid temples to Holy Mystra," he said. "The priests tend to be nose-in-the-air sorts who want to charge me coffers full of gold for casting—badly—what I can do myself with a few coppers of oddments."

Tabarast flapped a dismissive hand and replied, "Indeed, indeed, all too often . . . and I've my own quarrel with their snobbery—pimply younglings sneering down their noses at such as myself because we wear real, everyday, food-stained robes, and not silks and sashes and golden cross-garters, like rakes gone to town of an ardent evening. If they truly served wizards and not just awestruck young lasses who think they might have felt Mystra's kiss, awakening at midnight this tenday last,' they'd know all *true* mages look like rag heaps, not fashion-pretty popinjays!"

Beldrune looked hurt—again—and gestured down the front of his scarlet silk tunic. The gesture made it ripple glassily in the lamplight, its cloth-of-gold dragons gleaming, the glittering emeralds that served them as eyes a-winking, and the fine wire wrought into spirals that passed for their tongues bobbing. "And what am I? No true mage, I suppose?"

Tabarast passed a weary hand over his eyes. "Nay, nay, good Droon—present company excepted, of course. Your bright plumage doth so outshine mine aged eyes that I overlook it as a matter of course. Let us have no quarrel over your learning or able mastery of realm-shaking magics; you *are*, before all the gods, a 'true mage,' whatever by Mystra's gentle whispers *that* is. Let us by more heroic efforts resist the temptation to drift away into other matters, and—if discuss the forbidden we must—speak plainly. To whit: the priests of the Mantle say that the One Who Walks is free to act on his own; that is, to make just as bad a hash of things as you and I are free to do . . . moreover, that it is holy Mystra's will that he be left to blunder and choose and hurl recklessness on his own, to 'become what it is needful he become.' They want us all to pretend we don't know who or what he is, if we should meet with him."

Beldrune rested his chin on one hand, a fresh and smoking goblet raised in the other. "Just what is it that they say he must become?" he asked.

"That's where their usefulness ends," Tabarast snorted. "When one asks, they go to their knees and groan about 'not being worthy to know,' and 'the aims of the divine are beyond the comprehension of all mortals'—which tells me right there that *they* haven't figured it out yet—then they rush into an almost puppy-panting whirl of 'oh, but he's important! The signs! The signs!' "

Beldrune sipped deeply from his goblet, swallowed, and asked, "What signs?"

Tabarast resumed the ringing voice of doom that he'd used to delivered the lines from Broderick, and intoned: "In this Year of Laughter, the Blazing Hand of Sorcery ascends the starry night cloak, for the first time in centuries! Nine black tressym landed upon the sleeping princess Sharandra of the South and delivered themselves of four kittens each upon her very bosom! (Don't ask me how she slept through *that* or what she thought of the mess when she did wake!) The Walking Tower of Warglend has moved for the first time in a thousand years, taking itself from Tower Tor to the midst of a nearby lake! A talking frog has been found in Candlekeep, wherein also six pages in as many books have gone blank, and two books appeared that have never been seen by any Faerûnian scholar before! The Well of the Bonedance in Maraeda's run dry! The skeleton of the lich Buardrim has been seen dancing in—ah, *bah!* Enough! They can keep it up for hours!"

"Gullet Well's gone dry?"

Tabarast favored Beldrune with a look. "Yes," he said mildly. "Gullet Well *has* gone dry—for whatever real reason. I saw the dead horses to prove it. So there you have it. Tell me, good Droon, you get out and about more than I do, and hear more of the gossip—however paltry or deliberately fabricated it may be—among our fellow workers-of-Art. How say the mages about this One Who Walks? What do the trendy wizards think?"

It was Beldrune's turn to snort. "Trendy wizards *don't* think," he retorted, "or they'd take care never to be caught up in any trend. But as to what's being said . . . of him, less than nothing. What our colleagues seem to have heard out of whatever the priests have proclaimed can be boiled down to great secret excitement and preening over the chance to be named a Chosen of Mystra—and thereby get all sorts of special powers and inside knowledge. They seem to view it as the most exclusive club yet, and that someone is certain to privately contact them to join, any day now. If Mystra is selecting mortal mages to be Her personal servants, endowing them with spells mighty enough to shatter mountains and read minds, each and every mage wants to get into this oh-so-exclusive group without appearing in the slightest to be interested in such status."

Tabarast raised an eyebrow. "I see. How do you know I'm already not a Chosen and reading your mind even now?"

Beldrune gave his friend a wry smile. "If you were reading my mind, Baerast," he said, "you'd be trying to smite me down, right now—and blushing to boot!"

Tabarast lifted the other eyebrow to join the first. "Oh? Should I bother to venture further queries?" he asked. "I suspect not, but I'd like to be prepared if your incipient anger bids fair to goad you into muscular and daring feats that I must needs resist . . . You *do* feel incipient anger, don't you?"

"No; not a moment of it," Beldrune replied cheerfully. "Though I could probably work up to it, if you continue to guard that jar of halavan nuts so closely. Pass it over."

Tabarast did so, freely giving his colleague a sour look along with it and saying, "I value these nuts highly; one might even say they are precious to me. Conduct thy depredations accordingly."

The younger wizard smiled wryly. "All mages, I daresay, conduct their depredations while considering—if they take time to consider at all—what they're about to seize or destroy to be precious. Don't you?"

Tabarast looked thoughtful. "Yes," he murmured. "Yes, I do." He lifted an eyebrow. "How many of us, I wonder, fall so into exultation at our own power that we try to seize or destroy everything we deem precious?"

Beldrune scooped up a handful of nuts. "Most of us would consider a Chosen precious, would we not?" he asked.

Tabarast nodded. "The One Who Walks is going to have an interesting career in time soon to come," he predicted softly, his face very far from a smile. "Pour me something."

Beldrune did.

Lightning rose and snapped out, splitting the night with a bright flash of fury. El blinked and sat up. Blue arcs of deadly magic were leaping and crackling from dagger to dagger around his ring, and in the night beyond something was thrashing wetly—something that was being avoided by a score or more slinking, prowling things that looked like ragged shadows, but moved like hunting cats. Elminster came fully awake fast, peering all around and counting. The thrashing hadn't ended, and anything that could survive such a lash of lightning was something to be respected. Respected twenty-fold, it seemed.

He folded his cloak, slung it through the straps of the saddlebag in case hasty flight should be necessary, and stood up. The prowling shadows were moving around his roused ring from right to left, quickening their pace for a charge to come. Something was urging or goading them; something El could feel as a tension in the air, a growing, heavy, and fell presence with the force and fury of a hailstorm about to break. Shaking his hands and wriggling his fingers to leave them loose and ready for frantic casting to come, he peered into the night, trying to see his foe.

He could *feel* when he was facing it, its unseen gaze transfixing him like two hot sword tips, but he could see nothing but roiling darkness.

Perhaps the thing was cloaked in a wall of these prowling shadows. It might be best to conjure a high, glowing sphere of the sort folk called a "witchlight," just to see what he faced. Yet he had only one such spell. If his foe dashed it to darkness, El would be blinking and blinded for too long a time to keep his life against a concerted attack from many prowling things.

Should he—then it came. The shadows swerved and moved in at him on all sides in a soundless charge of rippling darkness.

His wards crackled and spat blue-white, leaping death into the night. Shadows stiffened, reared, and danced in agony amid racing, darting lightning. El spun around to make sure his ring had held in all places against this initial charge.

It had, but the shadow beasts weren't drawing back. Weeping as they perished, dwindling like smoke before the fury of the lightning crawling through them, they clawed and convulsed and tried to hurl themselves past the barrier. El watched and waited, as his lightning flickered and grew dim, dying with the creatures it was slaying. By the Lady, there were a lot of them.

It would not be long now before the spell failed utterly and he'd stand alone against the onslaught. He had one teleport spell that could snatch him from this peril, aye, but only to a place back along his wanderings, leaving these Lands of the Lady in front of him once more; and who knew how much a foe who was expecting him could muster for his second visit?

Here and there, as dying shadows roiled away into smoke, his spell was being brought to collapse: the daggers were rising from the ground, their cracklings and radiances fading, to leap at shadows. They would fly hungrily, points first, at anything outside the ring; he'd best stay where he was and hope they'd reap a good crop of shadow beasts before his unseen foe tried something else. Such as a spell of its own.

Green, many-clawed lightning was born in the night—in the hand of something manlike, bare-bodied, and stag-headed that juggled its conjuration in wickedly long fingers for a moment beside its hip, then hurled it at Elminster.

Snarling and expanding as it came, that ball of spell lightning burst through the last tatters of his ring shield without pause and rushed hungrily at the Athalantan, who was already muttering a swift phrase and angling his hand up, palm slanted out, in a curious gesture.

Lightning struck and rebounded, springing away as if it'd been struck, to go howling back the way it'd come. El could see red eyes watching him intently now and felt the weight of a mirthless smile that he could not see, as the figure simply stood and let the lightning flow back into it to be swallowed up as if it'd never been.

Elminster's raised, warding hand flickered with a radiance of its own, then was itself again. His spell still lurked, though, awaiting another attack . . . or two, if this stag-headed foe struck swiftly.

The last few slinking shadows rushed to the stag-headed being and seemed to flow up and *into* it. El used its moment of immobility to launch an attack of his own, tossing a dagger into the air that his Art made into thirty-three blades. He swept them all, whirling and darting, down upon his foe.

Antlers dipped swiftly as the figure of shadows ducked away, emitting what might have been a low growl or might have been an incantation. The thing stiffened and sent out a high, shrill cry that might have been a human woman taking a blade in the back (for Elminster had heard such a sound before, in the city of Hastarl, several centuries ago), as blades bit deep. There was a flash of unleashed magic, motes of light raining to the ground like water dashing off a warrior's shield in a heavy rain, and the whirling, stabbing blades were abruptly gone.

El pressed his advantage; winning this spell duel was certainly needful if he wanted to keep his life—no mage bent on capture hurls lightning—and it would be the act of a fool to stand idly awaiting the next spell Silent Antlers here wanted to bury him with.

He smiled thinly as his fingers traced an intricate pattern, their tips glowing as the casting concluded. Many, many of the things he'd done since that day when a mage-ridden dragon had pounced on Heldon and torn his life asunder could be viewed as acts of a fool.

"I'm a fool goaded by fools, it seems," he told his half-seen assailant pleasantly. "Do you attack all who pass this way, or is this a personal favor?"

His only answer was a loud hiss. He thought it ended with the stag-headed being spitting at him, but he couldn't be certain. His spell took effect then, with a roar that drowned out all other sounds for a time.

Blue flames blossomed around those night-black, spiderlike fingers and on the antlers beyond. The screams came in earnest this time.

El risked time enough to look all around, in case a lurking shadow was on the prowl—and so, glancing back over his own shoulder, he escaped being blinded when a counterspell set the night aflame.

It consumed his wardings in an instant, sending him staggering back among the smoke of shattered spells. Heat blistered his left cheek, and he heard hair sizzle as tears washed the sight from his left eye.

Softly and carefully through the pain, Elminster said the waiting word that awakened the final effect of the spell he'd already cast—and the blue flames cloaking the extremities of his foe blazed up in an exact echo of those that had just struck him.

The shriek that split the night was raw and awkward, born of real agony. El caught a brief glimpse of antlers thrashing back and forth before the flames died and heard harsh gasping receding eastward, amid the swish and crackle of grasses being trampled.

Something large fell in the grass, at least twice. When silence came at last El glided three quick steps to the west and crouched, listening intently to the night.

Nothing. He could hear the long grass stirring in the breeze, and the faint cry of some small wild creature dying in the jaws of another, far off to the south.

At length, El wearily drew the last enchanted dagger he owned—one that did nothing more than glow upon command—and threw it in the direction the sounds had gone, to strike and there illuminate the night.

He took care not to approach its glow too closely and to keep bent low over the grass . . . but nothing moved, and no spell or prowling shadow came leaping out of the night. When he looked where the dagger's light reached, all that could be seen was a broken trail leading a little way to a confused heap of crumbling and smoking bones, or antlers . . . or perhaps just branches. Something collapsed into ash as he drew nearer; something that had looked very much like a long, slim-fingered hand.

Dangling strips of paint quivered, fell, and were followed enthusiastically by the vaulted ceiling itself, leaping to the floor below with a deafening, dust—hurling crash. In its wake, the entire Ringyl shook.

Flung stones were still pattering down nearby buildings and crashing through bushes when the hall where an Athalantan had earlier seen stars rocked, groaned, and began to break apart. Gilded fruit shattered as the wall they were painted on burst asunder, splitting a dark oval and spitting sparkling stars into the night.

Sculpted stone lips quivered as if hesitant to speak, seemed to smile even more for an instant, then broke into many fragments as the widening crack reached them and spat stony pieces out to roll and crash across the trembling hall. The lips toppled, sighed into oblivion, and left a gaping hole in the wall where they'd been.

Echoes of the earth's fury that had caused this cleaving rolled on . . . and out of the hole in the wall, framed by a few surviving stars, something long and black and massive slid into view.

With a growing, grating roar, it canted over on the stony rubble and rattled out into the room: a black catafalque whose upthrust electrum arms held aloft a coffin and several scepters for a few impressive moments before toppling over on its side and crashing into and through the floor.

Shards of floor tile leaped into the air, chased by crawling purple lightning that spat out of the riven coffin. Electrum arms, smashed and twisted in the fall, melted as shattered scepters in their grasp died amid their own small and roiling magical blazes. One arm spat a scepter intact out onto the dust-choked pave an instant before failing protective magics flickered the length of the coffin, hung silent and grappling in the air for a long, tense time of silence, then collapsed in a small but sharp explosion that transformed coffin, catafalque, and all into dark dust and hurled it in all directions.

Amid the tumult, the scepter on the floor gave its own small sigh and collapsed into a neat outline of gently winking dust.

Silence fell in earnest upon the riven hall, and all was still save for the dust drifting down.

Not long afterward, the starlight grew stronger over Tresset's Ringyl, until a mote of blue-white radiance could clearly be seen drifting down out of the starry sky—descending smoothly, like a very large, bright, and purposeful will-o'-wisp, into the heart of the riven hall.

The light came to a smooth stop a handspan or so away from the floor and hung for a moment above the dust that had been the scepter—dust that winked and flickered like blown coals beneath its nearness.

There was a flash, a faint sound like bells struck at random, very far off, and the dust was a scepter once more—smooth and new-lustrous, glimmering with stored power.

A long-fingered, feminine hand suddenly appeared out of empty air, as if through a parted curtain, to grasp the scepter and take it up.

It flashed once like a winking star as it rose. As if in answer the hand grew an ivory-hued arm, the arm a bare shoulder that turned, allowing a glossy flood of dark hair to cascade over it, and rose into a neck, ear, line of jaw—then a beautiful, fine-boned face. Cold was her visage, serene and proud, as she turned dark eyes to look around at the ruined hall.

The scattered quartz stars glowed as if in greeting as the rest of the body grew or faded into view, turning with fearless, unconcerned grace to survey the shattered hall. A beautiful, dark-eyed sorceress held up her scepter like a warrior brandishing a blade in victory and smiled.

The scepter flashed and was gone, the sorceress with it, leaving sudden darkness behind, and only three glows flickering in that gloom: the scattered quartz stars. As the lengthening moments passed, those faint fires faded and went out, one by one, until lifeless darkness reigned in Tresset's Ringyl once more.

"Holy Lady," Elminster said to the stars, on his knees in what had once been his ring of daggers, with the sweat of spell battle still glistening on him, "I have come here, and fought—perhaps slain—at thy bidding. Guide me, I pray."

A gentle breeze rose and stirred the grasses. El watched it, wondering if it was a sign, or some evil thing his words had awakened, or simply uncaring wind, and continued, "I have dared to touch ye, and long to do so again. I have sworn to serve thee and will so, if ye will still have me—but show me, I pray, what I am to do in these haunted lands . . . for I would fain not blunder about, doing harm in ignorance. I have a horror of not knowing."

The response was immediate. Something blue-white seemed to snap and whirl behind his eyes, unfolding to reveal a scene in its smoky rifts: Elminster,

here and now, rising from his knees to take up pack and cloak and walk away
north and east, briskly and with some urgency . . . a scene that whirled away
to become daylight, falling upon an old, squat, untidy stone tower that seemed
more cone or mound than lofty cylinder. A large archway held an old, stout
wooden door that offered entrance with no moat or defenses to be seen—and
that arch displayed a sequence of relief-sculpted phases of the moon. Elminster
had never seen it before, but the vision was clear enough. Even as it faded, he
was leaning down to take up his belongings and begin his walk.

No more visions came to him. He nodded, spoke his thanks to the night,
and set off.

Not three hills had the last prince of Athalantar put at his back when a
chill, chiming wind whirled and danced through the Ringyl, like a flying snake
of frost, and climbed the grassy slopes to where Elminster's ring had been.

It recoiled from that place, a startled wisp of cold starlight arching and
twisting in the night air, then slowly advanced to trace the outline of the wards
that were now gone. Completing the circle, the wind leaped into its center
rather hesitantly, danced and swirled for a time over the spot where Elminster
had knelt to pray, then, very slowly, drifted off along the way El's feet had taken
him. It rose and flickered once as it went, almost as if looking around. Hungrily.

FIVE
ONE MORNING AT MOONSHORN

A mage can visit worlds and times in plenty by opening the right books. Unfortunately, they usually open the tomes full of spells instead, to find ready weapons to beat their own world and time into submission.

CLADDART OF CANDLEKEEP
FROM *THINGS I HAVE OBSERVED*
PUBLISHED CIRCA THE YEAR OF THE WAVE

Out of the dawn mists it rose, dark and old and misshapen, more like a gigantic, many-fissured tree stump than a tower. The sleepless and stumbling man silently cursed Mystra's dictate to use no needless magic for perhaps the hundredth time and winced at the blisters his boots were giving him. It had been a long and weary way hence from the lands of the Lady of Shadows.

Aye, this was it: Moonshorn Tower, just as Her vision had shown him: relief-carved phases of the moon proceeded around the worn stone arch that framed its massive black, many-strapped and bolted door.

As he approached, that door opened and a yawning man stepped out, shuffled a short distance away from the tower, and emptied a chamber pot into a ditch or cesspit somewhere in the tall grass. As the pot—emptier straightened, El saw that the man was of middling years and possessed of raven-dark hair, good looks framed by razor-edged sideburns, one normal—and deep brown—eye, and one eye that blazed like a distant star, white and glowing.

He saw Elminster and stiffened in wary surprise for a moment before striding back to bar passage through the open door. "Well met," he said, in carefully neutral tones. "Be it known that I am Mardasper, guardian of this shrine of Holy Mystra. Have you business here, traveler?"

Elminster was too tired to indulge in witty repartee, but he noted with some satisfaction that the state of the morning sunlight touching the tower matched the vision granted to him last night . . . or early this morn . . . or whenever. "I do," he replied simply.

"You venerate Holy Mystra, Lady of All Mysteries?"

Elminster smiled at the thought of how shocked this Mardasper would be if he knew just how intimately a certain falling-down-exhausted mage had venerated Mystra. "I do," he said again.

Mardasper gave him a hard look, that blazing eye stabbing out at the hawk-nosed Athalantan, and moved his hands in a tiny gesture that El knew to be a truth-sensing spell.

"All who enter here," the guardian said, gesturing with the chamber pot as if it was a scepter of office, "must obey me utterly and work no magic unbidden. Anyone who takes or damages even the smallest thing from within these walls forfeits his life, or at the least his freedom. You may rest within and take water from the fount, but no food or anything else is provided—and you must surrender to me your name and all written magic and enchanted items you carry, no matter how small or benign. They will be returned upon your departure."

"I agree to all this," El told him. "My name is Elminster Aumar. Here's my spellbook and the sole item of magic I yet carry: a dagger that can be made to glow as one desires, bright or dim. It can also purify water and edibles it touches and is guarded against rusting; I know of no other powers."

"This is all?" the fire-eyed guardian demanded, staring intently into Elminster's face as he accepted the book and the sheathed dagger. "And 'Elminster' is your true and usual name?"

"This is all, and aye, Elminster I am called," the Athalantan replied.

Mardasper gestured that he should enter, and they passed into a small chamber, dark after the bright sunlight, that held a lectern and much dust. The guardian wrote down Elminster's name and the date in a ledger as large as some doors El had seen, and waved at one of three closed doors behind the lectern.

"That stair leads to the upper levels, wherein are kept the writings you doubtless seek."

El inclined his head and replied wearily, "Have my thanks."

Writings I doubtless seek? he thought. *Well, perhaps so. . . .*

He turned, his hand upon the pull-ring of the door, and asked, "Why else would a mage come to Moonshorn Tower?"

Mardasper's head snapped up from the ledger, and his good eye blinked in surprise. The other one, El noticed, never closed.

"I know not," the guardian said, sounding almost embarrassed. "There's nothing else here."

"Why came ye here?" El asked gently.

The guardian locked eyes with him in silence for a time, then replied, "If my stewardship here is faithful and diligent for four years—two being already behind me—the priests of Mystra have promised to end the spell upon me that I cannot break." He pointed at his staring eye and added pointedly, "How I came to have this is a private matter. Ask no more on this, lest your welcome run out."

El nodded and opened the door. Probing magics sang and snarled around him for a moment. Then the darkness inside the door became a shrinking, receding web that melted away to reveal a smooth-worn, plain stone stair leading up. As the last prince of Athalantar set his hand upon its rail, an eye seemed to appear in the smooth stone just above his hand and wink at him . . . but perhaps it was just his over-weary imagination. He went on up the stair.

"To work!" The balding, bearded mage in the stained and patched robe threw up the shutter and set its support bar firmly in the socket, letting sunlight spill into the room.

"Aye, Baerast," the younger wizard agreed, wrapping his hands in a cloth to keep dust from them before he caught up the next support bar, "to work it is. We've much to do, to be sure."

Tabarast of the Three Sung Curses peered over his spectacles a trifle severely and said, "The last time you made such enthusiastic utterance, dearest Droon, you spent the entire day with some Netherese chiming-ball *child's* toy, trying to make it roll by itself!"

"As it was meant to do," Beldrune of the Bent Finger replied, looking hurt. "Is that not why we labor here thus, Baerast? Is restoring and making sense of the scraps of elder magic not an exalted calling? Doth not Holy Mystra Herself smile betimes upon us?"

"Yes, yes, and aye besides," Tabarast said dismissively, waving away the argument like three-day-old feast table scraps. "Though I doubt overmuch if she was impressed by a failed effort to resurrect a toy." He hefted the last support bar. "Yet, passing on from that trifle, let us recollect together."

He thrust the last bar into its socket, settled it with a slap, and turned to the vast and uneven table that filled most of the room, in several places almost touching the massive and crammed bookshelves ranked along the walls.

Sixty or more untidy piles of tomes rose here and there from a carpet of scrolls, scraps of old parchment, and more recent notes that completely covered the table; in places the writings were three layers deep. The papers were held flat by a motley assortment of gems, ornate and aged rings, scraps of intricate wire or wrought metal that had once been parts of larger items, candle-topped skulls, and stranger things.

The two mages thrust out their hands above the pages and moved them in slow circles, as if a tingling in their fingertips would locate a passage they were seeking. Tabarast said slowly, "Cordorlar, writing in the failing days of Netheril . . . the dragonsblood experiments . . ." His hand shot out to grasp a particular parchment. "Here!"

Beldrune, frowning, said, "I was tracing a triple-delayed-blast fireball magic some loosejaw named Olbert claimed to have made by combining earlier magics from Lhabbartan, Iliymbrim Sharnult, and—and . . . *agghh*, the name's gone now." He looked up. "So tell me: *what* dragonsblood experiments? Stirring the stuff into potions? Drinking it? Setting it aflame?"

"Introducing it into one's own blood in hopes that it would bring a human wizard longevity, increased vigor, the same immunity to certain perils that some dragons enjoy, or even full-blown draconic powers," Tabarast replied. "Various mages of the time claimed to have enjoyed successes in all of those areas. Not that any of them survived or left later evidence we've found yet, to bear out any such claims." He sighed. "We've *got* to get into Candlekeep."

Beldrune smote his forehead and said, "That again? Baerast, I agree, wholeheartedly and with every waking scrap of my brain. We do indeed have to be able to look at the tomes in Candlekeep—but we need to do so freely, whenever thoughts take us hence, not in a single or skulking visit. I somehow doubt they'll accept us as the new co-Keepers of Candlekeep if we march in there and demand such access."

It was Tabarast's turn to frown. "True, true," he said with a sigh. "Wherefore we've got to make the most of these salvaged scraps and forgotten oddments."

He sighed again. "No matter how untruthful and incomplete they may be."

He poked at one yellowing parchment with an almost accusatory forefinger, adding, "This worthy claimant boasts of *eating* an entire dragon, platter by platter. It took him a season, he says, and he hired the greatest cooks of the time to make it palatable fare by trading them its bones and scales. I began to doubt him when he said it was his *third* such dragon, and that he preferred red dragon meat to the flesh of blue dragons."

Beldrune smiled. "Ah, Baerast," he said. "Still clinging to this romantic delusion that folk who go to the trouble of writing are superior sorts who always set down the truth? Some folk lie even to their own diaries."

He waved at the ceiling and walls around them and added, "When all this was new, do you think the Netherese who dwelt or worked here were the great paragons some sages claim them to be—wiser than we, more mighty in all ways than the folk of today, and able to work almost any magic with a snap of the fingers? Not a bit of it! They were like us—a few bright minds, a lot of lazy-wits, and a few dark and devious twisters of truth who worked on folk around them to make others do as they desired. Sound familiar?"

Tabarast plucked up a falcon's head carved from a single palm-sized emerald an age ago and stroked its curved beak absently.

"I grant your point, Droon, yet I ask myself: what follows? Are we doomed to wallow in distortions and untruths as the years pass, with but seventeen spells to show for it—*seventeen?*"

Beldrune spread his hands. "That's seventeen more magics than some mages craft in a lifetime of working the Art," he reminded his colleague mildly. "And we share a task both of us love—and, moreover, are granted the occasional *personal* reward from Herself, remember?"

"How do we know She sends those dream-visions?" Tabarast said in a low voice. "How do we really know?"

Moonshorn Tower shook all around them for the briefest of instants, with a deep rumbling sound; somewhere a stack of books collapsed with a crash.

Beldrune smiled crookedly and said, "That's good enough for me. What do you want Her to do, Baerast? Dole out a spell a night, written across our brains in letters of everlasting fire?"

Tabarast snorted. "There's no need to be ridiculous, Droon." Then he smiled almost wistfully, and added, "Letters of fire would be nice, though, just once."

"Old cynic," the younger mage responded with an air of offended pomposity, "I am *never* ridiculous. I merely afford a degree of jollity that has never failed to please even more discerning audiences than yourself, or should I say *especially* more discerning audiences than yourself."

Tabarast mumbled something, then added more loudly, "This is why we accomplish so little, as the hours and days pass unheeded. Clever words, *clever words* we catch and hurl like small boys at skulltoss, and the work advances but little."

Beldrune gestured at the table. "So take up some new scrap, and let's begin," he challenged. "Today we'll work together rather than pursuing separate ends and see if the Lady smiles on us. Do start, old friend, and I shall keep us to the matter at hand. In this my vigilance shall be steadfast, but as nothing to my wroth."

"Isn't that 'wrath,' m'boy?" Tabarast asked, his hand hovering once more above the table.

"Lesser beings, dearest mage of my regard, may well indulge in wrath—I feel wroth," Beldrune replied loftily, then added with a snarl, "Now take up a paper, and let's be about it!"

Tabarast blinked in astonishment and took up a paper."—'That so surpasseth all mine previous . . . other mages decry such . . . Yet will I prevail, the truth being my guide and guardian,' methinks, methinks, methinks, ho ho hum . . . Hmmm. Someone writing in the South, before Myth Drannor but probably not all that long before, about a spell to put a mage's wits and all in the body of a beast, to make it prowl at his bidding for a night, or stay longer or forever within it should his own body be threatened or lost."

"Good, good," Beldrune responded. "Could it be Alavaernith, in the early days of working on his 'Threecats' spell? Or is it too effusive for that?"

"I suspect someone other than Alavaernith," Tabarast said slowly. "He was never so open with his secrets as this. . . ."

Neither of them noticed a red-eyed, hawk-nosed man step into the room and lean for a moment against the door sill with an air of utter weariness, looking around at everything as he listened to them.

"And does he say anything useful?" Beldrune pressed. "Or can we cast this aside on the heap in the barrel?"

Tabarast peered at the page, turned it over to make sure the back was blank, held it to the light seeking oddities in (or hidden under) the writing, and finally handed it to his colleague with a sound that was half sigh and half snort. "Nothing useful, beyond telling us what someone was working on or had thought of back then. . . ."

The hawk-nosed man stepped forward to peer at the gilt-lettered spines of tomes wedged tightly into the nearest bookshelf, then looked over at the table and carefully turned over a twisted, crumpled cage of wrought metal that had probably once held the shape of a globe. Examining it carefully, the stranger set it softly back down and peered at the writings beneath it.

"Now, *this* one," Tabarast said slowly, bent over the other side of the table, "is rather more interesting. No, we shan't be hurling this into the barrel quite so quickly." He held it up under his nose as he straightened, then paused as Elminster's boot made a slight sound and the dark-haired mage asked, "How goes it, Mardasper? Keeping an *eye* on things, as usual, hmmm?"

When there was no reply, he turned, and both mages stared across the room at the newcomer—who gave them a polite nod and smile, looked for a moment at an old and brittle scroll on the table, then stepped sideways, seeking more interesting writings.

Tabarast and Beldrune frowned at the stranger in unison, then turned their backs, drew in side by side, and continued their investigations in muttered tones.

El gave their eloquent backs and shoulders a wry, exhausted smile, then shrugged and peered at another parchment. It was something about crafting a spike-studded torture coffin so that folk latched into it were teleported elsewhere rather than suffering impalement, and it was written with that squaring of the letters that marked its origin as the south shore of the Sea of Fallen Stars. The glint of metallic inks shone back at him, and the page had reached that soft brown state just before crumbling begins . . . as old as he was, or older. El looked at the next page, sliding aside a Netherese ocular to do it.

He gave the beautiful item a second glance. The enchantments that would affix it over a wearer's eye were gone, but the gem would still, by the looks of it, afford vision of heat, and even through wood or stone a handspan thick or less. With the curled filigree around it, it looked like a giant, elegant tear that would glisten endlessly on a lady's cheek.

What a lot of work. Crafting far in excess of its usefulness, done for the sheer joy of mastering the Art and creating something that would last . . . and there must be a thousand times a thousand such items, scattered all over a world so rich in natural magic that all of them could be said to be frivolities.

And was Elminster Aumar, in truth, one more frivolity?

Perhaps, and perhaps he was destined to leave behind little more than these endless dusty scraps of parchment, the confused and unfinished ideas of centuries . . . yet that flow of mistakes and vain strivings and occasional triumphs or destructive disasters *was* the Art, with Mystra the gatekeeper of the Weave from which it all came and to which it all returned.

Enough. He was standing in a parchment-littered room in Moonshorn Tower, here and now, and the flow of magics or the very nature of Art were alike in their irrelevance. His world was a place of hunger, and thirst, feeling cold or hot—or feeling so gods-spitting tired that he could -barely keep his eyes open an instant longer.

Wait! There—he'd seen *that* writing before. The fine, flowing hand of Elenshaer, who'd been so good at crafting new and unusual wardings in Myth Drannor—until he'd been torn apart by a Phaerimm he'd rashly caged in too-feeble spells to do a little experimentation . . . a victim, some would say, of that arrogant assumption of elven superiority and of the ethical right to transform, mutilate, or tamper with "lesser beings," even if they're not truly lesser beings, that afflicts so many of his race. An unfortunate moment of misjudgment and another of carelessness, others would term it. And who was to say which view was right or if any of it truly mattered? Seeing the slender elf laughing and gesturing, fluted wineglass in hand, in his memory of a terrace that no longer stood, amid folk who no longer lived, El slid aside other writings to expose all of Elenshaer's missive.

It was a spell, of sorts. Or rather, the beginnings of a "hook" of Art that would allow an additional power to be added to an existing ward by the casting of another spell into the invisible hook—which would then draw the spell into the weaving of the ward and permit the caster to govern and adjust its effects. Elminster read the spell over silently until it approached its ending and stopped.

Elenshaer had followed a common elf mages' practice. He'd set down the crowning part of the casting on another paper, kept elsewhere. His abode would have held thousands of such papers, with Elenshaer's memory as the only link of what paper went with which. There'd even been a rogue mage in the City of Song, Twillist, who'd sought power by pilfering such "ends" of spells, trading them to young apprentices and others eager for more knowledge and power in exchange for lesser, but whole, magics.

The missing ending was almost obvious to a mage who'd had a hand in crafting mythals and studied with Cormanthan elves. A summation or linking bridge, probably "*Tanaethaert shurruna rae,*" a shaping gesture—thus—mirrored immediately and incorporated into the incantation with the utterance of "*Rahrada,*" then the declaration that would make the hook recede into the ward-weave and give its caster control of the spell effects it brought with it: "*Dannaras ouuhilim rabreivra, tonneth ootaha la, tabras torren ouliirym torrin, dalarabban yultah.*" A concluding gesture—thus—and it would be done.

He'd spoken those words aloud, though near—soundlessly, and was startled when something spun into being in the air before him, a little more than the length of his hand above Elenshaer's incomplete spell. A little glowing construction hung in the air above the page: lines of fire looping into a tiny knot that began to rotate as he watched it, to spin endlessly and silently.

Sigh. If there was such a thing as a needless magic, this was it. Unthinkingly he'd broken Mystra's decree, after enduring so much discomfort and danger to keep it. Gods *blast!*

As if that silent, savage thought had been a cue, the hook he'd created commenced to spit tiny sparks at the parchment beneath it. Oh, that was all he needed! In a room such as this, with dry and dusty paper inches deep on everything. . . .

His hands were already darting to shield the thickly strewn parchments against the sparks . . . too late. They landed, hopped, and—

Formed glowing words that were overlaying Elenshaer's writing as they advanced before his astonished eyes, leaving no smoke or sign of conflagration in their wake.

Leave. Now. Seek the Riven Stone.

The message flashed once, as if to make sure that he read it, blazed brightly, then slowly began to fade away.

El read them one more time and swallowed. He could barely stand, but the command couldn't be much clearer; he must leave this place without delay. He raised his head and looked regretfully around at all the lore he'd not be able to poke around in, now. No more sparks fell from the tiny whirling hook, and the two old wizards were still hunched against him on the far side of the room, mumbling secrets to each other so he'd not hear.

He looked down at the letters of magical flame again, found them just fading into invisibility, and watched until they were quite gone. Then he gave the room a deep, soundless sigh, followed it with a rueful grin, and crept out as softly as the thief in Hastarl he'd once been.

After the fourth page of unrelated lore, Tabarast murmured, "Will you look behind us and see where this stranger has got to? If he's wandered back to the door, or out of it, this guarding of tongues shall cease forthwith. I feel like a guilty servant gossiping in an outhouse."

"How can we discuss things if we can't speak freely?" Beldrune agreed, performing an elaborately casual glance back over his shoulder at the littered table. Then he swung right around, and said, "Baerast, he's gone."

Something in the younger mage's tone made Tabarast's head snap up. He turned around, too, to stare across the room where they'd labored for so long, and find it empty of strange mages, but now home to—

"The sign!" Beldrune gasped, voice unsteady in awe. "The sign! A Chosen was here among us!"

"After all these years," Tabarast murmured huskily, almost dazed. In an instant his life and his faith and all Toril around him had changed. "Who can it have been? That beak-nosed youngster? We must follow him!"

Slowly, as if they dared not disturb it, the two old mages advanced around the table. By unspoken agreement they walked in opposite directions, to come upon the spinning sigil from different directions—as if it might escape if they didn't pounce.

The little whirling knot of blazing lines was still there when they met in front of it to gape at it in awe. "It matches the vision completely," Tabarast murmured, as if there'd been some possibility of a mistake or counterfeit. "There can be no doubt."

He looked around the room at their piled, cluttered years of work. "I'm going to miss all of this," he said slowly.

"I'm not!" Beldrune replied, almost bowling the older mage over in his rush for the door. "Adventure—at last!"

Tabarast blinked at his fast-receding colleague and said, "Droon? Are you mad? This is exciting, yes, but our road's just beginning—it'll be a hard fall for you soon, if you're dancing this high in glee right now."

"The Dark Gods take your gloom, Baerast—we're going *adventuring!*" Beldrune shouted back up the stairway.

Tabarast winced and started descending steps, a sour expression settling onto his face. "You've never been on an adventure before, have you?"

Years of travel had made the hard-packed mud lane between Aerhiot's Field and Salopar's Field sink down into its own ditch, until now the tangled hedges almost met overhead, as disturbed birds and squirrels fretted and darted along in the perpetual gloom whenever anyone ventured along the lane.

The oxen were used to it, and so was Nuglar. He trudged along half asleep with his goad-stick in the crook of his arm, not expecting to have to use it, while the three massive beasts ambled along ahead of him, also half-asleep, hardly bothering to switch their tails against the biting buzzflies.

Something chimed nearby. Nuglar lifted one heavy eyelid and turned his head to see what could be making the sound . . . a wandering lamb, perhaps, collared with one of those tiny toy bells the priests of the Mother hung down their aspergilla? Several younglings?

He could see nothing but a sort of white, sparkling mist in the air, whirling tongues of it that trailed the chiming. It was all around him now, loud and somehow cruel, settling around him like a cold shawl . . . and around the oxen. One of them sobbed in sudden alarm as the chiming mist became a howling, tightening whirlwind encircling it.

Nuglar shouted, or thought he did, and stretched out a hand to that ox's rump—only to feel a deathly, searing chill, numbing in an instant like icy winter water. He drew back his arm.

It was a stump, blood streaming from where his hand should have been. He opened his mouth to scream, and a wisp of that deadly whirlwind spun out of nowhere to plunge down his throat.

Less than a breath later, Nuglar's jawbone dropped away from a wavering, wind-scoured skull—an instant before his skeleton collapsed into whirling dust, whipped together into crumbling oblivion with the three oxen.

With a loud, triumphant chorus of chiming, like many exultant bells being rung together, a larger, brighter whirlwind rose out of the lane and poured itself across Aerhiot's Field, leaving the muddy lane empty of all but a stout, well-worn goad-stick. It danced in the air in the whirling wake of the chiming mist for an eerie moment, then fell to the mud for other frightened farmers to find later.

A long time passed in the gloomy lane before squirrels meekly scampered and the birds dared to sing again.

The Riven Stone must be a place, or more likely a landmark—a rock cloven by a spring or winter ice. A feature he'd never heard of, but then there was a lot of Faerûn he knew nothing about, yet.

Was Mystra going to make him walk over every stride of it?

Almost reeling in exhaustion, Elminster trudged up a grassy slope, trying to keep in sight of the road that had brought him to the Tower . . . and was now taking him on away from it. Leaving the tower had been a matter of flat urgency, aye, but the Lady—or Azuth, speaking for her—knew he'd have to search for the Riven Stone. Well, then, he couldn't be expected to find it immediately.

That was good, because he could barely find the strength to put one foot in front of another any longer. El took another two clumsy steps, found himself sliding back down the slope to the roadside, stumbled, and a short rushing while later, fetched up hard against a duskwood tree.

It felt good to lean against the comforting bulk of the tree, when he was so gods-forsaken *weary* . . . bark burned against his cheek, and El caught himself halfway along a sliding fall. Sprawling a-snore in the road wouldn't be a wise thing, in this land of daggers ready for unprotected throats.

There was no branch handy to cling to, to climb the tree or even keep himself on his feet . . . and speaking of that, his knees were starting to buckle . . . ah, but wait. What had the Srinshee taught him about a treeshaping spell? Some simple change in the incantation of one of the spells he was carrying; Thoaloat's Variant, aye, that's what it had been called. "Doabro Thoaloat was a wily old goat"—and that little rhyme brought back the memory he needed: the change was *thus*.

It was possible that Elminster snored gently twice or thrice during the incantation, but the duskwood that appeared an instant later, leaning against an identical duskwood that had been there rather longer, preferred deep silence to snoring, and so peace fell by the roadside.

When he was in the steward's chamber, the wards always warned him. They almost blazed in great measure of approaching magic, this time, so Mardasper was through the door and standing behind his lectern with the diadem on his head, its eyepiece over his accursed eye, and the Lady Scepter on his head before the door opened—without any knock—and an elf mage stepped within, cloak swirling around him, and the gems set into the staff of living wood in his hand winking on and off in an ever-changing display. The elf met the steward's eye, let go of the staff—it hung upright in the air, its lights continuing to wink and twinkle—and watched for Mardasper's reaction with the faintest of sneers playing about his thin lips.

The steward took care not to look impressed or even interested and managed to add a faint air of dismissal to his visual examination of the newcomer. With elves, status and control were always issues. Push-push-shove, disdain, sniff, sneer . . . well, not this day, by Holy Mystra! He looked young, but Mardasper knew that even without spells to alter the body or appearance, one of the Fair Folk could look this green and vigorous for centuries. He looked haughty—but then they all did, didn't they?

"Well met," he said, in carefully neutral tones. "Be it known that I am Mardasper, guardian of this shrine of Holy Mystra. Have you business here, traveler?"

"I do," the elf said coldly, stepping forward. The steward willed the eyepiece to lift and gave the newcomer the full benefit of his blazing gaze. The elf slowed, eyes narrowing a trifle, then came to a smooth halt, hand not—quite—touching the butts of a trio of wands sheathed at his hip.

Mardasper resisted the urge to smile tightly and asked carefully, "You venerate Holy Mystra, Lady of All Mysteries?" He used the diadem to truth-read, saving his own spells for any unpleasantness that might prove necessary.

The elf hesitated. "Betimes," he said at last, and that was truth. Mardasper suspected the newcomer meant that he'd gone on his knees to Mystra a time or two in conditions of great privacy, in hopes of gaining an edge over rival elf mages. No matter; here, it would suffice.

"All who enter here," the guardian said, raising the tip of the Lady Scepter just enough to make an elven eye flicker, "must obey me utterly and work no magic unbidden. Anyone who takes or damages even the smallest thing from within these walls forfeits his life, or at the least his freedom. You may rest within, and take water from the fount, but no food or anything else is provided—and you must surrender to me your name, and all written magic and enchanted items you carry, no matter how small or benign. They will be returned upon your departure."

"I think not," the elf said scornfully. "I've no intention of ever becoming any man's slave, nor of yielding items entrusted to me, long venerated in my family, into the hands of anyone else—least of all a *human*. Do you know who I am, steward?"

"One of the Fair Folk, almost certainly a mage and probably of Cormanthan lineage, on the young side—and greatly lacking in both prudence and diplomacy," Mardasper replied bleakly. "Is there more I should know?" He caused the spell-gems on the diadem to awaken and flicker, reinforcing them with the aroused dazzle of the scepter. We may not all have blinking staves, youngling, he thought, but . . .

Elven eyes flashed green with anger and that thin mouth tightened like the jaws of a steel trap, but the elf said merely, "If I cannot proceed freely—no."

Mardasper shrugged, lifting his arms from the lectern to call the intruder's attention to the Lady Scepter once more. He did not want a spell battle even against a feeble foe, and he didn't need the ward-warnings or the hovering staff to tell him this was no feeble foe.

The elf shrugged elaborately, made his cloak swirl as he ostentatiously turned to go, and let his gaze fall way from the steward as if the man with the scepter were a piece of crumbling statuary. In doing so, his eyes fell across the open register—and suddenly blazed as brightly as Mardasper's own accursed eye.

The elf whirled around again, surging forward like a striking snake—and Mardasper practically thrust the Scepter into his nose, snapping, "Have a *care*, sir!"

"This man!" the elf spat, stabbing a daggerlike finger onto the last name entered in the book. "*Is he still here?*"

Mardasper looked into that incandescent gaze from inches away, trying to keep the fear out of his own eyes and knowing he was failing. He swallowed once then said—his voice surprisingly calm in his own ears—"No. He visited only briefly, this morn, departing not long ago. Headed west, I believe."

The elf snarled like an angry panther and whirled away again, heading for the door. The staff followed him, trailing black spell flames, two large green gems in its head coming alight to look uncannily like eyes.

"Would you like to leave a message for this Elminster, if he should stop at the tower again?" Mardasper asked in the grandest, most doom-laden voice he could manage, as the elf practically tore the door open. "Many do."

The elf turned in the doorway, and let the staff fly into his hand before he snapped, "Yes! Tell him Ilbryn Starym seeks him and would be pleased to find him prepared for our meeting." Then he stormed out, the door booming shut behind him. Its rolling thunders told the tale of the violence of its closing.

Mardasper stared at it until the wards told him the elf was gone. Then he ran a hand across his sweat—beaded brow and almost collapsed across the lectern in relief.

The Lady Scepter flashed once, and he almost dropped it. That had been a sign, for sure—but had it been one of reassurance? Or something else?

Mardasper shook the scepter slightly, hoping for something more, but, as he'd expected, nothing more happened. Ahh, tear in the Weave! Blast! By Mystra's Seven Secret Spells—!

He snarled incoherently for a moment, but resisted the urge to hurl the scepter. The last steward of Moonshorn Tower who'd done that had ended up as ashes paltry enough to fit in a man's palm. His, actually. Mardasper went back into his office under a heavy weight of gloom. Had he done the right thing? What did Mystra think of him? Should he have tried to stop the elf? Should he have allowed this Elminster fellow in at all? Of course the man couldn't have been *the* Elminster, the One Who Walks, could he? No, that one must be ancient by now, and only Mystra's—

Mardasper swallowed. He was going to fret over this all night and for days to come. He knew he was.

He set down the diadem and the scepter with exaggerated care, then sat back in his chair, sighed, and stared at the dark walls for a time. The priests of Mystra had been quite specific: a day in which strong drink of any sort passed his lips did not count in the marking of his service here.

Indeed. Quite deliberately he pulled out the three thick volumes at one end of the nearest bookshelf, reached into the darkness beyond, and came out with a large, dusty bottle. To the Abyss and beyond with the priests of Mystra and their niggling rules, too!

"Mystra," he asked aloud, as he uncorked the bottle, "how badly did I do?"

In his fingertips, the cork shone like a bright star for the briefest of instants—and shot back into the bottle so violently that his fingers and thumb were left bleeding and numb. Mardasper stared at them for a moment, then carefully put the bottle away again.

"So was that good . . . or bad?" he asked the gloom in bewilderment. "Oh, *where* are the priests when I need them?"

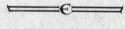

"Whoah!" Tabarast cried. "*Woaaaaah—*" His cry ended in a thump as his behind met the road hard, hurling dust in all directions. The mule came to a stop a pace farther on, gave him a reproachful look, and then stood waiting with a mournful air.

Beldrune sniggered as he overtook his winded colleague, urging it on with a small, feather-plumed whip, his splendid boots outthrust like tusks on either side of his mule. "You seem quite fond of fertile Faerûn beneath us this day, friend Baerast!" he observed jovially—an instant before his mule came to an abrupt stop beside the one Tabarast had lately been riding.

Overbalanced, Beldrune toppled helplessly over his mount's head with a startled yell, somersaulting onto the road with an impressive crash that made Tabarast wince, then sputter with repressed mirth as the two mules exchanged glances, seemed to come to some sort of agreement, and with one accord stepped forward, trampling the groaning Beldrune under hoof.

His groans turned to yells of rage and pain, and he flailed wildly with his arms until he was free of unwashed mule bodies and mud-caked mule hooves. "A rescue!" he cried. "For the love of Mystra, a rescue!"

"Get up," Tabarast said grimly, pulling at his hair. "This Chosen must be half the way to wherever he's going by now, and we can't even stay in the saddles of two smallish mules, by the Wand! Get *up*, Droon!"

"*Arrrgh!*" Beldrune yelled. "Let go of my hair!"

Tabarast did as he was bidden—and Beldrune's head fell back onto the road with a thump that sounded like a smaller echo of the one Tabarast had made earlier. The younger mage launched into a long and incoherent curse, but Tabarast ignored him, limping ahead to catch the bridles of their mules before the beasts got over the next rise in the road, and clean away.

"I've brought back your mule," he said to the still-snarling body on its back in the road. "I suggest we walk beside them for a time . . . we both seem to be a little out of practice at riding."

"If you mean we've been falling off all too often," Beldrune snarled, "then we are out of practice—but we won't get back in practice unless we mount up and ride!"

Suiting the action to the words, he hauled himself into the saddle of Tabarast's mule, hoping the change of mount would improve his ride a trifle.

The mule swiveled one eye to take in Tabarast standing beside it and someone else loudly occupying its back and didn't budge.

Beldrune yelled at it and hauled on the reins as if he was dragging in a monstrous fish. The mule's head was jerked up and back, but it started trying to twist the reins out of Beldrune's grasp, or draw them into its mouth by repeated chomping, rather than move even a single step forward.

Beldrune drew back his heels, wishing he was wearing spurs, and kicked the beast's flanks as hard as he could. Nothing happened, so he kicked again.

The mule shot forward, leaping up into the air and twisting as it did so.

Beldrune went over backward with what might have been a despairing sob, landed hard on one shoulder, and rolled helplessly back down the road. His splendid doublet was rapidly becoming a dung-stained rag as he tumbled along an impressive length of road before negotiating contact—a solid, leaf-shaking collision, to be precise—with one of a pair of duskwood trees by the roadside.

Tabarast snatched at the reins of the growling mule—until now, he hadn't known mules *could* growl—made sure he still had hold of the other mule's bridle, and looked back down the road. "Finished playing at bold knights on horseback?" he snapped. "We're on an important mission, remember?"

An upside-down Beldrune, who'd been staring at his booted feet a good way up the tree, above him, looked back at his colleague groggily for a moment, then slowly unfolded himself back into the road. When he was upright again, he raked showers of dust from his hair with one hand—wincing at the pains in his back this activity caused—and snarled, "With all the shouting you're doing, it's a safe bet that Elminster isn't within forty farms of here!"

The tree seemed to flicker for a moment, but neither of the two esteemed mages noticed.

SIX
AT THE RIVEN STONE

Let stones be riven and the world be changed,
When next two such as these meet,
With howling chaos in the sky
And deception a gliding serpent round their feet.

AUTHOR UNKNOWN
FROM THE BALLAD "MANY MEETINGS"
COMPOSED SOMETIME BEFORE THE YEAR OF THE TWELVERULE

Sunlight stabbed down, and Elminster smiled. He was still in lands he'd never seen before, but more than one farmer along this rising road had assured him he was heading toward the Riven Stone.

Out of habit El glanced back to see if anyone was following him, then up at the sky; taking bird-shape had been a favorite tactic of elf mages who didn't look with friendly eyes on the first human who'd walked into their cozy midst, and changed Cormanthyr forever. Right now, however, both places seemed empty of foes—or any living creature, for that matter.

Briefly El wondered how far along the road those two bumbling mages had gotten to yestereve on their recalcitrant mules. He chuckled. The way Mystra's whims ran, no doubt he'd find out soon enough.

The sky was blue and clear, and a brisk wind blew just this side of chilly; a grand day for walking, and the last prince of Athalantar was enjoying it. Rolling farm fields with rubblestone walls spread out on either side of the road; here and there, boulders too big to be moved thrust up out of the tillage like tomb markers or the snouts of gigantic, petrified monsters of the underearth. . . .

He was obviously remembering too many bards' ballads, and too few hours of plowing and haying. The air had that wet, earthy smell of fresh-plowed land, and if a certain Athalantan had to walk Toril alone, days like these at least made one feel alive and not a doddering survivor staggering toward a waiting grave.

The laughter of swift rushing water came to Elminster's ears from off to the left, and over the brow of the next rise its source came into view. A stream rushed past, cutting away across the fields in a small, deep-cut gorge. Ahead, it ran beside the road for a time, in its fall from what had to be a mill.

Ah, good. According to the last farmer, this must be Anthather's Mill. A tall fieldstone building, towering over a fork in the road. A fork, of course, which was bereft of any signs.

The stream rushed out of the pool below the mill dam, a creaking wheel turning endlessly in its wake. Men smudged white with flour were loading a cart by the roadside, adding bulging sacks to an already impressive pile. The horses were going to have a hard pull. One of the men saw El and murmured something. All of the men looked up, took their measure of the stranger, and looked back to their work, none of them halting in the hefting, tossing and heaving for a moment.

El spread his hands to show that he meant to draw no weapon, stopping beside the nearest man. "Well met," he said. "I seek the Riven Stone, and know not my road from here."

The man gave him an odd look, pointed up the left-hand road, and said, "'Tis easy enough to find, aye—straight along that, a good stride, until you're standing in the middle of it. But yon's just a stone, mind; there's nothing there."

El shrugged and smiled. "I go following a vow, of sorts," he said. "Have my thanks."

The miller nodded, waved, and looked down for the next sack. Somewhat reassured, Elminster strode on.

It took some hours of walking, but the Riven Stone was clear enough. Tall and as black as pitch, it rose out of scrub woods in a huge, helmlike cone—cloven neatly in half, with the road running through the gap. There were no farms nearby, and El suspected the Stone enjoyed the usual "haunted" or otherwise fell reputation such landmarks always attracted—if they weren't deemed holy by one faith or another.

No sigils, altars, or signs of habitation met his view as he came around the last bend and saw just how large the stone was. The cleft must have been six man-heights deep or more, and the way through it was long and dim. The inside surfaces of the stone were wet with seeping groundwater, and the faintest of mists drifted underfoot there in the gap.

There, where someone was standing awaiting him. Mystra provides.

Elminster walked steadily on into the gap, a pleasant smile on his face despite the stirrings in him that his freedom to wander would end here—and darker forebodings.

Those misgivings were not lessened by what met his eyes. The figure ahead was human and very female. Alone and cloakless, dark-gowned, tall and sleek of figure; in a word, dangerous.

Had Elminster been standing in a certain dark hall in Tresset's Ringyl as a scepter fell to dust, rather than panting on a hilltop over the remains of a stag-headed shadow, he'd have seen this beautiful, dark-eyed sorceress before. As it was, he was looking into a pair of proud, cold dark eyes—did they hold a hint of mischief? Or was that suppressed mirth . . . or triumph?—for the first time.

Her legs, in black boots, were almost impossibly long. Her glossy black hair fell in an unbound flood that was longer. Her skin was like ivory, her features fine; just the pleasant side of angular. She carried herself with serene fearlessness, one long-fingered hand playing almost idly with a wand. Aye, trouble. The sort of sorceress folk cowered away from.

"Well met," she said, making of those words both a challenge and a husky promise, as her eyes raked him leisurely from muddy boots to untidy hair. "Do you work"—her tongue darted into view for an instant between parted lips—"magic?"

Elminster kept his gaze steady on those dark eyes as he bowed. Mindful of Azuth's directive, he replied, "A little."

"Good," the dark lady replied, making the word almost a caress. She moved the wand in her hand ever so slightly to catch his eyes, smiled, and said, "I'm looking for an apprentice. A *faithful* apprentice."

El didn't fill the silence she left after those words, so she spoke again, just a trifle more briskly. "I am Dasumia, and you are—?"

"Elminster is my name, Lady. Just Elminster." Now for the polite dismissal. "I believe my days as an apprentice are over. I serve—"

Silver fire suddenly surged inside him, its flare bringing back an image of the cracked stone ceiling of the best bedchamber in Fox Tower, and words of silver fire writing themselves across the ceiling, vivid in the darkness: "Serve the one called Dasumia." El swallowed.

"—ye, if ye'll have me," he concluded his sentence, aware of amused dark eyes staring deep into his soul. "Yet I must tell ye: I serve Holy Mystra first and foremost."

The dark-eyed sorceress smiled almost lazily. "Yes, well—we all do," she said coyly, "don't we?"

"I'm sorry, Lady Dasumia," Elminster said gravely, "but ye must understand . . . I serve Her more closely than most. I am the One Who Walks."

Dasumia burst into silvery gales of laughter, throwing her head back and crowing her mirth until it echoed back off the stony walls flanking the two mages. "I'm sure you are," she said when she could speak again, gliding forward to pat Elminster's hand. "Do you know how many young mages seeking a reputation come to me claiming to be the One Who Walks? Well, I'll tell you—a dozen this last month, fully two score the month before that, snows and all, and one before you so far *this* month."

"Ah," Elminster replied, drawing himself up, "but they none of them were as handsome as me, were they?"

She burst out laughing again and impulsively hugged him. "A dream-vision told me to look for my apprentice here—but I never thought I'd find one who could make me laugh."

"Then ye'll have me?" El asked, giving no sign that he'd sensed her hug delivering many probing magics. More than one warm stirring in his innards told him Mystra's silver fire was hard at work countering hostile attempts to control and influence—and to leave behind at least three means of slaying him instantly by her uttering trigger words. Ah, but it was a wonderful thing to be a wizard. Almost as marvelous as being a Chosen.

Dasumia gave him a smile that held rather more triumph than welcome. "Body and soul I'll have you," she murmured. "Body and soul." She whirled away from him and looked back over her shoulder to purr provocatively, "Which shall we sample first, hmmm?"

"Now, *really*, Droon! I ask you: would we have had such widespread mastery of magic, such legions of capable or nearly capable mages, from sea unto sea and to the frozen wastes and uttermost east, if Myth Drannor still stood proud? Or would we have had closed, elite ranks of those who dwelt or had free admittance to the City of Song—and the rest of us left to fight for what scraps the glittering few deigned to toss to us, or that we could plunder from old tombs—and the liches lurking in them?" Tabarast turned in his saddle to make a point, almost fell out of it despite the tangle of sashes and belts he'd lashed himself on with, and thought it prudent to face forward again, merely gesturing airily with one hand. His mule sighed and kept on plodding.

"Come, come! We speak not of gems, Baerast," Beldrune replied, "nor yet cabbages—but magic! The Art! A ferrago of ideas, a feast of enchantments, an endless flood of new approaches and—"

"Free-flowing nonsense spoken by young mages," the older mage retorted. "Surely even you, young Droon, have seen enough years to know that generosity—truly open giving, not to an apprentice one can keep beholden or even spell-thralled—is a quality rarer and less cultivated in the ranks of wizards than in any other assembly of size or import in Faerûn today, save perhaps an orc horde. Pray weary my ears with rather less morology, if it troubles you not overmuch to do so."

Beldrune spread despairing hands. "Is any view that differs from your own but worthless idiocy?" he asked. "Or can it be—panoptic wind trumpet that you are—that some small shred of possibility remains that some truths the gods may not as yet have revealed unto wise old Tabarast, shrewd old Tabarast, *unthinking* old Tab—"

"Why is it that the young always resort so swiftly to personal offenses?" wise old Tabarast asked the world at large, loudly. "Name-calling and ridicule greet arguments that speak to a point, not foremost a person to attack or decry. Such a rude, unsettling approach makes a mountain of every monticule, a pernicious tempest of every chance exchange of remarks, and blackens the names of all who dare to hold recusant views. I disapprove strongly of it, Droon, I do. Such scrannel threats and blusterings are no worthy substitute for well-argued views—and all too often hold up a shield for jejune, even retrorse sciamachy, bereft of sense and waving bright purfle and clever verbiage where meaning has flown!"

"Uh, ah, ahem, yes," Beldrune said weakly. When Tabarast was riled, two words in ten was fair going. "We were speaking of the influence of fabled Myth Drannor on the practice of the Art across all Faerûn, I believe."

"We were," Tabarast confirmed almost severely, urging his mule over the summit of a monticule with a flourish of his tiny riding whip. The fact that it had broken in some past mishap, and now dangled uselessly from a point only inches above the handle, seemed to have utterly escaped his notice.

Beldrune waited for the torrent of grand but largely junkettaceous utterances that invariably accompanied any of Tabarast's observations of simple fact, but for once it did not come.

He raised his eyebrows in wonderment and said nothing as he followed his colleague over the hill. Hipsy—and plenty of it. 'Twas past time for hipsy. He slapped at the grand cloak rolled and belted at his hip, found the reassuring solid smoothness of his flask beneath it, and drew it forth. Tabarast had made this blend, and it was a mite watery for Beldrune's taste, but he didn't want to have to sit through *that* argument again. Next time, it'd be his turn, and there'd be more of the rare and heady concoction he'd heard called "brandy," and less water and wine.

Hmmm. Always assuming they both lived to see a next time. Adventure had seemed a grand thing a day ago—but he'd been thinking more of an adventure without mules. He'd be a hipshot, broken man if they had to ride many more days. Even with all the belts and sashes and lashings—which of course gave the demon-brained beasts a means of *dragging* mages who'd had the misfortune to fall out of their saddles helplessly along in the dirt until they could haul themselves hand-over-hand to the bridles, receiving regular kicks in the process—he'd fallen off more than twenty times thus far today.

Tabarast had managed an even more impressive Faerûn-kissing total, he reflected with a smirk, watching the old wizard bucketing down a steep descent with both legs sticking out like wobbling wings on either side of his patient mount. In another moment, he'd be—

Something that was dark and full of stars rushed past Beldrune like a vengeful wind, dealing his left leg a numbing blow and almost hurling him from his own saddle. He kept aboard the snorting, bucking mule only by digging his hands into its mane like claws and kicking out in a desperate, seesaw fight for balance.

Ahead of him, down the hill, he could see what was bearing down on poor, unwitting Tabarast: a slim, dark-cloaked elven rider bent low in the saddle of a ghostly horse, with a lightning-spitting staff floating along at his shoulder. Beldrune could see right through the silently churning hooves of the conjured mount as the elf swept down on Tabarast, swerved at the last instant to avoid a hard and direct collision, and stormed past, hurling mage and mule together over on their sides.

Beldrune hurried to his colleague's aid as swiftly as he dared, but Tabarast was working some magic or other that hoisted himself and the bewildered, feebly kicking mule upright again, and shouting, "Hircine lout! Lop-eared, fatuous, *rude* offspring of parents who should've known better! Ill-mannered tyrant of the road! *Careless* spellcaster! I shall impart some wisdom to your thumb-sized brain—see if I don't! It almost need not be said that I'll school you in humility—and safe riding—first!"

Ilbryn Starym heard some of those choice words, but didn't even bother to lift his sneer into a smile. *Humans.* Pale, blustering shadows of the one he was hunting. He must be getting close now.

Elminster Aumar—ugly hook nose, insolence *always* riding in the blue-gray eyes, hair as black and lank as that of a wet bear. That familiar, hungry tang rose into Ilbryn's mouth. Blood. He could almost taste the blood of this Elminster, who must die to wash clean the stain his filthy human hands had put on the bright honor of the Starym. As he topped a rise, Ilbryn stood up in the stirrups that weren't there and shouted to the world, "This Elminster must *die!*"

His shout rang back to him from the hilltops, but otherwise the world declined to answer.

Dusk almost always came down like a gentle curtain to close a glorious sunset at Moonshorn. Mardasper liked to be up on the crumbling battlements to see those sunsets, murmuring what words he could remember of lovelorn ballads and the chanted lays of the passing of heroes. It was the only time of the day—barring unpleasant visitors—when he let his emotions out, and dreamed of what he'd do out in Faerûn when his duty here was done.

Mardasper the Mighty he might become, stout-bearded, wise, and respected by lesser mages, rings of power glittering on his fingers as he crafted staves and tamed dragons and gave orders to kings that they dared not disobey.

Or he might rescue a princess or the daughter of a wealthy, haughty noble and ride away with her, using his magic to stay young and dashing but never taking up the robe and staff of a mage, keeping his powers as secret as possible as he carved out a little barony for himself, somewhere green.

Pleasant thoughts, soul-restoring and necessarily private . . . Wherefore Mardasper Oblyndrin was apt to grow very angry when something or someone interrupted his time alone, up on the battlements, to watch another day die into the west. He was angry now.

The wards warned him. The wards always warned him. Raw power, not held in check or under governance, always made them shriek as if in pain. Snarling at the happenstance, Mardasper was thundering down the long, narrow back stair before the intruder could have reached the doorstep. Precipitous it might be, but the back stair led directly to the third door in the entry hall; when the front door was hurled open, to bang against the wall and shudder at the impact, Mardasper was in place behind his lectern, white to his pinched lips and quivering in anger.

He stared out into the gathering night, but no one was there.

"Reveal," he said coldly, uttering aloud what he could have caused the wards to do silently, seeking to impress—or cause fear in—whoever was out there, playing pranks. It took magic of great power to force open the Tower door, with its intertwined glyphs, layers of active enchantments, and the runes set into its frame and graven on its hinges.

Too much power, he would have thought, to burn in any prank.

The wards showed him nothing lurking within their reach. Hmmph; perhaps that nose-in-the-air elf had left a timed magic behind and miscast on the timing. He couldn't think of anything fast enough to smite open a door and leave the reach of the wards so swiftly—and magic mighty enough to breach the door from afar would leave traces behind in the wards. So would a teleport or other translocation. The door's own magics should prevent a spell cast on it from surviving to take effect at any later time . . . so who—or what—had forced the door open?

Mardasper called on the power of the wards to close and seal the mighty door. After it had boomed shut, he stared at it thoughtfully without touching it for a long time, then murmured words he'd never used before, had never thought he'd have to use—the words that would force the awakened ward to expel any magic-wielding sentient in contact with it. The wards blazed white behind his eyes, finding nothing. If spellcasting beings were lurking nearby, they were either well out in the night-shrouded forest—

—or here, in the Tower, inside the wards already.

Mardasper looked at the door and swallowed, his throat suddenly dry. If there was an intruder in Moonshorn, he'd just sealed himself in with it.

Gods above. Well, perhaps it was time to earn his title as Guardian of the Tower. There was a lot of useful—and misunderstood, fragmentary, or forgotten—magic herein; potential realm-shattering weapons in the right unscrupulous hands. "Mystra be with me," he whispered, opened the door that led into the main stair, and started to climb.

The mist chimed only occasionally, and very softly, as it drifted across the parchment-strewn table like an eel ghosting its way among the rocks of an ocean reef. Occasionally it would pounce on a gem or a twisted filigree item placed as a paperweight by Tabarast and Beldrune, and a cold turquoise light would flare briefly. When the power drunk was very strong, the mist would swirl up in triumphant, flamelike bursts of white, winking motes of light that would dance above the table in triumph for a moment before dimming and dwindling into a drifting, serpentine mist once more.

From knickknack to gewgaw it darted, flaring as it drank, and growing ever larger. It was in mid-swirl when the door of the room suddenly opened, and the Guardian of the Tower peered in. Something in here had flashed, spilling a tongue of white light through the keyhole. . . .

Mardasper paused on the threshold and sent a seeking spell rolling out across the room. The mist faded and sank down behind the table, becoming nigh—invisible—and when the spell streamed through it, it allowed itself to be scattered rather than to resist and be found.

The spell washed into every corner of the room, then receded. In its wake, the wind sighed softly back together, not chiming even once.

Mardasper glared into the room, the flame from his blazing eye seeking what his spell could not see. There *must* be someone or something here; translocations wouldn't work inside Moonshorn.

His accursed eye saw it immediately: a breeze that was no breeze, but a living, drifting, incorporeal thing. In furious haste Mardasper lashed at it with a shatterstar spell—a magic designed to rend and burn ghostly and gaseous things.

The expected flames flared up, and the agonized scream with it. But the Guardian of the Tower was unprepared for what followed.

Instead of collapsing into sighing oblivion, the blazing, exploding mist drew together suddenly, rising with terrifying speed into the shape of a human head and shoulders—a head that was only eyes and long hair, trailing down onto a bust.

Mardasper took a pace back; who was this ghost-woman?

Fingers that were more smoke than flesh moved in intricate gestures, trailing the flames of the guardian's spell, and Mardasper frantically tried to think what spell he should use—this ghost that should not be able to withstand his shatterstar was casting magic!

An instant later, the ghostly outline of the sorceress grew a jaw and began to laugh—a high, shrill mirth that was almost lost in the sharp hiss of acid raining down on the guardian . . . and the shrieking death that followed.

Mardasper's melting, smoking bones tumbled to the floor amid a torrent of acid that made the floor erupt in smoke.

Over it all rose a cold, mirthless, triumphant laugh. Some might have judged that wild laughter to be almost a scream, but it had been a long time since the whirlwind had laughed aloud. It was a little out of practice.

SEVEN

DEADLY SPELLS FORBEAR THEE

Evil is no extravagance to those who serve themselves first.

THAELRYTHYN OF THAY
FROM *THE RED BOOK OF A THAYVIAN MAGE*
PUBLISHED CIRCA THE YEAR OF THE SADDLE

It was a cool day in late spring—the third greening of Toril to come and go since two mages had met in the Riven Stone—and the sky was ablaze in red, pink, and gold as the sun, in a leisurely manner, prepared to set. A tower rose like an indigo needle against that sky of flame, and out of the west something small and dark came flying to bank in a wide loop around that tower.

Heads looked up at it: a flying carpet, with two humans seated upon it, their figures dark against the fiery sky wherever the rays of the setting sun hadn't turned them the hue of beaten copper.

"Beautiful, is it not?" Dasumia purred, turning from surveying the tower. A green glint that El had long ago learned presaged danger was dancing in her eyes. She slid forward onto her elbows, cradling her chin in her hands, and regarded the tower with an almost satisfied air.

"Lady, it is," Elminster said carefully.

A teasing eye rolled up to stare into his own orbs. Ye gods, trouble indeed; Mystra defend.

His Lady Master pointed at the tower and said, "A wizard named Holivanter dwells there. A merry fellow; he taught the beasts he summoned to build it all sorts of comical songs and chants. He keeps talking frogs, and even gave a few of them wings with which to fly."

The carpet banked smoothly around the tower on its second orbit of the spire. The tower rose like a fairy-tale needle from neat, green walled gardens. Ruby-hued lamps glimmered in several of its windows, but it seemed otherwise tranquil, almost deserted.

"The house of Holivanter . . . pretty, isn't it?"

"Indeed, Lady," El agreed and meant it.

"Slay him," Dasumia snapped.

El blinked at her. She nodded, and pointed down at the slim tower with an imperious hand.

THE TEMPTATION OF ELMINSTER

601

El frowned. "Lady, I—"

Little flames seemed to flicker in Dasumia's eyes as she locked her gaze with his. One elegant eyebrow lifted.

"A friend of yours?"

"I know him not," El replied truthfully. There was no way he could send a warning, or a defense, or healing; the man was doomed. Why betray himself in futility?

Dasumia shrugged, drew forth a dark, smooth rod from a sheath on her hip, and extended it with languid grace. Something caused the air to curdle in a line, racing down, down . . .

. . . And the upper half of Holivanter's tower burst apart with a roar, spraying the sky with wreckage. Smaller purple, amber, and blue-green blasts followed as various scorched magics within the tower exploded in their turns. El stared at the conflagration as its echoes rolled back from nearby hills, and debris hurtled at them. Blackened fingers spun past the carpet, trailing flame. Holivanter was dead.

Dasumia rolled back onto one hip and propped herself up with one arm, the other toying with the rod. "So tell me," she told the sky, in silken-soft tones that made Elminster stiffen warily, "just why you disobeyed me. Does killing mages come hard to you?"

Fear stirred cold fingers within him. "It seems . . . unnecessary," El replied, choosing his words very carefully. "Does not Mystra say the use of magic should be encouraged, not jealously guarded or hampered?"

Ah, Mystra. Her word had led him here, to serve this beguiling evil. He'd almost forgotten what it felt like to be a Chosen of Mystra, but in his dreams, El often knelt and prayed, or repeated her decrees and advice, fearing it would entirely slip away from him if he did not. Sometimes he feared that the Lady Dasumia was stealing his memories with creeping magic or walling them away behind mists of forgetfulness, to make him entirely her creature. Whatever the cause, it was getting harder, as the months passed, to remember anything of his life before the Riven Stone. . . .

Dasumia laughed lightly. "Ah, I see. The priests of the Lady of Magic say such things, yes, to keep us from slaying thieves who steal scrolls . . . or disobedient apprentices. Yet I pay them little attention. Every mage who can rival me lessens my power. Why should I help such potential foes rise to challenge me? What gain I from that?"

She leaned forward to tap Elminster's knee with the rod. He tried not to look at the little green lights winking into life around it and wandering up and down its length almost lazily. "I've seen you on your knees to Mystra, of nights," she told him. "You pray and plead with her, yes, but tell me: how much does she talk to you?"

"Never, these days," El admitted, his voice as low and as small as the despair he felt. All he had to cling to were his small treacheries, and if she ever discovered those . . .

Dasumia smiled triumphantly. "There you are—alone, left to fend for yourself. If there is a Mystra who takes any interest in mortal mages, she watches while the strong help themselves, over the bodies of the weak. Never forget that, Elminster."

Her voice became more brisk. "I trust your labors haven't faltered in my absence," she commented, sitting up—and raising the rod to point at his face like a ready sword. "How many whole skeletons are ready?"

"Thirty-six," Elminster replied. She lifted that eyebrow again, obviously impressed, and leaned forward to peer into his eyes, dragging his gaze to meet hers by the sheer power of her presence. El tried not to wince or lean away. In some ways, the Lady Dasumia was as, as—well, *awesome* at close quarters and as irresistibly forceful in her presence—as Holy Lady Mystra Herself. How, a small voice in the back of his mind asked, could that possibly be?

"You *have* been hard at work," she said softly. "I'd thought you'd spend some time trying to get into my books and a little more poking around my tower before you got out the shovels. You please me."

El inclined his head, trying to keep satisfaction—and relief—from his face and voice. She must not have discovered his rescue work, then.

With his spells, her most obedient apprentice had healed a servant and whisked him to a land distant, laden with supplies and white with fear. She'd taken the man to her bed but tired of him as the Year of Mistmaidens began, and one morning she had turned him into a giant worm and left him impaled on one of the rusting spits behind the stables to die in slow, twisting agony. El had left the transformed body of a man who'd died of a fever in the servant's place. Restless and reckless meddling, perhaps. Doom-seeking lunacy; that, too. Yet he had to do such things, somehow, working small kindnesses to make up for her large, bold evils.

It hadn't been his first small treachery against her cruelty . . . but there was always the chance that it would be his last. "My honesty has always outstripped my ambition," he said gravely.

Her mockery returned. "A pretty speech, indeed," she said. "I can almost believe you follow Mystra's dictates to the letter."

She stretched like a large cat and used the rod over one shoulder to scratch her back, putting it within easy reach of Elminster. "You must have far more patience than I do," she admitted, her eyes very dark and steady upon him. "I could never serve such an arbitrary goddess."

"Is it permitted to ask whom ye do serve, Lady Master?" El asked, extending his hands in a mute offering to accept the enchanted rod.

She poked at her back once more, smiled, and put the rod into his hands. Two of the rings she wore blinked as she did so.

Dasumia smiled. "A little higher . . . ah, yessss." Her smile broadened as El carefully used the rod to scratch the indicated spot, but she kept her eyes fixed on his hands, and the rings that had winked a moment ago now flickered with a constant flame of readiness.

"It's no secret," she said casually. "I serve the Lord Bane. His gift to me was the dark fire that slays intruders and keeps more cautious mages at bay. Did you know there's some fool of an elf who tests my wards with a new spell every tenday? He's been at it for three seasons now, as regular as the calendar; almost as long as you've been with me." She smiled again. "Perhaps he wants your position. Should I order you to duel him?"

El spreads his hands and said, "If it's your wish, Lady. I'd as soon not slay anyone unnecessarily."

Dasumia stared at him in thoughtful silence for quite a long time as the carpet rushed on away from the smoking stump of the tower and the dying day, and finally murmuring, "And deprive me of the entertainment elven futility brings me? No fear."

She rose up on her knees in a single smooth motion, plucked the rod out of El's hand, resheathed it, and in the same continuous movement reached out with both hands to take hold of his shoulders. Her slender fingertips rested lightly upon him, yet Elminster suddenly felt that if he tried to move out of their grasp, he'd find them to be claws of unyielding iron. In three years, this was the closest contact between them.

He held still as his Lady Master brought her face close to his, their noses almost touching, and said, "Don't move or speak." Her breath was like hot mist on Elminster's cheeks and chin, and her eyes, very dark and very large, seemed to be staring right into the back of his head and seeing every last secret he kept there.

She leaned a little way forward, just for a moment, and their lips met. An imperious tongue parted his own lips—and something that burned and yet was icy raced into his mouth, roaring down his throat and coiling up his nose.

Agony—burning, shuddering, get-away-from-it agony! El sneezed, again and again, clawing at fabric in a desperate attempt to keep from falling, knowing his whole body was shuddering. He was convulsing and sprawling on the carpet, sobbing when he could find breath enough . . . and he was as helpless as a child.

Yellow mists cavorted and flowed before his eyes; the darkening sky overhead kept leaping and turning, and he was thrashing against claws that held him with painful, immovable force.

For what seemed an eternity he coughed and struggled against the yellow haze, drenched with sweat, until utter exhaustion left him able to spasm no more, and he could only lie moaning as the lessening surges of pain ebbed and clawed their ways through him.

He was Elminster. He was as weak as a dried, rolled-up leaf blown in the wind. He was—lying on his back on the flying carpet, and the only thing that had kept him from falling off it in his throes was the iron grip of the sorceress he served, the Lady Dasumia.

Her hands loosened on him, now. One left his bruised bicep—in which it had been sunk inches deep, like an anchor of iron throughout his thrashings—to trail across his brow, thrusting oceans of sweat away.

She bent over him in the gathering gloom of falling night, as the breezes of the lofty sky slid over them both, and said softly, "You have tasted the dark fire. Be warned; if ever you betray me, it shall surely slay you. As long as you worship Mystra more than you revere me, Bane's breath shall be agony to you. Three apprentices, down the years, have kissed me unbidden; none lived to boast of it."

Elminster stared up at her, unable to speak, agony still ruling him. She looked into his eyes, her own orbs two dark fires, and smiled slowly. "Your loyalty, however, outstrips theirs. You shall duel my worst foe for me and best him—when you are ready. You'll have to learn to kill first, though, swiftly and without reckoning the cost. He'll not give you much time for reflection."

At last El found the strength to speak. His voice was thick-tongued and halting, but it was speech nonetheless. "Lady, who is this foe?"

"A wizard Chosen by Mystra as her personal servant," the Lady Dasumia replied, looking away toward the last traces of the setting sun. Beneath them, the carpet started to descend. "He left my side to do so and though he could not follow the narrow path the Lady of Magic set for him and is now called the Rebel Chosen, he's not returned to me. Hah! Mystra must be unable to concede that anyone could turn from blind worship of her."

Her eyes were burning as she turned back to meet Elminster's gaze, and added in tones once more light and casual, "Nadrathen is his name. You shall slay him for me."

The last prince of Athalantar looked at the night sky rushing past and shivered once.

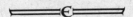

The rustling and croaking of night had begun in earnest in the thick stand of hiexel and thornwood and duskwood nearest the castle. As the flying carpet descended toward the tallest of the black towers, a pair of eyes blinked amid the fissured bark of a lightning-scarred duskwood and slowly sharpened into a coldly angry elven face. Roused anger glittered in Ilbryn Starym's eyes as he said softly, "Your wards may still my ears, proud Lady, but my spells work well enough when you are out over the wide world. Don't count overmuch on your apprentice. His life is mine."

He glowered at the tallest towers of the lady's castle long after the carpet was gone from view, until his glare slid suddenly into a calmer look; a frown of thoughtfulness rather than fury. "I wonder if anything in that mage's tower survived?" he asked the night. "It's worth the journey to see. . . ."

Dark-hued radiance flashed and curled like smoke, and the duskwood glared no more.

Dasumia's castle rose up into the sky above them in dark, forbidding ramparts. Tabarast watched the flying carpet disappear into its many-turreted heart and grunted. "Well, that was exciting," he said. "Another day of splendid and energetic furtherance of the Art, I must say."

Beldrune looked up from the tankard of magically warmed soup he was cradling and spoke in tones of some asperity. "My memory may be failing me from time to time, esteemed Baerast, but did we, or did we not, agree to moan no more about wasted time and -forgone opportunities? Our mission is, and remains, clear. Callow idiot this One Who Walks may be, but he—and what he chooses to do—are the most important developments in the Art in all Toril just now. I think we can afford to obey the dictates of a goddess—*the* goddess—and miss a few years of peering at fading, dusty writings in hopes of finding a new way of conjuring up floating lantern lights."

Tabarast merely grunted in wordless acknowledgment. A few lights blinked into life high in the turrets of Dasumia's castle, and the night noises resumed around them. They kept silent for a long time, crouched on little stools at the end of the hedgerow that marked the edge of the nearest tilled field to the Castle of the Lady, until Beldrune murmured, "Mardasper must have given us up for dead by now."

Tabarast shrugged and said, "He guards Moonshorn Tower, not we."

"Hmmph. Did he ever tell you about his fiery eye?"

"Aye. Something about a curse . . . he lost a spell duel to someone, and his service as guardian was payment to the priests of the Mysteries, to break the magic and restore him. Another poor mage-wits, driven into the service of the Lady who governs us all."

Beldrune lifted his head. "Do I hear the faith of Tabarast of the Three Sung Curses retunding? The divine graces of Holy Mystra losing their hold after all these years?"

"Of course not," Tabrast snapped. "Would I be sitting here the night through in all this cold damp if they were?" He thumbed the lid of his tankard open, took a long pull, and looked back at the castle towers in time to see one of the glimmering lights go out.

They sat and waited until their tankards were empty, but nothing else happened. The castle, it seemed, was asleep. Tabarast finally turned his gaze from it with a sigh. "We're all pawns of the Lady who minds the Weave, though—aren't we? It just comes down to whether you delude yourself into thinking you're free or not."

"Well, I *am* free," Beldrune snapped, his lips tightening. "By all means let these funny ideas prance through your head, Tabarast, and govern your days if you want them to, but kindly leave me out of the 'foolish puppet' drawer in your mind. You'll live longer if you grant that other mages might have scrambled out of it, too."

Tabarast turned to fix the younger mage with a wise and keen old glare. "*Which* other mages?"

"Oh, just the ones you meet," Beldrune grunted. "All of them."

Far from the turrets Tabarast and Beldrune were watching, and farther still from the shattered, smoking stump that had been the tower of Holivanter, another wizard's tower stood against the night sky.

This one was a modest roughstone affair studded with many small, loosely shuttered windows, sun boxes of herbs hanging from their sills. It stood alone in the wilderlands, bereft of village or muddy lane, and deer grazed contentedly around its very door—until a mist rising silently out of the grass settled upon them, and they sank down into oblivion, leaving only bones behind.

When there were no eyes left to see it, a chill, chiming whirlwind stole to the base of the tower and began to rise.

Floating up past climbing roses and ivy in eerie silence, it gathered itself in the air like a coiling snake—and lunged through a chink in a shutter halfway up the tower, pouring itself into the sleeping darkness beyond.

Dark chamber within opened into dark chamber, and the misty wind whirled, moaned as it gathered its might in that second room, a place of books and scroll-littered tables and dust—and became an upright, gliding thing of claws and jaws that slid out into the spiral stair at the heart of the tower, and up.

At the top of the tower, candlelight through an ill—fitting door danced reflections down the staircase, and an old and rough voice was speaking, alone, oblivious to the danger creeping closer, as clawed mists came gliding.

At the heart of a chalked symbol set with many candles, an old man in much-patched robes was on his knees, facing the chalk image of a pointing human hand. A blue radiance outlined the hand, and both it and the chalkwork were his doing, for he had dwelt long alone.

"For years I've served you, and the Great Lady, too," the wizard prayed. "I know how to smash things with spells and to raise them, too. Yet I know little of the world outside my walls and need your guidance now, O Azuth. Hear me, High One, and tell me, I pray: to whom should I pass on my magic?"

His last word seemed to echo, as if across a great gulf or chasm, and the blue conjured radiance suddenly shone almost blindingly bright.

Then it went out entirely as a wind rose out of the very floor, flowing from the chalked hand. The candles flared wildly, spat flames, and went out under its rushing onslaught, and out of the darkness that followed their deaths came a voice, deep and dry: "Guard yourself, faithful Yintras, for danger is very close to you now. I shall gather your Art unto me in the time of your passing . . . worry not."

With a crackle of leaking energy and a strange singing of the air, something blown on that wind flowed around the old wizard, winding around his trembling limbs to cloak him in warmth and vigor. With an ease and agility he hadn't felt in years, the old man sprang to his feet, raised his hands, and watched tiny lightnings crackle from one arm to the other with pleased wonder in his eyes, amid the gathering glimmer of unshed tears in his eyes. "Lord," he said roughly, "I am unworthy of such aid as this. I—"

Behind him, the door of the spell chamber split from top to bottom, shrieking its protest as more than a dozen claws literally tore it apart, tossing down the splinters to reveal an open, empty door frame.

Something that glowed with a pale, wavering ghostliness stood at the head of the stair—something large, menacing, and yet uncertain. A thing of claws and ever-shifting jaws and tentacles and cruelly barbed mandibles. A thing of menace and death, now advancing leisurely into the spell chamber at an almost gloating, slow pace.

Yintras Bedelmrin watched death come for him, floating over wards that would have seared limbs at a touch, and swallowed, trembling.

Lightning leaped within him, as if in reminder, and suddenly Yintras threw back his head, drew in a deep breath and spoke as loudly and as imperiously as he could. "I am armored by Azuth himself, and need fear no entity. Begone, whatever you are. Go from here, forever!"

The old wizard took a step toward the thing of claws, lightning still leaping from arm to arm. Ghostly radiance rose up in a menacing wall of claws and reaching tentacles—but even as it did so, it was flickering, trembling, and darkening. Holes were opening in its overreaching substance, holes that grew with it.

With horrifying speed it expanded to loom almost to the ceiling, towering over the old man in the many-patched robes. Yintras stood watching it, not knowing what to do and so doing nothing.

A fatal creed for an adventurer, and no better for wizards. He quailed, inwardly, knowing death could come in moments, horrified that he might embrace it when he could have escaped it—just by doing the right thing, or *something*.

Claws snatched at him in a horrible mass lunge that left him entirely unaware that a tentacle that had grown savage barbs and long-fanged jaws was snaking around through the darkness to stab at him from behind and below.

Lightning cracked, raged white-hot in the air of the spell chamber and was gone again, leaving—when his streaming eyes could see again—a feebly flickering gray mist cringing and writhing in the air by the door.

Yintras drew in a deep breath and did one of the bravest and most foolish things in his life thus far. He took a step toward the mist, chuckled, then took another step, raising his arms despite the lack of lightning or any feeling of surging or lurking power.

The mist gathered itself as if to do battle with him, rising and thickening into a small but solid mass, like a ready-raised shield trailing away into formlessness. The old wizard took another step, and the strange mist seemed to tremble.

He stretched forth a hand as if to grasp it. In a sudden wash of frigid air and a chiming of tiny, bell-like sounds, the mist broke into a swirling stream and was gone out the door in a flash, leaving only a mournful snarl in its wake.

Yintras watched it go and stared at the emptiness where it had been for a long anxious time. When at last he believed that it was truly gone, he went to his knees again to speak his thanks. All that came out were sobs, in a quickening rush that he found himself powerless to stop.

He crept forward in the darkness on knees and fingertips, trying to at least shape Azuth's name. Then he froze in surprise and awe. Where his tears had fallen, candle after candle was springing to life by itself, in a silently growing string of dancing warmth.

"Azuth," he managed to whisper at last. "My thanks!"

All of the candles went out in unison, then flared into life again. Yintras knelt in their midst, touched by glory and grateful for it. Sadness laced the edges of his bright delight too, and beneath all, he felt empty, utterly drained. He touched the smudged chalk that had once been the outline of a pointing hand and started to cry like a child.

EIGHT
THE SUNDERED THRONE

A throne is a prize that petty and cruel folk most often fight over. Yet, on bright mornings, 'tis but a chair.

RALDERICK HALLOWSHAW, JESTER
FROM *TO RULE A REALM, FROM TURRET TO MIDDEN*
PUBLISHED CIRCA THE YEAR OF THE BLOODBIRD

A shadow fell across the pages Elminster was frowning over. He did not have to look up to know who it was, even before a tress of glossy raven-black hair trailed across fading sketches and notations.

"Apprentice," Dasumia said beside his ear, in melodious, gentle tones that made El stiffen in alarm, "fetch the Orbrum, Prospaer on Nameless Horrors, and the Tome of Three Locks from my side table in the Blue Chamber, and bring them now to me in the Balcony Hall. Do off any items you may wear or carry that possess even the slightest dweomer, upon peril of your life."

"Aye, Lady Master," El murmured, glancing up to meet her eyes. She looked unusually stern, but there was no hint of anger or mischief about her eyes as she strode to a door that was seldom opened, stepped through it, and pulled it firmly closed behind her.

The solid click of its lock coincided with Elminster realizing he had to ask her what to do about the guardian of the Blue Chamber. Her spell-lock he could probably break—a test?—but the guardian would have to be slain if he was to do something so time—consuming as to cross the room, pick up three books, and attempt to carry them out again . . . or *it* would be the one doing the slaying.

If he slew it, she'd once told him, small malignant sentiences would be released from mirrors and orbs and tome-bindings all over the castle. They might rage for months before they were all recaptured and spellbound once more to obedience. Months of lost time she'd repay him for with the same duration of torment . . . and Elminster had tasted the Lady Dasumia's torments before.

Her favorite punishment seemed to be forcing him to fetch things on hands and knees that she'd thoroughly broken, so every movement was wobbling, grating agony, but sometimes—more often in recent days, as the Year of Mistmaidens abandoned spring for full summer—she preferred strapping El into a girdle of everhealing then stabbing him in succession with a slim sword tipped with poison, and a blade fashioned of jungle thorns as long as his forearm, dipped in flesh—eating acid. She seemed to enjoy the sounds of screaming.

These reflections took El only the few seconds needed to stride across the room and open the door Dasumia had passed through. Beyond it was the Long Gallery, a passage studded with alternating paintings and oval windows. It was an enclosed flying bridge the height of twenty men above a cobblestone courtyard, that linked the two tallest towers of the castle. Ever since two once-apprentices of the Lady had thought it a perfect venue for a duel and had slain each other amid conjured flames that threatened both attached towers, the Lady had caused the Gallery to be magic-dead: its very air quenched and quelled all spells, so Dasumia could do nothing but walk its considerable length; he'd have ample time to call out to her before she—

He snatched open the door, opened his mouth to speak—and stared in silence at a dark, lifeless, and very empty gallery.

Even if she'd been as swift as the fastest Calishite message-runners, and thrown dignity to the winds for a panting sprint the moment the door had closed, she'd have been no farther from him than mid-passage. There'd just not been time enough for anything else. Perhaps she'd banished the dead magic effect and not bothered to inform him. Perhaps—

He frowned and conjured light, directing it to appear at the midpoint of the passage. The casting was both simple and perfectly accomplished . . . but no light blossomed into being. The gallery was still death to magic.

Yet—no Lady Dasumia. Elminster turned away from that door looking very thoughtful.

El used the heavy, many-layered wards that the Lady had set upon the Blue Chamber to spin a modified maze spell that drew the guardian—a small, enthusiastic flying maelstrom of three barbed stingtails, raking claws, and a nasty disposition—into "otherwhere" for a long handful of moments. He was out and down the hall, with the door safely closed and the books under his arm, before it won its furiously hissing freedom.

Twice cobwebs brushed his face on his brisk jaunt along the Long Gallery, telling him the Lady Master hadn't passed this way recently—certainly not mere minutes ago.

The doors of the Balcony Hall stood open, star—studded smoke swirling gently out; the Lady had spun a spell-shield to protect her castle. This was to be a test, then, or a duel in earnest. He held the books in a stack out before him as he entered, and murmured, "I am come, Lady Master."

The books floated up out of his grasp toward the balcony, and from its height Dasumia said softly, "Close the doors and bar them, Apprentice."

El glanced up as he turned back to the doors. She was wearing a mask, and her hair was stirring about her shoulders as if winds were blowing through it. Spell-globes floated above and behind her; El saw much of her jewelry hanging in one, and the books were heading for another. Real magic was to be unleashed here.

He settled the bar and secured its chains without haste, giving her the time she needed to be absolutely ready. When facing the spells of a sorceress who can destroy you at will, it's best to give her little cause for irritation.

When he turned back into the room, the last glowspell had dimmed to a row of glimmering lights around the balcony rail; he could no longer see the sorceress who stood somewhere above him.

"It is time, and past time, Elminster, for me to assay this. Defend yourself as you're able—and strike back to slay, not gently."

Sudden light burst forth from on high: white, searing light that boiled forth at him from the face, bodice, and cupped hands of his Lady Master. Did she know of his treacheries?

Time enough to learn such things later . . . if he lived to enjoy a "later." El spun a hand vortex to catch it and sent it back at her, diving away when its fury proved too powerful for his defense, and broke his vortex apart in a snarling explosion that awakened short-lived fires here and there about the floor of the Hall. El spellsnatched one of them and threw it up at her, in hopes of spoiling another casting. It flickered as it plunged wide, but its brief radiance showed him Dasumia standing as rigid as a post, with silver bands of magic whipping about her—bands that became flailing chains as they rattled free of her and hurtled down upon him.

He danced across the Hall, to win himself the few moments they'd need to chase after him, then put his hands together in a spellburst that shattered them. He'd placed and angled himself so as to spit the unused fire of his spell up at the balcony, wondering how long his dozen or so defensive or versatile spells could serve him against the gathered might of her magic.

This time, some of it reached her; he heard her gasp, and saw her throw her head back, hair swirling, in the blazing moment when her spell-shield failed under the searing, clawing assault of his strike.

Then he glimpsed the flash of her teeth as she smiled, and felt the first cold whisper of fear. Now would come agony, if she could burst through his defenses to bring him down. And sooner or later—probably sooner—she would bring him down.

Purple lightning spat out of dark nothingness in a dozen places along the balcony rail, and lanced down into the Hall, ricocheting here, there, and everywhere. El spun a swift armoring spell but felt burning agony above one elbow, and in the opposing thigh—and crashed bruisingly to the stone floor, biting his tongue as he grunted back a scream. His body bounced and writhed helplessly as lightning surged through it; he fought to breathe now, not to weave spells or craft tactics. Yet perhaps the tatters of his failing, fading armoring could be used to hurl her lightning back—for she'd spent no time to raise another spell-shield for herself.

El crawled and rolled, blindly and agonizingly, seeking to be out of the searing surge of the lightning, to where he could gasp for breath and make his limbs obey.

A rising whistling sound just above his head told El his armoring had survived—and could turn lightning aside quite effectively. He willed it down to above his head, to break the lightning that was holding him in thrall, then moved it to one side, rolling to stay in its shadow.

Lightning clawed at his foot for a moment; then he was free once more. Murmuring a paltry incantation to make his armoring larger and longer lasting, El rose into a crouch to peer at the last few lightnings crawling about the Hall. It was the work of a few moments to deflect these so until they could all be cupped in his armoring and hurled back up at the balcony, raking it for the briefest of instants before they boiled away under the onslaught of the Lady Dasumia's next spell.

This one was a wall of green dust he'd seen before; short-lived and unstable, but turning all living things it touched briefly to stone. El cast a wall of force as fast as he knew how, bringing it into being curved like a cupped hand to scoop dust aside and spill it back up onto the balcony.

As his "hand" moved one way, he trotted in another direction, hurling magic missiles at where his Lady Master must be crouching, to keep her from moving away from the area wherein her dust would be delivered back to her.

A moment later, the glowing green cloud spilled across the balcony, and it was too late for Dasumia to flee. El had the satisfaction of seeing her stiffen and grow still.

An instant thereafter, he was shouting in startled pain as sharp, slicing blades materialized out of the air on all sides. He threw himself to the floor and rolled, shielding his face and throat with tight-curled arms as he willed his forcewall back down out of the balcony like a swooping falcon to batter aside blades and shield him.

Shrieking from overhead told him his tactic had worked; he gasped out one of his two dispel magic incantations to clear the air of flying, razor-sharp metal, then gaped in fresh surprise, as the disappearance of the blades caused a shimmering serpent of force to fade into view in midair and snap down, lashing at his forcewall until it shattered and failed.

As he dodged away from the magical whip, El stole a glance at Dasumia up on the balcony, still leaning stonily out with one hand raised. She hadn't moved an inch. These spells hitting him now must be linked, so that breaking or trammeling one awakens the next!

Was she unaware of the hall around her, in her petrified state? Or could she still exact some measure of control over her magics?

El vaulted a lash of the whip that struck the floor so close by that it left his arm and shoulder tingling and sprinted for the balcony stairs. The whip followed, coiling like a gigantic snake.

He took the broad steps three at a time, sprinting for all he was worth, and was able to dive behind Dasumia's stony feet before the whip could find him. It crashed down beside his face, the force of its strike swirling up remnants of green dust. El found himself growing numb . . . and struggling not to move slowly, as he entwined one arm around his Lady Master's legs and tried to climb her, whilst the whip raged in the air around him but did not strike ... and Elminster found he could not move at all.

The whip fell away into motes of fading light, and there was a moment of peaceful darkness in Balcony Hall.

"If my knees get chilled in future, I'll know who to summon," a familiar voice said from close above El's head, and he collapsed to Dasumia's ankles and the balcony floor, as his limbs were abruptly freed from thrall. She stepped away from him, turned with hands on hips, and looked down.

Their eyes met. Dasumia's held satisfaction and approval. "You're a sword ready enough to go into battle," she told him. "Go now, and sleep. When you're quite ready, you shall duel in earnest, elsewhere."

"Lady Master," Elminster asked, as he clambered to his feet, "is it permitted to ask whom I shall duel?"

Dasumia smiled and traced the line of his throat with one slender finger. "You," she said merrily, "are going to challenge Nadrathen, the Rebel Chosen, for me."

The Blood Unicorn flapped above the gates of Nethrar and the arched gate of the palace at its heart, telling every Galadornan that the King yet lived. As this bright summer day wore on, not a few eyes looked up at those standards again and again, seeking to learn if the ownership of the Unicorn Throne had changed.

For a season and more the aging, childless King Baerimgrim had lingered in the shadow of the tomb, kept alive after being savaged by the claws of the green dragon Arlavaunta only by his great strength and the Art of Court Mage Ilgrist. The once-mighty warrior was a thin and failing husk now, unable to sire children even with magical aid, and preoccupied by ever-present pain.

In the time of Baerimgrim's ailing, Galadorna had suffered under the skirmishes and mischief—crop-burning, and worse—of its five barons, all risen in ambition to be king after Baerimgrim. All had blood ties to the throne; all saw Galadorna as rightfully theirs ... and Galadornans hated and feared all of them.

Inside the House of the Unicorn this day the tension was a thing thick and heavy enough to be cut with a knife—and there was no shortage of knives held ready in its dim, tapestry-hung halls. The King was no longer expected to see nightfall and had been carried to his throne and tied in place there by servants, sitting with grim determination on his face and his crown slipping aslant upon his brow. The wizard Ilgrist stood guard over him like a tall, ever-present shadow, his own somber black robes overlaid by the linked crimson—unicorns mantle of his office, and suffered no hands but his own to straighten the crown or approach closely. There was good reason for his vigilance.

All five barons, like vultures circling to be in at a dying, were prowling the palace this day. Ilgrist had asked the eldest and most law-abiding among them, the huge and bearded warrior whom men called the Bear, to bring his seven best armsmen to bolster the throne guard, and Baron Belundrar had done so. He stood scowling around at the three doors of the throne room right now, hairy hands laced through the hilts of the many daggers at his belt. He was watching his men as they stared stonily, nose to nose, at the far more numerous troops of Baron Hothal, who like their master had come to court this day in full armor, fairly bristling with cross-scabbarded blades. At the heart of where they stood thickest lurked their master in his own full armor; some Galadornans said he never took it off save to don new, larger pieces.

Other armsmen were here too, though out of their armor—and looking as wary and uncomfortable over it as so many unshelled crabs, among all the battle-ready warriors. Some of them wore the purple tunics of Baron Maethor, the suave and ever-smiling master of a thousand intrigues and even more Galadornan bedchambers. "Purple poisoners," some folk of the realm called them, and not without cause. Other servants—some of whom looked suspiciously like battle-worn hireswords from other lands, not Galdornans at all—wore the scarlet of Baron Feldrin, the restless trickster who grew gold coins at the end of his fingertips every time he stretched out his hands to take things, it seemed . . . and his hands were outstretched often.

Last among this fellowship of ready death strolled the haughty magelings and quickblades of the baron some folk at court deemed the most dangerous threat to the freedoms enjoyed by all Galadornans: Tholone, the scarred would-be mage and accomplished swordsman, who styled himself "Lord" rather than Baron, and had largely ignored the decrees and writ of the Unicorn Throne for almost a decade. Some said Arlavaunta had been called forth from her lair to attack the king by his spells—because Baerimgrim had been riding with many armed knights at his back to demand Tholone's renewed loyalty, and long-withheld taxes, when the dragon's attack had come.

"A flock of vultures," the king muttered, watching the liveried lackeys drifting into the throne room. "None of them people I'd choose to have standing by, watching me die."

Court Mage Ilgrist smiled thinly and replied, "Your Majesty has the right of it, to be sure." He made a small hand sign to one of the throne guards who held the balconies this day, to make stone cold sure no baronial crossbowmen just happened to idly mount the back stairs to gain a better view of things. The officer nodded and sent three guards down those stairs, one bearing a horn and the other two walking with slow, measured tread, the banner of the Blood Unicorn borne stretched out in splendor between them. It showed the leaping crimson "horned horse" forever silhouetted against a full moon, on a glittering cloth-of-gold field. When the banner had been laid flat at the king's feet, the guard with the horn blew a single high, ringing note, to signify open court was now in session—and the king would entertain public deputations and entreaties from all folk, no matter how high or low.

There were a few commoners in the hall this day—folk who always watched the king, or who'd not have missed today's expected danger and excitement no matter what doom might confront them—but none of them dared push forward through the throngs of baronial men. The throne faced a half-ring of armsmen who were glaring hard-eyed in every direction whilst fondling the hilts of half-drawn daggers all the while; if he'd had the strength, King Baerimgrim would have risen and walked about mockingly introducing them all to each other.

As it was, he just sat and waited to see who of the five circling vultures was boldest. War would come no matter what was decided here today . . . but he could do Galadorna one last service and leave its throne as strongly held as possible, to keep the bloodshed, if the gods smiled, paltry.

The Bear would stand with him, if need be. No prize, but the best of a bad lot. He believed in laws and doing the right thing . . . but how much of that was rooted in his firm belief that as senior Baron among the five, and head of the oldest and largest noble house, the right thing meant Belundrar on the throne?

It was hard to say which was the most dangerous threat: Tholone's loose-leashed magelings, Maethor's spies and poisons, or Hothal's brute blades-enough-to-reap-all. And what sort of surprise blade had Feldrin's gold been used to hire . . . or was he supporting one of the others? Or were the Lords of Laothkund or other covetous foreign powers dealing with him?

Ah, it began. Striding out from among the tensely waiting warriors toward Baerimgrim came a young, black-bearded man in the green and silver of Hothal—one of the few who'd not come to court this day full-armored for battle.

The envoy bowed low before the throne, and said, "Most gracious Majesty, all Galadorna grieves at your condition. My Lord Hothal knows deep sorrow at the fate of royal Baerimgrim but grieves also for the future of fair Galadorna if the Unicorn Throne falls empty, to be fought over at this time—or worse, offers sitting room to one whose malice or blundering ignorance will lead the realm into ruin."

"You make your concerns clear enough, sir," the king said then, his dry tones awakening chuckles all over the room. "Bring you also solutions, I trust?"

The reddening envoy responded sharply, "Majesty, I do. I speak on behalf of Hothal, Baron of Galadorna, who begs leave to take the crown at this time, peaceably"—his voice rose to ride over sounds of derision and dispute from many in the chamber—"and with fair regard for the rights and desires of others. My lord requests this honor not idly; he has been most diligent on Galadorna's behalf and has bade me reveal thus: in return for promises that bright-visaged peace and fair-handed justice shall continue to flourish in the realm, he enjoys the full support of the most puissant lord Feldrin, Baron of Galadorna, which that noble personage shall himself confirm."

All eyes turned to Feldrin, who smiled in his customarily sly, sidelong way, his eyes meeting no one's gaze—and nodded, slowly and deliberately.

"Moreover," the envoy continued, "My lord hath spoken with the enemies of Galadorna, with an eye to keeping them from our borders and out of our purses, that the land remain free and prosperous, with no shadow of war-fear upon our thresholds. In return for most favored prices on silver and iron from our deep forest mines, the Lords of Laothkund have agreed to a treaty of mutual peace and border respect."

Cries of anger, oaths, and gasps of exaggerated horror made such a din in the chamber that the envoy paused for some time before adding, "My Lord Hothal submits that as he leads a force that can best keep the realm safe and prosperous, the crown should pass to him, and—for the good of Galadorna—his rule be proclaimed as legitimate by yourself, Grave Majesty."

There was another uproar, quelled in an instant by the deep rumble of Baron Belundrar as he lurched forward to stand beside the throne. With obvious reluctance in his tone and anger in his eyes, he said, "I share the anger of many here that any Galadornan would deal in secret with the wolves of Laothkund. Yet—"

He paused to sweep the room with his glare, his green eyes fierce under his bushy black brows and his battered nose jutting like a drawn blade, before he resumed, "Yet I will support this bid for the crown, scheming though it may seem, so long as the rule of law and right be upheld. Galadorna must be ruled by the strongest—and must not become a land of knifings and monthly intrigues or executions."

As the Bear stepped back to better survey all of the doors once more, a murmur of agreement arose at his words—but again the talk stilled in a moment as another baron stepped forth and purred, "A moment, brave Belundrar! You speak as if you see no acceptable alternative to this admitted scheming, to guard the safety of fair Galadorna in the years ahead. Well, then, listen to me, and I'll provide an offer unstained by dealing with enemies in secret."

Lord Tholone ignored Belundrar's instinctive snarl and continued, turning in a slow circle with his hand out, to survey all in the room. "You've heard very real and loyal concerns for the safety of our beloved realm. I share that love for Galadorna and worry for the security of us all. Unlike others, however, I've busied myself not with dark back-passage deals, but with assembling the finest company of mages this side of the sea!"

There was snorts and spitting as many warriors expressed their disgust at any reliance on wizards—and the presence of hired outlander mages here.

A cold-eyed Tholone raised his purring voice a notch and continued firmly, "Only my mages can guarantee the peace and prosperity we all seek. To those who mistrust magic, I ask this: if you truly want peace, do you hire and consort with battle-hungry warriors? Galadorna scarcely needs such bloody folk as its lords."

He left a little silence then for murmurs of agreement but heard instead, in that roomful of fearful courtiers and simmering warriors, only stony silence and quickly added, "I command magic enough to make Galadorna not only safe but great—and to deal with any traitors in this chamber who plan to put other interests before the security and rebuilding of the Realm of the Blood Unicorn."

"Bah! We'll have no twisted sorcerers ruling the realm!" someone shouted from the press of armored men around Baron Hothal, and several voices echoed, "Twisted sorcerers!" in tones of anger. The king and the Court Mage Ilgrist, who was standing by the royal shoulder, exchanged glances of rueful amusement.

The tumult, which had reached the point of daggers glinting here and there as they were drawn, fell abruptly still and silent once more.

The most handsome of the barons of Galadorna had stepped forth, the smile that charmed Galadornan ladies all too often flashing forth like a deft and graceful sword. Baron Maethor might well have been a crown prince, so richly was he dressed, so perfect his flowing mane of brown hair, and so smoothly confident his manner. "It grieves me, men of Galadorna," he said, "to see such anger and open lawlessness in this chamber. This blustering of those who walk around with ready swords, and the merciless will to use them, is the very thing that must be stopped if the Galadorna we all love is to be saved from sinking into . . . a land not worth saving or dwelling in; just another warlord's den."

He turned to look around the room, ruffled cloak swirling grandly, every eye upon him, and added, "Therefore, my duty to the realm stands clear. I must and shall support Lord Tholone—"

There was a gasp of surprise, and even Tholone's jaw dropped. Maethor and Tholone were considered the two strongest barons by many, and everyone in the realm knew they were far from friends.

"—the one man among us who can make a difference. I must go to bed this night knowing I have done my best for Galadorna . . . and I can only do that if Lord Tholone willingly gives the most trustworthy of us all, good Baron Belundrar, the post of seneschal of Nethrar, in sole charge of all justice throughout the realm."

There was an approving murmur; Belundrar blinked at Maethor. The pretty boy baron wasn't called "the Silver-Tongued Poisoner of Galadorna" for nothing. What was he up to?

Maethor gave everyone a last smile and glided quickly back within his protective ring of handsome aides in silks and leathers, with not-so-hidden daggers ready in their lace-wristed hands.

A stir of excited talk arose at this surprising—and to many, bright in promise—offer. A stir that rose sharply, only to fall away into tense silence once more, as the last baron slipped through his supporters to scuttle close to the throne, causing guards to stiffen and turn until Ilgrist waved them back.

Feldrin's big brown eyes roved around the chamber. His hands fluttered as nervously and as restlessly as always, as their thin, weak-looking owner bent near the ear of the king. Feldrin's fine but ill-fitting clothes were drenched with sweat, and his short black hair, usually straight—plastered to his skull, looked like a bird had been raking it for nesting material. He was almost dancing with fearful excitement as he whispered in the royal ear. On the other side of the throne, Ilgrist bent close to listen too, evoking one nervous glance from Feldrin—but only one.

"Most Just and Able Majesty," Feldrin breathed, along with a strong scent of parsley, "I too, in my not-so-bold way, love Galadorna and would at all costs see her escape the bloody ruin of war between us barons—moreover, I have good information that at least three ambitious lordlings of Laothkund will ride here with the best mercenaries they can muster if we do take up arms 'gainst each other, to carve away all of Galadorna that they can hold. These three have a pact; their men shall never turn on each other whilst any of us live."

"And so?" the king growled, sounding very much like Belundrar in his dislike of threats and whispered schemes. Feldrin wrung his hands nervously, his brown eyes very large as they darted this way and that, peering to see who might be close enough to hear. He lowered his voice still further and leaned close; Ilgrist pointedly raised one fist and let the ring on its middle finger gleam and glow for all to see. If Feldrin drew dagger on the king, it would be the last thing he ever did.

"I, too, will support Lord Tholone, if you, sire, can agree to my conditions—which you will appreciate must needs be kept secret. These are two: that Hothal be executed here and now—for he will never accept Tholone where you sit now, and will harry us all for years, spilling the best blood of the realm—"

"Including that of one Feldrin?" the king muttered, a smile almost creeping onto his face.

"I—I—well, yes, I do suppose, ahem-*hem*, and that brings us to the second hazard: the greater danger to Galadorna is the smiling snake yonder, Maethor. I need your royal promise that 'an accident' shall very soon befall him. He has been a tireless and always untrustworthy spinner of intrigues, master of lies and shadows and poison; the land has no need of him, no matter who holds the throne." Feldrin was almost panting now, streaming with sweat, out of fear at his own daring.

"And one Feldrin most assuredly has no need of such a pretty rival at scheming," Ilgrist murmured, so quietly that perhaps only the king heard.

King Baerimgrim thrust out a hand suddenly and caught hold of Feldrin's chin. He pulled, dragging the baron around to face him, and murmured, "I agree to these two conditions, so long as you stand steadfast and no one else dies by your hand, direction, or maneuverings. For your own good, I place one condition upon you, clever Feldrin: when you straighten up from here, look worried—not pleased."

The king thrust the whispering baron away, and raised a voice that held a quaver of enfeeblement, yet also the snap of command: "Lord Tholone! Attend us here, for the love of Galadorna!"

There was a momentary excited stir—in some corners of the throne room, almost a shout—then breathless silence.

Out of the heart of that waiting, watching stillness Lord Tholone came striding, face a pleasant mask, eyes wary. There was a faint singing in the air around him; his mages had been busy. No doubt daggers would prove futile fangs if thrown his way now or in the near hereafter.

If—given the number of wizards and warriors ready for battle and on edge with excitement—there would be a hereafter for anyone in this room.

The silence was utter as Tholone came to a stop before the Unicorn Throne, separated from the king only by the crimson and gold expanse of the Blood Unicorn banner.

"Kneel," Baerimgrim said hoarsely, "on the Unicorn."

There was a collective gasp of indrawn breath; such a bidding could mean only one thing. The king reached to his own head, and slowly—very slowly— did off the crown.

His hands did not tremble in the least as he raised it over Tholone's bent head—a head that had grown a triumphant, almost maniacal smile—and said, "Let all true Galadornans gathered here bear witness this day, that of my own free will, I name as my rightful heir thi—"

The crack of lightning that burst from the crown at that moment deafened men and hurled them back hard against the paneled walls. Baerimgrim and the Unicorn Throne were split in twain in a blackened, writhing instant, the crown ringing off the riven ceiling. As the blazing limbs of what had been the king slumped down amid the sagging wreckage of the throne, the golden unicorn's head that surmounted it sobbed aloud.

The court mage looked astonished for the first time, and snatched out a wand as he looked sharply at the painted wooden head . . . but whatever enchantment had made it speak had fled, and the head was cracking and collapsing into falling splinters.

Ilgrist glanced swiftly around the room. Feldrin was lying lifeless on the floor, his arms two scorched stumps and his face burned away, and Tholone was on his back, clawing feebly at gilding from the smoldering banner that had melted onto his face.

The court mage fired over them, calling forth the fury of the wand in his hand, and a veritable cloud of magic missiles sang and snarled their blue-white death around the room. Not a few of Tholone's magelings crumpled or slid down the wall, wisps of smoke issuing from their eyes and gaping mouths—then the air was full of curses and swords flashing in the hands of running men.

Fire leaped up in a circle around Ilgrist then, and the wand in his hand spat forth a last trio of magical bolts—they struck at mages who still stood, and one fell—before it crumbled.

The court mage let its ashes trickle from his hand as he looked calmly around the ring of angry armed men and said, "No, Galadorna is too important for me to allow such a mistake. Baerimgrim was a good king and my friend, but . . . one mistake is all that fells most kings. I trust the rest of you, gentlesirs, w—"

With a roar that shook the room, Belundrar the Bear launched himself through the flames, heedless of the pain, and leaped at Ilgrist.

The wizard coolly took a single step back, raising one hand. The knife in the baron's grasp, sweeping sidelong at Ilgrist's throat, struck something that broke it, amid sparks, and sent the Bear's arm springing back involuntarily, to hurl the hilt into the balconies. The fire that blossomed in the wizard's hand caught the Bear full in the face, and his roar became a gurgling for the brief instant before his blackened, flaming body crashed face first into the floor.

Ilgrist lifted a fastidious foot to let it slide, blazing, past. "Are there any more heroes here today?" he asked mildly. "I've plenty more death in these hands."

As if that had been a signal, the air filled with hurled daggers and swords, spinning at the court mage from roaring men on all sides—only to ring off an invisible barrier, every last one of them, and fall away.

Ilgrist looked down at the body of Belundrar, which had broken his circle of fire and was busily being burnt in two by its flames, and murmured "Blasted to smoking ruin. A true patriot—and see how much he accomplished, in the end? Come, gentlesirs! Let us have your submission. I shall be the new king of—"

"Never!" Baron Hothal thundered. "I'll die before I'll allow su—"

Ilgrist's mouth crooked. "But of course," he said.

He made a tiny gesture with two of his fingers, and the air was suddenly full of the twang and hum of crossbows firing, from the throne guard up in the balconies, their faces white and blank, their movements mechanical.

Warriors groaned, clutched vainly at quarrels sprouting in their faces or throats, and fell. Hitherto-concealed crossbows spat an answer from many baronial armsmen around the chamber—and the helmless Hothal, his head transfixed by many bolts, staggered, then toppled onto his side.

Baron Maethor would have tasted as many flying deaths had he not possessed an unseen barrier of his own that kept both hurled daggers and crossbow bolts from him. Many of his unarmored men fell, but others surged forward to drive daggers into the faces of Hothal's armored guardsmen or raced up balcony stairs to carve out a bloody revenge on Galadorna's throne guard.

The chamber erupted in a flurry of hacking, stabbing steel, the thunder of armored men running, and screams—all too many screams. There was fresh commotion at two of the throne room doors, as royal soldiers with halberds in their hands elbowed ways into the room—then a bright flash and roar that shook the chamber even more than the lightning had and left dazzled men blinking.

Into the ringing echoes of the blast he'd caused, transforming a score of Baron Hothal's best knights into so many bloody scraps of armor embedded in riven paneling, the court mage shouted, "All of you—hold! *Hold*, I say!"

Commoners, throne guards, and the men of Maethor who were left, with their master in their midst, all turned to look at the wizard. The ring of fire around Ilgrist was gone, and the mage was pointing across the chamber, at—

The burned and broken body of Lord Tholone, now struggling jerkily to sit upright, its legs still much-twisted ruin. It turned sightless, despairing eyes to the watching men and worked jaws that had already drooled much blood for some time before trembling lips said the horribly flat and rattling words, "Pay homage to King Ilgrist of Galadorna, as I do."

Bonelessly the body slumped—an instant before it burst apart in a blast that spattered many of the surviving warriors. One of them snarled, "Magecraft said those words, not Tholone!"

"Oh?" Ilgrist asked softly, as the twisted, blackened crown of Galadorna flew smoothly out of the wreckage into his hand. "And if so, what will you do?"

He straightened the crown with a sudden show of strength, and unseen spell-hands lifted the mantle of court mage from his shoulders. It fell unheeded to the floor as he stepped forward, settled the battered crown upon his brow, and said loudly, "So let all Galadornans kneel before their new king. I shall rule over Galadorna as Nadrathen, a name I've known rather longer than 'Ilgrist.' Bow down!"

The shocked silence was broken by the rustlings and scrapings of several armsmen going clumsily to their knees. One or two of Maethor's men knelt;

one was promptly knifed from behind by one of his fellows and fell on his face with a gurgling cry.

King Nadrathen regarded the knot of richly garbed men with a gentle smile and said to their midst, "Well, Maethor? Shall Galadorna lose all of its barons this day?"

There was a rustling from behind him. Nadrathen turned and stepped back in the same motion, protective magics plucking his feet from the floor, to drift gently down a good pace back—and stare in open-mouthed surprise.

The mantle of the Court Mage of Galadorna, let fall by Nadrathen scant moments ago, was rising from the floor again, to hang upright as though a rather tall man was wearing it.

As the wondering court watched, a body faded into view within the mantle—a hawk-nosed, raven-haired human wearing nondescript robes and a faint smile. "Nadrathen?" he asked. "Called the Rebel Chosen?"

"King Nadrathen of Galadorna, as it happens," came the cool reply. "And who might you be? The shade of a court mage past?"

"I am called Elminster—and by the Hand of Azuth and the Mercy of Mystra, I challenge thee to spell duel, here and now, in a circle of my rais—"

"Oh, by all the fallen *gods*," Nadrathen sighed, and black flames suddenly exploded out of his hands with a roar, racing in a thick cylinder, like a battering ram, at the newcomer.

"Die, and trouble my coronation no more," the new king of Galadorna told the sudden inferno of black flames that erupted where his spell had struck. All over the chamber murmuring armsmen were crouching low behind pillars and railings or slipping out doorways, and away.

Black flames howled up to the ceiling—and were gone, snarling up to some lofty otherwhere. The man in the mantle of court mage stood unchanged, save that one eyebrow was now raised in derision. "Ye have some aversion to rules of combat or defensive circles? Or were ye in some haste to remodel this part of thy castle?"

Nadrathen cursed—and stone blocks were suddenly raining down all around them, plunging down from empty air to shake the chamber with their thunderous landings. Stone shards sprayed in all directions as the floor shattered; more armsmen fled, shouting in fear.

No stones struck either Nadrathen or Elminster; it was the turn of the Rebel Chosen to lift his brows in surprise.

"You come well shielded," he granted grudgingly. "Ulmimber—or whatever your name is—do you know what I am?"

"An archmage of accomplished might," Elminster said softly, "named by Holy Mystra herself as one of her Chosen—and now turned to evil."

"I did not turn to evil, fool wizard. I am what I have always been; Mystra has known me for what I am from the first." The king of Galadorna regarded his challenger bleakly, and added, "You know what the outcome of our duel must be?"

El swallowed, started to nod, and then suddenly grinned. "Ye're going to talk me to death?"

Nadrathen snarled, "Enough! You had your chance, idiot, and now—"

The air above them was suddenly darker and full of a host of ghostly, faceless floating figures, cowled and robed, trailing away to nothingness as they swooped, thrusting cold and spectral blades at the hawk-nosed mage.

As those blades transfixed Elminster, they slid in without gore or resistance . . . and became dwindling smoke and sparks, taking their wielders with them.

Nadrathen gaped in astonishment. His words, when he could find them, came in a gasp. "You must be a Ch—"

Behind the self-styled king of Galadorna, unseen by either dueling mage, a long-fingered female hand had slid into view, protruding from the still-solid, upright back of the riven Unicorn Throne with blue motes of risen magic dancing around it. Those long, flexing fingers now leveled a deliberate finger at the back of the unwitting Rebel Chosen.

Nadrathen's eyes widened, bulging for one incredulous moment before all his glistening bones burst together out the front of his body. Behind them as they bounced, a bloody, shapeless mass of flesh slumped to the floor, spattering El's boots and the throne with gore.

El sprang back, gagging, but the bones and the horrible puddle that had been Nadrathen were already afire, blazing from within. Blue-white, wasted magic swirled above flames of bright silver as men cried out in disgust and fear all over the chamber. El watched a thread of silver rise straight up from those flames to pierce the ceiling and burn onward.

He never saw the sunlight stab down into the throne room from high above; he was staggering back to fall heavily on his knees by then, as magic that was not his own shocked into him, surging throughout his spasming, weeping body.

Baron Maethor swallowed. He dared not approach the man-high conflagration that had been "King" Nadrathen, but this challenger-mage was on his knees blindly vomiting silver flames onto the smoking floor. Galadorna could be free of over-ambitious mages yet.

"Hand me your blade," he murmured to an aide without looking, extending his hand for it. Just one throw would be enough, if—

A tall, slender feminine figure stepped from behind that conflagration, bare thighs above high black boots flashing through slashes in midnight-black robes. "I think I shall rule Galadorna," Dasumia said sweetly, blue motes still swirling about one of her hands. "Ascending my throne in this Year of Mistmaidens—this very hour, in fact. And you shall be my seneschal, Elminster of Galadorna. Rise, Court Mage, and bring me the fealty of yon surviving lords and barons—or an internal organ from each; whichever they prefer."

NINE
GLAD DAYS IN GALADORNA

The wise ruler leaves time among audiences and promenades for receptions of daggers—usually in the royal back.

RALDERICK HALLOWSHAW, JESTER
FROM *To Rule A Realm, From Turret To Midden*
PUBLISHED CIRCA THE YEAR OF THE BLOODBIRD

Dark fire snarled and spat, and the slender elf in dark robes staggered back, groaning. Ilbryn Starym's three hundredth or so encounter with the wards of dark fire around the Castle of the Lady had not gone well. Her power was still too great, even in her absence . . . and where by the Trees Everlasting was she, anyway?

He sighed, glared up at the dark, slender towers so high above him in the twilit sky, and—

Was sent almost sprawling by a hard and sudden impact. He whirled to do battle with whatever fell guardian had charged him and found himself staring at the receding boots of one of the two buffoon-mages who were also encamped outside the walls of Dasumia's fortress.

Beldrune's excited shout floated back to the furious elf. "Baerast! Hearken!"

Tabarast looked up from a fire that just wouldn't light, shaking his scorched fingertips, and asked somewhat testily, "What is it now?"

"I was scrying Nethrar," Beldrune of the Bent Finger panted, "as the dream bid me, and there's news! The Lady Dasumia has just taken the throne and named the Chosen One as her seneschal. Elminster is Court Mage of Galadorna now!"

Ilbryn stared at the trotting mage's back for a moment, then broke into a fluid dash that swiftly brought him abreast of Beldrune. He reached up, caught hold of one bobbing shoulder in its fashionable slashed and pleated claret-hued silk, and snapped, "*What?*"

Spun around to face blazing elven eyes by fingers that felt like talons of steel, Beldrune groaned, "Let go, longears! You've fingers like wolf jaws!"

Ilbryn shook him. "What did you say?"

Tabarast fumbled in a belt pouch, dropped a shower of small, sparkling items, and held one up between finger and thumb, muttering something.

A lance of shining nothingness coalesced out of the air and thrust forward, unerring and as swift as leaping lightning. It took Ilbryn right in his ribs, shattering his shielding spell in a cascade of small and wayward cracklings and snatching him off his feet.

He hit the phandar tree with brutal force; ribs snapped like dry kindling crushed in a forester's fist. Ilbryn sobbed and choked and writhed, fighting for breath, but the spell held him pinned to the trunk. If it had been a real lance, he'd have been cut in two . . . but that knowledge afforded him scant consolation. Through red mists of pain he glared almost pleadingly at the two human mages.

Tabarast regarded the trapped elf mage almost sorrowfully and shook his head. "The problem with young elves is they've got all the arrogance of the older ones, with nothing to back it up," he observed. "Now, Beldrune, speak up for the hasty youngling here. What did you say?"

Curthas and Halglond stood very straight and still, their pikes just so, for they knew their master's turret window overlooked this section of battlements . . . and that he liked to look out often on moonlit nights and see tranquility, not the gleam and flash of guards fidgeting at their posts.

They stood guard over one end of the arched bridge that linked the loftiest rooms of the Master's Tower with the encircling battlements. It was light enough duty. No thief or angry armsman for three realms distant would dare to come calling uninvited on Klandaerlas Glymril, Master of Wyverns. The dragonkin he held in spell-thrall were seldom unleashed; when they did come boiling out of their tower on swift wings, they were apt to be hungry, fearless, and savage of temper.

One guard risked a quick glance along the moonlit wall. The stout tower that imprisoned the wyverns stood, as usual, dark and silent. Like the rest of Glymril Gard, it had been raised by the Master's spells from the tumbled stones of an ancient keep, here on the end of a ridge that overlooked six towns and the meeting of two rivers.

It was moonlit and gloriously warm this night, even up on the ever-breezy battlements of Glymril Gard, and it was easy to drift into a reverie of other moonlit nights, without armor or guard duties, and—

Curthas stiffened and turned his head. Bells? What could be chiming up here on the battlements at this time of night?

He could see at a glance that the walls were deserted. Halglond was already peering down the walls and into the yards below, in case someone was climbing the walls or coming up the guard stairs. No. Perhaps someone's escaped falcon, still with its jesses, had perched nearby . . . but where?

The sound was faint, small—yet very close, not on the ground far below or in one of the towers. What by all the storm-loving gods could it *be*?

Now it seemed to be right under Halglond's nose, swirling. He could see a faint, ragged line of mist coiling and snaking in the air. He swept through it with his halberd, and small glowing motes of light gathered for a moment along its curved blade before winking out—like sparks without a fire.

The chiming wind curled away, moving along the battlements. He exchanged glances with Curthas, and they both trotted warily after it, watching it grow larger and brighter. From behind them came the faint squeal that heralded the shutters of the Master's turret window opening. Perhaps it was one of his spells . . . or not, but they'd best chase it down even so. This could well be a test of their diligence.

It led them to the Prow Tower at the end of the ridge, where rocks fell away in almost cliffs beneath the castle walls, and there it seemed to quicken its dancing and circling. Curthas and Halglond closed with it cautiously, separating to come at it from different directions, with halberds to the fore and crouching low to avoid being swept over the battlements into a fall, no matter how fierce the wind became.

The chiming rose to a loud and regular sound, almost annoying to the ears, and the mist that made it spiraled up into a vaguely human form taller than either of them. Both guards stabbed at it with their pikes, and suddenly it collapsed, falling to become a milky layer of radiance awash around their boots.

Curthas and Halglond traded looks again. Nothing met their probing pike thrusts, and the chiming was silent. They shrugged, took a last look around the curved tower battlements, and turned to head back to their posts, If the Master wanted to tell them what it had been, he would; if he kept silent about it, 'twould be best if they did, too, and—

Halglond pointed, and they both stared. Halfway back along the way they'd come, the mist was dancing along the battlements. It had a definite shape, now—and the shape was female, barefoot and in flowing skirts, with long hair flying free in her wake as she ran, a faint chiming in her wake. The guards could just see through her.

In unspoken accord they broke into a run. If she turned across the bridge they were supposed to be guarding . . .

She ran right past it, heading toward the binding-racks and bloodstains of Bloodtop Tower, where—when the Master had prisoners he no longer needed— the wyverns were sometimes allowed to feed. That was a good way off, and the ghostly lady seemed in no hurry; the pounding guards gained on her swiftly.

A dark-robed figure was coming across the bridge—the Master! Halglond hissed a curse, and Curthas felt like joining in, but the mage ignored them, turning to join the chase along the battlements well ahead of his two guards. He carried a wand in one hand.

The guards saw her turn, hair swirling in the moonlight, amid the binding-racks, and silently beckon the Master of Wyverns, as coyly as any lover in a minstrel's ballad. As he approached her, she danced away to the edge of the battlements. The hard-running guards saw him follow warily, wand raised and ready. Glymril looked back at them once, as if deciding whether or not to wait until they reached the Tower, and Curthas clearly saw amazement on his face.

Not of their master's making, then, and unexpected to boot. They did not slow in their now-panting sprint—but even so, Curthas knew the strange foreboding that precedes by instants the sure knowledge that one is going to be—just—too late.

The woman became a snakelike, formless thing, and the shocked guards heard a long, raw howl from Klandaerlas Glymril as something bright whirled around him in a swift spiral, climbing toward the moon.

An instant later the Master of Wyverns became a roaring column of flame that split the night with its sudden fury. Curthas clutched at Halglond's arm, and they came to a ragged, panting halt together, all too close to where the battlements joined Bloodtop Tower. There was a booming *thump*, and something exploded out of the pyre, trailing flames down into the inner courtyards: the wand.

The guards exchanged fearful looks, licked dry lips, and started to back away in fear. They had managed two strides before the stones beneath their feet rippled like waves on a beach and started to slump and fall.

They fell into oblivion with the gathering roar of Glymril Gard collapsing ringing in their ears.

As the moon saw that great fortress crash back down into the tumbled ruin it had been before Glymril's spells had rebuilt it, a bright and triumphant mist danced over the rising dust and fading screams, its chimes mixed with cold, echoing laughter.

The court mage looked at the guard captain's grim face and sighed. "Who was it this time?"

"Anlavas Jhoavryn, Lord Elminster: a merchant from somewhere south across the sea. Brass work, sundries; nothing important, but a lot of it. Many coins here over many seasons. His throat was cut."

Elminster sighed. "Maethor or one of the new barons?"

"L-lord, I know not, and hardly dare s—"

"Your *hunches*, loyal Rhoagalow."

The guard captain glanced nervously from side to side; El smiled crookedly and leaned over to put his ear right to the man's lips. "Limmator," the officer breathed hoarsely; El nodded and stepped back. No particular surprise if Rhoagalow was right; Limmator was the only baron—or lordling—in Galadorna busier in dark corners with bribe, threat, and ready knife than Maethor of the Many Whispers.

"Go and dine now," he told the exhausted guard officer. "We'll talk later."

Rhoagalow and his three armsmen hurried out; El took care not to sigh until the antechamber was quite empty.

He murmured something and moved two fingers a trifle. There was a faint thump behind one wall, as the spy there abruptly went to sleep. El gave the section of wall a mirthless smile and used the secret door he wanted to keep secret a little longer, taking the lightless passage beyond to one of the disused and dusty hidden rooms in the House of the Unicorn. A little time alone to think is a rare treasure some folk never seize for themselves . . . and others, the truly deprived in life, cannot.

Three barons had died so far this year, one of them with a dagger in his throat not two steps from entering the throne chamber, and six—no, seven— lesser lords. Galadorna had become a nest of vipers, striking at each other with their fangs bared whenever the whim took them, and the court mage was not a happy man. He had no friends; anyone he befriended soon ended up staring sightlessly at a ceiling of a morning. There were whisperings behind every door in the palace and never any true smiles when those doors opened. El was even getting used to the sight of dark ribbons of blood wandering out from behind closed doors; perhaps he should issue a decree commanding all doors in Nethrar be taken down and burned.

Hah to that. He was becoming what he knew they called him behind his back: "the Flapping Mouth That Spews Decrees." The barons and lordlings constantly tried to undercut royal authority, or even steal openly from the court, and his Lady Master was no help at all, using her spells too seldom to engender any fear that might in turn breed obedience.

There came a faint scratching sound from off to his left. Elminster pulled on the right knob and a panel slid open. Two young guardsmen peered into the dimness. "You sent for us, Lord Elminster?"

"Ye found the scrolls, Delver, and—?"

"Burned, and the ashes in the moat, lord, as you ordered, mixed with the dust you gave me. I used all of it."

Elminster nodded and reached out a hand to touch a forehead. "Forget all, loyal warrior," he said, "and so escape the doom we all fear."

The guard he'd touched shivered, eyes blank, then turned and hurried back into the darkness, unlacing his breeches as he went. He'd been heading for his quarters when the sudden, urgent need to use a garderobe had come upon him, and led him into the disused wing of the palace.

"Ingrath?" the court mage asked calmly.

"I found the Q—ah, *her* work in the Redshield Chamber and mixed in the white powder until I could see it no more. Then I said the words and got out."

El nodded and reached out his hand. "Ye and Delver are earning such handsome rewards. . . ." he murmured.

The guardsman chuckled. "Not the need to go to the jakes, please, lord. Let it be wandering trying to recall my youthful dalliances down here, eh?"

El smiled. "As ye wish," he said, as his fingers touched flesh. Ingrath's eyes flickered, and the forgetful warrior stepped around the still and silent mage, walked in a thoughtful circle around the room, found the panel, and trotted away again, his part in slowing Dasumia's evil forgotten once more.

Which might just keep him alive another month or two.

'Twould be safer if the two weren't friends and knew nothing of each other—but it had happened that the best warriors El could trust, after subtle but thorough mind-scrying, were fast friends. That should be no surprise, he supposed.

El paced the gloomy room, his mood dark enough to match it. Mystra's command to serve had been clear, but "serve in his own way" had always been Elminster's failing; if it was a flaw that was to doom him now, then let it be so. Some things a man must cling to, to remain a man.

Or a woman cleave to, to be herself ... and there was certainly one lady in Galadorna doing just as she pleased. Queen Dasumia always seemed to be laughing at him these days and certainly cared nothing for the duties of being queen; she was seldom to be found on the throne or even in the royal castle, leaving El to issue decrees in her stead. Galadorna could sink into war and thievery without her noticing ... and daily, as more slavers and unscrupulous merchants rushed in, knowing they'd be left more or less unrestricted in their dealings, the Lords of Laothkund were casting covetous eyes on the increasingly wealthy kingdom. One thing lawlessness among merchants does bring is full tax coffers.

El sighed again. The important thing was to make sure that with all this gold, lawlessness did not spread to the crown. Sweet Mystra forfend. Whatever would it be like to live in a land ruled by merchants?

Everyone ignored the splintering and crashing sounds of a table collapsing under two cursing men slugging each other and the shivering and tinkling sounds of breaking glass that followed as various nearby drinkers hurled bottles at the combatants, seeking to alter the odds of wagers just placed. Someone screamed from another room—a death cry that ended in a horrible, wet gurgle, and was answered by drunken applause. It was late, after all, and this was the Goblet of Shadows.

Nethrar had known wilder taverns in its time, but the days of golem dancers who ate their fees to enrich Ilgrist were gone, and the dens they'd done more than dance in were gone with them. The Goblet, however, was very much here—and those too afraid to brave its pleasures alone could always hire a trio of surly—looking warriors to guard them and make them—at least in their own eyes—seem a veteran member of a band of adventurers on dangerous business bent.

And there were the ladies. One such, a vision in blue silk and mock armor whose loops of chain and curves of leather did more to display than conceal, had just perched on the edge of a table not far from where Beldrune and Tabarast were nursing glasses of ruby-hued but raw heartsfire and grumbling, "Well aged? Six days, belike!" to each other.

Over their glasses, Beldrune and Tabarast watched the saucy beauty in the silks bending low over two young men at the table she'd chosen, giving them a view of the sort that older, more sober men have fallen headlong into before now. The two wizards cleared their throats in unison.

" 'Tis getting a might hot in here," Tabarast observed weakly, tugging at his collar.

"Over that side of the table, too?" Beldrune grunted, his eyes locked on the lady in blue. He flicked a finger, and through the din of chatter and laughter, singing and breaking glass, the two mages could suddenly hear a voice purring, as if it was speaking right in their ears: "Delver? Ingrath? Those names are . . . exciting. The names of daring men . . . of heroes. You *are* daring heroes, aren't you?"

The two young warriors chuckled and said something more or less in unison, and the saucy beauty in blue whispered, "How daring are you both feeling this night? And . . . how heroic?"

The two men laughed again, rather warily, and the beauty murmured, "Heroic enough to do a service for your queen? A—*personal* service?"

They saw her reach into her bodice and draw forth a long, heavy chain of linked gold coins that caught and held their hungry eyes as she flashed the unicorn-adorned Royal Ring of Galadorna.

Two sets of eyes widened, and looked slowly and more soberly up from the coins and the curves to the face above—where they found an impish grin followed by a tongue just darting into view between parted lips.

"Come," she said, "if you dare . . . to a place where we can . . . have more fun."

The watching wizards saw the two men hesitate and exchange glances. Then one of them said something, lifting his eyebrows in an exaggerated manner, and they both laughed rather nervously, drained their tankards, and rose. The queen looped her chain of coins around the wrist of one of them and towed him playfully off across the dim and crowded maze of tables, beaded curtains, and archways that formed the backbone of the Goblet.

Blue silk and supple leather swayed very close past the innocently tilted noses of Beldrune and Tabarast. When the second warrior had stalked past— hungry eyes, hairy arms and all—the two mages with one accord drained their heartsfires, turned to each other and turned red at the same time, tugged at their collars again, and cleared their throats once more.

Tabarast rumbled, "Ah—I think it's time to see the bottom of more than one tankard . . . don't you?"

"My thoughts exactly," Beldrune agreed. "After a keg or three of beer, now, mind you. . . ."

Deep in the dimness behind a pillar in the Goblet of Shadows, an elf whose face might have been cut from cold marble watched Queen Dasumia of Galadorna tow her two prizes out of the tumult. When they'd rounded a corner, out of sight, Ilbryn Starym turned his head to sneer down at the two blushing old wizards, who didn't see him. Then he glided off through the Goblet toward the exit he knew the queen would use, taking care to keep well back and well hidden.

Rhoagalow had brought word of another murder and a knifing whose victim might live. Elminster had handed him a hand keg of Burdym's Best from the royal cellar and told him to go somewhere safe and out of uniform to drink it.

Now the Court Mage of Galadorna was striding wearily bedward, looking forward to some solid hours of staring up into the darkness and getting some real thinking work done on the governance of a feud—festering little kingdom. Perhaps there'd be another assassination attempt in the wee hours. That would be jolly.

El's mood had a sword edge to it just now; an ache was already raging in his head from dealing with sharp-tongued merchants all day. Moreover, he couldn't seem to put an idea out of his mind—a rumor abroad in Nethrar courtesy of the two old bumbling mages from Moonshorn Tower, who seemed to have followed him here, that "Dasumia" was the name of the dread sorceress called the Lady of Shadows; could she and the queen somehow be related?

Hmmm. El sighed again, for perhaps the seven hundredth time this day, and out of habit glanced along the side corridor his passage had brought him to.

Then he came to a dead halt and peered long and hard. Someone very familiar was crossing the corridor farther down, using a passage parallel to his own. It was the queen, clad in blue silks and leather and chains like a tavern dancer—and she was leading two young men, warriors by their harness, whose hands and lips were hard at work upon her person as she led them along . . . out of view, and into a part of the House of the Unicorn Elminster had never yet visited. Cold fear stirred deep in his vitals as he recognized those two ardent men as his sometime tools against her, Delver and Ingrath.

His headache started to pound in earnest as he caught up his robes and sprinted as quietly but as swiftly as he could down the corridor toward the place where he'd seen Dasumia disappear. It was better not to use a concealment spell now, in case his Lady Master had a trailing spelltell active.

The queen was making no effort at stealth. The high, tinkling laugh she used as false flattery rang out as El reached the corner he thought was the right one and began hopping from pillar to pillar.

There followed the sounds of a slap, Delver's voice telling a jest he couldn't catch the words of, and more laughter. El abandoned stealth for haste as he saw the passage they'd used end at an archway. He was just in time to see the amorous trio leave the far end of that empty, echoing room through another arch.

One dark and disused chamber proved to lead into another, through a succession of open archways, and El took care to keep out of sight of anyone glancing back, and freeze whenever the sounds ahead ceased. He'd worked his way back to being a single chamber behind when some trick of eddying air currents made the voices of those he was following startlingly loud.

"Where by all the gods of battle are you *taking* us, woman?"

"Uh, *Your Majesty*, he meant to say. . . . This does look suspiciously like a way down to the dungeons."

Dasumia laughed again, a deep, hearty sound of pleasure this time. "Keep that hand right where it is, bold warrior . . . and no, don't-be-gentle-sirs, we're heading nowhere near the dungeons. You have a royal promise on that!"

El crept to the next archway like a hunting cat and peered around its edge—in time to hear the rattle of a beaded curtain, unseen around a corner, parting. Light flared out from beyond it; El took a chance, danced across the room to that corner, and took another chance: across the open, lit way they'd taken was another curtain. He could hide behind it and see into the lit area, if he just darted across the open way at the right moment not to be seen.

Now? He darted, halted, and tried to bring his breathing back to sound-lessness, all in a handful of instants. He used the next handful, and the next, to stare at where the queen had taken her catches.

The brightly lit area beyond the curtains was only an antechamber; an archway in its far wall opened into a place lit by a red, evil-looking radiance. Flanking that arch were two fully armored guardians, with their visors down and curving sabers raised in their gauntlets—warriors without feet, whose ankle stumps were gliding along inches above the stone floor without ever touching it. Helmed horrors, men called them; magically animated armor that could slay as surely as living armsmen.

El watched them start menacingly forward, only to halt at a gesture from the queen. Dasumia strode between them without stopping, towing her living warriors, and El stole along boldly in their wake, watching those raised sabers narrowly. Before he reached the helmed horrors, they wheeled around and floated along after the trio, sheathing their swords soundlessly. El brought up the rear, moving very cautiously now.

The chamber beyond was very large and very dark, its only light coming from a glowing ruby-hued tapestry at the far end, a tapestry that displayed a black device larger than many cottages El had seen: the Black Hand of Bane.

The aisle that ran down the center of the temple was lined with braziers. As Dasumia strode between each pair of them, they burst spontaneously into flame. Delver and Ingrath were obviously having second thoughts about their royal night of passion; El could clearly hear them gulping as they slowed and had to be dragged along by Dasumia.

There were pews on either side of the aisle, some of them occupied by slumped skeletons in robes, others by mummified or still-rotting corpses. El ducked into an empty row, crouching low to the floor; he knew what must be coming.

"No!" Ingrath cried suddenly, twisting free of the queen's grasp and whirling around to flee. He moaned despairingly, an instant before Delver tore free of the chain of coins, began his own sprint—and screamed.

The two helmed horrors had been floating right behind them, gauntleted hands out and ready to close on their throats. Those steely fingers beckoned to them now, as the empty helms leaned horribly closer.

Moaning in despair, the two guardsmen turned back to face the queen. Dasumia was lying on the altar, propped up on one elbow and wearing rather less than she'd entered the temple with. Laughingly she beckoned them.

Reluctantly, the two warriors stumbled forward.

TEN
TO TASTE DARK FIRE

The best thing an archmage can do with his spells? Use them to destroy another archmage, of course—and himself in the doing. We'll plant something useful in the ashes.

RADISHES, PERHAPS.
ALBRYNGUNDAR OF THE SINGING SWORD
FROM *THOUGHTS ON A BETTER FAERÛN*
PUBLISHED CIRCA THE YEAR OF THE LION

Unseen drums boomed and rolled, beginning an inexorable, unhurried beat that shook the temple. El watched narrowly as a large hand of Bane—a trifle taller than a man and seemingly carved of some black stone—rose into view behind the altar block. A halo of wispy red flames rose and fell around its fingers, and by their flickering light, as Dasumia leaped lightly back down from the altar, Elminster saw two long, metal-barbed black whips lying crossed upon the altar where she'd been lying.

The drumbeats quickened very slightly. Seeking a better view, El drew up the hood of his robes to hide his face in its cowl and slowly rose into a seated position on his pew, becoming just another slumped form among the many corpses. His decaying neighbors were no doubt onetime victims of rituals here. Delver and Ingrath—and one Elminster, too, for that matter—might well soon join them, if the Court Mage of Galadorna didn't act with precise timing and do just the right things in the moments just ahead.

The two warriors stood facing Dasumia, and they were trembling with fear. She took their hands and spoke to them. The words were lost to El in the sound of the drums, but she was obviously reassuring them. From time to time she embraced or kissed them, ignoring—as they could not—the hulking helmed horrors floating just behind their shoulders.

The queen turned, took up the whips, and handed one to each man. Leaning back against the altar, she snapped a command to them and held up her hands toward the dark, unseen ceiling in a gesture of summoning.

With great reluctance they swung the whips in her direction—with no force, so the barbed lengths simply brushed against her and bounced off harmlessly. Elminster heard Dasumia's angry order this time: "Strike! Strike or die!"

She held up her hands in a summoning once more, and the whips lashed out at her in earnest this time. Her body jerked under the blows, and a wisp of blue silk fell away. She hissed encouragement to Ingrath and Delver, who struck harder, their whips cracking. A lash wrapped around her, baring one of her breasts.

At their next blows, the first weals marked Dasumia, and she groaned at them to strike harder still. The guardsmen obeyed tentatively at first. Then with spirit as she shouted at them to strike ever harder, staring up at them as she had more than once overwhelmed Elminster with her will.

Delver and Ingrath reeled, then bent to their task, putting all their fear of dying here and resentment at her entrapping them behind each blow. Blood-drenched blue silk and smooth flesh beneath rapidly vanished under a rain of blows from whips that glistened dark with blood.

Abruptly Dasumia threw back her head and howled at them to stop. Delver, weeping hysterically, failed to do so—and the helmed horror behind him snaked out a gauntlet and caught his arm in a grip that halted his frantic flailing in mid-swing.

She looked more like a beast skinned for the roasting spit than a naked woman, now, but as Dasumia drew her arms down and put her hands on her hips to explain the next part of the ritual, she might have been imperiously gowned and giving orders to kneeling courtiers. She showed no trace of pain despite the blood coursing down her limbs, moving easily and with her usual wanton sway of the hips as she ordered Ingrath onto the altar, to lie on his back.

Anger was rising in Elminster. Anger and revulsion. He had to do something. He had to make this stop.

El tried to recall what he'd once heard a drunken worshiper of Bane say about this sort of ritual. Sacrifices being cut to death by priests flailing with sharp swords, was it? Or a floating Hand of Bane crushing sacrifices in its grip . . . aye, that was it.

Dasumia had mounted the guardsman on the altar and was crying out, "Strike! Strike!" to Delver, who was moving reluctantly forward with his whip to obey her, when El knew he could watch no longer.

The whip cracked down, trailing blood at each swing, and El found himself tingling with rage and with risen power—power throbbing at his very fingertips.

He was a Chosen of Mystra, however hazily he recalled what that had meant. "Mystra," he murmured, "guide me."

However evil his Lady Master had turned out to be, he could not watch her blood raining down any longer while he did nothing, and two good men drew closer and closer to their deaths. That black hand behind the altar would slowly rise, then reach out to crush them—as it was moving now!

Horrified, Elminster reached out with his will, using the one spell he could unleash without speaking or moving. Hopefully he could remain an anonymous corpse for a few moments more. He moved not against the hand—that would come next—but to disable the foes who were sure to come diving down on him the moment he was discovered. He could feel the webwork of linkages, now, coursing out from the altar. With infinite care he detached one linkage from a helmed horror, shifting it to a section of ceiling beyond the floating thing rather than severing it outright. If he could get one step further before being discovered. . . .

Dasumia stiffened and sat up, ignoring the continuing bite of the lash. She glared around the temple, seeking the intruder. El shrugged and broke the bindings of the second helmed horror with savage abruptness.

Dark and terrible eyes bored into him. Then, slowly, Dasumia's lips twisted into a smile. She sat back on the altar, reclining again on one elbow with an air of amusement, and watched him.

Silently, their limbs jerking, Delver and Ingrath began to shuffle toward Elminster. Obviously in thrall, they thrust the bloody whips they carried back over their shoulders, ready for the first lashing strike. The barbs that had so mutilated Dasumia glistened red with her blood as the guardsmen lurched nearer . . . and nearer. . . .

El's shearing spell was still active, and he was loathe to spend another magic when the duel of his life was waiting, sneering at him up on the altar. Yet what good would it do to break her thrall upon the warriors, when with another spell—no doubt to her a trifling magic—she could restore it?

Delver and Ingrath stumbled stiffly nearer, their faces locked and impassive, their eyes horrified and rolling, pleading with him for aid or mercy or release. . . .

El snapped the linkages that controlled them with brutal force. Ignoring their suddenly spasming bodies and uncontrolled spitting and ululating, he rode the shock of the magical backlash into their minds, feeling the same pain they did. It was he who cried out in agony—but they toppled bonelessly to the floor, senseless.

It had worked. El discovered he'd bitten his lip. He shot a glance at the altar, but Dasumia hadn't moved. She was still reclining at her ease, soundlessly laughing—and the blood and whip cuts were fading from her skin, melting away as if they'd never been.

El drew in a deep breath and glanced behind him to be sure there were no other helmed horrors, arriving Bane worshipers, or any other menace that might strike from behind. He found nothing. He thought he saw a movement among the corpses along the darkest row of pews, right at the back, but he could not be sure and could see nothing moving when he stared hard at that place. He dared not turn his back on Dasumia any longer.

Wheeling around, he found her still lying at ease on the altar, whole and healed now, her body quite bare. She laughed aloud, and El gritted his teeth against the rage now boiling up in his throat and with iron control worked his next magic with precision. Lady Master or no, he was going to bring that huge, hovering black hand of stone crashing down on the altar. He was—

The Hand resisted him utterly. Dasumia's laughter rose into real mirth as he snarled and strained to move it. He could feel the linkage, he could insinuate his will into its flows, to grasp at the magic—and it ignored him, remaining as rigid as an iron bar despite his best efforts to budge it. He was—he could . . . he could not.

As the Queen of Galadorna hooted at him, El abandoned the spell with a snarl and worked another magic, hiding his gestures from her, down below the back of the pew in front of him.

When he was ready, a seeming eternity later, he stood up and hurled his magic through her cruel laughter—not at the deadly, beautiful woman on the altar, or at the altar itself, a stone block that positively throbbed with ebbing and flowing magic he could not hope to overmaster. The floor beneath one end of it, however. . . .

Flagstones heaved, buckled, and shattered into shards, their cracks louder than those the whip had made. The floor rippled like a wave of stone, sending slivers of stone clattering against the back wall of the temple, and suddenly subsided, opening a huge pit. There must be cellars down there his magic could shove the earth and stone into, to clear a space so swiftly.

Dasumia sprang calmly off the altar to land on her feet, facing him. She smiled approvingly, saluted him, then turned to watch as the altar block shivered, teetered, and tipped over, sliding into the chasm with a thunderous crash.

"Shattered . . . how destructive of you," Dasumia observed merrily. "Care to destroy anything else?"

In grim, wordless answer Elminster snatched a stall-plate from the end of his pew and broke it across his knee, cracking the hand of Bane. Dying enchantments spat black sparks. He cast its wooden shards onto the floor and reached for the next plate.

Dasumia laughed. "So, has it come to a duel between us two at last, brave Elminster? Are you ready to dare me at last?"

"No," Elminster almost whispered. "Have ye forgotten what I told ye, when first we met at the Riven Stone? I serve Mystra first . . . and *then* Dasumia . . . then Galadorna. Tell me: who does Dasumia serve first?"

Dasumia laughed again. "Choices have prices," she said almost merrily. "Prepare to pay yours."

Her hands rose in a simple gesture, and almost immediately Elminster felt a tightness in his throat, a choking feeling that grew steadily worse. His legs and hips seemed to shift under him, his clothes began to feel tight . . . then more than tight.

El struggled to rise, and saw that his fingers were becoming stubby, bloated things, like mismatched, mottled sausages. So was the rest of him. Clothing began to split and disintegrate then, with tearing sounds like whip strikes.

The shredded remnants of the mantle of Court Mage of Galadorna fell away in tatters as El wallowed about, trying to rise on legs that kept changing in length and thickness. Dasumia was howling with laughter as he fell over to one side or another, growing steadily larger until he was pressed tight against the pew in front of his own in a grip that grew steadily more viselike. He was as fat as two cart barrels now, and still growing. He tried to spin the gestures of another spell with fingers that dangled and wobbled and were as long as his forearm—a forearm that was now as broad as his chest had been, before it, too, had started growing. . . .

Then his own spell took hold, and the tightness was suddenly gone as the pews in front of him, behind him, and under him all tore free of the floor, trailing dust as they rose—and tumbling him onto the floor, a grotesque mass of sliding, many-folded flesh that lay on its back, panting. El heaved and struggled, gasping for breath, and managed to get over onto one side, facing his foe.

The moment he could see her, three pews flashed through the air at her under his grim bidding, like gigantic lances. Dasumia ducked, rolled, then back flipped, turned as she landed, and in the same motion flexed her magnificent legs and sprang. All three pews missed, crashing into the floating black hand with a splintering fury that shook the room. One of the fingers broke off the hand, leaking magical radiances as it went.

Dasumia hissed something fast and harsh—and almost instantly El found himself rising into the air. Up and up he rose, uncontrollably, trying to see what was where around the temple as he went. Was she going to lift him and drop him, or—?

El caught sight of something lying in the aisle and got an idea. He worked the spell he needed in furious haste, knowing that a bruising impact with the cobwebbed stone ceiling was coming up fast.

He finished the spell just in time to throw one arm up in front of his face and turn his nose aside before slamming hard into the ceiling—sending startled bats screeching away in a wild flapping of wings—and finding that her magic was still pressing on him, pinning him against the dank stone.

He scrabbled with his arms and elbows, trying to roll over so he could see Dasumia—and not dark, dirty stone an inch from his eyelashes. He needed to be able to see, to work the spell he'd cast.

Grunting and gasping, he managed to roll his ponderous bulk over in time to see a tightly smiling Dasumia magically raise one of the shattered pews he'd hurled at her into the air—and send it right back at him.

Larger and larger it loomed as El scrambled along the ceiling trying to get out of its way, using his great bulk to catch and kick at vault ribs that would have been ten feet or more out of his reach if he'd been his proper size . . . El tried to concentrate on his own spell, down below, and ignore the oncoming pew.

He never saw the slim, dark-robed figure that stood up in the back pew to take calm, careful aim at him, fix his position in mind, then begin to cast its own deadly spell.

As El moved, the pew curved in the air to follow, Dasumia's smile broadening with anticipatory glee at the coming impact. The end that would strike Elminster was a splayed mass of jagged wooden splinters, most of them as long as a man was tall.

Dasumia took three swift steps sideways to get a better look at the situation—and that was all El needed. He rolled over a roof vault, wheezing like some great aerial whale, and in its lee called on his spell. Two whips rose from the aisle like eager, awakened snakes, to pounce on the Queen of Galadorna.

As the pew struck the ceiling with a crash that sent him bouncing off the ceiling tiles amid showers of dust, El had a brief glimpse of Dasumia's startled face as bloodied black leather whipped around one wrist and jerked down, throwing her onto her back. She struck her head on the floor and cried out in pain—and that was all the time the two whips needed. The wrist that had dragged her down was bound fast to her ankle, the other whip did the same on her other side, and one whip slapped its handle across her eyes, blinding her with tears, while the other thrust its handle into her open mouth, effectively gagging her.

Most of the pew broke away and showered the temple below with shards of wood as the gigantic missile cartwheeled away from the roof vault. Ilbryn Starym didn't even have time to flee as the rest of the pew plunged into the pew right in front of where he was sitting, sending riven wood in all directions and hurling him helplessly into the air, tumbling head over heels in the midst of his own conjured ball of magical flames to strike the back wall of the temple with a crash. He slid slowly and brokenly down that wall, his screams fading.

Abruptly El found himself plummeting to the ground. He grinned savagely; this must mean Dasumia was either falling unconscious or abandoning her spell in favor of something desperate. He sent the whips an urgent command to thrust their captive aloft, so he could give her the same sort of fall if she overcame him, or his own landing was too . . . hard.

Gods! El knew bones had shattered, even before he rolled over like some sort of agonized elephant and tried to scramble to his feet. Scrambling didn't work, but he did get upright by throwing his great bulk to one side, then trying to climb it with his clumsy legs. He got himself turned around in time to see his whips suddenly swinging empty, their captive gone from their entangling midst.

A moment later, a cold, cold pain slid into his side and out again, and he knew where she'd gone. He didn't bother to try to turn and face her, just to see a sword dripping with his own blood and to give her a better target to stab at, but concentrated on ignoring the pain and calling up another spell. The blade slid into him once more, but El knew his great bulk kept him safe from her slitting his throat—she couldn't reach it without so much climbing that he'd be able to simply topple over onto her to win this fight forever. He threw himself backward and heard her startled curse and the clangor of a dropped sword bouncing on stone. Now he did start to turn, heaving himself around. If the blade was close enough, he could throw himself on it and bury it.

He met Dasumia's startled eyes—and she brought one hand to her mouth, glanced down at the sword lying so close to him—and vanished, just moments before El completed his spell.

It was a blood magic incantation. El threw back his head and shrieked at the pain. As the magic healed his wounds, it felt like fire raging through his gigantic body—fire that flared, raged, then swiftly faded as the healing neared completion. It could also teleport him to wherever his freshly shed blood might be—on the floor beneath him, on the sword mere feet away . . . and on the hands of the queen, wherever she might be!

The spell flashed, the temple around him twisted, and he was suddenly behind the altar, where a crouching Dasumia was looking up at him in startled surprise. He reached out to clutch at her should she try to flee, and threw himself off-balance so as to fall on her. Dasumia back flipped again, her heels grazing the floating Black Hand of Bane—and El crashed down inches away from her frantically rolling form. He grabbed at her, but couldn't reach, and was still huffing and wallowing and trying to pivot his great bulk around so that his bloated and deformed arm could reach her when she fetched up against the back wall of the temple and cast another spell, favoring him with a catlike smile of triumph.

Something flashed. El turned his head in time to see one of the floating helmed horrors flow and twist, breaking apart into a whirling sphere of jagged metal shards—shards that came out of their dance in a stream that leaped right at him.

El threw one ponderous arm up in front of his eyes and throat, and with the other grabbed blindly, felt Dasumia's struggling form, closed his grasp mercilessly, and hauled her like a rag doll back up in front of him as a shield.

As searing shards cut into him in three places or more, El heard Dasumia gasp, a sound that was cut off sharply. When he lowered his shielding arm, he saw that she was biting her lip, blood trailing down her chin and eyes closed in her contorted face. Jagged shards had transfixed her in a dozen places, and she was shuddering. The blue-white motes of magic leaking from her might be contingencies . . . or might be something else. As he watched, a shard drooped, dangled, then broke off and fell, visibly smaller. Another seemed to be melting into her, and another—gods!

The sudden pain made Elminster drop his foe. Her ravaged body fell onto his great bulk—and the real pain began. A burning . . . smoke was rising from where she lay sprawled on his mounded flesh, and she was slowly sinking.

Acid! She'd turned her blood to acid, and it was eating away at him and at the shards. Well, the watching gods knew he'd spare flesh in plenty to lose, but he had to get clear of her. He snatched at her, threw her as hard as he could at the floating Hand of Bane, and had the satisfaction of seeing her strike it limply and stick for a moment before her own weight peeled her free, to fall from view behind the altar. Wisps of smoke curled up from the hand as a little left-behind acid ate at it, too.

El sat back grimly and sighed. Unconscious she might be, but he lacked the strength to crush her. Perhaps if he pushed her into the pit and shouldered those two loose pews into it on top of her . . .

Nay, he could not be so cruel. And so, when she awakened, Elminster Aumar would die. He was almost out of spells and still trapped in this grotesquely enlarged form, probably unable to fit through the passages that had brought him here. He could do little more to stop the evil Lady Master whom Mystra had sent him to serve. Her magic overmatched his, as his outstripped that of a novice. She would make a magnificent and able servant of Mystra, a better Chosen than he, if she were only biddable enough to obey anyone.

He shut his eyes against the banner of Bane and called up a mental image of the blue-white star of Mystra. "Lady of Mysteries," he said aloud, his voice echoing in the now-silent temple, "one who has been thy servant cries to ye in his need. I have failed thee, and failed in my service to the one called Dasumia, but see in her strength that could well serve thee in my place. Succor this Dasumia, I pray, and—"

Sudden, searing cold shocked him into an inarticulate cry. He could feel himself trembling uncontrollably as magic stronger than he'd ever felt before surged through him. Numbly he waited for whatever killing strike Dasumia would deal him, but it did not come. Instead, a warmth gently grew within the ice, and he felt himself relaxing, even as a strange crawling sensation swept over him. He was healed, he was growing smaller and lighter and himself again, and a face that he could barely see through flooding tears was bending over him.

Then he heard a voice speaking to him tenderly, a voice that belonged to the Queen of Galadorna but no longer held the cold cruelty of Dasumia. "So you pass the test, Elminster Aumar, and remain the first and dearest of my Chosen—even if your brains are too addled to recognize when a ritual of Bane is being perverted, bringing pleasure to his altar instead of pain, and shedding the blood of someone willing." A fond and musical laugh followed, then the words, "I am proud, this night."

Gentle arms enfolded him, and Elminster cried out in wonder as he felt himself lifted up, in a soaring flight that should have smashed them both into the ceiling but did not, reaching high and clear into the stars instead.

The roof of the House of the Unicorn burst apart, towers toppling, as a column of silver fire roared up into the night. As men on the battlements screamed and cursed, something chill and chiming that had been coiled hungrily around a spire close by their heads fled in a misty parabola, to drift away low over the streets of Nethrar, cowering in the night.

Silver fire danced on dark water, throwing feeble reflections onto purple-bordered tapestries of deepest black. High on those tapestries, in purple thread, were worked their sole adornments: cruel, somehow feminine smiles.

The inky waters of the scrying font rippled, and the scene of silver fire soaring up out of a castle was gone.

Someone close above the water said excitedly, "You saw? I know how we can use this."

"Tell me!" a cold voice snapped, sharp with excitement, then in lower tones, in another direction, said more calmly, "Cancel the Evenflame service. We'll be busy—and undisturbed, mark you, Sister Night—until further notice."

And so it was that Galadorna lost its queen and its court mage in the same night, less than a tenday before the armies of Laothkund rolled down from the tree-girt hills to set Nethrar ablaze, and shatter the Unicorn Kingdom forever.

PART II

SUNRISE ON A DARK ROAD

ELEVEN
MOONRISE, FROSTFIRE, AND DOOM

*Adventurers are best used to slay monsters. Sooner or later, they become your
worst monsters, and you have to hire new ones to do the obvious thing.*

RALDERICK HALLOWSHAW, JESTER
FROM *To Rule A Realm, From Turret To Midden*
PUBLISHED CIRCA THE YEAR OF THE BLOODBIRD

S eems peaceful enough, don't it?" the warrior rumbled, looking around from
the height of his saddle at the forest of hiexel, blueleaf, and gnarled old
phandar trees that flanked both sides of the road. Birds called in the distant
depths of its shade gloom, and small furry things scuttled here and there among
the dead leaves that carpeted its mossy stumps and mushroom-studded dead
falls. Golden shafts of sunlight stabbed down into the forest here and there,
lighting little clearings where shrubs fought each other for the light, and the
moss-draped creepers were fewer.

"Don't say such foolhead things, Arvas," one of his companions growled.
"They sound all too much like the sort of cues ambushing brigands like to follow.
That sentence of yours sounds like something that should end with an arrow
taking you in the throat—or the chunk of road your charger's standing on rising
up to be revealed as the head of some awakened titan or other."

"I'll take the 'or other,' you merry-faced killjoy," Arvas grunted. "I just meant
I don't see claw-sharpening marks on trees, bloodstains . . . that sort of thing—
which should make you even more cheerful."

"You can be sure the High Duke didn't hire us to block the Starmantle road
while we argue about things I'd rather other ears didn't hear about," a deeper
voice said sharply. "Arvas, Faldast—stow it!"

"Paeregur," Arvas said in weary tones, "have you looked up and down this
road recently? Do you see anyone—*anyone*—but us? Block the road from what,
may I ask? Since the deaths began, travel seems to have just about stopped along
here. Possibly about the same time you got this funny idea into your head that
you're somehow entitled to give the rest of us orders! Was it that new armor,
the heavy helm pressing hard on your brains? Or was it the new thrusting
codpiece with the—"

"Arvas, *enough!*" said someone else, in exasperation. "Gods, it's like having a
babbling drunk riding with us."

"Rolian," his halfling comrade said, from somewhere below the level of the humans' belts, "it is having a babbling drunk riding with us!"

There was a general roar of laughter—even echoed, albeit sarcastically, by Arvas himself—and the Frostfire Banner urged their mounts into a trot. They all wanted to find a good defensible place to camp before dark, or have time to get back to Starmantle if no such site offered itself, and it wouldn't be all that many hours, now, before the shadows grew long and the sun bright and low.

High Duke Horostos styled himself lord over the rich farmlands west of Starmantle, along a forested cliff of a coast that offered few harbors (and no good ones). As realms went, it was a quiet and safe land, plagued by the usual owlbears and stirges from time to time, the odd band of brigands, thieving peddlers; small problems that a few armsmen and foresters with good bows could handle.

Lately, it seemed, at about the time the worst winter snows ended and folk considered the useful part of the Year of the Awakening Wyrm to have begun, the High Duchy of Langalos had somehow acquired a big problem.

Something that left no tracks, but killed at will—passing merchants, woodcutters, farmers, livestock, and alert war bands of the Duke's best armsmen alike. Even a high-ranking priest of Tempus, traveling with a large mounted and well-armed bodyguard, had gone missing somewhere along the wooded road west of Starmantle, and was thought to have fallen afoul of the mysterious slayer. Could this be the "Awakening Wyrm" of the prophecies?

Perhaps, but hired griffon-riders flying over the area had found no sign of large caves, scorched or broken trees or any other marks of large beasts . . . or any sign of brigands or their encampments, for that matter. Nor had the few foresters who still dared to venture anywhere near the trees seen anything—and one by one, these were disappearing too. Their reports told of a land that seemed barren of any beast so large as a fox or hare; the game trails were grown over with ferns.

So the High Duke had reluctantly opened his coffers while he still had subjects to tax and refill them and had hired the classic solution: a band of adventurers—in this case, hireswords who'd been thrown out of service to wealthy Tethyrians for a variety of reasons, and gathered as the Frostfire Banner to seek their fortunes in more easterly lands, where their past indiscretions would be less well known.

The money offered by Horostos was both good and needed. The Banner were ten in all, and numbered among their ranks a pair apiece of mages and warrior-priests, yet they went warily. This was unfamiliar country to them—but death knows all lands, intimately and often.

So it was that cocked but unloaded crossbows hung across several saddles, though it was bad for the strings, and no one rode carelessly. The forest stayed lovely—and deserted.

"No stags," Arvas grunted once, and his companions, nodding their replies, realized how silent they'd fallen. Waiting for the blow to fall.

A goodly way west of Starmantle the road looped around and beneath an exposed spur of rock, an outcropping that pointed out to sea and upward like the prow of some great buried ship. Once the sun sank low and the Banner knew they had to turn around, they settled on the rocky prow as their camp.

"Yon's as good a place as the gods provide, short of bare hilltops. One to watch along the road and down the cliffs, and two to face the forest along the neck of it, here, tie up our horses below and be-damned to anyone trying to use the road by night, and we're set," Rolian grunted.

Paeregur gave a wordless grunt as his only answer. The tone of that grunt sounded unconvinced. The silence of fear hung heavy over the camp that night, and evenfeast was eaten in hushed tones.

"We're as close to death as we've ever been," the halfling muttered as they rolled themselves in their cloaks, laid weapons to hand, and watched the stars come out over the water.

"Will you belt up about dying?" Rolian hissed. "No one can come at us unseen, we've set a heavy watch, the dippers and the shields are ready for a fast wakening . . . what more can we do?"

"Ride out of here and go back to Tethyr," Avras said quietly—yet the camp had grown so still that most of them heard him. Several heads turned, wearing scowls . . . but no one said a word in reply.

Overhead, as deep night came down, the stars began to come out in earnest.

"What's that?" Rolian breathed, beside Paeregur's ear. "D'you hear it?"

"Of course I hear it," the warrior replied quietly, rising silently to his feet and turning slowly, his drawn blade glinting in the light of the new-risen moon. He could hear it best to the west, somewhere very close by, a thin, aimless chiming sound. A bridle? A bell on a minstrel's instrument, or on the harness of a wayward horse? Or—the little fey ones, come calling?

After a moment he took a few cautious crouching steps across the rock spur, picking his way between the still forms of his sleeping fellows. A thin thread of mist was drifting in the lee of the rock spur—strange, that, with the moon rising—but there was nothing to be seen. Not even seabirds, or an owl. In fact, that was why this was so eerie—the woods were still. No scuffling, no night cries or the shrieks of small animals being caught by larger prowlers . . . nothing. Paeregur shook his head in puzzlement, and turned slowly to go back. There it was again, that faint chiming.

He turned back to the west again and became a listening statue. After a time the chiming was gone. The tall warrior shrugged, glanced down at the horses below the prow—and froze.

Where were the horses? He took two quick strides to the other side of the prow, in case they'd all shifted to the east of the overhang—their lead-reins were long enough—but, no. They were gone. "Rolian," he growled, beckoning sharply, and ran along the prow to its very tip, where the still, cowled form of Avras sat facing out to sea, his sword across his knees. Hah! Some watch guard he'd turned out to be!

"Avras!" he hissed, clapping a heavy hand on the warrior's shoulder, "where are the horses? If you've been drinking again, so help me I'm g—"

The shoulder under his hand crumpled like a thing of dry leaves and kindling, and the faceless husk of Avras pivoted toward him for a moment before collapsing into ash. The man's skull tumbled out to bounce off Paeregur's boot before falling out and down to the road below with a dull clatter.

Paeregur almost fell off the spur recoiling in horror. Then he scrambled back along it to the first of his sleeping companions, and turned the blankets back with the point of his blade. A skull grinned up at him.

"Gods," he sobbed, slashing with his sword tip at the next cloak. His blade caught on the garment and dragged it half off; bones spilled out in a confusion of ash and collapse. Paeregur knew real gut-wrenching terror for the first time in his life. He wanted to run, anywhere, away from here.

Rolian was taking a damned long time to arrive.

Paeregur glanced along the spur to where Rolian had been sitting beside him, facing the forest—had been whispering to him, only a few breaths ago. Where had—?

The chiming, coming again—only this time, from among the wall of dark trees they'd been facing—sounded almost mocking. A little mist was curling around their trunks, and Rolian—

Rolian was standing in those trees with his sword in the crook of his arm and the laces of his codpiece in his hands, in the eternal wide-legged pose of men relieving themselves in the woods, facing away into the darkness. Paeregur started to relax, then fresh fear coiled in the pit of his stomach. Rolian was standing very still. Too still.

"Frostfire *awake!*" Paeregur roared, with all the volume he could muster; the very rocks rang back his shout, and an echo came back faintly from the depths of the forest. He was running as he bellowed, back along the spine of the spur toward Rolian . . . already knowing what he'd find.

He came to a stop behind that still form and tried to peer past it. Fangs? Eyes? Waiting blades? Nothing; the moonlight was enough to show him nothing but trees. He stretched out his sword gently. "Rolian?"

The warrior gave a long, formless sigh as he toppled forward into the trees. He broke into three pieces before he hit the ground, his blade bouncing away among dead leaves . . . and left Paeregur staring at a pair of empty boots and a tangle of slumped clothing. Ye bloody grave-sucking gods!

The tall warrior took two quick steps back from that place and spun around. Was he the only one left alive? Had any—but no. He almost shouted with relief: the mage Lhaerand was on his feet, face pinched with sleepy disapproval, as was the giant among them, slow-witted but loyal Phostral, his full plate armor make him a gleaming mountain in the moonlight. Two. Two of them all.

"Something has killed all the others," Paeregur told them tightly. "Something that can slay in a moment, and silently."

"Oh?" Lhaerand snarled. "Then what's that?"

It was the chiming again, only loud and insistent now, as if standing in triumph over them. Suddenly the mist was back, sliding past their feet and bringing its own chill with it as it drifted along the spur. Paeregur's eyes narrowed.

"Lhaerand," he said suddenly, "can you hurl fire?"

"Yes, of course," the mage snapped. "At who? I—"

"*At that!*" Paeregur shouted, fear making his voice almost a scream. "*Now!*"

And as if it could hear his words, the mist thickened into bright smoke, and struck, snakelike, at Phostral. The giant warrior had raised his blade and moved to challenge it even before Paeregur's cry; his companions could only see his back, and hear a faint sighing—was that a sizzle, at the heart of it? A gurgle?—in the instant before his blade fell from his hand. The gauntlet went with it, and nothing was left behind: the vambrace ended in a stump. Then, slowly, Phostral turned to face his companions.

His helm was empty, his head entirely burnt away, but something was filling it or at least holding it where it should be, above the armored wall of the warrior's chest. The thing that had been Phostral staggered toward them, moving slowly and tentatively. The mage stepped back and started to stammer out a spell.

Instantly the gigantic armored form turned toward him and toppled, crashing down on its face—or where its face had been—as a white whirlwind boiled up out of it, chiming. Paeregur shouted in fear, waving his sword and knowing it would avail him nothing—but Lhaerand shrieked and sprinted the length of the spur, with the mist-thing in cold and chiming pursuit.

The mage never tried to turn and fight. He ran as fast as he could and leaped, high and far, out over the road to somewhere above the cliffs beyond—where he howled all the way down to a wet and splintering end.

So that was a despairing death. Paeregur swallowed. What better would a heroic one be?

And how would any minstrel know, once he was bones and ash?

The whirlwind came back along the spur slowly, chiming almost coyly—as if it was toying with him.

The tall warrior set his jaw and raised his sword. When he judged the mist was near enough, he slashed at it and danced to one side, then planted himself to drive a vicious backhand back through its chiming whiteness.

Unsurprisingly, his blade met nothing, though its edge seemed to acquire a line of sparks. Even as he noticed them, in his frantic trot along the spur, they winked out.

He circled, tripping on someone's helm and almost falling, to lash out with his blade again. Once more he clove nothing, gasped his way aside from looming mist, and slashed through it again with the same utter lack of effect. The mist swirled, leaping over his head, and he dodged aside to avoid having it fall on him. It continued its sinuous rush, curving around his vainly thrusting blade to dart in along his sword arm.

At the last instant, it turned into him rather than grazing past—and blazing agony exploded through him. Paeregur was dazedly aware that he was screaming and staggering away vainly slapping at empty air with his arm.

His only arm.

Nothing remained on the other side but a twisted mass of seared flesh and leather, all melted together. There was no blood . . . but there was no arm left at all. His sword arm. Paeregur looked wildly about as the ribbon of mist floated almost mockingly past, and saw his sword lying atop a huddled mess that had once been a priest of Tymora. Much good Lady Luck had brought them all, to be sure. He ran unsteadily, not used to one side of him being a lot lighter than the other, over to his blade and scooped it up.

He was still straightening when the burning pain came again and he fell heavily onto his tailbone on the rock, watching an empty boot spin away. It had taken his leg.

He struggled to rise, to move at all, his remaining boot heel kicking vainly against the uneven stone, and waved his blade defiantly. The mist closed in and he made of himself a desperate whirlwind, spinning around and around with his blade constantly slashing the air. He rang it off the stone around him twice, once hard enough to chip the edge, and cared not. He was going to die here . . . what good is a pristine blade to a dead man?

The mist came at him again in an almost gloating dive, its chiming rising around him as he twisted and slashed desperately. When the burning came again, it was in his intact thigh and he was rolling helplessly over, flailing at nothing with his useless sword. One limb at a time—it *was* toying with him.

Was he going to be reduced to a helpless torso, unable to do anything but stare as it slew him very slowly?

A few panting breaths later, as he stared up at the uncaring stars through swimming eyes, he knew the answer was going to be—yes.

He wondered just how long the mist would make him suffer, then decided he was past caring. Almost his last thought was a rueful realization that all who die slowly enough to know what is happening must come to a place beyond caring.

He was . . . he was Paeregur Amaethur Donlas, and he had come to his cold end here on a rock in the wilderlands of the accursed High Duchy of Langalos in the early summer of the year seven hundred and sixty-seven (as Dalereckoning ran) with no one to mourn or mark his passing, and his dead comrades all around him.

Well, have my thanks, all you vigilant gods.

Paeregur's last thought was that he really should remember the name of that star . . . and that one, too. . . .

The Crypt of the Moondark family was overgrown with brambles, creepers, and contorted, curving trees deformed by warding enchantments that were still strong after centuries. The Moondark house, a happy mingling of elf and human blood, had been known for its fell sorcery, but no Moondarks had walked Faerûn for something like one hundred and sixteen winters . . . and Westgate was quite content about that. No more powerful spells that might challenge a king or discomfit self-styled nobles, and no more need to be polite to half-bloods who were graceful, handsome, learned, bright, all too merry—and all too insistent on fairness and honesty in ruling. There was even a sign, much more recent than the spell-locked gates: "Behold the ending of all who insist too much."

Elminster smiled grimly at that little moral notice. It was the first thing to crumble into dust at the touch of his most powerful spell. The long-untested wards beyond were the next thing. Dawn was almost upon Westgate, and he wanted to be safely inside the tomb-house before folk took to the streets.

The guards at the corner were still yawning and dozing against the outer wall of the crypt as Elminster slipped inside. On his short walk along the statue-flanked path to the doors of the pillared tomb house, El's magic burnt away an astonishing number of magical triggers and traps. An odd thing for one in the service of Mystra to practice . . . but then Mystra dealt in a healthy array of "odd things." What he was here to do was one of his most important tasks as a Chosen, one he spent a lot of time at these days. One that seemed to awaken an almost girlish glee in the Lady of Mysteries.

Elminster Aumar would do anything to see her smiling so.

The door wards, falling beam trap, and weave-of-jutting-blades traps were all to be expected, were anticipated, and were dealt with in but a few seconds. The fact that folk from time to time had to enter a family tomb for legitimate purposes—burials, not thefts—meant that such defenses had to be of a lesser order. In a matter of a few calm breaths Elminster was inside the dark chamber, with the door shut and spell-sealed behind him, and a radiance of his own making awakening everywhere along the low, cobwebbed ceiling.

Moondarks lay crumbling on all sides of him in stacked stone coffers that must have numbered nearly a hundred. The oldest ones were the largest, carved with ornate scenes along the sides, their lids effigies of the deceased; the more recent ones were plain stone boxes, some lacking even names. Thankfully none were stirring in undeath; he was running late as it was and never liked to hurry the fun part.

The bright and wealthy Moondarks had even been considerate enough to leave a funeral slab in the center of the crypt—a high table on which the coffin of the most recently dead could lie during a last service of remembrance, before it was muscled onto one of the stacks of the dead that lined the walls, to be left undisturbed forever. Or at least until a clever Chosen of Mystra happened along.

Elminster hummed a tune of lost Myth Drannor as he laid out his cloak on the empty slab—a large but nondescript lined leather cloak that wasn't much of any color anymore and sported more than the usual assortment of patches. The inside of the cloak bore several large, crude pockets, though they seemed flat and empty as El patted them affectionately then turned away to wander around the chamber peering at dark corners, particular caskets, and even the underside of the funeral slab.

When he returned from his stroll, he slid his fingers into an upper pocket and drew forth a lacing-wrapped flask full of an amber liquid. Holding it up, he murmured, "Mystra, to thee, as always. A pale shadow of the fire of thy touch."

A long, gasping pull later, El stoppered the flask, sighed contentedly, and put it away again—in a pocket that still looked empty.

He dug in the next empty pocket with both hands and drew forth a wand in a shabby, almost crumbling wyvernskin case. He'd spent two careful spells and a lot of running around trailing the case along the rough stone blocks of an old castle wall getting the case to look this elderly. He was even prouder of the wand, discolored by decades of handling that he'd accomplished in a few minutes with goose grease, sand, and soot. Now, Eaergladden Moondark had died destitute, begging his kin for a few coppers with which to buy a roasting-fowl . . . but who save one Elminster was still alive to remember that? So accomplished a mage as Eaergladden could quite well have had a wand, and of course a spellbook—El reached back into the empty pocket and pulled forth a worn and bulky tome with huge, much-battered brass corners—that he hadn't sold in his last year of life, after all. Not to mention the usual dagger enchanted so as not to rust or go dull, and to glow upon command; these enchantments were made to last, say, three centuries by a hire-cast elven longlook spell, from one of the poorer Myth Drannan apprentices. Aye, so.

El calmly lifted the lid of Eaergladden's casket, murmured, "Well met, Master Mage of the Moondarks," and gently laid the wand, dagger, and spellbook in the proper places around the mummified skeleton that had been Eaergladden. Then he closed the casket and went back to the cloak for a few scrolls—on carefully aged parchment—and a battered little book of magical observations, copied runes, and half-finished spells that should lead even a half-wit to the creation of a spell that would temporarily imbue the non-magically gifted with the ability to carry and cast a spell placed in them by a mage.

This work took up much of his time in the service of Mystra, these days; at her bidding, Elminster traveled Faerûn visiting ruins and the tombs of dead mages, planting "old" scrolls, spellbooks, minor enchanted items, and even the occasional staff for later folk to find—and all such leavings were in truth items he'd just finished crafting, and made to look old. Almost always, part of the treasures he left for others included notes that should lead anyone with a gift for magic to experiment and successfully create a "new" spell.

Mystra cared not overmuch who found these magics, or how they used them—so long as ever more magic was in use and ever more folk could wield it, rather than a few archwizards lording it over the spell-poor or magically barren, as had happened in the days of lost Netheril. El loved this sort of work and always had to fight a tendency to linger in the ruins and crypts, mischievously letting his lights and spell-effects be seen by others, to lure exploring adventurers toward his leavings.

"About as subtle as an orc horde," Mystra had once termed these tactics, pouting prettily, and El knew she was right. Wherefore today he firmly took up his cloak, worked the powerful spell Azuth had given him that obliterated all traces or magical echoes of his visit, and left in the form of a shadow. The thoughtful shadow restored a few of the wards and traps in his wake before he slipped back out onto the street, inches distant from the back of a guard whose attention was on a gold coin that seemed to have fallen from the sky moments before. Unnoticed, the shadow turned solid and strolled away.

The cloaked, hawk-nosed figure had been gone from sight around a corner for exactly the time it took to draw in a single good, deep breath when a dark horse came trotting through the steady stream of walking folk and clopped to a halt in front of the guard.

That worthy looked up, raising an eyebrow in both query and challenge, to see a young, maroon-robed elf in a rich cloak peering down at the coin in the guard's weathered palm.

The guard closed his fingers around it hastily and said, "Aye? What d'you want, outlander?"

"Myth Drannan, was it not?" the elf asked softly. "Found hereabouts?"

The guard flushed. "Paid to me fair and square, more like," he rumbled.

The elf nodded, his gaze now lingering long and considering on the overgrown crypt the guard was standing duty in front of. The Moondarks . . . that bastard house of dabbling mages. And all of them who'd found their way home to die now shared a stone tomb-house, such as humans favor. In good repair, by the looks of it, with its wards still up. It was closed up much too securely for inquisitive birds or scurrying squirrels to pluck up a gold coin and carry it outside the walls. His eyes narrowed, and his face grew as sharp as honed flint, causing the guard to warily raise his weapon and shrink back behind it.

Ilbryn Starym dropped the man a mirthless and absentminded smile and rode on toward the Stars and Sword.

Wizards who came to Westgate always stayed at the Sword, in hopes of being there when Alshinree wandered in and did her trance-dance. Alshinree was getting old and a bit gaunt, now; her dances weren't the affairs they'd once been, with the house crowded with hungrily staring men. Her dance, too, was usually just so much playacting and drunken mumbling . . . but sometimes, a little more often than once in a month, it happened. An entranced Alshinree uttered words of spells not known since Netheril fell, advice that might have come from the Lady of Mysteries herself, and detailed instructions as to the whereabouts, traps, and even contents of certain archmages' tombs, ruined schools of wizardry, sorcerous caches, and even long-forgotten abandoned temples to Mystra.

Bad things happened to mages who so much as spoke to Alshinree outside the Sword or who tried to coerce or pester her within its walls, so they contented themselves with booking rooms at the inn so often that some of them could be considered to have been living there. Even if a certain human mage—one Elminster, formerly Court Mage of Galadorna, before the fall of that realm—had not taken a room at the Sword, it held the best gathering of folk in Westgate who might just have seen him hereabouts or heard something of his deeds and current doings.

The hard looks thrown his way by every guard and many merchants he'd passed suddenly hit home; Ilbryn blinked, looked all around, and found that he was galloping his startled mount down the street, its hooves slipping and sliding on the cobbles. He reined in and settled the horse into a careful walk thereafter. The bright, sparkling spell-animated sign of the Stars and Sword loomed ahead, and the champion of Starym honor steered his mount through the bustling folk to—he hoped—some answers, or even the man he sought.

As he gathered the reins together in one hand to free the other for the bellpull that would summon hostelers to see to his horse, Ilbryn discovered that something he carried in a belt-pouch had found its way into his hand, and was now clenched there: a scrap of red cloth that had been part of the mantle of office of the Court Mage of Galadorna. Elminster's mantle.

The elf looked down at it, and although his hand remained rock steady, his handsome face slowly slipped into a stony, brooding mask. His eyes held such glittering menace that both hostelers recoiled and had to be coaxed back.

As he swung himself down from the saddle and reached for the handle of the Sword's finely carved front door, Ilbryn Starym smiled softly.

And as one of the hostelers put it, "That were worse than 'is glaring!"

Still smiling, Ilbryn put one hand—the one flickering with the risen radiance of a ready, deadly spell—behind his back, and with the other opened the door and went in.

The hostelers lingered, half-expecting to hear a terrific crash, or smoke, or even bodies hurled out through the windows . . . but their hoped-for entertainment never came.

TWELVE
THE EMPTY THRONE

It must bother most wizards a lot that for all their spells, they can't seize immortality. Many try to become gods, but few succeed. For this, let us all be very thankful.

SAMBRIN ULGRYTHYN, LORD SAGE OF SAMMARESH
FROM *THE VIEW FROM STORMWIND HILL*
PUBLISHED CIRCA THE YEAR OF THE GATE

Far to the east of Westgate, even as a smiling elf slipped into an inn expecting trouble, a mist drifted through an old, deep forest.

It was a mist that sparkled and chimed as it went, moving purposefully through the trees. Sometimes it rose up into an almost humanoid, striding form, bulking tall, thick and strong; at other times it moved like an ever-leaping, undulating snake. No birds called in the shade around it, and nothing rustled in the dead leaves underfoot. Only its own whirling breezes stirred the creepers and tatters of hanging moss it wound its way through; silence ruled the forest it traversed.

This was no wonder; earlier chiming hungers had left not a creature alive in that part of the forest to witness its haste. The chiming mist had left the graveyard of the Frostfire Banner far behind, moving for miles along the deserted road to a place where most eyes would have missed the sapling-studded, overgrown remnants of a lane turning off into the woods.

The mist drifted along the dips and turns of that road, passing like eager smoke across crumbling stone bridges that took the road across rivulets, to the deep green place where the road ended . . . and the ruins began.

The lines of gigantic old trees flanking the overgrown road gave way to a litter of creeper-shrouded, sagging wagons and coaches. Beyond lay thickets, at their hearts overgrown mounds that had once been stables and cottages. Beyond the thickets rose shadowtops so tall that their gloom choked away thickets and lay in endless shadow over the rotting ruin of a drawbridge across a deep, muddy cleft that had once been a moat . . . and the stone pillars or teeth within the moat, that had once been the stout buttresses of mostly fallen walls. Walls that had once frowned down on Faerûn from a great height, formed a massive keep.

The long-fallen fortress was more forest and tumbled stone, now, than a building. The mist moved purposefully through the tangle of leaning trees and creepers that grew in its inner spaces, as if it knew what chambers could be found where. As it went, the walls became taller. Here and there ceilings or roofing had survived, though all of the archways gaped open and doorless, and there were no signs that anyone—or anything—dwelt within.

The mist came to a gently chiming halt in a chamber that had once been large and grand indeed. Gaps in its walls showed the forest just outside, but there was still a ceiling, and even furniture. A rotting-canopied bed larger than many stable stalls, stood with ornate gilded bedposts and cloth of gold glinting among the green mildew-fur of its bedding. Close by stood a lounge, canted over where one leg had broken, and beyond that several stools were enthusiastically growing mushrooms. A little way farther on, across the cracked marble floor, a peeling, man-high oval mirror stood beside a sagging row of wardrobes. Water was dripping down onto what had once been a grand table in another part of the room—and beyond it, in the darkest, best-roofed rear of the chamber, stood a ring-shaped parapet. Within the knee-high circular wall was only deeper darkness . . . and when the mist began to move, it headed straight for this well.

As it approached, sudden flashes of light occurred in the air above the parapet.

The mist hesitated, rose a little higher, and ventured closer to the well.

The radiance reached for it, brightening, and was echoed by similar glows that crawled snakelike along the stone walls and the surrounding floor, outlining hitherto-invisible runes and symbols.

The mist danced for a moment among these flamelike tongues of silent light—then swooped, in a plunge that took it right down into the well. Elaborate traceries of magic flashed and flared into visibility for a moment as the mist arrowed past, seeming to lash and claw at it, but when it had disappeared down the well, these fading remnants of guardian spells lapsed into quiescence once more.

The shaft was a good distance across and fell straight down, a long and lightless way. It ended in a floor of uneven, natural stone—one end of a vast and dark natural cavern.

The mist moved into this velvet void with the confidence of someone who moves through utter darkness to a familiar spot. It chimed softly as its own faint radiance revealed something in the emptiness ahead: a tall, empty stone seat, facing it as it approached.

The mist stopped before it reached the man-sized throne, and hovered above a semicircle of large, complex runes that were graven into the floor in front of the throne. If the throne had been the center seat of a barge, facing ahead, the runes formed the rounded prow of the barge.

The mist seemed to linger for a time in thought, then the breeze of its movements suddenly quickened into a brisk whirlwind, spiraling around and around as it sparkled and chimed. As it swept up to violent speed, dust rose and whirled with it, pebbles rolled at its bidding, and the whirlwind rose into a horned, shifting column.

Arms it grew, and absorbed again, then humps or moving lumps that might have been heads or might have been other things, before it flashed once, then grew very dim.

No whirlwind or snake of mist now glowed in the darkness. Where the mist had been stood the translucent, ghostly shape of a tall, thin woman in a plain robe, her feet and arms bare, her hair a knee-length, unruly tangle, her eyes rather wild. She threw up her arms in triumph or glee, and mad laughter broke out of her, harsh and high and shrill, echoing back from dark and unseen stony crevices.

"You dare to doubt visions sent by our Lady Who Sings In Darkness?" the voice from behind the veil asked in dry tones. "That sounds perilously close to heresy—or even unbelief—to me."

"N-no, Dread Sister," a second female voice replied, a trifle too hastily. "My wits fail me—a personal flaw, no act of unbelief or discourtesy to the Nightsinger—and I cannot see why this shrine must be established in the depths of a wood, where none dwell and none will know of its existence or location."

"It is needful," the veiled voice replied. "Lie down upon the slab. You shall not be chained; your faith shall be demonstrated by your remaining in place upon it while the owlbear feeds. Offer yourself to it without resistance, and be free of fear. My spells shall keep you alive, whatever it devours of you—and no matter how painful it seems, no matter what wounds you sustain, you shall be restored wholly when the rite is done. I have survived such a ritual, in my day, and so have a select few here. To do this is a mark of true honor; the blood of someone so loyal is the best consecration we can offer the Dread Mistress Of All."

"Yes, Dread Sister," the underpriestess whispered, and the trembling of her body could be heard in her voice. "W-will I . . . will my mind be untouched by watching something eat me?" Her voice rose into what was almost a shrill shriek of horror at the thought.

"Well, Dread Sister," the veiled voice purred calmly, "that is up to you. The slab awaits. Dearest of those I've guided, make me proud this day, not ashamed. I shall be watching you—and so shall one who is far, far greater than any of us shall ever be."

"By Mystra's smile, that feels good!" Beldrune said wonderingly, as he stretched and wiggled his fingers experimentally. "I *do* feel younger; all the aches are gone." He swung himself up to a sitting position, rubbing at his face around his eyes, and from between his fingers fixed Tabarast with a level look.

"Truth time, trusted colleague of the arcane," he said firmly. "Wizards of a certain standing don't just 'find' new spells on hitherto-blank back pages of their spellbooks. Where did it really come from?"

Tabarast of the Three Sung Curses looked back over the tops of his thumb-smudged spectacles rather severely. "You grow not old gracefully, most highly regarded Droon. I detect a growing and decidedly unattractive tendency in yourself, to open disbelief in the testimony of your wiser elders. Crush this flaw, my boy, while yet you retain some friendly relations with folk who can serve as your wiser elders—for 'tis sure that, given your advancing age and wisdom, these are few, and shall be fewer henceforth."

The older wizard took a few thoughtful paces away, scratching the bridge of his nose. "I did indeed just find it, on a page that has always been blank, that I have looked to fill with a spell puissant enough to be worthy of the writing these last three decades. I know not how it came to be there, but I believe—I can only believe—that the sacred Hand of the Lady is involved somehow. Spare me the hearing, the spittle and drawn breath, of your usual lecture on Mystra's utter and everlasting refusal to give magic to mortals."

Beldrune blinked. Tabarast waited, carefully not smiling.

"Very well," the younger mage said after a pause that seemed longer than it truly was, "but you leave me, now, with very little to say. Some silences, I fear, are going to stretch."

Then Tabarast did smile—an instant before asking in innocent tones, "Is that a promise?"

Fortunately, a rejuvenated Beldrune of the Bent Finger proved to be every bit as bad a shot with hurled pillows as the old one had been.

Though not a living creature could be seen in the deep shade of the dusk-woods, here where their trunks stood so close together that they might have been gigantic blades of grass, the lone human could feel that someone was watching him. Someone very near. Swallowing, he decided to take a chance.

"Is this the place men call 'Tangletrees'?" he asked the air calmly, sitting down on the huge and moss—covered curve of a fallen tree trunk, and setting his smooth-worn staff aside.

"It is," came a grave reply, in a voice so light and melodious that it could only have been elven.

Umbregard, once of Galadorna, resisted his instinctive desire to turn toward where the voice seemed to have come from, to see who might be there. Instead, he smiled and held out his hands, empty palms upward. "I come in peace, without fire or any ill will or desire to despoil. I come seeking only answers."

A deep, liquid chuckle came to his ears, then the words, "So do we all, man—and the most fortunate of us find a few of them. Be my guest for a time, in safety and at ease. Rise and go around the two entwined trees to your right, down into the hollow. Its water, I suspect, will be the purest yet to pass your lips."

"My thanks," Umbregard replied, and meant it.

The hollow was cold and as dark as a cave; here the leaves met close overhead, and no sun at all touched the earth. Faintly glowing fungi gave off just enough light to see a stone at the edge of the little pool, and a crystal goblet waiting on it. "For my use?" the human mage asked.

"Of course," the calm voice replied, coming from everywhere and nowhere. "Do you fear enslaving enchantments, or elven trickery?"

"No," Umbregard replied. "Rather, I do not want to give offense by seizing things overboldly."

He took up the goblet—it was cool to the touch, and somehow softer in his fingers than it should have been—dipped it into the pool, and drank. As the ripples chased each other across the water, he thought he saw in them a sad, dark-eyed elf face regarding him for a moment . . . but if it had ever truly been there, it was gone in the next instant.

The water was good, and seemed at once both invigorating and soothing. The man let it slide down his throat, closed his eyes, and gave himself over to silent enjoyment.

Somewhere a bird called and was answered. It was all very peaceful . . . he sat up with a start, fearing for one awful moment that he had slept under an elven spell, and carefully set the goblet back on the stone where he'd found it.

"My thanks," he said again. "The water was every bit as you said it would be. Know that I am Umbregard, once of Galadorna, and have fled far since that realm fell. I work magic, though I can boast no great power, and I have prayed to Mystra—the goddess of magic humans venerate—often in my travels."

"And what have you prayed to her for?" the elven voice asked in tones of pleasant interest, sounding very close. Again Umbregard quelled the urge to turn and look at its source.

"Guidance in what good and fitting things magic can be used for, to build a life for one who is not interested in using spells as blades to threaten or thrust into others," he replied. "Galadorna, before its fall, had become a nest of spell-hurling vipers, each striving to bring rivals down and not caring what waste and ruin they wrought in the doing. I will not be like that."

"Well said," the elf said, and Umbregard heard the goblet being dipped then lifted up out of the pool. "Yet it is a long and hard wandering through the shadowed wood for one of your kind, to here. What brought you hence?"

"Mystra showed me the way, and this duskwood grove," Umbregard replied. "I knew not who I'd meet here, but I suspected it would be an elf, once of Myth Drannor . . . for such a one would know what it was to choose a path after the fall of your home and all you held dear."

He could clearly hear a wince in the elven voice as it replied, "You certainly have the gift of speaking plainly, Umbregard."

"I mean no offense," the human mage replied, turning quickly and offering his hand.

A moon elf male in a dark blue open-front shirt and high booted tight leather breeches was sitting perhaps another handspan away, the goblet raised in his hand. He seemed weaponless, though two small objects—black, teardrop-shaped gemstones that twinkled like two dark stars—floated in the air above his left shoulder.

He smiled into Umbregard's wonderstruck eyes and said, "I know. I am also known, among my folk, for my uncommon bluntness. I am called, in your tongue, Starsunder; a star fell from the sky at the moment of my birth, though I doubt whatever it heralded had anything at all to do with me."

The human mage gasped, shrank back, and said, "That's one of the . . ."

The elf's eyebrows lifted. "Yes?" he asked. "Or blurt you out a secret you must now try to keep?"

Umbregard blushed. "Ah, no . . . no," he said. "That's one of the sayings of the priests of Mystra. 'Seek you one for whom the stars fall, for he speaks truth.'"

Starsunder blinked. "Oh, dear. My role, it seems, is laid out for me," the elf said with a smile, drained the goblet, and set it down on the stone just as carefully as Umbregard had done. In soft silence, it promptly vanished.

"What truths have you come to hear?" the elf asked, and in that moment Umbregard came to understand that the lacing of laughter in an elf's voice is not always mockery.

He hesitated for a moment, then said, "Some in Galadorna whispered that the man Elminster, who was our last court mage, also lived in Myth Drannor long ago, and worked dark magic there. I know this is a human I ask about, and that I presume overmuch—why should you freely yield secrets to me, at all?—but I must know. If humans can live long years as elves do, how . . . and why? At what tasks should they spend all this time?"

Starsunder held up a hand. "The flood begins," he joked. "Hold at these for now, lest your remembrance of answers I give be lost in the rushing stream of your next query, and the one to follow, and so on." He smiled and leaned back against a tree root.

"To your first: yes, the same man named Elminster dwelt in Myth Drannor from before the laying of its mythal to some time after, learning and working much magic. Those who hated the idea of a human thrusting his way in among us elves—for he was the first, or among the first—and many folk who came to Myth Drannor, once it was open to all, and envied him his power, might have termed some of his castings 'dark,' but I cannot in truth judge them so, or his reasons for working this or that enchantment."

Umbregard opened his mouth to speak, but Starsunder chuckled and threw up a hand to still him. "Not yet, please; bald and important truths shouldn't be rushed."

Umbregard flushed, then smiled and sat back, gesturing to the elf to continue.

There was a twinkle in Starsunder's eyes as he spoke again. "Humans who master magic enough—or rather, *think* they've 'mastered' magic enough—try many ways to outlive their usual span of years. Most of these, from lichdom to elixirs, are flawed in that they twist the essential nature of persons using them. They become new—and many would judge, I among them, 'lesser'—beings in the process. If you ask me how you could live longer, I would say the only unstained way to do so . . . though it will change you as surely as the lesser ways . . . is the one Elminster has taken . . . or perhaps been led into. I know not if he ardently sought it and worked toward it, drifted into it, or was forced or pushed into it. He serves Mystra as a special servant, doing her bidding in exchange for longevity, special status, and powers to boot. I believe he is called a 'Chosen' of the goddess."

"How did he get to be chosen for this service?" Umbregard asked slowly. "Do you know?"

"I know not," Starsunder replied, "but I do know how he has continued it for what to humans is a very long time: love."

"Love? Mystra loves him?"

"And he loves her." There was disbelief or incredulity in the confusion written plainly on the human mage's face, so Starsunder added gently, "Yes, beyond fondness and friendship and the raging desires of the flesh; true, deep, and lasting love. It is hard to believe this until you've truly felt it, Umbregard, but listen to me. There is a power in love greater than most things that can touch humans . . . or elves, or orcs for that matter. A power for good and for ill. Like all things of such power, love is very dangerous."

"Dangerous?"

Starsunder smiled faintly and said, "Love is a flame that sets fire to things. It is a greater danger to mages than any miscast spell can ever hope to be."

He leaned forward to lay a hand on Umbregard's arm, and said almost fiercely, as they stared into each other's eyes, "Magic gone awry can merely kill a mage; love can remake him, and drive him to remake the world. Our Coronal's great love drove him to seek a way for Cormanthyr that remade it . . . and, most of my folk would say, in the end destroyed it. I was yet young one warm night, out swimming for a lark, with no magic of my own to be felt—something that probably kept me alive then—when the Great Lady of the Starym, Ildilyntra who had loved the Coronal and been loved by him, slew herself to try to bring about his death, driven by her love for our land, just as he was—and both of them seared in their striving by their denied yet thriving love for each other."

The moon elf sighed and shook his head. "You cannot feel the sadness that stirs in me when I hear them again in my head, arguing together—and you are the first human after Elminster to know of that night. Mind and mark, Umbregard: to speak of this secret to others of my kind may mean your swift death."

"I shall heed," Umbregard whispered. "Say on."

The elf smiled wryly and continued, "There's little more to say. Mystra chose this Elminster to serve her, and he has done well, where others have not. The gods make us all different, and more of us fail than succeed. Elminster has failed often—but his love has not, and he has remained at his task. Bravery, I think your bards term it."

"Bravery? How can one armored and aided by a god fear anything? Without fear to wrestle with and reconquer, again and again, where is bravery?" Umbregard asked, excitement making him bold.

Something like fondness danced in Starsunder's eyes as he replied, "There are many gods; divine favor marks a mortal for greater danger than his 'ordinary' fellow and is very seldom a sure defense against the perils of this world—or any other. Only fools trust in the gods so much that they set aside fear entirely, and dismiss or do not see the dangers. I have seen bravery among your kind often; it seems something humans are good at, though more often I see in them recklessness or foolish disregard for danger that others who see less well might term bravery."

"So what is bravery?" Umbregard asked. "Standing in the path of danger?"

"Yes. Staying at one's post or task, as diligent as ever, knowing that at any time the sword waiting overhead may fall, or seeing fast-approaching doom and not abandoning all to flee."

"Please know that I mean no disrespect, but I *must* know: if such is bravery, how is it," Umbregard whispered, fear in his own eyes at his own daring, "that Myth Drannor—Cormanthyr—fell, and you still live?"

Starsunder's answering smile held sadness. "A race and a realm need obedient fools to survive, even more than they need brave—and soon dead—heroes." He stood up, and made a movement with his hand that might have been a wave of farewell. "You can see which I must be. If ever you meet this Elminster of yours face to face, ask him which of the two he is—and bring back his answer to me. I must Know All; it is my failing." Like a graceful panther, he padded up out of the hollow into the duskwood grove above.

"Wait!" the human mage protested, rising and stumbling up into the trees in the elf's wake. "I've so much more to ask—must you go?"

"Only to prepare a place for a human to snore and a meal for us both," Starsunder replied. "You're welcome to stay and ask all the questions you can think of for as long as you want to tarry here. I've few friends left here among the living and this side of the Sundering Seas."

Umbregard found himself trembling. "I would be honored to be considered your friend," he said carefully and found himself trembling, "but I must ask this: how can you trust me so? We've but spoken for a few moments of your time, no more; how can you measure me? I could be a slayer of elves, a hunter of elven treasure—an elfbane. I give you my word I am no such thing . . . but I fear human promises to elves have all too often rung empty down the years."

Starsunder smiled. "This grove is sacred to two gods of my kind: Sehanine and Rillifane," he said. "They have judged you. Behold."

The eyes of the human wizard followed the elf's pointing hand to the moss-covered fallen tree and the wooden staff leaning there. Umbregard knew its familiar, well-worn length as well as he knew the hand that held it. That staff had accompanied him for thousands of miles, walking Faerûn, and was both old and fire-hardened, its ends bound shod with copper to keep them from splitting. Yet for all that, while he'd sat talking in the hollow, it had thrown forth green shoots in plenty up and down its length—and every shoot ended in a small, beautiful white flower, glowing in the shade.

In a colder darkness, a ghostly woman stopped laughing and let her hands fall. The echoes of her cold mirth rolled around the cavern for some time, while she looked around at its dark vastness almost as if seeing it for the first time, her eyes slowly becoming sharp and fierce and fiery.

They were two glittering flames when she moved at last, striding with catlike, confident grace to a particular rune. She touched the symbol firmly with one foot, watched it fill with a bright blue-white glow, then stood with arms folded, watching, as wisps of smoke rose from the radiance to form a cloud like a man-sized spark—a cloud that suddenly coalesced into something else. A legless, floating image of a youngish-looking man, eager and intense of manner, faced the empty throne, hanging in midair above the rune that had spawned it.

As the image began to speak, the ghostly woman strode around the runes to the throne, leaned on one arm of that seat, and watched the image's speech.

It wore robes of rich crimson trimmed with black, and golden rings gleamed on its fingers—their hue matched by the blazing gold of the man's eyes. He had tousled brown hair and the untidy beginnings of a beard, and his voice fairly leaped with eager confidence.

"I am Karsus, as you are Karsus. If you behold this, disaster has befallen me, the first Karsus—and you, the second, must carry on to glory."

The image seemed to pace forward but actually remained above the rune. It waved one hand restlessly and continued, "I know not what you recall of my—our—life; some say my mind is less than clear, these days. Know that many mages of our people have achieved great power; mightiest of these, the archwizards of Netheril, rule their own domains. Mine, like many, is a floating city; I named it for us. I am the most powerful of all the archwizards, the Arcanist Supreme. They call me Karsus the Great."

The image waved a dismissive hand, blazing eyes still fixed on the throne. The ghostly woman was murmuring along with the words she'd obviously heard many times before. Something that might have been a faint sneer played about her lips.

"Of course," the image went on, "given your awakening, none of that may mean anything. I may not have been slain by a rival or suffered a purely personal doom—Karsus the city and the glory of Netheril itself may have fallen in a great war or cataclysm; we have made many foes, the greatest of them ourselves. We war among ourselves, we Netherese, and some of us war within ourselves. My wits are not always wholly my own. You may well share this affliction; watch for it, and guard against it."

The image of Karsus smiled; arching a sardonic eyebrow, the ghostly woman smiled back. Karsus spoke on. "Perhaps you'll have no need of these recording spells of mine, but I've prepared one for each speculum you see on the floor in this place; a series of spellcasting lessons, lest you face the perils of this world lacking certain enchantments I've found crucial. Our work must continue; only through power absolute can I—we—find perfection . . . and Karsus exists, has always existed, to achieve perfection and transform all Toril."

The watching woman laughed at that, a short and unpleasant bark. "Mad indeed, Karsus! Destiny: reshape all Toril, Oh, you were certainly competent to do *that*."

"Your first need may now be for physical healing, and I have anticipated the recurrence of this need in time to come, in a life where you may lack loyal servant mages or anyone you can trust. Know, then, that touching the speculum that evoked this image of me, while speaking the word '*Dalabrindar,*' will heal all hurts. This power can be called upon as often as desired for so long as this rune remains unbroken, and can so serve anyone who speaks thus. The word is the name of the wizard who died so that this spell might live; truly, he has served us well, and—"

"Wasted words, Karsus!" the ghostly woman sneered. "Your clone was a headless mummy decorating this throne when I first saw it! Who slew it here, I wonder? Mystra? Azuth? Some rival? Or did the great and supreme sleeping Karsus fall to a passing adventurer-mage of puny spells, who thought he was beheading a lich?"

". . . many another spell will serve where these do not, but I have here preserved demonstrations of my casting of enchantments of lasting usefulness and . . ."

The ghostly woman turned away from the words she'd heard so many times before, nodding in satisfaction. "They'll do. They'll do indeed. I have here a lure no mage can resist." She strode across the rune again, and the image vanished in mid-word, the radiance winking out of the graven stone to let darkness rush back into the cavern.

"Now, how to let living mages know of it, without causing them to crowd in here by the elbowing thousands?" ghostly lips asked the utter darkness.

The darkness did not answer back.

A frowning ghost strode to the bottom of the shaft and began to blur, unraveling in a spiraling wind of her own making, until once more a whirlwind of flickering lights danced in the darkness, spiraling slowly up the shaft. "And how to keep my mage-catches here for more than one night?"

At the top of the shaft, the chiming whorl of lights hovered over the well ring, and a soft, echoing voice issued from it. "I must weave mighty spells, to be sure. The runes must respond only to me—and then only one a month, no matter what means are tried. That should cause a young mage to linger here long enough."

With sudden vigor the mist darted to one of the rents in the walls and plunged through it, snaking through the trees trailing wild laughter and the exultant shout, "Long enough for a good feed."

Thirteen
Kindness Scorches Stone

*Cruelty is a known scourge, too seldom clever—for which we should all thank
the gods. Kindness is the stronger blade, though more often scorned. Most folk
never learn that.*

Ralderick Hallowshaw, Jester
from *To Rule A Realm, From Turret To Midden*
published circa The Year of the Bloodbird

The tall, thin stranger who'd given them a cheerful smile as he'd gone into the
Maid was back out again in far less than the time it took to drain a tankard.

The two old men on the bench squinted up at him a mite suspiciously.
Folk seldom turned their way—which is why it was their favorite bench. It
sat in the full shadow of the increasingly ramshackle porch of the Fair Maid
of Ripplestones. A cold corner, but at least it wasn't in the full dazzle of the
morning sun.

The stranger was, though, his face outlined in gold as he tossed his nondescript cloak back to lay bare dark and dusty robes and breeches that bore no
badge or adornment, as—wonders of the Realms!—Alnyskavver came bustling
out with the best folding table, and a chair . . . and food!

The tavern master shuttled back and forth, puffing, as the two old men
watched a meal the likes of which they'd not seen in many a year accumulate
under their very noses: a tureen of the hot soup that'd been making two old bellies
rumble all morn, a block of the sharpest redruck cheese—and *three* grouse pies!

Baerdagh and Caladaster scratched at various itches and glared sourly at the
hawk-nosed stranger, wondering why by all the angry gods he'd had to choose
their bench as the place to set his mornfeast on. Everything they'd dreamed of
being able to afford for months now was steaming away under their noses. Just
who by the armpit of Tempus did he think he was, anyway?

The two old men exchanged looks as their all-too-empty bellies rumbled,
then with one accord stared the stranger up and down. No weapon . . . not
much wealth, either, by the looks of him, though his travel-scuffed boots were
very fine. An outlaw who'd had them off someone he knifed? Aye, that would
fit with all the money thrown out on a huge meal like this, coming down out
of the wilderlands a-starving and with stolen coins in plenty.

Now Alnyskavver was back with the haunch of venison they'd smelled
cooking all yestereve, all laid out cold amid pickled onions and sliced tongue

and suchlike, on the platter used when the High Duke came by ... it was too much to bear! Arrogant young bastard.

Shaking his head, Baerdagh spat pointedly into the dust by the stranger's boots and started to shift himself along the bench, to get out and away before this young glutton tucked into such a feast as this under their very noses and drove him and his empty vitals wild.

Caladaster was in the way, though, and slower to move, so the two old men were still shifting their behinds along the bench when the tavern master came back again with a keg of beer and tankards.

Three tankards.

The stranger sat down and grinned at Baerdagh as the old man looked up with the first glimmers of amazement dawning on his face.

"Well met, goodsirs," he said politely. "Please forgive my boldness, but I'm hungry, I hate to eat alone, and I need to talk to someone who knows a fair bit about the old days of Ripplestones. Ye look to have the wits and years enough ... what say we make a deal? We three share this—and eat freely, no stinting, ye keeping whatever we don't eat now—and ye give me, as best ye know, answers to a few questions about a lady who used to live hereabouts."

"Who are you?" Baerdagh asked bluntly, at about the same time as Caladaster said under his breath, "I don't like this. Meals don't just fall out of the sky. He must have paid Alnyskavver to get even a quarter of this out here on a table, but what's to say we won't have to pay summat, too?"

"Our thin purses," Baerdagh told his friend. "Alnyskavver knows just how poor we are. So does everyone else." He nodded his head toward the tavern windows. Caladaster looked, already knowing what he'd see. Near everyone in the place was crowded up against the dirty glass, watching as the hawk-nosed stranger poured two full tankards and slid them across the table, emptying eating forks and trencher knives out of the last tankard and sliding them across too.

Caladaster scratched his nose nervously, raked a hand down one of his untidy white-and-gray muttonchop whiskers—a sure sign of hurried, worried thought—and turned back to the stranger. "My friend asked who you are, an' I want to know too. I also want to know whatever little trick you've readied for us. I can leave your food an' just walk away, you know."

At that moment, his stomach chose to protest very loudly.

The stranger ran a hand through unruly black hair and leaned forward. "My name is Elminster, and I'm doing some work for my Lady Master; work that involves my finding and visiting old ruins and the tombs of wizards. I've been given money to spend as I need to, in plenty—see? I'll leave these coins on the table ... now, if I happen to vanish in a puff of smoke before ye pick up that tankard, there's enough here for ye to pay Alnyskavver yourselves."

Baerdagh looked down at the coins as if they were a handful of little sprites dancing under his nose, then back up at the stranger. "All right, that tale I'll grant," he said slowly, "but why us?"

Elminster poured his own tankard full, set it down, and asked, "Have ye any idea what weary work it is, spending days wandering around a town of increasingly suspicious folk, peeking over fences and looking for headstones and ruins? By the first nightfall, farmers always want to thrust hayforks through me. By the second, they're trying to do it in droves!"

Both old men barked short and snorting laughs at that.

"So I thought I'd save a lot of time and suspicion," the stranger added, "if I just shared a meal with some men I liked the look of, with years enough under their belts to know the old tales, and where so-and-so lies buried, and—"

"You're after Sharindala, aren't you?" Caladaster asked slowly, his eyes narrowing.

El nodded cheerfully. "I am," he said, "and before ye try to find the right words to ask me, know this: I will take nothing from her tomb, I'm not interested in opening her casket, performing any magic on her while I'm there, or digging up or burning down anything, and I'd be happy to have ye or someone else from Ripplestones along to watch what I do. I need to be able to look around thoroughly—in good bright daylight—and that's all."

"How do we know you're telling the truth?"

"Come with me," Elminster said, doling out platters and cutting into one of the pies. "See for thyselves."

Baerdagh almost moaned at the smell that came out of the opened pie with the rush of steam—but he'd no need to; his stomach took care of the utterance for him. His hands went out before he could stop himself. The stranger grinned and thrust the platter bearing the slice of pie into his hands.

"I'd rather not go about disturbing dead sorceresses," Caladaster replied, "an' I'm a bit old for clambering around on broken stones wondering when the roof's going to fall down on my head, but you can't miss Scorchstone Hall; you came—"

He broke off as Baerdagh kicked him under the table, but Elminster just grinned again and said, "Say on, please; I'm not going to whisk away the meal the moment I hear this!"

Caladaster ladled himself a bowl of soup with hands that he hoped weren't shaking with eagerness, and said thickly, "Friend Elminster, I want to warn you about her wards. That's why no one plundered the place long since, an' why you didn't see it. Trees and thorn bushes an' all have grown around it in a wall just outside the shimmering . . . but I recall, before they grew, seeing squirrels and foxes and even birds a-wing fall down dead when they so much as brushed Sharindala's wards. You came right past it on your way in, just after the bridge, where the road takes that big bend; it's bending around Scorchstone." He took a big bite of cheese, closed his eyes in momentary bliss, and added, "It burned after she died, mind; *she* didn't call it Scorchstone."

Baerdagh leaned close across the table to breathe beer conspiratorially all over Elminster and whisper roughly, "They say she walks there still, you know—a skeleton in the tatters of a fine gown, still able to slay with her spells."

El nodded. "Well, I'll try not to disturb her. What was she like in life, d'ye know?"

Baerdagh jerked his head in Caladaster's direction. The older man was blowing on his soup to cool it; he looked up, stroked his chin, and said, "Well, I was nobbut a lad then, do you see, and . . ."

One by one, overcome with curiosity, the folk of Ripplestones were drifting out of the Maid or down the street to listen—and, no doubt, to enthusiastically add their own warnings. Elminster grinned, sipped at his tankard, and waved at the two old men to continue. They were plowing through the food at an impressive rate; Baerdagh had already let out his belt once, and it lacked several hours to highsun, yet.

In the end, the two old men were content to let their good friend Elminster go alone up to Scorchstone Hall, though Caladaster gravely asked the hawk-nosed mage to stop by their neighboring cottages on his way out, if'n he needed a bed for the night, or just to let them know he'd fared safely. El as gravely promised he would, guessing he'd find deafening snores behind barred doors if he returned before the next morning. He helped the old men carry home the food their groaning-full bellies wouldn't let them eat and bought them each another keg of beer to wash it down with. They looked at him from time to time as if he was a god come calling in disguise but clasped his hand heartily enough in almost tearful thanks and wheezed their way indoors.

El smiled and went on his way, waving cheerfully to the scattering of Ripplestones children who came trailing after him—and the mothers who rushed to drag them back. He turned and walked straight into the thick-standing trees that hid Scorchstone Hall from view. The last watchers from afar, who'd wandered down from the Maid with their tankards in their hands, spat into the road thoughtfully, agreed that Ripplestones had seen the last of another madman, and turned away to drift back to the tavern or about their business.

The shimmering was as Caladaster had described it—but sighed into nothingness at the first passage spell El attempted. He became a shadow once more, in case more formidable traps awaited, and drifted quietly into the overgrown gardens of what had once been a fine mansion.

It had burned, but only a little. What must have been a tower at the eastern front corner was now only a blackened ring of stones among brambles, attached to the house beyond by a rock pile of its fallen walls—but the gabled house beyond seemed intact.

El found a place where a shutter sagged, and drifted into the gloom through a window that had never, it seemed, known glass. The dark mansion beyond had its share of leaks, mold, and rodent leavings, but it looked for all the world as if someone cleaned it regularly. The shadowy Chosen found no traps and soon reverted to solid form to poke and peer and open. He found sculptures, paintings smudged where someone had recently scrubbed mold away, and bookshelves full of travel journals, scholarly histories of kingdoms and prominent families, and even romantic novels. Nowhere in the house that he could see, however, was there any trace of magic. If this Sharindala had been a mage, all of her books and inks and spell-substances must have been destroyed in the fire that brought down her tower . . . and presumably the lady had perished therein, too.

El shrugged. Well, a searcher in days to come wouldn't know that if he did his work properly. A forgotten scroll on a shelf here, a wand in a wooden box hidden behind this tallchest, and a sheaf of incomplete spell notes thrust into that book *there*. Now to put a few more scrolls in the closets he'd seen up in the bedrooms, and his work here was done. Magic enough to set a mageling on the road to mastery, if shrewdly used, and—

He opened a closet door and something moved.

Cowered, actually, as handfire blazed between Elminster's fingers. Brown and gray bones shifted and shuffled into the deepest corner of the closet, holding a wobbling wand pointed at him. El saw glittering eyes, a wisp of cloth that might once have been part of a gown, and a snarl of long brown hair that was falling out of the shriveled remnant of a scalp as the skeleton brushed against the walls. He stepped back, holding up a hand in a "stop" gesture, hoping she'd not trigger that trembling wand.

"Lady Sharindala?" he asked calmly. "I am Elminster Aumar, once of Myth Drannor, and I mean no harm nor disrespect. Please come out and be at ease. I did not know ye still dwelt here. I'll pay ye proper respects, then withdraw from thy house and leave ye in peace."

He retreated to the door, put on his cloak and summoned up defenses in case the undead sorceress did use the wand, and waited, watching the open closet door.

After a long time, that dark-eyed skull peered out—and hastily withdrew. El leaned against the door frame and waited.

After a few moments more, the skeleton hesitantly shuffled out of the closet, looking in all directions for adventurers who might be waiting to pounce. She held the wand upward, not leveled upon him, and came to a stop halfway down the room, gazing at him in silence.

El offered her the chair beside him with a gesture. She didn't move, so he picked up the chair and carried it to her.

The wand came up, but he ignored it—even when magic missiles spat forth and streaked at him, trailing blue fire.

His spell defenses absorbed them harmlessly; El felt only gentle jolts as they struck. Pretending they'd never existed at all—or the second volley, that tore into his face from barely an arm's length away—the last prince of Athalantar set down the chair and gestured to the walking remains of Sharindala, then to the chair, offering it to her. Then he bowed and went back to the doorway.

After a long, silent moment, the skeleton went to the chair and sat down, crossing its legs at the ankles and leaning back on one arm of the chair out of long habit.

Elminster bowed again. "I apologize for my intrusion into thy home. I serve the goddess Mystra and am here on her bidding to leave magic for later searchers to find. I shall restore thy wards and trouble ye no more. Is there anything I can do for ye?"

After a long while, the skeleton shook its head, almost wearily.

"Would ye find lasting rest?" El asked gently. The wand shot up to menace him. He held up a staying hand and asked, "Do ye still work magic?"

The hair-shedding skull nodded, then shrugged, holding up the wand.

El nodded. "I've not searched for any magic ye may have hidden. I've only added, not taken away." A thought occurred to him, then, and he asked, "Would ye like to know new spells?"

The skeleton stiffened, made as if to rise, then nodded so emphatically that hair fell out in handfuls.

El reached into his cloak and drew forth a spellbook. Muttering a word over it, he strode back across the room, ignoring the hesitantly lifted wand—which spat nothing more at him—and gently placed the tome in her lap, holding it as her free hand came across to clasp it.

Her other hand dropped the wand and reached up impulsively to clasp his arm. Rather than pulling free, El reached out slowly to place his own hand over the dry, bony digits on his forearm and stroked them.

Sharindala trembled all over, and for a long time blue-gray eyes and dark points of light in the sockets of a fleshless skull stared into each other.

El withdrew his stroking hand and said, "Lady, I must go. I must place more magic elsewhere—but if I survive to return to Ripplestones in time to come, I'll stop and visit ye properly."

He received a slow but definite nod in answer.

"Lady, can ye speak?" El asked. The skeleton stiffened, then the hand on his arm became a fist that smashed down on the arm of the chair in frustration.

El bent over and tapped the book. "There's a spell in here, near the back, that can change that for ye. It requires no verbal component, obviously—but I want ye to remember something. When ye have some unbroken time to devote to things and have mastered that spell, I want ye to hold this tome and say aloud the words, 'Mystra, please.' Will ye remember?"

The skull nodded once more. El took hold of bony fingertips and brought them to his lips. "Then, Lady, fare thee well for now. I go, but shall return in time. Be happy."

He straightened, gave her a salute, and strode out of the room. The skeleton managed a wave at its last glimpse of his smiling face, then its hand fell to the book, cradling it as if it would never let go.

For a long time the skeleton that had been Sharindala sat in the chair, staring at the door and shuddering. The only sound in the room was a dry clicking as fleshless jaws worked. She was trying to weep.

"But there's *more!*" Beldrune hissed, creeping forward with his fingers held out like claws before him. Spellbound, the circle of pupils watched him with nary a titter at the appearance of an old and overweight wizard trying to tiptoe like an actor overplaying the part of a skulking thief. "This mighty mage has walked *these* very streets! Here—just outside, down yon alley, not three nights past—I saw him *myself!*"

"Think of it," Tabarast took up the telling excitedly, never knowing that the mage they were speaking of was at that moment kissing the fingertips of a skeleton. "We've walked with him, we studied magic at his very elbow in fabled Moonshorn Tower—and soon, just perhaps, you too may have this opportunity! To talk with the supreme sorcerer of the age—a man touched by a god!"

"Nay," Beldrune leered suggestively, "a man touched by a *goddess!*"

"Think of it!" Tabarast put in hastily, flashing a warning glare at young Droon. Don't the young ever think of anything *else?* "The great Elminster has lived for centuries! Some believe him to be a Chosen One, personally favored by the goddess Mystra—that's what my colleague was *trying* to say—and records are clear: he is a man who dwelt in fabled Myth Drannor when elven magic flowed like water, was respected enough to be accepted into a noble elf family there, advise their ruler, the Coronal—and even survive the darkness of its destruction at the hands of a shrieking army of foul fiends! Hard to believe? Ask the folk of Galadorna about Elminster's survival in the face of the fell magic of an archpriestess of Bane, while defying her in her very temple! This was before Galadorna's fall, when he was the court mage of that realm."

"Aye, all this is true," Beldrune agreed, taking up the tale. "And don't forget: he's been seen here—fearlessly strolling out of the tomb of the mage Taraskus in broad daylight!"

There were gasps at this last piece of news and many involuntary glances toward the windows.

A ghostly shape that had been floating outside one of those windows, listening intently, prudently fell away and dissolved into mists.

"I've lived for centuries, too," it murmured, chiming as it gathered speed to go elsewhere. "Perhaps this Elminster will make a fitting mate . . . if he's alive and human, and not some cleverly cloaked lich or crawling netherplanar spirit." Unaware that excited pupils were crowding the windows to glimpse her as a supposed magical manifestation of the very mage she was musing about, the sorceress drifted away, murmuring, "Elminster . . . 'tis time to go hunting Elminsters."

FOURTEEN
THE ELMINSTER HUNT

The deadliest sport among the Zhentarim is vying for supremacy within its dark ranks ... and in particular, the doom of the too young and nakedly ambitious: to be sent Elminster hunting. I'll wager that this has always been a perilous pastime. Some are wise enough, as I was, to use it as a chance to "die" our ways out of the Brotherhood. It was interesting—if a trifle depressing—to hear, while in disguise, what folk said of me, once they thought me safely dead. One day I'll return and haunt them all.

DESTRAR GULHALLOW
FROM *POSTHUMOUS MUSINGS OF A ZHENTARIM MAGELING*
PUBLISHED CIRCA THE YEAR OF THE MORNINGSTAR

The darkness never left Ilbryn Starym. It never would, not since the day when the last hunting lodge of the Starym had been torn apart in spells and flame, their proud halls in Myth Drannor already fallen, and the Starym had been shattered forever.

If any of his kin still lived, he'd never found trace of them. Once proud and mighty, the family that had led and defined Cormanthyr for an age was now reduced to one young and crippled cousin. If the Seldarine smiled, with his magic he might be able to sire children to carry on the family name ... but only if the Seldarine smiled.

Again, it had been the Accursed One, that grinning human Elminster, his spells splashing around the temple as he fought the queen of Galadorna. A thousand times Ilbryn had relived those searing instants of tumbling down the temple, broken and aflame. To work magic that would restore his leg and smooth his skin to be what it had once been would ruin spells he'd never mastered; the spells that had cost him so much, to keep his ravaged innards working. Years of agony—if he lived that long—lay ahead. Agony of the body to match the agony in his heart.

"Have my thanks, human," he snarled to the empty air. The horse promptly jostled him, sending stabbing pains through his twisted side, as it clopped across a worn and uneven bridge. Ahead, through the pain, he saw a signboard. On his sixth day out of Westgate, riding alone on a hard road, it was a welcome sight; it told him he was getting somewhere ... even if he didn't know quite where that *somewhere* was.

"Ripplestones," he read it aloud. "Another soaring human fortress of culture. How inspiring."

He drew his bitter sarcasm around himself like a dark cloak and urged his horse into a trot, sitting up in his saddle so as to look impressive when human eyes began their startled looks at him; an elf riding alone, all in black and wearing the swords and daggers of an adventurer, with—whenever he let the spell lapse—one side of his face a twisted, mottled mass of burn scar.

The weaponry was all for show, of course, to make his spells a surprise. Ilbryn dropped one hand to a smooth sword pommel and caressed it, keeping his face hard and grim, as the road rounded a thick stand of trees and Ripplestones spread out before him.

He was always wandering, always seeking Elminster. To hunt and slay Elminster Aumar was the burning goal that ruled his life—though there'd never be a House Starym to return to with triumphant news of avenging the family unless Ilbryn rebuilt it himself. He was close on Elminster's trail now; he could taste it.

He put out of his mind how many times he'd been this close before and at the end of the day had closed his fingers on nothing.

Ah, a tavern; The Fair Maid of Ripplestones. Probably the only tavern in this dusty farm town. Ilbryn stopped his horse, threw its reins over its head to enact the spell that would hold it like a statue until he spoke the right word, and began the bitter struggle to dismount without falling on his face.

As it was, his artificial leg clanked like a bouncing cartload of swords when he landed, and he clung to a saddle strap for long seconds before he could clear his face of the pain and straighten up.

The two old men on the bench just sat and watched him calmly, as if strange travelers rode up to the Fair Maid every day. Ilbryn spoke gently to them, but grasped the hilts of a blade and a throwing dagger as a sort of silent promise of trouble to come . . . if they wanted trouble.

"May this day find you in fortune," he said formally. "I hope you can help me. I'm seeking a friend of mine, to deliver an urgent message. I must catch him! Have you seen a human wizard who goes by the name of Elminster? He's tall, and thin, with dark hair and a hawk's nose . . . and he steps into every wizard's tomb he passes."

The two old men on the bench stared at him, frowning, but said not a word. A third man, standing in the tavern door, gave the two on the bench an even odder look than he'd given Ilbryn and said to the elf, "Oh, *him!* Aye, he went in Scorchstone right enough, and soon came out again, too. Headed east, he did, into the Dead Place."

"The Dead Place?"

"Aye; them as goes in comes not out. There's nary a squirrel or chipmunk 'tween Oggle's Stream and Rairdrun Hill, just this side of Starmantle. We go by boat, now, if'n we have to. No one takes the road, nor goes through the woods, neither. A tenday an' some back, some fancy adventuring band—an' not the first one, neither—hired by the High Duke hisself went in . . . and came not out again. Nor will they, or my name's not Jalobal—which, a-heh, 'tis. Mark you, they'll not be seen again, no. I hear there's another band of fools yet, jus' set out from Starmantle . . ."

The elf had already turned and begun the struggle up into his saddle again. With a grunt and a heave that brought a snarl of pain from between clenched teeth, he regained his seat on the high-backed saddle and took up his reins to head on east.

"Here!" Jalobal called. "Aren't you be stayin', then?"

Ilbryn twisted his lips into a grim smile. "I'll never catch him if I stop and rest wherever he's just moved on from."

"But yon's the Dead Place, like I told thee."

With two swift tugs, the elf undid the two silver catches on his hip that Baerdagh had thought were ornamental and peeled aside his breeches. Inside was no smooth skin, but a ridged mass of scars that looked like old tree bark, a sickly yellow where it wasn't already gray. The twisted burn-scarring extended from his knee to his armpit—and above the knee were the struts and lashings that held on a leg of metal and wood that the elf had not been born with.

"I'll probably feel at home there," the elf told the three gaping men thinly. "As you can see, I'm half dead already." Without another word or look in their direction, he pulled the catches closed and spurred his mount away.

In shocked silence, the three men watched the dust rise, and beyond it, the bobbing elf on his horse -dwindle from view along the overgrown road toward Oggle's Stream.

"Didj'ye see? Did d'ye see?" Jalobal asked the two silent men on the bench excitedly. They stared at him like two stones. He blinked at them then bustled back into the Maid to spread word about his daring confrontation with the scorched elf rider.

Baerdagh turned his head to look at Caladaster. "Did he say 'catch him up' or just 'catch him'?"

"He said 'catch him,'" Caladaster replied flatly. "I noticed that in particular."

Baerdagh shook his head. "I'd not like to walk in a mage's boots, for all their power. Crazed, the lot of them. Have you noticed?"

"Aye, I have," Caladaster replied, his voice deep and grim. "It passes, though, if you stop soon enough." And as if that had been a farewell, he got up from the bench and strode away toward his cottage.

Something flashed as he went, and the old man's hand was suddenly full of a stout, gem-studded staff that Baerdagh had never seen before.

Baerdagh closed his gaping mouth and rubbed his eyes to be sure he'd seen rightly. Aye, there it was, to be sure. He stared at Caladaster's back as his old comrade strode down the road home, but his friend never looked back.

Despite the gray sky and cool breezes outside, many a student had cast glances out the windows during this day's lesson. So many, in fact, that at one point Tabarast had been moved to comment severely, "I doubt very much that the great Elminster is going to perch like a pigeon on our windowsill just to hear what to him are the rudiments of magic. Those of you who desire to grasp a tenth of his greatness are advised to face front and pay attention to our admittedly less exciting teachings. All mages—even divine Azuth, the Lord of

Spells, who outstrips Elminster as he outstrips any of you, began in this way; learning mage-lore as words dropping from the lips of older, wiser wizards."

The glances back diminished noticeably after that, but Beldrune was still sighing in exasperation by the time Tabarast threw up his hands and snapped, "As the ability to focus one's concentration, that cornerstone of magecraft, seems today to utterly elude all too many of you, we'll conclude the class at this point, and begin—with fresh insight and interest, I trust—on the morrow. You are dismissed; homeward go, *without* playing spell pranks this time, Master Maglast."

"Yes sir," one handsome youth replied rather sullenly, amid the general tumult of scraping chairs, billowing cloaks, and hurrying bodies. Muttering, Tabarast turned to the hearth, to rake the coals out into a glittering bed and put another log on the fire. Beldrune glanced up at the smoke hanging and curling under the rafters—when things warmed up, that chimney would profit from a spell or two to blast it clean and hollow it out a trifle wider—then clasped his hands behind him and watched the class leave, just to make sure no demonstration daggers or spell notes accidentally fell into the sleeves, scrips, boots, or shirt fronts of students' clothing. As usual, Maglast was one of the last to depart. Beldrune met his gaze with a firm and knowing smile that sent the flushing youth hastily doorward, and only then became aware that a man who'd sat quietly in the back of the class with the air of someone whose thoughts are elsewhere—despite the gold piece he'd paid to be sitting there—was coming slowly forward. A first timer; perhaps he had some questions.

Beldrune asked politely, "Yes? And how may we help you, sir?"

The man had unkempt pale brown hair and washed-out brown eyes in a pleasantly forgettable face. His clothing was that of a down-at-heels merchant; dirty tunic and bulging-pocketed overtunic over patched and well-worn breeches and good but worn boots.

"I must find a man," he said in a very quiet voice, stepping calmly past Beldrune to where Tabarast was bending over the hearth, "and I'm willing to pay handsomely to be guided to him."

Beldrune stared at the man's back for a moment. "I think you misunderstand our talents, sir. We're not . . ." His voice trailed off as he saw what was being drawn in the hearth ashes.

The nondescript man had plucked up a kindling stick from beside the fire and was drawing a harp between the horns of a crescent moon, surrounded by four stars.

The man turned his head to make sure that both of the elderly mages had seen his design, then hastily raked ashes across it until his design was obliterated.

Beldrune and Tabarast exchanged looks, eyebrows raised and excitement tugging at the corners of their jaws. Tabarast leaned forward until his forehead almost touched Beldrune's and murmured, "A Harper. Elminster had a hand in founding them, you know."

"I do know, you dolt—*I'm* the one keeps his ears open for news, remember?" Beldrune replied a trifle testily, and turned to the Harper. "So who do you want us to find for you, anyway?"

"A wizard by the name of Elminster. Yes, our founder; *that* Elminster."

The pupils, had any returned to spy on the hearth with the same attention they'd paid to the windows, would at that moment have witnessed their two elderly, severe tutors squealing like excited children, hopping and shuffling in front of the fire as they clapped their hands in eagerness, then gabbling acceptances without any reference to fees or payments to the down-at-heels merchant, who was calmly returning the stick to where he'd found it in the center of the happy tumult.

Beldrune and Tabarast ran right into each other in their first eager rushes toward cupboards, laughed and clawed each other out of the way with equal enthusiasm, then rushed around snatching up whatever they thought might come in remotely useful on an Elminster hunt.

The worn-looking Harper leaned back against the wall with a smile growing on his face as the heap of "essentials" rapidly grew toward the rafters.

"What befell, Bresmer?" The High Duke's voice didn't hold much hope or eagerness; he wasn't expecting good news.

His seneschal gave him none. "Gone, sir, as near as we can tell. One dead horse, seen floating by fishermen. They took Ghaerlin out to see it; he was a horse tamer before he took service with you, lord. He said its eyes were staring and its hooves and legs all bloodied; he thinks it galloped right down the cliff, riderless, fleeing in fear. The boat guard report that the Banner didn't light the signal beacon or raise their pennant . . . I think they're all dead, lord."

Horostos nodded, hardly seeing the wineglass he was rolling between his fingers. "Have we found anyone else willing to take us on? Any word from Marskyn?"

Bresmer shook his head. "He thinks everyone in Westgate has heard all about the slayings—and so does Eltravar in Reth."

"Raise what we're offering," the High Duke said slowly. "Double the blood price."

"I've already done that, lord," the seneschal murmured. "Eltravar did that on his own, and I thought it prudent to confirm his offers with your ducal seal. Marskyn has being using the new offer for a tenday now . . . it's the doubled fee all of these mercenaries are refusing."

The High Duke grunted. "Well, we're seeing the measure of their spirit, at least, to know who not to hire when we've need in future."

"Or their prudence, lord," Bresmer said carefully. "Or their prudence."

Horostos looked up sharply, met his seneschal's eyes, then let his gaze fall again without saying anything. He brought his wineglass down to the table so hard it shattered into shards between his fingers, and snapped, "Well, we've got to do *something*! We don't even know what it is, and it'll be having whole villages next! I—"

"It already has, lord," Bresmer murmured. "Ayken's Stump, sometime last tenday."

"The woodcutters?" Horostos threw back his head and sighed at the ceiling. "I won't have a land to rule if this goes on much longer," he told it sadly. "The Slayer will be gnawing at the gates of this castle, with nothing left outside but the bones of the dead."

The ceiling, fully as wise as its long years, deigned not to answer.

Horostos brought his gaze back down to meet the eyes of his expressionless, carefully quiet seneschal, and asked, "Is there any hope? Anyone we can call on, before you and I up shields and ride out those gates together?"

"I did have a visit from one outlander, lord," Bresmer told the richly braided rug at his feet. "He said to tell you that the Harpers had taken an interest in this matter, lord, and they would report to you before the end of the season—if you could be found. I took that as a hint to tarry here until at least then, lord."

"Gods *blast* it, Bresmer! Sit like a babe trembling in a corner while my people look to me and say, 'There goes a coward, not a ruler'? Sit doing nothing while these mysterious wandering harpists murmur to me what's befalling in my land, and to stay out of it? Sit watching money flow out of the vault and men die still clutching it, while crops rot in the fields with no farmers left alive to tend them, or harvest them so we won't starve come winter? *What would you have me do?*"

"It's not my place to demand anything of you, lord," the seneschal said quietly. "You weep for your people and your land, and that is more than most rulers ever think to do. If you choose to ride out against the Slayer come morning, I'll ride with you . . . but I hope you'll give shelter to those who want to flee the forest, lord, and bide here, until a Harper comes riding in our gates to at least tell us what is destroying our land before we go up against it."

The High Duke stared at the shards of the wineglass in his lap and the blood running down his fingers, and sighed. "My thanks, Bresmer, for speaking sense to me. I'll tarry and be called a coward . . . and pray to Malar to call off this Slayer and spare my people." He rose, brushing glass aside impatiently, and acquired the ghost of a grin as he asked, "Any more advice, seneschal?"

"Aye, one thing more," Bresmer murmured. "Be careful where you do your hunting, lord."

A chill, chiming mist dived between two curving, moss-covered phandars, and slid snakelike through a rent in a crumbling wall. It made of itself a brief whirlwind in the chamber beyond, and became the shifting, semisolid outline of a woman once more.

She glanced around the ruined chamber, sighed, and threw herself down on the shabby lounge to think, tugging at hair that was little more than smoke as she reclined on one elbow and considered future victories.

"He must not see me," she mused aloud, "until he comes here and finds the runes himself. I must seem . . . *linked* to them, an attractive captive he must free, and solve some mystery about; not just how I came to be here, but who I am."

A slow smile grew across her face.

"Yes. Yes, I like that."

She whirled around and up into the air in a blurred whirlwind, to float gently down and stand facing the full-length, peeling mirror. Tall enough, yes . . . She turned this way and that, subtly altering her appearance to look more exotic and attractive—waist in, hips out, a little tilt to the nose, eyes larger . . .

"Yes," she told the glass at last, satisfaction in her voice. "A little better than Saeraede Lyonora was in life . . . and yet—no less deadly."

She drifted toward one of the row of wardrobes, made long, slender legs solid enough to walk; it had been a long time since she'd strutted across a dance floor, to say nothing of flouncing or mincing.

The wardrobe squealed as it opened, a damp door dropping away from the frame. Saeraede frowned and went to the next wardrobe where she'd put garments seized recently from wagons—and victims—on the road . . . when there had still been wagons.

Her smile became catlike at that thought, as she made her hands just solid enough to hold cloth, wincing at the empty feeling it caused within her. To become solid drained her so much.

As swiftly as she dared, she raked through the gowns, selecting three that most caught her eye, and draped them over the lounge. Rising up through the first, she became momentarily solid all over—and gasped at the cold emptiness that coiled within her. "Mustn't do this . . . for long," she gasped aloud, her breath hissing out to cloud the mirror. "Dare not use . . . too much, but these *must* fit. . . ."

The blue ruffles of the first gown were flattened and wrinkled from their visit to the wardrobe; the black one, with its daring slits all over, looked better but would tear and fall apart most easily. The last gown was red, and far more modest, but she liked the quality it shouted, with the gem-highlighted crawling dragons on its hips.

Her strength was failing fast. Gods, she needed to drain lives soon, or . . . With almost feverish speed she shifted her shape to fill out the three gowns most attractively, fixed their varying requirements in her mind, and thankfully collapsed into a whirlwind again, dumping the red gown to the ground in a puddle.

As mist she drifted over it, solidifying just her fingertips to carry it back to the wardrobe and hang it carefully away.

As she returned for the other two garments, an observer would have noticed that her twinkling lights had grown dim, and her mist was tattered and smaller than it had been.

By the time the wardrobe door closed behind the last gown, Saeraede had noticed that she was a little dimmer now. She sighed but couldn't resist coalescing back to womanly form for one last, critical look at herself in the mirror.

"You'll have to do, I suppose . . . and another thing, Saeraede," she chided herself. "Stop talking to yourself. You're lonely, yes, but not completely melt-witted."

"Try over there," a hoarse male voice said then, in what was probably intended to be a whisper. It was coming from the forest beyond the ruin, through one of the gaps in the walls. "I'm sure I saw a woman yonder, in a red gown. . . ."

The ghostly woman froze, head held high, then smiled wolfishly and collapsed into winking lights and mist once more.

"How thoughtful," she murmured to the mirror, her voice faint and yet echoing. "Just when I need them most."

Her laughter arose, as a merry tinkling. "I never thought I'd be around to see it, but adventurers are becoming almost . . . predictable."

She plunged out through a hole in the wall like a hungry eel. Seconds later, a hoarse scream rang out. It was still echoing back off the crumbling walls when there was another.

FIFTEEN
A DARK FLAME RISING

*And a dark flame shall rise, and scatter all before it, igniting red war, wild
magic, and slaughter. Just another quiet interlude before the fresh perils
of next month . . .*

CALDRAHAN MHELYMBRYN, SAGE OF MATTERS HOLY
FROM *A TASHLUTAN TRAVELER'S DAY-THOUGHTS*
PUBLISHED IN THE YEAR OF MOONFALL

Dread Brother Darlakhan.

It had a ring to it. It would go well with the branding and the whip
scars that crisscrossed his forearms. He'd worked hard with a paste of blood
and urine and black temple face paint to turn those scars into dark, permanent,
raised ridges. His eagerness to take branding in the temple rituals had not gone
unnoticed.

The wind off the Shaar was hot and dry this night, and he'd been looking
forward to a quiet evening of prostrate prayer on the cold stone of the cellar
floor—but the adeptress he'd paid to flog him first had come to him with a
harshly whispered mission instead: by Dread Sister Klalaera's command, he was
to immediately bear this platter of food and wine to the innermost chambers
of the House of Holy Night.

"I'm excited for you, Dread Brother," she'd whispered in his ear, before
she'd given him the customary slap across the face. Kneeling, he'd clawed at her
ankles with even more than the usual enthusiasm, his heart pounding with his
own excitement.

He'd *thought* the cruel Overmistress of the Acolytes had been eyeing him
rather closely for the last tenday or so; was this his chance at last?

When he was alone, he hastened to fix the mantle of shards around him,
tucking it up firmly between his thighs so as to make it draw blood before his
first step, instead of walking with infinite care to avoid its wounds, as most
did. Then he took up the platter, held it high, and made a silent prayer to the
all-seeing goddess.

Oh, holy Shar, forgive my presumption, but I would serve you as the dark
night wind, the barbed black blade, your scourge and trusted hand, not merely
as a temple puppet at Klalaera's whims.

"Shar," he breathed aloud, in case anyone was spying from behind panels
and thought he'd been quailing or daydreaming instead of praying. He raised

and lowered the platter in salute and set off briskly through the dimly torchlit halls of the temple. The smooth, black marble was cold under his bare feet, and his limbs tingled where threads of blood trickled down.

He walked straight and tall, never looking back at the naked novices crawling along in his wake, licking up his blood where it fell, and gave no sign he'd heard grunts and sobs and muffled screams behind the doors he passed, as the ambitious clergy of the House made their own pain sacrifices to Holy Shar.

He heard the rumble of the lone drum long before he reached the Inner Portal, and his excitement grew to an almost unbearable singing within him. A High Ritual, unannounced and unexpected, and he was to be part of it.

Dread Brother Darlakhan. Oh, yes. A measure of power at last. He was on his way to greatness.

Darlakhan rounded the last pillar and strode to the archway where the two priestesses crossed their razor-sharp black blades before him, then drew them back across his chest with the most delicate of strokes as he held the platter high out of the way. They turned toward him this night, and Darlakhan stopped, trembling, to receive their ultimate accolade: they let him watch as they shook his blood from the points of their swords into cupped palms, and brought it to their mouths.

He whispered, "As Shar wills," to them, making of his tone a thanks, then strode on down the last passage to the Inner Portal, the drumbeat growing louder before him.

He was surprised to find the Portal itself unguarded. A black curtain adorned with the Dark Disk hung in the customarily empty Portal Arch. Darlakhan slowed for a moment, wondering what to do, then decided he must follow the procedure all acolytes were trained in, as if nothing was occurring out of the ordinary.

He paused at the Portal, swept his elbows out to make the shards slash at him one last time—and to keep them out of the way as he knelt—and went to his knees, extending the platter at the full stretch of his arms and touching his forehead to the cold marble of the threshold.

Swift hands snatched the platter away, and others beheaded him with a single keen stroke.

A long, sleek arm snatched up the blood-gargling head by its hair. An oiled body stretched and thrust Darlakhan's head into a brazier, ignoring the flames that raced back down oiled flesh. "The last," that someone murmured, pain making the voice tight.

"Then know peace, Dread Sister," someone else said, touching her with the black Quenching Rod that drank all fire. The drum rolled one last time and fell silent, a long-nailed hand made a gesture, and black flames roared up out of a dozen braziers with a collective crackle and snarl.

Each brazier in the circle held a blackening, severed head. Each tongue of dark flame rose up in a twisting, flowing column to feed a dark sphere overhead.

The Sacred Chamber of Shar, the most holy room in the House of Holy Night, was crowded indeed. All of the cruel and powerful upper priestesses of

Shar were gathered here in their black and purple, beneath the sphere of roiling shadows. All of them streamed blood from open wounds, all of their eyes were bright with excitement, and all of their attention was now fixed on the sphere that loomed so large above their heads, as tall as six men.

Something swam into view briefly, within the sphere: a human arm, slender and feminine, white skinned and clawing vainly at nothing. Then an elbow was seen, and suddenly, the head and shoulders of a feebly struggling human female swam into view. All that could be seen of her was bare, and she was thrashing about in the fire, seemingly blind. Despair was written large across her face, the eyes dark, staring pools, the mouth open in an endless, soundless scream.

There was a murmur of puzzlement and surprise from among the gathered priestesses—and the tallest among them, resplendent in her horned black head-dress and her mantle of deepest purple, stepped forward and brought the long lash in her hand down with brutal force across the bare back of a man kneeling under the sphere. Sweat flew in all directions; he was drenched and gleaming.

"Explain, Dread Brother High," the Darklady of the House commanded, her voice sharp. "We were promised by you—and, in a sending, by the Flame of Darkness herself—that your striving would bring us great power and great opportunity. Even if this wench is some great queen of Faerûn, I see no power nor opportunity here save the grubby achievement of seizing a land and its coffers. Explain both well and speedily—and live."

The senior priest of the House looked at the struggling figure in the sphere as he let his hands fall to his sides, then slumped back to the marble floor, exhausted. Through his gasps, the priestesses saw the bright flash of his smile.

"It is a success, your Darkness," he said when he could find breath enough. "This is an avatar of the goddess Mystra, though of much less power than most she sends forth. We cannot harm it without unleashing magics too wild for all of us together to hope to control, but while we keep it trapped thus, we can tap the Weave whenever it strives to, gaining magic to power spells studied—and cast—as wizards do. This avatar must have been tainted by its flirtation with Bane . . . there is a lasting weakness here, I believe."

"Time enough for such musings later," said Darklady Avroana firmly. Her voice was still cold and biting, but the eagerness on her face and the tapping of her whip against her own thigh rather than across the face of High Brother Narlkond betrayed her excitement and approval. "Tell me of these spells. We sit and study as mages do, and fill our minds—and what then?"

"No power floods into those memorized patterns until our captive here seeks to touch the Weave," replied the senior priest, rolling over to face her on his knees, "which happens every few hours or so. It seems unable not to strive to, for that is its essential nature, and—"

"How long can we keep this up?" Avroana snapped, gesturing up at the sphere with her whip.

"So long as we have enthusiastic believers in the Dark Mother to furnish us with their heads."

"More have been called hither," said the Darklady, her lips shaping—for a very brief instant—a smile that was as cold as the glacial ice that seals shut a northern tomb. "They've been told we mount a holy crusade."

"Your Darkness," High Brother Narlkond replied, with a soft smile of his own, "we do."

"This is what in human speech would be called the Lookout Tree," said the moon elf, sitting down on a huge leaf—which promptly curled and flexed around him to form a couch that cupped him like a giant, gentle hand.

Umbregard stared around at the view between the great arched branches that split apart where they stood to soar still farther up into the thin, cold air. "By the gods," he said slowly, "those are clouds! We're looking down on the *clouds!*"

"Only the lowest sort of clouds," Starsunder said with a smile. "Oh, didn't you know? Yes, different shapes of clouds hang at different levels, just as fish in a lake seek levels in the water that suit them."

"Fish—?" the human mage asked, then grinned and said, "Never mind; we stray swiftly from my original questioning."

Starsunder grinned back. "Now do you see how it was that humans studied in Myth Drannor for centuries," he said, "and some of them still learned only a handful of the spells they came seeking? The best of them didn't even mind."

Umbregard shook his head. "Oh, to have been there," he whispered longingly, sitting down rather gingerly on another leaf. It promptly tumbled him into its center—he had time for only the briefest of startled murmurs—and folded itself around him, to leave him upright, enthroned in warm comfort.

"Well, ahem," he offered in pleased surprise, while Starsunder chuckled. "Nice, very nice." He looked at Starsunder's chair, still clearly alive and attached to the gigantic shadowtop tree they'd climbed so laboriously to the top of, up a spiral stair that had seemed endless. "I suppose there's no chance of getting a chair like this anywhere else but in the Elven Court?"

"None," Starsunder said with a wide smile, "at all. Sorry."

Umbregard snorted. "You don't sound sorry at all. Why did we have to sweat our weary ways up here, step after thousandth step; what's wrong with using spells to fly?"

"The tree needed to get to know you," his elf host explained. "Otherwise, when you sat down just now, it'd quite likely have hurled you off into yonder clouds like a catapult . . . and I'd have had no human wizards to chat with this evening."

Umbregard shuddered at the vision of being helplessly thrust out, out into the oh-so-empty air, before starting that terrible, long plunge . . .

"*Aghh!*" he shrieked, waving his hands to sweep away his mental vision. "Gods! Away, away! Let's get back to our converse! When we were eating—ohh, that treejelly! How d—no. Later, I'll ask that later. *Now* I want to know why you said, when we were eating, that Elminster stands in such danger just now—and stands also so close to being an even greater danger to us all . . . why?"

Starsunder looked out over miles of greenery toward the distant line of mountains for a moment before he said, "Any human mage who lives as many years as this Elminster outstrips most human foes of his own making; they die while he lives on. His very longevity and power make him a natural target for those of all races who would seize him, or his powers from him, or his supposed riches and enchanted items. Such perils confront all mages who've enjoyed any success."

Umbregard nodded, and his elf host continued.

"It's reasonable to suppose that a wizard of greater success attracts greater attention, and so greater foes, yes?"

Umbregard nodded again, sitting forward eagerly. "You're going to tell me about some great mysterious foes that Elminster's now facing?"

Starsunder smiled. "Such as the Phaerimm, the Malaugrym, and perhaps even the Sharn? No."

Umbregard frowned. "The Phaerr—?"

Starsunder chuckled. "If I tell you about them, they won't be mysterious any longer, will they? Moreover, you'll live the rest of your days in fear, and no one will believe you when you spread word of them. Each time you speak of them will increase the likelihood that one of their number will feel suffi- cient need to silence you—and so bring to a brutal and early end the life of Umbregard. No, forget them. It's good practice for mages, forgetting and letting go of things that interest them. Some of them never learn how, and die long before their time."

Umbregard frowned, opened his mouth to say something, and shut it again. Then it popped open once more, and he said almost angrily, "Well then, if we're to speak of no foes, what special danger does Elminster face?"

A small, tightly curled leaf at Starsunder's elbow opened then to reveal two glass bowls full of what looked like water. He passed one of the bowls over to Umbregard and they drank together.

It was water, and the coolest, clearest that Umbregard had yet tasted. As it slid down to every corner of his being, he felt suddenly fully awake and vigorous. He turned his head to exclaim about how he felt, looked into Starsunder's eyes, and saw sadness there. He hesitated in speaking just long enough for the moon elf to say deliberately, "Himself."

"Himself?" By the gods, had he been reduced to an echo? And was this his sixth evening here with Starsunder . . . or his seventh?

Yes. He was like a small child invited into the converse of adults, seeing a longer, graver view of Faerûn around him for the first time. With a sudden effort, Umbregard held his tongue and leaned forward to listen.

Starsunder rewarded him with a slight smile and added, "With all the friends, lovers, foes, and even realms of his youth gone, Elminster will feel increasingly alone—and as is the way of humans, lonely. He will cling to all he has left—his power and accomplishments of magecraft—and begin to chafe at the bargain that has robbed him of his youth, and of all the things he might have done, but did not . . . in short, he will become restless in the service of Mystra."

"No! You said so yourself: love—"

"It is the way of humans," Starsunder continued calmly, "and of us all, at differing times in our lives . . . but now it is I who digress. In short, Elminster will for the first time as a mature mage of power—as opposed to an ardent, easily-distracted youth—be ready to notice temptations."

"Temptations?"

"Chances to use his power as he sees fit, without the bidding of, or restrictions decreed by others. The desire to do just as he pleases, ignoring consequences for good or ill, smashing all who stand against him. To do whatever he's idly thought of doing, pursuing every whim."

"And so?"

"And so, while he's about it, every living creature on or under fair Toril must cower and hide—for what fate will Umbregard enjoy, if it strikes a passing Elminster that a handful of Umbregard tripes will make a good toy, or meal, for the next few minutes?"

The elf let his words hang in silence for a time, waiting for Umbregard to speak.

Soon enough the human wizard was unable to resist doing so. "Are you saying," he asked softly, "that we—I—or someone . . . must set out to destroy Elminster now, to save all Toril?"

Starsunder shook his head almost wearily. "Why is it that humans love that word so much? 'Destroy!'" He set his water bowl back into the leaf and asked with a smile, "If you succeeded, Umbregard the Mighty, tell me: who then would protect Toril from *you?*"

If I was a lurking Slayer, I would want a lair . . .

"Sweet Mystra," Elminster murmured, smiling despite himself, "whatever you do, stop me from *ever* trying to be a bard." He took another step along the crumbling wall of the ruin, the slight scrape of his boot on damp dead leaves seeming very loud in the eerie quiet of the empty forest.

Somehow he knew this crumbling keep had to be linked to whatever was killing folk and forest creatures hereabouts. He'd felt it clear out along the coast road, calling him here . . . calling him . . .

He stopped and glared up at the mossy stones. Could a spell be at work on him, drawing him here?

He'd have felt any simple charm or suggestion . . . wouldn't he?

Abruptly El wheeled around and started back across the sagging bridge, heading away from the ruins at a steady pace. He looked back once, just to be sure nothing was speeding toward his back, but all seemed as quiet as before. He still felt as if he was being watched, though.

He studied the toothlike remnants of walls for a long time, but nothing moved and nothing seemed to change. With a shrug, El turned around again and headed back down the road.

He hadn't gone far when he saw it—out of the corner of his eye, expected but yet not what he'd expected—a woman watching him from between two duskwood trees. He spun toward the trees, but there was no one there. He turned slowly on his heel, all around, but he saw no watching human, or anyone flitting from tree to tree or crouching in any hollow. He'd have heard the dead leaves rustling at any such movement, anyway.

With a little smile, El turned back to the road and an unhurried trudge along it back to the coast road. He suspected he'd not have to wait long before seeing that face peering at him again—for that was what it had been; no gowned figure, but a head and a neck. She could even be a floating ghost.

If she was the Slayer, that could well explain the lack of tracks to follow or creatures for the High Duke's men to corner. The manner of slaying even argu—

There she was again, peering at him from a tree ahead. This time El didn't rush forward but turned slowly to look in all directions . . . and as he'd expected, that face peered at him from a tree behind him, back toward the ruins, just long enough for their eyes to meet.

He smiled slowly and walked back to that second tree. He was only a few paces from it when a ghostly face turned to regard him from high in a tree a good distance closer to the ruins. Elminster gave her a cheery wave this time and allowed himself to be led back to the ruins. The sooner he got to the bottom of this, the sooner he could be away from here before dark, and on about the main task Mystra had set him.

He went the other way around the walls this time, just to cover new ground, and found himself looking, through gaps in the crumbling stonework, into a vast chamber that seemed to have furniture in it. He moved carefully nearer through the tangle of stunted shrubs and fallen stone, peering.

"There!" a voice snarled—human, rough, and not far away. As Elminster ducked low and spun around, he heard the familiar hum of approaching arrows. The life those arrows sought was his.

Ilbryn Starym reined in at the sentry's startled yell and held up an empty hand. "I come in peace," he began, "alone—"

By then javelins were whizzing his way and men with hastily-drawn swords in their hands and fear and astonishment warring on their faces were leaping through the trees on all sides. "Elves!" one of them roared. "I *told* you 'twas elves, all along—"

The elf sighed, threw off his cloak with the word that made the world dark, and backed his snorting mount to one side. Its sudden jerk told him one of the javelins had found a mark even before it reared up, spilling him out of his saddle, and came crashing down heavily on its side—inches away from Ilbryn. The elf rolled away as hard as he'd ever done anything in his life. A stray hoof numbed his good hip and had probably laid it open, too.

Bloody humans! Can't even ride along woodland trails without getting jumped by idiot adventurers arrogant enough to pitch their encampments *right* across the trail itself.

Ilbryn found his feet, stumbled awkwardly away until he ran into a tree, and propped himself against it. The humans were blundering around in the little corner of nightfall he'd made, hacking at each other—of course, the fools!—shouting in alarm, and generally despoiling their camp and the woods immediately around them. If these were the Slayers, they were more than inept . . . no, these must be one of the bands of hireswords—hah! They thought he was the Slayer!

Right, then . . .

Cloaked in darkness only he could see through, Ilbryn watched the fray rage for a time as he caught his breath and peered around, seeking mages or priests who might have the wits and power to end his spell. Once he unleashed another, his darkness would fall like a dropped cloak—so he wanted that spell to be a good one.

Two of this benighted band of adventurers were dead already at the hands of their fellows, and as Ilbryn watched, a third met a screaming end spitted on two javelins. The stronger of his slayers ran him back against a tree and left him pinned to it and vomiting his lifeblood away. The elf shook his head in disgust and kept looking . . . there!

That man by the tent, bent over the scrolls. Ilbryn readied his spell, then plucked up a stone from beside his tree, measured the throw with narrowed eyes—and threw. The stone bonged off the pot and spilled it into the fire.

The man with the scrolls whipped his head around to see what had befallen, and two other adventurers came loping back through the trees, employing that most favorite of human words, "What?" in the midst of many oaths.

A goodly group. Now, before they all ran off again! Ilbryn steadied himself against the tree, cast the spell as quietly as he could but with unhurried care, and was rewarded, an instant before its end, with the human mage hissing, "Hoy, all—*be still!* Listen!"

The seven-odd adventurers obediently stopped their shouting and rushing about, and they stood like statues as the darkness fell away—and waist-high whirling shards of steel melted out of the empty air and cut them all in half. A few of them even saw the elf standing against a tree sneering at them.

The crouching mage was beheaded, his blood exploding all over the scrolls as he slumped forward into the dirt. Seeing that, Ilbryn didn't bother to survey the slain any longer; he was listening hard now for the sounds of the living. At least two, and possibly as many as four, were still lurking close by.

One of them ran right past him, shrieking in horror as he sprinted into the bloody camp. Sweet trembling trees, were all humans this *stupid?*

Evidently they were; two others joined the first, weeping and yelling. Ilbryn sighed. It wouldn't be long before even fools such as these noticed a motionless elf standing against a tree. Almost regretfully he sent forth the spellburst that slew them.

THE TEMPTATION OF ELMINSTER

Its echoes were still ringing off the trees around when he heard the slight scrape of a boot that made him spin around—to stare at a lone, horror-struck human warrior three paces away, coming toward him with sword raised.

"*You're* the Slayer?" the man asked, face and knuckles white with fear.

"No," Ilbryn told him, backing away around the tree.

The man hesitated, then resumed his cautious advance. "Why did you kill my sword brothers?" he snarled, snatching out a dagger to give himself two ready fangs.

Ilbryn took another step back, keeping the tree between them, and shrugged. "You made a mistake," he told the human, as they started to slowly circle the tree, watching each other's eyes. "I was riding along the trail, at peace and intending no harm to you—and you attacked me, more than a dozen to one. Brigands? Adventurers? I'd no time to parley or see who you were. All I could do was defend myself. A little thought before swinging swords could have saved so much spilled blood." He smiled mockingly. "You should be more careful when you go out in the woods. It's dangerous out here."

That evoked the rage he'd hoped it would; humans were so predictable. With a wordless roar the warrior charged, hacking furiously. Ilbryn let the tree take most of the blows, waited until the blade got caught, then darted forward to snatch the man's dagger hand aside with one of his own hands—and press the other to the man's face, delivering the spell that would take his life.

Flesh smoked and melted; gurgling, the man went to his knees. By the despairing moan he made thereafter, he knew he was dying, even before he started clawing at his own flowing flesh, trying to get air.

"Not that I was unhappy to slay you all," Ilbryn told him lightly, "seeing as how you cost me a perfectly good horse." He stepped back and shot a look all around, in case other surviving adventurers—or the Slayer, whoever that might be—was approaching. No such peril seemed at hand.

The warrior made a last choking noise, then seemed to relax. "After all," Ilbryn told him, "This is the Dead Place, I'm told."

The elf turned away to walk through the camp and see if there was anything he might put to his own use. A few paces along he stopped, looked around again for foes, and bent rather stiffly and plucked up a good, slender blade from among the trodden leaves.

"Just in case," Ilbryn told the torn body of its dead, staring owner, whose fingers would forever be stretched out now toward the blade he'd let fall, the blade that now was no longer there. As the elf reached out with his own sword to cut free the scabbard from amongst the gory, tangled harness, he added almost merrily, "You never know when you'll need a good blade, after all."

SIXTEEN
IF MAGIC SHOULD FAIL

If magic should fail, Faerûn shall be changed forever—and not a few folk would welcome those changes. For one thing, the very land itself might tilt under the hurrying weight of the oppressed and aggrieved, chasing down now-powerless mages to settle old scores. I wonder what a river of wizards' blood would look like?

TAMMARAST TENGLOVES, BARD OF ELUPAR
FROM *THE STRINGS OF A SHATTERED LYRE*
PUBLISHED IN THE YEAR OF THE BEHIR

Begone! Mighty events shake all Faerûn, and the holy ones within cannot come out to speak to you now! For the love of Mystra, begone!"

The guard's voice was deep and powerful; it rolled out over the gathered crowd like a storm-driven wave crashing across the sands of a beach ... but when it died away, the people were still there. Fear made their voices high and their faces white, but they clung to the front steps of the House of the Ladystar as if for their very lives and would not be moved.

The guard made a last grand "get hence" gesture and stepped back off the balcony. "I'm sorry, Bright Master," he murmured. "They feel something is very wrong. It'd take the hounding spells of Mystra herself to shift them now."

"Do you dare to blaspheme *here*, in the holy place itself?" the high priest hissed, eyes blazing with fury. He drew back his hand as if to strike the guard—who stood a head taller than he, despite his own great height—then let it fall back to his side, looking dazed. "Lost," he said, lips trembling. "All is lost. . . ."

The guard enfolded the Lord of the House in a comforting embrace, as one holds a sobbing child, and said, "This shall pass, lord. Wait for nightfall; many shall leave then. Wait, know peace, and watch for some sign."

"You have some guidance for this counsel?" the high priest asked, almost desperately. He could not keep a quaver from his voice.

The guard patted his shoulders and stepped away with the grave reply, "Nay, lord—but look you; what else can we do?"

The Lord of the House managed a chuckle that was perilously close to a sob, and said, "My thanks, loyal Lhaerom." He drew in a deep breath, threw back his head as if donning his dignity like a mantle, and asked, "What do warriors do when they must wait and watch inside their walls, dawdling until a great blow falls on them?"

Lhaerom chuckled in return. "Many things, lord, most of which I leave to your wits to conjure up. There is one thing of comfort we undertake, which I

THE TEMPTATION OF ELMINSTER

687

suspect me your question seeks: we make soup. Pots and pots of it, as good and rich as we can manage. We let all partake, or at least smell if they cannot sup."

The high priest stared at him for a moment, then raised his hands in a "why not?" gesture and commanded the silently watching underpriests, "Get hence! To the kitchens, and make soup! Go!"

"You'll find, lord," the hulking guard added, "that—"

"Lhaerom," one of his fellow guards snapped, "fresh trouble." Without another word the guard turned away from the Lord of the House and ducked back out onto the balcony. The priest took two steps after him—only to find a guard barring his way. "no, lord," he said, face carefully expressionless. "'Twouldn't be wise. Some of them are throwing stones."

Outside, the bright sun fell on the closed bronze doors of the House of the Ladystar. Many fists fell thereon, too, and the guards and gatepriest had long since stopped answering knocks and cries for aid. They paced anxiously back and forth inside the gate, casting anxious glances at the bolts and bars, wondering if they'd hold. All of the spikes that could be found in the temple cellars had long since been driven between the stones to wedge the doors against being forced inward. The bright marks on those spikes told how often this morning the doors had already been sorely tested. The priest licked dry lips and asked, for perhaps the fortieth time, "And if this all gives way? What—"

The guard nearest him waved violently for him to fall silent. The priest frowned and opened his mouth to snap an angry response, then his eyes followed the guard's pointing hand to the doors and his jaw dropped almost to chest.

A man's hand was protruding *through* the bronze, magic crackling around his wrist where it passed through the thick metal. It was gesturing, forming the hand signs used between clergy of Mystra when enacting silent rituals.

The priest watched a few of them, then hissed, "Stay here!" and went pounding up the steps to a door that led into the barbican. He had to get onto that balcony. . . .

The hands of the tall man in the black cloak were trembling as he drew them back from the doors. He knew he'd been seen and knew the mood of the crowd pressing in behind him. "It's no use," he said loudly. "I can't get in."

"You're one of 'em, though, aren't ye?" a voice snarled, close by his ear.

"Aye, I saw him—used a spell, he did!" put in another, high with fear and anger—or rather, the angry need to lash out.

The man in the black cloak made no reply, but looked up at the balcony in desperate hope.

It was rewarded. Two burly guards came into view with long pikes in their hands—pikes fully able to reach down, into, and through anyone standing near the gate—and asked gruffly, more or less in unison, "Yes? You have lawful business in this holy house?"

"I do," the man in the black cloak told them, ignoring the angry mutterings that rose in a wave after his words. "Why are the gates closed?"

"Great doings on high demanding contemplation on the part of all ordained servants of Mystra," the guard thundered.

"Oh? Is there an orgy going on in there, or just a pig-wallowing feast?" someone called from the thick of the crowd, and there were roars of agreement and derision. "Aye, let us in! We want some too!"

"Begone!" the guards bellowed, straightening to face the entire crowd.

"Does Mystra live?" someone cried.

"Aye!" Others took up the call. "Does the goddess of magic yet breathe?"

The guard looked scornful. "Of *course* she does," he snarled. "Now go away!"

"Prove it!" someone yelled. "Cast a spell!"

The guard hefted his pike. "I don't cast spells, Roldo," he said menacingly. "Do you?"

"Get one of the priests—get 'em all!" Roldo called.

"Aye," someone else agreed. "And see if one of them—just *one* of them—can cast a spell!"

The roar of agreement that followed his words shook the very temple walls, but through it the man in the black cloak heard one of the guards mutter, "Aye, and make it a good big fireball, right about *there.*"

The other agreed, not smiling.

"Look," the man in the black cloak said to them, "I *must* speak to Kadeln. Kadeln Parosper. Tell him it's Tenthar."

The nearest guard leaned over. "No, *you* look," he said coldly. "I'm not opening these gates for anybody . . . short of holy Mystra herself. So if you can come back holding hands with her, and the two of you asking very nicely to come in, all right, but otherwise . . ."

A third figure was on the balcony, peering around the guard's shoulder. It wore the cloak and helm of a guard, but no gauntlets, and the helm—which was far too big for it—kept slipping forward over its face.

An impatient hand shoved the helm back up out of the way, and the white, worried face of Kadeln, Tomepriest of the Temple, stared down at his friend. "Tenthar," he hissed, "you shouldn't have come here. These people are wild with fear."

"You know," the man in the black cloak remarked almost casually, "standing down here with them, I'd begun to notice that." Then his control broke and he almost clawed his way up the wall to the balcony, ignoring a warning pike thrust. The dirty blade stopped inches from his nose and hung there warningly. Tenthar paid it not a blind bit of attention.

"Kadeln," Tenthar was snarling, "*what's going on?* Every last damned magic I work goes wild, and when I study—nothing. I can't *get* any new spells!"

"It's the same here," the white-faced priest whispered. "They're saying Mystra must have died, and—"

One of the guards hauled Kadeln away from the edge of the balcony, and the other jabbed viciously with his pike; Tenthar flung himself desperately back out of its reach and tumbled down the bronze doors to the ground.

The crowd melted away a few paces as if by magic, and he found himself lying in a little cleared space with the pike once more hanging a handspan above his throat. "Who are you?" the guard behind it demanded. "Answer, or die. I have new orders."

Tenthar sat up and thrust the pike head away with one contemptuous hand. When he scrambled to his feet, however, he took care to be a good two paces beyond its reach.

"Tenthar Taerhamoos is my name," he said sternly, opening his cloak to reveal rich robes, and a gem—studded medallion blazing on his chest. "Archmage of the Phoenix Tower. I'll be back."

And with that grim promise the archmage whirled around and pushed his way almost proudly through the crowd. All around him were murmurs of "It's *true!* Mystra's dead? Magic all undone?" and the like.

A stone spun out of somewhere and struck Tenthar on the shoulder. He did not stop or try to turn but struggled onward through bodies disinclined to let him pass. "An archmage?" someone cried. "With no spells?" another asked, close at hand. Another stone struck Tenthar, on the head this time, and he staggered.

There was a roar of mingled awe and exultant hunger all around him, and someone shrieked, "Get him!'

"Get him!" a thunderous chorus echoed. Tenthar went to his knees, looked up to see boots and sticks and hands coming at him from all sides, clutched his precious medallion to guard against the spell going wild, and said the words he'd hoped not to have to say.

Lightning crackled out in all directions, and Tenthar tried not to look at the dying folk dancing to its hungry surges around him. Chain lightning is a terrible thing even when unaugmented; with the medallion involved, well . . .

He sighed and stood up as the last of the screams died away, watching the bobbing heads of those who'd lived to flee grow smaller as they ran across the fields. He'd best be running, too, before some bloodthirsty idiot rallied them or the folk here who were only stunned and twitching recovered enough to seek revenge.

The smell of cooked flesh was strong; bodies were heaped on all sides. Tenthar gagged, then broke into a trot. He never even saw the pike hurled at him from the balcony; it fell well short and struck, quivering, in the dirt.

A blackened body rose from among the dead and tugged it free. "The thing I hate most about these little games," it remarked to the empty air, "is the *cost.* How many lives will be snuffed out before it's over, this time?"

Another blackened thing rose, shrugged, touched the pike, and said sadly, "There's always a price . . . all our power, and we can't change that."

There were two shimmerings in the air—and the two blackened bodies were gone. The pike winked out of sight an instant later.

"Are there archmages under every stone out yonder? Or just what bloody dancing gods were *those?*" the guard who'd thrown the pike barked, more fear than anger in his tones.

"Mystra and Azuth," the priest beside him whispered. The guards turned to look at Kadeln—and gasped in amazement. The missing pike had just appeared in the priest's shuddering hands. He stared at them, eyes full of wonder, and moaned, "Mystra and Azuth, they were. Standing right there, with the symbols they've granted us to know them by glowing above their heads—right *there!*"

He tried to point out into the litter of bodies, but decided to faint instead. He did it very well, eyes rolling up and body folding down. One of the guards caught him out of force of habit, and the other snatched hold of the pike.

If gods were going to come calling, he didn't want to be standing there unarmed.

"Mystra is dead!" the Darklady declared exultantly. "Her priests find their spells to be but flickering things, and mages study and find no power behind their words. Magic is now ours alone to command—ours to control!"

The purple flames that raged in the brazier before her cast strange lights on her face as she raised eyes that were very large and dark to gaze at them all. Around the flames sat her eager audience: the six priests of the Dark Lady who'd agreed to work as wizards, harnessing for their spells the power of what had already become known in the temple as the Secret in the Sphere. With them she could make the House of Holy Night the mightiest temple of Shar in all Faerûn—and the faith of the Nightbringer the most powerful in all Toril. It might not even take long.

"Most loyal Dreadspells," the high priestess told them, "you have a great opportunity to win the favor of Shar, and power for yourselves. Go forth into Faerûn and seek out the most capable mages and the largest holds of magic. Slay at will, and seize all you can. Bring back tomes, rare things, and anything that bears the tiniest glow of magic. You *must* slay any of those servants of Mystra called the Chosen if you meet with them. We here shall work most diligently with our spells to try to find them for you."

"Your Darkness?" one of the wizards asked hesitantly.

"Yes, Dread Brother Elryn?" Darklady Avroana's voice was silken; a clear warning to all that anyone who dared to interrupt her had better have a *very* good reason for doing so—or she'd soon give them one.

"My work involves farscrying our agents in Westgate," Elryn said quickly, "and rumor now abroad in that city speaks of many recent sightings of a Chosen in the vicinity of Starmantle . . . something about going into a 'Dead Place' . . ."

"I, too, have heard such tidings," the Darklady agreed eagerly. "My thanks for giving us a location, Elryn. All of you shall go there immediately—and there begin your holy task. Thrust your hands into the flames—oh, and *most* loyal Dreadspells, bear in mind that we can see and hear you always."

Six faces paled—and six hands were reluctantly extended into the flames. Darklady Avroana laughed delightedly at their fear and let them burn for a few moments ere she said the words that teleported them all elsewhere.

It was very peaceful in the woods around the shrine—and, since the killings had begun and fear had driven folks away, very quiet.

Most days Uldus Blackram was alone on his knees before the stone block, halfheartedly lashing himself a few times—gently, so as not to make much noise—and whispering prayers to the Nightsinger.

The shrine had been founded so nicely, consecrated with blood and a wild ritual that still made Uldus blush to remember it. Now there were no black-robed ladies to dance and whirl barefoot around the horned block and no one to lead him in the half-remembered prayers . . . so he did a lot of just thanking Shar for keeping him alive on his stealthy visits to the woods. He hoped she'd forgive him for not coming at night anymore.

"May your darkness keep me safe from the Slayer," Uldus breathed, his lips almost touching the dark stone. "May you guide me to power and exultation over mine enemies, and make of me a strong sword to cut where you need things cut, and slash where it is your will to slash. Oh, most holy Mistress of the Night, hear my prayer, the beseeching of your most loyal servant, Uldus Blackram. Shar, hear my prayer. Shar, answer my prayer. Shar, heed m—"

"Done, Uldus," said a voice from above him, crisply.

Uldus Blackram managed to strike his head on the altar, somersault over backward to get a good four paces away, and get to his feet all in one blurred flurry of movement.

When he froze, half turned to flee and panting hard, he was looking back at six bald-headed men in black and purple robes, standing in a semicircle around the altar facing him, with faint amusement on their faces.

"Lords of the Lady?" Uldus gasped. "Have my prayers been answered at last?"

"Uldus," the oldest of them said pleasantly, stepping forward, "they have. At last. Moreover, a fitting reward has been chosen for you. You're going to guide us into the Dead Place!"

"P-praise Shar!" Uldus replied, rolling his eyes wildly upward as he toppled to the turf in a dead faint.

"Revive him," Elryn commanded, not bothering to keep the contempt from his face or voice. "To think that such as this worship the Most Holy Lady of Loss."

"Well," one of the other wizards commented, bending over the fallen Uldus, "we all have to start somewhere."

The glowing spellsphere orbited the throne at an almost lazy pace. Saeraede gave it only casual attention, absorbed as she was in sending images of her peering self out into the trees to lure this bold Elminster back to her castle.

Aye, let us gently tease this fittingly powerful and somewhat attractive mage hence.

Yet the news was clear enough, from all the mages she covertly farscried. Word of the death of Mystra was spreading like wildfire, spells were going wild all over Faerûn, mages were shutting themselves up in towers before grudge-holding commoners could get to them—or tarrying too long, and getting caught on the ends of pitchforks in a dozen realms, and on and on.

It was time to move at last and make Saeraede Lyonora once more a name to be feared!

Abruptly something tore through one of her images. Saeraede sat up with a frown, and peered, trying to find out what it had been. The spellsphere abruptly lost its scene of city spires and flapping griffon wings beneath armored riders and acquired the dappled gloom of the forest above her. A forest that held a crouching Elminster, several of her floating faces, and—

Arrows snarled through her conjured visage and the dead leaves beyond, to thud into the forest loam and send Elminster scrambling around the other side of a tree.

Arrows?

"Damned adventurers!" she roared, her cry ringing back to her off the cavern roof, and sprang up from the throne. The spellsphere winked out as it fell, the radiance around the stone seat faded—but she was already whirling up the shaft, her eyes spitting flames of magefire. Were a bunch of blundering sword swingers going to shatter her long-nursed plans *now*?

The fittingly powerful and somewhat attractive Elminster boldly dodged another arrow, hurling himself on his face in wet moss and dead leaves as another dark shaft whined past his ear like an angry hornet and fetched up in the trunk of a nearby hiexel with a very solid thunk.

El scrambled up, drawing breath for a curse, and flung himself right back down on his face again. A second shaft hummed past low overhead, joining the first.

The hiexel didn't look to be enjoying these visitations too much, but Elminster hadn't time to survey its sadness—or do anything else but charge to his feet, leap over a fallen tree, and whirl around behind its rotting trunk. He bobbed up into view right away, betting that the two archers wouldn't have had time to put fresh arrows to their strings just yet. He had to see them.

Ah! There! He loosed a stream of magic missiles at one, then ducked down again, hearing the approaching thud of booted feet running hard in his direction.

It was time to get gone and be blessed quick about it!

He sprinted away, downhill and dodging from side to side, hearing crashing in his wake that heralded the coming of someone large, heavy, armored, and sword-waving. He didn't stop to exchange pleasantries, but whirled around a tree to let the grizzled armsman have some magic missiles full in the face. The man's head jerked back, wisps of smoke burst from his mouth and eyes, and he ran on blindly for another dozen paces before stumbling and crashing to the ground, dead or senseless.

"Dead or senseless." Hmm; 'twould do as a motto for some adventuring bands, to be sure, but . . .

It was time to circle around and take care of that second archer, or he'd be fleeing through the forest feeling phantom arrows between his shoulder blades for the rest of the day . . . or until they brought him down.

El trotted a goodly way off to the right and started to work his way back toward the ruin, keeping as low and as quiet as possible. It didn't matter if he spent hours worming his way closer, so long as he wasn't seen too soon. He had to get close enough to—

A grim-looking man in leathers, with a bow ready-strung in his hand, stepped into view around a gnarled phandar not twelve paces away. He couldn't help but see a certain hawk-nosed mage the moment he lifted his eyes from the arrow he'd just dropped. El lifted his hand to shoot forth his last magic missiles spell.

A moment later the archer exploded into whirling bones and fire. El had a brief glimpse of two dark eyes—if they were eyes—in a confused whirlwind of mist. Then whatever it was had gone, and scorched bones were thudding down onto the moss.

The Slayer?

It had to be. The talk had been all of something that burned its victims when it killed; this was it. "Well met," Elminster murmured to the empty woods, and went cautiously forward. He knew he'd already find nothing but ashes and bones of the rest of the adventurers, but just in case . . .

Sprawled garments, weapons, and bones were everywhere he looked, as he drew near the overgrown keep. The ruins seemed deserted again. A tense silence hung over them, almost as if something was waiting and watching for his approach. El stole back to the gaps in the wall he'd looked into before. That big chamber, where he'd seen the wardrobes and . . . a mirror? That would bear another look, to be sure.

He peered very cautiously into that vast room again and met those dark eyes once more, the mist they were at the heart of swirling around a wardrobe as its doors banged open. Then the mist flared into blinding brilliance and he couldn't see what was taken out of the wardrobe. Whatever it was, the whirlwind spun around and around it, almost as if deliberately hiding it from his view in its bright and chiming tatters, as it sped away across the room. El almost clambered in the gap after it to see better, but paused prudently when the glowing mist did.

It lingered in the farthest, darkest corner of the room for a moment, hovering above what looked like a well, then plunged down into that ring-shaped opening and out of sight.

"Ye want me to follow, do ye?" Elminster murmured, looking at the well. He glanced around the room, taking in the peeling mirror, the row of wardrobes—the open one holding an array of feminine apparel—the lounge, and the rest . . . then walked straight to the well.

"Very well," he said with a sigh. "Another reckless leap into danger. That does seem to be what this job most entails."

And he clambered over the edge of the well, dug his hands into the first of a row of handholds in the stone and tapped with the toes of his boots for another, found it, and started down. He might need his hellbent flying spell for getting back out again.

She laid out the three gowns on the stone at the bottom of the shaft as gently as a nurse stroking a sick child, and as gently set loose stones from the rubble over them. The exacting effort cost her much energy, but she worked swiftly, heedless of the cost, and darted away before her quarry got to the top of the shaft to look down.

A moment later she was sinking into one of the runes that sustained her, hiding her misty self entirely. She had been hungry too long, and the incessant chiming was even getting on *her* nerves.

Brandagaeris had been a mighty hero, tall and bronzed and strong; she had fed on him for three seasons, and he had come to love her and offer himself willingly . . . but in the end she had drained him and gone hungry again. That was her doom; once her own body had fallen to dust, what remained was a magic that needed to feed on the living—or dwell within, and necessarily burn out the innards of a young, strong, vital body. Brandagaeris had been one such, the sorcerer Sardon another . . . but somehow mages, clever as they were, lacked something she craved. Perhaps they had too little vitality.

She hoped this Elminster wouldn't be another such disappointment. Perhaps she could win his love, or at least his submission, and not have to fight him long to taste what power a Chosen held.

"Come to me," she whispered hungrily, her words no more than the faintest of sighings above the deep-graven rune. "Come to me, man-meal."

SEUENTEEN
A FINE DAY FOR TRAUEL

Travel broadens the mind and flattens the purse, they say. I've found it does rather more than that. It shatters the minds of the inflexible, and depletes the ranks of the surplus population. Perhaps rulers should decree that we all become nomads.

Then, of course, we could choose to stay only within the reach of those rulers we favor—and I can't conceive of the chaos and overburdened troops and officials that would be found in any realm in which folk could choose their rulers. Thankfully, I can't believe that any people would ever be crazed enough to do that. Not in this world, anyway.

YARYNOUS WHAELIDON
FROM *DISSENSIONS OF A CHESSENTAN*
PUBLISHED IN THE YEAR OF THE SPUR

Y ou're doing just fine, brave Uldus," Dreadspell Elryn said soothingly, prodding their trembling guide with the man's own sword. Brave Uldus arched away from the blade, but the noose around his neck—held tight and short-leashed in the fist of Dreadspell Femter—kept him from entirely missing its sharp reminder. Dreadspell Hrelgrath was walking along close by, too, his dagger held ready near the ribs of their unwilling guide.

"Shar is very pleased with you," Elryn told the man, as they went on along the almost invisible game trail, deeper into the Dead Place. "Now just show us this ruin ... oh, and Uldus, reassure me again: it is the *only* ruin or building or cave or construct you know about, anywhere in these woods, is it not?"

Choking around his noose, Uldus assured him that it was, oh, yes, Dread Lord, indeed it was, may the Nightbringer strike me down now if I lie, and all the watching gods bear witness—

Femter didn't wait for Elryn's sign this time before jerking the noose tight enough to cut Uldus off in mid-babble. The guide silently clawed at his throat, stumbling, until Femter relented enough to let him breathe again.

"Iyrindyl?" Elryn asked, without turning his head.

"I'm watching, Dread Lord," the youngest Dreadspell replied eagerly. "The first sign of walls or the like, I'll cry hold."

"It's not walls I'm seeing," the deep drawl of Dreadspell Daluth put in, a few strides later, "but an elf—alone, and walking with a drawn sword in his hand, yonder."

The Sharran priests stopped, unnecessarily clapping their hands over the mouth of their guide, and glared through the trees. A lone elf looked back at them, disgust written plain on his face.

A moment later, Elryn snarled, "Attack!" and the Sharrans surged forward, Elryn and Daluth standing still to hurl spells. They saw the elf sigh, take off his cloak and hurl it high over a tree branch, then turn to face them, crouching slightly. "Damned human adventurers!" he cried. "Haven't I killed enough of you *yet*?"

Ilbryn Starym watched the wizards run toward him—*charging* wizards? Truly, Faerûn was plunging deeper into madness with every passing day—took up the blade that was battle-booty from the last band of fools, and said a word over it. When he threw it like a dart at the onrushing men, it glowed, split into three, and leaped away like three falcons diving at separate targets.

At the same moment, a tree just behind the line of running wizards turned bright blue and tore itself up out of the earth with a deafening groan, hurling earth and stones in all directions. Someone cursed, sounding very surprised.

An instant later, a sheet of white lightning broke briefly over the running mages, and a man who seemed to have a noose around his neck convulsed, clawed at the air for a few moments and shrieked, "My *reward!*" and fell to earth in a twisted heap. The wizards ran on without pause, and Ilbryn sighed and prepared to blast them to nothingness. His three blades should have done *something*.

One of the running mages grunted, spun around, and went down with something glowing in his shoulder. Ilbryn smiled. One.

There was a flash, someone cried out in surprise and pain, and the three remaining wizards burst through the still-shimmering radiance and came on, one of them shaking fingers that trailed smoke. Ilbryn lost his smile. Some sort of barrier spell, and it had taken both of his other blades.

He raised his hands and waited. Sure enough, now that they were close enough to him that the army of Ilbryn and the army of half a dozen mages could count each other's teeth, the panting wizards were coming to a halt and preparing to hurl spells at him.

Ilbryn cloaked himself in a defensive sphere, leaving only a keyhole open for his next spell. If his measure of these dolts was correct, he'd not have over-much to fear in this battle . . . even with the wizard who'd taken his blade slowly crawling to his feet and the two who hadn't come running strolling slowly closer in the distance.

Abruptly the air in front of Ilbryn's sphere was filled with blue flowers, swirling about as they drifted to earth. An elf mouth crooked into a smile. By the startled oaths coming to his ears, *that* hadn't been supposed to happen. Perhaps he was caught up in some school of wizardry's battle test of the inept apprentices. He waited politely to see what else would come his way.

A moment later, he blinked with new respect. The earth was parting with a horrible ripping sound, between the boots of one of the mages—and racing toward Ilbryn, zigzagging only slightly as it came. Trees, boulders, and all were hurled aside in the chasm's swift advance, and Ilbryn readied his lone flight spell, just in case. He'd have to time this just right, collapsing the sphere and bounding aloft more or less in one smooth sequence.

The chasm swerved and snarled on past, trailing the awed yells of a wizard who seemed astonished he'd cast it. Ilbryn's eyes narrowed. What sort of madmen were these?

Well, he'd wasted more than enough time and magic on them already. He hurled a quick spell of his own out of the keyhole, and stood watching as the trunk of the shadowtop he'd shattered, a goodly distance above the wizards, spun about almost lazily, then came crashing down.

Wizards shouted and hurled themselves in all directions, but when the dancing, flailing branches receded to a shivering, one man lay broken like a discarded doll under a trunk ten times his girth.

Ilbryn risked another spell through the keyhole. Why not a volley of magic missiles? These idiots seemed almost like bewildered actors *playing* at being mages, not foes to fear at all.

He hoped, a moment later, that he hadn't just given the gods some sort of awful cue.

"If Mystra is dead, what's helping *his* spells?" Dreadspell Hrelgrath snarled, puffing his way back to where Elryn stood watching, cold-eyed.

"Whatever god of magic elves pray to, dolt," Daluth answered—an instant before blue-white bolts of force came racing their way.

"Back!" Elryn snapped, "I don't think these can miss, but *back*, anyway! This is costing us too much!"

Elryn's prediction proved to be right; none of the bolts missed. The Dreadspells grunted and staggered their ways back through the trees, hoping the elf wouldn't bother to follow them.

"Femter?" Elryn snapped.

A head snapped up. "I'll be all right, the next time the power surges into us," Femter replied grimly. "Some sort of magical blade. Can't use my arm, though."

"Our guide—dead?"

"Very," Femter said shortly, and there were a few dark chuckles.

"Iyrindyl?"

"Down. Forever. Half a tree fell on him."

Elryn drew in a deep breath and let it out in a ragged sigh, very conscious of the unseen eyes of Darklady Avroana upon him. "Right—consider that fiasco our first battle-practice. There'll be no more charging into any fray. From now on, we creep through these woods like shadows. When we find the ruin, we wait for the Weave to feed us once more, then—and only then, even if it takes all night—we advance. Out in these woods, only the Chosen really matters to us, and I'm not going to be caught off-guard again."

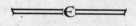

"*That's* a good plan," Ilbryn agreed sarcastically, as he let his clairaudience collapse, said farewell to the idiot wizards and their chatter, and cast the guidance spell that would take him to these ruins they'd been heading for. He bid it seek out man-touched stone, in any mass larger than four men—which should eliminate tombstones and the like—and in *this* general direction . . .

Almost immediately he felt the pull of the magic. Ilbryn followed it obediently, striding off through the woods along an invisible but unwavering line. Ah, but magic could be useful at times.

It had been cold and dark in Scorchstone Hall for many years. Too cold for the living.

A skeleton threw back the shutters of one window to let the sun in and went back to a table where a spellbook lay. Sitting down carefully in the stoutest chair left in the Hall, the skeleton took up the tome, clutched it to its ribcage with both bony arms enfolded around it, and called on the power of the spell it had cast earlier. The power that let it speak.

It said only two words, firmly enough that they echoed back from the dark corners of the room. "Mystra, please."

Blue-white fire burst forth from the book. The skeleton almost dropped the book in surprise, its bony fingertips clawing at its covers, as the flames that burned nothing washed over its bones, racing from the book to . . . her.

Sharindala shuddered as blue-white fire ran up and down her limbs, leaving something in its wake. She stared down at her glowing bones in wonder, then back at the book, feeling something rising in her throat.

Baerdagh stiffened at the sudden sound that came through the trees, and almost dropped his walking stick. He turned, to be absolutely sure that the faint weeping was coming from Scorchstone.

It was. In the very heart of that ruined mansion, a woman was sobbing—crying as if she'd never find breath to speak again. In dark, haunted Scorchstone, where the skeletal sorceress walked.

Baerdagh broke into a frantic shuffle, heading for the Maid—where strong drink, and plenty of it, would be waiting.

"Along here, it should be," Beldrune said, as they came around the bend and almost rode down an old man with a walking stick, who looked to have just taken up trotting, and was wheezing loudly to let the world know. "There! Up ahead, on the left—the Fair Maid of Ripplestones. We can get a good meal there, and decent beds a few doors on, and ask in both places about where Elminster's been hereabouts. I know he likes to look at old mages' towers."

"And their tombs, too," Tabarast put in. "It's been some years since I stopped here, but old Ralder, if he's still alive, used to roast a mean buck."

The down-at-heels Harper with the pale brown hair and eyes, riding between them, nodded pleasantly. "Sounds good," was all he said, as they slowed their horses at the ramshackle porch and rang the gong that would bring the stable boys.

An old man sitting on a bench deep in one corner of the porch looked at them sharply—especially at Tabarast—as they strode inside. After a moment, he got up and drifted into the Maid on their heels.

It seemed Caladaster was hungry enough for a second earlyevenfeast this day. By the time Baerdagh came puffing up to the front door of the Maid, Caladaster was sitting with the three horsemen who'd almost ridden him down as if they'd known each other for years.

"Aye, I know this Elminster, right enough," Caladaster was saying, "though a few days back I'd have answered you differently. He came walking up to this very tavern. Baerdagh—oh, hey! *This* is Baerdagh; come sit down with us, old dog—and I were warming yon bench, where you saw me just now, and he came striding up and bought us dinner—a huge feast it was, too!—in return for us telling him about Scorchstone Hall. Gods, but we ate like princes!"

"We can do no less," the youngest, poorest-looking of the three horsemen said then, saying his first quiet words since handing a stable boy some coins. "Eat hearty, both of you, and we'll trade information again."

"Oh, a-heh. Well enough . . . that's very kind of you, to be sure," Caladaster said heartily as he watched platters of steaming turtles and buttered snails brought to the table. Alnyskavver even winked at him as the tankards were set down beside them. Caladaster blinked. Gods, he was becoming a local lion!

"So where and what is Scorchstone Hall?" Beldrune asked almost jovially, plucking up a tankard and taking a long pull at it. Baerdagh didn't fail to notice the face the newcomer made at the taste of the brew or how quickly he set down the tankard again.

"A ruined mansion just back along the road a ways," he said quickly, determined to earn his share of the meal. "You passed it on your way in—the road bends around it, just this side of the bridge."

"It's warded," Caladaster said quietly. "You gentlesirs are mages, are you not?"

Three pairs of eyes lifted to him in brief silence until Tabarast sighed, took up a buttered snail that must have burned his fingers, and grunted, "It shows that badly, does it?"

Caladaster smiled. "I was a mage, years ago. Still am, I suppose. You have the look about you . . . eyes that see farther than the next hedge. Paunches and wrinkles, but yet fingers as nimble as a minstrel's. Not to mention the wardings on your saddlebags."

Beldrune chuckled, "All right, we're mages—two of us, at any rate."

"Not three?" Caladaster's brows rose.

The man with the pale brown eyes and the tousled hair smiled faintly and said, "Here and now, I harp."

"Ah," Caladaster said, carefully not glancing at the regulars in the Maid, who were bent almost out of their chairs straining not to miss a word of what passed between these travelers and the two old tankard-tossers. Wizards, now! And haunted Scorchstone! Mustn't miss this. . . .

A Harper and two wizards, hunting Elminster. Caladaster felt a little better, now, about telling them things. Hadn't Elminster had summat to do with starting the Harpers?

"Scorchstone Hall," Caladaster continued, in a voice so low that Baerdagh's sudden humming completely cloaked it from the ears of folk at other tables, "is the home of a local sorceress—a lady by the name of Sharindala. A good mage, and dead these many years. Of course, there are the usual tales of her being seen walking around past her windows, as a skeleton and all . . . but you'd have to be a damned good tree-climber to get to where you could just see a window of the Hall—let alone look through its closed shutters!"

He got smiles at that, and continued, "Whatever—Elminster asked us all about her, and we warned him about the wards, but it's my belief he went in there and did summat. We asked him to stop by our places—we live, Baerdagh an' I, in the two cottages hard by Scorchstone, 'twixt there and here—when he was done, so's we'd know he'd fared well—"

"And we wouldn't have to go in there looking for his body," Baerdagh growled and went back to his humming. Tabarast and the Harper exchanged amused glances.

Caladaster gave his old friend what some folks would call a dirty look and took up his tale again. "He did drop by to see us—looked right happy, too, though he had a little sadness about him, like folk get when they remember friends now gone, or see old ruins they remember as bright and bustling. He said he'd a 'task' to get on with, and had to head east. We warned him about the Slayer, o' course, but—"

"The Slayer?" the Harper asked quietly. Something about his words made the whole Maid fall silent, from door to rafters.

Alnyskavver, the tavern master, moved quickly forward. "It's not been seen here, lords," he said, "whatever it be. . . ."

"Aye, you're safe here," someone else grunted.

"Oh? Then why'd old Thaerlune pack up and move back to—"

"He *said* he was going to see his sister, her bein' sick an' all—"

Caladaster's open hand came down on the table with a crash. "*If* you don't mind," he said mildly into the little silence that followed and turned to the three travelers again.

"The Slayer is summat that has the High Duke, up in his castle Starmantle way, very worried. Summat is killing everything that lives in the forest, or travels the coast road past it, between Oggle's Stream—just beyond us here—and Rairdrun Hill. Cows, foxes, entire bands of hired adventurers, and several of 'em, too—everything. They've taken to calling it the Dead Place, this stretch of woods, but no one knows what's doing the killing. Some say the dead have been burned away to bones, others say other things, but no matter. We don't know what killer we're facing, so folk've been calling it the Slayer." He looked around the taproom. "Well enough? Said it all, didn't I?"

There were various grunts and grudging agreements, one or two hastily shushed dissenting opinions, and Caladaster smiled tightly and lowered his voice again. "Elminster walked straight into the Dead Place, he did, an' must be there now," he said. "I don't know right why he had to go there . . . but it's summat important, isn't it?"

There was a brief silence again. Then the Harper said, "I think so," at the same moment as Tabarast snapped, "*Everything* Elminster does is important."

"You're going after him?" Caladaster asked, in a voice that was barely above a whisper.

After a moment, the Harper nodded again.

"I'm going with you," Caladaster said, just as quietly. "That's a lot of woods, an' you'll need a guide. Moreover, I just might know where he was headed."

Beldrune stirred, "Well," he said gravely, "I don't know about that. You're a bit old to be going adventuring, and I'd not want to be—"

"Old? *Old?*" Caladaster asked, his jaw jutting. "What's *he*, then?" He pointed at Tabarast. "A blushing young lass?"

That old mage fixed Caladaster with a gaze that had made far mightier men quail, and snapped, " 'Just might know' where Elminster was heading to? What did he tell you—or are you guessing? *This* blushing young lass wants to know."

"There's a ruin in that forest," Caladaster said quietly, "in, off the road. You can tramp around in the trees all day waiting to get eaten by the Slayer while you search for it, or I can take you right to the ruin. If I'm wrong—well, at least you'll have one more old, overweight mage and his spells along for the jaunt."

"Overweight?" Tabarast snapped. "Who's overweight?"

"Ah," Beldrune said, clearing his throat and reaching for a dish of cheese stuffed mushrooms that Alnyskavver had just set down on the table, "that'd be me."

"I don't think it's a good idea to bring one more man along," Tabarast said sharply, "whom we may have to protect against the gods alone know what—"

"Ah," the Harper said quietly, laying a hand on Tabarast's arm, "but I think I'd very much like to have you along, Caladaster Daermree. If you can leave with us in the next few minutes, that is, and not need a night longer to prepare."

Caladaster pushed back his chair and got up. "I'm ready," he said simply. There was something like a smile deep in the Harper's eyes as he rose, set a stack of coins as tall as a tankard on the table—many eyes in the room bulged—and said, "Tavern master! Our horses—here's stabling for a tenday and for the feast. If we come not back to claim them by then, consider them yours. We'll walk from here. You set a good table."

Baerdagh was staring up at his old friend, his face pale. "C-Caladaster?" he asked. "Are you going yon, in truth—into the Dead Place?"

The old wizard looked at him. "Aye, but we can't take along an old warrior, so don't fear. Stay—we need you to eat all the rest of this for us!"

"I—I—" Baerdagh said, and his eyes fell to his tankard. "I wish I wasn't so old," he growled.

The Harper laid a hand on his shoulder. "It's never easy—but you've earned a rest. You were the Lion of Elversult, were you not?"

Baerdagh gaped up at the Harper as if he'd just grown three heads, and a crown on each one. "How did you know about that? *Caladaster* doesn't know about that!"

The Harper clapped his shoulder gently. "It's our business to remember heroes—forever. We're minstrels, remember?"

He strode to the door and said, "There's a very good ballad about you. . . ."

And then he was gone. Baerdagh half rose to follow, but Caladaster pushed him firmly back down. "You sit, and eat. If we don't come back, ask the next Harper through to sing it to you." He went to the door, then turned with a frown. "All those years," he said, scowling, "and you never told me you were the Lion! Just such a little thing it slipped your mind, huh?"

He went out the door. Tabarast and Beldrune followed. They just gave him shrugs and grins at the door, but Tabarast turned with his fingers on the handle and growled, "If it makes you feel better, you're not the only one who doesn't know what's going on!"

The door scraped shut, and Baerdagh stared at it blankly for a long while—long enough that everyone else had come back from the windows and watching the four men walk out of town, and sat down again. Alnyskavver lowered himself into the seat beside Baerdagh and asked hesitantly, "You were the Lion of Elversult?"

"A long time ago," Baerdagh said bitterly. "A long time ago."

"If you could go back to some moment, then," the tavern master asked a tankard in front of him softly, "what moment would it be?"

Baerdagh said slowly, "Well, there was a night in Suzail . . . We'd spent the early evening running through the castle, there, chasing young noble ladies who were trying to put their daggers into one another. Y'see, there was this dispute about—"

Turning to Alnyskavver to properly tell him the tale, Baerdagh suddenly realized how silent the room was. He lifted his eyes, and turned his head. All the folk of Ripplestones old enough to stand were crowded silently around him in a ring, waiting to hear.

Baerdagh turned very red and muttered, "Well, 'twas a long time ago. . . ."

"Is that when you got that medal?" Alnyskavver asked slyly, pointing at the chain that disappeared down Baerdagh's none-too-clean shirtfront.

"Well, no," the old warrior answered with a frown, "that was . . ."

He sat back, and blushed an even darker shade. "Oh, gods," he said.

The tavern master grinned and slid Baerdagh's tankard into the old warrior's hand. "You were in the castle in Suzail, chasing noble ladies up and down the corridors, and no doubt the Purple Dragons were chasing you, and—"

"Hah!" Baerdagh barked. "They were indeed—have you ever seen a man in full plate armor fall down a circular stair? Sounded like two blacksmiths, fighting in a forge! Why, we..."

One of the villagers clapped Alnyskavver's shoulder in silent thanks. The tavern master winked back as the old warrior's tale gathered speed.

"Not all that much more sun today," Caladaster grunted, "once we're in under the trees."

"Umm," Beldrune agreed. "Deep forest. Lots of rustlings, and weird hootings and such?"

Caladaster shook his head. "Not since the Slayer," he said. "Breezes through the leaves, is all—oh, and sometimes dead branches falling. Otherwise, 'tis silent as a tomb."

"Then we'll hear it coming all the easier," the Harper said calmly. "Lead on, Caladaster."

The old wizard nodded proudly as they strode on down the road together. They'd gone some miles and were almost at the place where the overgrown way to the ruins turned off the coast road, when a sudden thought struck him—as cold and as sudden as a bucket of lake water in the face.

He was very careful not to turn around, so that the Harper could see his face—this Harper who'd never given his own name. But from that moment on, he could feel the man's gaze on him—a cold lance tip touching the top of his spine, where his neck started.

The Harper had called him by his full name. Caladaster Daermree.

Caladaster *never* used his last name... and he hadn't told the Harper his last name; he never told anyone his last name. Baerdagh didn't know it—in fact, there was probably no one still alive who'd heard it.

So how was it that this Harper knew it?

EIGHTEEN
NO SHORTAGE OF VICTIMS

The one certainty in a coup, orc raid, or well-side gossip session is that there'll be no shortage of victims.

RALDERICK HALLOWSHAW, JESTER
FROM TO RULE A REALM, FROM TURRET TO MIDDEN
PUBLISHED CIRCA THE YEAR OF THE BLOODBIRD

I t was dark and silent, once the scrape of his boots had stilled. He was alone in the midst of cold, damp stone, the dust of ages sharp in his nostrils—and a feeling of tension as something watched him from the darkness, and waiting.

Elminster let himself grow as still as the stone handholds he still clung to, faced the aware and lurking darkness, and called up one of the powers Mystra had granted him. It was one he'd used far too little, because it required quiet concentration, and time . . . far more time than most of the beings he shared Faerûn with were ever willing to give him. Too often, these days, life seemed a headlong hurry.

His awareness ranged out through the waiting, listening darkness. Things both living and unliving he could not see, but magic, when El concentrated just . . . *so*, he could feel so keenly that he could make out surfaces on which dweomer clung, the tendrils of spell-bindings, and even the faint, fading traces of preservative magics that had failed.

All of those things lay before him. Faint magics swirled everywhere, none of them strong or precisely located, but outlining a large cavern or open space. A good way off, on the floor of this chamber or cavern—or down in a pit, he could not tell which—several closely clustered nodes of great, not-so-slumberous magical might throbbed and murmured ceaselessly. El blinked.

Trap or no trap, he had to see what waited here that could hold such magical might. He'd been led here; the swirling sentience that had done it was watching him or at least knew of his coming—so what was the point of stealth? El cast a stone-probing spell, seeking pits or seams ahead of him. Shrouded in its eerily faint blue glow, he stepped warily forward.

Great expanses of the floor were the natural rock of the cavern; as El proceeded, this gave way smoothly to a floor of huge stone slabs, smooth-polished and level; no mosses had stained them, but here and there, the fine white fur of salts leaching out of age-old rock trailed fingerlike across the stone.

A throne or seat of the same stone faced Elminster—empty of magic, surprisingly, though it was almost hidden from view behind the dazzle thrown off by the seven nodes of magic when he viewed it with his mage-sight. Thankfully, the seat was empty.

El sighed, threw back his head, and stepped forward. Seven nodes blinding in their magical might. Predictable or not, he could not ignore such power and remain Elminster. He smiled, shook his head ruefully—and took another step.

He might well die here, but he could not turn away.

The human was coming nearer. The Great Foe would soon be within reach—but also close to the runes that were too powerful to safely approach. Too close.

He would probably get only one chance, so it would have to be a shattering blow that even a great god-touched mage could not hope to survive. After all these years, a few days or even months more would matter not at all. The slaying stroke did.

The strike that would reveal him and harm the Foe all at once had to be one that destroyed—or at least ruined his foe into something powerless but aware—aware of the pain he would then deal to it at leisure, and of who was harming it during that long, dark time . . . and why.

So wait a bit more, like a patient ghost in the shadows.

Two dark eyes that blazed like two inky flames of fury peered from the depths of one of the darkest clefts in the rear of the cavern and watched the wary wizard step forward to his doom.

Years consumed by the ache to avenge, the gnawing need that ruled him night and day . . . years that had all come down to this.

"Yes, Vaelam?" Dreadspell Elryn asked, his voice dangerously soft and silky. A long, tense creeping advance to a ruin where powerful foes were almost certainly waiting for them had not improved his temper—especially after one of his boots had found its first muddy, water-filled old burrow hole. That had occurred three paces before his other boot found the second. He'd lost count, since then, of how many creeper thorns had torn at him and raked across his hands and face . . . and all of it, of course, watched sneeringly from afar by the cruel upperpriestesses of the House, among them the Darklady herself.

Vaelam was practically dancing with excitement, his eyes large and round. The foreguard of the Sharran "wizards" was a thin, soft-spoken priest, both careful and thorough in his duties. He was more excited, now, than Elryn had ever seen him.

"Dark Brother," he hissed excitedly, "I've found something."

"No," Elryn murmured, frowning, "Really? You *do* surprise me."

"It's a stone," Vaelam continued, astonishingly not catching Elryn's thick sarcasm at all—or displaying uncommonly swift skill at hiding his recognition of it. "A stone with writing on it."

"Writing that says . . . ?"

"Well, ah, just one letter actually—but one as long as a man is tall. It's a 'K'!"

"No!" Femter gasped sarcastically. "Could it be?"

"Brother, it is," Vaelam confirmed. He seemed genuinely oblivious to their derision.

"Show us," Elryn ordered curtly, and raised his voice a trifle. "Brothers, move slowly, keep apart, and watch the trees around. I don't want us crowded together when someone strikes from hiding. If we arrange things so that one fireball might take care of all of us, a hostile mage might not be able to resist his opportunity, hmm?"

"Aye," Daluth murmured, at the same time as someone else—Elryn couldn't tell who—muttered, "Thinks of everything, our Elryn."

Dark thoughts or not, the "wizards" of Shar reached the stone slab Vaelam had found without incident. It lay between two mossy banks, almost entirely covered with years of rotting, fallen leaves, but the K could clearly be seen. The deep-graven letter sprawled across a little more ground than one of the ornate temple chairs would cover; the stone slab seemed both old and huge.

Elryn leaned forward, not bothering to hide his own swift-rising excitement. Magic. This had to have something to do with magic, strong magic . . . and magic was what they were here for.

"Uncover it all," he ordered and stood back prudently to watch as this was done. The stone proved to be as long across, or longer, than a man laid out straight on his back, and twice that in the other direction, as well as being—at the one point where the ground dipped, along its edges—at least as thick as the length of a short sword.

When they were done uncovering it, the Sharrans stared at the massive slab . . . and it lay there patiently looking back at them.

It knew who would blink first.

After the silence grew uncomfortably long and the lesser priests started snatching sidelong glances at their leader, Elryn sighed and said, "Daluth, work the spell that wizards use to reveal magic. I can see no trigger to this—but there must be one."

Daluth nodded and did so. Elryn was as shocked as everyone else when he raised his head slowly and said, "No magic at all. None upon yon slab or around it. Nothing but what few things we carry, within reach of my spell."

"Impossible," Elryn snapped.

Daluth nodded. "I agree . . . but my spell cannot lie to me, can it?"

As Elryn stood glaring at him, there was a common gasp of relief—of held breaths let out—from the other Sharrans, and they strode forward to stand on the slab as if it had been calling to them.

Elryn whirled, a shout of warning rising to his lips—a shout that died unuttered. The priests under his command strode across the slab, scraped their boot heels on it, stomped and strolled, staring about at the trees as if the slab was an enspelled lookout that gave them some sort of special sight. No bolts of lightning burst from the stone to slay them, and none of them shifted shape, screamed, or acquired unusual expressions on their faces.

Instead, one by one, they shrugged and fell silent, blinking at each other and back at Elryn, until Hrelgrath said what they were all thinking: "But there must be *some* magic here, some purpose for this—and it can't be the lid of a tomb, or you'd need a dragon to lift it on and off."

Daluth raised a brow. "And because we have no dealings with dragons, no one does? What if this is some sort of storage box built by a dragon, for its own use?"

"In the midst of a forest? Right out in the open and down low, not girt about with rock? Admitting my unfamiliarity with wyrms, that still *feels* wrong to me," Femter replied. "No, this smacks of the work of men—or dwarves working for men, or mayhap even giants skilled at stonemasonry."

"So what or who doth the 'K' refer to?" Vaelam burst out. "A king, or a realm?"

"Or a god?" Daluth echoed quietly, and something in his voice brought all eyes upon him.

"Kossuth? In a forest?" Hrelgrath said in puzzled tones.

"Nay, nay," Vaelam said excitedly. "What was the name of that mage in the legend, who defied the gods to steal all magic and become himself lord over all magic? Klar . . . no, *Karsus.*"

And as that name left the young Sharran's mouth, he vanished, gone in the instant ere he could draw breath. The slab where he had stood, so close between Femter and Hrelgrath that they could easily have jostled elbows with him, was empty.

Those two brave and steadfast priests sprang and sprinted away from the slab with almost comical haste, as Daluth nodded grimly, his eyes fixed on the spot where Vaelam had stood, and Elryn said slowly, "Well, well . . ."

The four remaining priests stared at the slab in silence for a few tense moments before the most exalted Dreadspell said almost gently, "Daluth, stand upon the letter and utter the name Vaelam did."

Daluth cast a quick glance at Elryn, read in his face that this was a clear and firm order, and did as he was bid. Femter and Hrelgrath shifted uneasily as they watched their most capable comrade wink out of existence, and the appropriate one couldn't suppress a low groan of fear when Elryn said, "Now do likewise, -Hrelgrath."

Hrelgrath was trembling so with fear that he could barely shape the name "Karsus," but he vanished as swiftly and utterly as his predecessors. Femter shrugged and strode onto the slab without waiting for an order, looking back for Elryn's nod of assent when he'd planted his boots squarely in the center of the giant letter. The nod was given, and another false wizard disappeared.

Now alone, Elryn looked around at the trees, saw nothing moving or watching, shrugged, and followed his fellow Sharrans onto the slab.

Even before their battle with the elf who'd slain Iyrindyl with such casual ease, he'd thought this entire scheme of holy Sharrans trying to be mages was wrong—dangerously wrong. Dreadspells, indeed. Still, if by some miracle what lay at the other end of this teleport was not one huge trap, it just might lead to enough magic to win them Darklady Avroana's holy approval—and survival long enough to enjoy it. He smiled slowly at that thought, said, "Karsus," with slow deliberation, and watched the world whirl away.

A red radiance lit up the darkness, gleaming back from a hundred curves of metal and countless gems. The light was coming from the floor—wherever they'd walked, the boot prints were a-glow.

It was too late to cry out a warning about awakening guardian spells or beings—Vaelam was already wading through knee-deep, shifting wonders to pluck at a gauntlet whose rows of sapphires were winking with their own internal light: the lambent glow of awakened magic, echoed in sinister chatoyance from a dozen places around the crypt. The low-ceilinged room was crammed with heaped treasures, most of them strange to the eye, and all of them, by the looks of it, harboring magic.

Elryn managed to keep from gasping aloud, but he was conscious of the quick glance Daluth threw him and knew his awe and wonder must be written plainly on his face.

The junior Dreadspells certainly hadn't wasted any time. Hrelgrath seemed to be waltzing with an armored figure as he tried to wrest a gorget from it, and a row of sheathed wands slapped and dangled against Femter's right thigh, depending from a gem-encrusted belt that enwrapped his waist as if it had been made for him. It had altered to fit him, of course. The eager-eyed priest was already reaching into another heap of armbands and anklets, seeking out something else that had caught his eye. Vaelam was drawing on the gauntlet, now, his eyes already on something else.

Only Daluth stood empty-handed, his hands raised to deliver a quenching spell should one of the reckless younger Dreadspells unleash something that could doom them all.

Elryn darted glances in all directions, saw nothing moving by itself and no doors or other ways out of the stone-walled room, and asked quietly, "Oh most diligent Dreadspells, has anyone spared a thought for how we'll be able to leave this place?"

"Karsus," Hrelgrath said clearly, the gorget clutched triumphantly in his hands.

Nothing happened, but Vaelam was already pointing into the farthest, dimmest corner of the chamber. "Another 'K' in a clear spot of floor yonder," he reported. "That'll be it."

"Aye, but to take us back out—or in deeper, to somewhere else unknown?" Daluth asked.

"Moreover, if I was intending to slay thieves who found their way hence uninvited, the way out is where I'd place guards of one sort or another," Elryn added, then—having not moved a pace from where he'd appeared—said, "Karsus" carefully. No whirling before his eyes occurred again, but he was unsurprised.

Slithering metallic sounds heralded Vaelam's continued digging—and as Elryn watched, he saw Femter slip something into his robes, his fingers working at a hitherto-hidden underarm pouch.

"Take nothing you cannot carry," the senior Dreadspell warned, "and be fully prepared to surrender unto the Darklady every last item of magic we bear out of this place, no matter how trifling. We are not unobserved, now and always."

Femter's head snapped up, and he blushed as he found Elryn's eyes upon him. He opened his mouth to say something, but Daluth forestalled him by asking the room at large, "Has anyone found something whose powers are obvious?"

He was answered by shaken heads and frowns.

Elryn used the toe of his boot to open a small black coffer, lifted his eyebrows to the ceiling when he saw the row of rings it contained, snapped it shut again, then blinked at what had lain next to it.

"Daluth," he asked quietly, inclining his head toward the heap of gleaming mysteries by his boot, "that circlet—hasn't that symbol been used to mean healing?"

Daluth pounced on the diadem. It was of plain but massy gold over some more durable metal, and it bore the device of a gleaming sun cupped in two stylized hands. "Yes," he said excitedly. He held it up to show the others and snapped, "Find more of these. Leave off looking at other things for now."

The lesser Dreadspells did as they were bid, digging and tossing aside treasures, and rising, from time to time, with cries of satisfaction. Daluth took the items they proffered—four circlets and a bracer—and Elryn snapped, "Enough. All of you, take only so much as what you can wear or carry, and leave swords and helms and suchlike behind. We dare not try to awaken anything here. Gird yourselves as if for battle; I don't want to see anyone staggering under an armload of loose items."

He reached down and plucked up a number of scepters from among a litter of metal-bound tomes, platters and smaller boxes. Then, as if in afterthought, he casually picked up the black coffer, its dozen rings riding safely hidden inside it.

A few moments of work with the long thongs that always rode in his belt pouch, and the scepters were riding ready at his hip, the coffer hidden down the front of his breeches. Elryn was ready. He said briskly, "Vaelam, the honor is yours, I believe. Take us from this place."

The youngest Dreadspell looked at the clear space at the back of the crypt, waiting in silence for him, swallowed, and said, "You said there might be guards. . . ."

Elryn nodded. "I have every confidence that you'll deal with them quite capably," he said flatly, and waited.

Reluctantly the youngest priest-turned-wizard picked his way through the crowded room, slowing as he approached the letter on the floor. Four pairs of eyes watched him go, their owners crouching down behind heaps of unidentified magic. Vaelam sent them all a look of mingled anger and despair, drew himself erect, and snapped, "Karsus."

As swiftly and as silently as he'd first left them, Vaelam disappeared.

As if that had been a signal, something moved in the heap nearest to Hrelgrath, rising amid a clatter of many small things sliding and tumbling as the Sharran stumbled back, moaning in wordless alarm.

"Do nothing," Elryn snapped. In frozen silence the four men watched a glowing sword rise into view, its naked and glittering blade aimed somewhere between Daluth and Elryn. It seemed a good five or six feet long, its ornate hilt a-wink with many lustrous gems, an ever-changing array of runes and letters flickering momentarily up and down the blue flanks of its blade.

"Hrelgrath," Elryn ordered, "follow Vaelam. Keep low, and do nothing in haste. Go now."

When the second sweating Dreadspell winked elsewhere, the sword in the air seemed to shiver for a moment, but otherwise moved not. Elryn watched it for a while, then said slowly, "Femter, follow the others."

Again the sword stayed where it was. When only Daluth and Elryn were left, the senior Dreadspell asked his most capable comrade, "In case some spell prevents us from ever returning here, is there anything in particular we should bear with us?"

Daluth shrugged. "It'd take years to examine all that's here—and even then, we'd only know a few powers of each thing. This is utterly . . . fantastic. There's more magic crowded in here around us than I think all who worship Holy Shar, in their thousands, can muster. If I have to take just one thing—let it be that stand of staves, yonder. Four staves, I think; almost one for each of us, and all of them sure to hold some sort of magic we can wield in a battle. If we can awaken them, we can at least play convincingly at being archmages . . . for a little time."

"Let's hope it's long enough, a little time," Elryn agreed, "when it comes. Two each?"

They gave the floating sword another long look, slipped carefully past it, and Daluth took the two staves under one arm and pulled out a wand he'd found earlier in the other. The healing circlets bulged in his scrip.

Elryn looked down at Daluth's ready wand, smiled tightly, and quoted the saying, "We dare not trust anyone save Holy Shar herself." As he spoke, he raised the wand already in his own hand into view so that Daluth could see it.

"I mean this for perils I may find beyond the teleport," Daluth said carefully, "not for—closer dangers." His voice changed, sharpening in alarm. "'Ware the sword!"

Elryn whirled around to find the sword hanging just as before. He was still turning as he heard Daluth add calmly, "Karsus."

The senior Dreadspell sprang wildly sideways, just in case Daluth had found the urge to trigger his wand irresistible and sprawled on a heap of enspelled clothing. Glowing mesh flickered under him as he slithered painfully down it, traveling over an array of sharp points; hastily Elryn clawed his way upright, snatched another look at the sword, and found it still motionless.

He looked around the room, down at the red footprints already beginning to fade to the hue of old blood, around at the thankfully motionless heaps of treasure, and cast his gaze once more down at the clothes he'd fallen on. Surely that was a stomacher, such as haughty ladies wore ... he caught up one garment then another, feeling the tingling of powerful magic surging through his fingertips. They were all gowns, with cutouts in the meshes beneath ornate bodices.

Elryn of Shar looked at the shoulders of one, frowning in consideration ... then shrugged and began to strip off his own clothes. He'd best hurry, if he was to be swift enough to keep the others out of mischief—or, knowing this lot, just from wandering off without him. Struggling in the growing dimness while trying to keep his eye on the sword floating nearby, Elryn was briefly glad they'd found no mirror that he'd have to look at himself in. He could imagine Avroana's mirth as she watched him battling the unfamiliar garment—and when at last he stood on the letter on the floor, and with one wary eye on that floating blade, uttered the name "Karsus," it was just this snarled side of a heartfelt curse.

The smoking stump of what must have been an old and large duskwood gave mute testimony to the effectiveness of something one of the younger Dreadspells had awakened. Elryn stared at it with dark anger rising in him, but before he could say anything, Femter was thrusting a ring at him excitedly.

"Dark Brother, look! This ring—against the best seeking Brother Daluth can cast—completely cloaks the dweomers of all magic in contact with its wearer! One could go into the presence of a king armed for a beholder war and strike with impunity."

"Such bold stratagems are usually more effective in ballads than in real life," Elryn replied severely, "to say nothing of prudence." He looked for Daluth and found him carefully taking forth one circlet after another from his scrip.

"Ah," the leader of the Dreadspells announced in satisfaction, "a wiser way to spend time. Let us all heal ourselves, then devote a short time to examining wands and staves before resuming our journey to the ruins."

Several more trees suffered in the moments that followed. The healing items all proved to be of more effectiveness than a single use. Two of the staves proved to have no more battle worthy spells than the ability to spit forth the streaking bolts men called "magic missiles," but the others could unleash beams of ravening fire and explosive bursts of magic ... and two of those seemed able to drain touched magic items and even the spells of their wielders upon command, to power their most destructive attacks.

"What shining luck!" Vaelam laughed, blasting a helpless shadowtop sapling to ashes.

"Luck? Holy Shar led us to this spot, Dark Brother," Elryn said severely, playing to the priestesses watching from afar. "Shar guides us always ... you will do well never to forget that."

"Of course," Vaelam said hastily, then laughed heartily as the staff in his hands snarled again—and another tree vanished in roiling flames that fell away into streamers of smoke diving down to the leaf mold all around.

"Vaelam of Shar," Elryn said sharply, "stop that wasteful destruction at once. I'd rather not have this forest aflame around us or every druid and mage within a hundred miles appearing around us to give battle. Have you forgotten Iyrindyl's fate already?"

Vaelam grimaced, but he couldn't seem to stop fondling and hefting the staff, like a warrior who's just been handed a superb blade.

"My apologies, Dark Brother," he said, chastened, "I-I got caught up in its power." He licked his lips, firmly grounded the staff, and asked, as if seeking approval, "Do you know how tempting it is just to blast down everything that irritates or stands against you?"

"Yes, Vaelam, as a matter of fact, I do," Elryn replied, and wiggled the wand in his hand—the wand pointed at Vaelam's face—ever so slightly to draw the younger man's eyes. As Vaelam saw, and paled, the senior Dreadspell continued grimly, "It's just one of many such temptations."

Erlyn smiled tightly and thrust the wand back into his belt. "Aye," he added slowly, setting out at a steady pace in the direction of the ruins. "One of many."

He gestured curtly for the Dreadspells to follow. Reluctantly, they did so. Vaelam stopped to cast a longing look back at the stone slab, and the woods beyond it—and found himself looking right into the coldly smiling eyes and leveled staff of Daluth, who was watchfully bringing up the rear.

Vaelam managed a halfhearted smile, but Daluth's eyes grew no warmer. The youngest surviving Dreadspell swallowed, turned, and trudged off toward doom.

"Now, *this* curling of the leaf, on the other hand, tells you that this is a si—"

Starsunder paused in mid-word and straightened up suddenly, almost knocking his head against Umbregard's. The human mage stumbled hastily back out of the way as the elf threw out his hands.

Still standing dramatically stiff with his arms spread, the moon elf threw back his head and opened his mouth as if trying to taste the sky.

Silence fell. Umbregard watched his statuelike friend for what seemed like a very long time before he dared to ask, "Starsunder?"

"You expect someone else to jump into this body just because I stop moving?" came the mild reproof, as Starsunder turned his head, spun around, and took hold of Umbregard's arm all in one smooth motion. "Do you know of some body snatching, wizardly peril I'm unaware of?"

"W-where are we going?" Umbregard asked in lieu of a reply, as the slender moon elf practically dragged him around and between trees, dark green half cloak swirling.

"Where we're needed, and urgently," Starsunder said almost absently, urging the human he was towing into a trot.

"And where—" Umbregard was puffing now, even though they were descending a fern-covered slope rather than climbing, "—might *that* be?"

"In a forest almost as old as this one, across an arm of the sea," Starsunder replied, his voice as calm and his breathing as steady as if he'd been lounging at ease on a giant leaf rather than racing through the woods, leaping fallen trees and roots, and swinging around forest giants. "No place that humans remember a name for."

"Why?" Umbregard almost shouted, sprinting as fast as he ever had in all his life, with the slim elf still half a stride faster than he and threatening to drag his arm out of its socket.

"Trees are burning," Starsunder told him with a frown, "suddenly, as if struck by lightning or firestorm, where there's no storm in the sky to do such harm—and here we are!"

They plunged between two shadowtop trees that seemed perfectly matched, growing not three feet apart—and somewhere in the gloom between a blue haze plucked them and hurled them far away.

Umbregard's next step was in a different forest—one more dry and empty of calling birds and rustling animals. He gaped and tried to look behind him, but at that moment Starsunder let go of his arm and took hold of his chin. Staring into Umbregard's eyes from inches away, the moon elf murmured, "Make no unnecessary noise, and don't call out to anyone you see . . . even if they're old friends. Hmmm; especially if they're old friends."

"Why?" Umbregard asked, almost despairingly; why had he bothered to learn to speak any other word but "why"?

"You'll live longer," Starsunder said, laying two gentle fingers across the human mage's lips. "That's why."

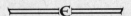

The Phoenix Tower was dark and cool and lonely. With his fortress ringed by thick thorns, jagged rubble, and a break neck chasm dug by his golems literally as they were falling apart, Tenthar felt secure from intrusion by all save the most persistent adventurers. If any such came calling, he'd just have to be very good at hiding . . . or dying.

The Archmage of the Phoenix Tower had long ago passed beyond loneliness into boredom—after all, how often can one read old and familiar spellbooks that one dare not try any castings out of? He was tired of trudging down to the cellars in the dark to gobble mushrooms like some sort of tomb beast. For that matter, he was tired of trudging everywhere rather than flying—and never leaving the Tower.

All he'd seen of Faerûn these last rides was the view his windows commanded. He lived from dawn to dusk, not daring to frivolously use any of the eight precious candle ends he'd found—he, Tenthar Taerhamoos, who was used to conjuring light as needed, almost without thinking. A light after dark might attract the attention of adventurers or hungry beasts that someone was in the shuttered tower. Not two days ago he'd slammed and bolted the shutters just in time. He'd spent most of the rest of the day crouched behind them, dry-mouthed in fear, listening to an angry peryton flap and slash with its horns at the old wood that he hoped would hold fast.

And if such foes got into the Tower, what could he do? He had no particular strength or skill at arms, and his spells failed him all the time, now—or at least, whenever he didn't bolster them with the precious power of his medallion, which was growing more feeble with each use.

He'd called on it too often in the early days of this spell-chaos, when he'd been frantic to find out what was happening, and why. Now he was just sitting in the endless gloom waiting for magic to obey him once more—or someone to force their way into the Phoenix Tower and kill him.

Each morning Tenthar went down into the underpantry, cast a simple spell from his memory, and grimly watched it turn the stone walls purple or make them start to melt or be goaded into a mad display of sprouting flowers—or whatever new idiocy struck Mystra's whimsy that day. Each morning he hoped spells would return to normal and he could begin life as the Archmage of the Phoenix Tower again.

Every day his visit to the underpantry disappointed him.

Every day he grimly climbed back up into the cold and lonely kitchens, boiled himself some beans and cut a little more green mold off the huge wheel of cheese under the marble hood before he climbed the stairs to the big window, to study anew the spell he'd miscast. Every day he grew a little more despairing.

It had almost gotten to the point where, given the right goad, he'd use his medallion to fly away from this place. He could find some distant realm where no one would know his face, seek work there as a scribe, and try to forget that he'd ever been an Archmage and summoned monsters from other worlds.

Aye, for the ghost of an excuse he'd—

Something shattered in the next room; it seemed a dozen bells rang amid the musical clatter of glass. Tenthar was up and through the door in an instant, peering—ah!

The spelltale he'd laid upon the elven tree-gate in the Tangletrees . . . someone had just used it to travel south to the woods near Starmantle. That was it. He was sick of hiding and doing nothing.

"The elves are on the move," Tenthar Taerhamoos told the glass shards at his feet grandly. "I must be there—at least I'll be able to learn as much about this chaos of spells as they do." He cut himself a large wedge of cheese with his dagger, wrapped it up in an old blanket with his traveling spellbook, and thrust the bundle into a battered old shoulder bag. Settling the blade back in its sheath, Tenthar called up the flickering power of his medallion, and cast a spell he'd had ready for a long time.

"Farewell, old stones," he told his Tower, casting what might be his last look around at it. "I'll return—if I can."

A moment later, the floor where he'd stood was empty. A moment after that, another spelltale shattered in the room where no one was left to hear.

All too often, an archmage's life is like that.

Excitement burned within her, leaping to the back of the throat she no longer had in a way it hadn't for years. *Gently, Saeraede. Lose nothing now out of haste . . . you're centuries past trembling like a maid, or should be.*

Like a wisp of dark smoke in the darkness, Saeraede flew up a thin crevice at the back of the cavern, back to the main room above.

She'd prepared this spell long ago, and he'd disturbed none of her preparations. In a trice it was done, gray smoke flowing out to settle like old stone over the top of the shaft. Its veil would seem like a raised stone floor to anyone on the surface, the well mouth completely concealed—and her quarry would be trapped beneath its web just as surely as if it was solid stone.

Saeraede gave herself a bare breath of time to gloat before plunging back down through the cold dark stone. *Now to let myself be freed by my savior prince . . . and bring him willingly to the slow slaughter.*

She plunged through the cavern like an arrow coming to earth; Elminster frowned and looked up, feeling some magical disturbance—but could sense nothing, and after a long, suspicious time of probing into the dusty darkness, he resumed his cautious advance. That was more than time enough for Saeraede to steal up into one of the runes through the cracked stone beneath, causing it to glow faintly.

Elminster stopped in front of it and stared at the unfamiliar curves and crossings. He didn't recognize any of these sigils. They looked both complex and old, and that of course suggested lost Netheril . . . or any of a score of its echoes, the fleeting realms that had followed its fall, with their self-styled sorcerer-kings; if any of the rotting old histories he'd read down the years had it right.

Only this one was glowing. El stared at it intently. "Sentience slumbreth here," he murmured, "but whose?"

Only silence answered him. The last prince of Athalantar acquired the ghost of a smile, sighed, and cast an unbinding.

The quiet echoes of his incantation were still rolling back to him from the walls all around when a ghostly head and shoulders erupted from the pale starry glow of the rune.

The eyes were dark and melting flecks in a head whose long and shapely neck yearned up from shoulders of striking beauty. Long hair flowed down over lush breasts, but it seemed his unbinding could free no more of this apparition from the grip of the now pulsing rune.

"Free me!" The voice was a tattered whisper, sighing from a lonely afar. "Oh, if the kindness and mercy of the gods mean anything to you, let me be *free!*"

"Who are ye?" El asked quietly, taking a pace back and kneeling to look more closely into the ghostly face, "and what are these runes?"

Ghostly lips seemed to tremble and gasp. When her voice soared out once more, it held the high, singing note of one who has triumphed over pain. "I am Saeraede . . . Saeraede Lyonora. I am bound here, so long I know not how many years have passed."

At the last few words, she seemed to grow dimmer and sank back into the rune as far as her shoulders.

"Who bound ye here?" Elminster asked, casting a quick look at the empty, watchful darkness all around. Aye, that was it; he could not shake the feeling that he was being watched . . . and not merely by the dark and spectral eyes floating near his feet.

"I was bound by the one who made these runes," the whispering shade told him. "Mine is the will and essence that empowers them, as the seasons pass."

"Why were ye bound?" El asked quietly, staring into eyes that seemed to hold tiny stars in their depths, as they melted pleadingly into his.

Her answer, when it came, was a sigh so soft that he barely heard it. Yet it came clearly: "Karsus was cruel."

The eyebrows of the last prince of Athalantar flew up. He knew that name. The Proudest Mage of All, who in his mad folly had dared to try to seize the power of godhood and suffered everlasting doom.

The name Karsus meant peril to any mage of sense. Elminster's eyes narrowed, and he stepped back and forthwith murmured a spell. Bound spirit, undead, wizardly shade or living woman, he would know truth when she spoke it—and falsehood. Of course, this Saeraede was likely to have been a sorceress of some accomplishment, perhaps an apprentice or rival of Karsus, for her to have been chosen for such a binding. She would know he'd just cast a truthtell.

Their eyes met in shared knowledge, and Elminster shrugged. She would answer as truthfully as she could, concealing only by her brevity. Like dueling swordsmen, they'd have to weigh each other's words and fence carefully. He cast a spell he should have used before entering the shaft, calling up a mantle of protection around himself, and stepped forward again.

Unseen beyond the faint shimmer of his mantle, fresh fury flared in eyes watching from the deep darkness at the back of the cavern.

"What will or must ye do, if freed?" El asked the head.

"Live again," she gasped. "Oh, man, free me!"

"What will freeing ye do to the runes?"

"Awaken them once each," the ghostly head moaned, "and they'll then be exhausted."

"What powers have the awakened runes?"

"They call up images of Karsus, who instructs all who view them in ways of magic. Karsus meant them for the education of his clone, hidden here."

"What became of it?" El asked sharply, hurrying to hear her answer as the truthtell ran out.

Dark, star-shot eyes stared steadfastly into his. "When awareness returned to me after my binding—a long time had passed, I think—I found it headless and wizened on the throne. I know not how it came to be that way."

His spell had failed before the second word had left those phantom lips, but somehow El believed her.

"Saeraede, how do I free ye?" he asked.

"If you have a spellquench or another unbinding, cast it upon me . . . not on the rune, but on me."

"And if I lack such magics?"

Those dark eyes flickered. "Stand over me, so that your mantle touches the rune, and I am within it. Then cast a magic missile, and let its target be the rune. In what follows, you should be unharmed—and I, freed. Be warned: 'twill cost you your mantle."

"Prepare thyself," Elminster told her, and stepped over her.

"Man, I have been waiting for an age, it seems; I am well prepared. Touch not the rune with your boots."

The last prince of Athalantar made sure his feet were clear of the glowing sigil, and made a careful casting. Blue-white radiance surged around him, roiling and tugging, the rune beneath him flared to blinding brilliance, and he heard Saeraede gasp.

Her breathing was ragged and swift as she surged up into the collapsing mantle beside him. As El stepped back, he saw wild delight in her face. All of the magic seemed to be rushing into her, and with each passing moment she grew more solid . . . more substantial. Her flickering, wraithlike form grew whole and acquired a dark gown. She was broad of shoulders, slim-waisted, and as tall or taller than he; her hair was an unbound, waist-length flow of velvet black, her brows startlingly dark tufts above eyes of leaping green. Her face was proud and lively—and very, very beautiful.

"Hail, savior mage," she said, eyes glowing with gratitude, as the last fires of magic fled into her. A single tongue of flame escaped from between her lips as she spoke. "Saeraede stands in your debt." She hesitated, reaching out one slender hand. "May I know your name?"

"Elminster, I am called," El told her, keeping a careful pace out of reach.

"Elminster," she breathed, eyes sparkling, "oh, have my *thanks!*"

She hugged herself, as if scarcely believing that she was whole and solid once more—and stepped forward off the rune. Her feet seemed to have grown spike-heeled, pointed black boots.

The moment she moved off it, the rune erupted. A column of white fire burst up from it, twice the height of a man, and smoke surged out in all directions from its snarling. Elminster took a pace back, eyes narrowing—and something unseen in the darkness of a deep crevice stirred and made as if to spring forth . . . but remained where it was, not all that far from the mage's unsuspecting back.

"Saeraede," El snapped, keeping his eyes on the unfolding magic, "what is this?"

"The magic of the rune," she replied, smiling at him. "Karsus prepared it to impress intruders. 'Tis harmless, a parade of illusions. Watch."

She turned to look at the column of flame, folding her arms, mild interest on her face. As she did so, the surging smoke seemed to freeze and thicken.

The archway of glowing runes solidified out of the smoke and air with startling swiftness. It occurred behind the fiery column, framing it, a wall that looked every bit as old and as solid as those of the cavern around—but hovered a few feet above the smooth stone floor. The runes around the arch matched those graven on the floor, save that all were afire, and even spitting lightning ... the risen lightning of awakened magic, now crawling between them almost continuously.

Saeraede stood calmly watching, and El, struck by a sudden thought, glided to her elbow and indicated the empty throne. "Will ye sit, lady?"

Saeraede gave him a dazzling smile, raised a hand in wordless thanks—not quite touching him—and sat upon the throne. No change in it, or her, was apparent to El's intent eyes. Hmmm, well. Nothing learned there.

As Saeraede crossed her legs and leaned back in ease upon the stone seat, the column of flame grew a face—a youthful face ringed by tousled hair and the stubble of a beard aborning, its eyes two points of blazing gold. They were fixed on the throne, and when Elminster swung his left arm in a sudden, wild flourish, the eyes did not move to follow it.

The air in the cavern was suddenly alive with a singing tension. The proud mouth opened, and the voice that issued from it crashed and rolled like thunder through Elminster's mind as well as through the cavern. "*I am Karsus!* Behold me, and fear. I am The Lord of Lords, a God Among Men, Arcanist Supreme. All magic is my domain, and all who work it or trifle with it without my blessing shall suffer. Begone, and live. Tarry, and the first and least of my curses shall begin its work upon you forthwith, gnawing memories from your brain until naught is left but a sighing shadow."

Elminster looked sharply at Saeraede at those last words, but she sat calmly watching as the hair on the flaming head spat a halo of lightning out to the runes, the echoes of its mighty voice still rolling around the cavern as they faded, leaving it shaking and dust—ridden. They burst into showers of sparks and fell, taking the illusion of the arch and its wall with them.

Still wearing its cruel smile, the face closed its eyes and shrank back into the column of flame, fading as it did so. In a few moments the flames fell back into the rune, and it winked out, becoming mere dark and lifeless grooves in the stone floor.

"Did that curse afflict ye?" Elminster demanded, striding around to where he could see Saeraede.

She lifted the edge of her beautiful mouth in a wry smile. "Never ... nor has it touched anyone, for 'tis all a bluff. Believe me; I've seen it many times down the years, whenever I grew overly lonely for the sight and sound of another human. 'Tis an empty warning, no more."

El nodded, almost trembling in his eagerness, and asked, "How can one see the scenes held by the other runes—and just what is in each?"

Saeraede pointed. "In this next rune lie two of the most destructive spells devised by Karsus—magics none else have attained since—as well as a defensive shielding of surpassing strength and a healing magic; he placed them thus in case his new self should have urgent need to do battle."

Her pointing finger moved. "The rune beyond holds another four magics, as powerful as the battle-spells but of more mundane usage. One creates a floating 'worldlet' to serve as a stronghold for the mage who uses magic to modify it further; one can stop and hold the waters of a river while digging out a new course for its bed; one can shield an area permanently against specific spells or schools of spells with precision—so that one can allow a lightning bolt but deny chain lightning, say; and the last can coddle and keep from harm a living human while permanently altering one limb or organ—Karsus most often used that to move heart or brain to an unexpected place, or graft beast claws where hands had been or extra eyeballs from others . . . he also gave some men gills to work under the sea for him, as I recall."

Saeraede waved her hand at the curving row of runes. "The others hold lesser magics, four in each—and Karsus himself demonstrates all castings, noting drawbacks, details, and effective strategies."

She watched the hunger in Elminster's face and suppressed a smile. She had seen this so many times before . . . even Chosen, it seemed, were like eager children when offered new toys. She waited for the question she knew would come.

Elminster licked lips that were suddenly dry, before he could swallow and say quietly, "I asked how one can awaken these runes, lady, to view what waits within . . . and ye've not answered that. Is there some secret here, some hazard or caution?"

Saeraede gave him a warm and welcoming smile. "Nay, sir. As you're not Karsus and able to work the magics that respond only to his blood, there's but a matter of time—and your patience."

El raised a questioning eyebrow, and her smile broadened and slid into sadness.

"Only I can activate the runes," the woman on the throne added softly, "and I can call forth the power of only one in a month, by means of a nameless spell bound into me by Karsus. 'Tis a spell I know not how to cast, nor can I teach it to another. I can only call on it when the time is right—and I have no doubt 'tis the sole reason I still exist."

Elminster opened his mouth to say something, his eyes alight with eager fire, but Saeraede held up a hand to stay his speech, and added, "You asked of a hazard? There is one, and 'tis thus: long years must have passed since I was bound here, for my powers have faded indeed. I can awaken one rune, and no more. To open another will destroy me—and all of the magic stored here will drain away and be lost; it cannot persist without me."

"So there is no way to see the spells Karsus stored here—or at least, more than one foursome of them?"

"There is a way," Saeraede said softly, her eyes on his. "If you use that last spell I spoke of, not to give me gills or a tail, but to pass magical strength into me . . . the magic of another spell that heals, or imparts vitality, or places the vital, flowing power of Art in items, to recharge them. All of these should work."

Elminster frowned in thought. "And we must bide here a month, to see the rune that holds that spell?"

Saeraede spread her hands. "You freed me and woke the first rune. I am yet able to awaken a rune, now—and I owe you my very life. Would you like to see the rune I spoke of, which holds the spell that will let me live to unlock the others for you?"

"I would," El said eagerly, striding forward.

Saeraede rose from the throne and held up her hands in warning.

"Remember," she said gravely, "you'll see Karsus instructing himself how to cast those spells, and the rune will then be dead forever, its spells—spells neither you nor any living mage may now be able to cast—lost with it."

She took two slow steps away from Elminster, then turned back to face him, pointing down at the rune. "If you want to preserve its power and be able to view it again hereafter, there is a way . . . but it will call greatly on your trust."

Elminster's brows rose again, but he said merely, "Say on."

Saeraede spread empty hands in the age-old gesture traders use to show they are unarmed, and said gently, "You can channel energy into the rune through me. Touch me as I stand upon the rune, and will your spell to seek the rune as its target. The bindings set within me by Karsus will keep me from harm and deliver the fury of your magic into the rune. One powerful spell ought to do it . . . or two lesser ones."

The eyes of the last prince of Athalantar narrowed. "Mystra forfend," he murmured, raising a reluctant hand.

"Elminster," Saeraede said beseechingly, "I owe you my life. I mean you no harm. Take whatever precautions you see fit—a blindfold, bindings, a gag." She extended her arms to him, wrists crossed over each other in a gesture of submission. "You have nothing to fear from me."

Slowly, Elminster stepped forward and took her cold hand in his.

NINETEEN
MORE BLOOD THAN THUNDER

The thunder of a king's tongue can always spill more blood than his own weight in gold before dawn the next morning.

MINTIPER MOONSILVER, BARD
FROM THE BALLAD GREAT CHANGES ABORNING
FIRST PERFORMED CIRCA THE YEAR OF THE SWORD AND STARS

Saeraede's touch was cold—colder than icy rivers he'd plunged into, colder even than the bite of blue glacial ice that had once seared his naked skin.

Gods! Elminster struggled to catch his breath, too shocked even to moan. The face so close to his held no hint of triumph, only anxious concern. El stared into those beautiful eyes and roared out his pain in a wordless shout that echoed around the cavern.

It was answered a moment later by a greater roar, a rumbling that shook the cavern and split its gloom with a flash of light—a flash that made all of the runes briefly catch fire, and sent a slim, stealthy figure shrinking back hastily into its crevice, unregarded.

One of her best spells, shattered like a glass goblet hurled to stones—and it could not be any doing of this helpless, shuddering mage in her hands. Oh, dark luck rule: were there spells on a Chosen that called for aid by themselves?

Saeraede straightened, eyes blazing, and snarled, "Who—?"

The light that stabbed down the shaft this time was no flash of destruction but a golden column of more lasting sorcery. Four figures rode its magic smoothly down into the cavern of the throne, boots first.

Three of the men in that column of light were old and stout and amazed. Caladaster, Beldrune, and Tabarast were all staring in awe at their companion. The quiet Harper had just broken a spell that had shaken the very trees around in its passing, and swept away a thick stone floor in the doing with a casual wave of his hand. He'd taken a few steps forward, smiled reassuringly at them, and another gesture had swept them up into waiting radiance and borne them down the shaft together in its glowing heart.

"Elminster," the fourth man said crisply, as his boots touched the stone floor as lightly as a falling feather kisses the earth, "stand away from yon runes. Mystra forbids us to do what you are attempting."

A gasping Elminster had only just then recovered the power of speech. He turned with a stiff, awkward lurch, limbs trembling, and said sharply through lips that were thin and blue, "Mystra forbids us to do, never to look. Who are you?"

The man smiled slightly, and his eyes became two lances of magical fire, stabbing across the cavern at Saeraede. "Call me—Azuth," he replied.

"The spell failed again, l-lord," the man in robes said, his voice not quite steady.

The Lord Esbre Felmorel nodded curtly. "You have our leave to withdraw. Go not where we cannot summon you in haste, if need be."

"Lord, it shall be so," the wizard murmured. He did not—quite—break into a run as he left the chamber, but the eyes of both guards at the door flickered as he passed.

"Nasmaerae?"

Lady Felmorel lifted unhappy eyes to his and said, "This is none of my doing, lord. Prayers to Most Holy Azuth are as close as I come to the Art now. This I swear."

A large and hairy hand closed over hers. "Be at ease, lady. I cannot forget that hard lesson any more than you can; I know you forget not, and transgress not. I have seen your blood upon the tiles before the altar, and seen you at prayer. You humiliate yourself as only one who truly believes can."

A smile touched his lips for a moment, and stole away again. "You frighten the men more now than you ever did when you ruled this castle by your sorcery, you know. They say you talk with Azuth every night."

"Esbre," his lady whispered, holding her eyes steady upon his despite the blush that had turned her face, throat, and beyond crimson, "I do. And I am more frightened right now than ever I was when Azuth stripped my Art from me before you. All magic is awry, all over the Realms. It will be down to the sharpest sword and the cunning of the wolf once more, and not one of our hired mages will be able to aid us!"

"And what is so bad about trusting only in sharp swords and the strong arms and cunning of warriors?"

"Esbre," the Lady Nasmaerae whispered, bringing her lips up to brush his—but too slowly for him to miss seeing the bright glimmer of unshed tears welling up in her eyes, "How long can you stand against foe after foe without the spells of our mages to hew them down for you? How many sharp swords and how much cunning does an orc horde have?"

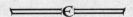

A chiming as of many bells rang out across the chamber. It nearly deafened Elminster, as the chill wind that carried it raced through him, searing him once more into frozen immobility. The ghostly mist that had been Saeraede was spiraling about him, coiling and twining—seemingly unharmed by the beams of fire Azuth had hurled, that roared through her into Elminster.

Ice, then fire—fire that lifted him off his feet in a whirlwind of battling mist and flames and set him down again staggering, too overwhelmed to do more than bleat in wordless pain.

"Here," Tabarast mumbled, through lips that were white and trembling with fear, "that's our Elminster you're smiting, sir—Your, er, Divineness, sir!"

"Break free of her," the Harper who was Azuth said quietly, his gaze no longer flaming—but now bent on the pain-narrowed eyes of Elminster, "or you are doomed."

"I'd say you're doomed anyway," a sneering voice said from above—and five staves spat in unison, hurling a rending rain of doom down the shaft.

The Overmistress of the Acolytes strode through the black curtain of hanging chains with every inch of the cruel authority that made her so feared among the underclergy. The cruel barbed lash rode upon her shoulder, ready to snap forward at the slightest act or omission that displeased her, and her face beneath the horned black mask wore a smile of cruel anticipation. Even the two guardian Priestesses of the Chamber shrank back from her; she ignored them as she strode on, the metal-shod heels of her thigh-high black boots clicking on the tiles, and shouldered through the three curtains of fabric into the innermost place of the Darklady's contemplation—the Pool of Shar.

A figure moved in the gloom beyond the pool: a figure in a familiar horned headdress and deep purple mantle. Dread Sister Klalaerla went to her knees immediately, holding forth her lash in both hands.

With leisurely tread the Darklady came around the inky waters and took it from her. The Overmistress immediately bowed forward to kiss the knife-blade toes of the Darklady's boots, holding her tongue against the cold, bloodstained metal until the lash came down across her own back.

It burned, despite the webwork of crossed lacings that were part of her own garb, but it was a mark of pride not to flinch or gasp; she held firm, waiting for the second blow that would mark her superior's displeasure, or the rain of cuts that meant Avroana's fury was aroused.

None came, and with a smooth motion that almost managed to conceal her relief, she straightened to a sitting position once more, for Avroana to put the lash to her lips. She kissed it, received it back, and relaxed. The ritual was satisfied.

"Your Darkness?" she asked, as was the custom.

"Klalaerla," the Darklady said, almost urgently—her familiarity made the Overmistress stiffen with excitement—"I need you to do something for me. Despite Narlkond's assurances, those five Dreadspells are going to fail us. You must be the striking hand that rewards them for their misdeeds. If they betray the House of Holy Night, you must bring the justice of the House to them, whatever the danger to yourself. I demand it. The Flame of Darkness *herself* demands it. Dearest of my believers, will you do this for me?"

"Gladly," Klalaerla said, and meant it. To travel outside the House once more! To breathe the free winds of Faerûn, out in the open, and see lands spread out before her once more! Oh, Avroana! "Lady most kind," she said, her voice trembling, "what must I do?"

The noise smote their ears like a blow. Dust curled up, the ground shuddered and heaved beneath their boots, and here and there around the ruins slabs of stone whirled aloft, thrust into the air by geysers of rocketing vapor.

The five Dreadspells exchanged awed, delighted glances, the roaring of their unleashed magic swallowing their shouts of excited approval, and poured down death until Elryn slapped at their arms and waved the scepters in his hands—weapons he'd snatched from his belt after his staff sputtered out.

When he had their attention, the senior Dark Brother aimed the scepters at an angle toward the floor beside the shaft. If their fire burst through into the cavern below, it would burn an angled path reaching to where Elryn's spying spell had shown him the staggering Chosen, near a throne and a ring or half-ring of runes that could perhaps, just perhaps, be made to explode.

The destruction of a Chosen was, after all, their holy mission. As Femter, Vaelam, and Hrelgrath aimed their staves with undaunted enthusiasm, Elryn stepped back a pace or two and saw Daluth, on the far side of the group, doing the same. They exchanged mirthless smiles. If there was a backlash, someone had to survive to take word to the distant Darklady—or, if it raced along the linkage she used to spy on them all, to see what fate she suffered. Perhaps it would even be one that would let two false wizards go their separate ways in Faerûn, so heavily laden with enchanted items that they could barely stand.

A more prudent time for such moondreams would come later—when they weren't standing in a haunted ruin near sunset, at the heart of a killing forest emptied of life, with a known Chosen and a madman who thought he was a god and the ghost of a sorceress locked in battle somewhere close by under their feet, hurling spells around and over old and powerful spell runes cut into the stone floor for some old and very important purpose.

The thunder of destructive magic roared on unabated as the junior Dreadspells laughed and exulted in the sheer rush of power under their command. Walls toppled, smashing wardrobes flat, as the floors that supported them melted away and tumbled into an ever-lengthening chasm. Trees all around groaned and creaked as the ground shifted.

Daluth kept his own wands trained straight down, at the self-styled Azuth and his companions. He'd seen the casual waves of a hand that had wrought what it took most archmages long and complicated rituals to achieve. God or avatar or boldly bluffing archmage, whatever it was must be destroyed.

Elryn aimed his scepters to fire through the opened, dust-choked space in the wake of the three staves—which were now, one by one, shuddering to exhaustion, to be tossed aside in favor of Netherese scepters whose blasts were almost as potent. Chosen or not, no lone wizard could stand unscathed in the face of such destruction. Elryn snarled as a scepter crumbled to dust, and snatched forth another to replace it. No, there was no chance at all that a man could survive this. Why, then, was he so uneasy?

The end of the cavern vanished in tumbling stones and the flash and rock spray of spell-wrought explosions. Floor slabs bounced upward as a shock wave rolled through them, toppling the throne. More rocks broke away and fell from the ceiling, bouncing amid the roiling fury there; on his knees, a dazed Elminster watched through pain-blurred eyes as the collapse of the ceiling continued in a rough line heading toward him, chunks of stone larger than he was crashing down or being hurled aside in an endless roaring tide.

Someone or something aloft must be trying to slay him, or destroy the runes . . . not that he faced any dearth of foes nearer at hand.

Saeraede, who must have lied to him about everything except who put the runes here, was riding him like a mounted knight, her claws around his throat and searing his back with talons of icy iron. He knew before he tried that no amount of rolling or smashing himself into a wall could harm or dislodge her; how can one crush or scrape away a wisp of ghostly mist?

Move he must, though, or be buried or torn apart by the snarling, smoking bolts and beams of magic that were gnawing their way through earth and stone to reach him. El groaned and crawled a little way along heaving stones—until the runes of Karsus erupted into white-hot columns of flame, one by one. As they licked and seared the collapsing ceiling, magic played all around the cavern, purple lightning dancing and strange half-seen shapes and images forming and collapsing and forming again in an endless parade.

The last prince of Athalantar smashed his nose and shoulder into a floor-slab that was heaving upward to meet him, and rolled over with a gasp of pain and despair. As he clawed at the edges of the stone with bloody, feeble fingers, trying to drag himself upright again, the stone melted away into smoke and rending magic burst into him.

Ah, well, this is it . . . forgive me, Mystra.

But no agony followed, and nothing plucked at his flesh, to melt and sear and reave. . . .

Instead, he was rolled over as if by the empty air, and glowing nothingness enclosed him in ropes of radiance. Dimly, through his tears and the roiling motes of light, Elminster saw magic rushing toward him from all sides, being drawn to him, veering in its dancing to race in.

Wild laughter rose around him, high and sharp and exultant. Saeraede!

She was wrapped around him, clinging in a web of glowing mists that grew thicker and brighter as she gorged herself on magic, a ghost of bright sorcery.

Sunlight was stabbing down into the riven cavern, now, but the dancing dust cloaked everything in gloom—everything but the rising giant built around Elminster's feebly writhing form. The rune-flames were twisting in midair to flow into Saeraede, and she was rising ever higher, a thing of crackling flame. El strained to look up at her—and two dark flecks among the magical fire became eyes that looked back at him in cold triumph . . . until a mouth swam out of the conflagration to join them and gave him a cruel smile.

"*You're mine now, fool,*" she whispered, in a hoarse hiss of fire, "*for the little while you'll last. . . .*"

"Lord Thessamel Arunder, the Lord of Spells," the steward announced grandly, as the doors swung wide. A wizard strode slowly through them, a cold sneer upon his sharp features. He wore a high-collared robe of unadorned black that made his thin frame look like a tomb obelisk, and a shorter, more lushly built lady in a gown of forest green clung to his arm, her large brown eyes dancing with lively mischief.

"Goodsirs," he began without courtesies, "why come you here to me once more this day? How many times must you hear my refusal before the words sink through your skulls?"

"Well met, Lord Arunder," said the merchant Phelbellow, in dry tones. "The morning finds you well, I trust?"

Arunder gave him a withering glare. "Spare me your toadying, rag seller. I'll *not* sell this house, raised by mighty magic, nor any wagon length of my lands, no matter how sweetly you grovel, or how much gold you offer. What need have I for coins? What need have I for gowns, for that matter?"

"Aye, I'll grant that," one of the other merchants grunted. "Can't see him looking like much in a good gown. No knees for it."

"No hips, neither," someone else added.

There were several sputters of mirth from the merchants crowded at the doorway; the wizard regarded them all with cold scorn, and said softly, "I weary of these insults. If you are not gone from my halls by the time I finish the Ghost Chant, the talons of my guardian ghosts shall—"

"Lady Faeya," Hulder Phelbellow asked, "has he not seen the documents?"

"Of course, Goodsir Phelbellow," the lady in green said in musical tones. Favoring them all with a smile, she stepped from her lord and drew forth a strip of folded vellum, "and he's signed them, too."

She proffered them to Phelbellow, who unfolded them eagerly, the men behind him crowding around to see.

The Lord of Spells gaped at the paper and the merchants, then at Faeya. "W-what befalls here?" he gasped.

"A sensible necessity, my lord," she replied sweetly. "I'm so glad you saw the good sense in signing it. A most handsome offer—enough to allow you to retire from your castings entirely, if you desire."

"I signed nothing," Arunder gasped, white-faced.

"Oh, but you did, lord—and so ardently, too," she replied, eyes dancing. "Have you forgotten? You remarked at the time upon the hardness and flatness of my belly that made your penmanship such ease. You signed it with quite a flourish, as I recall."

Arunder stiffened. "But . . . that was—"

"Base trickery?" one of the merchants chuckled. "Ah, well done, Faeya!"

Someone else barked with laughter, and a third someone contributed a murmur of, "That's rich, that is."

"Apprentice," the Lord of Spells whispered savagely, "*what have you done?*"

The Lady Faeya drew three swift paces away from him, into the heart of the merchants, who melted aside to make way for her like mist before flame, and turned back to face him, placing her hands on her hips.

"Among other things, Thessamel," she told him softly, "I've slain two men this last tenday, who came to settle old scores since your spells failed you—and word spread of it."

"*Faeya!* Are you *mad?* Telling these—"

"They know, Thess, they know," his lady told him with cold scorn. "The whole town knows. Every mage has his hands full of wild spells, not just you. If you paid one whit of attention to Faerûn outside your window, you'd know that already."

The Lord of Spells had turned as pale as old bones and was gaping at her, mouth working like a fish gasping out of water. Everyone waited for him to find his voice again; it took quite a while.

"But . . . your spells still work, then?" he managed to ask, at last.

"Not a one," she said flatly. "I killed them with this." She drew forth the tiny dagger from its sheath at her hip, then threw back her left sleeve to lay bare a long, angry-looking line of pine gum and wrapped linens. "That's how I got *this*."

"Were these merchants also coming to—to—?" Arunder asked faintly, swaying back on his heels. His hands were trembling like those of a sick old man.

"I went to them," Faeya told him in biting tones, "to beg them to make again the offer you so *charmingly* refused two months ago. They were good enough to oblige, when they could well have set their dogs on me: the apprentice of the man who turned three of them into pigs for a night."

There were angry murmurs of remembrance and agreement from among the merchants around her; Arunder stepped back and raised a hand to cast a spell out of sheer habit—before dropping it with a look of sick despair.

His lady drew herself up and said more calmly, "So now the deal's done. Your tower and all these lands, from high noon today henceforth, belong to this cabal of merchants, to use as they see fit."

"And-and what happens to me? Gods, woma—"

Faeya held up a hand, and the wizard's ineffectual gibbering ended as if cut off by a knife. Someone chuckled at that.

"We, my lord, are free to live unmolested in the South Spire, casting spells—so long as they harm or work ill upon no one upon this holding—as much as we desire . . . or are able to. You, Thess, receive two hundred thousand gold pieces—that's why all of these good men are here—all the firewood we require, and a dozen deer a year, prepared for the table."

Without a word, Hulder Phelbellow laid a sack upon the side table. It landed with the heavy clink of coins. Whaendel the butcher followed him, then, one by one, all of the others, the sacks building up until they were reaching up the wall, atop a table that creaked in protest.

Arunder's eyes bulged. "But . . . you can't have gold enough, none of you!"

His lady rejoined him in a graceful green shifting, and laid a comforting hand on his arm. "They have a backer, Thess. Now thank them politely. We've some packing to do—or you *will* be wearing my gowns."

"I-I—"

Her hitherto gentle hand thrust hard into his ribs.

"My lords," Arunder gulped, "I don't know how to thank you—"

"Thessamel," Phelbellow said genially, "you just did. Have our thanks, too—and fare thee well in the South Spire, eh?"

Arunder was still gulping as the merchants filed out, chuckling. The noises he was making turned to whimpers, however, when their withdrawal revealed the man who'd been sitting calmly behind them all the while, the faint glow of deadly magics playing along the naked broadsword that was laid across his knees. That blade was in the capable grasp of the large and hairy hands of the famous warrior Barundryn Harbright, whose smile, as he rose and looked straight into the wizard's eyes, was a wintry thing. "So we meet again, Arunder."

"You—!" the wizard's snarl was venomous.

"You're my tenant now, mage, so spare me the usual hissed curses and spittle. If you anger me enough, I'll take you under my arm down to the stream where the little ones play, and spank your behind until it's as red as a radish. I'm told that won't hamper your spellcasting one bit." One large, blunt-fingered hand waved casually through the air past Arunder's nose.

The wizard blinked in alarm. "What? Who—?"

"Told me so?" Harbright lifted his chin in a fond smile that was directed past Arunder's shoulder.

The Lord of Spells whirled around in time to see Faeya's catlike smile drifting out the door they'd come in by, together. The rest of her accompanied it, a vision in forest green.

Lord Thessamel Arunder moaned, swayed on his feet, and turned, on the verge of tears of rage, to run away from it all—only to come to an abrupt halt, with a squeak of real alarm, as he found himself about to run right into the edge of Harbright's glowing blade.

His eyes rose, slowly and unwillingly, from the steel that barred his way to the huge and hulking warrior who held it. There was something like pity in Barundryn Harbright's eyes as he rumbled, "Why are wizards, with all their wits, so slow to learn life's lessons?"

The blade swept down and away, seeking its sheath, and a large and steadying hand came down on the wizard's shaking shoulder. "Mages tend to live longer, Arunder," Harbright said gently, "if they manage to resist their most attractive temptations."

The Sharrans were beginning to sweat now, from the sheer strain of aiming and holding steady as the Art they wielded punched aside old stones and earth, to lay open a fortress and slay the beings below. Elryn watched Femter wince and shake the smoking fragments of a ring off one finger, as Hrelgrath tossed aside his third wand and Daluth slid one failing scepter back into his belt.

"Enough," Elryn bellowed, waving his hands. "Enough, Dreadspells of Shar!" Something had to be saved in case they met with other foes this day—or, gods above, there was someone still alive down there.

The priests-turned-wizards turned their heads in the sudden peace to blink at him, almost as if they'd forgotten who and where they were.

"We have a holy task, Dark Brothers," Elryn reminded them, letting them hear the regret in his voice, "and it is not melting away earth and stone in a forgotten ruin in the heart of a forest. Our quarry is the Chosen; how fares he?"

Three heads peered at roiling dust. All five looked down the shaft where they'd begun, where the dust was but a few flowing tongues. There was rubble down there, and—

One of the Sharrans cried out in disbelief.

The Harper who'd claimed to be Azuth was looking calmly back up at them, standing more or less where he'd been when their barrage began. The three old men, still blinking at him in awe, stood around him. He, they, and the floor around the bottom of the shaft seemed untouched.

"Finished?" he asked quietly, looking up at them with eyes of steady, storm-smoke gray.

Elryn felt cold fear catch at the back of his throat and slide slowly down into the pit of his stomach, but Femter snarled, "Shar take the man!" and snatched a wand from his belt.

Before Elryn or Daluth could stop him, Femter leaned over the well and snarled the word that sent a streak of flame down, down into the gloom below, straight at the upturned face of the gray-eyed man.

The Harper didn't move, but his mouth somehow stretched wider than a man's mouth should be able to—and the flames fell right into him. He shuddered for a moment as all of the fire plunged into his vitals. By the stumbling of the three old men around him, it seemed some sort of magic was keeping them at bay, moving them as he moved.

A moment later the fireball burst with a dull rumbling. The Harper stood with an unconcerned expression on his face as smoke whirled out of his ears.

He gave the watching Sharrans a reproving look and remarked, "Needs a little more pepper."

The Dreadspells were screaming and fleeing wildly even before Azuth lowered his head and looked again across the riven cavern at Elminster. "I mean what I say," he said gravely. "You must get free of her."

"I—can't," Elminster gasped, staring into the dark eyes of Saeraede, as she reared up over him in triumph like some sort of giant snake, twining around him in large and tightening coils.

"And you never will," she breathed triumphantly, her cold lips inches from his. He could feel the chilling frost of her breath on his face as she purred, "With the powers of a Chosen and all the might Karsus left here, I can defy even such as *him*."

She lifted her head to give Azuth a challenging glare as she clamped one giant hand of solid mist around El's throat. Other tentacles of mist rose around them both in a protective forest, undulating and lashing the tossed and shattered stone slabs.

The last prince of Athalantar struggled to breathe in her grasp, so throttled he couldn't speak or shout, as the ghostly sorceress leisurely turned the uppermost spire of her mists to a lush and very solid human torso, curvaceous and deadly.

Slim fingers grew fingernails like long talons, and when they were as long as Saeraede's hand, she reached almost lovingly for his mouth.

"We'll just have the tongue out, I think," she said aloud, "to forestall any nasty—ah, but wait a bit, Saeraede, you want him to tell you a few things before he's mute.... Hmmmm..."

Razor-sharp talons drifted just inches past Elminster's tightly constricted throat, to slice into the first flesh she found bared. Plowing deep gashes across the strangling mage's neck, she flicked his blood away in droplets that were caught in her whirling mists and held her bloody talons exultantly up to the sunlight.

"Ah, but I'm *alive* again," Saeraede hissed, "alive and whole! I breathe, I *feel!*" She brought that hand to her mouth, bit her own knuckles, and held the hand out toward the grimly watching avatar of Azuth to let him see the welling blood. "I bleed! I *live!*"

Then she screamed, swayed, and stared down, dark eyes widening in disbelief, at the gore-slick, smoking sword tip that had just burst through her breast from behind.

"Some people live far longer than they should," said Ilbryn Starym silkily from behind the hilt, as he stared gloating into the eyes of the mage still frozen in Saeraede's grasp. "Don't you agree, Elminster?"

A door was flung wide, to boom its broken song against a heavily paneled wall. It had been years since the tall, broad-shouldered woman who now stood in the doorway, her eyes snapping in alarm and anger, had worn the armor she hated so much—but as she stood glaring into the room, the half-drawn long sword at her hip gleaming, she looked every inch a warrior.

Sometimes Rauntlavon wished he was more handsome, strong, and about ten years older. He'd have given a lot for so magnificent a woman to smile at him.

Right now, she was doing anything *but* smiling. She was looking down at him as if she'd found a viper in her chamber pot—and his only consolation was that he wasn't the only mage rolling around on the floor under her dark displeasure; his master, the gruffly sardonic elf Iyriklaunavan, was gasping on the fine swanweave rug not a handspan away.

"Iyrik, by all the gods," the Ladylord Nuressa growled, "what befell *here?*"

"My farscrying spell went awry," the elf snarled back at her. "If it hadn't been for the lad, here, all those books'd be aflame now, and we'd be hurling water and running with buckets for our lives' worth!"

Rauntlavon's face flamed as the ladylord took a step forward and looked down at him with a rather kinder expression. "I-it was nothing, Great Lady," he stammered.

"Master Rauntlavon," she said gently, "an apprentice should never contradict his master-of-magecraft . . . nor belittle the judgment of any one of The Four Lords of the Castle."

Rauntlavon blushed as maroon as his robes and emitted the immortal words, "Yujus-yujus-er-ah-uhmmm, I, ah—"

"Yes, yes, boy, brilliantly explained as usual," Iyriklaunavan said dismissively, rolling to his elbows. "Now belt up and look around the room for me: is anything amiss? Anything broken? Smoldering? Aflame? Hop, now!"

Rauntlavon hopped, quite thankfully, but kept his attention more on what two of The Four Lords of the Castle were saying. They'd all been debonair and successful adventurers, less than a decade ago, and one never knew what wild and exciting things they might say.

Well, nothing about mating dragons *this* time.

"So tell me, Iyrik," the Ladylord was saying in her I-really-shouldn't-have-to-be-*this*-patient voice, "just *why* your farscrying spell blew up. Is it one of those magics you'd just be better off not trying? Or were you distracted by some nubile elf maid seen in your spying, perhaps?"

"Nessa," the elf growled—Rauntlavon had always admired the way he could look so agile and elegant and youthful, and yet be more gruff than any dwarf—as he rose and fixed her with one glaring that's-*quite*-enough eye, "this is serious. For us all, everywhere in Faerûn. Stop playing the swaggering warrior bitch for just a moment and listen. For once."

Rauntlavon froze, his head sunk between his shoulders, wondering if folk really survived the full fury of Great Lady Nuressa a-storming—and just how swiftly and brutally she'd notice him and have him removed from the room.

Very and with iron calm, it seemed.

"Master Rauntlavon," she said calmly, "you may leave us now. Close the door on your way out."

"Apprentice Rauntlavon," his master said, just as calmly, "it is my will that you abide with us. Send Master Rauntlavon out, and close the door behind him, remaining here with us."

Rauntlavon swallowed, drew in a deep breath, and turned around to face them, hardly daring to raise his eyes. "I-I've found nothing amiss at this end of the chamber," he announced, his voice higher and rather more unsteady than he wished it would be. "Shall I examine the other half of it now . . . or later?"

"Now will be fine, Rauntlavon," the ladylord said in a voice of velvet menace. "Pray proceed."

The apprentice actually shivered ere he bowed and mumbled, "As my Great Lady wishes."

"It's a wonderful thing to make men and boys fear you, Nessa, but does it really make up for your years under the lash? The escaped slave gets even by enslaving others?" His master's voice was biting; Rauntlavon tried not to let his momentary hesitation show. The ladylord had been a slave? Kneeling naked under a slaver's lash, in the dust and the heat? Gods, but he'd never have—

"Do you think we can leave my past careers in my own bedchamber closet, Iyrik?" the ladylord said almost gently. Her next sentence, however, was almost a battlefield shout. "Or is there some pressing need to *tell all the world?*"

"I won't tell anyone, I won't—I swear I won't!" Rauntlavon babbled, going to his knees on the rug.

He heard the Great Lady sigh and felt ironlike fingers on his shoulder, hauling him back to his feet. Other fingers took hold of his chin and turned his head as sharply as a whip is flicked. The apprentice found himself staring into the Lady Nuressa's smoky eyes from a distance of perhaps the length of his longest finger.

"Rauntlan," she said, addressing him as he liked his handful of friends to—a short name he'd had no idea any of the lords even knew about, "you know that one of the most essential skills any wizard can have is to keep the right secrets, and keep them well. So I shall test you now, to see if you're good enough to remain in the castle as a mage-in-training . . . or a wizard in your own right, in time to come. Keep my secret, and stay. Let it out—and be yourself shut out of our lands, chased to our borders with the flat of my blade finding your backside as often as I can land it."

Rauntlavon heard his master start to say something, but the ladylord made some sort of gesture he couldn't see behind her back, and Iyriklaunavan fell silent again.

"Do you understand, Rauntlan?"

Her voice was as calm and as gentle as if she'd been discussing haying a field; Rauntlavon swallowed, nodded, squirmed under the hard points of her gaze, and managed to say, "Great Lady, I swear to keep your secret. I shall abide by your testing . . . and if ever I let it slip, I shall come to you myself to admit the doing, so the chase can begin at your convenience."

Her dark brows rose. "Well said, Master Apprentice. Agreed, then."

She took a quick step back from him and lifted her gown unhurriedly to display a tanned, muscular leg so long and shapely that he swallowed twice, unable to tear his eyes from it. Somewhere far, far away, his master chuckled, but Rauntlavon was lost in the slow but continuing rise of fine fabric, up, up to her hip—he was swallowing hard, now, and knew his face must be as bright as a lamp—where his eyes locked on a purplish-white brand. The cruel design was burned deep into her flesh, just below the edge of the bone that made her hip jut out. She traced a circle around it with one long finger and asked in a dry voice, "Seen enough, Rauntlan?"

He almost choked, trying to swallow and nod fervently at the same time, and somewhere in the midst of his distress the gown went to her ankles again, her hand clapped his shoulders like a club crashing down, and her deep voice said in his ear, "So we have a secret to share now, you and I. Something to remember." She shoved him away gently and added, "I believe this end of the room hasn't been fully inspected yet, Master Apprentice."

Her voice was a brisk goad once more, but somehow Rauntlavon found himself almost grinning as he strode away to the end of the room and announced, "Inspection resumes, Great Lady—and sharing begins!"

His master laughed aloud, and after a moment Rauntlavon heard a low, thrilling murmur that must have been the ladylord chuckling.

She used the lash of her voice on Iyriklaunavan next, breaking off in mid-chuckle to snap, "Enough time wasted, mage. You frighten me up from my table with a map half drawn and my soup growing cold, then go all coy about why. What's so 'serious' that your apprentice must hear about it alongside me? Do you think you can get around to telling me about this oh-so-serious matter before, say, *nightfall?*"

"I meant it when I said this was serious, Nessa," Rauntlavon's master said quietly. "Put the edge of your tongue away for a moment and listen. Please."

He paused then, and—wonders! Rauntlavon even turned around to see, earning him an almost amused glance from the Great Lady—the Ladylord Nuressa gave him silence, waiting to hear him speak.

Iyriklaunavan blinked, seeming himself surprised, then said swiftly, "You know that magic—all magic not bolstered by draining a few sorts of enchanted items—is going wrong. Spells twisting to all sorts of results, untrustworthy and dangerous. Some mages are hiding in their towers, unable to defend themselves against anyone who might try to settle grudges. Magic has gone wild. If fewer folk knew about it, I'd say that this should be *our* secret—Rauntlavon's and mine own—for you to keep, or else. It will come as no surprise to you that many mages have been trying to find out why this darkness has befallen. I am one of them."

"And that's even less of a surprise," the Lady Nuressa said quietly. Rauntlavon's head snapped around to regard her somber face. He'd never heard her speak so gently before. She sounded almost . . . tender.

"I have no items to waste in bolstering my spells," Iyriklaunavan continued, "so the boy—Rauntlavon—has been my bulwark, using his spells to steady mine. Word has even come to us that some wizards—and even priests of the faiths of the Weave—believe divine Mystra and Azuth themselves have been corrupting magic deliberately, for some purpose mortals cannot even hazard."

"You worship our gods of magecraft?"

"Nessa," Iyriklaunavan said calmly, "I don't even *have* a bedchamber closet to keep *my* secrets in. I'm trying to hurry this, really I am; just listen."

Nuressa leaned back against one of the lamp-girt pillars that held up the ceiling of the spell chamber, and gestured for the elf mage to continue. She didn't even look irritated.

"Just now we were seeking but had not yet called up a place in our scrying, the enchantment being just complete," Iyriklaunavan continued, "when I felt one thing, and saw another. I think everyone in Faerûn who was attempting a scrying at the time felt what I did: the willful, reckless release of many wizards' staves at once, in one place, all directed at the same target."

"You mean mages everywhere feel it, whenever one wizard blasts another?" Nuressa's voice was incredulous. "No wonder you're all so difficult."

"No, we do not normally feel such things—nor have the violence of feeling anything strike us so hard that our own spells collapse into wildfire," Rauntlavon's master told her. "The reason we did this time was the target of this unleashing: the High One. I saw him, standing at the bottom of a shaft with three mortal mages, while magic seeking to destroy him rained down—and his attention was elsewhere."

"Azuth? Who was crazed enough to use magic to try to blast down a god of magic?" The ladylord looked -surprised.

"That I did not see," Iyriklaunavan replied. "I did, however, see what Azuth was regarding. A ghostly sorceress, who was trying to slay a Chosen of Mystra."

"What's that?" the Great Lady asked. "Some sort of servant of the goddess?"

"Yes," the elf mage said grimly, "and he was someone you might remember. Cast your thoughts back to a day when we fled from a tomb—a tomb furnished with pillars that erupted in eyes. A mage was hanging above us there, asleep or trapped, and came out after we fled. He asked you what year it was."

"Oh, yesss," the ladylord murmured, her eyes far away, "and I told him."

"And thereby we earned the favor of the goddess Mystra," Iyriklaunavan told her, "who delivered this castle into our hands."

The Lady Nuressa frowned. "I thought Amandarn won title to these lands while dicing with some merchant lords—hazarding all our coins in the process," she said.

Rauntlavon stood very still, not wanting to be ejected again now. Surely this was an even more dangerous secret than—

"Amandarn lost all our coins, Nessa. Folossan nearly killed him for it—and they had to flee when he stole a few bits back to buy a meal that night and got caught at it. The two of them hid in a shrine to Mystra—rolled right in under the altar and hid under its fine cloth. There they slept, though both of them swear magic must have dragged them into slumber, for they'd had little to drink and were all excited from their flight and the danger. When they awoke, all of our coins were back in Amandarn's pouch—along with the title to the castle."

The Great Lady's brow arched and she asked, "And you believe this tale?"

"Nessa, I used spells to glean every last detail of it out of both their heads, after they told me. It happened."

"I see," the Great Lady said calmly. "Rauntlavon, be aware that this is another secret shared between us here—and only us here, or you'll have to flee four Lords of the Castle, not merely one."

"Yes, Great Lady," the apprentice said, then swallowed and faced them both. "There's something I should say, now. If something happens to Great Azuth—or Most Holy Mystra—and magic keeps crumbling, we all share a grave problem."

"And what is that, Rauntlavon?" The Lady Nuressa asked, in almost kindly tones, her fingers caressing the pommel of her long sword.

Rauntlavon's eyes dropped to those fingers—whose fabled strength was one of the rocks upon which his world stood—then back up to meet her smoky eyes.

"I think we must pray for Azuth or find some way to aid him. The castle was built with much magic," he told the two lords, the words coming out in a rush. "If its spells fail, it will fall—and us with it."

The Great Lady's expression did not change. Her eyes turned to meet those of the Lord Iyriklaunavan. "Is this true?"

The elf merely nodded. Nuressa stared at him for a moment, her face still calm, but Rauntlavon saw that her hand was now closed around the hilt of the long sword and gripping so tightly that the knuckles were white. Her eyes swung back to his.

"Well, Rauntlavon—have you any plan for preventing such doom?"

Rauntlavon spread empty hands, wishing wildly that he could be the hero, and see love for him awaken in her eyes . . . wishing he could give her more than his despair. "No, Nuressa," he was astonished to hear himself calmly whispering. "I'm only an apprentice. But I will die for you, if you ask me."

He drew his blade out of the swaying sorceress with savage glee, to thrust it into the Great Foe he'd pursued for so long, the grasping, stinking human who'd dared to stain bright Cormanthyr with his presence and doom the House of Starym; now helpless before him, able to move just his eyes—fittingly—to see whence his doom came.

"Know as you die, human worm," Ilbryn hissed, "that the Starym aven—"

And those were the last words he ever spoke, as all the magic that the ancient sorceress had drawn into herself rushed out again, in a fiery flood of raw magical energy that consumed the blade that had spilled it and the elf whose hand held that blade, all in one raging wave that crashed against the far wall of the cavern and ate through solid rock as if it was soft cheese, thrusting onward until it found daylight on a slope beyond, and the groan of toppling trees and falling stones began in earnest.

Saeraede wailed, flames streaming from her mouth, and fell away from Elminster, her mists receding into a standing cloud whose dark and despairing eyes pleaded with his for a few fleeting moments before it collapsed and dwindled away to whirling dust.

El was still staggering and coughing, his hands at his ravaged throat, when Azuth strode forward and unleashed a magic whose eerie green glow flooded the runes and the dust that had been Saeraede alike.

Like a gentle wave rolling up a beach, the god's spell spread out to the crevice Ilbryn had hidden in and every other last corner of the ravaged cavern. Then it flickered, turned a lustrous golden hue that made Beldrune gasp, and rose from the floor, leaving scoured emptiness behind.

Azuth strode through the rising magic without pause, caught hold of the reeling Elminster by the shoulders, and marched him one step farther. In midstride they vanished together—leaving three old mages gaping at a fallen throne in a shaft of sunlight in a pit in the forest that was suddenly silent and empty.

They took a few steps toward the place where so much death and sorcery had swirled—far enough to see that the runes were now an arc of seven pits of shivered stone—then stopped and looked at each other.

"They're gone an' all, eh?" Beldrune said suddenly. "That's it—all that fury and struggle and in the space of a few breaths . . . that's it. All done, and us left behind an' forgotten."

Tabarast of the Three Sung Curses raised elegantly white tufted eyebrows and asked, "You expected things to be different, this once?"

"We were worthy of a god's personal protection," Caladaster almost whispered. "He walked with us and shielded us when we were endangered—danger he did not share, or he'd never have been able to deal with that fireball as he did."

"That was something, wasn't it?" Beldrune chuckled. "Ah, I can see myself telling the younglings that . . . a little more pepper, indeed."

"I believe that's why he did it," Tabarast told him. "Yes, we were honored—and we're still alive, unlike that ghost sorceress and the elf . . . that's an achievement, right there."

They looked at each other again, and Beldrune scratched at his chin, cleared his throat and said, "Yes—ahem. Well. I think we can just walk out, there at the end where the fire burst out of the cavern, that way."

"I don't want to leave here just yet," Caladaster replied, kicking at the cracked edge of one of the pits where a rune had been. "I've never stood with folk of real power before, at a spot where important things happen . . . and I guess I never will again. While I'm here, I feel . . . alive."

"Huh," Beldrune grunted, "*she* said that, an' look what happened to her."

Tabarast stumped forward and put his arms around Caladaster in a rough embrace, muttering, "I know just how you feel. We've got to go before dark, mind, and I'll want a tankard by then."

"A lot of tankards," Beldrune agreed.

"But somewhere quiet to sit and think, just us three," Tabarast added, almost fiercely. "I don't want to be sitting telling all the drunken farmers how we walked with a god this night, and have them laugh at us."

"Agreed," Caladaster said calmly, and turned away.

Beldrune stared at his back. "Where are you going?"

The old wizard reached the rubble-strewn bottom of the shaft and peered down at the stones. "I stood just here," he murmured, "and the god was . . . there." Though his voice was steady, even gruff, his cheeks were suddenly wet with tears.

"He protected us," he whispered. "He held back more magic than I've ever seen hurled before, in all my life, magic that turned the very rocks to empty air . . . for us, that we might live."

"Gods have to do that, y'see," Beldrune told him. "Someone has to see what they do and live to tell others. What's the good of all that power, otherwise?"

Caladaster looked at him with scorn, anger rising in his eyes, and stepped back from Beldrune. "Do you *dare* to *laugh* at divine—"

"Yes," Beldrune told him simply. "What's the good of being human, elsewise?"

Caladaster stared at him, mouth hanging open, for what seemed like a very long time. Then the old wizard swallowed deliberately, shook his head, and chuckled feebly. "I never saw things that way before," he said, almost admiringly. "Do you laugh at gods often?"

"One or twice a tenday," Beldrune said solemnly. "Thrice on high holy days, if someone reminds us when they are."

"Stand back, holy mocker," Tabarast said suddenly, waving at him. Beldrune raised his eyebrows in a silent question, but his old friend just waved a shooing hand at him and strode forward, adding, "Move those great booted hooves of yours, I said!"

"All right," Beldrune said easily, doing so, "so long as you tell me why."

Tabarast knelt in the rubble and tugged at something; a corner of bright cloth amid the stones. "Gems and scarlet fineweave?" he asked Faerûn at large. "What have we here?"

His wrinkled old hands were already plucking stones aside and uncovering cloth with dexterous speed, as Beldrune went to one knee with a grunt and joined him at the task. Caladaster stood over them anxiously, afraid that, somehow, a ghostly sorceress would rise from these rags to menace them anew.

Beldrune grunted in appreciation as the red gown, with gem-adorned dragons crawling over both hips, was laid out in full—but he promptly plucked it up and handed it to Caladaster, growling as he waved at more cloth, beneath, "There's more!"

The daring black gown was greeted with an even louder grunt, but when the blue ruffles came into view and Tabarast stirred around in the stones beneath enough to be sure that these three garments were all they were likely to find, Beldrune's grunts turned into low whispers of curiosity. "Being as Azuth wasn't wearing them, that I saw, these must have come from *her*," he said.

Tabarast and Caladaster exchanged glances. "Being older and wiser than you," his old friend told him kindly, "we'd figured out that much already."

Beldrune stuck out his tongue in response to that and held up the blue gown for closer scrutiny.

"Do these hold power, do you think?" Tabarast asked, the black gown dangling from his fingers as Caladaster suppressed a smirk.

"Hmmph. Power or not, I'm not wearing this backless number," Beldrune replied, turning the blue ruffles around again to face him. "It goes down far enough to give the cool drafts more'n a bit of help, if you know what I mean. . . ."

TWENTY
NEVER HAVE SO MANY
OWED SO MUCH

Never before in the history of this fair realm have so many owed so much to the
coffers of the king. Never fear but that he'll come collecting in short order—and
his price shall be the lives of his debtors, in some foreign war or other. He'll call
it a Crusade or something equally grand . . . but those who die in Cormyr's
colors will be just as dead as if he'd called it a Raid To Pillage, or a Head Col-
lecting Patrol. It is the way of kings to collect in blood. Only archmages can seize
such payments more swiftly and recklessly.

ALBAERTIN OF MARSEMBER
FROM *A SMALL BUT TREASONOUS CHAPBOOK*
PUBLISHED IN THE YEAR OF THE SERPENT

D oomtime," that deep voice boomed in Elminster's head. "Mind you make
the right choices." Somehow, the Athalantan knew that Azuth was gone,
and he *was* alone in the flood of blue sparks—the flood that he'd thought was
Azuth—whirling him over and over and down . . . to a place of darkness, with
a cold stone floor under his bare knees. He was naked, his gown and dagger and
countless small items of magery gone somewhere in the whirling.

"Robbed by a god," he murmured and chuckled. His mirth left no echo
behind, but what happened to it as it died away left him thinking he was
somewhere underground . . . somewhere not all that large. His good feeling
died soon after his chuckle; Elminster's innards felt—ravaged.

It was damp, and a chill was beginning to creep through him, but El did
not rise from his knees. He felt weak and sick, and—when he tried to seek
out magic or call up his spells—all of his powers as a Chosen and as a mage
seemed to be gone.

He was just a man again, on his knees in a dark chamber somewhere. He
knew that he should be despairing, but instead he felt at peace. He had seen far
more years than most humans and done—so far as he could judge, at least by
his own standards—fairly well. If it was time for death to come to him, so be it.

There were just the usual complaints: *was* it time for his death? What should
he be doing? What was going on? Who was going to stop by and furnish him
with answers to his every query—and when?

In all his life, there had only been one source for succor and guidance who
wasn't certain to be long dead by now, or entombed and asleep he knew not
where . . . and that one source was the goddess who made him her Chosen.

"Oh, Mystra, ye've been my lover, my mother, my soul guide, my savior, and
my teacher," Elminster said aloud. "Please, hear me now."

He hadn't really intended to pray . . . or perhaps he had, all along, but just
not admitted it to himself. "I've been honored to serve ye," he told the listening

darkness. "Ye've given me a splendid life, for which—as is the way of men—I've not thanked thee enough. I am content to face now whatever fate ye deem fitting for me, yet—as is the way of wizards—I wish to tell thee some things first."

He chuckled, and held up a hand. "Save thy spells and fury," he said. "'Tis only three things."

Elminster drew in a deep breath. "The first: thank ye for giving me the life ye have."

Was something moving in the gloom and shadows beyond where his eyes served him reliably?

He shrugged. What if something was? Alone, unclad, on his knees without magecraft to aid him; if something did approach him, this is how he'd have to greet it, and this was all he had to offer it.

"The second," El announced calmly. "Being thy Chosen is really what I want to spend out my days doing."

Those words echoed, where the darkness had muffled his words before. El frowned, then shrugged again and told the darkness earnestly, "The third, and most important to me to impart: Lady, I love thee."

As those words echoed, the darkness disgorged something that did move and reveal itself and loom all too clearly.

Something vast and monstrous and tentacled, slithered leisurely toward him.

"Was it a god?" Vaelam asked, white to the lips. Shrugs and panting were the first answers he got from his fellow Dreadspells, as they lay gasping in the hollow. Scraped and scratched by tree limbs in their run and thoroughly winded, they were only now shedding the heavy cloak of terror.

"God or no god," Femter muttered, "anyone who can withstand all we hurled down on his head—and *swallow* fireballs, for Shar's sake!—is someone I don't want to stand and face in battle."

"For Shar's sake, indeed, Dread Brother," someone said almost pleasantly from the far side of the hollow, where the ferns grew tall and they hadn't been yet. Five heads snapped around, eyes widening in alarm—

—and five jaws dropped, the throats beneath them swallowed noisily, and the eyes above them acquired a look of trapped fear.

The masked and cloaked lady floating in the air just above their reach, reclining at her ease on nothing, was all too familiar. "For there is a Black Flame in the Darkness," the cruel Overmistress of the Acolytes purred, in formal greeting.

"And it warms us, and its holy name is Shar," the five priests murmured in a reluctant, despairing chorus.

"You are far from the House of Holy Night, Dread Brothers, and unused to the ways of wizards—all too apt to stray, and in sore need of guidance," Dread Sister Klalaera observed, her voice a gentle honey of menace. "Wherefore our most caring and thoughtful Darklady Avroana has sent the House of Holy Night . . . to you."

"Hail, Dread Sister," Dreadspell Elryn said then, managing to keep his voice noncommittal. "What news?"

"News of the Darklady's deep displeasure at your leadership, most bold Elryn," the Overmistress said almost jovially, her eyes two spark-adorned flints. "And of her will: that you cease wandering Faerûn at your pleasure and return to the place from whence you so lately fled. Immense power lies there—and Shar means for us to have it. I know you'd not want to fail Most Holy Shar . . . or disappoint Darklady Avroana. So turn about and return thence, to serve Shar as capably as I know you can. I shall accompany you, to impart the Dark-lady's unfolding will as you return to the mission you were sent here for. Now rise, all of you!"

"Return?" Femter snarled, his hand darting to one of the wands still at his belt. "To duel with a god? Are you *mad*, Klalaera?"

The other Dreadspells watched silently, neither rising nor snarling defiance, as something unseen flashed between the Overmistress, at her ease with her head propped on her hand, and Femter Deldrannus, the wand still on its way out of his belt and not yet turned outward to menace anyone.

The priest shrieked and clutched at his head with both hands, hurling the wand away and staggering forward, his limbs trembling.

They watched him spasm and convulse and babble for what seemed like a very long time before Klalaera raised one languid hand and closed it in a casual gesture—and Femter collapsed in mid-word, falling in a sprawled and boneless heap like a dangle-puppet whose string had been cut.

"I can do the same to any of you—and all of you, at once," the Overmistress drawled. "Now rise, and return. You fear death at the hands of this 'god' you babble of—well, I can deliver you sure and certain death to set against one that may happen . . . or may not. Would any of you care to kneel and die here and now—in agony, and in the disfavor of Shar? Or will you show the Flame of Darkness just a little of the obedience she expects from those who profess to worship her?"

As Dread Sister Klalaera uttered these biting words, she descended smoothly to the ground, drawing from her belt the infamous barbed lash with which she disciplined the acolytes in her charge. The Dreadspells turned their faces reluctantly back toward the ruins they'd left so precipitously and began to trudge up out of the hollow—to the serenade of her whip crashing down on the defenseless back of the motionless Femter.

At the lip of the hollow, they turned in unspoken accord to look back—in time to see Femter, head lolling and eyes glazed, rise to his feet in the grip of fell magic and stagger after them, his back mere ribbons of flesh among an insect-buzzing welter of gore, his boots leaving bloody prints at every step. Klalaera shook drops of his dark blood from her saturated lash and gave them a soft smile. "Keep going," she said silkily. "I'll be right behind you."

Despite the floating menace of the Overmistress behind them, the five Dreadspells slowed cautiously as they climbed the last wooded ridge before the ruins. Blundering ahead blindly could mean swift doom . . . and a delay could well bring them to a shaft now empty of dangerous mages, leaving the ruins free for scavenging.

"Careful," Elryn murmured, the moment he heard the creak of leather that marked Dread Sister Klalaera bending forward to bring her lash down hard on someone's shoulders . . . probably his. "There's no need for anyone to strike alone in the fray, if we work together, and—"

"Avoid making pretty little speeches," Klalaera snapped. "Elryn, shut your mouth and lead the way! There's nothing between us and the ruins save a couple of stumps, a lot of waste lumber, your own fears, and—"

"Us," a musical voice murmured; an elven voice. Its owner rose up from the other side of the ridge, a scabbardless sword made of wood held in both his hands. "A walk in the woods these days holds so many dangers," Starsunder added. "My friend here, for instance."

The human mage Umbregard rose up from behind the ridge on cue and favored the Sharrans with a brief smile. He held a wand ready in either hand.

The Overmistress snapped, "Slay them!"

"Oh, well," Starsunder sighed theatrically, "if you *insist*." Magic roared out of him then in a roaring tide that swept aside wand-bolts, simple conjurations, and the lives of struggling Hrelgrath and dumbfounded Vaelam alike.

Femter screamed and fled blindly back into the trees—until Klalaera's unseen magic jerked him to a halt as if a noose had settled about his neck, and spun him around, thrashing and moaning, for the slow stagger back into the fray.

Beams of light were stabbing forth and wrestling in the roiling air as Elryn and a snarling Daluth sought to strike down the elf mage, and Umbregard used his own wands to disrupt and strike aside their attacks.

Daluth shouted in pain as an errant beam laid bare the bone of his shoulder, flesh, sinews, and clothing all boiling away in an instant. He staggered back a pace or two, at about the same time as Umbregard went over backward in a grunt and a shower of sparks, leaving the elf standing alone against the Sharrans.

The Overmistress of the Acolytes found her coldest, cruel smile and put it on. It widened slowly as Starsunder's shielding spell darkened, flickered, and began to shrink under the bolts and bursts streaming from the wands of the Dreadspells.

"I don't know who you are, elf," Klalaera remarked, almost pleasantly, "or why you chose to get in our way—but it's quite likely to be a fatal decision. I can slay you right now with a spell, but I'd rather have some answers. What is this place? What magic lies here that makes it worth you losing your life over?"

"The only thing that amazes me more about humans than their habit of splitting up fair Faerûn into separate 'places,' one seemingly having no connection to the next," Starsunder replied, as casually as if he'd been idly conversing with an old friend over a glass of moonwine, "is their need to gloat, threaten, and bluster in battle. If you *can* slay me, do so, and spare my ears. Otherwise—"

He sprang into the air as he spoke, leaving Sharran wand-blasts to ravage elfless stumps and ferns, and collapsed his shield into a net of deadly force that clawed at the Overmistress.

She writhed in the air, sobbing and snarling, until her desperate mental goading dragged the wild-eyed Femter over to stand beneath her. Then she collapsed her own defenses—and Starsunder's attack, still gnawing at them—down into the helpless Dreadspell, in a deadly flood that left him a tottering, blinded mass of blood and exposed bone.

The joints of Femter Deldrannus failed, and he sought his last, eternal embrace with the earth, ignored by all. He hadn't even been given time to scream.

A gasping Overmistress tumbled away through the air as her flight spell began to collapse.

Elryn roared in wordless victory as his wand-bursts found Starsunder at last, spinning the elf around in a swarm of biting bolts. Umbregard was struggling to rise, his face sick with pain as he watched his friend beset.

Daluth leveled his own wand at the human mage at point-blank range, across the smoking bodies of fallen fellow Dreadspells, and smiled a slow and soft smile at the horrified human.

Then he spun around and smashed Dread Sister Klalaera out of the air with all the might the wand in his hand could muster.

It crumbled away, leaving him holding nothing, as the lash all of the House of Holy Night hated and feared so much blazed from end to end and spun high into the trees, hurled by a spasming body in black leather that was crumpling into smoking ruin.

Crumpling—then snarling into a standing stance once more, surrounded by crackling black flames, the face that had been Klalaera's working and rippling beneath dead, staring eyes as her lips thundered, "Daluth, you shall die for that!"

The voice was thick and roaring, but the two surviving Dreadspells recognized it, Elryn's head snapping around from the task of rending the convulsing, darkening body of the elf mage.

"You are cast out of the favor of Shar—die friendless, false priest!" Darklady Avroana thundered, through the lips that were not hers.

The bolt of black flame that the body of the Overmistress vomited forth then swept away the errant wizard-priest, an old and mighty tree beyond him, and a stump that dwarfed them both, shaking the forest all around and hurling Elryn to the ground.

The last Dreadspell was still struggling to his feet as Klalaera's dangling body, still streaming black flames, floated forward. "Now let us be rid of meddling mages, elf and human both, and—"

The sphere of purple flame that came out of nowhere to hit what was left of the Overmistress tore her apart, spattering the trees around with tatters of black leather.

"Ah, fool, that's one thing none of us will ever be rid of," a new voice told the dwindling, collapsing sphere of black flames that hung where Klalaera had been.

Elryn gaped up at a human who stood holding a smoking, crumbling amulet in his hand, a black cloak swirling around him. "Faerûn will always have its meddling mages," the newcomer told the dying knot of flames in tones of grim satisfaction. "Myself, for instance."

Elryn put all of his might into a lunge at this new foe, swinging his belt mace viciously and jumping into the air to put all his weight behind the strike.

His target, however, wasn't there to meet the blurred rush of metal. The newcomer slid a knife into the priest's throat with almost delicate ease as he stepped around behind the last Dreadspell, and said politely, "Tenthar Taerhamoos, Archmage of the Phoenix Tower, at your service—eternally, it appears."

Choking over something ice cold in his throat that would not go away as the pleasant world of trees and dappled shade darkened around him, Elryn found he lacked the means to reply.

Purple flames exploded over the Altar of Shar with a sudden flourish, scorching the bowl of black wine there. The chosen acolyte held the glowing knife that was to be slaked in it aloft and kept fervently to his chanted prayer, not knowing that bursts of purple fire weren't part of this most holy ritual.

So intent was he on the flowing words of the incantation that he never saw the Darklady of the House stagger and fall past him across the altar, her limbs streaming purple fire. Wine hissed and sputtered under her as she thrashed, faceup and staring at the black, purple-rimmed circle that adorned the vaulted ceiling high above. Avroana was still arching her body and trying to find breath enough to scream as the prayer reached its last triumphal words . . . and the knife swept down.

With both hands the acolyte guided the consecrated blade, the runes on its dark flanks pulsing and glowing, down, down to the heart of the bowl, the very center of—Darklady Avroana's breast.

Their eyes met as the steel slid in, to the very hilt. Avroana had time to see triumphant glee dawning in the acolyte's eyes amid the wild horror of realizing his mistake before everything grew dim forever.

Gasping, Starsunder managed to raise himself on one arm, his face creased with pain. Large, weeping blisters covered all of his left flank—save where melted flesh glistened in dangling droplets and ropes of scorched sinew. Umbregard half staggered and half ran to his side, trying not to look at the Archmage of the Phoenix Tower, his foe of many years.

Fear of what Tenthar might do, standing so close at hand behind him, was written clearly on Umbregard's face as he knelt by Starsunder and carefully cast the most powerful healing spell he knew on the stricken elf. He was no priest, but even a fool could see that an unaided Starsunder hadn't long to live.

The elf mage shuddered in Umbregard's arms, seemed to sag a trifle, then breathed more easily, his eyes half closed. His side still looked the same, but the organs only partially hidden beneath the horrible seared wounds were no longer wrinkled or smoking. Still ...

A long hand reached past Umbregard, its fingers glowing with healing radiance, and touched Starsunder's flank. The glow flared, the elf shuddered, and the last fragments of something that had hung on a chain around the archmage's neck fell away into drifting dust. Tenthar rose hastily and stepped back, his hand going to his belt.

Umbregard looked up at the wand that hand had closed around, and hesitantly asked its owner, "Is there going to be violence between us?"

Tenthar shook his head. "When all Faerûn hangs in the balance," he replied, "personal angers must be set aside. I think I've grown up enough to set them aside for good." He extended his hand. "And you?"

Elminster knelt on the cold stone as the slithering, tentacled bulk drew nearer ... and nearer. With almost indolent ease a long, mottled blue-brown tentacle reached out for him, leathery strength curling around his throat. Icy flames of fear surged up his back, and El trembled as the tentacle tightened almost lovingly.

"Mystra," he whispered into the darkness, "I—"

A memory of holding a goddess in his arms as they flew through the air came to him unbidden, then, and he drew on the pride it awakened within him, forcing down his fear. "If I am to die under these tentacles, so be it. I've had a good life, and far more of it than most."

As his fear melted, so did the slithering monster, melting into nothingness. It hung like clinging smoke around him for a moment before sudden light washed over him. He turned his head to its source—and stared.

What his eyes had told him was probably a bare stone wall, though the cloak of gloom made it hard to see properly, was now a huge open archway. Beyond was a vast chamber awash in glowing golden coins, precious statuary, and gems—literally barrels full of glistening jewels.

Elminster looked at all its dazzle and just shrugged. His shoulders had barely fallen before the treasure chamber went dark, all of its riches melting away ... whereupon a trumpet sang out loudly behind him.

El whirled around to see another vast, grand, and warmly lit chamber. This one held no treasure, but instead a crowd of people ... royalty, by their glittering garb, crowns, and proud faces. Human kings and scaled, lizardlike emperors jostled with merfolk who were gasping in the air, all crowding forward to lay their crowns and scepters at his feet, murmuring endless variations on, "I submit me and all my lands, Great Elminster."

Princesses were removing their gem-studded gowns, now, and offering both gowns and themselves to him, prostrating themselves to clutch at his ankles. He felt their featherlike fingers upon him, stared into many worshiping, awed, and longing eyes, then shut his own firmly for a moment to gather the will he needed.

When he opened them, an eternity later, it was to say loudly and firmly: "My apologies, and I mean no offense by my refusal, but—no. I cannot accept ye, or any of this."

When he opened his eyes, everything was melting away amid growing dimness, and off to his right another light was growing, this one the dappled dance of true sunlight. Immeira of Buckralam's Starn was gliding forward across a bright room toward him, her arms outstretched and that eager smile on her face, offering herself to him. As she drew near, shaping his name soundlessly on her lips, she pulled open the bodice of her dark blue gown—and Elminster swallowed hard as the memories rose up in a sudden, warm surge.

The sun fell through the windows of Fox Tower and laid dappled fingers across the parchments Immeira was frowning over. Gods, how did anyone make sense of such as this? She sighed and slumped back in her chair—then, in a sort of dream, found herself rising to glide across the room, toward its darkest corner. Halfway there her fingers began to pluck at her catches and lacing, to tear open the front of her gown, as if offering herself to—empty air.

Immeira frowned. "Why—?" she murmured, then abruptly shivered, whirled around, and did up her gown again with shaking fingers.

Her busy fingers clenched into fists when she was done, and she peered in all directions around the deserted room, her face growing pale. "Wanlorn," she whispered. "Elminster? Do you need me?"

Silence was her answer. She was talking to an empty room, driven by her own fancies. Irritated, she strode back to her chair . . . and came to a halt in mid-stride, as a sudden feeling of being watched washed over her. It was followed by a surge of great peace and warmth.

Immeira found herself smiling at nothing, as contented as she'd ever felt. She beamed at the empty room around her and sat back down with a sigh. Dappled sun danced across her parchments, and she smiled at a memory of a slender, hawk-nosed man saving the Starn while she watched. Immeira sighed again, tossed her head to send her hair out of her eyes, and returned to the task of trying to decide who in the Starn should plant what, so that all might have food enough to last comfortably through the winter.

Her warm, yearning eagerness and hope, her delight . . . Elminster reached for Immeira, a broad smile growing on his own face—a smile that froze as the thought struck him: was this spirited young woman to be some sort of reward for him, to mark his retirement from Mystra's service?

He snatched back his hands from the approaching woman and told the darkness fiercely, "No. Long ago I made my choice . . . to walk the long road, the darker way, and know the sweep of danger and adventure and doom. I cannot turn back from it now, for even as I need Mystra, Mystra needs me."

At his words, Immeira and the sun-dappled room behind her melted away into falling motes of dwindling light that plunged down far below him in the great dark void he hung within, until his eyes could see them no more.

Abruptly fresh sunlight washed in from his right. Elminster turned toward it, and found himself gazing into a long chamber lined with rows of bookshelves that reached up to touch its high ceiling. Sunlit dust-motes hung thick in the air, and through their luster Elminster could see that the shelves were crammed with spell tomes, with not an inch of shelf left empty. Ribbons protruded from some of the spines; others glowed with mysterious runes.

A comfortable-looking armchair, footstool, and side table beckoned from the right-hand end of this library. The side table was piled high with books; El took a step forward to get a better look at them and found himself striding hungrily into the room.

Spells of Athalantar, gilt lettering on one spine said clearly. El extended an eager hand and let it fall back to his side, muttering, "No. It breaks my soul to refuse such knowledge, but . . . where's the fun of finding new magic, mastering it phrase by guess, and deduction by spell trial?"

The room didn't fall away into darkness as all the previous apparitions had done. El blinked around at more spellbooks than he could hope to collect in a century or more of doing nothing but hunting down and seizing books of magic, and swallowed. Then, as if in a dream, he took a step toward the nearest shelf, reaching for a particularly fat volume that bore the title *Galagard's Compendium of Spells Netherese.* It was . . . inches from his fingertips when El whirled around and snarled, "No!"

In the echoes of that exclamation his world went dark and empty again, the dusty room swept away in an instant, and he was standing in darkness and on darkness, alone once more.

A light approached out of black velvet nothingness, and became a man in ornate, high-collared robes, standing on a floor of stone slabs with a spell staff winking and humming in his hand. Not seeing Elminster, the man was staring grimly down at a dead woman sprawled on the stones before him, gentle smokes rising from her body, her face frozen in an eternal scream of fear.

"No," the man said wearily. "No more. I find that 'First among Her Chosen' has become an empty boast. Find another fool to be your slave down the centuries, lady. Everyone I loved—everyone I *knew*—is dead and gone, my work is swept away by each new grasping generation of spell hurlers, Faerûn fades into a pale shadow of the glory I saw in my youth—and most of all, I'm . . . so . . . damned . . . *tired.* . . ."

The man broke his staff with a sudden surge of strength, the muscles of his arms rippling. Blue light flared from the broken ends, swirling in the instant before a mighty explosion of released magic coalesced into a rushing wave. The despairing Chosen thrust one spearlike broken shaft end into his chest. He threw back his head in a soundless gasp or scream—and fell away into swirling dust, that convulsing jaw last, an instant before the outward rush of magic became blinding.

El turned his gaze away from that flash—only to find it mirrored in miniature elsewhere, in a hand-sized scrying sphere that a bald man in red robes was hunched over. The man shook his fist in triumph at what he saw in the depths of the crystal, and hissed, "Yes! *Yes!* Now I am First among Mystra's Chosen—and if they thought Elthaeris was overbearing, they'll learn well to kneel and quiver in fear beneath the spell—seizing scepter of Uirkymbrand! *Hahahaha!* The weak might just as well slay themselves right now, and yield their power to one more fitted to wield it—*me!*"

That mad shout was still ringing in Elminster's ears as that scene winked out, and a circle of light occurred right beside the last prince of Athalantar. Floating with it was a dagger—and as he recognized it, it slowly turned and rose, offering its hilt to his hand.

El looked down at it, smiled, and shook his head. "No. That's a way out I'll never take," he said.

The dagger winked out of existence—and promptly reappeared off to Elminster's left, in the hand of a robed man, his back to El, who promptly drove it into the back of another robed man. The victim stiffened as his wound spat forth a blue radiance, and the blade of the murderer's dagger flared up into a blue flame that swiftly consumed it. The dying man turned, his wound leaking a trail of tiny stars, and El saw that it was Azuth. Face convulsed in pain, the god clawed with his bare hands at the face of the man who stabbed him—and the radiance leaking out of him showed El the face of the recoiling murderer. The slayer of Azuth was ... Elminster.

"No!" El shouted, raking at the vision with his hands. "Away! *Awaaay!*" The two figures struggled with each other in the heart of a spreading cloud of blue stars, oblivious to him.

"Such ambitions are not mine," El snarled, "and shall never be, if Mystra grant it so. I am content to walk Faerûn, and know its ways more than I know the deep mysteries ... for how can I truly appreciate the one without the other?"

The dying Azuth swirled away, and out of the stars that had been his blood strode a man El knew from memories not his own, spell-shared with him once in Myth Drannor. It was Raumark, a sorcerer-king of Netheril who'd survived the fall of that decadent realm to become one of the founders of Halruaa. Raumark the Mighty stood alone in a hall of stout white pillars and vast echoing spaces, at the top of a high dais, and his face was both pale and grim.

Carefully he cast a spinning whorl of disintegration, testing it by dragging it through one of the giant pillars. The ceiling sagged as the top of the sheered-off pillar fell away into heavy crashing shards to the unseen floor below. Raumark watched the collapse, stone-faced, and brought the whorl back to spin in front of him, just beyond the lip of the dais.

He nodded down at it, as if satisfied—and jumped through it.

The scene died with Raumark, to be replaced by a view of a dusty tomb. A man El did not recognize but somehow knew was a Chosen of Mystra was taking an old and tattered grimoire out of a shoulder sack and placing it into an opened casket, the same task El had done so often for the Lady of Mysteries.

This Chosen, however, was in the grip of a seething fury, his eyes blazing with near madness. He plucked a cobwebbed skull up out of the casket, gazed into its sightless eye sockets, and snarled at it, "Spell after spell I just *give away*, while my body crumbles and grows deaf and stumbling. I'll end up like you in a few winters! Why should others taste the rewards I dole out, while I do not? Eh?"

He flung the skull back into its resting place and shoved the stone lid closed violently, the stony grating so loud that El winced. The Chosen strode forward with red fire in his eyes and said, "To live forever—why not? Seize a healthy body, snuff out its mind, ride it to ruin, then take the next. I've had the spells for a long time—why not use them?"

He resumed his determined walk, fading like a ghost through Elminster—but when the Athalantan turned his head to watch what happened to the Chosen, the man was gone, and the tomb he'd left fast fading behind him.

"Such a waste," El murmured, unshed tears glimmering in his eyes. "Oh, Mystra, Lady Mine, must this go on? Torment me no more, but give me some sign. Am I worthy to serve you henceforth? Or are ye so displeased with me that I should ask ye for death? Lady, tell me!"

It was a shock to feel the sudden tingling of lips upon his—Mystra's lips, they must be, for at their touch the thrill of raw power surged through him, making him feel alert and vigorous and mighty.

Elminster opened his eyes, lifting his arms to embrace her—but the Lady of the Weave was no more than a dwindling face of light, beyond his reach and receding swiftly into the void. "Lady?" he gasped almost despairingly, stretching out beseeching arms to her.

Mystra smiled. "You must be patient," her calm voice came quietly into his ear. "I shall visit you properly in time to come, but I must set you a task for me, first: a long one, perhaps the most important you'll ever undertake."

Her face changed, looking sad, and she added, "Though I can foresee at least one other task that might be judged as important."

"What task?" El blurted out. Mystra was little more than a twinkling star now.

"Soon," she said soothingly. "You shall know very soon. Now return to Faerûn—and heal the first wounded being you meet."

The darkness melted away, and El found himself in his clothes again, standing in the woods outside the ruins. A few paces away, two men were talking with an elf, all three of them sitting with their backs against the trunks of gnarled old trees. They broke off their converse to look up at him rather anxiously.

One of the mages suddenly sprouted a wand in his hand. Leveling it at Elminster, he asked coolly, "And you would be—?"

El smiled and said, "Dead long ago, Tenthar Taerhamoos, save for the fact that Mystra had other plans."

The three mages blinked at him, and the elf asked rather hesitantly, "You're the one they call Elminster, aren't you?"

"I am," El replied, "and the mission laid upon me is to heal ye." Ignoring a suddenly displayed arsenal of wands and winking rings, he cast a healing spell upon Starsunder, then another on Umbregard.

He and Tenthar locked gazes as he finished his castings, and El inclined his head toward the ruins and asked, "'Tis all done, then?"

"All but the drinking," Tenthar replied—and there was suddenly a dusty bottle of wine in his hand. He rubbed its label, peered into it suspiciously, drew out its cork, sniffed, and smiled.

"Magic seems to be reliable once more," he announced, holding out his other hand and watching four crystal goblets appear in it.

"Mystra's need is past, I think," El told him. "A testing is done, and many dark workers of magic have been culled."

Tenthar frowned and said, "It is the way of the cruel gods to take the best and brightest from us."

Umbregard shrugged as he accepted a glass and watched several other bottles appear out of thin air. "It is the way of gods to take us all," he added, "in the end."

Starsunder said then, "My thanks for the healing, Elminster. As to the way of gods, I believe none of us were made to live long. Elf, dwarf, human . . . even, I think, our gods themselves. The passage of too many years does things to us, makes us mad . . . the losses—friends, lovers, family, favorite places—and the loneliness. For my kind, a reward awaits, but that doesn't make the tarrying here any less wrenching; it only gives us something to look at, beyond present pain."

Elminster nodded slowly. "There may well be truth in thy words." He looked at Starsunder sidelong then and asked, "Did we meet, however briefly, in Myth Drannor?"

The moon elf smiled. "I was one of those who disagreed with the Coronal about admitting other races into the Fair City," the elf admitted. "I still do. It hastened our passing and gained us nothing but all our secrets stolen. And you were the one to break open the gates. I hated you and wished you dead. Had there been an easy, traceless way, I might have made things so."

"What stayed your hand?" El asked softly.

"I took your measure, several times, at revels and in the Mythal, and after. And you were as we—alone, and striving as best you knew how. I salute you, human. You resisted our goading, conducted yourself with dignity, and did well. Your good deeds will outlive you."

"My thanks," Elminster replied, his eyes bright with tears as he leaned over to embrace the elf. "To hear that means a lot."

The Fair Maid was elbow-to-elbow crowded. It seemed the High Duke's latest idea was to send huge armed caravans along the perilous road. Ripplestones looked like a drovers' yard, with beasts bawling and on the move everywhere. Inside, shielded a trifle from the dust if not the din, Beldrune, Tabarast, and Caladaster were sharing a table with a haughty mage from the Sword Coast, brimming tankards in every hand. The talk was of spells and fell monsters vanquished and wizards who would not die rising from their tombs, and folk were crowding around to listen.

"Why, that's *nothing!*" Beldrune was snarling. "Less than nothing! This very day, in the heart of the Dead Place, I stood beside the god *Azuth!*"

The mage from the Coast sneered in open disbelief, and thus goaded, Beldrune rushed on, "Oh, *yes*—Azuth, I tell you, an' . . ."

Caladaster and Tabarast exchanged silent looks, nodded, and with one accord rose and rummaged in Caladaster's pack while their comrade snarled on, jabbing a finger in the Coast mage's startled nose. "He needed our help, I tell you. *Our* spells saved the day—he said that!—an' he gave us to understand—"

"That we'd earned these magical robes!" Tabarast broke in triumphantly, holding up the daring black gown for all to see.

The roar of laughter that followed threatened to shake the very ceiling of the inn down on top of all the table-slapping, hooting drinkers, but as their laughter finally trailed away, a high-pitched chuckle joined in, from the doorway. Those who turned to see its source went very still.

"That almost looks as if it would fit me," Sharindala the sorceress told the four gaping mages brightly. "And I do need something to preserve my modesty, as you can see."

The Lady of Scorchstone Hall wore only her long, silken brown hair. It cloaked her breast and flanks as she strode forward, but no man there could fail to notice that aside from her tresses, she was bare to the world from the top of her head down to her hips—where her flesh ended, leaving bare bones from there to the floor.

"May I?" she asked, extending a hand for the garment. Around her, several folk slid down in their seats, fainting dead away, and there was a rush of booted feet for the door. Suddenly there was a small circle of empty space in the Fair Maid, ringed by men who were mostly white-faced and staring.

"I've got to get through a few more spells before I'll be able to eat or drink anything," Sharindala explained, "and it's rather embarrassing. . . ."

Tabarast snatched the gown out of her reach with a low growl of fear, but Caladaster stepped in front of him, tugging on his own robe. He had it over his head and off in a trice, to reveal a rotund and hairy body clad in breeches and braces that were stiff and shiny with age and dirt. "It's none too clean, lady," he said hesitantly, "and will probably hang on you as loose as any tent, but . . . take it; 'tis freely given."

A long, slender white arm took it, and a smile was given in return. "Caladaster? You were just a lad when I—oh, gods, has it been so long?"

Caladaster swallowed, red faced, and licked lips that seemed suddenly very dry. "What happened to you, Lady Sharee?"

"I died," she replied simply, and utter silence fell in the Maid. Then the sorceress shrugged on the offered robe, and smiled at the man who'd given it to her. "But I've come back. Mystra showed me the way."

There arose a murmur from the crowd. Sharindala took Caladaster's arm in one hand and his tankard in the other—her touch was cool and smooth and normal-seeming enough. She said gently, "Come, walk with me; we've much to talk about."

As they moved toward the door together, the half-skeletal sorceress paused in front of the mage from the Coast and added, "By the way, sir: everything that's been said about Azuth here this night is true. Whether you believe it or not."

They went out the door in a silence so deep that people had to gasp for air by the time they remembered to breathe again.

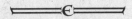

He seemed to have lost his boots again and to be walking barefoot on moonlight, somewhere in Faerûn where the sun of late afternoon should still have reigned. A breath ago he'd been talking with three mages in a forest, and the cheese had begun to arrive, to go with their wine—and now he was here, left with but a glimpse of their startled faces at the manner of his going.

So where exactly *was* here?

"Mystra?" he asked aloud, hopefully.

The moonlight surged up around him into silver flames that did not burn but instead sent the thrill of power through him, and those flames shaped themselves into arms that embraced him.

"Lady mine," Elminster breathed as he felt the soft brush of a familiar body against his—there went his clothes again; how did she *do* that?—and the tingling touch of her lips.

He kissed her back, hungrily, and silver fire swept through him as their bodies trembled together. He tried to caress soft, shifting flames—only to find himself holding nothing and standing in darkness once more, with Mystra standing like a pillar of silver fire not far away.

"Mystra?" El asked her, letting a little of the loneliness he'd felt into his voice.

"Please," the goddess whispered pleadingly, "This is as hard for me as it has been for you—I must not tarry. And you tempt me, Elminster . . . you tempt me so."

Silver flames swirled, and a hungry mouth closed on El's own for one long, glorious moment, fires crashing and charging through him, rising into splendor that made him weep and roar and writhe all at once.

"Elminster," that musical voice told him, as he floated in hazy bliss, "I'm sending you now to Silverhand Tower to rear three Chosen."

"Rear?" El asked, startled, his bliss washed away into alert alarm.

There seemed to be a laugh struggling to break through the tones of the goddess as she said, "You'll find three little girls waiting in the Tower, alone and uncertain. Be as a kindly uncle and tutor to them; feed them, clothe them, and teach them how to be and who to be."

Elminster swallowed, watching Mystra dwindle once more into a distant star. "You are forbidden to control their minds, or compel them save in emergencies most dire," she added. "As they grow older, let them forge forth to make their own lives. Your task then will be to watch over them covertly, and to ride in and pick up the pieces to ensure their survival from time to time, not to guide them unless they seek your advice . . . and we both know how often willful Chosen seek out the advice of others, don't we?"

"Mystra!" El cried despairingly, reaching out his arms for her.

"Oh by the Weave, man, don't make this any harder for me," Mystra murmured, and the kiss and caress that set him afire then also whirled him end over end, away.

EPILOGUE

Perhaps the greatest service Elminster has ever done for Faerûn is to be father and mother to the daughters of Mystra. Holding almost all of Mystra's magic and keeping Toril together with his very fingertips during the Time of Troubles—that was easy. Rearing little girls of clever wits, much energy, bewitching beauty, and mighty magical powers, and doing it well—now that's hard.

ANTARN THE SAGE
FROM *THE HIGH HISTORY OF FAERÛNIAN ARCHMAGES MIGHTY*
PUBLISHED CIRCA THE YEAR OF THE STAFF

S ilverhand Tower, when he found himself standing a little way off from it, blinking in the sunlight, was a riven shell, little more than a cottage attached to an empty ring of battlements and the gutted stump of a keep. Deep woods surrounded it, cloaked it, and were in the patient process of overwhelming it, hewn back only from an oval vegetable garden. A small, dirty face was peering doubtfully at him from its leafy green heart—a face that vanished, leaving only dancing leaves behind, once he smiled at it.

Elminster peered at the garden to see if he could catch sight of a little body scuttling anywhere. He could not, and soon shrugged and strolled toward the cottage, its straw roof a mass of bright flowers and nodding herbs.

"Ambara?" he called gently as he approached. "Ethena?"

The door seemed to be stuck fast—off the latch, but refusing to open. He nudged it with his knee, mindful of the fact that little bodies might be crouched behind it, and heard the faint protest of wood splintering. It had been pegged closed, into a dirt floor. Someone had a mallet or mace or axe to hand.

"Ambara?" he asked the darkness within. "Ethena? Anamanué?"

The wand spat so close behind him that he heard the young, light voice murmur the command word quite clearly before the rain of magic missiles tore into him, hurling him against the door. His body was still shuddering as something snatched the peg away and hurled the door open, spilling him into the dim interior, and something else drove an axe at his head, hard.

It struck his spellshield with a shower of sparks and glanced away, numbing hands that were too small for it and making their owner sob with pain. Without thinking El reached out and placed a healing on the small, barefoot slip of a girl who was trying not to cry . . . and became aware that an utter silence had fallen.

He drew his hand slowly back from the one he'd healed, seeing an intent face above a tightly clutched and dusty dagger, close by his left ear—and an equally intent face, over the ready-held wand, just out of reach to his right.

Long and tousled silver hair adorned all three heads, and all three of the faces, even in their dirty, alarmed, and childlike state, were breathtaking in their beauty.

"How is it you know our names?" the eldest one—with the wand—asked him fiercely. "Who are you?"

"Mystra told me," Elminster replied, giving her a grave smile, "and sent me to do for ye three what thy mother now cannot."

"Our mother's *dead!*" the girl with the wand told him fiercely.

Elminster nodded. "Ye're Ambara," he said, "aren't ye?"

"Nobody calls me *that*," the girl told him, tossing her head angrily. Gods, but she was beautiful.

"Ye're Ambara Dove, four summers old," El said gently. "What would ye like me to call ye?"

"Dove," the little girl told him. "And that's Storm. She can talk a little. Laer can't, yet—she just cries."

"She needs changing," El observed gravely.

"We all do," Dove told him severely, "after the fright you gave us. What we need most, though, is something to eat. I can't be wasting this precious thing"— she waved the wand with the air of a veteran battlemage—"blasting down any more little birds and beasts that make us sick to even look at them . . . and the things I know are safe to eat are *gone*."

"I'm not a great cook," El told her.

Dove sighed. "Why'd Mystra send *you*, then?" she asked rudely, then pointed with the wand. "We use *that* bit of the stream, below the stump, to wash, and drink from up here. You change Laer, and I'll go hunting. Storm'll be—"

"Watching you," Storm said suddenly, putting out a hand to take firm hold of Elminster's beard. "Shielding Laer. Be nice . . . like your beard. Nice."

Elminster grinned at her, found that he had a lump in his throat and tears threatening to burst forth. He swept them all into his arms and wept openly, knowing just a little of what a long, hard road lay before these three little ones, down the long years ahead.

Laeral gurgled with pleasure at being so close to the man who'd banished her pain, but Dove swatted him matter-of-factly on the side of the head and snapped, "Stop that cryin.' Night soon, and we've got to *eat*."

Elminster's tears turned to a chuckle, and suddenly he was rolling around on the dirt floor with three laughing, tumbling girls locked onto his hair and beard.

How many years was he going to be doing this?

The roast lizard was just bones and scorched scales and a pleasant smell, now. His crushed-berry sauce had been crude but a beginning, and he'd discovered that none of the girls had enough clothing to keep them warm as they slept, to say nothing of decent—but that his cloak would easily furnish three blankets just large enough to wrap them in. The sun was going down, and as El stared up at the twilit woods, he saw Mystra's dark eyes gazing down at him from among their tangled branches.

He stared into those eyes of deep mystery, as they sent him silent love and sympathy and fond admiration and sent back a silent prayer for guidance. He did not move until it was fully dark, and true night ruled the land.

A small hand captured one of his. Gods, but they could move silently, these three—or stealthily enough that an insect chorus could cloak their noises, at least.

Elminster looked down and whispered, "Shouldn't ye be getting off to sleep?" Dove pulled at his hand.

"Uncle Weirdbeard," she said insistently, "it's dark time, and I can't sleep until I know you're on guard against the wolves and all—else I have to stay up with my stick. I'm tired. Hadn't we better go in?"

He stared at her, found tears swimming in his eyes again, and quickly looked up at the brightening stars overhead.

"Sir," she asked almost sternly, pulling on his hand again, "Hadn't we better go in?"

El sighed, gave the stars a last look, his heart full. He knelt down, gave her a gentle kiss and a smile, and said, "Yes, I suppose we should. Why don't ye lead the way?"

ABOUT THE AUTHOR

ED GREENWOOD is the creator of the FORGOTTEN REALMS® fantasy world setting and the author of more than 170 books that have sold millions of copies worldwide in over two dozen languages. In real life, he's a Canadian librarian who lives in the Ontario countryside with his wife, a cat, and far too many books.